RANDOM
HOUSE
LARGE
PRINT

Spy

DANIELLE STEEL

Spy

A Novel

RANDOM HOUSE
LARGE PRINT

Published in the United States of America by Random House Large Print in association with Delacorte Press, an imprint of Random House, a division of Penguin Random House LLC, New York.

Cover design: Laura Klynstra
Cover photograph: Michael Nelson/Trevillion Images
Author photograph: © Brigitte Lacombe

The Library of Congress has established a Cataloging-in-Publication record for this title.

ISBN: 978-0-593-16818-9

www.penguinrandomhouse.com/large-print-format-books

FIRST LARGE PRINT EDITION

Printed in the United States of America

10 9 8 7 6 5 4 3 2 1

This Large Print edition published in accord with the standards of the N.A.V.H.

To my darling children,
Beatie, Trevor, Todd, Nick,
Samantha, Victoria, Vanessa,
Maxx, and Zara,

May you always be happy
    and safe, above all,
may your adventures be rewarding,
    your partners loving,
may you be wise, lucky, and blessed,
and may you lead long, happy lives.

With my greatest love,
Mom/d.s.

"Every great dream begins with a dreamer. Always remember, you have within you the strength, the patience, and the passion to reach for the stars to change the world."

—Source Unknown

Spy

Chapter 1

Thinking back on it later, the summer of 1939 was the last "normal" summer Alexandra Wickham remembered. It had been five years since her celebrated first London "Season" at eighteen, an event her parents had anticipated with excitement and expectation since she was a little girl. She had looked forward to it as the experience of a lifetime, a defining moment when she would be presented at court with all the other daughters of aristocratic families. It was her official entry into society, and since 1780 when the first Queen Charlotte's Ball was held by King George III to honor his wife, the purpose of "coming out" and being presented had been to allow aristocratic young ladies to catch the eye of future husbands. Marriage was supposed to be the result in a relatively short time. Although modern parents in the 1930s were less earnest about it, the hoped-for outcome hadn't changed.

Alex had been presented at court to King George V and Queen Mary, and had come out at Queen Charlotte's Ball, in an exquisite white lace and satin dress her mother had had made for her by Jean Patou in Paris. With her height and delicate blond looks, Alex had been a stunning beauty, and she didn't lack for suitors. Her older brothers, William and Geoffrey, had teased her mercilessly about being a debutante, and her subsequent failure to land a husband within the early months of the Season in London. Being at parties, balls, and social events was a major change for Alex, who had been horse-mad, like the rest of her family, since her earliest childhood. She'd been taunted into being a tomboy by her brothers, as a matter of survival. Wearing elegant gowns every night, and proper dresses at every luncheon in London, had been tiresome and sometimes even hard work for her.

She'd made many friends among the other debutantes, and most of them had been engaged by the end of the Season, and married shortly after. Alex couldn't imagine herself married to anyone at eighteen. She wanted to go to university, which her father thought unnecessary, and her mother inappropriate. Alex was an avid reader and student of history. A flock of diligent governesses had given her a thirst for knowledge and a love of literature, and honed her skills with watercolors and intricate embroidery and tapestry. Her own gift for languages had helped her learn French, German, and Italian almost flawlessly. She spoke French and German as well as she did English, which no one considered remarkable, and her Italian was almost as good. She enjoyed reading in French and German. She was also a graceful dancer, which made her a highly desirable partner at the balls she attended with her family.

But there was more to Alex than the quadrilles she danced effortlessly, her love of literature, and her gift for languages. She was what the men she met called "spirited." She wasn't afraid to voice her opinions, and had a wicked sense of humor. It made her a wonderful friend to her brothers' male companions, but few of them could imagine marrying her, despite her beauty. Those who wanted to accept the challenge, Alex found fatally boring. She had no desire to be locked away in Hampshire where her parents' manor house was located, doing needlepoint by the fire at night, like her mother, or raising a flock of unruly children, like her brothers had been. Maybe later, but surely not at eighteen.

The five years since her London Season in 1934 had flown by quickly, with Alex traveling abroad with her parents, riding in the local hunt or others she was invited to, visiting her friends who had married and even had several children by then, going to house parties, and helping her father on their estate. She had more interest in the land than her brothers, both of whom had fled to London. William, the oldest, led a gentleman's life and had a passion for flying machines. Geoffrey worked at a bank, went to parties every night, and was known as a heartbreaker. Her brothers were in no hurry to marry either.

Geoffrey was twenty-five, and William was twenty-seven and went to air races in England and France at every opportunity. He was a proficient pilot. Alex thought her brothers had a lot more fun than she did. She was something of a prisoner of the rules of society, and what was considered appropriate for a woman. She was the fastest rider in the county, which irritated her brothers and their friends, and her gift for languages came in handy on their family travels. By twenty-three, she had been to New York several times with her parents, and considered American men more liberal in their thinking and more fun than the Englishmen she'd met. She liked talking politics with her brothers and father, although they urged her not to do so at dinner parties, so she wouldn't frighten the men who might want to court her. Her response to her brothers' comments on the subject was sharp.

"I wouldn't want a man who didn't respect my opinions, or to whom I couldn't speak my mind."

"You'll wind up a spinster if you don't curb your tongue and your passion for horses," Geoffrey warned her, but both of her brothers were proud of how brave she was, how intelligent, and how bold and clear in her thinking. Their parents pretended not to notice, but they were secretly concerned that she hadn't found a husband yet, and didn't seem to want one.

She listened to all of Hitler's speeches in German on the radio, and had read several books about him. Long before the events of the summer of 1939, she had predicted that war would be inevitable. By that summer, her brothers and father agreed with her. It seemed unavoidable, and they were dismayed but not surprised when war was declared on September 3. They gathered to listen to King George's speech on the radio, urging Britons everywhere to be strong and courageous and defend their country. Like most of the population, the Wickhams' response was immediate. Both of Alex's brothers enlisted in the RAF, William in the Fighter Command, which suited him as an ace pilot, and Geoffrey in the Bomber Command. There was no hesitation. They reported for duty and training shortly after, as did most of their friends. It was what was expected of them, and they went willingly.

Alex remained quiet about it for several weeks, and then startled her parents when she announced that she had joined the voluntary First Aid Nursing Yeomanry shortly after Willie and Geoff had left for training. Her parents had made their own decision about how to contribute to the war effort. Her father was past the age of enlisting, but they had volunteered to accept twenty children from London into their home. The evacuation of children from the cities was being encouraged, and many parents were eager to find safe homes for their children in the country. Alex's mother, Victoria, was already busy preparing the building where they housed the household staff and stable hands. Their male staff would be greatly diminished by conscription anyway, and they had other quarters in the house for the women. They were setting up bunk rooms for the children. Three of the housemaids were going to help care for them, and two girls from the village, and two teachers from the local school were going to give them lessons. Victoria was going to teach them as well. She had been hoping that Alex would help her, but then Alex announced that she was going to London to drive lorries and ambulances, work as an aide in the local hospitals, and do whatever other assignments they gave her. Her parents were proud of her, but concerned about her being in London. Bombing raids were expected, and she would have been safer in the country, helping to take care of the children. The children the Wickhams would be housing were from poor and middle class backgrounds, and families all over the country were taking them in.

Alex had studied her options carefully before volunteering for the First Aid Nursing Yeomanry. She could have joined the Women's Voluntary Services to do clerical work, which didn't interest her, or the Air Raid Precautions, or worked on a female pump crew for the fire service. The Women's Voluntary Services was also organizing shelters, clothing exchanges, and mobile canteens. She could have joined the Women's Land Army to be trained in agricultural work, about which she already knew a great deal from their estate, but Alex didn't want to stay in Hampshire, and preferred to go to the city.

The Auxiliary Territorial Service offered more of what she hoped to do, with driving and general duties, but when she contacted them, they suggested clerical work, which would keep her cooped up in an office. She wanted more physical work. She had also spoken to the Women's Auxiliary Air Force, about deploying barrage balloons. But in the end the First Aid Nursing Yeomanry sounded as if it was the best suited to her skills, and they said there would be other opportunities for her once she joined.

Her brothers teased her about it when she wrote to them, and said they would keep an eye on her when they went to London. Her mother cried when she left Hampshire and made her promise to be careful, but she was already busy and had her hands full with the children billeted with them. The youngest was five, and the oldest was eleven, which Alex thought would be much harder work than whatever she would be assigned to do in London.

She arrived in town in October, a month after war had been declared. The king had spoken again, thanking the entire country for their response to the war effort. Alex felt like she was finally engaged in something important, and she thoroughly enjoyed her month of training with women of all ages, from all walks of life, and every part of the country. She felt that someone had thrown open the doors and windows of her life to a broader world, which was what she had hoped to find at university, and had longed for, for so long. She wrote letters to her parents and brothers constantly, telling them about what she was doing and learning.

Geoff came to London during a break in his own training and took her to dinner at Rules, one of their favorite restaurants. People smiled approvingly to see them both in uniform. She was excited when she informed Geoff about everything she'd been told. She already knew that she would be driving supply lorries as her first assignment, which would free up the men to do more important things.

"Just what I've always dreamed of," he teased her, "having a sister who's a lorry driver. It suits you, Alex. Thank God you never got married."

"Oh shut up," she said, grinning at him with eyes full of mischief. "And I didn't 'never' marry, I just haven't married yet. I probably will one day."

"Or you could drive a lorry after the war too. You may have found your true calling."

"What about you, when do you start flying?" she asked, with a look of concern, hidden by their constant teasing.

"Soon. I can't wait to bomb the hell out of the Germans." William was already flying missions. The two brothers had always been fiercely competitive, but William had more experience as a pilot than Geoff.

As always, they had a good time together, and Geoff dropped her off at her dorm after dinner. Blackout rules were already being enforced, and windows were covered. Shelters were being built. London was buzzing with activity and young people in uniform, as wartime regulations and conditions were announced. Food rationing hadn't begun yet, but they'd already been warned by the Ministry of Food that it would start with sugar, butter, and bacon in January. Everyone knew that life was going to change radically, but it hadn't yet. And holiday meals would remain much the same.

On their way back to Alex's dormitory, Geoff warned her of the dangers of fast men who would be trying to take advantage of young, innocent women, and that pregnancy or venereal disease could be the result. Alex laughed at what he said.

"Mama didn't mention any of that when I left home."

"She's too polite. She probably doesn't think she needs to, and that you're too well brought up to misbehave." He gave her a stern, brotherly look.

"And you think I'm not?" She raised an eyebrow at her brother.

"I know men. And if you fall in love with some randy bastard, he could talk you into something you'll regret."

"I'm not stupid," she said, looking mildly insulted.

"I just don't want anything to happen to you. You've never lived in the city, or met men like some of the ones you'll be meeting now. They can be pretty bold," he warned her again, determined to protect his baby sister.

"So can I," she said confidently.

"Well, just remember, if you get pregnant, I'll kill you . . . and you would break our parents' hearts."

"I'm not going to do anything like that," she said, shocked that he'd even suggested it. "I came here to work, not to find a man, or go to bars and get drunk." She knew that some of the girls in her dormitory flirted with every soldier they saw. It wasn't her style. "Maybe I should have joined the army, or the RAF like you and Willie. I thought about it. Maybe I will, eventually."

"You're doing enough as it is," he said, with a warm expression. "People say good things about the First Aid Nursing Yeomanry, and a lot of it's not about nursing. It's heavy work. Just don't get kicked out," he teased her again, "by mouthing off to a teacher or your superiors or something. I know what you can be like!"

"Just mind your back and make sure you get the Germans before they get you," she warned him. They hugged each other, and he left her outside her dormitory. He had to be at his base by midnight, and he had a ride back.

She was pleased to have seen him. She missed her

brothers, and her parents, but she was happy to be in London, being trained to be useful. She couldn't wait to start work. She had almost completed her training, and was proud to be part of the war effort, although she wondered if she should be doing more. Both of her brothers were part of the Advanced Air Striking Force of the RAF, and would be flying bombing missions over Germany. Reconnaissance missions had started as soon as war was declared, and Alex's lorry or ambulance driving seemed meager to her in comparison to her brothers' more dramatic contributions. But at least she wasn't sitting at home in Hampshire, she told herself.

She and Geoff had talked at dinner that night about going home for Christmas. All three of them had gotten leave to do so, and Geoff had said it might be the last chance they'd have. They were excited about it, and other men in Geoff's Bomber Command were going home too. Their superiors were being lenient with them for this first Christmas of the war. It was something to look forward to. There had been no major action, or very little, in the war so far. It was mostly preparations and plans, and getting ready for what was to come. Canadians, Australians, and Americans had come to volunteer too. There were even two Canadians and an Australian woman in Alex's group. Alex liked getting to know them. They all seemed much freer and more independent than the English girls Alex knew, and she admired them.

* * *

When Alex, Willie, and Geoff got back to Hampshire in time for Christmas, it looked no different than it had in other years. The countryside was as peaceful. The only change was that with blackout regulations, windows were covered so one couldn't see the Christmas tree lights shining brightly from the homes, or shop windows in the towns. And there was anti-blast tape on store windows in Lyndhurst, their favorite market town. Petrol rationing had been introduced, so people weren't traveling long distances to visit their families. But food was plentiful and Christmas celebrations were the same as before. Restaurants and hotels were full. People were in a festive mood despite the war.

Hundreds of thousands of children had been sent from London to homes in the country, and the government discouraged sending them back to London for the holidays, and urged the host families to keep them in the country, as many might not want to leave their parents in London again if they went home. Their parents were told not to visit them, for the same reason. And since railway travel was to be kept to a minimum, the children who had been sent away had to adjust to their first Christmas without their parents. Victoria and her helpers were determined to make it a happy time for them.

The Wickhams were making a big effort to entertain

the children and have Christmas be special. Victoria and the girls who helped care for them had knitted and bought gifts for all of them. Victoria had stayed up late every night herself sewing a teddy bear for each child. Alex joined her when she got home, helping her finish the final ones by tying bright red ribbons around their necks. Victoria had knitted a sweater for each child. She and almost every woman in the country were knitting constantly, and following the various government schemes about how to save money on clothes. Restraint was being encouraged but not enforced.

The Wickhams had two dinners on Christmas Eve. First, an early one for the children, where they received their gifts, and squealed with delight over the teddy bears. Miraculously, all the sweaters fit, the navy blue ones for the boys, and the red ones for the girls, and there were sweets for each of them from the shop in Lyndhurst. Later that night, the family had their traditional Christmas meal in the dining room. They dressed formally in black tie and evening gowns, as they always did. They exchanged gifts that had been thoughtfully picked out. Victoria had knitted a pink angora sweater for Alex and also gave her a pair of pale blue sapphire earrings, the same color as her eyes. They exchanged their gifts at midnight after dinner. Alex had bought her mother one of the stylish new large handbags in London. It would be practical for carrying ration books and

even her knitting. They were becoming very popular in London, one of the first noticeable fashion
changes of the war.

On Christmas morning, Alex shocked her family with another, when she appeared for Christmas
lunch wearing trousers, which were also the latest
rage in London. Her brothers looked horrified, and
her parents startled.

"**What** are **those**?" William asked with obvious
disapproval, when she walked into the drawing
room before lunch. She'd been riding her horse that
morning, and barely had time to change. "Is that
part of your uniform?"

"No, it's not," she said staunchly. "Don't be so
old-fashioned. Everyone is wearing them."

"Should I have worn a dress?" he asked.

"Only if you want to. Trousers are comfortable
and practical. Gabrielle Chanel has been wearing
them in Paris for several years. They're very fashion-
able. Besides, you wear them, why shouldn't I?"

"Can you imagine Mama wearing trousers?" he
said as though their mother weren't in the room.
Their father smiled.

"I hope not. Your mother looks lovely dressed as
she is." He glanced warmly at his wife. "If Alex wants
to try out a new fashion, she might as well do it here.
She's not hurting anyone," their father said generously, and William was upset, as Geoff laughed.

"Good one, Alex. Willie needs a little shaking
up," Geoff commented. Her hairdo was new too.

She was wearing her long blond hair in a bun, instead of the braid she'd worn since her childhood. There was a neat roll in the front, and she had on bright red lipstick, which was new too. After three months in London, she appeared more grown up and sophisticated, and even more beautiful.

"That's why women have uniforms," Willie persisted, "so they don't show up in ridiculous outfits like that. Trousers are for men, dresses and skirts for women. Alex seems to have gotten confused." William was stiff and disapproving. He was far more conservative than his younger brother.

"Don't be such a stuffed shirt," Geoff scolded him, and eventually William relaxed and they enjoyed the meal of pheasant and goose. In the civilized atmosphere of their dining room, with the family portraits gazing down at them, it was difficult to believe there was a war on. The only visible difference at their table was that all of the young men who worked for them had enlisted in the armed forces, and the maids were serving, which would have been considered improper before the war. It was a necessity now. All of the women were doing volunteer work in the neighboring towns, or had joined the Auxiliary Territorial Service, the Women's Voluntary Services, or the Observer Corps. Everyone was involved in some way in the war effort, but on a peaceful day like Christmas, nothing showed, except the blackout shades and fabric on the windows. The tree was brightly lit in the drawing room during the day, and the children had been brought in to admire it the day before. They were in awe of how tall it was, and how lavishly decorated with all the beautiful ornaments the family had used for years, with the antique angel at the top.

After lunch, the family took a walk together, and avoided talking about the war. Nothing new and dramatic had occurred since September except that the first German aircraft, a Heinkel He III bomber, had been shot down over Britain at the end of October. Winston Churchill had been consistently outspoken about what was to come.

But the Wickhams talked about local news as they walked the grounds of their estate. The boys bantered easily as they went ahead, and Alex joined them after staying with her parents at their pace for a while. Victoria was enjoying having children with them in Hampshire, although she admitted it was a lot of work to have so many young children to be responsible for. So far, they had given her no trouble and weren't as homesick as they had been in the beginning.

"What are you two talking about?" Alex asked Willie and Geoff as she caught up with them, still wearing the trousers that had outraged her oldest brother.

"Fast planes and loose women," Geoff quipped with a grin at his sister.

"Should I leave you to it?" she asked him.

"Not at all. Are you behaving yourself in London?"

"Of course," she said, remembering Geoff's advice. And in fact she was. She was busy with her volunteer work, and the assignments they gave her, mostly driving so far. She was responsible, reliable, and a good driver. She'd been driving in Hampshire for years, after one of the stable hands taught her when she was seventeen. "Are you behaving yourselves?" she asked her brothers, and William nodded, while Geoff hesitated.

"I'm not going to tell my baby sister about my love life," he said, laughing, and both his siblings rolled their eyes.

"Don't brag," Alex said, and that time William chuckled.

"His fantasy life, more likely. What woman would put up with him?"

"Scores of them," Geoff said confidently, and then chased them around the same trees they had played near as children. There was something so peaceful and restorative about being at their home in Hampshire. They all loved it. Alex thought it too dull when she lived there, but now that she was in London, coming home seemed like a gift, as it did to all of them.

Their parents watched them chasing one another like children and they smiled. It was a familiar scene, and Edward put an arm around his wife. For an instant, it panicked her, watching them, hoping they would all be safe, and Edward could sense his wife's thoughts. "They'll be fine," he whispered to her, and she nodded, with tears in her eyes. Her fears stuck in her throat like a fist. She hoped he was right.

They walked back to the house when it started to get dark, and then went to visit the children, who had had a good day, playing with the girls who took care of them. One of the teachers had spent the day with them too, since her own sons hadn't come home from their faraway bases for Christmas. The children from London were a blessing for them all.

William was the first to leave, three days after Christmas. He had to get back to his base. He wasn't allowed to tell them why. Geoff left the morning of New Year's Eve. He had plans in London that night, and was taking an early train. After thanking his parents and kissing his sister, he promised to take her to dinner again in London soon.

Alex left on New Year's Day. Her leave ended that night. Her mother held her close for a moment, and then looked in her daughter's eyes.

"Be careful, Mr. Churchill says things will get rough soon." Victoria believed him.

"I'm fine, Mama. They trained us for everything, and there are bomb shelters everywhere now, with wardens to get everyone underground as soon as the air raid sirens sound." Victoria nodded, with tears in her eyes. It had been a precious Christmas, for all of them, and she prayed it wouldn't be their last. In peaceful Hampshire, it was hard to believe there was a war on, and she couldn't bear the thought that her children would be in danger and she could lose one of them.

Alex hugged her again, and then waved, as one of their old farmers drove her to the station. Her parents stood outside her childhood home, waving at her, as the children from London came rushing out and stood around them, and Alex saw her mother stroking a little boy's hair with the gentleness that Alex loved about her. She knew the image would stay with her forever, wherever she went. Once the house was out of sight, she was excited about going back to London, where everything was happening. She could hardly wait. She waved to their old farmer once she boarded the train, and a few minutes later, it rolled slowly forward and the Lyndhurst station disappeared from view.

Chapter 2

The war began to gain momentum in the early days of 1940, like a slowly growing dragon, flashing its tail in warning. Missions were flown, planes were shot down on both sides, but no major battles were fought. Thousands of men were drafted into the army after the early volunteers of the months before. Alex was surprised when she was brought in by her superiors and questioned about her language skills. It had become apparent that she was completely at ease in French and German, and fluent to a considerable degree in Italian. She was asked if her parents were either German or French, and she said they weren't. When interrogated further, she explained that she had been taught all three languages by her governesses, growing up. Nothing further came of it, and she forgot about the interview. She assumed they just wanted to confirm her allegiance to Britain, and once they knew her parents were English, they felt no concern.

She had dinner with Geoff several times, and William once. She got home to Hampshire in April for a long weekend, but her brothers hadn't been back since Christmas. Her father particularly missed William's help running the estate. He had an older man to assist him, but Edward was essentially running it all alone now that William was in the war.

The children from London were thriving under her mother's watchful eye. Victoria knitted constantly the whole time Alex was there, making sweaters for them, for people at the hospital where she volunteered, and another sweater for Alex. It seemed to be a national pastime. Even in London, Alex saw women knitting everywhere.

Winston Churchill became prime minister, and told the country to be braced for attack. His warnings became all too real when the Battle of Britain began on July 10, and Hitler unleashed the demons of war on them with full force. The country held up staunchly and was well prepared. The bombing of London and other cities was constant, and Alex managed to call her parents to tell them that she was all right. She heard from both her brothers in the ensuing days. A month later, the Luftwaffe attempted to gain air superiority over Britain, with heavy losses on both sides, but more among the Germans, who failed in their mission. It had been a hellish few weeks since the Battle of Britain began. Churchill addressed the nation on the radio. Alex spent every night in the air raid shelter, with screaming babies, sweating men, and crying women, but there was a kind of solidarity between the people of London that she had never known before.

By day, she drove over rocks and rubble in the lorries and ambulances she was assigned, sometimes carrying the wounded to hospitals, at other times loads of bodies to where they would be identified and claimed. Buildings crumbled around her, the sight of the dead and injured became familiar, along with the stench of death and the plaster dust that choked her as she drove.

In August, two days after the Luftwaffe's fiercest attack when they failed to dominate the British in the air, the matron of her dormitory came to get her as she dressed for work. She asked Alex to come downstairs. When she followed her, she saw one of the leaders of William's fighter squadron waiting for her with a somber face. She knew the moment she caught sight of him, and fought not to show how violently she was shaking, trying not to faint. His words were quick, William had been shot down during the battle with the Luftwaffe on August 13. It had been declared a British victory. He had died a hero's death, at twenty-eight. She nodded and thanked the squadron leader, and went back upstairs to sit on her bed, feeling dazed. All she could think of were her parents, and how they would take the news. Their oldest son was dead. She wanted to talk to Geoff, but knew she couldn't reach him. He was flying missions every day, like William.

The matron gave her half an hour alone, and then came upstairs and told her that she had five days' leave, if she wanted it, to go home to see her parents, if she was able to get there. Alex nodded, with tears streaming down her cheeks, thanked her, and then packed a small bag and left a few minutes later.

She was able to get a slow train and arrived at Lyndhurst at dusk. She found a man with a car at the station, who was willing to drive her home for a small fee. It was dark when she got there and she knew her parents would know by then. The house seemed empty when she arrived. She walked into the library, and found her parents sitting like statues, too shocked to move, too brokenhearted to speak, until they saw her, and then all three of them sobbed in each other's arms. They had all known that people die in wartime, and William was a fighter pilot, but somehow they had been so confident in his abilities, he was so young and strong and sure of everything, that none of them had thought he would die. They sat together until midnight, and then went to the kitchen. Alex made them something to eat, but they weren't hungry. The vicar of the local church had come to see them earlier that night, Alex couldn't remember a word he had said. William was gone, in a stupid war that never should have started, caused by a lunatic in Germany. It made her realize now how many young men could die, and she still had one brother flying. Suddenly everything about the war seemed so wrong, no matter how brave they all were.

Alex put their untouched food in the icebox, and stayed with her parents until they went to bed. It was her mission to take care of them now. They were the children and she the parent. Word had spread of William's death, people in the area had brought food. The children they were housing had left little bunches of flowers on the front steps, not knowing what else to do. Some of them had already lost their parents in the bombing raids on London. Alex understood it all better now, the senselessness of war, and the losses they would sustain before it was over. It was all too real.

She laid down on her own bed after her parents retired for the night. She hoped that they would sleep, but doubted that they would. She lay there wide awake all night, thinking of William, how serious he had been, even as a young boy, the role of eldest son, which he took so much to heart, and the land and home and responsibilities he would inherit. Now Geoff, ever the clown and family jester, would have to step into his shoes, and take over from their father one day. Geoff had never prepared for it since William was the heir. Everything raced through her mind. She saw the sun come up, and heard the front door open and close. She tiptoed to the stairs, and looked down to see her brother standing there, thunderstruck, exhausted, with dark circles under his eyes as he looked up at her. They had given Geoff leave too. She raced down the stairs and flew into his arms, and clung to him as they both burst into tears.

She followed him into the kitchen, and made him something to eat. Rationing had finally begun to bite, and she used the eggs they still got from the farms on their property, toast with a little bit of the foul-smelling margarine they had now instead of butter, and the jam her mother made, with a cup of weak tea. He ate it as they talked about William and what happened. It seemed strange now that there were only the two of them, and not three. Their family seemed suddenly unbalanced, like a chair without a leg.

By the time Geoff finished eating, their parents joined them, and they sat together in the kitchen for a long time. The vicar was coming back to see them, and they were going to plan a small funeral service to be held at the church the next day, before Geoff and Alex had to go back to London. He would have been buried in the family cemetery on their estate, but there was no body. So in time a headstone in his memory would bear his name, with no remains beneath it.

Alex took their mother upstairs to help her bathe and put on a plain black dress, while Geoff and their father went outside to get some air and go for a walk. Edward tried to tell Geoff some things about the estate, since he would inherit it now. That possibility had never occurred to either of them before. Geoff couldn't bear listening to his father talk about it, it made William's death much too real to both of them. Geoff was relieved when he stopped.

Time was moving at a snail's pace, in slow motion. It all felt surreal. William was gone. Alex walked past his room on the way to her mother's, and was grateful that the door was closed. She couldn't have borne seeing all his familiar things just yet, not now.

When the vicar came, they arranged everything for the service. Victoria said what music they wanted. The vicar told her the choir would sing. Alex volunteered to arrange the flowers herself. After that, the rest of the day crawled by until it was evening again. Her father drank too much scotch before he retired for the night. Victoria went to bed as soon as the sun went down, and finally Geoff and Alex were left alone. He poured her a drink from what was left of the scotch, and one for himself.

"I hate this stuff," she said, making a face as she sipped it.

"It'll do you good." He drank his neat and poured himself a second one. "I figured I'd be the one to die in this war. He was such a good pilot. I was sure he could outrun every German."

"If you die, I'll kill you," Alex said grimly, taking another sip of the scotch, and he smiled at her.

"I'm not going to die, I'm just a gunner, dropping bombs out of a big bomber. There's no fancy footwork. They said William died a hero. What difference does that make? Who goddamn cares if he died a hero? He's gone. He took himself so seriously," he smiled at the memory, "even as a boy. He was the oldest son to the core. I don't even know how to run this place. He would have. He knew everything about it."

"You'll learn after the war," Alex said firmly. "Papa will teach you." He was eager to get started already now, with William barely gone.

"I don't want to learn. I want Willie to come back," he said and then started to sob, and Alex put her arms around him, wondering if any of them would ever be the same.

They sat together until three in the morning, until Geoff was thoroughly drunk, and Alex was exhausted. Then she walked him upstairs, and put him to bed with his clothes on. She went to her own room, lay down for a minute on her bed and fell sound asleep until the sun streamed into her room the next morning. As soon as she was fully awake, she realized what the day was. They had William's funeral to get through. Everything about the whole concept seemed so wrong. His funeral. Not his birthday, or something to celebrate. Her big brother Willie was dead. She'd always been so proud of him.

The family gathered in the front hall at ten o'clock that morning, her mother in another somber black dress, with red-rimmed eyes, clutching a handkerchief and wearing a hat Alex had never seen before.

Alex was wearing an old black dress, with black stockings. The day was unusually hot. Her father was wearing a dark blue suit, a white shirt, a black tie, and a homburg. Geoff looked severely hung-over and was in his uniform. Alex drove them to the church, and when they got there, they all stared for a minute. They hadn't expected anyone to be there. Word had spread from one family to another, and all of their employees and tenant farmers were there, all the families they knew, the locals William had grown up with, those who weren't in the army. And if they were away, their parents and sisters were there. There were easily three hundred people crowded into the tiny church and spilling out of it, while the Wickhams made their way through the silent crowd that stood there in respect for the family's loss and heartbreak. At the sight of them, the Wickhams had tears pouring down their cheeks, as the crowd parted and they made their way to the front pew, and took their places. Alex was relieved there was no casket. It would have put her over the edge, and killed their mother. It was easier not having anything.

The service was simple and respectful. The choir sang in their pure voices. Vicar Peterson spoke of William as a boy and a young man, of his skill as a pilot, and how much he would be missed by everyone. He reminded the assembled company that William had given his life for king and coun-try, and had been a hero to the end. He had no sweetheart that they were aware of when he died. Geoff knew he'd been seeing a girl in the Women's Auxiliary Air Force, at the base, but he didn't think it was serious. William hadn't wanted to get deeply involved with anyone after the war started, unlike Geoff who wanted to go out with all the women he could lay his hands on.

The vicar handed Victoria a single white rose from the arrangements Alex had carefully made the night before, and the family walked out of the church into the bright sunlight. Months later, there would be a new headstone in their family cemetery on the estate, but for now there was no reason to go there. They stood looking lost outside the church, as people filed by to shake their hands or embrace them, and when it was over, Alex drove them home. There were services like this one all over England, particularly since the Battle of Britain had begun a month before, and now they were part of the bereaved families who had lost their sons to this terrible war.

They got home at lunchtime, and the children had made a wreath of wildflowers and placed it on the door. Victoria smiled when she saw it. They went into the kitchen, and Geoff and Edward sat at the kitchen table, while Alex and Victoria made a simple lunch, which they attempted to eat but could barely swallow.

Victoria went to take a nap after that, and Edward walked upstairs with her. Alex and Geoff took a walk all the way to the pond at the far end of the property, where they had played as children and chased the ducks and geese.

"Remember when the bastard pushed me into the pond on New Year's Day when I was seven?" Geoff asked her and she nodded with a wintry smile.

"You cried all the way back to the house, and Papa shouted at him and said he could have drowned you. I was only five, but I still remember it perfectly." They both smiled at the memory, although it had seemed traumatic when it happened.

"I can't believe he's never coming back," Geoff said softly. "I keep expecting him to walk in and tell us it was all a mistake." They both wished it had been, but it was beginning to sink in.

The four of them stayed close together that night and the next day. The day after that, Geoff had to leave and report back to the air base. He and Alex clung to each other when he left, and their mother sobbed openly, begging him to be careful. Alex spent another day with them after Geoff went back, and then she had to leave too. She sat on the train, staring at her feet, and thinking about her brothers and her parents, when a man in uniform stepped into the first-class compartment and sat down. He was wearing the familiar RAF uniform she knew so well, and she avoided his eyes, once she recognized it. She didn't want to talk to a pilot, and have to explain about her brother. It was all too fresh to mention to a stranger, and he didn't speak to her either. He just sat down and stared out the window. Eventually he took a book out of the bag he was carrying. She didn't bother to look at what it was. But she noticed that he was tall, good looking, and had dark hair and warm brown eyes.

They'd been traveling for an hour, when they stopped at a station, and he glanced up from his book, saw the sign on the platform, and smiled at her. They were stopping at every station, which made the trip seem endless.

"It's going to be a long journey at this rate," he commented, "if you're going back to London too." She nodded, and he picked up the book again, and then closed it half an hour later. "Visiting friends or family in Hampshire?" She hadn't seen him when they had boarded the train, but he had noticed her. It would have been hard not to. A pretty blonde with a good figure. She was wearing her hair in a knot again, with the neatly pinned roll in front, and the bright red lipstick she wore every day now. It was her look ever since she'd moved to London. She was wearing a simple black suit, black stockings, and high heels, and wasn't in uniform, since wearing it off duty was optional because the First Aid Nursing Yeomanry was voluntary. She wore her uniform proudly at work, but rarely off duty, except when she went out to eat right after work with some of the other women.

"My parents," she answered his question. "I grew up in Hampshire," she said quietly.

"I came to visit friends, but they had to go to a

funeral while I was there," and as he said it, he noticed the black suit and black stockings and wondered if that was why she had gone home, and if
the funeral his friends had gone to was somehow
connected to her. They lapsed back into silence as
he glanced at her sympathetically, and then the train
stopped at another station a short time later. "I'm
sorry," he said softly, remembering that the funeral
had been for a young RAF pilot. "Your brother?"
he asked, and she nodded, as tears filled her eyes
and she looked away. He could easily imagine that
even his uniform was painful for her, and he wasn't
wrong. "I'm Richard Montgomery," he introduced
himself, and held out a hand. He didn't want to intrude on her, nor be rude either.

"Alexandra Wickham," she said politely as they
shook hands, which jogged his memory again. The
young pilot's name had been Wickham.

"It's an ugly war," he said with a hard look in
his eyes, and then he left her alone, and didn't talk
to her again. She fell asleep, and didn't wake until
they reached London. He helped her carry her bag
onto the platform. "Will you be all right on your
own?" He was worried about her, she looked so devastated. She nodded and then smiled at him.

"I'm fine. Thank you. Where are you stationed?"
she asked, just to be polite, and when he said it, it
was the same place Geoff was based.

"I have a brother there too, in Bomber Command.
My brother who died was a fighter pilot."

"I lead a fighter squadron." She could see that he was older than her brothers, though only by a few years. He was thirty-two.

"I'm with the First Aid Nursing Yeomanry," she said, and he nodded.

"You must work hard," he said, walking her into the station. Then he handed her her bag. "Take good care of yourself, Miss Wickham," he said kindly.

"You too."

"Maybe we'll run into each other again," he said with a hopeful look, but they both knew it was unlikely. London was a big city, teeming with people in chaotic circumstances now. "What's your brother's name in Bomber Command, in case I run into him at the base?"

"Geoff Wickham." He smiled at her again and they both walked away. He turned and waved at her, and then hurried for the exit, and she took a bus back to her dormitory. She was tired when she got there and signed in, and told the matron she would report for work the next day. She gave Alex a little pat on her shoulder and Alex went to her room. All the other girls were asleep in their bunks and she was grateful she didn't have to talk to anyone that night.

She reported for duty, in uniform, at six o'clock the next morning, for her assignment as an ambulance driver. It was an early shift. She finished work twelve hours later, too tired to think, which was a relief, and was surprised to find a note on the message board for her. It had a captain's name and a phone number. She didn't recognize the name, and wondered what it was about. It sounded official, but it was too late to call by then. She had a later shift the next day, so she tried the number the next morning before she left for work at eight A.M. She was back on ambulances again. The name on the message slip was Captain Bertram Potter. He answered the call on the first ring.

"Miss Wickham?" he asked, and she confirmed it. "Good of you to call me back. I'm calling from Special Operations Executive. We've been in existence for about a month, since we got Cabinet approval in July, and I'm sure you haven't heard of us yet. I'd like to have a chat with you, if you have the time. One of your superiors at the Yeomanry recommended you. You have some language skills that might be helpful to us. Do you have time to stop around sometime today?" She had no idea what he wanted, or why anyone had recommended her, but he sounded pleasant.

"I'll be working till about eight or nine tonight."

"What time do you start tomorrow?" he asked her.

"Eight A.M. if I'm on ambulances, slightly later if I'm driving lorries."

"Is a seven o'clock meeting too early for you?"

"No, it's fine," she sounded surprised that he was so eager to see her.

"Good. We're on Baker Street." He gave her the

address and told her to come to the second floor, and ask for him. "I'll have some strong coffee for you. Thank you for coming in at that hour. I like to get an early start."

"Not at all." After she hung up, she wondered if they wanted her to do translations for them, since he had mentioned her language skills. Other than that she knew nothing and had no idea what to expect. She asked the matron in her dormitory what the Special Operations Executive was, and she said she had no idea. There were so many special offices and volunteer bureaus being formed that she couldn't keep up with them.

Alex got up at five-thirty the next morning in order to get to Baker Street on time, and she was there promptly at seven, in her uniform. She had to report at lorries at eight-thirty, but it gave her an hour with Captain Potter before she'd have to leave, which ought to be enough if he wanted to give her some translating to do later. She could do it at night in her dorm, in bed with a torch, if the lights were out.

She asked a woman in uniform at a desk for Captain Potter and after she went to tell him Alex was there, he came out and escorted her to a small barren office with no windows and nothing on the walls. He was austere looking with thinning blond hair and piercing blue eyes. He looked to be about forty. He was wearing an old tweed jacket. She looked around and wondered what they did there. There was no clue in the decor.

"We just opened the office a month ago in July, as I told you on the phone. We're not fully set up yet, but we are efficiently staffed. We're a fairly large group of operatives, many of them women, who take on special assignments of a confidential nature. Some of it can be quite dangerous work, and some of it is less so. It can be as simple as translations, and we understand that you are flawlessly fluent in French and German, which could be very useful to us. You might be asked to translate radio transmission codes, fill out documents, or you could be asked to do forgeries, work in code or invisible ink. If you're willing, we may ask you to go behind enemy lines and bring back information, create reconnaissance maps, or get forms for us to fill out, to use as papers for our agents in the field." Alex was watching him closely in fascination, trying to understand what he was saying and where this was leading.

"How would I get behind enemy lines?" she asked in nearly a whisper.

"In a variety of ways, by train, or we might parachute you in, in certain instances. Some assignments are more extreme than others. Sometimes sabotage could be involved. You would be trained of course in weaponry, self-defense, and how to defend yourself specifically behind enemy lines. Mostly you would be sent on reconnaissance missions, to bring back information, and to aid Resistance groups in enemy areas and occupied zones." France had fallen to the Germans two months earlier.

"Are we talking about espionage?" Alex asked with a look of amazement. He didn't answer for a minute, and then he nodded.

"Yes, we are. You're a perfect candidate for us because of your excellent French and German. Does any of this sound interesting or possible to you? You would have to be unfailingly discreet, no one can know that you're working for us, or what you do. That could be awkward if you have a fiancé or a boyfriend, who would wonder where you disappear to periodically and question you. You would have to agree to keep your work for us a secret for twenty years, even from your family, or spouse, or children later on. We're a top-secret commando unit, and officially we do not exist. You would have a high security clearance, particularly if you'd be willing to go behind enemy lines for us. And of course, you'd have a cyanide pill, if things go too wrong. But, with a good set of papers, and your German skills, you're much less likely to run into trouble." Alex sat and stared at him for a long time.

"You're asking me to be a spy?" She didn't know if she should be flattered or terrified, or both.

"An agent," he corrected, "of the SOE. We have big plans for our branch, and a considerable number of operatives signed up already, recruited from other bureaus. We're getting them from the military and some of the volunteer groups. You fit our profile quite perfectly," he said coolly. "The beauty of what we're doing is that we can do things military personnel cannot. We have more leeway."

"My brother was just shot down and killed by the Germans," she said grimly.

"I'm sorry to hear it, but in a way that's immaterial in this job. We're asking you to perform missions with precision and training, not emotion. Your reasons for joining us are your own, but at no time can you allow your personal feelings to interfere with an assignment. You need to be clear about that before you start. If you want to work with us, that is."

"I've never thought of doing something like this. I volunteered with the Yeomanry because I wanted to help the war effort."

"I'm sure you are helping, but someone else can drive an ambulance or a lorry. Not everyone is able to do what you can, with your fluent French and German. You'd be the perfect operative to send behind enemy lines, if you can keep a cool head. But you and we will both know more about that once we train you. And if you work for the SOE, you would be paid in cash, so there is no trace of it. It's not an exorbitant amount given the risks. We don't want you suddenly having a large amount of money you can't account for. It's a reasonable sum. I assume you're supported by your parents." She nodded. Alex looked at her watch then and saw that it was almost time for her to leave for work, and she wasn't sure if he wanted her to make a decision on the spot. He was asking for a big commitment in an obviously high risk operation. She would have liked to discuss it with someone, like her father or brother, but the captain had made it clear that she couldn't. She would have to make her mind up on her own.

"You're welcome to give it some thought, if you feel you need to do that." He saw her hesitation. "There's no question, these aren't ordinary missions, and some of them can be dangerous. But they're exciting and interesting too, and you'd be making a **real** difference to the war effort, bringing us vital information we need, and wreaking havoc on their side. That's what we all want, and what we need to win the war." As he said it, in spite of his earlier warning, she thought of William shot down by the Germans, and suddenly she wanted to take the job he was offering, not as revenge, but for justice. The Germans could not, should not, win the war. And if she could help her country win it, she wanted to do that. Hitler had to be stopped, before half the children in Europe were dead or orphans.

"I'll do it," she said in a single breath. "I want to. When do I start?" There was a fire in her eyes that he had hoped to see, and now it was there burning brightly. It was passion, love of country, and wanting to do more than drive a lorry over what remained of a building. They needed people just like her, who were willing to die for their country, so others could be free. She looked like a brave girl to him. What he needed were agents with immense courage, determination, and a passion for freedom. After talking to her, something told him that Alexandra Wickham was just that kind of woman.

He stood up and shook hands with her then, more than pleased with their meeting. "Say nothing to anyone, Miss Wickham. If anyone asks, you can say I was looking for volunteer nurses' aides. And after this, do not discuss anything you heard today. Your friends and family don't need to know you've left the Yeomanry. If they discover it, you can say you're working with the pumpers on the street, helping to put out fires, or with the air raid wardens, getting people into shelters. They can never know you work for us from now on for the next twenty years, even after the war ends. Can you live with that kind of secret?" She nodded affirmatively and looked as though she meant it. It was for a good cause, the best one of all, the survival and freedom of England.

"Yes, I can. I don't need to tell anyone."

"We'll advise you when to report for training. You'll live with other female agents, in a barracks, all of whom appear to work for a variety of volunteer services, and all of whom will have top secret clearance like you. From now on, what you do, where you go, who you know, what you see is a secret. Even among other agents. And if you suspect someone you know or are related to is also an operative, you never ask. When you see an agent you know

is one on the street or anywhere, you never greet
them. You can expect to hear from us sometime in
the next month. We're putting a class together now.
We'll expect you to come within hours, after we call
you. And if you do have a boyfriend, you can't tell
him anything either. You need to come and go freely
with no explanations to anyone. Understood?"

"Yes, sir." She stood up, smiling at him, and wishing she could start at that moment, and not wait to
be called.

"Take care of yourself in the meantime." He sat
back down at his desk then, and she left his office,
stunned by everything that had happened. She was
twenty-four years old, and she had just become a
spy for the British government. All she knew was
that she was working for the SOE now. She hoped
that her brother would have been proud of her,
since there was not a soul in the world she could
tell. From now on, whatever happened, she was on
her own.

Chapter 3

As Alex had been instructed, she said nothing to anyone about her meeting with Bertram Potter. Geoff came to London to have dinner with her the following week, and he was still deeply depressed by their brother's death, and obsessed with killing Germans now. It was all he talked about, and Alex was sad after having dinner with him. He was suddenly bitter and angry, and fixated on revenge. He barely spoke of anything else.

The following night, she was lying in her bunk still awake at midnight, thinking about her meeting with Captain Potter and wondering when she'd be called, when the air raid sirens went off. They were all used to it by now, the blackouts and curfews, and air raids at night. She and fifty other women went rapidly down the stairs in their shoes and bathrobes to the shelter underground. It was always stifling and crowded. They all kept something by their bedsides to wear if they had to evacuate in a hurry. The important thing was wearing solid shoes, and she did. There were always rocks in the street now, and debris from buildings that had been bombed. She rushed down the stairs with the others in orderly fashion, left the building, and hurried up the street to the bomb shelter they went to almost every night. They could already hear the planes coming and the first bombs drop several miles away, as they arrived at the bomb shelter, where easily another hundred people had already found their way. Others had gone to the Tube stations underground, the subways, which had a greater capacity.

There were naked bulbs hanging from the ceiling, a floor of planks had been set down, there were benches throughout. Some volunteer group had left blankets because it got very cold and damp at night, and there were some toys for the children. Sometimes it was hours before the all clear would sound if the Luftwaffe pelted them all night. Alex thought of her brother in his downed plane again as she hurried down the stairs in an old pair of brogues she had worn ten years ago as a young girl. They were the most solid shoes she owned and she had brought them from home for this purpose. She sat on a bench with a group of other women, several of them had babies in their arms. A few of them nursed them to keep them quiet.

Most of the men sat on the wooden planks on the floor. She noticed a few men in uniform, who had obviously been out late, visiting someone, probably their girlfriends. She noticed a dark haired, broad shouldered RAF officer with his back to her, and paid no particular attention to him. It was late and everyone was tired, and there was always the question of what would remain of the houses they lived in. What if they came out of the shelter and found them destroyed? It was a possibility they had to face every day, the prospect of losing everything and even the people they loved. It made Alex long for Hampshire for a few minutes, and her parents' peaceful life there.

They could hear the bombs dropping and feel the walls of the shelter shake, and it was two full hours before the all clear finally sounded. The Luftwaffe had emptied their full load and were heading home.

There were fires everywhere when they came out of the shelter, and pumping crews doing their best to fight the flames. A building had collapsed and there was debris all over the street. Alex helped a woman with two children who said her husband was in the navy. And as she assisted one of the children to step over the rubble, and dodged an ambulance with its headlamps covered for the blackout, the dark haired man in uniform spoke to her.

"Miss Wickham?" She didn't know who he was at first, and then recognized him as the man on the train when she'd come back from Hampshire a few days before, after Willie's funeral service. He had said he hoped their paths would cross again and now they had. She looked up as she pulled her dressing gown around her, but she didn't recall his surname. He was Richard Something, but she couldn't remember what. She was too tired to search her memory now. She had to be at work in six hours.

"Oh, hello," she said, looking tired and distracted, as the mother reclaimed her child's hand, thanked Alex, and left. It had been a long night and that was familiar now.

"Richard Montgomery," he said, supplying his name for her. "Are you all right? Where do you live? I'll walk you back."

"Thank you, I live in a dormitory just down the street. I'll be fine." There were fire trucks trying to approach the scene, and crews shoveling the debris of the fallen building out of their path.

"It was a bad one tonight," he commented, as he took her arm to steady her, when she stumbled on a rock. "I was visiting a friend and about to head back to the base, when the sirens started. I have to be back in a few hours." She nodded, and wondered if he was flying a mission that day. Most of them were at night, unless they needed daylight to hit their target more precisely. There had been some mistakes made at night.

"We've lost three buildings on this street since I got back," she said, sounding tired. "They never let up." She felt desperately sorry for the people who lost their homes, or dug frantically through the rubble looking for people they loved who hadn't gotten out.

They were at her dormitory by then, which once again had been unharmed. It was no thing of beauty, but it was home for now. He looked at her when they got there.

"This is a terrible time and place to ask," he said, apologetic. "But I don't know how to reach you. Would you have dinner with me sometime? Say day after tomorrow?" She felt a shiver run down her spine as she realized that if he didn't show up, it would mean he had been shot down. But that was the way things were for now. You never knew who would die today or tomorrow, or still be alive next week, let alone in a year. He gazed at her pleadingly as though it was important to him, and she didn't have the heart to turn him down, although she had other things on her mind. This was no time for her to get involved with a man, with the job she had just accepted with the SOE as a spy. And what if they called her for training tomorrow night? Then she would stand him up.

"I'll try," she said. "Sometimes I get called in to work at the last minute, or have to work all night." It wasn't really true, but if the SOE called her and she didn't show up, she needed some excuse. She would have to start lying now and become good at it. "Is there somewhere I can leave you a message if

I can't make it?" He jotted a number on a piece of paper and handed it to her. She tore off a corner and wrote down the number of the dormitory and gave it back to him. "You can leave a message for me here if you need to. Where shall we meet?" He gave her the name of a fish restaurant she'd been to. It wasn't fancy, but it was clean, the food was good, and it was a quiet place to talk. It wasn't too crowded or too noisy, and they were open for dinner in spite of the blackouts and rationing. Some restaurants were only open for lunch now.

"Seven o'clock?" he suggested.

She nodded. "I finish at six. I'm starting at six in the morning that day."

"Don't worry, if you're late, I'll wait for you." She wanted to clean up at least a little before she met him. She was sorry he hadn't suggested her day off, when she'd have had time to wear a decent dress and heels. "See you then," he said smiling at her, and she saw that he had kind eyes. She had noticed that on the train too. There was a gentleness about him despite his obvious strength, the broad shoulders, and his height. He was handsome, but that seemed less important now. She waved as she disappeared into the dormitory, and hoped that his mission went well. If not, it would be one more loss to add to countless others. She already knew so many people who had died, not just her brother.

She reported for work a few hours later, and forced

herself not to think of Richard. She couldn't afford to invest much emotion in anyone now. Their lives were all too ephemeral, particularly his as a pilot, and hers when she went to work for the SOE.

There was no air raid that night, miraculously, and she worked a twelve-hour shift the next day driving an ambulance and barely had time to wash her face and brush her hair and put on a skirt and blouse with a red jacket before she met Richard at the fish restaurant. She looked pretty and young despite the haste with which she'd dressed, and he was happy to see her. His whole face lit up when she arrived. He was waiting for her when she got there, which meant he was still alive and hadn't been shot down, which was something to be grateful for. He looked just as relieved to see her.

"These days, you never know who's still going to be around from day to day," he said, and then was embarrassed when he remembered her brother. "I'm sorry, I shouldn't have said that."

"Why not? It's true," Alex said simply. "I don't like to think of it that way, but several of the girls I work with have been killed in air raids when buildings collapsed, and my brother . . . there's no predicting who's going to survive all this. I've seen people climb out of the rubble who you'd never have thought would survive it, like a man the other day who told me he was eighty-five. And then a bomb drops, and a hundred people are killed, including women and children."

"My sister, Jane, was killed in one of the first air raids," he said quietly. "She was on a pump crew, trying to fight a fire. She was a teacher, her students loved her. She was helping an elderly neighbor to the shelter, the woman could hardly walk. They never got there, and they were both killed. War teaches us a lot about destiny, and that you can't predict anything. I fly bombing missions over Germany almost every day, and I'm still alive, for now. And she's not."

"Your parents must be devastated," Alex said sympathetically, thinking of her own, still in shock over William's death just a week before.

"Both of my parents died before the war. Maybe it's just as well. They were killed in an accident, together. Maybe that was better than all this." There was something very serious about him, and his eyes were so gentle. "Tell me about yourself before the war," he said, smiling at her, and she laughed.

"There's not much to tell. A quiet life in Hampshire, too quiet for me. I rode my horse every day. I love to hunt with my brothers. We're all mad riders. I came out six years ago, and had a proper London Season, which seemed somewhat ridiculous to me, although some of it was fun. Lots of parties and balls and people to meet and pretty dresses, and then after six months it's all over. I failed to find a husband, and didn't want one, so I went back to Hampshire with my parents, which was something of a relief. Then boredom set in. Watercolors and needlepoint, and I have a passion for books. I know more about the crops on my father's property than he does, but I don't want to be a farmer either. I signed up as a volunteer and ran for London almost as soon as the war started, and I've been here for almost a year now. I'll have a hard time going back to Hampshire when it's over. I like the hustle bustle of London, and feeling useful driving a truck. I don't suppose that's a career I could embrace either, but I have no training for anything else. I wanted to go to university and study literature but my father wouldn't let me. I was brought up by governesses and tutors at home, and I always wanted to go to a normal school."

"If you have a passion for reading, you probably learned more at home than you would have at school," he said, smiling at her. His father had been a gentleman farmer, but after hearing about her London Season, and being schooled by governesses, he could tell that she far outranked him in the hierarchy of British society, and he suspected her parents wouldn't approve of him. They obviously had greater aspirations for their daughter, which she didn't seem to share. She seemed to be very pleased not to be married, and was enjoying her life in London, despite the perils of war. "Do you think you might stay in London afterward?" he asked, curious about her. He had a feeling she was headstrong, and had her own ideas, which didn't include languishing in Hampshire, especially now that she had tasted city life on her own. There were a number of young women in London like her, and Richard had a strong suspicion that society as they knew it was going to undergo some drastic changes after the war.

"I'll certainly try to stay," she said, "although my parents won't like it and will put up a fight for me to come home. They're willing to let me be here for king and country, as part of the war effort. But after that, they'll want me back where I was, and where they think I belong." It occurred to her as she said it that they certainly didn't expect her to join a top secret commando unit as part of her volunteer work, and become a spy.

"I think a lot of women will be in your situation. They're an important part of the workforce now, and they won't want to give that up when the men come home. They've gotten some independence, even if they're not paid as well as men. That's not fair, but at least they've gotten out of the kitchen, and into offices and factories. It's a big step for women." She was surprised by how liberal and modern he was. He seemed to like the idea of women working, if they wanted to.

"I'd have to go to university if I want a decent job," Alex said. "I don't think driving a lorry after the war would be challenging enough for me," she said and he laughed.

"I can see that would be the case." She was an extremely bright young woman with a fine mind and a number of ideas that didn't include sitting by the fire in Hampshire doing petit point and embroidery. But she hadn't figured out her future path yet, or how to get there. First, they all had to survive, which was by no means a sure thing at the moment. They were grateful to be alive every day.

They talked about the travel she'd done with her parents, and her visits to New York and Boston with them. They had gone to Egypt, on an archaeological study trip, and had toured extensively in Italy and Spain. She had never been to Asia but thought it would be fascinating.

Richard's life before the war had been much smaller, although he had gone to Cambridge after eight years in a boarding school in Scotland, which he said had been exactly like prison. His sister, Jane, had gone to a very good boarding school for young women. He had been properly brought up and educated, just not quite at the social level of her parents, which she didn't care about, but Richard felt sure they would. People of her parents' generation and background expected their daughters to marry within the aristocracy, and preferably someone with a title, not a gentleman farmer with a good education, no title or fortune and a very small farm. In their real world, after the war, he had nothing to offer her that they would approve of. Knowing that didn't stop him from wanting to spend time with her, and the war gave them opportunities to meet and get to know each other that they wouldn't have had otherwise. He was thirty-two, eight years older than Alex, which didn't seem like a problem to either of them.

They had a lovely evening together, and then he took her back to the dormitory, and she thanked him for dinner. He asked if she could dine with him again on Saturday, which was going to be his first full day off in a month, and she had the day off too. They agreed to go to Hyde Park together for a walk, and he suggested a restaurant she didn't know. It sounded wonderful to her, providing they were both alive by then, and he didn't get sent on an emergency mission so his day off would have to be canceled.

That didn't happen. He picked her up at her dormitory at noon on Saturday, and they stopped for fish and chips, which they ate sitting in the park. Then they went for a long walk, admiring the gardens and small pavilions, and rowed a small boat on a lake. He was impressed by how knowledgeable she was about art, particularly the French Impressionists and the artists of the Italian Renaissance, when she talked about it.

"You could teach art history," he said as he rowed her across the lake.

"Hardly. I don't have the education to teach. I know the kind of things governesses teach you. But I know nothing about science, and I'm terrible at math. I can do a perfect waltz, and dance a quadrille without missing a step. My brother Geoff worked at a bank before the war. He went to university. I didn't."

"You probably know more on certain subjects than most people who did."

"My French governess's father taught art history at the Sorbonne. She taught me all about French art. I learned about Italian art from books."

"I know nothing about art," he readily admitted. "I studied Chaucer and British literature at Cambridge. It's not very useful unless you want to teach."

"When did you learn to fly?" She wanted to know more about him too.

"My father was a flying ace in the Great War. He used to take me up in his plane with him from the time I was a young boy. I caught the bug from him. I spent all my time and money on flying planes. I suppose I could be a commercial pilot after the war. I made money giving flying lessons before the war when I finished at Cambridge. But you can't make much money at it. I couldn't have supported a family. I hadn't figured out what I wanted to be when I grew up, when war was declared and I enlisted. That's how I got to be a squadron leader. I've been flying for about fifteen years. Most of my pilots only learned recently. I have a few hot pilots, and I'm lucky to have them, but most of them are wet behind the ears, very green. I flew in air shows for prize money. What I learned saved my life more than a few times since we started flying missions."

"My brother William loved flying too. He probably wasn't as experienced as you, but planes were his passion," she said wistfully. "I still can't believe he's gone." Richard nodded and didn't say anything, but touched her hand, and she was moved by the gesture. He was a gentle person, and a nice man. He was respectful of her way of life, and her limited education, which he respected more than she did. She always felt like the victim of a society that didn't want women to be educated. She was hungry for knowledge, and soaked it up like a sponge.

"One day, I'll take you up in a plane, and we'll go flying together, after the war," he offered. She liked thinking that it was a possibility, although she wasn't counting on it. He wanted to. He had something to look forward to now. It helped soothe the pain of having lost his sister months before. They had that in common, they had each lost a sibling to the war.

Their dinner was perfect. The food was delicious and the atmosphere genteel, and he seemed perfectly at ease there with her. He was every inch a gentleman, by birth and education, but he had no fortune, and no blue blood in his veins. He was certain it would be a problem sooner or later, and she insisted it was nonsense. He knew better, and had been brushed off by the aristocratic parents of women he had gone out with before. He was respectable, but not thought to be worthy of their daughters. Alex wouldn't let him dwell on it, and dismissed his concerns as ridiculous. Besides, they weren't getting married. They were just having dinner, she reminded him.

The day they spent together was just what they had wanted it to be. It was magical for both of them, and a blessed relief from the pains of the last months and the constant stress of the war bearing down on them for the past year since it began. Hitler's war machine was functioning perfectly, although the RAF's victories had recently outnumbered the Luftwaffe's, which meant that more Germans had died than Allies, which was a grim way to look at it.

Richard didn't kiss her when he left her at the dormitory, though he wanted to. He was respectful and polite and good company, and seriously smitten with her. He would be flying missions over Germany every day for the next week, and he told her he'd call her when he had some time off again. They both hoped it would be soon.

Alex floated into the dormitory, and fell asleep thinking about him that night. Geoff called her on Sunday and she didn't tell him about Richard. She thought it was too soon, and nothing major had happened yet. Just two dates.

She went for a walk that afternoon with some of the other women, and when she got back, Captain Potter called her at six o'clock. He gave her the address of a barracks that had been set up for "volunteers," as he put it. And he told her who to report to there. She would be driven to their training center, Experimental Station 6, at Ashton Manor in Hertfordshire.

"You start training tomorrow. Report for duty at 0700 hours. Don't worry about the First Aid Nursing Yeomanry. We'll handle them. We've already taken several of their people into the SOE. Just tell them tonight that you can't work tomorrow. We'll call them in the morning, and release you. Good luck, Miss Wickham," he said, sounding very official, and as she hung up, her hand was shaking. She hoped she had done the right thing, agreeing to work for them. It was too late to change her mind now, and she wouldn't have anyway. Whatever it took, she was going to see it through.

She went upstairs to pack after that, before the other women came back from dinner. Her suitcase was packed by then, and she had slid it under her bed. She couldn't even say goodbye to the friends she'd made there. All she could say was that she'd been offered a place in another dormitory for volunteers. She had no idea whether or not she'd see any of them again. War was a time of constant losses and goodbyes, while pretending you believed you'd see each other again soon.

If Geoff or Richard called her, they wouldn't know where she had gone either. Captain Potter had said she would have a contact number at the SOE, but social contacts were discouraged during training, and she had a month of training ahead of her. She would just have to give them some excuse as to why she couldn't see them. Long hours, too much work, a series of emergencies, and maybe a bout of influenza. She'd think of something. Her life of mystery was about to begin, and she'd have to get used to lying to them, because she couldn't tell them when she went on missions. Geoff and Richard had the same constraints to deal with, but they were flying missions, not spying. Her life was about to become a web of lies, even to her family, and those she loved. If she and Richard continued to see each other, she'd be lying to him too, for a noble cause. She didn't regret it for a minute. Even if it was complicated, it was worth it.

She was about to become a spy for the SOE, with everything that entailed. She had no idea what that was yet. But she was about to find out, starting at seven A.M. the next day. Alex was still shaking with anticipation when she went to bed. She was glad Richard didn't call her that night. She wasn't ready to start lying to him yet. But she knew she would have to soon, and for a long, long time to come. Twenty years, if they both lived that long, and still knew each other then.

Chapter 4

Alex had no idea what she was getting into when she joined the SOE, but she learned rapidly. Everything moved at full speed, from the moment she arrived at the training center where she would spend the next month and dropped off her suitcase. She went to collect the uniforms they would wear during training. They were fatigues. There were eleven other women in her class. They were all given code names and not allowed to divulge their real names to anyone, even each other. Alex became the Cobra. An hour after they arrived, they were in a judo class, learning self-defense, with instructors who spared them no pain, and tossed each of the women on the mats as easily as flipping crepes. They tripped them, nearly strangled them, held them hostage, pitted them against each other and the instructors. Alex felt as though she was bruised from head to foot after two hours of it.

From there they went to a map-making class and were taught how to make precise maps and diagrams. After they diligently copied the maps they were shown, they had to destroy them and re-create them, meticulously, from memory. They did it again and again, and were told that in the next month they would hone their new skills to perfection.

"I can hardly walk after the judo class," the girl next to Alex whispered to her as they left the map class. After that they were taught how to falsify documents and do forgeries. They each made countless mistakes and had to start over again. And their final class of the day was on how to wield the small, lethal commando knife they were to keep on their person at all times from now on. It was small, as light as a feather, and looked like a child's toy, but they were told they could kill a man twice their size with it, once they learned to use it correctly. Two of the girls cut themselves with their knives during the exercises, and by the time they went back to their barracks, they were all mentally and physically drained.

Alex was too tired to eat dinner, and went to bed instead, as did several of the other women. They were woken at two A.M. for another judo class and expected to be instantly alert when attacked by army instructors. They were allowed to go to bed for two hours afterward, and were woken again at six for an exercise regimen, followed by a breakfast of porridge and then taken to a shooting gallery, where they were taught to use weapons, tiny pistols they would carry at all times, rifles, Sten guns, and submachine guns. The expert marksmen who were instructing them said that the Sten gun would be their most useful weapon. It was automatic and came apart, and was extremely lightweight.

They broke for lunch, and then came back to the shooting gallery for additional lessons. They ended the day with another forgery class. SOE had a department they called Station XIV, which did only forgeries with the precision of Old Masters. All the women in Alex's group felt clumsy as they tried to emulate the delicate work.

They had language instruction that night in both German and French. The instructors tried to trip them up and confuse them, and distract them into slipping into English, which all of them did as they got tired, except Alex who was able to think in both German and French.

In the days that followed they were taught espionage, sabotage, how to handle a grenade, how to kill a man or woman with their commando knives, and how to shoot their weapons accurately. Their memories were challenged constantly.

By the end of the first week, three of the women had dropped out, begging for mercy. They couldn't stand the extreme pressure, the demanding lessons, the challenges, and the mental and physical abuse. The women who remained were determined to stay the course, Alex among them, but every lesson pushed them to their limits and stretched them beyond what they thought possible to endure. They were taught to swim long distances underwater, how to remove a bullet and stitch their own skin. They were taught to transmit by radio and to use couriers. They learned various codes, and how to decode messages. They had to memorize whole pages of text and then reproduce them perfectly, in case they had to destroy a vital document and then re-create it when they returned from a mission. They were taught what to say if arrested. The judo lessons continued and were increasingly brutal. They were taught to shoot to kill with all of the guns they handled and how to land with a parachute.

It was the most terrifying, exhausting, challenging, excruciating month of Alex's life. The women hardly slept, and had to commit everything to memory. They had to strive beyond excellence to perfection. They could make no mistakes. Lives depended on it, theirs and others. They were taught how to conceal their cyanide pill, when to take it, and how. At the end of the month, Alex's brain felt like hamburger meat, her body like she'd been beaten to a pulp daily, but her maps and forgeries were impeccable, she could hit the bull's-eye with any of the guns they'd been taught to use. When she was asked to attack the judo instructor, she broke his nose, and he congratulated her. She had learned everything they taught her, and she had stretched her memory to its limits and could reproduce up to three pages of documents and decode everything they gave her to decipher. She only broke down and cried on the last day when they told her she had passed, which she found incredible. She was sure that they would reject her at the end of the course. She had never worked so hard in her entire life.

Alex had called and left messages for Geoff twice, and Richard once, to say she was working crazy double shifts at odd hours and couldn't see them for a few weeks, but assured them that she was fine. Geoff only called her once at the number she had left him for messages. Richard had called four times to say he was thinking of her and hoped she wasn't exhausted by her long hours, and he looked forward to seeing her when she was back to normal shifts.

At the end of the course, she was sent to a dormitory for lorry drivers, who were actually part of Military Intelligence and also worked as decoders. She was to tell anyone who asked that she only drove lorries now, and had to make deliveries throughout England and Scotland, to cover her absences, which they told her would be frequent, although usually brief. She was given three days off, and all she wanted to do was sleep, but she dutifully called Richard and her brother. Geoff was flying a mission when she called, and Richard called her back two hours later on her new contact number. He was relieved when he heard her voice.

"You must be exhausted, Alex. You've been working double shifts for four weeks and two days." He had kept careful count and sounded ecstatic to finally speak to her.

"I'm okay, just tired." There was no way she could have explained it all to him, even if she'd been allowed to. She had been transformed into a lethal machine to gather information, and destroy anyone who interfered with her. She wore a small pistol and her commando knife in a leather sheath at all times now, and knew how to use them as efficiently as any soldier. She concealed them in her clothing, strapped to her thigh, at her waist, anywhere that she could reach them quickly but they weren't seen. She was waiting for her first assignment, but had three days to recover, unwind, and absorb everything she'd been taught until it became part of her, like breathing or her heartbeat, without effort or thought.

"Do you have time for dinner?" Richard asked hopefully.

"I have time, but I might fall asleep on my plate. I'm not sure I'd be decent company, I strongly doubt it."

"I don't care. You can snore all through the meal. I just want to see you. I'm off tonight. Can you make it?" She just wanted to sleep, without having to fight off a judo instructor, or re-create a forgery while half asleep, but she wanted to see him too.

"Sure, I'd love to." He suggested a small Indian restaurant near her old dormitory, and she told him she'd moved to other housing for lorry drivers. She wasn't driving ambulances anymore. She would be making deliveries around England, Scotland, and Ireland, of materials to build bunkers in the countryside, and gun emplacements on the coast. She said they were driving stones from the debris of bombed-out houses in London to build airstrips elsewhere in England, which was true, although she wasn't doing it. It was her cover story now, and he sounded surprised.

"I thought you liked the ambulance work."

"I did, but they transferred me."

"Typical," he said, and told her the Indian restaurant was casual. She didn't have the energy to put on a dress, and wore trousers and a sweater instead. The SOE wanted her to wear her old Yeomanry uniform for work around London. She'd be in civilian clothes when she went on missions for the SOE. All of her outfits would be carefully chosen for her and packed in a suitcase, depending on the role she was supposed to play. But at home, in England, her Yeomanry volunteer work was her cover. Many of the women she had met during her training and in the dormitory had started, as she had, at the Yeomanry, or in the other volunteer services.

Richard was waiting for her at the restaurant when she got there. He looked as handsome as ever and was thrilled to see her. She could have been wearing her bathrobe and he wouldn't have noticed. He gave her a warm hug when she arrived, and held her hand all through dinner when they weren't eating. It was warm in the restaurant, and without thinking she pushed the sleeves of her sweater up to her elbows, and Richard stared at her arms in horror and touched them gently. She had bruises all the way up her arms from her judo classes and she pulled her sleeves down immediately. The rest of her body looked even worse, but she was relieved he couldn't see it.

"I'm sorry, I was carrying a load of cement blocks last week, and a couple of them fell on me. It looks worse than it is."

"I'm all for women doing war work," he said, frowning, as he held her hand again, "but they can't force you into unsafe conditions that really should be men's work. That's not right, Alex." She smiled at him, happy to see him again, and be in a civilized place, after the abuse of the past four weeks.

"How safe is your job?" she asked him gently. "We all do what we have to. And driving lorries is women's work for now, whatever the load is. I'm fine. Really." He acted as though he believed her but he was worried.

"I missed you, Alex. It felt like a year to me."

"It did to me too," she said, smiling at him. It had seemed like a century. She felt as though she'd been let out of prison, but she knew that everything they had taught her would serve her well, and possibly save her life when she started doing missions behind enemy lines for the SOE.

As soon as they left the restaurant after dinner, he

kissed her. There was an urgency now to his feelings, and how he touched her.

"The last month taught me that I don't want to miss a minute with you that we can spend together." And then he hesitated before asking her a question. "Would you ever go away with me somewhere, if we could get a couple of days off at the same time?" She thought about it for a minute and looked at him earnestly.

"I might, but not so soon. Let's get to know each other better, before we do something that risky." She didn't want to get pregnant, and she knew Geoff's warnings when she came to London had been right. Lots of girls away from home for the first time were getting pregnant, and found themselves in dire situations. She didn't want to be one of them.

"I'm in love with you," Richard whispered as he held her in his arms and they stood on the street.

"I love you too," she said gently, and meant it. "But I don't want to do anything foolish that we'll regret."

"If you get pregnant, I'll marry you," he said nobly, and she shook her head.

"If we ever get married, I want it to be because we want to, not because we have to." He nodded and knew she was right. He had been frantic without her for a month, and he wanted more with her than just dinner. But he agreed to wait.

He took her to her new dormitory, which was

even uglier than the last one he'd seen, and they stood outside kissing for a long time. "Can I see you in two days?" She knew it meant he was flying the next day but she didn't ask. They both had military secrets to respect.

"I'd like that. It's my last day off," she said, as he walked her up the steps and left her at the door. He wasn't allowed inside. It was a women's dormitory, and men weren't permitted, although she'd heard that girls snuck their boyfriends in sometimes. She didn't want to do that with him. "I'd like you to meet my parents one day, and my brother," she said. It still felt strange to her to realize that now she had only one.

"I will," he promised, and they kissed one last time. She was sound asleep when her head hit the pillow a few minutes later. She slept until the matron came to tell her that her brother was on the phone. She hurried downstairs to talk to him for the first time in a month.

"Where the hell have you been?" He sounded half worried and half angry at her. He didn't like not knowing where she was.

"Driving all over England, I'm on lorry duty now."

"What did you do? Get fired from the ambulances? You're a lousy driver, Alex." He laughed when he said it and sounded relieved. "Are you working today?"

"No, I'm off," she said sleepily, glancing at the bruises on her arms, and remembering how shocked Richard had been when he'd seen them.

"I'll come to see you later. I don't have to be back on the base until four."

They had lunch together at Rules, their favorite and reminiscent of their childhoods. It was only open for lunch now. Afterward, they walked around London between the ruined buildings in her new neighborhood. It felt as though the war would go on forever, and it had only been thirteen months. So many lives had been lost, including their brother's. But Geoff looked better than he had a month before and said he was seeing a new girl, a local who lived near the air base. Her father was a butcher, and he smuggled beef for them when Geoff had dinner at their house. She wanted to tell him about Richard, but it still felt too soon. They had not even known each other for two months, and she had been away for most of it. Things happened quickly in wartime. She had never told any man before that she loved him, but it felt right with Richard. And they were both acutely aware that every time they saw each other could be their last, which intensified everything.

Geoff left her in time to get back to the base, and she lay in bed that night, thinking about Richard, and wanting to be with him. She wondered when she would get her first assignment from the SOE. They had said it could be days or weeks, and in the meantime, they would make an honest woman of her, and have her drive a lorry from time to time, just on assignments around London so she'd be close at hand, if they needed her on short notice.

She wouldn't be able to warn Richard when she was leaving, or say where she'd been when she got back. But he wasn't supposed to tell her about the missions he flew either. The war was making liars of them all.

Their dinner the next night was as sweet as all their time together had been so far. Their kisses were getting longer and more heated, and he couldn't keep his hands off her body. She was hungry for him too. She barely managed to tear herself away. She wanted to go to a hotel room with him, like most of the young couples in London, but she wanted it to be right when it happened, and not at some seedy hotel, where they pretended to be married and the desk clerk sneered at them and knew it wasn't true. She wanted their first time to be a precious memory and not feel like a cheap trick. Richard understood and didn't press her about it, although his desire for her was intense, matched by hers.

He had no time off for the rest of the week, and she got a call from the woman designated as her contact at the SOE two days after she saw Richard. She told Alex to come in to the office on Baker Street the next day. Alex knew what that meant. She left the dormitory the next morning in a simple dress and jacket, and was at the SOE office half an hour later. They already had travel papers, a passport, and a suitcase packed for her. They were sending her into Germany to bring back a hundred forms, or as many as she could get, that the Germans used as their passes to travel in the country freely, with military stamps attached. A hundred of them would allow their SOE operatives easy entry and free passage around the country without question. They wanted a hundred but would be pleased with whatever they could get.

"That's it? You want me to bring back a stack of blank passes?" It didn't seem like a difficult mission to Alex. She would have to enter Germany from Switzerland with her forged documents, as a young German woman returning from Zurich.

"You'll have to talk your way into a police station, or a Gestapo office, and steal them when no one is looking. It may not be as easy as you think," her contact, whom she only knew as Marlene, which wasn't her real name, informed her.

The suitcase they had packed for her was filled with clothes that had been purchased in Germany, right down to her shoes, hat, and underwear. Her coat had a small fur collar. She was supposed to be a secretary in a medical office in Stuttgart, traveling to Berlin to see her sister. She was returning from a medical convention in Switzerland, sent by her employer. She had all the correct papers for it, and enough deutschmarks to look plausible. She was to go to the police station to report a suspicious occurrence and steal the forms while she was there. They had a special pouch for them that she could wear under her dress. She was to be as demure and charming as possible, in perfect German. And as soon as she got the forms they wanted, she was to backtrack into Switzerland, and return to England.

It sounded simple, but had the potential to get complicated, if any part of her story aroused suspicion, or her forged documents and passport were detected. Hopefully they wouldn't be, but she'd been taught that sometimes the easiest missions went awry, in which case Alex would be detained in Germany, possibly sent to jail, a labor camp, or even shot if they suspected her as an enemy agent. Anything was possible once she was in Germany. It had been made clear to her since the beginning that if she got in trouble, she was on her own. They would not get her out. She knew the conditions and had agreed to them. She left London that night, with a forged British passport she was to destroy in the train station bathroom in Zurich when she arrived. She was carrying a small vial of acid in a lipstick to dissolve the pages, and was to dispose of the remains of the passport in the trash. Once she applied the acid, the pages would melt. She was carrying a German passport taped to her body.

Alex sat awake on the train all night, her heart beating so loud she could hear it. They reached Zurich on schedule by morning, the trip took seventeen hours. She had a cup of coffee at the train station, went to the bathroom, destroyed the British passport she'd been using, and buried the traces of it deep in the trash. She changed her clothes then, taking the German passport and travel documents out of the pouch taped to her body, and emerged from the bathroom in time to catch the early morning train to Berlin, with a ticket she purchased for a second class compartment. The trip from Zurich to Berlin took all day, fourteen hours, and from the train station she went straight to the nearest police station she was directed to when she asked. She walked in looking slightly flustered and very young and innocent. She asked to speak to a police officer, and after a brief wait was led into the police sergeant's office. She smiled shyly at him, and just looking at her he nearly melted. He was old and tired and jaded, and had been shouting at his secretary when she arrived. He was just about to leave for his dinner.

"Yes, Fraulein?" He cheered up the moment Alex walked into his office. She told him her story, that a swarthy-looking man had tried to buy her German passport and travel papers, and she thought the police should know about it. She wanted to describe him to the police so he could be caught.

"Ahh, Gypsies!" he said, with a look of immense irritation. He told her that normally it wasn't even worth his while to write a report about it, it happened so frequently, but he seemed anxious to extend her time in his office, and said that for her, because she'd taken the trouble to come to see him, he would write a report, and she was a good German citizen to do her civic duty and expose him as an unsavory person. The sergeant excused himself for a moment to get the correct form, after checking several neat stacks on the windowsill, and as soon as he left the room, Alex walked over and spotted the travel forms with the official stamp on them immediately. She took a thick bunch of them, put them inside her blouse and slipped them into the pouch, buttoned her blouse again, and sat down in a chair to wait for him. He was back five minutes later, with his hair obviously freshly combed and pomaded and reeking of cheap cologne, as he beamed at her and told her what a pleasure it was to meet such a beautiful young woman.

He wrote his report with flourishes, an explanation of the incident, and a description of the man Alex had described to him, and had Alex sign it. She did so while smiling gratefully at the policeman, and told him it was so comforting to know that men like him were protecting the innocent. As she left his office, he gazed at her longingly, shouted at his secretary again before he left for dinner, and Alex hailed a cab and went back to the station. Mission accomplished. Or almost. She still had to get back to Zurich. There was a train leaving an hour later. She bought a ticket, and made one phone call to a number in Zurich before she boarded the train, and said what time the train would be arriving in the code she had been given for the trip. She got on the train then, settled in for half an hour, and it left on time for the fourteen hour trip back to Zurich. It arrived punctually in Zurich. She bought a magazine and some candy, and went to the restroom where she and an older woman collided just inside the doorway. Alex apologized politely and they backed away from each other. The exchange had been made so smoothly it was invisible. The older woman left with Alex's German passport and travel papers, and Alex had acquired a well-used British passport with her photograph in it. There was a ticket to London on the next train in the passport. It was leaving in half an hour. Alex boarded in plenty of time, put her suitcase in the rack, sat down in the compartment, and gave her ticket to the conductor when he asked for it. The train left the station right on time, as Alex's heart pounded, and eventually she calmed down.

When she arrived in London, Alex took a taxi to Baker Street, where Marlene was waiting for her. Alex handed over the travel forms she had taken from the police station, nearly a hundred of them. She stripped off her German clothes, left the suitcase, and put her own clothes on. Precisely two days and a few hours after she had left Baker Street, for Zurich, she had returned, with her first mission completed.

"You were lucky," Marlene said, to remind her that it didn't always happen that way.

"Beginners' luck," Alex said modestly, smiling at her. Marlene didn't return the smile. She was there to do a job, at any hour, not to make friends with the agents.

"We'll be in touch when we need you," was all she said as Alex left. There was a small feeling of victory that she had done the assignment well and it had gone smoothly, and a ripple of fear, thinking about what it might have been like if it hadn't. She could have been dead by then. She shuddered thinking of the fat, greasy policeman in Berlin, reeking of hair pomade and cheap cologne. But she was in it now. There was no turning back, and she didn't want to. She was an agent of British intelligence, and beyond the fear and victory and her own amazement, there was an overwhelming feeling of pride that she had done something for her country at last, something that mattered and would save lives. And she was willing to sacrifice her own life to do it.

Chapter 5

Alex felt dazed for two weeks after her first mission in Germany, as she thought about it and it became clear to her how daring and how fortunate she had been. If any part of the assignment had gone wrong, she could have been in serious trouble. But luckily for her, it had been as smooth as silk. It was daunting to realize what a huge risk she was taking. It seemed an important thing to do, and it was in fact a way to avenge her brother's death, to outsmart the Nazis on their home turf, but she wondered if at first she had decided to do it mostly for the challenge and the excitement. She knew only too well how devastated her parents would be, if anything happened to her. Geoff was flying bombing missions almost every day. And so was Richard, which worried her too. The most effective damage they could do to the Germans, whether on land or in the air, was on their home turf. But if anything went wrong while she was there, she knew that British intelligence would not rescue her. The various officials of the SOE had said it again and again. Trying to save her would put too many other lives in danger.

They sent her on various deliveries driving a lorry several times a week, while she waited to be called for her next mission. She and Richard saw each other whenever he had a free evening and he could get into the city. She was seeing nothing of Geoff. He was having too much fun with the butcher's daughter near the base. She knew he would have killed her if he'd had any idea what she was doing. Alex's seeming innocence and youth kept her above suspicion among the people she knew who didn't work for the SOE, and Richard never questioned her. He had his own worries as commander of a fighter squadron.

One of the things Alex liked best about her new line of work was the variety of women she met, in both her training class and the dormitory where she was billeted. There were a few women who had grown up as she had in a rarefied world of debutante balls, weekend house parties among aristocrats, and governesses who had taught them to do delicate watercolors and embroidery and speak French. And at the same time she was meeting young women who had grown up in much less genteel, and sometimes much rougher, circumstances. But all of them were intelligent, dedicated, amazingly brave, and willing to face the enemy and do all they could to disable them in enemy territory, risking their lives without a second thought. Women were taking on new challenges all over England, working in factories, driving buses and lorries, doing men's jobs, as well as their traditional roles as nurses, teachers, and secretaries.

She liked talking to the girls she lived with, all of whom were officially lorry drivers, and some of whom were still officially part of the First Aid Nursing Yeomanry as she was, although in fact their main job was for the Special Operations Executive, which worked closely with Military Intelligence. In fact, they were a house full of earnest, young, highly trained spies who were truly dangerous women, no matter what walk of life they came from originally. All of their parents would have been horrified by what they knew how to do now. But the SOE had broadened Alex's horizons and her world, and she was no longer constrained by the rules and traditions she had grown up with. When she thought about it, as seldom as possible, she had no idea how she would ever be able to go back to her peaceful country life in Hampshire after the war. Her life had become exciting in ways she could never have imagined, and she felt like a free, independent woman, as she and Richard got to know each other better. The woman he had fallen in love with was not the woman she had been brought up to be, or had been little more than a year before, when the war started. She had blossomed like a flower in summer after years she had thought of as barren and meaningless before. Her life had a purpose now, and nothing could stop her from carrying it out. And Richard didn't try, since he knew nothing about her espionage activities or her real job.

After her mission in Germany, Alex was brought in for a more advanced class as a wireless operator, for which she seemed to have a natural ability. She was also very good at deciphering codes.

She had just broken a particularly tricky code at the Baker Street office, when she was called in to help them and work along with some military decoders, all of them male, and she was sent to deliver a message to the prime minister himself. Her own security clearance with the SOE was high enough to make her eligible for the errand.

She was told to go to the New Public Offices, a government building at the corner of Horse Guards Road and Great George Street, near Parliament Square. She expected to find a normal office building, and to leave the large envelope from her superiors with a secretary outside the prime minister's office. It was an honor to be entrusted with it. She could easily imagine Mr. Churchill in a beautiful wood-paneled office, smoking a cigar while he made important decisions. Instead, when she arrived, she was sent to the basement by a soldier standing guard, and proceeded down many flights of stairs to a teeming underground collection of offices and conference rooms, with officers of high rank from the army, navy, and air force, striding in and out of rooms for meetings. She caught a rapid view of an enormous map room, communication rooms with countless wireless operators sitting in front of complicated panels, and a glimpse of the prime minister himself when someone opened his door and then closed it just as quickly. Alex instantly had the sense that the entire war and the government were being run from this highly efficient overpopulated basement facility, from which, in fact, the prime minister was directing Britain's participation in the war.

After asking for directions several times, Alex was finally directed to a serious-looking woman, older than herself, who took the envelope from her and promised to deliver it. It contained some crucial new information about codes, highly sensitive and related to national security. Alex was only a messenger but it felt like a sacred mission to her to be sent to the hub of the government's war room. The complex basement compound was far below ground so it would be safe during air raids and bombings, and so everyone there could work around the clock without concern. She was fascinated by it and wished she could tell Richard about it when she saw him for dinner that night, but she couldn't, and would never violate the secrets she now knew. And he would never understand why a volunteer with the First Aid Nursing Yeomanry would be sent on an errand like this. She had a hard time believing it herself.

"So what did you do today?" Richard asked, as they settled down at a small corner table at the Indian restaurant they both liked. She noticed that he looked tired, and she sensed that he'd had a hard day.

"We collected debris off the streets, and drove it away, for the airstrips they're building," she said innocently. So many buildings had collapsed in the constant bombings that numerous streets were now impassable and some of the residential areas were a maze of blocked streets, and occasionally they found bodies, as the bulldozers cleared the rubble away. It was a depressing job she had done often, but not that day.

"I wish they'd give you an easier job," he said. "Women were supposed to do clerical work, or work in factories. They seem to have most of you doing men's work now. Some of it is just too much for a woman to handle physically." If he had seen her training with the SOE, he would have been even more in awe, and terrified for her. "I hear they're going to have all civilian women register in a few months, even grandmothers. I think the cutoff will be sixty. It's with an eye to making conscription for women mandatory in the next year, if the war continues." It was obvious to all of them now that it would.

A number of Americans had come to volunteer with the RAF, and many American women had joined the British forces too, in spite of the fact that America had not joined the Allies so far, and President Roosevelt seemed determined to keep the United States out of the war. But they were getting support from individual Americans, as well as Canadians and Australians.

Several of the women Alex had met in the SOE were of other nationalities, French, Indian, Polish, and Alex was enjoying meeting them, and getting to know them. Some of the women in top security work kept to themselves, and no one on the outside would have guessed that they were spies, just as they wouldn't have with Alex, who appeared to be an innocent young woman who had never seen anything more dangerous than a ballroom. She looked like what she was, a well-born young woman, but Richard had already discovered that she was much more than that, her interests and passions were much deeper, and her powers of observation were more acute than many of the men he worked with. The notion that women weren't able to handle the same responsibilities as men was a concept he found absurd. In fact, he found many of the women he knew even smarter than most men. His open-mindedness on the subject endeared him to Alex. He was surprisingly fair and modern in his thinking, unlike her father and brothers who thought that women should stay home, and that even driving an ambulance was too much for them to cope with.

They sat at dinner late that night, sharing their

views about Winston Churchill. Richard felt sure he was going to win the war for them, and thought him brilliant. Alex ached to say she had caught a glimpse of him through an open door only that afternoon, but she couldn't. There were no exceptions to the rules, and the high security clearance she had now reflected how trustworthy she was. She also had a permit to carry weapons, which Richard was unaware of.

The air raid sirens began just as they left the restaurant, and they hurried to the nearest shelter and spent two hours among crying children and their tired parents as the bombs fell and destroyed their homes. When they left the shelter, they walked past a small hotel, and Richard cast her a pleading look.

"I don't want to leave you, Alex. Can't we just spend a few hours there together?" She wanted that as much as he did, and was about to say no, and this time something stopped her. What if something happened to either of them? Their life now was about seizing the moment. It might never come again. With her work and his fighter missions, every day they had was a gift. And instead of declining, she nodded. They'd seen the hotel several times, it looked small and clean, and not the kind of tawdry place she wanted to avoid, and where others she knew went routinely.

She followed him into the hotel cautiously, and Richard spoke to the clerk at the desk. He had just come back from the shelter himself, with their handful of guests. He seemed as worn-out as they were.

Richard spoke quietly to the man at the desk, and his rank showed on his uniform. Almost every man in London was in uniform now, but Richard was no mere private with a floozy on his arm for the night.

"Our building suffered damage in the raid tonight. My wife and I need a place to stay until morning," Richard said, appearing upset and apologetic, and the clerk was immediately sympathetic.

"Do you have children?" the clerk asked, noticing how respectable Alex looked. She was wearing a simple black coat and a gray dress, and there was plaster dust in her hair just from walking down the street.

"They're in Hampshire," Richard said creatively and the clerk nodded, as Alex forced herself not to giggle. The clerk handed them a key, and Richard paid him, and they walked up the stairs together.

"That was quick thinking about the children," Alex whispered and he smiled at her.

"The children **are** in Hampshire, they're just not ours," he whispered back, as they found the room and he unlocked the door. It was small and sparsely furnished but clean. There was a white chenille bedspread on the bed, and pink satin curtains, a chair and a desk and a chest of drawers with a mirror that had cracked during one of the bombings. But the building was still standing, and it was their home for what remained of their first night together. There was a sink in the room, and a bathroom down the hall. And without waiting another instant, Richard turned to her, took her in his arms, and kissed her as he carefully removed her clothes. He knew this was her first time and he was gentle with her.

She was standing in her underwear and stocking feet moments later, shaking, as she unbuttoned his shirt, and he took it off, and then his trousers. With the utmost tenderness he lifted her onto the bed, and she moaned as his hands discovered her, their bodies pressed together. Alex had no hesitation now, she had made up her mind, as she did with all things, and once decided she moved forward and never looked back.

"I love you so much, Alex," he said, as she pulled out her hairpins, set them on the night table, and her blond hair tumbled past her shoulders and down her back, as he kissed and caressed every inch of her. He tried to be as gentle as he could when he entered her, but passion swept them both away, as Alex tensed with fear at first, and then relaxed in his arms. It was all over moments later as they lay panting on the bed, and he pulled her tightly against him. "I will love you forever," he promised in a voice raw with emotion, and she knew he meant it. She just hoped that forever wouldn't come too soon for either or both of them. Neither was sure anymore.

"I love you too," she whispered with tears in her eyes, and he was praying she had no regrets and that she wouldn't get pregnant just yet. They hadn't expected to give in to passion that night and he wasn't prepared, and they had decided to risk it this one time. He wanted to have children with her one day, but not now, in a world torn asunder by war. And he wanted their children to be safe when they were born. He never doubted for a minute that he would marry her, if she would have him. He was still concerned that her parents wouldn't accept him as a suitable husband for her. He felt unworthy himself given the difference in their circumstances, but he knew for certain that no one would ever love her more. She believed that too, and she loved him just as much.

She wanted to stay awake all night to savor every instant with him, but finally fell asleep in his arms. She awoke with the early winter sunlight filtering into the room when he opened the blackout curtains, as he gently touched her cheek and she smiled.

"Did I dream last night?" she whispered to him.

"If you did, we had the same dream," he whispered back.

They made love again before she was even fully awake, and he pulled out to make sure there would be no mistake, as he had the night before. He hadn't expected her to give in to him. They took turns tiptoeing to the bathroom, nervous about running into other guests, but there was no one in the halls. When Alex got back, he admired her as she put her clothes on and he watched. It was like a striptease in reverse as she put her garter belt on, and aroused him just as much. He didn't have to be back at the base until that afternoon, and she had no assignment that day, so they were in no hurry. But reluctantly they finally left the room with a last kiss, and returned the key at the desk.

They went out to eat breakfast at a nearby restaurant, and then he took her back to her dormitory. Alex could already sense that everything had changed once they'd made love. She felt as though she truly belonged to him now, and he looked sad when it came time to leave her. Most of the women who lived there had gone to work by then, and they lingered on the stairs, kissing and standing close together, remembering the night before.

"I'm busy tonight, but I'll call you tomorrow," he said and she nodded and looked into his eyes. "Be careful, Alex. If anything happens to you . . ." He couldn't finish the sentence, but it was everyone's fear now for those they loved. A bomb could fall out of the sky at any moment, a building could collapse, his plane could be shot down, or they could send her on a mission into Germany from which she'd never return, which she knew better than he. His appeared to be the more dangerous job, but that was no longer true since she'd gone to work for the SOE.

"I love you," she whispered softly, and then ran up the stairs with a wave, as he turned and walked away. Every time he left her, he felt as though his heart would fly out of his chest. He had never loved anyone as he did her. But it was impossible to envision the future now, there were too many dangers and too many unknowns.

When she walked past the desk, Alex noticed a message for her pinned to the bulletin board. She opened it and saw that it was from Bertram Potter. She called him back immediately.

"I need to see you this afternoon at three," he said without further information, which could mean anything. A mission, a meeting, another class they wanted her to take. She was not to ask questions, just do as she was told.

She dressed carefully, thinking of Richard, wondering what the future had in store for them. She wanted to invite him to spend Christmas in Hampshire with her parents. Geoff had already said he didn't have Christmas off this year, so she would be alone with them, and she wanted Richard to meet them, and see where she'd grown up, at Wickham Manor.

She arrived at the SOE offices on Baker Street a few minutes before three, ready for whatever they assigned her. There was always a thrill of excitement when they called. Every sense was alert, as she waited outside Captain Potter's office, and he called her in immediately.

"We need you as a chaperone on a reconnaissance mission in Germany. We have a recon expert we need to send in. He doesn't speak German and you're going to be his wife. You're flying to Zurich tonight. We have a car waiting for you there. You'll drive to a small town where there's a munitions factory. He'll make the maps. You're just along for the ride, as a cover."

"How's that going to work if he doesn't speak German?" She hadn't worked with a male counterpart yet.

"War veteran. A nasty wound to the throat. He has the appropriate scar. You're his wife and you'll speak for him. You're there to visit relatives in the Ruhr region, which happens to be their main industrial center. We want you both in and out quickly. He'll make the maps, you'll drive, and talk if you get stopped. You'll drive across the Swiss border. The whole thing shouldn't take more than a day or two. You can stay in a hotel if you have to, in the same room obviously." It reminded her of the night she had just spent with Richard, and now she'd be spending a night at a hotel with a strange man as part of her job. "We have clothes for both of you. The other operative should be here in a few minutes. You leave in an hour. No names please, except those on the passports waiting for you in Zurich. You can turn all your British papers in to the agent who gives you the car. And from the moment you walk out of this office, he doesn't talk. Is that clear? We'll give you a map of the area you'll be traveling to. You can study it once you're in the car. It should take you about eight hours to drive to Essen from Zurich. You live in Berlin, you're a schoolteacher, he was a lawyer before the war. He gets veteran's benefits now. He has a limp as well." She didn't know if that was real or not and didn't ask. "Your suitcase has a false bottom, there's a gun with a silencer in it. You may need it. There's a submachine gun in his."

What he told her made it clear that the mission was dangerous. She had her pistol in a hidden pocket in her purse, and when they left the office, she'd have her commando knife strapped to her upper thigh. She had had that in her purse too when Richard undressed her the night before, along with her pistol, which she always carried now.

When she left the captain's office to change clothes, she passed a tall thin man in the hall. He didn't smile at her, and she noticed that he walked with a limp when he entered the office after her and closed the door.

Marlene told her they would be given deutschmarks in Zurich when they got their passports and travel papers. Alex changed into German clothes again. She wore a drab brown coat, with a matching hat, scuffed shoes with thick heels, and a gray shirt and sweater. The cuffs of the coat were frayed, and it was clear that they weren't people with money. Marlene handed her a wedding ring in the right size and Alex slipped it on her finger, and for an instant she wished it was Richard's, and that she'd had it the night before when they checked into the hotel. The SOE had taken all her measurements and had all her sizes. When Alex was finished dressing, she looked like a schoolteacher, had her blond hair pulled back in a severe bun, wore no makeup and put on glasses. She was still beautiful, but much less noticeably so. She looked plain.

Her partner for the mission joined her ten minutes later. They were Heinrich and Ursula Schmitt. Her nickname was Ushi. She had already memorized the details of their biography. He looked as dreary as she did, in baggy trousers, a heavy gray wool coat, and a battered hat. And like hers, his shoes were scuffed. He carried a cane to go with his limp, and there was a radio transmitter in it. He had paper in a hidden pocket for the map.

They left the office carrying their suitcases. Heinrich, or whatever his real name was, nodded to her, and after that, they took a bus to the airport, and caught their flight to Zurich, a nondescript, badly dressed, and not particularly attractive couple. The unflattering hat, severe hairdo, absence of makeup, and glasses had quashed even Alex's usually striking beauty.

The flight was uneventful, and only a few minutes late. Alex noticed that Heinrich had sketched small drawings in a pocket-sized notebook on the flight, and she wondered if in real life he was an artist. The drawings were very good, of several flowers in detail, and a landscape, all in miniature.

They took a bus at the Zurich airport, and got off at the first stop, walked a quarter of a mile to a restaurant, where the agent was waiting for them with their papers and the car. The whole exchange of British documents for German ones took less than a minute. They got the keys to the old tired German car, and a moment later they took off with Alex driving. She and Heinrich hadn't exchanged a word so far and she knew they weren't supposed to.

She turned to him as they drove off and spoke to him in German, asking if everything was all right. He understood the gist of it, and nodded. They drove on into the night, and stopped at a small inn just after midnight. She explained to the innkeeper that she and her husband needed a room. He showed no interest in them. Alex paid for the room and he handed her a key, and Heinrich limped up the stairs to join her in a room that smelled musty with a narrow bed. The sheets were clean but the rest of the room was dirty. She lay down on the bed with her clothes on, and Heinrich pointed to her and shook his head. If the authorities came into the room to check them, they would find it suspicious that she was fully dressed, no matter how dirty the room was. She nodded, and reluctantly put on her nightgown, and Heinrich changed into pajamas. He wasn't an engaging traveling companion, and had a sour look about him. She could see the scar on his neck, supposed to be a war wound, and didn't know if it was real or not, but it was convincing.

She cautiously got into bed next to him, staying

as close to the edge as she could without falling out. And her fellow operative did the same and acted as though she wasn't there. He ignored her completely.

She lay awake for the rest of the night, got up and dressed at six in the morning. At seven they went downstairs and had ersatz sausages for breakfast, and watery fake coffee. The Germans were under severe rationing. They left shortly after, for the drive to the industrial area in the Ruhr region as a light snow began to fall. It was freezing. They drove all day, it took longer due to the weather, and they reached their destination at nightfall, but it was too dark for Heinrich to study the area or make his maps. They checked into another hotel, which was as unappealing as the one the previous night, and were lucky to get a double bed this time. The next morning two soldiers stopped them on the road and checked their papers.

Heinrich had all the documents he needed to prove he was a veteran wounded in the war, and no longer on active duty. The soldier who read his papers nodded, and waved them on, as Alex silently let out a breath and a billow of frost in the cold morning air. After that they drove to a spot at the right angle for him to make his maps. There was no one around, and they were some distance from the factories, and no one stopped them, or inquired what they were doing there. Heinrich had almost finished when a soldier appeared out of nowhere and approached them, as Alex appeared casual but caught her breath. He asked to see what Heinrich was doing, and he handed him a sketchpad with gentle rolling hills and a church steeple, everything they saw in front of them, minus the factories. The map he'd been working on was already in his coat pocket. He handed him his veteran's certificate as well.

The soldier studied the sketchpad for a moment, and then nodded and handed it back to Heinrich, and then studied Alex. He was thinking that she would almost be attractive if they weren't so poor and her clothes weren't so shabby. He could see that she was young, but she had the fatigue of an old woman in her eyes. It occurred to him that being married to a mute invalid couldn't be a pleasant life for her, but he said nothing, and waved them on. Alex thanked him, put the car in gear and drove away. She glanced at Heinrich and asked him in German as simply as she could if he was finished, and he nodded. He had everything they needed. He had memorized the rest. She saw him put the meticulous map inside his hollow cane, and they drove in silence the way they had come, and reached the Swiss border by late that night. Two soldiers came out to check their papers, and Alex explained that they were going to see a doctor in Zurich for her husband's throat. They had permission from the Reich to do so, which she showed them as well, since the army doctors had not been able to help him or repair his vocal cords. The two soldiers stepped away from the car and conferred for a minute, and then nodded, and let them through.

They drove to a house on a back road on the way to Zurich, exchanged their documents for British ones, and the agent followed them to the airport on a bicycle, and took the car from them when they got there an hour later. They walked away without looking back. With their papers were two plane tickets from Zurich to London. They boarded without drawing attention to themselves, put their small suitcases in the overhead rack, with their weapons in them, which fortunately they hadn't had to use, although they were prepared to kill any soldiers who stopped them if they had to. Heinrich's cane disappeared, telescoped into an inside pocket of his coat, and when he disembarked from the plane in London, he no longer limped, and after a trip to the restroom, there was no sign of the scar on his throat. Alex quietly took off her glasses and put them in her pocket, and looked instantly prettier without the heavy frames.

In London, they took a bus into the city, keeping their valises close to them. They got off at the stop nearest Baker Street, and walked the rest of the way, still without a word to each other, and Heinrich walking normally in long strides that Alex had to hurry to keep up with. This time, despite the late hour, Captain Potter was waiting for them, and looked expectantly at Heinrich.

"Well?"

The man Alex only knew as Heinrich handed him the cane. "Done. I got what you wanted." Captain Potter's tense face melted into a broad smile. Alex thought the intensity of his work had aged him. He had none of the appearance of youth, or even his forty years. He had the soul of an old man and the world on his shoulders.

"They're waiting for this at the War Office. Thank you both," Potter said, as both agents visibly relaxed. "No problems?"

"Not really. We got checked by soldiers a couple of times, and the border patrol studied me carefully, but Ursula here put them at ease, saying we were going to see a doctor for my throat. And we had the permission slip for it." He turned to Alex then. "Well done." And then he turned back to Bertram Potter. "The car was crap, by the way. I don't know how she got it that far." He smiled and Alex noticed that he had a deep voice and a heavy Scottish brogue. "She was a fine partner, never slipped or broke the rules once, and her German is perfect. I understand it, but my accent is pure Glasgow, not Berlin." He laughed and Alex smiled at the compliment as Captain Potter saluted him and she realized that her partner outranked the captain. Her fellow agent on the trip was a high-ranking officer in Military Intelligence, and Captain Potter seemed impressed by his praise for her and gave her a warm glance, which was rare for him.

She went to change into her own clothes then,

and "Heinrich" was gone when she returned. Their mission had been accomplished. Captain Potter left for the War Office, despite the late hour, and Alex left Baker Street alone, thinking about the past two days, realizing again how differently things might have gone. There was always that feeling that they had escaped the lion's jaws by the skin of their teeth. But they had made it.

She took the bus to the dormitory, and there was no message from Richard when she got there. Once again, she had disappeared without warning or explanation, but she wouldn't have to invent a plausible reason when she spoke to him the next day, since he hadn't called. She was sure he was busy too.

He didn't call the next day either, and at the end of the afternoon, she dialed a number he had given her, for information if anything ever happened to him. She felt a little foolish calling, with no real reason for concern, but he hadn't contacted her in three days, which wasn't like him. His missions were shorter than hers and only lasted a few hours.

She hesitantly asked for information about him, and they told her to wait, which she did, for a long time. It was a full five minutes before the voice at the base came back on the line and told her that Captain Montgomery's plane had been shot down during a mission. He hadn't come back with the others, and there had been no message from him so far. She knew that he carried a small transmitter to send messages if he was on the ground in enemy territory.

"Did anyone see . . . was he . . ." she choked on the words, wanting to know if any of the other pilots had seen him shot and killed.

"That's all we know, madam," the voice said formally. "He's missing in action. He may turn up in a few days or weeks, depending on whether he's injured, or has been captured." He was cut and dry.

"Thank you," she said in a whisper, as terror rose in her throat. Richard's plane had gone down, and he was missing in action, but at least no one had seen him get killed. She just prayed that wherever he was, he would find his way out of enemy territory. He had been shot down over Germany, and he was out there somewhere, dead or dying, maybe gravely injured, or alone. Her hand was shaking as she set down the phone. She had survived her mission, and now Richard was lost. It struck her again how their lives could change in an instant, and hers just had.

She went to her room, which she shared with a dozen other women, and lay down on her bed and sobbed as quietly as she could. Her life wouldn't be worth living without him. She had already lost a brother, and all she could do now was pray she wouldn't lose the only man she had ever loved. Or that he wasn't already dead.

Chapter 6

The six weeks between when Richard was shot down and Christmas were the longest of her life. She tried not to call the base too often, and she finally asked Captain Potter to call the War Office and see what he could find out. He reported that they knew no more than they had already told her. For the moment, Richard was missing in action, and presumed dead. But Alex knew others had survived getting shot down over Germany. Perhaps he'd been captured and sent to a prisoner of war camp, or maybe he had died from his injuries. Others had walked across Germany, and crossed the Swiss border on foot.

She had two more missions in Germany in November, and one in France in early December, pursuing information and documents. She was in a daze each time, and wanted to try to find him herself, but she knew she couldn't get him out alone, without papers, even if she did, especially if he was injured. And she knew trying to do that would be a violation of one of the most stringent rules of the SOE. There were no personal missions. Each time she left Germany, it tore her heart out, knowing that she was leaving him there, either dead or alive. She ached to know which it was, but there was not a single message from him in any form.

Her heart felt like a rock as she took the train to Hampshire at Christmas. She had another shock when she got there. She knew her brother Geoffrey wasn't coming home for Christmas, and hadn't been able to get leave, but she wasn't prepared for how severely her parents had aged since Willie's death in August. Her mother looked ravaged and was suddenly an old woman and her father looked even worse. They cried every time they spoke of Willie and insisted on showing Alex the new marble headstone in their cemetery the moment she arrived. If anything, they seemed more depressed than they had been when it first happened. The reality had finally sunk in that William was never coming back. Her father was running the estate and it had become a burden not a joy. His spirit was broken.

She felt the same way now about Richard. She couldn't tell herself fairy stories anymore, that they would hear from him any day, or he would run, crawl, or walk out of Germany across the Swiss border. It appeared that his categorization as "presumed dead" had been the right assumption. It broke her heart to think it, and there was no one she could talk to about it, since no one knew about them. She grieved in silence and mourned him every day. Alex had given up hope by Christmas, and was trying to face his death as bravely as possible. She was even disappointed when she realized she wasn't pregnant. She would have gladly gone through the shame of an illegitimate child, in order to have his baby, but that wasn't to be either.

She never said a word about him to her parents. There was no point now if he was dead.

The only thing that cheered her were the children from London. It was their second Christmas with them, and it had been a hard year for the Wickhams, after losing William. But the children they were housing always brought a smile to her mother's face, and her father had been trying to teach some of the slightly older boys to play cricket. Her mother had made them all Christmas gifts by then, and once again the government had strongly discouraged the children from going home for Christmas, for fear that their parents wouldn't part with them again after the holidays, and it was safer for them in the country. The parents had been urged not to visit them, or as seldom as possible, so as not to torment the children when they didn't bring them home. And most parents couldn't afford to come anyway. Many of them knew that they were orphans now, with parents who had died in the bombings in London, or fathers who had died in the war.

It was a quiet Christmas for Alex and her parents, without her brothers. Alex's own spirits were dragging with no news of Richard, and the almost certainty now that he was dead after a month and a half behind enemy lines. It was unlikely he had survived.

She tried to cheer up her parents while she was there, but it had been an exhausting holiday, attempting to buoy their spirits without success, and who could blame them. They were disappointed not to see Geoffrey, and constantly worried about him. Alex had spent the whole holiday trying to reassure them about Geoff, and looking for interesting topics of conversation to distract them. She was successful at neither.

She felt defeated on New Year's Day, when she left to go back to London, and they looked as sad as they had when she'd arrived. There were some things you couldn't compensate them for, losing their beloved oldest son was one of them. They loved Alex too, but it was different. All their hopes and the future of the family had rested on William. Alex couldn't imagine them being happy again. Or herself, if Richard was in fact dead. She was trying to accept it, but everything she thought of that had once delighted her made her sad. She dreaded going back to work after the holidays, and doing another mission in Germany. She hated the Germans with a passion now. She knew her work was not meant to be a personal vendetta but it was becoming that way, after William died and Richard was shot down.

She could only get on a slow train back to London, and remembered that she had met him on a train just like it.

The dormitory was deserted when she got there, the women were either asleep after too much reveling the night before, or they were out with friends. None of them were working that day, and she was grateful she wasn't either.

She put away the clothes she had brought back from Hampshire, and hadn't bothered to pack a pretty dress her mother had given her for Christmas. It had been one of hers. Alex had no one to wear it for now, or to go out with. The last thing she wanted to do was celebrate anything with Richard almost certainly dead.

She lay on her bunk staring at the ceiling. Geoff had said he might come by but he hadn't called her, and she wanted to be left alone anyway. For a week, she had done nothing but try to cheer up her parents, now she just wanted to vegetate for a while and not speak to anyone.

It was almost dinnertime, when one of the girls came home, stuck her head in the door, and spoke to Alex.

"Gentleman downstairs to see you," she said. So Geoff had come to see her after all, Alex thought. She hoped he wasn't coming to tell her the butcher's daughter was pregnant and he was getting married, or already had. It would kill their parents if he did. She went down the stairs, feeling beaten, and opened the door to the visiting room. There was only one person in it. A man with a bandage on his head, a cast on his arm, and leaning on a cane. It took a second for it to register who he was, and then she flew into his arms and nearly knocked him over. It was Richard!

"Oh my God! Oh my God . . . you're alive! I thought you were dead. . . ." she said breathlessly, sobbing as she kissed him and he clutched her to him. He had been missing for seven weeks, and she felt like she was dreaming.

"Take it easy, take it easy," he said, as he let himself down gingerly into a chair. "I'm still a little battered." He pulled her down on his lap and she put her arms around him and kissed him.

"Where were you?"

"Skiing in the Alps," he teased her and looked at her as though he couldn't believe he was there either, and this wasn't a dream. "I went down after we bombed some of the factories." In fact, she hadn't been far from him, she realized, on one of her recent missions. "I got banged up pretty badly and hit my head when I landed. A farmer took me in and hid me under his barn. They brought me in at night or I'd have frozen by morning. They even got a doctor from another village. I had a nasty bump on the head, and didn't know where I was for a few days, and eventually it got better. I broke my arm and my ankle and the doctor set them, but they haven't fully healed yet. The farmer got me to the border, where

I stayed with friends of theirs until I got stronger. The doctor did a good job and as soon as my ankle was strong enough, I started walking through the foothills and forests toward Switzerland. They gave me enough basic food supplies to keep me going and I drank melted snow. I didn't think I'd make it, but I had to try." She could see what it had cost him. He looked ten years older. "It took me about a month. I called from Switzerland two days ago, and they came and got me yesterday. I'll be in the hospital for a few days getting checked out, my arm hasn't healed yet, but I wanted to see you. I didn't want to call you. I wanted to surprise you." She was laughing and crying all at once and so was he. It was a miracle that he had survived and had walked so far in the condition he was in. No one had stopped him, or helped him. He hadn't seen another human in a month. He had slept in caves, and lived by his wits and sheer endurance. He told her he had refused to die and all he wanted was to come back to her. It had kept him alive, when he wanted to give up. The food the farmer had given him was enough to nourish him, although he had lost a shocking amount of weight. And his face was dark and leathery from the elements. "I want to go back and see them after the war, to thank them," he said, looking deeply moved. And then he lowered his voice to ask her a question. "Are you pregnant?" She shook her head, visibly disappointed.

"When you were shot down, I hoped I was. Before that, I was terrified I might be. But I wasn't."

"We'll fix that at the appropriate moment. But not just yet. We have a war to win first." He smiled at her.

"When do you go back to active duty?" She was worried, she could see the worn look in his eyes and he could hardly stand up. He leaned heavily on the cane. He said the final days had been the hardest.

"As soon as I can fly a plane. Not long, I suspect." His feet had been numb from the cold. They were all pushing hard, and taking chances. It was the nature of the times they lived in. "I'll have a little time off now. I hope they don't send you driving all over England. Maybe you can come and visit me at the hospital while I'm there." She nodded, the question was more if they were going to send her back to Germany on a mission immediately, which was possible on any given day.

"I will whenever I'm not working," she promised. He spent an hour with her, and then he had to go back to the base. They had given him a car and a young airman as a driver so he could come to see her, since he had no other family. They kissed and talked for a long time. She was drinking in the joy of knowing he was alive and hadn't died when he was shot down.

She helped him into the car, and he went back to the base. She promised to visit him the next day, and prayed they wouldn't send her on a mission. But no one from the SOE called her the day after New Year's. She took a bus out to the air base, and spent hours with Richard after they reset his arm. The ankle had healed correctly, as he said. They told him he couldn't fly for a month until he was stronger and had recovered. A number of the pilots he commanded had come to see him, and were thrilled he was alive. He was the hero of the squadron now.

When Alex returned to her dormitory that night, basking in the joy of having Richard back, there was a message for her. She had to report to Baker Street at noon the next day. She didn't know what she'd tell Richard, but she had to think of something. She thought of asking to be relieved of the mission, but didn't want to do that either. She hadn't refused a single assignment since she'd joined them, and didn't think she should. She was with the SOE to help save her country and win the war. She had to go back to work.

Her assignment the next day, when she went to the SOE office, was to go to Paris to gather information. The German high command there had plans to launch a two pronged attack on England, and Military Intelligence wanted to know more about it. She was the perfect candidate to find out. Once they got her into Paris, they wanted her to attend several parties, hobnob with the wives and mistresses of the German officers, and meet the officers themselves. They knew that she could play the role to perfection. She was the obvious choice. They were putting a wardrobe together for her, and were going to have her stay at an elegant hotel. Paris was full of beautiful women, many eager to collaborate with the Germans, and Alex was going to be one of them.

"When do I leave?" she asked, unhappy to be obliged to leave Richard so soon after he got back. But she had no official role in his life since she wasn't his wife.

"You leave tomorrow. We're going to parachute you in to an operative just outside Paris. He'll take you the rest of the way." She hadn't been parachuted in before and was nervous about it. What if she got hurt? Or stuck in a tree, and shot down by the Germans. With Richard's miraculous safe return, she didn't want to reenact it herself. "Is there a problem?" Captain Potter looked at her, sensing her reluctance.

"No, none," she said, without a quiver in her voice.

At least she could see Richard that night, and explain to him that she would be gone for a few days. She could tell him she was driving up to Scotland, and it would take her time to get back. They wanted her in Paris for three days, and didn't want her to stay too long. And if something went wrong, she could leave Paris sooner. They wanted to gather as much information as they could, without taking too many risks and losing a good agent. She had become a valuable operative for them, in Germany, and now in France. Her language skills had proven to be as useful as they'd hoped.

She took the bus out to see Richard at the hospital on the base that night, and he was happy to see her. His face lit up when she walked into the room. Nearly his whole squadron had dropped by in the past two days, including some new faces who came to pay their respects to the legendary squadron leader. And he was even more of a hero now after his recent escape, and long trek back.

Alex told him casually that she had a long drive to Scotland and back in the next few days.

"What, they don't have enough rocks in Scotland, they need ours too?" he teased her. He was sorry she had to go, but she'd be back soon, and he wasn't worried about her. He would have been if he had known what she was really going to do.

She left in a small military plane from a tiny airport the next day, so as not to draw attention when they arrived. She carried all her clothes in a heavy pack on her back, but had carried more in training, and wore an airman's flying suit and combat boots to make the jump. She had all the arms she needed, an arsenal of small weapons on her person, her commando knife, a Sten gun in her backpack, her cyanide pill in her pocket, and a wardrobe worthy of any high-ranking SS officer's wife or mistress, including a white mink jacket to wear at night.

Their clothing sources had gone all out to find it, and had borrowed it from a British colonel's wife, who happened to be French and had bought it in Paris before the war. They had warned her it might not come back, but was for a good cause, so she had agreed to lend it. Alex had tried it on. It fit perfectly and she loved it.

"Can I get paid in mink this time?" she asked when she saw it, and Captain Potter laughed. What she was paid in cash monthly wouldn't have covered any of the wardrobe. They kept the pay of the SOE workers modest, so as not to arouse suspicion with a noticeable influx of funds.

"The person who lent it to us wants it back. So you'd better come back in one piece, with the mink," the captain teased her. He had grown to like and respect her. She was brave and there was nothing she wouldn't do for them.

"I'm going to love being a collaborator. They're so well-dressed," she joked as she preened, still wearing the jacket. Her mother had a black one like it from before the war. But the white one was more stylish.

"Apparently," he said and moved on to the more serious aspects of the mission, and gave her a list of all the information they wanted. They expected it to take several days. And when she was ready, they would get her out, using the same agent outside Paris to help her escape. They were going to pick her up by plane, it was risky on the ground, but they trusted their agents, and flying her in and out was faster, once they cleared the range of the anti-aircraft guns in the area. Alex was well aware of the risks. In some ways, it was more dangerous than what she'd done in Germany so far, but a lot more exciting. She loved the role she had to play and felt like Mata Hari, or a very glamorous modern-day spy.

When the plane lifted off the ground carrying Alex toward France, she was tense as she thought about her mission and how to accomplish it. The weather and visibility were poor, which gave them a certain amount of cover. And it didn't take them long to reach the countryside near Paris. They knew precisely where their agent was expecting them to drop her, and at the exact moment, the co-pilot of the plane slid open the door as they lost altitude as far as they dared, and he told her to jump.

"Shit!" was the last thing she said in English. She hadn't done a parachute jump since her training and it had terrified her then as it did now. She dropped the short distance into a clump of trees, and within minutes her parachute had caught on a tree branch, and she was dangling like a paper doll and being buffeted by the wind. It was how many of their operatives in other places had gotten shot, and Alex knew how important it was to get down quickly.

"Allo?" She heard a whispered voice just below here. "Pompadour?" It was her code name for the mission, after Madame de Pompadour, the courtesan.

"Oui," she responded affirmatively. "I'm caught." They were speaking French, and like her missions in German, there would be no English. Her French documents said she was born in Lyon and had previously lived in Paris, in the sixteenth arrondissement, one of the chicest neighborhoods. She was allegedly a young widow, living in the South of France now.

"I'll come up and get you," he said, but Alex was faster, she slid her commando knife out of her sleeve and removed it from its sheath, shimmied up the tree, holding fast with one arm, like a monkey, and started cutting the cords of the parachute with the razor sharp blade. She was down to the last cord in seconds and looked below her. All she could see was a shadowy form in the darkness.

"Catch me!" she said as she cut the last cord. The operative caught her, and they both fell onto the grass unharmed. "We have to get the parachute," she said quickly, as they both shimmied back up the tree, pulled it down toward them, rolled it into a tight ball, and took it with them. He led her through some bushes moving quickly, and they traveled a considerable distance on foot until she saw a farmhouse. All the lights were out, but she knew there was a Resistance cell based there, and they were meeting there tonight. The local agents were expecting her and knew she would be going to Paris in the morning. There was a car in the barn waiting for her, which had been stolen for the occasion, and had the license plates changed. Alex would be entering Paris in style.

She followed the operative to the farmhouse, and he led her through a door in the kitchen floor down to a cellar where she would spend the night. He went back upstairs then and moved a rug and table into place over it. He hoped there wouldn't be too many rats down there tonight. He had left her something to eat and a bottle of wine, and heard no sound from below until he went to bed, and he led Alex back up in the morning at the first light of day.

"Thank you for the wine, I slept like a rock." She smiled at him.

"No rats?" He grinned at her.

"Oh God, don't tell me now." He was about her age, slight, in a heavy black sweater and baggy dark blue pants, and he lit a cigarette and put it between his lips and then offered her a cup of coffee, the evil brew that was all they could get in England now too. She declined it. She had gotten out of the flight suit the night before, and left it in the cellar with the parachute. She was carrying a backpack, and still wearing the combat boots with military trousers and a heavy sweater. It was freezing and there was no heat in the farmhouse.

An old woman came out to the kitchen shortly after. He said that she was his grandmother, and that they shared the house with his brother, who had gone to Brittany. He said his parents had died before the war, and only he and his brother and grandmother were left. His grandmother poured herself a cup of the nearly undrinkable coffee and went back to her room shortly after. She took no interest in what they were doing, and had probably seen worse things happening before. This was one of the most important cells of the Resistance outside Paris.

"Can I see the car?" Alex asked him. His code name was Brouillard, Fog, because he was able to disappear so quickly. He led her into the barn then, and slid open the door with a grin. There stood an impeccable, astoundingly beautiful, shiny black Duesenberg in mint condition. "Oh my God, where did you get it?" Alex was stunned.

"We stole it," he said proudly. "In Nice, last week. It belongs to an American. He left it here before the war. I suppose he'll come back for it someday. We borrowed it in the meantime. My brother knew about it. He worked for him one summer. We're going to have one of the boys in the area drive you. He has a clean record. You can't use any of us for that."

"Does he know how to drive it?" It was a spectacular machine, for her triumphant entry into Paris.

"We taught him. He's not so smooth, but he's learning." She laughed at what he said. The plan Military Intelligence had concocted was that she was to make a splashy entrance, dazzle all the men who saw her, find out everything she could from members of the high command, and make a rapid exit before anyone exposed her. It was a daring plan, and Alex liked it. It was going to be very different from her German missions, and hopefully successful. In some ways, the bolder the better. Who would suspect her of trying to hide anything in a car like that?

Brouillard told her she had a suite reserved at an excellent, discreet small hotel. Several of the mistresses of German officers lived there. Le Meurice had been taken over as headquarters by the Germans. The Ritz was only for officers of high rank, and the only civilian who stayed there was Gabrielle Chanel, the designer, a known collaborator. The smaller hotel would suit them. Alex had to get dressed then and Brouillard told her to use his bedroom, upstairs. She took her heavy backpack up with her, and emerged twenty minutes later like Cinderella, transformed. She wore an exquisitely cut navy blue Dior suit which showed off her figure with an elegant dark blue fur hat, high-heeled black shoes with silk stockings, and an alligator bag. She was wearing long navy blue suede gloves, and diamond earrings that weren't real but looked it. The rest of what she had was in the backpack, and Brouillard had managed to find two white alligator suitcases which she packed with her wardrobe, and he put in the trunk of the car.

Alex had done her makeup to perfection, with bright red lipstick, and she looked dazzling, as the young boy Brouillard had enlisted appeared in a black suit, and a chauffeur's cap they'd found in the car. Alex looked like a movie star as they drove the car out of the barn, and she got in, ready for her triumphant arrival in Paris. It was a daring plan, but no one would suspect her of hiding anything. She was having fun as she thanked Brouillard and they took off for Paris, with an occasional bump and grind of the gears, as she told her neophyte chauffeur how to drive it. She would have driven it herself, but that would have aroused suspicions.

They sailed right into Paris through the Porte Dauphine, drove around the Place de la Concorde with the Arc de Triomphe in plain view, and then through the Place Vendôme to her hotel on the rue Cambon, right behind the Ritz and next to Chanel. There were several beautiful, elegant young women in the lobby chatting with each other, and they watched Alex with interest as she checked in. She looked like one of them, but they didn't know her, which intrigued them.

Alex went to Chanel, Dior, and Cartier that afternoon and looked around, while salespeople scurried to serve her, but she bought nothing. The name on her papers was Mme. Florence de Lafayette, and one of their best forgers had done them. They were flawless. And then she went back to the hotel to rest and change. They had forged an invitation to a very grand party that night and she planned to make an entrance. She languished in the bath for half an hour, and put on a white evening gown that fit her like a second skin, with the white mink jacket, and a big diamond ring that was another fake but would fool anyone who saw it on her finger. Florence de Lafayette was easily one of the most beautiful women in the room when she entered the ballroom where the party was being held. It was in honor of Hermann Goering, who was visiting Paris, and considered himself a connoisseur of all fine things, particularly women and art. Every important general was there, mostly with their mistresses, or on the hunt for a new one. "Florence" stood gazing at the scene from the top of a grand staircase that led into the ballroom, and two men approached her almost the moment she walked in. One was a general recently arrived from Berlin, the other was a colonel based in Paris whose name she was familiar with. Both were important men.

The colonel was the first to offer her his arm down the grand staircase. He was a strikingly handsome man in his early forties, very tall, and as blond and blue-eyed as Alex. He never left her side, handed her a glass of champagne, and invited her to dance as soon as the music started. She circled the dance floor gracefully with him as he looked bewitched by her, and she silently thanked her governesses for the endless dancing lessons she had hated, which had finally paid off. The general cut in very quickly. He was portly and much older. Both men spent the evening courting her and vying for her attention as she teased them both and flirted with them shamelessly.

The general invited her to lunch with him the

next day at Le Meurice, and said he had a marvelous chef he had stolen from the Ritz. And the
colonel invited her to dinner at La Tour d'Argent
the following night and to another party afterward.
All eyes were on Alex for most of the night. She
looked stunning, and was breathtakingly smooth in
her performance, as a woman seeking a new lover
from among the high command. Her intentions
were plain, the outcome, whom she would choose,
not yet sure. At one o'clock, she smiled enticingly at
the colonel, whispered that she would see him the
next day, and disappeared back to her hotel in the
stolen Duesenberg with the farm boy at the wheel.
The plan was unfolding just as she and her superiors
wanted. Already that night, she had gleaned some
interesting information, and made notes in code,
which she put in the lining of the suitcase, where
her Sten gun was too, for emergencies. She had her
tiny pistol inside one thigh, and her commando
knife attached to the other. These were dangerous
men she was playing with, and she knew it. They
could turn on her in an instant, and might before
the charade was over.

Lunch with the general the next day at Le Meurice
was elegant and informative. She titillated him
with funny stories and teased him, while pretending not to care about anything serious. He bragged
about some of their plans for Paris, and how soon
they would be in London, after they crushed the
English. He tried to kiss her and she wouldn't let

him. When she got back to her own hotel, her room was filled with flowers from both her suitors, and a third one she hadn't noticed. When the colonel arrived to pick her up for dinner, she was wearing a very daring silver gown with almost no back and he looked incredibly handsome in his uniform, he bowed and clicked his heels as he kissed Alex's hand, and handed her a box from Van Cleef & Arpels with a diamond bracelet in it. This was serious business. He was playing for high stakes, and so was she. He was far more discreet than the general and not quite so liberal with information, and he made it clear to her by the end of the evening that he would be honored if she would decide to become his companion on a regular basis, and of course the SS would provide her with an apartment. He said they had commandeered several truly beautiful ones, and she could choose among them. He complimented her on the Duesenberg and said that she was obviously a woman with exquisite taste who deserved only the finest things. She told him how bored she had been in Paris after her husband died, and she had been living in Cap d'Antibes more recently, and felt that the time was ripe to come back to Paris. She didn't give him an answer about the apartment, but she was exquisitely seductive, and he was completely under her spell, and wise enough not to be crude about it. He didn't force her hand or rush her, which the general would have.

They talked more seriously about the war at the

end of the evening, and she shared with him that she had read all of Adolf Hitler's writings, which was true because she thought him a madman, but she didn't say that, and she praised Gabrielle Chanel's impeccable talent, taste, and courage, to let him know that she approved of collaborators. He got the message clearly, and kissed her lightly on the lips when he dropped her off at her hotel. More than that would have panicked her, but so far it was all manageable, and she was having fun, taunting and teasing them, and gathering more information than they realized. While they protected their major secrets, which British Military Intelligence knew from breaking their codes, she was pulling miles and miles of smaller secrets from them, like a clown pulling silk scarves from his sleeve, or taking coins from someone's ear. She knew she was playing a dangerous game, but it was addictive.

She got more flowers the next day, and she didn't know what to do about the diamond bracelet. She would insult the colonel profoundly if she refused to accept it, particularly if she wanted him to think she was open to being his mistress, but she could hardly keep it and return to England with spoils of war of that value. She herself was the trophy the colonel wanted, as did the general, but he was a less ardent and convincing suitor. Alex actually enjoyed the colonel's company, and their intelligent conversations. She felt like a courtesan in the days of Louis XIV, playing with palace intrigues.

The plum she had come for fell into her lap that night, when the colonel decided that treating her as his established mistress would convince her to accept his offer, and he shared some of the more intimate details of his job with her, including the bombings he knew were planned for Europe in the coming months, and that they were planning to plunder France before they left it, which was why Hermann Goering was there. He had already shipped several trainloads of France's greatest art treasures to Berlin, and he was here for more. They were going to empty the Louvre eventually and give its contents to Hitler, although he was less of an art enthusiast than Goering. The Führer wanted power and control over all of Europe. Goering wanted their art. It was a lethal combination and made Alex's blood boil to hear it. France was already in their clutches, and they wanted to strip her to the bone. It took all her self-control not to react, and simply listen, and he trusted her enough to brag to her about future bombing missions. He respected her discretion and intelligence, and in real life, he wasn't wrong. But this wasn't real to her, it was a game.

Alex was wearing a black satin gown that night, held by a tiny string of rhinestones to her neck, and he warned her that with a single tiny tug on the string, he could leave her standing naked in the nightclub where they were dancing, and had been talking for hours, while drinking champagne. She drank far less than he did.

"Why would you want to have me stand naked here?" she said innocently, as he looked as though he might grab her, he could no longer resist her tantalizing charms and teasing.

"Because I would like to see you naked, my dear. And I don't want to wait much longer." He was normally not a patient man and was used to taking what he wanted. She was making him work for it.

"You won't have to," she said softly.

"Tonight?" He looked as though he were going to eat her alive as his eyes lit up, and she could sense how dangerous he could be. She was playing with fire and she knew it, and she already had all the information the SOE wanted, and more. Now she was just taunting the lion to see how far she could go. And he was a dangerous predator.

"It's not the right time," she said shyly, and he nodded.

"I understand. I've acquired a very beautiful boat in the South of France, in Cannes. Would you like to join me on it? We could pick your apartment when we come back. I have just the right one in mind. It's a smaller Versailles, with its own ballroom. It would suit you. Should we go to my boat in a few days?" he said, running a finger slowly up her arm, and barely brushing past her breast as he gazed into her eyes.

"I'd like that very much," she whispered.

"We'll fly to Nice on Friday, and spend a few days on the boat."

"How did you get it?" She couldn't resist asking him, looking young and innocent.

"Ah . . . we have our ways, you know. . . . Its owners had to go away, and left everything behind. I'm very fond of the sea. The boat was given to me. It's quite marvelous, with a crew of twenty-three." She could perfectly imagine how he had gotten it, and the thought of it turned her stomach. There was no doubt in her mind now. It was time to go. She had all she needed, and the game was too dangerous. It was time for Cinderella to leave the ball.

They went on talking for a while longer, and she smiled at him and said she was tired. She said she had fittings at Dior the next morning. Many of the women of the officers of the high command bought their gowns there.

"Next time I will come with you, and I will pick what I would like to see you wear." She nodded as though she was touched and pleased. And he kissed her lightly on the lips when he left her. She had also gleaned from him that night that he had a wife and five children in Munich, which didn't seem to slow him down in Paris. They were a special breed of men, conquerors to their cores, of women and priceless objects and art. They had to possess it all. "I can't wait until the boat on Friday," he said, barely able to contain himself as she drifted into the hotel with a smile and a wave.

As soon as she got to her room, she started packing her gowns and the white mink jacket. She had had

everything she needed, her wardrobe had been perfect, and she wore it well. She left out one chic black
suit to wear as she left the hotel the next day, allegedly for her fittings at Dior. After she packed, she
wrote down all the information again, in code, and
put it in the suitcase Brouillard had gotten her with
the tricky lining, which suited her purposes.

She settled her hotel bill the next morning at
nine o'clock, before anyone was up, and the lobby
was empty. She left a handsome tip for the maid,
and got in the car ten minutes later with all her
belongings and the farm boy at the wheel. She
asked the concierge not to let anyone know she had
left until that night and slipped him an enormous
tip. He said he understood, and she was sure he
didn't. He had no idea who he was dealing with.

She arrived at Brouillard's house before ten in the
morning in her fancy suit, and he told the boy to
put the car in the barn. She gave Brouillard a coded
message to send, which meant to pick her up that
night, and she smiled at him.

"Time to go."

"It went well?" She had been in Paris for three days.

"Yes, but I don't want to push my luck." The ruse
had worked, but you had to know when to stop.

She put her belongings in the backpack, and the
coded information in a pouch on her body, and
had the boy put the empty alligator luggage in
the Duesenberg. She changed into her flight suit
and combat boots, and waited in the cellar all day.

Brouillard had gone to another farm to send the coded message and came back with the response which she decoded and nodded at him.

"Nine o'clock pickup."

"We'll be ready," he assured her. Four or five of his operatives would have to shine torches to guide the plane in, and she'd be ready to run for it from the tree line. The mission wasn't over until she was back in London, and they weren't there yet, by any means. She handed him the box from Van Cleef then with a piece of notepaper from the hotel.

"Do you have a courier who can get this back to Le Meurice tomorrow after I'm gone, without causing your man any trouble? I'm returning something to a colonel there."

"We'll manage it," he said, looking unconcerned. She wasn't sure if it was bravado or real, but she handed it to him. The note said simply, "It turns out that I'm just a small town girl after all. I'm going back to the provinces, where I belong. Thank you for a wonderful time! Florence." It was the elegant ladylike thing to do, no matter that he was a German and an SS officer, and they were enemies. She wasn't going to steal a diamond bracelet to prove a point, and God only knew who it belonged to and how he had gotten it. She addressed the package to Colonel Klaus von Meissen, and knew she would remember him. She could have been a highly paid mistress if she chose. The thought made her smile. It was a story to tell her grandchildren one day.

It was a long day waiting in the cellar, and finally at eight-thirty that night, they went out to the clearing in the trees where the plane would come in. They had their torches ready for when they heard the plane. Four of his friends had come, and Alex had her heavy backpack on. It was cold that night and they were all shivering, and she suddenly wondered if Klaus knew yet that she was gone. They were supposed to have dinner that night, and she had begged off lunch with the general. It had been an extraordinarily odd few days compared to her real life, and in sharp contrast to the agonies of war that she saw every day.

They heard the plane coming, as Brouillard's collaborators lit their torches, and just as they did, powerful arms reached out and grabbed Alex and pulled her backward with a hand over her mouth, and Brouillard saw it happen. A German soldier had snuck up on them and had been watching from the bushes. Alex struggled for an instant, and would have grabbed him, but the backpack was in her way. The young soldier pulled his gun from his holster as the plane approached. With no warning that anything was wrong, and with a flick of her wrist, Alex slipped her commando knife out of her sleeve and unsheathed it, and without hesitating, she plunged it backward into the German's stomach. He gave a gasp, dropped his gun, looking wild-eyed. Brouillard realized what had happened, and what she'd done, as the soldier fell to the ground dead.

"I'm really sorry," she said to Brouillard, cleaning the blade on the grass, and sheathing it again, as she slipped it in her sleeve. "Now what are you going to do?" She hated to leave him with a German corpse to dispose of, as a souvenir of her visit.

"Don't worry, one Boche more or less. We'll take care of it. They won't find him. He'll just disappear." The plane landed as he said it, and she had to run. "You're quite a woman." He smiled at her. "Can you do that in an evening gown and high heels?"

"I've never tried, but I'm sure I could. Thank you. Take care of yourself. Are you going to keep the car?"

"For a while." She laughed in answer, waved, and ran for the plane, before other soldiers discovered them with their torches. They turned them off as an airman pulled her in, and she fell onto the floor of the plane as he closed the door. They were already racing through the clearing and lifted off a minute later. There was no sound of gunfire. The young soldier had been alone. The plane gained altitude and headed toward London, in the cold French night and a sky full of stars. It had been a heady experience and a strange few days. It was the first time any man had given her a diamond bracelet, and the first time she had killed anyone. And in her current line of work, possibly not the last. The soldier had been young, but he was her enemy, and she felt no guilt at all.

Chapter 7

Richard got a pass from the hospital, and he and Alex had dinner two days after she got back from Paris, and he asked her what she'd been doing since he last saw her.

"The usual," she said, smiling at him. Captain Potter had been very pleased with the results of the Paris trip. "Just driving rocks around."

"Why is it that I sometimes get the feeling you do a lot more than that, and don't tell me?" But so did he. They all had to be secretive.

"Oh, sure," she countered with a grin, "like spending a few days in Paris, having fittings at Dior and ordering new clothes, going to parties, wearing ball gowns, dancing with handsome officers, getting diamond bracelets from my admirers." She had summed up the Paris mission perfectly, and he laughed when she said it.

"All right, all right. I wasn't suggesting anything

that extreme. I just think they ought to use your talents better than they do. We need lorry drivers, but you're capable of so much more than that."

"I'm glad you think so. At least I'm not stuck in Hampshire, knitting. I'll take driving rocks over that any day."

"There must be something in between."

"Maybe so," she said, and they moved on to other subjects. He was being released from the hospital earlier than they thought originally. He was healthy and young, in spite of his long trek, and he had arranged to borrow a small apartment from a friend so they could spend another night together. The opportunities to do so were few and far between. One of them was always working, and he flew night missions most of the time. She had her unaccountable absences to cover for. She wondered at times if he was suspicious, but he didn't seem to be.

The air strikes Colonel Klaus van Meissen had boasted to her about when she was in Paris turned out to be real. Thanks to her, they were forewarned, so much better prepared for them. Her superiors at the SOE were amazed by how much information she'd come back with. The air strikes continued while London took a beating, and the RAF retaliated. There were constant bombing missions, and Alex knew Geoff went on many of them. He seemed stressed and tired whenever she saw him.

The war was wearing everyone down. It had gone on for eighteen months when she got a call at the dormitory from her mother, and luckily she wasn't away on a mission. Her mother could barely speak she was so hysterical, and it took Alex fully five minutes to understand that the War Office had sent someone to tell them that Geoff had been killed on one of their bombing raids over Germany.

The news hit Alex like a bomb too. Both of her brothers were dead now. And she and Geoff had always been so close. William had been more stand-offish and responsible, the perfect big brother. Geoff had been her best friend and partner in crime when they were younger. She couldn't imagine life without him. She requested an immediate leave from the SOE, and told Captain Potter about her brother. He was deeply sympathetic and very kind to her, as she sat and cried in his office. He had grown very fond of her. So far, she had been an exceptional agent and she had earned his respect.

"You know, you have the opportunity to opt out now, honorably," he said quietly. "As the last sur- viving child in your family, you don't need to do dangerous missions for the SOE anymore. It would be a tremendous hardship for your parents if some- thing should happen to you too. Maybe you need to think about that, and decide what you want to do. I know your parents aren't aware that you're work- ing for intelligence now. But you know it. Maybe you need to work in a factory or something more suitable than going on sabotage missions in enemy territory where your life is at stake. Think about it, Alex." She had confessed to Captain Potter about killing the German soldier when she left France in January, and he had been calm and understanding about it. He said that the first time you took someone's life, it was a shock. But he pointed out that if she hadn't, he would have shot five people in the Resistance cell that was helping her, and he would have shot her. She had had no other choice except to use her commando knife on him. "And even if you'd left him unconscious and still alive, he would have reported them to the authorities as soon as you left."

"I know. I knew it was the only thing to do. I just wanted you to know I did it. It was a strange feeling. I thought I should feel guilty, but I didn't."

"That's why you're a good agent. You know what you have to do, and you do it, whatever it takes. We've all done something like it at some point. It goes with the kind of work we do. Sometimes we have to kill people to save ourselves or others. It's part of the nature of war. And then we have to make our peace with it and leave it behind us." He wasn't unfeeling about it, but he was matter-of-fact and reasonable, which set the tone for her too. He was her role model, and she knew she didn't want to give up SOE work now because Geoff had died. The Germans had killed both her brothers, and she also knew that what Captain Potter said about her parents was true. It would kill them if something happened to her too. And she couldn't tell them and ask their advice, or even Richard's. She could tell no one about her work in espionage. It was one of the conditions of her job. She had sworn to twenty years of silence about her wartime experience and the SOE.

She took a two-week leave to be with her parents in Hampshire, left a message for Richard, and left that afternoon, feeling dazed. Once she was home, she no longer felt like an espionage agent. In the setting where they grew up, she was a girl who had lost both her brothers.

Her parents were even more devastated now than they had been at Christmas, mourning only William. They had lost two sons, and looked destroyed. They had another funeral without a body or a casket to bury. The whole county came to the simple service they arranged for their second son, and Alex did all she could to help her mother. She wondered if the twenty children from London were too much for her now, but Alex also thought they cheered her up. She tried to talk to her father about all of it a few days after the funeral, when they were out walking together.

"Do you want me to come home, Papa?" she offered bravely.

"And what would you do here?" he said, smiling sadly at his daughter, his last remaining child. This wasn't how he had expected his family to turn out, with both of their sons gone, and Alex living in London. It was a high price of war for them all. "You've led a bigger life now. Could you really come back here and sit knitting with your mother night after night? There are no able bodied young men left in the county. They're all at war. You'd be alone with us, and you'd be unhappy, Alex. We miss you terribly, but it would be selfish of us to expect you to come home." Her eyes filled with tears at the thought of how generous he was, and he was right. She would have hated coming home now. Maybe after the war, but even then it would be hard. And for now there was nothing to come home to except her parents. It wasn't a life for a girl her age, and her father knew it too. She was twenty-four years old, and Hampshire would be a tomb for her. Her childhood home was all about loss now, not action, where she knew she was truly making a difference for the war effort.

She decided to broach another subject with him then, she wasn't sure if the timing was right, but she had been putting it off for months.

"There's someone I'd like you to meet sometime, Papa. A friend in London. Maybe he could come down and visit sometime." It was the first time she had mentioned Richard to them.

"A young man?" He searched her eyes and she nodded. "Is he important to you?"

"Yes, he is."

"Then we should meet him. What do you know about him?" It was a good question, and her father wanted to know. He thought Alex was inexperienced in the ways of the world and about men. Geoff had thought so too.

"He loves to fly planes and has since he was a little boy." She smiled at her father. "He's gentle and kind and intelligent. He went to boarding school in Scotland, and Cambridge after. He's afraid you won't like him because his background isn't quite as . . ." she searched for the right word, "social as ours. He thinks that because I made my debut at Queen Charlotte's Ball, and was presented at court, you won't think he's good enough for me. His father was a gentleman farmer, but I think it was quite a small farm."

"Do **you** care if he's less aristocratic than we are?"

"No, I don't," she said. "I love him. He's good to me, and he would take good care of me."

"Do you want to marry him?" Her father looked surprised. He didn't think she was that serious about anyone. They'd heard nothing about him.

"Not now, during the war. We both want the war to be over before we think about it. Everything is too insecure now. It colors everything."

"Yes, it does," he agreed with her, thinking of his sons. Their family was altered forever without them. "That's wise of you. This war is going to change everything after it's over. The last one did too. The Great War shook up the whole social order of the British aristocracy, and destroyed the economy. But this war has thrown people together who would never have met before. There's very little left of the old ways, and maybe there will be nothing at all left of it once the war is over. People used to marry within their acquaintanceship, they married the people they grew up with, they stayed in their counties, and married the sons and daughters of their parents' friends. Now so many of the young men will be gone after the war, and you meet many more different kinds of people than you would have if the war had never happened. The son of a gentleman farmer doesn't sound so bad to me now. Twenty years ago, I wouldn't have liked it. But now? What's left? Nothing of the old order and the old rules. I'd like to meet your young man. Tell him he's welcome here whenever you come home, if he can get leave." Edward was intelligent about it and knew there was no fighting change, and he wanted her to be happy.

"Thank you, Papa," she said, grateful for his open mind. "Do you think Mama will feel that way too? I know she wanted me to get married when I came out, and she'd like me to have a title. But I never met anyone I fell in love with. And I don't care about a title."

"And you're really in love with this young man?" He still looked startled since it was the first he'd heard of it.

"I am," she said quietly.

"Then we should meet him soon. He'll think we're savages if I don't meet the man my daughter is in love with. What command is he with? He's RAF, I assume, if he likes to fly."

"He's the commander of a fighter squadron in the RAF."

Her father shook his head. "Tell him to try to stay alive till the end of the war. We've had enough heartbreak in this family, we don't need more. And I think your mother will understand too. She would have loved to see you married to an earl or a duke. But a good man is all you need. You don't need a title," he looked at the land around him, "and one day all this will be yours. You'll inherit everything," he said sadly, because it meant that both of his sons were gone, but he loved her too. "Does he like the land?"

"I think so, Papa. I'm not sure. He likes the skies and everything in them."

"Maybe he'll come to love the land too," he said hopefully as they walked back to the house, quiet and lost in thought. He was thinking of William and Geoff and how different things might be if they were alive.

It was a peaceful visit although a sad one, and they were sorry to see her go back to London after two weeks. She hadn't solved her dilemma about the SOE, if it was too unkind to her parents to continue working for them and risking her life. But she could be killed in a bombing raid in her dormitory in London too. No one and no location was entirely safe anymore.

She was still wrestling with her conscience about what she should do about the SOE when she got a call from Captain Potter himself, at her dormitory. She was in her room at the time and she came downstairs to talk to him on the phone in the hall.

"Have you made a decision yet?"

"I haven't," she said. "I want to keep on with it. But you're right too, if something happens to me, it might kill my parents. Losing my second brother just now has been very hard on them, on all of us," she admitted.

"I'm going to make it even harder for you, I'm afraid," he said. He felt bad for her but he needed her. Alex had become one of their best operatives and they had a dicey situation on their hands. "Whatever you choose in the end, I need you for a big mission in a few days. Could you come in and talk to me about it tomorrow?" He wouldn't discuss it on the phone and she didn't expect him to.

She met with him the next day in his office, and he told her what it was about. They wanted reconnaissance information on a munitions factory in Germany. He knew how precise she was, and how diligent. She didn't need a partner but if something went wrong, she could easily be trapped in Germany, and killed or sent to a prison camp, the former being more likely. It was a cruel thing to ask her to do on the heels of her brother's death.

Bertram Potter was willing to respect whatever she wanted to do. But the war wouldn't wait. She had never turned down a mission, and he needed her more than ever. This assignment would require split-second precision, or she wouldn't get out. They wanted her to transmit some critical information and then they were going to blow up the munitions factory immediately. They were going to airlift her in, as they had in France. And this was no genteel mission. This was hardcore, and she knew it as he described it to her. But he had no one else right for the job. He trusted her completely.

"Can I think about it tonight?" she asked him.

"Yes, and I'll respect whatever you decide. If you don't want to do it, I won't push you, and we'll get someone else, though maybe not someone as good." She never failed. He smiled at her. She had turned into someone he could rely on. He hoped she'd agree to do the job. "Maybe you can retire after this one."

"I probably won't want to," she said seriously. "This kind of work becomes an addiction. I think I might already be hooked." But this wasn't going to be the kind of fun she had in Paris, toying with the enemy, enjoying every minute of it, and going to parties in glamorous gowns. This would be using her wits from the moment she hit the ground. She told Captain Potter she would call him in the morning. She wanted to sleep on it.

She was supposed to have dinner with Richard that night and she was relieved when he had to cancel. Two of his pilots were sick and he was going to fly a mission himself that he hadn't planned to. She wanted time to think.

She was awake most of the night and called Captain Potter in the morning.

"I'll do it," she said simply. "When do I leave?"

"In two days, on Friday. I need you to come in and be briefed all day tomorrow. We're getting our directions directly from the prime minister and the War Office." It was a very big deal and she had to tell Richard that she couldn't see him for the next few days. She said she was going back to Scotland.

All she really knew was that she was going to parachute into Germany and they estimated that she'd be there for five days, and then she had to get out. It was the kind of mission people often didn't return from. She knew she had to, for her parents' sake, if nothing else. And she didn't feel she could turn Captain Potter, or her country, down. She had to do this, even if she retired afterward.

She spent all of the next day in briefings, and particularly studied the list of requests from the War Office. She saw a memo from the prime minister himself. This was no small mission. It was huge. And it was an honor that they wanted her to do it.

She had dinner with Richard the night before she left. She was leaving early the next morning and she told him she couldn't go to a hotel with him, but she would when she got back, and she wanted to plan a trip to Hampshire with him when they both had leave. He was touched that she had spoken to her parents about him, and thought it was a good sign. She had said that her father was aware that the world was changing and didn't hold it against Richard that he didn't have a title, which was something of a relief.

"Will you be all right going to Scotland tomorrow?" he asked her gently. "You seem tense." He always noticed her every little mood and nuance and paid close attention to it.

"I probably am," she said casually. "You know how the roads are. They're a mess all the way up there and back."

"I wish I thought it was just the roads you're worried about. But whatever it is, just take care of yourself. Your parents and I need you." She nodded and said very little that night. She couldn't. She had too much on her mind. She had forged papers, would be switching between three passports, travel documents that were also forgeries, maps to learn, signals to send and decode, sabotage if possible. It was a massive assignment, and a very delicate one. She hit the ground running, literally, when she parachuted in the next day. Everything went smoothly, and she met her first contact in the place she was meant to, and got the documents she needed. She was going to be spending all five days in the vicinity of the munitions factory and she didn't want to be recognized, or become a familiar face either, which would be dangerous for her then and in future.

She slept with her Sten gun under her pillow at the hotel, and carried her pistol in her pocket at all times. She had her commando knife on her, and was on the alert day and night. She slept little, and sent encoded messages through couriers a local agent sent her. This was a highly coordinated combined effort, and by the fourth day, she had gathered all the information they needed in the war room. She was to be airlifted out the next day.

That night a bomb exploded at the munitions factory, placed there by a random group trying to sabotage the factory, and all hell broke loose. She contacted London through a local operative and asked what they wanted her to do. They told her to leave anyway. They had all their own sabotage mechanisms in place, and felt that their operation could go forward. They didn't care that someone else had planted a bomb too. But it had drawn countless German troops to the area and heightened vigilance.

She went to the meeting place for the plane that was due to pick her up. She was precisely on time, and heard the engines purring in the distance, and when the plane got close enough to land, an anti-aircraft gun behind her ripped through it, the plane crashed, and the pilot and gunner were killed. She disappeared into the brush and headed for some distant hills before going back to her contact. The

Germans didn't find her, but she had no idea how to get out and back to England now. She had valid though forged German travel documents so she could move around Germany, but she was going to need to make an exchange for a British passport to get back into England. And she couldn't walk home. It was too dangerous to go back to the local operatives after the explosion. The Germans would be covering every inch of the area for the saboteurs who had done it.

She hid in the hills and waited until the munitions factory exploded on schedule the next day. It was blown to smithereens, and the result of Alex's work was complete, but escaping didn't seem possible for the moment. She was stuck hiding in the forest. She retreated into the hills for four days after the explosion, and took refuge in a cave with some supplies she had with her, which sustained her. She sat up the entire time listening and trying to stay awake and be alert. And then she made her way back into town and contacted one of their operatives using a drop and a code. He was stunned that she was still there. They arranged for a plane to pick her up that night, and that time it worked without a problem. The Germans were searching the area, and she had to hide right up until the time she left at ten o'clock that night. Alex had been gone for nine days instead of five, and they had been tense ones. But she had cleverly avoided being captured by the Germans.

She reported to the SOE office on Baker Street

when she got back to London, and Captain Potter was waiting for her to congratulate her on an extraordinarily successful mission. She had had a lot of time to think while hiding in the hills, about what she wanted to do.

"Are you going to retire now?" he asked quietly. He hoped she wouldn't. Her calm sangfroid under pressure was of great value to the SOE.

"No," she said with a sigh. "I suppose I'm in forever. What do spies do when they get old?" She was beginning to wonder.

"They keep spying until they can't remember who's on what team anymore. Some operatives stay in forever. I probably will," he said, smiling at her, grateful that she was staying. She had accomplished her mission with infinite precision.

"Maybe I will too. Anyway, I'm going to bed now. At least I didn't kill anyone this time." But they both knew something like it would happen again one day. It was the nature of their work, along with ingenuity and courage. And she had plenty of both.

"So how was Scotland?" Richard asked her when she saw him for dinner the next day. She looked more rested after a good night's sleep. There was no visible sign of what she'd been through for nine days.

"Oh you know, pretty tiring, the usual . . . the same."

"I will do you the honor of not asking you anything

more about it," he smiled at her, "and spare you the embarrassment of lying to the man you love."

She didn't try to convince him otherwise. She just let it go. She was too tired to convince anyone of anything. All she wanted to do was sleep. She had spent the afternoon in the War Office, telling them what had happened in minute detail, and everyone was pleased with the end result and how they had achieved it. The munitions factory had been utterly destroyed in the second explosion, the mission she had been in charge of that was nearly bungled. The prime minister's secretary made due note of the identity of the agent who had parachuted into Germany and stayed there until all her goals had been accomplished.

"Can I talk you into going to bed with me tonight?" Richard asked her after dinner, but she looked exhausted.

"Can we put it off just a bit? I'm too tired to move," she said, smiling at him.

"I think you've gone off me," he teased her.

"I promise I haven't. I'm just tired."

"That's what you get for driving rocks all over Great Britain."

"I suppose so," she said, and melted into his arms when he kissed her.

Chapter 8

Richard and Alex finally managed a trip to Hampshire that summer, in August. It was the first anniversary of William's death, so the family spent some quiet time in the cemetery and Richard joined them. There was a marker there for Geoff now too. But the rest of the weekend was easy and pleasant. Alex showed Richard all her favorite spots where she had played with her brothers, every tree she had climbed, or almost, the tree house they had built together when Willie was fifteen, Geoff thirteen, and she was eleven.

He spent time with her parents, and took a long walk with her father. Edward didn't ask him what his intentions were, he already knew from Alex, but he wanted to get a sense of the man she wanted to marry one day, and he liked him. Richard was polite, well brought up, and well educated. He didn't come from an important family or have a great deal of money, but he was a gentleman and a kind person and he loved Alex. Her parents could see it. Her mother was still a little disappointed that Alex didn't care about marrying within the aristocracy, but Alex said it meant nothing to her. And most of the men she had known growing up were dead now.

She was happy with Richard, and they insisted they wouldn't get engaged until after the war. They didn't want to jinx themselves by making plans before it was all over. The war had been going on in Europe for almost two years.

The Americans came into the war in December of that year, 1941, after the Japanese attacked Pearl Harbor in Hawaii. Their joining the war gave the Allies fresh energy, and they needed it.

Alex and Richard spent Christmas with her parents in Hampshire, which was different now with neither of her brothers present, but Richard added a new male element, and he was wonderful with the children from London.

Alex was surprised by how much they had grown in the last two years. Some of the older ones were teenagers now. Richard thanked her parents profusely for letting him join them, and they went back to London on New Year's Day as Alex always did.

In the spring, Alex hardly saw him.

A thousand bombers were sent to bomb Cologne in May, another thousand to bomb Essen in June, and a little later in the month, another thousand bombed Bremen and the Focke-Wulf aircraft factory. The bombings continued all through 1942, and in 1943, the British concentrated on destroying the German industrial base. While Richard was fighting them from the air, Alex was in and out of Germany frequently for the SOE. In November 1943, the Allies began a four-month bombing campaign to destroy Berlin.

In March of the following year, 1944, Alex parachuted into Germany to help a handful of RAF officers escape the German Stalag Luft III prisoner of war camp, a hundred miles southeast of Berlin, and successfully made it across the border with three of them. With the help of several operatives, she got them back to England. Seventy-six prisoners had escaped the camp, of which fifty were murdered, twenty-three were captured and put back in prison, and three made it to freedom and came back. The camp had been thought to be escape-proof. Alex had only been able to save three of them.

Two months later she was a frequent visitor to the war room and had become a familiar face as plans for D-Day, the invasion of Normandy, got under way. She supplied all the information she could, was parachuted into France twice, and successfully got back to England. When the actual battle began on June 6, Richard's squadron was involved from the air, while the U.S. Marines and the army landed on the beaches.

Alex no longer made excuses to Richard for her frequent disappearances. He was used to them by then. Even the king and queen hadn't been to Scotland as often as Alex claimed she had been. All he cared about was that she was safe and came back quickly each time after she'd disappeared. They both had parts of their jobs that they couldn't discuss with each other, but their goals were the same, to win the war, and have it end.

By the time the invasion of Normandy began on D-Day, Alex was twenty-eight, Richard was thirty-six, and they had been in love for almost four years. Her parents were used to him by then, and enjoyed his company. Even Victoria had stopped regretting the fact that Alex was not going to marry a peer of the realm, and have a title. She was perfectly content to have Alex become Richard's wife one day, if they both survived the war.

For the next year after Normandy, most of Alex's missions were in France and no longer Germany. She met with Resistance cells in the countryside, and became proficient with explosives. She had frequently been obliged to defend herself by then, when caught in tight situations, and her commando knife had proven to be more useful than her pistol, which had its purposes too. She never discussed the weaponry she used with Richard, although on one occasion, in an amorous moment, he slipped his hand under her skirt into her garter belt and removed it holding her pistol. He didn't question her about it. He knew better, but the nature of the dangers she faced and the risks he suspected she took worried him constantly. When he found the pistol in her garter belt, he handed it to her with a bemused expression.

"I assume you use this to help with your driving. Do you shoot other lorry drivers if they get in your way?" he asked with a raised eyebrow.

"Something like that." She smiled at him and offered no further explanation.

"Pretty little weapon, though. It's so small. Does it really work?"

"Would you like me to show you?" she said wryly.

"Actually no, I wouldn't." He had come across her commando knife once and hadn't said anything about it. He had never seen the submachine gun she concealed in her belongings, which would have truly shocked him. She had recently gotten a new one with a silencer, the latest model Sten gun, which was extremely useful. When they were fooling around on the lawn one day during a visit to her parents in Hampshire, she flipped him on his back with a judo move that knocked the wind out of him, and left him breathless on the grass for several minutes as he looked up at her in amazement. "You're a dangerous woman, Alex Wickham."

"I try not to be," she said demurely.

"Did they teach you that when you were driving ambulances, or when you got your license for the lorries?" He was curious about what she did, but didn't press her. He knew better than to pry.

"A little of both." He had sensed for several years that there were things about her he didn't want to know, and couldn't. Just as there were things about his missions that he couldn't share with her. It didn't matter. They knew enough about each other, and their love deepened year by year. They trusted each other completely.

In the final days of the war, both of them were constantly running from one assignment to the next. Alex was working closely with Military Intelligence, while still receiving assignments from the SOE, and Richard's squadron was in the air more than it was on the ground.

Eleven months after the invasion of Normandy, it was finally over, on May 8, 1945. Both she and Richard had been instrumental in the final days of the war, and a week after Germany surrendered, Richard's commanding officer informed him that he was to be awarded the Distinguished Flying Cross. Alex was enormously proud of him, and expected no recognition herself. What she had done for the past five years, she had done for love of country, and to speed up the end of the war. It had been a long time coming, after almost six years of war in Europe. She would get no acknowledgment for her clandestine activities as a spy, unlike Richard, who was a war hero.

Her mother was busy then locating the parents who hadn't visited the children for several years. A few had, but not many, either following government recommendations, or because they couldn't afford it or it was too difficult. And many had died, which they knew. Victoria had stayed in touch with the parents for the most part, but at the end of the war, eleven of the twenty children were orphans, and only nine had families and homes to return to.

Victoria had a lengthy discussion with Edward about it, and they consulted Alex too. They wanted to continue to offer a home to the eleven children who had virtually grown up there and no longer had families. Alex agreed. It seemed like the right thing to do, and the children were thrilled. The youngest would turn eighteen in seven years, and Victoria felt taking care of them would occupy her since both of her sons were gone, and she doubted that Alex would move back from London, even now. She was happy that Richard and Alex visited as frequently as they could.

The nine children whose parents were still alive went back to London within two weeks of peace being declared, and everyone cried when they left. They promised to write and visit often. The Wickhams had been wonderful to them. The children called their benefactors Aunt Victoria and Uncle Ed.

In the final days after the war ended, Alex met with Bertram Potter, and they shared a sandwich in his office. He had papers on his desk stacked up nearly to the ceiling.

"What happens now?" she asked him. After five

years of working together, he was still her boss but they were also friends.

"I suppose they'll shut us down eventually," he said. "We've served our purpose. The war is over."

"There are no peacetime spies?" she said, smiling at him.

"There are, but that's all run by the military. We were separate and independent, even though we co-operated with them. We had fun, didn't we?" He looked nostalgic about it.

"Sometimes," she admitted, "at other times I was scared to death." Alex had done things she had never thought herself capable of, but working for the SOE had always seemed like the right thing to do. She had only questioned it briefly after Geoff's death, for her parents' sake, but had stayed in anyway. She was willing to die for her country.

"What are you going to do now? Go back to Hampshire?" Bertram asked her.

"I thought I'd go for the summer, to help my mother. She's decided to keep eleven of the children. They're all orphans. The other nine just went home. It won't feel like home to them after six years. Anyway, after the summer, I suppose I'll look for a job, hopefully in London. Hampshire is too quiet for me. It always was. And you?" She knew he had no wife or children. His whole life was his work, and the people he knew there.

"It will take me about a year to get through the paperwork, and get everything in order before we can officially close our doors." He looked around his office, and Alex could easily believe it would take him a year to get through it all, maybe two. "You can always help me with the clerical work if you want to. There's enough to keep a dozen people busy."

"I might." She looked as though the idea appealed to her, she liked working for him, and Bertram clearly liked the idea too. "I'll call you in September when I'm ready to come back. I want to get Richard to stay in Hampshire for a while too."

"What's he going to do without a squadron of fighter pilots to command? He's got flying in his blood. He won't give that up easily."

"It's a good question. He hasn't found the answer yet himself. Flying lessons aren't really enough to keep him busy. And nearly everyone knows how to fly now, at least those who want to. The others hope to never hear the sound of planes again. It will remind them of the war."

Two weeks later, while she was cooking lamb chops for dinner in the apartment they occasionally borrowed from a friend, she turned around to see Richard behind her, perched on one knee on the floor, with a determined expression.

"Are you all right?" She had no idea what he was doing, and then it dawned on her. He had a purposeful expression on his face. "Now? While I'm cooking?"

"Yes, now. I've waited long enough. I've waited nearly five years for this moment." She stopped what she was doing, took off her apron, and turned off the stove. "Alexandra Victoria Edwina Wickham, will you do me the honor of marrying me and becoming my wife?" She hadn't expected it to affect her that way, but her eyes filled with tears immediately, and she nodded, and answered.

"Yes, I will," she said solemnly, and then he surprised her even more. He reached for her hand and slipped a small diamond engagement ring on her finger. It was beautiful and she stared at it in disbelief. "Oh my God, when did you do that?"

"Yesterday," he said proudly. "I went to Asprey. It's an antique." It fit perfectly, and he stood up then and kissed her. She thought of something after he did. "Did you ask my father?"

"Three or four years ago. I told him we wouldn't get engaged until after the war." Richard looked very pleased with himself and the lamb chops were forgotten.

He was still living at the base, and she in the dormitory, and she knew she had to move out soon. They used their friend's apartment when they wanted to spend a night together and didn't want to go to a hotel. The apartment felt more like a home. The couple who'd been living there were getting divorced and weren't using it for now. She had met someone while he was stationed elsewhere.

Alex warmed up the lamb chops again, and they

sat down to dinner at the table in the kitchen. The apartment was really too small for them, but they loved being able to spend occasional nights together. That would have never been possible for Alex before the war. But after six years of freedom, air raids, and sabotage missions, no one paid any attention to what others did, and most of the old rules had fallen by the wayside. They couldn't live together without being married, but they could spend nights together as long as they were discreet and no one knew.

"When do you want to get married?" she asked him, as they ate dinner.

"Soon. Yesterday. Four years ago," he said, smiling at her. "Do you want to get married here?"

"Let's do it in Hampshire with my parents. In July?"

"Perfect. I should be out of the RAF by then. And then I have to find a job. I have some ideas."

"I need to get a dress," she said dreamily, and he smiled at her. He was glad that they'd waited. Now they could plan their future together, without worrying about who would be dead the next day, or if she'd be widowed in the first month of their marriage.

They called her parents that night and told them the news. They were delighted. They would have the wedding at the church, and a reception at the house for friends in the neighborhood. Richard thought a few of his RAF friends would come too. He wanted one of them to be his best man. Alex wanted her parents as her witnesses, and her father would walk her down the aisle.

She wanted to find a dress before she left for Hampshire, and her mother offered hers from thirty-four years before, which meant more to her. Victoria had come down the grand staircase in her parents' home in 1911. They had moved into Edward's family home after that, with his mother still living in the dower house at the time. It was unoccupied now. They'd been saving it for Alex one day, but eventually the entire estate would be hers, with her brothers gone.

Richard still owned his father's farm, but rented it to a tenant farmer and hadn't been there in years. The farmer was very responsible and Richard liked deriving a small income from it, although he didn't want to live there. And like Alex, it was his now, as the only survivor. Alex would own her father's entire estate one day. The war had decimated their families and killed all their siblings. It had happened to so many.

Alex left for Hampshire two weeks later. She had emptied what she had at the dormitory and was taking it on the train to Hampshire with her, in two suitcases. Richard was going to join her there in a week. They were to be married at the end of July and Richard said he had people to see in London in the meantime, about their future. He was being slightly mysterious about it, and Alex let him. She knew he would tell her when he was ready.

For their honeymoon, they were going to the South of France. They had talked about going to Venice, but Italy was still in turmoil, although Venice had come through the war relatively unscathed. They had only been attacked once when a hundred planes had bombed the harbor and destroyed all the German ships there, but the city had been untouched. In other areas, many of the roads had been bombed, and there was rubble everywhere. Parts of Italy were in ruins. They were going to Cannes on the Riviera instead, to lie on a beach for a week, and soak up the sun together and then go back to Hampshire for the rest of the summer. Alex had assured him that he'd earned this, after six years of flying fighter planes and commanding a squadron.

She felt like a princess when she got home. Her mother fussed over her, and had gotten their best guest room ready for her and Richard. Her childhood room was too small for them. And in the guest room they would be in the opposite wing from her parents.

She and her mother spent the next two weeks getting ready for the wedding. They chose the flowers at the nursery, set the menu, and hired a caterer for the lunch. They invited fifty friends from neighboring homes and farms, and a few good friends from London. With rationing still in effect, they couldn't have a big wedding or serve more people. But they were happy with close friends. They had both lost so many. And her mother altered the wedding dress for Alex. It fit perfectly.

Victoria hired a small local band so there would be dancing. At last they were having a celebration. There was something joyful to share with their friends, not a tragedy. The war was over, and at last, Alex was getting married. She only wished her brothers could have been there.

Chapter 9

The wedding her parents gave for them was exactly what Richard and Alex wanted. Small, elegant, intimate, but more informal than most weddings of the past. It was a beautiful sunny day for an outdoor reception in her parents' garden. The music in the church was what they had selected. Victoria had arranged the flowers herself, and Alex carried an exquisite trailing bouquet of tiny white orchids and lily of the valley, which grew in the greenhouse of her parents' estate.

The food was delicious. Some things were still difficult to get, but there was enough and it was beautifully prepared and served, and the dance music was wonderfully romantic. Richard danced with Victoria, and Alex with her father, and he could see how happy she was. Their eleven foster children had been Alex's only attendants, all dressed in white. Victoria made their clothes, and they were proud to be part of the ceremony. They had preceded her into the church and looked adorable. At the end of the day, when the last guest had left, after enjoying quantities of champagne, malt whiskey, and the excellent food, and dancing until nearly midnight, the bride and groom went to their room, which Victoria had decorated with white orchids.

The next day, after breakfast, the couple boarded a train, which would ultimately get them to Nice in the South of France for their honeymoon. Richard had reserved a suite for them at the Carlton, with a balcony and a view of the Mediterranean. The elegant hotel on the Croisette had been used as a military hospital during the war, and was being restored to its original use now, and already open as a hotel. For the next week, they ate in intimate restaurants, walked along the Croisette, swam in the sea, and lay on the beach and reveled in finally being a couple in peacetime. Alex had carefully locked all her weapons of war in a trunk and moved them to the attic in Hampshire before their wedding. It was the past now.

Their honeymoon was everything Alex had dreamed of and always wanted, and they returned to Hampshire suntanned and relaxed. Alex wore a simple gold ring with her engagement ring, and Victoria and Edward were happy to see them.

A few days after they got back, at dinner with Alex's parents, Richard shared his plans for the future. He had been to the Foreign Office before he came to Hampshire for the wedding. He had tried to think about what he would be good at, and would provide an interesting life for them. Neither of them wanted to settle down in Hampshire, at least not yet, and he couldn't imagine himself as a banker, or even a teacher. The only training he'd had was as a pilot, and he couldn't see himself supporting a family on what he'd made giving lessons before the war. He didn't want to be a commercial pilot and be away from Alex all the time. The thought of flying commercially made him feel like a bus driver.

"This may sound crazy to you," he said cautiously, "but I thought the diplomatic corps could be interesting. We'd be assigned to a foreign country for four years, and then move on somewhere else. And at the end of it, I would have a respected position in the Foreign Office." He looked at Alex after he suggested the idea, and she was smiling. He had said it with considerable trepidation. What they had described to him sounded very exotic, and with Alex's gift for languages she would be the perfect diplomat's wife, and he had a feeling she would entertain beautifully, after what he had seen of the way Alex had grown up. She had the background and the training. "What do you think?" He looked at his wife as he said it. "Would you mind living all over the world for a number of years, before we settle down in England?"

"We were hoping you'd want to move back to

Hampshire," Edward said, sounding disappointed. "It's a wonderful place to raise children."

"I'm sure we'll end up here eventually," Richard said politely, "but it would also be an extraordinary experience for children to grow up in different countries and cultures before that, and for us too."

"I love the idea," Alex said when she spoke up. "We'd never be bored and we'd meet so many interesting people." It was the perfect counterpoint to her past five years as a spy, which she had some qualms about giving up. Life was going to seem very quiet, even dull, without her harrowing missions. Richard was thrilled that she liked his idea, and hadn't run screaming from the room. She was the ideal partner for an adventure of that kind. She had a thirst for new experiences, people, places, and languages.

"They said I would spend six or nine months at the Foreign Office, getting trained, and then we'd be given our first assignment. It could be someplace quite unusual." Alex's parents were startled, it had never occurred to them that they would want to be jaunting around the world, changing homes and countries every four years. But Victoria had to admit it suited them, and she thought it was very enterprising of Richard to have thought of it. Alex was full of admiration for him too, and she couldn't think of anything better or that she'd like more.

"You're brilliant!" she said to him when they were alone in their bedroom a little while later.

"Would it be too difficult bringing up children in different countries and moving every four years?" It had been his only hesitation, and they both wanted children.

"I don't think so," Alex said, thinking about it. "It would broaden their life experience immensely. And we'd have so much help provided by the embassies. We'd get very spoiled." She smiled at him. It was the perfect plan.

"If you agree, I'll start at the Foreign Office in September, and they'll send us to our first post next spring. We could start a baby now, if you want, and then it would be born before we leave," he said with a twinkle in his eyes. He was eager to have children.

"I think that would be hard, taking a very young baby to some exotic place. Let's settle in first and get to know the country, and then have children." It sounded like a much better plan to her, rather than taking a newborn to some far off country that might be primitive, or even hostile. "I love the idea of being in the diplomatic corps, though. My darling, you're a genius!" She put her arms around his neck and kissed him, and a little while later, they found their way to the bed, and made love. They had the time and opportunity now, a summer when neither of them had to work, and they were married. Alex had never been happier, and Richard was thrilled that she liked his plan for their future. The problem was solved.

* * *

It was mid-August when Alex was opening the mail that had been forwarded to her from her dormitory. She'd received an official-looking letter, and her eyes widened in surprise as she read it. Her parents had just come in from a walk, Richard was about to go fishing, and Alex had promised to go and play with the children.

"I'm to receive two medals," she said in amazement as she looked up at them with the letter still in her hand. The George Medal and the OBE. They were civil medals and not military, because the SOE was not officially part of Military Intelligence.

"What for?" her mother asked.

"My war work," she said, smiling at Richard.

"For driving a lorry?" Her father looked skeptical.

"Well, not exactly. I did a bit more than that." Richard was smiling at her, remembering the pistol and the commando knife he had discovered, and he had suspected for several years that she was doing more than she admitted for the war effort, probably a lot more, although he couldn't even begin to guess the extent of it, or the training she had received to do it.

"How much more than that?" her mother questioned her. They weren't awarding her two medals for a minor contribution.

"Oh, not a lot," Alex said vaguely, unable to say

more, even now. "Richard is the war hero, I'm not." She was well aware of her promise not to reveal her espionage activities for twenty years. It had been a solemn vow.

"You must have done something if they're giving you a medal." Her father was perplexed but she couldn't tell them or anyone of the reconnaissance and sabotage missions she'd carried out, and the frequent assignments behind enemy lines assisting Resistance groups in occupied Europe and in Germany. Bertram had reminded her of her sworn promise recently. She remembered it well.

"I translated a lot of documents for the Yeomanry," Alex said as Richard watched her intently and sensed there was much more to the story than she could tell them or ever would. He remembered her frequent absences, supposedly delivering rocks to other parts of Great Britain. He suspected the truth might have amazed them but he didn't insist. Her parents were baffled and afterward she looked at Richard gratefully.

"Thank you for not pressing me," she said to him.

"I understand, and I'm proud of you," he said in a tender voice. Without knowing the details, he suspected that there was a great deal more to his wife than any of them would ever know. He could only guess, and wondered if she had worked for Military Intelligence for the entire war. And if so, she would never be able to tell them. "All those times you disappeared, Alex, that was part of it, wasn't it?" She nodded but couldn't say more. "I thought so," he said quietly.

She still had her weapons locked in the attic. They hadn't asked her to return them. She wanted to keep them, if they'd let her. Captain Potter hadn't told her to give them back, so she hadn't.

"I'm just grateful you weren't killed," Richard said with feeling. And so was she, about both of them. Richard was only sorry that she couldn't tell them more. "I thought you were up to some mischief, I just hoped it wasn't too serious," he said, relieved. "I don't know what medals they're giving you," he said solemnly, "but I'm sure you deserve them, Alex, and you earned them." She nodded and was grateful that he respected her silence and didn't push her about it.

"I hope I did," she said with a serious look.

"I'm going fishing," he said then, letting it go. He kissed her and they walked out of the house together so she could play with the children as she'd promised.

"What do you suppose she did to get those medals?" Victoria asked Edward as they sat in the library together, after the two young people went out.

"Maybe we wouldn't want to know," he said wisely. "There were a lot of secret activities during the war."

"I hope she didn't do anything dangerous," Victoria said, but at least she had come through it and the war was over.

On his way to go fishing Richard was thinking

about how little they knew Alex. She was a brave woman, he had always sensed that about her.

And as Victoria glanced out the window, she saw Alex playing tag with the children in the garden, like any other young woman her age. She wondered what they couldn't guess about her, and decided it was best they didn't know.

Chapter 10

The small ceremony in September awarding Alex the two medals she was being given was a modest event in the offices of the SOE with Bertram Potter presiding, and a minor official from the War Office present. Bertram made a short speech, and his respect for Alex and affection for her shone through. The War Office representative pinned the medals on her, and shook her hand. No one else was there to see it and she was sorry Richard and her parents couldn't be there. Marlene served port and cookies afterward, which Betram had purchased himself to make the occasion more festive.

He spoke of Alex's courage and passion for her country, her determination to accomplish every mission, no matter how dangerous or challenging. He said that she had never refused or balked at a single assignment, and had gone behind enemy lines again and again in frightening conditions, without a moment's hesitation. He said she had been one of their best operatives, and richly deserved the medals and the appreciation of her country. He spoke of her loyalty, her bravery and willingness to do everything in her power and beyond to help win the war. Alex was deeply touched by what he said.

Bertram acknowledged that there were too many unsung and unknown heroes like her, who had acted in secret, followed every order, risked their lives, and in too many cases lost them to the enemy. It had been a costly war for the entire country.

Alex had already agreed to come in to the office twice a week to help Bertram organize his mountain of papers, so there was no need to say goodbye to him. And she was sad to hear that there was already talk of closing the office. There was no reason for the SOE to exist once the war was over, and there were no further assignments anticipated. Their operatives had already been disbanded. From now on, MI5 would be overseeing any intelligence missions domestically, and MI6 would handle anything international. SOE had become obsolete in peacetime, which made everyone who had worked for them sad to know that it would soon disappear into the annals of history. It made putting Bertram's files into the archives in good order that much more important, and Alex was happy to help him do it.

After the ceremony, which Richard couldn't attend, he took her to dinner at Rules, where they hadn't been since the war. It was their favorite restaurant. They had just found a small apartment in Kensington, and rented it furnished for six months, since they knew they would be leaving for Richard's first assignment in the spring. They still didn't know where it would be. The country was struggling to get on its feet, with massive rebuilding and restoration projects to face. In many areas, the city had been gutted, as had others in Europe. Germany was in shambles, and Italy not much better. France had suffered less damage by capitulating so quickly to the enemy. Their art treasures had been plundered and stolen in vast quantities by the occupying army, and members of the SS high command who had come to Paris strictly for that purpose. It was known now that the French had been clever about hiding many of their treasures underground, and the Resistance had been instrumental in helping them dig tunnels and caves, where their most valuable art was stored. But much had been lost and taken into enemy territory, and would be difficult to trace and even harder to retrieve. French museum officials were determined to do it, and many artifacts were already being brought back from the tunnels and returned to the Louvre.

Alex remembered Colonel von Meissen referring to Goering's many trips to France to bring trainloads of France's art treasures back to Germany. It was all too real now that the war was over and the enormous losses they had suffered were being revealed. Alex wondered if the colonel was still alive and had survived the war. She wondered too if he had just thought her a shy, unwilling young woman, or if he had realized that he had been duped. She knew she had gotten out just in time, but it had been one of her more entertaining missions, the only one of its kind, and a successful one. She had gotten all the information the War Office wanted.

By October, Richard had settled into his job at the Foreign Office, preparing him for his role in post-war diplomacy. He was carefully monitoring world news, while trying to guess where he would be sent for his first assignment, and he remained open to all possibilities. He and Alex would discuss world politics late into the night. Europe was still in turmoil, with every country severely marked by the war. Food was still scarce in England, crops limited, and the economy suffering with so much to rebuild. Asia had its own troubles. Richard didn't think he'd be sent there. Russia had taken over eastern Germany, slicing right through Berlin. A post in the Eastern Bloc countries would be challenging. They too were ravaged by the war and destitute, with people starving. And there were problems throughout the British Empire.

There had been trouble in India since the viceroy at the time war was declared, the unlikeable and unpopular Lord Linlithgow, had declared war on behalf of India without consulting India's nationalist politicians. As a result, their left wing congressmen opposed the war, and the most vocal among them, Jawaharlal Nehru, was sent to prison for three years, and had only recently been released. Imperial India was being torn apart by constant battles between the Hindus and the Muslims, with demands to split the country, frequent bloodshed, and a risk of civil war. Two million Indians had served in the British armed forces, most of whom would return to India now, to add to the dissent and confusion. It appeared to be an insoluble problem, and while they were focused on the war in Europe, the British had lost power and control elsewhere in the empire. British India's days appeared to be numbered, which Richard was studying intently.

It was February of 1946 when the Foreign Office finally informed Richard of his assignment, as deputy counselor to the viceroy, a respectable position, which would provide him a front row seat to the changes that would be inevitable in the coming months, and a valuable training ground for him. There had been a mutiny of the Royal Indian Air Force a month before. And a few weeks previously there had been demonstrations in Calcutta, in which many of the participants had been killed, and then further strikes to protest their deaths within a day. They had just been notified in the Foreign Office of a mutiny of the Royal Indian Navy as well, and of another strike in Bombay where two hundred had been killed.

"These are troubled times in imperial India, Montgomery. You won't have an easy task. We believe that Indian independence will be inevitable, and we'd like that to happen with as little bloodshed as possible, which may not be feasible. Partition may be inevitable too. Nehru will be an important player in the future. Krishna Menon is a trouble-maker of the worst sort, and Mahatma Gandhi is their spiritual leader. There are extraordinary economic opportunities there, Karachi and Bangalore are booming, while they're starving in other areas. You'll be briefed on all of it of course now that we know where you're going," the Foreign Office official said, smiling at him.

"Living conditions are exceptionally good, just as always, with many servants. We have a quite pleasant house for you there, and there are a multitude of social events in the British and international communities. It has always been a post that our people have enjoyed. I'm sure you will too. And lots of other women to keep your wife amused. You leave in four weeks, by ship. It's a long journey, but passenger ships are being returned to service by the navy, and refitted for peacetime use. It will be an adventure, Montgomery. Best of luck to you. Your briefing sessions start in three days.

"Viscount Wavell is the viceroy, he's a good chap. I've worked with him myself, very fair. He's the right man for you to start your career with. Four years in India, particularly at this time, will teach you a great deal. I'm sure you'll make ambassador on the next round. Four years go faster than one realizes. It's enough time to settle in and really get to know the country, but not so long that you won't want to move on to the next post." Richard nodded, trying to absorb everything he had been told.

What stuck out in his mind was that they were leaving in four weeks, and he wanted to tell Alex so she could start getting ready. He knew she wanted to spend time with her parents in Hampshire before they left. He had a lot to do, and wanted to advise his tenant on his own farm that he would be in India for the next four years. It sounded like a lifetime right now. But his tenant was solid and reliable so that was one less worry for him. Richard smiled as he wondered how many children they would have by the time they moved on to their next post. And aside from the political issues which would keep him busy, it would be a comfortable life for them, far more so than in their tiny flat in London, or even life on her parents' estate. After the war, it was nearly impossible to get help. No one wanted to be a servant anymore. They all preferred to work in factories and offices, and so many of the young men hadn't returned from the war.

He was waiting for Alex when she got home from her work with Bertram that night. She had stayed later than usual, struggling to create an archival system for him. He was a brilliant leader, but not adept at creating records, or keeping files updated, and they had a lot of catching up to do, since they knew the players and the assignments so well.

The minute Alex saw the excitement in Richard's eyes, she knew that there was news. He told her as soon as she took off her hat and coat, before she even had time to sit down.

"We're leaving in four weeks," he blurted out like a schoolboy with something important to report. "We're going to India. I'll be deputy counselor to the viceroy, which isn't an important post. But I have a lot to learn." She could see how happy he was, as he threw his arms around her and lifted her off the ground.

"That's very exciting!" She was happy too. India sounded fascinating, she had been reading about it extensively. "I wonder if they'll get independence while we're there."

"It sounds like it, although that's not going to be a simple change, with the Hindus and the Muslims. The Muslims want partition and their own state. There will almost surely be bloodshed over that. But we'll be safe in New Delhi. They said we have a very pleasant house. So we're off and running. Your pilot husband has a real job, and we have some exciting years ahead of us. Thank you for being such a good sport," he said and then kissed her. "Let's go out to dinner to celebrate." They went to a neighborhood pub they frequented and had bangers and mash. The sausages were still a bit thin, but they were tasty.

Alex was already thinking of everything she had

to do in the coming weeks, and what she wanted to pack. What she didn't need, she was going to leave with her parents. She knew she'd need evening clothes in India, for the social life they'd lead there, and she wanted to be properly dressed and make Richard proud of her. Her evening gowns from her London Season eleven years before looked tired and outdated now. She hadn't bought any new ones since. Her mother had said she would give Alex some of hers. She had to give Bertram notice that she was leaving, so he could hire someone else to help with the files. Marlene was overwhelmed. They still called her by her code name, although her real name was Vivian Spence.

When Alex told Bertram the news the next day, he looked crestfallen. He had known that they were waiting for Richard's foreign assignment, but he had hoped it wouldn't be so soon.

"In four weeks?" He was visibly dismayed.

"I hate to do it, but I really need to leave in two. I have to pack and get everything organized, and I want to spend time with my parents. It's a long way for them to come, and I'm not sure how often they'll get out there to see us. It's going to be hard for them when we leave." She was dreading it for them, now that she was their only child. But she had to follow Richard, as his wife, and they hadn't complained. It would be painful for them, though. She was even more grateful now that they had the foster children to distract them.

"We'll have to work more quickly then, and do all we can in the next two weeks," Bertram said with an air of determination mixed with panic. There was so much left to do. And he had just been given notice that the SOE office would close in June, only four months away. He didn't see how they could finish by then, but they would have to. The SOE was history, it was over.

Alex was working earnestly at her desk in the tiny office she'd been assigned, and she was diligently closing file after file, and packing them chronologically into boxes as she finished. It was all to be delivered to the archives of the War Office when SOE closed.

Bertram walked into her office with a serious expression as she put another folder into a box that was already half full. It would be easy for anyone to understand her system if they ever wanted to exhume the files from the archives, and she was making a careful inventory for a master list, with the names of every operative, and each assignment had a file number they could cross-reference.

"I hate to interrupt you, but could you come into my office for a minute?" Bertram asked her.

"Of course," she said, stopping what she was doing. "Is something wrong? Did I forget something?"

"Not at all. There's someone here to see you." She followed him into his office, and a tall lean man with gray hair was standing at the window, looking out, and turned to smile at them as they walked in. Bertram introduced them. His name was Lyle Bridges, he was very distinguished looking, and had eyes that took everything in. Alex could sense that he was scrutinizing her as she sat down across the desk from Bertram, and Lyle Bridges sat down in the chair next to her. He got right to the point, and the purpose of his visit.

"I've heard a great deal about you, Mrs. Montgomery, and Captain Potter has allowed me to read your file. It's very impressive. I wish you'd been working for us for all these years, in Military Intelligence, but you did indirectly. Thanks to operatives like you, we won the war." She smiled at what he said. "The country needs more people like you. Sometimes I think women are our best agents. They're more practical than men, and sometimes more fearless. They don't talk about it, they just go in and do the job. I understand that you'll be going to India soon," he said.

"My husband has joined the diplomatic corps," she said cautiously. "India will be our first assignment. We're very excited about it."

"It's an interesting time there, with independence in the offing, and possibly partition. You won't have a dull moment." He smiled at her. She still had no idea why Bertram had introduced them, or what Lyle Bridges wanted with her. The war was over, and so was her job with the SOE, and they were leaving in four weeks. She had understood that he'd been with Military Intelligence during the war, but all of that was over now. It was history, for her anyway. "You must be wondering why I wanted to meet you. The war is over, for most people. But we are the watchdogs who never sleep. MI5 keeps track of national security domestically, and MI6 is the foreign branch. We have operatives all over the world, even in peacetime. And your going to India now is a very interesting situation, for you and for us, and an opportunity for you to continue to serve your king and your country, and to protect our fellow countrymen from threats of any kind, sometimes even before they happen.

"I've seen and read about the kind of dedication you brought to your work for the SOE, and you caught the attention of some of my colleagues during sessions you attended in the war room, particularly before D-Day. Nothing goes unnoticed there." He smiled at her, and his eyes were needle sharp, watching her reaction to what he said. "If you joined us, we wouldn't expect you to take an active role, as you did in the war. But you have an opportunity to gather information from the people you meet, the things you hear or observe. India is far from London, sometimes people have a tendency to be more outspoken in the colonies, even if India is about to not be one, and become an independent nation, which makes it even more important to keep a finger on its pulse. You will meet many of the Indian officials who interest us, as the result of your husband's job with the viceroy. We would like to ask you if you would be our eyes and ears in India, and simply report to us what you see and who you meet, what you hear, who attends the dinner parties you go to, or who you invite to your home. You might even receive some direction from us on that. Lunch with the wife of an important official could give you a wealth of information. We're interested in all of it," he admitted.

"And how would I share the information with you?"

"We'll give you a small radio transmitter, disguised as a first aid kit, and you can send us messages in code. There's no risk to your transmitting, there's no danger now of someone intercepting it and shooting you, as there was during the war behind enemy lines. It's just an information flow between you and MI6, and a way for you to continue serving your country, if you agree to do it. There is no risk. But your security clearance would remain the same as it is now, in case you come across sensitive information. You haven't been deactivated in our files yet, so there would be nothing additional to do. You could contact us once a week if there's nothing going on, or after every social event, to give us a list of who you met. It's very low key compared to what you've been doing for the last five years. And it would take very little of your time. I imagine your husband will keep you busy with all the events you have to attend as part of his job. That's why your current situation will be so interesting to us." She nodded, and didn't say anything as she thought about it.

"Would I be able to tell my husband?" she asked. She didn't want to keep secrets from him again, as she had to about the SOE and couldn't even tell him now. An open flow of information and honest exchange between them seemed important.

"I'm afraid not," Bridges answered. "Just to be on the safe side. We consider it top secret, in case you come across something important to national security. It's best, in fact obligatory, that he doesn't know." Alex nodded again. "Will you give it some thought?"

"I will," she said quietly. What he wanted from her was clear. Even if the stakes and consequences weren't as severe, he wanted her to continue being a spy, and she wasn't sure she wanted to do that. For the past eight months, she had considered that chapter of her life closed. And now they wanted her to open it again, and lie to Richard. What they wanted didn't sound difficult, but it put her in an awkward situation. She **did** like the idea of having something more important to do than just having lunch with other women and going to parties with Richard at night. As long as they didn't have children yet, she had time on her hands.

"You would be paid by MI6 this time. Not a fortune. We pay a very average sum into a bank account each month. Too much money would draw attention, so we keep it to an amount you don't have to explain, as we did before."

It was all swirling around in her head as the man from MI6 shook hands with them and left, and she looked at Bertram across his desk.

"Did you contact them, or did they initiate it?" she asked, curious about it.

"I got a call from MI6 yesterday. This was entirely their idea. They must have seen Richard's file in the Foreign Office. They see everything."

"What do you think I should do?" She was troubled.

"I think you should do it," he said without hesitating. "You're not the sort of woman to just spend your life dressing up and putting on makeup, and chatting with other women. You need something more important to do. And this isn't just about you, Alex. You love your country, so do I. People like us need to find a way to serve. What else is there? Where would England be without us?" He smiled at her.

"It can't be that important telling them who I meet at parties."

"You never know. They wouldn't ask you if it wasn't, and India is a hotbed of intrigue and political conflict right now. It could turn into a real mess if they don't handle it right, particularly with partition. The Muslims want a piece of India to make their own country, Pakistan. India is mostly Hindu, and they want the Muslims out too." Alex had been reading about it for months. "There could be a full-scale religious war there, the likes of which we've never seen."

"What are you going to do?" She had wondered about it but hadn't asked him recently.

"I'm going back to MI5, to keep the country safe at home," he smiled, "while you junket around the world and have a dozen servants to dress you and serve you breakfast in bed. It won't be a bad life," he said affectionately. Life in the colonies had always been luxurious and pleasant.

"There's more to India than that, a lot more," she said. "I want to visit the shrines, and try to understand the religious issues better between the Hindus, the Muslims, and the Sikhs." She sounded naïve but well-meaning to him as she said it.

"That alone is a life's work. It's a magical place. I served in the army there years ago. But there's a cruel side to it too. Be careful of that."

"Do you think I'd be in danger if I take the job?" she asked him candidly, trusting him to be honest with her.

"No, I don't. This is the tame side of spying, what they're proposing to you. You'd be an information source for MI6, nothing more. They have thousands of them all over the world. They don't expect you to solve their problems out there. The issues are too big for that. They just want names and places and what people say. It might be fun." She thought so too. She just wasn't sure if she wanted to be a spy again. She had enjoyed not working since peace was declared, but she did want to find something to do in India, or she knew she'd be bored. "Think about it tonight," he suggested and she sighed.

"I hate lying to Richard."

Bertram laughed at that. "Most women do, about far less worthy things than national security. And you wouldn't be lying to him. He's not going to ask you if you're still a spy. It would never occur to him." That was true. He might have suspected something about her wartime activities but he had never asked and wouldn't. If he did suspect, he knew she couldn't tell him. "Sleep on it tonight. MI6 is very anxious to have you. They said as much when they called me. They'll wait."

Alex went home after that, her thoughts filled with the conversation with the representative from MI6 that afternoon, and Richard noticed that she seemed distracted. She said she had a headache from going through dusty files all day.

"Well, that's almost over." He smiled at her. "You'll be a lady of leisure with an army of servants to wait on you soon." He was proud to be able to provide that for her through his job.

"That sounds sinfully indolent," she said, looking embarrassed. "I'll have to do something to keep busy."

"Have babies," he said, smiling tenderly at her again. "It would be easier for you there, with so much help." She nodded. She liked the idea too, once they settled in, which was their plan. She wondered if spies had children. She supposed they did. She felt less guilty as she thought about it now. Her love for her country hadn't diminished with the end of the war. And working for MI6 would be a way to be useful, with no great risk to her, as Bertram said. There were no dangers to the job. And what harm would it do if she told them who she saw at dinner parties and what they said? It was so little to do for her country. She had almost made up her mind when she fell asleep that night.

She awoke the next morning to a beautiful day. Richard talked about the political situation in India over breakfast, and she found all of it fascinating now.

By the time she got to the SOE office, she had made up her mind, and no longer felt guilty about it. Richard was serving their country in his own way. She had hers, even if it was more clandestine. Her conscience was clear.

She walked into Bertram's office as soon as she arrived.

"I'm going to do it," she said in one breath, and he looked up with a smile.

"Good girl. I knew you would. It's very little effort, with some possible benefit to national security, and no risk to you." That was her conclusion too.

She called Lyle Bridges from her office a few minutes later, and he sounded pleased. "Welcome to MI6, Mrs. Montgomery. You should have been one of ours all along. I don't know how we missed you.

We should have snatched you from SOE at the start of the war. We'll need a day to brief you. You don't need training from us. I read your training scheme. You won't need any of that now, but it's good to know. I assume you still have your 'accessories.'" He meant her weapons and she understood.

"Yes, I do."

"Keep them. They're always good to have. We'll give you the transmitter when you come in to be briefed." They set a date for her to come to their offices before she left for Hampshire for her last two weeks in England. She walked back in to see Bertram to tell him.

"Brava, my dear. Once a spy always a spy," he said and laughed. "There's no reason for you not to do this," he said more seriously. "And MI6 is a good branch. The best."

"Thank you for the advice," she said, and she was walking out of his office when he spoke again.

"Call me Bertie," he said softly and she looked at him and smiled. He wasn't her boss anymore. They were colleagues, and there was a nice feeling to it, like graduating, or growing up.

"Thank you, Bertie," she said and walked back to her office. She sat down at her desk, still smiling. She was a spy again. It felt much better than she thought it would. It gave special meaning to her life. And Bertie was right. Richard didn't need to know.

Chapter 11

Alex's two weeks in Hampshire with her parents flew by, and Richard joined her for the last few days. He had finished all his briefings by then. She had done hers with MI6 in a single day, before she left for Hampshire, but no one knew except Bertie. She had a last lunch with him before she went, and he promised to stay in touch. She was going to miss him and his wise advice.

Edward and Victoria came to see them off on the boat when they sailed from Southampton. The Foreign Office had booked passage for them in first class on the SS **Aronda,** a ship of the British India Steam Navigation Company. It was five years old, there were forty-five passengers in first class, a hundred and ten in second, and two thousand two hundred and seventy-eight "unberthed deck passengers." It was a very comfortable ship though not as luxurious as some of the European or even

British ships. The food was known to be excellent and first-class passengers dressed fashionably and formally in the evening. The ship carried cargo as well, and the journey would take four weeks, which seemed long, but they had both brought a stack of books and articles to read, for work and pleasure, mostly about India. There was so much to learn, and Alex wanted to know all she could when she got there. There were going to be social events to attend on the boat in the evening too. Alex had brought several trunks with her, mostly of summer clothes to wear in the crushing heat. They had no plans to return to England in the next few years. Her parents had said they would try to come in about a year, and Alex hoped they would. They might even have a grandchild by then, in which case she was sure they would come.

Their final parting was as painful as Alex had feared it would be. Victoria was sobbing, and Edward had tears in his eyes when he hugged Alex, who could barely speak. Richard felt acutely guilty for taking her away from them, but the opportunities in the diplomatic corps were limitless and too tempting, and Alex had wanted to go too. She just hated to leave her parents now that her brothers were gone. She was their last surviving child, which they all still found unimaginable. And the pain of loss seemed so fresh.

The boat horn sounded and her parents got off and waved from the dock for as long as Alex could see them, and then she turned to Richard standing at the railing next to her in the brisk March breeze.

"Are you all right?" he asked her, worried, as he put his arms around her. "I'm sorry, Alex." He felt as though he had stolen her from them.

"Don't be. We're going to have a wonderful life in India," she said generously, wiping the last tears off her cheeks with the handkerchief her mother had given her. It smelled of her perfume.

They went to explore the ship after that, and reserved a table in the dining saloon. The sea was choppy as they left Southampton, and the sky was gray. It was a suitable way to leave England, but it smoothed out after that, and that night Alex wore a simple black evening gown of her mother's, and Richard played billiards afterward. It felt like a honeymoon to them.

They lay on deck chairs and read most days, with blankets covering them and deck stewards in attendance, serving them bouillon and biscuits, for those who were seasick, although not many passengers were. It had been a smooth voyage so far. They had dinner in the dining saloon every night, and played shuffleboard in the daytime. They chatted with other couples making the trip, and felt like old friends by the time they docked in India four weeks later.

Alex could hardly sleep the night before, waiting for the mysteries of India to unfold, and Richard was eager to get to work, and meet the viceroy and the counselor, his direct superior, the man that he would be working for.

Two Anglo-Indian assistants came to meet them at the dock in Calcutta, with a car provided by Government House, and another vehicle for their luggage. As Richard watched their trunks come off, Alex looked around at the people, the women in gem colored saris, with their heads covered and bindis on their foreheads. There were beggars in the streets near the dock, and children with missing limbs who tore at her heart. And threaded among them there were colorful carts, pedicabs, a palace in the distance, the smell of flowers and spices heavy in the air. It was everything she had thought it would be. The roads were choked with people as they drove away from the dock and she stared out the window at the sights as they went past. She hardly spoke to Richard, she was so intrigued by everything around them, and he was watching intently too.

They were driven from the dock to the train then for the nine hundred mile journey to New Delhi where they would live. The first-class compartment was comfortable and luxurious. They had a thirty-hour journey ahead of them.

The trip to New Delhi was long and tedious, and when they finally arrived they were driven to the Lodhi Estate area, near the Lodhi Gardens. It was the most recent residential area built during the British raj, where government officials lived. They entered a gate, and drove down a narrow driveway past a riot of colorful flowers, and a garden and lawn that were perfectly tended. There were big trees shading the house, which looked like a small Victorian palace, and was referred to as a "bungalow." Half a dozen servants were standing outside, all dressed in white, waiting to greet them as they arrived. It was even more beautiful than anything Alex had imagined. Young boys came running from the back of the house to help the drivers with the luggage, and an Indian man in western dress came forward and bowed deeply.

"I am Sanjay, your butler, sir. My wife, Isha, and I are at your service." He bowed again to Alex, and a graceful-looking woman came to stand next to him. He introduced her to their new employers, as she bowed too.

Alex's trunks were being carried into the house at a rapid rate, as a flock of young men and women appeared. There were at least a dozen of them, and four men tending the immaculate garden. Richard and Alex walked into the house then, and the beauty of it took her breath away. The ceilings were at least fifteen feet high in two large reception rooms and a dining room, each with a wide balcony. The fragrance of exotic flowers was heavy in the air in the house, and enormous fans were circling lazily on the ceiling, moving very little air, but the rooms were relatively cool. A handsome staircase off to the side led up to the bedrooms. There were two huge bedrooms on the second floor, with dressing rooms for each of them, and on the floor above were half a dozen guest rooms. Isha explained that the servants were housed in a separate building. She offered to show Alex the kitchen then, and Alex followed her down the back stairs to the main floor, and through a narrow passage to an enormous room where half a dozen people were working and a male cook was giving them orders in Hindi, a language Alex had not tried to master yet. The most common choices here were Hindi, Urdu, or Punjabi. And there were numerous other dialects around the country.

The chef was dressed in white Indian dress and bowed low to Alex and spoke to her in rapid Hindi, assuring her of his deepest respect and dedication, as translated by Isha.

"Please tell him thank you." Alex was not used to speaking through an interpreter but here she had no other choice, and Richard was planning to use interpreters too.

"How many people work here, in the house?" Alex asked Isha.

"Only fourteen in the house, ma'am, but many of them have children or family who come to help in the day." Alex had counted at least twenty people rushing around so far. And she suspected that all of them were poorly paid, but they looked happy and cheerful, and grateful to be there. There wasn't a sour, unhappy face in the lot, they were all clean and tidy, and the house was immaculate.

Their bedroom was decorated in pale blue satin,

with curtains to match the bedspread and furniture, enormous windows looking out over the balconies, and shutters for when the days were too hot. It was already warm, and it was only April, she could imagine how hot it might get in August. Alex had read that men always complained about their dinner jackets and tailcoats and the heavy winter uniforms they had to wear for state occasions and formal functions, particularly in the case of visiting royalty, which until now had happened often, and perhaps would occur less once they achieved independence, which was becoming more and more likely. Independence was bound to affect how people lived in India, if it was no longer a colony of the British Empire. They would be following Indian traditions then, and not British, as had been the case for the past two hundred years.

When Alex went back upstairs, she found Richard on their bedroom balcony, admiring their surroundings. Everything around them felt exotic, and it was easy to see, even at a glance, why people loved living here. Nearly twenty domestics and a beautiful house for the deputy counselor of the viceroy seemed extraordinary. But it was what they had heard about before.

"I should go to the office and introduce myself," Richard said to her.

"The house is so beautiful," she whispered as she stood next to him, and he put an arm around her. "And so many servants I won't know what to do with them." Isha had explained that there were two laundresses, one for her and one for Richard, a duster, three cleaners in the house, the cook and his two assistants, and sometimes many more when they entertained, two footmen to serve at table for only her and her husband, and a woman whose grandmother had been trained as a ladies' maid in London to help Alex dress if she wished it, and Isha and Sanjay. And that did not include the four gardeners and a chauffeur, and extra people who were added for special occasions. In all, there were nineteen people to wait on them, and Alex could easily understand why people who had lived in India for most of their lives, or a long period of time, had trouble adjusting when they came back to England. That kind of opulence and service hadn't existed in England for half a century.

The cook had prepared a light meal for them by then, and Isha led them to the dining room where Sanjay was waiting, and introduced them to the two footmen, Avi and Ram.

Two places were set at the table with embroidered linens, silver, and crystal, and a moment later, Avi and Ram served them a light Indian meal, under the stern supervision of Sanjay, worthy of any English butler. He had already explained to Richard that he had worked in the viceroy's palace as a young boy. Richard could only imagine what that looked like, if the deputy had a house like this with nineteen servants.

Richard left quickly after lunch to meet the viceroy and the first counselor, and Alex went upstairs to find three women and her lady's maid unpacking her trunks with Isha. Alex wanted to do it herself but was afraid to offend them, so after studying the closets, she told them where she wanted things put away, and she instructed them to leave the final locked valise for her to deal with. Richard wasn't aware that she had brought them, but she had her weapons in there. She hadn't carried them in nearly a year, but given her new assignment with MI6, she had brought them. The very small radio transmitter they had given her was in the same case. She found a locked cupboard with the key in the lock in her closet. After she closed the closet door behind her, so no one could observe her, she put her weapons away there, locked the door, and put the key in her pocket. She didn't want anyone coming across her Sten gun, especially Richard.

Richard came home that evening, as pleased with his two superiors as Alex was with the lovely house they had been assigned. Richard had expressed to them how comfortable and luxurious their living quarters were, and Counselor Aubrey Watson-Smith said with a broad grin that theirs was even bigger, and his wife had become totally spoiled. He said she hadn't stopped having babies since they got there and would have a rude awakening when they went back to England, and she had to take care of four children herself, which made Richard smile. And, he said, she was expecting another.

"We're hoping to do the same," he said in an undervoice. Alex had said she wanted to wait until they got settled, but Richard couldn't see that it would take long, given how they would be living.

He'd had a serious meeting with the viceroy, whom Richard found very impressive, and he liked Aubrey, his immediate superior, who invited him to join the local cricket team made up of the British men who worked there. There was to be a formal dinner at the viceroy's palace the following week, and he and Alex were expected to be there, and would meet everyone then. Their life in India had begun.

For the next three months, their social life was a constant round of parties and formal dinners. If anything, the social gatherings were even more formal than those in London, from what Richard knew of it. People in England had lost most of their servants after the war and couldn't replace them. The style now for extremely formal living had begun to relax ever so slightly, even among the upper classes, whereas in India nothing had changed. Those who lived there wanted to show that they were more British than the British, so everything was lavishly, beautifully done, and extremely formal and elegant. They had an army of servants to help them maintain a lifestyle that was faltering or had disappeared everywhere else. Alex felt like her mother in the old days, as she dressed in an evening gown every night and Sanjay laid out Richard's dinner jacket and black tie, since Sanjay doubled as butler and valet.

"I've never had a valet in my life," Richard said, when he came into Alex's dressing room as she put her lipstick on. She was wearing an exquisite pale pink evening gown, and looked like a young queen.

"And you probably never will have a valet again," she teased him, "nor I a lady's maid. I feel like a character in a nineteenth-century novel. It's fun, though, isn't it?" He smiled, pleased that she was enjoying their exotic new life so much. And she liked the women she had met so far. She had met Samantha Watson-Smith, the counselor's wife, and liked her, but she was eight months pregnant, and said she was going into hiding soon. She could hardly move, and was terrified she was having twins. She said she was twice the size she'd been with the last one. She had four boys and was hoping for a girl.

The formal dinner and reception at the viceroy's palace was spectacular, and very British. The next day Alex dutifully sent a list of all the guests she remembered meeting with a brief synopsis of their conversations. She did that every morning, after the social events of the night before. She used her radio transmitter as soon as Richard left for work.

In May, Jawaharlal Nehru was elected the leader of the Congress Party, which she reported to her superiors at MI6 immediately, although they would know that themselves from other sources. Alex reported it when she met him at the next state dinner at the Viceroy's House in June and she had a chance to chat with him. Nehru spoke to her of the end of British rule, and the importance of independence for India. He also mentioned partition. He felt strongly that the Muslims in India should be moved to what would become the dominion of Pakistan, and the four million Hindus in Pakistan should return to India, a massive and complicated undertaking. She transmitted what he said verbatim to her contact at MI6, whom she knew only by a code number and not a name. Meeting Nehru was the most important encounter she had had so far. She waited until she received confirmation that they had gotten her message, which she sent in code, and then she put the transmitter away in her locked closet. The ritual never took long and her transmissions were all benign. There was none of the urgency of the war in what she had to relay to them. It was as easy as Lyle Bridges had said it would be, and took almost no time at all. Her messages to MI6 were simple.

Everything about their life in India was easy and exceedingly pleasant, until August when violence between Hindus and Muslims left at least four thousand dead in a Calcutta bloodbath, which Alex reported to MI6 immediately, along with everything she heard about it. They were far from the violence in New Delhi, nine hundred miles from Calcutta.

She had been visiting Samantha Watson-Smith

and her new babies, twin boys as she had feared, when she heard the news. Samantha commented that Aubrey was afraid that there would be more violence in the near future. The Hindu population was afraid of extreme violence if the British agreed to an independent India and pulled out too quickly. The twins were three months old by then, and as she handed them to two Indian amahs, she said to Alex that they really had to stop. They had six boys now, and she would never be able to cope with them if Aubrey ever got transferred back to England. Alex laughed when she said it. It seemed to be the opinion of most of the women she met there, who enjoyed a lifestyle they couldn't have had anywhere else. And even in India, that life was about to disappear, or would eventually, with the end of British rule.

"I can see how one would get incredibly spoiled here," Alex admitted. She had described it in detail to her mother, who said she wished she had some of that at home. She was managing all eleven of the foster children with only one girl to help her now, since the other one had gone to London to find better-paid work.

Two weeks after the violence in Calcutta, an interim government was formed, and Nehru became vice president, which set off more violence two days later between Hindus and Muslims in Bombay.

In the fall, there was an atmosphere of unrest

throughout the country, and skirmishes between Hindus and Muslims were constantly occurring. Alex and Richard talked about it at night, and whatever information she gleaned, or insights into the problems, she passed on to MI6 rapidly, in a steady stream of daily commentary about the problems in India, all relating to the eventual independence of India, and possible partition from Pakistan.

On several occasions, Richard expressed concern that there would be violence in New Delhi, and without saying anything to him, Alex began wearing her commando knife again, and carrying her tiny pistol in her purse. She wasn't frightened of the violence herself, but the reports of the riots were concerning, with Hindus and Sikhs wielding sabers and swords, and massive bloodshed in the streets. The Sikhs were neither Muslim nor Hindu, but a separate religion entirely. They were monotheistic, believing in one God, originated in the Punjab region, and broke from Hinduism due to their rejection of the caste system.

But in their British circles all was peaceful. Viscount Wavell's Christmas party was the most extraordinary event Alex had ever attended, with elephants lining the drive to the viceroy's palace, and caged Bengal tigers decorating the front lawn. She described all of it in her letters to her mother, and sent lists and reports of everyone she met and spoke with to MI6 on her radio transmitter. Everyone she talked to with some knowledge of the subject felt

certain that there would be more bloodshed between the Hindus and Muslims, and more strikes
and riots, before India achieved independence, and
Richard felt sure they were right.

As the year ended, the only disappointment they
had experienced since coming to India eight months
before was that Alex had been trying unsuccessfully
to conceive a baby almost since they arrived, and
so far it hadn't happened. Richard was less concerned about it than she was. Alex was afraid that
something might be wrong. She visited a doctor
Samantha Watson-Smith recommended, a kind old
Englishman who had delivered all of Samantha's
babies, and he told Alex to relax, that coming to
India was a big change, and when he heard something of her war experiences, he told her that her
body needed time to adjust to peacetime and her
new environment. She had lived through six years
of stress and trauma during the war, and the loss of
two brothers. Now she was living in a foreign culture
with the drumroll of violence in the background.
It was hardly the right atmosphere to conceive a
baby, which didn't explain why Samantha had been
pregnant non-stop almost since she'd arrived, but
she had nothing else on her mind. She was a sweet
woman, but parties, and wearing pretty clothes and
seducing her husband, and then giving birth, were
her only concerns. Alex was far more involved and

interested in local politics, while appearing not to be, and following the news closely was of greater interest to her. She liked talking to the men at the parties they went to, not to flirt with them, as most of the women did, but to hear what they had to say and then report it to Military Intelligence at home.

But whatever the reason, Alex was still not pregnant at the end of the year. She shared her concerns with her mother, who said the same thing as the doctor and told her to relax, which was Richard's theory too.

The clashes between Hindus and Muslims continued, and erupted in March in Punjab. And just before that, in February, Viscount Wavell stepped down as viceroy, and was replaced by Viscount Mountbatten of Burma, great-grandson of Queen Victoria, uncle of Prince Philip, and protégé of Winston Churchill. He was greatly favored and much admired, and it was hoped that he would help make the transition to Indian independence smoother, and put an end to the violence that was spreading across the country. He had a warm relationship with many of the princes of India. He also had an absolutely dazzling wife, Edwina, who charmed everyone, became a close friend of Vice President Nehru, and was frequently seen with him. Viscount Mountbatten seemed to be off to a good start from the moment he arrived. People adored them both and were in awe of them.

It made a great change for Richard, as he had

enjoyed working for Viscount Wavell, and Viscount Mountbatten made stronger social demands on all of them. He and the spectacularly beautiful and charming Edwina entertained constantly, and Richard and Alex were expected to be there. Although Richard found it tiresome after a while, Alex found it very useful, and met scores of new people, and influential men in politics, which she reported to MI6 diligently. They rarely asked her for additional information. She supplied so much of it, about people and politics and key players, that they got a very clear picture of the state of India on the ground.

When she arrived, Alex had wanted to spend some time visiting the shrines of India, but with the increasing unrest, Richard had asked her not to, and she spent most of her time with social pursuits, meeting people, going out at night with Richard, and writing coded reports to MI6. Her lady's maid had seen her pistol and commando knife on her dressing table one morning while she was dressing, and had pointed to them and told Alex she was very wise. Alex put a finger to her lips, urging her not to tell, and the woman nodded immediately. She understood, but Indians were worried these days about what independence would cost them, and how many lives would be lost in the process.

The great moment finally came after years of negotiation and months of violence and riots. India

won her independence and became the Dominion
of India, free of British rule, on the fourteenth of
August 1947, fifteen months after Richard and Alex
had come to India, and on the fifteenth of August,
Pakistan became independent of India, and became
a dominion. India was largely Hindu, and Pakistan
Muslim. The exchange of many millions between
the two countries had not happened and would be
virtually impossible to implement.

Jawaharlal Nehru was made the first prime minister of the Dominion of India, and stood on the ram-
parts of the Red Fort, on the day of independence,
and unfurled the Indian tricolor flag to mark the
end of British colonial rule, and Lord Mountbatten
moved out of Viceroy's House, all of which Alex
reported to MI6. It was the end of two hundred
years of British history and the beginning of India's
freedom as an independent country. And Viscount
Mountbatten, no longer viceroy, at the request of
the new Indian leaders, became governor-general of
the Union of India.

Mohammed Ali Jinnah became the governor-
general of Pakistan, and Liaquat Ali Khan became
the prime minister.

For the next three months, there were massacres
and migrations of Hindus and Muslims between
India and Pakistan. The violence was unspeakably
brutal, with murders, arson, mass abductions, and
rapes. Seventy-five thousand women were raped
and most of them disfigured or dismembered in the

process. Villages were burned to the ground. Old women and infants and children were savagely murdered and hacked into bits. Pregnant women were viciously killed and babies set on fire and killed. The violence was unthinkable and unimaginable to civilized people, with extreme atrocities. It was in fact a religious war no one could stop.

As the months wore on, fifteen million people, mostly Muslims, had been forced from their homes, and close to two million were dead.

As viceroy, Viscount Mountbatten had agreed to India's independence ten months before it had been provisionally scheduled to happen, and people wondered if the violence would have been less extreme if the British had stayed in power longer, and made the transition more slowly, all of which Alex reported to MI6.

In September, a month after independence had been declared and the partition of Pakistan had taken place, Prime Minister Nehru asked for four million Hindus to be removed from Pakistan and sent to India, and an equal four million Muslims in India to relocate to Pakistan. Both countries were in an uproar and at the end of October war broke out between India and Pakistan. Alex wore both her pistol and her commando knife all the time now whenever she went out. Although most of the violence was in Punjab, India was becoming a dangerous place. She kept her Sten gun where she could reach it quickly, in case she ever needed to defend herself or their home. So far, they weren't in danger in New Delhi, and they were far from most of the violence, but that could always change. Her parents were worried about her, and she always assured them that they were safe.

Also a month after independence was declared, the Watson-Smiths were transferred and Richard became counselor, no longer deputy, an important promotion for him.

The turmoil in India continued into 1948. In January, the country was shaken when their spiritual leader Mahatma Gandhi was assassinated. For the rest of the year various princely states seceded from India to join Pakistan, or the reverse. The Indo-Pakistani war continued insolubly. In June, Viscount Mountbatten gave up his position as governor-general of the Union of India, after less than a year in office. The position of viceroy had disappeared with independence, and the position of governor-general was taken over by an Indian, while Jawaharlal Nehru staunchly remained prime minister, with a firm grip on the country.

Richard's position in India was more delicate after Viscount Mountbatten left, and Richard quietly remained below the radar, making himself available for British subjects still living in India, and attempting to pour oil on troubled waters wherever possible. But life in India wasn't nearly as pleasant as it had been when they arrived. They still had the same luxuries and remained in the same house, but

Alex had her small weapons on her at all times, and Richard caught a glimpse of them one day while she was getting dressed.

"How long have you been wearing those?" he asked her, surprised to see them again. He thought she'd put them away after the war.

"For a while," she said quietly. "Old habits die hard. I wore them night and day for five years." But he knew she had stopped carrying them before they came to India.

"Are you afraid here?" He was concerned and trusted her judgment and evaluation of the situation.

"Not really," she said thoughtfully. "But I like to be cautious. Things can get heated in religious wars." The fighting was geographically far from them, but they no longer had the status in India that they once had, now that colonial rule was over.

A year later, Nehru changed that, or altered it somewhat, declaring that despite becoming a republic, they could remain part of the British Commonwealth. The Indians and Pakistanis had agreed to a ceasefire in January, and signed a peace treaty in July. And in November, the man who had assassinated Mahatma Gandhi was executed. India was finally returning to some semblance of order more than two years after they'd won independence. Richard and Alex enjoyed a peaceful Christmas, and the best Christmas present of all was that three days before Christmas, the doctor confirmed what she suspected. Alex was pregnant at last.

Chapter 12

Alex was surprised by how ill she felt in the early months of her pregnancy. It was worse than she'd expected and she went out less than she had in the more than three years they'd been there. They had come to India at a historic time, and it had been a roller coaster ride being there, but all of that was eclipsed now by the joy she felt over the baby she was carrying, and Richard's delight. Her own joy was dampened somewhat by the misery of feeling ill from the moment she woke up, until she fell asleep at night. She went out with Richard in the evening whenever possible, but the rest of the time she stayed in bed, and Isha tried every Indian remedy she knew for the nausea of pregnancy and so far nothing had worked. Alex felt sick all the time.

The baby was due in July 1950, and they were to be transferred before then. Their four years in India were almost over, and Alex was worried about having to move to another assignment, and another country, shortly before the baby came. They had no idea yet where they would be going. Richard had had feedback from the Foreign Office in London that his superiors were pleased with him, and had promised him a good post on the next round. He and Alex both loved India and the people, and they had been heartbroken over the violence that had cost so many lives.

Alex began to feel better in January, and only days after the intense nausea had begun to wane, she received a letter from her mother that devastated her. Her father had died the day after Christmas, and Victoria sounded shattered. He was only sixty-three years old, had had a heart attack and died instantly. Alex was convinced that his sons' deaths had shortened his life. She was crushed over the loss. Alex was in the living room waiting for Richard when he came home.

"Are you all right?" She was so pale that he was worried, although he was used to it by now. She had been deathly sick since November, although she had concealed it from him at first, until she was sure she was pregnant. And now she was sheet white again.

"My father . . ." she said and couldn't finish the sentence. He'd been dead for nearly a month by then, and she hadn't known it. While they were celebrating Christmas, and rejoicing over the baby they were going to have, her mother had buried her father in the family cemetery, all alone, with none of her children present to support her. "I have to go home to be with her," Alex said, stunned by her father's death, and worried about her mother.

"You can't," Richard said fervently. "You're not well enough."

"I don't have malaria." She smiled weakly at him. "I'm pregnant."

"You'll lose the baby," and they had waited so long for it to happen. They had been trying for three years.

"No, I won't. Women have been taking ships while they're pregnant for centuries." But it would be a long journey, and would take weeks to get there. "Maybe I could fly."

"Ask the doctor. That might be worse, with the altitude." He didn't want her to make the trip at all.

"Flying would be faster. I want to spend a few weeks with my mother. I have to, Richard. She's all alone. She sounds overwhelmed by everything she has to handle now." It was the first time that Alex truly regretted their having left England. Before, they had each other. Now her mother was alone at sixty-one, and hadn't expected to be widowed. Going home to be with her for a while seemed like the least Alex could do. She was the only child Victoria had left.

She went to the doctor the next day and explained the situation to him. He didn't love the idea of her traveling so far, but the first trimester was over, and he thought flying might be less traumatic for her than a long journey by ship.

Richard reluctantly made the arrangements for her. She would fly BOAC and change planes several times. The whole journey would take nearly forty hours, and would be exhausting, but she would have more time with her mother that way, rather than wasting weeks going by boat, and she was determined to go. Richard had gotten her a seat on the plane for the next day. They lay together that night, while he held her and she cried for her father, and he feared she would lose the baby from the long trip.

"Just take care of yourself, please. I'll be worried sick about you."

"Don't be. I'll be fine." She got up, finished packing, and appeared in their bedroom carrying her Sten gun, and he gave a start when he saw it.

"What are you doing with that?" He sat up straight in bed.

"It's my old friend." She grinned at him. "I thought you should have it while I'm gone. You never know when you'll need it."

"I'm married to a mercenary. You're the only woman I know who travels with weapons, and your own submachine gun."

She grinned at him again. "Where do you want me to put this?" It was another reminder to Richard that whatever Alex said, she had done more during the war than drive rocks from England to Scotland to build airstrips. She didn't need a gun for that.

"Where's that been for the past four years?"

"Locked in my closet." She was carrying a box of the bullets too, and he shook his head.

"Leave it where it was, just give me the key." She left to put it away and handed him the key when she came to bed, and he shook his head again as he looked at her. "Sometimes I think I don't know you. You're always stronger than I think. I was in the same war you were, and I don't run around with a submachine gun, or a pistol and that nasty little knife of yours."

"I relied on them for five years. You were in a plane," she said simply, and he leaned over and kissed her.

"I'd hate to see you use them, you're probably a better shot than I am."

"I doubt it." She wondered what he would think if he knew she was working for MI6. He wouldn't like it. She had radioed them that day, and explained the situation, that she was returning to England for a few weeks, after the death of her father, and would make contact with them when she was there. She would have nothing to report in the meantime. Things had been quiet lately anyway, and she had gone out very little, feeling so ill.

Richard took her to the airport the next day, for the first leg of her trip. He kissed her and held her for a long time before he let her go, and she waved as she walked to the plane. She was sad, but strong, and anxious to see her mother. He watched her until she boarded, and then watched as the plane took off. He prayed that she and the baby would come back to him safely. He didn't want anything to happen to either of them. And as his driver took him to the office, he smiled at the memory of her, looking like a young girl in their bedroom the night before, holding her old gun. She was a remarkable woman, and he was just sorry she had to go home alone. But he couldn't leave India right now, he was too busy.

The flight to London seemed interminable although she slept a lot. Alex had been traveling for forty hours when she arrived in London.

She took a bus from the airport to the train station, and caught the train to Hampshire. Her mother had no idea she was coming. Alex got a cab at the train station and walked into the house carrying her suitcase, just as her mother was leaving for the market with a basket over her arm. She screamed when she saw Alex and looked like she was going to faint.

"What are you doing here? You're in New Delhi, and you're pregnant."

"I'm pregnant," she smiled at her mother and hugged her, "but I'm here now. I came to see you." And with that, her mother burst into tears, and they walked into the library and sat down. She told Alex all the details of how it had happened. He'd had a sudden terrible pain in his chest, and then he just collapsed and he was gone. Alex held her mother's hand and had an arm around her. Her mother was stunned and grateful she had come.

"I don't think Papa ever recovered from losing Willie and Geoff. It was too much for him. He had such high hopes for both of them," Alex said sadly. He had had far fewer expectations for his daughter, except about who she married. But in the end, he had liked Richard and by the time they married, he was very fond of him.

"I think you're right. How are things in India?" her mother asked her.

"Better. The country is settling down. It was a mess for a while. I think they did it all too soon. We're almost through there. Richard is waiting for our next assignment."

"I wish they'd send you home for a while," Victoria said wistfully.

"They won't." She didn't want to mislead her mother, and give her false hope. "They don't send us home between assignments. But at least I'm here now."

"Are you exhausted? You must have flown for days!"

"Forty hours. And I'm a bit tired, but I slept on the planes. Do you want me to go to the market with you?"

"I'll go. I won't be long. You have a bath and a cup of tea, and I'll be back as fast as I can." She looked better just seeing Alex.

"How are the children?" Alex asked, and her mother looked wistful about them too.

"There are only three left. The others are working at jobs in London. One of them is in Liverpool, and one in Manchester. One of them is at university in Edinburgh. They're lovely kids. They all came home for Christmas." Alex smiled. It had been a wonderful thing to do. Her parents had never had any regrets about them. "I'll be back quickly," Victoria said and picked up her market basket, and walked out the front door. Alex wanted to visit her father's grave with her mother, but she wasn't ready for it yet.

Alex walked to the phone as soon as her mother left. She sent a telegram to Richard that she had arrived safely, and was in Hampshire. And then she called her contact at MI6 for when she was in country. She reported where she was and how to reach her, and said she'd call again before she went back to New Delhi. And then she called Bertie at MI5. He was happy to hear from her, and sorry to hear about her father. He said he was fine, and enjoying the work. She brought him up to speed on India in a nutshell and none of it surprised him.

She thought about calling Samantha Watson-Smith when she hung up. They'd been back in England for a year, living in a tiny flat outside London with no help, and she was hating every minute of it. They were hoping for a plush assignment where they'd be comfortable. They had exchanged a few letters since they'd left, but she was so busy with the boys, she rarely had time to write.

Alex went upstairs to her old room then, and decided to stay there, since she was alone this time. She had bathed and changed into a black sweater and skirt and black stockings by the time her mother came back. She was wearing black out of respect for her father.

She went to help her mother with the groceries when she heard her come in. It felt good being there to lend a hand.

"How are you feeling, by the way?" her mother asked her.

"Better now. I was sick as a dog for the first few months."

"I was sick with you. I never was with the boys." She smiled at Alex.

"It's due in July. We'll have transferred by then."

"I hope to someplace decent with a good hospital," her mother said, and made lunch for both of them.

Alex went to bed early that night, exhausted from the trip, but she was happy to be home, and she knew it made a big difference to her mother. She still couldn't believe her father was gone. She wished he had lived long enough to know about the baby. He was too young to die, but so were her brothers. And now she had a new life inside her. She was thinking about how strange life was, with its losses and gifts, and then she fell asleep.

* * *

It was snowing when she woke up, and after breakfast, she and her mother went out to where her father was buried. There was no headstone yet. They stood there for a long time, holding hands, with the snow falling on their hair and shoulders, and walked back to the house for a cup of hot tea. Alex built a fire for them in the library and it felt strange to be home, but warm and comfortable too. They had been living in India for so long, and their life was so different there.

They played cards that night, and took the children to the cinema on the weekend. Several of the neighbors dropped by to check on Victoria, and they were surprised, and pleased for her, to see that Alex was home.

Alex stayed with her for three weeks, which gave them time to discuss who would manage the estate now, since Victoria didn't feel equal to it and Alex was so far away. The man who'd been helping Edward was willing to do it, and he was going to stay in touch with Alex on bigger decisions. And then she had to go back. It was even harder to leave than it had been the first time. She hadn't been home in four years. Her parents had promised to come out to India, but never had. And she knew her mother would never come alone, so she didn't know when she'd see her again. She didn't want to go years without seeing her, especially now, with her father gone and her mother alone.

"I want you to come and see your grandchild," she said in a husky voice as she was leaving.

"I will. I promise. And your letters are wonderful," Victoria said, as tears spilled onto her cheeks. Alex wouldn't let her come to the airport. It would have been too hard for both of them, and she wouldn't have her husband to go home with now. It would be a long, lonely train ride back to Hampshire.

"I'll send you pictures of the baby. If it's a boy, we'll name him after Papa." Hearing it only made Victoria cry more, and finally Alex tore herself away, and got into the car waiting to take her to the train station to get to London, and from there to the airport by bus. Her long journey back had begun.

Her mother stood in the doorway waving to her, until the car was out of sight, and then she sat down in the kitchen and cried. She wondered if she would ever see her daughter again, or the baby she was carrying. Wherever they went now on Richard's next assignment, it would still be so far away.

Alex thought about her mother all the way to London, considering the same things. She felt so guilty leaving her, but she had to get back to Richard. Her home was with him now, and they would have to move soon. She was glad she had come to see her mother. The trip seemed even longer on the way back.

She had sent Richard a telegram with her arrival time in Delhi. She didn't know if he'd come to the airport, but she hoped he would. You could see the small swell of the baby now. She was four months pregnant. She had gone to see her old doctor in Hampshire, and he said everything seemed fine, and the baby was the right size.

Alex slept on the last flight until the plane landed in Delhi, and walked down the steps with her hand luggage. Her mother had knitted a little sweater and cap for the baby and she'd brought them with her in her valise.

She was dazed from the long trip as she walked toward the terminal. She saw Richard as soon as she stepped into it, and he came toward her and held her close in his powerful arms.

"Oh my God, I missed you so much," he said as he held her for a long time and then they walked out of the airport together. His car and driver were waiting, and he handed Raghav Alex's suitcase, and got into the car next to her.

"Did you shoot anyone with my gun?" she whispered and he laughed.

"I never touched it. You're a menace. How's your mother?" he asked.

"Sad." He nodded. How else could she be? "I felt terrible leaving her. She's going to be so lonely now. I hope she comes to see the baby, wherever we are."

He looked troubled when she said it, and Alex had the feeling something was wrong. He looked happy to see her, but as though something else was bothering him. She didn't ask him until they were alone in their bedroom when they got home. Isha had brought her a tray with some soup and little things to tempt her to eat, and Alex thanked her warmly. "What's wrong?" she asked him immediately.

"Nothing, really. I got my new assignment. I was hoping for a change from here. Europe maybe, now that the country is recovering." She would have liked that too, especially now with her mother alone.

"What did we get?" She wondered if they were being sent to the wilds of Africa, or someplace primitive.

"Pakistan." His disappointment showed on his face, and in his eyes. "We've been here for a long time, and it isn't much of a change. They feel that I know the situation so well here by now, having been here for the transition, that they want to move me over to the other side. It's really the flip side of the same coin, and things won't be as comfortable for you in Pakistan as they are here. They say they're giving us a nice house in Karachi. I'm sorry, Alex. They promised me a plum job next time. They made me deputy high commissioner this time, which is a step up."

"A very nice step up." She smiled at him. It was like being ambassador somewhere else. Inside the British Commonwealth, they had high commissioners, not ambassadors. "When do we go?"

"May." It was in three months. She'd be seven months pregnant by then. "Do you mind having the baby there?"

"It's as good as anywhere else." It didn't worry her.

"The embassy has its own doctor, at least he's British. So you won't have some guy speaking Urdu or Bengali delivering the baby." She laughed at the thought.

"I don't think the baby will care," she said and he laughed.

"You're a trouper. I'm sorry I didn't get a more glamorous assignment."

"I don't need glamour," she said and kissed him. "I just need you."

"I'm a lucky man," he said and meant it. "Even if you do carry a lot of weapons around." They both laughed at that.

They were sad to leave the friends they had made in New Delhi, but a number of them had already left. The diplomatic community was always a group of ever-changing faces, which also made life interesting. Alex had come to love it and Richard did too.

Alex was particularly sad to leave Isha and Sanjay when they left New Delhi. They had been loyal and gentle and kind. She promised to stay in touch with them, and to send them pictures of the baby.

They had already sent most of their things to Karachi and Alex was pleasantly surprised when she saw the house there. It wasn't as pretty and luxurious as the house in New Delhi, or as lavishly staffed, but it was large and pleasant and peaceful, and there were enough people working there to keep them well served. Alex picked a room for the nursery almost as soon as they arrived. She ventured into the market-place the following week with her driver, to buy a cradle. She found a pretty one that was hand carved.

Richard liked the high commissioner he was working for, Sir Laurence Grafftey-Smith, who had been there since the partition and Pakistan's inde-pendence. He would be leaving in a year.

The social life in Karachi was much quieter than in New Delhi, which suited Alex for the moment. Once she got their new house in order, she was too tired to go out. She went to a few cocktail par-ties with Richard, and one official dinner, and by then she was eight months pregnant, and felt like a beached whale in the heat. The baby was big now and she was exhausted.

She met the local British doctor, and he thought the baby was large, but she'd had no problems ex-cept nausea in the beginning. There was a maternity clinic the wives of European diplomats used, and she was planning to give birth there. All the nurses were English or French.

Their house in Karachi had a wide porch that got a nice breeze at night. She was lying there with Richard a week before her due date, when her water broke. They called the doctor, and he sent them to the clinic and said he'd come later. Labor hadn't started yet, and traditionally first babies took a long time. Richard drove her there himself. He had already checked to see where it was. The clinic was spotless when they walked in. They examined Alex and said nothing had started and let Richard sit with her for a while. For the first time, she wished she were at home in England, with her mother. She suddenly felt far from home, and scared. She had braved the enemy a hundred times, and been in situations most men would have been afraid to face, but now, about to have a baby, she didn't feel equal to the task. He could see the fear in her eyes.

"Did you bring your gun?" he whispered to her, and she laughed. He had a way of lightening the moment, and making everything seem okay, even when it wasn't.

"My pistol's in my purse," she whispered back.

"You can always shoot the doctor if you don't like him."

"I wish I were home with my mum," she said sadly, as a tear crept down her cheek. She suddenly looked young and afraid.

"I wish they'd let me stay with you," he said, worried, but they'd already asked and been refused. There was a waiting room for fathers, or he could go home and come back later, after the baby was born, which most men did. The nurses said they would call him when the baby came, but he had promised Alex he wouldn't leave.

She dozed for a while after that, and woke up

around midnight when the pains started. They came hard and fast, and Richard could tell things were moving quickly, when the doctor arrived and he left the room. He assured Richard it wouldn't be long.

"The nurses tell me your baby's in a hurry." He smiled and closed the door, and Richard thought he heard Alex shout in pain after that. He paced the halls for an hour waiting for news. They had taken Alex to the delivery room a few minutes after the doctor arrived. Finally Richard sat down in the waiting room in despair. All the nurses would say was that they would notify him as soon as the baby was born.

She'd been in the delivery room for two hours when the doctor came to find him in the waiting room with a broad smile.

"You have a handsome son, Mr. Montgomery. Your wife did very well. You have a big boy, nine pounds." Richard almost winced when he said it. It sounded painful to him.

"When can I see Alex?"

"She'll be back in her room in a little while." He didn't tell Richard that he had just finished stitching her up. She was badly torn by a baby that size, and labor had been difficult and fast. A nurse brought the baby to show him then. He had a round face and Alex's blond hair. He looked like a chubby duck with pale peach fuzz on his head, and Richard's heart melted the minute he saw him. He was wrapped in a blue blanket, and they took him to the nursery as soon as his father had seen him. The doctor had left by then.

It was another two hours before Alex came back to the room. She was groggy from the ether they had given her when they stitched her up, and a shot afterward for the pain. When Richard walked into her room, she looked like she'd been hit by a truck, with dark circles under her eyes.

"Are you okay?" he asked as he bent to kiss her.

"I think so." She didn't want to tell him how bad it had been, but he could see it. They hadn't given her anything for the pain, until the stitches, and it was much worse than she'd been told it would be. Samantha always said it was like shelling peas, which was a bold-faced lie, she knew now. Her mother had hinted it might be hard the first time, but didn't want to scare her.

"He's so beautiful, and so are you." Richard kissed her, and sat next to her bed, holding her hand until she went back to sleep. As she lay there, the sun came up, and streamed into the room, and it felt like a blessing, as he watched his sleeping wife. They had a son. And he knew as he sat there that it was the most precious moment of his life.

Chapter 13

They named the baby Edward William Geoffrey Montgomery as she had promised her mother they would. Richard took a picture of Alex holding him, to send to her. They let Alex leave the clinic after a week. She was nursing him, and he was a hungry baby. He looked three months old when he was only a week old.

Richard was settling into the job, and getting to know the city. They were still dealing with religious issues, the fallout of partition, and the exchange of four million Muslims for four million Hindus, an immense undertaking which was nearly impossible to accomplish and still wasn't fully complete. Those they moved had nowhere to go.

Alex was happy to see him when he came home at night. She was on her feet again in a few weeks, enjoying the baby, and she had cut back her social life radically from what it had been in New Delhi. But she realized that she had to get back to it soon so she could report to MI6. The social life in Karachi wasn't as intense. She was enjoying being home with the baby and didn't feel like going out.

She started joining Richard for diplomatic social events again in October. She was very impressed when she met the prime minister, Liaquat Ali Khan. He was one of the great leaders of Pakistan, a champion of independent rule. He was a statesman, lawyer, and political theorist. He had been the finance minister of India's interim government, the first defense minister of Pakistan and the prime minister, and also served as the minister of Commonwealth and Kashmir affairs. Alex admired him and found him to be a fascinating person when she talked to him. She sent a report about their meeting to MI6, with high praise for the prime minister, who was much loved in Pakistan.

The rest of the year slipped by without event.

The new high commissioner, Sir Gilbert Laithwaite, Richard's new boss, arrived after the first of the year. He was British-Irish, born in Dublin, and a war hero from World War I. He had been in India for more than thirty years, on various commissions with the India office, as principal private secretary to the viceroy. He had also been deputy undersecretary of state for India and had just returned from a tour of duty as ambassador to Ireland. Now he was high commissioner to Pakistan. Richard liked him from the moment he met him, and knew that he had a lot to learn from him. It would make his appointment to Pakistan that much more worthwhile. It had been uneventful so far, which in some ways was a relief after India.

In February a failed coup d'état caught everyone's attention. After a relatively peaceful year, the country was badly shaken on October 16, 1951, by the assassination of Prime Minister Liaquat Ali Khan, whom Alex had met and been so impressed by. It was viewed as a tragedy and he was called the Martyr of the Nation. Khan was shot twice in the chest and his assassin was killed on the spot, and said to be a professional killer for hire. The country mourned their prime minister's death intensely. Richard and the high commissioner met with Pakistani leaders several times.

The relatively peaceful year before that had given Alex and Richard time to enjoy their son, who had turned a year old that July, and started walking a few weeks after that. He was a happy, bouncy toddler, and Richard spent every moment he could with him and Alex when he wasn't working. Alex was trying to convince her mother to come and see him, without success so far. She didn't want to travel on her own, although she missed Alex terribly and wanted to see her grandson. But not enough to leave home. And she hadn't been well. She had become increasingly retiring since her husband's death, and didn't even venture to London, let alone Pakistan.

Little Edward was fifteen months old the week

after the prime minister's death when he came down with a flu of some kind and a high fever. Alex wasn't sure what it was, but they took him to the hospital the same night. He was delirious when they got there, and Richard and Alex were frantic. They were told by the doctor who examined him that he had cholera, which was common in both Pakistan and India at the time. He was unconscious half an hour after they got him to the hospital, and nothing brought down the fever as they sat with him through the night and Alex and the nurses bathed him with cool cloths. He was deep in a coma by morning, with Alex and Richard sitting next to his bed and holding him. Little Edward died at noon.

Alex held him in her arms after he died, and the doctor assured them that nothing could have been done for him. They were inconsolable, and held a funeral for him two days later. He was cremated after that, and Alex kept the little urn with his ashes next to her bed. She lay there day and night with her eyes closed, thinking of him, running the film of his short life through her head. And the last terrible night when they could do nothing to save him. She felt as though she had died herself.

Alex called a friend of her mother's in Hampshire, and asked her to go and tell Victoria in person what had happened. She didn't want her mother reading it in a telegram when she was alone.

Victoria called Alex in Karachi as soon as she'd heard, and tried to offer what consolation she could, having lost two sons herself. She felt terrible that she hadn't come to see him, but she hadn't been well herself. She had started having heart problems after Alex's father died, and was afraid of the long trip. And now she had lost a grandson she had never met.

Alex talked to her mother for a long time, and cried the whole time on the phone. A week later, Richard found her in their son's room when he got home, packing the baby's things. She hadn't touched any of it until then. But he wasn't coming back. Richard stood with her and they both cried as they folded all his clothes and put them with his toys in a big box. She wanted to save them, but couldn't stand seeing them every day. And she gently closed the door to his room after everything was packed. She didn't go in for months. It was too painful. Whenever Richard came home from work, she looked as though she'd been crying. She went out with him to important social events, but anything she could avoid, she did. She couldn't imagine being happy again. The death of King George VI provided some distraction, although everything seemed remote and unimportant to her now.

A month later, five months after Edward's death, Alex was shocked when she discovered that she was pregnant. They wanted another baby sometime in the future, but not so soon. She was still mourning Edward and knew she always would. She didn't feel ready to open her heart to another baby just yet. But fate had made the decision for her.

She wasn't sick this time, but her spirit wasn't in it. She acted as though nothing was happening, and never spoke of the baby or the pregnancy. She didn't want to fall in love with another child and have the fates steal it away.

"Do you want to go home to have the baby this time?" Richard asked her gently, and she shook her head. She was still sending coded messages to MI6, and she went out with Richard occasionally, but she had been depressed ever since Edward died, and Richard didn't know what to do. He had spoken to the doctor about it, and he said that she'd feel better after the new baby came, but Richard wasn't so sure. In all the years he'd known her, he had never seen her like this. He was wondering if he should take her home and leave her with her mother for a while. Alex barely spoke to him. The baby was due in October 1952, almost exactly a year after Edward's death. She was still depressed.

They went through the motions of sharing a normal life with each other, but Richard knew Alex wasn't there. She hadn't been for a year.

He took her to New Delhi for a party the high commissioner was giving. He thought it would do her good to see her old friends, and New Delhi was livelier than Karachi. The party was lovely and Alex looked beautiful, but he could tell that she didn't care about any of it. Something in her had died with little Edward, and Richard couldn't find a way to bring her back. He could feel the baby kick at night when they lay close together, and Alex never said a word. She never put his hand on her belly, or smiled when the baby kicked, as she had the first time. She seemed to be disconnected from everything in her life now, even Richard.

Alex had been in a fog all year. He wondered if she'd ever be the same. He got her to help him entertain, reluctantly, and he almost had to drag her out of bed to do it. Two weeks from her due date, she had still done nothing for the new baby. They were totally unprepared. They had put away Edward's cradle with his things, and they didn't even have a basket or a crib for the baby to sleep in. She had given Edward's crib away to someone who needed it.

She was putting something away in the nursery when her water broke, and she panicked, and suddenly there was a lake around her feet.

She looked at Richard with terror in her eyes, as though she was going to bolt and run.

"I'm not ready . . . I can't . . . I can't do that again," she whispered to him.

"It's going to be all right." The delivery had been fine the last time. Edward's death had nothing to do with the delivery.

When Richard called the doctor at home, his wife said he was out but would be back soon. He went to tell Alex, and she was lying on their bed, staring into space.

"We should go to the clinic," he said quietly, "the doctor is out, but his wife said he'll be back soon." He was worried about her.

"I don't care. I'm not going to that place again." Richard looked frightened by what she said, and the vehemence with which she said it. He could see how panicked she was.

"Well, you can't have the baby at home," he said reasonably, but there was nothing reasonable about Alex. She was a cornered animal, and she looked like she was ready to attack him, or run.

"Yes, I can have it at home. Everyone does here."

"Everyone we know goes to the same clinic we went to before."

"I hated it. I won't. And Pakistani women don't go there. They have their babies at home." He didn't want to remind her that Pakistan and India had among the highest infant and maternal mortality rates in the world.

"I won't let you do that. It's not safe for you or the baby to have it here." He could see from the expression on her face that the pains had started, and he didn't want to waste time arguing with her, but he wasn't sure how to get her out of the house if she refused to go. "I have some say in this too."

"No, you don't. It's my body, and I'll do what I want."

"It's our baby, Alex. Please don't take a chance with this. I wouldn't know what to do if something goes wrong, for you or the baby."

"I don't want to go back to where he was born," she said, sobbing. "It's too soon, I'll expect to see him there. I'm not ready for this baby, I can't do it again," and between sobs, she was writhing in pain. "What if this baby dies too?"

"It won't," he said, his eyes pleading with her even more than his words.

"You don't know that. It could get sick, just like Edward did." He had died in a matter of hours and there was nothing they could do.

"Please, Richard . . . I want it to be different . . . I don't want this baby to die too." All the pain and anguish and terror of the past year were pouring out of her like a tidal wave and she was finally reaching out to him, but he couldn't let her have it at home. What if everything went wrong? Then this baby would die too.

She hadn't been ready for this baby, and now he knew it, but the baby was coming anyway. They hadn't even tried to get pregnant this time. It happened with no effort on their part.

"What if I stay with you this time?" he asked, feeling desperate. They were losing time, and the clinic was twenty minutes away.

"They won't let you," she said through clenched teeth. "They refused last time."

"I'll refuse to leave you. I swear." As he said it, he scooped her up in his arms, and she didn't fight him. She was in too much pain. It was happening even faster than the last time. He ran down the stairs carrying her, as one of their servants came running to help him. "Get Amil," he said, asking for the driver, who came immediately. He'd been in the kitchen talking to the others. "We're going to the clinic," he told him, and ran toward the car with Alex. One of the maids rushed toward him and handed him a stack of towels. But by then Alex had stopped arguing with him, and Richard wasn't sure they'd make it to the hospital before the baby was born. It had been less than an hour since her water had broken. "Drive quickly," he told the driver, who took him at his word, as Alex lay against him in the backseat, and smiled up at him.

"I'm sorry I've been so difficult. I've been so broken."

"I know," he said gently, as another pain tore through her and she clutched his arm.

"I think I'm having the baby," she said, as he stared at her in panic.

"Now?"

"Soon." But just from the look in her eyes, he could see that she was back. Heartbroken over Edward, but sane again. She hadn't been in months. And he'd been at his wits' end.

She didn't make a sound for the rest of the drive to the clinic, but she had his arm in a vise-like grip. And the moment they got to the clinic, Amil opened the door, Richard scooped her up, and rushed inside carrying her.

"My wife is about to deliver," he said to the nurse

at the desk, and she rushed toward them, pressed a buzzer, and led them to an exam room at a dead run, as four nurses came flying out to help them. He lay Alex gently down on the exam table, as two nurses took off her clothes as quickly as they could. "You may leave now," the oldest of the nurses said in an imperious tone.

"I'm not going to. Just so we have that clear. My wife had a traumatic experience. I'm not leaving her for a minute." He looked fiercely at the head nurse.

"Her baby was very big. I was at the delivery."

"He died a year ago. I'm not leaving her alone." The nurse was shocked and didn't say another word. It was obvious that Richard wasn't going anywhere. And Alex was lying naked on the exam table and let out a hideous scream, as two of the nurses rushed to see what was going on, and the third covered her with a thin drape, and put her feet in stirrups. But as soon as the pain had passed, Alex looked at him and smiled.

"Thank you. I can do this if you're here," she said softly.

"I'm not going anywhere." Another pain seized her then, and she started pushing with a look of anguish on her face.

"Stop," one of the nurses commanded her. "The doctor isn't here yet." Alex paid no attention to her and went on pushing as she held Richard's hand. She let out another scream, and there was a wail between her legs, as one of the nurses checked under the drape, and lifted up the baby with the cord between its legs so they couldn't see what it was, but Richard didn't care, just so it was healthy. It was the most beautiful sight he had ever seen, and Alex lay back smiling, exhausted from the effort but looking victorious at what she'd done.

"It's a girl!" one of the nurses said, as the doctor walked in.

"What's going on here? And what are **you** doing here?" he asked Richard with a frown.

"Watching my daughter be born," Richard said with a broad grin. And the shock of the baby coming had finally shaken Alex out of her depressed and nearly catatonic state. She was crying as she saw the baby. She looked nothing like Edward. She had dark hair and dark eyes like Richard, which was a relief. If she had looked just like Edward, it would have been too hard, and too much of a déjà vu. Everything had been different this time, and it was a girl.

"May I examine your wife now?" he said to Richard, indicating that he should leave.

"You may, but I'm not going anywhere." The doctor turned to examine Alex and she was worn-out but happy. Richard was deeply moved by what he'd seen. "What are we calling her?" he asked Alex when they were alone, and she looked thoughtful.

"How does Sophie sound to you?"

"I like it," he said as he bent to kiss his wife. "You were spectacular, by the way. You deserve a medal for this too." She laughed at what he said, and for an instant there was a sad look in her eyes, and he understood and kissed her again, and spoke softly to her. "He was beautiful too. But this is the little angel we were meant to have." She nodded and squeezed his hand as a tear slid down her cheek. One of the nurses walked into the room and handed the baby to her, all cleaned up and in a pink blanket. She was the most beautiful sight they had ever seen. The doctor had left the room, and the nurses left them alone with Sophie, who peered at them as though she had seen them before. And, as Alex looked into her daughter's eyes, for the first time in a year she felt alive and at peace.

Chapter 14

When they left Pakistan for their next assignment in April of 1954, Sophie was eighteen months old, running everywhere, and full of life. All the servants and everyone who saw her loved her. Their time in Pakistan had been difficult for Alex, losing her father and little Edward, and her depression afterward. But Pakistan had been less turbulent than their years in India, although less interesting too. Their life in New Delhi had been more exciting and more fun. One of the highlights of their time in Pakistan was the spectacular party they'd given for the coronation of Queen Elizabeth II ten months earlier. It had been a glorious occasion and people were still talking about the party nearly a year later. They had gone all out to honor the young queen and no one would ever forget the party at the embassy, with a ball in white tie and tails for the men, and the women in exquisite evening gowns and magnificent jewels.

This time, they were happy to be going to Morocco, somewhere so different from anyplace they knew. After eight years in India and Pakistan, which were so closely related, they were ready for something new. Alex had promised to visit her mother with Sophie as soon as she could. The last of the foster children had left for university while they were in Pakistan, so Victoria was entirely alone. Morocco was close enough to England that Alex hoped her mother would finally visit them. Victoria had never been to India or Pakistan in all the years they were there, and Alex had only been home to see her when her father died. They wrote to each other a great deal but that wasn't the same as visiting would have been.

This time, after eight years in the diplomatic corps, Richard was going to Morocco as the ambassador, which was a huge step up for him, and Alex was very proud.

She had advised MI6 of their transfer to Morocco, and they had expressed considerable interest in what was going on there.

Once again, they were going to an assignment in a country that wanted its independence. In this case from France and Spain. Morocco had been divided into a French and a Spanish protectorate since 1912. There had been considerable dissent and unrest in Morocco for the past two years, before Richard and Alex got there. In December of 1952, a Tunisian labor leader had been murdered, and riots had broken out in Casablanca. The French government's response had been to ban the new Moroccan Communist Party and the Istiqlal, or Independence Party, which was conservative and royalist. A year after the banning of the two political parties by the French, they had aggravated the situation further by exiling Morocco's much loved and deeply respected Sultan Mohammed V. They had sent him to Madagascar, and replaced him with the very unpopular Mohammed Ben Arafa. The sultan was considered a religious leader, and the Moroccans objected strenuously to his exile. By the time Richard arrived in Rabat, the capital, as ambassador, Moroccan citizens were demanding the sultan's return, and responding with violence to France's reluctance to bring him out of exile. They now wanted independence as well.

Everything about Alex and Richard's arrival in Morocco was exciting. The embassy was an exquisite building with the Moorish architecture that Alex found exotic and appealing. The British ambassador's residence was a maze-like palace that she found fascinating, and she couldn't wait to entertain there. The diplomatic community was warm and welcoming, and Richard loved his very efficient staff. At the same time, they were living in a warm coastal city with a festive atmosphere that the French regularly flocked to as a vacation spot.

The ambassador's palace, like almost every house and villa in the city, was surrounded by beautiful gardens with lush flowers in a riot of colors. Some of the architecture dated back to the seventh century, and had originally been built by Spanish Muslims who had been expelled from Spain, hence its Moorish influence. The French had come much later in 1912.

Alex loved everything about the city. The medina in the older part of the city, in the center of town, was a conglomeration of shops and small inviting restaurants and cafés that Alex couldn't wait to explore, along with the nearby city of Salé, which had originally been built by the Romans. There were Roman ruins in many areas, and two major Roman roads. The city was rich with history. Everyone spoke French, which was an advantage for Alex, and she had already decided to study Arabic, and add it to her repertoire of languages. She was pleased that Sophie would learn French here once she started talking.

Alex had bought miles of sari fabric before she left India, and wanted to find a local dressmaker to turn it into harem pants, and flowing dresses to wear when they gave dinner parties. She felt as though she could be more daring in her dress here than she had been in Pakistan. Both were Muslim countries, but Pakistan was more conservative and traditional. Everything from the music to the history of the architecture delighted her about Morocco. Richard was going to be busy watching the evolution of their demands for independence from France, and their efforts to regain control over the areas still ruled by the Spanish.

The first order of business as far as the Moroccans were concerned was the return of Sultan Mohammed V from Madagascar. He had been there for a year when the Montgomerys arrived, and moved into the British ambassador's palace.

Morocco provided precisely the kind of exotic experience Alex had hoped to have when Richard joined the diplomatic corps. She enjoyed it even more than India, where the situation had been so dire at various times, and there had been so much bloodshed at the end of British rule, although Alex had loved India too. Once again, they had an army of servants to attend to them, and a flock of lovely young women to help care for Sophie.

In the first months of their residency, Alex visited all the historical sites and told Richard about them, since he had no time to explore them with her. She had visited the Roman ruins, the city of Salé, and the areas where the Phoenicians and Carthaginians had lived on the banks of the Bou Regreg River, right next to where the Romans had built Salé. She already knew the medina intimately after their first month there, and had found treasures in the shops.

She had sent her mother a beautiful antique hand-embroidered caftan to wear around the house, and found fun blouses for herself with little bells on them, and wonderful Moorish leather slippers with bells on them as well.

Alex was busy moving the furniture around and freshening up the ambassador's palace. She filled it with flowers every day. Richard commented that he had never seen her so happy, and they discussed the political situation when they met at night. Richard felt certain that ultimately Morocco would win its independence, without the bloodbath that had occurred in India and Pakistan. The situation was much more manageable here. It was a wonderful place to bring up Sophie in balmy weather most of the year. She was enjoying playing in their gardens, and had begun to say her first words in French by that summer. Alex's lessons in Arabic were proceeding well. As usual, Richard was vastly impressed by Alex's ability to jump in and adjust to a new culture and environment almost immediately. She had fallen in love with the country, and was perfectly suited to the demands of a diplomatic life.

Richard broached the subject of another baby with her shortly after they got there. Rabat seemed like an ideal place for them to have another child, and Sophie was such an easy happy little girl that another baby appealed to Richard more than ever. Alex was thirty-eight by then, and less enthusiastic about having another child. She was enjoying

Sophie, and felt too old to try again. Richard said that was ridiculous. She looked ten years younger than she was, but she didn't feel it. She had suffered so painfully over Edward's death that she didn't want to risk having another child where something might go wrong. Sophie felt like enough to her and was a gift. Her parents adored her.

They went to numerous social events, entertained frequently at the residence, and rapidly became the most popular hosts in Rabat. Alex liked the wife of the French ambassador, who had been in the Resistance during the war, and they had much in common.

Six months after they'd arrived, Alex could hold her own in Arabic. She wasn't fluent yet, but she was working on it, and took lessons every day. Sophie was chattering in French by then, as well as English.

They had been there for a year, when the French government finally brought Sultan Mohammed V back from exile, and reinstated him. Richard had discreetly been part of the negotiations to convince the French to do so. Just before the sultan's triumphant return, Alex received a coded message from MI6, requesting that she meet with a high up member of the Communist Party, at a café in the medina. They wanted his assurance that there would not be riots if the sultan returned. They had set up the meeting through their operatives in country, and wanted her to see him face-to-face. It was the first time they had asked her to meet with anyone since she had started working for them nine years before. She felt she couldn't turn them down. She just hoped that no one would see her with a strange man at a café in the medina. The coded message said that she was to carry a blue book and wear a red sweater, go to a specific café and sit down, and he would find her.

The meeting was set for the following day, and she had to change some appointments, her Arabic lesson and a haircut, to do it. The next day, she was at the designated place on time. As she walked through the medina to the café, it suddenly reminded her of her clandestine meetings in Germany to receive stolen papers or forged passports, while working for the SOE.

A nondescript man sat down across from her two minutes later, and she guessed that he'd watched her arrive. They exchanged their agreed upon code greeting so she knew it was him, and she asked him what MI6 wanted to know. He assured her there wouldn't be any trouble. The riots two years before had been about the murder of a Tunisian labor leader. They had no objections to the sultan, and thought his return to power would be a good thing, and help the country get independence from the French.

She thanked him and he left a few minutes later. She ordered a mint tea, and afterward wandered through several shops, looking unconcerned, didn't buy anything, and then left. It had been an easy mission to accomplish, and she sent her coded report of the meeting to MI6 as soon as she got home. They confirmed that they received it.

She ran into the French ambassador's wife at the hairdresser later that afternoon. She gave Alex an odd look and then asked her in an undervoice if she had met a man in a café at the medina that morning. She had seen her, and Alex laughed.

"Hardly, I stopped for a cup of tea, and he tried to sell me a watch or something, probably stolen. I told him I wasn't interested, and he left." She brushed it off and her French friend looked relieved.

"You shouldn't go to the cafés there alone. There are some very odd people around, and women sometimes get kidnapped in Morocco and sold into the sex trade. Be careful, my dear. We don't want to lose you." They both laughed then, but it was good to know that she'd been seen. If Richard had asked, she wouldn't have known what to say. She hadn't had reason to lie to him in years.

The sultan returned to Rabat three days later, and once back, he successfully negotiated independence, with French-Moroccan cooperation and interdependence. He instituted reforms that transformed Morocco into a constitutional monarchy with a democratic form of government.

In February of 1956, Morocco was granted home rule, to a certain degree. And on March 2, full independence was achieved with the French-Moroccan agreement. Mohammed V took an active role in modernizing the country's government and he remained leery of both the Independence Party and the Communists. Alex had much to report to MI6 in their first two years there. And as always, she culled great information from dinner parties and the people she met and entertained.

A month after the French-Moroccan agreement, Spain also recognized Moroccan independence, and over the next two years, Morocco eventually regained control over a number of the Spanish-ruled areas. Tangier was reintegrated later in 1956, and the sultan became king the following year, with lavish celebrations, which Richard and Alex attended.

Once again, they were in residence for an era of great changes in Morocco, all of them considered positive, and effected peacefully.

Richard felt he had accomplished a great deal there, and had been successful at assisting with the delicate negotiations for independence. He had done well, and they had spent a wonderful four years there when they left Rabat in 1958. They had made friends they would never forget, both among the other diplomats and the Moroccans.

Alex was able to spend a month in Hampshire with her mother and Sophie, at the end of Richard's ambassadorship in Morocco, before they went to their new post in Hong Kong. Her mother seemed even more frail than before, which saddened Alex.

Alex had every intention of learning to speak Mandarin or Cantonese while she was in Hong Kong. Mandarin was the most common dialect spoken in China, although Cantonese was spoken in Hong Kong. Sophie was five and a half when they left Rabat, and totally bilingual in French and English. Alex's Arabic was fluent by then. They had bought many treasures while they were there, and interesting objects she'd found in the medina. She'd never been asked to have another meeting for MI6, but she wondered if she would be again someday, depending on where Richard was posted. He was excited about Hong Kong, and so was she, but nothing had prepared her for the vibrant, bustling over-crowded city they encountered from the moment they landed at Hong Kong's international airport, Kai Tak.

The war years had been brutal for the residents of Hong Kong, during the Japanese occupation. Those who could had fled and those who lived through it had experienced harsh treatment by the Japanese, and malnutrition to the point of near starvation. The Communists winning the civil war and taking control of mainland China four years later had caused an influx into Hong Kong of displaced immigrants fleeing Communist rule. This added masses of available cheap labor. In the thirteen years since the end of the war, the population of Hong Kong had quadrupled to over two million. Business was booming, and the British colony had flourished. Money, business, and large investments had moved from Shanghai to Hong Kong. Those who had fled before the Japanese occupation returned after the war. Skyscrapers had sprung up. Money was plentiful. The textile industry had taken hold, as well as several others. It was a center for business under British rule, although only a stone's throw from Communist mainland China. Hong Kong was an extremely valuable trade center, and did business with the new government in Beijing. The government was committed to making Hong Kong a center of business, trade, and manufacturing. It provided a trade bridge between Communist China and the rest of the world.

There had been riots two years before Richard and Alex arrived, due to low wages, long working hours, and overcrowded conditions among the poorer population, but by 1958, when Richard was assigned to Hong Kong as high commissioner, all was peaceful, and business of every sort was thriving. Hong Kong was against Communist policies, and defined capitalism at its best.

Those in power were mostly British, or European, with a strong Scottish influence among the old established firms. In true British style, club life was extremely important to the men doing business in Hong Kong. The Hong Kong Club was the most venerable and prestigious, and the Royal Hong Kong Yacht Club was almost as important. Richard had automatic membership at both. As high commissioner of Hong Kong, he would be working closely with the British governor of Hong Kong, Sir Robert Brown Black, during his stay there.

In some ways, Hong Kong was more British than Britain itself, as happened sometimes in the colonies, and there was a close trade relationship with the Chinese as well. Unlike the Old Guard in England, made up of aristocrats with rapidly diminishing funds, but who still frowned on "trade" and "commerce" no matter how desperate their financial situation, in Hong Kong, money and business were king, and vast quantities of money changed hands in important deals. Social events were an opportunity to make new connections. The British in Hong Kong were not afraid to pursue major financial deals, or amass large fortunes, and there was enormous wealth in the city when Richard and Alex arrived.

Social life was extremely important, with business motives just below the surface. People sometimes went to two or three parties a night, and occasionally a cocktail party provided just the impetus needed to close a deal. The city was seething with activity, economic, industrial, and social, and some saw that the future of industry was in using cheap Chinese labor to produce products at a fraction of the cost of making them elsewhere. The marriage of business and social life was working extremely well, in ways that might have been frowned on in England, but were hotly pursued in Hong Kong. There were sports clubs, traditional clubs, dining clubs, night clubs, parties were constant, all the key players were British, with no Chinese visible on the Hong Kong club scene. There were also fabulous restaurants, and the shopping opportunities for antiques, jewelry, and clothing were supreme.

There were apartments in the tall buildings that had gone up all over the city, and the beautiful old homes, and some important new ones were on the Peak, which was where Richard and Alex would be living in the high commissioner's residence. The governor's mansion was there too.

All social events except cocktail parties were black tie, and there was dancing at almost every party. The French ambassador's wife in Morocco had given Alex the address of a fabulous little dressmaker, who could copy any Paris gown for next to nothing, and Alex was eager to see her for the extensive wardrobe she would need for their busy social life in Hong Kong. Having Paris fashions copied in Hong Kong was common, and every woman had a skilled seamstress to recommend. Their life in Rabat had been slightly more relaxed, and less formal than colonial life in Hong Kong.

The only problems that required closer supervision were those caused by the triads, groups of Communist gangsters originally from mainland China, who worked sub rosa and infiltrated Hong Kong whenever they could, operating with threats and violence to achieve their ends. They were the criminal element in Hong Kong.

The British Red Cross was very active in Hong Kong, and it had been subtly suggested that Alex might like to volunteer, as some of the more social women did. It was considered an appropriate activity, since women were not welcome in any of the clubs, except for special events.

Many dialects of Chinese were spoken in Hong Kong, Cantonese being the most common among the populace and local workers. Mandarin was more widely spoken among Chinese elsewhere. Alex ambitiously wanted to attempt to learn both. She had mastered Arabic and was fluent after her four years in Rabat. Chinese would be a bigger challenge, but as always, she was undaunted, and thought it might be useful for Richard socially, and even for herself, running their home, if she learned Chinese. Knowing her, he was sure she would master it in no time.

They were thrilled when they saw their home on the Peak, with a view of the harbor. They had a full staff, many of whom had come from mainland China after the civil war, and all of whom had been impeccably trained in proper British service by their predecessors. They all spoke English. There were maids, housemen, a butler, an excellent chef who had worked at a French restaurant, and a nanny for Sophie, who looked like a child herself, and was a very sweet young girl. The service they provided was more polished than what Alex and Richard had had before, but Alex still missed the kindness and warmth of Sanjay and Isha in New Delhi. Their help in Rabat had been less formally trained, but they were very kind, and adored Sophie. She spoke to her new nanny Yu Li in French at first. Yu Li giggled and spoke to Sophie in English, and Alex hoped Sophie would learn Chinese as well. She thought a variety of languages would always be useful for her, whatever she chose to do in later life. It had served Alex well so far.

As she always did, Alex reported to MI6 diligently from the day they arrived, and was startled when they almost instantly requested that she take a more active role. Other than her one meeting with the Communist leader in the medina in Rabat, she had never been asked to make contacts in the local population, only to report on who she met and what she heard and saw. This time her contact at MI6 sent her a list of people they wanted her to be on the lookout for, three they wanted her to try to meet, and several they wanted her to include in their dinner parties. Only one of the names was Chinese, the others were British, and all were men, which required some delicacy and ingenuity on her part, so she didn't acquire the reputation of being a flirt or a loose woman. She didn't have access to them in their clubs. It would all have to happen at the cocktail parties they went to, or the dinners they were invited to, and the ones they gave themselves.

Alex was busy setting up the house the way she wanted and she included two of the names on the guest list for the first dinner party they planned to give three weeks after they arrived. The local socialites, businessmen, and diplomats were eager to meet the new high commissioner and his wife, and they had already received a dozen invitations within days of their arrival. Richard wanted her to accept as many as they could attend, sometimes with a cocktail party or two preceding a formal dinner elsewhere afterward. Within a month, their life was a social whirl, and Alex hardly had time for anything else. She had committed to memory the names she was to look out for, and those MI6 wanted her to invite.

She ran into two of the people whose names were on the list at the first cocktail party they went to. One was a Scotsman who worked at the Hongkong and Shanghai Banking Corporation, commonly called "the Bank" by everyone in Hong Kong, and the other was an Irish manufacturer who had made a fortune in textiles since the war. The Scotsman, Ronald MacDuffy, was her father's age, drank straight scotch, and eyed her with interest. He wasn't particularly talkative except about banking. The other, Patrick Kelly, was an effusive Irishman about her own age. He invited her to lunch when they met, which she declined. Afterward she stood behind him and listened to him talk to a friend of his about a deal he was working on in Beijing. She committed both conversations to memory, and sent them to MI6 in code that night, and then she joined Richard in bed, who was reading reports from his office. He was trying to get up to speed on all the most important dealers and players in Hong Kong, as well as the political issues with Communist China, which was so close at hand.

The two men MI6 had told her to invite both came to their first official dinner party with their wives, neither of whom were very interesting, but beautiful and fashionably dressed. Both men were very influential in Hong Kong, had lived there before the war, returned to England during the occupation, and gone back to Hong Kong as soon as the Japanese surrendered. They had heavy investments in Hong Kong, and one of them quietly invited Alex for drinks the following night. She accepted, based on an instinct that it was what MI6 would have wanted, and she was right. When she reported the invitation to them, they asked her to meet him, and see what he had to say. She had to come up with an excuse to give Richard for skipping a cocktail party they were invited to that night, and meeting him later at the dinner they had accepted at the French consulate. The French were active in Hong Kong too, but not as much as the British.

Richard was so busy at the office that he didn't question her being unable to join him at the cocktail party, with the thin excuse that she had a late meeting at the Red Cross to discuss a blood drive with them that she had agreed to run.

She was wearing a sleek black evening gown when she met Arthur Beringer at the bar at the Peninsula Hotel, and she was mildly reminded of her brief brush with the SS colonel in Paris. He even looked a little like him and was a very attractive man. There was a subtle sexual undertone as he greeted her, and complimented her on her sexy black dress, courtesy of Marie-Laure's Chinese dressmaker who had copied it from a photograph in a magazine in two days. In addition to being ridiculously inexpensive in Hong Kong, they were fast, and the copies were impeccable.

Beringer ordered her a glass of champagne without asking what she wanted. He was drinking gin on the rocks.

"I know you're new to Hong Kong, but I wanted to make you aware of some of the opportunities we have here. There are fortunes to be made. We'll all be rich when we go back to England if we play our cards right." He went straight to the heart of the matter, and the allegory was a good one, since she had heard that he was a serious gambler, and had taken some huge risks to make his fortune. He was a fearless investor and was said to have a few dubious connections. "There are some very interesting deals here, if you're not afraid of unorthodox alliances. Our friends in Beijing understand the merits of capitalism, if conducted discreetly." He wasn't afraid to let her know that he was dealing with the Communist Chinese, which was bold of him. He had no idea whether he could trust her or not, but she looked like an innocent woman, and he saw her as a conduit to the connections she would be making as the wife of the high commissioner. Reaching out to her was a gamble on his part, but could be a good one, and profitable for them both.

"I'm afraid my husband and I aren't in a position to make investments," she said demurely, smiling at him, as she remembered the diamond bracelet she had given back in Paris during the war. In some ways, this was no different. Arthur Beringer was an opportunist said to stop at nothing to get what he wanted.

"I assumed as much," Beringer said smoothly. Most diplomats were not wealthy but extremely well connected with people in high places. "But you'll be meeting many people. If you steer the right ones in my direction, there would be a commission for you, perhaps even a very considerable amount, depending on the results afterward." He had put his cards on the table, and she looked intrigued as she glanced back at him.

"And how would I explain that to my husband?"

"There are banks here that maintain discreet accounts, numbered or in another name. Leave that to me. Trust me, you could be a rich woman by the time you leave Hong Kong."

"I'll have to think about it, Mr. Beringer, but your proposal is certainly intriguing. As long as no one would ever know." She appeared innocent, beautiful, and trusting.

"I have friends in low places," he said, smiling at his own joke. "You have no idea how useful that can be at times."

"The triads?" she asked, referring to what amounted to Chinese gangs, whom she had been told dealt in prostitution, paid assassins, and drug trafficking.

"Perhaps," he said, and signaled for another drink. "You don't need to worry about the details. Lead the sheep to me, and the money will magically appear in your numbered account. No one will ask questions, and your husband will never know." She wondered how many people in their circle did business with him. Possibly more than she would ever suspect. Hong Kong was teeming with honest and dishonest people pursuing their fortunes, some with methods like the ones Beringer had mentioned. All he was suggesting was a commission for her, which could have been honest, except for the numbered account and the fact that she couldn't tell her husband, and his talk of "friends in Beijing" and allusion to the feared triads of Hong Kong. She glanced at her watch, then slowly picked up her evening bag, smiled at him, and said she had to go.

"Let me know about my offer after you give it some thought. And perhaps we could have lunch sometime." He was too smooth to be blatant about pursuing her sexually as well, but it was implied in the look he gave her, and the way he touched her bare shoulder before she left. There was something dangerous and frightening about him, particularly if he was involved in the underworld of Hong Kong, and it appeared he was.

Her driver took her to the French consulate after that, in the Rolls provided for her, and as soon as she found Richard, she saw Beringer walk in with his wife. She was moderately attractive, slightly older than Alex, dripping with diamonds, and flirted with the French consul all night. Arthur Beringer greeted Alex and Richard with a polite nod, but didn't approach, and there was nothing to suggest that he and Alex had been drinking champagne at the Peninsula half an hour earlier, or that he had any interest in her, business or social. He was a masterful poker player and it showed.

The dinner at the French consulate lasted until one in the morning, and Richard was tired on the way home, after a long day. They talked about the people they had met, and she asked him what he thought of Arthur Beringer and his wife.

"He looks like a shady guy to me," he said without any particular interest, "and she appears to be on the hunt for a little too much fun." Alex smiled at his assessment, and agreed. Richard went right to bed when they got home, and she took her time in her dressing room, as she often did when she felt that her messages for MI6 were pressing. After she undressed, she took out the transmitter she kept hidden in a locked drawer, and sent MI6 the full report of her meeting with Beringer at the Peninsula before dinner. They confirmed receipt of the information with no further comment. She had done her job, and all she had to do now was tell him that she had considered his offer, but felt it best to decline.

When she got up the next morning, she had a message from MI6. She always checked after Richard left for the office. It was part of her daily routine, even if she'd had nothing to report to them the night before. She also checked for messages every night before she went to bed.

The message from her contact was brief. "Don't respond immediately. Stall him for a while." It was easy enough to do. She heard nothing further from them after that, and Beringer called her himself a week later, mid-morning when he knew Richard would be out. He was clever about when to call married women, and Alex suspected he did it a lot.

"Have you given any further thought to our conversation?" he asked, sounding languid and as though it didn't matter to him either way. But he must have cared somewhat or he wouldn't have been calling to press her for a response.

"I have," she said, sounding timid and uncertain. "I just don't want to create a problem for my husband if it ever came out."

"Don't worry. I'm not careless about business matters. No one will ever know."

"And if they do? The Colonial Office is quite adamant about maintaining anti-Communist policies in the colony. You mentioned your 'friends in Beijing.'

My husband could lose his job if it became known that I was involved in deals that involved them."

"And his wife could make a fortune. He won't need his job if we do this right, and you can be sure I will." He was pressuring her, which she found interesting. She wondered if later on, blackmail would be part of the deal, with what they'd have at stake. She wouldn't put it past him. "Think about it for a few more days." He hesitated for an instant, and tried to tempt her again. "You could end up with millions if you work on this with me. You'd be wise not to turn it down." Was it a threat? She wasn't sure. She reported the conversation to MI6, and then went out to lunch. She checked for a response from them after her Cantonese lesson that afternoon, and the message was clear.

"Keep stalling or meet him again. Don't let the fish swim away. Do not decline the offer, nor accept, remain ambiguous." They wanted her to play a game with him, which she sensed could be dangerous. He didn't seem like a patient man. She called him in the office, and said that she was tempted, but afraid. She implied that she needed reassurance, and he was happy to provide it.

"Have lunch with me," he said sounding sensual and persuasive, and she agreed, managing to sound innocent and flirtatious. It had been a long time since she had used those wiles in her line of work, and she almost found it amusing, but she didn't want Richard to discover her games. It was different doing espionage work for Military Intelligence, now that she was married. It had been simple reporting who she met, but was becoming more complicated engaging with a man like Beringer. She didn't want Richard to get hurt, or find out. He would never trust her again if he did.

She met Arthur Beringer for lunch the following day at a discreet restaurant he suggested. He was wearing an impeccably cut dark blue suit which looked more Savile Row than Hong Kong, and he never mentioned his offer once. Instead he tried to seduce her and several times brushed her hand, and then finally over tea at the end, he brought up his business proposal to her again, and she sensed a faint desperation in his voice.

"I need someone no one will suspect to work with me, Alex." They had progressed to first names. "You're clean here. I want to move a large sum of money from Shanghai into an account here, which some extremely well-placed people can access without problem. I'm willing to give you a sizable piece of it if you do this for me, simply as a gift. Commissions will come later." She wondered if Communist officials from Beijing would be using the account, and receiving payment from him, or someone in the triads. "I need to do it quickly, in the next few days." She feigned nervousness as he said it, and wondered how far MI6 wanted her to go in stringing him along. Listening to him, she had the feeling that there was a lot at stake, and some very important people involved, whom MI6 were obviously interested in, not just Beringer.

"Give me another day," she said, as he reached for her hand under the table and caressed it, and then rested his on her knee, as she prayed he wouldn't go any farther. He was dangerously close to the edge of her skirt as she met his eyes. "I'm married, Arthur," she said softly, with all that it implied and meant to her.

"So am I. Your husband is too busy to pay attention to you. And he'll have his share of offers too. Hong Kong corrupts people. You haven't understood that yet." She didn't want to. She knew Richard would never be vulnerable to men like Arthur Beringer. "I want to go to bed with you," he said too softly for anyone else to hear him. "You're a beautiful woman and I want you." She wanted to tell him that he couldn't buy her, but knew that silence was the wisest course. This was a job, for both of them. He wanted to convince her, and it was espionage for her, following orders from MI6. It wasn't personal, for either of them. And on his side, it was just a ploy to get her to do what he wanted. If he had dared, he would have forced her and preferred it. She could see violence in his eyes.

She thanked him for lunch then, and stood up, and he grabbed her wrist as she was leaving. "Just do it. You won't regret it," he said intensely. She nodded and walked away, praying no one would tell Richard they had seen her having lunch with another man. She could hardly concentrate on her Chinese lesson that afternoon, and she was quiet when she went out with Richard that night. She had wanted to spend time with Sophie before they left, but they were rushed, and she was happy with her new nanny. Alex felt as though she'd hardly seen Sophie since they'd been in Hong Kong. There were so many other demands on her as the high commissioner's wife.

"Tired?" Richard asked her in the car on the way to dinner. "We go out an awful lot here, don't we?" But he was enjoying the varied facets of his position in Hong Kong and the complex situations that arose more than she was, with Arthur Beringer breathing down her neck. She was grateful that they weren't at the same dinner party that night.

She got a shock when she read the morning paper the next day at breakfast. Arthur Beringer had been murdered by an unknown assassin, possibly linked to the triads. There was a long article in the paper about him, his unsavory connections, some of his more suspicious deals, and his vast fortune. The police called her after Richard left for the office, and asked for a moment of her time in the afternoon. Her heart was pounding when she asked what it was about, and they said that they wanted to speak to anyone who had met with him in the last twenty-four hours of his life, and they had reason to believe that they had met for lunch.

She didn't confirm or deny it, agreed to a five o'clock meeting with them at her home, and flew to her dressing room to send a message to MI6 and hoped they'd respond quickly. She told them that the police wanted to interview her about her lunch with Beringer the previous day. It was sure to cause a scandal if word got out. It was a small city, and there was constant gossip in the circles they moved in, and would be plenty about the high commissioner's wife, if any connection with Beringer was implied. It almost made her want to resign from MI6. They had never said that she would be used as bait, or have face-to-face meetings with dangerous subjects. She was meant to be an information gatherer and nothing more. That had been their agreement and they were stretching that now beyond her comfort level. And this was not wartime, where risking her life seemed right to her. Nor did she want to risk her marriage or Richard's career.

The response they sent her was almost immediate. "We'll handle it from here. Mission complete." An hour later she got a call from the secretary of the chief of police, canceling the appointment, apologizing, and saying that they had made a mistake. They sincerely regretted any inconvenience, and that was the end of it. A month later, there was an article in the paper, saying that Beringer had been laundering money for both the triads and the Communists, and had gotten exposed in a double cross between the two, presumably for a vast amount of money.

Richard said he'd had a bad feeling about him, and Alex nodded, grateful that MI6 hadn't let her down, and had gotten her out of the police investigation. It was the closest she'd ever come to being exposed. She never saw Beringer's wife again. Word was that she had left Hong Kong immediately after his death, and disappeared. And MI6 hadn't asked her to meet with anyone since. They appeared to be content with the reports she sent, and only asked her occasionally to include people at their dinner parties that they wouldn't have invited otherwise, but all of them seemed like respectable businessmen and bankers, despite MI6's interest in them. For now Alex was safe, and glad she was. Richard had no idea how close she came to being involved in a major scandal. It reminded her that her spying activities were dangerous, even in peacetime and even if no one was holding a knife to her throat. The unseen risks could be just as lethal.

Chapter 15

Nine months after they'd arrived in Hong Kong, Alex got another request from MI6 to meet with someone, a Chinese woman this time. The woman had started a massive textile business with factories near Shanghai, and they wanted to know how closely involved she was with the Communists. Alex was fascinated by her when they met. She was somewhere in her thirties, her father had been a major landowner in mainland China and had fled the Communists, but there was concern that she might have maintained or renewed ties with them. Alex only met her once, but it became clear later on that she was the mistress of an important member of the Communist Party, who was facilitating her business. He eventually lost his position and disappeared, and she fled China and moved to England, possibly as a result of the information Alex had deduced from talking to her. She was extremely beautiful and everything about her screamed danger and intrigue.

It was months before Alex was asked to meet anyone again, and each time she did, she had to lie and make excuses to Richard. Only once did she feel that she was in a dangerous situation, with a suspected member of the triads. She had gone to the meeting armed with her pistol and her knife and never had to use them, but she would have if needed. The rest of the time she played the role of gracious hostess and devoted wife, and by their second year there, she had mastered both Cantonese and Mandarin surprisingly well, which impressed everyone who heard her speak them. Only Richard wasn't surprised. He knew how brilliant and talented she was.

And MI6 continued to ask her to meet people of interest from time to time. Hong Kong was teeming with intrigue.

Two years after they arrived in Hong Kong, Victoria wasn't well. Alex went home for a month, and took Sophie with her. Sophie was bored in Hampshire. She said there were too many bugs there, and there was nothing to do. She didn't like riding as her mother had as a child, or any of the classic English pursuits. The foster children were long gone, although they stayed in touch with Victoria, but she was alone now, with only a housekeeper and a man to help around the house. The man running the estate for her came to see her once a week and sent written reports to Alex as well. And Richard always gave her good advice.

Victoria was seventy-two then, and in delicate health. Alex felt guilty about how seldom she saw her, but she was busy as the high commissioner's wife and Hong Kong was far away. Victoria had been widowed for eleven years, and whenever Alex invited her to Hong Kong, she said she didn't like to travel without Edward. She seemed older than her years. Alex was forty-four and thriving in the interesting life she led with Richard. They both loved Hong Kong, and wished they'd never have to leave. They talked about moving back there one day when he retired. Sophie was eight years old and was still bilingual in French and English. Her mother spoke to her in French most of the time to maintain it, and Sophie had picked up Cantonese from the women who took care of her. Being in Hampshire made Alex realize that her daughter had no real ties to England except by nationality. She'd only been there three times in her lifetime, as a small child, and other than her grandmother, she had no one there. Pakistan, where she was born, Morocco, and Hong Kong were the only homes and cultures she knew. It was an enviable life in many ways, particularly for Alex and Richard, but in some ways it was odd for Sophie to grow up steeped in so many cultures that were not her own. Alex's mother thought so too.

"You'll inherit all this one day," she said wistfully about the manor house and their estate, "and maybe you'll come back to live in England then, and enjoy it. You grew up here. And Richard grew up on his parents' farm and in a Scottish boarding school. You both have roots here. But what will Sophie be attached to? She knows nothing of English life, except in the colonies and that's not the same." They all knew people who had grown up in India and other places, and were more English than anyone who had grown up at home, but there was a false quality to it, when you had grown up with an elephant in the backyard, or a camel, her mother insisted. Sophie had loved the camels when they were in Morocco, and she'd probably never go back to Morocco. And Hampshire was more foreign to her than any of the places she'd lived.

"It's an odd way to grow up. But I suppose it's a nice life for all of you, with big houses and many servants. But none of it belongs to you. This does," she reminded her. Alex thought about it sometimes too, and she missed it, but she couldn't imagine living in Hampshire now, and not for a very long time. "I hope you don't sell it. It's been in your father's family for three hundred years, and he loved it so." It was an awesome responsibility, and Alex knew that even if she did keep it, wherever they were living at the time, Sophie might not want the estate when she grew up. If she was living halfway around the world, a house in Hampshire would mean nothing to her. In fact, she couldn't wait to go back to Hong Kong, which was more familiar to her, and Alex felt that way too. It was the downside of the life they had chosen, which suited them so well. They lost their emotional ties to their original homes.

Alex enjoyed the month with her mother and was sad to leave her. Each time she saw her now, her mother had gotten thinner, older, and more fragile, and she was afraid she'd never see her again. She hoped her mother would still be alive when Richard retired and they moved back to England, but that was still a long time away. He was only fifty-two years old and far from retirement. He would spend the last few years in the Foreign Office, after his last post. But they expected to be living abroad for at least another ten years. She wasn't sure her mother would live that long, and hoped she would. She had given up trying to convince her mother to visit them wherever they were posted, and she was an unfamiliar figure in Sophie's life, having spent so little time with her. Being an only child weighed heavily on Alex now. She felt guilty about her mother all the time. Letters and photographs were no substitute for human contact. She saw that her mother saved every one of her letters in boxes, and had for all the years she'd been gone.

Despite the sadness of leaving her mother, Alex was glad to get back to Hong Kong. Richard had been busy, and as always, the parties seemed to multiply. She continued reporting to MI6, and had the occasional meeting at their request, and they never put her in an awkward or dangerous position again. After several meetings at MI6 in London, they sensed that it could prove to be dangerous for her husband, and had chosen to respect that, for now anyway. The last two years flew by faster than Richard and Alex had expected, or wanted them to.

They had dozens of friends in Hong Kong when they left, and this time Alex only had a brief week to spend with her mother in Hampshire. They wanted them settled in their new post quickly. Richard's predecessor had left due to illness, and it was going to be a challenging but plum post for him, one of the more important ones. He was going to be the British ambassador to the Soviet Union, living in Moscow.

It sounded extremely interesting to both of them, though Sophie wasn't happy about it. She wanted to stay in Hong Kong, and Alex promised they'd come back one day. Sophie was nearly ten when they left Hong Kong, and after a week with her grandmother, she flew to Moscow with her mother, where Richard was waiting for them. He told Alex that the ambassador's house was respectable, and had been a luxurious home before the revolution, but forty-five years later, it was a symbol of fallen grandeur, in a Communist country, with a population composed of battered, tired, poor, starving, suppressed people, closely watched by the KGB. It was going to be a challenging, fascinating four years, and as they walked into the house in the same area where all the nicer embassies were, in the Arbat district, and saw the battered furniture, the faded curtains, and threadbare rugs, Alex knew she had work to do. The house was inadequately heated, it was a cold, dreary winter day, and Sophie burst into tears and turned on her mother when she saw it. She hated Moscow on sight. Alex saw it as an important step in Richard's career, and interesting for her too. Sophie was just a child having to adjust to a whole new way of life, again, in an unfamiliar, inhospitable country.

"I hate you for bringing me here!" she shouted at her parents, as Alex and Richard exchanged a look over her head. It wasn't going to be easy. They had known that when they left Hong Kong, which had been the jewel of his career so far, and this might prove to be his greatest challenge.

MI6 was extremely pleased with where Alex had landed, and her contact told her the day they arrived that they had lots for her to do. She wondered if this would prove to be their undoing. She hoped not, and Richard hoped not too, and prayed that he was equal to the task.

Chapter 16

Alex and Richard had been sent to Moscow in 1962, at one of the most interesting times since the Russian Revolution. The Cold War was in full swing, and had been for several years, and the situation had gotten markedly more tense since 1960, when the Russians shot down an American U-2 spy plane, and captured the pilot, Gary Powers. Since then, relations had been strained between the United States and Russia. The incident had threatened to cancel the summit meeting planned in Paris two weeks later. They went forward anyway, with Premier Khrushchev demanding an apology from the American president. When President Eisenhower refused, Khrushchev left the meeting.

Two years later when Richard arrived in Moscow, relations remained tense, and the Cold War had intensified, not only between Russia and the United States, but with Britain as well.

Great Britain had had its own problems with the Russians, who had recruited a number of well-placed English scientists and even diplomats to spy for them, with double agents complicating matters even further by spying for both sides. There was considerable bitterness on the British side about the traitors and defectors who sold everything from highly sensitive secrets to missiles to the Russians.

Spying was an extremely dangerous practice, as Alex had been told by the SOE, and later by MI6. If caught, there was no hope of being rescued. And prison or execution were the norm in Russia for Western spies who were apprehended. Those who chose to spy on Britain for the Soviets, working for the KGB, their secret police, were sentenced to equally unpleasant punishments in England, if caught by the British. The Soviets were known to pay a high price for traitors who defected to the east.

The Cambridge Five were among the most famous spies with high positions in the British establishment, which gave them access to secrets with a major impact on national security. Seven years before Richard arrived in Moscow, the naval attaché at the British embassy in Moscow had been imprisoned in England with an eighteen-year sentence for spying for the Soviet Union.

Nuclear technology was vital to the British, the Americans, and the Soviets. Fortunes changed hands for anyone who would defect to either side.

A year before Richard became the British

ambassador in Moscow, a British intelligence agent was sentenced to forty-two years in prison for spying for the Soviets and the British, as a double agent.

The KGB was particularly energetic about trying to steal agents of MI5 and MI6, who were considered a prize. They succeeded in a number of instances. British Military Intelligence was extremely sensitive about it. The game of stealing spies and intelligence agents and luring them from one side to the other had become an almost common feature of the Cold War.

In spite of it, the appearance of diplomacy continued, with the ball being carried vigorously by the Americans whose embassy, Spaso House, hosted many of the most glittering social events in Moscow, and whose invitations were the most prized. Their July Fourth party every year was legendary. In 1935, they had added a ballroom onto the house where they held balls, dances, concerts, movie screenings, and some of the best diplomatic parties in Moscow. Premier Khrushchev was notorious for showing up and attending every event he was invited to by the Americans, although the KGB spied on them relentlessly.

The American ambassador and his wife were Richard and Alex's first visitors the day after they arrived. Alex was trying to decide how to make the house more attractive for the receptions they planned to hold there. She had found some extra furniture and rugs rolled up in the basement, and when the Americans arrived, Alex apologized for how she looked.

"You look lovely, my dear," the ambassador said warmly, as his wife handed Alex a beautifully wrapped gift, and he pointed to the street outside, as he spoke to her, and Richard immediately understood and nodded. The American ambassador put a finger to his lips as he looked at Alex. "Why don't you let us show you your neighborhood. There are some charming old houses you'll enjoy seeing." He smiled at her, and his wife nodded, smiling at them.

"I'll get our coats," Richard said and disappeared, and returned a minute later, and handed Alex her coat, as he put on his own. Sophie was getting acquainted with the young girl at the embassy who was to care for her. She was Russian but spoke relatively good English, and Sophie hadn't warmed to her yet. They were unpacking some of her toys in her large, chilly bedroom upstairs, where Sophie had taped movie posters to the walls.

They were on the street a moment later, appearing to stroll toward Arbat Square. "I'm sorry to kidnap you," the ambassador said, smiling at Richard, as his bodyguard followed at a discreet distance behind them. "I'm sure you've been warned by your own government, but our homes are riddled with listening devices, put there by the KGB. We found over a hundred microphones and cameras when we combed it when we moved in. In fireplaces, in plants, under couches, in the walls, in the air vents, in the garden, they're everywhere. You can't say anything in the house you don't want the Soviets to hear. I thought you should know how extensive it is." Alex and his wife were chatting as they walked, and she invited the newcomers to a formal dinner at Spaso House the following week, and Alex thanked her.

"They're always after our operatives from MI5 and MI6, quite successfully at times, unfortunately," Richard said wryly.

"We all have the same problems," the American said. "They'll have bugs in your daughter's room, and don't trust any of your servants. It's an entire nation of people taught to spy and report on each other. It's quite sad really," but the Crisis in Suez and the American U-2 disaster had intensified the Cold War. "And they'll go through your personal belongings several times a day."

They discussed the diplomatic situation in Moscow then as they walked. British and American goals were much the same. To provide information about Soviet domestic and foreign policy, to promote British trade, and American in their case, and develop scientific and cultural exchanges, and to influence Soviet foreign policy on broader international issues. It was all very straightforward, but when you added espionage and counter-espionage to the mix, it became complicated. And being an ambassador to the Soviet Union, from whatever country, was both an honor and a challenge.

They walked around the square in a leisurely way

for about half an hour and then the Americans left them.

Before they did, the ambassador had offered to lend them their "decorator," who was actually a superb agent trained in detecting listening devices and debugging the house whenever possible. Richard accepted gratefully. The agent brought in a team that claimed to be "interior decorators," a clever ruse the KGB hadn't caught on to.

"Thank you for sharing the information," Richard said pleasantly. He had heard much of it before, but the American ambassador had added to it very usefully.

"You'll get used to it. We all do. And it's a good group here, in the foreign community. We all got here for a reason. If we do well enough everywhere else, they reward us by punishing us here." The American laughed and Richard smiled ruefully. "They like to have a good time though. And they love coming to the embassy."

"We've got some work to do with ours," Richard said. He knew Alex wasn't happy with the condition they had found the house in, and Sophie hated it. The transition was difficult, particularly coming from the luxurious comforts and sophisticated delights of Hong Kong, which was infinitely more civilized than the conditions in Russia.

He and Alex walked for a few more minutes once they were alone, and she tried not to show how discouraged she was. "You might want to hide your pistol, Alex, if they haven't seen it already." He was worried about it. "They might wonder why you have it."

"I thought of that too. That and my knife are in a safe place." She smiled at him.

"Where's that?" He was puzzled. Nowhere was safe, if they searched their belongings constantly, as the American ambassador said.

"On my body." They weren't allowed to search a diplomat's wife, by reciprocal agreement, unless they had proof that she was a spy, which they didn't.

"And your bigger, uh . . . accessory . . . ?" he asked her, referring to the Sten gun she said she kept as a souvenir of the war.

"It comes apart and folds up nicely in a leather bound Bible." He looked impressed and smiled at her.

"Why do you still need to carry that? You're not a volunteer in wartime anymore." He didn't know if she'd ever used it and thought it unlikely.

"You never know when it might come in handy. I got it during the war and I just kept it all. You may be glad I have that one day."

"You don't want the Russians to think you're a spy," he warned her.

"I'm not a spy," she lied to him, "I'm just careful."

"Just make sure no one finds it. I guess I should be grateful you left your other submachine gun with your mother," he teased her. He had never believed that when she said it. And how could she have one?

The Sten gun she had with her was ominous enough and some kind of fetish for Alex, along with her pistol and knife.

"It's annoying that the house is so heavily bugged," Alex said thoughtfully. "I'll warn Sophie. How will you work if your office is bugged too?"

"That's for our technicians to solve. It's what they get paid to do." And he told her about the team of decorators the American ambassador had offered. "It's all a big game here, about who is spying on whom." And everything they could find out or overhear went straight to the secret police in Moscow, the KGB.

They discovered that night that their cook was surprisingly good, although he had never left Russia. They had a fine meal and went to bed early. Richard had a lot to think about and read late into the night, trying to get up to speed. His post in Moscow was the greatest challenge of his diplomatic career so far. The next morning Alex had a message from MI6. It gave her a time and a name, in code, for a meeting, and a code phrase that would tell her the person was a British operative, but didn't mention a meeting place. She decided to wait to see what would happen.

At precisely eleven A.M., as she sat at her desk in the small office she was going to use at the residence, one of the Russian maids came to tell her that the wife of the Finnish ambassador had come to visit. The name matched the one she'd received from MI6. And she went downstairs to be handed a bouquet of flowers by a pretty blond woman.

"I love daisies in the winter, don't you?" she said to Alex with a warm smile. It was the code phrase, and Alex was intrigued to realize that she was a British agent for MI6 too. She was English, and the wife of an ambassador. They had much in common.

"Yes, I do. That's so kind of you." Alex smiled at her as a knowing look passed between them. They exchanged pleasantries and womanly information about Moscow, where Alex could get her hair done, where the best shopping was. Sophie was going to be tutored at the embassy, and Alex was planning to take Russian lessons. Many of the diplomatic families hadn't brought their children to Russia but Alex didn't want to leave Sophie with her mother, where she'd be lonely and unhappy, nor put her in boarding school, so they had brought her. Alex wanted to take Russian lessons with her. It would keep them both occupied.

After they chatted for a while, Alex walked the wife of the Finnish ambassador back to her car. On the way, Prudence Mikki said softly, "Don't trust anyone or anything, not even in your car. I think our friends in London will keep you busy. They do me. There's a lot to do here." Alex didn't comment, but she hoped not. Soviet Russia was the last place on earth where she wanted to make a mistake, and be imprisoned as a spy. The thought of it made her shudder. They kissed on both cheeks, and Alex waved with a smile as Prudence was driven away by her chauffeur, and Alex called after her thanking her for the flowers. At least she had a friend here.

Alex was able to buy some fabric at a market Richard's secretary told her about and got new curtains made for the reception rooms, and she discovered that there was more furniture in a warehouse. The last ambassador hadn't liked it, and they had brought their own. What was stored was infinitely better than what was in the residence now. She made a list of things to ask her mother for. She rolled out the carpets she'd found, and brought some of the spare furniture to the house, and asked the housekeeper to order flowers for them twice a week. The residence started to look better. She asked Richard's secretary for the most recent embassy guest lists, and planned their first dinner party. As they had in Hong Kong, MI6 gave her a list of who they wanted her to entertain. The list was long here. Alex didn't question it, she just added the names, and she knew the KGB would see a copy of the list anyway. She planned to invite most of the members of the diplomatic community to their first party, and they had room for dancing if they moved the furniture. The wife of the American ambassador had said Alex could use their band. It seemed vital to meet the most important people as soon as possible, although entertaining seemed clumsier here, and more awkward, than in Hong Kong where everyone was so social, and it all went smoothly. Hong Kong was far more sophisticated than the Soviet Union, but she had expected that.

A week before the party, MI6 added two more names to the list. Richard and Alex were going to the party at the American embassy that night and she was looking forward to it, and Richard said he was too when he came home to change.

When they got there two very proper Chinese butlers were checking in the guests, worthy of Buckingham Palace in their precision and decorum. The ambassador's wife had told her about them. They were Chinese, married to Russians, and couldn't get visas to leave the country, so they were trapped there, and worked for the Americans. They were well known in Moscow, and Alex envied how smooth and professional they were. The help at the British residence was far less efficient, and seemed more intent on listening to them and spying on them than providing proper service.

The atmosphere at the party at Spaso House was a breath of fresh air. The house was beautifully decorated in an elegant, modern American way. The ambassador and his wife had brought their own paintings, and everyone seemed relaxed just being there, as though they weren't even in Russia. It set an example that Alex wanted to emulate. She wanted to show the locals and the rest of the diplomatic community what a proper British home looked like, and how it was run. She decided to give a series of high teas, proper luncheons for women, and cocktail parties like the ones in Hong Kong, as well as formal dinner parties for important guests. She had a dozen new ideas when they left the party that night, and she had loved their band and planned to use it. There was a singer who sang jazz like Billie Holiday.

"You look happy," Richard said, pleased. He had enjoyed meeting so many of his fellow ambassadors in one room, and a number of important Soviet officials, whom he had wanted to meet.

"I'm planning our social life for the next six months," she said. They never spoke of anything more important anymore unless they were walking down a street. They tried to take a walk together every day so they could catch up on what really mattered. "I loved the singer."

"I did too. Maybe we should try for something a little more British," he suggested and Alex dismissed the idea.

"When the Americans get it right, they really do." It had been a beautiful evening.

She was in great spirits until she retrieved her encoded messages, and was given the name of someone they wanted her to meet with, within the next few days. She had to hire him as a guide at a museum. It was all she knew, that and his name. She looked much less happy when she got to bed. Richard was already half asleep. The man she was supposed to meet had a Russian name. MI6 was putting her to work, and it was delicate here. They hadn't pressed her about many meetings in Hong Kong after the Beringer incident, but in Moscow, they needed all their agents to be active. They had warned her of it when Richard was transferred, and they were already moving into action.

She went to the museum the next day, and asked if they had any guides who spoke English, before she asked for him by name. They called someone on the phone, and a short thin man appeared, gave his name, and it was the same name she'd been given by MI6, which seemed fortunate. He was carrying a recording device in his hand, he explained after she introduced herself. And he said he had the entire tour recorded in English on the machine, but would accompany her to explain it. She nodded, and they began their tour of the museum, and he turned the machine on for her when they reached the first room and she put on headphones. All of the art dated from after the Bolshevik revolution and had themes of work. Most of it was in a crude style, and none of it was pretty. And as she looked at the first paintings, the recording began. It had nothing to do with the art. It was a lengthy message for MI6 about nuclear arms meetings that were taking place, in violation of a recent treaty. She showed no reaction or surprise, and continued to listen to the recording and look at the art, as they went from room to room.

The recording ended long before they finished the tour, and she pretended she was still listening, and when they reached the last room, she thanked him and handed the machine and earphones to him. She had committed all of it to memory, as she'd been trained to do, and the tour guide erased the message as soon as she handed back the machine. She had listened to it a second time to be certain that she would remember it all. He was obviously one of the Russians who was spying for the British, and could even have been a double agent. Although she was sure that MI6 knew he was secure, if they had her meet with him, given her delicate position because of Richard.

It wasn't up to her to evaluate the information, only to pass it on. She left the museum, went back to the residence, and encoded the entire recording she had committed to memory verbatim, naming the source before she did so. He had offered to give her the recording and she had refused it, so he erased it instead. It was too dangerous for him to keep. She had been trained for this, the transmittal of information. It was what she had done during the war, and it had been no more or less dangerous than this.

She waited for a response after she sent it. She had turned the taps on in her bathroom as though she were running a bath, to drown out any minor sound of her tapping on the transmitter. The response came two minutes later.

"Received. Well done. Thank you." She stared at the transmitter for a minute, hating what she had gotten herself into, yet still compelled to do it.

"To hell with you too," she said softly, as she put the tiny machine away, in its case, which looked like a first aid kit. No one would have guessed what was in it, what it was, or what it could do. Like Alex herself, it looked entirely innocent, and was anything but. The lives of the people affected by it, and her own, were on the line every day. She realized now that their stay in Moscow was going to be much more dangerous than she'd expected.

Chapter 17

Realizing how delicate her situation was, and not wanting her to quit, MI6 didn't ask her to do too many missions for them. Fewer than they had others do. They saved the really important meetings and inquiries for her, so they didn't waste her with risks that weren't crucial. Mostly, they stuck to their agreement of having her gather information she gleaned socially in diplomatic circles, but every now and then, they sent her out to meet someone she assumed was an operative of MI6. She never saw the man from the museum again. But there were others. She had to meet one woman in a butcher's shop and stand in line with her for hours, and she was late for a dinner party they were going to at the Turkish embassy. Richard was annoyed with her for being late and having to change when she got home. She said she had gone to the butcher to pick their meat herself since the cook bought such poor cuts on his own. He complained that she could have done it in the morning, and she didn't argue with him. He was tired and stressed a lot of the time, trying to maintain the balance between defending Britain's interests and not adding to the hostility of the Cold War, which was a juggling act at best, particularly knowing that the KGB was watching them at all times. It was a constant source of stress, even for Sophie.

Within six months, Alex was speaking Russian, which was even more useful for the eavesdropping she did for MI6. Richard couldn't get the hang of it and had a translator with him constantly. He used several of them, all sent from England with Russian skills, but he never fully trusted them. He believed his secretary to be trustworthy but anyone in Russia could be a double agent, and many were. He didn't even fully trust the Brits there, which added constant stress to his job. He could see why his predecessor had gotten sick. One had to be on the alert every moment of the day and night. Alex felt that way too. MI6 was in constant contact with her, and she hated hearing from them here. Every time she did an assignment for them, however small, she felt the weight of responsibility on her shoulders, and was torn between her duty to her country, and responsibility to her husband, and was afraid of hurting him in some unseen way that would blow up in their faces later. but quite remarkably, nothing did. It all went smoothly, however tense things were.

The year after they arrived, in November of 1963, the assassination of John F. Kennedy shocked the world, and dreams were broken when he died. An innocence had been lost, if it had ever existed. The days of Camelot seemed more than ever like an illusion now. Alex cried with the rest of the world at the tragic face of Jacqueline Kennedy behind her widow's veil as she held her young children's hands.

It reminded everyone of the evil forces that came into play every day. Even the Soviets were deeply moved by his murder. It was hard not to be. The American ambassador and his wife had gone to Washington for the funeral.

Their time in Russia seemed to pass more quickly than any of their other posts, because the days were so chock full, the stakes were so high, the tension so constant. It was like living in a minefield, and Alex was glad when their next assignment came, and Richard admitted privately that he was too. Russia was one of the most important posts the Foreign Office could assign, and he knew he was close to his last ones before they brought him home. He had been assigned from one foreign post to another for exactly twenty years. Alex had just turned fifty, and Richard was fifty-eight. He guessed that he would have one more assignment, and then they would assign him to a desk job in the Foreign Office for a few years, offering sage counsel based on experience until he retired. But they had one more post coming their way, and he smiled when he read the communique. He had earned it, and he was gratified that his superiors recognized it. He had won their gratitude and respect for his four years in Russia. His next assignment, and probably his last, was Washington, D.C. He told Alex after dinner when they took their nightly walk around the square.

"I have something to tell you," he said, tucking her hand tightly into his arm. He loved their few private moments together and valued her advice.

"You're in love with your secretary," she said, grinning at him.

"Please God, no. Have you looked at her?"

"You're joining a religious order?"

"I would if we stayed here much longer. No, we're going to Washington."

"For a holiday?" She looked pleased, and he laughed.

"Do you think I re-enlisted here?" They couldn't do that anyway, but he would have died first. Four years was enough. "No, my darling. I think it's probably our last assignment, given my age, and they saved the best for last. Or one of the best. It's a plum post, and will be a taste of Heaven after Moscow, the Cold War, and the KGB."

"You're going to be the British ambassador to Washington?" She almost screamed it, as he nodded, stopped walking, and hugged her close. For all the difficult moments, and sometimes frightening times and occasional disappointments, they were closer than ever, and their marriage had stayed solid.

The diplomatic corps had torn asunder more than one marriage. It was not an easy life, and infidelity was common, but Alex was well suited to Richard's career and they had grown to love it over the years.

"I am going to be the ambassador to Washington. And we are going to eat hamburgers and go to baseball games, and probably go to dinner at the White House from time to time. Happy days are here again." He beamed at her, and they walked back to the house to tell Sophie. Richard didn't want the KGB knowing before it was officially announced, so Alex wrote it on a piece of paper and handed it to Sophie, and she screamed when she read it. She was almost fourteen years old and thought that America was the coolest place on earth, although she'd never been there. She loved Elvis and had all his records, although she loved the Beatles too, Nat King Cole, and Frank Sinatra, Rock Hudson, and Doris Day.

"When?" Sophie whispered.

"In a few weeks, I imagine."

"And for once, I speak the language, thank God." Sophie still remembered her Cantonese, her Russian was awkward and she hated it, and her French was perfect. She hoped never to use any of it again, except maybe French. She grabbed the paper out of her mother's hand, and scribbled on it rapidly. "Can I go to a normal American high school?"

"Yes." Her mother smiled at her, and went back to Richard. Sophie wanted to start packing that night. Russia had not won her heart.

"You have a **very** happy daughter," she said.

"She'll never want to leave once we get there," he said, looking worried. "I want her in England with us, when we go home."

"That won't be a problem. She's English, not American."

"She's never lived there," he said.

"All colonials go back 'home' eventually. So will she."

"Don't be so sure. But at least she'll have fun for the next four years." Russia had been dreary for all of them. Alex was leaving the residence in better shape than she'd found it, and he had done a good job as ambassador, but they were very ready to leave.

Alex sent a message to MI6 that night to inform them that they would be transferring to Washington shortly, she wasn't sure if MI6 had been advised yet. Their response came back swiftly.

"Congratulations to the ambassador. Well done."

She went to bed that night dreaming of Washington, and the delights waiting for them there.

There were countless dinners for them at all the embassies before they left. It was a closed community, particularly in Moscow, and they were all sorry to see Richard and Alex leave.

The Russian officials came to visit him one by one, and thanked him for his help in trying to achieve detente. He couldn't ask for more. And he thanked his entire staff warmly when he left. He had been respected and admired in every part. He spent two days with the new ambassador to brief him, left everything in good order, and then they departed.

They flew from Moscow to London, spent a few days there so Richard could be briefed by the Foreign Office, and stayed with Victoria in Hampshire for a few days. Alex did some shopping in London with Sophie, and then they flew to New York on BOAC. It felt like a dream to all three of them.

The embassy on Massachusetts Avenue, designed by Lutyens with extensive gardens, was magnificent. It was built in 1930 with primarily British materials, marble, wood, glazing, with new offices in a building in front of it, completed only two years before they arrived. The staff was superb. Richard paid an official visit to President Johnson, and the White House was even more impressive than he had imagined. The previous ambassador had left everything in impeccable order. They settled into the ambassador's residence. Alex assumed that she would have very little to do for MI6 for the next four years. The British did not spy on the Americans, they didn't need to. They shared information liberally. It was an enormous relief not to be in a hostile country, surrounded by danger and risk.

Alex and Sophie went to look at schools days after they arrived. She hadn't been in a proper school since Hong Kong and had been tutored for four years in Moscow by an English teacher married to a Russian.

She fell in love with the Sidwell Friends School, one of the finest private schools in Washington. Richard went to see it too. He wanted to be sure that she went to a school that would prepare her for the British university system when they went back. But they all agreed that it was a wonderful school, and she passed the equivalency and entrance exams without problems, in all subjects. They accepted her, despite her previously unorthodox schooling. She would be starting a "real American high school" in September, just as she had wanted to. Her parents had never seen her happier, and Alex was just as happy. She felt as though she had dropped a thousand pound weight off her shoulders when they left Russia. She had worried about every one of her missions there, and had been afraid of being caught and arrested as a spy. But she had stuck it out anyway. She was planning to leave MI6 in four years when they went back to London, after thirty years of espionage work. It was a more than respectable career as a spy.

The time had expired on her twenty-year vow of silence on her work for the SOE while they were in Russia. Technically, she could have told Richard and was tempted to but since she was still working for MI6, she decided not to, so as not to arouse his suspicions.

As they had in Hong Kong, they were caught up in the social whirl of Washington immediately, and went to embassy dinners, state functions, parties of every kind almost every night. The highlight of their social life there came in the form of the invitation to Luci Johnson's, the president's daughter, wedding to Patrick Nugent, two weeks after they arrived. The reception in the East Room for seven hundred guests was dazzling, and Richard and Alex thoroughly enjoyed it.

They made friends easily in the international community in Washington, and among the locals, some of them the parents of the girls Sophie went to school with. Sophie was thriving in an American school. It was like her reward for the odd upbringing she'd had from Pakistan to Morocco, China, and Russia. She never talked about it to her friends. She told Alex she wanted to forget about it, and settle down in one place for the rest of her life.

Alex's work for MI6 in Washington was almost negligible, which was a relief too, and felt like a vacation. She told them about the politicians and diplomats she met, and dinners at the White House. It was all very tame, with no crisis whose resolution rested on her.

They were privileged to attend their second White House wedding when President Johnson's daughter Lynda Bird married Charles Robb sixteen months after her sister's wedding just after Alex and Richard had arrived. There were six hundred and fifty guests, and Alex and Richard knew most of them by then. They were frequent guests at the White House, for state dinners, and smaller, more intimate ones.

The time went too quickly. They had a battle royal with Sophie when she was a senior in high school, and it wasn't one Richard wanted to lose. She wanted to go to an American college like her friends. She didn't want to go back to England with her parents, and go to university there. She said she felt American now and wanted to stay.

"That's absurd," her father argued with her. "You're not American, you're English. You've only been here for three years."

"I don't care. I want to stay here. I don't know anyone in London. I don't want to live with Grandmama in Hampshire. I don't want to go to an English university. I want to go to college here. I have to apply this year, Papa." She pleaded with him, and begged her mother to convince him. But Alex didn't like the idea of leaving her in the States either.

"We have no relatives here. What if you get sick?" Sophie was headstrong. Alex wanted to be near at hand to guide and watch her.

"Then you can come over and be with me. Please don't make me go back, Mama. I want to stay here." She'd had assorted minor boyfriends by then, but that wasn't her reason for staying. She loved her friends, and everything about America, and all her friends were applying to college in the States. She thought England was dreary and felt no bond to it since she'd never lived there. Being English was just a passport to her and nothing more.

Alex and Richard talked about it constantly, and he offered a compromise.

"You can go to college here, if you get in. But after you graduate, you come back to England and go to work there, without question. I don't want you staying here, and I'm not going to live three thousand miles from my only daughter in my old age," he said firmly, and after Sophie left the room, squealing with delight, Alex turned to him with a serious expression.

"That's what my mother did. She's been alone, thousands of miles from her only daughter, for twenty-three years, and totally alone ever since my father died." She felt sad as she said it.

"We'll be home in a year. You can make it up to her," he said gently. But Alex knew she couldn't give her mother the years back. She and Richard had been gone for all that time in the diplomatic corps. It had been a good decision for them, but not for her mother, and she felt terrible about it.

The final months flew by. They were leaving in June, right after Sophie's high school graduation. She was planning to travel around California with friends, and spend August with one of them in Martha's Vineyard. The girl's parents had a house there.

She had been accepted at almost every school she'd applied to, and decided to go to Barnard at Columbia University in New York. She was going to live in the dorms. She would be seventeen when she started college in September, and turn eighteen in December. She was coming back to England for Christmas and her eighteenth birthday, and Alex was going to visit her in school in the fall for a parents' weekend. She already missed her and hated the idea of her being three thousand miles away. It gave her a taste of what her mother's life had been like.

Richard and Alex had one last dinner at the White House. Richard Nixon had become president, and Richard had a good rapport with him.

Sophie's graduation was bittersweet for them, but joyous for Sophie. She couldn't wait to leave for California with her friends. She left Washington before they did, and the morning she left, Alex turned to Richard. They were packing to leave themselves.

"I feel as though I've lost her," Alex said with tears brimming in her eyes, and he put an arm around her.

"You haven't. She'll come home after all this, like a good English girl." Alex wondered if her father had said that to her mother when she and Richard left for India. But she'd been married, which was different. She had to follow her husband. Sophie was following her dreams, which was more dangerous.

Two weeks later, they left Washington and flew to London. She and Richard stayed at Claridge's for a few days, and found an apartment. He had the summer off, before he had to report to the Foreign

Office, and Alex had promised her mother they would spend the summer with her, except for a few short trips they wanted to take around England to visit old friends, and maybe a short trip to Italy or France. Richard hadn't seen his farm in years, and didn't even know the renters anymore. A management service at the local realtor handled it for him. He was thinking of selling it. The property wasn't valuable, and he was never going to live there. There was no point hanging on to it.

They drove down to Hampshire, and Alex was shocked when she saw her mother. She was thin and pale and emaciated, and could barely walk. It was obvious that she was ill. Alex went to see her mother's doctor, who told Alex that she had stomach cancer. She hadn't wanted to tell Alex and worry her, and had been sick alone for months. She talked to her mother about it when she got home.

"Why didn't you tell me? I would have come home." Her mother seemed peaceful about it, as she looked lovingly at her daughter.

"You couldn't leave Richard and Sophie alone in Washington," her mother said generously. So she had been alone here. The housekeeper took care of her, but she'd been alone at night and insisted she didn't mind.

She slept a lot once Alex was home. They walked in the garden together, and visited her father's grave, and her brothers'. Her mother was eighty-two, and most of her friends were gone. But at least Alex was home. At last. Her mother had waited so long for this, and now it was so close to the end. They had missed more than two decades together. It was Alex's greatest regret about her life. That and the little boy she had lost. It had been a good life other than that.

Victoria died in her sleep, peacefully, three weeks after Alex came home. It was as though she had waited for her. And once she saw her again, she could leave.

Alex called Sophie to tell her, and she flew back from California for her grandmother's funeral. Only a few people were there in the small church. Sophie stayed until her friends got to Martha's Vineyard, and then she flew to Boston to join them. Alex took her to the airport, and hugged her tight before her flight.

"Be careful. I love you, Sophie." As she watched her go, running to catch her plane, her dark hair flying behind her, Alex realized for the first time that a mother's greatest gift was to let her children pursue their dreams, wherever they took them. Seeing Sophie go was one of the hardest things she'd ever done. It gave her new respect for her mother, who had lost two sons and let her only daughter fly away to the other side of the world.

Alex drove to London after that. She had an appointment she'd been planning to keep for a long time. She had nothing left to do for them. She had done very little for the past four years. She had spent the war years working for the SOE, and had worked for MI6 for twenty-four years after that. It was long enough. The money they had paid her had never been remarkable, intentionally. She had done it for the love of queen and country. There was no other reason to do it.

She handed in her letter of resignation, and her contact shook her hand and thanked her.

"You've done a fine job for us for a long time." It seemed odd that thirty years as a spy ended with a letter and a handshake, but she had done her job. It was up to others now.

She drove back to Hampshire feeling nostalgic but lighter, and as though she had come full circle. She still missed her mother, and all the years they hadn't had together, but she had followed Richard on his path, and had had her own too. She had managed both, and had been there for Sophie too.

He was just coming back from the lake with his fishing pole when she got home, and he looked like a boy playing hooky as she smiled at him.

"Was her flight delayed?" he asked Alex. She was late coming home.

"I had a meeting in London. Long overdue."

"Medical?" He looked worried, and she shook her head. It was time to be honest with him at last. She had kept secrets from him for most of their life together, but she'd had no other choice.

"I retired from MI6 today," she said, expecting him to look shocked. But he wasn't surprised. "I've worked for them for thirty years." There were tears gleaming in her eyes as she said it. And she knew she would miss it. It had given added meaning to her life for so long. More than half her life.

"I always knew." He smiled. "I just prayed that you wouldn't get arrested, or get us thrown out of wherever we were living at the time. You scared the pants off me in Moscow a few times."

"I scared myself too," she admitted and laughed. He knew her better than she thought. "You never said anything?"

"I thought it was bad form to ask my wife if she was a spy. Most women don't drag a submachine gun around or carry a pistol. I suspected something during the war, but I knew you couldn't tell me."

"I worked for the SOE then. Espionage and sabotage behind enemy lines. It was much rougher stuff."

"I hate to think of it," he said seriously. He walked over and kissed her then. "So you're not a spy anymore?" She shook her head. "Well, that will be different. You'll have to tell Sophie about it one day."

"Maybe. I'm not sure she'd want to know." She had her own life to lead now. Her own secrets to keep.

"You're quite a woman," he said as they walked into the house that was hers now. They had some repairs to do, and a few things Alex wanted to change. They had a good man managing the estate. They were planning to live in London during the week, and use it on weekends. Alex had been involved in running it for many years, and Richard took an interest in it too. It would be easier dealing with it at close range now that they were back. "You'll have to find something else to do now, without weapons, I hope." She had loved the house and considered it home all her life, no matter where she had lived in the world. She regretted that Sophie had never gotten attached to it. Maybe when she was older she would.

Alex could feel her parents near her at the Hampshire house. She and Richard had had a fabulous life together, living all over the world, but she was glad they were home. And she hoped Sophie would consider it home one day too.

Chapter 18

Alex's predictions about her daughter were more accurate than Richard's. She graduated from Barnard and didn't want to come home to England. Her friends were all in the States now, from Washington and Columbia. She wanted to stay in New York, at least for another year. She had fallen in love with a boy who graduated from Columbia Law School when she got her undergraduate degree, and the romance looked serious to Alex.

They met Steve Bennett at Sophie's graduation, and had lunch with him and his parents. Steve's father was a West Point general, and Steve was an only child and had been an army brat, and had grown up all over the world too, and he had hated it as much as Sophie had their travels. He had just joined a law firm in New York and wanted to live in one place now too. Richard enjoyed talking to Sam Bennett, Steve's father, about their war experiences, and the places they had lived. And his mother was a warm woman, who had followed her husband around the world whenever possible. Sam was still in the military, currently stationed at the Pentagon, and they lived in Washington, D.C. He was four years younger than Alex, and a dozen years younger than Richard, and a vital, dynamic man. They both enjoyed him and his wife and liked his son.

Steve represented stability to Sophie. They wanted the same things, a solid life, in one place forever. Steve seemed overwhelmed by his father, and had hated what he'd seen of the military, which his father privately admitted to Richard had been a disappointment to him. Sam was third generation West Point. But Steve had done well in law school and had joined an excellent firm.

Sophie had already lined up a job for herself at the United Nations after graduation, as a French-English translator, and had listed Chinese and Russian as languages she spoke adequately. Steve was enormously impressed with how mature she was, as were his parents. He was twenty-seven, and had worked at a bank for two years before going to law school. He had gotten a joint law and MBA degree, and was obviously solid and serious and just as in love with her as she was with him. They were young, but mature for their ages and crazy about each other.

Richard strenuously objected to her staying in New York, but it was a losing battle and Alex knew

it. She convinced Richard that they had to let Sophie
do what she wanted. She was almost twenty-two,
and knew her own mind, just as Alex had when she
left Hampshire and moved to London at twenty-
three, and never came home to live again.

"That was different, there was a war on."

"I'm not sure that would have made a difference
to me. I was ready to leave the nest. It was a good
excuse. She's ready too," Alex said with resignation.

Steve and Sophie came to Hampshire for two
weeks in August, and Steve spoke to Richard, and
asked his permission to ask for Sophie's hand in marriage, and there were tears in Richard's eyes when he
gave him his blessing. He hated the idea of her staying in the States but knew he couldn't stop her. He
hated that Alex was right.

They got engaged at Christmas and married the
following summer in New York. Alex and Richard
wanted her to get married in Hampshire, but all
of their friends were in New York, so they agreed
to let them get married there. They liked his parents, they were good, solid, respectable people with
good values. Steve and Sophie seemed so young to
get married, but Alex pointed out to Richard that
they would have gotten married sooner too if there
hadn't been a war on.

"Instead we snuck around to cheap hotels, pretending to be married, terrified every day that one
of us would get killed. I'd rather see them happily
married," she said with a sigh. "She is young, but

she knows her mind. I think we frightened her, dragging her all over the world because that was what we wanted to do. All she wants is to put down roots and never move again. It's what's right for her." And Steve felt that way too after his own childhood. Both sets of parents had chosen lives and careers that didn't suit their children, even if it had been interesting, filled with rich experiences.

"The diplomatic corps was the only job I could think of after the war," Richard said apologetically to Alex.

"It was right for us. I don't think it was for her. She's happier now. And Steve will be good to her. He's a nice boy. She doesn't want the adventures we had. And he doesn't want the life his father had in the military." Listening to her, Richard knew she was right. She so often was, and knew their daughter well.

They married in June 1975, a year after they both graduated. She was twenty-two, and he was twenty-eight. It seemed young, but not too young. And their babies came quickly after that. Steve and Sophie felt ready for it. His parents had married young too. Steve and Sophie had three daughters, Sabrina was born a year to the day after they got married. Alex flew to New York the minute the baby came. She looked just like Sophie, and was a beautiful baby, and they were proud and ecstatic. Alex cried when she held her. She hadn't expected to feel as much for a grandchild as she did.

Elizabeth was born two years later, with blond angelic looks, like a princess in a fairytale. And Charlotte was an accident, but warmly welcomed, a year after Elizabeth was born. They had three children in four years, and moved to a house in Connecticut. Steve was doing well at the law firm. Sophie hadn't worked since her first pregnancy, and Steve didn't want her to. She was happy at home with her babies, and a young Irish girl to help her. Sophie loved her husband, her babies, and their home. She became an American citizen after Charlotte was born, which really broke Richard's heart. But she maintained dual nationality, which appeased him somewhat.

Alex wished they lived closer, but New York was only a plane ride away. She wasn't going to make the same mistake her own mother had made, never visiting them, but they had been in more difficult places halfway around the world. New York was an easy trip. And it warmed her heart to see Sophie looking happy and fulfilled. She finally had the life she had always wanted, that suited her, and she was at peace.

Sophie dutifully brought the girls to visit her parents in Hampshire for a month every summer, and Steve came for two weeks. He worked hard, and they liked spending time in Maine every year after Hampshire. Alex loved her time with her granddaughters, and visited them in New York two or three times during the year. She thoroughly enjoyed how different they were, with distinct personalities from the moment they were born. Sabrina was very serious, and seemed very conservative and traditional as she was growing up. She was as horse-mad as Alex had been as a young girl. She spent as much time as she could on the horses Alex and Richard had bought when they moved back to England. Alex still rode a great deal herself, and rode with Sabrina when she visited.

Elizabeth was the princess in the family. Her sisters teased her about it. She loved pretty clothes, going to parties, having fun. She always had a flock of boyfriends and admirers and said she wanted to get married and wear a beautiful gown. She loved going through Alex's photographs of her presentation at Queen Charlotte's Ball, which Alex thought looked ridiculously old fashioned now, but Lizzie loved them, and wished she could do it. Sophie had come out at the International Ball in Washington her freshman year in college and her parents had flown over for it.

Charlotte was the adventurer in the group, always up to mischief, daring, afraid of nothing, wanting to explore beyond the horizons of her world. As she got older, she loved hearing her grandfather talk about the places they had lived. She thought it was exotic and exciting.

The girls were fourteen, twelve, and eleven when Richard told them and their mother one summer during their annual visit that their grandmother had been a spy for thirty years. They were stunned and fascinated and wanted to know all about it. Sophie was horrified and realized how little she knew her own mother. Sabrina was filled with admiration for her. Elizabeth thought it sounded scary and awful, and Charlotte drank it all in, and hounded Alex to tell her about it. She wanted all the details. Their mother was shocked by some of the stories, particularly of the SOE during the war. She'd had no idea that her mother had been an intelligence agent during her father's entire diplomatic career, although she knew a little about her war experiences. But Alex had always underplayed it.

"Why didn't I know about all that?" Sophie asked her mother about her years with MI6.

"You weren't supposed to. I couldn't tell anyone about the SOE for twenty years. Your father didn't know either, or I thought he didn't. I told him when I retired from MI6 after we came home from Washington, and he said he'd known all along. He never told me." At Richard's insistence, Alex showed the girls her war medals, which made it more real to them.

Richard was eighty-two and retired then, but still healthy and strong. They had kept the apartment in London, but didn't go often anymore. He preferred life in Hampshire, and Alex went to the city alone sometimes, to shop or see old friends. Bertie had died a few years before but they had stayed good friends and had had lunch from time to time.

Alex had the leisure time to do things now that she hadn't for years. At seventy-four, she looked ten years younger. She enjoyed her month with Sophie and her granddaughters every summer, although she could see that Sophie had no real attachment to the house in Hampshire. It was a place she visited and dutifully brought her daughters to see her parents. But her heart was with Steve and in the States. And she felt more American than English. It was her country, by choice, and she'd lived there since she was fourteen, after they left Moscow.

It was Sabrina who loved coming to England, and ultimately went to Oxford. She came to see her grandparents regularly, and spent weekends with them, and eventually brought the boy she had met at Oxford and fallen in love with along with her. He was the classic British aristocrat, and everything Alex's mother had wanted her to marry. It had taken two more generations for that to happen. His father was a marquess, and he had a big family property of his own, and a title, that he would inherit as the oldest son.

Like her mother, Sabrina married young, and she married at Wickham Manor, much to Alex and Richard's delight. She was twenty-two when she married, and Anthony twenty-five. Having their wedding in Hampshire meant the world to Alex. Richard had just turned ninety, and was slowly becoming frail, and going to New York for the wedding would have been too much for him. But he could be at his granddaughter's wedding, since she had it at Wickham Manor.

Not to be outdone, Elizabeth married a year later. She seemed less serious and more frivolous than her older sister. Sabrina was taking a course for a master's degree in archaeology at Oxford. Elizabeth married a man ten years older who treated her like a princess, and spoiled her. Her husband, Matthew, was from a New York banking family, and Sophie had to plan an enormous New York wedding for four hundred. She enjoyed it, and had nothing else to do. Elizabeth had just finished college and wanted to sail straight into marriage, before going to work for a fashion magazine in the fall. Matthew worked at the family bank and Lizzie wanted a huge wedding. They were in all the magazines regularly as the golden couple, and Sophie sent all the clippings to her mother. Elizabeth had grown up to be very much like Sophie as a little girl.

Alex and Richard both agreed that he wasn't strong enough to attend the wedding in New York. A society wedding for four hundred people would have been too much for him, and he urged Alex to go to see their granddaughter married.

She spent a week in New York helping Sophie before the wedding, and stayed for two days after. It gave Alex a chance to spend time with Charlotte, who had just finished her last year at Harvard, graduating a year early. She had been in a rush to do things all her life.

"Don't tell me you're getting married too," Alex said when she arrived in New York, and Charlotte laughed.

"Not a chance, Grandmama. I have other plans. I want to travel. Actually, I have an idea. Would you go to Hong Kong with me one day? I want to see where you and Grandfather lived, and my mom grew up, or one of the places anyway. She still remembers it, and she loved it. She hated Russia."

"We all did," Alex admitted. "I'll go with you one day, but I don't think I should leave your grandfather right now." Charlotte nodded. He was ninety-one, and had seemed very frail at Sabrina's wedding. She and Anthony were living in London, and flying in for Lizzie's wedding. "What are your plans?" Alex asked her youngest granddaughter. Charlotte was the boldest and most adventuresome of her granddaughters. She had majored in political science at Harvard.

"I want to get a job in Beijing," she said without hesitating. Interesting things were happening there, and China was the wave of the future. Charlotte had taken Chinese in college and spoke Mandarin very well. "I want to go there, and to Hong Kong with you one day."

"I never went to Beijing when I lived there. It wasn't open then. I'd like to see it with you," Alex said thoughtfully. At eighty-three she was still hungry to travel, but Richard wasn't up to it anymore. He didn't even like going to London. They hadn't used their apartment there all year, but Alex liked having it, in case she wanted to go to town and spend the night, although she worried about leaving Richard. Their housekeeper took good care of him, but Alex didn't like leaving him for more than a few hours.

Sophie joined them then with her table seating charts for the wedding in her hand. "What are you two up to?" she asked them, looking distracted.

"Planning a trip to China," Charlotte answered.

"Now?" She looked surprised.

"I can't leave your father. We're just dreaming." Alex smiled at Sophie.

"Maybe next year," Charlotte said hopefully, as her mother looked at Alex intently.

"Do you mind sitting next to my father-in-law, Mama?" Her mother-in-law had died the year before, shortly after Sabrina's wedding. "You'll both be alone. I have nightmares every night about the seating."

"That would be fine," Alex said easily. "You can seat me wherever you like." They had rented an enormous estate in the Hamptons, and were tenting the lawn for the reception. And there were buses to take people back and forth to the city so they didn't have to drive. The logistics were like planning an invasion. Alex said it reminded her of D-Day but Sophie had it well in hand and enjoyed it.

The wedding was as beautiful as Alex knew it would be. Elizabeth wore a dress made for her in

Paris and she really did look like a fairy princess as she came down the aisle on her father's arm. It had none of the British country feeling that had characterized Sabrina's wedding in Hampshire. Lizzie's wedding was pure Hollywood glamour. She wore a slinky white satin dress that showed off her figure, with a twenty-foot train behind her, and a lace veil. She looked like a movie star, and everyone gasped when they saw her. **Vogue** was covering the wedding. Both of her sisters were bridesmaids wearing pale blue satin gowns. Sophie was wearing emerald green organza, and Alex had worn navy lace that showed off her trim figure too, but was appropriate for her age. The groom's mother was more theatrical, and was wearing gold.

It was a seven o'clock black-tie wedding, and everything was perfection. There was a twelve-piece dance band for the beginning of the evening, and a disco with a famous DJ was being set up later in a separate tent. The lighting and sound system alone had taken two days to set up, and the white orchids on every table were exquisite. Alex smiled when she saw Sophie dancing with Steve at the wedding. They were still in love after twenty-four years. Alex and Richard had been married for fifty-four years.

Alex enjoyed her seat at the wedding. General Bennett, Steve's father and grandfather of the bride, was good company. He had retired from the army a few years earlier, but still consulted at the Pentagon, and was on numerous military councils. He had taught a class at West Point the year before, which he told Alex he had thoroughly enjoyed.

"Our granddaughter Charlotte told me something interesting last year," he said, smiling at Alex, pleased with his seat too. It had been an adjustment losing his wife the year before, and he said he was keeping busy.

"Charlotte always tells me interesting things," Alex said, smiling. "She was trying to talk me into a trip to Hong Kong and Beijing with her when I arrived. I loved it in Hong Kong when we lived there. I think it's the only place we lived that Sophie enjoyed, other than Washington. She's American at heart."

"Charlotte tells me you were a spy," he said with a smile. "Is that true?" He wasn't sure if she'd been exaggerating or not.

"I suppose so," she said, looking mildly embarrassed. "I worked for the SOE during the war, doing espionage and clandestine missions behind enemy lines. And I worked for MI6 in British Army intelligence from 1946 until 1970."

"Did Richard know?" He looked profoundly impressed. He'd heard a lot about the SOE in military circles and had collaborated with MI6.

"Not when I worked for the SOE, he said he always suspected when I told him when I retired from MI6. They recruited me when I married Richard, and he joined the diplomatic corps. They approached me right before we left for India, and I agreed, but he didn't know for certain until after I retired. I couldn't tell him. He suspected. He knows me too well. And I suppose the submachine gun I was rather fond of was a clue." She laughed.

"That's an interesting time to have been working for Military Intelligence," Sam commented. "The independence of India and Pakistan, and later, the Cold War."

"I scared myself a few times in Russia," she admitted with a grin. "I was always afraid I'd get caught and shot as a spy. There were a lot of defectors from England then, some of them working as double agents for the Russians. It was impossible to know who you could trust. We were both relieved when he got transferred to Washington. That was great fun."

"Working behind enemy lines during the war can't have been easy either."

"It wasn't," she confirmed, but offered no details.

"I don't think I've ever known a spy," he said, smiling at her, "at least I wasn't aware of it. I always think of spies as men."

"There were some astoundingly good female agents during the war," Alex said staunchly.

"Charlotte says you have two medals." Alex was embarrassed then. She wasn't used to talking about it. She never had before except to Richard, Sophie, and her grandchildren.

"Bouncing around in a drawer somewhere," she said about her medals.

"You should be very proud of your service to your

country," he said respectfully, and she was touched by how earnestly he said it.

"Coming from a general, that's very generous of you. I'm sure my contribution was far less impressive than yours."

"I doubt that. Would you like to discuss it on the dance floor? I'd like to get a dance in, before they switch to the disco." She laughed at what he said, and joined him on the dance floor. He was an excellent dancer and she had a good time. He was seventy-nine years old, looked younger, and was in great shape. They talked about politics and the many places they had both lived, and they rode one of the buses back to the city together that evening and he dropped her off at the St. Regis Hotel in a cab.

"I enjoyed the evening, Alex," he said. "There aren't a lot of women I can discuss espionage with, or who understand about living through a war."

"It's all a long time ago now." She smiled at him, but she had enjoyed it too. "Call us if you ever come to England."

"I will." He was still living in Washington, and enjoyed the consulting he still did at the Pentagon. It kept his hand in on military affairs.

There was a brunch for family and close friends at the Carlyle the next day, which Alex attended. Sam had gone back to Washington, and the bride and groom left for their honeymoon early that morning. They were going to Paris and the South of France.

Alex congratulated Sophie on putting together a beautiful wedding. The next day, Alex flew back to London, and arrived in Hampshire just as Richard was going to bed. She had called him the day before with all the details.

"I missed you," she said as she kissed him, and he smiled.

"Who did you sit next to?"

"Steve's father. He said to say hello. Charlotte had told him about my work for the SOE and MI6, so it gave us something to talk about."

"He had no problem finding something to talk to you about last year at Sabrina's wedding. He has an eye for you, my dear."

"Don't be silly. I'm an old woman. He's not chasing after me."

"I'm sure he would."

"I hope this means you're jealous. That would be much more interesting to me," she said, kissed him again, and helped him up the stairs. She didn't like how tired he seemed. He had been slowly running out of steam for several months. He was like a candle beginning to flicker, which tore at her heart. She helped him get ready for bed, and then told him more about the wedding as they lay there together, and while she was talking to him, he fell asleep, and she lay next to him, holding his hand.

He seemed better the next morning, and they went for a nice walk. Richard's mind was still crystal clear, but his body was failing. The eight-year age difference between them now seemed vast, when it never had before.

The following week he caught a cold and stayed in bed. She called the doctor, who came to see him, and said he was fine, and to keep warm and rest for a few days. Alex made him stay in bed, and brought his meals up on a tray. Day by day he seemed to be growing weaker. She was frightened when she looked at him. He seemed to have aged years in a matter of weeks. She sat by his bed in the afternoons and read quietly while he slept, and she stayed close and kept an eye on him, and was right there next to him if he needed anything. But mostly, he slept.

"Let's go for a walk tomorrow," he said one night as she helped him back into bed. "I'm tired of lying around here." He looked very pale and thin.

"Good. We'll go for a walk tomorrow," Alex said as she tucked him in. She kissed him on the cheek, and he held her hand when she got into bed. She could hear him breathing softly a few minutes later. She lay next to him, wishing she could give him back some of his energy and vitality, or give him some of hers. She gently stroked his cheek, and then fell asleep herself. When she woke in the morning, he looked peaceful, and he was gone. Richard had slipped away in the night, lying next to her. She'd been at his side until the last moment, and she was grateful he hadn't died when she was in New York for Lizzie's wedding. She lay next to him for a little while longer, and then she got up, kissed his cheek, and quietly left the room. She had known this moment would come, but she wasn't ready for it, and knew she never would be. After fifty-four years, she couldn't imagine a life without him. They had been so perfectly suited to each other. It took the breath out of her, thinking of going on without him.

She sat down in the kitchen and called Sophie, and told her what had happened.

She was shocked, not prepared for it either.

"I'm so sorry, Mama. I'll fly out today." Alex nodded, as the tears rolled down her cheeks.

"I can't imagine my life without him. I never could." The pain of it reminded her suddenly of when they had lost Edward, only this was infinitely worse. They had been life partners for more than half a century.

Alex called the vicar and the funeral home after that. She stood by in a plain black dress when they took him away. She went for a long walk after they left, all the way to the lake, and she could feel him with her. She knew he always would be, they had shared so much, and she was going to miss him so terribly. It was a deep pain and a loss like no other.

Chapter 19

Alex slept alone in their bed that night, for the first time in years. She got up at six and made herself a cup of tea. Sophie arrived a few hours later. She had taken the night flight from New York, and Charlotte was with her. Sabrina had promised to come down from London that afternoon, with Anthony. And Lizzie and Matthew were flying in from Paris from their honeymoon. Steve was coming from New York in time for the funeral, to be with Sophie. And by that night, the house was filled with voices and people, her daughter and granddaughters, her son-in-law and two grandsons-in-law. She wished that Richard were there too. It was how the house was meant to be, alive and vibrant with youth. She was glad they were there. Two days later, they buried him next to her father and mother, and the headstones for her brothers. She'd had a small one put there for Edward when they came back from Pakistan. Her grandparents were there too.

After the burial, they went back to the house and had lunch. Sophie organized it with the house-keeper, and the girls helped. They chattered and talked and they all took a walk that afternoon, just as Richard had wanted to right before he died. They stayed another day, and the house was agonizingly empty when they all left.

For the next six months, Alex felt like a marble in a shoebox, rolling around the empty house, not sure what to do with herself, without him. She went up to London, and used the apartment, and that felt strange too. It still felt unbelievable that he was no longer there. She couldn't get used to it and not having Richard to talk to. Sophie invited her to New York for Christmas, but she decided to stay home, with her memories of Richard.

A year later, Charlotte got a master's degree from Harvard in political science. Alex was very proud of her, and went to the ceremony.

Sam Bennett was there too and asked how she was doing. He told her how sorry he was about Richard.

"I'm all right," she said halfheartedly.

"It's strange at first. And very hard. The world feels off kilter without them, and then you get used to it and you go on living," he said wisely and she nodded. He had described it perfectly, and had gone through it when he had lost his wife two years before. Alex was eighty-four then, and Sam was eighty. They were each half of what had once been whole, and now no longer existed.

"When are we going to China, Grandmama?" Charlotte asked her at lunch after graduation, and Alex looked wistful. She wondered if it would be too painful now to go. "I'm starting a job in Beijing in November," she said, and Alex was startled. "I have some training to do before I leave. We should go over this summer." It would be hot then, and Alex was curious about her job in Beijing.

"What kind of job?" she asked her.

"With a newspaper," Charlotte said vaguely. "They had a spot for one foreigner and I got it. If you don't want to go now, you can visit me when I'm there, working. I could meet you in Hong Kong."

"I might do that," Alex said, looking intrigued. "What sort of training will you be doing?" Charlotte looked away as she answered.

"You know, the usual kind of thing, before you take a job in a foreign country."

"Your Chinese is fluent," Alex reminded her as she watched her granddaughter's face. And she saw Sam watching her too. Their eyes met for a minute afterward. Charlotte went off to talk to some of her friends then, and Sam and Alex were alone for a minute. "What sort of job is it?" she asked him quietly, and he smiled at her.

"Your security clearance was probably higher

than mine, so I guess I can tell you. She's going to Quantico."

"Quantico?" It rang a bell, but she wasn't sure what it was for a minute.

"CIA," he said so no one else could hear them, and Alex looked shocked. "They train FBI agents there too, but she's interested in international, not domestic. Like your MI5 and MI6."

"She's training for the CIA?" she whispered, and he laughed at her.

"You of all people should understand. I think it's genetic. She's following in your footsteps," he said gently.

"But that's so dangerous!"

"And it wasn't for you? They all have to follow their own paths, just as we did. Steve hated the idea of West Point, and Sophie hated growing up all over the world, and cares nothing about England. Sabrina is more English than the English and her children will be too, with Anthony. And Lizzie wants a glamorous life in New York, which you and I don't care about. Now Charlotte wants to be an agent of some kind, maybe a spy, just like you. And who knows, maybe one day we'll have a great-grandson who will go to West Point. They are who they are, in spite of us, not because of us. But of all of them, Charlotte is the most like you. She's a bold, brave, passionate, incredibly bright girl, and if she is a spy, she'll be a damned good one, like you were. And whatever it is she's doing in Beijing, she's not going to tell us much about it, just like you never did." As she listened to him, Alex knew he was right, and if Charlotte was going to work for the CIA, she'd be a terrific agent. Alex was proud of her just thinking about it. And when Charlotte came back to the table, Alex smiled at her.

"I think I'll come and see you once you're working in Beijing. It's too hot there now. We'll go to Hong Kong if you can take a few days off." She didn't ask her any more questions. She knew now.

Charlotte came to see her that afternoon at her hotel before she left, and Alex turned to her with a smile. "I have a graduation present for you." She had already given her a small pair of diamond earrings, which Charlotte was wearing, and Alex reached into her purse, and handed her something from the palm of her hand. Charlotte saw immediately what it was and looked shocked. "Is that yours?" It was the pistol Alex always had on her person or in her purse.

"I've been carrying it for more than fifty years. It's an antique, like me. Now it's yours." She handed her the bullets separately. She had removed them when she got back to the hotel. "Good luck at Quantico," she said softly.

"How did you know?" Charlotte asked her, cradling the small pistol in her hand.

"Your grandfather told me. I was a spy, not a clairvoyant. It actually shoots quite well, by the way. I've always been a fairly good shot." She sounded young again as she said it, and Charlotte laughed. "And whatever you do, don't do anything to be like me. Follow your own dreams, and your own heart."

"I've always wanted to do something like this, especially once Grandpapa told us about your being a spy. I'm not ready to settle down like my sisters, and I don't think I will be for a long time. I've got a lot of flying to do and I'm ready to spread my wings." She looked at the pistol again then and at her grandmother. "You don't need it, Grandmama?"

"I think at my age, it would be a little unseemly if I go around shooting people. My judo is still pretty good." Alex was grinning at her, proud to be her grandmother.

"You're dangerous, Grandmama." It was a compliment and Alex took it that way.

"I used to be. I don't need to be dangerous anymore. Just be careful. Learn your lessons well, and always follow your instincts." It was good advice for life, not just espionage. Alex kissed her then, and Charlotte left a few minutes later, with the pistol and bullets in her purse. Her grandmother still amazed her. She wished she knew more about her life, but probably no one ever would. It was her personality, and the nature of her work.

Alex flew back to London that night, and was back in Hampshire on a beautiful summer day.

She went for long walks every day, and felt better by the end of the summer. Her granddaughters didn't come in the summer anymore. They had their own lives to lead, their partners, and their careers. Charlotte was in Quantico in training, which her parents didn't know. Sam and Alex were the only ones who knew, and the "newspaper" job in Beijing was a cover for her first job with the CIA.

Alex was thinking about it one afternoon when the phone rang. It was Sam Bennett, calling from London.

"What are you doing here?" She was surprised to hear his voice.

"I'm speaking at the Royal Military Academy, on the war in Vietnam, and where we went wrong. Can I buy you dinner?" She liked the idea. They always enjoyed talking to each other at family events. Richard had liked him too.

"You can. We can trade war stories. Would you like to come to Hampshire after that? You've seen my friendly old place here, with hundreds of years of family history to bore you, some good walks, and a lake." He had been there for Sabrina's wedding, and liked it a lot.

"It seems like a very nice place for two old warhorses like us to hang out. I'd like to come. The girls love it, and even Sophie grudgingly admits that she does too. Dinner in town tomorrow?"

"It sounds wonderful. I have a flat in Kensington, so I'll spend the night. Where are you staying?"

"The Connaught." It was a very distinguished, small, elegant hotel, suitable for a general.

"I'll pick you up at your hotel, if you like," she offered.

"Perfect. Eight o'clock?"

"Wonderful. And, Sam, thank you. For the good advice about Charlotte and letting her spread her wings and do what she wants . . . for taking me to dinner . . . I was getting bored here."

"We have lots to talk about," he said, sounding buoyant. "The general and the spy. It sounds like a plot for a book."

"I'm not sure I still have a book in me." She laughed. "But a chapter or two perhaps."

"We'll just see where the story goes. I've waited a long time for this. I've had my eye on you since Sophie and Steven's wedding, but my wife was a good woman and your husband was a good man." Richard was right. He had said that Sam had an eye for her, and he wasn't wrong. She didn't know where it would lead. Maybe nowhere, but he had questions to ask her, and she had stories to tell, and she wanted to hear his. "Tomorrow at eight then."

"I won't be armed. I gave Charlotte my pistol as a graduation present. I still have an old Sten gun here somewhere." She was laughing.

"I come in peace." He was laughing too. They were having fun, and there was no harm in that.

"So do I," she assured him.

"See you tomorrow, Alex."

"Thank you, Sam." She smiled as she hung up.

About the Author

DANIELLE STEEL has been hailed as one of the world's most popular authors, with almost a billion copies of her novels sold. Her many international bestsellers include **Child's Play, The Dark Side, Lost and Found, Blessing in Disguise, Silent Night, Turning Point, Beauchamp Hall,** and other highly acclaimed novels. She is also the author of **His Bright Light,** the story of her son Nick Traina's life and death; **A Gift of Hope,** a memoir of her work with the homeless; **Pure Joy,** about the dogs she and her family have loved; and the children's books **Pretty Minnie in Paris** and **Pretty Minnie in Hollywood.**

Daniellesteel.com
Facebook.com/DanielleSteelOfficial
Twitter: @daniellesteel
Instagram: @officialdaniellesteel

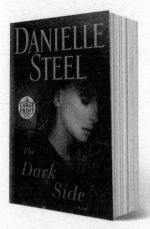

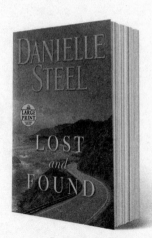

PLAYS FOR THE THEATRE

A DRAMA ANTHOLOGY

PLAYS FOR THE THEATRE

A DRAMA ANTHOLOGY

Sixth Edition

Edited by

Oscar G. Brockett

HARCOURT BRACE COLLEGE PUBLISHERS
Fort Worth Philadelphia San Diego New York Orlando Austin San Antonio
Toronto Montreal London Sydney Tokyo

Publisher	Ted Buchholz
Editor in Chief	Christopher P. Klein
Acquisitions Editor	Barbara J.C. Rosenberg
Developmental Editor	Cathlynn Richard
Project Editor	Laura J. Hanna
Production Manager	Jane Tyndall Ponceti
Art Director	Vicki Whistler

Cover artwork by David Hockney
Detail, *Parade Curtain after Picasso,* 1980
Oil on canvas, 48 x 60 inches
© David Hockney

Requests for permission to make copies of any
part of the work should be mailed to:
Permissions Department
Harcourt Brace & Company
6277 Sea Harbor Drive
Orlando, Florida 32887-6777

Some material in this work previously appeared in
PLAYS FOR THE THEATRE,
Fifth Edition, copyright © 1988, 1984, 1979, 1974, 1967
by Holt, Rinehart and Winston, Inc.
All rights reserved.

Address for Editorial Correspondence:
Harcourt Brace College Publishers
301 Commerce Street
Suite 3700
Fort Worth, Texas 76102

Address for Orders:
Harcourt Brace & Company
6277 Sea Harbor Drive
Orlando, Florida 32887

Printed in the United States of America
Library of Congress Catalog Card Number: 95-79645

ISBN: 0-15-501581-8
5 6 7 8 9 0 1 2 3 4 090 9 8 7 6 5 4 3 2 1

Preface

This sixth edition of *Plays for the Theatre* is a very substantial revision of earlier versions. Although it contains fourteen plays, as did the fifth edition, eight of the plays are new to this anthology.

Selecting plays for an anthology is always risky business. For each play chosen many others, perhaps equally worthy, must be rejected. In choosing plays for inclusion in the present edition, my goal has been to provide a selection both of representative plays from the past and of recent culturally diverse plays.

The works included in the present edition are drawn from many periods, ranging through ancient Greece, the Middle Ages, the seventeenth century, the late nineteenth century, and the twentieth century. They include works from the past by major playwrights—Sophocles, Shakespeare, Molière, Ibsen, O'Neill, Brecht, Williams, and Beckett—as well as an anonymous medieval mystery play and a commedia dell'arte scenario. The recent plays—one each by an African American, an Asian American, and a Latina—have been chosen both for their cultural and gender diversity and their dramatic power. Additional diversity is achieved by the inclusion of four plays that touch on Gay subjects, although none is specifically a Gay or Lesbian play.

Each of the plays is discussed at some length in a companion book, *The Essential Theatre*, Sixth Edition, published by Harcourt Brace College Publishers. This companion volume places each play within its historical and cultural context. Although each book can stand alone, together they provide a much fuller understanding of the plays than either volume does when used alone.

I would like to thank the reviewers who took the time to provide insight and guidance on this project: Gary Faircloth, East Carolina University; Elizabeth C. Ramírez, University of Oregon; LaLonnie Lehman, Texas Christian University; Ron Thronson, Chapman University; and Julia Allacdice Gagne, Valencia Community College.

Contents

Sophocles (495–406 B.C.)

Oedipus Rex (c. 430 B.C.)

Oedipus Rex was first performed in Athens at the City Dionysia (a major religious and civic festival held annually in honor of Dionysus, the god of wine and fertility) in competition with works by two other playwrights. Each dramatist presented three tragedies and one satyr play each time they competed before the audience of approximately fifteen thousand spectators. Sophocles was awarded first prize for the group of plays that included *Oedipus Rex*, considered by the Greek philosopher Aristotle an ideal example of tragic form.

The most striking feature of Greek tragedy is the alternation of dramatic episodes with choral passages. In Sophocles' day, the tragic chorus included fifteen performers who sang (or recited) and danced the choral passages to musical accompaniment. Other typical features of Greek tragedy are the small number of individualized characters, the restriction of the action to a single place, the tightly unified plot, the serious and philosophic tone, and the poetic language.

The action of *Oedipus Rex* is extremely concentrated: A complete reversal of the protagonist's fortune takes place in a single day. The story follows Oedipus, king of Thebes, as he attempts to discover the murderer of Laïos, the former king, after an oracle declares that the plague now destroying the city will not be lifted until the guilty one is cast out. Oedipus' search gradually uncovers terrible truths about the past and his own origins. The initial suspicion that Oedipus himself may be the slayer of Laïos is rapidly followed by other electrifying moments (among them Iocaste's recognition that she is not only Oedipus' wife but also his mother), and the ultimate outcome: blindness, exile, and anguish for the once-powerful king.

Sophocles is admired particularly for his skillful management of extensive plot materials: He accomplishes the gradual unveiling of mystery after mystery and a steady increase in dramatic tension with the utmost economy of means. Although, like most great plays, *Oedipus Rex* is open to many interpretations, most critics have agreed that a central concern is the uncertainty of fate and humanity's helplessness in the face of destiny.

Sophocles

Oedipus Rex

English Version by Dudley Fitts and Robert Fitzgerald

PERSONS REPRESENTED

OEDIPUS

A PRIEST

CREON

TEIRESIAS

IOCASTE [JOCASTA]

MESSENGER

SHEPHERD OF LAÏOS

SECOND MESSENGER

CHORUS OF THEBAN ELDERS

THE SCENE———*Before the palace of* OEDIPUS, *King of Thebes. A central door and two lateral doors open onto a platform which runs the length of the façade. On the platform, right and left, are altars; and three steps lead down into the "orchestra," or chorus-ground. At the beginning of the action these steps are crowded by suppliants who have brought branches and chaplets of olive leaves and who lie in various attitudes of despair.* OEDIPUS *enters.*

PROLOGUE

OEDIPUS: My children, generations of the living
In the line of Kadmos, nursed at his ancient hearth:
Why have you strewn yourselves before these altars
In supplication, with your boughs and garlands?
The breath of incense rises from the city
With a sound of prayer and lamentation.
                                        Children,
I would not have you speak through messengers,
And therefore I have come myself to hear you—
I, Oedipus, who bear the famous name.
    [*To a* PRIEST.]
You, there, since you are eldest in the company,
Speak for them all, tell me what preys upon you,
Whether you come in dread, or crave some blessing:
Tell me, and never doubt that I will help you

In every way I can; I should be heartless
Were I not moved to find you suppliant here.
PRIEST: Great Oedipus, O powerful King of Thebes!
    You see how all the ages of our people
Cling to your altar steps: here are boys
Who can barely stand alone, and here are priests
By weight of age, as I am a priest of God,
And young men chosen from those yet unmarried;
As for the others, all that multitude,
They wait with olive chaplets in the squares,
At the two shrines of Pallas, and where Apollo
Speaks in the glowing embers.
                       Your own eyes
Must tell you: Thebes is tossed on a murdering sea
And can not lift her head from the death surge.
A rust consumes the buds and fruits of the earth;
The herds are sick; children die unborn,
And labor is vain. The god of plague and pyre
Raids like detestable lightning through the city,
And all the house of Kadmos is laid waste,
All emptied, and all darkened; Death alone
Battens upon the misery of Thebes.

You are not one of the immortal gods, we know;
Yet we have come to you to make our prayer
As to the man surest in mortal ways
And wisest in the ways of God. You saved us
From the Sphinx, that flinty singer, and the tribute
We paid to her so long; yet you were never
Better informed than we, nor could we teach you:
It was some god breathed in you to set us free.

Therefore, O mighty King, we turn to you:
Find us our safety, find us a remedy,
Whether by counsel of the gods or men.
A king of wisdom tested in the past
Can act in a time of troubles, and act well.
Noblest of men, restore
Life to your city! Think how all men call you
Liberator for your triumph long ago;
Ah, when your years of kingship are remembered,
Let them not say *We rose, but later fell—*
Keep the State from going down in the storm!
Once, years ago, with happy augury,
You brought us fortune; be the same again!
No man questions your power to rule the land:

But rule over men, not over a dead city!
Ships are only hulls, citadels are nothing,
When no life moves in the empty passageways.
OEDIPUS: Poor children! You may be sure I know
All that you longed for in your coming here.
I know that you are deathly sick; and yet,
Sick as you are, not one is as sick as I.
Each of you suffers in himself alone
His anguish, not another's; but my spirit
Groans for the city, for myself, for you.

I was not sleeping, you are not waking me.
No, I have been in tears for a long while
And in my restless thought walked many ways.
In all my search, I found one helpful course,
And that I have taken: I have sent Creon,
Son of Menoikeus, brother of the Queen,
To Delphi, Apollo's place of revelation,
To learn there, if he can,
What act or pledge of mine may save the city.
I have counted the days, and now, this very day,
I am troubled, for he has overstayed his time.
What is he doing? He has been gone too long.
Yet whenever he comes back, I should do ill
To scant whatever duty God reveals.
PRIEST: It is a timely promise. At this instant
They tell me Creon is here.
OEDIPUS: O Lord Apollo!
May his news be fair as his face is radiant!
PRIEST: It could not be otherwise: he is crowned with bay,
The chaplet is thick with berries.
OEDIPUS: We shall soon know;
He is near enough to hear us now.
          [*Enter* CREON.]
                                        O Prince:
Brother: son of Menoikeus:
What answer do you bring us from the god?
CREON: A strong one. I can tell you, great afflictions
Will turn out well, if they are taken well.
OEDIPUS: What was the oracle? These vague words
Leave me still hanging between hope and fear.
CREON: Is it your pleasure to hear me with all these
Gathered around us? I am prepared to speak,
But should we not go in?
OEDIPUS: Let them all hear it.
It is for them I suffer, more than for myself.
CREON: Then I will tell you what I heard at Delphi.

In plain words
The god commands us to expel from the land of Thebes
An old defilement we are sheltering.
It is a deathly thing, beyond cure;
We must not let it feed upon us longer.

OEDIPUS: What defilement? How shall we rid ourselves of it?

CREON: By exile or death, blood for blood. It was
Murder that brought the plague-wind on the city.

OEDIPUS: Murder of whom? Surely the god has named him?

CREON: My lord: long ago Laïos was our king,
Before you came to govern us.

OEDIPUS: I know;
I learned of him from others; I never saw him.

CREON: He was murdered; and Apollo commands us now
To take revenge upon whoever killed him.

OEDIPUS: Upon whom? Where are they? Where shall we find a clue
To solve that crime, after so many years?

CREON: Here in this land, he said
                                   If we make enquiry,
We may touch things that otherwise escape us.

OEDIPUS: Tell me: Was Laïos murdered in his house,
Or in the fields, or in some foreign country?

CREON: He said he planned to make a pilgrimage.
He did not come home again.

OEDIPUS: And was there no one,
No witness, no companion, to tell what happened?

CREON: They were all killed but one, and he got away
So frightened that he could remember one thing only.

OEDIPUS: What was that one thing? One may be the key
To everything, if we resolve to use it.

CREON: He said that a band of highwaymen attacked them,
Outnumbered them, and overwhelmed the King.

OEDIPUS: Strange, that a highwayman should be so daring—
Unless some faction here bribed him to do it.

CREON: We thought of that. But after Laïos' death
New troubles arose and he had no avenger.

OEDIPUS: What troubles could prevent your hunting down the killers?

CREON: The riddling Sphinx's song
Made us deaf to all mysteries but her own.

OEDIPUS: Then once more I must bring what is dark to light.
It is most fitting that Apollo shows,
As you do, this compunction for the dead.
You shall see how I stand by you, as I should,
To avenge the city and the city's god,
And not as though it were for some distant friend,
But for my own sake, to be rid of evil.
Whoever killed King Laïos might—who knows?—

Decide at any moment to kill me as well.
By avenging the murdered king I protect myself.
Come, then, my children: leave the altar steps,
Lift up your olive boughs!
                    One of you go
And summon the people of Kadmos to gather here.
I will do all that I can; you may tell them that.
        [*Exit a* PAGE.]
So, with the help of God,
We shall be saved—or else indeed we are lost.
PRIEST: Let us rise, children. It was for this we came,
And now the King has promised it himself.
Phoibos has sent us an oracle; may he descend
Himself to save us and drive out the plague.
        [*Exeunt* OEDIPUS *and* CREON *into the palace by the central door. The* PRIEST
        and the SUPPLIANTS *disperse R and L. After a short pause the* CHORUS *en-
        ters the orchestra.*]

                    PARODOS

CHORUS: What is God singing in his profound   [STROPHE 1]
        Delphi of gold and shadow?
        What oracle for Thebes, the sunwhipped city?

        Fear unjoints me, the roots of my heart tremble.

        Now I remember, O Healer, your power, and wonder:
        Will you send doom like a sudden cloud, or weave it
        Like nightfall of the past?

        Speak, speak to us, issue a holy sound:
        Dearest to our expectancy: be tender!

        Let me pray to Athenê, the immortal daughter of Zeus, [ANTISTROPHE 1]
        And to Artemis her sister
        Who keeps her famous throne in the market ring,
        And to Apollo, bowman at the far butts of heaven—

        O gods, descend! Like three streams leap against
        The fires of our grief, the fires of darkness;
        Be swift to bring us rest!

        As in the old time from the brilliant house
        Of air you stepped to save us, come again!

        Now our afflictions have no end,   [STROPHE 2]
        Now all our stricken host lies down
        And no man fights off death with his mind;

The noble plowland bears no grain,
And groaning mothers can not bear—

See, how our lives like birds take wing,
Like sparks that fly when a fire soars,
To the shore of the god of evening.

The plague burns on, it is pitiless,   [ANTISTROPHE 2]
Though pallid children laden with death
Lie unwept in the stony ways,

And old gray women by every path
Flock to the strand about the altars

There to strike their breasts and cry
Worship of Phoibos in wailing prayers:
Be kind, God's golden child!

There are no swords in this attack by fire,   [STROPHE 3]
No shields, but we are ringed with cries.
Send the besieger plunging from our homes
Into the vast sea-room of the Atlantic
Or into the waves that foam eastward of Thrace—

For the day ravages what the night spares—

Destroy our enemy, lord of the thunder!
Let him be riven by lightning from heaven!

Phoibos Apollo, stretch the sun's bowstring,   [ANTISTROPHE 3]
That golden cord, until it sing for us,
Flashing arrows in heaven!
                              Artemis, Huntress,
Race with flaring lights upon our mountains!

O scarlet god, O golden-banded brow,
O Theban Bacchos in a storm of Maenads,
    [*Enter* OEDIPUS, *C.*]
Whirl upon Death, that all the Undying hate.
Come with blinding torches, come in joy!

SCENE I

OEDIPUS: Is this your prayer? It may be answered. Come,
        Listen to me, act as the crisis demands,
        And you shall have relief from all these evils.

        Until now I was a stranger to this tale,
        As I had been a stranger to the crime.
        Could I track down the murderer without a clue?

But now, friends,
As one who became a citizen after the murder,
I make this proclamation to all Thebans:
If any man knows by whose hand Laïos, son of Labdakos,
Met his death, I direct that man to tell me everything,
No matter what he fears for having so long withheld it.
Let it stand as promised that no further trouble
Will come to him, but he may leave the land in safety.

Moreover: If anyone knows t'he murderer to be foreign,
Let him not keep silent: he shall have his reward from me.
However, if he does conceal it; if any man
Fearing for his friend or for himself disobeys this edict,
Hear what I propose to do:

I solemnly forbid the people of this country,
Where power and throne are mine, ever to receive that man
Or speak to him, no matter who he is, or let him
Join in sacrifice, lustration, or in prayer.
I decree that he be driven from every house,
Being, as he is, corruption itself to us: the Delphic
Voice of Zeus has pronounced this revelation.
Thus I associate myself with the oracle
And take the side of the murdered king.

As for the criminal, I pray to God—
Whether it be a lurking thief, or one of a number—
I pray that that man's life be consumed in evil and wretchedness.
And as for me, this curse applies no less
If it should turn out that the culprit is my guest here,
Sharing my hearth.
                        You have heard the penalty.
I lay it on you now to attend to this
For my sake, for Apollo's, for the sick
Sterile city that heaven has abandoned.
Suppose the oracle had given you no command:
Should this defilement go uncleansed for ever?
You should have found the murderer: your king,
A noble king, had been destroyed!
                        Now I,
Having the power that he held for me,
Having his bed, begetting children there
Upon his wife, as he would have, had he lived—
Their son would have been my children's brother,
If Laïos had had luck in fatherhood!
(But surely ill luck rushed upon his reign)—
I say I take the son's part, just as though
I were his son, to press the fight for him

And see it won! I'll find the hand that brought
Death to Labdakos' and Polydoros' child,
Heir to Kadmos' and Agenor's line.
And as for those who fail me,
May the gods deny them the fruit of the earth,
Fruit of the womb, and may they rot utterly!
Let them be wretched as we are wretched, and worse!

For you, for loyal Thebans, and for all
Who find my actions right, I pray the favor
Of justice, and of all the immortal gods.
CHORAGOS: Since I am under oath, my lord, I swear
    I did not do the murder, I can not name
    The murderer. Might not the oracle
    That has ordained the search tell where to find him?
OEDIPUS: An honest question. But no man in the world
    Can make the gods do more than the gods will.
CHORAGOS: There is one last expedient—
OEDIPUS: Tell me what it is.
    Though it seem slight, you must not hold it back.
CHORAGOS: A lord clairvoyant to the lord Apollo,
    As we all know, is the skilled Teiresias.
    One might learn much about this from him, Oedipus.
OEDIPUS: I am not wasting time:
    Creon spoke of this, and I have sent for him—
    Twice, in fact; it is strange that he is not here.
CHORAGOS: The other matter—that old report—seems useless.
OEDIPUS: Tell me. I am interested in all reports.
CHORAGOS: The King was said to have been killed by highwaymen.
OEDIPUS: I know. But we have no witnesses to that.
CHORAGOS: If the killer can feel a particle of dread,
    Your curse will bring him out of hiding!
OEDIPUS: No.
    The man who dared that act will fear no curse.
        [*Enter the blind seer* TEIRESIAS, *led by a* PAGE.]
CHORAGOS: But there is one man who may detect the criminal.
    This is Teiresias, this is the holy prophet
    In whom, alone of all men, truth was born.
OEDIPUS: Teiresias: seer: student of mysteries,
    Of all that's taught and all that no man tells,
    Secrets of Heaven and secrets of the earth:
    Blind though you are, you know the city lies
    Sick with plague; and from this plague, my lord,
    We find that you alone can guard or save us.

    Possibly you did not hear the messengers?
    Apollo, when we sent to him,

Sent us back word that this great pestilence
Would lift, but only if we established clearly
The identity of those who murdered Laïos.
They must be killed or exiled.

                         Can you use
Birdflight or any art of divination
To purify yourself, and Thebes, and me
From this contagion? We are in your hands.
There is no fairer duty
Than that of helping others in distress.

TEIRESIAS: How dreadful knowledge of the truth can be
    When there's no help in truth! I knew this well,
    But made myself forget. I should not have come.

OEDIPUS: What is troubling you? Why are your eyes so cold?

TEIRESIAS: Let me go home. Bear your own fate, and I'll
    Bear mine. It is better so: trust what I say.

OEDIPUS: What you say is ungracious and unhelpful
    To your native country. Do not refuse to speak.

TEIRESIAS: When it comes to speech, your own is neither temperate
    Nor opportune. I wish to be more prudent.

OEDIPUS: In God's name, we all beg you—

TEIRESIAS: You are all ignorant.
    No; I will never tell you what I know.
    Now it is my misery; then, it would be yours.

OEDIPUS: What! You do know something, and will not tell us?
    You would betray us all and wreck the State?

TEIRESIAS: I do not intend to torture myself, or you.
    Why persist in asking? You will not persuade me.

OEDIPUS: What a wicked old man you are! You'd try a stone's
    Patience! Out with it! Have you no feeling at all?

TEIRESIAS: You call me unfeeling. If you could only see
    The nature of your own feelings . . .

OEDIPUS: Why,
    Who would not feel as I do? Who could endure
    Your arrogance toward the city?

TEIRESIAS: What does it matter!
    Whether I speak or not, it is bound to come.

OEDIPUS: Then, if "it" is bound to come, you are bound to tell me.

TEIRESIAS: No, I will not go on. Rage as you please.

OEDIPUS: Rage? Why not!

                  And I'll tell you what I think:
    You planned it, you had it done, you all but
    Killed him with your own hands: if you had eyes,
    I'd say the crime was yours, and yours alone.

TEIRESIAS: So? I charge you, then,
    Abide by the proclamation you have made:
    From this day forth

Never speak again to these men or to me;
You yourself are the pollution of this country.
OEDIPUS: You dare say that! Can you possibly think you have
Some way of going free, after such insolence?
TEIRESIAS: I have gone free. It is the truth sustains me.
OEDIPUS: Who taught you shamelessness? It was not your craft.
TEIRESIAS: You did. You made me speak. I did not want to.
OEDIPUS: Speak what? Let me hear it again more clearly.
TEIRESIAS: Was it not clear before? Are you tempting me?
OEDIPUS: I did not understand it. Say it again.
TEIRESIAS: I say that you are the murderer whom you seek.
OEDIPUS: Now twice you have spat out infamy. You'll pay for it!
TEIRESIAS: Would you care for more? Do you wish to be really angry?
OEDIPUS: Say what you will. Whatever you say is worthless.
TEIRESIAS: I say you live in hideous shame with those
Most dear to you. You can not see the evil.
OEDIPUS: It seems you can go on mouthing like this for ever.
TEIRESIAS: I can, if there is power in truth.
OEDIPUS: There is:
But not for you, not for you,
You sightless, witless, senseless, mad old man!
TEIRESIAS: You are the madman. There is no one here
Who will not curse you soon, as you curse me.
OEDIPUS: You child of endless night! You can not hurt me
Or any other man who sees the sun.
TEIRESIAS: True: it is not from me your fate will come.
That lies within Apollo's competence.
As it is his concern.
OEDIPUS: Tell me.
Are you speaking for Creon, or for yourself?
TEIRESIAS: Creon is no threat. You weave your own doom.
OEDIPUS: Wealth, power, craft of statesmanship!
Kingly position, everywhere admired!
What savage envy is stored up against these,
If Creon, whom I trusted, Creon my friend,
For this great office which the city once
Put in my hands unsought—if for this power
Creon desires in secret to destroy me!

He has bought this decrepit fortune-teller, this
Collector of dirty pennies, this prophet fraud—
Why, he is no more clairvoyant than I am!
                                                    Tell us.
Has your mystic mummery ever approached the truth?
When that hellcat the Sphinx was performing here,
What help were you to these people?
Her magic was not for the first man who came along:

It demanded a real exorcist. Your birds—
What good were they? or the gods, for the matter of that?
But I came by,
Oedipus, the simple man, who knows nothing—
I thought it out for myself, no birds helped me!
And this is the man you think you can destroy,
That you may be close to Creon when he's king!
Well, you and your friend Creon, it seems to me,
Will suffer most. If you were not an old man,
You would have paid already for your plot.
CHORAGOS: We can not see that his words or yours
　　　Have been spoken except in anger, Oedipus,
　　　And of anger we have no need. How can God's will
　　　Be accomplished best? That is what most concerns us.
TEIRESIAS: You are a king. But where argument's concerned
　　　I am your man, as much a king as you.
　　　I am not your servant, but Apollo's.
　　　I have no need of Creon to speak for me.

　　　Listen to me. You mock my blindness, do you?
　　　But I say that you, with both your eyes, are blind:
　　　You can not see the wretchedness of your life,
　　　Nor in whose house you live, no, nor with whom.
　　　Who are your father and mother? Can you tell me?
　　　You do not even know the blind wrongs
　　　That you have done them, on earth and in the world below.
　　　But the double lash of your parents' curse will whip you
　　　Out of this land some day, with only night
　　　Upon your precious eyes.
　　　Your cries then—where will they not be heard?
　　　What fastness of Kithairon will not echo them?
　　　And that bridal-descant of yours—you'll know it then,
　　　The song they sang when you came here to Thebes
　　　And found your misguided berthing.
　　　All this, and more, that you can not guess at now,
　　　Will bring you to yourself among your children.

　　　Be angry, then. Curse Creon. Curse my words.
　　　I tell you, no man that walks upon the earth
　　　Shall be rooted out more horribly than you.
OEDIPUS: Am I to bear this from him?—Damnation
　　　Take you! Out of this place! Out of my sight!
TEIRESIAS: I would not have come at all if you had not asked me.
OEDIPUS: Could I have told that you'd talk nonsense, that
　　　You'd come here to make a fool of yourself, and of me?
TEIRESIAS: A fool? Your parents thought me sane enough.
OEDIPUS: My parents again!—Wait: who were my parents?
TEIRESIAS: This day will give you a father, and break your heart.

OEDIPUS: Your infantile riddles! Your damned abracadabra!
TEIRESIAS: You were a great man once at solving riddles.
OEDIPUS: Mock me with that if you like; you will find it true.
TEIRESIAS: It was true enough. It brought about your ruin.
OEDIPUS: But if it saved this town?
TEIRESIAS: [*to the* PAGE] Boy, give me your hand.
OEDIPUS: Yes, boy; lead him away.
                                        —While you are here
     We can do nothing. Go; leave us in peace.
TEIRESIAS: I will go when I have said what I have to say.
     How can you hurt me? And I tell you again:
     The man you have been looking for all this time,
     The damned man, the murderer of Laïos,
     That man is in Thebes. To your mind he is foreign-born,
     But it will soon be shown that he is Theban,
     A revelation that will fail to please.
                                        A blind man,
     Who has his eyes now; a penniless man, who is rich now;
     And he will go tapping the strange earth with his staff
     To the children with whom he lives now he will be
     Brother and father—the very same; to her
     Who bore him, son and husband—the very same
     Who came to his father's bed, wet with his father's blood.

     Enough. Go think that over.
     If later you find error in what I have said,
     You may say that I have no skill in prophecy.
          [*Exit* TEIRESIAS, *led by his* PAGE. OEDIPUS *goes into the palace.*]

                              ODE I

CHORUS: The Delphic stone of prophecies   [STROPHE 1]
     Remembers ancient regicide
     And a still bloody hand.
     That killer's hour of flight has come.
     He must be stronger than riderless
     Coursers of untiring wind,
     For the son of Zeus armed with his father's thunder
     Leaps in lightning after him;
     And the Furies follow him, the sad Furies.

     Holy Parnassos' peak of snow   [ANTISTROPHE 1]
     Flashes and blinds that secret man,
     That all shall hunt him down:
     Though he may roam the forest shade
     Like a bull wild from pasture
     To rage through glooms of stone.
     Doom comes down on him; flight will not avail him;

For the world's heart calls him desolate,
And the immortal Furies follow, for ever follow.

But now a wilder thing is heard [STROPHE 2]
From the old man skilled at hearing Fate in the wingbeat of a bird.
Bewildered as a blown bird, my soul hovers and can not find
Foothold in this debate, or any reason or rest of mind.
But no man ever brought—none can bring
Proof of strife between Thebes' royal house,
Labdakos' line, and the son of Polybos;
And never until now has any man brought word
Of Laïos' dark death staining Oedipus the King.

Divine Zeus and Apollo hold [ANTISTROPHE 2]
Perfect intelligence alone of all tales ever told;
And well though this diviner works, he works in his own night;
No man can judge that rough unknown or trust in second sight,
For wisdom changes hands among the wise.
Shall I believe my great lord criminal
At a raging word that a blind old man let fall?
I saw him, when the carrion woman faced him of old,
Prove his heroic mind! These evil words are lies.

SCENE II

CREON: Men of Thebes:
   I am told that heavy accusations
   Have been brought against me by King Oedipus.

I am not the kind of man to bear this tamely.

If in these present difficulties
He holds me accountable for any harm to him
Through anything I have said or done—why, then,
I do not value life in this dishonor.
It is not as though this rumor touched upon
Some private indiscretion. The matter is grave.
The fact is that I am being called disloyal
To the State, to my fellow citizens, to my friends.
CHORAGOS: He may have spoken in anger, not from his mind.
CREON: But did you not hear him say I was the one
   Who seduced the old prophet into lying?
CHORAGOS: The thing was said; I do not know how seriously.
CREON: But you were watching him! Were his eyes steady?
   Did he look like a man in his right mind?
CHORAGOS: I do not know.
   I can not judge the behavior of great men.
   But here is the King himself.

[*Enter* OEDIPUS.]

OEDIPUS: So you dared come back.
Why? How brazen of you to come to my house,
You murderer!
                              Do you think I do not know
That you plotted to kill me, plotted to steal my throne?
Tell me, in God's name: am I coward, a fool,
That you should dream you could accomplish this?
A fool who could not see your slippery game?
A coward, not to fight back when I saw it?
You are the fool, Creon, are you not? hoping
Without support or friends to get a throne?
Thrones may be won or bought: you could do neither.

CREON: Now listen to me. You have talked; let me talk, too.
You can not judge unless you know the facts.

OEDIPUS: You speak well: there is one fact; but I find it hard
To learn from the deadliest enemy I have.

CREON: That above all I must dispute with you.

OEDIPUS: That above all I will not hear you deny.

CREON: If you think there is anything good in being stubborn
Against all reason, then I say you are wrong.

OEDIPUS: If you think a man can sin against his own kind
And not be punished for it, I say you are mad.

CREON: I agree. But tell me: what have I done to you?

OEDIPUS: You advised me to send for that wizard, did you not?

CREON: I did. I should do it again.

OEDIPUS: Very well. Now tell me:
How long has it been since Laïos—

CREON: What of Laïos?

OEDIPUS: Since he vanished in that onset by the road?

CREON: It was long ago, a long time.

OEDIPUS: And this prophet,
Was he practicing here then?

CREON: He was; and with honor, as now.

OEDIPUS: Did he speak of me at that time?

CREON: He never did:
At least, not when I was present.

OEDIPUS: But . . . the enquiry?
I suppose you held one?

CREON: We did, but we learned nothing.

OEDIPUS: Why did the prophet not speak against me then?

CREON: I do not know; and I am the kind of man
Who holds his tongue when he has no facts to go on.

OEDIPUS: There's one fact that you know, and you could tell it.

CREON: What fact is that? If I know it, you shall have it.

OEDIPUS: If he were not involved with you, he could not say
That it was I who murdered Laïos.

CREON: If he says that, you are the one that knows it!—
    But now it is my turn to question you.
OEDIPUS: Put your questions. I am no murderer.
CREON: First, then: You married my sister?
OEDIPUS: I married your sister.
CREON: And you rule the kingdom equally with her?
OEDIPUS: Everything that she wants she has from me.
CREON: And I am the third, equal to both of you?
OEDIPUS: That is why I call you a bad friend.
CREON: No. Reason it out, as I have done.

    Think of this first: Would any sane man prefer
    Power, with all a king's anxieties,
    To that same power and the grace of sleep?
    Certainly not I.
    I have never longed for the king's power—only his rights.
    Would any wise man differ from me in this?
    As matters stand, I have my way in everything
    With your consent, and no responsibilities.
    If I were king, I should be a slave to policy.

    How could I desire a scepter more
    Than what is now mine—untroubled influence?
    No, I have not gone mad; I need no honors,
    Except those with the perquisites I have now.
    I am welcome everywhere; every man salutes me,
    And those who want your favor seek my ear,
    Since I know how to manage what they ask.
    Should I exchange this case for that anxiety?
    Besides, no sober mind is treasonable.
    I hate anarchy
    And never would deal with any man who likes it.

    Test what I have said. Go to the priestess
    At Delphi, ask if I quoted her correctly.
    And as for this other thing: if I am found
    Guilty of treason with Teiresias,
    Then sentence me to death! You have my word
    It is a sentence I should cast my vote for—
    But not without evidence!
                       You do wrong
    When you take good men for bad, bad men for good.
    A true friend thrown aside—why, life itself
    Is not more precious!
                      In time you will know this well:
    For time, and time alone, will show the just man,
    Though scoundrels are discovered in a day.
CHORAGOS: This is well said, and a prudent man would ponder it.
    Judgments too quickly formed are dangerous.

OEDIPUS: But is he not quick in his duplicity?
    And shall I not be quick to parry him?
    Would you have me stand still, hold my peace, and let
    This man win everything, through my inaction?
CREON: And you want—what is it, then? To banish me?
OEDIPUS: No, not exile. It is your death I want,
    So that all the world may see what treason means.
CREON: You will persist, then? You will not believe me?
OEDIPUS: How can I believe you?
CREON: Then you are a fool.
OEDIPUS: To save myself?
CREON: In justice, think of me.
OEDIPUS: You are evil incarnate.
CREON: But suppose that you are wrong?
OEDIPUS: Still I must rule.
CREON: But not if you rule badly.
OEDIPUS: O city, city!
CREON: It is my city, too!
CHORAGOS: Now, my lords, be still, I see the Queen,
    Iocastê, coming from her palace chambers;
    And it is time she came, for the sake of you both.
    This dreadful quarrel can be resolved through her.
        [*Enter* IOCASTE.]
IOCASTE: Poor foolish men, what wicked din is this?
    With Thebes sick to death, is it not shameful
    That you should rake some private quarrel up?
        [*To* OEDIPUS:]
    Come into the house.

                        —And you, Creon, go now:
    Let us have no more of this tumult over nothing.
CREON: Nothing? No, sister: what your husband plans for me
    Is one of two great evils: exile or death.
OEDIPUS: He is right.
                    Why, woman, I have caught him squarely
    Plotting against my life.
CREON: No! let me die
    Accurst if ever I have wished you harm!
IOCASTE: Ah, believe it, Oedipus!
    In the name of the gods, respect this oath of his
    For my sake, for the sake of these people here!
                                                    [STROPHE 1]
CHORAGOS: Open your mind to her, my lord. Be ruled by her, I beg you!
OEDIPUS: What would you have me do?
CHORAGOS: Respect Creon's word. He has never spoken like a fool,
    And now he has sworn an oath.
OEDIPUS: You know what you ask?
CHORAGOS: I do.

OEDIPUS: Speak on, then.
CHORAGOS: A friend so sworn should not be baited so,
      In blind malice, and without final proof.
OEDIPUS: You are aware, I hope, that what you say
      Means death for me, or exile at the least.
CHORAGOS: No, I swear by Helios, first in Heaven!   [STROPHE 2]
      May I die friendless and accurst,
      The worst of deaths, if ever I meant that!
         It is the withering fields
            That hurt my sick heart:
         Must we bear all these ills,
            And now your bad blood as well?
OEDIPUS: Then let him go. And let me die, if I must,
      Or be driven by him in shame from the land of Thebes.
      It is your unhappiness, and not his talk,
      That touches me.
                        As for him—
      Wherever he goes, hatred will follow him.
CREON: Ugly in yielding, as you were ugly in rage!
      Natures like yours chiefly torment themselves.
OEDIPUS: Can you not go? Can you not leave me?
CREON: I can.
      You do not know me; but the city knows me,
      And in its eyes, I am just, if not in yours.
         [*Exit* CREON.]
                                                         [ANTISTROPHE 1]
CHORAGOS: Lady Iocastê, did you not ask the King to go to his chambers?
IOCASTE: First tell me what has happened.
CHORAGOS: There was suspicion without evidence: yet it rankled
      As even false charges will.
IOCASTE: On both sides?
CHORAGOS: On both.
IOCASTE: But what was said?
CHORAGOS: Oh let it rest, let it be done with!
      Have we not suffered enough?
OEDIPUS: You see to what your decency has brought you:
      You have made difficulties where my heart saw none.
CHORAGOS: Oedipus, it is not once only I have told you—   [ANTISTROPHE 2]
         You must know I should count myself unwise
      To the point of madness, should I now forsake you–
            You, under whose hand,
               In the storm of another time,
            Our dear land sailed out free.
            But now stand fast at the helm!
IOCASTE: In God's name, Oedipus, inform your wife as well:
      Why are you so set in this hard anger?
OEDIPUS: I will tell you, for none of these men deserves
      My confidence as you do. It is Creon's work,

His treachery, his plotting against me.

IOCASTE: Go on, if you can make this clear to me.

OEDIPUS: He charges me with the murder of Laïos.

IOCASTE: Has he some knowledge? Or does he speak from hearsay?

OEDIPUS: He would not commit himself to such a charge,
But he has brought in that damnable soothsayer
To tell his story.

IOCASTE: Set your mind at rest.
If it is a question of soothsayers, I tell you
That you will find no man whose craft gives knowledge
Of the unknowable.

Here is my proof.

An oracle was reported to Laïos once
(I will not say from Phoibos himself, but from
His appointed ministers, at any rate)
That his doom would be death at the hands of his own son—
His son, born of his flesh and of mine!

Now, you remember the story: Laïos was killed
By marauding strangers where three highways meet.
But his child had not been three days in this world
Before the King had pierced the baby's ankles
And left him to die on a lonely mountainside.

Thus, Apollo never caused that child
To kill his father, and it was not Laïos' fate
To die at the hands of his son, as he had feared.
This is what prophets and prophecies are worth!
Have no dread of them.
It is God himself
Who can show us what he wills, in his own way.

OEDIPUS: How strange a shadowy memory crossed my mind,
Just now while you were speaking; it chilled my heart.

IOCASTE: What do you mean? What memory do you speak of ?

OEDIPUS: If I understand you, Laïos was killed
At a place where three roads meet.

IOCASTE: So it was said;
We have no later story.

OEDIPUS: Where did it happen?

IOCASTE: Phokis, it is called: at a place where the Theban Way
Divides into the roads toward Delphi and Daulia.

OEDIPUS: When?

IOCASTE: We had the news not long before you came
And proved the right to your succession here.

OEDIPUS: Ah, what net has God been weaving for me?

IOCASTE: Oedipus! Why does this trouble you?
OEDIPUS: Do not ask me yet.
　　First, tell me how Laïos looked, and tell me
　　How old he was.
IOCASTE: He was tall, his hair just touched
　　With white; his form was not unlike your own.
OEDIPUS: I think that I myself may be accurst
　　By my own ignorant edict.
IOCASTE: You speak strangely.
　　It makes me tremble to look at you, my King.
OEDIPUS: I am not sure that the blind man can not see.
　　But I should know better if you were to tell me—
IOCASTE: Anything—though I dread to hear you ask it.
OEDIPUS: Was the King lightly escorted, or did he ride
　　With a large company, as a ruler should?
IOCASTE: There were five men with him in all: one was a herald,
　　And a single chariot, which he was driving.
OEDIPUS: Alas, that makes it plain enough!
                                                    But who—
　　Who told you how it happened?
IOCASTE: A household servant,
　　The only one to escape.
OEDIPUS: And is he still
　　A servant of ours?
IOCASTE: No; for when he came back at last
　　And found you enthroned in the place of the dead king,
　　He came to me, touched my hand with his, and begged
　　That I would send him away to the frontier district
　　Where only the shepherds go—
　　As far away from the city as I could send him.
　　I granted his prayer; for although the man was a slave,
　　He had earned more than this favor at my hands.
OEDIPUS: Can he be called back quickly?
IOCASTE: Easily.
　　But why?
OEDIPUS: I have taken too much upon myself
　　Without enquiry; therefore I wish to consult him.
IOCASTE: Then he shall come.
                                        But am I not one also
　　To whom you might confide these fears of yours?
OEDIPUS: That is your right; it will not be denied you,
　　Now least of all; for I have reached a pitch
　　Of wild foreboding. Is there anyone
　　To whom I should sooner speak?

　　Polybos of Corinth is my father.
　　My mother is a Dorian: Meropê.

I grew up chief among the men of Corinth
Until a strange thing happened—
Not worth my passion, it may be, but strange.

At a feast, a drunken man maundering in his cups
Cries out that I am not my father's son!

I contained myself that night, though I felt anger
And a sinking heart. The next day I visited
My father and mother, and questioned them. They stormed,
Calling it all the slanderous rant of a fool;
And this relieved me. Yet the suspicion
Remained always aching in my mind;
I know there was talk; I could not rest;
And finally, saying nothing to my parents,
I went to the shrine at Delphi.
The god dismissed my question without reply;
He spoke of other things.
                              Some were clear,
Full of wretchedness, dreadful, unbearable:
As, that I should lie with my own mother, breed
Children from whom all men would turn their eyes;
And that I should be my father's murderer.

I heard all this, and fled. And from that day
Corinth to me was only in the stars
Descending in that quarter of the sky,
As I wandered farther and farther on my way
To a land where I should never see the evil
Sung by the oracle. And I came to this country
Where, so you say, King Laïos was killed.

I will tell you all that happened there, my lady.
There were three highways
Coming together at a place I passed;
And there a herald came towards me, and a chariot
Drawn by horses, with a man such as you describe
Seated in it. The groom leading the horses
Forced me off the road at his lord's command;
But as this charioteer lurched over towards me
I struck him in my rage. The old man saw me
And brought his double goad down upon my head
As I came abreast.
                      He was paid back, and more!
Swinging my club in this right hand I knocked him
Out of his car, and he rolled on the ground.
                                      I killed him.

I killed them all.
Now if that stranger and Laïos were—kin,
Where is a man more miserable than I?
More hated by the gods? Citizen and alien alike
Must never shelter me or speak to me—
I must be shunned by all.
                              And I myself
Pronounced this malediction upon myself!
Think of it: I have touched you with these hands,
These hands that killed your husband. What defilement!

Am I all evil, then? It must be so,
Since I must flee from Thebes, yet never again
See my own countrymen, my own country,
For fear of joining my mother in marriage
And killing Polybos, my father.
                                        Ah,
If I was created so, born to this fate,
Who could deny the savagery of God?

O holy majesty of heavenly powers!
May I never see that day! Never!
Rather let me vanish from the race of men
Than know the abomination destined me!
CHORAGOS: We, too, my lord, have felt dismay at this.
    But there is hope: you have yet to hear the shepherd.
OEDIPUS: Indeed, I fear no other hope is left me.
IOCASTE: What do you hope from him when he comes?
OEDIPUS: This much:
    If his account of the murder tallies with yours,
    Then I am cleared.
IOCASTE: What was it that I said
    Of such importance?
OEDIPUS: Why, "marauders," you said,
    Killed the King, according to this man's story.
    If he maintains that still, if there were several,
    Clearly the guilt is not mine: I was alone.
    But if he says one man, singlehanded, did it,
    Then the evidence all points to me.
IOCASTE: You may be sure that he said there were several;
    And can he call back that story now? He can not.
    The whole city heard it as plainly as I.
    But suppose he alters some detail of it:
    He can not ever show that Laïos' death
    Fulfilled the oracle: for Apollo said
    My child was doomed to kill him; and my child—
    Poor baby!—it was my child that died first.

No. From now on, where oracles are concerned,
I would not waste a second thought on any.
OEDIPUS: You might be right.
                              But come: let someone go
For the shepherd at once. This matter must be settled.
IOCASTE: I will send for him.
I would not wish to cross you in anything,
And surely not in this.—Let us go in.
        [*Exeunt into the palace.*]

ODE II

CHORUS: Let me be reverent in the ways of right,   [STROPHE 1]
        Lowly the paths I journey on;
        Let all my words and actions keep
        The laws of the pure universe
        From highest Heaven handed down.
        For Heaven is their bright nurse,
        Those generations of the realms of light;
        Ah, never of mortal kind were they begot,
        Nor are they slaves of memory, lost in sleep;
        Their Father is greater than Time, and ages not.

        The tyrant is a child of Pride   [ANTISTROPHE 1]
        Who drinks from his great sickening cup
        Recklessness and vanity,
        Until from his high crest headlong
        He plummets to the dust of hope.
        That strong man is not strong.
        But let no fair ambition be denied;
        May God protect the wrestler for the State
        In government, in comely policy,
        Who will fear God, and on His ordinance wait.

        Haughtiness and the high hand of disdain   [STROPHE 2]
        Tempt and outrage God's holy law;
        And any mortal who dares hold
        No immortal Power in awe
        Will be caught up in a net of pain;
        The price for which his levity is sold.
        Let each man take due earnings, then,
        And keep his hands from holy things,
        And from blasphemy stand apart—
        Else the crackling blast of heaven
        Blows on his head, and on his desperate heart;
        Though fools will honor impious men,
        In their cities no tragic poet sings.
        Shall we lose faith in Delphi's obscurities,   [ANTISTROPHE 2]

We who have heard the world's core
Discredited, and the sacred wood
Of Zeus at Elis praised no more?
The deeds and the strange prophecies
Must make a pattern yet to be understood.
Zeus, if indeed you are lord of all,
Throned in light over night and day,
Mirror this in your endless mind:
Our masters call the oracle
Words on the wind, and the Delphic vision blind!
Their hearts no longer know Apollo,
And reverence for the gods has died away.

SCENE III

    [*Enter* IOCASTE.]
IOCASTE: Princes of Thebes, it has occurred to me
To visit the altars of the gods, bearing
These branches as a suppliant, and this incense.
Our King is not himself: his noble soul
Is overwrought with fantasies of dread,
Else he would consider
The new prophecies in the light of the old.
He will listen to any voice that speaks disaster,
And my advice goes for nothing.
    [*She approaches the altar, R.*]
                         To you, then, Apollo,
Lycean lord, since you are nearest, I turn in prayer.
Receive these offerings, and grant us deliverance
From defilement. Our hearts are heavy with fear
When we see our leader distracted, as helpless sailors
Are terrified by the confusion of their helmsman.
    [*Enter* MESSENGER.]
MESSENGER: Friends, no doubt you can direct me:
Where shall I find the house of Oedipus,
Or, better still, where is the King himself?
CHORAGOS: It is this very place, stranger; he is inside.
This is his wife and mother of his children.
MESSENGER: I wish her happiness in a happy house,
Blest in all the fulfillment of her marriage.
IOCASTE: I wish as much for you: your courtesy
Deserves a like good fortune. But now, tell me:
Why have you come? What have you to say to us?
MESSENGER: Good news, my lady, for your house and your husband.
IOCASTE: What news? Who sent you here?
MESSENGER: I am from Corinth.
The news I bring ought to mean joy for you,
Though it may be you will find some grief in it.

IOCASTE: What is it? How can it touch us in both ways?
MESSENGER: The word is that the people of the Isthmus
    Intend to call Oedipus to be their king.
IOCASTE: But old King Polybos—is he not reigning still?
MESSENGER: No. Death holds him in his sepulchre.
IOCASTE: What are you saying? Polybos is dead?
MESSENGER: If I am not telling the truth, may I die myself.
IOCASTE: [*to a* MAIDSERVANT:] Go in, go quickly; tell this to your master.
    O riddlers of God's will, where are you now!
    This was the man whom Oedipus, long ago,
    Feared so, fled so, in dread of destroying him—
    But it was another fate by which he died.
        [*Enter* OEDIPUS, *C.*]
OEDIPUS: Dearest Iocastê, why have you sent for me?
IOCASTE: Listen to what this man says, and then tell me
    What has become of the solemn prophecies.
OEDIPUS: Who is this man? What is his news for me?
IOCASTE: He has come from Corinth to announce your father's death!
OEDIPUS: Is it true, stranger? Tell me in your own words.
MESSENGER: I can not say it more clearly: the King is dead.
OEDIPUS: Was it by treason? Or by an attack of illness?
MESSENGER: A little thing brings old men to their rest.
OEDIPUS: It was sickness, then?
MESSENGER: Yes, and his many years.
OEDIPUS: Ah!
    Why should a man respect the Pythian hearth, or
    Give heed to the birds that jangle above his head?
    They prophesied that I should kill Polybos,
    Kill my own father; but he is dead and buried,
    And I am here—I never touched him, never,
    Unless he died of grief for my departure,
    And thus, in a sense, through me. No. Polybos
    Has packed the oracles off with him underground.
    They are empty words.
IOCASTE: Had I not told you so?
OEDIPUS: You had; it was my faint heart that betrayed me.
IOCASTE: From now on never think of those things again.
OEDIPUS: And yet—must I not fear my mother's bed?
IOCASTE: Why should anyone in this world be afraid,
    Since Fate rules us and nothing can be foreseen?
    A man should live only for the present day.

    Have no more fear of sleeping with your mother:
    How many men, in dreams, have lain with their mothers!
    No reasonable man is troubled by such things.
OEDIPUS: That is true; only—
    If only my mother were not still alive!
    But she is alive. I can not help my dread.

IOCASTE: Yet this news of your father's death is wonderful.
OEDIPUS: Wonderful. But I fear the living woman.
MESSENGER: Tell me, who is this woman that you fear?
OEDIPUS: It is Meropê, man; the wife of King Polybos.
MESSENGER: Meropê? Why should you be afraid of her?
OEDIPUS: An oracle of the gods, a dreadful saying.
MESSENGER: Can you tell me about it or are you sworn to silence?
OEDIPUS: I can tell you, and I will.

    Apollo said through his prophet that I was the man
    Who should marry his own mother, shed his father's blood
    With his own hands. And so, for all these years
    I have kept clear of Corinth, and no harm has come—
    Though it would have been sweet to see my parents again.
MESSENGER: And is this the fear that drove you out of Corinth?
OEDIPUS: Would you have me kill my father?
MESSENGER: As for that
    You must be reassured by the news I gave you.
OEDIPUS: If you could reassure me, I would reward you.
MESSENGER: I had that in mind, I will confess: I thought
    I could count on you when you returned to Corinth.
OEDIPUS: No: I will never go near my parents again.
MESSENGER: Ah, son, you still do not know what you are doing—
OEDIPUS: What do you mean? In the name of God tell me!
MESSENGER: —If these are your reasons for not going home.
OEDIPUS: I tell you, I fear the oracle may come true.
MESSENGER: And guilt may come upon you through your parents?
OEDIPUS: That is the dread that is always in my heart.
MESSENGER: Can you not see that all your fears are groundless?
OEDIPUS: How can you say that? They are my parents, surely?
MESSENGER: Polybos was not your father.
OEDIPUS: Not my father?
MESSENGER: No more your father than the man speaking to you.
OEDIPUS: But you are nothing to me!
MESSENGER: Neither was he.
OEDIPUS: Then why did he call me son?
MESSENGER: I will tell you:
    Long ago he had you from my hands, as a gift.
OEDIPUS: Then how could he love me so, if I was not his?
MESSENGER: He had no children, and his heart turned to you.
OEDIPUS: What of you? Did you buy me? Did you find me by chance?
MESSENGER: I came upon you in the crooked pass of Kithairon.
OEDIPUS: And what were you doing there?
MESSENGER: Tending my flocks.
OEDIPUS: A wandering shepherd?
MESSENGER: But your savior, son, that day.
OEDIPUS: From what did you save me?
MESSENGER: Your ankles should tell you that.
OEDIPUS: Ah, stranger, why do you speak of that childhood pain?

MESSENGER: I cut the bonds that tied your ankles together.
OEDIPUS: I have had the mark as long as I can remember.
MESSENGER: That was why you were given the name you bear.
OEDIPUS: God! Was it my father or my mother who did it?
    Tell me!
MESSENGER: I do not know. The man who gave you to me
    Can tell you better than I.
OEDIPUS: It was not you that found me, but another?
MESSENGER: It was another shepherd gave you to me.
OEDIPUS: Who was he? Can you tell me who he was?
MESSENGER: I think he was said to be one of Laïos' people.
OEDIPUS: You mean the Laïos who was king here years ago?
MESSENGER: Yes; King Laïos; and the man was one of his herdsmen.
OEDIPUS: Is he still alive? Can I see him?
MESSENGER: These men here
    Know best about such things.
OEDIPUS: Does anyone here
    Know this shepherd that he is talking about?
    Have you seen him in the fields, or in the town?
    If you have, tell me. It is time things were made plain.
CHORAGOS: I think the man he means is that same shepherd
    You have already asked to see. Iocastê perhaps
    Could tell you something.
OEDIPUS: Do you know anything
    About him, Lady? Is he the man we have summoned?
    Is that the man this shepherd means?
IOCASTE: Why think of him?
    Forget this herdsman. Forget it all.
    This talk is a waste of time.
OEDIPUS: How can you say that?
    When the clues to my true birth are in my hands?
IOCASTE: For God's love, let us have no more questioning!
    Is your life nothing to you?
    My own is pain enough for me to bear.
OEDIPUS: You need not worry. Suppose my mother a slave,
    And born of slaves: no baseness can touch you.
IOCASTE: Listen to me, I beg you: do not do this thing!
OEDIPUS: I will not listen; the truth must be made known.
IOCASTE: Everything that I say is for your own good!
OEDIPUS: My own good
    Snaps my patience, then; I want none of it.
IOCASTE: You are fatally wrong! May you never learn who you are!
OEDIPUS: Go, one of you, and bring the shepherd here.
    Let us leave this woman to brag of her royal name.
IOCASTE: Ah, miserable!
    That is the only word I have for you now.
    That is the only word I can ever have.
       [*Exit into the palace.*]

CHORAGOS: Why has she left us, Oedipus? Why has she gone
    In such a passion of sorrow? I fear this silence:
    Something dreadful may come of it.
OEDIPUS: Let it come!
    However base my birth, I must know about it.
    The Queen, like a woman, is perhaps ashamed
    To think of my low origin. But I
    Am a child of Luck; I can not be dishonored.
    Luck is my mother; the passing months, my brothers,
    Have seen me rich and poor.
                      If this is so,
    How could I wish that I were someone else?
    How could I not be glad to know my birth?

ODE III

CHORUS: If ever the coming time were known   [STROPHE]
    To my heart's pondering,
    Kithairon, now by Heaven I see the torches
    At the festival of the next full moon,
    And see the dance, and hear the choir sing
    A grace to your gentle shade:
    Mountain where Oedipus was found,
    O mountain guard of a noble race!
    May the god who heals us lend his aid,
    And let that glory come to pass
    For our king's cradling-ground.

    Of the nymphs that flower beyond the years,   [ANTISTROPHE]
    Who bore you, royal child,
    To Pan of the hills or the timberline, Apollo,
    Cold in delight where the upland clears,
    Or Hermês for whom Kyllenê's heights are piled?
    Or flushed as evening cloud,
    Great Dionysos, roamer of mountains,
    He—was it he who found you there,
    And caught you up in his own proud
    Arms from the sweet god-ravisher
    Who laughed by the Muses' fountains?

SCENE IV

OEDIPUS: Sirs: though I do not know the man,
    I think I see him coming, this shepherd we want:
    He is old, like our friend here, and the men
    Bringing him seem to be servants of my house.
    But you can tell, if you have ever seen him.
        [*Enter* SHEPHERD *escorted by servants.*]

CHORAGOS: I know him, he was Laïos' man. You can trust him.

OEDIPUS: Tell me first, you from Corinth: is this the shepherd
    We were discussing?

MESSENGER: This is the very man.

OEDIPUS: [*to* SHEPHERD] Come here. No, look at me. You must answer
    Everything I ask.—You belonged to Laïos?

SHEPHERD: Yes: born his slave, brought up in his house.

OEDIPUS: Tell me: what kind of work did you do for him?

SHEPHERD: I was a shepherd of his, most of my life.

OEDIPUS: Where mainly did you go for pasturage?

SHEPHERD: Sometimes Kithairon, sometimes the hills nearby.

OEDIPUS: Do you remember ever seeing this man out there?

SHEPHERD: What would he be doing there? This man?

OEDIPUS: This man standing here. Have you ever seen him before?

SHEPHERD: No. At least, not to my recollection.

MESSENGER: And that is not strange, my lord. But I'll refresh
    His memory: he must remember when we two
    Spent three whole seasons together, March to September,
    On Kithairon or thereabouts. He had two flocks;
    I had one. Each autumn I'd drive mine home
    And he would go back with his to Laïos' sheepfold.—
    Is this not true, just as I have described it?

SHEPHERD: True, yes; but it was all so long ago.

MESSENGER: Well, then: do you remember, back in those days,
    That you gave me a baby boy to bring up as my own?

SHEPHERD: What if I did? What are you trying to say?

MESSENGER: King Oedipus was once that little child.

SHEPHERD: Damn you, hold your tongue!

OEDIPUS: No more of that!
    It is your tongue needs watching, not this man's.

SHEPHERD: My King, my Master, what is it I have done wrong?

OEDIPUS: You have not answered his question about the boy.

SHEPHERD: He does not know . . . He is only making trouble . . .

OEDIPUS: Come, speak plainly, or it will go hard with you.

SHEPHERD: In God's name, do not torture an old man!

OEDIPUS: Come here, one of you; bind his arms behind him.

SHEPHERD: Unhappy king! What more do you wish to learn?

OEDIPUS: Did you give this man the child he speaks of?

SHEPHERD: I did.
    And I would to God I had died that very day.

OEDIPUS: You will die now unless you speak the truth.

SHEPHERD: Yet if I speak the truth, I am worse than dead.

OEDIPUS: Very well; since you insist upon delaying—

SHEPHERD: No! I have told you already that I gave him the boy.

OEDIPUS: Where did you get him? From your house? From somewhere else?

SHEPHERD: Not from mine, no. A man gave him to me.

OEDIPUS: Is that man here? Do you know whose slave he was?

SHEPHERD: For God's love, my King, do not ask me any more!
OEDIPUS: You are a dead man if I have to ask you again.
SHEPHERD: Then . . . Then the child was from the palace of Laïos.
OEDIPUS: A slave child? or a child of his own line?
SHEPHERD: Ah, I am on the brink of dreadful speech!
OEDIPUS: And I of dreadful hearing. Yet I must hear.
SHEPHERD: If you must be told, then . . .

                             They said it was Laïos' child;
    But it is your wife who can tell you about that.
OEDIPUS: My wife!—Did she give it to you?
SHEPHERD: My lord, she did.
OEDIPUS: Do you know why?
SHEPHERD: I was told to get rid of it.
OEDIPUS: An unspeakable mother!
SHEPHERD: There had been prophecies . . .
OEDIPUS: Tell me.
SHEPHERD: It was said that the boy would kill his own father.
OEDIPUS: Then why did you give him over to this old man?
SHEPHERD: I pitied the baby, my King.
    And I thought that this man would take him far away
    To his own country.
                  He saved him—but for what a fate!
    For if you are what this man says you are,
    No man living is more wretched than Oedipus.
OEDIPUS: Ah God!
    It was true!
        All the prophecies!
                 —Now,
    O, Light, may I look on you for the last time!
    I, Oedipus,
    Oedipus, damned in his birth, in his marriage damned,
    Damned in the blood he shed with his own hand!
     [*He rushes into the palace.*]

ODE IV

CHORUS: Alas for the seed of men.   [STROPHE 1]

    What measure shall I give these generations
    That breathe on the void and are void
    And exist and do not exist?

    Who bears more weight of joy
    Than mass of sunlight shifting in images,
    Or who shall make his thought stay on
    That down time drifts away?

    Your splendor is all fallen.

O naked brow of wrath and tears,
O change of Oedipus!
I who saw your days call no man blest—
Your great days like ghósts góne.

That mind was a strong bow.   [ANTISTROPHE 1]

Deep, how deep you drew it then, hard archer,
At a dim fearful range,
And brought dear glory down!

You overcame the stranger—
The virgin with her hooking lion claws—
And though death sang, stood like a tower
To make pale Thebes take heart.

Fortress against our sorrow!

True king, giver of laws,
Majestic Oedipus!
No prince in Thebes had ever such renown,
No prince won such grace of power.

And now of all men ever known   [STROPHE 2]
Most pitiful is this man's story:
His fortunes are most changed, his state
Fallen to a low slave's
Ground under bitter fate.

O Oedipus, most royal one!
The great door that expelled you to the light
Gave at night—ah, gave night to your glory:
As to the father, to the fathering son.

All understood too late.

How could that queen whom Laïos won,
The garden that he harrowed at his height,
Be silent when that act was done?

But all eyes fail before time's eye,   [ANTISTROPHE 2]
All actions come to justice there.
Though never willed, though far down the deep past,
Your bed, your dread sirings,
Are brought to book at last.
Child by Laïos doomed to die,
Then doomed to lose that fortunate little death,
Would God you never took breath in this air
That with my wailing lips I take to cry:

For I weep the world's outcast.

I was blind, and now I can tell why:
Asleep, for you had given ease of breath
To Thebes, while the false years went by.

ÉXODOS

[*Enter, from the palace,* SECOND MESSENGER.]
SECOND MESSENGER: Elders of Thebes, most honored in this land,
What horrors are yours to see and hear, what weight
Of sorrow to be endured, if, true to your birth,
You venerate the line of Labdakos!
I think neither Istros nor Phasis, those great rivers,
Could purify this place of the corruption
It shelters now, or soon must bring to light—
Evil not done unconsciously, but willed.

The greatest griefs are those we cause ourselves.
CHORAGOS: Surely, friend, we have grief enough already;
What new sorrow do you mean?
SECOND MESSENGER: The Queen is dead.
CHORAGOS: Iocastê? Dead? But at whose hand?
SECOND MESSENGER: Her own.
The full horror of what happened you can not know,
For you did not see it; but I, who did, will tell you
As clearly as I can how she met her death.

When she had left us,
In passionate silence, passing through the court,
She ran to her apartment in the house,
Her hair clutched by the fingers of both hands.
She closed the doors behind her; then, by that bed
Where long ago the fatal son was conceived—
That son who should bring about his father's death—
We hear her call upon Laïos, dead so many years,
And heard her wail for the double fruit of her marriage,
A husband by her husband, children by her child.

Exactly how she died I do not know:
For Oedipus burst in moaning and would not let us
Keep vigil to the end: it was by him
As he stormed about the room that our eyes were caught.
From one to another of us he went, begging a sword,
Cursing the wife who was not his wife, the mother
Whose womb had carried his own children and himself.
I do not know: it was none of us aided him,
But surely one of the gods was in control!
For with a dreadful cry

He hurled his weight, as though wrenched out of himself,
At the twin doors: the bolts gave, and he rushed in.
And there we saw her hanging, her body swaying
From the cruel cord she had noosed about her neck.
A great sob broke from him, heartbreaking to hear,
As he loosed the rope and lowered her to the ground.

I would blot out from my mind what happened next!
For the King ripped from her gown the golden brooches
that were her ornament, and raised them, and lunged them down
Straight into his own eyeballs, crying, "No more,
No more shall you look on the misery about me,
The horrors of my own doing! Too long you have known
The faces of those whom I should never have seen,
Too long been blind to those for whom I was searching!
From this hour, go in darkness!" And as he spoke,
He struck at his eyes—not once, but many times;
And the blood spattered his beard,
Bursting from his ruined sockets like red hail.

So from the unhappiness of two this evil has sprung,
A curse on the man and woman alike. The old
Happiness of the house of Labdakos
Was happiness enough: where is it today?
It is all wailing and ruin, disgrace, death—all
The misery of mankind that has a name—
And it is wholly and for ever theirs.
CHORAGOS: Is he in agony still? Is there no rest for him?
SECOND MESSENGER: He is calling for someone to lead him to the gates
So that all the children of Kadmos may look upon
His father's murderer, his mother's—no,
I can not say it!
                              And then he will leave Thebes,
Self-exiled, in order that the curse
Which he himself pronounced may depart from the house.
He is weak, and there is none to lead him,
So terrible is his suffering.
                              But you will see:
Look, the doors are opening; in a moment
You will see a thing that would crush a heart of stone.
        [*The central door is opened;* OEDIPUS, *blinded, is led in.*]
CHORAGOS: Dreadful indeed for men to see.
Never have my own eyes
Looked on a sight so full of fear.

Oedipus!
What madness came upon you, what daemon
Leaped on your life with heavier
Punishment than a mortal man can bear?

No: I can not even
Look at you, poor ruined one.
And I would speak, question, ponder,
If I were able. No.
You make me shudder.
OEDIPUS: God.   God.
  Is there a sorrow greater?
  Where shall I find harbor in this world?
  My voice is hurled far on a dark wind.
  What has God done to me?
CHORAGOS: Too terrible to think of, or to see.
OEDIPUS: O cloud of night,   [STROPHE 1]
  Never to be turned away: night coming on,
  I can not tell how: night like a shroud!

  My fair winds brought me here.
                              O God. Again
  The pain of the spikes where I had sight,
  The flooding pain
  Of memory, never to be gouged out.
CHORAGOS: This is not strange.
  You suffer it all twice over, remorse in pain,
  Pain in remorse.
OEDIPUS: Ah dear friend   [ANTISTROPHE 1]
  Are you faithful even yet, you alone?
  Are you still standing near me, will you stay here,
  Patient, to care for the blind?
                              The blind man!
  Yet even blind I know who it is attends me,
  By the voice's tone—
  Though my new darkness hide the comforter.
CHORAGOS: Oh fearful act!
  What god was it drove you to rake black
  Night across your eyes?
OEDIPUS: Apollo. Apollo. Dear   [STROPHE 2]
  Children, the god was Apollo.
  He brought my sick, sick fate upon me.
  But the blinding hand was my own!
  How could I bear to see
  When all my sight was horror everywhere?
CHORAGOS: Everywhere; that is true.
OEDIPUS: And now what is left?
  Images? Love? A greeting even,
  Sweet to the senses? Is there anything?
  Ah, no, friends: lead me away.
  Lead me away from Thebes.
                              Lead the great wreck
  And hell of Oedipus, whom the gods hate.

CHORAGOS: Your fate is clear, you are not blind to that.
　　　Would God you had never found it out!
OEDIPUS: Death take the man who unbound   [ANTISTROPHE 2]
　　　My feet on that hillside
　　　And delivered me from death to life! What life?
　　　If only I had died,
　　　This weight of monstrous doom
　　　Could not have dragged me and my darlings down.
CHORAGOS: I would have wished the same.
OEDIPUS: Oh never to have come here
　　　With my father's blood upon me! Never
　　　To have been the man they call his mother's husband!
　　　Oh accurst! Oh child of evil,
　　　To have entered that wretched bed—
　　　　　　　　　　　　　　　　　the selfsame one!
　　　More primal than sin itself, this fell to me.

CHORAGOS: I do not know how I can answer you.
　　　You were better dead than alive and blind.
OEDIPUS: Do not counsel me any more. This punishment
　　　That I have laid upon myself is just.
　　　If I had eyes,
　　　I do not know how I could bear the sight
　　　Of my father, when I came to the house of Death,
　　　Or my mother: for I have sinned against them both
　　　So vilely that I could not make my peace
　　　By strangling my own life.
　　　　　　　　　　　　　Or do you think my children,
　　　Born as they were born, would be sweet to my eyes?
　　　Ah never, never! Nor this town with its high walls,
　　　Nor the holy images of the gods.
　　　　　　　　　　　For I,
　　　Thrice miserable!—Oedipus, noblest of all the line
　　　Of Kadmos, have condemned myself to enjoy
　　　These things no more, by my own malediction
　　　Expelling that man whom the gods declared
　　　To be a defilement in the house of Laïos.
　　　After exposing the rankness of my own guilt,
　　　How could I look men frankly in the eyes?
　　　No, I swear it,
　　　If I could have stifled my hearing at its source,
　　　I would have done it and made all this body
　　　A tight cell of misery, blank to light and sound:
　　　So I should have been safe in a dark agony
　　　Beyond all recollection.
　　　　　　　　　　　Ah Kithairon!
　　　Why did you shelter me? When I was cast upon you,
　　　Why did I not die? Then I should never

Have shown the world my execrable birth.

Ah Polybos! Corinth, city that I believed
The ancient seat of my ancestors: how fair
I seemed, your child! And all the while this evil
Was cancerous within me!
                              For I am sick
In my daily life, sick in my origin.

O three roads, dark ravine, woodland and way
Where three roads met: you, drinking my father's blood,
My own blood, spilled by my own hand: can you remember
The unspeakable things I did there, and the things
I went on from there to do?
                              O marriage, marriage!
The act that engendered me, and again the act
Performed by the son in the same bed—
                              Ah, the net
Of incest, mingling fathers, brothers, sons,
With brides, wives, mothers: the last evil
That can be known by men: no tongue can say
How evil!
              No. For the love of God, conceal me
Somewhere far from Thebes; or kill me; or hurl me
Into the sea, away from men's eyes for ever.

Come, lead me. You need not fear to touch me.
Of all men, I alone can bear this guilt.
       [*Enter* CREON.]
CHORAGOS: We are not the ones to decide; but Creon here
       May fitly judge of what you ask. He only
       Is left to protect the city in your place.
OEDIPUS: Alas, how can I speak to him? What right have I
       To beg his courtesy whom I have deeply wronged?
CREON: I have not come to mock you, Oedipus,
       Or to reproach you either.
              [*To* ATTENDANTS:]—You, standing there:
       If you have lost all respect for man's dignity,
       At least respect the flame of Lord Helios:
       Do not allow this pollution to show itself
       Openly here, an affront to the earth
       And Heaven's rain and the light of day. No, take him
       Into the house as quickly as you can.
       For it is proper
       That only the close kindred see his grief.
OEDIPUS: I pray you in God's name, since your courtesy
       Ignores my dark expectation, visiting

With mercy this man of all men most execrable:
Give me what I ask—for your good, not for mine.
CREON: And what is it that you would have me do?
OEDIPUS: Drive me out of this country as quickly as may be
     To a place where no human voice can ever greet me.
CREON: I should have done that before now—only,
     God's will had not been wholly revealed to me.
OEDIPUS: But his command is plain: the parricide
     Must be destroyed. I am that evil man.
CREON: That is the sense of it, yes; but as things are,
     We had best discover clearly what is to be done.
OEDIPUS: You would learn more about a man like me?
CREON: You are ready now to listen to the god.
OEDIPUS: I will listen. But it is to you
     That I must turn for help. I beg you, hear me.
     The woman in there—
     Give her whatever funeral you think proper:
     She is your sister.
                    —But let me go, Creon!
     Let me purge my father's Thebes of the pollution
     Of my living here, and go out to the wild hills,
     To Kithairon, that has won such fame with me,
     The tomb my mother and father appointed for me,
     And let me die there, as they willed I should.
     And yet I know
     Death will not ever come to me through sickness
     Or in any natural way: I have been preserved
     For some unthinkable fate. But let that be.

     As for my sons, you need not care for them.
     They are men, they will find some way to live.
     But my poor daughters, who have shared my table,
     Who never before have been parted from their father—
     Take care of them. Creon; do this for me.
     And will you let me touch them with my hands
     A last time, and let us weep together?
     Be kind, my lord.
     Great prince, be kind!
                         Could I but touch them,
     They would be mine again, as when I had my eyes.
          [*Enter* ANTIGONE *and* ISMENE, *attended.*]
     Ah, God!
     Is it my dearest children I hear weeping?
     Has Creon pitied me and sent my daughters?
CREON: Yes, Oedipus: I knew that they were dear to you
     In the old days, and know you must love them still.
OEDIPUS: May God bless you for this—and be a friendlier
     Guardian to you than he has been to me!

Children, where are you?
Come quickly to my hands: they are your brother's—
Hands that have brought your father's once clear eyes
To this way of seeing—
                         Ah dearest ones,
I had neither sight nor knowledge then, your father
By the woman who was the source of his own life!
And I weep for you—having no strength to see you—,
I weep for you when I think of the bitterness
That men will visit upon you all your lives.
What homes, what festivals can you attend
Without being forced to depart again in tears?
And when you come to marriageable age,
Where is the man, my daughters, who would dare
Risk the bane that lies on all my children?
Is there any evil wanting? Your father killed
His father; sowed the womb of her who bore him;
Engendered you at the fount of his own existence!
That is what they will say of you
                                    Then, whom
Can you ever marry? There are no bridegrooms for you,
And your lives must wither away in sterile dreaming.

O Creon, son of Menoikeus!
You are the only father my daughters have,
Since we, their parents, are both of us gone for ever.
They are your own blood: you will not let them
Fall into beggary and loneliness;
You will keep them from the miseries that are mine!
Take pity on them; see, they are only children,
Friendless except for you. Promise me this,
Great Prince, and give me your hand in token of it.
     [CREON *clasps his right hand.*]
Children:
I could say much, if you could understand me,
But as it is, I have only this prayer for you:
Live where you can, be as happy as you can—
Happier, please God, than God has made your father!
CREON: Enough. You have wept enough. Now go within.
OEDIPUS: I must; but it is hard.
CREON: Time eases all things.
OEDIPUS: But you must promise—
CREON: Say what you desire.
OEDIPUS: Send me from Thebes!
CREON: God grant that I may!
OEDIPUS: But since God hates me . . .
CREON: No, he will grant your wish.
OEDIPUS: You promise?

CREON: I can not speak beyond my knowledge.
OEDIPUS: Then lead me in.
CREON: Come now, and leave your children.
OEDIPUS: No! Do not take them from me!
CREON: Think no longer
    That you are in command here, but rather think
    How, when you were, you served your own destruction.
       [*Exeunt into the house all but the* CHORUS; *the* CHORAGOS *chants directly to
       the audience:*]
CHORAGOS: Men of Thebes: look upon Oedipus.

    This is the king who solved the famous riddle
    And towered up, most powerful of men.
    No mortal eyes but looked on him with envy,
    Yet in the end ruin swept over him.

    Let every man in mankind's frailty
    Consider his last day; and let none
    Presume on his good fortune until he find
    Life, at his death, a memory without pain.

Anonymous

Noah and His Sons (A.D. 1425–1450)

Noah and His Sons was presented at Wakefield (England), the third of the thirty-two short plays that together dramatized the biblical account of human existence from Creation to the Last Judgment. The entire cycle was presented out of doors during the Corpus Christi festival, a religious celebration of the sacrament of bread and wine (the body and blood of Christ), the union of the human and divine in the person of Christ, and the promise of redemption through His sacrifice.

The central feature of the Corpus Christi festival was a procession (which included representatives from every rank and profession) through the town with the consecrated bread and wine. This procession may have been the inspiration for the staging of the cycle; mounting plays on wagons and performing them at various stops along a processional route. Each play was assigned to a different trade guild that was then responsible for mounting and financing its play. The overall cycle was under the supervision of the town council, and the scripts had to be approved by the church.

Noah and His Sons is one of five plays identified as the work of the "Wakefield Master," works considered far superior to the other plays in the same cycle. *Noah* is noted in part for the variety achieved through the comic bickering of the title character and his wife, an element that locates the action in a world familiar to the medieval audience. The play is short (558 lines), made up of sixty-two nine-line stanzas. The structure of the stanzas suggests a formalized delivery by the performers.

The play is divided into three parts of approximately equal length: the opening expository scene with God and Noah establishing justification for the flood; two scenes of bickering between Noah and his wife; and the scenes showing first the building of the ark and then the time on board. It is clear, entertaining, and didactic.

Wakefield Cycle—Anonymous
(A.D. 1425–1450)

Noah and His Sons

CHARACTERS

NOAH
GOD
NOAH'S WIFE
FIRST SON
SECOND SON
THIRD SON
FIRST WIFE
SECOND WIFE
THIRD WIFE

Note: Many obsolete words have been retained so as not to alter unduly the rhyme scheme. The first four lines of each nine-line stanza use both end and mid-line rhymes; the fifth and ninth lines rhyme, as do lines six through eight. To clarify obsolete words, modern equivalents have been placed in brackets immediately following the words they clarify.

NOAH: Mightful god veray [truly], Maker of all that is,
  Three persons, none say nay, one god in endless bliss,
  Thou made both night and day, beast, fowl, and fish,
  All creatures that live may, wrought thou at thy wish,
   As thou well might;
  The sun, the moon, verament [truly],
  Thou made; the firmament,
  The stars also, full fervent,
   To shine thou made full bright.

  Angels thou made full even, all orders that is,
  To have the bliss in heaven. This did thou more and less,
  Full marvelous to neven [tell]; yet was there unkindness,
  More by folds seven than I can well express;
   For why?
  Of all angels in brightness
  God gave Lucifer most lightness,
  Yet proudly he fled his dais,
   And set him even Him by.

  He thought himself as worthy as Him that him made;
  In brightness, in beauty, therefore God did him degrade;

Put him in a low degree soon after, in a brade [minute],
Him and all his menye [minions], where he may be unglad
   For ever.
Shall they never win away,
Hence unto doomsday,
But burn in hell for aye,
    Shall they depart never.

Soon after, that gracious lord in His likeness made man,
That place to be restored, even as he began,
Of the Trinity by accord, Adam and Eve, that woman,
To multiply without discord, in paradise put He them,
   And sayeth to both
Gave in commandment,
On the tree of life to lay no hand;
But yet the false fiend
   Made Him with man wroth,

Enticed man to gluttony, stirred him to sin in pride;
But in paradise securely might no sin abide,
And therefore man full hastily was put out, in that tide [time],
In woe and wretchedness for to be, in pains full cried,
   To know,
First on earth, and then in hell
With fiends for to dwell,
But He his mercy mell [dispenses]
   To those that will Him trow [swear allegiance].

Oil of mercy He has hight [promised], as I have heard said,
To every living wight that would love Him and dread;
But now before His sight every living leyde [person],
Most party day and night, sin in word and deed
   Full bold;
Some in pride, ire, and envy,
Some in covetousness and gluttony,
Some in sloth and lechery,
   And otherwise manifold.

Therefore I dread lest God on us will take vengeance
For sin is now allowed without any repentance;
Six hundred years and odd have I, without distance [dispute],
On earth, as any sod, lived with great grievance
   Always;
And now I wax old,
Sick, sorry, and cold,
As muck upon mold
   I wither away;

But yet will I cry for mercy and call;
Noah thy servant, am I, Lord over all!
Lest me and my fry shall also fall;
Save from villainy and bring to Thy hall
    In heaven;
And keep me from sin,
This world within;
Comely king of mankind,
    I pray Thee, hear my stevyn [voice]!

      [GOD *appears above.*]
GOD: Since I have made all thing that is liffand [living],
Duke, emperor, and king, with mine own hand,
For to have their liking by sea and by sand,
Every man to my bidding should be bound
    Full fervent;
That made man such a creature,
Fairest of favor,
Man must love me par-amour,
    By reason, and repent.

Methought I showed man love when I made him to be
All angels above, like to the Trinity;
And now in great reproof full low lies he,
On earth himself to stuff with sin that displeases me
    Most of all;
Vengeance will I take,
In earth for sin's sake,
My anger thus will I wake,
    Both of great and small.

I repent full sore that ever I made man,
By me he sets no store, and I am his sovereign;
I will destroy, therefore, both beast, man and woman,
All shall perish, less and more; that bargain may they ban [regret],
    That ill has done.
In earth I see right naught
But sin that is unsought [unrepented];
Of those that well has wrought
    Find I almost none.

Therefore shall I undo [destroy] all this middle erd [earth]
With floods that shall flow and run with hideous rerd [noise];
I have good cause thereto: of me no man is afeard,
As I say, shall I do: of vengeance draw my sword,
    And make end
Of all that bears life,

Save Noah and his wife,
For they would never strive
    With me nor me offend.

To him to great win [joy] hastily will I go,
To Noah my servant, ere I blyn [stop] to warn him of his woe.
In earth I see but sin running to and fro,
Among both more and min [less], each the other's foe;
    With all their intent;
They shall I forego [destroy]
With floods that shall flow,
I shall work them woe,
    That will not repent.

              [GOD *descends and comes to* NOAH.]
GOD: Noah, my friend, I thee command, from cares thee dispel,
A ship I do demand of nail and board full well.
Thou was e'er a trusty man, to me true as steel,
To my bidding obedient; friendship shall thou feel
    To mede [in reward].
Of length thy ship be
Three hundred cubits, warn I thee,
Of height even thirty,
    Of fifty also in brede [breadth].

Anoint thy ship with pitch and tar without and also within,
The water out to spar [keep] this is a helpful gyn [means];
Look no man thee mar. Three tiers of chambers begin,
Thou must spend many a spar, this work ere thou win
    To end fully.
Make in thy ship also,
Parlors one or two,
And other houses mo [more],
    For beasts that there must be.

One cubit in height a window shall thou make;
On the side a doore with slyght [skill] beneath shall thou take;
With thee shall no man fight, nor do thee any kind of hate.
When all is done thus right, thy wife, that is thy mate,
    Take in to thee;
Thy sons of good fame,
Shem, Japhet, and Ham,
Take in also them,
    Their wives also three.

For all shall be undone [destroyed] that live on land but ye,
With floods that from above shall fall, and that plentily;

It shall begin full soon to rain incessantly,
After seven days 'twill come, and endure days forty,
   Without fail.
Take to thy ship also
Of each kind, beasts two,
Male and female, but no more,
   Ere thou pull up thy sail.

For they may thee avail when all this thing is wrought;
Stuff thy ship with victual, for hunger that ye perish nought;
Of beasts, fowl, and cattle, for them have thou in thought,
For them in my counsel, that some succor be sought,
   In haste;
They must have corn and hay,
And other meat alway;
Do now as I thee say,
   In the name of the Holy Ghost.

NOAH: Ah! Benedicite! What art thou that thus
   Tells afore that shall be? Thou art full marvelous!
   Tell me, for charity, thy name so gracious.
GOD: My name is of dignity and also full glorious
     To know.
   I am God most mighty,
   One God in Trinity,
   Made thee and each man to be;
     To love me well thou owe.

NOAH: I thank thee, lord so dear, that would vouch safe
   Thus low to appear to a simple knave;
   Bless us, lord, here, for charity I it crave,
   The better may we steer the ship that we shall have,
     Certain.
GOD: Noah, to thee and thy fry
   My blessing grant I;
   Ye shall wax and multiply,
     And fill the earth again,

When all these floods are past and fully gone away.
NOAH: Lord, homeward will I haste as fast as that I may;
   My wife will I frast [ask] what she will say, [*Exit* GOD]
   And I am aghast that we get some fray
     Betwixt us both;
   For she is full testy,
   For little oft angry,
   If anything wrong be,
     Soon is she wroth. [*He goes to his wife.*]

God speed, dear wife, how fare ye?

WIFE: Now, as ever I might thrive, the worst is I see thee;
    Do tell me belife [quickly] where has thou thus long be?
    To death may we drive, or live for thee [for all you care],
        For want indeed.
    When we sweat or swink [labor],
    Thou does what thou think,
    Yet of meat and of drink
        Have we great need.

NOAH: Wife, we are hard stead with tidings new.

WIFE: But thou were worthy be clad in Stafford blue [be beaten blue];
    For thou art always afraid, be it false or true;
    But God knows I am led, and that may I rue,
        For ill;
    For I dare be thy borrow [pledge],
    From even unto morrow,
    Thou speaks ever of sorrow;
        God send thee once thy fill!

We women may wary [curse] all ill husbands;
I have one, by Mary, that loosed me of my bands;
If he be troubled I must tarry, how so ever it stands,
With semblance full sorry, wringing both my hands
    For dread.
But yet other while,
With pleasure and with guile,
I shall smite and smile,
    And quit him his mede [give him what he deserves].

NOAH: Well! hold thy tongue ram-skyt, or I shall thee still!

WIFE: By my thrift, if thou smite, I shall turn thee until!

NOAH: We shall assay as tight! Have at thee, Gill!
    Upon the bone shall it bite!

WIFE: Ah, so, marry! thou smitest ill!
    But I suppose
I shall not in thy debt,
Flee from this flett [floor]!
Take thee there a langett [thong]
    To tie up thy hose!

NOAH: A! wilt thou so? Marry, that is mine.

WIFE: Thou shall three for two, I swear by God's pain!

NOAH: And I shall return them though, in faith, ere syne [long].

WIFE: Out upon thee, ho!

NOAH: Thou can both bite and whine,
    with a rerd [noise];
    For all if she strike,

　　　Yet fast will she shriek,
　　　In faith I hold none like
　　　　　In all middle-earth;

　　　But I will keep charity, for I have work to do.
WIFE: Here shall no man tarry thee. I pray thee go to!
　　　Full well may we miss thee as ever have I ro [peace];
　　　To spin will I dress me.
NOAH:　　　　　　　　　　Well, farewell, lo!
　　　　　But wife,
　　　Pray for me busily,
　　　Till again I come unto thee.
WIFE: Even as thou prays for me,
　　　　　As ever might I thrive. [*Exit* WIFE.]

NOAH: I tarry full long from my work, I trow;
　　　Now my gear will I fang [take] and thitherward draw;
　　　I may full ill gang [go], the truth for to know,
　　　But if God help not among, I may sit down daw [melancholy]
　　　　　To ken;
　　　Now assay will I
　　　How I can of wrightry [workmanship],
　　　In nomine patris et filii, et spiritus sancti,
　　　　　Amen.

　　　To begin of this tree, my bones will I bend,
　　　I trust from the Trinity succor will be sent;
　　　It fares full fair, think me, this work to my hand;
　　　Now blessed be he that this can amend.
　　　　　Lo, here the length,
　　　Three hundred cubits evenly,
　　　Of breadth, lo, is it fifty,
　　　The height is even thirty
　　　　　Cubits full strength.

　　　Now my gown will I cast, and work in my coat,
　　　Make will I the mast ere I shift one foot,
　　　A! my back, I trow, will burst! This is a sorry note!
　　　It is wonder that I last, such an old dote
　　　　　All dulled,
　　　To begin such a work!
　　　My bones are so stark [stiff],
　　　No wonder if they wark [ache],
　　　　　For I am full old.

　　　The top and the sail both will I make,
　　　The helm and the castle also will I take;
　　　To drive each single nail will I not forsake;

This gear may never fail, that dare I undertake
    At once.
This is a noble gin [device]
These nails so they run,
Through more and min [less],
    These boards each one;

Window and door, even as he said,
Three chief chambers, they are well made;
Pitch and tar full sure thereupon laid,
This will ever endure, thereof am I paid;
    for why?
It is better wrought
Than I could have thought;
Him that made all of nought
    I thank only.

Now will I hie me and nothing be lither [slow],
My wife and my meneye [family], to bring even hither.
Attend hither tidily wife, and consider,
Hence must us flee, all of us together,
    In haste.
WIFE: Why, sir, what ails you?
Who is't that assails you?
To flee it avails you,
    And ye be aghast [afraid].

NOAH: [*seeing his wife spinning*] There is yarn on the reel other, my dame.
WIFE: Tell me that each deal, else get ye blame.
NOAH: He that cares may keill [cool] blessed be his name!
He has for our seyll [happiness] to shield us from shame,
    And said,
All this world about
With floods so stout,
That shall run on a route,
    Shall be overlaid.

He said all shall be slain but only we,
Our sons that are bayn [obedient] and their wives three;
A ship he bade me ordain, to save us and our fee [property],
Therefore with all our main, thank we that free
    Healer of bayll [sorrow];
Hie us fast, go we thither.
WIFE: I know never whither,
I am dazed and I dither
    For fear of that tale.

NOAH: Be not afeard, have done. Pack up our gear,
>That we be there ere noon without more dere [hindrance].
FIRST SON: It shall be done full soon. Brothers, help to bear.
SECOND SON: Full long shall I not hoyne [delay] to do my share,
>Brother Shem.
THIRD SON: Without any yelp,
>With my might shall I help.
WIFE: Yet for dread of a skelp [blow]
>Help well thy dam.

NOAH: Now are we there as we should be;
>To get in our gear, our cattle and fee,
>In this vessel here, my children free.
WIFE: I was never shut up ere, as now might I be,
>In such an hostel as this,
>In faith I can not find
>Which is before, which is behind.
>But shall we here be confined,
>Noah, as have thou bliss?

NOAH: Dame, as it is skill [reason], here must us abide grace;
>Therefore, wife, with good will come into this place.
WIFE: Sir, for Jack nor for Jill will I turn my face
>Till I have on this hill spun a space
>on my rok [distaff];
>Well were he, might get me,
>Now will I down set me,
>Yet reede [warn] I no man let me [stop me],
>For dread of a knock.

NOAH: Behold from the heaven the cararacts all,
>That are open full even, great and small,
>And the planets seven gone from their stall,
>These thunders and levyn [lightning] down make fall
>Full stout,
>Both halls and bowers,
>Castles and towers;
>Full sharp are these showers,
>That rain about;

Therefore, wife, have done. Come into ship fast.
WIFE: Yea, Noah, go patch thy shone [shoes] the better will they last.
FIRST WIFE: Good mother, come in soon, for all is overcast,
>Both the sun and the moon.
SECOND WIFE: And many winds blast
>Full sharp.
>These floods so thay run,
>Therefore, mother, come in.

WIFE: In faith, yet will I spin;
    All in vain ye carp.

THIRD WIFE: If ye like ye may spin, Mother, in the ship.
NOAH: Now is this twice. Come in, dame, on my friendship.
WIFE: Whether I lose or I win, in faith, for thy fellowship
    Care I not a pin. This spindle will I slip
      Upon this hill,
    Ere I stir one foot.
NOAH: Peter! I trow we dote;
    Without any more note
      Come in if ye will.

WIFE: Yea, water nighs so near that I sit not dry;
    Into the ship with a byr [rush] therefore will I hie
    For dread that I drown here.
NOAH: Dame, securely,
    It be bought full dear, ye abode so long by
      Out of the ship.
WIFE: I will not, for thy bidding,
    Go from door to midding [dunghill; do whatever you demand].
NOAH: In faith, and for your long tarrying
      Ye shall taste of the whip.

WIFE: Spare me not, I pray thee, but even as thou think,
    These great words shall not flay me.
NOAH: Abide, dame, and drink,
    For beaten shall thou be, with this staff till thou stink;
    Are the strokes good? say me.
WIFE: What say ye, Wat Wynk?
NOAH: Speak!
    Cry me mercy, I say!
WIFE: Thereto say I nay.
NOAH: Unless thou do, by this day,
      Thy head shall I break.

        [To women in the audience.]
WIFE: Lord, I were at rest and heartily full whole,
    Might I once have a mess of widow's coyll [fare];
    For thy soul, without jest, should I deal penny doyll [alms],
    So would more, no frese [fear], that I see in this sole [place]
      Of wives that are here
    For the life they have led
    Would their husbands were dead
    For, as ever ate I bread,
      So would I our sire were.

[*To men in the audience.*]

NOAH: Ye men who have wives whilst they are young,
    If you love your lives, chastise their tongue:
    Methinks my heart rives, both liver and lung,
    To see such strifes, wedmen among;
        But I,
    As have I bliss,
    Shall chastise this.
WIFE: Yet may you miss,
        Nicholl Neddy!

NOAH: I shall make thee still as stone, beginner of blunder!
    I shall beat thee back and bone and break all asunder.
        [*They fight.*]
WIFE: Oh, alas, I am gone! Out upon thee, man's wonder!
NOAH: See how she can groan, and I lie under!
        But, wife,
    In this haste let us ho [stop],
    For my back is near in two.
WIFE: And I am beat so blue
        That I may not thrive.
        [*They enter the ark.*]

FIRST SON: Ah! why fare ye thus? Father and mother both!
SECOND SON: Ye should not be so spitus [spiteful] standing in such a
    woth [danger].
THIRD SON: These weathers are so hidus [hideous] with many a cold
    coth [disease].
NOAH: We will do as ye bid us. We will no more be wroth,
        Dear bairns!
    Now to the helm will I hent [go],
    And to my ship tend.
WIFE: I see on the firmament,
        Methinks, the seven stars.

NOAH: This is a great flood, wife, take heed.
WIFE: So me thought, as I stood. We are in great dread;
    These waves are so wode [wild].
NOAH: Help, God, in this need!
    As thou art steerman good and best, as I rede [counsel],
        Of all;
    Thou rule us in this race,
    As thou me promised has.
WIFE: This is a perilous case:
        Help, God, when we call!

NOAH: Wife, attend the steer-tree, and I shall assay
    The deepness of the sea that we bear, if I may.

WIFE: That shall I do full wisely. Now go thy way,
　　For upon this flood have we floated many a day,
　　　　With pain.
NOAH: Now the water will I sound
　　Ah! it is far to the ground;
　　This travail I expound
　　　　Had I to tyne [lose].

　　Above all hills bedeyn [completely] the water is risen late
　　Cubits fifteen, but in a higher state
　　It may not be, I ween, for this well I wate [know],
　　This forty days has rain been. It will therefore abate
　　　　Full lele [loyal].
　　This water in haste,
　　Eft will I test;
　　Now am I aghast,
　　　　It is waned a great deal.

　　Now are the weathers ceased and cataracts quit,
　　Both the most and the least.
WIFE: Methink, by my wit,
　　The sun shines in the east. Lo, is not yond it?
　　We should have a good feast were these floods flit
　　　　So spytus [malicious].
NOAH: We have been here, all we,
　　Three hundred days and fifty.
WIFE: Yea, now wanes the sea;
　　　　Lord, well is us!

NOAH: The third time will I prove [test] what deepness we bear.
WIFE: How long shall thou heave. Lay in thy line there.
NOAH: I may touch with my lufe [hand] the ground even here.
WIFE: Then begins to grufe [grow] to us merry cheer;
　　　　But, husband,
　　What ground may this be?
NOAH: The hills of Armenia.
WIFE: Now blessed be he
　　　　That thus for us ordained!

NOAH: I see tops of hills he [high] many at a sight,
　　Nothing to hinder me, the weather is so bright.
WIFE: These are of mercy, tokens full right.
NOAH: Dame, thou counsel me what fowl best might
　　　　And cowth [could],
　　With flight of wing
　　Bring, without tarrying,
　　Of mercy some tokening
　　　　Either by north or south.

For this is the first day of the tenth moon.
WIFE: The raven, dare I lay, will come again soon;
As fast as thou may cast him forth, have done,
He may happen to day come again ere noon
Without delay.
NOAH: I will cast out also
Doves one or two:
Go your way, go,
God send you some prey!

Now are these fowls flown into separate country;
Pray we fast each one, kneeling on our knee,
To him that is alone worthiest of degree,
That he would send anon our fowls some fee
To glad us.
WIFE: They may not fail of land,
The water is so wanand [waning].
NOAH: Thank we God all weldand [wielding],
That lord that made us.

It is a wondrous thing, me thinks soothly,
They are so long tarrying, the fowls that we
Cast out in the morning.
WIFE: Sir, it may be
They tarry till they bring.
NOAH: The raven is a-hungry
Alway;
He is without any reason,
If he find any carrion,
As peradventure may befon [befall],
He will not away;

The dove is more gentle, her trust I unto,
Like unto the turtle, for she is ay true.
WIFE: Hence but a little. She comes, lew, lew!
She brings in her bill some novels [signs] new;
Behold!
It is of an olive tree
A branch, thinkest me.
NOAH: It is so, perde [par dieu; by our God],
Right so is it called.

Dove, bird full blest, fair might thee befall!
Thou art true for to trust as stone in the wall;
Full well I it wist [knew] thou would come to thy hall,
WIFE: A true token is't we shall be saved all;
For why?
The water, since she come,

Of deepness plumb,
Is fallen a fathom,
   And more hardily [certainly].

FIRST SON: These floods are gone. Father, behold!
SECOND SON: There is left right none, and that be ye bold.
THIRD SON: As still as a stone, our ship is stalled.
NOAH: Upon land here anon that we were, fain I would;
   My childer dear,
Shem, Japhet, and Ham,
With glee and with gam [sport],
Come we all sam [together],
   We will no longer abide here.

WIFE: Here have we been, Noah, long enough,
With trouble and with teyn [grief], and endured much woe.
NOAH: Behold on this green neither cart nor plough
Is left, as I ween, neither tree nor bough,
   Nor other thing,
But all is away;
Many castles, I say,
Great towns of array,
   Flit [destroyed] has this flowyng [flood].

WIFE: These floods, not afright, all this world so wide
Has moved with might, on sea and by side.
NOAH: To death are they dyght [gone], proudest of pride,
Every wight that ever was spied,
   With sin,
All are they slain,
And put unto pain.
WIFE: From thence again
   May they never win.

NOAH: Win? no, I-wis, but He that might has
Would remember their mys [misery] and admit them to
   grace;
As He in misfortune is bliss, I pray Him in this space,
In heaven high with His, to secure us a place,
   That we,
With His saints in sight,
And His angels bright,
May come to His light:
   Amen, for charity.

William Shakespeare (1564–1616)

Hamlet, Prince of Denmark (c. 1600)

During the sixteenth century, when religious drama was forbidden, the groups that had financed and staged the cycle plays ceased their support of theatre, disapproving of the professional and commercial role that theatre had been forced to adopt in order to survive. The necessity of attracting a paying audience motivated acting companies to offer a different play each day (though the same play might be repeated at intervals during a season) and thus they created an ongoing demand for new plays. Partially for this reason, the years between 1585 and 1610 produced an exceptional number of outstanding English playwrights, among whom William Shakespeare is universally acknowledged the greatest, and possibly the greatest playwright the world has known.

In addition to being a playwright, Shakespeare was an actor, as well as a shareholder (part owner) both in his acting company and in the theatre in which they performed. As the company's principal playwright, he wrote an average of two plays each season. Among his thirty-eight surviving plays, *Hamlet* is one of the most admired.

Hamlet, like *Oedipus Rex*, has as its protagonist a man who is charged with punishing the murderer of a king. But Shakespeare uses a much broader canvas than Sophocles does and includes within his drama more facets of his story, more characters, and a wider sweep of time and place. Shakespeare's play develops chronologically and places all important incidents on stage. The only important events that precede the play's opening (Claudius' seduction of his brother's wife and his murder of his brother) are replicated in the play-within-the-play. The rapid shifts in time and place are made possible by theatrical conventions that establish locale and other significant conditions through spoken passages ("spoken decor") that localize as needed the fixed facade against which the action occurred.

Hamlet is thematically rich: the pervasiveness of betrayal (brother of brother, wife of husband, parent of child, friend of friend); the opposing demands made on Hamlet (that he revenge his father's murder and that he adhere to Christian doctrine against murder); the nature of kingship and the need to rule oneself before ruling others; and several other themes. Shakespeare's dramatic poetry is generally conceded to be the finest in the English language. The basic medium is blank verse, which allows the flexibility of ordinary speech while elevating it through imagery and rhythm.

Because of its compelling story, powerful characters, and great poetry, *Hamlet* is one of the world's finest achievements in drama. Although it embodies many ideas typical of its time, it transcends the limitations of a particular era. It continues to move spectators in the theatre as it has since its first presentation around 1600.

William Shakespeare

Hamlet, Prince of Denmark

DRAMATIS PERSONAE

CLAUDIUS, *King of Denmark*
HAMLET, *son to the former and nephew to the present King*
POLONIUS, *Lord Chamberlain*
HORATIO, *friend to Hamlet*
LAERTES, *son to Polonius*
VOLTEMAND
CORNELIUS
ROSENCRANTZ   } *courtiers*
GUILDENSTERN
OSRIC
A GENTLEMAN
A PRIEST
MARCELLUS } *officers*
BERNARDO
FRANCISCO, *a soldier*
REYNALDO, *servant to Polonius*
PLAYERS
TWO CLOWNS, *grave-diggers*
FORTINBRAS, *Prince of Norway*
A NORWEGIAN CAPTAIN
ENGLISH AMBASSADORS
GERTRUDE, *Queen of Denmark, and mother of Hamlet*
OPHELIA, *daughter to Polonius*
GHOST *of Hamlet's father*
LORDS, LADIES, OFFICERS, SOLDIERS, SAILORS, MESSENGERS, AND
   ATTENDANTS

SCENE——*Denmark.*

ACT I

SCENE I——*Elsinore. The guard-platform of the Castle.*

[FRANCISCO *at his post. Enter to him* BERNARDO.]
BERNARDO: Who's there?

FRANCISCO: Nay, answer me. Stand and unfold* yourself.
BERNARDO: Long live the king!
FRANCISCO: Bernardo?
BERNARDO: He.   5
FRANCISCO: You come most carefully upon your hour.
BERNARDO: 'Tis now struck twelve; get thee to bed, Francisco.
FRANCISCO: For this relief much thanks. 'Tis bitter cold,
    And I am sick at heart.
BERNARDO: Have you had quiet guard?   10
FRANCISCO: Not a mouse stirring.
BERNARDO: Well; good night.
    If you do meet Horatio and Marcellus,
    The rivals* of my watch, bid them make haste.
    [*Enter* HORATIO *and* MARCELLUS.]
FRANCISCO: I think I hear them. Stand, ho! Who is there?
HORATIO: Friends to this ground.
MARCELLUS: And liegemen to the Dane.*   15
FRANCISCO: Give you good night.
MARCELLUS: O, farewell, honest soldier!
    Who hath reliev'd you?
FRANCISCO: Bernardo hath my place.
    Give you good night.   [*Exit.*]
MARCELLUS: Holla, Bernardo!
BERNARDO: Say—
    What, is Horatio there?
HORATIO: A piece of him.
BERNARDO: Welcome, Horatio; welcome, good Marcellus.   20
HORATIO: What, has this thing appear'd again to-night?
BERNARDO: I have seen nothing.
MARCELLUS: Horatio says 'tis but our fantasy,
    And will not let belief take hold of him
    Touching this dreaded sight, twice seen of us;   25
    Therefore I have entreated him along
    With us to watch the minutes of this night,
    That, if again this apparition come,
    He may approve* our eyes and speak to it.
HORATIO: Tush, tush, 'twill not appear.
BERNARDO: Sit down awhile,   30
    And let us once again assail your ears,
    That are so fortified against our story,
    What we have two nights seen.

---

* indicates a note identified by line number. The textual reference is given in bold type, its clarifica-   35
tion in roman type.
[1,i,2] **unfold** identify
[13] **rivals** companions
[15] **liegemen to the Dane** loyal subjects to the king of Denmark
[28] **approve** confirm

HORATIO: Well, sit we down,
    And let us hear Bernardo speak of this.
BERNARDO: Last night of all,   35
    When yond same star that's westward from the pole
    Had made his course t' illume that part of heaven
    Where now it burns, Marcellus and myself,
    The bell then beating one—
        [*Enter* GHOST.]
MARCELLUS: Peace, break thee off; look where it comes again.   40
BERNARDO: In the same figure, like the King that's dead.
MARCELLUS: Thou art a scholar; speak to it, Horatio.
BERNARDO: Looks 'a not like the King? Mark it, Horatio.
HORATIO: Most like. It harrows me with fear and wonder.
BERNARDO: It would be spoke to.
MARCELLUS: Question it, Horatio.   45
HORATIO: What art thou that usurp'st this time of night
    Together with that fair and warlike form
    In which the majesty of buried Denmark*
    Did sometimes march? By heaven I charge thee, speak!
MARCELLUS: It is offended.   50
BERNARDO: See, it stalks away.
HORATIO: Stay! speak, speak! I charge thee, speak!
        [*Exit* GHOST.]
MARCELLUS: 'Tis gone, and will not answer.
BERNARDO: How now, Horatio! You tremble and look pale.
    Is not this something more than fantasy?
    What think you on't?   55
HORATIO: Before my God, I might not this believe
    Without the sensible and true avouch*
    Of mine own eyes.
MARCELLUS: Is it not like the King?
HORATIO: As thou art to thyself:
    Such was the very armour he had on   60
    When he the ambitious Norway* combated;
    So frown'd he once when, in an angry parle,*
    He smote the sledded Polacks* on the ice.
    'Tis strange.
MARCELLUS: Thus twice before, and jump* at this dead hour,   65
    With martial stalk hath he gone by our watch.
HORATIO: In what particular thought to work I know not;
    But, in the gross and scope* of mine opinion,

---

[48] **buried Denmark** buried king of Denmark
[57] **avouch** proof
[61] **Norway** king of Norway
[62] **parle** parley
[63] **sledded Polacks** Poles on sleds
[65] **jump** just
[68] **gross and scope** general drift

This bodes some strange eruption to our state.
MARCELLUS: Good now, sit down, and tell me, he that knows,
  Why this same strict and most observant watch
  So nightly toils the subject* of the land;
  And why such daily cast of brazen cannon,
  And foreign mart* for implements of war;
  Why such impress* of shipwrights, whose sore task   75
  Does not divide the Sunday from the week;
  What might be toward,* that this sweaty haste
  Doth make the night joint-labourer with the day:
  Who is't that can inform me?
HORATIO: That can I;
  At least, the whisper goes so. Our last King,   80
  Whose image even but now appear'd to us,
  Was, as you know, by Fortinbras of Norway,
  Thereto prick'd on by a most emulate pride,
  Dar'd to the combat; in which our valiant Hamlet—
  For so this side of our known world esteem'd him— 85
  Did slay this Fortinbras; who, by a seal'd compact,
  Well ratified by law and heraldry,*
  Did forfeit, with his life, all those his lands
  Which he stood seiz'd of,* to the conqueror;
  Against the which a moiety competent*   90
  Was gaged* by our King; which had return'd
  To the inheritance of Fortinbras,
  Had he been vanquisher; as, by the same comart*
  And carriage of the article design'd,*
  His fell to Hamlet. Now, sir, young Fortinbras,   95
  Of unimproved* mettle hot and full,
  Hath in the skirts* of Norway, here and there,
  Shark'd up a list of lawless resolutes,*
  For food and diet, to some enterprise
  That hath a stomach in't,* which is no other,   100
  As it doth well appear unto our state,
  But to recover of us, by strong hand

---

[72] **nightly toils the subject** citizens work by night (as well as by day)
[74] **mart** trade
[75] **impress** forced service
[77] **toward** in preparation
[87] **law and heraldry** heraldic law
[89] **seiz'd of** in possession of
[90] **moiety competent** like portion
[91] **gaged** pledged
[93] **comart** agreement
[94] **carriage of the article design'd** provisions of the pact
[96] **unimproved** unproved
[97] **skirts** borders, outskirts
[98] **shark'd up a list of lawless resolutes** enlisted a force of desperate men
[100] **hath a stomach in't** requires courage

And terms compulsatory, those foresaid lands
So by his father lost; and this, I take it,
Is the main motive of our preparations,   105
The source of this our watch, and the chief head*
Of this post-haste and romage* in the land.
BERNARDO: I think it be no other but e'en so.
      Well may it sort,* that this portentous figure
      Comes armed through our watch; so like the King   110
      That was and is the question of these wars.
HORATIO: A mote it is to trouble the mind's eye.
      In the most high and palmy state of Rome,
      A little ere the mightiest Julius fell,
      The graves stood tenantless, and the sheeted dead   115
      Did squeak and gibber in the Roman streets;
      As, stars with trains of fire, and dews of blood,
      Disasters* in the sun; and the moist star*
      Upon whose influence Neptune's empire* stands
      Was sick almost to doomsday with eclipse;   120
      And even the like precurse* of fear'd events,
      As harbingers preceding still the fates
      And prologue to the omen coming on,
      Have heaven and earth together demonstrated
      Unto our climatures* and countrymen.   125
            [*Reenter* GHOST.]
      But, soft, behold! Lo, where it comes again!
      I'll cross it,* though it blast me. Stay, illusion.
            [GHOST *spreads its arms.*]
      If thou hast any sound or use of voice,
      Speak to me.
      If there be any good thing to be done,   130
      That may to thee do ease and grace to me,
      Speak to me.
      If thou art privy to thy country's fate,
      Which happily* foreknowing may avoid,
      O, speak!   135
      Or if thou hast uphoarded in thy life
      Extorted treasure in the womb of earth,

---

106 **chief head** principal reason
107 **romage** bustling activity
109 **sort** turn out
118 **disasters** threatening signs
118 **moist star** the moon
119 **Neptune's empire** the ocean (the Roman god Neptune's domain)
121 **precurse** foreshadowing
125 **climatures** regions
127 **cross it** cross its path
134 **happily** haply, perhaps

For which, they say, you spirits oft walk in death,
    [*The cock crows.*]
Speak of it. Stay, and speak. Stop it, Marcellus.
MARCELLUS: Shall I strike at it with my partisan?*   140
HORATIO: Do, if it will not stand.
BERNARDO: 'Tis here!
HORATIO: 'Tis here!
MARCELLUS: 'Tis gone!   [*Exit* GHOST.]
    We do it wrong, being so majestical,
    To offer it the show of violence;
    For it is, as the air, invulnerable,   145
    And our vain blows malicious mockery.
BERNARDO: It was about to speak, when the cock crew.
HORATIO: And then it started like a guilty thing
    Upon a fearful summons. I have heard
    The cock, that is the trumpet to the morn,   150
    Doth with his lofty and shrill-sounding throat
    Awake the god of day; and at his warning,
    Whether in sea or fire, in earth or air,
    Th' extravagant and erring* spirit hies
    To his confine; and of the truth herein   155
    This present object made probation.*
MARCELLUS: It faded on the crowing of the cock.
    Some say that ever 'gainst* that season comes
    Wherein our Saviour's birth is celebrated,
    This bird of dawning singeth all night long;   160
    And then, they say, no spirit dare stir abroad,
    The nights are wholesome, then no planets strike,*
    No fairy takes, nor witch hath power to charm,
    So hallowed and so gracious is that time.
HORATIO: So have I heard, and do in part believe it.   165
    But look, the morn, in russet mantle clad,
    Walks o'er the dew of yon high eastward hill.
    Break we our watch up; and, by my advice,
    Let us impart what we have seen to-night
    Unto young Hamlet; for, upon my life,   170
    This spirit, dumb to us, will speak to him.
    Do you consent we shall acquaint him with it,
    As needful in our loves, fitting our duty?
MARCELLUS: Let's do't, I pray; and I this morning know
    Where we shall find him most convenient.   175
    [*Exeunt.*]

---

140 **partisan** pike (weapon)
154 **extravagant and erring** wandering outside its proper realm
156 **made probation** gives proof
158 **ever 'gainst** just before
162 **strike** exert evil influence

SCENE II———*Elsinore. The Castle.*

[*Flourish.* Enter* CLAUDIUS KING OF DENMARK, GERTRUDE THE QUEEN,
and COUNCILLORS, *including* POLONIUS, *his son* LAERTES, VOLTEMAND,
CORNELIUS, *and* HAMLET.]

KING: Though yet of Hamlet our dear brother's death
       The memory be green; and that it us befitted
       To bear our hearts in grief, and our whole kingdom
       To be contracted in one brow of woe;
       Yet so far hath discretion fought with nature   5
       That we with wisest sorrow think on him,
       Together with remembrance of ourselves.
       Therefore our sometime sister,* now our queen,
       Th' imperial jointress* to this warlike state,
       Have we, as 'twere with a defeated joy,   10
       With an auspicious and a dropping eye,
       With mirth in funeral, and with dirge in marriage,
       In equal scale weighing delight and dole,
       Taken to wife; nor have we herein barr'd
       Your better wisdoms, which have freely gone   15
       With this affair along. For all, our thanks.
       Now follows that you know: young Fortinbras,
       Holding a weak supposal of our worth,
       Or thinking by our late dear brother's death
       Our state to be disjoint and out of frame,*   20
       Co-leagued with this dream of his advantage*—
       He hath not fail'd to pester us with message
       Importing the surrender of those lands
       Lost by his father, with all bands of law,
       To our most valiant brother. So much for him.   25
       Now for ourself, and for this time of meeting,
       Thus much the business is: we have here writ
       To Norway, uncle of young Fortinbras—
       Who, impotent and bed-rid, scarcely hears
       Of this his nephew's purpose—to suppress   30
       His further gait* herein, in that the levies,
       The lists, and full proportions,* are all made
       Out of his subject;* and we here dispatch
       You, good Cornelius, and you, Voltemand,
       For bearers of this greeting to old Norway;   35

I,ii (stage direction) **Flourish** trumpet fanfare
[8] **our sometime sister** my former sister-in-law
[9] **jointress** joint ruler
[20] **frame** order
[21] **advantage** superior power
[31] **gait** proceeding
[32] **proportions** war supplies
[33] **out of his subject** out of the Norwegian king's subjects

Giving to you no further personal power
To business with the King more than the scope
Of these dilated articles* allow.
Farewell; and let your haste commend your duty.

CORNELIUS: ⎫ In that and all things will we show our duty. 40
VOLTEMAND: ⎰

KING: We doubt it nothing; heartily farewell.
        [*Exeunt* VOLTEMAND *and* CORNELIUS.]
And now, Laertes, what's the news with you?
You told us of some suit; what is't, Laertes?
You cannot speak of reason to the Dane
And lose your voice.* What wouldst thou beg, Laertes, 45
That shall not be my offer, not thy asking?
The head is not more native* to the heart,
The hand more instrumental to the mouth,
Than is the throne of Denmark to thy father.
What wouldst thou have, Laertes?

LAERTES: My dread lord, 50
Your leave and favour to return to France;
From whence though willingly I came to Denmark
To show my duty in your coronation,
Yet now, I must confess, that duty done,
My thoughts and wishes bend again toward France, 55
And bow them to your gracious leave and pardon.

KING: Have you your father's leave? What says Polonius?

POLONIUS: 'A hath, my lord, wrung from me my slow leave
By laboursome petition; and at last
Upon his will I seal'd my hard consent.* 60
I do beseech you, give him leave to go.

KING: Take thy fair hour, Laertes; time be thine,
And thy best graces spend it at thy will!
But now, my cousin* Hamlet, and my son—

HAMLET: [*aside*] A little more than kin, and less than kind. 65

KING: How is it that the clouds* still hang on you?

HAMLET: Not so, my Lord; I am too much in the sun.

QUEEN: Good Hamlet, cast thy nighted colour off,
And let thine eye look like a friend on Denmark.
Do not for ever with thy vailed lids* 70
Seek for thy noble father in the dust.
Thou know'st 'tis common—all that lives must die,
Passing through nature to eternity.

---

[38] **dilated articles** detailed documents
[45] **lose your voice** waste your breath
[47] **native** related
[60] **hard consent** reluctantly gave consent
[64] **cousin** kinsman
[66] **clouds** grief; mourning dress
[70] **vailed lids** lowered eyes

HAMLET: Ay, madam, it is common.
QUEEN: If it be,
    Why seems it so particular with thee?   75
HAMLET: Seems, madam! Nay, it is; I know not seems.
    'Tis not alone my inky cloak, good mother,
    Nor customary suits of solemn black,
    Nor windy suspiration* of forc'd breath,
    No, nor the fruitful river in the eye,   80
    Nor the dejected haviour of the visage,
    Together with all forms, moods, shapes of grief,
    That can denote me truly. These, indeed, seem;
    For they are actions that a man might play;
    But I have that within which passes show—   85
    These but the trappings and the suits of woe.
KING: 'Tis sweet and commendable in your nature, Hamlet,
    To give these mourning duties to your father;
    But you must know your father lost a father;
    That father lost, lost his; and the survivor bound,   90
    In filial obligation, for some term
    To do obsequious* sorrow. But to persever
    In obstinate condolement* is a course
    Of impious stubbornness; 'tis unmanly grief;
    It shows a will most incorrect to heaven,   95
    A heart unfortified, a mind impatient,
    An understanding simple and unschool'd;
    For what we know must be, and is as common
    As any the most vulgar thing to sense,
    Why should we in our peevish opposition   100
    Take it to heart? Fie! 'tis a fault to heaven,
    A fault against the dead, a fault to nature,
    To reason most absurd; whose common theme
    Is death of fathers, and who still hath cried,
    From the first corse* till he that died to-day,   105
    'This must be so.' We pray you throw to earth
    This unprevailing* woe, and think of us
    As of a father; for let the world take note
    You are the most immediate to our throne;
    And with no less nobility of love   110
    Than that which dearest father bears his son
    Do I impart toward you. For your intent
    In going back to school in Wittenberg,
    It is most retrograde* to our desire;

79 **windy suspiration** heavy sighs
92 **obsequious** funereal
93 **condolements** mourning
105 **corse** corpse
107 **unprevailing** unavailing
114 **retrograde** contrary

And we beseech you bend you* to remain   115
Here, in the cheer and comfort of our eye,
Our chiefest courtier, cousin, and our son.
QUEEN: Let not thy mother lose her prayers, Hamlet:
I pray thee stay with us; go not to Wittenberg.
HAMLET: I shall in all my best obey you, madam.   120
KING: Why, 'tis a loving and a fair reply.
Be as ourself in Denmark. Madam, come;
This gentle and unforc'd accord of Hamlet
Sits smiling to my heart; in grace whereof,
No jocund health that Denmark drinks to-day   125
But the great cannon to the clouds shall tell
And the King's rouse* the heaven shall bruit* again,
Re-speaking earthly thunder. Come away.
        [*Flourish. Exeunt all but* HAMLET.]
HAMLET: O, that this too too solid flesh would melt,
Thaw, and resolve itself into a dew!   130
Or that the Everlasting had not fix'd
His canon* 'gainst self-slaughter! O God! God!
How weary, stale, flat, and unprofitable,
Seem to me all the uses of this world!
Fie on't! Ah, fie! 'tis an unweeded garden,   135
That grows to seed; things rank and gross in nature   *grief*
Possess it merely.* That it should come to this!
But two months dead! Nay, not so much, not two.
So excellent a king that was to this
Hyperion* to a satyr, so loving to my mother,   140
That he might not beteem* the winds of heaven
Visit her face too roughly. Heaven and earth!
Must I remember? Why, she would hang on him
As if increase of appetite had grown
By what it fed on; and yet, within a month—   145
Let me not think on't. Frailty, thy name is woman!—
A little month, or ere those shoes were old
With which she followed my poor father's body,
Like Niobe,* all tears—why she, even she—
O God! a beast that wants discourse of reason*   150
Would have mourn'd longer—married with my uncle,
My father's brother; but no more like my father
Than I to Hercules. Within a month,

115 **bend you** agree
127 **rouse** drinking, carousing
127 **bruit** noisily announce
132 **canon** law
137 **merely** completely
140 **Hyperion** the sun god noted for beauty
141 **beteem** permit
149 **Niobe** mother in Greek mythology who wept without stopping for the death of her children
150 **wants discourse of reason** lacks reasoning power

Ere yet the salt of most unrighteous tears
Had left the flushing in her galled eyes,   155
She married. O, most wicked speed, to post*
With such dexterity to incestuous* sheets!
It is not, nor it cannot come to good.
But break, my heart, for I must hold my tongue.
    [*Enter* HORATIO, MARCELLUS, *and* BERNARDO.]
HORATIO: Hail to your lordship!
HAMLET: I am glad to see you well.   160
    Horatio—or I do forget myself.
HORATIO: The same, my lord, and your poor servant ever.
HAMLET: Sir, my good friend. I'll change* that name with you.
    And what make you from Wittenberg, Horatio?
    Marcellus?   165
MARCELLUS: My good lord!
HAMLET: I am very glad to see you. [*to* BERNARDO] Good even, sir.—
    But what, in faith, make you from Wittenberg?
HORATIO: A truant disposition, good my lord.
HAMLET: I would not hear your enemy say so;   170
    Nor shall you do my ear that violence,
    To make it truster* of your own report
    Against yourself. I know you are no truant.
    But what is your affair in Elsinore?
    We'll teach you to drink deep ere you depart.   175
HORATIO: My lord, I came to see your father's funeral.
HAMLET: I prithee do not mock me, fellow-student;
    I think it was to see my mother's wedding.
HORATIO: Indeed, my lord, it followed hard upon.
HAMLET: Thrift, thrift, Horatio! The funeral bak'd-meats   180
    Did coldly furnish forth the marriage tables.
    Would I had met my dearest* foe in heaven
    Or ever I had seen that day, Horatio!
    My father—methinks I see my father.
HORATIO: Where, my lord?
HAMLET: In my mind's eye, Horatio.
HORATIO: I saw him once; 'a was a goodly king.   185
HAMLET: 'A* was a man, take him for all in all,
    I shall not look upon his like again.
HORATIO: My lord, I think I saw him yesternight.
HAMLET: Saw who?
HORATIO: My lord, the King your father.   190
HAMLET: The King my father!

---

156 **post** hasten
157 **incestuous** incestuous because the church considered a sister-in-law equivalent to being a sister
163 **change** exchange
172 **truster** believer
182 **dearest** most hated
186 **'A** he

HORATIO: Season your admiration* for a while
    With an attent ear, till I may deliver,
    Upon the witness of these gentlemen,
    This marvel to you.
HAMLET: For God's love, let me hear.   195
HORATIO: Two nights together had these gentlemen,
    Marcellus and Bernardo, on their watch,
    In the dead waste and middle of the night,
    Been thus encount'red. A figure like your father,
    Armed at point exactly, cap-a-pe,*   200
    Appears before them, and with solemn march
    Goes slow and stately by them; thrice he walk'd
    By their oppress'd and fear-surprised eyes,
    Within his truncheon's length,* whilst they, distill'd*
    Almost to jelly with the act of fear,   205
    Stand dumb and speak not to him. This to me
    In dreadful* secrecy impart they did;
    And I with them the third night kept the watch;
    Where, as they had delivered, both in time,
    Form of the thing, each word made true and good,   210
    The apparition comes. I knew your father;
    These hands are not more like.
HAMLET: But where was this?
MARCELLUS: My lord, upon the platform where we watch.
HAMLET: Did you not speak to it?
HORATIO: My lord, I did;
    But answer made it none; yet once methought   215
    It lifted up its head and did address
    Itself to motion, like as it would speak;
    But even then the morning cock crew loud,
    And at the sound it shrunk in haste away
    And vanish'd from our sight.
HAMLET: 'Tis very strange.   220
HORATIO: As I do live, my honour'd lord, 'tis true;
    And we did think it writ down in our duty
    To let you know of it.
HAMLET: Indeed, indeed, sirs, but this troubles me.
    Hold you the watch to-night?
ALL: We do, my lord.   225
HAMLET: Arm'd, say you?
ALL: Arm'd, my lord.
HAMLET: From top to toe?
ALL: My lord, from head to foot.

---

[192] **Season your admiration** control your wonder
[200] **cap-a-pe** head to foot
[204] **truncheon's length** space of a short club
[204] **distill'd** reduced
[207] **dreadful** terrified

HAMLET: Then saw you not his face?

HORATIO: O yes, my lord; he wore his beaver* up.   230

HAMLET: What, look'd he frowningly?

HORATIO: A countenance more in sorrow than in anger.

HAMLET: Pale or red?

HORATIO: Nay, very pale.

HAMLET: And fix'd his eyes upon you?

HORATIO: Most constantly.

HAMLET: I would I had been there.   235

HORATIO: It would have much amaz'd you.

HAMLET: Very like, very like. Stay'd it long?

HORATIO: While one with moderate haste might tell* a hundred.

BOTH: Longer, longer.

HORATIO: Not when I saw't.

HAMLET: His beard was grizzl'd*—no?   240

HORATIO: It was, as I have seen it in his life,
    A sable silver'd.*

HAMLET: I will watch to-night;
    Perchance 'twill walk again.

HORATIO: I warr'nt it will.

HAMLET: If it assume my noble father's person.
    I'll speak to it, though hell itself should gape   245
    And bid me hold my peace, I pray you all,
    If you have hitherto conceal'd this sight,
    Let it be tenable* in your silence still;
    And whatsoever else shall hap to-night,
    Give it an understanding, but no tongue;   250
    I will requite your loves. So, fare you well—
    Upon the platform, 'twixt eleven and twelve,
    I'll visit you.

ALL: Our duty to your honour.

HAMLET: Your loves, as mine to you; farewell.
    [*Exeunt all but* HAMLET.]
    My father's spirit in arms! All is not well.   255
    I doubt* some foul play. Would the night were come!
    Till then sit still, my soul. Foul deeds will rise,
    Though all the earth o'erwhelm them, to men's eyes.   [*Exit.*]

SCENE III——*Elsinore. The house of* POLONIUS.

[*Enter* LAERTES *and* OPHELIA *his sister.*]

LAERTES: My necessaries are embark'd. Farewell.
    And, sister, as the winds give benefit

230 **beaver** visor, face guard
238 **tell** count
240 **grizzl'd** gray
242 **sable silver'd** black mixed with gray
248 **tenable** held
256 **doubt** suspect

And convoy* is assistant, do not sleep,
But let me hear from you.
OPHELIA: Do you doubt that?
LAERTES: For Hamlet, and the trifling of his favour, 5
Hold it a fashion and a toy* in blood,
A violet in the youth of primy* nature,
Forward* not permanent, sweet not lasting,
The perfume and suppliance* of a minute;
No more.
OPHELIA: No more but so?
LAERTES: Think it no more; 10
For nature crescent* does not grow alone
In thews* and bulk, but as this temple* waxes,
The inward service of the mind and soul
Grows wide withal. Perhaps he loves you now,
And now no soil nor cautel* doth besmirch 15
The virtue of his will; but you must fear,
His greatness weigh'd,* his will is not his own;
For he himself is subject to his birth:
He may not, as unvalued* persons do,
Carve for himself; for on his choice depends 20
The sanity and health of this whole state;
And therefore must his choice be circumscrib'd
Unto the voice and yielding of that body
Whereof he is the head. Then if he says he loves you,
It fits your wisdom so far to believe it 25
As he in his particular act and place
May give his saying deed; which is no further
Than the main voice of Denmark goes withal.
Then weigh what loss your honour may sustain,
If with too credent* ear you list his songs, 30
Or lose your heart, or your chaste treasure open
To his unmast'red importunity.
Fear it, Ophelia, fear it, my dear sister;
And keep you in the rear of your affection,
Out of the shot and danger of desire. 35
The chariest maid is prodigal enough

I,iii,3 **convoy** conveyance
[6] **toy** idle fancy
[7] **primy** youthful, spring-like
[8] **Forward** premature
[9] **suppliance** diversion
[11] **crescent** increasing
[12] **thews** sinews
[12] **temple** the body
[15] **cautel** deceit
[17] **greatness weigh'd** high rank considered
[19] **unvalued** of low rank
[30] **credent** credulous

William Shakespeare

If she unmask her beauty to the moon.
Virtue itself scapes not calumnious strokes;
The canker* galls the infants of the spring
Too oft before their buttons* be disclos'd;   40
And in the morn and liquid dew of youth
Contagious blastments are most imminent.
Be wary, then; best safety lies in fear:
Youth to itself rebels, though none else near.
OPHELIA: I shall the effect of this good lesson keep   45
    As watchman to my heart. But, good my brother,
    Do not, as some ungracious* pastors do,
    Show me the steep and thorny way to heaven,
    Whiles, like a puff'd and reckless libertine,
    Himself the primrose path of dalliance treads   50
    And recks not his own rede.*
LAERTES: O, fear me not!
        [*Enter* POLONIUS.]
    I stay too long. But here my father comes.
    A double blessing is a double grace;
    Occasion smiles upon a second leave.
POLONIUS: Yet here, Laertes! Aboard, aboard, for shame!   55
    The wind sits in the shoulder of your sail,
    And you are stay'd for. There—my blessing with thee!
    And these few precepts in thy memory
    Look thou character.* Give thy thoughts no tongue,
    Nor any unproportion'd* thought his act.   60
    Be thou familiar, but by no means vulgar.
    Those friends thou hast, and their adoption tried,
    Grapple them to thy soul with hoops of steel;
    But do not dull thy palm with entertainment
    Of each new-hatch'd, unfledg'd comrade. Beware   65
    Of entrance to a quarrel; but, being in,
    Bear't that th' opposed may beware of thee.
    Give every man thy ear, but few thy voice;
    Take each man's censure, but reserve thy judgment.
    Costly thy habit as thy purse can buy,   70
    But not express'd in fancy; rich, not gaudy;
    For the apparel oft proclaims the man;
    And they in France of the best rank and station
    Are of a most select and generous choice in that.
    Neither a borrower nor a lender be;   75
    For loan oft loses both itself and friend,

---

[39] **canker** worm
[40] **buttons** buds
[47] **ungracious** without themselves being in God's grace
[51] **recks not his own rede** doesn't heed his own advice
[59] **character** inscribe
[60] **unproportion'd** unconsidered

And borrowing dulls the edge of husbandry.*
This above all—to thine own self be true,
And it must follow, as the night the day,
Thou canst not then be false to any man.   80
Farewell; my blessing season* this in thee!
LAERTES: Most humbly do I take my leave, my lord.
POLONIUS: The time invites you; go, your servants tend.*
LAERTES: Farewell, Ophelia; and remember well
    What I have said to you.
OPHELIA: 'Tis in my memory lock'd,   85
    And you yourself shall keep the key of it.
LAERTES: Farewell.
POLONIUS: What is't, Ophelia, he hath said to you?
OPHELIA: So please you, something touching the Lord Hamlet.
POLONIUS: What is't, Ophelia, he hath said to you?
OPHELIA: So please you, something touching the Lord Hamlet.
POLONIUS: Marry,* well bethought!   90
    'Tis told me he hath very oft of late
    Given private time to you; and you yourself
    Have of your audience been most free and bounteous.
    If it be so—as so 'tis put on me,
    And that in way of caution—I must tell you   95
    You do not understand yourself so clearly
    As it behoves my daughter and your honour.
    What is between you? Give me up the truth.
OPHELIA: He hath, my lord, of late made many tenders
    Of his affection to me.   100
POLONIUS: Affection! Pooh! You speak like a green girl,
    Unsifted* in such perilous circumstance.
    Do you believe his tenders, as you call them?
OPHELIA: I do not know, my lord, what I should think.
POLONIUS: Marry, I will teach you: think yourself a baby   105
    That you have ta'en these tenders for true pay
    Which are not sterling. Tender yourself more dearly;
    Or—not to crack the wind of the poor phrase,
    Running it thus—you'll tender me a fool.*
OPHELIA: My lord, he hath importun'd me with love   110
    In honourable fashion.
POLONIUS: Ay, fashion you may call it; go to, go to.
OPHELIA: And hath given countenance to his speech, my lord,
    With almost all the holy vows of heaven.

---

⁷⁷ **husbandry** thrift
⁸¹ **season** make fruitful
⁸³ **tend** await
⁹⁰ **Marry** By the Virgin Mary
¹⁰² **Unsifted** untried
¹⁰⁹ **tender me a fool** present me with a baby

POLONIUS: Ay, springes to catch woodcocks!* I do know,   115
    When the blood burns, how prodigal the soul
    Lends the tongue vows. These blazes, daughter,
    Giving more light than heat—extinct in both,
    Even in their promise, as it is a-making—
    You must not take for fire. From this time   120
    Be something scanter of your maiden presence;
    Set your entreatments* at a higher rate
    Than a command to parle. For Lord Hamlet,
    Believe so much in him, that he is young,
    And with a larger tether may he walk   125
    Than may be given you. In few, Ophelia,
    Do not believe his vows; for they are brokers,*
    Not of that dye* which their investments* show,
    But mere implorators* of unholy suits,
    Breathing like sanctified and pious bonds,*   130
    The better to beguile. This is for all—
    I would not, in plain terms, from this time forth
    Have you so slander* any moment leisure
    As to give words or walk with the Lord Hamlet.
    Look to't, I charge you. Come your ways.   135
OPHELIA: I shall obey, my lord.   *[Exeunt.]*

    SCENE IV——*Elsinore. The guard-platform of the Castle.*

    [Enter HAMLET, HORATIO, *and* MARCELLUS.*]*
HAMLET: The air bites shrewdly;* it is very cold.
HORATIO: It is a nipping and an eager* air.
HAMLET: What hour now?
HORATIO: I think it lacks of twelve.
MARCELLUS: No, it is struck.
HORATIO: Indeed? I heard it not. It then draws near the season   5
    Wherein the spirit held his wont to walk.
    [A flourish of trumpets, and two pieces go off.]
    What does this mean, my lord?
HAMLET: The King doth wake* to-night and takes his rouse,*
    Keeps wassail, and the swagg'ring up-spring* reels,

115 **springes to catch woodcocks** snares to catch unwary birds
122 **entreatments** conversations
127 **brokers** procurers
128 **dye** kind
128 **investments** outer garments
129 **implorators** solicitors
130 **bonds** pledges
133 **slander** disgrace
I,iv,1 **shrewdly** bitterly
2 **eager** sharp
8 **wake** revel
8 **rouse** carouses
9 **up-spring** dance

And, as he drains his draughts of Rhenish* down, 10
The kettledrum and trumpet thus bray out
The triumph of his pledge.*
HORATIO: Is it a custom?
HAMLET: Ay, marry, is't;
But to my mind, though I am native here
And to the manner born, it is a custom 15
More honour'd in the breach than the observance.
This heavy-headed revel east and west
Makes us traduc'd and tax'd of* other nations;
They clepe* us drunkards, and with swinish phrase
Soil our addition,* and, indeed, it takes 20
From our achievements, though perform'd at height,
The pith and marrow of our attribute.*
So, oft it chances in particular men
That, for some vicious mole* of nature in them,
As in their birth, wherein they are not guilty, 25
Since nature cannot choose his origin;
By the o'ergrowth of some complexion,*
Oft breaking down the pales* and forts of reason;
Or by some habit that too much o'er-leavens*
The form of plausive* manners—that these men, 30
Carrying, I say, the stamp of one defect,
Being nature's livery or fortune's star,*
His virtues else, be they as pure as grace,
As infinite as man may undergo,
Shall in the general censure* take corruption 35
From that particular fault. The dram of eale
Doth all the noble substance of a doubt
To his own scandal.
          [*Enter* GHOST.]
HORATIO: Look, my lord, it comes.
HAMLET: Angels and ministers of grace defend us!
Be thou a spirit of health* or goblin damn'd, 40
Bring with thee airs from heaven or blasts from hell,

---

10 **Rhenish** Rhine wine
12 **the triumph of his pledge** drinking a glass of wine in one draught
18 **tax'd of** accused by
19 **clepe** call
20 **addition** honor
22 **attribute** reputation
24 **mole** blemish
27 **complexion** natural disposition
28 **pales** walls
29 **o'er-leavens** overdoes, corrupts
30 **plausive** pleasing
32 **nature's livery or fortune's star** determined by nature or by the stars
35 **general censure** popular judgment
40 **spirit of health** good spirit

Be thy intents wicked or charitable,
Thou com'st in such a questionable* shape
That I will speak to thee. I'll call thee Hamlet,
King, father, royal Dane. O, answer me!   45
Let me not burst in ignorance, but tell
Why thy canoniz'd* bones, hearsed in death,
Have burst their cerements;* why the sepulchre
Wherein we saw thee quietly enurn'd
Have op'd his ponderous and marble jaws   50
To cast thee up again. What may this mean
That thou, dead corse, again in complete steel
Revisits thus the glimpses of the moon,
Making night hideous, and we fools of nature
So horridly to shake our disposition*   55
With thoughts beyond the reaches of our souls?
Say, why is this? wherefore? What should we do?
      [GHOST *beckons* HAMLET.]
HORATIO: It beckons you to go away with it,
  As if some impartment* did desire
  To you alone.
MARCELLUS: Look with what courteous action   60
  It waves you to a more removed ground.
  But do not go with it.
HORATIO: No, by no means.
HAMLET: It will not speak; then I will follow it.
HORATIO: Do not, my lord.
HAMLET: Why, what should be the fear?
  I do not set my life at a pin's fee;   65
  And for my soul, what can it do to that,
  Being a thing immortal as itself?
  It waves me forth again; I'll follow it.
HORATIO: What if it tempt you toward the flood, my lord,
  Or to the dreadful summit of the cliff   70
  That beetles* o'er his base into the sea,
  And there assume some other horrible form,
  Which might deprive your sovereignty of reason
  And draw you into madness? Think of it:
  The very place puts toys* of desperation,   75
  Without more motive, into every brain
  That looks so many fathoms to the sea

---

[43] **questionable** of dubious identity
[47] **canoniz'd** buried according to church rules
[48] **cerements** burial garments
[55] **shake our disposition** unsettle our minds
[59] **impartment** message to impart
[71] **beetles** juts out
[75] **toys** notions

And hears it roar beneath.
HAMLET: It waves me still.
    Go on; I'll follow thee.
MARCELLUS: You shall not go, my lord.
HAMLET: Hold off your hands.
HORATIO: Be rul'd; you shall not go.   80
HAMLET: My fate cries out,
    And makes each petty arture* in this body
    As hardy as the Nemean lion's nerve.*   [GHOST *beckons.*]
    Still am I call'd. Unhand me, gentlemen.
    By heaven, I'll make a ghost of him that lets* me.
    I say, away! Go on; I'll follow thee.   85
       [*Exeunt* GHOST *and* HAMLET.]
HORATIO: He waxes desperate with imagination.
MARCELLUS: Let's follow; 'tis not fit thus to obey him.
HORATIO: Have after. To what issue will this come?
MARCELLUS: Something is rotten in the state of Denmark.
HORATIO: Heaven will direct it.   90
MARCELLUS: Nay, let's follow him.   [*Exeunt.*]

      SCENE V ———— *Elsinore. The battlements of the Castle.*

    [*Enter* GHOST *and* HAMLET.]
HAMLET: Whither wilt thou lead me? Speak. I'll go no further.
GHOST: Mark me.
HAMLET: I will.
GHOST: My hour is almost come,
    When I to sulph'rous and tormenting flames
    Must render up myself.
HAMLET: Alas, poor ghost!
GHOST: Pity me not, but lend thy serious hearing
    To what I shall unfold.   5
HAMLET: Speak; I am bound to hear.
GHOST: So art thou to revenge, when thou shalt hear.
HAMLET: What?
GHOST: I am thy father's spirit,   *is he?*
    Doom'd for a certain term to walk the night,
    And for the day confin'd to fast in fires,   10
    Till the foul crimes done in my days of nature
    Are burnt and purg'd away. But that I am forbid
    To tell the secrets of my prison-house,
    I could a tale unfold whose lightest word
    Would harrow up thy soul, freeze thy young blood,   15
    Make thy two eyes, like stars, start from their spheres,

---

[82] **arture** artery
[83] **Nemean lion's nerve** sinews of the mythical lion slain by Heracles
[85] **lets** hinders

Thy knotted and combined locks to part,
And each particular hair to stand an end,
Like quills upon the fretful porpentine.*   20
But this eternal blazon* must not be
To ears of flesh and blood. List, list, O, list!
If thou didst ever thy dear father love—
HAMLET: O God!
GHOST: Revenge his foul and most unnatural murder.   25
HAMLET: Murder!
GHOST: Murder most foul, as in the best it is;
        But this most foul, strange, and unnatural.
HAMLET: Haste me to know't, that I, with wings as swift
        As meditation or the thoughts of love,   30
        May sweep to my revenge.
GHOST: I find thee apt;
        And duller shouldst thou be than the fat weed
        That roots itself in ease on Lethe wharf,*
        Wouldst thou not stir in this. Now, Hamlet, hear:
        'Tis given out that, sleeping in my orchard,   35
        A serpent stung me; so the whole ear of Denmark
        Is by a forged process* of my death
        Rankly abus'd; but know, thou noble youth,
        The serpent that did sting thy father's life
        Now wears his crown.
HAMLET: O my prophetic soul!   40
        My uncle!
GHOST: Ay, that incestuous, that adulterate* beast,
        With witchcraft of his wits, with traitorous gifts—
        O wicked wit and gifts that have the power
        So to seduce!—won to his shameful lust   45
        The will of my most seeming virtuous queen.
        O Hamlet, what a falling off was there,
        From me, whose love was of that dignity
        That it went hand in hand even with the vow
        I made to her in marriage; and to decline   50
        Upon a wretch whose natural gifts were poor
        To those of mine!
        But virtue, as it never will be moved,
        Though lewdness court it in a shape of heaven,
        So lust, though to a radiant angel link'd,   55
        Will sate itself in a celestial bed
        And prey on garbage.
        But soft! methinks I scent the morning air.

1,v,20 **fretful porpentine** fearful porcupine
21 **eternal blazon** revelation about eternity
33 **Lethe wharf** bank of the river of forgetfulness in Hades
37 **forged process** false account
42 **adulterate** adulterous

Brief let me be. Sleeping within my orchard,
My custom always of the afternoon,   60
Upon my secure* hour thy uncle stole,
With juice of cursed hebona* in a vial,
And in the porches of my ears did pour
The leperous distilment; whose effect
Holds such an enmity with blood of man   65
That swift as quicksilver it courses through
The natural gates and alleys of the body;
And with a sudden vigour it doth posset*
And curd, like eager* droppings into milk,
The thin and wholesome blood. So did it mine;   70
And a most instant tetter* bark'd about,
Most lazar-like,* with vile and loathsome crust,
All my smooth body.
Thus was I, sleeping, by a brother's hand
Of life, of crown, of queen, at once dispatch'd;   75
Cut off even in the blossoms of my sin,
Unhous'led, disappointed, unanel'd;*
No reck'ning made, but sent to my account
With all my imperfections on my head.
O, horrible! O, horrible! most horrible!   80
If thou hast nature in thee, bear it not;
Let not the royal bed of Denmark be
A couch for luxury* and damned incest.
But howsoever thou pursuest this act,
Taint not thy mind, nor let thy soul contrive   85
Against thy mother aught; leave her to heaven,
And to those thorns that in her bosom lodge
To prick and sting her. Fare thee well at once.
The glowworm shows the matin* to be near,
And gins to pale his uneffectual fire.   90
Adieu, adieu, adieu! Remember me.   [*Exit.*]
HAMLET: O all you host of heaven! O earth! What else?
And shall I couple hell? O, fie! Hold, hold, my heart;
And you, my sinews, grow not instant old,
But bear me stiffly up. Remember thee!   95
Ay, thou poor ghost, whiles memory holds a seat

---

61 **secure** unsuspecting
62 **hebona** poisonous plant
68 **posset** curdle
69 **eager** acid
71 **tetter** inflammation of the skin
72 **lazar-like** leper-like
77 **Unhous'led, disappointed, unanel'd** without the sacrament of communion, unabsolved of sin, without extreme unction
83 **luxury** lust
89 **matin** morning

In this distracted globe.* Remember thee!
Yea, from the table* of my memory
I'll wipe away all trivial fond* records,
All saws* of books, all forms, all pressures* past,   100
That youth and observation copied there,
And thy commandment all alone shall live
Within the book and volume of my brain,
Unmix'd with baser matter. Yes, by heaven!
O most pernicious woman!   105
O villain, villain, smiling, damned villain!
My tables—meet it is I set it down
That one may smile, and smile, and be a villain;
At least I am sure it may be so in Denmark. [*writing*]
So, uncle, there you are. Now to my word: 110
It is 'Adieu, adieu! Remember me.'
I have sworn't.
HORATIO: [*within*] My lord, my lord!
          [*Enter* HORATIO *and* MARCELLUS.]
MARCELLUS: Lord Hamlet!
HORATIO: Heavens secure him!
HAMLET: So be it!
MARCELLUS: Illo, ho, ho,* my lord!   115
HAMLET: Hillo, ho, ho, boy! Come, bird, come.
MARCELLUS: How is't, my noble lord?
HORATIO: What news, my lord?
HAMLET: O, wonderful!
HORATIO: Good my lord, tell it.
HAMLET: No; you will reveal it.
HORATIO: Not I, my lord, by heaven!
MARCELLUS: Nor I, my lord.   120
HAMLET: How say you, then; would heart of man once think it?
          But you'll be secret?
BOTH: Ay, by heaven, my lord!
HAMLET: There's never a villain dwelling in all Denmark
          But he's an arrant knave.
HORATIO: There needs no ghost, my lord, come from the grave   125
          To tell us this.
HAMLET: Why, right; you are in the right;
          And so, without more circumstance* at all,
          I hold it fit that we shake hands and part;
          You, as your business and desire shall point you—

⁹⁷ **globe** head
⁹⁸ **table** tablet
⁹⁹ **fond** foolish
¹⁰⁰ **saws** maxims
¹⁰⁰ **pressures** impressions
¹¹⁵ **Illo, ho, ho** falconer's call to his hawk
¹²⁷ **circumstance** details

> For every man hath business and desire,   130
>   Such as it is; and for my own poor part,
>   Look you, I will go pray.
> HORATIO: These are but wild and whirling words, my lord.
> HAMLET: I am sorry they offend you, heartily;
>   Yes, faith, heartily.
> HORATIO: There's no offence, my lord.   135
> HAMLET: Yes, by Saint Patrick, but there is, Horatio,
>   And much offence, too. Touching this vision here—
>   It is an honest ghost,* that let me tell you.   — *he decides*
>   For your desire to know what is between us,
>   O'ermaster't as you may. And now, good friends,   140
>   As you are friends, scholars, and soldiers,
>   Give me one poor request.
> HORATIO: What is't, my lord? We will.
> HAMLET: Never make known what you have seen to-night.
> BOTH: My lord, we will not.
> HAMLET: Nay, but swear't.
> HORATIO: In faith,   145
>   My lord, not I.
> MARCELLUS: Nor I, my lord, in faith.
> HAMLET: Upon my sword.
> MARCELLUS: We have sworn, my lord, already.
> HAMLET: Indeed, upon my sword, indeed.
> GHOST: [*cries under the stage*] Swear.
> HAMLET: Ha, ha, boy! say'st thou so? Art thou there, true-penny?*   150
>   Come on. You hear this fellow in the cellarage:
>   Consent to swear.
> HORATIO: Propose the oath, my lord.
> HAMLET: Never to speak of this that you have seen,
>   Swear by my sword.
> GHOST: [*beneath*] Swear.   155
> HAMLET: Hic et ubique?* Then we'll shift our ground.
>   Come hither, gentlemen,
>   And lay your hands again upon my sword.
>   Swear by my sword
>   Never to speak of this that you have heard.   160
> GHOST: [*beneath*] Swear, by his sword.
> HAMLET: Well said, old mole! Canst work i' th' earth so fast?
>   A worthy pioneer!* Once more remove, good friends.
> HORATIO: O day and night, but this is wondrous strange!
> HAMLET: And therefore as a stranger give it welcome.   165
>   There are more things in heaven and earth, Horatio,
>   Than are dreamt of in your philosophy.

138 **honest ghost** true ghost of his father rather than a demon
150 **true-penny** honest fellow
156 **Hic et ubique** Here and everywhere
163 **pioneer** miner

But come.
Here, as before, never, so help you mercy,
How strange or odd soe'er I bear myself—   170
As I perchance hereafter shall think meet
To put an antic disposition* on—
That you, at such times, seeing me, never shall,
With arms encumb'red* thus, or this head-shake,
Or by pronouncing of some doubtful phrase,   175
As 'Well, well, we know' or 'We could, an if we would'
Or, 'If we list to speak' or 'There be, an if they might'
Or such ambiguous giving out, to note
That you know aught of me—this do swear,
So grace and mercy at your most need help you.   180
GHOST: [*beneath*] Swear.
HAMLET: Rest, rest, perturbed spirit! So, gentlemen,
With all my love I do commend me* to you;
And what so poor a man as Hamlet is
May do t'express his love and friending to you,   185
God willing, shall not lack. Let us go in together;
And still your fingers on your lips, I pray.
The time is out of joint. O cursed spite,
That ever I was born to set it right!
Nay, come, let's go together.   [*Exeunt.*] 190

ACT II

SCENE I————*Elsinore. The house of* POLONIUS.

[*Enter* POLONIUS *and* REYNALDO.]
POLONIUS: Give him this money and these notes, Reynaldo.
REYNALDO: I will, my lord.
POLONIUS: You shall do marvellous wisely, good Reynaldo,
Before you visit him, to make inquire
Of his behaviour.
REYNALDO: My lord, I did intend it.   5
POLONIUS: Marry, well said; very well said. Look you, sir,
Enquire me first what Danskers* are in Paris;
And how, and who, what means, and where they keep,*
What company, at what expense; and finding
By this encompassment and drift of question   10
That they do know my son, come you more nearer
Than your particular demands will touch it.
Take you, as 'twere, some distant knowledge of him;

---

172 **antic disposition** strange behavior
174 **encumb'red** folded
183 **commend me** entrust myself
II,i,7 **Danskers** Danes
8 **keep** dwell

As thus: 'I know his father and his friends,
And in part him.' Do you mark this, Reynaldo?   15
REYNALDO: Ay, very well, my lord.
POLONIUS: 'And in part him—but' you may say 'not well;
     But if 't be he I mean, he's very wild;
     Addicted so and so'; and there put on him
     What forgeries you please; marry, none so rank   20
     As may dishonour him; take heed of that;
     But, sir, such wanton, wild, and usual slips
     As are companions noted and most known
     To youth and liberty.
REYNALDO: As gaming, my lord.
POLONIUS: Ay, or drinking, fencing, swearing, quarrelling.   25
     Drabbing*—you may go so far.
REYNALDO: My lord, that would dishonour him.
POLONIUS: Faith, no; as you may season it in the charge.
     You must not put another scandal on him,
     That he is open to incontinency;   30
     That's not my meaning. But breathe his faults so quaintly*
     That they may seem the taints of liberty;
     The flash and outbreak of a fiery mind,
     A savageness in unreclaimed blood,
     Of general assault.*
REYNALDO: But, my good lord—   35
POLONIUS: Wherefore should you do this?
REYNALDO: Ay, my lord,
     I would know that.
POLONIUS: Marry, sir, here's my drift,
     And I believe it is a fetch of warrant:*
     You laying these slight sullies on my son,
     As 'twere a thing a little soil'd wi' th' working,   40
     Mark you,
     Your party in converse, him you would sound,
     Having ever seen in the prenominate crimes*
     The youth you breathe of guilty, be assur'd
     He closes with you in this consequence—*   45
     'Good sir' or so, or 'friend' or 'gentleman'
     According to the phrase or the addition*
     Of man and country.
REYNALDO: Very good, my lord.

---

[26] **drabbing** womanizing
[31] **quaintly** ingeniously
[35] **of general assault** common to all men
[38] **fetch of warrant** justifiable device
[43] **having ... crimes** if he has ever seen the aforementioned crimes
[45] **He closes ... this consequence** agrees with you
[47] **addition** title

POLONIUS: And then, sir, does 'a *this—'a does—What was I
    about to say? By the mass, I was about to say something;   50
    where did I leave?
REYNALDO: At 'closes in the consequence,' at 'friend or so' and 'gentleman.'
POLONIUS: At 'closes in the consequence'—ay, marry,
    He closes thus: 'I know the gentleman;   55
    I saw him yesterday, or t'other day,
    Or then, or then; with such, or such; and, as you say,
    There was 'a gaming; there o'ertook in's rouse;
    There falling out at tennis'; or perchance
    'I saw him enter such a house of sale,'   60
    Videlicet,* a brothel, or so forth. See you now
    Your bait of falsehood take this carp of truth;
    And thus do we of wisdom and of reach,
    With windlasses and with assays of bias,*   65
    By indirections find directions out;
    So, by my former lecture and advice,
    Shall you my son. You have me, have you not?
REYNALDO: My lord, I have.
POLONIUS: God buy ye; fare ye well.
REYNALDO: Good my lord!   70
POLONIUS: Observe his inclination in yourself.*
REYNALDO: I shall, my lord.
POLONIUS: And let him ply his music.
REYNALDO: Well, my lord.
POLONIUS: Farewell!   [*Exit* REYNALDO.]
    [*Enter* OPHELIA.]
    How now, Ophelia! What's the matter?
OPHELIA: O my lord, my lord, I have been so affrighted!   75
POLONIUS: With what, i' th' name of God?
OPHELIA: My lord, as I was sewing in my closet,*
    Lord Hamlet, with his doublet all unbrac'd,*
    No hat upon his head, his stockings fouled,
    Ungart'red and down-gyved* to his ankle;   80
    Pale as his shirt, his knees knocking each other,
    And with a look so piteous in purport
    As if he had been loosed out of hell
    To speak of horrors—he comes before me.
POLONIUS: Mad for thy love?
OPHELIA: My lord, I do not know,   85
    But truly I do fear it.

---

[49] 'a he
[61] **videlicet** namely
[65] **windlasses . . . bias** indirect means
[71] **in yourself** for yourself
[77] **closet** private room
[78] **doublet all unbrac'd** jacket entirely unlaced/open
[80] **down-gyved** hanging down

POLONIUS: What said he?
OPHELIA: He took me by the wrist, and held me hard;
    Then goes he to the length of all his arm,
    And, with his other hand thus o'er his brow,
    He falls to such a perusal of my face   90
    As 'a would draw it. Long stay'd he so.
    At last, a little shaking of mine arm,
    And thrice his head thus waving up and down,
    He rais'd a sigh so piteous and profound
    As it did seem to shatter all his bulk   95
    And end his being. That done, he lets me go,
    And, with his head over his shoulder turn'd,
    He seem'd to find his way without his eyes;
    For out adoors he went without their help
    And to the last bended their light on me.   100
POLONIUS: Come, go with me. I will go seek the King.
    This is the very ecstasy* of love,
    Whose violent property fordoes* itself,
    And leads the will to desperate undertakings
    As oft as any passion under heaven   105
    That does afflict our natures. I am sorry—
    What, have you given him any hard words of late?
OPHELIA: No, my good lord; but, as you did command,
    I did repel his letters, and denied
    His access to me.
POLONIUS: That hath made him mad.   110
    I am sorry that with better heed and judgment
    I had not quoted him.* I fear'd he did but trifle,
    And meant to wreck thee; but beshrew my jealousy!*
    By heaven, it is as proper to our age
    To cast beyond ourselves in our opinions   115
    As it is common for the younger sort
    To lack discretion. Come, go we to the King.
    This must be known; which, being kept close, might move
    More grief to hide than hate to utter love.*   120
    Come.   *[Exeunt.]*

SCENE II———*Elsinore. The Castle.*

[*Flourish. Enter* KING, QUEEN, ROSENCRANTZ, GUILDENSTERN, *and attendants.*]

KING: Welcome, dear Rosencrantz and Guildenstern!
    Moreover that we much did long to see you,

---

[102] **ecstasy** madness
[103] **property fordoes** quality destroys
[112] **quoted** noted
[113] **beshrew my jealousy** curse on my suspicions
[117–19] **come, go . . . utter love** telling the king may anger him, but not telling him might anger him more

⏑ / ⏑ / ⏑ / ⏑ / ⏑ /
The need we have to use you did provoke
Our hasty sending. Something have you heard
Of Hamlet's transformation; so I call it,   5
Sith* nor th' exterior nor the inward man
Resembles that it was. What it should be,
More than his father's death, that thus hath put him
So much from th' understanding of himself,
I cannot deem of. I entreat you both   10
That, being of so* young days brought up with him,
And sith so neighboured to his youth and haviour,
That you vouchsafe your rest* here in our court
Some little time; so by your companies
To draw him on to pleasures, and to gather,   15
So much as from occasion you may glean,
Whether aught to us unknown afflicts him thus
That, open'd,* lies within our remedy.
QUEEN: Good gentlemen, he hath much talk'd of you;
And sure I am two men there is not living   20
To whom he more adheres. If it will please you
To show us so much gentry* and good will
As to expend your time with us awhile
For the supply and profit of our hope,
Your visitation shall receive such thanks   25
As fits a king's remembrance.
ROSENCRANTZ: Both your Majesties
Might, by the sovereign power you have of us,
Put your dread pleasures more into command
Than to entreaty.
GUILDENSTERN: But we both obey,
And here give up ourselves, in the full bent,*   30
To lay our service freely at your feet,
To be commanded.
KING: Thanks, Rosencrantz and gentle Guildenstern.
QUEEN: Thanks, Guildenstern and gentle Rosencrantz.
And I beseech you instantly to visit   35
My too much changed son. Go, some of you,
And bring these gentlemen where Hamlet is.
GUILDENSTERN: Heavens make our presence and our practices
Pleasant and helpful to him!
QUEEN: Aye amen! [*Exeunt* ROSENCRANTZ, GUILDENSTERN, *and some attendants.*]
        [*Enter* POLONIUS.]

II,ii,6 **sith** since
11 **of so** from such
13 **vouchsafe your rest** consent to remain
18 **open'd** revealed
22 **gentry** courtesy
30 **in the full bent** entirely

POLONIUS: Th' ambassadors from Norway, my good lord,   40
    Are joyfully return'd.
KING: Thou still hast been the father of good news.
POLONIUS: Have I, my lord? I assure you, my good liege,
    I hold my duty, as I hold my soul,
    Both to my God and to my gracious King;   45
    And I do think—or else this brain of mine
    Hunts not the trail of policy so sure
    As it hath us'd to do—that I have found
    The very cause of Hamlet's lunacy.
KING: O, speak of that; that do I long to hear.   50
POLONIUS: Give first admittance to th' ambassadors;
    My news shall be the fruit to that great feast.
KING: Thyself do grace to them, and bring them in.
    [*Exit* POLONIUS.]
    He tells me, my dear Gertrude, he hath found
    The head and source of all your son's distemper.   55
QUEEN: I doubt it is no other but the main,
    His father's death and our o'erhasty marriage.
KING: Well, we shall sift him.
    [*Reenter* POLONIUS, *with* VOLTEMAND *and* CORNELIUS.]
    Welcome, my good friends!
    Say, Voltemand, what from our brother Norway?
VOLTEMAND: Most fair return of greetings and desires.   60
    Upon our first,* he sent out to suppress
    His nephew's levies; which to him appear'd
    To be a preparation 'gainst the Polack;
    But, better look'd into, he truly found
    It was against your Highness. Whereat griev'd,   65
    That so his sickness, age, and impotence,
    Was falsely borne in hand,* sends out arrests
    On Fortinbras; which he, in brief, obeys;
    Receives rebuke from Norway; and, in fine,
    Makes vow before his uncle never more   70
    To give th' assay of arms against your Majesty.
    Whereon old Norway, overcome with joy,
    Gives him threescore thousand crowns in annual fee,
    And his commission to employ those soldiers,
    So levied as before, against the Polack;   75
    With an entreaty, herein further shown, [*gives a paper*]
    That it might please you to give quiet pass
    Through your dominions for this enterprise,
    On such regards of safety and allowance
    As therein are set down.
KING: It likes us well;   80
    And at our more considered time we'll read,

---

61 **first** first meeting
67 **borne in hand** deceived

Answer, and think upon this business.
Meantime we thank you for your well-took labour.
Go to your rest; at night we'll feast together.
Most welcome home!   [*Exeunt* AMBASSADORS *and attendants.*]
POLONIUS: This business is well ended.   85
  My liege, and madam, to expostulate
  What majesty should be, what duty is,
  Why day is day, night night, and time is time,
  Were nothing, but to waste night, day, and time.
  Therefore, since brevity is the soul of wit,   90
  And tediousness the limbs and outward flourishes,
  I will be brief. Your noble son is mad.
  Mad call I it; for, to define true madness,
  What is't but to be nothing else but mad?
  But let that go.   95
QUEEN: More matter with less art.
POLONIUS: Madam, I swear I use no art at all.
  That he's mad, 'tis true: 'tis true 'tis pity;
  And pity 'tis 'tis true. A foolish figure!
  But farewell it, for I will use no art.
  Mad let us grant him, then; and now remains   100
  That we find out the cause of this effect;
  Or rather say the cause of this defect,
  For this effect defective comes by cause.
  Thus it remains, and the remainder thus.
  Perpend.*   105
  I have a daughter—have while she is mine —
  Who in her duty and obedience, mark,
  Hath given me this. Now gather, and surmise. [*reads*]
  'To the celestial, and my soul's idol, the most beautified Ophelia.' That's an ill
    phrase, a vile phrase; 'beautified' is a vile phrase. But you shall hear.
    Thus: [*reads*]
  'In her excellent white bosom, these, &c.'
QUEEN: Came this from Hamlet to her?
POLONIUS: Good madam, stay awhile; I will be faithful. [*reads*]   115
  'Doubt thou the stars are fire;
    Doubt that the sun doth move;
  Doubt* truth to be a liar;
    But never doubt I love.
  'O dear Ophelia, I am ill at these numbers.* I have not art to reckon my groans;
    but that I love thee best, O most best, believe it. Adieu.
                  'Thine evermore, most dear lady, whilst
                        this machine is to him,
                              HAMLET.'

---

105 **perpend** consider carefully
118 **doubt** suspect
120 **ill at these numbers** unskilled at versifying

This, in obedience, hath my daughter shown me; 125
And more above,* hath his solicitings,
As they fell out by time, by means, and place,
All given to mine ear.
KING: But how hath she
Receiv'd his love?
POLONIUS: What do you think of me?
KING: As of a man faithful and honourable. 130
POLONIUS: I would fain prove so. But what might you think,
When I had seen this hot love on the wing,
As I perceiv'd it, I must tell you that,
Before my daughter told me—what might you,
Or my dear Majesty your Queen here think, 135
If I had play'd the desk or table-book;*
Or given my heart a winking,* mute and dumb;
Or look'd upon this love with idle sight—
What might you think? No, I went round to work,
And my young mistress thus I did bespeak: 140
'Lord Hamlet is a prince out of thy star;
This must not be.' And then I prescripts gave her,
That she should lock herself from his resort,
Admit no messengers, receive no tokens.
Which done, she took the fruits of my advice; 145
And he repelled, a short tale to make,
Fell into a sadness, then into a fast,
Thence to a watch,* thence into a weakness,
Thence to a lightness,* and, by this declension,
Into the madness wherein now he raves 150
And all we mourn for.
KING: Do you think 'tis this?
QUEEN: It may be, very like.
POLONIUS: Hath there been such a time—I would fain know that—
That I have positively said ''Tis so,'
When it prov'd otherwise?
KING: Not that I know. 155
POLONIUS: Take this from this,* if this be otherwise.
If circumstances lead me, I will find
Where truth is hid, though it were hid indeed
Within the centre.*
KING: How may we try it further?

---

126 **above** besides
136 **play'd the desk or table-book** been a passive receiver of secrets
137 **winking** closed my eyes
148 **watch** wakefulness
149 **lightness** mental derangement
156 **this from this** (indicating by pointing) head from body
159 **centre** center of the earth

POLONIUS: You may know sometimes he walks four hours together,   160
    Here in the lobby.
QUEEN: So he does, indeed.
POLONIUS: At such a time I'll loose my daughter to him.
    Be you and I behind an arras* then;
    Mark the encounter: if he love her not,
    And be not from his reason fall'n thereon,   165
    Let me be no assistant for a state,
    But keep a farm and carters.
KING: We will try it.
        [Enter HAMLET, *reading on a book.]*
QUEEN: But look where sadly the poor wretch comes reading.
POLONIUS: Away, I do beseech you, both away:
    I'll board him presently.* O, give me leave.   170
        [Exeunt KING *and* QUEEN.]
    How does my good Lord Hamlet?
HAMLET: Well, God-a-mercy.
POLONIUS: Do you know me, my lord?
HAMLET: Excellent well; you are a fishmonger.*
POLONIUS: Not I, my lord.   175
HAMLET: Then I would you were so honest a man.
POLONIUS: Honest, my lord!
HAMLET: Ay, sir; to be honest, as this world goes, is to be one man pick'd out of
    ten thousand.
POLONIUS: That's very true, my lord.   180
HAMLET: For if the sun breed maggots in a dead dog, being a good kissing
    carrion—Have you a daughter?
POLONIUS: I have, my lord.
HAMLET: Let her not walk i' th' sun. Conception* is a blessing. But as your daugh-
    ter may conceive—friend, look to't.   185
POLONIUS: How say you by that? *[aside]* Still harping on my daughter. Yet he
    knew me not at first; 'a said I was a fishmonger. 'A is far gone, far gone. And
    truly in my youth I suff'red much extremity for love. Very near this. I'll
    speak to him again.—What do you read, my lord?
HAMLET: Words, words, words.   190
POLONIUS: What is the matter, my lord?
HAMLET: Between who?
POLONIUS: I mean, the matter that you read, my lord.
HAMLET: Slanders, sir; for the satirical rogue says here that old men have grey
    beards; that their faces are wrinkled; their eyes purging thick amber and
    plum-tree gum; and that they have a plentiful lack of wit, together with   195
    most weak hams—all which, sir, though I most powerfully and potently be-
    lieve, yet I hold it not honesty to have it thus set down; for you yourself, sir,
    shall grow old as I am, if, like a crab, you could go backward.

163 **arras** tapestry
170 **board him presently** accost him at once
174 **fishmonger** dealer in fish (slang for procurer)
184 **conception** understanding; becoming pregnant

POLONIUS: [*aside*] Though this be madness, yet there is method in't.—Will you 200
    walk out of the air, my lord?

HAMLET: Into my grave?

POLONIUS: Indeed, that's out of the air. [*aside*] How pregnant sometimes his
    replies are! a happiness that often madness hits on, which reason and sanity
    could not so prosperously be delivered of. I will leave him, and suddenly
    contrive the means of meeting between him and my daughter.—My lord. I 205
    will take my leave of you.

HAMLET: You cannot, sir, take from me anything that I will more willingly part
    withal—except my life, except my life, except my life.

        [*Enter* ROSENCRANTZ *and* GUILDENSTERN.]

POLONIUS: Fare you well, my lord. 210

HAMLET: These tedious old fools!

POLONIUS: You go to seek the Lord Hamlet; there he is.

ROSENCRANTZ: [*to* POLONIUS] God save you, sir!

        [*Exit* POLONIUS.]

GUILDENSTERN: My honour'd lord!

ROSENCRANTZ: My most dear lord! 215

HAMLET: My excellent good friends! How dost thou, Guildenstern? Ah, Rosen-
    crantz! Good lads, how do you both?

ROSENCRANTZ: As the indifferent* children of the earth.

GUILDENSTERN: Happy in that we are not over-happy;
        On fortune's cap we are not the very button. 220

HAMLET: Nor the soles of her shoe?

ROSENCRANTZ: Neither, my lord.

HAMLET: Then you live about her waist, or in the middle of her favours?

GUILDENSTERN: Faith, her privates we.

HAMLET: In the secret parts of Fortune? O, most true; she is a strumpet. What 225
    news?

ROSENCRANTZ: None, my lord, but that the world's grown honest.

HAMLET: Then is doomsday near. But your news is not true. Let me question
    more in particular. What have you, my good friends, deserved at the hands
    of Fortune, that she sends you to prison hither?

GUILDENSTERN: Prison, my lord! 230

HAMLET: Denmark's a prison.

ROSENCRANTZ: Then is the world one.

HAMLET: A goodly one; in which there are many confines, wards, and dungeons,
        Denmark being one o' th' worst.

ROSENCRANTZ: We think not so, my lord. 235

HAMLET: Why, then, 'tis none to you; for there is nothing either good or bad, but
    thinking makes it so. To me it is a prison.

ROSENCRANTZ: Why, then your ambition makes it one; 'tis too narrow for your
    mind.

HAMLET: O God, I could be bounded in a nutshell and count myself a king of 240
    infinite space, were it not that I have bad dreams.

---

²¹⁸ **indifferent** ordinary

GUILDENSTERN: Which dreams indeed are ambition; for the very substance of the ambitious is merely the shadow of a dream.

HAMLET: A dream itself is but a shadow.

ROSENCRANTZ: Truly, and I hold ambition of so airy and light a quality that it is   245
but a shadow's shadow.

HAMLET: Then are our beggars bodies, and our monarchs and oustretch'd heroes the beggars' shadows. Shall we to th' court? for, by my fay,* I cannot reason.

BOTH: We'll wait upon you.

HAMLET: No such matter. I will not sort you with the rest of my servants; for, to   250
speak to you like an honest man, I am most dreadfully attended. But, in the beaten way of friendship, what make you at Elsinore?

ROSENCRANTZ: To visit you, my lord; no other occasion.

HAMLET: Beggar that I am, I am even poor in thanks; but I thank you; and sure, dear friends, my thanks are too dear a half-penny.* Were you not sent for? Is   255
it your own inclining? It is a free visitation? Come, come, deal justly with me. Come, come; nay, speak.

GUILDENSTERN: What should we say, my lord?

HAMLET: Why, any thing. But to th' purpose: you were sent for; and there is a kind of confession in your looks, which your modesties have not craft enough to   260
colour; I know the good King and Queen have sent for you.

ROSENCRANTZ: To what end, my lord?

HAMLET: That you must teach me. But let me conjure you by the rights of our fellowship, by the consonancy of our youth, by the obligation of our ever-preserved love, and by what more dear a better proposer can charge you   265
withal, be even and direct with me, whether you were sent for or no?

ROSENCRANTZ: [*aside to* GUILDENSTERN] What say you?

HAMLET: [*aside*] Nay, then, I have an eye of you.—If you love me, hold not off.

GUILDENSTERN: My lord, we were sent for.

HAMLET: I will tell you why; so shall my anticipation prevent your discovery,* and   270
your secrecy to the King and Queen moult no feather. I have of late—but wherefore I know not—lost all my mirth, forgone all custom of exercises; and indeed it goes so heavily with my disposition that this goodly frame, the earth, seems to me a sterile promontory; this most excellent canopy the air, look you, this brave o'er-hanging firmament, this majestical roof fretted*   275
with golden fire—why, it appeareth no other thing to me than a foul and pestilent congregation of vapours. What a piece of work is man! How noble in reason! how infinite in faculties! in form and moving, how express* and admirable! in action, how like an angel! in apprehension, how like a god! the beauty of the world! the paragon of animals! And yet, to me, what is this quintessence of dust? Man delights not me—no, nor woman neither,   280
though by your smiling you seem to say so.

ROSENCRANTZ: My lord, there was no such stuff in my thoughts.

HAMLET: Why did ye laugh, then, when I said 'Man delights not me'?

---

²⁴⁸ **fay** faith

²⁵⁵ **too dear a half-penny** not worth a half-penny

²⁷⁰ **prevent your discovery** forestall your disclosure

²⁷⁵ **fretted** adorned

²⁷⁸ **express** exact

ROSENCRANTZ: To think, my lord, if you delight not in man, what lenten enter- 285
tainment the players shall receive from you. We coted* them on the way;
and hither are they coming to offer you service.

HAMLET: He that plays the king shall be welcome—his Majesty shall have tribute on me; the adventurous knight shall use his foil and target;* the lover
shall not sigh gratis; the humorous man shall end his part in peace; the
clown shall make those laugh whose lungs are tickle o' th' sere;* and the lady 290
shall say her mind freely, or the blank verse shall halt* for't. What players
are they?

ROSENCRANTZ: Even those you were wont to take such delight in—the tragedi-
ans of the city.

HAMLET: How chances it they travel? Their residence, both in reputation and 295
profit, was better both ways.

ROSENCRANTZ: I think their inhibition* comes by the means of the late in-
novation.*

HAMLET: Do they hold the same estimation they did when I was in the city? Are
they so followed?

ROSENCRANTZ: No, indeed, are they not. 300

HAMLET: How comes it? Do they grow rusty?

ROSENCRANTZ: Nay, their endeavour keeps in the wonted pace; but there is, sir,
an eyrie* of children, little eyases that cry out on the top of question,* and
are most tyrannically clapp'd* for't. These are now the fashion, and so be-
rattle the common stages*—so they call them—that many wearing rapiers 305
are afraid of goose quills* and dare scarce come thither.

HAMLET: What, are they children? Who maintains 'em? How are they escoted?*
Will they pursue the quality* no longer than they can sing? Will they not
say afterwards, if they should grow themselves to common players — as it is
most like, if their means are no better—their writers do them wrong to 310
make them exclaim against their own succession?*

ROSENCRANTZ: Faith, there has been much to-do on both sides; and the nation
holds it no sin to tarre* them to controversy. There was for a while no
money bid for argument,* unless the poet and the player went to cuffs in the
question.

---

²⁸⁶ **coted** overtook
²⁸⁹ **target** shield
²⁹¹ **tickle o' th' sere** on a hair trigger
²⁹² **halt** limp
²⁹⁷ **inhibition** hindrance
²⁹⁷ **innovation** probably a reference to the boys' theatre companies that were at this time offering se-
rious competition to the adult companies
³⁰³ **eyrie** nest
³⁰³ **little eyases ... question** young hawks that cry shrilly above others in a debate
³⁰⁴ **tyrannically clapp'd** violently applauded
^{304–05} **berattle the common stages** put down the public theatres
³⁰⁶ **goose quills** pens (of those who satirize the public theatres and their audiences)
³⁰⁷ **escoted** financially supported
³⁰⁸ **quality** profession of acting
³¹¹ **succession** future profession
³¹³ **tarre** incite
³¹⁴ **argument** for a playscript

HAMLET: Is't possible?   315
GUILDENSTERN: O, there has been much throwing about of brains.
HAMLET: Do the boys carry it away?
ROSENCRANTZ: Ay, that they do, my lord—Hercules and his load,* too.
HAMLET: It is not very strange; for my uncle is King of Denmark, and those that
    would make mows at him while my father lived give twenty, forty, fifty, a   320
    hundred ducats apiece for his picture in little. 'Sblood, there is something in
    this more than natural, if philosophy could find it out.
       [A flourish.]
GUILDENSTERN: There are the players.
HAMLET: Gentlemen, you are welcome to Elsinore. Your hands, come then; th'
    appurtenance of welcome is fashion and ceremony. Let me comply* with   325
    you in this garb;* lest my extent* to the players, which, I tell you, must show
    fairly outwards, should more appear like entertainments than yours. You are
    welcome. But my uncle-father and aunt-mother are deceived.
GUILDENSTERN: In what, my dear lord?
HAMLET: I am but mad north-north-west; when the wind is southerly I know a   330
    hawk from a handsaw.
       [Reenter POLONIUS.]
POLONIUS: Well be with you, gentlemen!
HAMLET: Hark you, Guildenstern, and you, too—at each ear a hearer: that great
    baby you see there is not yet out of his swaddling clouts.
ROSENCRANTZ: Happily* he is the second time come to them; for they say an old   335
    man is twice a child.
HAMLET: I will prophesy he comes to tell me of the players; mark it. You say
    right, sir: a Monday morning; 'twas then indeed.
POLONIUS: My lord, I have news to tell you.
HAMLET: My lord, I have news to tell you. When Roscius was an actor in   340
    Rome—
POLONIUS: The actors are come hither, my lord.
HAMLET: Buzz, buzz!
POLONIUS: Upon my honour—
HAMLET: They came each actor on his ass—
POLONIUS: The best actors in the world, either for tragedy, comedy, history,   345
    pastoral, pastoral-comical, historical-pastoral, tragical-historical, tragical-
    comical-historical-pastoral, scene individable, or poem unlimited. Seneca
    cannot be too heavy nor Plautus too light. For the law of writ and the lib-
    erty,* these are the only men.
HAMLET: O Jephthah, judge of Israel, what a treasure hadst thou!   350
POLONIUS: What a treasure had he, my lord?

---

[318] **Hercules and his load** reference to the Globe Theatre, whose sign showed Hercules carrying the globe on his shoulders
[325] **comply** be courteous
[326] **garb** outward show
[326] **extent** behavior
[335] **happily** perhaps
[348] **law of writ and the liberty** sticking to the text and improvising

HAMLET: Why—
> *'One fair daughter, and no more,*
> *The which he loved passing well.'*

POLONIUS: [*aside*] Still on my daughter.

HAMLET: Am I not i' th' right, old Jephthah?   355

POLONIUS: If you call me Jephthah, my lord, I have a daughter that I love passing well.

HAMLET: Nay, that follows not.

POLONIUS: What follows then, my lord?

HAMLET: Why—   360
> *'As by lot, God wot'*

and then, you know,
> *'It came to pass, as most like it was.'*

The first row of the pious chanson* will show you more; for look where my
abridgement* comes.   365

[*Enter the* PLAYERS.]

You are welcome, masters; welcome all.—I am glad to see thee well.— Welcome, good friends.—O, my old friend! Why thy face is valanc'd* since I
saw thee last; com'st thou to beard me in Denmark?—What, my young
lady* and mistress! By'r lady, your ladyship is nearer to heaven than when I
saw you last by the altitude of a chopine.* Pray God, your voice, like a piece 370
of uncurrent gold, be not crack'd within the ring.*—Masters, you are all
welcome. We'll e'en to't like French falconers, fly at anything we see. We'll
have a speech straight. Come, give us a taste of your quality; come, a passionate speech.

FIRST PLAYER: What speech, my good lord?

HAMLET: I heard thee speak me a speech once, but it was never acted; or, if it was, 375
not above once; for the play, I remember, pleas'd not the million; 'twas
caviary to the general.* But it was—as I received it, and others whose judgments in such matters cried in the top of mine*—an excellent play, well di-
gested in the scenes, set down with as much modesty as cunning.* I remember one said there were no sallets* in the lines to make the matter savoury, 380
nor no matter in the phrase that might indict the author of affectation; but
call'd it an honest method, as wholesome as sweet, and by very much more
handsome than fine.* One speech in it I chiefly lov'd; 'twas Aeneas' tale to
Dido; and thereabout of it especially where he speaks of Priam's slaughter.
If it live in your memory, begin at this line—let me see: 385

---

364 **first row of the pious chanson** first stanza of a religious song
365 **abridgement** interruption
367 **valanc'd** furnished with a beard
368 **young lady** boy who played female roles
369 **chopine** thick-soled shoe
371 **crack'd within the ring** comparing a boy's breaking voice with a cracked coin (which it was illegal
to use)
377 **caviary to the general** too rich for the common audience
378 **top of mine** agreed with or exceeded mine
379 **modesty as cunning** restraint as cleverness
380 **sallets** salads (spicy jests)
382 **more handsome than fine** well proportioned rather than ornamented

> '*The rugged Pyrrhus, like th' Hyrcanian beast,*'*
'Tis not so; it begins with Pyrrhus.
>> '*The rugged Pyrrhus, he whose sable* arms,*
>> *Black as his purpose, did the night resemble*
>> *When he lay couched in the ominous horse,**   390
>> *Hath now this dread and black complexion smear'd*
>> *With heraldry more dismal; head to foot*
>> *Now is he total gules, horridly trick'd**
>> *With blood of fathers, mothers, daughters, sons,*
>> *Bak'd and impasted* with the parching streets,*   395
>> *That lend a tyrannous and damned light*
>> *To their lord's murder. Roasted in wrath and fire,*
>> *And thus o'er-sized* with coagulate gore,*
>> *With eyes like carbuncles, the hellish Pyrrhus*
>> *Old grandsire Priam seeks.*'   400
> So proceed you.

POLONIUS: Fore God, my lord, well spoken, with good accent and good discretion.

FIRST PLAYER: '*Anon he finds him*
>> *Striking too short at Greeks; his antique sword,*
>> *Rebellious to his arm, lies where it falls,*   405
>> *Repugnant to command. Unequal match'd,*
>> *Pyrrhus at Priam drives, in rage strikes wide;*
>> *But with the whiff and wind of his fell sword*
>> *Th' unnerved father falls. Then senseless Ilium,**
>> *Seeming to feel this blow, with flaming top*   410
>> *Stoops to his base,* and with a hideous crash*
>> *Takes prisoner Pyrrhus' ear. For, lo! his sword,*
>> *Which was declining on the milky head*
>> *Of reverend Priam, seem'd i' th' air to stick.*
>> *So, as a painted tyrant, Pyrrhus stood*   415
>> *And, like a neutral to his will and matter,*
>> *Did nothing.*
>> *But as we often see, against* some storm,*
>> *A silence in the heavens, the rack* stand still,*
>> *The bold winds speechless, and the orb below*   420
>> *As hush as death, anon the dreadful thunder*
>> *Doth rend the region; so, after Pyrrhus' pause,*
>> *A roused vengeance sets him new a-work;*

---

[386] **Hyrcanian beast** tiger
[388] **sable** black
[390] **ominous horse** the wooden horse used in taking Troy
[393] **total gules, horridly trick'd** entirely red, horridly adorned
[395] **impasted** encrusted
[398] **o'er-sized** smeared over
[409] **Ilium** Troy
[411] **stoops to his base** collapses
[418] **against** before
[419] **rack** clouds

And never did the Cyclops' hammers fall
*On Mars' armour, forg'd for proof eterne,** 425
With less remorse than Pyrrhus' bleeding sword
Now falls on Priam.
Out, out, thou strumpet, Fortune! All you gods,
In general synod, take away her power;*
Break all the spokes and fellies from her wheel,* 430
And bowl the round nave down the hill of heaven,*
As low as to the fiends.'

POLONIUS: This is too long.

HAMLET: It shall to the barber's, with your beard. Prithee say on. He's for a jig, or
a tale of bawdry, or he sleeps. Say on; come to Hecuba. 435

FIRST PLAYER: *'But who, ah, who had seen the mobled* queen—'*

HAMLET: 'The mobled queen'?

POLONIUS: That's good; 'mobled queen' is good.

FIRST PLAYER: *'Run barefoot up and down, threat'ning the flames*
With bisson rheum; a clout* upon that head* 440
Where late the diadem stood, and for a robe,
*About her lank and all o'er-teemed loins,**
A blanket, in the alarm of fear caught up—
Who this had seen, with tongue in venom steep'd,
'Gainst Fortune's state would treason have pronounc'd. 445
But if the gods themselves did see her then,
When she saw Pyrrhus make malicious sport
In mincing with his sword her husband's limbs,
The instant burst of clamour that she made—
Unless things mortal move them not at all— 450
Would have made milch the burning eyes of heaven,*
And passion in the gods.'

POLONIUS: Look whe'er* he has not turn'd his colour, and has tears in 's eyes.
Prithee no more.

HAMLET: 'Tis well; I'll have thee speak out the rest of this soon.—Good my lord, 455
will you see the players well bestowed? Do you hear: let them be well used;
for they are the abstract and brief chronicles of the time; after your death
you were better have a bad epitaph than their ill report while you live.

POLONIUS: My lord, I will use them according to their desert.

HAMLET: God's bodykins, man, much better. Use every man after his desert, and 460
who shall 'scape whipping? Use them after your own honour and dignity;
the less they deserve, the more merit is in your bounty. Take them in.

425 **proof eterne** to last forever
429 **synod** council
430 **fellies** rims
431 **nave** hub
436 **mobled** muffled
440 **bisson rheum** blinding tears
440 **clout** rag
442 **o'er-teemed loins** exhausted with childbearing
451 **milch** moist
453 **whe'er** whether

POLONIUS: Come, sirs.

HAMLET: Follow him, friends. We'll hear a play to-morrow. Dost thou hear me,
old friend; can you play 'The Murder of Gonzago'?   465

FIRST PLAYER: Ay, my lord.

HAMLET: We'll ha't to-morrow night. You could, for a need, study a speech of
some dozen or sixteen lines which I would set down and insert in't, could
you not?

FIRST PLAYER: Ay, my lord.

HAMLET: Very well. Follow that lord; and look you mock him not. [*Exeunt* POLO-   470
NIUS *and* PLAYERS.] My good friends, I'll leave you till night. You are welcome to Elsinore.

ROSENCRANTZ: Good my lord!

       [*Exeunt* ROSENCRANTZ *and* GUILDENSTERN.]

HAMLET: Ay, so God buy to you! Now I am alone.

    O, what a rogue and peasant slave am I!   475
    Is it not monstrous that this player here,
    But in a fiction, in a dream of passion,
    Could force his soul so to his own conceit*
    That from her working all his visage wann'd;
    Tears in his eyes, distraction in's aspect,   480
    A broken voice, and his whole function* suiting
    With forms* to his conceit? And all for nothing!
    For Hecuba!
    What's Hecuba to him or he to Hecuba,
    That he should weep for her? What would he do,   485
    Had he the motive and the cue for passion
    That I have? He would drown the stage with tears,
    And cleave the general ear with horrid speech;
    Make mad the guilty, and appal* the free,
    Confound the ignorant, and amaze indeed   490
    The very faculties of eyes and ears.
    Yet I,
    A dull and muddy-mettl'd* rascal, peak,
    Like John-a-dreams,* unpregnant of* my cause,
    And can say nothing; no, not for a king   495
    Upon whose property and most dear life
    A damn'd defeat was made. Am I a coward?
    Who calls me villain, breaks my pate across,
    Plucks off my beard and blows it in my face,
    Tweaks me by the nose, gives me the lie i' th' throat   500
    As deep as to the lungs? Who does me this?
    Ha!

478 **conceit** imagination
481 **function** action
482 **forms** bodily expressions
489 **appal the free** terrify the guiltless
493 **muddy-mettl'd** weak spirited
493–94 **peak, like John-a-dreams** mope like a dreamer
494 **unpregnant of** unmoved by

'Swounds, I should take it; for it cannot be
But I am pigeon-liver'd* and lack gall
To make oppression bitter, or ere this   505
I should 'a fatted all the region kites*
With this slave's offal. Bloody, bawdy villain!
Remorseless, treacherous, lecherous, kindless* villain!
O, vengeance!
Why, what an ass am I! This is most brave,   510
That I, the son of a dear father murder'd,
Prompted to my revenge by heaven and hell,
Must, like a whore, unpack my heart with words,
And fall a-cursing like a very drab,*
A scullion!* Fie upon't! foh!   515
About,* my brains. Hum—I have heard
That guilty creatures, sitting at a play,
Have by the very cunning of the scene
Been struck so to the soul that presently*
They have proclaim'd their malefactions;   520
For murder, though it have no tongue, will speak
With most miraculous organ. I'll have these players
Play something like the murder of my father
Before mine uncle. I'll observe his looks;
I'll tent* him to the quick. If 'a do blench,*   525
I know my course. The spirit that I have seen
May be a devil; and the devil hath power
T'assume a pleasing shape; yea and perhaps
Out of my weakness and my melancholy,
As he is very potent with such spirits,   530
Abuses me to damn me. I'll have grounds
More relative* than this. The play's the thing
Wherein I'll catch the conscience of the King.   [*Exit.*]

ACT III

SCENE I———*Elsinore. The Castle.*

[*Enter* KING, QUEEN, POLONIUS, OPHELIA, ROSENCRANTZ, *and* GUILD-
ENSTERN.]

KING: And can you by no drift of conference*

504 **pigeon-liver'd** a coward
506 **kites** scavenger birds
508 **kindless** unnatural
514 **drab** prostitute
515 **scullion** kitchen servant
516 **About** to work
519 **presently** immediately
525 **tent** probe
525 **blench** blanch
532 **relative** certain
III,i,1 **conference** conversation

Get from him why he puts on this confusion,
Grating so harshly all his days of quiet
With turbulent and dangerous lunacy?
ROSENCRANTZ: He does confess he feels himself distracted,   5
    But from what cause 'a will by no means speak.
GUILDENSTERN: Nor do we find him forward to be sounded;*
    But, with a crafty madness, keeps aloof
    When we would bring him on to some confession
    Of his true state.
QUEEN: Did he receive you well?   10
ROSENCRANTZ: Most like a gentleman.
GUILDENSTERN: But with much forcing of his disposition.*
ROSENCRANTZ: Niggard of question; but of our demands
    Most free in his reply.
QUEEN: Did you assay* him
    To any pastime?   15
ROSENCRANTZ: Madam, it so fell out that certain players
    We o'er-raught* on the way. Of these we told him;
    And there did seem in him a kind of joy
    To hear of it. They are here about the court,
    And, as I think, they have already order   20
    This night to play before him.
POLONIUS: 'Tis most true;
    And he beseech'd me to entreat your Majesties
    To hear and see the matter.
KING: With all my heart; and it doth much content me
    To hear him so inclin'd.   25
    Good gentlemen, give him a further edge,
    And drive his purpose into these delights.
ROSENCRANTZ: We shall, my lord.
        [*Exeunt* ROSENCRANTZ *and* GUILDENSTERN.]
KING: Sweet Gertrude, leave us, too;
    For we have closely* sent for Hamlet hither,
    That he, as 'twere by accident, may here
    Affront* Ophelia.   30
    Her father and myself—lawful espials*—
    Will so bestow ourselves that, seeing unseen,
    We may of their encounter frankly judge,
    And gather by him, as he is behav'd,   35
    If't be th' affliction of his love or no
    That thus he suffers for.

7**forward to be sounded** willing to be questioned
12**forcing of his disposition** effort
14**assay** tempt
17**o'er-raught** overtook
29**closely** secretly
31**affront** meet face to face
32**espials** observers

QUEEN: I shall obey you;
  And for your part, Ophelia, I do wish
  That your good beauties be the happy cause
  Of Hamlet's wildness; so shall I hope your virtues   40
  Will bring him to his wonted way again,
  To both your honours.
OPHELIA: Madam, I wish it may.   [*Exit* QUEEN.]
POLONIUS: Ophelia, walk you here.—Gracious, so please you,
  We will bestow ourselves.—Read on this book;
  That show of such an exercise may colour*   45
  Your loneliness.—We are oft to blame in this:
  'Tis too much prov'd, that with devotion's visage
  And pious action we do sugar o'er
  The devil himself.
KING: [*aside*] O, 'tis too true!
  How smart a lash that speech doth give my conscience!   50
  The harlot's cheek, beautied with plast'ring art,
  Is not more ugly to the thing that helps it
  Than is my deed to my most painted word.
  O heavy burden!
POLONIUS: I hear him coming; let's withdraw, my lord.   55
     [*Exeunt* KING *and* POLONIUS.]
     [*Enter* HAMLET.]
HAMLET: To be, or not to be—that is the question;
  Whether 'tis nobler in the mind to suffer
  The slings and arrows of outrageous fortune,
  Or to take arms against a sea of troubles,
  And by opposing end them? To die, to sleep—   60
  No more; and by a sleep to say we end
  The heart-ache and the thousand natural shocks
  That flesh is heir to. 'Tis a consummation
  Devoutly to be wish'd. To die, to sleep;
  To sleep, perchance to dream. Ay, there's the rub;*   65
  For in that sleep of death what dreams may come,
  When we have shuffled off this mortal coil,*
  Must give us pause. There's the respect*
  That makes calamity of so long life;
  For who would bear the whips and scorns of time,   70
  Th' oppressor's wrong, the proud man's contumely,
  The pangs of despis'd love, the law's delay,
  The insolence of office, and the spurns
  That patient merit of th' unworthy takes,
  When he himself might his quietus* make   75

45 **colour** give an excuse for
65 **rub** impediment
67 **shuffled off this mortal coil** separated body from soul
68 **respect** consideration
75 **quietus** end

With a bare bodkin?* Who would these fardels* bear,
To grunt and sweat under a weary life,
But that the dread of something after death —
The undiscover'd country, from whose bourn*
No traveller returns—puzzles the will,   80
And makes us rather bear those ills we have
Than fly to others that we know not of?
Thus conscience does make cowards of us all;
And thus the native hue of resolution
Is sicklied o'er with pale cast* of thought,   85
And enterprises of great pitch and moment,
With this regard, their currents turn awry
And lose the name of action.—Soft you now!
The fair Ophelia.—Nymph, in thy orisons*
Be all my sins rememb'red.
OPHELIA: Good my lord,   90
   How does your honour for this many a day?
HAMLET: I humbly thank you; well, well, well.
OPHELIA: My lord, I have remembrance of yours
   That I have longed to re-deliver.
   I pray you now receive them.
HAMLET: No, not I;   95
   I never gave you aught.
OPHELIA: My honour'd lord, you know right well you did,
   And with them words of so sweet breath compos'd
   As made the things more rich; their perfume lost,
   Take these again; for to the noble mind   100
   Rich gifts wax poor when givers prove unkind.
   There, my lord.
HAMLET: Ha, Ha! Are you honest?*
OPHELIA: My lord?
HAMLET: Are you fair?   105
OPHELIA: What means your lordship?
HAMLET: That if you be honest and fair, your honesty should admit no discourse
   to your beauty.
OPHELIA: Could beauty, my lord, have better commerce than with honesty?
HAMLET: Ay, truly; for the power of beauty will sooner transform honesty from 110
   what it is to a bawd* than the force of honesty can translate beauty into his
   likeness. This was sometime a paradox, but now the time gives it proof. I
   did love you once.
OPHELIA: Indeed, my lord, you made me believe so.

---

[76] **bodkin** dagger
[76] **fardels** burdens
[79] **bourn** region
[85] **cast** color
[89] **orisons** prayers
[103] **are you honest?** are you modest; chaste; truthful
[111] **bawd** procurer

HAMLET: You should not have believ'd me; for virtue cannot so inoculate our old 115
stock but we shall relish of it.* I loved you not.

OPHELIA: I was the more deceived.

HAMLET: Get thee to a nunnery. Why wouldst thou be a breeder of sinners? I am
myself indifferent honest,* but yet I could accuse me of such things that it
were better my mother had not borne me: I am very proud, revengeful, am- 120
bitious; with more offences at my beck than I have thoughts to put them in,
imagination to give them shape, or time to act them in. What should such
fellows as I do crawling between earth and heaven? We are arrant knaves,
all; believe none of us. Go thy ways to a nunnery. Where's your father?

OPHELIA: At home, my lord. 125

HAMLET: Let the doors be shut upon him, that he may play the fool nowhere but
in's own house. Farewell.

OPHELIA: O, help him, you sweet heavens!

HAMLET: If thou dost marry, I'll give thee this plague for thy dowry: be thou as
chaste as ice, as pure as snow, thou shalt not escape calumny. Get thee to a 130
nunnery, go, farewell. Or, if thou wilt needs marry, marry a fool; for wise
men know well enough what monsters* you make of them. To a nunnery
go; and quickly, too. Farewell.

OPHELIA: O heavenly powers, restore him!

HAMLET: I have heard of your paintings, too, well enough; God hath given you 135
one face, and you make yourselves another. You jig and amble, and you lisp,
and nickname God's creatures, and make your wantonness your ignorance.*
Go to, I'll no more on't; it hath made me mad. I say we will have no more
marriage: those that are married already, all but one, shall live; the rest shall
keep as they are. To a nunnery, go. 140
          [*Exit.*]

OPHELIA: O, what a noble mind is here o'erthrown!
The courtier's, soldier's, scholar's, eye, tongue, sword;
Th' expectancy and rose* of the fair state,
The glass of fashion and the mould of form,*
Th' observ'd of all observers—quite, quite down! 145
And I, of ladies most deject and wretched,
That suck'd the honey of his music vows,
Now see that noble and most sovereign reason,
Like sweet bells jangled, out of time and harsh;
That unmatch'd form and feature of blown* youth 150
Blasted with ecstasy.* O, woe is me
T' have seen what I have seen, see what I see!
          [*Reenter* KING *and* POLONIUS.]

---

115 **virtue cannot . . . relish of it** virtue cannot shield us from still desiring sinful pleasures
119 **indifferent honest** modestly virtuous
132 **monsters** cuckolds
137 **make your wantonness your ignorance** excuse your wantonness by pretending ignorance
143 **expectancy and rose** hope
144 **mould of form** pattern of excellent behavior
150 **blown** blooming
151 **ecstasy** madness

KING: Love! His affections do not that way tend;
    Nor what he spake, though it lack'd form a little,
    Was not like madness. There's something in his soul   155
    O'er which his melancholy sits on brood;
    And I do doubt* the hatch and the disclose
    Will be some danger; which to prevent
    I have in quick determination
    Thus set it down: he shall with speed to England   160
    For the demand of our neglected tribute.
    Haply the seas and countries different,
    With variable objects, shall expel
    This something-settled matter in his heart
    Whereon his brains still beating puts him thus   165
    From fashion of himself. What think you on't?
POLONIUS: It shall do well. But yet do I believe
    The origin and commencement of his grief
    Sprung from neglected love. How now, Ophelia!
    You need not tell us what Lord Hamlet said;   170
    We heard it all. My lord, do as you please;
    But if you hold it fit, after the play
    Let his queen mother all alone entreat him
    To show his grief. Let her be round* with him;
    And I'll be placed, so please you, in the ear   175
    Of all their conference. If she find him not,*
    To England send him; or confine him where
    Your wisdom best shall think.
KING: It shall be so:
    Madness in great ones must not unwatch'd go.   180
      [*Exeunt.*]

SCENE II———*Elsinore. The Castle.*

[*Enter* HAMLET *and three of the* PLAYERS.]

HAMLET: Speak the speech, I pray you, as I pronounc'd it to you, trippingly on
the tongue; but if you mouth it, as many of our players do, I had as lief the
towncrier spoke my lines. Nor do not saw the air too much with your hand,
thus, but use all gently; for in the very torrent, tempest, and, as I may say,
whirlwind of your passion, you must acquire and beget a temperance that   5
may give it smoothness. O, it offends me to the soul to hear a robustious
periwig-pated* fellow tear a passion to tatters, to very rags, to split the ears
of the groundlings,* who, for the most part, are capable of nothing* but

---

¹⁵⁷**doubt** fear
¹⁷⁴ **round** blunt
¹⁷⁶ **find him not** doesn't find out what is bothering him
^{III,ii,6–7}**periwig-pated** wig-wearing
⁸**groundlings** spectators who stood in the space surrounding the stage; presumably the poorest and
least-educated spectators
⁸**are capable of nothing** understand nothing

inexplicable dumb shows* and noise. I would have such a fellow whipp'd for
o'erdoing Termagant; it out-herods Herod.* Pray you avoid it.   10

FIRST PLAYER: I warrant your honour.

HAMLET: Be not too tame neither, but let your own discretion be your tutor. Suit
the action to the word, the word to the action; with this special observance,
that you o'erstep not the modesty of nature; for anything so o'erdone is
from* the purpose of playing, whose end, both at the first and now, was and   15
is to hold, as 'twere, the mirror up to nature; to show virtue her own feature,
scorn her own image, and the very age and body of the time his form and
pressure.* Now, this overdone or come tardy off, though it makes the un-
skilful laugh, cannot but make the judicious grieve; the censure of the which
one must, in your allowance, o'erweigh a whole theatre of others. O, there   20
be players that I have seen play—and heard others praise, and that highly—
not to speak it profanely, that, neither having th' accent of Christians, nor
the gait of Christian, pagan, nor man, have so strutted and bellowed that I
have thought some of Nature's journeymen* had made men, and not made
them well, they imitated humanity so abominably.   25

FIRST PLAYER: I hope we have reform'd that indifferently* with us, sir.

HAMLET: O, reform it altogether. And let those that play your clowns speak no
more than is set down for them; for there be of them that will themselves
laugh, to set on some quantity of barren spectators to laugh, too, though in
the meantime some necessary question of the play be then to be considered.   30
That's villainous, and shows a most pitiful ambition in the fool that uses it.
Go, make you ready.

    [*Exeunt* PLAYERS.]

    [*Enter* POLONIUS, ROSENCRANTZ, *and* GUILDENSTERN.]

How now, my lord! Will the King hear this piece of work?

POLONIUS: And the Queen, too, and that presently.

HAMLET: Bid the players make haste.   [*Exit* POLONIUS.]   35

    Will you two help to hasten them?

ROSENCRANTZ: Ay, my lord.   [*Exeunt they two.*]

HAMLET: What, ho, Horatio!

    [*Enter* HORATIO.]

HORATIO: Here, sweet lord, at your service.   40

HAMLET: Horatio, thou art e'en as just a man
    As e'er my conversation cop'd withal.*

HORATIO: O my dear lord!

HAMLET: Nay, do not think I flatter;
    For what advancement may I hope from thee,   45
    That no revenue hast but thy good spirits
    To feed and clothe thee? Why should the poor be flatter'd?

---

⁹ **dumb shows** silent miming (used, as later in this scene, as prologues to plays)
¹⁰ **Termagant ... Herod** exaggeratedly overacted roles in medieval mystery plays
¹⁴ **from** contrary to
¹⁷ **pressure** image
²⁴ **journeymen** workers not yet masters of their craft
²⁶ **indifferently** mostly
⁴² **cop'd withal** met with

No, let the candied* tongue lick absurd pomp,
And crook the pregnant hinges of the knee*
Where thrift* may follow fawning. Dost thou hear?   50
Since my dear soul was mistress of her choice
And could of men distinguish her election,
S'hath seal'd thee* for herself; for thou hast been
As one, in suff'ring all, that suffers nothing;
A man that Fortune's buffets and rewards   55
Hast ta'en with equal thanks; and blest are those
Whose blood* and judgment are so well commingled
That they are not a pipe for Fortune's finger
To sound what stop she please. Give me that man
That is not passion's slave, and I will wear him   60
In my heart's core, ay, in my heart of heart,
As I do thee. Something too much of this.
There is a play to-night before the King;
One scene of it comes near the circumstance
Which I have told thee of my father's death.   65
I prithee, when thou seest that act afoot,
Even with the very comment* of thy soul
Observe my uncle. If his occulted* guilt
Do not itself unkennel in one speech,
It is a damned ghost that we have seen,   70
And my imaginations are as foul
As Vulcan's stithy.* Give him heedful note;
For I mine eyes will rivet to his face;
And, after, we will both our judgments join
In censure of his seeming.*   75
HORATIO: Well, my lord.
    If 'a steal aught the whilst this play is playing,
    And 'scape detecting, I will pay the theft.
        [*Enter trumpets and kettledrums. Danish march. Sound a flourish. Enter*
        KING, QUEEN, POLONIUS, OPHELIA, ROSENCRANTZ, GUILDENSTERN, *and*
        other LORDS *attendant, with the guard carrying torches.*]
HAMLET: They are coming to the play; I must be idle.*
    Get you a place.   80
KING: How fares our cousin Hamlet?

---

[48] **candied** sugared, flattering
[49] **pregnant hinges of the knee** quick to curtsy and kneel
[50] **thrift** profit
[53] **S'hath seal'd thee** my soul has chosen you
[57] **blood** feelings
[67] **very comment** deepest wisdom
[68] **occulted** hidden
[72] **Vulcan's stithy** forge of the Greek god
[75] **censure of his seeming** judgment on his response
[79] **be idle** play the fool

HAMLET: Excellent, i' faith; of the chameleon's dish.* I eat the air promise-cramm'd; you cannot feed capons so.

KING: I have nothing with this answer, Hamlet; these words are not mine.

HAMLET: No, nor mine now. [*to* POLONIUS] My lord, you play'd once in th' uni- 85
versity, you say?

POLONIUS: That did I, my lord, and was accounted a good actor.

HAMLET: What did you enact?

POLONIUS: I did enact Julius Caesar; I was kill'd i' th' Capitol; Brutus kill'd me.

HAMLET: It was a brute part of him to kill so capital a calf there. Be the players 90
ready?

ROSENCRANTZ: Ay, my lord; they stay upon your patience.

QUEEN: Come hither, my dear Hamlet, sit by me.

HAMLET: No, good mother; here's metal more attractive.*

POLONIUS: [*to the* KING] O, ho! do you mark that?

HAMLET: Lady, shall I lie in your lap? [*lying down at* OPHELIA's *feet*] 95

OPHELIA: No, my lord.

HAMLET: I mean, my head upon your lap?

OPHELIA: Ay, my lord.

HAMLET: Do you think I meant country matters?*

OPHELIA: I think nothing, my lord. 100

HAMLET: That's a fair thought to lie between maids' legs.

OPHELIA: What is, my lord?

HAMLET: Nothing.

OPHELIA: You are merry, my lord.

HAMLET: Who, I? 105

OPHELIA: Ay, my lord.

HAMLET: O God, your only jig-maker!* What should a man do but be merry?
For look you how cheerfully my mother looks, and my father died within's
two hours.

OPHELIA: Nay, 'tis twice two months, my lord. 110

HAMLET: So long? Nay then, let the devil wear black, for I'll have a suit of sables.
O heavens! die two months ago, and not forgotten yet? Then there's hope a
great man's memory may outlive his life half a year; but, by'r lady, 'a must
build churches, then; or else shall 'a suffer not thinking on, with the hobby-
horse,* whose epitaph is 'For O, for O, the hobby-horse is forgot!' 115

[*The trumpet sounds. Hautboys play. The Dumb Show enters.*]
[*Enter a* KING *and a* QUEEN, *very lovingly; the* QUEEN *embracing him and
he her. She kneels, and makes a show of protestation unto him. He takes her
up, and declines his head upon her neck. He lies him down upon a bank
of flowers; she, seeing him asleep, leaves him. Anon comes in a* FELLOW, *takes
off his crown, kisses it, pours poison in the sleeper's ears, and leaves him.
The* QUEEN *returns; finds the* KING *dead, and makes passionate action. The*

---

⁸²**chameleon's dish** air (on which chameleons were thought to live)

⁹³**attractive** magnetic

⁹⁹**country matters** (a sexual innuendo)

¹⁰⁷**jig-maker** composer of songs and dances (jigs were often performed as afterpieces in the theatre,
and often by the fool)

¹¹⁴**hobby-horse** mock horse worn by a performer in mummers plays

POISONER, *with some two or three* MUTES, *comes in again, seeming to condole with her. The dead body is carried away. The* POISONER *woos the* QUEEN *with gifts: she seems harsh awhile, but in the end accepts his love. Exeunt.*]

OPHELIA: What means this, my lord?

HAMLET: Marry, this is miching mallecho;* it means mischief.

OPHELIA: Belike this show imports the argument* of the play.
[*Enter* PROLOGUE.]

HAMLET: We shall know by this fellow: the players cannot keep counsel; they'll   120
tell all.

OPHELIA: Will 'a tell us what this show meant?

HAMLET: Ay, or any show that you show him. Be not you asham'd to show, he'll
not shame to tell you what it means.

OPHELIA: You are naught, you are naught.* I'll mark the play.

PROLOGUE: *For us, and for our tragedy,*   125
   Here stooping to your clemency,
   We beg your hearing patiently.
   [*Exit.*]

HAMLET: Is this a prologue, or the posy of a ring?*

OPHELIA: 'Tis brief, my lord.

HAMLET: As woman's love.   130
[*Enter the* PLAYER KING *and* QUEEN.]

PLAYER KING: *Full thirty times hath Phoebus' cart* gone round*
   Neptune's salt wash and Tellus'* orbed ground,*
   And thirty dozen moons with borrowed sheen
   About the world have times twelve thirties been,
   Since love our hearts and Hymen did our hands*   135
   Unite comutual in most sacred bands.

PLAYER QUEEN: *So many journeys may the sun and moon*
   Make us again count o'er ere love be done!
   But, woe is me, you are so sick of late,
   So far from cheer and from your former state,   140
   That I distrust you. Yet, though I distrust,*
   Discomfort you, my lord, it nothing must;
   For women fear too much even as they love,
   And women's fear and love hold quantity,
   In neither aught, or in extremity.   145
   Now, what my love is, proof hath made you know;
   And as my love is siz'd, my fear is so.

---

[117] **miching mallecho** sneaky mischief
[118] **argument** plot
[124] **naught** naughty
[128] **posy of a ring** sentiment inscribed in a ring
[131] **Phoebus' cart** the sun god's chariot
[132] **Neptune's salt wash** the sea
[132] **Tellus** Roman goddess of the Earth
[135] **Hymen** god of marriage
[141] **distrust** am anxious about

> *Where love is great, the littlest doubts are fear;*
> *Where little fears grow great, great love grows there.*

PLAYER KING: *Faith, I must leave thee, love, and shortly, too:* 150
> *My operant* powers their functions leave to do;*
> *And thou shalt live in this fair world behind,*
> *Honour'd, belov'd; and haply one as kind*
> *For husband shalt thou—*

PLAYER QUEEN: *O, confound the rest!* 155
> *Such love must needs be treason in my breast.*
> *In second husband let me be accurst!*
> *None wed the second but who kill'd the first.*

HAMLET: That's wormwood, wormwood.*

PLAYER QUEEN: *The instances* that second marriage move** 160
> *Are base respects of thrift,* but none of love.*
> *A second time I kill my husband dead,*
> *When second husband kisses me in bed.*

PLAYER KING: *I do believe you think what now you speak;*
> *But what we do determine oft we break.* 165
> *Purpose is but the slave to memory,*
> *Of violent birth, but poor validity;**
> *Which now, the fruit unripe, sticks on the tree;*
> *But fall unshaken when they mellow be.*
> *Most necessary 'tis that we forget* 170
> *To pay ourselves what to ourselves is debt.*
> *What to ourselves in passion we propose,*
> *The passion ending, doth the purpose lose.*
> *The violence of either grief or joy*
> *Their own enactures* with themselves destroy.* 175
> *Where joy most revels grief doth most lament;*
> *Grief joys, joy grieves, on slender accident.*
> *This world is not for aye; nor 'tis not strange*
> *That even our loves should with our fortunes change;*
> *For 'tis a question left us yet to prove,* 180
> *Whether love lead fortune or else fortune love.*
> *The great man down, you mark his favourite flies;*
> *The poor advanc'd makes friends of enemies.*
> *And hitherto doth love on fortune tend;*
> *For who not needs shall never lack a friend,* 185
> *And who in want a hollow friend doth try,*
> *Directly seasons* him his enemy.*

---

[151] **operant** active
[159] **wormwood** a bitter herb
[160] **instances** motives
[160] **move** induce
[161] **base respects of thrift** considerations of profit
[167] **validity** strength
[175] **enactures** acts
[187] **seasons** ripens him into

> But, orderly to end where I begun,
> Our wills and fates do so contrary run
> That our devices still are overthrown;   190
> Our thoughts are ours, their ends none of our own.
> So think thou wilt no second husband wed;
> But die thy thoughts when thy first lord is dead.

PLAYER QUEEN: Nor earth to me give food, nor heaven light,
> Sport and repose lock from me day and night,   195
> To desperation turn my trust and hope,
> An anchor's* cheer in prison be my scope,
> Each opposite that blanks* the face of joy
> Meet what I would have well, and it destroy,
> Both here and hence pursue my lasting strife,   200
> If, once a widow, ever I be wife!

HAMLET: If she should break it now!

PLAYER KING: 'Tis deeply sworn. Sweet, leave me here awhile;
> My spirits grow dull, and fain I would beguile
> The tedious day with sleep.   [Sleeps.] 205

PLAYER QUEEN: Sleep rock thy brain,
> And never come mischance between us twain!

HAMLET: Madam, how like you this play?

QUEEN: The lady doth protest too much, methinks.

HAMLET: O, but she'll keep her word.   210

KING: Have you heard the argument?* Is there no offence in't?

HAMLET: No, no; they do but jest, poison in jest; no offence i' th' world.

KING: What do you call the play?

HAMLET: 'The Mouse-trap.' Marry, how? Tropically.* This play is the image of a murder done in Vienna: Gonzago is the duke's name; his wife, Baptista. 215 You shall see anon. 'Tis a knavish piece of work; but what of that? Your Majesty, and we that have free* souls, it touches us not. Let the galled jade* wince, our withers are unwrung.
> [Enter LUCIANUS.]
> This is one Lucianus, nephew to the King.

OPHELIA: You are as good as a chorus, my lord.   220

HAMLET: I could interpret* between you and your love, if I could see the puppets dallying.

OPHELIA: You are keen, my lord, you are keen.

HAMLET: It would cost you a groaning to take off mine edge.*

OPHELIA: Still better, and worse.   225

---

¹⁹⁷ **anchor's** anchorite, hermit
¹⁹⁸ **opposite that blanks** adverse thing that makes the face blanch
²¹¹ **argument** plot
²¹⁴ **tropically** figuratively
²¹⁷ **free** souls free of guilt
²¹⁷ **galled jade** chafed horse
²²¹ **interpret** explain like a puppet master if he could see the puppets playing wantonly
²²⁴ **cost . . . edge** (a sexual reference)

HAMLET: So you mis-take* your husbands.—Begin, murderer; pox, leave thy 225
damnable faces and begin. Come; the croaking raven doth bellow for
revenge.

LUCIANUS: *Thoughts black, hands apt, drugs fit, and time agreeing;*
Confederate season,* else no creature seeing;
Thou mixture rank, of midnight weeds collected, 230
With Hecate's ban* thrice blasted, thrice infected.
Thy natural magic and dire property*
On wholesome life usurps immediately.
[*Pours the poison in his ears.*]

HAMLET: 'A poisons him i' th' garden for his estate. His name's Gonzago. The
story is extant, and written in very choice Italian. You shall see anon how 235
the murderer gets the love of Gonzago's wife.

OPHELIA: The King rises.

HAMLET: What, frighted with false fire!*

QUEEN: How fares my lord?

POLONIUS: Give o'er the play. 240

KING: Give me some light. Away!

POLONIUS: Lights, lights, lights!
[*Exeunt all but* HAMLET *and* HORATIO.]

HAMLET: Why, let the strucken deer go weep,
The hart ungalled play;
For some must watch, while some must sleep; 245
Thus runs the world away.
Would not this, sir, and a forest of feathers*—if the rest of my fortunes turn
Turk* with me—with two Provincial roses on my raz'd shoes,* get me a fel-
lowship in a cry of players,* sir?

HORATIO: Half a share. 250

HAMLET: A whole one, I.
For thou dost know, O Damon dear,
This realm dismantled was
Of Jove himself; and now reigns here
A very, very—peacock. 255

HORATIO: You might have rhym'd.

HAMLET: O good Horatio, I'll take the ghost's word for a thousand pound. Didst
perceive?

HORATIO: Very well, my lord.

HAMLET: Upon the talk of the poisoning. 260

HORATIO: I did very well note him.

---

²²⁶ **mis-take** err in taking
²²⁹ **confederate season** the opportunity offered me
²³¹ **Hecate's ban** the goddess of sorcery's curse
²³² **property** nature
²³⁸ **false fire** blank firing of a gun
²⁴⁷ **forest of feathers** costume with feathers
²⁴⁸ **turn Turk** go badly
²⁴⁸ **raz'd shoes** shoes ornamented with slashes
²⁴⁹ **cry of players** company of actors

HAMLET: Ah, ha! Come, some music. Come, the recorders.
    For if the King like not the comedy,
    Why, then, belike he likes it not, perdy.*
    Come, some music.   265
            [*Reenter* ROSENCRANTZ *and* GUILDENSTERN.]
GUILDENSTERN: Good my lord, vouchsafe me a word with you.
HAMLET: Sir, a whole history.
GUILDENSTERN: The King, sir—
HAMLET: Ay, sir, what of him?
GUILDENSTERN: Is, in his retirement, marvellous distemp'red.   270
HAMLET: With drink, sir?
GUILDENSTERN: No, my lord, rather with choler.*
HAMLET: Your wisdom should show itself more richer to signify this to his doc-
    tor; for for me to put him to his purgation would perhaps plunge him into
    far more choler.   275
GUILDENSTERN: Good my lord, put your discourse into some frame,* and start
    not so wildly from my affair.
HAMLET: I am tame, sir. Pronounce.
GUILDENSTERN: The Queen, your mother, in most great affliction of spirit, hath
    sent me to you.   280
HAMLET: You are welcome.
GUILDENSTERN: Nay, good my lord, this courtesy is not of the right breed. If it
    shall please you to make me a wholesome answer, I will do your mother's
    commandment; if not, your pardon and my return shall be the end of my
    business.   285
HAMLET: Sir, I cannot.
ROSENCRANTZ: What, my lord?
HAMLET: Make you a wholesome* answer; my wit's diseas'd. But, sir, such answer
    as I can make, you shall command: or rather, as you say, my mother. There-
    fore no more, but to the matter: my mother, you say—
ROSENCRANTZ: Then thus she says: your behaviour hath struck her into amaze-   290
    ment and admiration.*
HAMLET: O wonderful son, that can so stonish a mother! But is there no sequel
    at the heels of this mother's admiration? Impart.
ROSENCRANTZ: She desires to speak with you in her closet ere you go to bed.
HAMLET: We shall obey, were she ten times our mother. Have you any further   295
    trade with us?
ROSENCRANTZ: My lord, you once did love me.
HAMLET: And do still, by these pickers and stealers.*
ROSENCRANTZ: Good my lord, what is your cause of distemper? You do surely bar
    the door upon your own liberty, if you deny your griefs to your friend.   300

---

²⁶⁴ **perdy** by God (par dieu)
²⁷² **choler** anger
²⁷⁶ **frame** order, control
²⁸⁷ **wholesome** sane
²⁹¹ **admiration** wonder
²⁹⁸ **pickers and stealers** hands

HAMLET: Sir, I lack advancement.*

ROSENCRANTZ: How can that be, when you have the voice of the King himself for your succession in Denmark?

HAMLET: Ay, sir, but 'While the grass grows'—the proverb* is something musty. [*Reenter the* PLAYERS, *with recorders.*]

O, the recorders! Let me see one. To withdraw* with you—why do you go 305 about to recover the wind of me,* as if you would drive me into a toil?*

GUILDENSTERN: O my lord, if my duty be too bold, my love is too unmannerly.*

HAMLET: I do not well understand that. Will you play upon this pipe?

GUILDENSTERN: My lord, I cannot.

HAMLET: I pray you. 310

GUILDENSTERN: Believe me, I cannot.

HAMLET: I do beseech you.

GUILDENSTERN: I know no touch of it, my lord.

HAMLET: It is as easy as lying: govern these ventages* with your fingers and thumb, give it breath with your mouth, and it will discourse most eloquent 315 music. Look you, these are the stops.

GUILDENSTERN: But these cannot I command to any utterance of harmony; I have not the skill.

HAMLET: Why, look you now, how unworthy a thing you make of me! You would play upon me; you would seem to know my stops; you would pluck out the 320 heart of my mystery; you would sound me from my lowest note to the top of my compass;* and there is much music, excellent voice, in this little organ,* yet cannot you make it speak. 'Sblood, do you think I am easier to be play'd on than a pipe? Call me what instrument you will, though you can fret me, yet you cannot play upon me. 325
[*Reenter* POLONIUS.]

God bless you, sir!

POLONIUS: My lord, the Queen would speak with you, and presently.

HAMLET: Do you see yonder cloud that's almost in shape of a camel?

POLONIUS: By th' mass, and 'tis like a camel indeed.

HAMLET: Methinks it is like a weasel. 330

POLONIUS: It is back'd like a weasel.

HAMLET: Or like a whale?

POLONIUS: Very like a whale.

HAMLET: Then I will come to my mother by and by. [*aside*] They fool me to the top of my bent.*—I will come by and by. 335

---

301 **advancement** promotion

304 **proverb** (the rest of the proverb is "the horse starveth")

305 **withdraw** speak privately

306 **recover the wind of me** get on the windward side of me

306 **toil** snare

307 **duty . . . unmannerly** if I have seemed rude it is because my love for you leads me beyond good manners

314 **ventages** vents, stops on a musical instrument

322 **compass** range

322 **organ** the recorder

334–35 **fool me . . . my bent** they force me to play the fool to the fullest

POLONIUS: I will say so.   [*Exit* POLONIUS.]
HAMLET: 'By and by' is easily said. Leave me, friends.
    [*Exeunt all but* HAMLET.]
    'Tis now the very witching time of night,
    When churchyards yawn, and hell itself breathes out
    Contagion to this world. Now could I drink hot blood,   340
    And do such bitter business as the day
    Would quake to look on. Soft! now to my mother.
    O heart, lose not thy nature; let not ever
    The soul of Nero* enter this firm bosom.
    Let me be cruel, not unnatural: 345
    I will speak daggers to her, but use none.
    My tongue and soul in this be hypocrites—
    How in my words somever she be shent,*
    To give them seals* never, my soul, consent!
    [*Exit.*]

SCENE III——*Elsinore. The Castle.*

    [*Enter* KING, ROSENCRANTZ, *and* GUILDENSTERN.]
KING: I like him not; nor stands it safe with us
    To let his madness range. Therefore prepare you;
    I your commission will forthwith dispatch,
    And he to England shall along with you.
    The terms* of our estate may not endure   5
    Hazard so near's as doth hourly grow
    Out of his brows.
GUILDENSTERN: We will ourselves provide.
    Most holy and religious fear it is
    To keep those many many bodies safe   10
    That live and feed upon your Majesty.
ROSENCRANTZ: The single and peculiar* life is bound
    With all the strength and armour of the mind
    To keep itself from noyance;* but much more
    That spirit upon whose weal depends and rests   15
    The lives of many. The cease of majesty
    Dies not alone, but like a gulf* doth draw
    What's near it with it. It is a massy wheel,
    Fix'd on the summit of the highest mount,
    To whose huge spokes ten thousand lesser things   20
    Are mortis'd and adjoin'd; which when it falls,
    Each small annexment, petty consequence,

344 **Nero** Roman emperor who killed his mother
348 **shent** rebuked
349 **give them seals** confirm them with deeds
III,iii,5 **terms** conditions
12 **peculiar** private
14 **noyance** injury
17**gulf** whirlpool

       Attends the boist'rous ruin. Never alone
       Did the king sigh, but with a general groan.
KING: Arm* you, I pray you, to this speedy voyage;
       For we will fetters put about this fear,   25
       Which now goes too free-footed.
ROSENCRANTZ: We will haste us.
           [*Exeunt* ROSENCRANTZ *and* GUILDENSTERN.]
           [*Enter* POLONIUS.]
POLONIUS: My lord, he's going to his mother's closet.
       Behind the arras I'll convey myself   30
       To hear the process.* I'll warrant she'll tax him home;*
       And, as you said, and wisely was it said,
       'Tis meet that some more audience than a mother,
       Since nature makes them partial, should o'erhear
       The speech, of vantage.* Fare you well, my liege.   35
       I'll call upon you ere you go to bed,
       And tell you what I know.
KING: Thanks, dear my lord.   [*Exit* POLONIUS.]
       O, my offence is rank, it smells to heaven;
       It hath the primal eldest curse* upon't—   40
       A brother's murder! Pray can I not,
       Though inclination be as sharp as will.
       My stronger guilt defeats my strong intent,
       And, like a man to double business bound,
       I stand in pause where I shall first begin,   45
       And both neglect. What if this cursed hand
       Were thicker than itself with brother's blood,
       Is there not rain enough in the sweet heavens
       To wash it white as snow? Whereto serves mercy
       But to confront the visage of offence?   50
       And what's in prayer but this twofold force,
       To be forestalled ere we come to fall,
       Or pardon'd being down? Then I'll look up;
       My fault is past. But, O, what form of prayer
       Can serve my turn? 'Forgive me my foul murder'!   55
       That cannot be; since I am still possess'd
       Of those effects* for which I did the murder—
       My crown, mine own ambition, and my queen.
       May one be pardon'd and retain th' offence?
       In the corrupted currents of this world   60
       Offence's gilded hand may shove by justice;
       And oft 'tis seen the wicked prize itself

[24] **arm** prepare
[31] **process** proceedings
[31] **tax him home** rebuke him sharply
[35] **of vantage** from some advantageous place
[40] **primal eldest curse** oldest curse (Cain's murder of his brother Abel)
[57] **effects** things gained

Buys out the law. But 'tis not so above:
There is no shuffling;* there the action lies
In his true nature; and we ourselves compell'd,   65
Even to the teeth and forehead of our faults,
To give in evidence. What then? What rests?*
Try what repentance can. What can it not?
Yet what can it when one cannot repent?
O wretched state! O bosom black as death!   70
O limed* soul, that, struggling to be free,
Art more engag'd!* Help, angels. Make assay:
Bow, stubborn knees; and, heart, with strings of steel,
Be soft as sinews of the new-born babe.
All may be well.   [*He kneels.*] 75
       [*Enter* HAMLET.]
HAMLET: Now might I do it pat, now 'a is a-praying;
And now I'll do't—and so 'a goes to heaven,
And so am I reveng'd. That would be scann'd.*
A villain kills my father; and for that,   80
I, his sole son, do this same villain send
To heaven.
Why, this is hire and salary, not revenge.
'A took my father grossly, full of bread,*
With all his crimes broad blown, as flush* as May;   85
And how his audit* stands who knows save heaven?
But in our circumstance and course of thought
'Tis heavy with him; and am I then reveng'd
To take him in the purging of his soul,
When he is fit and season'd for his passage?   90
No.
Up, sword, and know thou a more horrid hent.
When he is drunk asleep, or in his rage;
Or in th' incestuous pleasure of his bed;
At game, a-swearing, or about some act   95
That has no relish of salvation in't—
Then trip him, that his heels my kick at heaven,
And that his soul may be as damn'd and black
As hell, whereto it goes. My mother stays.
This physic* but prolongs thy sickly days.   [*Exit.*] 100
KING: [*rising*] My words fly up, my thoughts remain below.
Words without thoughts never to heaven go.   [*Exit.*]

Handwritten marginal notes:
regicide = decide
wants and knows is not well

---

64 **shuffling** trickery
67 **rests** remains
71 **limed** trapped (birds were caught by liming tree limbs with a sticky substance)
72 **engag'd** entrapped
79 **would be scann'd** needs to be thought about
84 **full of bread** worldly gratifications
85 **crimes . . . flush** sins in full bloom as flowers in May
86 **audit** account
100 **physic** (to Claudius) this medicine (prayer)

SCENE IV——— *The* QUEEN'*s closet.*

[*Enter* QUEEN *and* POLONIUS.]

POLONIUS: 'A will come straight. Look you lay home* to him;
Tell him his pranks have been too broad* to bear with,
And that your Grace hath screen'd and stood between
Much heat and him. I'll silence me even here.
Pray you be round with him.   5

HAMLET: [*within*] Mother, mother, mother!

QUEEN: I'll warrant you. Fear me not.
Withdraw, I hear him coming.
[POLONIUS *goes behind the arras.*]
[*Enter* HAMLET.]

HAMLET: Now, mother, what's the matter?   10

QUEEN: Hamlet, thou hast thy father much offended.

HAMLET: Mother, you have my father much offended.

QUEEN: Come, come, you answer with an idle* tongue.

HAMLET: Go, go, you question with a wicked tongue.

QUEEN: Why, how now, Hamlet!   15

HAMLET: What's the matter now?

QUEEN: Have you forgot me?

HAMLET: No, by the rood,* not so:
You are the Queen, your husband's brother's wife;
And—would it were not so!—you are my mother.   20

QUEEN: Nay then, I'll set those to you that can speak.

HAMLET: Come, come, and sit you down; you shall not budge.
You go not till I set you up a glass*
Where you may see the inmost part of you.

QUEEN: What wilt thou do? Thou wilt not murder me?   25
Help, help, ho!

POLONIUS: [*behind*] What, ho! help, help, help!

HAMLET: [*draws*] How now! a rat?
Dead, for a ducat, dead!
[*kills* POLONIUS *with a pass through the arras*]

POLONIUS: [*behind*] O, I am slain!   30

QUEEN: O me, what hast thou done?

HAMLET: Nay, I know not:
Is it the King?

QUEEN: O, what a rash and bloody deed is this!

HAMLET: A bloody deed!—almost as bad, good mother,   35
As kill a king and marry with his brother.

QUEEN: As kill a king!

HAMLET: Ay, lady, it was my word. [*parting the arras*]
Thou wretched, rash, intruding fool, farewell!

III,iv,1 **lay home** rebuke him sharply
2 **broad** unrestrained
13 **idle** foolish
18 **rood** cross
23 **glass** mirror

I took thee for thy better. Take thy fortune;   40
Thou find'st to be too busy is some danger.
Leave wringing of your hands. Peace; sit you down,
And let me wring your heart; for so I shall,
If it be made of penetrable stuff;
If damned custom have not braz'd* it so   45
That it be proof and bulwark against sense.*

QUEEN: What have I done that thou dar'st wag thy tongue
       In noise so rude against me?

HAMLET: Such an act
       That blurs the grace and blush of modesty;   50
       Calls virtue hypocrite; takes off the rose
       From the fair forehead of an innocent love,
       And sets a blister there,* makes marriage-vows
       As false as dicers' oaths. O, such a deed
       As from the body of contraction* plucks   55
       The very soul, and sweet religion makes
       A rhapsody* of words. Heaven's face does glow
       O'er this solidity and compound mass
       With heated visage, as against the doom—
       Is thought-sick at the act.   60

QUEEN: Ay me, what act,
       That roars so loud and thunders in the index?*

HAMLET: Look here upon this picture and on this,
       The counterfeit presentment* of two brothers.
       See what a grace was seated on this brow;   65
       Hyperion's curls; the front* of Jove himself;
       An eye like Mars, to threaten and command;
       A station* like the herald Mercury
       New lighted on a heaven-kissing hill—
       A combination and a form indeed   70
       Where every god did seem to set his seal,
       To give the world assurance of a man.
       This was your husband. Look you now what follows:
       Here is your husband, like a mildew'd ear
       Blasting his wholesome brother. Have you eyes?   75
       Could you on this fair mountain leave to feed,
       And batten* on this moor? Ha! have you eyes?
       You cannot call it love; for at your age

---

⁴⁵ **braz'd** hardened
⁴⁶ **proof . . . sense** armored against feeling
⁵³ **sets a blister** brands (as a harlot)
⁵⁵ **contraction** marriage contract
⁵⁷ **rhapsody** senseless string
⁶² **index** prologue
⁶⁴ **counterfeit presentment** represented image
⁶⁶ **front** forehead
⁶⁸ **station** bearing
⁷⁷ **batten** feed gluttonously

The heyday in the blood is tame, it's humble,
And waits upon the judgment; and what judgment   80
Would step from this to this? Sense, sure, you have,
Else could you not have motion; but sure that sense
Is apoplex'd;* for madness would not err,
Nor sense to ecstasy* was ne'er so thrall'd
But it reserv'd some quantity of choice   85
To serve in such a difference. What devil was't
That thus hath cozen'd you at hoodman-blind?*
Eyes without feeling, feeling without sight.
Ears without hands or eyes, smelling sans* all,
Or but a sickly part of one true sense   90
Could not so mope.* O shame! where is thy blush?
Rebellious hell,
If thou canst mutine in a matron's bones,
To flaming youth let virtue be as wax
And melt in her own fire; proclaim no shame
When the compulsive ardour gives the charge,   95
Since frost itself as actively doth burn,
And reason panders will.*

QUEEN: O Hamlet, speak no more!
Thou turn'st my eyes into my very soul;   100
And there I see such black and grained spots
As will not leave their tinct.*

HAMLET: Nay, but to live
In the rank sweat of an enseamed* bed,
Stew'd in corruption, honeying and making love   105
Over the nasty sty!

QUEEN: O, speak to me no more!
These words like daggers enter in my ears;
No more, sweet Hamlet.

HAMLET: A murderer and a villain!   110
A slave that is not twentieth part the tithe*
Of your precedent lord; a vice* of kings;
A cutpurse of the empire and the rule,
That from a shelf the precious diadem stole
And put it in his pocket!   115

QUEEN: No more!

---

[83] **apoplex'd** paralyzed
[84] **ecstasy** madness
[87] **hoodman-blind** cheated you at blindman's buff
[89] **sans** without
[91] **so mope** be so stupid
[98] **reason panders will** reason acts as a panderer for desire
[102] **tinct** color
[104] **enseamed** rumpled
[111] **tithe** tenth part
[112] **vice** wicked character in medieval plays

[*Enter* GHOST.]

HAMLET: A king of shreds and patches—
　　　Save me, and hover o'er me with your wings,
　　　You heavenly guards! What would your gracious figure?

QUEEN: Alas, he's mad!   120

HAMLET: Do you not come your tardy son to chide,
　　　That, laps'd in time and passion, lets go by
　　　Th' important acting of your dread command?
　　　O, say!

GHOST: Do not forget; this visitation   125
　　　Is but to whet thy almost blunted purpose.
　　　But look, amazement on thy mother sits.
　　　O, step between her and her fighting soul!
　　　Conceit* in weakest bodies strongest works.
　　　Speak to her, Hamlet.   130

HAMLET: How is it with you, lady?

QUEEN: Alas, how is't with you,
　　　That you do bend your eye on vacancy,
　　　And with th' incorporal* air do hold discourse?
　　　Forth at your eyes and spirits wildly peep;   135
　　　And, as the sleeping soldiers in th' alarm,
　　　Your bedded* hairs like life in excrements*
　　　Start up and stand an end. O gentle son,
　　　Upon the heat and flame of thy distemper
　　　Sprinkle cool patience! Whereon do you look?   140

HAMLET: On him, on him! Look you how pale he glares.
　　　His form and cause conjoin'd, preaching to stones,
　　　Would make them capable.*—Do not look upon me,
　　　Lest with this piteous action you convert
　　　My stern effects;* then what I have to do   145
　　　Will want true colour—tears perchance for blood.

QUEEN: To whom do you speak this?

HAMLET: Do you see nothing there?

QUEEN: Nothing at all; yet all that is I see.

HAMLET: Nor did you nothing hear?   150

QUEEN: No, nothing but ourselves.

HAMLET: Why, look you there. Look how it steals away.
　　　My father, in his habit* as he liv'd!
　　　Look where he goes even now out at the portal.
　　　　　[*Exit* GHOST.]

129 **conceit** imagination
134 **incorporal** empty, bodiless
137 **bedded** flat-lying
137 **excrements** outgrowths
143 **capable** receptive
145 **convert my stern effects** divert my serious purpose
153 **habit** garment

QUEEN: This is the very coinage of your brain.   155
    This bodiless creation ecstasy
    Is very cunning in.
HAMLET: Ecstasy!
    My pulse as yours doth temperately keep time.
    And makes as healthful music. It is not madness   160
    That I have utt'red. Bring me to the test,
    And I the matter will re-word which madness
    Would gambol* from. Mother, for love of grace,
    Lay not that flattering unction* to your soul,
    That not your trespass but my madness speaks: 165
    It will but skin and film the ulcerous place,
    Whiles rank corruption, mining* all within,
    Infects unseen. Confess yourself to heaven;
    Repent what's past; avoid what is to come;
    And do not spread the compost on the weeds,   170
    To make them ranker. Forgive me this my virtue;
    For in the fatness of these pursy* times
    Virtue itself of vice must pardon beg,
    Yea, curb* and woo for leave to do him good.   175
QUEEN: O Hamlet, thou hast cleft my heart in twain.
HAMLET: O, throw away the worser part of it,
    And live the purer with the other half.
    Good night—but go not to my uncle's bed;
    Assume a virtue, if you have it not.
    That monster custom, who all sense doth eat,   180
    Of habits devil, is angel yet in this,
    That to the use* of actions fair and good
    He likewise gives a frock or livery
    That aptly is put on. Refrain to-night;
    And that shall lend a kind of easiness   185
    To the next abstinence; the next more easy;
    For use almost can change the stamp of nature,
    And either curb the devil, or throw him out,
    With wondrous potency. Once more, good night;
    And when you are desirous to be blest,   190
    I'll blessing beg of you. For this same lord
    I do repent; but Heaven hath pleas'd it so,
    To punish me with this, and this with me,
    That I must be their scourge and minister.
    I will bestow him, and will answer well   195

[163] **gambol** start away
[164] **unction** ointment
[167] **mining** undermining
[172] **pursy** bloated
[174] **curb** bow low
[182] **use** practice

The death I gave him. So, again, good night.
I must be cruel only to be kind;
Thus bad begins and worse remains behind.
One word more, good lady.
QUEEN: What shall I do?
HAMLET: Not this, by no means, that I bid you do: 200
Let the bloat King tempt you again to bed;
Pinch wanton on your cheek; call you his mouse;
And let him, for a pair of reechy* kisses,
Or paddling in your neck with his damn'd fingers,   205
Make you to ravel all this matter out,
That I essentially am not in madness,
But mad in craft. 'Twere good you let him know;
For who that's but a queen, fair, sober, wise,
Would from a paddock,* from a bat, a gib,*
Such dear concernings hide? Who would do so?   210
No, in despite of sense and secrecy,
Unpeg the basket on the house's top,
Let the birds fly, and, like the famous ape,
To try conclusions,* in the basket creep   215
And break your own neck down.
QUEEN: Be thou assur'd, if words be made of breath
And breath of life, I have no life to breathe
What thou hast said to me.
HAMLET: I must to England; you know that?   220
QUEEN: Alack,
I had forgot. 'Tis so concluded on.
HAMLET: There's letters seal'd; and my two school-fellows,
Whom I will trust as I will adders fang'd—
They bear the mandate;* they must sweep my way   225
And marshal me to knavery. Let it work;
For 'tis the sport to have the engineer
Hoist with his own petar;* and't shall go hard
But I will delve one yard below their mines
And blow them at the moon, O, 'tis most sweet   230
When in one line two crafts* directly meet.
This man shall set me packing.
I'll lug the guts into the neighbour room.
Mother, good night. Indeed, this counsellor
Is now most still, most secret, and most grave,   235

204 **reechy** foul
209 **paddock** toad
209 **gib** tomcat
215 **try conclusions** make experiments
225 **mandate** command
228 **petar** bomb
231 **crafts** intrigues

Who was in life a foolish prating knave.
Come, sir, to draw toward an end with you.
Good night, mother.
  [*Exeunt severally;* HAMLET *tugging in* POLONIUS.]

ACT IV

SCENE I———*Elsinore. The Castle.*

[*Enter* KING, QUEEN, ROSENCRANTZ, *and* GUILDENSTERN.]
KING: There's matter in these sighs, these profound heaves,
 You must translate; 'tis fit we understand them.
 Where is your son?
QUEEN: Bestow this place on us a little while.
  [*Exeunt* ROSENCRANTZ *and* GUILDENSTERN.]
 Ah, mine own lord, what have I seen to-night!   5
KING: What, Gertrude? How does Hamlet?
QUEEN: Mad as the sea and wind, when both contend
 Which is the mightier. In his lawless fit,
 Behind the arras hearing something stir,
 Whips out his rapier, cries 'A rat, a rat!'   10
 And in this brainish apprehension* kills
 The unseen good old man.
KING: O heavy deed!
 It had been so with us had we been there.
 His liberty is full of threats to all—   15
 To you yourself, to us, to every one.
 Alas, how shall this bloody deed be answer'd?
 It will be laid to us, whose providence*
 Should have kept short, restrain'd, and out of haunt,*
 This mad young man. But so much was our love,   20
 We would not understand what was most fit;
 But, like the owner of a foul disease,
 To keep it from divulging, let it feed
 Even on the pith of life. Where is he gone?
QUEEN: To draw apart the body he hath kill'd;   25
 O'er whom his very madness, like some ore
 Among a mineral of metals base,*
 Shows itself pure: 'a weeps for what is done.
KING: O Gertrude, come away!
 The sun no sooner shall the mountains touch   30
 But we will ship him hence; and this vile deed
 We must with all our majesty and skill
 Both countenance and excuse. Ho Guildenstern!

IV,i,11 **brainish apprehension** mad imagination
18 **providence** foresight
19 **out of haunt** away from association with others
26–27 **ore . . . base** like gold among baser metals

[*Reenter* ROSENCRANTZ *and* GUILDENSTERN.]
Friends, both go join you with some further aid:
Hamlet in madness hath Polonius slain,   35
And from his mother's closet hath he dragg'd him;
Go seek him out; speak fair, and bring the body
Into the chapel. I pray you haste in this.
　　　[*Exeunt* ROSENCRANTZ *and* GUILDENSTERN.]
Come, Gertrude, we'll call up our wisest friends
And let them know both what we mean to do   40
And what's untimely done; so haply slander—
Whose whisper o'er the world's diameter,
As level as the cannon to his blank,*
Transports his pois'ned shot—may miss our name,
And hit the woundless* air. O, come away!   45
My soul is full of discord and dismay.   [*Exeunt.*]

SCENE II ———— *Elsinore. The Castle.*

　　　[*Enter* HAMLET.]
HAMLET: Safely stow'd.
GENTLEMEN: [*within*] Hamlet! Lord Hamlet!
HAMLET: But soft! What noise? Who calls on Hamlet? O, here they come!
　　　[*Enter* ROSENCRANTZ *and* GUILDENSTERN.]
ROSENCRANTZ: What have you done, my lord, with the dead body?
HAMLET: Compounded it with dust, whereto 'tis kin.   5
ROSENCRANTZ: Tell us where 'tis, that we may take it thence. And bear it to the
　　chapel.
HAMLET: Do not believe it.
ROSENCRANTZ: Believe what?
HAMLET: That I can keep your counsel, and not mine own. Besides, to be de-   10
　　manded of* a sponge—what replication* should be made by the son of a
　　king?
ROSENCRANTZ: Take you me for a sponge, my lord?
HAMLET: Ay, sir; that soaks up the King's countenance,* his rewards, his author-
　　ities. But such officers do the King best service in the end: he keeps them,
　　like an ape an apple in the corner of his jaw; first mouth'd to be last swal-   15
　　lowed; when he needs what you have glean'd, it is but squeezing you and,
　　sponge, you shall be dry again.
ROSENCRANTZ: I understand you not, my lord.
HAMLET: I am glad of it; a knavish speech sleeps in a foolish ear.
ROSENCRANTZ: My lord, you must tell us where the body is, and go with us to the   20
　　King.
HAMLET: The body is with the King, but the King is not with the body. The King
　　is a thing—

---

[43] **blank** white center of a target
[45] **woundless** invulnerable
[IV,ii,10–11] **demanded of** questioned by
[11] **replication** reply
[13] **countenance** favor

GUILDENSTERN: A thing, my lord!

HAMLET: Of nothing. Bring me to him. Hide fox, and all after.* [*Exeunt.*] 25

SCENE III——*Elsinore. The Castle.*

[*Enter* KING, *attended.*]

KING: I have sent to seek him, and to find the body.
How dangerous is it that this man goes loose!
Yet must not we put the strong law on him:
He's lov'd of the distracted* multitude,
Who like not in their judgment but their eyes; 5
And where 'tis so, th' offender's scourge is weigh'd,
But never the offence. To bear* all smooth and even,
This sudden sending him away must seem
Deliberate pause.* Diseases desperate grown
By desperate appliance are reliev'd, 10
Or not at all.

[*Enter* ROSENCRANTZ.]

How now! what hath befall'n?

ROSENCRANTZ: Where the dead body is bestow'd, my lord,
We cannot get from him.

KING: But where is he? 15

ROSENCRANTZ: Without, my lord; guarded, to know your pleasure.

KING: Bring him before us.

ROSENCRANTZ: Ho, Guildenstern! bring in the lord.

[*Enter* HAMLET *and* GUILDENSTERN.]

KING: Now, Hamlet, where's Polonius?

HAMLET: At supper. 20

KING: At supper! Where?

HAMLET: Not where he eats, but where 'a is eaten; a certain convocation of politic* worms are e'en at him. Your worm is your only emperor for diet: we fat all creatures else to fat us, and we fat ourselves for maggots; your fat king and your lean beggar is but variable service*—two dishes, but to one table. 25 That's the end.

KING: Alas, alas!

HAMLET: A man may fish with the worm that hath eat of a king, and eat of the fish that hath fed of that worm.

KING: What dost thou mean by this? 30

HAMLET: Nothing but to show you how a king may go a progress through the guts of a beggar.

KING: Where is Polonius?

---

25 **hide fox, and all after** call in game (as in hide-and-seek)
IV,iii,4 **distracted** confused
7 **bear** carry out
9 **pause** planning
22 **politic** statesmanlike
25 **variable service** different courses

HAMLET: In heaven; send thither to see; if your messenger find him not there,
seek him i' th' other place yourself. But if, indeed, you find him not within   35
this month, you shall nose him as you go up the stairs into the lobby.
KING: [*to attendants*] Go seek him there.
HAMLET: 'A will stay till you come.   [*Exeunt attendants.*]
KING: Hamlet, this deed, for thine especial safety—
Which we do tender,* as we dearly grieve   40
For that which thou hast done—must send thee hence
With fiery quickness. Therefore prepare thyself;
The bark is ready, and the wind at help,
Th' associates tend,* and everything is bent
For England.   45
HAMLET: For England!
KING: Ay, Hamlet.
HAMLET: Good!
KING: So is it, if thou knew'st our purposes.
HAMLET: I see a cherub that sees them. But, come; for England! Farewell, dear   50
mother.
KING: Thy loving father, Hamlet.
HAMLET: My mother: father and mother is man and wife; man and wife is one
flesh; and so, my mother. Come, for England.   [*Exit.*]
KING: Follow him at foot;* tempt him with speed aboard;   55
Delay it not; I'll have him hence to-night.
Away! for everything is seal'd and done
That else leans* on th' affair. Pray you make haste.
[*Exeunt all but the* KING.]
And, England, if my love thou hold'st at aught—
As my great power thereof may give thee sense,   60
Since yet thy cicatrice* looks raw and red
After the Danish sword, and thy free awe*
Pays homage to us—thou mayst not coldly set
Our sovereign process;* which imports at full,
By letters congruing to that effect,   65
The present* death of Hamlet. Do it, England:
For like the hectic* in my blood he rages,
And thou must cure me. Till I know 'tis done,
Howe'er my haps,* my joys were ne'er begun.   [*Exit.*]

40 **tender** hold dear
44 **tend** wait
55 **at foor** closely
58 **leans** depends
61 **cicatrice** scar
62 **free awe** uncompelled submission
63–64 **coldly set our sovereign process** disregard our royal command
66 **present** immediate
67 **hectic** fever
69 **haps** fortunes

SCENE IV——*A plain in Denmark.*

[*Enter* FORTINBRAS *with his army over the stage.*]
FORTINBRAS: Go, Captain, from me greet the Danish king.
    Tell him that by his license Fortinbras
    Craves the conveyance of a promis'd march
    Over his kingdom. You know the rendezvous.
    If that his Majesty would aught with us,   5
    We shall express our duty in his eye;*
    And let him know so.
CAPTAIN: I will do't, my lord.
FORTINBRAS: Go softly* on.   [*Exeunt all but the* CAPTAIN.]
    [*Enter* HAMLET, ROSENCRANTZ, GUILDENSTERN, *and others.*]
HAMLET: Good sir, whose powers are these?   10
CAPTAIN: They are of Norway, sir.
HAMLET: How purpos'd, sir, I pray you?
CAPTAIN: Against some part of Poland.
HAMLET: Who commands them, sir?
CAPTAIN: The nephew to old Norway, Fortinbras.   15
HAMLET: Goes it against the main* of Poland, sir,
    Or for some frontier?
CAPTAIN: Truly to speak, and with no addition,
    We go to gain a little patch of ground
    That hath in it no profit but the name.   20
    To pay five ducats, five, I would not farm it;
    Nor will it yield to Norway or the Pole
    A ranker* rate should it be sold in fee.*
HAMLET: Why, then the Polack never will defend it.
CAPTAIN: Yes, it is already garrison'd.   25
HAMLET: Two thousand souls and twenty thousand ducats
    Will not debate* the question of this straw.
    This is th' imposthume* of much wealth and peace,
    That inward breaks, and shows no cause without
    Why the man dies. I humbly thank you, sir.
CAPTAIN: God buy you, sir.   30
ROSENCRANTZ: Will't please you go, my lord?
HAMLET: I'll be with you straight. Go a little before.
    [*Exeunt all but* HAMLET.]
    How all occasions do inform against me,
    And spur my dull revenge! What is a man,   35
    If his chief good and market* of his time

IV,iv,6 **in his eye** in his presence
9 **softly** slowly
16 **main** main part
23 **ranker** higher
23 **in fee** outright
27 **debate** settle
28 **imposthume** ulcer
36 **market** profit

Be but to sleep and feed? A beast, no more!
Sure he that made us with such large discourse,*
Looking before and after, gave us not
That capability and godlike reason   40
To fust* in us unus'd. Now, whether it be
Bestial oblivion, or some craven scruple
Of thinking too precisely on th' event—
A thought which, quarter'd, hath but one part wisdom
And ever three parts coward—I do not know   45
Why yet I live to say 'This thing's to do,'
Sith I have cause, and will, and strength, and means,
To do't. Examples gross* as earth exhort me:
Witness this army, of such mass and charge,*
Led by a delicate and tender prince,   50
Whose spirit, with divine ambition puff'd,
Makes mouths at the invisible event,*
Exposing what is mortal and unsure
To all that fortune, death, and danger dare,
Even for an egg-shell. Rightly to be great   55
Is not to stir without great argument,*
But greatly* to find quarrel in a straw,
When honour's at the stake. How stand I, then,
That have a father kill'd, a mother stain'd,
Excitements* of my reason and my blood,   60
And let all sleep, while to my shame I see
The imminent death of twenty thousand men
That, for a fantasy and trick of fame,
Go to their graves like beds, fight for a plot
Whereon the numbers cannot try the cause,   65
Which is not tomb enough and continent*
To hide the slain? O, from this time forth,
My thoughts be bloody, or be nothing worth!   *[Exit.]*

SCENE V———*Elsinore. The Castle.*

[*Enter* QUEEN, HORATIO, *and a* GENTLEMAN.]
QUEEN: I will not speak with her.
GENTLEMAN: She is importunate, indeed distract.
    Her mood will needs be pitied.
QUEEN: What would she have?

---

38 **discourse** understanding
41 **fust** grow moldy
48 **gross** large
49 **charge** expense
52 **makes mouths ... event** scorns the outcome
56 **argument** reason
57**greatly** nobly
60 **excitements** incentives
66 **continent** container

GENTLEMAN: She speaks much of her father; says she hears   5
    There's tricks i' th' world, and hems, and beats her heart;
    Spurns enviously at straws;* speaks things in doubt,*
    That carry but half sense. Her speech is nothing,
    Yet the unshaped use of it doth move
    The hearers to collection;* they yawn* at it,   10
    And botch the words up fit to their own thoughts;
    Which, as her winks and nods and gestures yield them,
    Indeed would make one think there might be thought,
    Though nothing sure, yet much unhappily.
HORATIO: 'Twere good she were spoken with; for she may strew   15
    Dangerous conjectures in ill-breeding minds.
QUEEN: Let her come in.   [*Exit* GENTLEMAN.]
    [*aside*] To my sick soul, as sin's true nature is,
    Each toy seems prologue to some great amiss.*
    So full of artless jealousy* is guilt,   20
    It spills* itself in fearing to be spilt.
        [*Enter* OPHELIA *distracted.*]
OPHELIA: Where is the beauteous Majesty of Denmark?
QUEEN: How now, Ophelia!
OPHELIA: [*sings*]

          How should I your true love know
            From another one?   25
          By his cockle hat and staff,
            *And his sandal shoon.**

QUEEN: Alas, sweet lady, what imports this song?
OPHELIA: Say you? Nay, pray you, mark.   [*sings*]
          He is dead and gone, lady,
            He is dead and gone;   30
          At his head a grass-green turf,
            At his heels a stone.

    O, ho!
QUEEN: Nay, but, Ophelia—   35
OPHELIA: Pray you, mark.   [*sings*]
        White his shroud as the mountain snow—
       [*Enter* KING.]
QUEEN: Alas, look here, my lord.
OPHELIA: *Larded** with sweet flowers;*
          Which bewept to the grave did not go   40
           With true-love showers.

IV,v,7 **spurns . . . straws** objects to insignificant matters
7 **in doubt** uncertainly
10 **collection** gather and listen
10 **yawn** gape
19 **amiss** misfortune
20 **artless jealousy** crude suspicion
21 **spills** destroys
27 **shoon** shoes
39 **larded** decorated

KING: How do you, pretty lady?

OPHELIA: Well, God dild* you! They say the owl was a baker's daughter. Lord, we
     know that we are, but know not what we may be. God be at your table!

KING: Conceit* upon her father.   45

OPHELIA: Pray let's have no words of this; but when they ask you what it means,
     say you this: [*sings*]

> To-morrow is Saint Valentine's day,
>   All in the morning betime,
> And I a maid at your window,   50
>   To be your Valentine.
> Then up he rose, and donn'd his clothes,
>   And dupp'd* the chamber-door;
> Let in the maid, that out a maid
>   Never departed more.   55

KING: Pretty Ophelia!

OPHELIA: Indeed, la, without an oath, I'll make an end on't.   [*sings*]

> By Gis* and by Saint Charity,
>   Alack, and fie for shame!
> Young men will do't, if they come to't;   60
>   By Cock, they are to blame.
> Quoth she 'Before you tumbled me,
>   You promis'd me to wed.'

He answers:

> 'So would I 'a done, by yonder sun,   65
>   An thou hadst not come to my bed.'

KING: How long hath she been thus?

OPHELIA: I hope all will be well. We must be patient; but I cannot choose but
     weep to think they would lay him i' th' cold ground. My brother shall know
     of it; and so I thank you for your good counsel. Come, my coach! Good   70
     night, ladies; good night, sweet ladies, good night, good night.
          [*Exit.*]

KING: Follow her close; give her good watch, I pray you.
          [*Exeunt* HORATIO *and* GENTLEMAN.]
     O, this is the poison of deep grief; it springs
     All from her father's death. And now behold—
     O Gertrude, Gertrude!   75
     When sorrows come, they come not single spies,
     But in battalions! First, her father slain;
     Next, your son gone, and he most violent author
     Of his own just remove; the people muddied,*
     Thick and unwholesome in their thoughts and whispers   80
     For good Polonius' death; and we have done but greenly*

---

43 **dild** reward
45 **conceit** brooding
53 **dupp'd** opened
58 **Gis** Jesus
79 **muddied** confused
81 **greenly** foolishly

In hugger-mugger* to inter him; poor Ophelia
Divided from herself and her fair judgment,
Without the which we are pictures, or mere beasts;
Last, and as much containing as all these, 85
Her brother is in secret come from France;
Feeds on his wonder,* keeps himself in clouds,
And wants not buzzers* to infect his ear
With pestilent speeches of his father's death;
Wherein necessity, of matter beggar'd,* 90
Will nothing stick* our person to arraign
In ear and ear. O my dear Gertrude, this,
Like to a murd'ring piece,* in many places
Gives me superfluous death. [*A noise within.*]
QUEEN: Alack, what noise is this? 95
KING: Attend!
     [*Enter a* GENTLEMAN.]
Where are my Switzers!* Let them guard the door.
What is the matter?
GENTLEMAN: Save yourself, my lord:
The ocean, overpeering of his list,* 100
Eats not the flats with more impetuous haste
Than young Laertes, in a riotous head,*
O'erbears your officers. The rabble call him lord;
And, as the world were now but to begin,
Antiquity forgot, custom not known, 105
The ratifiers and props of every word,
They cry 'Choose we; Laertes shall be king.'
Caps, hands, and tongues, applaud it to the clouds,
'Laertes shall be king, Laertes king.'
QUEEN: How cheerfully on the false trail they cry! 110
     [*Noise within.*]
O, this is counter, you false Danish dogs!
KING: The doors are broke.
     [*Enter* LAERTES, *with others, in arms.*]
LAERTES: Where is this king?—Sirs, stand you all without.
ALL: No, let's come in.
LAERTES: I pray you give me leave. 115
ALL: We will, we will.
     [*Exeunt.*]

---

[82] **hugger-mugger** secret haste
[87] **wonder** suspicion
[88] **buzzers** tale-bearers
[90] **beggar'd** lacking facts
[91] **will nothing stick** will not hesitate
[93] **murd'ring piece** cannon
[97] **Switzers** Swiss guards
[100] **list** shore
[102] **in a riotous head** with a rebellious mob

LAERTES: I thank you. Keep the door.—O thou vile king,
    Give me my father!
QUEEN: Calmly, good Laertes.
LAERTES: That drop of blood that's calm proclaims me bastard;   120
    Cries cuckold to my father; brands the harlot
    Even here, between the chaste unsmirched brow
    Of my true mother.
KING: What is the cause, Laertes,
    That thy rebellion looks so giant-like?   125
    Let him go, Gertrude; do not fear our person:
    There's such divinity doth hedge a king
    That treason can but peep to what it would,
    Acts little of his will. Tell me, Laertes,
    Why thou art thus incens'd. Let him go, Gertrude.   130
    Speak, man.
LAERTES: Where is my father?
KING: Dead.
QUEEN: But not by him.
KING: Let him demand his fill.   135
LAERTES: How came he dead? I'll not be juggled with.
    To hell, allegiance! Vows, to the blackest devil!
    Conscience and grace, to the profoundest pit!
    I dare damnation. To this point I stand,
    That both the worlds I give to negligence,*   140
    Let come what comes; only I'll be reveng'd
    Most thoroughly for my father.
KING: Who shall stay you?
LAERTES: My will, not all the world's.
    And for my means, I'll husband them* so well   145
    They shall go far with little.
KING: Good Laertes,
    If you desire to know the certainty
    Of your dear father, is't writ in your revenge
    That, swoopstake,* you will draw both friend and foe,   150
    Winner and loser?
LAERTES: None but his enemies.
KING: Will you know them, then?
LAERTES: To his good friends thus wide I'll ope my arms
    And, like the kind life-rend'ring pelican,   155
    Repast* them with my blood.
KING: Why, now you speak
    Like a good child and a true gentleman.
    That I am guiltless of your father's death,
    And am most sensibly in grief for it,   160

---

[140] **both the worlds . . . negligence** I care not what may happen to me in this world or the next
[145] **husband them** use them economically
[150] **swoopstake** in a full sweep
[155–56] **pelican, repast** (pelicans were thought to use their own blood to feed their young)

It shall as level to your judgment 'pear
As day does to your eye.   [*A noise within:* 'Let her come in.']
LAERTES: How now! What noise is that?
        [*Reenter* OPHELIA.]
O, heat dry up my brains! tears seven times salt
Burn out the sense and virtue* of mine eye!   165
By heaven, thy madness shall be paid with weight
Till our scale turn the beam.* O rose of May!
Dear maid, kind sister, sweet Ophelia!
O heavens! is't possible a young maid's wits
Should be as mortal as an old man's life?   170
Nature is fine* in love; and where 'tis fine
It sends some precious instance* of itself
After the thing it loves.
OPHELIA: [*sings*]
                 They bore him barefac'd on the bier;
                 Hey non nonny, nonny, hey nonny;   175
                 And in his grave rain'd many a tear—
Fare you well, my dove!
LAERTES: Hadst thou thy wits, and didst persuade revenge,
        It could not move thus.
OPHELIA: You must sing 'A-down, a-down,' an you call him a-down-a. O, how 180
        the wheel becomes it! It is the false steward, that stole his master's daughter.
LAERTES: This nothing's more than matter.*
OPHELIA: There's rosemary, that's for remembrance; pray you, love, remember.
        And there is pansies, that's for thoughts.
LAERTES: A document* in madness—thoughts and remembrance fitted.   185
OPHELIA: There's fennel for you, and columbines. There's rue for you; and here's
        some for me. We may call it herb of grace a Sundays. O, you must wear your
        rue with a difference. There's a daisy. I would give you some violets, but they
        wither'd all when my father died. They say 'a made a good end.
        [*sings*] *For bonny sweet Robin is all my joy.*   190
LAERTES: Thought and affliction, passion, hell itself,
        She turns to favour* and to prettiness.
OPHELIA: [*sings*]
                 And will 'a not come again?
                 And will 'a not come again?
                 No, no, he is dead,   195
                 Go to thy death-bed,
                 He never will come again.

---

165 **virtue** power
167 **scale down the beam** weigh down the balance of a scale
171 **fine** refined
172 **instance** sample
182 **nothing's ... matter** this nonsense contains more meaning than does a statement of great matter
185 **document** lesson
192 **favour** to beauty

> *His beard was as white as snow,*
> *All flaxen was his poll;**
>   *He is gone, he is gone,*   200
>   *And we cast away moan:*
> *God-a-mercy on his soul!*

And of all Christian souls, I pray God. God buy you.
   [*Exit.*]

LAERTES: Do you see this, O God?

KING: Laertes, I must commune with your grief,   205
   Or you deny me right. Go but apart,
   Make choice of whom your wisest friends you will,
   And they shall hear and judge 'twixt you and me.
   If by direct or by collateral* hand
   They find us touch'd,* we will our kingdom give,   210
   Our crown, our life, and all that we call ours,
   To you in satisfaction; but if not,
   Be you content to lend your patience to us,
   And we shall jointly labour with your soul
   To give it due content.   215

LAERTES: Let this be so.
   His means of death, his obscure funeral—
   No trophy, sword, nor hatchment,* o'er his bones,
   No noble rite nor formal ostentation*—
   Cry to be heard, as 'twere from heaven to earth,   220
   That I must call't in question.

KING: So you shall;
   And where th' offence is, let the great axe fall.
   I pray you go with me.
      [*Exeunt.*]

                SCENE VI ———— *Elsinore. The Castle.*

      [*Enter* HORATIO *with an* ATTENDANT.]

HORATIO: What are they that would speak with me?

ATTENDANT: Sea-faring men, sir; they say they have letters for you.

HORATIO: Let them come in.   [*Exit* ATTENDANT.]
   I do not know from what part of the world
   I should be greeted, if not from Lord Hamlet.   5
      [*Enter* SAILORS.]

SAILOR: God bless you, sir.

HORATIO: Let Him bless thee, too.

SAILOR: 'A shall, sir, an't please Him. There's a letter for you, sir; it came from th'
   ambassador that was bound for England—if your name be Horatio, as I am
   let to know it is.   10

199 **flaxen was his poll** his hair was white
209 **collateral** indirect
210 **touch'd** implicated
218 **hatchment** stone bearing coat of arms
219 **ostentation** ceremony

HORATIO: [*reads*] 'Horatio, when thou shalt have overlook'd* this, give these fellows some means to the King: they have letters for him. Ere we were two days old at sea, a pirate of very warlike appointment gave us chase. Finding ourselves too slow of sail, we put on a compelled valour; and in the grapple I boarded them. On the instant they got clear of our ship; so I alone became their prisoner. They have dealt with me like thieves of mercy; but they knew what they did; I am to do a good turn for them. Let the King have the letters I have sent; and repair thou to me with as much speed as thou wouldest fly death. I have words to speak in thine ear will make thee dumb; yet are they much too light for the bore of the matter. These good fellows will bring thee there I am. Rosencrantz and Guildenstern hold their course for England; of them I have much to tell thee. Farewell.

                          'He that thou knowest thine, HAMLET.'

Come, I will give you way for these your letters,
And do't the speedier that you may direct me   25
To him from whom you brought them.   [*Exeunt.*]

          SCENE VII——*Elsinore. The Castle.*

    [*Enter* KING *and* LAERTES.]
KING: Now must your conscience my acquittance seal,
And you must put me in your heart for friend,
Sith you have heard, and with a knowing ear,
That he which hath your noble father slain
Pursu'd my life.   5
LAERTES: It well appears. But tell me
Why you proceeded not against these feats,
So crimeful and so capital* in nature,
As by your safety, wisdom, all things else,
You mainly were stirr'd up.   10
KING: O, for two special reasons,
Which may to you, perhaps, seem much unsinew'd,*
But yet to me th' are strong. The Queen his mother
Lives almost by his looks; and for myself,
My virtue or my plague, be it either which—   15
She is so conjunctive* to my life and soul
That, as the star moves not but in his sphere,
I could not but by her. The other motive,
Why to a public count I might not go,
Is the great love the general gender* bear him;   20
Who, dipping all his faults in their affection,
Work like the spring that turneth wood to stone,
Convert his gyves* to graces; so that my arrows,

IV,vi,11 **overlook'd** read
IV,vii,8 **capital** deserving death
12 **unsinew'd** weak
16 **conjunctive** closely united
20 **general gender** common people
23 **gyves** fetters

Too slightly timber'd* for so loud a wind,
Would have reverted to my bow again,   25
But not where I have aim'd them.
LAERTES: And so have I a noble father lost;
A sister driven into desp'rate terms,
Whose worth, if praises may go back again,
Stood challenger on mount of all the age   30
For her perfections. But my revenge will come.
KING: Break not your sleeps for that. You must not think
That we are made of stuff so flat and dull
That we can let our beard be shook with danger,
And think it pastime. You shortly shall hear more.   35
I lov'd your father, and we love our self;
And that, I hope, will teach you to imagine—
    [*Enter a* MESSENGER *with letters.*]
How now! What news?
MESSENGER: Letters, my lord, from Hamlet:
These to your Majesty; this to the Queen.   40
KING: From Hamlet! Who brought them?
MESSENGER: Sailors, my lord, they say; I saw them not.
They were given me by Claudio; he receiv'd them
Of him that brought them.
KING: Laertes, you shall hear them.   45
Leave us.   [*Exit* MESSENGER.]
[*reads*] 'High and Mighty. You shall know I am set naked* on your king-
dom. To-morrow shall I beg leave to see your kingly eyes; when I shall, first
asking your pardon thereunto, recount the occasion of my sudden and more
strange return.   50
                                                    HAMLET.'

What should this mean? Are all the rest come back?
Or is it some abuse,* and no such thing?
LAERTES: Know you the hand?
KING: 'Tis Hamlet's character. 'Naked'!
And in a postscript here, he says 'alone.'   55
Can you devise* me?
LAERTES: I am lost in it, my lord. But let him come;
It warms the very sickness in my heart
That I shall live and tell him to his teeth
'Thus didest thou.'   60
KING: If it be so, Laertes—
As how should it be so, how otherwise?—
Will you be rul'd by me?
LAERTES: Ay, my lord;
So you will not o'errule me to a peace.   65

²⁴ **timber'd** shafted
⁴⁷**naked** destitute
⁵² **abuse** deception
⁵⁶ **devise** advise

KING: To thine own peace. If he be now return'd,
　　　As checking at* his voyage, and that he means
　　　No more to undertake it, I will work him
　　　To an exploit now ripe in my device,
　　　Under the which he shall not choose but fall; 70
　　　And for his death, no wind of blame shall breathe;
　　　But even his mother shall uncharge the practice
　　　And call it accident.
LAERTES: My lord, I will be rul'd
　　　The rather, if you could devise it so 75
　　　That I might be the organ.
KING: 　　　　　　　　　　　　　It falls right.
　　　You have been talk'd of since your travel much,
　　　And that in Hamlet's hearing, for a quality
　　　Wherein they say you shine. Your sum of parts
　　　Did not together pluck such envy from him 80
　　　As did that one; and that, in my regard,
　　　Of the unworthiest siege.*
LAERTES: What part is that, my lord?
KING: A very riband in the cap of youth,
　　　Yet needful, too; for youth no less becomes 85
　　　The light and careless livery that it wears
　　　Than settled age his sables and his weeds,*
　　　Importing health and graveness. Two months since
　　　Here was a gentleman of Normandy—
　　　I have seen myself, and serv'd against, the French, 90
　　　And they can well on horseback; but this gallant
　　　Had witchcraft in't; he grew into his seat,
　　　And to such wondrous doing brought his horse,
　　　As had he been incorps'd and demi-natur'd
　　　With the brave beast. So far he topp'd my thought, 95
　　　That I, in forgery* of shapes and tricks,
　　　Come short of what he did.
LAERTES: 　　　　　　　　　　A Norman was't?
KING: A Norman.
LAERTES: 　　　　Upon my life, Lamord.
KING: 　　　　　　　　　　　The very same.
LAERTES: I know him well. He is the brooch* indeed
　　　And gem of all the nation. 100
KING: He made confession* of you;
　　　And gave you such a masterly report
　　　For art and exercise in your defence,

⁶⁷**checking at** abandoning
⁸²**siege** rank
⁸⁷**weeds** sober attire
⁹⁶**forgery** invention
⁹⁹**brooch** ornament
¹⁰¹**confession** report

And for your rapier most especial,
That he cried out 'twould be a sight indeed   105
If one could match you. The scrimers* of their nation
He swore had neither motion, guard, nor eye,
If you oppos'd them. Sir, this report of his
Did Hamlet so envenom with his envy
That he could nothing do but wish and beg   110
Your sudden coming o'er, to play with you.
Now out of this—
LAERTES: What out of this, my lord?
KING: Laertes, was your father dear to you?
Or are you like the painting of a sorrow,   115
A face without a heart?
LAERTES: Why ask you this?
KING: Not that I think you did not love your father;
But that I know love is begun by time,
And that I see, in passages of proof,*
Time qualifies* the spark and fire of it.   120
There lives within the very flame of love
A kind of wick or snuff that will abate it;
And nothing is at a like goodness still;
For goodness, growing to a pleurisy,*
Dies in his own too much. That we would do,   125
We should do when we would; for this 'would' changes,
And hath abatements and delays as many
As there are tongues, are hands, are accidents;
And then this 'should' is like a spendthrift's sigh
That hurts by easing. But to the quick* of th' ulcer: 130
Hamlet comes back; what would you undertake
To show yourself in deed your father's son
More than in words?
LAERTES: To cut his throat i' th' church.
KING: No place, indeed, should murder sanctuarize;*   135
Revenge should have no bounds. But, good Laertes,
Will you do this? Keep close within your chamber.
Hamlet return'd shall know you are come home.
We'll put on those shall praise your excellence,
And set a double varnish on the fame   140
The Frenchman gave you; bring you, in fine,* together,
And wager on your heads. He, being remiss,
Most generous, and free from all contriving,

---

¹⁰⁶ **scrimers** fencers
¹¹⁹ **passages of proof** proved cases
¹²⁰ **qualifies** diminishes
¹²⁴ **pleurisy** excess
¹³⁰ **quick** sensitive part
¹³⁵ **sanctuarize** protect
¹⁴¹ **in fine** finally

Will not peruse the foils; so that with ease
Or with a little shuffling, you may choose 145
A sword unbated,* and, in a pass of practice,*
Requite him for your father.
LAERTES: I will do't;
And for that purpose I'll anoint my sword.
I bought an unction of a mountebank,
So mortal that but dip a knife in it, 150
Where it draws blood no cataplasm* so rare,
Collected from all simples* that have virtue
Under the moon, can save the thing from death
That is but scratch'd withal. I'll touch my point
With this contagion, that, if I gall him slightly, 155
It may be death.
KING: Let's further think of this;
Weigh what convenience both of time and means
May fit us to our shape.* If this should fail,
And that our drift look through* our bad performance,
'Twere better not assay'd, therefore this project 160
Should have a back or second, that might hold
If this did blast in proof.* Soft! let me see.
We'll make a solemn wager on your cunnings—
I ha't.
When in your motion you are hot and dry— 165
As make your bouts more violent to that end—
And that he calls for drink, I'll have preferr'd him
A chalice for the nonce,* whereon but sipping,
If he by chance escape your venom'd stuck,*
Our purpose may hold there. But stay; what noise? 170
          [*Enter* QUEEN.]
QUEEN: One woe doth tread upon another's heel,
So fast they follow. Your sister's drown'd, Laertes.
LAERTES: Drown'd? O, where?
QUEEN: There is a willow grows aslant the brook
That shows his hoar* leaves in the glassy stream; 175
Therewith fantastic garlands did she make
Of crowflowers, nettles, daisies, and long purples
That liberal* shepherds give a grosser name,

---

146 **unbated** not blunted
146 **pass of practice** treacherous thrust
151 **cataplasm** poultice
152 **simples** medicinal herbs
158 **shape** role
159 **drift look through** purpose show through
162 **blast in proof** fail in performance
168 **nonce** occasion
169 **stuck** thrust
175 **hoar** silver-gray
178 **liberal** coarse-mouthed

But our cold maids do dead men's fingers call them.
There, on the pendent boughs her coronet weeds   180
Clamb'ring to hang, an envious sliver broke;
When down her weedy trophies and herself
Fell in the weeping brook. Her clothes spread wide
And, mermaid-like, awhile they bore her up;
Which time she chanted snatches of old lauds,*   185
As one incapable* of her own distress,
Or like a creature native and indued*
Unto that element; but long it could not be
Till that her garments, heavy with their drink,
Pull'd the poor wretch from her melodious lay   190
To muddy death.
LAERTES: Alas, then she is drown'd!
QUEEN: Drown'd, drown'd.
LAERTES: Too much of water hast thou, poor Ophelia,
And therefore I forbid my tears; but yet
It is our trick,* nature her custom holds,   195
Let shame say what it will. When these are gone,
The woman* will be out. Adieu, my lord.
I have a speech o' fire that fain would blaze
But that this folly douts it.   [*Exit.*]
KING: Let's follow, Gertrude.   200
How much I had to do to calm his rage!
Now fear I this will give it start again;
Therefore let's follow.   [*Exeunt.*]

ACT V

[*Enter two* CLOWNS *with spades and picks.*]

FIRST CLOWN: Is she to be buried in Christian burial when she wilfully seeks her
    own salvation?
SECOND CLOWN: I tell thee she is; therefore make her grave straight.* The crowner*
    hath sat on her, and finds it Christian burial.
FIRST CLOWN: How can that be, unless she drown'd herself in her own defence?   5
SECOND CLOWN: Why, 'tis found so.
FIRST CLOWN: It must be 'se offendendo';* it cannot be else. For here lies the
    point: if I drown myself wittingly, it argues an act; and an act hath

---

185 **lauds** hymns
186 **incapable** unaware
187 **indued** in harmony with
195 **trick** way
197 **woman** womanly part
V,i,3 **straight** straight way
3 **crowner** coroner
7**se offendendo** false Latin, instead of "se defendendo" meaning "in self-defense"

three branches—it is to act, to do, to perform; argal,* she drown'd herself wittingly.

SECOND CLOWN: Nay, but hear you, Goodman Delver. 10

FIRST CLOWN: Give me leave. Here lies the water; good. Here stands the man; good. If the man go to this water and drown himself, it is, will he, nill he, he goes—mark you that; but if the water come to him and drown him, he drowns not himself. Argal, he that is not guilty of his own death shortens not his own life. 15

SECOND CLOWN: But is this law?

FIRST CLOWN: Ay, marry, is't; crowner's quest* law.

SECOND CLOWN: Will you ha' the truth an't? If this had not been a gentlewoman, she should have been buried out a Christian burial.

FIRST CLOWN: Why, there thou say'st; and the more pity that great folk should 20 have count'nance* in this world to drown or hang themselves more than their even Christen.* Come, my spade. There is no ancient gentlemen but gard'ners, ditchers, and grave-makers; they hold up* Adam's profession.

SECOND CLOWN: Was he a gentleman?

FIRST CLOWN: 'A was the first that ever bore arms.*

SECOND CLOWN: Why, he had none. 25

FIRST CLOWN: What, art a heathen? How dost thou understand the Scripture? The Scripture says Adam digg'd. Could he dig without arms? I'll put another question to thee. If thou answerest me not to the purpose, confess thyself—

SECOND CLOWN: Go to. 30

FIRST CLOWN: What is he that builds stronger than either the mason, the shipwright, or the carpenter?

SECOND CLOWN: The gallows-maker; for that frame outlives a thousand tenants.

FIRST CLOWN: I like thy wit well; in good faith the gallows does well; but how does it well? It does well to those that do ill. Now thou dost ill to say the gallows is built stronger than the church; argal, the gallows may do well to 35 thee. To't again, come.

SECOND CLOWN: Who builds stronger than a mason, a shipwright, or a carpenter?

FIRST CLOWN: Ay, tell me that, and unyoke.*

SECOND CLOWN: Marry, now I can tell. 40

FIRST CLOWN: To 't.

SECOND CLOWN: Mass, I cannot tell.

[*Enter* HAMLET *and* HORATIO, *afar off.*]

FIRST CLOWN: Cudgel thy brains no more about it, for your dull ass will not mend his pace with beating; and when you are ask'd this question next, say 'a grave-maker': the house he makes lasts till doomsday. Go, get thee to Yaughan; fetch me a stoup* of liquor. [*Exit* SECOND CLOWN.] 45

⁹ **argal** false Latin for "ergo" ("therefore")
¹⁷ **crowner's quest** coroner's inquest
²¹ **count'nance** privilege
²¹⁻²² **even Christen** fellow Christian
²³ **hold up** keep up
²⁴ **bore arms** had a coat of arms
³⁹ **unyoke** quit work for the day
⁴⁶ **stoup** tankard

[*digs and sings*]
> In youth, when I did love, did love
>> Methought it was very sweet,
> To contract-o-the time for-a my behove,*
> O, methought there-a-was nothing-a meet.   50

HAMLET: Has this fellow no feeling of his business, that 'a sings in grave-making?

HORATIO: Custom hath made it in him a property of easiness.*

HAMLET: 'Tis e'en so; the hand of little employment hath the daintier sense.

FIRST CLOWN: [*sings*]
> But age, with his stealing steps,
>> Hath clawed me in his clutch,   55
> And hath shipped me intil the land,
>> As if I had never been such.

[*throws up a skull*]

HAMLET: That skull had a tongue in it, and could sing once. How the knave jowls* it to the ground, as if 'twere Cain's jawbone, that did the first murder! This might be the pate of a politician, which this ass now o'erreaches; one   60
that would circumvent God, might it not?

HORATIO: It might, my lord.

HAMLET: Or of a courtier; which could say 'Good morrow, sweet lord! How dost thou, sweet lord?' This might be my Lord Such-a-one, that praised my Lord Such-a-one's horse, when 'a meant to beg it—might it not?   65

HORATIO: Ay, my lord.

HAMLET: Why, e'en so; and now my Lady Worm's, chapless,* and knock'd about the mazard* with a sexton's spade. Here's fine revolution, an we had the trick to see't. Did these bones cost no more the breeding but to play at log-gats* with them? Mine ache to think on't.   70

FIRST CLOWN: [*sings*]
> A pick-axe and a spade, a spade
>> For and a shrouding sheet:
> O, a pit of clay for to be made
>> For such a guest is meet.

[*throws up another skull*]

HAMLET: There's another. Why may not that be the skull of a lawyer? Where be   75
his quiddities* now, his quillets,* his cases, his tenures,* and his tricks? Why does he suffer this rude knave now to knock him about the sconce* with a dirty shovel, and will not tell him of his action of battery? Hum! This fellow might be in's time a great buyer of land, with his statutes, his recognizances, his fines,* his double vouchers, his recoveries. Is this the fine* of his fines,

---

and the recovery of his recoveries, to have his fine pate full of fine dirt? Will 80
his vouchers vouch him no more of his purchases, and double ones, too,
than the length and breadth of a pair of indentures?* The very conveyances
of his lands will scarcely lie in this box; and must th' inheritor himself have
no more, ha? 85

HORATIO: Not a jot more, my lord.

HAMLET: Is not parchment made of sheep-skins?

HORATIO: Ay, my lord, and of calves' skins, too.

HAMLET: They are sheep and calves which seek out assurance in that. I will speak
to this fellow. Whose grave's this, sirrah?

FIRST CLOWN: Mine, sir. [*sings*] 90

> *O, a pit of clay for to be made*
> *For such a guest is meet.*

HAMLET: I think it be thine indeed, for thou liest in't.

FIRST CLOWN: You lie out on't, sir, and therefore 'tis not yours. For my part, I do
not lie in't, yet it is mine. 95

HAMLET: Thou dost lie in't, to be in't and say it is thine; 'tis for the dead, not for
the quick; therefore thou liest.

FIRST CLOWN: 'Tis a quick lie, sir; 'twill away again from me to you.

HAMLET: What man dost thou dig it for?

FIRST CLOWN: For no man, sir. 100

HAMLET: What woman, then?

FIRST CLOWN: For none neither.

HAMLET: Who is to be buried in't?

FIRST CLOWN: One that was a woman, sir; but, rest her soul, she's dead.

HAMLET: How absolute* the knave is! We must speak by the card,* or equivoca- 105
tion will undo us. By the Lord, Horatio, this three years I have took note of
it: the age is grown so picked* that the toe of the peasant comes so near the
heel of the courtier, he galls his kibe.* How long hast thou been a grave-
maker?

FIRST CLOWN: Of all the days i' th' year, I came to't that day that our last King
Hamlet overcame Fortinbras. 110

HAMLET: How long is that since?

FIRST CLOWN: Cannot you tell that? Every fool can tell that: it was that very day
that young Hamlet was born—he that is mad, and sent into England.

HAMLET: Ay, marry, why was he sent into England?

FIRST CLOWN: Why, because 'a was mad: 'a shall recover his wits there; or, if 'a do 115
not, 'tis no great matter there.

HAMLET: Why?

FIRST CLOWN: 'Twill not be seen in him there: there the men are as mad as he.

HAMLET: How came he mad?

FIRST CLOWN: Very strangely, they say. 120

HAMLET: How strangely?

---

83 **indentures** contracts
105 **absolute** positive, certain
105 **card** exactly
107 **picked** refined
108 **kibe** sore on the heel

FIRST CLOWN: Faith, e'en with losing his wits.

HAMLET: Upon what ground?

FIRST CLOWN: Why, here in Denmark. I have been sexton here, man and boy, thirty years.   125

HAMLET: How long will a man lie i' th' earth ere he rot?

FIRST CLOWN: Faith, if 'a be not rotten before 'a die—as we have many pocky corses* now-a-days that will scarce hold the laying in—'a will last you some eight year or nine year. A tanner will last you nine year.

HAMLET: Why he more than another?   130

FIRST CLOWN: Why, sir, his hide is so tann'd with his trade that 'a will keep out water a great while; and your water is a sore decayer of your whoreson dead body. Here's a skull now; this skull has lien you i' th' earth three and twenty years.

HAMLET: Whose was it?

FIRST CLOWN: A whoreson mad fellow's it was. Whose do you think it was?   135

HAMLET: Nay, I know not.

FIRST CLOWN: A pestilence on him for a mad rogue! 'A poured a flagon of Rhenish on my head once. This same skull, sir, was, sir, Yorick's skull, the King's jester.

HAMLET: This?

FIRST CLOWN: E'en that.   140

HAMLET: Let me see. [*takes the skull*] Alas, poor Yorick! I knew him, Horatio: a fellow of infinite jest, of most excellent fancy; he hath borne me on his back a thousand times. And now how abhorred in my imagination it is! My gorge rises at it. Here hung those lips that I have kiss'd I know not how oft. Where be your gibes now, your gambols, your songs, your flashes of merri- 145 ment that were wont to set the table on a roar? Not one now to mock your own grinning—quite chap-fall'n?* Now get you to my lady's chamber, and tell her, let her paint an inch thick, to this favour* she must come; make her laugh at that. Prithee, Horatio, tell me one thing.

HORATIO: What's that, my lord?   150

HAMLET: Dost thou think Alexander look'd o' this fashion i' th' earth?

HORATIO: E'en so.

HAMLET: And smelt so? Pah!   [*throws down the skull*]

HORATIO: E'en so, my lord.

HAMLET: To what base uses we may return, Horatio! Why may not imagination 155 trace the noble dust of Alexander till 'a find it stopping a bung-hole?

HORATIO: 'Twere to consider too curiously* to consider so.

HAMLET: No, faith, not a jot; but to follow him thither with modesty enough, and likelihood to lead it, as thus: Alexander died, Alexander was buried, Alexander returneth to dust; the dust is earth; of earth we make loam, and why of that loam whereto he was converted might they not stop a beer- 160 barrel?

---

127 **pocky corses** corpses of those with syphilis
147 **chap-fall'n** jawless (down in the mouth)
148 **favour** appearance, condition
157 **curiously** minutely

    Imperious Caesar, dead and turn'd to clay,
    Might stop a hole to keep the wind away.
    O, that that earth which kept the world in awe
    Should patch a wall t' expel the winter's flaw!* 165
But soft! but soft! awhile. Here comes the King.
[Enter the KING, QUEEN, LAERTES, *in funeral procession after the coffin,*
with PRIEST *and* LORDS *attendant.]*
The Queen, the courtiers. Who is this they follow?
And with such maimed* rites? This doth betoken
The corse they follow did with desperate hand
Fordo it own life. 'Twas of some estate.* 170
Couch* we awhile and mark.   *[retiring with* HORATIO]
LAERTES: What ceremony else?
HAMLET: That is Laertes, a very noble youth. Mark.
LAERTES: What ceremony else?
PRIEST: Her obsequies have been so far enlarg'd
    As we have warrantise. Her death was doubtful; 175
    And, but that great command o'ersways the order,
    She should in ground unsanctified have lodg'd
    Till the last trumpet; for charitable prayers,
    Shards, flints, and pebbles, should be thrown on her;
    Yet here she is allow'd her virgin crants,* 180
    Her maiden strewments, and the bringing home
    Of bell and burial.
LAERTES: Must there no more be done?
PRIEST: No more be done.
    We should profane the service of the dead 185
    To sing sage requiem and such rest to her
    As to peace-parted souls.
LAERTES: Lay her i' th' earth;
    And from her fair and unpolluted flesh
    May violets spring! I tell thee, churlish priest, 190
    A minist'ring angel shall my sister be
    When thou liest howling.
HAMLET: What, the fair Ophelia!
QUEEN: Sweets to the sweet; farewell! *[scattering flowers]*
    I hop'd thou shouldst have been my Hamlet's wife; 195
    I thought thy bride-bed to have deck'd, sweet maid,
    And not have strew'd thy grave.
LAERTES: O, treble woe
    Fall ten times treble on that cursed head
    Whose wicked deed thy most ingenious sense*

---

165 **flaw** gust
168 **maimed** curtailed
170 **estate** high rank
171 **couch** hide
180 **crants** garlands
199 **ingenious sense** finely endowed mind

Depriv'd thee of! Hold off the earth awhile,   200
Till I have caught her once more in mine arms.
    [*leaps into the grave*]
Now pile your dust upon the quick and dead,
Till of this flat a mountain you have made
T' o'er-top old Pelion or the skyish head
Of blue Olympus.   205
HAMLET: [*advancing*] What is he whose grief
    Bears such an emphasis, whose phrase of sorrow
    Conjures the wand'ring stars, and makes them stand
    Like wonder-wounded hearers? This is I,
    Hamlet, the Dane.   [*leaps into the grave*] 210
LAERTES: The devil take thy soul! [*grappling with him*]
HAMLET: Thou pray'st not well.
    I prithee take thy fingers from my throat;
    For, though I am not splenitive* and rash,
    Yet have I in me something dangerous,   215
    Which let thy wiseness fear. Hold off thy hand.
KING: Pluck them asunder.
QUEEN: Hamlet! Hamlet!
ALL: Gentlemen!
HORATIO: Good my lord, be quiet.
    [*The attendants part them, and they come out of the grave.*]
HAMLET: Why, I will fight with him upon this theme
    Until my eyelids will no longer wag.   220
QUEEN: O my son, what theme?
HAMLET: I lov'd Ophelia: forty thousand brothers
    Could not, with all their quantity of love
    Make up my sum. What wilt thou do for her?
KING: O, he is mad, Laertes.   225
QUEEN: For love of God, forbear him.
HAMLET: 'Swounds, show me what th'owt do:
    Woo't weep, woo't fight, woo't fast, woo't tear thyself,
    Woo't drink up eisel,* eat a crocodile?
    I'll do't. Dost come here to whine?   230
    To outface me with leaping in her grave?
    Be buried quick with her, and so will I;
    And, if thou prate of mountains, let them throw
    Millions of acres on us, till our ground,
    Singeing his pate against the burning zone,*   235
    Make Ossa like a wart! Nay, an thou'lt mouth,
    I'll rant as well as thou.
QUEEN: This is mere madness;
    And thus awhile the fit will work on him;
    Anon, as patient as the female dove

---

214 **splenitive** fiery spirited
229 **eisel** vinegar
235 **burning zone** the sun

When that her golden couplets are disclos'd*   240
His silence will sit drooping.

HAMLET: Hear you, sir:
What is the reason that you use me thus?
I lov'd you ever. But it is no matter.
Let Hercules himself do what he may,
The cat will mew, and dog will have his day.   [*Exit.*] 245

KING: I pray thee, good Horatio, wait upon him.

          [*Exit* HORATIO.]

[*to* LAERTES] Strengthen your patience in our last night's speech;
We'll put the matter to the present push.*—
Good Gertrude, set some watch over your son.—
This grave shall have a living* monument.   250
An hour of quiet shortly shall we see;
Till then in patience our proceeding be.   [*Exeunt.*]

SCENE II———Elsinore. The Castle.

[*Enter* HAMLET *and* HORATIO.]

HAMLET: So much for this, sir; now shall you see the other. You do remember all
    the circumstance?

HORATIO: Remember it, my lord!

HAMLET: Sir, in my heart there was a kind of fighting
That would not let me sleep. Methought I lay   5
Worse than the mutines in the bilboes.* Rashly,
And prais'd be rashness for it—let us know,
Our indiscretion sometime serves us well,
When our deep plots do pall,* and that should learn us
There's a divinity that shapes our ends,
Rough-hew them how we will.   10

HORATIO: That is most certain.

HAMLET: Up from my cabin,
My sea-gown scarf'd about me, in the dark
Grop'd to find out them; had my desire;
Finger'd* their packet, and in fine withdrew   15
To mine own room again, making so bold,
My fears forgetting manners, to unseal
Their grand commission; where I found, Horatio,
Ah, royal knavery! an exact command,
Larded* with many several sorts of reasons,   20
Importing Denmark's health and England's, too,

---

[240] **golden couplets are disclos'd** doves were thought to lay only two eggs; here the reference is to young, just-hatched doves
[248] **present push** immediate test
[250] **living** lasting
[V,ii,6] **mutines in the bilboes** mutineers in chains
[8] **pall** fail
[15] **finger'd** stole
[20] **larded** enriched

With, ho! such bugs and goblins in my life*—
That, on the supervise,* no leisure bated,*
No, not to stay the grinding of the axe,
My head should be struck off.   25
HORATIO: Is't possible?
HAMLET: Here's the commission; read it at more leisure.
　　　But wilt thou hear now how I did proceed?
HORATIO: I beseech you.
HAMLET: Being thus benetted round with villainies—   30
　　　Ere I could make a prologue to my brains,
　　　They had begun the play—I sat me down;
　　　Devis'd a new commission; wrote it fair.
　　　I once did hold it, as our statists* do,
　　　A baseness to write fair,* and labour'd much   35
　　　How to forget that learning; but sir, now
　　　It did me yeoman's service. Wilt thou know
　　　Th' effect* of what I wrote?
HORATIO: Ay, good my lord.
HAMLET: An earnest conjuration from the King,
　　　As England was his faithful tributary,   40
　　　As love between them like the palm might flourish,
　　　As peace should still her wheaten garland wear
　　　And stand a comma* tween their amities,
　　　And many such like as's of great charge,
　　　That, on the view and knowing of these contents,   45
　　　Without debatement further more or less,
　　　He should those bearers put to sudden death,
　　　Not shriving-time* allow'd.
HORATIO: How was this seal'd?
HAMLET: Why, even in that was heaven ordinant.*
　　　I had my father's signet in my purse,   50
　　　Which was the model of that Danish seal;
　　　Folded the writ up in the form of th' other;
　　　Subscrib'd it, gave't th' impression, plac'd it safely,
　　　The changeling never known. Now, the next day
　　　Was our sea-fight; and what to this was sequent   55
　　　Thou knowest already.
HORATIO: So Guildenstern and Rosencrantz go to't.
HAMLET: Why, man, they did make love to this employment;
　　　They are not near my conscience; their defeat

22 **bugs . . . my life** imagined terrors if I were allowed to live
23 **supervise** reading
23 **leisure baited** delay allowed
34 **statists** statesmen
35 **fair** clearly
38 **effect** purport
43 **comma** link
48 **shriving-time** time to be absolved of sin
49 **ordinant** on my side

Does by their own insinuation* grow: 60
'Tis dangerous when the baser nature comes
Between the pass and fell* incensed points
Of mighty opposites.
HORATIO: Why, what a king is this!
HAMLET: Does it not, think thee, stand me now upon*—
He that hath kill'd my king and whor'd my mother;   65
Popp'd in between th' election* and my hopes;
Thrown out his angle for my proper life,*
And with such coz'nage*—is't not perfect conscience
To quit* him with this arm? And is't not to be damn'd
To let this canker of our nature come   70
In further evil?
HORATIO: It must be shortly known to him from England
What is the issue of the business there.
HAMLET: It will be short; the interim is mine.
And a man's life's no more than to say 'one.'   75
But I am very sorry, good Horatio,
That to Laertes I forgot myself;
For by the image of my cause I see
The portraiture of his. I'll court his favours.
But sure the bravery of his grief did put me   80
Into a tow'ring passion.
HORATIO: Peace; who comes here?
          [*Enter young* OSRIC.]
OSRIC: Your lordship is right welcome back to Denmark.
HAMLET: I humbly thank you, sir. [*aside to* HORATIO] Dost know this water-fly?
HORATIO: [*aside to* HAMLET] No, my good lord.
HAMLET: [*aside to* HORATIO] Thy state is the more gracious; for 'tis a vice to know   85
him. He hath much land, and fertile. Let a beast be lord of beasts, and his
crib shall stand at the king's mess!* 'Tis a chough,* but, as I say, spacious* in
the possession of dirt.
OSRIC: Sweet lord, if your lordship were at leisure, I should impart a thing to you
from his Majesty.   90
HAMLET: I will receive it, sir, with all diligence of spirit. Put your bonnet to his
right use, 'tis for the head.
OSRIC: I thank your lordship; it is very hot.
HAMLET: No, believe me, 'tis very cold; the wind is northerly.

---

[60] **insinuation** meddling
[62] **pass and fell** thrust and cruel
[64] **stand me now upon** became incumbent on me
[66] **election** selection to be king
[67] **angle for my proper life** tried to end my own life
[68] **coz'nage** trickery
[69] **quit** pay back
[87] **mess** table
[87] **chough** chatterer
[87] **spacious** well off

OSRIC: It is indifferent cold, my lord, indeed.   95

HAMLET: But yet methinks it is very sultry and hot for my complexion.*

OSRIC: Exceedingly, my lord; it is very sultry, as 'twere—I cannot tell how. But, my lord, his Majesty bade me signify to you that 'a has laid a great wager on your head. Sir, this is the matter—

HAMLET: I beseech you, remember.   100

      [HAMLET *moves him to put on his hat.*]

OSRIC: Nay, good my lord; for my ease, in good faith. Sir, here is newly come to court Laertes; believe me, an absolute gentleman, full of most excellent differences,* of very soft society and great showing. Indeed, to speak feelingly of him, he is the card* or calendar of gentry, for you shall find in him the continent* of what part a gentleman would see.   105

HAMLET: Sir, his definement* suffers no perdition* in you; though, I know, to divide him inventorially would dozy* th' arithmetic of memory, and yet but yaw neither in respect of his quick sail. But, in the verity of extolment, I take him to be a soul of great article, and his infusion of such dearth and rareness, as to make true diction of him, his semblable is his mirror, and who else would trace him, his umbrage, nothing more.   110

OSRIC: Your lordship speaks most infallibly of him.

HAMLET: The concernancy,* sir? Why do we wrap the gentleman in our more rawer breath?

OSRIC: Sir?   115

HORATIO: [*aside to* HAMLET] Is't not possible to understand in another tongue? You will to't, sir, really.

HAMLET: What imports the nomination of this gentleman?

OSRIC: Of Laertes?

HORATIO: [*aside*] His purse is empty already; all's golden words are spent.   120

HAMLET: Of him, sir.

OSRIC: I know you are not ignorant—

HAMLET: I would you did, sir; yet, in faith, if you did, it would not much approve* me. Well, sir.

OSRIC: You are not ignorant of what excellence Laertes is—   125

HAMLET: I dare not confess that, lest I should compare with him in excellence; but to know a man well were to know himself.

OSRIC: I mean, sir, for his weapon; but in the imputation* laid on him by them, in his meed* he's unfellowed.

HAMLET: What's his weapon?   130

OSRIC: Rapier and dagger.

---

⁹⁶ **complexion** temperament
¹⁰² **differences** distinguishing characteristics
¹⁰⁴ **card** model
¹⁰⁴ **continent** summary
¹⁰⁶ **definement** description
¹⁰⁶ **perdition** loss (this entire speech mocks Osric's use of overblown language)
¹⁰⁷ **dozy** dizzy
¹¹³ **concernancy** meaning
¹²³ **approve** commend
¹²⁸ **imputation** reputation
¹²⁹ **meed** merit

HAMLET: That's two of his weapons—but well.

OSRIC: The King, sir, hath wager'd him with six Barbary horses; against the which he has impon'd,* as I take it, six French rapiers and poniards, with their assigns,* as girdle, hangers, and so—three of the carriages, in faith, are very dear to fancy, very responsive to the hilts, most delicate carriages, and 135 of very liberal conceit.

HAMLET: What call you the carriages?

HORATIO: [*aside to* HAMLET] I knew you must be edified by the margent* ere you had done.

OSRIC: The carriages, sir, are the hangers. 140

HAMLET: The phrase would be more germane to the matter if we could carry a cannon by our sides. I would it might be hangers till then. But on: six Barbary horses against six French swords, their assigns, and three liberal conceited carriages; that's the French bet against the Danish. Why is this all impon'd, as you call it? 145

OSRIC: The King, sir, hath laid, sir, that in a dozen passes between yourself and him he shall not exceed you three hits; he hath laid on twelve for nine, and it would come to immediate trial if your lordship would vouchsafe the answer.

HAMLET: How if I answer no?

OSRIC: I mean, my lord, the opposition of your person in trial. 150

HAMLET: Sir, I will walk here in the hall. If it please his Majesty, it is the breathing time of day* with me; let the foils be brought, the gentlemen willing, and the King hold his purpose, I will win for him an I can; if not, I will gain nothing but my shame and the odd hits.

OSRIC: Shall I redeliver you e'en so? 155

HAMLET: To this effect, sir, after what flourish your nature will.

OSRIC: I commend my duty to your lordship.

HAMLET: Yours, yours. [*Exit* OSRIC.] He does well to commend it himself; there are no tongues else for's turn.

HORATIO: This lapwing runs away with the shell on his head. 160

HAMLET: 'A did comply, sir, with his dug before 'a suck'd it.* Thus has he, and many more of the same bevy, that I know the drossy age dotes on, only got the tune of the time and outward habit of encounter*—a kind of yesty* collection, which carries them through and through the most fann'd and winnowed opinions; and do but blow them to their trial, the bubbles are out.* 165
[*Enter a* LORD.]

LORD: My lord, his Majesty commended him to you by young Osric, who brings back to him that you attend him in the hall. He sends to know if your pleasure hold to play with Laertes, or that you will take longer time.

---

¹³⁴**impon'd** wagered
¹³⁴**assigns** accompaniments
¹³⁸**margent** exaggerated terminology
^{151–52}**breathing time of day** time when I do my exercises
¹⁶¹**'A did comply . . . suck'd it** He was ceremoniously polite to his mother's breast before he sucked it
¹⁶³**habit of encounter** superficial way of talking to people
¹⁶³**yesty** frothy
¹⁶⁵**blow them . . . bubbles are out** question them and they are at a loss

HAMLET: I am constant to my purposes; they follow the king's pleasure: if his fitness speaks, mine is ready now—or whensoever, provided I be so able 170 as now.

LORD: The King and Queen and all are coming down.

HAMLET: In happy time.

LORD: The Queen desires you to use some gentle entertainment* to Laertes before you fall to play.

HAMLET: She well instructs me.   [*Exit* LORD.] 175

HORATIO: You will lose this wager, my lord.

HAMLET: I do not think so; since he went into France I have been in continual practice. I shall win at the odds. But thou wouldst not think how ill all's here about my heart; but it is no matter.

HORATIO: Nay, good my lord—   180

HAMLET: It is but foolery; but it is such a kind of gaingiving* as would perhaps trouble a woman.

HORATIO: If your mind dislike anything, obey it. I will forestall their repair hither, and say you are not fit.

HAMLET: Not a whit, we defy augury: there is a special providence in the fall of a 185 sparrow. If it be now, 'tis not to come; if it be not to come, it will be now; if it be not now, yet it will come—the readiness is all. Since no man owes of aught he leaves, what is't to leave betimes?* Let be.

> [*A table prepared. Trumpets, drums, and officers with cushions, foils, and daggers. Enter* KING, QUEEN, LAERTES, *and all the state.*]

KING: Come, Hamlet, come, and take this hand from me.

> [*The* KING *puts* LAERTES' *hand into* HAMLET's.]

HAMLET: Give me your pardon, sir. I have done you wrong;   190
But pardon't, as you are a gentleman.
This presence* knows,
And you must needs have heard how I am punish'd
With a sore distraction. What I have done
That might your nature, honour, and exception,*   195
Roughly awake, I here proclaim was madness.
Was't Hamlet wrong'd Laertes? Never Hamlet.
If Hamlet from himself be ta'en away,
And when he's not himself does wrong Laertes,
Then Hamlet does it not, Hamlet denies it.   200
Who does it, then? His madness. If't be so,
Hamlet is of the faction* that is wrong'd;
His madness is poor Hamlet's enemy.
Sir, in this audience,
Let my disclaiming from a purpos'd evil   205
Free me so far in your most generous thoughts

---

¹⁷³ **gentle entertainment** be courteous
¹⁸¹ **gaingiving** misgiving
¹⁸⁸ **betimes** early
¹⁹² **presence** assembly
¹⁹⁵ **exception** disapproval
²⁰² **faction** group

That I have shot my arrow o'er the house
And hurt my brother.
LAERTES: I am satisfied in nature,
Whose motive in this case should stir me most
To my revenge; but in my terms of honour   210
I stand aloof, and will no reconcilement
Till by some elder masters of known honour
I have a voice and precedent of peace
To keep my name ungor'd—but till that time
I do receive your offer'd love like love,   215
And will not wrong it.
HAMLET: I embrace it freely;
And will this brother's wager frankly play.
Give us the foils. Come on.
LAERTES: Come, one for me.
HAMLET: I'll be your foil, Laertes; in mine ignorance
Your skill shall, like a star i' th' darkest night,   220
Stick fiery* off indeed.
LAERTES: You mock me, sir.
HAMLET: No, by this hand.
KING: Give them the foils, young Osric. Cousin Hamlet,
You know the wager?
HAMLET: Very well, my lord;
Your Grace has laid the odds a' th' weaker side.   225
KING: I do not fear it: I have seen you both;
But since he's better'd,* we have therefore odds.
LAERTES: This is too heavy; let me see another.
HAMLET: This likes me well. These foils have all a length?
      [*They prepare to play.*]
OSRIC: Ay, my good lord.   230
KING: Set me the stoups of wine upon that table.
If Hamlet give the first or second hit,
Or quit in answer of the third exchange,
Let all the battlements their ordnance fire;
The King shall drink to Hamlet's better breath,   235
And in the cup an union* shall he throw,
Richer than that which four successive kings
In Denmark's crown have worn. Give me the cups;
And let the kettle* to the trumpet speak,
The trumpet to the cannoneer without,   240
The cannons to the heavens, the heaven to earth,
'Now the King drinks to Hamlet.' Come, begin—
And you, the judges, bear a wary eye.

---

221 **stick fiery off** stand out brilliantly
227 **better'd** improved
236 **union** pearl
239 **kettle** kettledrum

HAMLET: Come on, sir.

LAERTES: Come, my lord.   [*They play.*]

HAMLET: One.

LAERTES: No.

HAMLET: Judgment?   245

OSRIC: A hit, a very palpable hit.

LAERTES: Well, again.

KING: Stay, give me drink. Hamlet, this pearl is thine;
    Here's to thy health. [*Drum, trumpets, and shot.*] Give him the cup.

HAMLET: I'll play this bout first; set it by awhile.
    Come. [*They play.*] Another hit; what say you?   250

LAERTES: A touch, a touch, I do confess't.

KING: Our son shall win.

QUEEN: He's fat,* and scant of breath.
    Here, Hamlet, take my napkin, rub thy brows.
    The Queen carouses to thy fortune, Hamlet.

HAMLET: Good madam!

KING: Gertrude, do not drink.   255

QUEEN: I will, my lord; I pray you pardon me.

KING: [*aside*] It is the poison'd cup; it is too late.

HAMLET: I dare not drink yet, madam; by and by.

QUEEN: Come, let me wipe thy face.

LAERTES: My lord, I'll hit him now.

KING: I do not think't.   260

LAERTES: [*aside*] And yet it is almost against my conscience.

HAMLET: Come, for the third. Laertes, you do but dally;
    I pray you pass with your best violence;
    I am afeard you make a wanton* of me.

LAERTES: Say you so? Come on.   [*They play.*] 265

OSRIC: Nothing, neither way.

LAERTES: Have at you now!

    [LAERTES *wounds* HAMLET; *then, in scuffling, they change rapiers, and*
        HAMLET *wounds* LAERTES.]

KING: Part them; they are incens'd.

HAMLET: Nay, come again.   [*The* QUEEN *falls.*]

OSRIC: Look to the Queen there, ho!   270

HORATIO: They bleed on both sides. How is it, my lord?

OSRIC: How is't, Laertes?

LAERTES: Why, as a woodcock, to mine own springe,* Osric;
    I am justly kill'd with mine own treachery.

HAMLET: How does the Queen?

KING: She swoons to see them bleed.

QUEEN: No, no, the drink, the drink! O my dear Hamlet!   275
    The drink, the drink! I am poison'd.   [*dies*]

---

252 **fat** sweaty
264 **wanton** spoiled child
272 **springe** snare

HAMLET: O, villainy! Ho! let the door be lock'd.
　　Treachery! Seek it out.   [LAERTES *falls*.]
LAERTES: It is here, Hamlet. Hamlet, thou art slain;
　　No med'cine in the world can do thee good;   280
　　In thee there is not half an hour's life;
　　The treacherous instrument is in thy hand,
　　Unbated and envenom'd. The foul practice*
　　Hath turn'd itself on me; lo, here I lie,
　　Never to rise again. Thy mother's poison'd.   285
　　I can no more. The King, the King's to blame.
HAMLET: The point envenom'd, too!
　　Then, venom, to thy work.   [*stabs the* KING]
ALL: Treason! treason!
KING: O, yet defend me, friends; I am but hurt.   290
HAMLET: Here, thou incestuous, murd'rous, damned Dane,
　　Drink off this potion. Is thy union here?
　　Follow my mother.   [KING *dies*.]
LAERTES: He is justly serv'd:
　　It is a poison temper'd* by himself.   295
　　Exchange forgiveness with me, noble Hamlet.
　　Mine and my father's death come not upon thee,
　　Nor thine on me!   [*dies*]
HAMLET: Heaven make thee free of it! I follow thee.
　　I am dead, Horatio. Wretched Queen, adieu!
　　You that look pale and tremble at this chance,   300
　　That are but mutes or audience to this act,
　　Had I but time, as this fell sergeant Death
　　Is strict in his arrest, O, I could tell you—
　　But let it be. Horatio, I am dead:
　　Thou livest; report me and my cause aright   305
　　To the unsatisfied.
HORATIO:　　　　　　　Never believe it.
　　I am more an antique Roman* than a Dane;
　　Here's yet some liquor left.
HAMLET:　　　　　　　　　As th'art a man,
　　Give me the cup. Let go. By heaven, I'll ha't.
　　O good Horatio, what a wounded name,   310
　　Things standing thus unknown, shall live behind me!
　　If thou didst ever hold me in thy heart,
　　Absent thee from felicity awhile,
　　And in this harsh world draw thy breath in pain,
　　To tell my story. [*March afar off, and shot within.*] What warlike noise   315
　　is this?

---

283 **foul practice** deception
295 **temper'd** mixed
307 **antique Roman** given to suicide

OSRIC: Young Fortinbras, with conquest come from Poland,
    To th' ambassadors of England gives
    This warlike volley.
HAMLET: O, I die, Horatio!
    The potent poison quite o'er-crows* my spirit.
    I cannot live to hear the news from England,   320
    But I do prophesy th' election lights
    On Fortinbras; he has my dying voice.
    So tell him, with th' occurrents,* more and less,
    Which have solicited*—the rest is silence.
        [*dies*]
HORATIO: Now cracks a noble heart. Good night, sweet prince,   325
    And flights of angels sing thee to thy rest!   [*March within.*]
    Why does the drum come hither?
       [*Enter* FORTINBRAS *and* ENGLISH AMBASSADORS, *with drum, colours, and*
       attendants.]
FORTINBRAS: Where is this sight?
HORATIO: What is it you would see?
    If aught of woe or wonder, cease your search.
FORTINBRAS: This quarry* cries on havoc.* O proud death,   330
    What feast is toward* in thine eternal cell
    That thou so many princes at a shot
    So bloodily hast struck?
FIRST AMBASSADOR: The sight is dismal;
    And our affairs from England come too late: 335
    The ears are senseless that should give us hearing
    To tell him his commandment is fulfill'd
    That Rosencrantz and Guildenstern are dead.
    Where should we have our thanks?
HORATIO: Not from his* mouth,   340
    Had it th' ability of life to thank you:
    He never gave commandment for their death.
    But since, so jump* upon this bloody question,
    You from the Polack wars, and you from England,
    And here arrived, give order that these bodies   345
    High on a stage* be placed to the view;
    And let me speak to th' yet unknowing world
    How these things came about. So shall you hear
    Of carnal, bloody, and unnatural acts;

---

319 **o'er-crows** overpowers
323 **occurrents** occurrences
324 **solicited** incited
330 **quarry** heap of slain bodies
330 **cries on havoc** proclaims general slaughter
331 **toward** in preparation
340 **his** Claudius'
343 **jump** precisely
346 **stage** platform

Of accidental judgments, casual* slaughters; 350
Of deaths put on by cunning and forc'd cause;
And, in this upshot, purposes mistook
Fall'n on th' inventors' heads—all this can I
Truly deliver.
FORTINBRAS: Let us haste to hear it,
And call the noblest to the audience. 355
For me, with sorrow I embrace my fortune;
I have some rights of memory* in this kingdom,
Which now to claim my vantage doth invite me.
HORATIO: Of that I shall have also cause to speak,
And from his mouth whose voice will draw on more.* 360
But let this same be presently perform'd,
Even while men's minds are wild, lest more mischance
On* plots and errors happen.
FORTINBRAS: Let four captains
Bear Hamlet like a soldier to the stage;
For he was likely, had he been put on, 365
To have prov'd most royal; and for his passage*
The soldier's music and the rite of war
Speak loudly for him.
Take up the bodies. Such a sight as this
Becomes the field, but here shows much amiss. 370
Go, bid the soldiers shoot.
          [*Exeunt marching. A peal of ordnance shot off.*]

350 **casual** unplanned
357 **rights of memory** past claims
360 **voice will draw on more** vote will influence others
363 **on** on top of earlier
366 **passage** death

A Commedia dell'Arte Scenario
Recorded by Flaminio Scala in 1611

The Dentist

Much of the innovative theatrical activity in Renaissance Italy occurred in the privacy of the courts of rulers. Alongside these performances, another type, *commedia dell'arte* (comedy of professional artists), catered to the general public. First mentioned in historical records in the 1560s, commedia rapidly became the most popular theatrical entertainment in Italy, as well as throughout much of Europe after troupes began to tour. It remained popular until the mid-eighteenth century and influenced many of Europe's major dramatists.

Adaptability was one of commedia's primary assets. Though it made use of scenery and theatre buildings when they were available, it could as easily be performed without scenery in a town square. Each company had a set of stock characters, each with his or her own distinctive costume and (for some characters) masks, who appeared in all productions. There were three major groups of actors: the lovers (attractive young people who dressed fashionably and did not wear masks); the masters, all of them masked (Pantalone, an elderly Venetian merchant; Dottore, an academic or doctor of law; and the Capitano, a braggart soldier); and the *zanni* or servants, also masked (at least two males—one clever and one stupid—and one female, maid to an inamorata). The scripts were scenarios that merely summarized, scene by scene, the situations, complications, and outcome. The actors improvised the dialogue and fleshed out the action. The scripts left room for *lazzi,* elaborate bits of stage business, most of which could be used in a number of different productions.

The Dentist is a typical scenario, probably from the repertory of the Gelosi ("zealous") company. It takes place out of doors in a space readily accessible to all the characters. Like many other scripts, it shows the servants intriguing against their masters and assisting the young lovers. The action is loosely organized, leaving considerable latitude for improvisation of dialogue and stage business. The reader of a commedia scenario, like its performers, must fill in much that is indicated only in bare outline. That companies were able to do this to great acclaim over a period of 200 years says much about the performers of this unique theatrical form.

156

A Commedia dell'Arte Scenario
Recorded by Flaminio Scala in 1611

The Dentist

ARGUMENT

Pantalone lived in Rome with his son Oratio and daughter Flaminia. Oratio was in love with a well-to-do young widow named Isabella, who was also in love with him. Pantalone also loved Isabella, and being rejected by her, he decided to get rid of his son as a rival by sending him away to school. Isabella discovered the plan and, disapproving of it, decided to prevent it. She consulted an old friend who confided that she had a potion that, mixed into candy, would make whoever ate it lose their reason, and another potion that would cure the madness. Isabella decided to use the secret potion on Oratio, hoping that it would prevent Pantalone from sending him away. What followed will become clear in the play.

CHARACTERS IN THE PLAY

PANTALONE
ORATIO, *his son*
FLAMINIA, *his daughter*
PEDROLINO, *his servant*
FLAVIO
ISABELLA, *his widowed sister*
FRANCESCHINA, *her maidservant*
ARLECCHINO, *her servant*
DOTTORE
CAPITANO SPAVENTO
PASQUELLA, *an old woman*

PROPERTIES

Two boxes of candy
A dentist's costume
A pair of pliers
A chair

SETTING

ROME. *(All the action takes place in a street, or open space, between two houses. One house belongs to Pantalone, the other to Isabella.)*

ACT ONE

PANTALONE *and* PEDROLINO *enter. Pantalone is telling Pedrolino that he loves the young widow Isabella. Suspecting that his son Oratio is his rival for Isabella's love, he declares his intention to get Oratio out of the way by sending him to school in Perugia. Pedrolino defends Oratio and chastises Pantalone. They begin an argument that develops into an exchange of blows and ends with Pantalone biting Pedrolino on the arm. Threatening Pedrolino with further punishment,* PANTALONE *leaves, saying he will report Pedrolino's insubordination to Franceschina, Isabella's maid with whom Pedrolino is in love. Pedrolino promises revenge on Pantalone for biting him.*

FRANCESCHINA *enters. She has been sent by Isabella to look for Oratio. Pedrolino tells her about the bite he has received from Pantalone. To get revenge on Pantalone, they contrive a plan to make Pantalone believe that his breath stinks.* FRANCESCHINA *exits into the house.*

FLAVIO *enters. Speaking to Pedrolino about his love for Flaminia, Flavio gets carried away and slaps Pedrolino on his wounded arm. Pedrolino, exaggerating his pain, is able to enlist Flavio in his plan to make Pantalone think his breath stinks.* FLAVIO *exits.*

DOTTORE *enters. He is seeking Pantalone to collect twenty-five scudi that Pantalone owes him. While expressing his exasperation with Pantalone, Dottore seizes Pedrolino by his wounded arm, and Pedrolino exaggerates his pain even more than in the preceding scene. Dottore agrees to assist in the trick on Pantalone in return for Pedrolino's promise to help him collect his debt.* DOTTORE *exits, and* PEDROLINO *leaves to look for Oratio.*

CAPITANO SPAVENTO *enters, telling of his love for Isabella and boasting about his brave deeds. Isabella's servant,* ARLECCHINO, *enters and there follows a ridiculous scene with Capitano before* ARLECCHINO *leaves to call Isabella as Capitano has demanded. Meanwhile,* FLAMINIA, *looking out of her window, has seen Capitano, with whom she is in love. She now addresses him, begging him to return her love but he rejects her.* ISABELLA *comes out, believing that it is Oratio who has sent for her. In a three-way scene, Capitano begs Isabella to love him, while Flaminia begs Capitano to love her. Finally,* ISABELLA *leaves, expressing her scorn for Capitano, even as Capitano expresses his scorn for Flaminia.* CAPITANO *exits, leaving Flaminia lamenting his rejection.*

PEDROLINO *appears, telling Flaminia that he has overheard her exchange with Capitano and threatening to tell her father unless she cooperates in playing the stinking-breath trick on Pantalone. After acceding to his demand,* FLAMINIA *leaves. Pedrolino, exaggerating even more how much his arm hurts, wishes that he were a doctor so he could avenge himself.*

ARLECCHINO *enters and as they talk a new plan takes shape in Pedrolino's mind. Pedrolino bribes Arlecchino to disguise himself as a dentist.* ARLECCHINO *leaves to dress himself for his new role.*

ORATIO *enters. Pedrolino reveals that Pantalone is Oratio's rival for Isabella's love, and that Pantalone is going to send him away to school in Perugia. Stricken by this news, Oratio pleads with Pedrolino to help him. Pedrolino promises to do so if Oratio will reciprocate by cooperating in the trick of the stinking breath. Oratio agrees. He then expresses his desire to talk with Isabella. Pedrolino calls her and* ISABELLA *comes outside. Oratio tells her that he loves her but that he is being sent away. She is very sad.*

Pantalone is heard calling loudly. Hearing him, ISABELLA *goes into her house. Pedrolino tries to persuade Oratio not to go to Perugia.* PANTALONE *enters, sees his son, and orders him to go prepare himself to leave immediately for Perugia. Submissively,* ORATIO *enters the house. Pedrolino, while talking to Pantalone, suddenly cries out, "Phew, Master, your breath stinks terribly." Pantalone laughs.* FRANCESCHINA *enters and, after expressing disgust at his breath, tells Pantalone that if his breath wasn't so repulsive, Isabella would love him. When* FRANCESCHINA *leaves, Pantalone wonders if what she has said is true.*

FLAVIO, *passing by, is given a signal by Pedrolino. He comes to talk to Pantalone but, complaining of Pantalone's breath,* FLAVIO *leaves hastily. Pantalone is beginning to be concerned about these complaints.* DOTTORE *arrives and Pedrolino gives him the sign. After expressing disgust with Pantalone's breath,* DOTTORE *exits. Pantalone decides that he will ask Flaminia if his breath really stinks. He calls her and when* FLAMINIA *comes out she tells her father that his breath stinks something awful.* FLAMINIA *goes back in.*

ORATIO *enters and verifies what the others have said.* ORATIO *leaves quickly. Pantalone decides that the problem is a bad tooth and decides to have the tooth pulled. After ordering Pedrolino to find a dentist,* PANTALONE *goes into the house. Before Pedrolino can leave,* ARLECCHINO *arrives in his disguise as a dentist. After telling Arlecchino to pull all of Pantalone's teeth because they are decayed,* PEDROLINO *hides. Arlecchino begins calling out under the windows for anyone who needs help because of bad teeth.*

After calling down to him from a window, PANTALONE *comes out. Arlecchino takes out a great variety of comically inappropriate tools, calling them by ridiculous names. He makes Pantalone sit in a chair and, using a very large pair of pliers, pulls out four good teeth. In great pain, Pantalone grabs for anything within reach. Finally he gets hold of the dentist's beard which, being false, comes off in his hand.* ARLECCHINO *runs away, and Pantalone throws the chair after him. Groaning with pain,* PANTALONE *goes into the house as the first act ends.*

ACT TWO

Isabella's elderly friend PASQUELLA *comes to visit. When she knocks,* ISABELLA *comes out and tells her of her love for Oratio and how his father is sending him away. Pasquella promises to help her if she will use Pasquella's secret potions, which she conceals in candy. Isabella agrees to send Arlecchino to get the doctored candy.* PASQUELLA *leaves. Isabella expresses her happiness.*

PEDROLINO *enters, congratulating himself on the success of the trick played on Pantalone. He tells Isabella that Pantalone is stubborn and that he is determined to send Oratio away.* PANTALONE *comes in with* ORATIO, *saying that he is sticking with Oratio to make certain that he leaves immediately. After greeting Isabella,* PANTALONE *drags* ORATIO *into the house. Before he disappears, Oratio makes a sign for Isabella to talk to Pedrolino. Isabella tells Pedrolino to come back within the hour.*

FLAVIO *enters and, seeing Pedrolino with Isabella, his sister, he suspects something is up. He sends* ISABELLA *into the house and threatens Pedrolino. Pedrolino placates him by suggesting that he can help Flavio marry Flaminia by getting Flavio into the house with Flaminia. Flavio bites, and Pedrolino tells him that, to get into Pantalone's house,*

Flavio must disguise himself as a dentist. Unaware that a fake dentist has pulled Pantalone's teeth, FLAVIO *leaves to secure the disguise. Laughing,* PEDROLINO *goes off to find Oratio.*

ARLECCHINO *enters, congratulating himself on how well things went with the trick on Pantalone.* ISABELLA, *calling down from her window, sends him to Pasquella's house for the candy. Before Arlecchino can leave,* PEDROLINO *arrives laughing about the trick played on Pantalone.* CAPITANO *enters and threatens Arlecchino, who says Isabella has told Pedrolino what Capitano must do to get into her house. When Capitano turns to Pedrolino,* ARLECCHINO *runs off. Pedrolino at first says he knows nothing about it, but eventually he tells Capitano that he must dress himself as a Venetian, like Pantalone, and that Pedrolino will then get Capitano into Isabella's house. Now happy, the* CAPITANO *goes off to find a disguise.*

Having seen Pedrolino talking to Capitano, FLAMINIA *comes out and asks what is going on. Pedrolino says that this evening he will bring her lover to her, disguised as a woman, and asks for one of her dresses. After gladly bringing him one,* FLAMINIA *exits as* DOTTORE *enters, declaring heatedly that he will get the twenty-five scudi promised by Pantalone. Pedrolino, momentarily intimidated, hands him the dress just as* PANTALONE *arrives. Seeing Dottore with the dress, Pantalone calls him a thief and hits him. Pedrolino joins in the beating, paying no attention to Dottore's protests. Having given Dottore a thorough beating,* PANTALONE *and* PEDROLINO *go into the house. Outraged,* DOTTORE *leaves, shouting that he will have the law on them.*

Coming to say farewell to Isabella before he leaves, ORATIO *enters and knocks on her door.* ISABELLA *comes out, and they have a love scene. Isabella tells Oratio that she is going to send him some candy, which she makes him promise to eat before he leaves.* ORATIO *and* ISABELLA *go into their separate houses. Dressed as a dentist as Pedrolino has instructed him,* FLAVIO *enters and shouts under Pantalone's window. Hearing him,* PANTALONE *rushes out and beats Flavio, thinking it is the fake dentist who has pulled his teeth.* PANTALONE *reenters his house, and* FLAVIO *runs off. Dressed like Pantalone,* CAPITANO *enters.* FLAVIO *returns and, believing that Capitano is Pantalone, gives him a thorough beating. As* CAPITANO *and* FLAVIO *run off, the second act ends.*

ACT THREE

ARLECCHINO *enters with the boxes of candy.* ISABELLA *comes out, takes both boxes, and then hands one box back to Arlecchino with instructions to give it to Oratio. Keeping the other box,* ISABELLA *goes into the house.* PEDROLINO *arrives, and Arlecchino, to save himself work, asks Pedrolino to give the candy to Oratio.* ARLECCHINO *goes into the house as Pedrolino puts some of the candy into his pocket.*

ORATIO *enters and Pedrolino gives him the box of candy. After* ORATIO *leaves, Pedrolino eats the candy he had hidden in his pocket and immediately loses his wits.* CAPITANO *enters, swearing that he will kill Pedrolino for talking him into dressing as Pantalone. When Pedrolino responds nonsensically and seems to be insane, the amazed Capitano decides to forego his plan.* PEDROLINO *wanders off.*

FLAMINIA *enters and once more confesses her love; rejecting her,* CAPITANO *leaves. Declaring that she is now determined to love Flavio,* FLAMINIA *goes into her house.* DOTTORE *returns, shouting that justice will prevail. When* PEDROLINO *arrives, Dottore threatens him, but Pedrolino's madness frightens him.* DOTTORE *runs away.*

FRANCESCHINA *enters to speak to Pedrolino, but he continues to act like a madman. When* PEDROLINO *leaves,* FRANCESCHINA *follows him.*

ARLECCHINO *enters looking desperate and knocks at Isabella's door. When* ISABELLA *comes out, he tells her that Oratio, after eating the candy, has gone mad. She tells Arlecchino to bring Oratio to her, and* ARLECCHINO *leaves to do so.* FLAVIO *enters and asks Isabella what the matter is. She tells him all that has happened, of how she has induced Oratio's madness, and of how she has the secret to make him well. Declaring his love for Oratio's sister, Flavio promises to help straighten everything out.* ISABELLA *goes into the house and* FLAVIO *exits to find Pantalone.*

PANTALONE *enters wondering whether Oratio has left for Perugia.* PEDROLINO *enters and responds strangely to Pantalone.* ORATIO *arrives wearing a long gown and acting mad. Both* ORATIO *and* PEDROLINO *exit, leaving Pantalone in despair.* FLAVIO *returns to tell Pantalone that Oratio's health is in the hands of Isabella. Pantalone asks him to call her.* ISABELLA *enters and offers to cure Oratio, but in return she asks two favors: first, that Flaminia marry her brother Flavio; and second, that Oratio marry whomever Isabella chooses. Pantalone accepts her conditions and calls Flaminia.* FLAMINIA *comes out and agrees to marry Flavio.*

Seemingly mad and speaking nonsense, ORATIO *enters.* FLAVIO *takes him into the house and returns shortly to announce that Oratio has regained his sanity. Then,* ORATIO *enters with* ISABELLA, *who asks her second favor of Pantalone: that she be allowed to marry Oratio. Pantalone consents. At that moment,* DOTTORE *enters, chased by the mad* PEDROLINO. FLAVIO *takes* PEDROLINO *into the house to cure him. When* FLAVIO *and* PEDROLINO *come back out, Pedrolino confesses to Pantalone the conspiracy he has used to get revenge for Pantalone's bite. He also acknowledges the other tricks he has played on various characters and begs pardon of anyone who has been offended. All forgive him, and the comedy ends in laughter.*

Molière (Jean-Baptiste Poquelin, 1622–1673)

Tartuffe (1664, 1667, 1669)

While English drama of Shakespeare's time owed much to medieval conventions, French dramatists after the 1630s looked back to Greece and Rome for their standards. This conscious imitation of the classics gave rise to a set of literary standards summed up in the term *neoclassicism*. These included the unities of time, place, and action; strict distinction between tragedy and comedy, with no intermingling of the two; the use of universalized character types; and the demand that drama teach moral lessons. Many of the plays written in compliance with these demands now seem lifeless, but the tragedies of Racine and the comedies of Molière, written in France during the last half of the seventeenth century, reached a peak of artistry in the neoclassical mode. Unlike plays of earlier eras, these were written for the proscenium-arch stage and for perspective settings composed of wings, drops, and borders.

Molière is one of the most skillful and inventive comic dramatists of all times, and *Tartuffe* is one of his most admired plays. Within the restricted frame of one room, one day, and one main story, using a limited number of characters and little physical action, Molière creates an excellent comedy of character. The action of *Tartuffe*, divided into five acts, develops through five stages: the demonstration of Tartuffe's complete hold over Orgon; the unmasking of Tartuffe; Tartuffe's attempted revenge; the foiling of Tartuffe's plan; and the happy resolution. Molière has been criticized for delaying Tartuffe's first appearance until the third act, but he makes skillful use of this delay by having all the other characters establish his hypocrisy and Orgon's gullibility in trusting Tartuffe. The resolution, in which Tartuffe is suddenly discovered to be a notorious criminal, has also been criticized as overly contrived, but it is emotionally satisfying because it punishes Tartuffe and reestablishes the norm.

In *Tartuffe* Molière uses the verse form that by that time had become standard in French tragedy—the alexandrine (twelve-syllable lines, with each pair of adjacent lines rhyming). Richard Wilbur's translation, used here, is generally considered one of the finest now available both for its accuracy and for its rendition of Molière's verse.

When *Tartuffe* was written in 1664, it was immediately denounced as an attack on religious piety. The controversy was so intense that Louis XIV forbade the play's production. Molière rewrote it in 1667, only to have it banned once more. Finally, in 1669 he was able to gain permission for its production. It has remained in the repertory continuously since that time. It is still performed more often than any other play by Molière.

Molière

Tartuffe

Translated into English Verse by Richard Wilbur

CHARACTERS

MME. PERNELLE, *Orgon's mother*
ORGON, *Elmire's husband*
ELMIRE, *Orgon's wife*
DAMIS, *Orgon's son, Elmire's stepson*
MARIANE, *Orgon's daughter, Elmire's stepdaughter, in love with Valère*
VALÈRE, *in love with Mariane*
CLÉANTE, *Orgon's brother-in-law*
TARTUFFE, *a hypocrite*
DORINE, *Mariane's lady's-maid*
M. LOYAL, *a bailiff*
A POLICE OFFICER
FLIPOTE, *Mme. Pernelle's maid*

The scene throughout: ORGON'S *house in Paris*

ACT I

SCENE I

MADAME PERNELLE: Come, come, Flipote; it's time I left this place.
ELMIRE: I can't keep up, you walk at such a pace.
MADAME PERNELLE: Don't trouble, child; no need to show me out.
    It's not your manners I'm concerned about.
ELMIRE: We merely pay you the respect we owe.
    But, Mother, why this hurry? Must you go?
MADAME PERNELLE: I must. This house appals me. No one in it
    Will pay attention for a single minute.
    Children, I take my leave much vexed in spirit.
    I offer good advice, but you won't hear it.
    You all break in and chatter on and on.
    It's like a madhouse with the keeper gone.
DORINE: If . . .
MADAME PERNELLE: Girl, you talk too much, and I'm afraid
    You're far too saucy for a lady's-maid.
    You push in everwhere and have your say.
DAMIS: But . . .

MADAME PERNELLE: You, boy, grow more foolish every day.
    To think my grandson should be such a dunce!
    I've said a hundred times, if I've said it once,
    That if you keep the course on which you've started,
    You'll leave your worthy father broken-hearted.
MARIANE: I think . . .
MADAME PERNELLE: And you, his sister, seem so pure,
    So shy, so innocent, and so demure.
    But you know what they say about still waters.
    I pity parents with secretive daughters.
ELMIRE: Now, Mother . . .
MADAME PERNELLE: And as for you, child, let me add
    That your behavior is extremely bad,
    And a poor example for these children, too.
    Their dear, dead mother did far better than you.
    You're much too free with money, and I'm distressed
    To see you so elaborately dressed.
    When it's one's husband that one aims to please,
    One has no need of costly fripperies.
CLÉANTE: Oh, Madam, really . . .
MADAME PERNELLE: You are her brother, Sir,
    And I respect and love you; yet if I were
    My son, this lady's good and pious spouse,
    I wouldn't make you welcome in my house.
    You're full of worldly counsels which, I fear,
    Aren't suitable for decent folk to hear.
    I've spoken bluntly, Sir; but it behooves us
    Not to mince words when righteous fervor moves us.
DAMIS: Your man Tartuffe is full of holy speeches . . .
MADAME PERNELLE: And practices precisely what he preaches.
    He's a fine man, and should be listened to.
    I will not hear him mocked by fools like you.
DAMIS: Good God! Do you expect me to submit
    To the tyranny of that carping hypocrite?
    Must we forgo all joys and satisfactions
    Because that bigot censures all our actions?
DORINE: To hear him talk—and he talks all the time—
    There's nothing one can do that's not a crime.
    He rails at everything, your dear Tartuffe.
MADAME PERNELLE: Whatever he reproves deserves reproof.
    He's out to save your souls, and all of you
    Must love him, as my son would have you do.
DAMIS: Ah no, Grandmother, I could never take
    To such a rascal, even for my father's sake.
    That's how I feel, and I shall not dissemble.
    His every action makes me seethe and tremble
    With helpless anger, and I have no doubt
    That he and I will shortly have it out.

DORINE: Surely it is a shame and a disgrace
    To see this man usurp the master's place—
    To see this beggar who, when first he came,
    Had not a shoe or shoestring to his name
    So far forget himself that he behaves
    As if the house were his, and we his slaves.

MADAME PERNELLE: Well, mark my words, your souls would fare far better
    If you obeyed his precepts to the letter.

DORINE: You see him as a saint. I'm far less awed;
    In fact, I see right through him. He's a fraud.

MADAME PERNELLE: Nonsense!

DORINE: His man Laurent's the same, or worse;
    I'd not trust either with a penny purse.

MADAME PERNELLE: I can't say what his servant's morals may be;
    His own great goodness I can guarantee.
    You all regard him with distaste and fear
    Because he tells you what you're loath to hear,
    Condemns your sins, points out your moral flaws,
    And humbly strives to further Heaven's cause.

DORINE: If sin is all that bothers him, why is it
    He's so upset when folk drop in to visit?
    Is Heaven so outraged by a social call
    That he must prophesy against us all?
    I'll tell you what I think: if you ask me,
    He's jealous of my mistress' company.

MADAME PERNELLE: Rubbish! [*to* ELMIRE] He's not alone, child, in complaining
    Of all of your promiscuous entertaining.
    Why, the whole neighborhood's upset, I know,
    By all these carriages that come and go,
    With crowds of guests parading in and out
    And noisy servants loitering about.
    In all of this, I'm sure there's nothing vicious;
    But why give people cause to be suspicious?

CLÉANTE: They need no cause, they'll talk in any case.
    Madam, this world would be a joyless place
    If, fearing what malicious tongues might say,
    We locked our doors and turned our friends away.
    And even if one did so dreary a thing,
    D'you think those tongues would cease their chattering?
    One can't fight slander; it's a losing battle;
    Let us instead ignore their tittle-tattle.
    Let's strive to live by conscience's clear decrees,
    And let the gossips gossip as they please.

DORINE: If there is talk against us, I know the source:
    It's Daphne and her little husband, of course.
    Those who have greatest cause for guilt and shame
    Are quickest to besmirch a neighbor's name.
    When there's a chance for libel, they never miss it;

When something can be made to seem illicit
They're off at once to spread the joyous news,
Adding to fact what fantasies they choose.
By talking up their neighbor's indiscretions
They seek to camouflage their own transgressions,
Hoping that others' innocent affairs
Will lend a hue of innocence to theirs,
Or that their own black guilt will come to seem
Part of a general shady color-scheme.

MADAME PERNELLE: All that is quite irrelevant. I doubt
That anyone's more virtuous and devout
Than dear Orante; and I'm informed that she
Condemns your mode of life most vehemently.

DORINE: Oh, yes, she's strict, devout, and has no taint
Of worldliness; in short, she seems a saint.
But it was time which taught her that disguise;
She's thus because she can't be otherwise.
So long as her attractions could enthrall,
She flounced and flirted and enjoyed it all,
But now that they're no longer what they were
She quits a world which fast is quitting her,
And wears a veil of virtue to conceal
Her bankrupt beauty and her lost appeal.
That's what becomes of old coquettes today:
Distressed when all their lovers fall away,
They see no recourse but to play the prude,
And so confer a style on solitude.
Thereafter, they're severe with everyone,
Condemning all our actions, pardoning none,
And claiming to be pure, austere, and zealous
When, if the truth were known, they're merely jealous,
And cannot bear to see another know
The pleasures time has forced them to forgo.

MADAME PERNELLE: [*initially* to ELMIRE] That sort of talk is what you like
        to hear;
Therefore you'd have us all keep still, my dear,
While Madam rattles on the livelong day.
Nevertheless, I mean to have my say.
I tell you that you're blest to have Tartuffe
Dwelling, as my son's guest, beneath this roof;
That Heaven has sent him to forestall its wrath
By leading you, once more, to the true path;
That all he reprehends is reprehensible,
And that you'd better heed him, and be sensible.
These visits, balls, and parties in which you revel
Are nothing but inventions of the Devil.
One never hears a word that's edifying:
Nothing but chaff and foolishness and lying,

As well as vicious gossip in which one's neighbor
Is cut to bits with épée, foil, and saber.
People of sense are driven half-insane
At such affairs, where noise and folly reign
And reputations perish thick and fast.
As a wise preacher said on Sunday last,
Parties are Towers of Babylon, because
The guests all babble on with never a pause;
And then he told a story which, I think . . .
[*to* CLÉANTE] I heard that laugh, Sir, and I saw that wink!
Go find your silly friends and laugh some more!
Enough; I'm going; don't show me to the door.
I leave this household much dismayed and vexed;
I cannot say when I shall see you next.
[*slapping* FLIPOTE] Wake up, don't stand there gaping into space!
I'll slap some sense into that stupid face.
Move, move, you slut.

SCENE II

CLÉANTE: I think I'll stay behind;
    I want no further pieces of her mind.
    How that old lady . . .
DORINE: Oh, what wouldn't she say
    If she could hear you speak of her that way!
    She'd thank you for the *lady*, but I'm sure
    She'd find the *old* a little premature.
CLÉANTE: My, what a scene she made, and what a din!
    And how this man Tartuffe has taken her in!
DORINE: Yes, but her son is even worse deceived;
    His folly must be seen to be believed.
    In the late troubles, he played an able part
    And served his king with wise and loyal heart,
    But he's quite lost his senses since he fell
    Beneath Tartuffe's infatuating spell.
    He calls him brother, and loves him as his life,
    Preferring him to mother, child, or wife.
    In him and him alone will he confide;
    He's made him his confessor and his guide;
    He pets and pampers him with love more tender
    Than any pretty mistress could engender,
    Gives him the place of honor when they dine,
    Delights to see him gorging like a swine,
    Stuffs him with dainties till his guts distend,
    And when he belches, cries "God bless you, friend!"
    In short, he's mad; he worships him; he dotes;
    His deeds he marvels at, his words he quotes;

Thinking each act a miracle, each word
Oracular as those that Moses heard.
Tartuffe, much pleased to find so easy a victim,
Has in a hundred ways beguiled and tricked him,
Milked him of money, and with his permission
Established here a sort of Inquisition.
Even Laurent, his lackey, dares to give
Us arrogant advice on how to live;
He sermonizes us in thundering tones
And confiscates our ribbons and colognes.
Last week he tore a kerchief into pieces
Because he found it pressed in a *Life of Jesus:*
He said it was a sin to juxtapose
Unholy vanities and holy prose.

SCENE III

ELMIRE: [*to* CLÉANTE] You did well not to follow; she stood in the door
And said *verbatim* all she'd said before.
I saw my husband coming. I think I'd best
Go upstairs now, and take a little rest.
CLÉANTE: I'll wait and greet him here; then I must go.
I've really only time to say hello.
DAMIS: Sound him about my sister's wedding, please.
I think Tartuffe's against it, and that he's
Been urging Father to withdraw his blessing.
As you well know, I'd find that most distressing.
Unless my sister and Valère can marry,
My hopes to wed *his* sister will miscarry,
And I'm determined . . .
DORINE: He's coming.

SCENE IV

ORGON: Ah, Brother, good-day.
CLÉANTE: Well, welcome back. I'm sorry I can't stay.
How was the country? Blooming, I trust, and green?
ORGON: Excuse me, Brother; just one moment.
[*to* DORINE] Dorine . . .
[*to* CLÉANTE] To put my mind at rest, I always learn
The household news the moment I return.
[*to* DORINE] Has all been well, these two days I've been gone?
How are the family? What's been going on?
DORINE: Your wife, two days ago, had a bad fever,
And a fierce headache which refused to leave her.
ORGON: Ah. And Tartuffe?
DORINE: Tartuffe? Why, he's round and red,
Bursting with health, and excellently fed.
ORGON: Poor fellow!

DORINE: That night, the mistress was unable
  To take a single bite at the dinner-table.
  Her headache-pains, she said, were simply hellish.
ORGON: Ah. And Tartuffe?
DORINE: He ate his meal with relish,
  And zealously devoured in her presence
  A leg of mutton and a brace of pheasants.
ORGON: Poor fellow!
DORINE: Well, the pains continued strong,
  And so she tossed and tossed the whole night long,
  Now icy-cold, now burning like a flame.
  We sat beside her bed till morning came.
ORGON: Ah. And Tartuffe?
DORINE: Why, having eaten, he rose
  And sought his room, already in a doze,
  Got into his warm bed, and snored away
  In perfect peace until the break of day.
ORGON: Poor fellow!
DORINE: After much ado, we talked her
  Into dispatching someone for the doctor.
  He bled her, and the fever quickly fell.
ORGON: Ah. And Tartuffe?
DORINE: He bore it very well.
  To keep his cheerfulness at any cost,
  And make up for the blood *Madame* had lost,
  He drank, at lunch, four beakers full of port.
ORGON: Poor fellow!
DORINE: Both are doing well, in short.
  I'll go and tell *Madame* that you've expressed
  Keen sympathy and anxious interest.

SCENE V

CLÉANTE: That girl was laughing in your face, and though
  I've no wish to offend you, even so
  I'm bound to say that she had some excuse.
  How can you possibly be such a goose?
  Are you so dazed by this man's hocus-pocus
  That all the world, save him, is out of focus?
  You've given him clothing, shelter, food, and care;
  Why must you also . . .
ORGON: Brother, stop right there.
  You do not know the man of whom you speak.
CLÉANTE: I grant you that. But my judgment's not so weak
  That I can't tell, by his effect on others . . .
ORGON: Ah, when you meet him, you two will be like brothers!
  There's been no loftier soul since time began.
  He is a man who . . . a man who . . . an excellent man.

To keep his precepts is to be reborn,
And view this dunghill of a world with scorn.
Yes, thanks to him I'm a changed man indeed.
Under his tutelage my soul's been freed
From earthly loves, and every human tie:
My mother, children, brother, and wife could die,
And I'd not feel a single moment's pain.

CLÉANTE: That's a fine sentiment, Brother; most humane.

ORGON: Oh, had you seen Tartuffe as I first knew him,
Your heart, like mine, would have surrendered to him.
He used to come into our church each day
And humbly kneel nearby, and start to pray.
He'd draw the eyes of everybody there
By the deep fervor of his heartfelt prayer;
He'd sigh and weep, and sometimes with a sound
Of rapture he would bend and kiss the ground;
And when I rose to go, he'd run before
To offer me holy-water at the door.
His serving-man, no less devout than he,
Informed me of his master's poverty;
I gave him gifts, but in his humbleness
He'd beg me every time to give him less.
"Oh, that's too much," he'd cry, "too much by twice!
I don't deserve it. The half, Sir, would suffice."
And when I wouldn't take it back, he'd share
Half of it with the poor, right then and there.
At length, Heaven prompted me to take him in
To dwell with us, and free our souls from sin.
He guides our lives, and to protect my honor
Stays by my wife, and keeps an eye upon her;
He tells me whom she sees, and all she does,
And seems more jealous than I ever was!
And how austere he is! Why, he can detect
A mortal sin where you would least suspect;
In smallest trifles, he's extremely strict.
Last week, his conscience was severely pricked
Because, while praying, he had caught a flea
And killed it, so he felt, too wrathfully.

CLÉANTE: Good God, man! Have you lost your common sense—
Or is this all some joke at my expense?
How can you stand there and in all sobriety . . .

ORGON: Brother, your language savors of impiety.
Too much free-thinking's made your faith unsteady,
And as I've warned you many times already,
'Twill get you into trouble before you're through.

CLÉANTE: So I've been told before by dupes like you:
Being blind, you'd have all others blind as well;
The clear-eyed man you call an infidel,

And he who sees through humbug and pretense
Is charged, by you, with want of reverence.
Spare me your warnings, Brother; I have no fear
Of speaking out, for you and Heaven to hear,
Against affected zeal and pious knavery.
There's true and false in piety, as in bravery,
And just as those whose courage shines the most
In battle, are the least inclined to boast,
So those whose hearts are truly pure and lowly
Don't make a flashy show of being holy.
There's a vast difference, so it seems to me,
Between true piety and hypocrisy:
How do you fail to see it, may I ask?
Is not a face quite different from a mask?
Cannot sincerity and cunning art,
Reality and semblance, be told apart?
Are scarecrows just like men, and do you hold
That a false coin is just as good as gold?
Ah, Brother, man's a strangely fashioned creature
Who seldom is content to follow Nature,
But recklessly pursues his inclination
Beyond the narrow bounds of moderation,
And often, by transgressing Reason's laws,
Perverts a lofty aim or noble cause.
A passing observation, but it applies.
ORGON: I see, dear Brother, that you're profoundly wise;
You harbor all the insight of the age.
You are our one clear mind, our only sage,
The era's oracle, its Cato, too,
And all mankind are fools compared to you.
CLÉANTE: Brother, I don't pretend to be a sage,
Nor have I all the wisdom of the age.
There's just one insight I would dare to claim:
I know that true and false are not the same;
And just as there is nothing I more revere
Than a soul whose faith is steadfast and sincere,
Nothing that I more cherish and admire
Than honest zeal and true religious fire,
So there is nothing that I find more base
Than specious piety's dishonest face—
Than these bold mountebanks, these histrios
Whose impious mummeries and hollow shows
Exploit our love of Heaven, and make a jest
Of all that men think holiest and best;
These calculating souls who offer prayers
Not to their Maker, but as public wares,
And seek to buy respect and reputation
With lifted eyes and sighs of exaltation;

These charlatans, I say, whose pilgrim souls
Proceed, by way of Heaven, toward earthly goals,
Who weep and pray and swindle and extort,
Who preach the monkish life, but haunt the court,
Who make their zeal the partner of their vice—
Such men are vengeful, sly, and cold as ice,
And when there is an enemy to defame
They cloak their spite in fair religion's name,
Their private spleen and malice being made
To seem a high and virtuous crusade,
Until, to mankind's reverent applause,
They crucify their foe in Heaven's cause.
Such knaves are all too common; yet, for the wise,
True piety isn't hard to recognize,
And happily, these present times provide us
With bright examples to instruct and guide us.
Consider Ariston and Périandre;
Look at Oronte, Alcidamas, Clitandre;
Their virtue is acknowledged; who could doubt it?
But you won't hear them beat the drum about it.
They're never ostentatious, never vain,
And their religion's moderate and humane;
It's not their way to criticize and chide:
They think censoriousness a mark of pride,
And therefore, letting others preach and rave,
They show, by deeds, how Christians should behave.
They think no evil of their fellow man,
But judge of him kindly as they can.
They don't intrigue and wangle and conspire;
To lead a good life is their one desire;
The sinner wakes no rancorous hate in them;
It is the sin alone which they condemn;
Nor do they try to show a fiercer zeal
For Heaven's cause than Heaven itself could feel.
These men I honor, these men I advocate
As models for us all to emulate.
Your man is not their sort at all, I fear:
And, while your praise of him is quite sincere,
I think that you've been dreadfully deluded.

ORGON: Now then, dear Brother, is your speech concluded?

CLÉANTE: Why, yes.

ORGON: Your servant, Sir. [*He turns to go.*]

CLÉANTE: No, Brother; wait.
There's one more matter. You agreed of late
That young Valère might have your daughter's hand.

ORGON: I did.

CLÉANTE: And set the date, I understand.

ORGON: Quite so.

CLÉANTE: You've now postponed it; is that true?
ORGON: No doubt.
CLÉANTE: The match no longer pleases you?
ORGON: Who knows?
CLÉANTE: D'you mean to go back on your word?
ORGON: I won't say that.
CLÉANTE: Has anything occurred
     Which might entitle you to break your pledge?
ORGON: Perhaps.
CLÉANTE: Why must you hem and haw, and hedge?
     The boy asked me to sound you in this affair . . .
ORGON: It's been a pleasure.
CLÉANTE: But what shall I tell Valère?
ORGON: Whatever you like.
CLÉANTE: But what have you decided?
     What are your plans?
ORGON: I plan, Sir, to be guided
     By Heaven's will.
CLÉANTE: Come, Brother, don't talk rot.
     You've given Valère your word; will you keep it, or not?
ORGON: Good day.
CLÉANTE: This looks like poor Valère's undoing;
     I'll go and warn him that there's trouble brewing.

ACT II

SCENE I

ORGON: Mariane.
MARIANE: Yes, Father?
ORGON: A word with you; come here.
MARIANE: What are you looking for?
ORGON: [*peering into a small closet*] Eavesdroppers, dear.
     I'm making sure we shan't be overheard.
     Someone in there could catch our every word.
     Ah, good, we're safe. Now, Mariane, my child,
     You're a sweet girl who's tractable and mild,
     Whom I hold dear, and think most highly of.
MARIANE: I'm deeply grateful, Father, for your love.
ORGON: That's well said, Daughter; and you can repay me
     If, in all things, you'll cheerfully obey me.
MARIANE: To please you, Sir, is what delights me best.
ORGON: Good, good. Now, what d'you think of Tartuffe, our guest?
MARIANE: I, Sir?
ORGON: Yes. Weigh your answer; think it through.
MARIANE: Oh, dear. I'll say whatever you wish me to.
ORGON: That's wisely said, my Daughter. Say of him, then,

That he's the very worthiest of men,
And that you're fond of him, and would rejoice
In being his wife, if that should be my choice.
Well?
MARIANE: What?
ORGON: What's that?
MARIANE: I . . .
ORGON: Well?
MARIANE: Forgive me, pray.
ORGON: Did you not hear me?
MARIANE: Of *whom*, Sir, must I say
That I am fond of him, and would rejoice
In being his wife, if that should be your choice?
ORGON: Why, of Tartuffe.
MARIANE: But, Father, that's false, you know.
Why would you have me say what isn't so?
ORGON: Because I am resolved it shall be true.
That it's my wish should be enough for you.
MARIANE: You can't mean, Father . . .
ORGON: Yes, Tartuffe shall be
Allied by marriage to this family,
And he's to be your husband, is that clear?
It's a father's privilege . . .

SCENE II

ORGON: [*to* DORINE] What are you doing in here?
Is curiosity so fierce a passion
With you, that you must eavesdrop in this fashion?
DORINE: There's lately been a rumor going about—
Based on some hunch or chance remark, no doubt—
That you mean Mariane to wed Tartuffe.
I've laughed it off, of course, as just a spoof.
ORGON: You find it so incredible?
DORINE: Yes, I do.
I won't accept that story, even from you.
ORGON: Well, you'll believe it when the thing is done.
DORINE: Yes, yes, of course. Go on and have your fun.
ORGON: I've never been more serious in my life.
DORINE: Ha!
ORGON: Daughter, I mean it; you're to be his wife.
DORINE: No, don't believe your father; it's all a hoax.
ORGON: See here, young woman . . .
DORINE: Come, Sir, no more jokes;
You can't fool us.
ORGON: How dare you talk that way?
DORINE: All right, then: we believe you, sad to say.

But how a man like you, who looks so wise
And wears a moustache of such splendid size,
Can be so foolish as to . . .
ORGON: Silence, please!
My girl, you take too many liberties.
I'm master here, as you must not forget.
DORINE: Do let's discuss this calmly; don't be upset.
You can't be serious, Sir, about this plan.
What should that bigot want with Mariane?
Praying and fasting ought to keep him busy.
And then, in terms of wealth and rank, what is he?
Why should a man of property like you
Pick out a beggar son-in-law?
ORGON: That will do.
Speak of his poverty with reverence.
His is pure and saintly indigence
Which far transcends all worldly pride and pelf.
He lost his fortune, as he says himself,
Because he cared for Heaven alone, and so
Was careless of his interests here below.
I mean to get him out of his present straits
And help him to recover his estates—
Which, in his part of the world, have no small fame.
Poor though he is, he's a gentleman just the same.
DORINE: Yes, so he tells us; and, Sir, it seems to me
Such pride goes very ill with piety.
A man whose spirit spurns this dungy earth
Ought not to brag of lands and noble birth;
Such worldly arrogance will hardly square
With meek devotion and the life of prayer.
. . . But this approach, I see, has drawn a blank;
Let's speak, then, of his person, not his rank.
Doesn't it seem to you a trifle grim
To give a girl like her to a man like him?
When two are so ill-suited, can't you see
What the sad consequence is bound to be?
A young girl's virtue is imperilled, Sir,
When such a marriage is imposed on her;
For if one's bridegroom isn't to one's taste,
It's hardly an inducement to be chaste,
And many a man with horns upon his brow
Has made his wife the thing that she is now.
It's hard to be a faithful wife, in short,
To certain husbands of a certain sort,
And he who gives his daughter to a man she hates
Must answer for her sins at Heaven's gates.
Think, Sir, before you play so risky a role.
ORGON: This servant-girl presumes to save my soul!

DORINE: You would do well to ponder what I've said.
ORGON: Daughter, we'll disregard this dunderhead.
     Just trust your father's judgment. Oh, I'm aware
     That I once promised you to young Valère;
     But now I hear he gambles, which greatly shocks me;
     What's more, I've doubts about his orthodoxy.
     His visits to church, I note, are very few.
DORINE: Would you have him go at the same hours as you,
     And kneel nearby, to be sure of being seen?
ORGON: I can dispense with such remarks, Dorine.
          [*to* MARIANE]
     Tartuffe, however, is sure of Heaven's blessing,
     And that's the only treasure worth possessing.
     This match will bring you joys beyond all measure;
     Your cup will overflow with every pleasure;
     You two will interchange your faithful loves
     Like two sweet cherubs, or two turtle-doves.
     No harsh word shall be heard, no frown be seen,
     And he shall make you happy as a queen.
DORINE: And she'll make him a cuckold, just wait and see.
ORGON: What language!
DORINE: Oh, he's a man of destiny;
     He's *made* for horns, and what the stars demand
     Your daughter's virtue surely can't withstand.
ORGON: Don't interrupt me further. Why can't you learn
     That certain things are none of your concern?
DORINE: It's for your own sake that I interfere.
          [*She repeatedly interrupts* ORGON *just as he is turning to speak to his
          daughter.*]
ORGON: Most kind of you. Now, hold your tongue, d'you hear?
DORINE: If I didn't love you . . .
ORGON: Spare me your affection.
DORINE: I'll love you, Sir, in spite of your objection.
ORGON: Blast!
DORINE: I can't bear, Sir, for your honor's sake,
     To let you make this ludicrous mistake.
ORGON: You mean to go on talking?
DORINE: If I didn't protest
     This sinful marriage, my conscience couldn't rest.
ORGON: If you don't hold your tongue, you little shrew . . .
DORINE: What, lost your temper? A pious man like you?
ORGON: Yes! Yes! You talk and talk. I'm maddened by it.
     Once and for all, I tell you to be quiet.
DORINE: Well, I'll be quiet. But I'll be thinking hard.
ORGON: Think all you like, but you had better guard
     That saucy tongue of yours, or I'll . . . [*turning back to* MARIANE] Now,
          child,
     I've weighed this matter fully.

DORINE: [*aside*] It drives me wild
    That I can't speak.
        [ORGON *turns his head, and she is silent.*]
ORGON: Tartuffe is no young dandy,
    But, still, his person . . .
DORINE: [*aside*] Is as sweet as candy.
ORGON: Is such that, even if you shouldn't care
    For his other merits . . .
        [*He turns and stands facing* DORINE, *arms crossed.*]
DORINE: [*aside*] They'll make a lovely pair.
    If I were she, no man would marry me
    Against my inclination, and go scot-free.
    He'd learn, before the wedding-day was over,
    How readily a wife can find a lover.
ORGON: [*to* DORINE] It seems you treat my orders as a joke.
DORINE: Why, what's the matter? 'Twas not to you I spoke.
ORGON: What *were* you doing?
DORINE: Talking to myself, that's all.
ORGON: Ah! [*aside*] One more bit of impudence and gall,
    And I shall give her a good slap in the face.
        [*He puts himself in position to slap her;* DORINE, *whenever he glances at her,*
        stands immobile and silent.]
    Daughter, you shall accept, and with good grace,
    The husband I've selected . . . Your wedding-day . . .
    [*to* DORINE] Why don't you talk to yourself?
DORINE: I've nothing to say.
ORGON: Come, just one word.
DORINE: No thank you, Sir. I pass.
ORGON: Come, speak; I'm waiting.
DORINE: I'd not be such an ass.
ORGON: [*turning to* MARIANE] In short, dear Daughter, I mean to be obeyed,
    And you must bow to the sound choice I've made.
DORINE: [*moving away*] I'd not wed such a monster, even in jest.
        [ORGON *attempts to slap her, but misses.*]
ORGON: Daughter, that maid of yours is a thorough pest;
    She makes me sinfully annoyed and nettled.
    I can't speak further; my nerves are too unsettled.
    She's so upset me by her insolent talk,
    I'll calm myself by going for a walk.

SCENE III

DORINE: [*returning*] Well, have you lost your tongue, girl? Must I play
    Your part, and say the lines you ought to say?
    Faced with a fate so hideous and absurd,
    Can you not utter one dissenting word?
MARIANE: What good would it do? A father's power is great.

DORINE: Resist him now, or it will be too late.

MARIANE: But . . .

DORINE: Tell him one cannot love at a father's whim;
    That you shall marry for yourself, not him;
    That since it's you who are to be the bride,
    It's you, not he, who must be satisfied;
    And that if his Tartuffe is so sublime,
    He's free to marry him at any time.

MARIANE: I've bowed so long to Father's strict control,
    I couldn't oppose him now, to save my soul.

DORINE: Come, come, Mariane. Do listen to reason, won't you?
    Valère has asked your hand. Do you love him, or don't you?

MARIANE: Oh, how unjust of you! What can you mean
    By asking such a question, dear Dorine?
    You know the depth of my affection for him;
    I've told you a hundred times how I adore him.

DORINE: I don't believe in everything I hear;
    Who knows if your professions were sincere?

MARIANE: They were, Dorine, and you do me wrong to doubt it;
    Heaven knows that I've been all too frank about it.

DORINE: You love him, then?

MARIANE: Oh, more than I can express.

DORINE: And he, I take it, cares for you no less?

MARIANE: I think so.

DORINE: And you both, with equal fire,
    Burn to be married?

MARIANE: That is our one desire.

DORINE: What of Tartuffe, then? What of your father's plan?

MARIANE: I'll kill myself, if I'm forced to wed that man.

DORINE: I hadn't thought of that recourse. How splendid!
    Just die, and all your troubles will be ended!
    A fine solution. Oh, it maddens me
    To hear you talk in that self-pitying key.

MARIANE: Dorine, how harsh you are! It's most unfair.
    You have no sympathy for my despair.

DORINE: I've none at all for people who talk drivel
    And, faced with difficulties, whine and snivel.

MARIANE: No doubt I'm timid, but it would be wrong . . .

DORINE: True love requires a heart that's firm and strong.

MARIANE: I'm strong in my affection for Valère,
    But coping with my father is his affair.

DORINE: But if your father's brain has grown so cracked
    Over his dear Tartuffe that he can retract
    His blessing, though your wedding-day was named,
    It's surely not Valère who's to be blamed.

MARIANE: If I defied my father, as you suggest,
    Would it not seem unmaidenly, at best?
    Shall I defend my love at the expense

Of brazenness and disobedience?
Shall I parade my heart's desires, and flaunt . . .
DORINE: No, I ask nothing of you. Clearly you want
To be Madame Tartuffe, and I feel bound
Not to oppose a wish so very sound.
What right have I to criticize the match?
Indeed, my dear, the man's a brilliant catch.
Monsieur Tartuffe! Now, there's a man of weight!
Yes, yes, Monsieur Tartuffe, I'm bound to state,
Is quite a person; that's not to be denied;
'Twill be no little thing to be his bride.
The world already rings with his renown;
He's a great noble—in his native town;
His ears are red, he has a pink complexion,
And all in all, he'll suit you to perfection.
MARIANE: Dear God!
DORINE: Oh, how triumphant you will feel
At having caught a husband so ideal!
MARIANE: Oh, do stop teasing, and use your cleverness
To get me out of this appalling mess.
Advise me, and I'll do whatever you say.
DORINE: Ah no, a dutiful daughter must obey
Her father, even if he weds her to an ape.
You've a bright future; why struggle to escape?
Tartuffe will take you back where his family lives,
To a small town aswarm with relatives—
Uncles and cousins whom you'll be charmed to meet.
You'll be received at once by the elite,
Calling upon the bailiff's wife, no less—
Even, perhaps, upon the mayoress,
Who'll sit you down in the *best* kitchen chair.
Then, once a year, you'll dance at the village fair
To the drone of bagpipes—two of them, in fact—
And see a puppet-show, or an animal act.
Your husband . . .
MARIANE: Oh, you turn my blood to ice!
Stop torturing me, and give me your advice.
DORINE: [*threatening to go*] Your servant, Madam.
MARIANE: Dorine, I beg of you . . .
DORINE: No, you deserve it; this marriage must go through.
MARIANE: Dorine!
DORINE: No.
MARIANE: Not Tartuffe! You know I think him . . .
DORINE: Tartuffe's your cup of tea, and you shall drink him.
MARIANE: I've always told you everything, and relied . . .
DORINE: No. You deserve to be tartuffified.
MARIANE: Well, since you mock me and refuse to care,
I'll henceforth seek my solace in despair:

Despair shall be my counsellor and friend,
And help me bring my sorrows to an end.
    [*She starts to leave.*]
DORINE: There now, come back; my anger has subsided.
    You do deserve some pity, I've decided.
MARIANE: Dorine, if Father makes me undergo
    This dreadful martyrdom, I'll die, I know.
DORINE: Don't fret; it won't be difficult to discover
    Some plan of action . . . But here's Valère, your lover.

SCENE IV

VALÈRE: Madam, I've just received some wondrous news
    Regarding which I'd like to hear your views.
MARIANE: What news?
VALÈRE: You're marrying Tartuffe.
MARIANE: I find
    That Father does have such a match in mind.
VALÈRE: Your father, Madam . . .
MARIANE: . . . has just this minute said
    That it's Tartuffe he wishes me to wed.
VALÈRE: Can he be serious?
MARIANE: Oh, indeed he can;
    He's clearly set his heart upon the plan.
VALÈRE: And what position to you propose to take,
    Madam?
MARIANE: Why—I don't know.
VALÈRE: For heaven's sake—
    You don't know?
MARIANE: No.
VALÈRE: Well, well!
MARIANE: Advise me, do.
VALÈRE: Marry the man. That's my advice to you.
MARIANE: That's your advice?
VALÈRE: Yes.
MARIANE: Truly?
VALÈRE: Oh, absolutely.
    You couldn't choose more wisely, more astutely.
MARIANE: Thanks for this counsel; I'll follow it, of course.
VALÈRE: Do, do; I'm sure 'twill cost you no remorse.
MARIANE: To give it didn't cause your heart to break.
VALÈRE: I gave it, Madam, only for your sake.
MARIANE: And it's for your sake that I take it, Sir.
DORINE: [*withdrawing to the rear of the stage*]
    Let's see which fool will prove the stubborner.
VALÈRE: So! I am nothing to you, and it was flat
    Deception when you . . .

MARIANE: Please, enough of that.
    You've told me plainly that I should agree
    To wed the man my father's chosen for me,
    And since you've deigned to counsel me so wisely,
    I promise, Sir, to do as you advise me.
VALÈRE: Ah, no, 'twas not by me that you were swayed.
    No, your decision was already made;
    Though now, to save appearances, you protest
    That you're betraying me at my behest.
MARIANE: Just as you say.
VALÈRE: Quite so. And I now see
    That you were never truly in love with me.
MARIANE: Alas, you're free to think so if you choose.
VALÈRE: I choose to think so, and here's a bit of news:
    You've spurned my hand, but I know where to turn
    For kinder treatment, as you shall quickly learn.
MARIANE: I'm sure you do. Your noble qualities
    Inspire affection . . .
VALÈRE: Forget my qualities, please.
    They don't inspire you overmuch, I find.
    But there's another lady I have in mind
    Whose sweet and generous nature will not scorn
    To compensate me for the loss I've borne.
MARIANE: I'm no great loss, and I'm sure that you'll transfer
    Your heart quite painlessly from me to her.
VALÈRE: I'll do my best to take it in my stride.
    The pain I feel at being cast aside
    Time and forgetfulness may put an end to.
    Or if I can't forget, I shall pretend to.
    No self-respecting person is expected
    To go on loving once he's been rejected.
MARIANE: Now, that's fine, high-minded sentiment.
VALÈRE: One to which any sane man would assent.
    Would you prefer it if I pined away
    In hopeless passion till my dying day?
    Am I to yield you to a rival's arms
    And not console myself with other charms?
MARIANE: Go then: console yourself; don't hesitate.
    I wish you to; indeed, I cannot wait.
VALÈRE: You wish me to?
MARIANE: Yes.
VALÈRE: That's the final straw.
    Madam, farewell. Your wish shall be my law.
        [*He starts to leave, and then returns: this repeatedly.*]
MARIANE: Splendid.
VALÈRE: [*coming back again*] This breach, remember, is of your making;
    It's you who've driven me to the step I'm taking.

MARIANE: Of course.

VALÈRE: [*coming back again*] Remember, too, that I am merely
　　　Following your example.

MARIANE: I see that clearly.

VALÈRE: Enough. I'll go and do your bidding, then.

MARIANE: Good.

VALÈRE: [*coming back again*] You shall never see my face again.

MARIANE: Excellent.

VALÈRE: [*walking to the door, then turning about*] Yes?

MARIANE: What?

VALÈRE: What's that? What did you say?

MARIANE: Nothing. You're dreaming.

VALÈRE: Ah. Well, I'm on my way.
　　　Farewell, *Madame.*
　　　　　[*He moves slowly away.*]

MARIANE: Farewell.

DORINE: [*to* MARIANE] If you ask me,
　　　Both of you are as mad as mad can be.
　　　Do stop this nonsense, now. I've only let you
　　　Squabble so long to see where it would get you.
　　　Whoa there, Monsieur Valère!
　　　　　[*She goes and seizes Valère by the arm; he makes a great show of resis-
　　　　　tance.*]

VALÈRE: What's this, Dorine?

DORINE: Come here.

VALÈRE: No, no, my heart's too full of spleen.
　　　Don't hold me back; her wish must be obeyed.

DORINE: Stop!

VALÈRE: It's too late now; my decision's made.

DORINE: Oh, pooh!

MARIANE: [*aside*] He hates the sight of me, that's plain.
　　　I'll go, and so deliver him from pain.

DORINE: [*leaving* VALÈRE, *running after* MARIANE] And now *you* run away!
　　　Come back.

MARIANE: No, no.
　　　Nothing you say will keep me here. Let go!

VALÈRE: [*aside*] She cannot bear my presence, I perceive.
　　　To spare her further torment, I shall leave.

DORINE: [*leaving* MARIANE, *running after* VALÈRE] Again! You'll not escape, Sir;
　　　　don't you try it.
　　　Come here, you two. Stop fussing, and be quiet.
　　　　　[*She takes* VALÈRE *by the hand, then* MARIANE, *and draws them together.*]

VALÈRE: [*to* DORINE] What do you want of me?

MARIANE: [*to* DORINE] What is the point of this?

DORINE: We're going to have a little armistice.
　　　[*to* VALÈRE] Now, weren't you silly to get so overheated?

VALÈRE: Didn't you see how badly I was treated?

DORINE: [*to* MARIANE] Aren't you a simpleton, to have lost your head?

MARIANE: Didn't you hear the hateful things he said?

DORINE: [*to* VALÈRE] You're both great fools. Her sole desire, Valère,
    Is to be yours in marriage. To that I'll swear.
      [*to* MARIANE] He loves you only, and he wants no wife
      But you, Mariane. On that I'll stake my life.

MARIANE: [*to* VALÈRE] Then why you advised me so, I cannot see.

VALÈRE: [*to* MARIANE] On such a question, why ask advice of *me?*

DORINE: Oh, you're impossible. Give me your hands, you two.
      [*to* VALÈRE] Yours first.

VALÈRE: [*giving* DORINE *his hand*] But why?

DORINE: [*to* MARIANE] And now a hand from you.

MARIANE: [*also giving* DORINE *her hand*] What are you doing?

DORINE: There: a perfect fit.
    You suit each other better than you'll admit.
      [VALÈRE *and* MARIANE *hold hands for some time without looking at each
      other.*]

VALÈRE: [*turning toward* MARIANE] Ah, come, don't be so haughty. Give a man
    A look of kindness, won't you, Mariane?
      [MARIANE *turns toward* VALÈRE *and smiles.*]

DORINE: I'll tell you, lovers are completely mad!

VALÈRE: [*to* MARIANE] Now come, confess that you were very bad
    To hurt my feelings as you did just now.
    I have a just complaint, you must allow.

MARIANE: *You* must allow that you were most unpleasant . . .

DORINE: Let's table that discussion for the present;
    Your father has a plan which must be stopped.

MARIANE: Advise us, then; what means must we adopt?

DORINE: We'll use all manner of means, and all at once.
    [*to* MARIANE] Your father's addled; he's acting like a dunce.
    Therefore you'd better humor the old fossil.
    Pretend to yield to him, be sweet and docile,
    And then postpone, as often as necessary,
    The day on which you have agreed to marry.
    You'll thus gain time, and time will turn the trick.
    Sometimes, for instance, you'll be taken sick,
    And that will seem good reason for delay;
    Or some bad omen will make you change the day—
    You'll dream of muddy water, or you'll pass
    A dead man's hearse, or break a looking-glass
    If all else fails, no man can marry you
    Unless you take his ring and say "I do."
    But now, let's separate. If they should find
    Us talking here, our plot might be divined.
    [*to* VALÈRE] Go to your friends, and tell them what's occurred,
    And have them urge her father to keep his word.
    Meanwhile, we'll stir her brother into action,
    And get Elmire, as well, to join our faction.
    Good-bye.

VALÈRE: [*to* MARIANE] Though each of us will do his best,
  It's your true heart on which my hopes shall rest.
MARIANE: [*to* VALÈRE] Regardless of what Father may decide,
  None but Valère shall claim me as his bride.
VALÈRE: Oh, how those words content me! Come what will . . .
DORINE: Oh, lovers, lovers! Their tongues are never still.
  Be off, now.
VALÈRE: [*turning to go, then turning back*] One last word . . .
DORINE: No time to chat:
  You leave by this door; and *you* leave by that.
    [DORINE *pushes them, by the shoulders, toward opposing doors.*]

ACT III

SCENE I

DAMIS: May lightning strike me even as I speak,
  May all men call me cowardly and weak,
  If any fear or scruple holds me back
  From settling things, at once, with that great quack!
DORINE: Now, don't give way to violent emotion.
  Your father's merely talked about this notion,
  And words and deeds are far from being one.
  Much that is talked about is left undone.
DAMIS: No, I must stop that scoundrel's machinations;
  I'll go and tell him off; I'm out of patience.
DORINE: Do calm down and be practical. I had rather
  My mistress dealt with him—and with your father.
  She has some influence with Tartuffe, I've noted.
  He hangs upon her words, seems most devoted,
  And may, indeed, be smitten by her charm.
  Pray Heaven it's true! 'Twould do our cause no harm.
  She sent for him, just now, to sound him out
  On this affair you're so incensed about;
  She'll find out where he stands, and tell him, too
  What dreadful strife and trouble will ensue
  If he lends countenance to your father's plan.
  I couldn't get in to see him, but his man
  Says that he's almost finished with his prayers.
  Go, now. I'll catch him when he comes downstairs.
DAMIS: I want to hear this conference, and I will.
DORINE: No, they must be alone.
DAMIS: Oh, I'll keep still.
DORINE: Not you. I know your temper. You'd start a brawl,
  And shout and stamp your foot and spoil it all.
  Go on.
DAMIS: I won't; I have a perfect right . . .

DORINE: Lord, you're a nuisance! He's coming; get out of sight.
  [DAMIS *conceals himself in a closet at the rear of the stage.*]

SCENE II

TARTUFFE: [*observing* DORINE, *and calling to his manservant offstage*] Hang up my
    hair-shirt, put my scourge in place,
  And pray, Laurent, for Heaven's perpetual grace.
  I'm going to the prison now, to share
  My last few coins with the poor wretches there.
DORINE: [*aside*] Dear God, what affectation! What a fake!
TARTUFFE: You wished to see me?
DORINE: Yes . . .
TARTUFFE: [*taking a handkerchief from his pocket*] For mercy's sake,
  Please take this handkerchief, before you speak.
DORINE: What?
TARTUFFE: Cover that bosom, girl. The flesh is weak,
  And unclean thoughts are difficult to control.
  Such sights as that can undermine the soul.
DORINE: Your soul, it seems, has very poor defenses,
  And flesh makes quite an impact on your senses.
  It's strange that you're so easily excited;
  My own desires are not so soon ignited,
  And if I saw you naked as a beast,
  Not all your hide would tempt me in the least.
TARTUFFE: Girl, speak more modestly; unless you do,
  I shall be forced to take my leave of you.
DORINE: Oh, no, it's I who must be on my way;
  I've just one little message to convey.
  Madame is coming down, and begs you, Sir,
  To wait and have a word or two with her.
TARTUFFE: Gladly.
DORINE: [*aside*] *That* had a softening effect!
  I think my guess about him was correct.
TARTUFFE: Will she be long?
DORINE: No: that's her step I hear.
  Ah, here she is, and I shall disappear.

SCENE III

TARTUFFE: May heaven, whose infinite goodness we adore,
  Preserve your body and soul forevermore,
  And bless your days, and answer thus the plea
  Of one who is its humblest votary.
ELMIRE: I thank you for that pious wish. But please,
  Do take a chair and let's be more at ease.
    [*They sit down.*]
TARTUFFE: I trust that you are once more well and strong?

ELMIRE: Oh, yes: the fever didn't last for long.

TARTUFFE: My prayers are too unworthy, I am sure,
> To have gained from Heaven this most gracious cure;
> But lately, Madam, my every supplication
> Has had for object your recuperation.

ELMIRE: You shouldn't have troubled so. I don't deserve it.

TARTUFFE: Your health is priceless, Madam, and to preserve it
> I'd gladly give my own, in all sincerity.

ELMIRE: Sir, you outdo us all in Christian charity.
> You've been most kind. I count myself your debtor.

TARTUFFE: 'Twas nothing, Madam. I long to serve you better.

ELMIRE: There's a private matter I'm anxious to discuss.
> I'm glad there's no one here to hinder us.

TARTUFFE: I, too, am glad; it floods my heart with bliss
> To find myself alone with you like this.
> For just this chance I've prayed with all my power—
> But prayed in vain, until this happy hour.

ELMIRE: This won't take long, Sir, and I hope you'll be
> Entirely frank and unconstrained with me.

TARTUFFE: Indeed, there's nothing I had rather do
> Than bare my inmost heart and soul to you.
> First, let me say that what remarks I've made
> About the constant visits you are paid
> Were prompted not by any mean emotion,
> But rather by a pure and deep devotion,
> A fervent zeal . . .

ELMIRE: No need for explanation.
> Your sole concern, I'm sure, was my salvation.

TARTUFFE: [*taking* ELMIRE's *hand and pressing her fingertips*] Quite so; and such
> great fervor do I feel . . .

ELMIRE: Ooh! Please! You're pinching!

TARTUFFE: 'Twas from excess of zeal.
> I never meant to cause you pain, I swear.
> I'd rather . . . [*He places his hand on* ELMIRE's *knee.*]

ELMIRE: What can your hand be doing there?

TARTUFFE: Feeling your gown; what soft, fine-woven stuff!

ELMIRE: Please, I'm extremely ticklish. That's enough.
> [*She draws her chair away;* TARTUFFE *pulls his after her.*]

TARTUFFE: [*fondling the lace collar of her gown*] My, my, what lovely lacework on
> your dress!
> The workmanship's miraculous, no less.
> I've not seen anything to equal it.

ELMIRE: Yes, quite. But let's talk business for a bit.
> They say my husband means to break his word
> And give his daughter to you, Sir. Had you heard?

TARTUFFE: He did once mention it. But I confess
> I dream of quite a different happiness.

It's elsewhere, Madam, that my eyes discern
The promise of that bliss for which I yearn.
ELMIRE: I see: you care for nothing here below.
TARTUFFE: Ah, well—my heart's not made of stone, you know.
ELMIRE: All your desires mount heavenward, I'm sure,
In scorn of all that's earthly and impure.
TARTUFFE: A love of heavenly beauty does not preclude
A proper love for earthly pulchritude;
Our senses are quite rightly captivated
By perfect works our Maker has created.
Some glory clings to all that Heaven has made;
In you, all Heaven's marvels are displayed.
On that fair face, such beauties have been lavished,
The eyes are dazzled and the heart is ravished;
How could I look on you, O flawless creature,
And not adore the Author of all Nature,
Feeling a love both passionate and pure
For you, his triumph of self-portraiture?
At first, I trembled lest that love should be
A subtle snare that Hell had laid for me;
I vowed to flee the sight of you, eschewing
A rapture that might prove my soul's undoing;
But soon, fair being, I became aware
That my deep passion could be made to square
With rectitude, and with my bounden duty.
I thereupon surrendered to your beauty.
It is, I know, presumptuous on my part
To bring you this poor offering of my heart,
And it is not my merit, Heaven knows,
But your compassion on which my hopes repose.
You are my peace, my solace, my salvation;
On you depends my bliss—or desolation;
I bide your judgment and, as you think best,
I shall be either miserable or blest.
ELMIRE: Your declaration is most gallant, Sir,
But don't you think it's out of character?
You'd have done better to restrain your passion
And think before you spoke in such a fashion.
It ill becomes a pious man like you . . .
TARTUFFE: I may be pious, but I'm human, too:
With your celestial charms before his eyes,
A man has not the power to be wise.
I know such words sound strangely, coming from me,
But I'm no angel, nor was meant to be,
And if you blame my passion, you must needs
Reproach as well the charms on which it feeds.
Your loveliness I had no sooner seen

Than you became my soul's unrivalled queen;
Before your seraph glance, divinely sweet,
My heart's defenses crumbled in defeat,
And nothing fasting, prayer, or tears might do
Could stay my spirit from adoring you.
My eyes, my sighs have told you in the past
What now my lips make bold to say at last,
And if, in your great goodness, you will deign
To look upon your slave, and ease his pain,—
If, in compassion for my soul's distress,
You'll stoop to comfort my unworthiness,
I'll raise to you, in thanks for that sweet manna,
An endless hymn, an infinite hosanna.
With me, of course, there need be no anxiety,
No fear of scandal or of notoriety.
These young court gallants, whom all the ladies fancy,
Are vain in speech, in action rash and chancy;
When they succeed in love, the world soon knows it;
No favor's granted them but they disclose it
And by the looseness of their tongues profane
The very altar where their hearts have lain.
Men of my sort, however, love discreetly,
And one may trust our reticence completely.
My keen concern for my good name insures
The absolute security of yours;
In short, I offer you, my dear Elmire,
Love without scandal, pleasure without fear.

ELMIRE: I've heard your well-turned speeches to the end,
And what you urge I clearly apprehend.
Aren't you afraid that I may take a notion
To tell my husband of your warm devotion,
And that, supposing he were duly told,
His feelings toward you might grow rather cold?

TARTUFFE: I know, dear lady, that your exceeding charity
Will lead your heart to pardon my temerity;
That you'll excuse my violent affection
As human weakness, human imperfection;
And that—O fairest!—you will bear in mind
That I'm but flesh and blood, and am not blind.

ELMIRE: Some women might do otherwise, perhaps,
But I shall be discreet about your lapse;
I'll tell my husband nothing of what's occurred
If, in return, you'll give your solemn word
To advocate as forcefully as you can
The marriage of Valère and Mariane,
Renouncing all desire to dispossess
Another of his rightful happiness,
And . . .

SCENE IV

DAMIS: [*emerging from the closet where he has been hiding*] No! We'll not hush up
    this vile affair;
    I heard it all inside that closet there,
    Where Heaven, in order to confound the pride
    Of this great rascal, prompted me to hide.
    Ah, now I have my long-awaited chance
    To punish his deceit and arrogance,
    And give my father clear and shocking proof
    Of the black character of his dear Tartuffe.

ELMIRE: Ah no, Damis; I'll be content if he
    Will study to deserve my leniency.
    I've promised silence—don't make me break my word;
    To make a scandal would be too absurd.
    Good wives laugh off such trifles, and forget them;
    Why should they tell their husbands, and upset them?

DAMIS: You have your reasons for taking such a course,
    And I have reasons, too, of equal force.
    To spare him now would be insanely wrong.
    I've swallowed my just wrath for far too long
    And watched this insolent bigot bringing strife
    And bitterness into our family life.
    Too long he's meddled in my father's affairs,
    Thwarting my marriage-hopes, and poor Valère's.
    It's high time that my father was undeceived,
    And now I've proof that can't be disbelieved—
    Proof that was furnished me by Heaven above.
    It's too good not to take advantage of.
    This is my chance, and I deserve to lose it
    If, for one moment, I hestitate to use it.

ELMIRE: Damis . . .

DAMIS: No, I must do what I think right.
    Madam, my heart is bursting with delight,
    And, say whatever you will, I'll not consent
    To lose the sweet revenge on which I'm bent.
    I'll settle matters without more ado;
    And here, most opportunely, is my cue.

SCENE V

DAMIS: Father, I'm glad you've joined us. Let us advise you
    Of some fresh news which doubtless will surprise you.
    You've just now been repaid with interest
    For all your loving-kindness to our guest.
    He's proved his warm and grateful feelings toward you;
    It's with a pair of horns he would reward you.
    Yes, I surprised him with your wife, and heard

His whole adulterous offer, every word.
She, with her all-too-gentle disposition,
Would not have told you of his proposition;
But I shall not make terms with brazen lechery,
And feel that not to tell you would be treachery.
ELMIRE: And I hold that one's husband's peace of mind
Should not be spoilt by tattle of this kind.
One's honor doesn't require it: to be proficient
In keeping men at bay is quite sufficient.
These are my sentiments, and I wish, Damis,
That you had heeded me and held your peace. [*Exit.*]

SCENE VI

ORGON: Can it be true, this dreadful thing I hear?
TARTUFFE: Yes, Brother, I'm a wicked man, I fear:
A wretched sinner, all depraved and twisted,
The greatest villain that has ever existed.
My life's one heap of crimes, which grows each minute;
There's naught but foulness and corruption in it;
And I perceive that Heaven, outraged by me,
Has chosen this occasion to mortify me.
Charge me with any deed you wish to name;
I'll not defend myself, but take the blame.
Believe what you are told, and drive Tartuffe
Like some base criminal from beneath your roof;
Yes, drive me hence, and with a parting curse:
I shan't protest, for I deserve far worse.
ORGON: [*to* DAMIS] Ah, you deceitful boy, how dare you try
To stain his purity with so foul a lie?
DAMIS: What! are you taken in by such a bluff?
Did you not hear . . . ?
ORGON: Enough, you rogue, enough!
TARTUFFE: Ah. Brother, let him speak: you're being unjust.
Believe his story; the boy deserves your trust.
Why, after all, should you have faith in me?
How can you know what I might do, or be?
Is it on my good actions that you base
Your favor? Do you trust my pious face?
Ah, no, don't be deceived by hollow shows;
I'm far, alas, from being what men suppose;
Though the world takes me for a man of worth,
I'm truly the most worthless man on Earth.
[*to* DAMIS] Yes, my dear son, speak out now: call me the chief
Of sinners, a wretch, a murderer, a thief;
Load me with all the names men most abhor;
I'll not complain; I've earned them all, and more;

I'll kneel here while you pour them on my head
As a just punishment for the life I've led.
ORGON: [*to* TARTUFFE] This is too much, dear Brother.
    [*to* DAMIS] Have you no heart?
DAMIS: Are you so hoodwinked by this rascal's art . . . ?
ORGON: Be still, you monster.
    [*to* TARTUFFE] Brother, I pray you, rise.
    [*to* DAMIS] Villain!
DAMIS: But . . .
ORGON: Silence!
DAMIS: Can't you realize . . . ?
ORGON: Just one word more, and I'll tear you limb from limb.
TARTUFFE: In God's name, Brother, don't be harsh with him.
    I'd rather far be tortured at the stake
    Than see him bear one scratch for my poor sake.
ORGON: [*to* DAMIS] Ingrate!
TARTUFFE: If I must beg you, on bended knee,
    To pardon him . . .
ORGON: [*falling to his knees, addressing* TARTUFFE] Such goodness cannot be!
    [*to* DAMIS] Now, *there's* true charity!
DAMIS: What, you . . . ?
ORGON: Villain, be still!
    I know your motives; I know you wish him ill:
    Yes, all of you—wife, children, servants, all—
    Conspire against him and desire his fall,
    Employing every shameful trick you can
    To alienate me from this saintly man.
    Ah, but the more you seek to drive him away,
    The more I'll do to keep him. Without delay,
    I'll spite this household and confound its pride
    By giving him my daughter as his bride.
DAMIS: You're going to force her to accept his hand?
ORGON: Yes, and this very night, d'you understand?
    I shall defy you all, and make it clear
    That I'm the one who gives the orders here.
    Come, wretch, kneel down and clasp his blessed feet,
    And ask his pardon for your black deceit.
DAMIS: I ask that swindler's pardon? Why, I'd rather . . .
ORGON: So! You insult him, and defy your father!
    A stick! A stick! [*to* TARTUFFE] No, no—release me, do.
        [*to* DAMIS]
    Out of my house this minute! Be off with you,
    And never dare set foot in it again.
DAMIS: Well, I shall go, but . . .
ORGON: Well, go quickly, then.
    I disinherit you; an empty purse
    Is all you'll get from me—except my curse!

SCENE VII

ORGON: How he blasphemed your goodness! What a son!
TARTUFFE: Forgive him, Lord, as I've already done.
          [*to* ORGON] You can't know how it hurts when someone tries
          To blacken me in my dear Brother's eyes.
ORGON: Ahh!
TARTUFFE: The mere thought of such ingratitude
          Plunges my soul into so dark a mood . . .
          Such horror grips my heart . . . I gasp for breath,
          And cannot speak, and feel myself near death.
ORGON: [*He runs, in tears, to the door through which he has just driven his son.*]
          You blackguard! Why did I spare you? Why did I not
          Break you in little pieces on the spot?
          Compose yourself, and don't be hurt, dear friend.
TARTUFFE: These scenes, these dreadful quarrels, have got to end.
          I've much upset your household, and I perceive
          That the best thing will be for me to leave.
ORGON: What are you saying!
TARTUFFE: They're all against me here;
          They'd have you think me false and insincere.
ORGON: Ah, what of that? Have I ceased believing in you?
TARTUFFE: Their adverse talk will certainly continue,
          And charges which you now repudiate
          You may find credible at a later date.
ORGON: No, Brother, never.
TARTUFFE: Brother, a wife can sway
          Her husband's mind in many a subtle way.
ORGON: No, no.
TARTUFFE: To leave at once is the solution;
          Thus only can I end their persecution.
ORGON: No, no, I'll not allow it; you shall remain.
TARTUFFE: Ah, well; 'twill mean much martyrdom and pain,
          But if you wish it . . .
ORGON: Ah!
TARTUFFE: Enough; so be it.
          But one thing must be settled, as I see it.
          For your dear honor, and for our friendship's sake,
          There's one precaution I feel bound to take.
          I shall avoid your wife, and keep away . . .
ORGON: No, you shall not, whatever they may say.
          It pleases me to vex them, and for spite
          I'd have them see you with her day and night.
          What's more, I'm going to drive them to despair
          By making you my only son and heir;
          This very day, I'll give to you alone
          Clear deed and title to everything I own.
          A dear, good friend and son-in-law-to-be

Is more than wife, or child, or kin to me.
     Will you accept my offer, dearest son?
TARTUFFE: In all things, let the will of Heaven be done.
ORGON: Poor fellow! Come, we'll go draw up the deed.
     Then let them burst with disappointed greed!

ACT IV

SCENE I

CLÉANTE: Yes, all the town's discussing it, and truly,
     Their comments do not flatter you unduly.
     I'm glad we've met, Sir, and I'll give my view
     Of this sad matter in a word or two.
     As for who's guilty, that I shan't discuss;
     Let's say it was Damis who caused the fuss;
     Assuming, then, that you have been ill-used
     By young Damis, and groundlessly accused,
     Ought not a Christian to forgive, and ought
     He not to stifle every vengeful thought?
     Should you stand by and watch a father make
     His only son an exile for your sake?
     Again I tell you frankly, be advised:
     The whole town, high and low, is scandalized;
     This quarrel must be mended, and my advice is
     Not to push matters to a further crisis.
     No, sacrifice your wrath to God above,
     And help Damis regain his father's love.
TARTUFFE: Alas, for my part I should take great joy
     In doing so. I've nothing against the boy.
     I pardon all, I harbor no resentment;
     To serve him would afford me much contentment.
     But Heaven's interest will not have it so:
     If he comes back, then I shall have to go.
     After his conduct—so extreme, so vicious—
     Our further intercourse would look suspicious.
     God knows what people would think! Why, they'd describe
     My goodness to him as a sort of bribe;
     They'd say that out of guilt I made pretense
     Of loving-kindness and benevolence—
     That, fearing my accuser's tongue, I strove
     To buy his silence with a show of love.
CLÉANTE: Your reasoning is badly warped and stretched,
     And these excuses, Sir, are most farfetched.
     Why put yourself in charge of Heaven's cause?
     Does Heaven need our help to enforce its laws?
     Leave vengeance to the Lord, Sir; while we live,
     Our duty's not to punish, but forgive;

And what the Lord commands, we should obey
Without regard to what the world may say.
What! Shall the fear of being misunderstood
Prevent our doing what is right and good?
No, no; let's simply do what Heaven ordains,
And let no other thoughts perplex our brains.

TARTUFFE: Again, Sir, let me say that I've forgiven
Damis, and thus obeyed the laws of Heaven;
But I am not commanded by the Bible
To live with one who smears my name with libel.

CLÉANTE: Were you commanded, Sir, to indulge the whim
Of poor Orgon, and to encourage him
In suddenly transferring to your name
A large estate to which you have claim?

TARTUFFE: 'Twould never occur to those who know me best
To think I acted from self-interest.
The treasures of this world I quite despise;
Their specious glitter does not charm my eyes;
And if I have resigned myself to taking
The gift which my dear Brother insists on making,
I do so only, as he well understands,
Lest so much wealth fall into wicked hands,
Lest those to whom it might descend in time
Turn it to purposes of sin and crime,
And not, as I shall do, make use of it
For Heaven's glory and mankind's benefit.

CLÉANTE: Forget these trumped-up fears. Your argument
Is one the rightful heir might well resent;
It *is* a moral burden to inherit
Such wealth, but give Damis a chance to bear it.
And would it not be worse to be accused
Of swindling, than to see that wealth misused?
I'm shocked that you allowed Orgon to broach
This matter, and that you feel no self-reproach;
Does true religion teach that lawful heirs
May freely be deprived of what is theirs?
And if the Lord has told you in your heart
That you and young Damis must dwell apart,
Would it not be the decent thing to beat
A generous and honorable retreat,
Rather than let the son of the house be sent,
For your convenience, into banishment?
Sir, if you wish to prove the honesty
Of your intentions . . .

TARTUFFE: Sir, it is half-past three.
I've certain pious duties to attend to,
And hope my prompt departure won't offend you.

CLÉANTE: [*alone*] Damn.

SCENE II

DORINE: Stay, Sir, and help Mariane, for Heaven's sake!
    She's suffering so, I fear her heart will break.
    Her father's plan to marry her off tonight
    Has put the poor child in a desperate plight.
    I hear him coming. Let's stand together, now,
    And see if we can't change his mind, somehow,
    About this match we all deplore and fear.

SCENE III

ORGON: Hah! Glad to find you all assembled here.
    [*to* MARIANE] This contract, child, contains your happiness,
    And what it says I think your heart can guess.
MARIANE: [*falling to her knees*] Sir, by that Heaven which sees me here
        distressed,
    And by whatever else can move your breast,
    Do not employ a father's power, I pray you,
    To crush my heart and force it to obey you,
    Nor by your harsh commands oppress me so
    That I'll begrudge the duty which I owe—
    And do not so embitter and enslave me
    That I shall hate the very life you gave me.
    If my sweet hopes must perish, if you refuse
    To give me to the one I've dared to choose,
    Spare me at least—I beg you, I implore—
    The pain of wedding one whom I abhor;
    And do not, by a heartless use of force,
    Drive me to contemplate some desperate course.
ORGON: [*feeling himself touched by her*] Be firm, my soul. No human weakness,
        now.
MARIANE: I don't resent your love for him. Allow
    Your heart free rein, Sir; give him your property,
    And if that's not enough, take mine from me;
    He's welcome to my money; take it, do,
    But don't, I pray, include my person, too.
    Spare me, I beg you; and let me end the tale
    Of my sad days behind a convent veil.
ORGON: A convent! Hah! When crossed in their amours,
    All lovesick girls have the same thought as yours.
    Get up! The more you loathe the man, and dread him,
    The more ennobling it will be to wed him.
    Marry Tartuffe, and mortify your flesh!
    Enough; don't start that whimpering afresh.
DORINE: But why . . . ?
ORGON: Be still, there. Speak when you're spoken to.
    Not one more bit of impudence out of you.
CLÉANTE: If I may offer a word of counsel here . . .

ORGON: Brother, in counseling you have no peer;
        All your advice is forceful, sound, and clever;
        I don't propose to follow it, however.
ELMIRE: [*to* ORGON] I am amazed, and don't know what to say;
        Your blindness simply takes my breath away.
        You are indeed bewitched, to take no warning
        From our account of what occurred this morning.
ORGON: Madam, I know a few plain facts and one
        Is that you're partial to my rascal son;
        Hence, when he sought to make Tartuffe the victim
        Of a base lie, you dared not contradict him.
        Ah, but you underplayed your part, my pet;
        You should have looked more angry, more upset.
ELMIRE: When men make overtures, must we reply
        With righteous anger and a battle-cry?
        Must we turn back their amorous advances
        With sharp reproaches and with fiery glances?
        Myself, I find such offers merely amusing,
        And make no scenes and fusses in refusing;
        My taste is for good-natured rectitude,
        And I dislike the savage sort of prude
        Who guards her virtue with her teeth and claws,
        And tears men's eyes out for the slightest cause:
        The Lord preserve me from such honor as that,
        Which bites and scratches like an alley-cat!
        I've found that a polite and cool rebuff
        Discourages a lover quite enough.
ORGON: I know the facts, and I shall not be shaken.
ELMIRE: I marvel at your power to be mistaken.
        Would it, I wonder, carry weight with you
        If I could *show* you that our tale was true?
ORGON: Show me?
ELMIRE: Yes.
ORGON: Rot.
ELMIRE: Come, what if I found a way
        To make you see the facts as plain as day?
ORGON: Nonsense.
ELMIRE: Do answer me; don't be absurd.
        I'm not now asking you to trust our word.
        Suppose that from some hiding-place in here
        You learned the whole sad truth by eye and ear—
        What would you say of your good friend, after that?
ORGON: Why, I'd say . . . nothing, by Jehoshaphat!
        It can't be true.
ELMIRE: You've been too long deceived,
        And I'm quite tired of being disbelieved.
        Come now: let's put my statements to the test,
        And you shall see the truth made manifest.

ORGON: I'll take that challenge. Now do your uttermost.
    We'll see how you make good your empty boast.
ELMIRE: [*to* DORINE] Send him to me.
DORINE: He's crafty; it may be hard
    To catch the cunning scoundrel off his guard.
ELMIRE: No, amorous men are gullible. Their conceit
    So blinds them that they're never hard to cheat.
    Have him come down. [*to* CLÉANTE *and* MARIANE] Please leave us, for a bit.

SCENE IV

ELMIRE: Pull up this table, and get under it.
ORGON: What?
ELMIRE: It's essential that you be well-hidden.
ORGON: Why there?
ELMIRE: Oh, Heavens! Just do as you are bidden.
    I have my plans; we'll soon see how they fare.
    Under the table, now; and once you're there,
    Take care that you are neither seen nor heard.
ORGON: Well, I'll indulge you, since I gave my word
    To see you through this infantile charade.
ELMIRE: Once it is over, you'll be glad we played.
    [*to her husband, who is now under the table*]
    I'm going to act quite strangely, now, and you
    Must not be shocked at anything I do.
    Whatever I may say, you must excuse
    As part of that deceit I'm forced to use.
    I shall employ sweet speeches in the task
    Of making that impostor drop his mask;
    I'll give encouragement to his bold desires,
    And furnish fuel to his amorous fires.
    Since it's for your sake, and for his destruction,
    That I shall seem to yield to his seduction,
    I'll gladly stop whenever you decide
    That all your doubts are fully satisfied.
    I'll count on you, as soon as you have seen
    What sort of man he is, to intervene,
    And not expose me to his odious lust
    One moment longer than you feel you must.
    Remember: you're to save me from my plight
    Whenever . . . He's coming! Hush! Keep out of sight!

SCENE V

TARTUFFE: You wish to have a word with me, I'm told.
ELMIRE: Yes. I've a little secret to unfold.
    Before I speak, however, it would be wise
    To close that door, and look for spies.
    [TARTUFFE *goes to the door, closes it, and returns.*]

The very last thing that must happen now
Is a repetition of this morning's row.
I've never been so badly caught off guard.
Oh, how I feared for you! You saw how hard
I tried to make that troublesome Damis
Control his dreadful temper, and hold his peace.
In my confusion, I didn't have the sense
Simply to contradict his evidence;
But as it happened, that was for the best,
And all has worked out in our interest.
This storm has only bettered your position;
My husband doesn't have the least suspicion,
And now, in mockery of those who do,
He bids me be continually with you.
And that is why, quite fearless of reproof,
I now can be alone with my Tartuffe,
And why my heart—perhaps too quick to yield—
Feels free to let its passion be revealed.

TARTUFFE: Madam, your words confuse me. Not long ago,
    You spoke in quite a different style, you know.

ELMIRE: Ah, Sir, if that refusal made you smart,
    It's little that you know of woman's heart,
    Or what that heart is trying to convey
    When it resists in such a feeble way!
    Always, at first, our modesty prevents
    The frank avowal of tender sentiments;
    However high the passion which inflames us,
    Still, to confess its power somehow shames us.
    Thus we reluct, at first, yet in a tone
    Which tells you that our heart is overthrown,
    That what our lips deny, our pulse confesses,
    And that, in time, all noes will turn to yesses.
    I fear my words are all too frank and free,
    And a poor proof of woman's modesty;
    But since I'm started, tell me, if you will—
    Would I have tried to make Damis be still,
    Would I have listened, calm and unoffended,
    Until your lengthy offer of love was ended,
    And be so very mild in my reaction,
    Had your sweet words not given me satisfaction?
    And when I tried to force you to undo
    The marriage-plans my husband has in view,
    What did my urgent pleading signify
    If not that I admired you, and that I
    Deplored the thought that someone else might own
    Part of a heart I wished for mine alone?

TARTUFFE: Madam, no happiness is so complete

As when, from lips we love, come words so sweet;
Their nectar floods my every sense, and drains
In honeyed rivulets through all my veins.
To please you is my joy, my only goal;
Your love is the restorer of my soul;
And yet I must beg leave, now, to confess
Some lingering doubts as to my happiness.
Might this not be a trick? Might not the catch
Be that you wish me to break off the match
With Mariane, and so have feigned to love me?
I shan't quite trust your fond opinion of me
Until the feelings you've expressed so sweetly
Are demonstrated somewhat more concretely,
And you have shown, by certain kind concessions,
That I may put my faith in your professions.

ELMIRE: [*She coughs, to warn her husband.*] Why be in such a hurry? Must my heart
Exhaust its bounty at the very start?
To make that sweet admission cost me dear,
But you'll not be content, it would appear,
Unless my store of favors is disbursed
To the last farthing, and at the very first.

TARTUFFE: The less we merit, the less we dare to hope,
And with our doubts, mere words can never cope.
We trust no promised bliss till we receive it;
Not till a joy is ours can we believe it.
I, who so little merit your esteem,
Can't credit this fulfillment of my dream,
And shan't believe it, Madam, until I savor
Some palpable assurance of your favor.

ELMIRE: My, how tyrannical your love can be,
And how it flusters and perplexes me!
How furiously you take one's heart in hand,
And make your every wish a fierce command!
Come, must you hound and harry me to death?
Will you not give me time to catch my breath?
Can it be right to press me with such force,
Give me no quarter, show me no remorse,
And take advantage, by your stern insistence,
Of the fond feelings which weaken my resistance?

TARTUFFE: Well, if you look with favor upon my love,
Why, then, begrudge me some clear proof thereof?

ELMIRE: But how can I consent without offense
To Heaven, toward which you feel such reverence?

TARTUFFE: If Heaven is all that holds you back, don't worry.
I can remove that hindrance in a hurry.
Nothing of that sort need obstruct our path.

ELMIRE: Must one not be afraid of Heaven's wrath?
TARTUFFE: Madam, forget such fears, and be my pupil,
      And I shall teach you how to conquer scruple.
      Some joys, it's true, are wrong in Heaven's eyes;
      Yet Heaven is not averse to compromise;
      There is a science, lately formulated,
      Whereby one's conscience may be liberated,
      And any wrongful act you care to mention
      May be redeemed by purity of intention.
      I'll teach you, Madam, the secrets of that science;
      Meanwhile, just place on me your full reliance.
      Assuage my keen desires, and feel no dread:
      The sin, if any, shall be on my head.
          [ELMIRE *coughs, this time more loudly.*]
      You've a bad cough.
ELMIRE: Yes, yes. It's bad indeed.
TARTUFFE: [*producing a little paper bag*] A bit of licorice may be what you need.
ELMIRE: No, I've a stubborn cold, it seems. I'm sure it
      Will take much more than licorice to cure it.
TARTUFFE: How aggravating.
ELMIRE: Oh, more than I can say.
TARTUFFE: If you're still troubled, think of things this way:
      No one shall know our joys, save us alone,
      And there's no evil till the act is known;
      It's scandal, Madam, which makes it an offense,
      And it's no sin to sin in confidence.
ELMIRE: [*having coughed once more*] Well, clearly I must do as you require,
      And yield to your importunate desire.
      It is apparent, now, that nothing less
      Will satisfy you, and so I acquiesce.
      To go so far is much against my will;
      I'm vexed that it should come to this; but still,
      Since you are so determined on it, since you
      Will not allow mere language to convince you,
      And since you ask for concrete evidence, I
      See nothing for it, now, but to comply.
      If this is sinful, if I'm wrong to do it,
      So much the worse for him who drove me to it.
      The fault can surely not be charged to me.
TARTUFFE: Madam, the fault is mine, if fault there be,
      And . . .
ELMIRE: Open the door a little, and peek out;
      I wouldn't want my husband poking about.
TARTUFFE: Why worry about the man? Each day he grows
      More gullible; one can lead him by the nose.
      To find us here would fill him with delight,
      And if he saw the worst, he'd doubt his sight.

ELMIRE: Nevertheless, do step out for a minute
    Into the hall, and see that no one's in it.

SCENE VI

ORGON: [*coming out from under the table*] That man's a perfect monster, I must
        admit!
    I'm simply stunned. I can't get over it.
ELMIRE: What, coming out so soon? How premature!
    Get back in hiding, and wait until you're sure.
    Stay till the end, and be convinced completely;
    We mustn't stop till things are proved concretely.
ORGON: Hell never harbored anything so vicious!
ELMIRE: Tut, don't be hasty. Try to be judicious.
    Wait, and be certain that there's no mistake.
    No jumping to conclusions, for Heaven's sake!
        [*She places* ORGON *behind her, as* TARTUFFE *reenters.*]

SCENE VII

TARTUFFE: [*not seeing* ORGON] Madam, all things have worked out to perfection;
    I've given the neighboring rooms a full inspection;
    No one's about; and now I may at last . . .
ORGON: [*intercepting him*] Hold on, my passionate fellow, not so fast!
    I should advise a little more restraint.
    Well, so you thought you'd fool me, my dear saint!
    How soon you wearied of the saintly life—
    Wedding my daughter, and coveting my wife!
    I've long suspected you, and had a feeling
    That soon I'd catch you at your double-dealing.
    Just now, you've given me evidence galore;
    It's quite enough; I have no wish for more.
ELMIRE: [*to* TARTUFFE] I'm sorry to have treated you so slyly,
    But circumstances forced me to be wily.
TARTUFFE: Brother, you can't think . . .
ORGON: No more talk from you;
    Just leave this household, without more ado.
TARTUFFE: What I intended . . .
ORGON: That seems fairly clear.
    Spare me your falsehoods and get out of here.
TARTUFFE: No, I'm the master, and you're the one to go!
    This house belongs to me, I'll have you know,
    And I shall show you that you can't hurt *me*
    By this contemptible conspiracy,
    That those who cross me know not what they do,
    And that I've means to expose and punish you,
    Avenge offended Heaven, and make you grieve
    That ever you dared order me to leave.

ELMIRE: What was the point of all that angry chatter?
ORGON: Dear God, I'm worried. This is no laughing matter.
ELMIRE: How so?
ORGON: I fear I understood his drift.
    I'm much disturbed about that deed of gift.
ELMIRE: You gave him . . . ?
ORGON: Yes, it's all been drawn and signed.
    But one thing more is weighing on my mind.
ELMIRE: What's that?
ORGON: I'll tell you; but first let's see if there's
    A certain strong-box in his room upstairs.

ACT V

SCENE I

CLÉANTE: Where are you going so fast?
ORGON: God knows!
CLÉANTE: Then wait;
    Let's have a conference, and deliberate
    On how this situation's to be met.
ORGON: That strong-box has me utterly upset;
    This is the worst of many, many shocks.
CLÉANTE: Is there some fearful mystery in that box?
ORGON: My poor friend Argas brought that box to me
    With his own hands, in utmost secrecy;
    'Twas on the very morning of his flight.
    It's full of papers which, if they came to light,
    Would ruin him—or such is my impression.
CLÉANTE: Then why did you let it out of your possession?
ORGON: Those papers vexed my conscience, and it seemed best
    To ask the counsel of my pious guest.
    The cunning scoundrel got me to agree
    To leave the strong-box in his custody,
    So that, in case of an investigation,
    I could employ a slight equivocation
    And swear I didn't have it, and thereby,
    At no expense to conscience, tell a lie.
CLÉANTE: It looks to me as if you're out on a limb.
    Trusting him with that box, and offering him
    That deed of gift, were actions of a kind
    Which scarcely indicate a prudent mind.
    With two such weapons, he has the upper hand,
    And since you're vulnerable, as matters stand,
    You erred once more in bringing him to bay.
    You should have acted in some subtler way.

ORGON: Just think of it: behind that fervent face,
 A heart so wicked, and a soul so base!
 I took him in, a hungry beggar, and then . . .
 Enough, by God! I'm through with pious men:
 Henceforth I'll hate the whole false brotherhood,
 And persecute them worse than Satan could.
CLÉANTE: Ah, there you go—extravagant as ever!
 Why can you not be rational? You never
 Manage to take the middle course, it seems,
 But jump, instead, between absurd extremes.
 You've recognized your recent grave mistake
 In falling victim to a pious fake;
 Now, to correct that error, must you embrace
 An even greater error in its place,
 And judge our worthy neighbors as a whole
 By what you've learned of one corrupted soul?
 Come, just because one rascal made you swallow
 A show of zeal which turned out to be hollow,
 Shall you conclude that all men are deceivers,
 And that, today, there are no true believers?
 Let atheists make that foolish inference;
 Learn to distinguish virtue from pretense,
 Be cautious in bestowing admiration,
 And cultivate a sober moderation.
 Don't humor fraud, but also don't asperse
 True piety; the latter fault is worse,
 And it is best to err, if err one must,
 As you have done, upon the side of trust.

SCENE II

DAMIS: Father, I hear that scoundrel's uttered threats
 Against you; that he pridefully forgets
 How, in his need, he was befriended by you,
 And means to use your gifts to crucify you.
ORGON: It's true, my boy. I'm too distressed for tears.
DAMIS: Leave it to me, Sir; let me trim his ears.
 Faced with such insolence, we must not waver.
 I shall rejoice in doing you the favor
 Of cutting short his life, and your distress.
CLÉANTE: What a display of young hotheadedness!
 Do learn to moderate your fits of rage.
 In this just kingdom, this enlightened age,
 One does not settle things by violence.

SCENE III

MADAME PERNELLE: [*entering with* ELMIRE *and* MARIANE]
 I hear strange tales of very strange events.

ORGON: Yes, strange events which these two eyes beheld.
    The man's ingratitude is unparalleled.
    I save a wretched pauper from starvation,
    House him, and treat him like a blood relation,
    Shower him every day with my largesse,
    Give him my daughter, and all that I possess;
    And meanwhile the unconscionable knave
    Tries to induce my wife to misbehave;
    And not content with such extreme rascality,
    Now threatens me with my own liberality,
    And aims, by taking base advantage of
    The gifts I gave him out of Christian love,
    To drive me from my house, a ruined man,
    And make me end a pauper, as he began.

DORINE: Poor fellow!

MADAME PERNELLE: No, my son, I'll never bring
    Myself to think him guilty of such thing.

ORGON: How's that?

MADAME PERNELLE: The righteous always were maligned.

ORGON: Speak clearly, Mother. Say what's on your mind.

MADAME PERNELLE: I mean that I can smell a rat, my dear.
    You know how everybody hates him, here.

ORGON: That has no bearing on the case at all.

MADAME PERNELLE: I told you a hundred times, when you were small,
    That virtue in this world is hated ever;
    Malicious men may die, but malice never.

ORGON: No doubt that's true, but how does it apply?

MADAME PERNELLE: They've turned you against him by a clever lie.

ORGON: I've told you, I was there and saw it done.

MADAME PERNELLE: Ah, slanderers will stop at nothing, Son.

ORGON: Mother, I'll lose my temper . . . For the last time,
    I tell you I was witness to the crime.

MADAME PERNELLE: The tongues of spite are busy night and noon,
    And to their venom no man is immune.

ORGON: You're talking nonsense. Can't you realize
    I saw it; saw it; saw it with my eyes?
    Saw, do you understand me? Must I shout it
    Into your ears before you'll cease to doubt it?

MADAME PERNELLE: Appearances can deceive, my son. Dear me,
    We cannot always judge by what we see.

ORGON: Drat! Drat!

MADAME PERNELLE: One often interprets things awry;
    Good can seem evil to a suspicious eye.

ORGON: Was I to see his pawing at Elmire
    As an act of charity?

MADAME PERNELLE: Till his guilt is clear
    A man deserves the benefit of the doubt.
    You should have waited, to see how things turned out.

ORGON: Great God in Heaven, what more proof did I need?
    Was I to sit there, watching, until he'd . . .
    You drive me to the brink of impropriety.
MADAME PERNELLE: No, no, a man of such surpassing piety
    Could not do such a thing. You cannot shake me.
    I don't believe it, and you shall not make me.
ORGON: You vex me so that, if you weren't my mother,
    I'd say to you . . . some dreadful thing or other.
DORINE: It's your turn now, Sir, not to be listened to;
    You'd not trust us, and now she won't trust you.
CLÉANTE: My friends, we're wasting time which should be spent
    In facing up to our predicament.
    I fear that scoundrel's threats weren't made in sport.
DAMIS: Do you think he'd have the nerve to go to court?
ELMIRE: I'm sure he won't: they'd find it all too crude
    A case of swindling and ingratitude.
CLÉANTE: Don't be too sure. He won't be at a loss
    To give his claims a high and righteous gloss;
    And clever rogues with far less valid cause
    Have trapped their victims in a web of laws.
    I say again that to antagonize
    A man so strongly armed was most unwise.
ORGON: I know it; but the man's appalling cheek
    Outraged me so, I couldn't control my pique.
CLÉANTE: I wish to Heaven that we could devise
    Some truce between you, or some compromise.
ELMIRE: If I had known what cards he held, I'd not
    Have roused his anger by my little plot.
ORGON: [*to* DORINE, *as* M. LOYAL *enters*] What is that fellow looking for? Who
    is he?
    Go talk to him—and tell him that I'm busy.

SCENE IV

MONSIEUR LOYAL: Good day, dear sister. Kindly let me see
    Your master.
DORINE: He's involved with company,
    And cannot be disturbed just now, I fear.
MONSIEUR LOYAL: I hate to intrude; but what has brought me here
    Will not disturb your master, in any event.
    Indeed, my news will make him most content.
DORINE: Your name?
MONSIEUR LOYAL: Just say that I bring greetings from
    Monsieur Tartuffe, on whose behalf I've come.
DORINE: [*to* ORGON] Sir, he's a very gracious man, and bears
    A message from Tartuffe, which, he declares,
    Will make you most content.
CLÉANTE: Upon my word,
    I think this man had best be seen, and heard.

ORGON: Perhaps he has some settlement to suggest.
    How shall I treat him? What manner would be best?
CLÉANTE: Control your anger, and if he should mention
    Some fair adjustment, give him your full attention.
MONSIEUR LOYAL: Good health to you, good Sir. May Heaven confound
    Your enemies, and may your joys abound.
ORGON: [*aside, to* CLÉANTE] A gentle salutation: it confirms
    My guess that he is here to offer terms.
MONSIEUR LOYAL: I've always held your family most dear;
    I served your father, Sir, for many a year.
ORGON: Sir, I must ask your pardon; to my shame,
    I cannot now recall your face or name.
MONSIEUR LOYAL: Loyal's my name; I come from Normandy,
    And I'm a bailiff, in all modesty.
    For forty years, praise God, it's been my boast
    To serve with honor in that vital post,
    And I am here, Sir, if you will permit
    The liberty, to serve you with this writ . . .
ORGON: To—*what?*
MONSIEUR LOYAL: Now, please, Sir, let us have no friction:
    It's nothing but an order of eviction.
    You are to move your goods and family out
    And make way for new occupants, without
    Deferment or delay, and give the keys . . .
ORGON: I? Leave this house?
MONSIEUR LOYAL: Why yes, Sir, if you please.
    This house, Sir, from the cellar to the roof,
    Belongs now to the good Monsieur Tartuffe,
    And he is lord and master of your estate
    By virtue of a deed of present date,
    Drawn in due form, with clearest legal phrasing . . .
DAMIS: Your insolence is utterly amazing!
MONSIEUR LOYAL: Young man, my business here is not with you,
    But with your wise and temperate father, who,
    Like every worthy citizen, stands in awe
    Of justice, and would never obstruct the law.
ORGON: But . . .
MONSIEUR LOYAL: Not for a million, Sir, would you rebel
    Against authority; I know that well.
    You'll not make trouble, Sir, or interfere
    With the execution of my duties here.
DAMIS: Someone may execute a smart tattoo
    On that black jacket of yours, before you're through.
MONSIEUR LOYAL: Sir, bid your son be silent. I'd much regret
    Having to mention such a nasty threat
    Of violence, in writing my report.
DORINE: [*aside*] This man Loyal's a most disloyal sort!

MONSIEUR LOYAL: I love all men of upright character,
    And when I agreed to serve these papers, Sir,
    It was your feelings that I had in mind.
    I couldn't bear to see the case assigned
    To someone else, who might esteem you less
    And so subject you to unpleasantness.
ORGON: What's more unpleasant than telling a man to leave
    His house and home?
MONSIEUR LOYAL: You'd like a short reprieve?
    If you desire it, Sir, I shall not press you,
    But wait until tomorrow to dispossess you.
    Splendid. I'll come and spend the night here, then,
    Most quietly, with half a score of men.
    For form's sake, you might bring me, just before
    You go to bed, the keys to the front door.
    My men, I promise, will be on their best
    Behavior, and will not disturb your rest.
    But bright and early, Sir, you must be quick
    And move out all your furniture, every stick:
    The men I've chosen are both young and strong,
    And with their help it shouldn't take you long.
    In short, I'll make things pleasant and convenient,
    And since I'm being so extremely lenient,
    Please show me, Sir, a like consideration,
    And give me your entire cooperation.
ORGON: [*aside*] I may be all but bankrupt, but I vow
    I'd give a hundred louis, here and now,
    Just for the pleasure of landing one good clout
    Right on the end of that complacent snout.
CLÉANTE: Careful; don't make things worse.
DAMIS: My bootsole itches
    To give that beggar a good kick in the breeches.
DORINE: Monsieur Loyal, I'd love to hear the whack
    Of a stout stick across your fine broad back.
MONSIEUR LOYAL: Take care: a woman, too, may go to jail if
    She uses threatening language to a bailiff.
CLÉANTE: Enough, enough, Sir. This must not go on.
    Give me that paper, please, and then begone.
MONSIEUR LOYAL: Well, *au revoir*. God give you all good cheer!
ORGON: May God confound you, and him who sent you here!

SCENE V

ORGON: Now, Mother, was I right or not? This writ
    Should change your notion of Tartuffe a bit.
    Do you perceive his villainy at last?
MADAME PERNELLE: I'm thunderstruck. I'm utterly aghast.

DORINE: Oh, come, be fair. You mustn't take offense
>   At this new proof of his benevolence.
>   He's acting out of selfless love, I know.
>   Material things enslave the soul, and so
>   He kindly has arranged your liberation
>   From all that might endanger your salvation.
ORGON: Will you not ever hold your tongue, you dunce?
CLÉANTE: Come, you must take some action, and at once.
ELMIRE: Go tell the world of the low trick he's tried.
>   The deed of gift is surely nullified
>   By such behavior, and public rage will not
>   Permit the wretch to carry out his plot.

SCENE VI

VALÈRE: Sir, though I hate to bring you more bad news,
>   Such is the danger that I cannot choose.
>   A friend who is extremely close to me
>   And knows my interest in your family
>   Has, for my sake, presumed to violate
>   The secrecy that's due to things of state,
>   And sends me word that you are in a plight
>   From which your salvation lies in flight.
>   That scoundrel who's imposed upon you so
>   Denounced you to the King an hour ago
>   And, as supporting evidence, displayed
>   The strong-box of a certain renegade
>   Whose secret papers, so he testified,
>   You had disloyally agreed to hide.
>   I don't know just what charges may be pressed,
>   But there's a warrant out for your arrest;
>   Tartuffe has been instructed, furthermore,
>   To guide the arresting officer to your door.
CLÉANTE: He's clearly done this to facilitate
>   His seizure of your house and your estate.
ORGON: That man, I must say, is a vicious beast!
VALÈRE: Quick, Sir; you mustn't tarry in the least.
>   My carriage is outside, to take you hence;
>   This thousand louis should cover all expense.
>   Let's lose no time, or you shall be undone;
>   The sole defense, in this case, is to run.
>   I shall go with you all the way, and place you
>   In a safe refuge to which they'll never trace you.
ORGON: Alas, dear boy, I wish that I could show you
>   My gratitude for everything I owe you.
>   But now is not the time; I pray the Lord
>   That I may live to give you your reward.
>   Farewell, my dears; be careful . . .

CLÉANTE: Brother, hurry.
  We shall take care of things; you needn't worry.

SCENE VII

TARTUFFE: Gently, Sir, gently; stay right where you are.
  No need for haste; your lodging isn't far.
  You're off to prison, by order of the Prince.
ORGON: This is the crowning blow, you wretch; and since
  It means my total ruin and defeat,
  Your villainy is now at last complete.
TARTUFFE: You needn't try to provoke me; it's no use.
  Those who serve Heaven must expect abuse.
CLÉANTE: You are indeed most patient, sweet, and blameless.
DORINE: How he exploits the name of Heaven! It's shameless.
TARTUFFE: Your taunts and mockeries are all for naught;
  To do my duty is my only thought.
MARIANE: Your love of duty is most meritorious,
  And what you've done is little short of glorious.
TARTUFFE: All deeds are glorious, Madam, which obey
  The sovereign Prince who sent me here today.
ORGON: I rescued you when you were destitute;
  Have you forgotten that, you thankless brute?
TARTUFFE: No, no, I well remember everything;
  But my first duty is to serve my King.
  That obligation is so paramount
  That other claims, beside it, do not count;
  And for it I would sacrifice my wife,
  My family, my friend, or my life.
ELMIRE: Hypocrite!
DORINE: All that we most revere, he uses
  To cloak his plots and camouflage his ruses.
CLÉANTE: If it is true that you are animated
  By pure and loyal zeal, as you have stated,
  Why was this zeal not roused until you'd sought
  To make Orgon a cuckold, and been caught?
  Why weren't you moved to give your evidence
  Until your outraged host had driven you hence?
  I shan't say that the gift of all his treasure
  Ought to have damped your zeal in any measure;
  But if he is a traitor, as you declare,
  How could you condescend to be his heir?
TARTUFFE: [*to the* OFFICER] Sir, spare me all this clamor; it's growing shrill.
  Please carry out your orders, if you will.
OFFICER: Yes, I've delayed too long, Sir. Thank you kindly.
  You're just the proper person to remind me.
  Come, you are off to join the other boarders
  In the King's prison, according to his orders.

TARTUFFE: Who? I, Sir?

OFFICER: Yes.

TARTUFFE: To prison? This can't be true!

OFFICER: I owe an explanation, but not to you.
   [*to* ORGON] Sir, all is well; rest easy, and be grateful.
   We serve a Prince to whom all sham is hateful,
   A Prince who sees into our inmost hearts,
   And can't be fooled by any trickster's arts.
   His royal soul, though generous and human,
   Views all things with discernment and acumen;
   His sovereign reason is not lightly swayed,
   And all his judgments are discreetly weighed.
   He honors righteous men of every kind,
   And yet his zeal for virtue is not blind,
   Nor does his love of piety numb his wits
   And make him tolerant of hypocrites.
   'Twas hardly likely that this man could cozen
   A King who's foiled such liars by the dozen.
   With one keen glance, the King perceived the whole
   Perverseness and corruption of his soul,
   And thus high Heaven's justice was displayed:
   Betraying you, the rogue stood self-betrayed.
   The King soon recognized Tartuffe as one
   Notorious by another name, who'd done
   So many vicious crimes that one could fill
   Ten volumes with them, and be writing still.
   But to be brief: our sovereign was appalled
   By this man's treachery toward you, which he called
   The last, worst villainy of a vile career,
   And bade me follow the impostor here
   To see how gross his impudence could be,
   And force him to restore your property.
   Your private papers, by the King's command,
   I hereby seize and give into your hand.
   The King, by royal order, invalidates
   The deed which gave this rascal your estates,
   And pardons, furthermore, your grave offense
   In harboring an exile's documents.
   By these decrees, our Prince rewards you for
   Your loyal deeds in the late civil war,
   And shows how heartfelt is his satisfaction
   In recompensing any worthy action,
   How much he prizes merit, and how he makes
   More of men's virtues than of their mistakes.

DORINE: Heaven be praised!

MADAME PERNELLE: I breathe again, at last.

ELMIRE: We're safe.

MARIANE: I can't believe the danger's past.
ORGON: [*to* TARTUFFE] Well, traitor, now you see . . .
CLÉANTE: Ah, Brother, please,
    Let's not descend to such indignities.
    Leave the poor wretch to his unhappy fate,
    And don't say anything to aggravate
    His present woes; but rather hope that he
    Will soon embrace an honest piety,
    And mend his ways, and by a true repentance
    Move our just King to moderate his sentence.
    Meanwhile, go kneel before your sovereign's throne
    And thank him for the mercies he has shown.
ORGON: Well said: let's go at once and, gladly kneeling,
    Express the gratitude which all are feeling.
    Then, when that first great duty has been done,
    We'll turn with pleasure to a second one,
    And give Valère, whose love has proven so true,
    The wedded happiness which is his due.

Henrik Ibsen (1828–1906)

A Doll's House (1879)

Ibsen's early plays (beginning in 1850) were poetic dramas about Norwegian legend or history. In the 1870s, he deliberately abandoned his earlier approach to write prose plays about contemporary life. *A Doll's House* and *Ghosts* made Ibsen the most controversial playwright in Europe, for the former was thought to attack the institution of marriage and the family, and the latter brought the taboo subject of venereal disease to the stage. Ibsen's prose plays were thought to epitomize realism, a new movement then under way. Subsequently, his prose works were said to have initiated the modern drama.

Undergirding *A Doll's House* is the basic assumption that character and action are determined by hereditary and environmental forces. What each character is and does is explained by information about background, upbringing, and experience. During the course of the action, we learn enough about all the characters to understand how they have arrived at where they are. Ibsen could have made his play melodramatic by depicting Krogstad as villain and Nora as persecuted heroine. Instead, all of the characters strive for what they consider right. Thus instead of a type, each character appears to be a complex, fallible human being.

A Doll's House is usually read today as a play about the status of women in the late nineteenth century. It pleases Torvald to think of Nora as incapable of making decisions, even about what she should wear to a party. The play also shows that women are legally reduced to the state of childhood (or doll) because a wife was required to have her husband's consent in almost all matters, whereas her husband could act wholly independently, even disposing of property orignally hers without her consent or knowledge. At the end of the play, Nora's alienation is not only from her husband but also from society in general. She chooses to leave her husband and children because, finding herself in disagreement with both law and public opinion and not yet certain of her own convictions, she does not believe herself ready to meet her responsibilities as a wife and mother. It was this ending that made the play so controversial, for it challenged the status quo.

A Doll's House could serve as a model of cause-to-effect dramatic structure. The first act sets up masterfully and with seeming naturalness all of the conditions out of which the subsequent action grows logically and seemingly inexorably.

Henrik Ibsen

A Doll's House

Translated *by* William Archer (*with* emendations *by the* Editor)

CHARACTERS

TORVALD HELMER
NORA, *his wife*
DOCTOR RANK
MRS. LINDE
NILS KROGSTAD
THE HELMERS' THREE YOUNG CHILDREN
ANNE, *their nurse*
A HOUSEMAID
A PORTER

The action of the play takes place in the Helmers' house.

ACT I

SCENE——*A room furnished comfortably and tastefully but not extravagantly. At the back, a door to the right leads to the entrance-hall, another to the left leads to* HELMER'S *study. Between the doors stands a piano. In the middle of the left-hand wall is a door, and beyond it a window. Near the window are a round table, armchairs and a small sofa. In the right-hand wall, at the farther end, another door; and on the same side, nearer the footlights, a stove, two easy chairs and a rockingchair; between the stove and the door, a small table. Engravings on the walls; a cabinet with china and other small objects; a small book-case with well-bound books. The floors are carpeted, and a fire burns in the stove. It is winter.*

A bell rings in the hall; shortly afterwards the door is heard to open. Enter NORA, *humming a tune and in high spirits. She is in out-door dress and carries a number of parcels; these she lays on the table to the right. She leaves the outer door open after her, and through it is seen a* PORTER *who is carrying a Christmas Tree and a basket, which he gives to the* MAID, *who has opened the door.*

NORA: Hide the Christmas Tree carefully, Helen. Be sure the children don't see it till this evening, when it is trimmed [*to the* PORTER *taking out her purse*] How much?

PORTER: A half-crown.

NORA: There's a crown. No, keep the change. [*The* PORTER *thanks her, and goes out.* NORA *shuts the door. She is laughing to herself, as she takes off her hat and coat. She takes a packet of macaroons from her pocket and eats one or two; then goes cautiously to her husband's door and listens*] Yes, he is in. [*Still humming, she goes to the table on the right.*]

HELMER: [*calls out from his room*] Is that my little lark twittering out there?

NORA: [*busy opening some of the parcels*] Yes, it is!

HELMER: Is it my little squirrel bustling about?

NORA: Yes!

HELMER: When did my squirrel come home?

NORA: Just now. [*puts the bag of macaroons into her pocket and wipes her mouth*] Come in here, Torvald, and see what I have bought.

HELMER: Don't disturb me. [*A little later he opens the door and looks into the room, pen in hand*] Bought, did you say? All these things? Has my little spend-thrift been wasting money again?

NORA: Yes, but, Torvald, this year we really can let ourselves go a little. This is the first Christmas that we have not needed to economise.

HELMER: Still, you know, we can't spend money recklessly.

NORA: Yes, Torvald, we may be a wee bit more reckless now, mayn't we? Just a tiny wee bit! You are going to have a big salary and earn lots and lots of money.

HELMER: Yes, after the New Year; but then it will be a whole quarter before the salary is due.

NORA: Pooh! we can borrow till then.

HELMER: Nora! [*goes up to her and takes her playfully by the ear*] The same little featherhead! Suppose, now, that I borrowed one thousand crowns to-day, and you spent it all in the Christmas week, and then on New Year's Eve a roof tile fell on my head and killed me, and—

NORA: [*putting her hands over his mouth*] Oh! don't say such horrid things.

HELMER: Still, suppose that happened,—what then?

NORA: If that were to happen, I don't suppose I should care whether I owed money or not.

HELMER: Yes, but what about the people who had lent it?

NORA: They? Who would care about them? I wouldn't know who they were.

HELMER: How like a woman! But seriously, Nora, you know what I think about that. No debt, no borrowing. There can be no freedom or beauty about a home that depends on borrowing and debt. We two have kept bravely on the straight road so far, and we will go on the same way for the short time left.

NORA: [*moving towards the stove*] As you please, Torvald.

HELMER: [*following her*] Come, come, my little skylark must not droop her wings. What is this! Is my little squirrel sulking? [*taking out his purse*] Nora, what do you think I've got here?

NORA: [*turning round quickly*] Money!

HELMER: There you are. [*gives her some money*] Do you think I don't know what a lot is needed for housekeeping at Christmas-time?

NORA: [*counting*] One-two-three! Thank you, thank you, Torvald; that will keep me going for a long time.

HELMER: Indeed it must.

NORA: Yes, yes, it will. But come here and let me show you what I have bought. And all so cheap! Look, here is a new suit for Ivar, and a sword; and a horse and trumpet for Bob; and a doll and a doll's bed for Emmy,—they are very plain, but anyway she'll soon break them. And here are dress materials and handkerchiefs for the maids; old Anne ought really to have something better.

HELMER: And what is in this parcel?

NORA: [*crying out*] No, no! you mustn't see that till this evening.

HELMER: Very well. But now tell me, you extravagant little person, what would you like for yourself?

NORA: For myself? Oh, I'm sure I don't want anything.

HELMER: Yes, but you must. Tell me something reasonable that you would particularly like to have.

NORA: No, I really can't think of anything—unless, Torvald—

HELMER: Well?

NORA: [*playing with his coat buttons, and without raising her eyes to his*] if you really want to give me something, you might—you might—

HELMER: Well, out with it!

NORA: [*speaking quickly*] You might give me money, Torvald. Only just as much as you can afford; and then one of these days I will buy something with it.

HELMER: But, Nora—

NORA: Oh, do! dear Torvald; please, please do! Then I will wrap it up in beautiful gold paper and hang it on the Christmas Tree. Wouldn't that be fun?

HELMER: What are little people called that are always wasting money?

NORA: Spendthrifts—I know. Let's do what you suggest, Torvald, and then I shall have time to think what I need most. That is a very sensible plan, isn't it?

HELMER: [*smiling*] Indeed it is—that is to say, if you were really to save out of the money I give you, and then really buy something for yourself. But if you spend it all on the housekeeping and any number of unnecessary things, then I merely have to pay up again.

NORA: Oh but, Torvald—

HELMER: You can't deny it, my dear little Nora. [*puts his arm around her waist*] It's a sweet little spendthrift, but she uses up a lot of money. One would hardly believe how expensive such little persons are!

NORA: It's a shame to say that. I do really save all I can.

HELMER: [*laughing*] That's very true,—all you can. But you can't save anything!

NORA: [*smiling quietly and happily*] You haven't any idea how many expenses we skylarks and squirrels have, Torvald.

HELMER: You are an odd little soul. Very like your father. You always find some new way of wheedling money out of me, and, as soon as you have got it, it seems to melt in your hands. You never know where it has gone. Still, one must take you as you are. It is in the blood; for indeed it is true that you can inherit these things, Nora.

NORA: Ah, I wish I had inherited many of papa's qualities.

HELMER: And I would not wish you to be anything but just what you are, my sweet little skylark. But, do you know, it strikes me that you are looking rather—what shall I say—rather guilty to-day?

NORA: Do I?

HELMER: You do, really. Look straight at me.

NORA: [*looks at him*] Well?

HELMER: [*wagging his finger at her*] Hasn't Miss Sweet-Tooth been breaking rules in town to-day?

NORA: No; what makes you think that?

HELMER: Hasn't she paid a visit to the pastry shop?

NORA: No, I assure you, Torvald—

HELMER: Not been nibbling sweets?

NORA: No, certainly not.

HELMER: Not even taken a bite at a macaroon or two?

NORA: No, Torvald, I assure you really—

HELMER: There, there, of course I was only joking.

NORA: [*going to the table on the right*] I wouldn't think of going against your wishes.

HELMER: No, I am sure of that; besides, you gave me your word—[*going up to her*] Keep your little Christmas secrets to yourself, my darling. They will all be revealed to-night when the Christmas Tree is lit, no doubt.

NORA: Did you remember to invite Doctor Rank?

HELMER: No. But there is no need; he will come to dinner with us as he always does. However, I will ask him when he comes in this morning. I have ordered some good wine. Nora, you can't think how I am looking forward to this evening.

NORA: So am I! And how the children will enjoy themselves, Torvald!

HELMER: It is splendid to feel that one has a secure job and a big enough income. It's delightful to think of, isn't it?

NORA: It's wonderful.

HELMER: Do you remember last Christmas? For a full three weeks beforehand you shut yourself up every evening till long after midnight, making ornaments for the Christmas Tree and all the other fine things that were to be a surprise to us. It was the dullest three weeks I ever spent!

NORA: I didn't find it dull.

HELMER: [*smiling*] But there was precious little to show for it, Nora.

NORA: Oh, you shouldn't tease me about that again. How could I help the cat's getting in and tearing everything to pieces?

HELMER: Of course you couldn't, poor little girl. You had the best of intentions to please us all, and that's the main thing. But it is a good thing that our hard times are over.

NORA: Yes, it is really wonderful.

HELMER: This time I needn't be all alone and bored and you needn't ruin your dear eyes and and your pretty little hands—

NORA: [*clapping her hands*] No, Torvald, I don't have to any longer, do I! It's wonderful to hear you say so! [*taking his arm*] Now I will tell you how I have been thinking we ought to arrange things, Torvald. As soon as Christmas is over—[*a bell rings in the hall*] There's the doorbell. [*she tidies the room a little*] There's someone at the door. What a nuisance!

HELMER: If it is a caller, remember I am not at home.

MAID: [*in the doorway*] A lady to see you, ma'am,—a stranger.

NORA: Ask her to come in.

MAID: [*to* HELMER] The doctor came at the same time, sir.

HELMER: Did he go straight into my study?

MAID: Yes, sir.

> [HELMER *goes into his room. The* MAID *ushers in* MRS. LINDE, *who is in travelling clothes and shuts the door.*]

MRS. LINDE: [*in a dejected and timid voice*] How do you do, Nora?

NORA: [*doubtfully*] How do you do—

MRS. LINDE: You don't recognise me, I suppose.

NORA: No, I'm afraid—yes, to be sure, I seem to—[*suddenly*] Yes! Christine! Is it really you?

MRS. LINDE: Yes, it is I.

NORA: Christine! To think of my not recognising you! And yet how could I— [*in a gentle voice*] How you've changed, Christine!

MRS. LINDE: Yes, I have indeed. In nine, ten long years—

NORA: Is it so long since we met? I suppose it is. The last eight years have been a happy time for me, I can tell you. And so now you have come into town, and have taken this long journey in winter—that was brave of you.

MRS. LINDE: I arrived by boat this morning.

NORA: To have some fun at Christmas-time, of course. How delightful! We will have such fun together! But take off your things. You are not cold, I hope. [*helps her*] Now we will sit down by the stove, and be comfortable. No, take this armchair; I will sit here in the rockingchair. [*takes her hands*] Now you look like your old self again; it was only the first moment—You are a little paler, Christine, and perhaps a little thinner.

MRS. LINDE: And much, much older, Nora.

NORA: Perhaps a little older; very, very little; certainly not much. [*stops suddenly and speaks seriously*] What a thoughtless creature I am, chattering away like this. My poor, dear Christine, do forgive me.

MRS. LINDE: What do you mean, Nora?

NORA: [*gently*] Poor Christine, you are a widow.

MRS. LINDE: Yes; it is three years ago now.

NORA: Yes, I know; I saw it in the papers. I assure you, Christine, I meant to write to you at the time, but I always put it off and something always prevented me.

MRS. LINDE: I quite understand, dear.

NORA: It was very bad of me, Christine. Poor thing, how you must have suffered. And he left you nothing?

MRS. LINDE: No.

NORA: And no children?

MRS. LINDE: No.

NORA: Nothing at all, then?

MRS. LINDE: Not even sorrow or grief to live upon.

NORA: [*looking incredulously at her*] But, Christine, is that possible?

MRS. LINDE: [*smiles sadly and strokes her hair*] It sometimes happens, Nora.

NORA: So you are quite alone. How dreadfully sad that must be. I have three lovely children. You can't see them just now, for they are out with their nurse. But now you must tell me everything.

MRS. LINDE: No, no; I want to hear about you.

NORA: No, you must begin. I mustn't be selfish to-day; to-day I must only think of your affairs. But there is one thing I must tell you. Have you heard about our great piece of good luck?

MRS. LINDE: No, what is it?

NORA: Just imagine, my husband has been made manager of the Bank!

MRS. LINDE: Your husband? What good luck!

NORA: Yes, tremendous! A lawyer's profession is such an uncertain thing, especially if he won't undertake unsavoury cases; and naturally Torvald has never been willing to do that, and I quite agree with him. You may imagine how pleased we are! He'll begin his job in the Bank at the New Year, and then he'll have a big salary and lots of commissions. For the future we can live quite differently—we can do just as we like. I feel so relieved and so happy, Christine! It will be splendid to have heaps of money and not need to have any anxiety, won't it?

MRS. LINDE: Yes, anyhow I think it would be delightful to have what one needs.

NORA: No, not only what one needs, but heaps and heaps of money.

MRS. LINDE: [*smiling*] Nora, Nora, haven't you learnt sense yet? In our schooldays you were a great spendthrift.

NORA: [*laughing*] Yes, that is what Torvald says now. [*wags her finger at her*] But "Nora, Nora" isn't so silly as you think. We have not been in a position for me to waste money. We have both had to work.

MRS. LINDE: You, too!

NORA: Yes; odds and ends, needlework, crochetings, embroidery, and that kind of thing. [*dropping her voice*] And other things as well. You know Torvald left his office when we were married? There was no prospect of promotion there, and he had to try and earn more than before. But during the first year he overworked himself dreadfully. You see, he had to make money every way he could, and he worked early and late; but he couldn't stand it, and fell dreadfully ill, and the doctors said it was necessary for him to go south.

MRS. LINDE: You spent a whole year in Italy, didn't you?

NORA: Yes. It was no easy matter to get away, I can tell you. It was just after Ivar was born; but naturally we had to go. It was a wonderfully beautiful trip and it saved Torvald's life. But it cost a tremendous lot of money, Christine.

MRS. LINDE: So I should think.

NORA: It cost about forty-eight hundred crowns. That's a lot, isn't it?

MRS. LINDE: Yes, and in emergencies like that it is lucky to have the money.

NORA: We got the money from papa.

MRS. LINDE: Oh, I see. It was just about that time that he died, wasn't it?

NORA: Yes; and just think of it, I couldn't go and nurse him. I was expecting little Ivar's birth every day and I had my poor sick Torvald to look after. My dear, kind father—I never saw him again, Christine. That was the saddest time I have known since our marriage.

MRS. LINDE: I know how fond you were of him. And then you went off to Italy?

NORA: Yes; you see, we had money then, and the doctors insisted on our going, so we started a month later.

MRS. LINDE: And your husband came back quite well?

NORA: As sound as a bell!

MRS. LINDE: But—the doctor?

NORA: What doctor?

MRS. LINDE: I thought your maid said the gentleman who arrived here just as I did, was the doctor?

NORA: Yes, that was Doctor Rank, but he doesn't come here professionally. He is our closest friend, and comes in at least once every day. No, Torvald has not had an hour's illness since then, and our children are strong and healthy and so am I. [*jumps up and claps her hands*] Christine! Christine! it's good to be alive and happy!—But how horrid of me; I am talking of nothing but my own affairs. [*sits on a stool near her, and rests her arms on her knees*] You mustn't be angry with me. Tell me, is it really true that you did not love your husband? Why did you marry him?

MRS. LINDE: My mother was alive then, and was bedridden and helpless, and I had to provide for my two younger brothers; so I didn't think I was justified in refusing his offer.

NORA: No, perhaps you were quite right. He was rich at that time, then?

MRS. LINDE: I believe he was quite well off. But his business was a precarious one; and, when he died, it all went to pieces and there was nothing left.

NORA: And then?—

MRS. LINDE: Well, I had to turn my hand to anything I could find—first a small shop, then a small school, and so on. The last three years have seemed like one long working-day, with no rest. Now it is at an end, Nora. My poor mother needs me no more, for she is gone; and the boys don't need me either; they have got jobs and can shift for themselves.

NORA: What a relief you must feel—

MRS. LINDE: No, indeed; I only feel my life unspeakably empty. No one to live for any more. [*gets up restlessly*] That was why I could not stand the life in my little backwater any longer. I hope it may be easier here to find something which will busy me and occupy my thoughts. If only I could have the good luck to get some regular work—office work of some kind—

NORA: But, Christine, that is so frightfully tiring, and you look tired out now. You had far better go away to some watering-place.

MRS. LINDE: [*walking to the window*] I have no father to give me money for a journey, Nora.

NORA: [*rising*] Oh, don't be angry with me.

MRS. LINDE: [*going up to her*] It is you that mustn't be angry with me, dear. The worst of a position like mine is that it makes one so bitter. No one to work for, and yet obliged to be always on the look-out for chances. One must live, and so one becomes selfish. When you told me of the happy turn your fortunes have taken—you will hardly believe it—I was delighted not so much on your account as on my own.

NORA: How do you mean?—Oh, I understand. You mean that perhaps Torvald could get you something to do.

MRS. LINDE: Yes, that was what I was thinking of.

NORA: He must, Christine. Just leave it to me; I will broach the subject very cleverly—I will think of something that will please him very much. It will make me so happy to be of some use to you.

MRS. LINDE: How kind you are, Nora, to be so anxious to help me! It is doubly kind in you, for you know so little of the burdens and troubles of life.

NORA: I—? I know so little of them?

MRS. LINDE: [*smiling*] My dear! Small household cares and that sort of thing! You are a child, Nora.

NORA: [*tosses her head and crosses the stage*] You ought not to be so superior.

MRS. LINDE: No!

NORA: You are just like the others. They all think that I am incapable of anything really serious—

MRS. LINDE: Come, come—

NORA: —that I have gone through nothing in this world of cares.

MRS. LINDE: But, my dear Nora, you have just told me all your troubles.

NORA: Pooh!—those were trifles. [*lowering her voice*] I have not told you the important thing.

MRS. LINDE: The important thing! What do you mean?

NORA: You look down on me, Christine—but you shouldn't. You are proud, aren't you, of having working so hard and so long for your mother?

MRS. LINDE: Indeed, I don't look down on any one. But it is true that I am proud and glad to think that I was privileged to make the end of my mother's life almost free from care.

NORA: And you are proud to think of what you have done for your brothers.

MRS. LINDE: I think I have the right to be.

NORA: I think so, too. But now, listen to this; I, too, have something to be proud and glad of.

MRS. LINDE: I have no doubt you have. But what do you refer to?

NORA: Speak low. Suppose Torvald were to hear! He mustn't on any account—no one in the world must know, Christine, except you.

MRS. LINDE: But what is it?

NORA: Come here. [*pulls her down on the sofa beside her*] Now I'll show you that I also have something to be proud and glad of. It was I who saved Torvald's life.

MRS. LINDE: "Saved"? How?

NORA: I told you about our trip to Italy. Torvald would never have recovered if he had not gone there—

MRS. LINDE: Yes, but your father gave you the necessary funds.

NORA: [*smiling*] Yes, that is what Torvald and all the others think, but—

MRS. LINDE: But—

NORA: Papa didn't give us a crown. It was I who procured the money.

MRS. LINDE: You? All that large sum?

NORA: Forty-eight hundred crowns. What do you think of that?

MRS. LINDE: But, Nora, how could you possibly do it? Did you win a prize in the Lottery?

NORA: [*contemptuously*] In the Lottery? There would have been no credit in that.

MRS. LINDE: But where did you get it then?

NORA: [*humming and smiling with an air of mystery*] Hm, hm! Aha!

MRS. LINDE: Because you couldn't have borrowed it.

NORA: Couldn't I? Why not?

MRS. LINDE: No, a wife cannot borrow without her husband's consent.

NORA: [*tossing her head*] Oh, if it's a wife who has any head for business—a wife who has the wit to be a little bit clever—

MRS. LINDE: I don't understand it at all, Nora.

NORA: There is no need you should. I never said I had borrowed the money. I may have got it some other way. [*lies back on the sofa*] Perhaps I got it from some admirer. When you're as attractive as I am—

MRS. LINDE: You're mad.

NORA: Now, you know you're full of curiosity, Christine.

MRS. LINDE: Listen to me, Nora dear. Haven't you been a little bit foolish?

NORA: [*sits up straight*] Is it foolish to save your husband's life?

MRS. LINDE: It seems to me foolish without his knowledge, to—

NORA: But it was absolutely necessary that he not know! My goodness, can't you understand that? It was necessary he should have no idea what a dangerous condition he was in. It was to me that the doctors came and said that his life was in danger, and that the only thing to save him was to live in the south. Do you suppose I didn't try, first of all, to get what I wanted as if it were for myself? I told him how much I should love to travel abroad like other young wives; I tried tears and entreaties with him; I told him that he ought to remember the condition I was in, and that he ought to be kind and indulgent to me; I even hinted that he might raise a loan. That nearly made him angry, Christine. He said I was thoughtless, and that it was his duty as my husband not to indulge me in my whims and caprices—as I believe he called them. Very well, I thought, you must be saved—and that was how I came to devise a way out of the difficulty—

MRS. LINDE: And did your husband never find out from your father that the money hadn't come from him?

NORA: No, never. Papa died just at that time. I had meant to let him into the secret and beg him never to reveal it. But he was so ill then—unfortunately there was no need to tell him.

MRS. LINDE: And since then have you never told your secret to your husband?

NORA: Good Heavens, no! How could you think that? A man who has such strong opinions about these things! And besides, how painful and humiliating it would be for Torvald, with his male pride, to know that he owed me anything! It would upset our relationship altogether; our beautiful happy home would no longer be the same.

MRS. LINDE: Do you mean never to tell him about it?

NORA: [*meditatively, and with a half smile*] Yes—some day, perhaps, after many years, when I'm no longer as attractive as I am now. Don't laugh at me! I mean, of course, when Torvald is no longer as devoted to me as he is now; when my dancing and dressing-up and reciting have palled on him; then it may be a good thing to have something in reserve—[*breaking off*] What nonsense! That time will never come. Now, what do you think of my great secret, Christine? Do you still think I am of no use? I can tell you, too, that this affair has caused me a lot of worry. It has been by no means easy for me to meet my payments punctually. I may tell you that there is something that is called, in business, quarterly interest, and another thing called payment in installments, and it is always so dreadfully difficult to manage them. I have had to save a little here and there, where I could, you understand. I have not been able to put aside much from my housekeeping money, for Torvald must have a good table. I couldn't let my children be shabbily dressed; I have felt obliged to use up all he gave me for them, the sweet little darlings!

MRS. LINDE: So it has all had to come out of your own expenses, poor Nora?

NORA: Of course. Besides, I was the one responsible for it. Whenever Torvald has given me money for new dresses and such things, I have never spent more than half of it; I have always bought the simplest and cheapest things. Thank Heaven, any clothes look good on me, and so Torvald has never noticed it. But it was often very hard on me, Christine—because it is delightful to be really well dressed, isn't it?

MRS. LINDE: Quite so.

NORA: Well, then I have found other ways of earning money. Last winter I was lucky enough to get a lot of copying to do; so I locked myself up and sat writing every evening until quite late at night. Many a time I was desperately tired; but all the same it was a tremendous pleasure to sit there working and earning money. It was like being a man.

MRS. LINDE: How much have you been able to pay off in that way?

NORA: I can't tell you exactly. You see, it is very difficult to keep an account of a business matter of that kind. I only know that I have paid every penny that I could scrape together. Many a time I was at my wits' end. [*smiles*] Then I used to sit here and imagine that a rich old gentleman had fallen in love with me—

MRS. LINDE: What! Who was it?

NORA: —that he had died; and that when his will was opened it contained, written in big letters, the instruction: "The lovely Mrs. Nora Helmer is to have all I possess paid over to her at once in cash."

MRS. LINDE: But, my dear Nora—who could the man be!

NORA: Good gracious, can't you understand? There was no old gentleman at all; it was only something that I used to sit here and imagine, when I couldn't think of any way of getting money. But it's all the same now; the tiresome old person can stay where he is, as far as I am concerned; I don't care about him or his will, either, for I am free from care now. [*jumps up*] My goodness, it's delightful to think of, Christine! Free from care! To be able to be free from care, quite free from care; to be able to play and romp with the children; to be able to keep the house beautifully and have everything just as Torvald likes it! And, think of it, soon the spring will come and the big blue sky! Perhaps we shall be able to take a little trip—perhaps I shall see the sea again! Oh, it's a wonderful thing to be alive and be happy. [*a bell is heard in the hall*]

MRS. LINDE: [*rising*] There's the doorbell; perhaps I had better go.

NORA: No, don't go; no one will come in here; it is sure to be for Torvald.

SERVANT: [*at the hall door*] Excuse me, ma'am—there is a gentleman to see the master, and as the doctor is with him—

NORA: Who is it?

KROGSTAD: [*at the door*] It is I, Mrs. Helmer. [MRS. LINDE *starts, trembles, and turns to the window.*]

NORA: [*takes a step towards him, and speaks in a strained, low voice*] You? What is it? What do you want to see my husband about?

KROGSTAD: Bank business—in a way. I have a small post in the Bank, and I hear your husband is to be our chief now—

NORA: Then it is—

KROGSTAD: Nothing but dry business matters, Mrs. Helmer; absolutely nothing else.

NORA: Be so good as to go into the study, then. [*She bows indifferently to him and shuts the door into the hall; then comes back and makes up the fire in the stove.*]

MRS. LINDE: Nora—who was that man?

NORA: A lawyer named Krogstad.

MRS. LINDE: Then it really was he.

NORA: Do you know the man?

MRS. LINDE: I used to—many years ago. At one time he was a solicitor's clerk in our town.

NORA: Yes, he was.

MRS. LINDE: He is greatly altered.

NORA: He made a very unhappy marriage.

MRS. LINDE: He is a widower now isn't he?

NORA: With several children. There now, it's burning. [*shuts the door of the stove and moves the rockingchair aside*]

MRS. LINDE: They say he carries on various kinds of business.

NORA: Really! Perhaps he does; I don't know anything about it. But don't let's think of business: it is so boring.

DOCTOR RANK: [*Comes out of* HELMER's *study. Before he shuts the door he calls to him.*] No, my dear fellow, I won't disturb you; I would rather go in to your wife for a little while. [*shuts the door and sees* MRS. LINDE] I beg your pardon; I'm afraid I'm disturbing you, too.

NORA: No, not at all. [*introducing him*] Doctor Rank, Mrs. Linde.

RANK: I have often heard Mrs. Linde's name mentioned here. I think I passed you on the stairs when I arrived, Mrs. Linde?

MRS. LINDE: Yes, I go up very slowly; I can't manage stairs well.

RANK: Ah! some slight internal weakness?

MRS. LINDE: No, the fact is I have been overworking myself.

RANK: Nothing more than that? Then I suppose you have come to town to amuse yourself with our entertainments?

MRS. LINDE: I have come to look for work.

RANK: Is that a good cure for overwork?

MRS. LINDE: One must live, Doctor Rank.

RANK: Yes, the general opinion seems to be that it's necessary.

NORA: Look here, Doctor Rank—you know you want to live.

RANK: Certainly. However wretched I may feel, I want to prolong the agony as long as possible. All my patients are like that. And so are those who are morally sick—one of them, and a bad case, too, is at this very moment with Helmer—

MRS. LINDE: [*sadly*]. Ah!

NORA: Whom do you mean?

RANK: A lawyer, Krogstad, a fellow you don't know at all. He suffers from a diseased moral character, Mrs. Helmer; but even he began talking about it being highly important that he should live.

NORA: Did he? What did he want to speak to Torvald about?

RANK: I have no idea; I only heard that it was something about the Bank.

NORA: I didn't know this—what's his name—Krogstad had anything to do with the Bank.

RANK: Yes, he has some sort of appointment there. [*to* MRS. LINDE] I don't know whether you find also in your part of the world that there are certain people who go zealously sniffing about to smell out moral corruption, and, as soon as they have found some, put the person concerned into some lucrative position where they can keep their eye on him. Healthy natures are left out in the cold.

MRS. LINDE: Still I think the sick are those who most need taking care of.

RANK: [*shrugging his shoulders*] Yes, there you are. That is the sentiment that is turning Society into a hospital.

> [NORA, *who has been absorbed in her thoughts, breaks out into smothered laughter and claps her hands.*]

RANK: Why do you laugh at that? Have you any notion what Society really is?

NORA: What do I care about tiresome Society? I am laughing at something quite different, something extremely amusing. Tell me, Doctor Rank, are all the people who are employed in the Bank dependent on Torvald now?

RANK: Is that what you find so extremely amusing?

NORA: [*smiling and humming*] That's my affair! [*walking about the room*] It's perfectly glorious to think that we have—that Torvald has so much power over so many people. [*takes the packet from her pocket*] Doctor Rank, what do you say to a macaroon?

RANK: What, macaroons? I thought they were forbidden here.

NORA: Yes, but these are some Christine gave me.

MRS. LINDE: What! I?

NORA: Oh, well, don't be alarmed! You couldn't know that Torvald had forbidden them. I must tell you that he's afraid they will spoil my teeth. But—once in a while—That's so, isn't it, Doctor Rank? Here [*puts a macaroon into his mouth*] you must have one, too, Christine. And I shall have one, just a little one—or at most two. [*walking about*] I am tremendously happy. There is just one thing in the world now that I should dearly love to do.

RANK: Well, what is that?

NORA: It's something I should dearly love to say so Torvald could hear me.

RANK: Well, why can't you say it?

NORA: No, I daren't; it's so shocking.

MRS. LINDE: Shocking?

RANK: Well, I should not advise you to say it. Still, with us you might. What is it you would so much like to say so Torvald could hear?

NORA: I should just love to say—Well, I'm damned!

RANK: Are you mad?

MRS. LINDE: Nora, dear—!

RANK: Say it, here he is!

NORA: [*hiding the packet*] Hush! Hush! Hush! [HELMER *comes out of his room, with his coat over his arm and his hat in his hand.*]

NORA: Well, Torvald dear, have you got rid of him?

HELMER: Yes, he's gone.

NORA: Let me introduce you—this is Christine, who has come to town.

HELMER: Christine—? Excuse me, but I don't know—

NORA: Mrs. Linde, dear; Christine Linde.

HELMER: Of course. A school friend of my wife, I presume?

MRS. LINDE: Yes, we've known each other since then.

NORA: And just think, she's taken a long journey in order to see you.

HELMER: What do you mean?

MRS. LINDE: No, really I—

NORA: Christine is tremendously clever at office work and she's frightfully anxious to work under some clever man, so as to improve—

HELMER: Very sensible, Mrs. Linde.

NORA: And when she heard you had been appointed manager of the Bank—the news was telegraphed, you know—she travelled here as quick as she could, Torvald, I'm sure you will be able to do something for Christine, for my sake, won't you?

HELMER: Well, it is not altogether impossible. I presume you are a widow, Mrs. Linde?

MRS. LINDE: Yes.

HELMER: And have had some experience of office work?

MRS. LINDE: Yes, a fair amount.

HELMER: Ah! well, it's very likely I may be able to find something for you.

NORA: [*clapping her hands*] What did I tell you? What did I tell you?

HELMER: You have just come at a fortunate moment, Mrs. Linde.

MRS. LINDE: How am I to thank you?

HELMER: There's no need. [*puts on his coat*] But to-day you must excuse me—

RANK: Wait a minute, I'll come with you. [*brings his fur coat from the hall and warms it at the fire*]

NORA: Don't be long away, Torvald dear.

HELMER: About an hour, not more.

NORA: Are you going, too, Christine?

MRS. LINDE: [*putting on her cloak*] Yes, I must go and look for a room.

HELMER: Oh, well then, we can walk together.

NORA: [*helping her*] What a pity it is we are so short of space here; I am afraid it is impossible for us—

MRS. LINDE: Please don't think of it! Good-bye, Nora dear, and many thanks.

NORA: Good-bye for the present. Of course you will come back this evening. And you, too, Dr. Rank. What do you say? If you are well enough? Oh, you must be! Wrap yourself up well. [*They go to the door all talking together. Children's voices are heard on the staircase.*]

NORA: There they are. There they are! [*she runs to open the door. The* NURSE *comes in with the children.*] Come in! Come in! [*stoops and kisses them*] Oh, you sweet blessings! Look at them, Christine! Aren't they darlings?

RANK: Don't let's stand here in the draught.

HELMER: Come along, Mrs. Linde; the place will only be bearable for a mother now! [RANK, HELMER, *and* MRS. LINDE *go downstairs. The* NURSE *comes forward with the children;* NORA *shuts the hall door.*]

NORA: How fresh and well you look! Such red cheeks!—like apples and roses. [*The children all talk at once while she speaks to them.*] Have you had great fun? That's splendid! What, you pulled both Emmy and Bob along on the sled?—both at once?—that *was* good. You are a clever boy, Ivar. Let me take her for a little, Anne. My sweet little baby doll! [*takes the baby from the* MAID *and dances it up and down*] Yes, yes, mother will dance with Bob, too. What! Have you been snowballing? I wish I had been there, too! No, no, I will take their things off, Anne; please let me do it, it's such fun. Go in now, you look half frozen. There's some hot coffee for you on the stove.

[*The* NURSE *goes into the room on the left.* NORA *takes off the children's things and throws them about, while they all talk to her at once.*]

NORA: Really! Did a big dog run after you? But it didn't bite you? No, dogs don't bite nice little dolly children. You mustn't look at the parcels, Ivar. What are they? Ah, I daresay you would like to know. No, no—it's something nasty! Come, let us have a game! What shall we play? Hide-and-Seek? Yes, we'll play Hide-and-Seek. Bob shall hide first. Must I hide? Very well, I'll hide first. [*She and the children laugh and shout, and romp in and out of the room; at last* NORA *hides under the table, the children rush in and look for her, but do not see her; they hear her smothered laughter, run to the table, lift up the cloth and find her. Shouts of laughter. She crawls forward and pretends to frighten them. Fresh laughter. Meanwhile there has been a knock at the hall door, but none of them has noticed it. The door is half opened, and* KROGSTAD *appears. He waits a little; the game goes on.*]

KROGSTAD: Excuse me, Mrs. Helmer.

NORA: [*with a stifled cry, turns round and gets up on to her knees*] Ah! what do you want?

KROGSTAD: Excuse me, the outer door was ajar; I suppose someone forgot to shut it.

NORA: [*rising*] My husband is out, Mr. Krogstad.

KROGSTAD: I know that.

NORA: What do you want here, then?

KROGSTAD: A word with you.

NORA: With me?—[*to the children, gently*] Go in to nurse. What? No, the strange man won't do mother any harm. When he's gone we will have another game. [*She takes the children into the room on the left, and shuts the door after them.*] You want to speak to me?

KROGSTAD: Yes, I do.

NORA: To-day? It is not the first of the month yet.

KROGSTAD: No, it is Christmas Eve, and it will depend on yourself what sort of a Christmas you will spend.

NORA: What do you want? To-day it is absolutely impossible for me—

KROGSTAD: We won't talk about that till later on. This is something different. I presume you can give me a moment?

NORA: Yes—yes, I can—although—

KROGSTAD: Good. I was in Olsen's Restaurant and saw your husband going down the street—

NORA: Yes?

KROGSTAD: With a lady.

NORA: What then?

KROGSTAD: May I make so bold as to ask if it was a Mrs. Linde?

NORA: It was.

KROGSTAD: Just arrived in town?

NORA: Yes, to-day.

KROGSTAD: She's a great friend of yours, isn't she?

NORA: She is. But I don't see—

KROGSTAD: I knew her, too, once upon a time.

NORA: I'm aware of that.

KROGSTAD: Are you? So you know all about it; I thought as much. Then I can ask you, without beating about the bush—is Mrs. Linde to have an appointment in the Bank?

NORA: What right have you to question me, Mr. Krogstad?—You, one of my husband's subordinates! But since you ask, you shall know. Yes, Mrs. Linde *is* to have an appointment. And it was I who pleaded her cause, Mr. Krogstad, let me tell you that.

KROGSTAD: I was right in what I thought, then.

NORA: [*walking up and down*] Sometimes one has a tiny little bit of influence, I should hope. Because one is a woman, it doesn't necessarily follow that—. When anyone is in a subordinate position, Mr. Krogstad, they should really be careful to avoid offending anyone who—who—

KROGSTAD: Who has influence?

NORA: Exactly.

KROGSTAD: [*changing his tone*] Mrs. Helmer, you will be so good as to use your influence on my behalf.

NORA: What? What do you mean?

KROGSTAD: You will be so kind as to see that I am allowed to keep my subordinate position in the Bank.

NORA: What do you mean by that? Who proposes to take your post away from you?

KROGSTAD: Oh, there is no necessity to keep up the pretence of ignorance. I can quite understand that your friend is not very anxious to expose herself to the chance of rubbing shoulders with me; and I quite understand, too, whom I have to thank for being discharged.

NORA: But I assure you—

KROGSTAD: Very likely; but, to come to the point, the time has come when I should advise you to use your influence to prevent that.

NORA: But, Mr. Krogstad, I *have* no influence.

KROGSTAD: Haven't you? I thought you said yourself just now—

NORA: Naturally I didn't mean you to put that construction on it. I! What should make you think I have any influence of that kind with my husband?

KROGSTAD: Oh, I have known your husband from our student days. I don't suppose he's any more unassailable than other husbands.

NORA: If you speak slightingly of my husband, I shall turn you out of the house.

KROGSTAD: You are bold, Mrs. Helmer.

NORA: I'm not afraid of you any longer. As soon as the New Year comes, I shall in a very short time be free of the whole thing.

KROGSTAD: [*controlling himself*] Listen to me, Mrs. Helmer. If necessary, I am prepared to fight for my small post in the Bank as if I were fighting for my life.

NORA: So it seems.

KROGSTAD: It's not only for the sake of the money; indeed, that weighs least with me in the matter. There's another reason—well, I may as well tell you. My position is this. I daresay you know, like everybody else, that once, many years ago, I was guilty of an indiscretion.

NORA: I think I've heard something of the kind.

KROGSTAD: The matter never came into court; but every way seemed to be closed to me after that. So I took to the business that you know of. I had to do something; and, honestly, I don't think I've been one of the worst. But now I must cut myself free from all that. My sons are growing up; for their sake I must try and win back as much respect as I can in the town. This post in the Bank was like the first step up for me—and now your husband is going to kick me downstairs again into the mud.

NORA: But you must believe me, Mr. Krogstad; it's not in my power to help you at all.

KROGSTAD: Then it's because you haven't the will; but I have means to compel you.

NORA: You don't mean that you will tell my husband that I owe you money?

KROGSTAD: Hm!—suppose I were to tell him?

NORA: It would be shameful of you. [*sobbing*] To think of his learning my secret, which has been my joy and pride, in such an ugly, clumsy way—that he should learn it from you! And it would put me in a horribly disagreeable position—

KROGSTAD: Only disagreeable?

NORA: [*impetuously*] Well, do it, then!—and it will be the worse for you. My husband will see for himself what a blackguard you are, and you certainly won't keep your post then.

KROGSTAD: I asked you if it was only a disagreeable scene at home that you were afraid of?

NORA: If my husband does get to know of it, of course he will at once pay you what is still owing, and we shall have nothing more to do with you.

KROGSTAD: [*coming a step nearer*] Listen to me, Mrs. Helmer. Either you have a very bad memory or you know very little of business. I shall be obliged to remind you of a few details.

NORA: What do you mean?

KROGSTAD: When your husband was ill, you came to me to borrow forty-eight hundred crowns.

NORA: I didn't know any one else to go to.

KROGSTAD: I promised to get you that amount—

NORA: Yes, and you did so.

KROGSTAD: I promised to get you that amount, on certain conditions. Your mind was so taken up with your husband's illness, and were so anxious to get the money for your journey, that you seem to have paid no attention to the conditions of our bargain. Therefore it will not be amiss if I remind you of them. Now, I promised to get the money on the security of a bond which I drew up.

NORA: Yes, and which I signed.

KROGSTAD: Good. But below your signature there were a few lines constituting your father a surety for the money; those lines your father should have signed.

NORA: Should? He did sign them.

KROGSTAD: I had left the date blank; that is to say your father should himself have inserted the date on which he signed the paper. Do you remember that?

NORA: Yes, I think I remember—

KROGSTAD: Then I gave you the bond to send by post to your father. Is that not so?

NORA: Yes.

KROGSTAD: And you naturally did so at once, because five or six days afterwards you brought me the bond with your father's signature. And then I gave you the money.

NORA: Well, haven't I been paying it off regularly?

KROGSTAD: Fairly so, yes. But—to come back to the matter in hand—that must have been a very trying time for you, Mrs. Helmer?

NORA: It was, indeed.

KROGSTAD: Your father was very ill, wasn't he?

NORA: He was very near his end.

KROGSTAD: And died soon afterwards?

NORA: Yes.

KROGSTAD: Tell me, Mrs. Helmer, can you by any chance remember what day your father died?—on what day of the month, I mean.

NORA: Papa died on the 29th of September.

KROGSTAD: That is correct; I have ascertained it for myself. And, as that is so, there is a discrepancy [*taking a paper from his pocket*] which I cannot account for.

NORA: What discrepancy? I don't know—

KROGSTAD: The discrepancy consists, Mrs. Helmer, in the fact that your father signed this bond three days after his death.

NORA: What do you mean? I don't understand—

KROGSTAD: Your father died on the 29th of September. But, look here; your father has dated his signature the 2nd of October. It is a discrepancy, isn't it? [*NORA is silent*] Can you explain it to me? [*NORA is still silent*] It is a remarkable thing, too, that the words "2nd of October," as well as the year, are not written in your father's handwriting but in one that I think I know. Well, of course it can be explained; your father may have forgotten to date his signature, and someone else may have dated it before they knew of his death. There is no harm in that. It all depends on the signature of the name; and *that* is genuine, I suppose, Mrs. Helmer? It was your father himself who signed his name here?

NORA: [*after a short pause, throws her head up and looks defiantly at him*] No, it was not. It was I that wrote papa's name.

KROGSTAD: Are you aware that is a dangerous confession?

NORA: In what way? You'll have your money soon.

KROGSTAD: Let me ask you a question; why did you not send the paper to your father?

NORA: It was impossible; papa was so ill. If I'd asked him for his signature, I should have had to tell him what the money was to be used for; and when he was so ill himself I couldn't tell him that my husband's life was in danger—it was impossible.

KROGSTAD: It would have been better for you if you had given up your trip abroad.

NORA: No, that was impossible. That trip was to save my husband's life; I couldn't give that up.

KROGSTAD: But did it never occur to you that you were committing a fraud on me?

NORA: I couldn't take that into account; I didn't trouble myself about you at all. I couldn't bear you, because you put so many heartless difficulties in my way, although you knew what a dangerous condition my husband was in.

KROGSTAD: Mrs. Helmer, you evidently do not realise clearly what it is that you have been guilty of. But I can assure you that my one false step, which lost me all my reputation, was nothing more or nothing worse than what you have done.

NORA: You? Do you ask me to believe that you were brave enough to run a risk to save your wife's life?

KROGSTAD: The law cares nothing about motives.

NORA: Then it must be a very foolish law.

KROGSTAD: Foolish or not, it is the law by which you will be judged, if I produce this paper in court.

NORA: I don't believe it. Is a daughter not to be allowed to spare her dying father anxiety and care? Is a wife not to be allowed to save her husband's life? I don't know much about law; but I am certain that there must be laws permitting such things as that. Have you no knowledge of such laws—you who are a lawyer? You must be a very poor lawyer, Mr. Krogstad.

KROGSTAD: Maybe. But matters of business—such business as you and I have had together—do you think I don't understand that? Very well. Do as you please. But let me tell you this—if I lose my position a second time, you shall lose yours with me. [*He bows, and goes out through the hall.*]

NORA: [*appears buried in thought for a short time, then tosses her head*] Nonsense! Trying to frighten me like that!—I am not so silly as he thinks. [*begins to busy herself putting the children's things in order*] And yet—? No, it's impossible! I did it for love's sake.

THE CHILDREN: [*in the doorway on the left*] Mother, the stranger has gone out through the gate.

NORA: Yes, dears, I know. But, don't tell anyone about the stranger. Do you hear? Not even papa.

CHILDREN: No, mother; but will you come and play again?

NORA No, no,—not now.

CHILDREN: But, mother, you promised.

NORA: Yes, but I can't now. Go in; I have such a lot to do. Go in, my sweet little darlings. [*She gets them into the room by degrees and shuts the door on them; then sits down on the sofa, takes up a piece of needlework and sews a few stitches, but soon stops.*] No! [*throws down the work, gets up, goes to the hall door and calls out*] Helen! bring the Tree in. [*goes to the table on the left, opens a drawer, and stops again*] No, no! it is quite impossible!

MAID [*coming in with the Tree*] Where shall I put it, ma'am?

NORA: Here, in the middle of the floor.

MAID: Shall I get you anything else?

NORA: No, thank you. I have all I want.

      [*exit* MAID]

NORA: [*begins dressing the tree*] A candle here—and flowers here—. The horrible man! It's all nonsense—there's nothing wrong. The Tree shall be splendid! I'll do everything I can think of to please you, Torvald!—I'll sing for you, dance for you—[HELMER *comes in with some papers under his arm.*] Oh! are you back already?

HELMER: Yes. Has anyone been here?

NORA: Here? No.

HELMER: That's strange. I saw Krogstad going out of the gate.

NORA: Did you? Oh yes, I forgot, Krogstad was here for a moment.

HELMER: Nora, I can see from your manner that he has been here begging you to say a good word for him.

NORA: Yes.

HELMER: And you were to appear to do it of your own accord; you were to conceal from me the fact of his having been here; didn't he beg that of you, too?

NORA: Yes, Torvald, but—

HELMER: Nora, Nora, and you would be a party to that sort of thing? To have any talk with a man like that, and give him any sort of promise? And to to tell me a lie into the bargain?

NORA: A lie—?

HELMER: Didn't you tell me no one had been here? [*shakes his finger at her*] My little song-bird must never do that again. A song-bird must have a clean beak to chirp with—no false notes! [*puts his arm round her waist*] That's so, isn't it? Yes, I'm sure it is. [*lets her go*] We will say no more about it. [*sits down by the stove*] How warm and snug it is here! [*turns over his papers*]

NORA: [*after a short pause, during which she busies herself with the Christmas Tree*] Torvald!

HELMER: Yes.

NORA: I am looking forward tremendously to the fancy dress ball at the Stenborgs' the day after to-morrow.

HELMER: And I'm tremendously curious to see what you're going to surprise me with.

NORA: It was very silly of me to want to do that.

HELMER: What do you mean?

NORA: I can't hit upon anything that will do; everything I think of seems so silly and insignificant.

HELMER: Does my little Nora acknowledge that at last?

NORA: [*standing behind his chair with her arms on the back of it*] Are you very busy, Torvald?

HELMER: Well—

NORA: What are all those papers?

HELMER: Bank business.

NORA: Already?

HELMER: I have got authority from the retiring manager to undertake the necessary changes in the staff and in the reorganization of the work; and I must make use of the Christmas week for that, so as to have everything in order for the new year.

NORA: Then that was why this poor Krogstad—

HELMER: Hm!

NORA: [*leans against the back of his chair and strokes his hair*] If you hadn't been so busy I should have asked you a tremendously big favour, Torvald.

HELMER: What's that? Tell me.

NORA: There is no one has such good taste as you. And I do so want to look nice at the costume ball. Torvald, couldn't you take me in hand and decide what I shall go as, and what sort of a dress I shall wear?

HELMER: Aha! so my obstinate little woman is obliged to get someone to come to her rescue?

NORA: Yes, Torvald, I can't get along at all without your help.

HELMER: Very well, I'll think it over, we shall manage to hit on something.

NORA: That *is* nice of you. [*Goes to the Christmas Tree. A short pause.*] How pretty the red flowers look—. But, tell me, was it really something very bad that this Krogstad was guilty of?

HELMER: He forged someone's name. Have you any idea what that means?

NORA: Isn't it possible that he was driven to do it by necessity?

HELMER: Yes; or, as in so many cases, by imprudence. I am not so heartless as to condemn a man altogether because of a single false step of that kind.

NORA: No, you wouldn't, would you, Torvald?

HELMER: Many a man has been able to retrieve his character, if he has openly confessed his fault and taken his punishment.

NORA: Punishment—?

HELMER: But Krogstad did nothing of that sort; he got himself out of it by a cunning trick, and that is why he has gone under altogether.

NORA: But do you think it would—?

HELMER: Just think how a guilty man like that has to lie and play the hypocrite with everyone, how he has to wear a mask in the presence of those near and dear to him, even before his own wife and children. And about the children—that's the most terrible part of it all, Nora.

NORA: How?

HELMER: Because such an atmosphere of lies infects and poisons the whole life of a home. Each breath the children take in such a house is full of the germs of evil.

NORA: [*coming nearer him*] Are you sure of that?

HELMER: My dear, I have often seen it in the course of my life as a lawyer. Almost everyone who has gone to the bad early in life has had a deceitful mother.

NORA: Why do you only say—mother?

HELMER: It seems most commonly to be the mother's influence, though naturally a bad father's would have the same result. Every lawyer is familiar with the fact. This Krogstad, now, has been persistently poisoning his own children with lies and dissimulation; that's why I say he has lost all moral character. [*holds out his hands to her*] That's why my sweet little Nora must promise me not to plead his cause. Give me your hand on it. Come, come, what's this? Give me your hand. There now, that's settled. I assure you it would be quite impossible for me to work with him; I literally feel physically ill when I am in the company of such people.

NORA: [*takes her hand out of his and goes to the opposite side of the Christmas Tree*] How hot it is in here; and I have such a lot to do.

HELMER: [*getting up and putting his papers in order*] Yes, and I must try and read through some of these before dinner; and I must think about your costume, too. And it's just possible I may have something ready in gold paper to hang up on the Tree. [*puts his hand on her head*] My precious little singing-bird! [*He goes into his room and shuts the door after him.*]

NORA: [*after a pause, whispers*] No, no—it isn't true. It's impossible; it must be impossible.

[*The* NURSE *opens the door on the left.*]

NURSE: The little ones are begging so hard to be allowed to come in to mamma.

NORA: No, no, no! Don't let them come in to me! You stay with them, Anne.

NURSE: Very well, ma'am. [*shuts the door*]

NORA: [*pale with terror*] Deprave my little children? Poison my home? [*A short pause. Then she tosses her head.*] It's not true. It can't possibly be true.

ACT II

THE SAME SCENE———— *The Christmas Tree is in the corner by the piano, stripped of its ornaments and with burnt-down candle-ends on its dishevelled branches.* NORA's *cloak and hat are lying on the sofa. She is alone in the room, walking about uneasily. She stops by the sofa and takes up her cloak.*

NORA: [*drops the cloak*] Someone is coming now! [*goes to the door and listens*] No— it's no one. Of course, no one will come to-day, Christmas Day—nor to-morrow, either. But, perhaps—[*opens the door and looks out*] No, nothing in the mail box; it's quite empty. [*comes forward*] What rubbish! Of course he can't be in earnest about it. Such a thing couldn't happen; it's impossible— I have three little children.

[*Enter the* NURSE *from the room on the left, carrying a big cardboard box.*]

NURSE: At last I've found the box with the fancy dress.

NORA: Thanks; put it on the table.

NURSE: [*doing so*] But it's very much in want of mending.

NORA: I should like to tear it into a hundred thousand pieces.

NURSE: What an idea! It can easily be put in order—just a little patience.

NORA: Yes, I'll go and get Mrs. Linde to come and help me with it.

NURSE: What, out again? In this horrible weather? You'll catch cold, ma'am, and make yourself ill.

NORA: Well, worse than that might happen. How are the children?

NURSE: The poor little souls are playing with their Christmas presents, but—

NORA: Do they ask much for me?

NURSE: You see, they're so accustomed to have their mamma with them.

NORA: Yes, but, nurse, I shan't be able to be so much with them now as I was before.

NURSE: Oh well, young children easily get accustomed to anything.

NORA: Do you think so? Do you think they would forget their mother if she went away altogether?

NURSE: Good heavens!—went away altogether?

NORA: Nurse, I want you to tell me something I have often wondered about— how could you have the heart to put your own child out among strangers?

NURSE: I was obliged to, if I wanted to be little Nora's nurse.

NORA: Yes, but how could you be willing to do it?

NURSE: What, when I was going to get such a good place by it? A poor girl who has got into trouble should be glad to. Besides, that wicked man didn't do a single thing for me.

NORA: But I suppose your daughter has quite forgotten you.

NURSE: No, indeed she hasn't. She wrote to me when she was confirmed, and when she was married.

NORA: [*putting her arms around her neck*] Dear old Anne, you were a good mother to me when I was little.

NURSE: Little Nora, poor dear, had no other mother but me.

NORA: And if my little ones had no other mother, I'm sure you would— What nonsense I'm talking! [*opens the box*] Go in to them. Now I must—. You will see to-morrow how charming I'll look.

NURSE: I'm sure there will be no one at the ball so charming as you, ma'am. [*goes into the room on the left*]

NORA: [*begins to unpack the box, but soon pushes it away from her*] If only I dared go out. If only no one would come. If only I could be sure nothing would happen here in the meantime. Stuff and nonsense! No one will come. Only I mustn't think about it. I'll brush my muff. What lovely, lovely gloves! Out of my thoughts, out of my thoughts! One, two, three, four, five, six—[*screams*] Ah! there is someone coming—. [*makes a movement towards the door, but stands irresolute*]

[*Enter* MRS. LINDE *from the hall, where she has taken off her cloak and hat.*]

NORA: Oh, it's you, Christine. There is no one else out there, is there? How good of you to come!

MRS. LINDE: I heard you were up asking for me.

NORA: Yes, I was passing by. As a matter of fact, it's something you could help me with. Let us sit down here on the sofa. Look here. To-morrow evening there is to be a costume ball at the Stenborgs', who live above us; and Torvald wants me to go as a Neapolitan fisher-girl, and dance the Tarantella that I learned on Capri.

MRS. LINDE: I see; you're going to perform a character.

NORA: Yes, Torvald wants me to. Look, here's the dress; Torvald had it made for me there, but now it's all so torn, and I haven't any idea—.

MRS. LINDE: We'll easily put that right. It's only some of the trimming come unsewn here and there. Needle and thread? Now then, that's all we need.

NORA: It *is* nice of you.

MRS. LINDE: [*sewing*] So you're going to be dressed up to-morrow, Nora. I'll tell you what—I'll come in for a moment and see you in your fine feathers. But

I have completely forgotten to thank you for a delightful evening yesterday.

NORA: [*gets up, and crosses the stage*] Well, I don't think yesterday was as pleasant as usual. You ought to have come to town a little earlier, Christine. Certainly Torvald does understand how to make a house attractive.

MRS. LINDE: And so do you, it seems to me; you are not your father's daughter for nothing. But tell me, is Doctor Rank always as depressed as he was yesterday?

NORA: No; yesterday it was very noticeable. I must tell you that he suffers from a very dangerous disease. He has tuberculosis of the spine, poor creature. His father was a horrible man who committed all sorts of excesses; and that's why his son was sickly from childhood, do you understand?

MRS. LINDE: [*dropping her sewing*] But my dearest Nora, how do you know anything about such things?

NORA: [*walking about*] Pooh! When you have three children, you get visits now and then from—from married women, who know something of medical matters, and they talk about one thing and another.

MRS. LINDE: [*goes on sewing. A short silence*] Does Doctor Rank come here every day?

NORA: Every day regularly. He's Torvald's best friend, and a great friend of mine, too. He's just like one of the family.

MRS. LINDE: But tell me this—is he perfectly sincere? I mean, isn't he the kind of man that is very anxious to make himself agreeable?

NORA: Not in the least. What makes you think that?

MRS. LINDE: When you introduced him to me yesterday, he declared he had often heard my name mentioned in this house; but afterwards I noticed that your husband hadn't the slightest idea who I was. So how could Doctor Rank—?

NORA: That's quite right, Christine. Torvald is so absurdly fond of me that he wants me absolutely to himself, as he says. At first he used to seem almost jealous if I mentioned any of my friends back home, so naturally I gave up doing so. But I often talk about such things with Doctor Rank, because he likes hearing about them.

MRS. LINDE: Listen to me, Nora. You are still very like a child in many things, and I'm older than you in many ways and have a little more experience. Let me tell you this—you ought to make an end of it with Doctor Rank.

NORA: What ought I to make an end of?

MRS. LINDE: Of two things, I think. Yesterday you talked some nonsense about a rich admirer who was to leave you money—

NORA: An admirer who doesn't exist, unfortunately! But what then?

MRS. LINDE: Is Doctor Rank well off?

NORA: Yes, he is.

MRS. LINDE: And has no one to provide for?

NORA: No, no one; but—

MRS. LINDE: And comes here every day?

NORA: Yes, I told you so.

MRS. LINDE: But how can this well-bred man be so tactless?

NORA: I don't understand you at all.

MRS. LINDE: Don't pretend, Nora. Do you suppose I don't guess who lent you the forty-eight hundred crowns?

NORA: Are you out of your senses? How can you think of such a thing! A friend of ours, who comes here every day! Do you realize what a horribly painful position that would be?

MRS. LINDE: Then it really isn't he?

NORA: No certainly not. It would never have entered my head for a moment. Besides, he had no money to lend then; he came into his money afterwards.

MRS. LINDE: Well, I think that was lucky for you, my dear Nora.

NORA: No, it would never have come into my head to ask Doctor Rank. Although I am quite sure that if I had asked him—

MRS. LINDE: But of course you won't.

NORA: Of course not. I have no reason to think it could possibly be necessary. But I'm quite sure that if I told Doctor Rank—

MRS. LINDE: Behind your husband's back?

NORA: I must make an end of it with the other one, and that will be behind his back, too. I must make an end of it with him.

MRS. LINDE: Yes, that's what I told you yesterday, but—

NORA: [*walking up and down*] A man can put a thing like that straight much easier than a woman—

MRS. LINDE: One's husband, yes.

NORA: Nonsense! [*standing still*] When you pay off a debt you get your bond back, don't you?

MRS. LINDE: Yes, as a matter of course.

NORA: And can tear it into a hundred thousand pieces, and burn it—the nasty dirty paper!

MRS. LINDE: [*looks hard at her, lays down her sewing and gets up slowly*] Nora, you are keeping something from me.

NORA: Do I look as if I were?

MRS. LINDE: Something has happened to you since yesterday morning. Nora, what is it?

NORA: [*going nearer to her*] Christine! [*listens*] Hush! there's Torvald come home. Do you mind going in to the children for the present? Torvald can't bear to see dressmaking going on. Let Anne help you.

MRS. LINDE: [*gathering some of the things together*] Certainly—but I'm not leaving till we've had it out with one another. [*She goes into the room on the left, as Helmer comes in from the hall.*]

NORA: [*going up to HELMER*] I have wanted you so much, Torvald dear.

HELMER: Was that the dressmaker?

NORA: No, it was Christine; she is helping me to put my costume in order. You will see I shall look quite smart.

HELMER: Wasn't that a happy thought of mine, now?

NORA: Splendid! But don't you think it's nice of me, too, to do as you wish?

HELMER: Nice?—because you do as your husband wishes? Well, well, you little rogue, I'm sure you did not mean it in that way. But I'm not going to disturb you; you will want to be trying on your costume, I expect.

NORA: I suppose you're going to work.

HELMER: Yes. [*shows her a bundle of papers*] Look at that. I have just been to the Bank. [*turns to go into his room*]

NORA: Torvald.

HELMER: Yes.

NORA: If your little squirrel were to ask you something very, very prettily—?

HELMER: What then?

NORA: Would you do it?

HELMER: I should like to hear what it is, first.

NORA: Your squirrel would run about and do all her tricks if you would be nice, and do what she wants.

HELMER: Speak plainly.

NORA: Your skylark would chirp about in every room, with her song rising and falling—

HELMER: Well, my skylark does that anyhow.

NORA: I'd be a fairy and dance for you in the moonlight, Torvald.

HELMER: Nora—you surely don't mean that request you made of me this morning?

NORA: [*going near him*] Yes, Torvald, I beg you so earnestly—

HELMER: Have you really the nerve to bring up that question again?

NORA: Yes, dear, you *must* do as I ask; you *must* let Krogstad keep his post in the Bank.

HELMER: My dear Nora, it is his post that I have arranged for Mrs. Linde to have.

NORA: Yes, you've been awfully kind about that; but you could just as well dismiss some other clerk instead of Krogstad.

HELMER: This is simply incredible obstinacy! Because you chose to give him a thoughtless promise that you would speak for him, I am expected to—

NORA: That isn't the reason, Torvald. It is for your own sake. This fellow writes in the most scurrilous newspapers; you've told me so yourself. He can do you an unspeakable amount of harm. I am frightened to death of him—

HELMER: Ah, I understand; it is recollections of the past that scare you.

NORA: What do you mean?

HELMER: Naturally you are thinking of your father.

NORA: Yes—yes, of course. Just recall in your mind what these malicious creatures wrote in the papers about papa, and how horribly they slandered him. I believe they would have procured his dismissal if the Department had not sent you over to inquire into it, and if you had not been so kindly disposed and helpful to him.

HELMER: My little Nora, there is an important difference between your father and me. Your father's reputation as a public official was not above suspicion. Mine is, and I hope it will continue to be so, as long as I hold my office.

NORA: You never can tell what mischief these men may contrive. We ought to be so well off, so snug and happy here in our peaceful home, and have no cares—you and I and the children, Torvald! That's why I beg you so earnestly—

HELMER: And it's just by interceding for him that you make it impossible for me to keep him. It's already known at the Bank that I mean to dismiss Krogstad. Is it to get about now that the new manager has changed his mind at his wife's bidding—

NORA: And what if it did?

HELMER: Of course!—if only this obstinate little person can get her way! Do you suppose I'm going to make myself ridiculous before my entire staff, to let people think that I am a man to be swayed by all sorts of outside influence? I should very soon feel the consequences of that, I can tell you! And besides, there is something that makes it quite impossible for me to have Krogstad in the Bank as long as I am manager.

NORA: Whatever is that?

HELMER: His moral failings I might perhaps have overlooked, if necessary—

NORA: Yes, you could—couldn't you?

HELMER: And I hear he is a good worker, too. But I knew him when we were boys. It was one of those rash friendships that so often prove an embarrassment later in life. I may as well tell you plainly, we were once on first-name terms with one another. But this tactless fellow lays no restraint on himself when other people are present. On the contrary, he thinks it gives him the right to adopt a familiar tone with me, and every minute it is "I say, Helmer, old fellow!" and that sort of thing. It's extremely painful for me. He would make my position in the Bank intolerable.

NORA: Torvald, I don't believe you mean that.

HELMER: Don't you? Why not?

NORA: Because it is such a petty way of looking at things.

HELMER: What are you saying? Petty? Do you think I'm petty?

NORA: No, just the opposite, dear—it's exactly for that reason.

HELMER: It's the same thing. You say my point of view is petty, so I must be so, too. Petty. Very well—I must put an end to this. [*goes to the hall door and calls*] Helen!

NORA: What are you going to do?

HELMER: [*looking among his papers*] Settle it. [*enter* MAID] Look here; take this letter and go downstairs with it at once. Find a messenger and tell him to deliver it, and be quick. The address is on it, and here is the money.

MAID: Very well, sir. [*exit with the letter*]

HELMER: [*putting his papers together*] Now then, little Miss Obstinate.

NORA: [*breathless*] Torvald—what was that letter?

HELMER: Krogstad's dismissal.

NORA: Call her back, Torvald! There is still time. Oh Torvald, call her back! Do it for my sake—for your own sake—for the children's sake! Do you hear me, Torvald? Call her back! You don't know what that letter can bring upon us.

HELMER: It's too late.

NORA: Yes, it's too late.

HELMER: My dear Nora, I can forgive the anxiety you are in, although really it is an insult to me. It is, indeed. Isn't it an insult to think that I should be afraid of a starving journalist's vengeance? But I forgive you nevertheless, because it's such eloquent witness to your great love for me. [*takes her in his arms*] And that's as it should be, my own darling Nora. Come what will, you may be sure I'll have both courage and strength if they be needed. You'll see I am man enough to take everything upon myself.

NORA: [*in a horror-stricken voice*] What do you mean by that?

HELMER: Everything, I say—

NORA: [*recovering herself*] You'll never have to do that.

HELMER: That's right. Well, we'll share it, Nora, as man and wife should. That's how it should be. [*caressing her*] Are you happy now? There, there!—not these frightened dove's eyes! The whole thing is only the wildest fantasy— Now, you must go and play through the Tarantella and practise with your tambourine. I'll go into the inner office and shut the door, and I'll hear nothing; you can make as much noise as you please. [*turns back at the door*] And when Rank comes, tell him where he can find me. [*nods to her, takes his papers and goes into his room and shuts the door after him*]

NORA: [*bewildered with anxiety, stands as if rooted to the spot, and whispers*] He was capable of doing it. He will do it. He will do it in spite of everything—No, not that! Never, never! Anything rather than that! Oh, for some help, some way out of it! [*the doorbell rings*] Doctor Rank! Anything rather than that— anything, whatever it is! [*She puts her hands over her face, pulls herself together, goes to the door and opens it. RANK is standing without, hanging up his coat. During the following dialogue it begins to grow dark.*]

NORA: Good-day, Doctor Rank. I knew your ring. But you mustn't go into Torvald now; I think he is busy with something.

RANK: And you?

NORA: [*brings him in and shuts the door after him*] Oh, you know very well I always have time for you.

RANK: Thank you. I shall make use of as much of it as I can.

NORA: What do you mean by that? As much of it as you can?

RANK: Well, does that alarm you?

NORA: It was such a strange way of putting it. Is anything likely to happen?

RANK: Nothing but what I've long been prepared for. But I certainly didn't expect it to happen so soon.

NORA: [*gripping him by the arm*] What have you found out? Doctor Rank, you must tell me.

RANK: [*sitting down by the stove*] It's all up with me. And it can't be helped.

NORA: [*with a sigh of relief*] Is it about yourself?

RANK: Who else? It's no use lying to one's self. I am the most wretched of all my patients, Mrs. Helmer. Lately I've been taking stock of my internal economy. Bankrupt! Probably within a month I shall lie rotting in the churchyard.

NORA: What an ugly thing to say!

RANK: The thing itself is cursedly ugly, and the worst of it is that I'll have to face so much more that is ugly before that. I'll only make one more examination of myself; when I have done that, I'll know pretty certainly when the horrors of dissolution will begin. There's something I want to tell you. Helmer's sensitivity makes him disgusted at everything that is ugly; I won't have him in my sickroom.

NORA: Oh, but, Doctor Rank—

RANK: I won't have him there. Not on any account. I bar my door to him. As soon as I'm quite certain that the worst has come, I'll send you my card with a black cross on it, and then you will know that the loathsome end has begun.

NORA: You are quite absurd to-day. And I wanted you so much to be in a really good humour.

RANK: With death stalking beside me?—To have to pay this penalty for another man's sin! Is there any justice in that? And in every single family, in one way or another, some such inexorable retribution is being exacted—

NORA: [*putting her hands over her ears*] Rubbish! Do talk of something cheerful.

RANK: Oh, it's a mere laughing matter, the whole thing. My poor innocent spine has to suffer for my father's youthful amusements.

NORA: [*sitting at the table on the left*] I suppose you mean that he was too partial to asparagus and paté de foie gras, don't you?

RANK: Yes, and to truffles.

NORA: Truffles, yes. And oysters, too, I suppose?

RANK: Oysters, of course, that goes without saying.

NORA: And heaps of port and champagne. It is sad that all these nice things should take their revenge on our bones.

RANK: Especially that they should revenge themselves on the unlucky bones of those who have not had the satisfaction of enjoying them.

NORA: Yes, that's the saddest part of it all.

RANK: [*with a searching look at her*] Hm!—

NORA: [*after a short pause*] Why did you smile?

RANK: No, it was you that laughed.

NORA: No, it was you that smiled, Doctor Rank!

RANK: [*rising*] You're a bigger tease than I thought.

NORA: I'm in a silly mood to-day.

RANK: So it seems.

NORA: [*putting her hands on his shoulders*] Dear, dear Doctor Rank, death mustn't take you away from Torvald and me.

RANK: It's a loss you would easily recover from. Those who are gone are soon forgotten.

NORA: [*looking at him anxiously*] Do you believe that?

RANK: People form new ties, and then—

NORA: Who will form new ties?

RANK: Both you and Helmer, when I'm gone. You yourself are already on the high road to it, I think. What did Mrs. Linde want here last night?

NORA: Oho!—you don't mean to say you're jealous of poor Christine?

RANK: Yes, I am. She'll be my successor in this house. When I'm done for, this woman will—

NORA: Hush! don't speak so loud. She's in that room.

RANK: To-day again. There, you see.

NORA: She's only come to sew my costume for for me. Bless my soul, how unreasonable you are! [*sits down on the sofa*] Be nice now, Doctor Rank, and to-morrow you will see how beautifully I shall dance, and you can imagine I'm doing it all for you—and for Torvald, too, of course. [*takes various things out of the box*] Doctor Rank, come and sit down here, and I'll show you something.

RANK: [*sitting down*] What is it?

NORA: Just look at those!

RANK: Silk stockings.

NORA: Flesh-coloured. Aren't they lovely? It is so dark here now, but tomorrow—. No, no, no! you must only look at the feet. Oh well, you may have leave to look at the legs, too.

RANK: Hm!—

NORA: Why are you looking so critical? Don't you think they will fit me?

RANK: I have no means of forming an opinion about that.

NORA: [*looks at him for a moment*] For shame! [*hits him lightly on the ear with the stockings*] That's to punish you. [*folds them up again*]

RANK: And what other nice things am I to be allowed to see?

NORA: Not a single thing more, for being so naughty. [*she looks among the things, humming to herself*]

RANK: [*after a short silence*] When I'm sitting here, talking to you as intimately as this, I can't imagine for a moment what would have become of me if I had never come into this house.

NORA: [*smiling*] I believe you do feel thoroughly at home with us.

RANK: [*in a lower voice, looking straight in front of him*] And to be obliged to leave it all—

NORA: Nonsense, you're not going to leave it.

RANK: [*as before*] And not be able to leave behind one the slightest token of one's gratitude, scarcely even a fleeting regret—nothing but an empty place which the first comer can fill as well as any other.

NORA: And if I asked you now for a—? No!

RANK: For what?

NORA: For a big proof of your friendship—

RANK: Yes, yes!

NORA: I mean a tremendously big favour—

RANK: Would you really make me so happy for once?

NORA: Ah, but you don't know what it is yet.

RANK: No—but tell me.

NORA: I really can't, Doctor Rank. It's something out of all reason; it means advice, and help, and a favour—

RANK: The bigger the better. I can't conceive what it is you mean. Do tell me. Haven't I your confidence?

NORA: More than anyone else. I know you are my truest and best friend, and so I'll tell you what it is. Well, Doctor Rank, it's something you must help me to prevent. You know how devotedly, how inexpressibly deeply Torvald loves me; he would never for a moment hesitate to give his life for me.

RANK: [*leaning towards her*] Nora—do you think he is the only one—?

NORA: [*with a slight start*] The only one—?

RANK: The only one who would gladly give his life for your sake.

NORA: [*sadly*] Is that it?

RANK: I was determined you should know it before I went away, and there'll never be a better opportunity than this. Now you know it, Nora. And now you know, too, that you can trust me as you would trust no one else.

NORA: [*rises, deliberately and quietly*] Let me pass.

RANK: [*makes room for her to pass him, but sits still*] Nora!

NORA: [*at the hall door*] Helen, bring in the lamp. [*goes over to the stove*] Dear Doctor Rank, that was really horrid of you.

RANK: To have loved you as much as anyone else does? Was that horrid?

NORA: No, but to go and tell me so. There was really no need—

RANK: What do you mean? Did you know—? [MAID *enters with lamp, puts it down on the table, and goes out*] Nora—Mrs. Helmer—tell me, had you any idea of this?

NORA: Oh, how do I know whether I had or whether I hadn't? I really can't tell you—To think you could be so clumsy, Doctor Rank! We were getting on so nicely.

RANK: Well, at all events you know now that you can command me, body and soul. So won't you speak out?

NORA: [*looking at him*] After what happened?

RANK: I beg you to let me know what it is.

NORA: I can't tell you anything now.

RANK: Yes, yes. You mustn't punish me in that way. Let me have permission to do for you whatever a man may do.

NORA: You can do nothing for me now. Besides, I really don't need any help at all. You will find the whole thing is merely fancy on my part. It really is so—of course it is! [*Sits down in the rockingchair, and looks at him with a smile.*] You are a nice man, Doctor Rank!—don't you feel ashamed of yourself, now the lamp has come!

RANK: Not a bit. But perhaps I had better go—for ever?

NORA: No, indeed, you shall not. Of course you must come here just as before. You know very well Torvald can't do without you.

RANK: Yes, but you?

NORA: Oh I'm always tremendously pleased when you come.

RANK: It's just that, that put me on the wrong track. You are a riddle to me. I've often thought that you'd almost as soon be in my company as in Helmer's.

NORA: Yes—you see there are some people one loves best, and others whom one would almost always rather have as companions.

RANK: Yes, there is something in that.

NORA: When I was at home, of course I loved papa best. But I always thought it tremendous fun if I could steal down into the maids' room, because they never moralised at all, and talked to each other about such entertaining things.

RANK: I see—it is *their* place I have taken.

NORA: [*jumping up and going to him*] Oh, dear, nice Doctor Rank, I never meant that at all. But surely you can understand that being with Torvald is a little like being with papa—

[*Enter* MAID *from the hall.*]

MAID: If you please, ma'am. [*whispers and hands her a card*]

NORA: [*glancing at the card*] Oh! [*puts it in her pocket*]

RANK: Is there anything wrong?

NORA: No, no, not in the least. It's only something—it's my new dress—

RANK: What? Your dress is lying there.

NORA: Oh, yes, that one; but this is another. I ordered it. Torvald mustn't know about it—

RANK: Oho! Then that was the great secret.

NORA: Of course. Just go in to him; he is sitting in the inner room. Keep him as long as—

RANK: Make your mind easy; I won't let him escape. [*Goes into* HELMER's *room.*]

NORA: [*to the* MAID] And he's waiting in the kitchen?

MAID: Yes; he came up the back stairs.

NORA: But didn't you tell him no one was in?

MAID: Yes, but it was no good.

NORA: He won't go away?

MAID: No; he says he won't until he has seen you, ma'am.

NORA: Well, let him come in—but quietly. Helen, you mustn't say anything about it to anyone. It's a surprise for my husband.

MAID: Yes, ma'am, I quite understand. [*exit*]

NORA: This dreadful thing is going to happen! It will happen in spite of me! No, no, no, it can't happen—it shan't happen! [*she bolts the door of* HELMER's *room. The* MAID *opens the hall door for* KROGSTAD *and shuts it after him. He is wearing a fur coat, high boots, and a fur cap.*]

NORA: [*advancing towards him*] Speak low—my husband is at home.

KROGSTAD: No matter about that!

NORA: What do you want of me?

KROGSTAD: An explanation.

NORA: Make haste then. What is it?

KROGSTAD: You know, I suppose, that I've got my dismissal.

NORA: I couldn't prevent it, Mr. Krogstad. I fought as hard as I could on your side, but it was no good.

KROGSTAD: Does your husband love you so little, then? He knows what I can expose you to, and yet he ventures—

NORA: How can you suppose that he has any knowledge of the sort?

KROGSTAD: I didn't suppose so at all. It would not be the least like our dear Torvald Helmer to show so much courage—

NORA: Mr. Krogstad, a little respect for my husband, please.

KROGSTAD: Certainly—all the respect he deserves. But since you have kept the matter so carefully to yourself, I make bold to suppose that you have a little clearer idea, than you had yesterday, of what it actually is that you have done?

NORA: More than you could ever teach me.

KROGSTAD: Yes, bad lawyer that I am.

NORA: What is it you want of me?

KROGSTAD: Only to see how you were, Mrs. Helmer. I have been thinking about you all day long. A mere cashier, hackwriter, a—well, a man like me—even he has a little of what is called feeling, you know.

NORA: Show it, then; think of my little children.

KROGSTAD: Have you and your husband thought of mine? But never mind about that. I only wanted to tell you that you need not take this matter too seriously. In the first place there will be no accusation made on my part.

NORA: No, of course not; I was sure of that.

KROGSTAD: The whole thing can be arranged amicably; there is no reason why anyone should know anything about it. It will remain a secret between us three.

NORA: My husband must never get to know anything about it.

KROGSTAD: How will you be able to prevent it? Am I to understand that you can pay the balance that's owing?

NORA: No, not just at present.

KROGSTAD: Or perhaps that you have some means of raising the money soon?

NORA: None that I mean to make use of.

KROGSTAD: Well, in any case, it would've been of no use to you now. If you stood there with ever so much money in your hand, I would never part with your bond.

NORA: Tell me what purpose you mean to put it to.

KROGSTAD: I shall only preserve it—keep it in my possession. No one who is not concerned in the matter shall have the slightest hint of it. So that if the thought of it has driven you to any desperate resolution—

NORA: It has.

KROGSTAD: If you had it in your mind to run away from your home—

NORA: I had.

KROGSTAD: Or even something worse—

NORA: How could you know that?

KROGSTAD: Give up the idea.

NORA: How did you know I had thought of *that?*

KROGSTAD: Most of us think of that at first. I did, too—but I hadn't the courage.

NORA: [*faintly*] No more had I.

KROGSTAD: [*in a tone of relief*] No, that's it, isn't it—you hadn't the courage, either?

NORA: No, I haven't—I haven't.

KROGSTAD: Besides, it would have been a great piece of folly. Once the first storm at home is over—. I have a letter for your husband in my pocket.

NORA: Telling him everything?

KROGSTAD: In as lenient a manner as I possibly could.

NORA: [*quickly*] He mustn't get that letter. Tear it up. I will find some means of getting money.

KROGSTAD: Excuse me, Mrs. Helmer, but I think I told you just now—

NORA: I am not speaking of what I owe you. Tell me what sum you are asking my husband for, and I will get the money.

KROGSTAD: I am not asking your husband for a penny.

NORA: What do you want, then?

KROGSTAD: I will tell you. I want to rehabilitate myself, Mrs. Helmer; I want to get on; and in that your husband must help me. For the last year and a half I have not had a hand in anything dishonourable, and all that time I have been struggling in most restricted circumstances. I was content to work my way up step by step. Now I'm turned out, and I'm not going to be satisfied with merely being taken into favour again. I want to get on, I tell you. I want to get into the Bank again, in a higher position. Your husband must make a place for me—

NORA: That he will never do!

KROGSTAD: He will; I know him; he dare not protest. And as soon as I'm in there again with him, then you will see! Within a year I shall be the manager's right hand. It will be Nils Krogstad and not Torvald Helmer who manages the Bank.

NORA: That's a thing you will never see!

KROGSTAD: Do you mean that you will—?

NORA: I have courage enough for it now.

KROGSTAD: Oh, you can't frighten me. A fine, spoilt lady like you—

NORA: You'll see, you'll see.

KROGSTAD: Under the ice, perhaps? Down into the cold, coal-black water? And then, in the spring, to float up to the surface, all horrible and unrecognisable, with your hair fallen out—

NORA: You can't frighten me.

KROGSTAD: Nor you me. People don't do such things, Mrs. Helmer. Besides, what use would it be? I should have him completely in my power all the same.

NORA: Afterwards? When I am no longer—

KROGSTAD: Have you forgotten that it is I who have the keeping of your reputation? [*Nora stands speechlessly looking at him.*] Well, now, I've warned you. Don't do anything foolish. When Helmer has received my letter, I shall expect a message from him. And be sure you remember that it's your husband himself who has forced me into such ways as this again. I'll never forgive him for that. Good-bye, Mrs. Helmer. [*exit through the hall*]

NORA: [*goes to the hall door, opens it slightly and listens*] He's going. He's not putting the letter in the box. Oh no, no! that's impossible! [*opens the door by degrees*] What's that? He's standing outside. He's not going downstairs. Is he hesitating? Can he—? [*A letter drops into the box; then* KROGSTAD's *footsteps are heard, till they die away as he goes downstairs.* NORA *utters a stifled cry, and runs across the room to the table by the sofa. A short pause.*]

NORA: In the mail box. [*steals across to the hall door*] There it lies—Torvald, Torvald, there is no hope for us now!

[MRS. LINDE *comes in from the room on the left, carrying the dress.*]

MRS. LINDE: There, I can't see anything more to mend now. Would you like to try it on—?

NORA: [*in a hoarse whisper*] Christine, come here.

MRS. LINDE: [*throwing the dress down on the sofa*] What's the matter with you? You look so upset.

NORA: Come here. Do you see that letter? There, look—you can see it through the glass in the box.

MRS. LINDE: Yes, I see it.

NORA: That letter is from Krogstad.

MRS. LINDE: Nora—it was Krogstad who lent you the money!

NORA: Yes, and now Torvald will know all about it.

MRS. LINDE: Believe me, Nora, that's the best thing for both of you.

NORA: You don't know all. I forged a name.

MRS. LINDE: Good heavens—!

NORA: I only want to say this to you, Christine—you must be my witness.

MRS. LINDE: Your witness? What do you mean? What am I to—?

NORA: If I should go out of my mind—and it might easily happen—

MRS. LINDE: Nora!

NORA: Or if anything else should happen to me—anything, for instance, that might prevent my being here—

MRS. LINDE: Nora! Nora! You're quite out of your mind.

NORA: And if it should happen that there were someone who wanted to take all the responsibility, all the blame, you understand—

MRS. LINDE: Yes, yes—but how can you suppose—?

NORA: Then you must be my witness, that it's not true, Christine. I'm not out of my mind at all. I'm in my right senses now, and I tell you no one else has known anything about it; I, and I alone, did the whole thing. Remember that.

MRS. LINDE: I will, indeed. But I don't understand all this.

NORA: How should you understand it? A miracle is going to happen.

MRS. LINDE: A miracle?

NORA: Yes, a miracle.—But it's so terrible, Christine; it *mustn't* happen, not for all the world.

MRS. LINDE: I will go at once and see Krogstad.

NORA: Don't go to him; he will do you some harm.

MRS. LINDE: There was a time when he would gladly do anything for my sake.

NORA: He?

MRS. LINDE: Where does he live?

NORA: How should I know—? Yes [*feeling in her pocket*] here is his card. But the letter, the letter—!

HELMER: [*calls from his room, knocking at the door*] Nora!

NORA: [*cries out anxiously*] Oh, what's that? What do you want?

HELMER: Don't be so frightened. We are not coming in; you have locked the door. Are you trying on your dress?

NORA: Yes, that's it. I look so nice, Torvald.

MRS. LINDE: [*who has read the card*] I see he lives at the corner here.

NORA: Yes, but it's no use. It's hopeless. The letter is lying there in the box.

MRS. LINDE: And your husband keeps the key?

NORA: Yes, always.

MRS. LINDE: Krogstad must ask for his letter back unread, he must find some pretence—

NORA: But it's just at this time that Torvald generally—

MRS. LINDE: You must delay him. Go in to him in the meantime. I'll come back as soon as I can. [*She goes out hurriedly through the hall door.*]

NORA: [*goes to* HELMER'S *door, opens it and peeps in*] Torvald!

HELMER: [*from the inner room*] Well? May I venture at last to come into my own room again? Come along, Rank, now you'll see—[*halting in the doorway*] But what is this?

NORA: What is what, dear?

HELMER: Rank led me to expect a splendid transformation.

RANK: [*in the doorway*] I understood so, but evidently I was mistaken.

NORA: Yes, nobody is to have the chance of admiring me in my costume until to-morrow.

HELMER: But, my dear Nora, you look so worn out. Have you been practising too much?

NORA: No, I have not practised at all.

HELMER: But you will need to—

NORA: Yes, indeed I shall, Torvald. But I can't get on a bit without you to help me; I have absolutely forgotten the whole thing.

HELMER: Oh, we'll soon work it up again.

NORA: Yes, help me, Torvald. Promise that you will! I'm so nervous about it—all the people—. You must give yourself up to me entirely this evening. Not the tiniest bit of business—you mustn't even take a pen in your hand. Will you promise, Torvald dear?

HELMER: I promise: This evening I'll be wholly and absolutely at your service, you helpless little thing. But, first of all I'll just—[*goes towards the hall door.*]

NORA: What are you going to do there?

HELMER: Only see if any letters have come.

NORA: No, no! don't do that, Torvald!

HELMER: Why not?

NORA: Torvald, please don't. There is nothing there.

HELMER: Well, let me look. [*Turns to go to the letterbox.* NORA, *at the piano, plays the first bars of the Tarantella.* HELMER *stops in the doorway.*] Aha!

NORA: I can't dance to-morrow if I don't practise with you.

HELMER: [*going up to her*] Are you really so afraid of it, dear?

NORA: Yes, so dreadfully afraid of it. Let me practise at once; there is time now, before we go to dinner. Sit down and play for me, Torvald dear; coach me, and correct me as you play.

HELMER: With great pleasure, if you wish me to. [*Sits down at the piano.*]

NORA: [*Takes out of the box a tambourine and a long variegated shawl. She hastily drapes the shawl round her. Then she springs to the front of the stage and calls out.*] Now play for me! I'm going to dance!

> [HELMER *plays and* NORA *dances.* RANK *stands by the piano behind* HELMER, *and looks on.*]

HELMER: [*as he plays*] Slower, slower!

NORA: I can't do it any other way.

HELMER: Not so violently, Nora!

NORA: This is the way.

HELMER: [*stops playing*] No, no—that's not a bit right.

NORA: [*laughing and swinging the tambourine*] Didn't I tell you so?

RANK: Let me play for her.

HELMER: [*getting up*] Yes, do. I can correct her better then.

> [RANK *sits down at the piano and plays.* NORA *dances more and more wildly.* HELMER *has taken up a position beside the stove, and during her dance gives her frequent instructions. She does not seem to hear him; her hair comes down and falls over her shoulders; she pays no attention to it, but goes on dancing. Enter* MRS. LINDE.]

MRS. LINDE: [*standing as if spellbound in the doorway*] Oh!—

NORA: [*as she dances*] Such fun, Christine!

HELMER: My dear darling Nora, you are dancing as if your life depended on it.

NORA: So it does.

HELMER: Stop, Rank; this is sheer madness. Stop, I tell you! [RANK *stops playing, and* NORA *suddenly stands still.* HELMER *goes up to her.*] I could never have believed it. You have forgotten everything I taught you.

NORA: [*throwing away the tambourine*] There, you see.

HELMER: You'll want a lot of coaching.

NORA: Yes, you see how much I need it. You must coach me up to the last minute. Promise me that, Torvald!

HELMER: You can depend on me.

NORA: You must not think of anything but me, either to-day or to-morrow; you mustn't open a single letter—not even open the mail box—

HELMER: Ah, you're still afraid of that fellow—

NORA: Yes, indeed I am.

HELMER: Nora, I tell from your looks that there is a letter from him lying there.

NORA: I don't know; I think there is; but you must not read anything of that kind now. Nothing horrid must come between us till this is all over.

RANK: [*whispers to* HELMER] You mustn't contradict her.

HELMER: [*taking her in his arms*] The child shall have her way. But to-morrow night, after you've danced—

NORA: Then you will be free. [*The* MAID *appears in the doorway to the right.*]

MAID: Dinner is served, ma'am.

NORA: We will have champagne, Helen.

MAID: Very good, ma'am. [*exit*]

HELMER: Hullo!—are we going to have a banquet.?

NORA: Yes, a champagne banquet till the small hours. [*calls out*] And a few macaroons, Helen—lots, just for once!

HELMER: Come, come, don't be so wild and nervous. Be my own little skylark.

NORA: Yes, dear, I will. But go in now and you, too, Doctor Rank. Christine, you must help me to do up my hair.

RANK: [*whispers to* HELMER *as they go out*] I suppose there's nothing—she is not expecting anything?

HELMER: Far from it, my dear fellow; it is simply nothing more than this childish nervousness I was telling you of. [*They go into the right-hand room.*]

NORA: Well!

MRS. LINDE: Gone out of town.

NORA: I could tell from your face.

MRS. LINDE: He's coming home to-morrow evening. I wrote a note for him.

NORA: You should have let it alone; you must prevent nothing. After all, it is splendid to be waiting for a wonderful thing to happen.

MRS. LINDE: What is it that you are waiting for?

NORA: Oh, you wouldn't understand. Go in to them, I will come in a moment. [MRS. LINDE *goes into the dining-room.* NORA *stands still for a little while, as if to compose herself. Then she looks at her watch.*] Five o'clock. Seven hours till midnight; and then twenty-four hours till the next midnight. Then the Tarantella will be over. Twenty-four and seven? Thirty-one hours to live.

HELMER: [*from the doorway on the right*] Where's my little skylark?

NORA: [*going to him with her arms outstretched*] Here she is!

ACT III

THE SAME SCENE———*The table has been placed in the middle of the stage, with chairs round it. A lamp is burning on the table. The door into the hall stands open. Dance music is heard in the room above.* MRS. LINDE *is sitting at the table idly turning over the leaves of a book she tries to read, but does not seem able to collect her thoughts. Every now and then she listens intently for a sound at the outer door.*

MRS. LINDE: [*looking at her watch*] Not yet—and the time is nearly up. If only he doesn't—. [*listens again*] Ah, there he is. [*Goes into the hall and opens the outer door carefully. Light footsteps are heard on the stairs. She whispers.*] Come in. There's no one here.

KROGSTAD: [*in the doorway*] I found a note from you at home. What does this mean?

MRS. LINDE: It's absolutely necessary that I have a talk with you.

KROGSTAD: Really! And is it absolutely necessary that it should be here?

MRS. LINDE: It's impossible where I live; there's no private entrance to my rooms. Come in; we're quite alone. The maid's asleep and the Helmers are at the dance upstairs.

KROGSTAD: [*coming into the room*] Are the Helmers really at a dance to-night?

MRS. LINDE: Yes, why not?

KROGSTAD: Certainly—why not?

MRS. LINDE: Now, Nils, let's have a talk.

KROGSTAD: Can we two have anything to talk about.

MRS. LINDE: We have a great deal to talk about.

KROGSTAD: I shouldn't have thought so.

MRS. LINDE: No, you have never properly understood me.

KROGSTAD: Was there anything else to understand except what was obvious to all the world—a heartless woman jilts a man when a better catch turns up.

MRS. LINDE: Do you believe I'm as absolutely heartless as all that? And do you believe that I did it with a light heart?

KROGSTAD: Didn't you?

MRS. LINDE: Nils, did you really think that?

KROGSTAD: If it were as you say, why did you write to me as you did at that time?

MRS. LINDE: I could do nothing else. As I had to break with you, it was my duty also to put an end to all that you felt for me.

KROGSTAD: [*wringing his hands*] So that was it. And all this—only for the sake of money!

MRS. LINDE: You must not forget that I had a helpless mother and two little brothers. We couldn't wait for you, Nils; your prospects seemed hopeless then.

KROGSTAD: That may be so, but you had no right to throw me over for any one else's sake.

MRS. LINDE: Indeed I don't know. Many a time did I ask myself if I had the right to do it.

KROGSTAD: [*more gently*] When I lost you, it was as if all the solid ground went from under my feet. Look at me now—I'm a shipwrecked man clinging to a bit of wreckage.

MRS. LINDE: But help may be near.

KROGSTAD: It *was* near; but then you came and stood in my way.

MRS. LINDE: Unintentionally, Nils. It was only to-day that I learned it was your place I was going to take in the Bank.

KROGSTAD: I believe you, if you say so. But now that you know it, are you not going to give it up to me?

MRS. LINDE: No, because that would not benefit you in the least.

KROGSTAD: Oh, benefit, benefit—I would have done it whether or no.

MRS. LINDE: I have learned to act prudently. Life, and hard, bitter necessity have taught me that.

KROGSTAD: And life has taught me not to believe in fine speeches.

MRS. LINDE: Then life has taught you something very reasonable. But deeds you must believe in?

KROGSTAD: What do you mean by that?

MRS. LINDE: You said you were like a shipwrecked man clinging to some wreckage.

KROGSTAD: I had good reason to say so.

MRS. LINDE: Well, I am like a shipwrecked woman clinging to some wreckage— no one to mourn for, no one to care for.

KROGSTAD: It was your own choice.

MRS. LINDE: There was no other choice—then.

KROGSTAD: Well, what now?

MRS. LINDE: Nils, how would it be if we two shipwrecked people could join forces?

KROGSTAD: What are you saying?

MRS. LINDE: Two on the same piece of wreckage would stand a better chance than each on their own.

KROGSTAD: Christine!

MRS. LINDE: What do you suppose brought me to town?

KROGSTAD: Do you mean that you gave me a thought?

MRS. LINDE: I couldn't endure life without work. All my life, as long as I can remember, I have worked, and it's been my greatest and only pleasure. But now I'm quite alone in the world—my life is so dreadfully empty and I feel so forsaken. There is not the least pleasure in working for one's self. Nils, give me someone and something to work for.

KROGSTAD: I don't trust that. It's nothing but a woman's overstrained sense of generosity that prompts you to make such an offer of yourself.

MRS. LINDE: Have you ever noticed anything of the sort in me?

KROGSTAD: Could you really do it? Tell me—do you know all about my past life?

MRS. LINDE: Yes.

KROGSTAD: And do you know what they think of me here?

MRS. LINDE: You seemed to me to imply that with me you might have been quite another man.

KROGSTAD: I'm certain of it.

MRS. LINDE: Is it too late now?

KROGSTAD: Christine, are you saying this deliberately? Yes, I'm sure you are. I see it in your face. Have you really the courage, then—?

MRS. LINDE: I want to be a mother to someone, and your children need a mother. We two need each other. Nils, I have faith in your real character—I can dare anything together with you.

KROGSTAD: [*grasps her hand*] Thanks, thanks, Christine! Now I shall find a way to clear myself in the eyes of the world. Ah, but I forgot—

MRS. LINDE: [*listening*] Hush! The Tarantella! Go, go!

KROGSTAD: Why? What is it?

MRS. LINDE: Do you hear them up there? When that is over, we may expect them back.

KROGSTAD: Yes, yes—I will go. But it's all no use. Of course you're not aware what steps I've taken in the matter of the Helmers.

MRS. LINDE: Yes, I know all about that.

KROGSTAD: And in spite of that have you the courage to—?

MRS. LINDE: I understand very well to what lengths a man like you might be driven by despair.

KROGSTAD: If I could only undo what I've done!

MRS. LINDE: You cannot. Your letter is lying in the mail box now.

KROGSTAD: Are you sure of that?

MRS. LINDE: Quite sure, but—

KROGSTAD: [*with a searching look at her*] Is that what it all means?—that you want to save your friend at any cost? Tell me frankly. Is that it?

MRS. LINDE: Nils, a woman who has once sold herself for another's sake, doesn't do it a second time.

KROGSTAD: I'll ask for my letter back.

MRS. LINDE: No, no.

KROGSTAD: Yes, of course I will. I'll wait here till Torvald comes; I will tell him he must give me my letter back—that it only concerns my dismissal—that he's not to read it.

MRS. LINDE: No, Nils, you must not recall your letter.

KROGSTAD: But, tell me, wasn't it for that very purpose that you asked me to meet you here?

MRS. LINDE: In my first moment of fright, it was. But twenty-four hours have elapsed since then, and in that time I've witnessed incredible things in this house. Torvald must know all about it. This unhappy secret must be disclosed; they must have a complete understanding between them, which is impossible with all this concealment and falsehood going on.

KROGSTAD: Very well, if you will take the responsibility. But there's one thing I can do in any case, and I shall do it at once.

MRS. LINDE: [*listening*] You must be quick and go! The dance is over; we are not safe a moment longer.

KROGSTAD: I'll wait for you below.

MRS. LINDE: Yes, do. You must see me back to my door.

KROGSTAD: I have never had such an amazing piece of good fortune in my life! [*Goes out through the outer door. The door between the room and the hall remains open.*]

MRS. LINDE: [*tidying up the room and laying her hat and cloak ready*] What a difference! what a difference! Someone to work for and live for—a home to bring comfort into. That I will do, indeed. I wish they would be quick and come—[*listens*] Ah, there they are now. I must put on my things. [*Takes up her hat and cloak.* HELMER'S *and* NORA'S *voices are heard outside; a key is turned, and* HELMER *brings* NORA *almost by force into the hall. She is in an Italian costume with a large black shawl around her; he is in evening dress, and a black cloak which is flying open.*]

NORA: [*hanging back in the doorway, and struggling with him*] No, no, no!—don't take me in. I want to go upstairs again; I don't want to leave so early.

HELMER: But, my dearest Nora—

NORA: Please, Torvald dear—please, *please*—only an hour more.

HELMER: Not a single minute, my sweet Nora. You know that was our agreement. Come along into the room; you are catching cold standing there. [*He brings her gently into the room, in spite of her resistance.*]

MRS. LINDE: Good-evening.

NORA: Christine!

HELMER: You here, so late, Mrs. Linde?

MRS. LINDE: Yes, you must excuse me; I was so anxious to see Nora in her dress.

NORA: Have you been sitting here waiting for me?

MRS. LINDE: Yes, unfortunately I came too late, you had already gone upstairs; and I thought I couldn't go away again without having seen you.

HELMER: [*taking off* NORA's *shawl*] Yes, take a good look at her. I think she's worth looking at. Isn't she charming, Mrs. Linde?

MRS. LINDE: Yes, indeed she is.

HELMER: Doesn't she look remarkably pretty? Everyone thought so at the dance. But she is terribly self-willed, this sweet little person. What are we to do with her? You will hardly believe that I had almost to bring her away by force.

NORA: Torvald, you will repent not having let me stay, even if it were only for half an hour.

HELMER: Listen to her, Mrs. Linde! She had danced her Tarantella, and it had been a tremendous success, as it deserved—although possibly the performance was a trifle too realistic—a little more so, I mean, than was strictly compatible with propriety. But never mind about that! The chief thing is, she had made a success—she had made a tremendous success. Do you think I was going to let her remain there after that, and spoil the effect? No, indeed! I took my charming little Capri maiden—my capricious little Capri maiden, I should say—on my arm; took one quick turn around the room; a curtsy on either side, and, as they say in novels, the beautiful apparition disappeared. An exit ought always to be effective, Mrs. Linde; but that's what I cannot make Nora understand. Pooh! this room is hot. [*throws his cloak on a chair, and opens the door of his room*] Hullo! it's all dark in here. Oh, of course—excuse me—[*He goes in, and lights some candles.*]

NORA: [*in a hurried and breathless whisper*] Well?

MRS. LINDE: [*in a low voice*] I have had a talk with him.

NORA: Yes, and—

MRS. LINDE: Nora, you must tell your husband all about it.

NORA: [*in an expressionless voice*] I knew it.

MRS. LINDE: You have nothing to be afraid of as far as Krogstad is concerned; but you must tell him.

NORA: I won't tell him.

MRS. LINDE: Then the letter will.

NORA: Thank you, Christine. Now I know what I must do. Hush—!

HELMER: [*coming in again*] Well, Mrs. Linde, have you admired her?

MRS. LINDE: Yes, and now I will say good-night.

HELMER: What, already? Is this yours, this knitting?

MRS. LINDE: (*taking it*) Yes, thank you, I had very nearly forgotten it.

HELMER: So you knit?

MRS. LINDE: Of course.

HELMER: Do you know, you ought to embroider.

MRS. LINDE: Really? Why?

HELMER: Yes, it's far more becoming. Let me show you. You hold the embroidery thus in your left hand, and use the needle with the right—like this—with a long, easy sweep. Do you see?

MRS. LINDE: Yes, perhaps—

HELMER: But in the case of knitting—that can never be anything but ungraceful; look here—the arms close together, the knitting-needles going up and down—it has a sort of Chinese effect—. That was really excellent champagne they gave us.

MRS. LINDE: Well,—good-night, Nora, and don't be stubborn any more.

HELMER: That's right, Mrs. Linde.

MRS. LINDE: Good-night, Mr. Helmer.

HELMER: [*accompanying her to the door*] Good-night, good-night. I hope you'll get home all right. I should be very happy to—but you haven't any great distance to go. Good-night, good-night. [*She goes out; he shuts the door after her, and comes in again.*] Ah!—at last we have got rid of her. She is a frightful bore, that woman.

NORA: Aren't you very tired, Torvald?

HELMER: No, not in the least.

NORA: Nor sleepy?

HELMER: Not a bit. On the contrary, I feel extraordinarily lively. And you?—you really look both tired and sleepy.

NORA: Yes, I'm very tired. I want to go to sleep at once.

HELMER: There, you see it was quite right of me not to let you stay there any longer.

NORA: Everything you do is quite right, Torvald.

HELMER: [*kissing her on the forehead*] Now my little skylark is speaking reasonably. Did you notice what good spirits Rank was in this evening?

NORA: Really? Was he? I didn't speak to him at all.

HELMER: And I very little, but I haven't seen him in such good form for a long time. [*Looks for a while at her and then goes nearer to her.*] It's delightful to be at home by ourselves again, to be all alone with you—you fascinating, charming little darling!

NORA: Don't look at me like that, Torvald.

HELMER: Why shouldn't I look at my dearest treasure?—at all the beauty that's mine, all mine?

NORA: [*going to the other side of the table*] You mustn't say things like that to me to-night.

HELMER: [*following her*] You have still got the Tarantella in your blood, I see. And it makes you more captivating than ever. Listen—the guests are beginning to leave now. [*in a lower voice*] Nora—soon the whole house will be quiet.

NORA: Yes, I hope so.

HELMER: Yes, my own darling Nora. Do you know when I'm out at a party with you like this, why I speak so little to you, keep away from you, and only send a stolen glance in your direction now and then?—do you know why I do that? It's because I make believe that we are secretly in love, and you are my secretly promised bride, and that no one suspects there is anything between us.

NORA: Yes, yes—I know very well you're thinking about me all the time.

HELMER: And when we are leaving, and I am putting the shawl over your beautiful young shoulders—on your lovely neck—then I imagine that you are my bride and that we have just come from the wedding, and I am bringing you for the first time into our home—to be alone with you for the first time— quite alone with my shy little darling! All this evening I have longed for nothing but you. When I watched the seductive figures of the Tarantella, my blood was on fire; I could endure it no longer, and that was why I brought you down so early—

NORA: Go away, Torvald! You must let me go. I won't—

HELMER: What's that? You're teasing, my little Nora! You won't—you won't? Am I not your husband—? [*A knock is heard at the outer door.*]

NORA: [*starting*] Did you hear—?

HELMER: [*going into the hall*] Who is it?

RANK: [*outside*] It is I. May I come in for a moment?

HELMER: [*in a fretful whisper*]. Oh, what does he want now? [*aloud*] Wait a minute? [*unlocks the door*] Come, that's kind of you not to pass by our door.

RANK: I thought I heard your voice, and felt as if I should like to look in. [*with a swift glance round*] Ah, yes!—these dear familiar rooms. You are very happy and cozy in here, you two.

HELMER: It seems to me that you looked after yourself pretty well upstairs, too.

RANK: Excellently. Why shouldn't I? Why shouldn't one enjoy everything in this world?—at any rate as much as one can, and as long as one can. The wine was capital—

HELMER: Especially the champagne.

RANK: So you noticed that, too? It's almost incredible how much I managed to put away!

NORA: Torvald drank a great deal of champagne to-night, too.

RANK: Did he?

NORA: Yes, and he is always in such good spirits afterwards.

RANK: Well, why should one not enjoy a merry evening after a well-spent day?

HELMER: Well spent: I'm afraid I can't take credit for that.

RANK: [*clapping him on the back*] But I can, you know!

NORA: Doctor Rank, you must have been occupied with some scientific investigation to-day.

RANK: Exactly.

HELMER: Just listen!—little Nora talking about scientific investigations!

NORA: And may I congratulate you on the result?

RANK: Indeed you may.

NORA: Was it favourable, then?

RANK: The best possible, for both doctor and patient—certainty.

NORA: [*quickly and searchingly*] Certainty?

RANK: Absolute certainty. So wasn't I entitled to make a merry evening of it after that?

NORA: Yes, you certainly were, Doctor Rank.

HELMER: I think so, too, so long as you don't have to pay for it in the morning.

RANK: Oh well, one can't have anything in this life without paying for it.

NORA: Doctor Rank—are you fond of masked balls?

RANK: Yes, if there's a fine lot of pretty costumes.

NORA: Tell me—what shall we two wear at the next?

HELMER: Little featherbrain!—are you thinking of the next already?

RANK: We two? Yes. I can tell you. You shall go as a good fairy—

HELMER: Yes, but what do you suggest as an appropriate costume for that?

RANK: Let your wife go dressed just as she is in everyday life.

HELMER: That was really very prettily turned. But can't you tell us what you'll be?

RANK: Yes, my dear friend, I have quite made up my mind about that.

HELMER: Well?

RANK: At the next fancy-dress ball I shall be invisible.

HELMER: That's a good joke!

RANK: There is a big black hat—have you never heard of hats that make you invisible? If you put one on, no one can see you.

HELMER: [*suppressing a smile*] Yes, you're quite right.

RANK: But I am clean fogetting what I came for. Helmer, give me a cigar—one of the dark Havanas.

HELMER: With the greatest pleasure. [*Offers him his case.*]

RANK: [*takes a cigar and cuts off the end*] Thanks.

NORA: [*striking a match*] Let me give you a light.

RANK: Thank you. [*She holds the match for him to light his cigar.*] And now good-bye!

HELMER: Good-bye, good-bye, dear old man!

NORA: Sleep well, Doctor Rank.

RANK: Thank you for that wish.

NORA: Wish me the same.

RANK: You? Well, if you want me to sleep well! And thanks for the light. [*He nods to them both and goes out.*]

HELMER: [*in a subdued voice*] He has drunk more than he ought.

NORA: [*absently*] Maybe. [HELMER *takes a bunch of keys out of his pocket and goes into the hall.*] Torvald! what are you going to do there?

HELMER: Empty the mail box; it's quite full; there will be no room for the newspaper, to-morrow morning.

NORA: Are you going to work to-night?

HELMER: You know quite well I'm not. What is this? Some one has been at the lock.

NORA: At the lock—?

HELMER: Yes, someone has. What can it mean? I should never have thought the maid—Here is a broken hairpin. Nora, it is one of yours.

NORA: [*quickly*] Then it must have been the children—

HELMER: Then you must get them out of those ways. There, at last I have got it open. [*Takes out the contents of the mail box, and calls to the kitchen.*] Helen!—Helen, put out the light over the front door. [*Goes back into the room and shuts the door into the hall. He holds out his hand full of letters.*] Look at that—look what a heap of them there are. [*turning them over*] What on earth is that?

NORA: [*at the window*] The letter—No! Torvald, no!

HELMER: Two cards—of Rank's.

NORA: Of Doctor Rank's?

HELMER: [*looking at them*] Doctor Rank. They were on the top. He must have put them in when he went out.

NORA: Is there anything written on them?

HELMER: There is a black cross over the name. Look there—what an uncomfortable idea! It looks as if he were announcing his own death.

NORA: It's just what he's doing.

HELMER: What? Do you know anything about it? Has he said anything to you?

NORA: Yes. He told me that when the cards came it would be his leave-taking from us. He means to shut himself up and die.

HELMER: My poor old friend. Certainly I knew we should not have him very long with us. But so soon! And so he hides himself away like a wounded animal.

NORA: If it has to happen, it's best it should be without a word—don't you think so, Torvald?

HELMER: [*walking up and down*] He had so grown into our lives. I can't think of him as having gone out of them. He, with his sufferings and his loneliness, was like a cloudy background to our sunlit happiness. Well, perhaps it's best so. For him, anyway. [*Standing still.*] And perhaps for us, too, Nora. We two are thrown quite upon each other now. [*Puts his arms round her.*] My darling wife, I don't feel as if I could hold you tight enough. Do you know, Nora, I've often wished that you might be threatened by some great danger, so I might risk my life's blood, and everything, for your sake.

NORA: [*disengages himself, and says firmly and decidedly*] Now you must read your letters, Torvald.

HELMER: No, no; not to-night. I want to be with you, my darling wife.

NORA: With the thought of your friend's death—

HELMER: You are right, it has affected us both. Something ugly has come between us—the thought of the horrors of death. We must try and rid our minds of that. Until then—we'll each go to our own room.

NORA: [*hanging on his neck*] Good-night, Torvald—Good-night!

HELMER [*kissing her on the forehead*] Good-night, my little singing-bird. Sleep sound, Nora. Now I'll read my letters through. [*He takes his letters and goes into his room, shutting the door after him.*]

NORA: [*gropes distractedly about, seizes* HELMER's *cloak, throws it round her, while she says in quick, hoarse, spasmodic whispers*] Never to see him again. Never! Never! [*Puts her shawl over her head.*] Never to see my children again, either—never again. Never! Never!—Ah! the icy, black water—the unfathomable depths—if only it were over! He has got it now—now he is reading it. Good-bye, Torvald and my children! [*She is about to rush out through the hall, when* HELMER *opens his door hurriedly and stands with an open letter in his hand.*]

HELMER: Nora!

NORA: Ah!—

HELMER: What's this? Do you know what's in this letter?

NORA: Yes, I know. Let me go! Let me get out!

HELMER: [*holding her back*] Where are you going?

NORA: [*trying to get free*] You shan't save me, Torvald!

HELMER: [*reeling*] True? Is this true, that I read her? Horrible! No, no—it's impossible that it can be true.

NORA: It's true. I have loved you above everything else in the world.

HELMER: Oh, don't let us have any silly excuses.

NORA: [*taking a step towards him*] Torvald—!

HELMER: Miserable creature—what have you done?

NORA: Let me go. You shall not suffer for my sake. You shall not take it upon yourself.

HELMER: No tragedy airs, please. [*locks the hall door*] Here you shall stay and give me an explanation. Do you understand what you've done? Answer me? Do you understand what you've done?

NORA: [*looks steadily at him and says with a growing look of coldness in her face*] Yes, now I am beginning to understand thoroughly.

HELMER: [*walking about the room*] What a horrible awakening! All these eight years—she who was my joy and pride—a hypocrite, a liar—worse, worse—a criminal! The unutterable ugliness of it all!—For shame! For shame! [NORA *is silent and looks steadily at him. He stops in front of her.*] I ought to have suspected that something of the sort would happen. I ought to have foreseen it. All your father's lack of principle—be silent!—all your father's lack of principle has come out in you. No religion, no morality, no sense of duty—. How I'm punished for having winked at what he did! I did it for your sake, and this is how you repay me.

NORA: Yes, that's just it.

HELMER: Now you have destroyed all my happiness. You've ruined my entire future. It is horrible to think of! I'm in the power of an unscrupulous man; he can do what he likes with me, ask anything he likes of me, give me any orders he pleases—I dare not refuse. And I must sink to such miserable depths because of a silly woman!

NORA: When I'm out of the way, you'll be free.

HELMER: No fine speeches, please. Your father had always plenty of those ready, too. What good would it be to me if you were out of the way, as you say? Not the slightest. He can make the affair known everywhere; and if he does, I may be falsely suspected of having been a party to your criminal action. Very likely people will think I was behind it all—that it was I who prompted you! and I have to thank you for all this—you whom I have cherished during the whole of our married life. Do you understand now what it is you have done to me?

NORA: [*coldly and quietly*] Yes.

HELMER: It's so incredible that I can't take it in. But we must come to some understanding. Take off that shawl. Take it off, I tell you. I must try and appease him some way or another. The matter must be hushed up at any cost. And as for you and me, it must appear as if everything between us were just as before—but naturally only in the eyes of the world. You will still remain in my house, that is a matter of course. But I shall not allow you to bring up the children; I dare not trust them to you. To think that I should be obliged to say so to one whom I have loved dearly, and whom I still—. No, that's all over. From this moment happiness is not the question; all that concerns us is to save the remains, the fragments, the appearance— [*A ring is heard at the front-door bell.*]

HELMER: [*with a start*] What's that? So late! Can the worst—? Can he—? Hide yourself, Nora. Say you are ill.

[NORA *stands motionless.* HELMER *goes and unlocks the hall door.*]

MAID: [*half-dressed, comes to the door*] A letter for the mistress.

HELMER: Give it to me. [*takes the letter, and shuts the door*] Yes, it's from him. You shall not have it; I will read it myself.

NORA: Yes, read it.

HELMER: [*standing by the lamp*] I scarcely have the courage to do it. It may mean ruin for both of us. No, I must know. [*Tears open the letter, runs his eye over a few lines, looks at a paper enclosed, and gives a shout of joy.*] Nora! [*She looks at him questioningly.*] Nora!—No, I must read it once again—. Yes, it's true! I'm saved! Nora, I'm saved!

NORA: And I?

HELMER: You, too, of course; we are both saved, both you and I. Look, he sends you your bond back. He says he regrets and repents—that a happy change in his life—never mind what he says! We are saved, Nora! No one can do anything to you. Oh, Nora, Nora!—no, first I must destroy these hateful things. Let me see—. [*Takes a look at the bond*] No, no, I won't look at it. The whole thing shall be nothing but a bad dream to me. [*Tears up the bond and both letters, throws them all into the stove, and watches them burn.*] There—now it doesn't exist any longer. He says that since Christmas Eve you—. These must have been three dreadful days for you, Nora.

NORA: I have fought a hard fight these three days.

HELMER: And suffered agonies, and seen no way out but—. No, we won't call any of the horrors to mind. We'll only shout with joy, and keep saying, "It's all over! It's all over!" Listen to me, Nora. You don't seem to realise that it is all over. What is this?—such a cold, set face! My poor little Nora, I quite understand; you don't feel that I have forgiven you. But it's true, Nora, I swear it; I've forgiven you everything. I know that what you did, you did out of love for me.

NORA: That's true.

HELMER: You have loved me as a wife ought to love her husband. Only you hadn't sufficient knowledge to judge of the means you used. But do you suppose you are any the less dear to me, because you don't understand how to act on your own responsibility? No, no; only lean on me; I will advise you and direct you. I should not be a man if this womanly helplessness did not just give you a double attractiveness in my eyes. You mustn't think any more about the hard things I said in my first moment of consternation, when I thought everything was going to overwhelm me. I've forgiven you, Nora; I swear to you I've forgiven you.

NORA: Thank you for your forgiveness. [*She goes out through to the door to the right.*]

HELMER: No, don't go—[*looks in*] What are you doing in there?

NORA: [*from within*] Taking off my costume.

HELMER: [*standing at the open door*] Yes, do. Try and calm yourself, and make your mind easy again, my frightened little singing-bird. Be at rest, and feel secure; I have broad wings to shelter you under. [*walks up and down by the door*] How warm and cozy our home is, Nora. Here is shelter for you; here I'll protect you like a hunted dove that I have saved from a hawk's claws: I'll bring peace to your poor beating heart. It will come, little by little, Nora, believe me. To-morrow morning you will look upon it all quite differently; soon everything will be just as it was before. Very soon you won't need me to assure you that I've forgiven you; you will feel the certainty that I've done so. Can you suppose I should ever think of such a thing as repudiating you, or even reproaching you? You have no idea what a true man's heart is like, Nora. There is something so indescribably sweet and satisfying, to a man, in the knowledge that he has forgiven his wife—forgiven her freely, and with all his heart. It seems as if that had made her, as it were, doubly his own; he has given her a new life, so to speak; and she has in a way become both wife and child to him. So you shall be for me after this, my little scared, helpless darling. Have no anxiety about anything, Nora; only be frank and open with me, and I'll serve as will and conscience both to you—. What's this? Not gone to bed? Have you changed your clothes?

NORA: [*in everyday dress*] Yes, Torvald, I have changed my clothes now.

HELMER: But what for?—so late as this.

NORA: I shall not sleep to-night.

HELMER: But, my dear Nora—

NORA: [*looking at her watch*] It's not so very late. Sit down here, Torvald. You and I have much to say to one another. [*She sits down at one side of the table.*]

HELMER: Nora—what's this?—this cold, set face!

NORA: Sit down. It'll take some time; I have a lot to talk over with you.

HELMER: [*sits down at the opposite side of the table*] You alarm me, Nora!—and I don't understand you.

NORA: No, that's just it. You don't understand me, and I've never understood you, either—before to-night. No, you mustn't interrupt me. You must simply listen to what I say. Torvald, this is a settling of accounts.

HELMER: What do you mean by that?

NORA: [*after a short silence*] Isn't there any thing that strikes you as strange in our sitting here like this?

HELMER: What is that?

NORA: We've been married now eight years. Doesn't it occur to you that this is the first time we two, you and I, husband and wife, have had a serious conversation?

HELMER: What do you mean by "serious"?

NORA: In all these eight years—longer than that—from the beginning of our acquaintance, we've never exchanged a word on any serious subject.

HELMER: Was it likely that I would be continually and for ever telling you about worries that you couldn't help me with?

NORA: I'm not speaking about business matters. I say that we have never sat down in earnest together to try and get at the bottom of anything.

HELMER: But, dearest Nora, would it have been any good to you?

NORA: That's just it; you've never understood me. I have been greatly wronged, Torvald—first by papa and then by you.

HELMER: What! By us two—by us two, who've loved you better than anyone else in the world?

NORA: [*shaking her head*] You've never loved me. You've only thought it pleasant to be in love with me.

HELMER: Nora, what do I hear you saying?

NORA: It's perfectly true, Torvald. When I was at home with papa, he told me his opinion about everything, and so I had the same opinions; and if I differed from him I concealed the fact, because he wouldn't have liked it. He called me his doll-child, and he played with me just as I used to play with my dolls. And when I came to live with you—

HELMER: What sort of an expression is that to use about our marriage?

NORA: [*undisturbed*] I mean that I was simply transferred from papa's hands into yours. You arranged everything according to your own taste, and so I got the same tastes as you—or else I pretended to. I'm really not quite sure which—I think sometimes the one and sometimes the other. When I look back on it, it seems to me as if I'd been living here like a poor woman—just from hand to mouth. I've existed merely to perform tricks for you, Torvald. But you would have it so. You and papa have committed a great sin against me. It's your fault that I have made nothing of my life.

HELMER: How unreasonable and how ungrateful you are, Nora! Have you not been happy here?

NORA: No, I have never been happy. I thought I was, but it's never really been so.

HELMER: Not—not happy!

NORA: No, only merry. And you've always been so kind to me. But our home has been nothing but a playroom. I've been your doll-wife, just as at home I was papa's doll-child; and here the children have been my dolls. I thought it great fun when you played with me, just as they thought it great fun when I played with them. That's what our marriage has been, Torvald.

HELMER: There is some truth in what you say—exaggerated and strained as your view of it is. But for the future it'll be different. Playtime shall be over, and lesson-time shall begin.

NORA: Whose lessons? Mine, or the children's?

HELMER: Both yours and the children's, my darling Nora.

NORA: Alas, Torvald, you're not the man to educate me into being a proper wife for you.

HELMER: And you can say that?

NORA: And I—how am I fitted to bring up the children?

HELMER: Nora!

NORA: Didn't you say so yourself a little while ago—that you dare not trust me to bring them up?

HELMER: In a moment of anger! Why do you pay any heed to that?

NORA: Indeed, you were perfectly right. I'm not fit for the task. There is another task I must undertake first. I must try and educate myself—you're not the man to help me in that. I must do that for myself. And that's why I'm going to leave you now.

HELMER: [*springing up*] What do you say?

NORA: I must stand quite alone, if I'm to understand myself and everything about me. It's for that reason that I cannot remain with you any longer.

HELMER: Now, Nora!

NORA: I'm going away from here now, at once. I'm sure Christine will take me in for the night—

HELMER: You're out of your mind! I won't allow it! I forbid you!

NORA: It's no use forbidding me anything any longer. I'll take with me what belongs to myself. I'll take nothing from you, either now or later.

HELMER: What sort of madness is this!

NORA: To-morrow I'll go home—I mean, to my old home. It will be easiest for me to find something to do there.

HELMER: You blind, foolish woman!

NORA: I must try and get some sense, Torvald.

HELMER: To desert your home, your husband, and your children! And you don't consider what people will say!

NORA: I can't consider that at all. I only know that it is necessary for me.

HELMER: It's shocking. This is how you would neglect your most sacred duties.

NORA: What do you consider my most sacred duties?

HELMER: Do I need to tell you that? Are they not your duties to your husband and your children?

NORA: I have other duties just as sacred.

HELMER: That you have not. What duties could those be?

NORA: Duties to myself.

HELMER: Before all else, you are a wife and a mother.

NORA: I don't believe that any longer. I believe that before all else I'm a reasonable human being, just as you are—or, at all events, that I must try and become one. I know quite well, Torvald, that most people would think you right, and that views of that kind are to be found in books; but I can no longer content myself with what most people say, or with what's found in books. I must think over things for myself and get to understand them.

HELMER: Can't you understand your place in your own home? Haven't you a reliable guide in such matters as that?—have you no religion?

NORA: I'm afraid, Torvald, I do not exactly know what religion is.

HELMER: What're you saying?

NORA: I know nothing but what the clergyman said, when I went to be confirmed. He told us that religion was this, and that, and the other. When I'm away from all this, and am alone, I'll look into that matter, too. I'll see if what the clergyman said is true, or at all events if it is true for me.

HELMER: This is unheard of in a woman of your age! But if religion cannot touch you, let me try and awaken your conscience. I suppose you have some moral sense? Or—answer me—am I to think you have none?

NORA: I assure you, Torvald, that is not an easy question to answer. I really don't know. The thing puzzles me altogether. I only know that you and I look at it in quite a different light. I'm learning, too, that the law is quite another thing from what I supposed; but I find it impossible to convince myself that the law is right. According to it a woman has no right to spare her old dying father, or to save her husband's life. I can't believe that.

HELMER: You talk like a child. You don't understand the conditions of the world in which you live.

NORA: No, I don't. But now I'm going to try. I'm going to see if I can make out who is right, the world or I.

HELMER: You're ill, Nora; you're delirious; I almost think you're out of your mind.

NORA: I've never felt my mind so clear and certain as to-night.

HELMER: And is it with a clear and certain mind that you forsake your husband and your children?

NORA: Yes, it is.

HELMER: Then there is only one possible explanation.

NORA: What is that?

HELMER: You don't love me any more.

NORA: No, that's just it.

HELMER: Nora!—and you can say that?

NORA: It gives me great pain, Torvald, for you have always been so kind to me, but I can't help it. I don't love you any more.

HELMER: [*regaining his composure*] Is that a clear and certain conviction, too?

NORA: Yes, absolutely clear and certain. That's the reason why I'll not stay here any longer.

HELMER: And can you tell me what I've done to forfeit your love?

NORA: Yes, indeed I can. It was to-night, when the wonderful thing did not happen; then I saw you were not the man I had thought you.

HELMER: Explain yourself better—I don't understand you.

NORA: I've waited so patiently for eight years; for, goodness knows, I knew very well that wonderful things don't happen every day. Then this horrible misfortune came upon me; and then I felt quite certain that the wonderful thing was going to happen at last. When Krogstad's letter was lying out there, never for a moment did I imagine that you would consent to accept this man's conditions. I was so absolutely certain that you would say to him: Publish the thing to the whole world. And when that was done—

HELMER: Yes, what then?—when I had exposed my wife to shame and disgrace?

NORA: When that was done, I was so absolutely certain, you would come forward and take everything upon yourself, and say I'm the guilty one.

HELMER: Nora—!

NORA: You mean that I would never have accepted such a sacrifice on your part? No, of course not. But what would my assurances have been worth against yours? That was the wonderful thing which I hoped for and feared; and it was to prevent that, that I wanted to kill myself.

HELMER: I would gladly work night and day for you, Nora—bear sorrow and want for your sake. But no man would sacrifice his honour for the one he loves.

NORA: Millions of women have done it.

HELMER: Oh, you think and talk like a heedless child.

NORA: Maybe. But you neither think nor talk like the man I could bind myself to. As soon as your fear was over—and it was not fear for what threatened me, but for what might happen to you—when the whole thing was past, as far as you were concerned it was exactly as if nothing at all had happened. Exactly as before, I was your little skylark, your doll, which you would in future treat with doubly gentle care, because it was so brittle and fragile. [*getting up*] Torvald—it was then it dawned on me that for eight years I'd been living here with a strange man, and had borne him three children—. Oh, I can't bear to think of it! I could tear myself into little bits!

HELMER: [*sadly*] I see, I see. An abyss has opened between us—there's no denying it. But, Nora, wouldn't it be possible to fill it up?

NORA: As I am now, I'm no wife for you.

HELMER: I have it in me to become a different man.

NORA: Perhaps—if your doll is taken away from you.

HELMER: But to part!—to part from you! No, no. Nora, I can't understand that idea.

NORA: [*going out to the right*] That makes it all the more certain that it must be done. [*She comes back with her cloak and hat and a small bag, which she puts on a chair by the table.*]

HELMER: Nora, Nora, not now! Wait till to-morrow.

NORA: [*putting on her cloak*] I can't spend the night in a strange man's room.

HELMER: But can't we live here like brother and sister—?

NORA: [*putting on her hat*] You know very well that wouldn't last long. [*Puts the shawl round her.*] Good-bye, Torvald. I won't see the little ones. I know they are in better hands than mine. As I am now, I can be of no use to them.

HELMER: But some day, Nora—some day?

NORA: How can I tell? I have no idea what is going to become of me.

HELMER: But you are my wife, whatever becomes of you.

NORA: Listen, Torvald. I have heard that when a wife deserts her husband's house, as I'm doing now, he is legally freed from all obligations towards her. In any case I set you free from all your obligations You're not to feel yourself bound in the slightest way, any more than I shall. There must be perfect freedom on both sides. See, here is your ring back. Give me mine.

HELMER: That, too?

NORA: That, too.

HELMER: Here it is.

NORA: That's right. Now it's all over. I've put the keys here. The maids know all about everything in the house—better than I do. To-morrow, after I've left her, Christine will come here and pack up my own things that I brought with me from home. I'll have them sent to me.

HELMER: All over! all over!—Nora, shall you never think of me again?

NORA: I know I'll often think of you and the children and this house.

HELMER: May I write to you, Nora?

NORA: No—never. You must not do that.

HELMER: But at least let me send you—

NORA: Nothing—nothing—

HELMER: Let me help you if you're in want.

NORA: No. I can receive nothing from a stranger.

HELMER: Nora—can I never be anything more than a stranger to you?

NORA: [*taking her bag*] Ah, Torvald, the most miraculous thing of all would have to happen.

HELMER: Tell me what that would be!

NORA: Both you and I would have to be so changed that—Oh, Torvald, I don't
believe any longer in miracles happening.

HELMER: But I will believe in it. Tell me? So changed that—?

NORA: That our life together would be a real wedlock. Good-bye. [*She goes out
through the hall.*]

HELMER: [*sinks down on a chair at the door and buries his face in his hands*] Nora!
Nora! [*looks round, and rises*] Empty. She is gone. [*A hope flashes across his
mind.*] The most miraculous thing of all—?

    [*The sound of a door shutting is heard from below.*]

Eugene O'Neill (1888–1953)

"The Hairy Ape" (1921)

Eugene O'Neill was the first American dramatist to win widespread international fame. He experimented with many dramatic forms and styles in his twenty-five full-length plays. In "*The Hairy Ape*" he adopted many conventions of expressionism, an artistic movement that emerged in Germany just prior to World War I. The expressionists proclaimed the supreme importance of the human spirit, which they believed was being crushed or distorted by materialism and industrialism.

"*The Hairy Ape*" shows the influence of expressionism on American drama. The unity of the play derives from a central theme: humanity's frustrated search for identity in a hostile environment. In the first scene, Yank is confident that he and his fellow stokers are the only ones who belong because it is they who make the ship go (and by extension the factories and machines of modern industrialized society). But when the shipowner's pampered, anemic daughter (who represents power, money, and influence) calls Yank "a hairy ape," his confidence is shattered. Seeking to reestablish his identity, he first visits Fifth Avenue, the home territory of the rich and powerful, where he proclaims his superiority by physically attacking the men, only to have his very existence go unacknowledged. Thrown into jail, he decides that the answer lies in destroying the steel and machinery over which he originally thought he had power. In jail he learns that the International Workers of the World (IWW) opposes the owners of factories and ships and, when he is released, he offers to blow up the IWW's enemies. Rejected there, too, Yank visits the apes in the zoo, but when he releases a gorilla it crushes him, and he dies without having achieved a sense of belonging. Yank is symbolic of modern humanity in an industrialized society—cut off from a past when human beings had an integral relationship with the natural environment and now little better than cogs in the industrial machine.

"*The Hairy Ape*" is representative of the outlook and techniques of expressionism. The episodic structure and distorted visual elements are typical of the movement, as is the longing for fulfillment, which suggests the need to change society so that the individual can find a coherent, satisfying relationship with the environment.

Eugene O'Neill

"The Hairy Ape"

CHARACTERS

ROBERT SMITH, "YANK"
PADDY
LONG
MILDRED DOUGLAS
HER AUNT
SECOND ENGINEER
A GUARD
A SECRETARY OF AN ORGANIZATION
STOKERS, LADIES, GENTLEMEN, ETC.

SCENES

Scene I: The firemen's forecastle of an ocean liner—an hour after sailing from New York.
Scene II: Section of promenade deck, two days out—morning.
Scene III: The stokehole. A few minutes later.
Scene IV: Same as Scene I. Half an hour later.
Scene V: Fifth Avenue, New York. Three weeks later.
Scene VI: An island near the city. The next night.
Scene VII: In the city. About a month later.
Scene VIII: In the city. Twilight of the next day.

SCENE I

The firemen's forecastle of a transatlantic liner an hour after sailing from New York for the voyage across. Tiers of narrow, steel bunks, three deep, on all sides. An entrance in rear. Benches on the floor before the bunks. The room is crowded with men, shouting, cursing, laughing, singing—a confused, inchoate uproar swelling into a sort of unity, a meaning—the bewildered, furious, baffled defiance of a beast in a cage. Nearly all the men are drunk. Many bottles are passed from hand to hand. All are dressed in dungaree pants, heavy, ugly shoes. Some wear singlets, but the majority are stripped to the waist.

The treatment of this scene, or of any other scene in the play, should by no means be naturalistic. The effect sought after is a cramped space in the bowels of a ship, imprisoned by white steel. The lines of bunks, the uprights supporting them, cross each other like the steel framework of a cage. The ceiling crushes down upon the men's heads. They cannot stand upright. This accentuates the natural stooping posture which shoveling coal and the resultant overdevelopment of back and shoulder muscles have given them. The men themselves should resemble those pictures in which the appearance of Neanderthal Man is guessed at. All are hairy-chested, with long arms of tremendous power, and low,

266

receding brows above their small, fierce, resentful eyes. All the civilized white races are represented, but except for the slight differentiation in color of hair, skin, eyes, all these men are alike.

The curtain rises on a tumult of sound. YANK *is seated in the foreground. He seems broader, fiercer, more truculent, more powerful, more sure of himself than the rest. They respect his superior strength—the grudging respect of fear. Then, too, he represents to them a self-expression, the very last word in what they are, their most highly developed individual.*

VOICES: Gif me trink dere, you!
　　　'Ave a wet!
　　　Salute!
　　　Gesundheit!
　　　Skoal!
　　　Drunk as a lord, God stiffen you!
　　　Here's how!
　　　Luck!
　　　Pass back that bottle, damn you!
　　　Pourin' it down his neck!
　　　Ho, Froggy! Where the devil have you been?
　　　La Touraine.
　　　I hit him smash in yaw, py Gott!
　　　Jenkins—the First—he's a rotten swine—
　　　And the coppers nabbed him—and I run—
　　　I like peer better. It don't pig head gif you.
　　　A slut, I'm sayin'! She robbed me aslape—
　　　To hell with 'em all!
　　　Your're a bloody liar!
　　　Say dot again!
　　　　　[*Commotion. Two men about to fight are pulled apart.*]
　　　No scrappin' now!
　　　Tonight—
　　　See who's the best man!
　　　Bloody Dutchman!
　　　Tonight on the for'ard square.
　　　I'll bet on Dutchy.
　　　He packa da wallop, I tella you!
　　　Shut up, Wop!
　　　No fightin', maties. We're all chums, ain't we?
　　　　　[*A voice starts bawling a song.*]
　　　　　　　Beer, beer, glorious beer!
　　　　　　　Fill yourselves right up to here.
YANK: [*for the first time seeming to take notice of the uproar about him, turns around threateningly—in a tone of contemptuous authority*] Choke off dat noise! Where d'yuh get dat beer stuff? Beer, hell! Beer's for goils—and Dutchmen. Me for somep'n wit a kick to it! Gimme a drink, one of youse guys. [*Several bottles are eagerly offered. He takes a tremendous gulp at one of them; then, keeping the bottle in his hand, glares belligerently at the owner, who hastens*

to acquiesce in this robbery by saying.] All righto, Yank. Keep it and have another. [YANK *contemptuously turns his back on the crowd again. For a second there is an embarrassed silence. Then—*]

VOICES: We must be passing the Hook.
    She's beginning to roll to it.
    Six days in hell—and then Southampton.
    Py Yesus, I vish somepody take my first vatch for me!
    Gittin seasick, Square-head?
    Drink up and forget it!
    What's in your bottle?
    Gin.
    Dot's nigger trink.
    Absinthe? It's doped. You'll go off your chump, Froggy!
    Cochon!
    Whisky, that's the ticket!
    Where's Paddy?
    Going asleep.
    Sing us that whisky song, Paddy.
       [*They all turn to an old, wizened Irishman who is dozing, very drunk, on the benches forward. His face is extremely monkey-like with all the sad, patient pathos of that animal in his small eyes.*]
    Singa da song, Caruso Pat!
    He's gettin' old. The drink is too much for him.
    He's too drunk.

PADDY: [*blinking about him, starts to his feet resentfully, swaying, holding on to the edge of a bunk*] I'm never too drunk to sing. 'Tis only when I'm dead to the world I'd be wishful to sing at all. [*with a sort of sad contempt*] "Whisky Johnny," ye want? A chanty, ye want? Now that's a queer wish from the ugly like of you, God help you. But no matther. [*He starts to sing in a thin, nasal, doleful tone.*]

       Oh, whisky is the life of man!
         Whisky! O Johnny! [*They all join in on this.*]
       Oh, whisky is the life of man!
         Whisky for my Johnny! [*Again chorus.*]
       Oh, whisky drove my old man mad!
         Whisky! O Johnny!
       Oh, whisky drove my old man mad!
         Whisky for my Johnny!

YANK: [*again turning around scornfully*] Aw hell! Nix on dat old sailing ship stuff! All dat bull's dead, see? And you're dead, too, yuh damned old Harp, on'y yuh don't know it. Take it easy, see. Give us a rest. Nix on de loud noise. [*with a cynical grin*] Can't youse see I'm tryin to t'ink?

ALL: [*repeating the word after him as one with the same cynical amused mockery*] Think! [*The chorused word has a brazen metallic quality as if their throats were phonograph horns. It is followed by a general uproar of hard, barking laughter.*]

VOICES: Don't be cracking your head wit ut, Yank.
    You gat headache, py yingo!
    One thing about it—it rhymes with drink!

Ha, ha, ha!
Drink, don't think!
Drink, don't think!
Drink, don't think!
[*A whole chorus of voices has taken up this refrain, stamping on the floor, pounding on the benches with fists.*]
YANK: [*taking a gulp from his bottle—good-naturedly*] Aw right. Can de noise. I got yuh de foist time. [*The uproar subsides. A very drunken sentimental tenor begins to sing.*]

> Far away in Canada,
> Far across the sea,
> There's a lass who fondly waits
> Making a home for me—

YANK: [*fiercely contemptuous*] Shut up, yuh lousy boob! Where d'yuh get dat tripe? Home? Home, hell! I'll make a home for yuh! I'll knock yuh dead. Home! T'hell wit home! Where d'yuh get dat tripe? Dis is home, see? What d'yuh want wit home? [*proudly*] I runned away from mine when I was a kid. On'y too glad to beat it, dat was me. Home was lickings for me, dat's all. But yuh can bet your shoit no one ain't never licked me since! Wanter try it, any of youse? Huh! I guess not. [*in a more placated but still contemptuous tone*] Goils waitin' for yuh, huh? Aw, hell! Dat's all tripe. Dey don't wait for no one. Dey'd double-cross yuh for a nickel. Dey're all tarts, get me? Treat 'em rough, dat's me. To hell wit 'em. Tarts, dat's what, de whole bunch of 'em.
LONG: [*very drunk, jumps on a bench excitedly, gesticulating with a bottle in his hand*] Listen 'ere, Comrades! Yank 'ere is right. 'E says this 'ere stinkin' ship is our 'ome. And 'e says as 'ome is 'ell. And 'e's right! This is 'ell. We lives in 'ell, Comrades—and right enough we'll die in it. [*raging*] And who's ter blame, I arsks yer? We ain't. We wasn't born this rotten way. All men is born free and ekal. That's in the bleedin' Bible, maties. But what d'they care for the Bible—them lazy, bloated swine what travels first cabin? Them's the ones. They dragged us down 'til we're on'y wage slaves in the bowels of a bloody ship, sweatin', burnin' up, eatin' coal dust! Hit's them's ter blame—the damned Capitalist clarss!
[*There had been a gradual murmur of contemptuous resentment rising among the men until now he is interrupted by a storm of catcalls, hisses, boos, hard laughter.*]
VOICES: Turn it off!
Shut up!
Sit down!
Closa da face!
Tamn fool! [*Etc.*]
YANK: [*standing up and glaring at* LONG] Sit down before I knock yuh down! [LONG *makes haste to efface himself.* YANK *goes on contemptuously.*] De Bible, huh? De Cap'tlist class, huh? Aw nix on dat Salvation Army–Socialist bull. Git a soapbox! Hire a hall! Come and be saved, huh? Jerk us to Jesus, huh? Aw g'wan! I've listened to lots of guys like you, see. Yuh're all wrong. Wanter know what I t'ink? Yuh ain't no good for no one. Yuh're de bunk. Yuh ain't got no noive, get me? Yuh're yellow, dat's what. Yellow, dat's you. Say!

What's dem slobs in de foist cabin got to do wit us? We're better men dan dey are, ain't we? Sure! One of us guys could clean up de whole mob wit one mitt. Put one of 'em down here for one watch in de stokehole, what'd happen? Dey'd carry him off on a stretcher. Dem boids don't amount to nothin'. Dey're just baggage. Who makes dis old tub run? Ain't it us guys? Well den, we belong, don't we? We belong and dey don't. Dat's all. [*A loud chorus of approval.* YANK *goes on.*] As for dis bein' hell—aw, nuts! Yuh lost your noive, dat's what. Dis is a man's job, get me? It belongs. It runs dis tub. No stiffs need apply. But yuh're a stiff, see? Yuh're yellow, dat's you.

VOICES: [*with a great hard pride in them*]
    Righto!
    A man's job!
    Talk is cheap, Long.
    He never could hold up his end.
    Divil take him!
    Yank's right. We make it go.
    Py Gott, Yank say right ting!
    We don't need no one cryin' over us.
    Makin' speeches.
    Throw him out!
    Yellow!
    Chuck him overboard!
    I'll break his jaw for him!
    [*They crowd around* LONG *threateningly.*]

YANK: [*half good-natured again—contemptuously*] Aw, take it easy. Leave him alone. He ain't woith a punch. Drink up. Here's how, whoever owns dis. [*He takes a long swallow from his bottle. All drink with him. In a flash all is hilarious amiability again, back-slapping, loud talk, etc.*]

PADDY: [*who has been sitting in a blinking, melancholy daze—suddenly cries out in a voice full of old sorrow*] We belong to this, you're saying? We make the ship to go, you're saying? Yerra then, that Almighty God have pity on us! [*His voice runs into the wail of a keen, he rocks back and forth on his bench. The men stare at him, startled and impressed in spite of themselves.*] Oh, to be back in the fine days of my youth, ochone! Oh, there was fine beautiful ships them days—clippers wid tall masts touching the sky—fine strong men in them—men that was sons of the sea as if 'twas the mother that bore them. Oh, the clean skins of them, and the clear eyes, the straight backs and full chests of them! Brave men they was, and bold men surely! We'd be sailing out, bound down round the Horn maybe. We'd be making sail in the dawn, with a fair breeze, singing a chanty song wid no care to it. And astern the land would be sinking low and dying out, but we'd give it no heed but a laugh, and never a look behind. For the day that was, was enough, for we was free men—and I'm thinking 'tis only slaves do be giving heed to the day that's gone or the day to come—until they're old like me. [*with a sort of religious exaltation*] Oh, to be scudding south again wid the power of the Trade Wind driving her on steady through the nights and the days! Full sail on her! Nights and days! Nights when the foam of the wake would be flaming wid fire, when the sky'd be blazing and winking wid stars. Or the full of the moon maybe. Then you'd see her driving through the gray night, her sails stretching aloft all silver and white, not a sound on the deck, the lot of us dreaming dreams, till you'd believe 'twas no real ship at all you was on but a ghost ship like the *Flying Dutchman* they say does be roaming the seas forevermore widout touching a port. And there was the days, too. A warm sun on the clean decks. Sun warming the blood of you, and wind over the miles of shiny green ocean like strong drink to your lungs. Work—aye, hard work—but who'd mind that at all? Sure, you worked under the sky and 'twas work wid skill and daring to it. And wid the day done, in the dog watch, smoking me pipe at ease, the lookout would be raising land maybe, and we'd see the mountains of South Americy wid the red fire of the setting sun painting their white tops and the clouds floating by them! [*His tone of exaltation ceases. He goes on mournfully.*] Yerra, what's the use of talking? 'Tis a dead man's whisper. [*to* YANK *resentfully*] 'Twas them days men belonged to ships, not now. 'Twas them days a ship was part of the sea, and a man was part of a ship, and the sea joined all together and made it one. [*scornfully*] Is it one wid this you'd be, Yank—black smoke from the funnels smudging the sea, smudging the decks—the bloody engines pounding and throbbing and shaking—wid divil a sight of sun or a breath of clean air—choking our lungs wid coal dust—breaking our backs and hearts in the hell of the stoke-hole—feeding the bloody furnace—feeding our lives along wid the coal, I'm thinking—caged in by steel from a sight of the sky like bloody apes in the zoo! [*with a harsh laugh*] Ho-ho, divil mend you! Is it to belong to that you're wishing? Is it a flesh and blood wheel of the engines you'd be?

YANK: [*who has been listening with a contemptuous sneer, barks out the answer*] Sure ting! Dat's me. What about it?

PADDY: [*as if to himself—with great sorrow*] Me time is past due. That a great wave wid sun in the heart of it may sweep me over the side sometime I'd be dreaming of the days that's gone!

YANK: Aw, yuh crazy Mick! [*He springs to his feet and advances on* PADDY *threateningly—then stops, fighting some queer struggle within himself—lets his hands fall to his sides—contemptuously.*] Aw, take it easy. Yuh're aw right, at dat. Yuh're bugs, dat's all—nutty as a cuckoo. All dat tripe yuh been pullin'— Aw, dat's all right. On'y it's dead, get me? Yuh don't belong no more, see. Yuh don't got de stuff. Yuh're too old. [*disgustedly*] But aw say, come up for air onct in a while, can't yuh? See what's happened since yuh croaked. [*He suddenly bursts forth vehemently, growing more and more excited.*] Say! Sure! Sure I meant it! What de hell—Say, lemme talk! Hey! Hey, you old Harp! Hey, youse guys! Say, listen to me—wait a moment—I gotter talk, see. I belong and he don't. He's dead but I'm livin'. Listen to me! Sure I'm part of de engines! Why de hell not! Dey move, don't dey? Dey're speed, ain't dey? Dey smash trou, don't dey! Twenty-five knots a hour! Dat's goin' some! Dat's new stuff! Dat belongs! But him, he's too old. He gets dizzy. Say, listen. All dat crazy tripe about nights and days; all dat crazy tripe about stars and moons; all dat crazy tripe about suns and winds, fresh air and de rest of it—Aw hell, dat's all a dope dream! Hittin' de pipe of de past, dat's what he's doin'. He's old and don't belong no more. But me, I'm young! I'm in de pink! I move wit it! It, get me! I mean de ting dat's de guts of all dis. It ploughs trou all de tripe he's been sayin'. It blows dat up! It knocks dat dead! It slams dat offen de face of de Oith! It, get me! De engines and de coal and de smoke and all de rest of it! He can't breathe and swallow coal dust, but I kin, see? Dat's fresh air for me! Dat's food for me! I'm new, get me? Hell in de stokehole? Sure! It takes a man to work in hell. Hell, sure, dat's my fav'rite climate. I eat it up! I git fat on it! It's me make it hot! It's me makes it roar! It's me makes it move! Sure, on'y for me everyting stops. It all goes dead, get me? De noise and smoke and all de engines movin' de woild, dey stop. Dere ain't nothin' no more! Dat's what I'm sayin'. Everyting else dat makes de woild move, somep'n makes it move. It can't move without somep'n else, see? Den yuh get down to me. I'm at de bottom, get me! Dere ain't nothin' foither. I'm de end! I'm de start! I start somep'n and de woild moves! It—dat's me!—de new dat's moiderin' de old! I'm de ting in coal dat makes it boin; I'm steam and oil for de engines; I'm de ting in noise dat makes yuh hear it; I'm smoke and express trains and steamers and factory whistles; I'm de ting in gold dat makes it money! And I'm what makes iron into steel! Steel, dat stands for de whole ting! And I'm steel—steel—steel! I'm de muscles in steel, de punch behind it! [*As he says this he pounds with his fist against the steel bunks. All the men, roused to a pitch of frenzied self-glorification by his speech, do likewise. There is a deafening metallic roar, through which* YANK's *voice can be heard bellowing.*] Slaves, hell. We run de whole woiks. All de rich guys dat tink dey're somep'n, dey ain't nothin'! Dey don't belong. But us guys, we're in de move, we're at de bottom, de whole ting is us! [PADDY *from the start of* YANK's *speech has been taking one gulp after another from his bottle, at first frightenedly, as if he were afraid to listen, then desperately, as if to drown his senses, but finally has achieved complete indifferent, even amused, drunkenness.* YANK *sees his lips moving. He quells the uproar with a shout.*] Hey, youse guys, take it easy! Wait a moment! de nutty Harp is sayin' somep'n.

PADDY: [*is heard now—throws his head back a mocking burst of laughter*] Ho-ho-ho-ho-ho—

YANK: [*drawing back his fist, with a snarl*] Aw! Look out who yuh're givin' the bark!

PADDY: [*begins to sing the "Miller of Dee" with enormous good nature*]
              I care for nobody, no, not I,
              And nobody cares for me.

YANK: [*good-natured himself in a flash, interrupts* PADDY *with a slap on the bare back like a report*] Dat's de stuff! Now yuh're gettin' wise to somep'n. Care for nobody, dat's de dope! To hell wit 'em all. And nix on nobody else carin'. I kin care for myself, get me! [*Eight bells sound, muffled, vibrating through the steel walls as if some enormous brazen gong were imbedded in the heart of the ship. All the men jump up mechanically, file through the door silently close upon each other's heels in what is very like a prisoners' lockstep.* YANK *slaps* PADDY *on the back.*] Our watch, yuh old Harp! [*mockingly*] Come on down in hell. Eat up de coal dust. Drink in de heat. It's it, see! Act like yuh liked it, yuh better—or croak yuhself.

PADDY: [*with jovial defiance*] To the divil wid it! I'll not report this watch. Let thim log me and be damned. I'm no slave the like of you. I'll be sittin' here at me ease, and drinking, and thinking, and dreaming dreams.

YANK: [*contemptuously*] Tinkin' and dreamin', what'll that get yuh? What's tinkin' got to do wit it? We move, don't we? Speed, ain't it? Fog, dat's all you stand for. But we drive trou dat, don't we? We split dat up and smash trou— twenty-five knots a hour! [*turns his back on* PADDY *scornfully*] Aw, yuh make me sick! Yuh don't belong! [*He strides out the door in rear.* PADDY *hums to himself, blinking drowsily.*]

CURTAIN

SCENE II

Two days out. A section of the promenade deck. MILDRED DOUGLAS *and her aunt are discovered reclining in deck chairs. The former is a girl of twenty, slender, delicate, with a pale, pretty face marred by a self-conscious expression of disdainful superiority. She looks fretful, nervous, and discontented, bored by her own anemia. Her aunt is a pompous and proud—and fat—old lady. She is a type even to the point of a double chin and lorgnettes. She is dressed pretentiously, as if afraid her face alone would never indicate her position in life.* MILDRED *is dressed all in white.*

The impression to be conveyed by this scene if one of the beautiful, vivid life of the sea all about—sunshine on the deck in a great flood, the fresh sea wind blowing across it. In the midst of this, these two incongruous, artificial figures, inert and disharmonious, the elder like a gray lump of dough touched up with rouge, the younger looking as if the vitality of her stock had been sapped before she was conceived, so that she is the expression not of its life energy but merely of the artificialities that energy had won for itself in the spending.

MILDRED: [*looking up with affected dreaminess*] How the black smoke swirls back against the sky! Is it not beautiful?

AUNT: [*without looking up*] I dislike smoke of any kind.

MILDRED: My great-grandmother smoked a pipe—a clay pipe.

AUNT: [*ruffling*] Vulgar!

MILDRED: She was too distant a relative to be vulgar. Time mellows pipes.

AUNT: [*pretending boredom but irritated*] Did the sociology you took up at college teach you that—to play the ghoul on every possible occasion, excavating old bones? Why not let your great-grandmother rest in her grave?

MILDRED: [*dreamily*] With her pipe beside her—puffing in Paradise.

AUNT: [*with spite*] Yes, you are a natural-born ghoul. You are even getting to look like one, my dear.

MILDRED: [*in a passionless tone*] I detest you, Aunt. [*looking at her critically*] Do you know what you remind me of? Of a cold pork pudding against a background of linoleum tablecloth in the kitchen of a—but the possibilities are wearisome. [*She closes her eyes*]

AUNT: [*with a bitter laugh*] Merci for your candor. But since I am and must be your chaperon—in appearance, at least—let us patch up some sort of armed truce. For my part you are quite free to indulge any pose of eccentricity that beguiles you—as long as you observe the amenities—

MILDRED: [*drawling*] The inanities?

AUNT: [*going on as if she hadn't heard*] After exhausting the morbid thrills of social service work on New York's East Side—how they must have hated you, by the way, the poor that you made so much poorer in their own eyes!—you are now bent on making your slumming international. Well, I hope Whitechapel will provide the needed nerve tonic. Do not ask me to chaperon you there, however. I told your father I would not. I loathe deformity. We will hire an army of detectives and you may investigate everything—they allow you to see.

MILDRED: [*protesting with a trace of genuine earnestness*] Please do not mock at my attempts to discover how the other half lives. Give me credit for some sort of groping sincerity in that at least. I would like to help them. I would like to be some use in the world. Is it my fault I don't know how? I would like to be sincere, to touch life somewhere. [*with weary bitterness*] But I'm afraid I have neither the vitality nor integrity. All that was burnt out in our stock before I was born. Grandfather's blast furnaces, flaming to the sky, melting steel, making millions—then father keeping those home fires burning, making more millions—and little me at the tail-end of it all. I'm a waste product in the Bessemer process—like the millions. Or rather, I inherit the acquired trait of the by-product, wealth, but none of the energy, none of the strength of the steel that made it. I am sired by gold and damned by it, as they say at the race track—damned in more ways than one. [*She laughs mirthlessly.*]

AUNT: [*unimpressed—superciliously*] You seem to be going in for sincerity today. It isn't becoming to you, really—except as an obvious pose. Be as artificial as you are, I advise. There's a sort of sincerity in that, you know. And, after all, you must confess you like that better.

MILDRED: [*again affected and bored*] Yes, I suppose I do. Pardon me for my outburst. When a leopard complains of its spots, it must sound rather grotesque. [*in a mocking tone*] Purr, little leopard. Purr, scratch, tear, kill, gorge yourself and be happy—only stay in the jungle where your spots are camouflage. In a cage they make you conspicuous.

AUNT: I don't know what you are talking about.

MILDRED: It would be rude to talk about anything to you. Let's just talk. [*She looks at her wristwatch.*] Well, thank goodness, it's about time for them to come for me. That ought to give me a new thrill, Aunt.

AUNT: [*affectedly troubled*] You don't mean to say you're really going? The dirt—the heat must be frightful—

MILDRED: Grandfather started as a puddler. I should have inherited an immunity to heat that would make a salamander shiver. It will be fun to put it to the test.

AUNT: But don't you have to have the captain's—or someone's—permission to visit the stokehole?

MILDRED: [*with a triumphant smile*] I have it—both his and the chief engineer's. Oh, they didn't want to at first, in spite of my social service credentials. They didn't seem a bit anxious that I should investigate how the other half lives and works on a ship. So I had to tell them that my father, the president of Nazareth Steel, chairman of the board of directors of this line, had told me it would be all right.

AUNT: He didn't.

MILDRED: How naïve age makes one! But I said he did, Aunt. I even said he had given me a letter to them—which I had lost. And they were afraid to take the chance that I might be lying. [*excitedly*] So it's ho! for the stokehole. The second engineer is to escort me. [*looking at her watch again*] It's time. And here he comes, I think.

> [*The* SECOND ENGINEER *enters. He is a husky, fine-looking man of thirty-five or so. He stops before the two and tips his cap, visibly embarrassed and ill-at-ease.*]

SECOND ENGINEER: Miss Douglas?

MILDRED: Yes. [*throwing off her rugs and getting to her feet*] Are we all ready to start?

SECOND ENGINEER: In just a second, ma'am. I'm waiting for the Fourth. He's coming along.

MILDRED: [*with a scornful smile*] You don't care to shoulder this responsibility alone, is that it?

SECOND ENGINEER: [*forcing a smile*] Two are better than one. [*disturbed by her eyes, glances out to sea—blurts out*] A fine day we're having.

MILDRED: Is it?

SECOND ENGINEER: A nice warm breeze—

MILDRED: It feels cold to me.

SECOND ENGINEER: But it's hot enough in the sun—

MILDRED: Not hot enough for me. I don't like Nature. I was never athletic.

SECOND ENGINEER: [*forcing a smile*] Well, you'll find it hot enough where you're going.

MILDRED: Do you mean hell?

SECOND ENGINEER: [*flabbergasted, decides to laugh*] Ho-ho! No, I mean the stokehole.

MILDRED: My grandfather was a puddler. He played with boiling steel.

SECOND ENGINEER: [*all at sea—uneasily*] Is that so? Hum, you'll excuse me, ma'am, but are you intending to wear that dress?

MILDRED: Why not?

SECOND ENGINEER: You'll likely rub against oil and dirt. It can't be helped.

MILDRED: It doesn't matter. I have lots of white dresses.

SECOND ENGINEER: I have an old coat you might throw over—

MILDRED: I have fifty dresses like this. I will throw this one into the sea when I come back. That ought to wash it clean, don't you think?

SECOND ENGINEER: [*doggedly*] There's ladders to climb down that are none too clean—and dark alleyways—

MILDRED: I will wear this very dress and none other.

SECOND ENGINEER: No offense meant. It's none of my business. I was only warning you—

MILDRED: Warning? That sounds thrilling.

SECOND ENGINEER: [*looking down the deck—with a sigh of relief*] There's the Fourth now. He's waiting for us. If you'll come—

MILDRED: Go on. I'll follow you. [*He goes.* MILDRED *turns a mocking smile on her aunt.*] An oaf—but a handsome, virile oaf.

AUNT: [*scornfully*] Poser!

MILDRED: Take care. He said there were dark alleyways—

AUNT: [*in the same tone*] Poser!

MILDRED: [*biting her lips angrily*] You are right. But would that my millions were not so anemically chaste!

AUNT: Yes, for a fresh pose I have no doubt you would drag the name of Douglas in the gutter!

MILDRED: From which it sprang. Good-by, Aunt. Don't pray too hard that I may fall into the fiery furnace.

AUNT: Poser!

MILDRED: [*viciously*] Old hag! [*She slaps her aunt insultingly across the face and walks off, laughing gaily.*]

AUNT: [*screams after her*] I said "poser"!

CURTAIN

SCENE III

The stokehole. In the rear, the dimly-outlined bulks of the furnaces and boilers. High overhead one hanging electric bulb sheds just enough light through the murky air laden with coal dust to pile up masses of shadows everywhere. A line of men, stripped to the waist, is before the furnace doors. They bend over, looking neither to right nor left, handling their shovels as if they were part of their bodies, with a strange, awkward, swinging rhythm. They use the shovels to throw open the furnace doors. Then from these fiery round holes in the black a flood of terrific light and heat pours full upon the men who are outlined in silhouette in the crouching, inhuman attitudes of chained gorillas. The men shovel with a rhythmic motion, swinging as on a pivot from the coal which lies in heaps on the floor behind to hurl it into the flaming mouths before them. There is a tumult of noise—the brazen clang of the furnace doors as they are flung open or slammed shut, the grating, teeth-gritting grind of steel against steel, of crunching coal. This clash of sounds stuns one's ears with its rending dissonance. But there is order in it, rhythm, a mechanical regulated recurrence, a tempo. And rising above all, making the air hum with the quiver of liberated energy, the roar of leaping flames in the furnaces, the monotonous throbbing beat of the engines.

As the curtain rises, the furnace doors are shut. The men are taking a breathing spell. One or two are arranging the coal behind them, pulling it into more accessible heaps. The others can be dimly made out leaning on their shovels in relaxed attitudes of exhaustion.

PADDY: [*from somewhere in the line—plaintively*] Yerra, will this divil's own watch nivir end? Me back is broke. I'm destroyed entirely.

YANK: [*from the center of the line—with exuberant scorn*] Aw, yuh make me sick! Lie down and croak, why don't yuh? Always beefin', dat's you! Say, dis is a cinch! Dis was made for me! It's my meat, get me! [*A whistle is blown—a thin, shrill note from somewhere overhead in the darkness.* YANK *curses without resentment.*] Dere's de damn engineer crackin' de whip. He tinks we're loafin'.

PADDY: [*vindictively*] God stiffen him!

YANK: [*in an exultant tone of command*] Come on, youse guys! Git into de game! She's gittin' hungry. Pile some grub in her. Trow it into her belly! Come on now, all of youse! Open her up!

> [*At this last all the men, who have followed his movements of getting into position, throw open their furnace doors with a deafening clang. The fiery light floods over their shoulders as they bend round for the coal. Rivulets of sooty sweat have traced maps on their backs. The enlarged muscles form bunches of highlight and shadow.*]

YANK: [*chanting a count as he shovels without seeming effort*] One—two—tree— [*his voice rising exultantly in the joy of battle*] Dat's de stuff! Let her have it! All togedder now! Sling it into her! Let her ride! Shoot de piece now! Call de toin on her! Drive her into it! Feel her move! Watch her smoke! Speed, dat's her middle name! Give her coal, youse guys! Coal, dat's her booze! Drink it up, baby! Let's see yuh sprint! Dig in and gain a lap! Dere she go-o-es.

> [*This last in the chanting formula of the gallery gods at the six-day bike race. He slams his furnace door shut. The others do likewise with as much unison as their wearied bodies will permit. The effect is of one fiery eye after another, being blotted out with a series of accompanying bangs.*]

PADDY: [*groaning*] Me back is broke. I'm bate out—bate—

> [*There is a pause. Then the inexorable whistle sounds again from the dim regions above the electric light. There is a growl of cursing rage from all sides.*]

YANK: [*shaking his fist upward—contemptuously*] Take it easy dere, you! Who d'yuh tink's runnin' dis game, me or you? When I git ready, we move. Not before! When I git ready, get me!

VOICES: [*approvingly*]
That's the stuff!
Yank tal him, py golly!
Yank ain't affeerd.
Goot poy, Yank!
Give 'im hell!
Tell 'im 'e's a bloody swine!
Bloody slave-driver!

YANK: [*contemptuously*] He ain't got no noive. He's yellow, get me? All de engineers is yellow. Dey got streaks a mile wide. Aw, to hell wit him! Let's move, youse guys. We had a rest. Come on, she needs it! Give her pep! It ain't for him. Him and his whistle, dey don't belong. But we belong, see! We gotter feed de baby! Come on!

> [*He turns and flings his furnace door open. They all follow his lead. At this instant the SECOND and FOURTH ENGINEERS enter from the darkness on the left with MILDRED between them. She starts, turns paler, her pose is crumbling, she shivers with fright in spite of the blazing heat, but forces herself to leave the ENGINEERS and take a few steps nearer the men. She is right behind YANK. All this happens quickly while the men have their backs turned.*]

YANK: Come on, youse guys! [*He is turning to get coal when the whistle sounds again in a peremptory, irritating note. This drives YANK into a sudden fury. While the other men have turned full around and stopped dumbfounded by the spectacle of* MILDRED *standing there in her white dress,* YANK *does not turn far enough to see her. Besides, his head is thrown back, he blinks upward through the murk trying to find the owner of the whistle, he brandishes his shovel murderously over his head in one hand, pounding on his chest, gorilla-like, with the other, shouting.*] Toin off dat whistle! Come down outa dere, yuh yellow, brass-buttoned, Belfast bum, yuh! Come down and I'll knock yer brains out! Yuh lousy, stinkin', yellow mut of a Catholic-moiderin' bastard! Come down and I'll moider yuh! Pullin' dat whistle on me, huh? I'll show yuh! I'll crash yer skull in! I'll drive yer teet' down yer troat! I'll slam yer nose trou de back of yer head! I'll cut yer guts out for a nickel, yuh lousy boob, yuh dirty crummy, muck-eatin' son of a—[*Suddenly he becomes conscious of all the other men staring at something directly behind his back. He whirls defensively with a snarling, murderous growl, crouching to spring, his lips drawn back over his teeth, his small eyes gleaming ferociously. He sees* MILDRED, *like a white apparition in the full light from the open furnace doors. He glares into her eyes, turned to stone. As for her, during his speech she has listened, paralyzed with horror, terror, her whole personality crushed, beaten in, collapsed, by the terrific impact of this unknown, abysmal brutality, naked and shameless. As she looks at his gorilla face, as his eyes bore into hers, she utters a low, choking cry and shrinks away from him, putting both hands up before her eyes to shut out the sight of his face, to protect her own. This startles* YANK *to a reaction. His mouth falls open, his eyes grow bewildered.*]

MILDRED: [*about to faint—to the* ENGINEERS, *who now have her one by each arm— whimperingly*] Take me away! Oh, the filthy beast!

[*She faints. They carry her quickly back, disappearing in the darkness at the left, rear. An iron door clangs shut. Rage and bewildered fury rush back on* YANK. *He feels himself insulted in some unknown fashion in the very heart of his pride. He roars.*]

YANK: God damn yuh! [*and hurls his shovel after them at the door which has just closed. It hits the steel bulkhead with a clang and falls clattering on the steel floor. From overhead the whistle sounds again in a long, angry, insistent command.*]

CURTAIN

SCENE IV

The firemen's forecastle. YANK'S *watch has just come off duty and had dinner. Their faces and bodies shine from a soap-and-water scrubbing but around their eyes, where a hasty dousing does not touch, the coal dust sticks like black makeup, giving them a queer, sinister expression.* YANK *has not washed either face or body. He stands out in contrast to them, a blackened, brooding figure. He is seated forward on a bench in the exact attitude of Rodin's "The Thinker." The others, most of them smoking pipes, are staring at* YANK *half-apprehensively, as if fearing an outburst; half-amusedly as if they saw a joke somewhere that tickled them.*

VOICES: He ain't ate nothin'.
Py golly, a fallar gat to gat grub in him.
Divil a lie.
Yank feeda da fire, no feeda da face.

Ha-ha.

He ain't even washed hisself.

He's forgot.

Hey, Yank you forgot to wash.

YANK: [*sullenly*] Forgot nothin'! To hell wit washin'.

VOICES: It'll stick to you.

It'll get under your skin.

Give yer the bleedin' itch, that's wot.

It makes spots on you—like a leopard.

Like a piebald nigger, you mean.

Better wash up, Yank.

You sleep better.

Wash up, Yank.

Wash up! Wash up!

YANK: [*resentfully*] Aw say, youse guys. Lemme alone. Can't youse see I'm tryin' to tink?

ALL: [*repeating the word after him as one with cynical mockery*] Think! [*The word has a brazen, metallic quality as if their throats were phonograph horns. It is followed by a chorus of hard, barking laughter.*]

YANK: [*springing to his feet and glaring at them belligerently*] Yes, tink! Tink, dat's what I said! What about it?

[*They are silent, puzzled by his sudden resentment at what used to be one of his jokes.* YANK *sits down again in the same attitude of "The Thinker."*]

VOICES: Leave him alone.

He's got a grouch on.

Why wouldn't he?

PADDY: [*with a wink at the others*] Sure I know what's the matther. 'Tis aisy to see. He's fallen in love, I'm telling you.

ALL: [*repeating the word after him as one with cynical mockery*] Love! [*The word has a brazen, metallic quality as if their throats were phonograph horns. It is followed by a chorus of hard, barking laughter.*]

YANK: [*with a contemptuous snort*] Love, hell! Hate, dat's what. I've fallen in hate, get me?

PADDY: [*philosophically*] 'Twould take a wise man to tell one from the other. [*with a bitter, ironical scorn, increasing as he goes on*] But I'm telling you it's love that's in it. Sure what else but love for us poor bastes in the stokehole would be bringing a fine lady, dressed like a white quane, down a mile of ladders and steps to be havin' a look at us? [*A growl of anger goes up from all sides.*]

LONG: [*jumping on a bench—hectically*] Hinsultin' us! Hinsultin' us, the bloody cow! And them bloody engineers! What right 'as they got to be exhibitin' us's if we was bleedin' monkeys in a menagerie? Did we sign for hinsults to our dignity as 'onest workers? Is that in the ship's articles? You kin bloody well bet it ain't! But I knows why they done it. I arsked a deck steward 'o she was and 'e told me. 'Er old man's a bleedin' millionaire, a bloody Capitalist! 'E's got enuf bloody gold to sink this bleedin' ship! 'E makes arf the bloody steel in the world! 'E owns this bloody boat! And you and me, Comrades, we're 'is slaves! And the skipper and mates and engineers, they're 'is slaves! And she's 'is bloody daughter and we're all 'er slaves, too! And she gives 'er orders as 'ow she wants to see the bloody animals below decks and down they takes 'er!

[*There is a roar of rage from all sides.*]

YANK: [*blinking at him bewilderedly*] Say! Wait a moment! Is all dat straight goods?

LONG: Straight as string! The bleedin' steward as waits on 'em, 'e told me about 'er. And what're we goin' ter do, I arsks yer? 'Ave we got ter swaller 'er hinsults like dogs? It ain't in the ship's articles. I tell yer we got a case. We kin go to law—

YANK: [*with abysmal contempt*] Hell! Law!

ALL: [*repeating the word after him as one with cynical mockery*] Law! [*The word has a brazen, metallic quality as if their throats were phonograph horns. It is followed by a chorus of hard, barking laughter.*]

LONG: [*feeling the ground slipping from under his feet—desperately*] As voters and citizens we kin force the bloody governments—

YANK: [*with abysmal contempt*] Hell! Governments!

ALL: [*repeating the word after him as one with cynical mockery*] Governments! [*The word has a brazen, metallic quality as if their throats were phonograph horns. It is followed by a chorus of hard, barking laughter.*]

LONG: [*hysterically*] We're free and equal in the sight of God—

YANK: [*with abysmal contempt*] Hell! God!

ALL: [*repeating the word after him as one with cynical mockery*] God! [*The word has a brazen, metallic quality as if their throats were phonograph horns. It is followed by a chorus of hard, barking laughter.*]

YANK: [*witheringly*] Aw, join de Salvation Army!

ALL: Sit down! Shut up! Damn fool! Sea-lawyer!

[LONG *slinks back out of sight.*]

PADDY: [*continuing the trend of his thoughts as if he had never been interrupted—bitterly*] And there she was standing behind us, and the Second pointing at us like a man you'd hear in a circus would be saying: In this cage is a queerer kind of baboon than ever you'd find in darkest Africy. We roast them in their own sweat—and be damned if you won't hear some of thim saying they like it! [*He glances scornfully at* YANK.]

YANK: [*with a bewildered uncertain growl*] Aw!

PADDY: And there was Yank roarin' curses and turning round wid his shovel to brain her—and she looked at him, and him at her—

YANK: [*slowly*] She was all white. I tought she was a ghost. Sure.

PADDY: [*with heavy, biting sarcasm*] 'Twas love at first sight, divil a doubt of it! If you'd seen the endearin' look on her pale mug when she shriveled away with her hands over her eyes to shut out the sight of him! Sure, 'twas as if she'd seen a great hairy ape escaped from the Zoo!

YANK: [*stung—with a growl of rage*] Aw!

PADDY: And the loving way Yank heaved his shovel at the skull of her, only she was out the door! [*a grin breaking over his face*] 'Twas touching, I'm telling you! It put the touch of home, swate home in the stokehole. [*There is a roar of laughter from all.*]

YANK: [*glaring at* PADDY *menacingly*] Aw, choke dat off, see!

PADDY: [*not heeding him—to the others*] And her grabbin' at the Second's arm for protection. [*with a grotesque imitation of a woman's voice*] Kiss me, Engineer dear, for it's dark down here and me old man's in Wall Street making money! Hug me tight, darlin', for I'm afeerd in the dark and me mother's on deck makin' eyes at the skipper! [*Another roar of laughter.*]

YANK: [*threateningly*] Say! What yuh tryin' to do, kid me, yuh old Harp?

PADDY: Divil a bit! Ain't I wishin' myself you'd brained her?

YANK: [*fiercely*] I'll brain her! I'll brain her yet, wait 'n' see! [*coming over to* PADDY—*slowly*] Say, is dat what she called me—a hairy ape?

PADDY: She looked it at you if she didn't say the word itself.

YANK: [*grinning horribly*] Hairy ape, huh? Sure! Dat's de way she looked at me, aw right. Hairy ape! So dat's me, huh? [*bursting into rage—as if she were still in front of him*] Yuh skinny tart! Yuh white-faced bum, yuh! I'll show yuh who's a ape! [*turning to the others, bewilderment seizing him again*] Say, youse guys. I was bawlin' him out for pullin' de whistle on us. You heard me. And den I seen youse lookin' at somep'n and I tought he'd sneaked down to come up in back of me, and I hopped round to knock him dead wit de shovel. And dere she was wit de light on her! Christ, yuh coulda pushed me over with a finger! I was scared, get me? Sure! I tought she was a ghost, see? She was all in white like dey wrap around stiffs. You seen her. Kin yuh blame me? She didn't belong, dat's what. And den when I come to and seen it was a real skoit and seen de way she was lookin' at me—like Paddy said— Christ, I was sore, get me? I don't stand for dat stuff from nobody. And I flung de shovel—on'y she'd beat it. [*furiously*] I wished it'd banged her! I wished it'd knocked her block off!

LONG: And be 'anged for murder or 'lectrocuted? She ain't bleedin' well worth it.

YANK: I don't give a damn what! I'd be square wit her, wouldn't I? Tink I wanter let her put somep'n over on me? Tink I'm goin' to let her git away wit dat stuff? Yuh don't know me! No one ain't never put nothin' over on me and got away wit it, see!—not dat kind of stuff—no guy and no skoit neither! I'll fix her! Maybe she'll come down again—

VOICE: No chance, Yank. You scared her out of a year's growth.

YANK: I scared her? Why de hell should I scare her? Who de hell is she? Ain't she de same as me? Hairy ape, huh? [*with his old confident bravado*] I'll show her I'm better'n her, if she on'y knew it. I belong and she don't, see! I move and she's dead! Twenty-five knots a hour, dat's me! Dat carries her but I make dat. She's on'y baggage. Sure! [*again bewilderedly*] But, Christ, she was funny lookin'! Did yuh pipe her hands? White and skinny. Yuh could see de bones through 'em. And her mush, dat was dead white, too. And her eyes, dey was like dey'd seen a ghost. Me, dat was! Sure! Hairy ape! Ghost, huh? Look at dat arm! [*He extends his right arm, swelling out the great muscles.*] I coulda took her wit dat, wit just my little finger even, and broke her in two. [*again bewilderedly*] Say, who is dat skoit, huh? What is she? What's she come from? Who made her? Who give her de noive to look at me like dat? Dis ting's got my goat right. I don't get her. She's new to me. What does a skoit like her mean, huh? She don't belong, get me! I can't see her. [*with growing anger*] But one ting I'm wise to, aw right, aw right! Youse all kin bet your shoits I'll git even wit her. I'll show her if she tinks she—She grinds de organ and I'm on de string, huh? I'll fix her! Let her come down again and I'll fling her in de furnace! She'll move den! She won't shiver at nothin', den! Speed, dat'll be her! She'll belong den! [*He grins horribly.*]

PADDY: She'll never come. She's had her bellyful, I'm telling you. She'll be in bed now, I'm thinking, wid ten doctors and nurses feedin' her salts to clean the fear out of her.

YANK: [*enraged*] Yuh tink I made her sick, too, do yuh? Just lookin' at me, huh? Hairy ape, huh? [*in a frenzy of rage*] I'll fix her! I'll tell her where to git off! She'll git down on her knees and take it back or I'll bust de face offen her! [*shaking one fist upward and beating on his chest with the other*] I'll find yuh! I'm comin', d'yuh hear? I'll fix yuh, God damn yuh! [*He makes a rush for the door.*]

VOICES: Stop him!
He'll get shot!
He'll murder her!
Trip him up!
Hold him!
He's gone crazy!
Gott, he's strong!
Hold him down!
Look out for a kick!
Pin his arms!

> [*They have all piled on him and, after a fierce struggle, by sheer weight of numbers have borne him to the floor just inside the door.*]

PADDY: [*who has remained detached*] Kape him down till he's cooled off. [*scornfully*] Yerra, Yank, you're a great fool. Is it payin' attention at all you are to the like of that skinny sow widout one drop of rale blood in her?

YANK: [*frenziedly, from the bottom of the heap*] She done me doit! She done me doit, didn't she? I'll get square wit her! I'll get her some way! Git offen me, youse guys! Lemme up! I'll show her who's a ape!

CURTAIN

SCENE V

Three weeks later. A corner of Fifth Avenue in the Fifties on a fine Sunday morning. A general atmosphere of clean, well-tidied, wide street; a flood of mellow, tempered sunshine; gentle, genteel breezes. In the rear, the show windows of two shops, a jewelry establishment on the corner, a furrier's next to it. Here the adornments of extreme wealth are tantalizingly displayed. The jeweler's window is gaudy with glittering diamonds, emeralds, rubies, pearls, etc., fashioned in ornate tiaras, crowns, necklaces, collars, etc. From each piece hangs an enormous tag from which a dollar sign and numerals in intermittent electric lights wink out the incredible prices. The same in the furrier's. Rich furs of all varieties hang there bathed in a downpour of artificial light. The general effect is of a background of magnificence cheapened and made grotesque by commercialism, a background in tawdry disharmony with the clear light and sunshine on the street itself.

Up the side street YANK *and* LONG *come swaggering.* LONG *is dressed in shore clothes, wears a black Windsor tie, cloth cap.* YANK *is in his dirty dungarees. A fireman's cap with black peak is cocked defiantly on the side of his head. He has not shaved for days and around his fierce, resentful eyes—as around those of* LONG *to a lesser degree—the black smudge of coal dust still sticks like makeup. They hesitate and stand together at the corner, swaggering, looking about them with a forced, defiant contempt.*

LONG: [*indicating it all with an oratorical gesture*] Well, 'ere we are, Fif' Avenoo. This 'ere's their bleedin private lane, as yer might say. [*bitterly*] We're trespassers 'ere. Proletarians keep orf the grass!

YANK: [*dully*] I don't see no grass, yuh boob. [*staring at the sidewalk*] Clean, ain't it? Yuh could eat a fried egg offen it. The white wings got some job sweepin' dis up. [*looking up and down the avenue—surlily*] Where's all de white-collar stiffs yuh said was here—and de skoits—*her* kind?

LONG: In church, blast 'em! Arskin' Jesus to give 'em more money.

YANK: Choich, huh? I uster go to choich onct—sure—when I was a kid. Me old man and woman, dey made me. Dey never went demselves, dough. Always got too big a head on Sunday mornin', dat was dem. [*with a grin*] Dey was scrappers for fair, bot' of dem. On Satiday nights when dey bot' got a skinful dey could put up a bout oughter been staged at de Garden. When dey got trough dere wasn't a chair or table wit a leg under it. Or else dey bot' jumped on me for somep'n. Dat was where I loined to take punishment. [*with a grin and a swagger*] I'm a chip offen de old block, get me?

LONG: Did yer old man follow the sea?

YANK: Naw. Worked along shore. I runned away when me old lady croaked wit de tremens. I helped at truckin' and in de market. Den I shipped in de stokehole. Sure. Dat belongs. De rest was nothin'. [*looking around him*] I ain't never seen dis before. De Brooklyn waterfront, dat was where I was dragged up. [*taking a deep breath*] Dis ain't so bad at dat, huh?

LONG: Not bad? Well, we pays for it wiv our bloody sweat, if yer wants to know!

YANK: [*with sudden angry disgust*] Aw, hell! I don't see no one, see—like her. All dis gives me a pain. It don't belong. Say, ain't dere a back room around dis dump? Let's go shoot a ball. All dis is too clean and quiet and dolled-up, get me! It gives me a pain.

LONG: Wait and yer'll bloody well see—

YANK: I don't wait for no one. I keep on de move. Say, what yuh drag me up here for, anyway? Tryin' to kid me, yuh simp, yuh?

LONG: Yer wants to get back at 'er, don't yer? That's what yer been sayin' every bloomin' hour since she hinsulted yer.

YANK: [*vehemently*] Sure ting I do! Didn't I try to get even wit her in Southampton? Didn't I sneak on de dock and wait for her by de gangplank? I was goin' to spit in her pale mug, see! Sure, right in her pop-eyes! Dat woulda made me even, see? But no chanct. Dere was a whole army of plainclothes bulls around. Dey spotted me and gimme de bum's rush. I never seen her. But I'll git square wit her yet, you watch! [*furiously*] De lousy tart! She tinks she kin get away wit moider—but not wit me! I'll fix her! I'll tink of a way!

LONG: [*as disgusted as he dares to be*] Ain't that why I brought yer up 'ere—to show yer? Yer been lookin' at this 'ere 'ole affair wrong. Yer been actin' an' talkin' 's if it was all a bleedin' personal matter between yer and that bloody cow. I wants to convince yer she was on'y a representative of 'er clarss. I wants to awaken yer bloody clarss consciousness. Then yer'll see it's 'er clarss yer've got to fight, not 'er alone. There's a 'ole mob of 'em like 'er, Gawd blind 'em!

YANK: [*spitting on his hands—belligerently*] De more de merrier when I gits started. Bring on de gang!

LONG: Yer'll see 'em in arf a mo', when that church lets out. [*He turns and sees the window display in the two stores for the first time.*] Blimey! Look at that, will yer? [*They both walk back and stand looking in the jeweler's.* LONG *flies into a fury.*] Just look at this 'ere bloomin' mess! Just look at it! Look at the bleedin' prices on 'em—more 'n our 'ole bloody stokehole makes in ten voyages sweatin' in 'ell! And they—'er and 'er bloody clarss—buys 'em for toys to dangle on 'em! One of these 'ere would buy scoff for a starvin' family for a year!

YANK: Aw, cut de sob stuff! T'hell wit de starvin' family. Yuh'll be passin' de hat to me next. [*with naïve admiration*] Say, dem tings is pretty, huh? Bet yuh dey'd hock for a piece of change aw right. [*then turning away, bored*] But, aw hell, what good are dey? Let her have 'em. Dey don't belong no more'n she does. [*with a gesture of sweeping the jeweler's into oblivion*] All dat don't count, get me?

LONG: [*who has moved to the furrier's—indignantly*] And I s'pose this 'ere don't, neither—skins of poor, 'armless animals slaughtered so as 'er and 'ers can keep their bleedin' noses warm!

YANK: [*who has been staring at something inside—with queer excitement*] Take a slant at dat! Give it de once-over! Monkey fur—two t'ousand bucks! [*bewilderedly*] Is dat straight goods—monkey fur? What de hell—?

LONG: [*bitterly*] It's straight enuf. [*with grim humor*] They wouldn't bloody well pay that for a 'airy ape's skin—no, nor for the 'ole livin' ape with all 'is 'ead, and body, and soul thrown in!

YANK: [*clenching his fists, his face growing pale with rage as if the skin in the window were a personal insult*] Trowin' it up in my face! Christ! I'll fix her!

LONG: [*excitedly*] Church is out. 'ere they come, the bleedin' swine. [*after a glance at* YANK's *lowering face—uneasily*] Easy goes, Comrade. Keep yer bloomin' temper. Remember force defeats itself. It ain't our weapon. We must impress our demands through peaceful means—the votes of the onmarching proletarians of the bloody world!

YANK: [*with abysmal contempt*] Votes, hell! Votes is a joke, see. Votes for women! Let dem do it!

LONG: [*still more uneasily*] Calm, now. Treat 'em wiv the proper contempt. Observe the bleedin' parasites but 'old yer 'orses.

YANK: [*angrily*] Git away from me! Yuh're yellow, dat's what. Force, dat's me! De punch, dat's me every time, see!

[*The crowd from church enter from the right, sauntering slowly and affectedly, their heads held stiffly up, looking neither to right nor left, talking in toneless, simpering voices. The women are rouged, calcimined, dyed, overdressed to the nth degree. The men are in Prince Alberts, high hats, spats, canes, etc. A procession of gaudy marionettes, yet with something of the relentless horror of Frankensteins in their detached, mechanical unawareness.*]

VOICES: Dear Doctor Caiaphas! He is so sincere!
What was the sermon? I dozed off.

About the radicals, my dear—and the false doctrines that are being
   preached.
We must organize a hundred percent American bazaar.
And let everyone contribute one one-hundredth percent of their income tax.
What an original idea!
We can devote the proceeds to rehabilitating the veil of the temple.
But that has been done so many times.

YANK: [*glaring from one to the other of them—with an insulting snort of scorn*] Huh!
Huh! [*Without seeming to see him, they make wide detours to avoid the spot
where he stands in the middle of the sidewalk.*]

LONG: [*frightenedly*] Keep yer bloomin' mouth shut, I tells yer.

YANK: [*viciously*] G'wan! Tell it to Sweeney! [*He swaggers away and deliberately
lurches into a top-hatted gentleman, then glares at him pugnaciously.*] Say, who
d'yuh tink yuh're bumpin'? Tink yuh own de Oith?

GENTLEMAN: [*coldly and affectedly*] I beg your pardon. [*He has not looked at* YANK
and passes on without a glance, leaving him bewildered.]

LONG: [*rushing up and grabbing* YANK's *arm*] 'Ere! Come away! This wasn't what I
meant. Yer'll 'ave the bloody coppers down on us.

YANK: [*savagely—giving him a push that sends him sprawling*] G'wan!

LONG: [*picks himself up—hysterically*] I'll pop orf then. This ain't what I meant.
And whatever 'appens, yer can't blame me. [*He slinks off left.*]

YANK: T' hell wit youse! [*He approaches a lady—with a vicious grin and a smirking
wink.*] Hello, Kiddo. How's every little ting? Got anyting on for tonight? I
know an old boiler down to de docks we kin crawl into. [*The lady stalks by
without a look, without a change of pace.* YANK *turns to others—insultingly.*]
Holy smokes, what a mug! Go hide yuhself before de horses shy at yuh.
Gee, pipe de heinie on dat one! Say, youse, yuh look like de stoin of a ferry-
boat. Paint and powder! All dolled up to kill! Yuh look like stiffs laid out for
de boneyard! Aw, g'wan, de lot of youse! Yuh give me de eye-ache. Yuh
don't belong, get me! Look at me, why don't youse dare? I belong, dat's me!
[*pointing to a skyscraper across the street which is in process of construction—
with bravado*] See dat building goin' up dere? See de steel work? Steel, dat's
me! Youse guys lives on it and tink yuh're somep'n. But I'm *in* it, see! I'm
de hoistin' engine dat makes it go up! I'm it—de inside and bottom of it!
Sure! I'm steel and steam and smoke and de rest of it! It moves—speed—
twenty-five stories up—and me at de top and bottom—movin'! Youse
simps don't move. Yuh're on'y dolls I winds up to see 'm spin. Yuh're de
garbage, get me—de leavins—de ashes we dump over de side! Now, what
'a' yuh gotta say? [*But as they seem neither to see nor hear him, he flies into a
fury.*] Bums! Pigs! Tarts! Bitches! [*He turns in a rage on the men, bumping viciously into them but not jarring them the least bit. Rather it is he who recoils after each collision. He keeps growling.*] Git off de Oith! G'wan, yuh bum! Look
where yuh're goin', can't yuh? Git outa here! Fight, why don't yuh? Put up
yer mitts! Don't be a dog! Fight or I'll knock yuh dead!

   [*But, without seeming to see him, they all answer with mechanical affected
   politeness:*]

I beg your pardon. [*Then at a cry from one of the women, they all scurry to the
furrier's window.*]

THE WOMAN: [*ecstatically, with a gasp of delight*] Monkey fur! [*The whole crowd of men and women chorus after her in the same tone of affected delight.*] Monkey fur!

YANK: [*with a jerk of his head back on his shoulders, as if he had received a punch full in the face—raging*] I see yuh, all in white! I see yuh, yuh white-faced tart, yuh! Hairy ape, huh? I'll hairy ape yuh!

> [*He bends down and grips at the street curbing as if to pluck it out and hurl it. Foiled in this, snarling with passion, he leaps to the lamppost on the corner and tries to pull it up for a club. Just at that moment a bus is heard rumbling up. A fat, high-hatted, spatted gentleman runs out from the side street. He calls out plaintively:*] Bus! Bus! Stop there! [*and runs full tilt into the bending, straining* YANK, *who is bowled off his balance*]

YANK: [*seeing a fight—with a roar of joy as he springs to his feet*] At last! Bus, huh? I'll bust yuh! [*He lets drive a terrific swing, his fist landing full on the fat gentleman's face. But the gentleman stands unmoved as if nothing had happened.*]

GENTLEMAN: I beg your pardon. [*then irritably*] You have made me lose my bus. [*He claps his hands and begins to scream.*] Officer! Officer!

> [*Many police whistles shrill out on the instant and a whole platoon of policemen rush in on* YANK *from all sides. He tries to fight but is clubbed to the pavement and fallen upon. The crowd at the window have not moved or noticed this disturbance. The clanging gong of the patrol wagon approaches with a clamoring din.*]

CURTAIN

SCENE VI

Night of the following day. A row of cells in the prison on Blackwells Island. The cells extend back diagonally from right front to left rear. They do not stop, but disappear in the dark background as if they ran on, numberless, into infinity. One electric bulb from the low ceiling of the narrow corridor sheds its light through the heavy steel bars of the cell at the extreme front and reveals part of the interior. YANK *can be seen within, crouched on the edge of his cot in the attitude of Rodin's "The Thinker." His face is spotted with black and blue bruises. A blood-stained bandage is wrapped around his head.*

YANK: [*suddenly starting as if awakening from a dream, reaches out and shakes the bars—aloud to himself, wonderingly*] Steel. Dis is de zoo, huh? [*A burst of hard, barking laughter comes from the unseen occupants of the cells, runs back down the tier, and abruptly ceases.*]

VOICES: [*mockingly*] The zoo? That's a new name for this coop—a damn good name!
Steel, eh? You said a mouthful. This is the old iron house.
Who is that boob talkin'?
He's the bloke they brung in out of his head. The bulls had beat him up fierce.

YANK: [*dully*] I musta been dreamin'. I tought I was in a cage at de zoo—but de apes don't talk, do dey?

VOICES: [*with mocking laughter*] You're in a cage aw right.

A coop!

A pen!

A sty!

A kennel! [*Hard laughter—a pause.*]

Say, guy! Who are you? No, never mind lying. What are you?

Yes, tell us your sad story. What's your game?

What did they jug yuh for?

YANK: [*dully*] I was a fireman—stokin' on de liners. [*then with sudden rage, rattling his cell bars*] I'm a hairy ape, get me? And I'll bust youse all in de jaw if yuh don't lay off kiddin' me.

VOICES: Huh! You're a hard-boiled duck, ain't you!

When you spit, it bounces! [*Laughter.*]

Aw, can it. He's a regular guy. Ain't you?

What did he say he was—a ape?

YANK: [*defiantly*] Sure ting! Ain't dat what youse all are—apes?

[*A silence. Then a furious rattling of bars from down the corridor.*]

A VOICE: [*thick with rage*] I'll show yuh who's a ape, yuh bum!

VOICES: Ssshh! Nix!

Can de noise!

Piano!

You'll have the guard down on us!

YANK: [*scornfully*] De guard? Yuh mean de keeper, don't yuh?

[*Angry exclamations from all the cells.*]

VOICE: [*placatingly*] Aw, don't pay no attention to him. He's off his nut from the beatin'-up he got. Say, you guy! We're waitin' to hear what they landed you for—or ain't yuh tellin'?

YANK: Sure, I'll tell youse. Sure! Why de hell not? On'y—youse won't get me. Nobody gets me but me, see? I started to tell de judge and all he says was: "Toity days to tink it over." Tink it over! Christ, dat's all I been doin' for weeks! [*after a pause*] I was tryin' to git even wit someone, see?—someone dat done me doit.

VOICES: [*cynically*] De old stuff, I bet. Your goil, huh?

Give yuh the double-cross, huh?

That's them every time!

Did yuh beat up de odder guy?

YANK: [*disgustedly*] Aw, yuh're all wrong! Sure dere was a skoit in it—but not what youse mean, not dat old tripe. Dis was a new kind of skoit. She was dolled up all in white—in de stokehole. I tought she was a ghost. Sure. [*A pause.*]

VOICES: [*whispering*] Gee, he's still nutty.

Let him rave. It's fun listenin'.

YANK: [*unheeding—groping in his thoughts*] Her hands—dey was skinny and white like dey wasn't real but painted on somep'n. Dere was a million miles from me to her—twenty-five knots a hour. She was like some dead ting de cat brung in. Sure, dat's what. She didn't belong. She belonged in de window of a toy store, or on de top of a garbage can, see! Sure! [*He breaks out angrily.*] But would yuh believe it, she had de noive to do me doit. She lamped me like she was seein' somep'n broke loose from de menagerie.

Christ, yuh'd oughter seen her eyes! [*He rattles the bars of his cell furiously.*]
But I'll get back at her yet, you watch! And if I can't find her I'll take it out
on de gang she runs wit. I'm wise to where dey hangs out now. I'll show her
who belongs! I'll show her who's in de move and who ain't. You watch
my smoke!

VOICES: [*serious and joking*] Dat's de talkin'!
Take her for all she's got!
What was this dame anyway? Who was she, eh?

YANK: I dunno. First cabin stiff. Her old man's a millionaire, dey says—name of
Douglas.

VOICES: Douglas? That's the president of the Steel Trust, I bet.
Sure. I seen his mug in de papers.
He's filthy with dough.

VOICE: Hey, feller, take a tip from me. If you want to get back at that dame, you
better join the Wobblies. You'll get some action then.

YANK: Wobblies? What de hell's dat?

VOICE: Ain't you ever heard of the I.W.W.?

YANK: Naw. What is it?

VOICE: A gang of blokes—a tough gang. I been readin' about 'em today in the paper. The guard give me the *Sunday Times.* There's a long spiel about 'em. It's
from a speech made in the Senate by a guy named Senator Queen. [*He is in
the cell next to* YANK's. *There is a rustling of paper.*] Wait'll I see if I got light
enough and I'll read you. Listen. [*He reads.*] "There is a menace existing in
the country today which threatens the vitals of our fair Republic—as foul a
menace against the very life-blood of the American Eagle as was the foul
conspiracy of Cataline against the eagles of ancient Rome!"

VOICE: [*disgustedly*] Aw, hell! Tell him to salt de tail of dat eagle!

VOICE: [*reading*] "I refer to that devil's brew of rascals, jailbirds, murderers and
cutthroats who libel all honest working men by calling themselves the Industrial Workers of the World; but in the light of their nefarious plots, I call
them the Industrious *Wreckers* of the World!"

YANK: [*with vengeful satisfaction*] Wreckers, dat's de right dope! Dat belongs! Me
for dem!

VOICE: Ssshh! [*reading*] "This fiendish organization is a foul ulcer on the fair
body of our Democracy—"

VOICE: Democracy, hell! Give him the boid, fellers—the raspberry! [*They do.*]

VOICE: Ssshh! [*reading*] "Like Cato I say to this Senate, the I. W. W. must be destroyed! For they represent an ever-present dagger pointed at the heart of
the greatest nation the world has ever known, where all men are born free
and equal, with equal opportunities to all, where the Founding Fathers have
guaranteed to each one happiness, where Truth, Honor, Liberty, Justice,
and the Brotherhood of Man are a religion absorbed with one's mother's
milk, taught at our father's knee, sealed, signed, and stamped upon the glorious Constitution of these United States!" [*A perfect storm of hisses, catcalls,
boos, and hard laughter.*]

VOICES: [*scornfully*] Hurrah for de Fort' of July!
Pass de hat!
Liberty!

Justice!
Honor!
Opportunity!
Brotherhood!

ALL: [*with abysmal scorn*] Aw, hell!

VOICE: Give that Queen Senator guy the bark! All togedder now—one—two—tree—[*A terrific chorus of barking and yapping.*]

GUARD: [*from a distance*] Quiet there, youse—or I'll git the hose. [*The noise subsides.*]

YANK: [*with growling rage*] I'd like to catch dat senator guy alone for a second. I'd loin him some trute!

VOICE: Ssshh! Here's where he gits down to cases on the Wobblies. [*reads*] "They plot with fire in one hand and dynamite in the other. They stop not before murder to gain their ends, nor at the outraging of defenseless womanhood. They would tear down society, put the lowest scum in the seats of the mighty, turn Almighty God's revealed plan for the world topsy-turvy, and make of our sweet and lovely civilization a shambles, a desolation where man, God's masterpiece, would soon degenerate back to the ape!"

VOICE: [*to* YANK] Hey, you guy. There's your ape stuff again.

YANK: [*with a growl of fury*] I got him. So dey blow up tings, do dey? Dey turn tings round, do dey? Hey, lend me dat paper, will yuh?

VOICE: Sure. Give it to him. On'y keep it to yourself, see. We don't wanter listen to no more of that slop.

VOICE: Here you are. Hide it under your mattress.

YANK: [*reaching out*] Tanks. I can't read much but I kin manage. [*He sits, the paper in the hand at his side, in the attitude of Rodin's "The Thinker." A pause. Several snores from down the corridor. Suddenly* YANK *jumps to his feet with a furious groan as if some appalling thought had crashed on him—bewilderedly.*] Sure—her old man—president of de Steel Trust—makes half de steel in de world—steel—where I tought I belonged—drivin' trou—movin'—in dat—to make *her*—and cage me in for her to spit on! Christ! [*He shakes the bars of his cell door till the whole tier trembles. Irritated, protesting exclamations from those awakened or trying to get to sleep.*] He made dis—dis cage! Steel! *It* don't belong, dat's what! Cages, cells, locks, bolts, bars—dat's what it means!—holdin' me down wit him at de top! But I'll drive trou! Fire, dat melts it! I'll be fire—under de heap—fire dat never goes out—hot as hell—breakin' out in de night—[*While he has been saying this last he has shaken his cell door to a clanging accompaniment. As he comes to the "breakin' out" he seizes one bar with both hands and, putting his two feet up against the others so that his position is parallel to the floor like a monkey's, he gives a great wrench backwards. The bar bends like a licorice stick under his tremendous strength. Just at this moment the* PRISON GUARD *rushes in, dragging a hose behind him.*]

GUARD: [*angrily*] I'll loin youse bums to wake me up! [*sees* YANK] Hello, it's you, huh? Got the D. Ts., hey? Well, I'll cure 'em. I'll drown your snakes for yuh! [*noticing the bar*] Hell, look at dat bar bended! On'y a bug is strong enough for dat!

YANK: [*glaring at him*] Or a hairy ape, yuh big yellow bum! Look out! Here I come! [*He grabs another bar.*]

GUARD: [*scared now—yelling off left*] Toin de hose on, Ben—Full pressure! And call de others—and a straitjacket!

> [*The curtain is falling. As it hides* YANK *from view, there is a splattering smash as the stream of water hits the steel of* YANK'*s cell.*]

CURTAIN

SCENE VII

Nearly a month later. An I. W. W. local near the waterfront, showing the interior of a front room on the ground floor, and the street outside. Moonlight on the narrow street, buildings massed in black shadow. The interior of the room, which is general assembly room, office, and reading room, resembles some dingy settlement boys' club. A desk and high stool are in one corner. A table with papers, stacks of pamphlets, chairs about it, is at center. The whole is decidedly cheap, banal, commonplace and unmysterious as a room could well be. The SECRETARY *is perched on the stool making entries in a large ledger. An eye shade casts his face into shadows. Eight or ten men, longshoremen, ironworkers, and the like, are grouped about the table. Two are playing checkers. One is writing a letter. Most of them are smoking pipes. A big signboard is on the wall at the rear, "Industrial Workers of the World—Local No. 57."*

> [YANK *comes down the street outside. He is dressed as in Scene Five. He moves cautiously, mysteriously. He comes to a point opposite the door; tiptoes softly up to it, listens, is impressed by the silence within, knocks carefully, as if he were guessing at the password to some secret rite. Listens. No answer. Knocks again a bit louder. No answer. Knocks impatiently, much louder.*]

SECRETARY: [*turning around on his stool*] What the hell is that—someone knocking? [*shouts*] Come in, why don't you?

> [*All the men in the room look up.* YANK *opens the door slowly, gingerly, as if afraid of an ambush. He looks around for secret doors, mystery, is taken aback by the commonplaceness of the room and the men in it, thinks he may have gotten in the wrong place, then sees the signboard on the wall and is reassured.*]

YANK: [*blurts out*] Hello.

MEN: [*reservedly*] Hello.

YANK: [*more easily*] I tought I'd bumped into de wrong dump.

SECRETARY: [*scrutinizing him carefully*] Maybe you have. Are you a member?

YANK: Naw, not yet. Dat's what I come for—to join.

SECRETARY: That's easy. What's your job—longshore?

YANK: Naw. Fireman—stoker on de liners.

SECRETARY: [*with satisfaction*] Welcome to our city. Glad to know you people are waking up at last. We haven't got many members in your line.

YANK: Naw. Dey're all dead to de woild.

SECRETARY: Well, you can help to wake 'em. What's your name? I'll make out your card.

YANK: [*confused*] Name? Lemme tink.

SECRETARY: [*sharply*] Don't you know your own name?

YANK: Sure; but I been just Yank for so long—Bob, dat's it—Bob Smith.

SECRETARY: [*writing*] Robert Smith. [*fills out the rest of card*] Here you are. Cost you half a dollar.

YANK: Is dat all—four bits? Dat's easy. [*gives the* SECRETARY *the money*]

SECRETARY: [*throwing it in drawer*] Thanks. Well, make yourself at home. No introductions needed. There's literature on the table. Take some of those pamphlets with you to distribute aboard ship. They may bring results. Sow the seed, only go about it right. Don't get caught and fired. We got plenty out of work. What we need is men who can hold their jobs—and work for us at the same time.

YANK: Sure. [*But he still stands, embarrassed and uneasy.*]

SECRETARY: [*looking at him—curiously*] What did you knock for? Think we had a coon in uniform to open doors?

YANK: Naw. I tought it was locked—and dat yuh'd wanter give me the once-over trou a peep-hole or somep'n to see if I was right.

SECRETARY: [*alert and suspicious but with an easy laugh*] Think we were running a crap game? That door is never locked. What put that in your nut?

YANK: [*with a knowing grin, convinced that this is all camouflage, a part of the secrecy*] Dis burg is full of bulls, ain't it?

SECRETARY: [*sharply*] What have the cops got to do with us? We're breaking no laws.

YANK: [*with a knowing wink*] Sure. Youse wouldn't for woilds. Sure. I'm wise to dat.

SECRETARY: You seem to be wise to a lot of stuff none of us knows about.

YANK: [*with another wink*] Aw, dat's aw right, see. [*then made a bit resentful by the suspicious glances from all sides*] Aw, can it! Youse needn't put me trou de toid degree. Can't youse see I belong? Sure! I'm reg'lar. I'll stick, get me? I'll shoot de woiks for youse. Dat's why I wanted to join in.

SECRETARY: [*breezily, feeling him out*] That's the right spirit. Only are you sure you understand what you've joined? It's all plain and above board; still, some guys get a wrong slant on us. [*sharply*] What's your notion of the purpose of the I.W.W.?

YANK: Aw, I know all about it.

SECRETARY: [*sarcastically*] Well, give us some of your valuable information.

YANK: [*cunningly*] I know enough not to speak outa my toin. [*then resentfully again*] Aw, say! I'm reg'lar. I'm wise to de game. I know yuh got to watch your step wit a stranger. For all youse know, I might be a plainclothes dick, or somep'n, dat's what yuh're tinkin', huh? Aw, forget it! I belong, see? Ask any guy down to de docks if I don't

SECRETARY: Who said you didn't?

YANK: After I'm 'nitiated, I'll show yuh.

SECRETARY: [*astounded*] Initiated? There's no initiation.

YANK: [*disappointed*] Ain't there no password—no grip nor nothin'?

SECRETARY: What'd you think this is—the Elks—or the Black Hand?

YANK: De Elks, hell! De Black Hand, dey're a lot of yellow back-stickin' Ginees. Naw. Dis is a man's gang, ain't it?

SECRETARY: You said it! That's why we stand on our two feet in the open. We got no secrets.

YANK: [*surprised but admiringly*] Yuh mean to say yuh always run wide open—like dis?

SECRETARY: Exactly.

YANK: Den yuh sure got your noive wit youse!

SECRETARY: [*sharply*] Just what was it made you want to join us? Come out with that straight.

YANK: Yuh call me? Well, I got noive, too! Here's my hand. Yuh wanter blow tings up, don't yuh? Well, dat's me! I belong!

SECRETARY: [*with pretended carelessness*] You mean change the unequal conditions of society by legitimate direct action—or with dynamite?

YANK: Dynamite! Blow it offen de Oith—steel—all de cages—all de factories, steamers, buildings, jails—de Steel Trust and all dat makes it go.

SECRETARY: So—that's your idea, eh? And did you have any special job in that line you wanted to propose to us? [*He makes a sign to the men, who get up cautiously one by one and group behind* YANK.]

YANK: [*boldly*] Sure, I'll come out wit it. I'll show youse I'm one of de gang. Dere's dat millionaire guy, Douglas—

SECRETARY: President of the Steel Trust, you mean? Do you want to assassinate him?

YANK: Naw, dat don't get yuh nothin'. I mean blow up de factory, de woiks, where he makes de steel. Dat's what I'm after—to blow up de steel, knock all de steel in de woild up to de moon. Dat'll fix tings! [*eagerly, with a touch of bravado*] I'll do it by me lonesome! I'll show yuh! Tell me where his woiks is, how to get there, all de dope. Gimme de stuff, de old butter—and watch me do de rest! Watch de smoke and see it move! I don't give a damn if dey nab me—long as it's done! I'll soive life for it—and give 'em de laugh! [*half to himself*] And I'll write her a letter and tell her de hairy ape done it. Dat'll square tings.

SECRETARY: [*stepping away from* YANK] Very interesting. [*He gives a signal. The men, huskies all, throw themselves on* YANK *and before he knows it they have his legs and arms pinioned. But he is too flabbergasted to make a struggle, anyway. They feel him over for weapons.*]

MAN: No gat, no knife. Shall we give him what's what and put the boots to him?

SECRETARY: No. He isn't worth the trouble we'd get into. He's too stupid. [*He comes closer and laughs mockingly in* YANK's *face.*] Ho-ho! By God, this is the biggest joke they've put up on us yet. Hey, you Joke! Who sent you—Burns or Pinkerton? No, by God, you're such a bonehead I'll bet you're in the Secret Service! Well, you dirty spy, you rotten agent-provocator, you can go back and tell whatever skunk is paying you blood-money for betraying your brothers that he's wasting his coin. You couldn't catch a cold. And tell him that all he'll ever get on us, or ever has got, is just his own sneaking plots that he's framed up to put us in jail. We are what our manifesto says we are, neither more nor less—and we'll give him a copy of that any time he calls. And as for you—[*He glares scornfully at* YANK, *who is sunk in an oblivious stupor.*] Oh, hell, what's the use of talking? You're a brainless ape.

YANK: [*aroused by the word to fierce-but-futile struggles*] What's dat, yuh Sheeny bum, yuh!

SECRETARY: Throw him out, boys.

> [*In spite of his struggles, this is done with gusto and éclat. Propelled by sev-*
> *eral parting kicks,* YANK *lands sprawling in the middle of the narrow cob-*
> *bled street. With a growl he starts to get up and storm the closed door, but*
> *stops bewildered by the confusions in his brain, pathetically impotent. He sits*
> *there brooding, in as near to the attitude of Rodin's "The Thinker" as he can*
> *get in his position.*]

YANK: [*bitterly*] So dem boids don't tink I belong, neider. Aw, to hell wit 'em!
Dey're in de wrong pew—de same old bull—soapboxes and Salvation
Army—no guts! Cut out an hour offen de job a day and make me happy!
Gimme a dollar more a day and make me happy! Tree square a day, and
cauliflowers in de front yard—ekal rights—a woman and kids—a lousy
vote—and I'm all fixed for Jesus, huh? Aw, hell! What does dat get yuh?
Dis ting's in your inside, but it ain't your belly. Feedin' your face—sinkers
and coffee—dat don't touch it. It's way down—at de bottom. Yuh can't
grab it, and yuh can't stop it. It moves, and everything moves. It stops and
de whole woild stops. Dat's me now—I don't tick, see?—I'm a busted In-
gersoll, dat's what. Steel was me, and I owned de woild. Now I ain't steel,
and de woild owns me. Aw, hell! I can't see—it's all dark, get me? It's all
wrong! [*He turns a bitter mocking face up like an ape gibbering at the moon.*]
Say, youse up dere, Man in de Moon, yuh look so wise, gimme de answer,
huh? Slip me de inside dope, de information right from de stable—where
do I get off at, huh?

A POLICEMAN: [*who has come up the street in time to hear this last—with grim*
humor] You'll get off at the station, you boob, if you don't get up out of
that and keep movin'.

YANK: [*looking up at him—with a hard, bitter laugh*] Sure! Lock me up! Put me in
a cage! Dat's de on'y answer yuh know. G'wan, lock me up!

POLICEMAN: What you been doin'?

YANK: Enuf to gimme life for! I was born, see? Sure, dat's de charge. Write it in
de blotter. I was born, get me!

POLICEMAN: [*jocosely*] God pity your old woman! [*then matter-of-fact*] But I've
no time for kidding. You're soused. I'd run you in but it's too long a walk to
the station. Come on now, get up, or I'll fan your ears with this club! Beat it
now! [*He hauls* YANK *to his feet.*]

YANK: [*in a vague mocking tone*] Say, where do I go from here?

POLICEMAN: [*giving him a push—with a grin, indifferently*] Go to hell.

CURTAIN

SCENE VIII

Twilight of the next day. The monkey house at the zoo. One spot of clear gray light falls
on the front of one cage so that the interior can be seen. The other cages are vague,
shrouded in shadow from which chatterings pitched in a conversational tone can be
heard. On the one cage a sign from which the word "gorilla" stands out. The gigantic an-
imal himself is seen squatting on his haunches on a bench in much the same attitude as

Rodin's "The Thinker." YANK *enters from the left. Immediately a chorus of angry chattering and screeching breaks out. The gorilla turns his eyes but makes no sound or move.*

YANK: [*with a hard, bitter laugh*] Welcome to your city, huh? Hail, hail, de gang's all here! [*At the sound of his voice the chattering dies away into an attentive silence.* YANK *walks up to the gorilla's cage and, leaning over the railing, stares in at its occupant, who stares back at him, silent and motionless. There is a pause of dead stillness. Then* YANK *begins to talk in a friendly, confidential tone, half-mockingly, but with a deep undercurrent of sympathy.*] Say, yuh're some hard-lookin' guy, ain't yuh? I seen lots of tough nuts dat de gang called gorillas, but yuh're de foist real one I ever seen. Some chest yuh got, and shoulders, and dem arms and mitts! I bet yuh got a punch in eider fist dat'd knock 'em silly! [*This with genuine admiration. The gorilla, as if he understood, stands upright, swelling out his chest and pounding on it with his fist.* YANK *grins sympathetically.*] Sure, I get yuh. Yuh challenge de whole woild, huh? Yuh got what I was sayin' even if yuh muffed de woids. [*then bitterness creeping in*] And why wouldn't yuh get me? Ain't we both members of de same club— de Hairy Apes? [*They stare at each other—a pause—then* YANK *goes on slowly and bitterly.*] So yuh're what she seen when she looked at me, de white-faced tart! I was you to her, get me? On'y outa de cage—broke out—free to moider her, see? Sure! Dat's what she tought. She wasn't wise dat I was in a cage, too—worser'n yours—sure—a damn sight—'cause you got some chanct to bust loose—but me—[*He grows confused.*] Aw, hell! It's all wrong, ain't it? [*a pause*] I s'pose yuh wanter know what I'm doin' here, huh? I been warmin' a bench down to de Battery—ever since last night. Sure. I seen de sun come up. Dat was pretty, too—all red and pink and green. I was lookin' at de skyscrapers—steel—and all de ships comin' in, sailin' out, all over de Oith—and dey was steel, too. De sun was warm, dey wasn't no clouds, and dere was a breeze blowin'. Sure, it was great stuff. I got it aw right—what Paddy said about dat bein' de right dope—on'y I couldn't get *in* it, see? I couldn't belong in dat. It was over my head. And I kept tinkin'—and den I beat it up here to see what youse was like. And I waited till dey was all gone to git yuh alone. Say, how d'yuh feel sittin' in dat pen all de time, havin' to stand for 'em comin' and starin' at yuh—de white-faced, skinny tarts and de boobs what marry 'em—makin' fun of yuh, laughin' at yuh, gittin' scared of yuh—damn 'em! [*He pounds on the rail with his fist. The gorilla rattles the bars of his cage and snarls. All the other monkeys set up an angry chattering in the darkness.* YANK *goes on excitedly.*] Sure! Dat's de way it hits me, too. On'y yuh're lucky, see? Yuh don't belong wit 'em and yuh know it. But me, I belong wit 'em—but I don't, see? Dey don't belong wit me, dat's what. Get me? Tinkin' is hard—[*He passes one hand across his forehead with a painful gesture. The gorilla growls impatiently.* YANK *goes on gropingly.*] It's dis way, what I'm drivin' at. Youse can sit and dope dream in de past, green woods, de jungle, and de rest of it. Den yuh belong and dey don't. Den yuh kin laugh at 'em, see? Yuh're de champ of de woild. But me—I ain't got no past to tink in, nor nothin' dat's comin', on'y what's now—and dat don't belong. Sure, you're de best off ! Yuh can't tink, can yuh? Yuh can't talk, neider. But I kin make a bluff at talkin' and tinkin'—a'most git away wit it—a'most!—

and dat's where de joker comes in. [*He laughs.*] I ain't on Oith and I ain't in heaven, get me? I'm in de middle tryin' to separate 'em, takin' all de woise punches from bot' of 'em. Maybe dat's what dey call hell, huh? But you, yuh're at de bottom. You belong! Sure! Yuh're de on'y one in de woild dat does, yuh lucky stiff! [*The gorilla growls proudly.*] And dat's why dey gotter put yuh in a cage, see? [*The gorilla roars angrily.*] Sure! Yuh get me. It beats it when you try to tink it or talk it—it's way down—deep—behind—you 'n' me we feel it. Sure! Bot' members of dis club! [*He laughs—then in a savage tone.*] What de hell! T' hell wit it! A little action, dat's our meat! Dat belongs! Knock 'em down and keep bustin' 'em till dey croak yuh wit a gat—wit steel! Sure! Are yuh game? Dey've looked at youse, ain't dey—in a cage? Wanter git even? Wanter wind up like a sport 'stead of croakin' slow in dere? [*The gorilla roars an emphatic affirmative.* YANK *goes on with a sort of furious exultation.*] Sure! Yuh're reg'lar! You'll stick to de finish! Me 'n' you, huh?—bot' members of this club! We'll put up one last star bout dat'll knock 'em offen deir seats! Dey'll have to make de cages stronger after we're trou! [*The gorilla is straining at his bars, growling, hopping from one foot to the other.* YANK *takes a jimmy from under his coat and forces the lock on the cage door. He throws this open.*] Pardon from de governor! Step out and shake hands. I'll take yuh for a walk down Fif' Avenoo. We'll knock 'em offen de Oith and croak wit' de band playin'. Come on, Brother. [*The gorilla scrambles gingerly out of his cage. Goes to* YANK *and stands looking at him.* YANK *keeps his mocking tone—holds out his hand.*] Shake—de secret grip of our order. [*Something, the tone of mockery, perhaps, suddenly outrages the animal. With a spring he wraps his huge arms around* YANK *in a murderous hug. There is a cracking snap of crushed ribs—a gasping cry, still mocking, from* YANK.] Hey, I didn't say kiss me! [*The gorilla lets the crushed body slip to the floor, stands over it uncertainly, considering; then picks it up, throws it in the cage, shuts the door, and shuffles off menacingly into the darkness at left. A great uproar of frightened chattering and whimpering comes from the other cages. Then* YANK *moves, groaning, opening his eyes, and there is silence. He mutters painfully.*] Say—dey oughter match him—wit Zybszko. He got me, aw right. I'm trou. Even him didn't tink I belonged. [*then, with sudden passionate despair*] Christ, where do I get off at? Where do I fit in? [*checking himself as suddenly*] Aw, what de hell! No squawkin', see! No quittin', get me! Croak wit your boots on! [*He grabs hold of the bars of the cage and hauls himself painfully to his feet—looks around him bewilderedly—forces a mocking laugh.*] In de cage, huh? [*in the strident tones of a circus broker*] Ladies and gents, step forward and take a slant at de one and only—[*his voice weakening*]—one and original—Hairy Ape from de wilds of—

[*He slips in a heap on the floor and dies. The monkeys set up a chattering, whimpering wail. And, perhaps, the Hairy Ape at last belongs.*]

CURTAIN

Bertolt Brecht (1891–1956)

The Good Woman of Setzuan (1940)

The expressionists' idealistic dream of transforming humanity foundered in disillusionment during the 1920s. Some writers came to believe that society could be improved only by adopting a program of concrete political action, and in the theatre they sought to focus attention on the great difference between human needs and existing conditions. Attempts to use the theatre as a weapon took several forms, but the most significant was Epic Theatre, exemplified in the plays of Bertolt Brecht. Brecht used many of the devices of expressionist drama, such as episodic structure, unity derived from theme or thesis, and nonillusionistic visual elements. But Brecht, unlike the expressionists, did not suggest that external appearance is untruthful or insignificant; rather, he wished to provoke audiences to reflect on the immediate world and its injustices, and he believed that he could do so most effectively if his audience remained conscious that it was in a theatre. Rejecting the theatre of illusion on the basis that it merely lulls the spectator's critical faculties, Brecht devised several techniques (such as projected captions, songs, and presentational acting) to interrupt the empathetic response and intensify the spectator's awareness of social, economic, and political injustices. It was his hope that the spectator would become aware of the need for change outside the theatre.

The Good Woman of Setzuan is a parable about the difficulties of remaining good under existing social and economic conditions. The "good" person, Shen Te, is generous and well-intentioned, but she soon finds herself exploited and betrayed. Her solution is to disguise herself as her cousin Shui Ta—that is, to let the exploitative side of her character direct her actions. As time passes, she finds herself more and more frequently forced into taking on the role of the ruthless capitalist. Brecht uses this device to suggest the progressive deterioration of morality. The play ends in a stalemate, for the gods leave Shen Te with the same simplistic message they delivered in the prologue—"Be good"—and she is no nearer to knowing how to accomplish this under the present economic system. Throughout the play Brecht skillfully and persistently reminds the audience that Shen Te's predicament is a universal human condition—and one that might be solved by taking the right economic and political action.

Bertolt Brecht

The Good Woman of Setzuan

Revised English Version by Eric Bentley

CHARACTERS

WONG, *a water seller*
THREE GODS
SHEN TE, *a prostitute, later a shopkeeper*
MRS. SHIN, *former owner of Shen Te's shop*
A FAMILY OF EIGHT (*husband, wife, brother, sister-in-law, grandfather, nephew, niece, boy*)
AN UNEMPLOYED MAN
A CARPENTER
MRS. MI TZU, *Shen Te's landlady*
YANG SUN, *an unemployed pilot, later a factory manager*
AN OLD WHORE
A POLICEMAN
AN OLD MAN
AN OLD WOMAN, *his wife*
MR. SHU FU, *a barber*
MRS. YANG, *mother of Yang Sun*
GENTLEMEN, VOICES, CHILDREN (*three*), *etc.*

PROLOGUE

At the gates of the half-Westernized city of Setzuan. Evening.

[WONG *the water seller introduces himself to the audience.*]

WONG: I sell water here in the city of Setzuan. It isn't easy. When water is scarce, I have long distances to go in search of it, and when it is plentiful, I have no income. But in our part of the world there is nothing unusual about poverty. Many people think only the gods can save the situation. And I hear from a cattle merchant—who travels a lot—that some of the highest gods are on their way at this very moment. Informed sources have it that heaven is quite disturbed at all the complaining. I've been coming out here to the city gates for three days now to bid these gods welcome. I want to be the first to greet them. What about those fellows over there? No, no, they *work*. And that one there has ink on his fingers, he's no god, he must be a clerk from the cement factory. *Those* two are another story. They look as though they'd like to beat you. But gods don't need to beat you, do they?

[THREE GODS *appear.*]

What about those three? Old-fashioned clothes—dust on their feet—they *must be gods!* [*he throws himself at their feet*] Do with me what you will, illustrious ones!

FIRST GOD: [*with an ear trumpet*] Ah! [*he is pleased*] So we are expected?

WONG: [*giving them water*] Oh, yes. And I *knew* you'd come.

FIRST GOD: We need somewhere to stay the night. You know of a place?

WONG: The whole town is at your service, illustrious ones! What sort of a place would you like?

[*The* GODS *eye each other.*]

FIRST GOD: Just try the first house you come to, my son.

WONG: That would be Mr. Fo's place.

FIRST GOD: Mr. Fo.

WONG: One moment! [*He knocks at the first house.*]

VOICE FROM MR. FO'S: No!

[WONG *returns a little nervously.*]

WONG: It's too bad. Mr. Fo isn't in. And his servants don't dare do a thing without his consent. He'll have a fit when he finds out who they turned away, won't he?

FIRST GOD: [*smiling*] He will, won't he?

WONG: One moment! The next house is Mr. Cheng's. Won't he be thrilled!

FIRST GOD: Mr. Cheng.

[WONG *knocks.*]

VOICE FROM MR. CHENG'S: Keep your gods. We have our own troubles!

WONG: [*back with the* GODS] Mr. Cheng is very sorry, but he has a houseful of relations. I think some of them are a bad lot, and naturally, he wouldn't like you to see them.

THIRD GOD: Are we so terrible?

WONG: Well, only with bad people, of course. Everyone knows the province of Kwan is always having floods.

SECOND GOD: Really? How's that?

WONG: Why, because they're so irreligious.

SECOND GOD: Rubbish. It's because they neglected the dam.

FIRST GOD: [*to* SECOND] Sh! [*to* WONG] You're still in hopes, aren't you, my son?

WONG: Certainly. All Setzuan is competing for the honor! What happened up to now is pure coincidence. I'll be back. [*He walks away, but then stands undecided.*]

SECOND GOD: What did I tell you?

THIRD GOD: It *could* be pure coincidence.

SECOND GOD: The same coincidence in Shun, Kwan, and Setzuan? People just aren't religious any more, let's face the fact. Our mission has failed!

FIRST GOD: Oh come, we might run into a good person any minute.

THIRD GOD: How did the resolution read? [*unrolling a scroll and reading from it*] "The world can stay as it is if enough people are found [*at the word "found"* *he unrolls it a little more*] living lives worthy of human beings." Good people, that is. Well, what about this water seller himself? *He's* good, or I'm very much mistaken.

SECOND GOD: You're very much mistaken. When he gave us a drink, I had the impression there was something odd about the cup. Well, look! [*He shows the cup to the* FIRST GOD.]

FIRST GOD: A false bottom!

SECOND GOD: The man is a swindler.

FIRST GOD: Very well, count *him* out. That's one man among millions. And as a matter of fact, we only need one on *our* side. These atheists are saying, "The world must be changed because no one can *be* good and *stay* good." No one, eh? I say: let us find one—just one—and we have those fellows where we want them!

THIRD GOD: [*to* WONG] Water seller, is it so hard to find a place to stay?

WONG: Nothing could be easier. It's just me. I don't go about it right.

THIRD GOD: Really?

    [*He returns to the others. A* GENTLEMAN *passes by.*]

WONG: Oh dear, they're catching on. [*He accosts the* GENTLEMAN.] Excuse the intrusion, dear sir, but three gods have just turned up. Three of the very highest. They need a place for the night. Seize this rare opportunity—to have real gods as your guests!

GENTLEMAN: [*laughing*] A new way of finding free rooms for a gang of crooks.

    [*Exit* GENTLEMAN.]

WONG: [*shouting at him*] Godless rascal! Have you no religion, gentleman of Setzuan? [*pause*] Patience, illustrious ones! [*pause*] There's only one person left. Shen Te, the prostitute. She *can't* say no. [*calls up to a window*] Shen Te!

    [SHEN TE *opens the shutters and looks out.*]

WONG: Shen Te, it's Wong. *They're* here, and nobody wants them. Will you take them?

SHEN TE: Oh, no, Wong, I'm expecting a gentleman.

WONG: Can't you forget about him for tonight?

SHEN TE: The rent has to be paid by tomorrow or I'll be out on the street.

WONG: This is no time for calculation, Shen Te.

SHEN TE: Stomachs rumble even on the Emperor's birthday, Wong.

WONG: Setzuan is one big dunghill!

SHEN TE: Oh, very well! I'll hide till my gentleman has come and gone. Then I'll take them. [*She disappears.*]

WONG: They mustn't see her gentleman or they'll know what she is.

FIRST GOD: [*who hasn't heard any of this*] I think it's hopeless.

    [*They approach* WONG.]

WONG: [*jumping, as he finds them behind him*] A room has been found, illustrious ones! [*He wipes sweat off his brow.*]

SECOND GOD: Oh, good.

THIRD GOD: Let's see it.

WONG: [*nervously*] Just a minute. It has to be tidied up a bit.

THIRD GOD: Then we'll sit down here and wait.

WONG: [*still more nervous*] No, no! [*holding himself back*] Too much traffic, you know.

THIRD GOD: [*with a smile*] Of course, if you *want* us to move.

> [*They retire a little. They sit on a doorstep.* WONG *sits on the ground.*]

WONG: [*after a deep breath*] You'll be staying with a single girl—the finest human being in Setzuan!

THIRD GOD: That's nice.

WONG: [*to the audience*] They gave me such a look when I picked up my cup just now.

THIRD GOD: You're worn out, Wong.

WONG: A little, maybe.

FIRST GOD: Do people have a hard time of it?

WONG: The good ones do.

FIRST GOD: What about yourself?

WONG: You mean I'm not good. That's true. And I don't have an easy time, either!

> [*During this dialogue, a* GENTLEMAN *has turned up in front of* SHEN TE'S *house, and has whistled several times. Each time* WONG *has given a start.*]

THIRD GOD: [*to* WONG, *softly*] Psst! I think he's gone now.

WONG: [*confused and surprised*] Ye-e-es.

> [*the* GENTLEMAN *has left now, and* SHEN TE *has come down in the street.*]

SHEN TE: [*softly*] Wong!

> [*Getting no answer, she goes off down the street.* WONG *arrives just too late, forgetting his carrying pole.*]

WONG: [*softly*] Shen Te! Shen Te! [*to himself*] So she's gone off to earn the rent. Oh dear, I can't go to the gods *again* with no room to offer them. Having failed in the service of the gods, I shall run to my den in the sewer pipe down by the river and hide from their sight!

> [*He rushes off.* SHEN TE *returns, looking for him, but finding the* GODS. *She stops in confusion.*]

SHEN TE: You are the illustrious ones? My name is Shen Te. It would please me very much if my simple room could be of use to you.

THIRD GOD: Where is the water seller, Miss . . . Shen Te?

SHEN TE: I missed him, somehow.

FIRST GOD: Oh, he probably thought you weren't coming, and was afraid of telling us.

THIRD GOD: [*picking up the carrying pole*] We'll leave this with you. He'll be needing it.

> [*Led by* SHEN TE, *they go into the house. It grows dark, then light. Dawn. Again escorted by* SHEN TE, *who leads them through the half-light with a little lamp, the* GODS *take their leave.*]

FIRST GOD: Thank you, thank you, dear Shen Te, for your elegant hospitality! We shall not forget! And give our thanks to the water seller—he showed us a good human being.

SHEN TE: Oh, *I'm* not good. Let me tell you something: when Wong asked me to put you up, I hesitated.

FIRST GOD: It's all right to hesitate if you then go ahead! And in giving us that room you did much more than you knew. You proved that good people still exist, a point that has been disputed of late—even in heaven. Farewell!

SECOND GOD: Farewell!

THIRD GOD: Farewell!

SHEN TE: Stop, illustrious ones! I'm not sure you're right. I'd like to be good, it's true, but there's the rent to pay. And that's not all: I sell myself for a living. Even so I can't make ends meet, there's too much competition. I'd like to honor my father and mother and speak nothing but the truth and not covet my neighbor's house. I should love to stay with one man. But how? How is it done? Even breaking a few of your commandments, I can hardly manage.

FIRST GOD: [*clearing his throat*] These thoughts are but, um, the misgivings of an unusually good woman!

THIRD GOD: Good-bye, Shen Te! Give our regards to the water seller!

SECOND GOD: And above all: be good! Farewell!

FIRST GOD: Farewell!

THIRD GOD: Farewell!

[*They start to wave good-bye.*]

SHEN TE: But everything is so expensive. I don't feel sure I can do it!

SECOND GOD: That's not in our sphere. We never meddle with economics.

THIRD GOD: One moment. [*They stop.*] Isn't it true she might do better if she had more money?

SECOND GOD: Come, come! How could we ever account for it Up Above?

FIRST GOD: Oh, there are ways. [*They put their heads together and confer in dumb show. To* SHEN TE, *with embarrassment:*] As you say you can't pay your rent, well, um, we're not paupers, so of course we *insist* on paying for our room. [*Awkwardly thrusting money into her hand.*] There! [*quickly*] But don't tell anyone! The incident is open to misinterpretation.

SECOND GOD: It certainly is!

FIRST GOD: [*defensively*] But there's no law against it! It was never decreed that a god mustn't pay hotel bills!

[*The* GODS *leave.*]

SCENE I———*A small tobacco shop. The shop is not as yet completely furnished and hasn't started doing business.*

SHEN TE: [*to the audience*] It's three days now since the gods left. When they wanted to pay for the room, I looked down at my hand, and there was more than a thousand silver dollars! I bought a tobacco shop with the money, and moved in yesterday. I don't own the building, of course, but I can pay the rent, and I hope to do a lot of good here. Beginning with Mrs. Shin, who's just coming across the square with her pot. She had the shop before me, and yesterday she dropped in to ask rice for her children. [*Enter* MRS. SHIN. *Both women bow.*] How do you do, Mrs. Shin.

MRS. SHIN: How do you do, Miss Shen Te. You like your new home?

SHEN TE: Indeed, yes. Did your children have a good night?

MRS. SHIN: In that hovel? The youngest is coughing already.

SHEN TE: Oh, dear!

MRS. SHIN: You're going to learn a thing or two in these slums.

SHEN TE: Slums? That's not what you said when you sold me the shop!

MRS. SHIN: Now don't start nagging! Robbing me and my innocent children of their home and then calling it a slum! That's the limit! [*She weeps.*]

SHEN TE: [*tactfully*] I'll get your rice.

MRS. SHIN: And a little cash while you're at it.

SHEN TE: I'm afraid I haven't sold anything yet.

MRS. SHIN: [*screeching*] I've got to have it. Strip the clothes from my back and then cut my throat, will you? I know what I'll do: I'll dump my children on your doorstep! [*She snatches the pot out of* SHEN TE's *hands.*]

SHEN TE: Please don't be angry. You'll spill the rice.

[*Enter an elderly* HUSBAND *and* WIFE *with their shabbily dressed* NEPHEW.]

WIFE: Shen Te, dear! You've come into money, they tell me. And we haven't a roof over our heads! A tobacco shop. We had one, too. But it's gone. Could we spend the night here, do you think?

NEPHEW: [*appraising the shop*] Not bad!

WIFE: He's our nephew. We're inseparable!

MRS. SHIN: And who are these . . . ladies and gentlemen?

SHEN TE: They put me up when I first came in from the country. [*to the audience*] Of course, when my small purse was empty, they put me out on the street, and they may be afraid I'll do the same to them. [*to the newcomers, kindly*] Come in, and welcome, though I've only one little room for you—it's behind the shop.

HUSBAND: That'll do. Don't worry.

WIFE: [*bringing* SHEN TE *some tea*] We'll stay over here, so we won't be in your way. Did you make it a tobacco shop in memory of your first real home? We can certainly give you a hint or two! That's one reason we came.

MRS. SHIN: [*to* SHEN TE] Very nice! As long as you have a few customers, too!

HUSBAND: Sh! A customer!

[*Enter an* UNEMPLOYED MAN, *in rags.*]

UNEMPLOYED MAN: Excuse me. I'm unemployed.

[MRS. SHIN *laughs.*]

SHEN TE: Can I help you?

UNEMPLOYED MAN: Have you any damaged cigarettes? I thought there might be some damage when you're unpacking.

WIFE: What nerve, begging for tobacco! [*rhetorically*] Why don't they ask for bread?

UNEMPLOYED MAN: Bread is expensive. One cigarette butt and I'll be a new man.

SHEN TE: [*giving him cigarettes*] That's very important—to be a new man. You'll be my first customer and bring me luck.

[*The* UNEMPLOYED MAN *quickly lights a cigarette, inhales, and goes off, coughing.*]

WIFE: Was that right, Shen Te, dear?

MRS. SHIN: If this is the opening of a shop, you can hold the closing at the end of the week.

HUSBAND: I bet he had money on him.

SHEN TE: Oh, no, he said he hadn't!

NEPHEW: How d'you know he wasn't lying?

SHEN TE: [*angrily*] How do you know he was?

WIFE: [*wagging her head*] You're too good, Shen Te, dear. If you're going to keep this shop, you'll have to learn to say no.

HUSBAND: Tell them the place isn't yours to dispose of. Belongs to . . . some relative who insists on all accounts being strictly in order . . .

MRS. SHIN: That's right! What do you think you are—a philanthropist?

SHEN TE: [*laughing*] Very well, suppose I ask you for my rice back, Mrs. Shin?

WIFE: [*combatively, at* MRS. SHIN] So that's *her* rice?

[*Enter the* CARPENTER, *a small man.*]

MRS. SHIN: [*who, at the sight of him, starts to hurry away*] See you tomorrow, Miss Shen Te! [*Exit* MRS. SHIN.]

CARPENTER: Mrs. Shin, it's you I want!

WIFE: [*to* SHEN TE] Has she some claim on you?

SHEN TE: She's hungry. That's a claim.

CARPENTER: Are you the new tenant? And filling up the shelves already? Well, they're not yours till they're paid for, ma'am. I'm the carpenter, so I should know.

SHEN TE: I took the shop "furnishings included."

CARPENTER: You're in league with that Mrs. Shin, of course. All right. I demand my hundred silver dollars.

SHEN TE: I'm afraid I haven't got a hundred silver dollars.

CARPENTER: Then you'll find it. Or I'll have you arrested.

WIFE: [*whispering to* SHEN TE] That relative, make it a cousin.

SHEN TE: Can't it wait till next month?

CARPENTER: No!

SHEN TE: Be a little patient, Mr. Carpenter, I can't settle all claims at once.

CARPENTER: Who's patient with me? [*He grabs a shelf from the wall.*] Pay up—or I take the shelves back!

WIFE: Shen Te! Dear! Why don't you let your . . . cousin settle this affair? [*to* CARPENTER] Put your claim in writing. Shen Te's cousin will see you get paid.

CARPENTER: [*derisively*] Cousin, eh?

HUSBAND: Cousin, yes.

CARPENTER: I know these cousins!

NEPHEW: Don't be silly. He's a personal friend of mine.

HUSBAND: What a man! Sharp as a razor!

CARPENTER: All right. I'll put my claim in writing. [*Puts shelf on floor, sits on it, writes out bill.*]

WIFE: [*to* SHEN TE] He'd tear the dress off your back to get his shelves. Never recognize a claim. That's my motto.

SHEN TE: He's done a job, and wants something in return. It's shameful that I can't give it to him. What will the gods say?

HUSBAND: You did your bit when you took *us* in.

[*Enter the* BROTHER, *limping, and the* SISTER-IN-LAW, *pregnant.*]

BROTHER: [*to* HUSBAND *and* WIFE] So this is where you're hiding out! There's family feeling for you! Leaving us on the corner!

WIFE: [*embarrassed, to* SHEN TE] It's my brother and his wife. [*to them*] Now stop grumbling, and sit quietly in that corner. [*to* SHEN TE] It can't be helped. She's in her fifth month.

SHEN TE: Oh yes. Welcome!

WIFE: [*to the couple*] Say "thank you." [*They mutter something.*] The cups are there. [*to* SHEN TE] Lucky you bought this shop when you did!

SHEN TE: [*laughing and bringing tea*] Lucky indeed!

[*Enter* MRS. MI TZU, *the landlady.*]

MRS. MI TZU: Miss Shen Te? I am Mrs. Mi Tzu, your landlady. I hope our relationship will be a happy one. I like to think I give my tenants modern, per-
sonalized service. Here is your lease. [*to the others, as* SHEN TE *reads the lease*]
There's nothing like the opening of a little shop, is there? A moment of
true beauty! [*she is looking around*] Not very much on the shelves, of course.
But everything in the gods' good time! Where are your references, Miss
Shen Te?

SHEN TE: Do I *have* to have references?

MRS. MI TZU: After all, I haven't a notion who you are!

HUSBAND: Oh, *we'd* be glad to vouch for Miss Shen Te! We'd go through fire
for her!

MRS. MI TZU: And who may you be?

HUSBAND: [*stammering*] Ma Fu, tobacco dealer.

MRS. MI TZU: Where is your shop, Mr. . . . Ma Fu?

HUSBAND: Well, um, I haven't got a shop—I've just sold it.

MRS. MI TZU: I see. [*to* SHEN TE] Is there no one else that knows you?

WIFE: [*whispering to* SHEN TE] Your cousin! Your cousin!

MRS. MI TZU: This is a respectable house, Miss Shen Te. I never sign a lease without certain assurances.

SHEN TE: [*slowly, her eyes downcast*] I have . . . a cousin.

MRS. MI TZU: On the square? Let's go over and see him. What does he do?

SHEN TE: [*as before*] He lives . . . in another city.

WIFE: [*prompting*] Didn't you say he was in Shung?

SHEN TE: That's right. Shung.

HUSBAND: [*prompting*] I had his name on the tip of my tongue, Mr. . . .

SHEN TE: [*with an effort*] Mr. . . . Shui . . . Ta.

HUSBAND: That's it! Tall, skinny fellow!

SHEN TE: Shui Ta!

NEPHEW: [*to* CARPENTER] *You* were in touch with him, weren't you? About the
shelves?

CARPENTER: [*surlily*] Give him this bill. [*He hands it over.*] I'll be back in the
morning. [*Exit* CARPENTER.]

NEPHEW: [*calling after him, but with his eyes on* MRS. MI TZU] Don't worry! Mr.
Shui Ta pays on the nail!

MRS. MI TZU: [*looking closely at* SHEN TE] I'll be happy to make his acquaintance,
Miss Shen Te. [*Exit* MRS. MI TZU.]
        [*Pause.*]

WIFE: By tomorrow morning she'll know more about you than you do yourself.

SISTER-IN-LAW: [*to* NEPHEW] This thing isn't built to last.
        [*Enter* GRANDFATHER.]

WIFE: It's Grandfather! [*to* SHEN TE] Such a good old soul!
        [*The* BOY *enters.*]

BOY: [*over his shoulder*] Here they are!

WIFE: And the boy, how he's grown! But he always could eat enough for ten.
        [*Enter the* NIECE.]

WIFE: [*to* SHEN TE] Our little niece from the country. There are more of us now
than in your time. The less we had, the more there were of us; the more

there were of us, the less we had. Give me the key. We must protect our-selves from unwanted guests. [*She takes the key and locks the door.*] Just make yourself at home. I'll light the little lamp.

NEPHEW: [*a big joke*] I hope her cousin doesn't drop in tonight! The strict Mr. Shui Ta!

[SISTER-IN-LAW *laughs.*]

BROTHER: [*reaching for a cigarette*] One cigarette more or less . . .

HUSBAND: One cigarette more or less.

[*They pile into the cigarettes. The* BROTHER *hands a jug of wine round.*]

NEPHEW: Mr. Shui Ta'll pay for it!

GRANDFATHER: [*gravely, to* SHEN TE] How do you do?

[SHEN TE, *a little taken aback by the belatedness of the greeting, bows. She has the* CARPENTER'*s bill in one hand, the landlady's lease in the other.*]

WIFE: How about a bit of song? To keep Shen Te's spirits up?

NEPHEW: Good idea. Grandfather, you start!

SONG OF THE SMOKE

GRANDFATHER:
>   I used to think (before old age beset me)
>   That brains could fill the pantry of the poor.
>   But where did all my cerebration get me?
>   I'm just as hungry as I was before.
>   So what's the use?
>   See the smoke float free
>   Into ever colder coldness!
>   It's the same with me.

HUSBAND:
>   The straight and narrow path leads to disaster
>   And so the crooked path I tried to tread.
>   That got me to disaster even faster.
>   (They say we shall be happy when we're dead.)
>   So what's the use?
>   See the smoke float free
>   Into ever colder coldness!
>   It's the same with me.

NIECE:
>   You older people, full of expectation,
>   At any moment now you'll walk the plank!
>   The future's for the younger generation!
>   Yes, even if that future is a blank.
>   So what's the use?
>   See the smoke float free
>   Into ever colder coldness!
>   It's the same with me.

NEPHEW: [*to the* BROTHER] Where'd you get that wine?

SISTER-IN-LAW: [*answering for the* BROTHER] He pawned the sack of tobacco.

HUSBAND: [*stepping in*] What? That tobacco was all we had to fall back on! You pig!

BROTHER: *You'd* call a man a pig because your wife was frigid! Did you refuse to drink it?

> [*They fight. The shelves fall over.*]

SHEN TE: [*imploringly*] Oh don't! Don't break everything! Take it, take it, take it all, but don't destroy a gift from the gods!

WIFE: [*disparagingly*] This shop isn't big enough. I should never have mentioned it to Uncle and the others. When *they* arrive, it's going to be disgustingly overcrowded.

SISTER-IN-LAW: And did you hear our gracious hostess? She cools off quick!

> [*Voices outside. Knocking at the door.*]

UNCLE'S VOICE: Open the door!

WIFE: Uncle! Is that you, Uncle?

UNCLE'S VOICE: Certainly, it's me. Auntie says to tell you she'll have the children here in ten minutes.

WIFE: [*to* SHEN TE] I'll have to let him in.

SHEN TE: [*who scarcely hears her*]
> The little lifeboat is swiftly sent down
> Too many men too greedily
> Hold on to it as they drown.

SCENE Ia ———— WONG's *den in a sewer pipe.*

WONG: [*crouching there*] All quiet! It's four days now since I left the city. The gods passed this way on the second day. I heard their steps on the bridge over there. They must be a long way off by this time, so I'm safe. [*Breathing a sigh of relief, he curls up and goes to sleep. In his dream the pipe becomes transparent, and the* GODS *appear. Raising an arm, as if in self-defense:*] I know, I know, illustrious ones! I found no one to give you a room—not in all Setzuan! There, it's out. Please continue on your way!

FIRST GOD: [*mildly*] But you did find someone. Someone who took us in for the night, watched over us in our sleep, and in the early morning lighted us down to the street with a lamp.

WONG: It was . . . Shen Te that took you in?

THIRD GOD: Who else?

WONG: And I ran away! "She isn't coming," I thought, "she just can't afford it."

GODS: [*singing*]
> *O you feeble, well-intentioned, and yet feeble chap*
> *Where there's need the fellow thinks there is no goodness!*
> *When there's danger he thinks courage starts to ebb away!*
> *Some people only see the seamy side!*
> *What hasty judgment! What premature desperation!*

WONG: I'm *very* ashamed, illustrious ones.

FIRST GOD: Do us a favor, water seller. Go back to Setzuan. Find Shen Te, and give us a report on her. We hear that she's come into a little money. Show interest in her goodness—for no one can be good for long if goodness is not in de-

mand. Meanwhile we shall continue the search, and find other good people. After which, the idle chatter about the impossibility of goodness will stop!
[*The* GODS *vanish.*]

SCENE II

[*A knocking*]

WIFE: Shen Te! Someone at the door. Where is she, anyway?

NEPHEW: She must be getting the breakfast. Mr. Shui Ta will pay for it.
[*The* WIFE *laughs and shuffles to the door. Enter* MR. SHUI TA *and the* CARPENTER.]

WIFE: Who is it?

SHUI TA: I am Miss Shen Te's cousin.

WIFE: What?

SHUI TA: My name is Shui Ta.

WIFE: Her cousin?

NEPHEW: Her cousin?

NIECE: But that was a joke. She hasn't got a cousin.

HUSBAND: So early in the morning?

BROTHER: What's all the noise?

SISTER-IN-LAW: This fellow says he's her cousin.

BROTHER: Tell him to prove it.

NEPHEW: Right. If you're Shen Te's cousin, prove it by getting the breakfast.

SHUI TA: [*whose regime begins as he puts out the lamp to save oil; loudly, to all present, asleep or awake*] Would you all please get dressed! Customers will be coming! I wish to open my shop!

HUSBAND: *Your* shop? Doesn't it belong to our good friend Shen Te?
[SHUI TA *shakes his head.*]

SISTER-IN-LAW: So we've been cheated. Where is the little liar?

SHUI TA: Miss Shen Te has been delayed. She wishes me to tell you there will be nothing she can do—now I am here.

WIFE: [*bowled over*] I thought she was good!

NEPHEW: Do you have to believe *him*?

HUSBAND: I don't.

NEPHEW: Then do something.

HUSBAND: Certainly! I'll send out a search party at once. You, you, you, and you, go out and look for Shen Te. [*as the* GRANDFATHER *rises and makes for the door*] Not you, Grandfather, you and I will hold the fort.

SHUI TA: You won't find Miss Shen Te. She has suspended her hospitable activity for an unlimited period. There are too many of you. She asked me to say: this is a tobacco shop, not a gold mine.

HUSBAND: Shen Te never said a thing like that. Boy, food! There's a bakery on the corner. Stuff your shirt full when they're not looking!

SISTER-IN-LAW: Don't overlook the raspberry tarts.

HUSBAND: And don't let the policeman see you.
[*The* BOY *leaves.*]

SHUI TA: Don't you depend on this shop now? Then why give it a bad name by stealing from the bakery?

NEPHEW: Don't listen to him. Let's find Shen Te. She'll give him a piece of her mind.

SISTER-IN-LAW: Don't forget to leave us some breakfast.
[BROTHER, SISTER-IN-LAW, *and* NEPHEW *leave.*]

SHUI TA: [*to the* CARPENTER] You see, Mr. Carpenter, nothing has changed since the poet, eleven hundred years ago, penned these lines:
A governor was asked what was needed
To save the freezing people in the city.
He replied:
"A blanket ten thousand feet long
to cover the city and all its suburbs."
[*He starts to tidy up the shop.*]

CARPENTER: Your cousin owes me money. I've got witnesses. For the shelves.

SHUI TA: Yes, I have your bill. [*he takes it out of his pocket*] Isn't a hundred silver dollars rather a lot?

CARPENTER: No deductions! I have a wife and children.

SHUI TA: How many children?

CARPENTER: Three.

SHUI TA: I'll make you an offer. Twenty silver dollars.
[*The* HUSBAND *laughs.*]

CARPENTER: You're crazy. Those shelves are real walnut.

SHUI TA: Very well, take them away.

CARPENTER: What?

SHUI TA: They cost too much. Please take them away.

WIFE: Not bad! [*And she, too, is laughing.*]

CARPENTER: [*a little bewildered*] Call Shen Te, someone! [*to* SHUI TA] She's *good!*

SHUI TA: Certainly. She's ruined.

CARPENTER: [*provoked into taking some of the shelves*] All right, you can keep your tobacco on the floor.

SHUI TA: [*to the* HUSBAND] Help him with the shelves.

HUSBAND: [*grins and carries one shelf over to the door where the* CARPENTER *now is*] Good-bye, shelves!

CARPENTER: [*to the* HUSBAND] You dog! You want my family to starve?

SHUI TA: I repeat my offer. I have no desire to keep my tobacco on the floor. Twenty silver dollars.

CARPENTER: [*with desperate aggressiveness*] One hundred!
[SHUI TA *shows indifference, looks through the window. The* HUSBAND *picks up several shelves.*]

CARPENTER: [*to* HUSBAND] You needn't smash them against the doorposts, you idiot! [*to* SHUI TA] These shelves were made to measure. They're no use anywhere else!

SHUI TA: Precisely.
[*The* WIFE *squeals with pleasure.*]

CARPENTER: [*giving up, sullenly*] Take the shelves. Pay what you want to pay.

SHUI TA: [*smoothly*] Twenty silver dollars.
[*He places two large coins on the table. The* CARPENTER *picks them up.*]

HUSBAND: [*brings the shelves in*] And quite enough, too!

CARPENTER: [*slinking off*] Quite enough to get drunk on.

HUSBAND: [*happily*] Well, we got rid of him!

WIFE: [*weeping with fun, gives a rendition of the dialogue just spoken*] "Real walnut," says he. "Very well, take them away," says his lordship. "I have three children," says he. "Twenty silver dollars," says his lordship. "They're no use anywhere else," says he. "Pre-cisely," said his lordship! [*She dissolves into shrieks of merriment.*]

SHUI TA: And now: go!

HUSBAND: What's that?

SHUI TA: You're thieves, parasites. I'm giving you this chance. Go!

HUSBAND: [*summoning all his ancestral dignity*] That sort deserves no answer. Besides, one should never shout on an empty stomach.

WIFE: Where's that boy?

SHUI TA: Exactly. The boy. I want no stolen goods in this shop. [*very loudly*] I strongly advise you to leave! [*But they remain seated, noses in the air. Quietly.*] As you wish. [SHUI TA *goes to the door.* A POLICEMAN *appears.* SHUI TA *bows.*] I am addressing the officer in charge of this precinct?

POLICEMAN: That's right, Mr., um, what was the name, sir?

SHUI TA: Mr. Shui Ta.

POLICEMAN: Yes, of course, sir.
      [*They exchange a smile.*]

SHUI TA: Nice weather we're having.

POLICEMAN: A little on the warm side, sir.

SHUI TA: Oh, a little on the warm side.

HUSBAND: [*whispering to the* WIFE] If he keeps it up till the boy's back, we're done for. [*Tries to signal* SHUI TA.]

SHUI TA: [*ignoring the signal*] Weather, of course, is one thing indoors, another out on the dusty street!

POLICEMAN: Oh, quite another, sir!

WIFE: [*to the* HUSBAND] It's all right as long as he's standing in the doorway—the boy will see him.

SHUI TA: Step inside for a moment! It's quite cool indoors. My cousin and I have just opened the place. And we attach the greatest importance to being on good terms with the, um, authorities.

POLICEMAN: [*entering*] Thank you, Mr. Shui Ta. It *is* cool.

HUSBAND: [*whispering to the* WIFE] And now the boy won't see him.

SHUI TA: [*showing* HUSBAND *and* WIFE *to the* POLICEMAN] Visitors, I think my cousin knows them. They were just leaving.

HUSBAND: [*defeated*] Ye-e-es, we were . . . just leaving.

SHUI TA: I'll tell my cousin you couldn't wait.
      [*Noise from the street. Shouts of* "Stop, Thief!"]

POLICEMAN: What's that?
      [*The* BOY *is in the doorway with cakes and buns and rolls spilling out of his shirt. The* WIFE *signals desperately to him to leave. He gets the idea.*]

POLICEMAN: No, you don't! [*he grabs the* BOY *by the collar*] Where's all this from?

BOY: [*vaguely pointing*] Down the street.

POLICEMAN: [*grimly*] So that's it. [*Prepares to arrest the* BOY.]

WIFE: [*stepping in*] And we knew nothing about it. [*to the* BOY] Nasty little thief!

POLICEMAN: [*dryly*] Can you clarify the situation, Mr. Shui Ta?

[SHUI TA *is silent.*]

POLICEMAN: [*who understands silence*] Aha. You're all coming with me—to the station.

SHUI TA: I can hardly say how sorry I am that my establishment . . .

WIFE: Oh, he saw the boy leave not ten minutes ago!

SHUI TA: And to conceal the theft asked a policeman in?

POLICEMAN: Don't listen to her, Mr. Shui Ta. I'll be happy to relieve you of their presence one and all! [*to all three*] Out! [*He drives them before him.*]

GRANDFATHER: [*leaving last, gravely*] Good morning!

POLICEMAN: Good morning!

[SHUI TA, *left alone, continues to tidy up.* MRS. MI TZU *breezes in.*]

MRS. MI TZU: You're her cousin, are you? Then have the goodness to explain what all this means—police dragging people from a respectable house! By what right does your Miss Shen Te turn my property into a house of assignation? Well, as you see, I know all!

SHUI TA: Yes. My cousin has the worst possible reputation: that of being poor.

MRS. MI TZU: No sentimental rubbish, Mr. Shui Ta. Your cousin was a common . . .

SHUI TA: Pauper. Let's use the uglier word.

MRS. MI TZU: I'm speaking of her conduct, not her earnings. But there must have *been* earnings, or how did she buy all this? Several elderly gentlemen took care of it, I suppose. I repeat: this is a respectable house! I have tenants who prefer not to live under the same roof with such a person.

SHUI TA: [*quietly*] How much do you want?

MRS. MI TZU: [*he is ahead of her now*] I beg your pardon.

SHUI TA: To reassure yourself. To reassure your tenants. How much will it cost?

MRS. MI TZU: You're a cool customer.

SHUI TA: [*picking up the lease*] The rent is high. [*He reads on.*] I assume it's payable by the month?

MRS. MI TZU: Not in her case.

SHUI TA: [*looking up*] What?

MRS. MI TZU: Six months' rent payable in advance. Two hundred silver dollars.

SHUI TA: Six . . . ! Sheer usury! And where am I to find it?

MRS. MI TZU: You should have thought of that before.

SHUI TA: Have you no heart, Mrs. Mi Tzu? It's true Shen Te acted foolishly, being kind to all those people, but she'll improve with time. I'll see to it she does. She'll work her fingers to the bone to pay her rent, and all the time be as quiet as a mouse, as humble as a fly.

MRS. MI TZU: Her social background . . .

SHUI TA: Out of the depths! She came out of the depths! And before she'll go back there, she'll work, sacrifice, shrink from nothing. . . . Such a tenant is worth her weight in gold, Mrs. Mi Tzu.

MRS. MI TZU: It's silver dollars we were talking about, Mr. Shui Ta. Two hundred silver dollars or . . .

[*Enter the* POLICEMAN.]

POLICEMAN: Am I intruding, Mr. Shui Ta?

MRS. MI TZU: This tobacco shop is well known to the police, I see.

POLICEMAN: Mr. Shui Ta has done us a service, Mrs. Mi Tzu. I am here to present our official felicitations!

MRS. MI TZU: That means less than nothing to me, sir. Mr. Shui Ta, all I can say is: I hope your cousin will find my terms acceptable. Good day, gentlemen. [*Exit.*]

SHUI TA: Good day, ma'am.
    [*Pause.*]

POLICEMAN: Mrs. Mi Tzu a bit of a stumbling block, sir?

SHUI TA: She wants six months' rent in advance.

POLICEMAN: And you haven't got it, eh? [SHUI TA *is silent.*] But surely you can get it, sir? A man like you?

SHUI TA: What about a woman like Shen Te?

POLICEMAN: You're not staying, sir?

SHUI TA: No, and I won't be back. Do you smoke?

POLICEMAN: [*taking two cigars, and placing them both in his pocket*] Thank you, sir—I see your point. Miss Te—let's mince no words—Miss Shen Te lived by selling herself. "What else could she have done?" you ask. "How else was she to pay the rent?" True. But the fact remains, Mr. Shui Ta, it is not respectable. Why not? A very deep question. But, in the first place, love— love isn't bought and sold like cigars, Mr. Shui Ta. In the second place, it isn't respectable to go waltzing off with someone that's paying his way, so to speak—it must be for love! Thirdly, and lastly, as the proverb has it: not for a handful of rice but for love! [*Pause. He is thinking hard.*] "Well," you may say, "and what good is all this wisdom if the milk's already spilt?" Miss Shen Te is what she is. Is *where* she is. We have to face the fact that if she doesn't get hold of six months' rent pronto, she'll be back on the streets. The question then as I see it—everything in this world is a matter of opinion—the question as I see it is: *how* is she to get hold of this rent? How? Mr. Shui Ta: I don't know. [*Pause.*] I take that back, sir. It's just come to me. A husband. We must find her a husband!
    [*Enter a little* OLD WOMAN.]

OLD WOMAN: A good cheap cigar for my husband, we'll have been married forty years tomorrow and we're having a little celebration.

SHUI TA: Forty years? And you still want to celebrate?

OLD WOMAN: As much as we can afford to. We have the carpet shop across the square. We'll be good neighbors, I hope?

SHUI TA: I hope so, too.

POLICEMAN: [*who keeps making discoveries*] Mr. Shui Ta, you know what we need? We need capital. And how do we acquire capital? We get married.

SHUI TA: [*to* OLD WOMAN] I'm afraid I've been pestering this gentleman with my personal worries.

POLICEMAN: [*lyrically*] We can't pay six months' rent, so what do we do? We marry money.

SHUI TA: That might not be easy.

POLICEMAN: Oh, I don't know. She's a good match. Has a nice, growing business. [*to the* OLD WOMAN] What do you think?

OLD WOMAN: [*undecided*] Well—

POLICEMAN: Should she put an ad in the paper?

OLD WOMAN: [*not eager to commit herself*] Well, if *she* agrees—

POLICEMAN: I'll write it for her. *You* lend us a hand, and *we* write an ad for you! [*He chuckles away to himself, takes out his notebook, wets the stump of a pencil between his lips, and writes away.*]

SHUI TA: [*slowly*] Not a bad idea.

POLICEMAN: "What . . . *respectable* . . . man . . . with small capital . . . widower . . . not excluded . . . desires . . . marriage . . . into flourishing . . . tobacco shop?" And now let's add: "Am . . . pretty . . ." No! . . . "Prepossessing appearance."

SHUI TA: If you don't think that's an exaggeration?

OLD WOMAN: Oh, not a bit. I've seen her.

[*The* POLICEMAN *tears the page out of his notebook, and hands it over to* SHUI TA.]

SHUI TA: [*with horror in his voice*] How much luck we need to keep our heads above water! How many ideas! How many friends! [*to the* POLICEMAN] Thank you, sir, I think I see my way clear.

SCENE III——*Evening in the municipal park. Noise of a plane overhead.*

[YANG SUN, *a young man in rags, is following the plane with his eyes: one can tell that the machine is describing a curve above the park.* YANG SUN *then takes a rope out of his pocket, looking anxiously about him as he does so. He moves toward a large willow. Enter two prostitutes, one the* OLD WHORE, *the other the* NIECE *whom we have already met.*]

NIECE: Hello. Coming with me?

YANG SUN: [*taken aback*] If you'd like to buy me a dinner.

OLD WHORE: Buy you a dinner! [*to the* NIECE] Oh, we know him—it's the unemployed pilot. Waste no time on him!

NIECE: But he's the only man left in the park. And it's going to rain.

OLD WHORE: Oh, how do you know?

[*And they pass by,* YANG SUN *again looks about him, again takes his rope, and this time throws it round a branch of the willow tree. Again he is interrupted. It is the two prostitutes returning—and in such a hurry they don't notice him.*]

NIECE: It's going to pour!

[*Enter* SHEN TE.]

OLD WHORE: There's that *gorgon* Shen Te! That *drove* your family out into the cold!

NIECE: It wasn't her. It was that cousin of hers. She offered to pay for the cakes. I've nothing against her.

OLD WHORE: I have, though. [*so that* SHEN TE *can hear*] Now where would the little lady be off to? She may be rich now but that won't stop her snatching our young men, will it?

SHEN TE: I'm going to the tearoom by the pond.

NIECE: Is it true what they say? You're marrying a widower—with three children?

SHEN TE: Yes. I'm just going to see him.

YANG SUN: [*his patience at breaking point*] Move on there! This is a park, not a whorehouse!

OLD WHORE: Shut your mouth!
> [*But the two prostitutes leave.*]

YANG SUN: Even in the farthest corner of the park, even when it's raining, you can't get rid of them! [*He spits.*]

SHEN TE: [*overhearing this*] And what right have you to scold them? [*But at this point she sees the rope.* Oh!

YANG SUN: Well, what are you staring at?

SHEN TE: That rope. What is it for?

YANG SUN: Think! Think! I haven't a penny. Even if I had, I wouldn't spend it on you. I'd buy a drink of water.
> [*The rain starts.*]

SHEN TE: [*still looking at the rope*] What is the rope for? You mustn't!

YANG SUN: What's it to you? Clear out!

SHEN TE: [*irrelevantly*] It's raining.

YANG SUN: Well, don't try to come under this tree.

SHEN TE: Oh, no. [*She stays in the rain.*]

YANG SUN: Now go away. [*pause*] For one thing, I don't like your looks, you're bowlegged.

SHEN TE: [*indignantly*] That's not true!

YANG SUN: Well, don't show 'em to me. Look, it's raining. You better come under this tree.
> [*Slowly, she takes shelter under the tree.*]

SHEN TE: Why did you want to do it?

YANG SUN: You really want to know? [*pause*] To get rid of you! [*pause*] You know what a flyer is?

SHEN TE: Oh yes, I've met a lot of pilots. At the tearoom.

YANG SUN: You call *them* flyers? Think they know what a machine is? Just 'cause they have leather helmets? They gave the airfield director a bribe, that's the way *those* fellows got up in the air! Try one of them out sometime. "Go up to two thousand feet," tell them, "then let it fall, then pick it up again with a flick of the wrist at the last moment." Know what he'll say to that? "It's not in my contract." Then again, there's the landing problem. It's like landing on your own backside. It's no different, planes are human. Those fools don't understand. [*pause*] And I'm the biggest fool for reading the book on flying in the Peking school and skipping the page where it says, "We've got enough flyers and we don't need you." I'm a mail pilot with no mail. You understand that?

SHEN TE: [*shyly*] Yes. I do.

YANG SUN: No, you don't. You'd never understand that.

SHEN TE: When we were little we had a crane with a broken wing. He made friends with us and was very good-natured about our jokes. He would strut along behind us and call out to stop us going too fast for him. But every spring and autumn when the cranes flew over the villages in great swarms, he got quite restless. [*pause*] I understand that. [*She bursts out crying.*]

YANG SUN: Don't!

SHEN TE: [*quieting down*] No.

YANG SUN: It's bad for the complexion.

SHEN TE: [*sniffing*] I've stopped.

[*She dries her tears on her big sleeve. Leaning against the tree, but not look-ing at her, he reaches for her face.*]

YANG SUN: You can't even wipe your own face. [*He is wiping it for her with his handkerchief. Pause.*]

SHEN TE: [*still sobbing*] I don't know *anything!*

YANG SUN: You interrupted me! What for?

SHEN TE: It's such a rainy day. You only wanted to do . . . *that* because it's such a rainy day. [*To the audience:*]
    In our country
    The evenings should never be somber
    High bridges over rivers
    The gray hour between night and morning
    And the long, long winter:
    Such things are dangerous
    For, with all the misery,
    A very little is enough
    And men throw away an unbearable life.
        [*Pause.*]

YANG SUN: Talk about yourself for a change.

SHEN TE: What about me? I have a shop.

YANG SUN: [*incredulous*] You have a shop, have you? Never thought of walking the streets?

SHEN TE: I did walk the streets. Now I have a shop.

YANG SUN: [*ironically*] A gift of the gods, I suppose!

SHEN TE: How did you know?

YANG SUN: [*even more ironically*] One fine evening the gods turned up saying: here's some money!

SHEN TE: [*quickly*] One fine morning.

YANG SUN: [*fed up*] This isn't much of an entertainment.
        [*Pause.*]

SHEN TE: I can play the zither a little. [*pause*] And I can mimic men. [*pause*] I got the shop, so the first thing I did was to give my zither away. So I can be as stupid as a fish now, I said to myself, and it won't matter.
    I'm rich now, I said
    I walk alone, I sleep alone
    For a whole year, I said
    I'll have nothing to do with a man.

YANG SUN: And now you're marrying one! The one at the tearoom by the pond?
        [SHEN TE *is silent.*]

YANG SUN: What do you know about love?

SHEN TE: Everything.

YANG SUN: Nothing. [*pause*] Or d'you just mean you enjoyed it?

SHEN TE: No.

YANG SUN: [*again without turning to look at her, he strokes her cheek with his hand*] You like that?

SHEN TE: Yes.

YANG SUN: [*breaking off*] You're easily satisfied, I must say. [*pause*] What a town!

SHEN TE: You have no friends?

YANG SUN: [*defensively*] Yes, I have! [*change of tone*] But they don't want to hear I'm still unemployed. "What?" they ask. "Is there still water in the sea?" You have friends?

SHEN TE: [*hesitating*] Just a . . . cousin.

YANG SUN: Watch him carefully.

SHEN TE: He only came once. Then he went away. He won't be back. [YANG SUN *is looking away.*] But to be without hope, they say, is to be without goodness!
[*Pause.*]

YANG SUN: Go on talking. A voice is a voice.

SHEN TE: Once, when I was a little girl, I fell, with a load of brushwood. An old man picked me up. He gave me a penny, too. Isn't it funny how people who don't have very much like to give some of it away? They must like to show what they can do, and how could they show it better than by being kind? Being wicked is just like being clumsy. When we sing a song, or build a machine, or plant some rice, we're being kind. You're kind.

YANG SUN: You make it sound easy.

SHEN TE: Oh, no. [*little pause*] Oh! A drop of rain!

YANG SUN: Where'd you feel it?

SHEN TE: Right between the eyes.

YANG SUN: Near the right eye? Or the left?

SHEN TE: Near the left eye.

YANG SUN: Oh, good. [*he is getting sleepy*] So you're through with men, eh?

SHEN TE: [*with a smile*] But I'm not bowlegged.

YANG SUN: Perhaps not.

SHEN TE: Definitely not.
[*Pause.*]

YANG SUN: [*leaning wearily against the willow*] I haven't had a drop to drink all day, I haven't eaten anything for *two* days. I couldn't love you if I tried.
[*Pause.*]

SHEN TE: I like it in the rain.
[*Enter* WONG *the water seller, singing.*]

THE SONG OF THE WATER SELLER IN THE RAIN

> *"Buy my water," I am yelling*
> *And my fury restraining*
> *For no water I'm selling*
> *'Cause it's raining, 'cause it's raining!*
> *   I keep yelling: "Buy my water!"*
> *   But no one's buying*
> *   Athirst and dying*
> *   And drinking and paying!*
> *   Buy water!*
> *   Buy water, you dogs!*
>
> *Nice to dream of lovely weather!*
> *Think of all the consternation*

> *Were there no precipitation*
> *Half a dozen years together!*
> > *Can't you hear them shrieking: "Water!"*
> > *Pretending they adore me?*
> > *They all would go down on their knees before me!*
> > *Down on your knees!*
> > *Go down on your knees, you dogs!*
>
> *What are lawns and hedges thinking?*
> *What are fields and forests saying?*
> *"At the cloud's breast we are drinking!*
> *And we've no idea who's paying!"*
> > *I keep yelling: "Buy my water!"*
> > *But no one's buying*
> > *Athirst and dying*
> > *And drinking and paying!*
> > *Buy water*
> > *Buy water, you dogs!*

[*The rain has stopped now.* SHEN TE *sees* WONG *and runs toward him.*]

SHEN TE: Wong! You're back! Your carrying pole's at the shop.

WONG: Oh, thank you, Shen Te. And how is life treating *you?*

SHEN TE: I've just met a brave and clever man. And I want to buy him a cup of your water.

WONG: [*bitterly*] Throw back your head and open your mouth and you'll have all the water you need—

SHEN TE: [*tenderly*]

> *I want* your *water, Wong*
> *That water that has tired you so*
> *The water that you carried all this way*
> *The water that is hard to sell because*
> > *it's been raining.*
> *I need it for the young man over there—he's a flyer!*
> > *A flyer is a bold man:*
> > *Braving the storms*
> > *In company with the clouds*
> > *He crosses the heavens*
> > *And brings to friends in faraway lands*
> > *The friendly mail!*

[*She pays* WONG, *and runs over to* YANG SUN *with the cup. But* YANG SUN *is fast asleep.*]

SHEN TE: [*calling to* WONG, *with a laugh*] He's fallen asleep! Despair and rain and I have worn him out!

SCENE IIIa———WONG's *den.*

[*The sewer pipe is transparent, and the* GODS *again appear to* WONG *in a dream.*]

WONG: [*radiant*] I've seen her, illustrious ones! And she hasn't changed!

FIRST GOD: That's good to hear.

WONG: She loves someone.

FIRST GOD: Let's hope the experience gives her the strength to stay good!

WONG: It does. She's doing good deeds all the time.

FIRST GOD: Ah? What sort? What sort of good deeds, Wong?

WONG: Well, she has a kind word for everybody.

FIRST GOD: [*eagerly*] And then?

WONG: Hardly anyone leaves her shop without tobacco in his pocket—even if he can't pay for it.

FIRST GOD: Not bad at all. Next?

WONG: She's putting up a family of eight.

FIRST GOD: [*gleefully, to the* SECOND GOD] Eight! [*to* WONG] And that's not all, of course!

WONG: She bought a cup of water from me even though it was raining.

FIRST GOD: Yes, yes, yes, all these smaller good deeds!

WONG: Even they run into money. A little tobacco shop doesn't make so much.

FIRST GOD: [*sententiously*] A prudent gardener works miracles on the smallest plot.

WONG: She hands out rice every morning. That eats up half her earnings.

FIRST GOD: [*a little disappointed*] Well, as a beginning . . .

WONG: They call her the Angel of the Slums—whatever the carpenter may say!

FIRST GOD: What's this? A carpenter speaks ill of her?

WONG: Oh, he only says her shelves weren't paid for in full.

SECOND GOD: [*who has a bad cold and can't pronounce his* n's *and* m's] What's this? Not paying a carpenter? Why was that?

WONG: I suppose she didn't have the money.

SECOND GOD: [*severely*] One pays what one owes, that's in our book of rules! First the letter of the law, then the spirit.

WONG: But it wasn't Shen Te, illustrious ones, it was her cousin. She called *him* in to help.

SECOND GOD: Then her cousin must never darken her threshold again!

WONG: Very well, illustrious ones! But in fairness to Shen Te, let me say that her cousin is a businessman.

FIRST GOD: Perhaps we should inquire what is customary? I find business quite unintelligible. But everybody's doing it. Business! Did the Seven Good Kings do business? Did King the Just sell fish?

SECOND GOD: In any case, such a thing must not occur again!

> [*The* GODS *start to leave.*]

THIRD GOD: Forgive us for taking this tone with you, Wong, we haven't been getting enough sleep. The rich recommended us to the poor, and the poor tell us they haven't enough room.

SECOND GOD: Feeble, feeble, the best of them!

FIRST GOD: No great deeds! No heroic daring!

THIRD GOD: On such a *small* scale.

SECOND GOD: Sincere, yes, but what is actually *achieved?*

> [*One can no longer hear them.*]

WONG: [*calling after them*] I've thought of something, illustrious ones: Perhaps you shouldn't ask—too—much—all—at—once!

SCENE IV———*The square in front of* SHEN TE's *tobacco shop. Besides* SHEN TE's *place, two other shops are seen: the carpet shop and a barber's. Morning.*

> [*Outside* SHEN TE's *the* GRANDFATHER, *the* SISTER-IN-LAW, *the* UNEM-PLOYED MAN, *and* MRS. SHIN *stand waiting.*]

SISTER-IN-LAW: She's been out all night again.

MRS. SHIN: No sooner did we get rid of that crazy cousin of hers than Shen Te herself starts carrying on! Maybe she does give us an ounce of rice now and then, but can you depend on her? Can you depend on her?

> [*Loud voices from the barber's.*]

VOICE OF SHU FU: What are you doing in my shop? Get out—at once!

VOICE OF WONG: But, sir. They all let me sell . . .

> [WONG *comes staggering out of the barber's shop pursued by* MR. SHU FU, *the barber, a fat man carrying a heavy curling iron.*]

SHU FU: Get out, I said! Pestering my customers with your slimy old water! Get out! Take your cup!

> [*He holds out the cup.* WONG *reaches out for it.* MR. SHU FU *strikes his hand with the curling iron, which is hot.* WONG *howls.*]

SHU FU: You had it coming, my man!

> [*Puffing, he returns to his shop. The* UNEMPLOYED MAN *picks up the cup and gives it to* WONG.]

UNEMPLOYED MAN: You can report that to the police.

WONG: My hand! It's smashed up!

UNEMPLOYED MAN: Any bones broken?

WONG: I can't move my fingers.

UNEMPLOYED MAN: Sit down. I'll put some water on it.

> [WONG *sits.*]

MRS. SHIN: The water won't cost you anything.

SISTER-IN-LAW: You might have got a bandage from Miss Shen Te till she took to staying out all night. It's a scandal.

MRS. SHIN: [*despondently*] If you ask me, she's forgotten we ever existed!

> [*Enter* SHEN TE *down the street, with a dish of rice.*]

SHEN TE: [*to the audience*] How wonderful to see Setzuan in the early morning! I always used to stay in bed with my dirty blanket over my head afraid to wake up. This morning I saw the newspapers being delivered by little boys, the streets being washed by strong men, and fresh vegetables coming in from the country on ox carts. It's a long walk from where Yang Sun lives, but I feel lighter at every step. They say you walk on air when you're in love, but it's even better walking on the rough earth, on the hard cement. In the early morning, the old city looks like a great heap of rubbish! Nice, though, with all its little lights. And the sky, so pink, so transparent, before the dust comes and muddies it! What a lot you miss if you never see your city rising from its slumbers like an honest old craftsman pumping his lungs full of air and reaching for his tools as the poet says! [*cheerfully, to her waiting guests*] Good morning, everyone, here's your rice! [*Distributing the rice, she comes upon* WONG.] Good morning, Wong, I'm quite lightheaded today. On my way over, I looked at myself in all the shop windows. I'd love to be beautiful.

> [*She slips into the carpet shop.* MR. SHU FU *has just emerged from his shop.*]

SHU FU: [*to the audience*] It surprises me how beautiful Miss Shen Te is looking today! I never gave her a passing thought before. But now I've been gazing upon her comely form for exactly three minutes! I begin to suspect I am in love with her. She is overpoweringly attractive! [*crossly, to* WONG] Be off with you, rascal!

> [*He returns to his shop.* SHEN TE *comes back out of the carpet shop with the* OLD MAN, *its proprietor, and his wife—whom we have already met—the* OLD WOMAN. SHEN TE *is wearing a shawl. The* OLD MAN *is holding up a looking glass for her.*]

OLD WOMAN: Isn't it lovely? We'll give you a reduction because there's a little hole in it.

SHEN TE: [*looking at another shawl on the* OLD WOMAN s *arm*] The other one's nice, too.

OLD WOMAN: [*smiling*] Too bad there's no hole in that!

SHEN TE: That's right. My shop doesn't make very much.

OLD WOMAN: And your good deeds eat it all up! Be more careful, my dear. . . .

SHEN TE: [*trying on the shawl with the hole*] Just now, I'm lightheaded! Does the color suit me?

OLD WOMAN: You'd better ask a man.

SHEN TE: [*to the* OLD MAN] Does the color suit me?

OLD MAN: You'd better ask your young friend.

SHEN TE: I'd like to have your opinion.

OLD MAN: It suits you very well. But wear it this way: the dull side out.

> [SHEN TE *pays up.*]

OLD WOMAN: If you decide you don't like it, you can exchange it. [*She pulls* SHEN TE *to one side.*] Has he got money?

SHEN TE: [*with a laugh*] Yang Sun? Oh, no.

OLD WOMAN: Then how're you going to pay your rent?

SHEN TE: I'd forgotten about that.

OLD WOMAN: And next Monday is the first of the month! Miss Shen Te, I've got something to say to you. After we [*indicating her husband*] got to know you, we had our doubts about that marriage ad. We thought it would be better if you'd let *us* help you. Out of our savings. We reckon we could lend you two hundred silver dollars. We don't need anything in writing—you could pledge us your tobacco stock.

SHEN TE: You're prepared to lend money to a person like me?

OLD WOMAN: It's folks like you that need it. We'd think twice about lending anything to your cousin.

OLD MAN: [*coming up*] All settled, my dear?

SHEN TE: I wish the gods could have heard what your wife was just saying, Mr. Ma. They're looking for good people who're happy—and helping me makes you happy because you know it was love that got me into difficulties!

> [*The* OLD COUPLE *smile knowingly at each other.*]

OLD MAN: And here's the money, Miss Shen Te.

> [*He hands her an envelope.* SHEN TE *takes it. She bows. They bow back. They return to their shop.*]

SHEN TE: [*holding up her envelope*] Look, Wong, here's six months' rent! Don't you believe in miracles now? And how do you like my new shawl?

WONG: For the young fellow I saw you with in the park?
[SHEN TE *nods.*]
MRS. SHIN: Never mind all that. It's time you took a look at his hand!
SHEN TE: Have you hurt your hand?
MRS. SHIN: That barber smashed it with his curling iron. Right in front of our eyes.
SHEN TE: [*shocked at herself*] And I never noticed! We must get you to a doctor this minute or who knows what will happen?
UNEMPLOYED MAN: It's not a doctor he should see, it's a judge. He can ask for compensation. The barber's filthy rich.
WONG: You think I have a chance?
MRS. SHIN: [*with relish*] If it's really good and smashed. But is it?
WONG: I think so. It's very swollen. Could I get a pension?
MRS. SHIN: You'd need a witness.
WONG: Well, you all saw it. You could all testify.
[*He looks around. The* UNEMPLOYED MAN, *the* GRANDFATHER, *and the* SISTER-IN-LAW *are all sitting against the wall of the shop eating rice. Their concentration on eating is complete.*]
SHEN TE: [*to* MRS. SHIN] You saw it yourself.
MRS. SHIN: I want nothing to do with the police. It's against my principles.
SHEN TE: [*to* SISTER-IN-LAW] What about you?
SISTER-IN-LAW: Me? I wasn't looking.
SHEN TE: [*to the* GRANDFATHER, *coaxingly*] Grandfather, *you'll* testify, won't you?
SISTER-IN-LAW: And a lot of good that will do. He's simple-minded.
SHEN TE: [*to the* UNEMPLOYED MAN] You seem to be the only witness left.
UNEMPLOYED MAN: My testimony would only hurt him. I've been picked up twice for begging.
SHEN TE: Your brother is assaulted, and you shut your eyes?
He is hit, cries out in pain, and you are silent?
The beast prowls, chooses, and seizes his victim, and you say:
"Because we showed no displeasure, he has spared us."
If no one present will be a witness, I will. I'll say
I saw it.
MRS. SHIN: [*solemnly*] The name for that is perjury.
WONG: I don't know if I can accept that. Though maybe I'll have to. [*looking at his hand*] Is it swollen enough, do you think? The swelling's not going down?
UNEMPLOYED MAN: No, no. The swelling's holding up well.
WONG: Yes. It's *more* swollen if anything. Maybe my wrist is broken after all. I'd better see a judge at once.
[*Holding his hand very carefully, and fixing his eyes on it, he runs off.* MRS. SHIN *goes quickly into the barber's shop.*]
UNEMPLOYED MAN: [*seeing her*] She is getting on the right side of Mr. Shu Fu.
SISTER-IN-LAW: You and I can't change the world, Shen Te.
SHEN TE: Go away! Go away, all of you!
[*The* UNEMPLOYED MAN, *the* SISTER-IN-LAW, *and the* GRANDFATHER *stalk off, eating and sulking.*]
[*To the audience:*]
They've stopped answering

They stay put
They do as they're told
They don't care
Nothing can make them look up
But the smell of food.

    [*Enter* MRS. YANG, YANG SUN's *mother, out of breath.*]

MRS. YANG: Miss Shen Te. My son has told me everything. I am Mrs. Yang, Sun's mother. Just think. He's got an offer. Of a job as a pilot. A letter has just come. From the director of the airfield in Peking!

SHEN TE: So he can fly again? Isn't that wonderful!

MRS. YANG: [*less breathlessly all the time*] They won't give him the job for nothing. They want five hundred silver dollars.

SHEN TE: We can't let money stand in his way, Mrs. Yang!

MRS. YANG: If only you could help him out!

SHEN TE: I have the shop. I can try! [*She embraces* MRS. YANG.] I happen to have two hundred with me now. Take it. [*She gives her the old couple's money.*] It was a loan but they said I could repay it with my tobacco stock.

MRS. YANG: And they were calling Sun the Dead Pilot of Setzuan! A friend in need!

SHEN TE: We must find another three hundred.

MRS. YANG: How?

SHEN TE: Let me think. [*slowly*] I know someone who can help. I didn't want to call on his services again, he's hard and cunning. But a flyer must fly. And I'll make this the last time.

    [*Distant sound of a plane.*]

MRS. YANG: If the man you mentioned can do it . . . Oh, look, there's the morning mail plane, heading for Peking!

SHEN TE: The pilot can see us, let's wave!

    [*They wave. The noise of the engine is louder.*]

MRS. YANG: You know that pilot up there?

SHEN TE: Wave, Mrs. Yang! I know the pilot who will be up there. He gave up hope. But he'll do it now. One man to raise himself above the misery, above us all.

    [*To the audience:*]
Yang Sun, my lover:
Braving the storms
In company with the clouds
Crossing the heavens
And bringing to friends in faraway lands
The friendly mail!

SCENE IVa———*In front of the inner curtain.*

    [*Enter* SHEN TE, *carrying* SHUI TA's *mask. She sings:*]

THE SONG OF DEFENSELESSNESS

       In our country
       A useful man needs luck

Only if he finds strong backers
Can he prove himself useful.
The good can't defend themselves and
Even the gods are defenseless.

Oh, why don't the gods have their own ammunition
And launch against badness their own expedition
Enthroning the good and preventing sedition
And bringing the world to a peaceful condition?

Oh, why don't the gods do the buying and selling
Injustice forbidding, starvation dispelling
Give bread to each city and joy to each dwelling?
Oh, why don't the gods do the buying and selling?
[*She puts on* SHUI TA's *mask and sings in his voice.*]
You can only help one of your luckless brothers
By trampling down a dozen others.

Why is it the gods do not feel indignation
And come down in fury to end exploitation
Defeat all defeat and forbid desperation
Refusing to tolerate such toleration?

Why is it?

SCENE V————SHEN TE's *tobacco shop.*

[*Behind the counter,* MR. SHUI TA, *reading the paper.* MRS. SHIN *is cleaning up. She talks and he takes no notice.*]

MRS. SHIN: And when certain rumors get about, what *happens* to a little place like this? It goes to pot. *I* know. So, if you want my advice, Mr. Shui Ta, find out just what has been going on between Miss Shen Te and that Yang Sun from Yellow Street. And remember: a certain interest in Miss Shen Te has been expressed by the barber next door, a man with twelve houses and only one wife, who, for that matter, is likely to drop off at any time. A certain interest has been expressed. He was even inquiring about her means and, if *that* doesn't prove a man is getting serious, what would? [*Still getting no response, she leaves with her bucket.*]

YANG SUN'S VOICE: Is that Miss Shen Te's tobacco shop?

MRS. SHIN'S VOICE: Yes, it is, but it's Mr. Shui Ta who's here today.

[SHUI TA *runs to the mirror with the short, light steps of* SHEN TE, *and is just about to start primping, when he realizes his mistake, and turns away, with a short laugh. Enter* YANG SUN. MRS. SHIN *enters behind him and slips into the back room to eavesdrop.*]

YANG SUN: I am Yang Sun. [SHUI TA *bows*] Is Shen Te in?

SHUI TA: No.

YANG SUN: I guess you know our relationship? [*He is inspecting the stock.*] Quite a place! And I thought she was just talking big. I'll be flying again, all right.

[*He takes a cigar, solicits and receives a light from* SHUI TA.] You think we can squeeze the other three hundred out of the tobacco stock?

SHUI TA: May I ask if it is your intention to sell at once?

YANG SUN: It was decent of her to come out with the two hundred, but they aren't much use with the other three hundred still missing.

SHUI TA: Shen Te was overhasty promising so much. She might have to sell the shop itself to raise it. Haste, they say, is the wind that blows the house down.

YANG SUN: Oh, she isn't a girl to keep a man waiting. For one thing or the other, if you take my meaning.

SHUI TA: I take your meaning.

YANG SUN: [*leering*] Uh, huh.

SHUI TA: Would you explain what the five hundred silver dollars are for?

YANG SUN: Want to sound me out? Very well. The director of the Peking airfield is a friend of mine from flying school. I give him five hundred: he gets me the job.

SHUI TA: The price is high.

YANG SUN: Not as these things go. He'll have to fire one of the present pilots— for negligence. Only the man he has in mind isn't negligent. Not easy, you understand. You needn't mention that part of it to Shen Te.

SHUI TA: [*looking intently at* YANG SUN] Mr. Yang Sun, you are asking my cousin to give up her possessions, leave her friends, and place her entire fate in your hands. I presume you intend to marry her?

YANG SUN: I'd be prepared to.

[*Slight pause.*]

SHUI TA: Those two hundred silver dollars would pay the rent here for six months. If you were Shen Te wouldn't you be tempted to continue in business?

YANG SUN: What? Can you imagine Yang Sun the flyer behind a counter? [*in an oily voice*] "A strong cigar or a mild one, worthy sir?" Not in this century!

SHUI TA: My cousin wishes to follow the promptings of her heart, and, from her own point of view, she may even have what is called the right to love. Accordingly, she has commissioned me to help you to this post. There is nothing here that I am not empowered to turn immediately into cash. Mrs. Mi Tzu, the landlady, will advise me about the sale.

[*Enter* MRS. MI TZU.]

MRS. MI TZU: Good morning, Mr. Shui Ta, you wish to see me about the rent? As you know it falls due the day after tomorrow.

SHUI TA: Circumstances have changed, Mrs. Mi Tzu: my cousin is getting married. Her future husband here, Mr. Yang Sun, will be taking her to Peking. I am interested in selling the tobacco stock.

MRS. MI TZU: How much are you asking, Mr. Shui Ta?

YANG SUN: Three hundred sil—

SHUI TA: Five hundred silver dollars.

MRS. MI TZU: How much did she pay for it, Mr. Shui Ta?

SHUI TA: A thousand. And very little has been sold.

MRS. MI TZU: She was robbed. But I'll make you a special offer if you'll promise to be out by the day after tomorrow. Three hundred silver dollars.

YANG SUN: [*shrugging*] Take it, man, take it.

SHUI TA: It is not enough.

YANG SUN: Why not? Why not? Certainly, it's enough.

SHUI TA: Five hundred silver dollars.

YANG SUN: But why? We only need three!

SHUI TA: [*to* MRS. MI TZU] Excuse me. [*takes* YANG SUN *on one side*] The tobacco stock is pledged to the old couple who gave my cousin the two hundred.

YANG SUN: Is it in writing?

SHUI TA: No.

YANG SUN: [*to* MRS. MI TZU] Three hundred will do.

MRS. MI TZU: Of course, I need an assurance that Miss Shen Te is not in debt.

YANG SUN: Mr. Shui Ta?

SHUI TA: She is not in debt.

YANG SUN: When can you let us have the money?

MRS. MI TZU: The day after tomorrow. And remember: I'm doing this because I have a soft spot in my heart for young lovers! [*Exit.*]

YANG SUN: [*calling after her*] Boxes, jars, and sacks—three hundred for the lot and the pain's over! [*to* SHUI TA] Where else can we raise money by the day after tomorrow?

SHUI TA: Nowhere. Haven't you enough for the trip and the first few weeks?

YANG SUN: Oh, certainly.

SHUI TA: How much, exactly.

YANG SUN: Oh, I'll dig it up, even if I have to steal it.

SHUI TA: I see.

YANG SUN: Well, don't fall off the roof. I'll get to Peking somehow.

SHUI TA: Two people can't travel for nothing.

YANG SUN: [*not giving* SHUI TA *a chance to answer*] I'm leaving *her* behind. No millstones round *my* neck!

SHUI TA: Oh.

YANG SUN: Don't look at me like that!

SHUI TA: How precisely is my cousin to live?

YANG SUN: Oh, you'll think of something.

SHUI TA: A small request, Mr. Yang Sun. Leave the two hundred silver dollars here until you can show me two tickets for Peking.

YANG SUN: You learn to mind your own business, Mr. Shui Ta.

SHUI TA: I'm afraid Miss Shen Te may not wish to sell the shop when she discovers that . . .

YANG SUN: You don't know women. She'll want to. Even then.

SHUI TA: [*a slight outburst*] She is a human being, sir! And not devoid of common sense!

YANG SUN: Shen Te is a woman: she *is* devoid of common sense. I only have to lay my hand on her shoulder, and church bells ring.

SHUI TA: [*with difficulty*] Mr. Yang Sun!

YANG SUN: Mr. Shui Whatever-it-is!

SHUI TA: My cousin is devoted to you . . . because . . .

YANG SUN: Because I have my hands on her breasts. Give me a cigar. [*He takes one for himself, stuffs a few more in his pocket, then changes his mind and takes the whole box.*] Tell her I'll marry her, then bring me the three hundred. Or let her bring it. One or the other. [*Exit.*]

MRS. SHIN: [*sticking her head out of the back room*] Well, he has your cousin under his thumb, and doesn't care if all Yellow Street knows it!

SHUI TA: [*crying out*] I've lost my shop! And he doesn't love me! [*He runs berserk through the room, repeating these lines incoherently. Then stops suddenly, and addresses* MRS. SHIN.] Mrs. Shin, you grew up in the gutter, like me. Are we lacking in hardness? I doubt it. If you steal a penny from me, I'll take you by the throat till you spit it out! You'd do the same to me. The times are bad, this city is hell, but we're like ants, we keep coming, up and up the walls, however smooth! Till bad luck comes. Being in love, for instance. One weakness is enough, and love is the deadliest.

MRS. SHIN: [*emerging from the back room*] You should have a little talk with Mr. Shu Fu, the barber. He's a real gentleman and just the thing for your cousin. [*She runs off.*]

SHUI TA: A caress becomes a stranglehold
A sigh of love turns to a cry of fear
Why are there vultures circling in the air?
A girl is going to meet her lover.
    [SHUI TA *sits down and* MR. SHU FU *enters with* MRS. SHIN.]

SHUI TA: Mr. Shu Fu?

SHU FU: Mr. Shui Ta.
    [*They both bow.*]

SHUI TA: I am told that you have expressed a certain interest in my cousin Shen Te. Let me set aside all propriety and confess: she is at this moment in grave danger.

SHU FU: Oh, dear!

SHUI TA: She has lost her shop, Mr. Shu Fu.

SHU FU: The charm of Miss Shen Te, Mr. Shui Ta, derives from the goodness, not of her shop, but of her heart. Men call her the Angel of the Slums.

SHUI TA: Yet her goodness has cost her two hundred silver dollars in a single day: we must put a stop to it.

SHU FU: Permit me to differ, Mr. Shui Ta. Let us, rather, open wide the gates to such goodness! Every morning, with pleasure tinged by affection, I watch her charitable ministrations. For they are hungry, and she giveth them to eat! Four of them, to be precise. Why only four? I ask. Why not four hundred? I hear she has been seeking shelter for the homeless. What about my humble cabins behind the cattle run? They are at her disposal. And so forth. And so on. Mr. Shui Ta, do you think Miss Shen Te could be persuaded to listen to certain ideas of mine? Ideas like these?

SHUI TA: Mr. Shu Fu, she would be honored.
    [*Enter* WONG *and the* POLICEMAN. MR. SHU FU *turns abruptly away and studies the shelves.*]

WONG: Is Miss Shen Te here?

SHUI TA: No.

WONG: I am Wong the water seller. You are Mr. Shui Ta?

SHUI TA: I am.

WONG: I am a friend of Shen Te's.

SHUI TA: An intimate friend, I hear.

WONG: [*to the* POLICEMAN] You see? [*to* SHUI TA] It's because of my hand.

POLICEMAN: He hurt his hand, sir, that's a fact.

SHUI TA: [*quickly*] You need a sling, I see. [*He takes a shawl from the back room, and throws it to* WONG.]

WONG: But that's her new shawl!

SHUI TA: She has no more use for it.

WONG: But she bought it to please someone!

SHUI TA: It happens to be no longer necessary.

WONG: [*making the sling*] She is my only witness.

POLICEMAN: Mr. Shui Ta, your cousin is supposed to have seen the barber hit the water seller with a curling iron.

SHUI TA: I'm afraid my cousin was not present at the time.

WONG: But she was, sir! Just ask her! Isn't she in?

SHUI TA: [*gravely*] Mr. Wong, my cousin has her own troubles. You wouldn't wish her to add to them by committing perjury?

WONG: But it was she that told me to go to the judge!

SHUI TA: Was the judge supposed to heal your hand?

[MR. SHU FU *turns quickly around.* SHUI TA *bows to* SHU FU, *and vice versa.*]

WONG: [*taking the sling off, and putting it back*] I see how it is.

POLICEMAN: Well, I'll be on my way. [*to* WONG] And you be careful. If Mr. Shu Fu wasn't a man who tempers justice with mercy, as the saying is, you'd be in jail for libel. Be off with you!

[*Exit* WONG, *followed by* POLICEMAN.]

SHUI TA: Profound apologies, Mr. Shu Fu.

SHU FU: Not at all, Mr. Shui Ta. [*pointing to the shawl*] The episode is over?

SHUI TA: It may take her time to recover. There are some fresh wounds.

SHU FU: We shall be discreet. Delicate. A short vacation could be arranged. . . .

SHUI TA: First, of course, you and she would have to talk things over.

SHU FU: At a small supper in a small, but high-class, restaurant.

SHUI TA: I'll go and find her. [*Exit into back room.*]

MRS. SHIN: [*sticking her head in again*] Time for congratulations, Mr. Shu Fu?

SHU FU: Ah, Mrs. Shin! Please inform Miss Shen Te's guests they may take shelter in the cabins behind the cattle run!

[MRS. SHIN *nods, grinning.*]

SHU FU: [*to the audience*] Well? What do you think of me, ladies and gentlemen? What could a man do more? Could he be less selfish? More farsighted? A small supper in a small but . . . Does that bring rather vulgar and clumsy thoughts into your mind? Ts, ts, ts. Nothing of the sort will occur. She won't even be touched. Not even accidentally while passing the salt. An exchange of ideas only. Only the flowers on the table—white chrysanthemums, by the way [*he writes down a note of this*]—yes, over the white chrysanthemums, two young souls will . . . shall I say "find each other"? We shall *not* exploit the misfortune of others. Understanding? Yes. An offer of assistance? Certainly. But quietly. Almost inaudibly. Perhaps with a single glance. A glance that could also—also mean more.

MRS. SHIN: [*coming forward*] Everything under control, Mr. Shu Fu?

SHU FU: Oh, Mrs. Shin, what do you know about this worthless rascal Yang Sun?

MRS. SHIN: Why, he's the most worthless rascal . . .

SHU FU: Is he really? You're sure? [*as she opens her mouth*] From now on, he doesn't exist! Can't be found anywhere!

> [*Enter* YANG SUN]

YANG SUN: What's been going on here?

MRS. SHIN: Shall I call Mr. Shui Ta, Mr. Shu Fu? He wouldn't want strangers in here!

SHU FU: Mr. Shui Ta is in conference with Miss Shen Te. Not to be disturbed.

YANG SUN: Shen Te here? I didn't see her come in. What kind of conference?

SHU FU: [*not letting him enter the back room*] Patience, dear sir! And if by chance I have an inkling who you are, pray take note that Miss Shen Te and I are about to announce our engagement.

YANG SUN: What?

MRS. SHIN: You didn't expect that, did you?

> [YANG SUN *is trying to push past the barber into the back room when* SHEN TE *comes out.*]

SHU FU: My dear Shen Te, ten thousand apologies! Perhaps you . . .

YANG SUN: What is it, Shen Te? Have you gone crazy?

SHEN TE: [*breathless*] My cousin and Mr. Shu Fu have come to an understanding. They wish me to hear Mr. Shu Fu's plans for helping the poor.

YANG SUN: Your cousin wants to part us.

SHEN TE: Yes.

YANG SUN: And you've agreed to it?

SHEN TE: Yes.

YANG SUN: They told you I was bad. [SHEN TE *is silent.*] And suppose I am. Does that make me need you less? I'm low, Shen Te, I have no money, I don't do the right thing but at least I put up a fight! [*He is near her now, and speaks in an undertone.*] Have you no eyes? Look at him. Have you forgotten already?

SHEN TE: No.

YANG SUN: How it was raining?

SHEN TE: No.

YANG SUN: How you cut me down from the willow tree? Bought me water? Promised me money to fly with?

SHEN TE: [*shakily*] Yang Sun, what do you want?

YANG SUN: I want you to come with me.

SHEN TE: [*in a small voice*] Forgive me, Mr. Shu Fu, I want to go with Mr. Yang Sun.

YANG SUN: We're lovers you know. Give me the key to the shop. [SHEN TE *takes the key from around her neck.* YANG SUN *puts it on the counter. To* MRS. SHIN:] Leave it under the mat when you're through. Let's go, Shen Te.

SHU FU: But this is rape! Mr. Shui Ta!

YANG SUN: [*to* SHEN TE] Tell him not to shout.

SHEN TE: Please don't shout for my cousin, Mr. Shu Fu. He doesn't agree with me, I know, but he's wrong. [*To the audience:*]

> I want to go with the man I love
> I don't want to count the cost
> I don't want to consider if it's wise
> I don't want to know if he loves me
> I want to go with the man I love.

YANG SUN: That's the spirit.
      [*And the couple leave.*]

SCENE Va——— *In front of the inner curtain.*

      [SHEN TE *in her wedding clothes, on the way to her wedding.*]
SHEN TE: Something terrible has happened. As I left the shop with Yang Sun, I
      found the old carpet dealer's wife waiting on the street, trembling all over.
      She told me her husband had taken to his bed sick with all the worry and
      excitement over the two hundred silver dollars they lent me. She said it
      would be best if I gave it back now. Of course, I had to say I would. She said
      she couldn't quite trust my cousin Shui Ta or even my fiancé Yang Sun.
      There were tears in her eyes. With my emotions in an uproar, I threw my-
      self into Yang Sun's arms, I couldn't resist him. The things he'd said to Shui
      Ta had taught Shen Te nothing. Sinking into his arms, I said to myself:

      To let no one perish, not even oneself
      To fill everyone with happiness, even oneself
      Is so good

      How could I have forgotten those two old people? Yang Sun swept me away
      like a small hurricane. But he's not a bad man, and he loves me. He'd rather
      work in the cement factory than owe his flying to a crime. Though, of
      course, flying *is* a great passion with Sun. Now, on the way to my wedding,
      I waver between fear and joy.

SCENE VI——— *The "private dining room" on the upper floor of a cheap restaurant in a
poor section of town.*

      [*With* SHEN TE: *the* GRANDFATHER, *the* SISTER-IN-LAW, *the* NIECE, MRS.
      SHIN, *the* UNEMPLOYED MAN. *In a corner, alone, a* PRIEST. *A* WAITER
      pouring wine. Downstage, YANG SUN *talking to his* MOTHER. *He wears a
      dinner jacket.*]
YANG SUN: Bad news, Mamma. She came right out and told me she can't sell the
      shop for me. Some idiot is bringing a claim because he lent her the two
      hundred she gave you.
MRS. YANG: What did you say? Of course, you can't marry her now.
YANG SUN: It's no use saying anything to *her.* I've sent for her cousin, Mr. Shui Ta.
      He said there was nothing in writing.
MRS. YANG: Good idea. I'll go and look for him. Keep an eye on things.
      [*Exit* MRS. YANG. SHEN TE *has been pouring wine.*]
SHEN TE: [*to the audience, pitcher in hand*] I wasn't mistaken in him. He's bearing
      up well. Though it must have been an awful blow—giving up flying. I do
      love him so. [*calling across the room to him*] Sun, you haven't drunk a toast
      with the bride!
YANG SUN: What do we drink to?
SHEN TE: Why, to the future!
YANG SUN: When the bridegroom's dinner jacket won't be a hired one!
SHEN TE: But when the bride's dress will still get rained on sometimes!

YANG SUN: To everything we ever wished for!

SHEN TE: May all our dreams come true!
  [*They drink.*]

YANG SUN: [*with loud conviviality*] And now, friends, before the wedding gets under way, I have to ask the bride a few questions. I've no idea what kind of wife she'll make, and it worries me. [*wheeling on* SHEN TE] For example. Can you make five cups of tea with three tea leaves?

SHEN TE: No.

YANG SUN: So I won't be getting very much tea. Can you sleep on a straw mattress the size of that book? [*He points to the large volume the* PRIEST *is reading.*]

SHEN TE: The two of us?

YANG SUN: The one of you.

SHEN TE: In that case, no.

YANG SUN: What a wife! I'm shocked!
  [*While the audience is laughing, his* MOTHER *returns. With a shrug of her shoulders, she tells* YANG SUN *the expected guest hasn't arrived. The* PRIEST *shuts the book with a bang, and makes for the door.*]

MRS. YANG: Where are *you* off to? It's only a matter of minutes.

PRIEST: [*watch in hand*] Time goes on, Mrs. Yang, and I've another wedding to attend to. Also a funeral.

MRS. YANG: [*irately*] D'you think we planned it this way? I was hoping to manage with one pitcher of wine, and we've run through two already. [*Points to empty pitcher. Loudly*] My dear Shen Te, I don't know where your cousin can be keeping himself!

SHEN TE: My cousin?!

MRS. YANG: Certainly. I'm old-fashioned enough to think such a close relative should attend the wedding.

SHEN TE: Oh, Sun, is it the three hundred silver dollars?

YANG SUN: [*not looking her in the eye*] Are you deaf? Mother says she's old-fashioned. And I say I'm considerate. We'll wait another fifteen minutes.

HUSBAND: Another fifteen minutes.

MRS. YANG: [*addressing the company*] Now you all know, don't you, that my son is getting a job as a mail pilot?

SISTER-IN-LAW: In Peking, too, isn't it?

MRS. YANG: In Peking, too! The two of us are moving to Peking!

SHEN TE: Sun, tell your mother Peking is out of the question now.

YANG SUN: Your cousin'll tell her. If he agrees. I don't agree.

SHEN TE: [*amazed, and dismayed*] Sun!

YANG SUN: I hate this godforsaken Setzuan. What people! Know what they look like when I half close my eyes? Horses! Whinnying, fretting, stamping, screwing their necks up! [*loudly*] And what is it the thunder says? They are su-per-flu-ous! [*he hammers out the syllables*] They've run their last race! They can go trample themselves to death! [*pause*] I've got to get out of here.

SHEN TE: But I've promised the money to the old couple.

YANG SUN: And since you always do the wrong thing, it's lucky your cousin's coming. Have another drink.

SHEN TE: [*quietly*] My cousin can't be coming.

YANG SUN: How d'you mean?

SHEN TE: My cousin can't be where I am.

YANG SUN: Quite a conundrum!

SHEN TE: [*desperately*] Sun, I'm the one that loves you. Not my cousin. He was thinking of the job in Peking when he promised you the old couple's money—

YANG SUN: Right. And that's why he's bringing the three hundred silver dollars. Here—to my wedding.

SHEN TE: He is not bringing the three hundred silver dollars.

YANG SUN: Huh? What makes you think that?

SHEN TE: [*looking into his eyes*] He says you only bought one ticket to Peking. [*Short pause.*]

YANG SUN: That was yesterday. [*He pulls two tickets part way out of his inside pocket, making her look under his coat.*] Two tickets. I don't want Mother to know. She'll get left behind. I sold her furniture to buy these tickets, so you see . . .

SHEN TE: But what's to become of the old couple?

YANG SUN: What's to become of me? Have another drink. Or do you believe in moderation? If I drink, I fly again. If you drink, you may learn to understand me.

SHEN TE: You want to fly. But I can't help you.

YANG SUN: "Here's a plane, my darling—but it's only got one wing!"
        [*The* WAITER *enters.*]

WAITER: Mrs. Yang!

MRS. YANG: Yes?

WAITER: Another pitcher of wine, ma'am?

MRS. YANG: We have enough, thanks. Drinking makes me sweat.

WAITER: Would you mind paying, ma'am?

MRS. YANG: [*to everyone*] Just be patient a few moments longer, everyone, Mr. Shui Ta is on his way over! [*to the* WAITER] Don't be a spoilsport.

WAITER: I can't let you leave till you've paid your bill, ma'am.

MRS. YANG: But they know me here!

WAITER: That's just it.

PRIEST: [*ponderously getting up*] I humbly take my leave. [*And he does.*]

MRS. YANG: [*to the others, desperately*] Stay where you are, everybody! The priest says he'll be back in two minutes!

YANG SUN: It's no good, Mamma. Ladies and gentlemen, Mr. Shui Ta still hasn't arrived and the priest has gone home. We won't detain you any longer.
        [*They are leaving now.*]

GRANDFATHER: [*in the doorway, having forgotten to put his glass down*] To the bride! [*He drinks, puts down the glass, and follows the others.*]
        [*Pause.*]

SHEN TE: Shall I go, too?

YANG SUN: You? Aren't you the bride? Isn't this your wedding? [*he drags her across the room, tearing her wedding dress*] If we can wait, you can wait. Mother calls me her falcon. She wants to see me in the clouds. But I think it may be St. Nevercome's Day before she'll go to the door and see my plane thunder by. [*Pause. He pretends the guests are still present.*] Why such a lull in the conversation, ladies and gentlemen? Don't you like it here? The ceremony is only slightly postponed—because an important guest is expected at any moment. Also because the bride doesn't know what love is. While we're waiting, the bridegroom will sing a little song. [*He does so:*]

THE SONG OF ST. NEVERCOME'S DAY

> *On a certain day, as is generally known,*
> *One and all will be shouting: Hooray, hooray!*
> *For the beggar maid's son has a solid-gold throne*
> *And the day is St. Nevercome's Day*
> *On St. Nevercome's, Nevercome's, Nevercome's Day*
> *He'll sit on his solid-gold throne*
>
> *Oh, hooray, hooray! That day goodness will pay!*
> *That day badness will cost you your head!*
> *And merit and money will smile and be funny*
> *While exchanging salt and bread*
> *On St. Nevercome's, Nevercome's, Nevercome's Day*
> *While exchanging salt and bread*
>
> *And the grass, oh, the grass will look down at the sky*
> *And the pebbles will roll up the stream*
> *And all men will be good without batting an eye*
> *They will make of our Earth a dream*
> *On St. Nevercome's, Nevercome's, Nevercome's Day*
> *They will make of our Earth a dream*
>
> *And as for me, that's the day I shall be*
> *A flyer and one of the best*
> *Unemployed man, you will have work to do*
> *Washerwoman, you'll get your rest*
> *On St. Nevercome's, Nevercome's, Nevercome's Day*
> *Washerwoman you'll get your rest*

MRS. YANG: It looks like he's not coming.
[*The three of them sit looking at the door.*]

SCENE VIa————WONG's *den.*

[*The sewer pipe is again transparent and again the* GODS *appear to* WONG *in a dream.*]

WONG: I'm so glad you've come, illustrious ones. It's Shen Te. She's in great trouble from following the rule about loving thy neighbor. Perhaps she's *too* good for this world!

FIRST GOD: Nonsense! You are eaten up by lice and doubts!

WONG: Forgive me, illustrious one, I only meant you might deign to intervene.

FIRST GOD: Out of the question! My colleague here intervened in some squabble or other only yesterday. [*He points to the* THIRD GOD, *who has a black eye.*] The results are before us!

WONG: She had to call on her cousin again. But not even he could help. I'm afraid the shop is done for.

THIRD GOD: [*a little concerned*] Perhaps we should help after all?

FIRST GOD: The gods help those that help themselves.

WONG: What if we *can't* help ourselves, illustrious ones?

[*Slight pause.*]

SECOND GOD: Try, anyway! Suffering ennobles!

FIRST GOD: Our faith in Shen Te is unshaken!

THIRD GOD: We certainly haven't found any *other* good people. You can see where we spend our nights from the straw on our clothes.

WONG: You might help her find her way by—

FIRST GOD: The good man finds his own way here below!

SECOND GOD: The good woman, too.

FIRST GOD: The heavier the burden, the greater her strength!

THIRD GOD: We're only onlookers, you know.

FIRST GOD: And everything will be all right in the end, O ye of little faith!

[*They are gradually disappearing through these last lines.*]

SCENE VII———*The yard behind* SHEN TE's *shop. A few articles of furniture on a cart.*

[SHEN TE *and* MRS. SHIN *are taking the washing off the line.*]

MRS. SHIN: If you ask me, you should fight tooth and nail to keep the shop.

SHEN TE: How can I? I have to sell the tobacco to pay back the two hundred silver dollars today.

MRS. SHIN: No husband, no tobacco, no house and home! What are you going to live on?

SHEN TE: I can work. I can sort tobacco.

MRS. SHIN: Hey, look. Mr. Shui Ta's trousers! He must have left here stark naked!

SHEN TE: Oh, he may have another pair, Mrs. Shin.

MRS. SHIN: But if he's gone for good as you say, why has he left his pants behind?

SHEN TE: Maybe he's thrown them away.

MRS. SHIN: Can I take them?

SHEN TE: Oh, no.

[*Enter* MR. SHU FU, *running.*]

SHU FU: Not a word! Total silence! I know all. You have sacrificed your own love and happiness so as not to hurt a dear old couple who had put their trust in you! Not in vain does this district—for all its malevolent tongues—call you the Angel of the Slums! That young man couldn't rise to your level, so you left him. And now, when I see you closing up the little shop, that veritable heaven of rest for the multitude, well, I cannot, I cannot let it pass. Morning after morning I have stood watching in the doorway not unmoved— while you graciously handed out rice to the wretched. Is that never to happen again? Is the good woman of Setzuan to disappear? If only you would allow *me* to assist you! Now don't say anything! No assurances, no exclamations of gratitude! [*He has taken out his checkbook.*] Here! A blank check. [*He places it on the cart.*] Just my signature. Fill it out as you wish. Any sum in the world. I herewith retire from the scene, quietly, unobtrusively, making no claims, on tiptoe, full of veneration, absolutely selflessly . . . [*He has gone.*]

MRS. SHIN: Well! You're saved. There's always some idiot of a man. . . . Now hurry! Put down a thousand silver dollars and let me fly to the bank before he comes to his senses.

SHEN TE: I can pay you for the washing without any check.

MRS. SHIN: What? You're not going to cash it just because you might have to marry him? Are you crazy? Men like him *want* to be led by the nose! Are you still thinking of that flyer? All Yellow Street knows how he treated you!

SHEN TE: When I heard his cunning laugh, I was afraid
But when I saw the holes in his shoes, I loved him dearly.

MRS. SHIN: Defending that good-for-nothing after all that's happened!

SHEN TE: [*staggering as she holds some of the washing*] Oh!

MRS. SHIN: [*taking the washing from her, dryly*] So you feel dizzy when you stretch and bend? There couldn't be a little visitor on the way? If that's it, you can forget Mr. Shu Fu's blank check: it wasn't meant for a christening present!

[*She goes to the back with a basket.* SHEN TE's *eyes follow* MRS. SHIN *for a moment. Then she looks down at her own body, feels her stomach, and a great joy comes into her eyes.*]

SHEN TE: O joy! A new human being is on the way. The world awaits him. In the cities the people say: he's got to be reckoned with, this new human being! [*She imagines a little boy to be present, and introduces him to the audience.*] This is my son, the well-known flyer!
Say: "Welcome"
To the conqueror of unknown mountains and unreachable regions
Who brings us our mail across the impassable deserts!

[*She leads him up and down by the hand.*]

Take a look at the world, my son. That's a tree. Tree, yes. Say: "Hello, tree!" And bow. Like this. [*She bows.*] Now you know each other. And, look, here comes the water seller. He's a friend, give him your hand. A cup of fresh water for my little son, please. Yes, it *is* a warm day. [*handing the cup*] Oh dear, a policeman, we'll have to make a circle round *him*. Perhaps we can pick a few cherries over there in the rich Mr. Pung's garden. But we mustn't be seen. You want cherries? Just like children with fathers. No, no, you can't go straight at them like that. Don't pull. We must learn to be reasonable. Well, have it your own way. [*She has let him make for the cherries.*] Can you reach? Where to put them? Your mouth is the best place. [*She tries one herself.*] Mmm, they're good. But the policeman, we must run! [*They run.*] Yes, back to the street. Calm now, so no one will notice us. [*Walking the street with her child, she sings.*]

> Once a plum—'twas in Japan—
> Made a conquest of a man
> But the man's turn soon did come
> For he gobbled up the plum

[*Enter* WONG, *with a* CHILD *by the hand. He coughs.*]

SHEN TE: Wong!

WONG: It's about the carpenter, Shen Te. He's lost his shop, and he's been drinking. His children are on the streets. This is one. Can you help?

SHEN TE: [*to the* CHILD] Come here, little man. [*Takes him down to the footlights.*

To the audience:]
You there! A man is asking you for shelter!
A man of tomorrow says: what about today?
His friend the conqueror, whom you know,
Is his advocate!
[*to* WONG] He can live in Mr. Shu Fu's cabins. I may have to go there my-
self. I'm going to have a baby. That's a secret—don't tell Yang Sun—we'd
only be in his way. Can you find the carpenter for me?

WONG: I knew you'd think of something. [*to the* CHILD] Good-bye, son, I'm going
for your father.

SHEN TE: What about your hand, Wong? I wanted to help, but my cousin . . .

WONG: Oh, I can get along with one hand, don't worry. [*He shows how he can
handle his pole with his left hand alone.*]

SHEN TE: But your right hand! Look, take this cart, sell everything that's on it,
and go to the doctor with the money . . .

WONG: She's still good. But first I'll bring the carpenter. I'll pick up the cart when
I get back. [*Exit* WONG.]

SHEN TE: [*to the* CHILD] Sit down over here, son, till your father comes. [*The*
CHILD *sits cross-legged on the ground. Enter the* HUSBAND *and* WIFE, *each dragging a large, full sack.*]

WIFE: [*furtively*] You're alone, Shen Te, dear?
[SHEN TE *nods. The* WIFE *beckons to the* NEPHEW *offstage. He comes on
with another sack.*]

WIFE: Your cousin's away? [SHEN TE *nods*] He's not coming back?

SHEN TE: No. I'm giving up the shop.

WIFE: That's why we're here. We want to know if we can leave these things in
your new home. Will you do us this favor?

SHEN TE: Why, yes, I'd be glad to.

HUSBAND: [*cryptically*] And if anyone asks about them, say they're yours.

SHEN TE: Would anyone ask?

WIFE: [*with a glance at her husband*] Oh, someone might. The police, for instance.
They don't seem to like us. Where can we put it?

SHEN TE: Well, I'd rather not get in any more trouble . . .

WIFE: Listen to her. The good woman of Setzuan!
[SHEN TE *is silent.*]

HUSBAND: There's enough tobacco in those sacks to give us a new start in life.
We could have our own tobacco factory!

SHEN TE: [*slowly*] You'll have to put them in the back room.
[*The sacks are taken offstage, while the* CHILD *is alone. Shyly glancing about
him, he goes to the garbage can, starts playing with the contents, and eating
some of the scraps. The others return.*]

WIFE: We're counting on you, Shen Te!

SHEN TE: Yes. [*She sees the* CHILD *and is shocked.*]

HUSBAND: We'll see you in Mr. Shu Fu's cabins.

NEPHEW: The day after tomorrow.

SHEN TE: Yes. Now, go. Go! I'm not feeling well.
[*Exeunt all three, virtually pushed off.*]
He is eating the refuse in the garbage can!

Only look at his little gray mouth!
[*Pause. Music.*]
As this is the world *my* son will enter
I will study to defend him.
To be good to you, my son,
I shall be a tigress to all others
If I have to.
And I shall have to.
[*She starts to go.*]
One more time, then. I hope really the last.
[*Exit* SHEN TE, *taking* SHUI TA's *trousers.* MRS. SHIN *enters and watches her with marked interest. Enter the* SISTER-IN-LAW *and the* GRAND-FATHER.]

SISTER-IN-LAW: So it's true, the shop has closed down. And the furniture's in the back yard. It's the end of the road!

MRS. SHIN: [*pompously*] The fruit of high living, selfishness, and sensuality! Down the primrose path to Mr. Shu Fu's cabins—with you!

SISTER-IN-LAW: Cabins? Rat holes! He gave them to us because his soap supplies only went moldy there!
[*Enter the* UNEMPLOYED MAN.]

UNEMPLOYED MAN: Shen Te is moving?

SISTER-IN-LAW: Yes. She was sneaking away.

MRS. SHIN: She's ashamed of herself, and no wonder!

UNEMPLOYED MAN: Tell her to call Mr. Shui Ta or she's done for this time!

SISTER-IN-LAW: Tell her to call Mr. Shui Ta or *we're* done for this time.
[*Enter* WONG *and* CARPENTER, *the latter with a* CHILD *on each hand.*]

CARPENTER: So we'll have a roof over our heads for a change!

MRS. SHIN: Roof? Whose roof?

CARPENTER: Mr. Shu Fu's cabins. And we have little Feng to thank for it. [FENG, *we find, is the name of the* CHILD *already there; his* FATHER *now takes him. To the other two:*] Bow to your little brother, you two!
[*The* CARPENTER *and the two new arrivals bow to* FENG. *Enter* SHUI TA.]

UNEMPLOYED MAN: Sst! Mr. Shui Ta!
[*Pause.*]

SHUI TA: And what is this crowd here for, may I ask?

WONG: How do you do, Mr. Shui Ta? This is the carpenter. Miss Shen Te promised him space in Mr. Shu Fu's cabins.

SHUI TA: That will not be possible.

CARPENTER: We can't go there after all?

SHUI TA: All the space is needed for other purposes.

SISTER-IN-LAW: You mean we have to get out? But we've got nowhere to go.

SHUI TA: Miss Shen Te finds it possible to provide employment. If the proposition interests you, you may stay in the cabins.

SISTER-IN-LAW: [*with distaste*] You mean *work*? Work for Miss Shen Te?

SHUI TA: Making tobacco, yes. There are three bales here already. Would you like to get them?

SISTER-IN-LAW: [*trying to bluster*] We have our own tobacco! We were in the tobacco business before you were born!

SHUI TA: [*to the* CARPENTER *and the* UNEMPLOYED MAN] You *don't* have your own
tobacco. What about you?
    [*The* CARPENTER *and the* UNEMPLOYED MAN *get the point, and go for the
sacks. Enter* MRS. MI TZU.]
MRS. MI TZU: Mr. Shui Ta? I've brought you your three hundred silver dollars.
SHUI TA: I'll sign your lease instead. I've decided not to sell.
MRS. MI TZU: What? You don't need the money for that flyer?
SHUI TA: No.
MRS. MI TZU: And you can pay six months' rent?
SHUI TA: [*takes the barber's blank check from the cart and fills it out*] Here is a check
for ten thousand silver dollars. On Mr. Shu Fu's account. Look! [*He shows
her the signature on the check.*] Your six months' rent will be in your hands by
seven this evening. And now, if you'll excuse me.
MRS. MI TZU: So it's Mr. Shu Fu now. The flyer has been given his walking pa-
pers. These modern girls! In my day they'd have said she was flighty. That
poor, deserted Mr. Yang Sun!
    [*Exit* MRS. MI TZU. *The* CARPENTER *and the* UNEMPLOYED MAN *drag the
three sacks back on the stage.*]
CARPENTER: [*to* SHUI TA] I don't know why I'm doing this for you.
SHUI TA: Perhaps your children want to eat, Mr. Carpenter.
SISTER-IN-LAW: [*catching sight of the sacks*] Was my brother-in-law here?
MRS. SHIN: Yes, he was.
SISTER-IN-LAW: I thought as much. I know those sacks! That's our tobacco!
SHUI TA: Really? I thought it came from my back room! Shall we consult the
police on the point?
SISTER-IN-LAW: [*defeated*] No.
SHUI TA: Perhaps you will show me the way to Mr. Shu Fu's cabins?
    [*Taking* FENG *by the hand,* SHUI TA *goes off, followed by the* CARPENTER
and his two older children, the SISTER-IN-LAW, *the* GRANDFATHER, *and
the* UNEMPLOYED MAN. *Each of the last three drags a sack. Enter* OLD MAN
and OLD WOMAN.]
MRS. SHIN: A pair of pants—missing from the clothesline one minute—and next
minute on the honorable backside of Mr. Shui Ta.
OLD WOMAN: We thought Miss Shen Te was here.
MRS. SHIN: [*preoccupied*] Well, she's not.
OLD MAN: There was something she was going to give us.
WONG: She was going to help me, too. [*looking at his hand*] It'll be too late soon.
But she'll be back. This cousin has never stayed long.
MRS. SHIN: [*approaching a conclusion*] No, he hasn't, has he?

SCENE VIIa———*The sewer pipe.*

    [WONG *asleep. In his dream, he tells the* GODS *his fears. The* GODS *seem tired
from all their travels. They stop for a moment and look over their shoulders
at the water seller.*]
WONG: Illustrious ones. I've been having a bad dream. Our beloved Shen Te was
in great distress in the rushes down by the river—the spot where the bodies
of suicides are washed up. She kept staggering and holding her head down

as if she was carrying something and it was dragging her down into the mud. When I called out to her, she said she had to take your book of rules to the other side, and not get it wet, or the ink would all come off. You had talked to her about the virtues, you know, the time she gave you shelter in Setzuan.

THIRD GOD: Well, but what do you suggest, my dear Wong?

WONG: Maybe a little relaxation of the rules, Benevolent One, in view of the bad times.

THIRD GOD: As for instance?

WONG: Well, um, goodwill, for instance, might do instead of love?

THIRD GOD: I'm afraid that would create new problems.

WONG: Or instead of justice, good sportsmanship?

THIRD GOD: That would only mean more work.

WONG: Instead of honor, outward propriety?

THIRD GOD: Still more work! No, no! The rules will have to stand, my dear Wong!
[*Wearily shaking their heads, all three journey on.*]

SCENE VIII———SHUI TA's *tobacco factory in* SHU FU's *cabins.*

[*Huddled together behind bars, several families, mostly women and children. Among these people the* SISTER-IN-LAW, *the* GRANDFATHER, *the* CARPENTER, *and his* THREE CHILDREN. *Enter* MRS. YANG *followed by* YANG SUN.]

MRS. YANG: [*to the audience*] There's something I just *have* to tell you: strength and wisdom are wonderful things. The strong and wise Mr. Shui Ta has transformed my son from a dissipated good-for-nothing into a model citizen. As you may have heard, Mr. Shui Ta opened a small tobacco factory near the cattle runs. It flourished. Three months ago—I shall never forget it—I asked for an appointment, and Mr. Shui Ta agreed to see us—me and my son. I can see him now as he came through the door to meet us. . . .
[*Enter* SHUI TA *from a door.*]

SHUI TA: What can I do for you, Mrs. Yang?

MRS. YANG: This morning the police came to the house. We find you've brought an action for breach of promise of marriage. In the name of Shen Te. You also claim that Sun came by two hundred silver dollars by improper means.

SHUI TA: That is correct.

MRS. YANG: Mr. Shui Ta, the money's all gone. When the Peking job didn't materialize, he ran through it all in three days. I know he's a good-for-nothing. He sold my furniture. He was moving to Peking without me. Miss Shen Te thought highly of him at one time.

SHUI TA: What do *you* say, Mr. Yang Sun?

YANG SUN: The money's gone.

SHUI TA: [*to* MRS. YANG] Mrs. Yang, in consideration of my cousin's incomprehensible weakness for your son, I am prepared to give him another chance. He can have a job—here. The two hundred silver dollars will be taken out of his wages.

YANG SUN: So it's the factory or jail?

SHUI TA: Take your choice.

YANG SUN: May I speak with Shen Te?

SHUI TA: You may not.
  [*Pause.*]
YANG SUN: [*sullenly*] Show me where to go.
MRS. YANG: Mr. Shui Ta, you are kindness itself: the gods will reward you! [*to
  YANG SUN*] And honest work will make a man of you, my boy. [YANG SUN
  follows SHUI TA *into the factory.* MRS. YANG *comes down again to the footlights.*]
  Actually, honest work didn't agree with him—at first. And he got no op-
  portunity to distinguish himself till—in the third week—when the wages
  were being paid . . .
    [SHUI TA *has a bag of money. Standing next to his foreman—the former*
    UNEMPLOYED MAN—*he counts out the wages. It is* YANG SUN'*s turn.*]
UNEMPLOYED MAN: [*reading*] Carpenter, six silver dollars. Yang Sun, six silver
  dollars.
YANG SUN: [*quietly*] Excuse me, sir. I don't think it can be more than five. May I
  see? [*He takes the foreman's list.*] It says six working days. But that's a mis-
  take, sir. I took a day off for court business. And I won't take what I haven't
  earned, however miserable the pay is!
UNEMPLOYED MAN: Yang Sun. Five silver dollars. [*to* SHUI TA] A rare case, Mr.
  Shui Ta!
SHUI TA: How is it the book says six when it should say five?
UNEMPLOYED MAN: I must've made a mistake, Mr. Shui Ta. [*with a look at* YANG
  SUN] It won't happen again.
SHUI TA: [*taking* YANG SUN *aside*] You don't hold back, do you? You give your all
  to the firm. You're even honest. Do the foreman's mistakes always favor the
  workers?
YANG SUN: He does have . . . friends.
SHUI TA: Thank you. May I offer you any little recompense?
YANG SUN: Give me a trial period of one week, and I'll prove my intelligence is
  worth more to you than my strength.
MRS. YANG: [*still down at the footlights*] Fighting words, fighting words! That
  evening, I said to Sun: "If you're a flyer, then fly, my falcon! Rise in the
  world!" And he got to be foreman. Yes, in Mr. Shui Ta's tobacco factory, he
  worked real miracles.
    [*We see* YANG SUN *with his legs apart standing behind the workers who are
    handing along a basket of raw tobacco above their heads.*]
YANG SUN: Faster! Faster! You, there, d'you think you can just stand around, now
  you're not foreman any more? It'll be your job to lead us in song. Sing!
    [UNEMPLOYED MAN *starts singing. The others join in the refrain.*]

SONG OF THE EIGHTH ELEPHANT

> *Chang had seven elephants—all much the same—*
> *But then there was Little Brother*
> *The seven, they were wild, Little Brother, he was tame*
> *And to guard them Chang chose Little Brother*
> *Run faster!*
> *Mr. Chang has a forest park*

Which must be cleared before tonight
And already it's growing dark!

When the seven elephants cleared that forest park
Mr. Chang rode high on Little Brother
While the seven toiled and moiled till dark
On his big behind sat Little Brother
Dig faster!
Mr. Chang has a forest park
Which must be cleared before tonight
And already it's growing dark!

And the seven elephants worked many an hour
Till none of them could work another
Old Chang, he looked sour, on the seven he did glower
But gave a pound of rice to Little Brother
What was that?
Mr. Chang has a forest park
Which must be cleared before tonight
And already it's growing dark!

And the seven elephants hadn't any tusks
The one that had the tusks was Little Brother
Seven are no match for one, if the one has a gun!
How old Chang did laugh at Little Brother!
Keep on digging!
Mr. Chang has a forest park
Which must be cleared before tonight
And already it's growing dark!

[*Smoking a cigar,* SHUI TA *strolls by.* YANG SUN, *laughing, has joined in the refrain of the third stanza and speeded up the tempo of the last stanza by clapping his hands.*]

MRS. YANG: And that's why I say: strength and wisdom are wonderful things. It took the strong and wise Mr. Shui Ta to bring out the best in Yang Sun. A real superior man is like a bell. If you ring it, it rings, and if you don't, it don't, as the saying is.

SCENE IX——SHEN TE's *shop, now an office with club chairs and fine carpets. It is raining.*

[SHUI TA, *now fat, is just dismissing the* OLD MAN *and* OLD WOMAN. MRS. SHIN, *in obviously new clothes, looks on, smirking.*]

SHUI TA: No! I can *not* tell you when we expect her back.

OLD WOMAN: The two hundred silver dollars came today. In an envelope. There was no letter, but it must be from Shen Te. We want to write and thank her. May we have her address?

SHUI TA: I'm afraid I haven't got it.

OLD MAN: [*pulling* OLD WOMAN'*s sleeve*] Let's be going.

OLD WOMAN: She's got to come back some time!
> [*They move off, uncertainly, worried.* SHUI TA *bows.*]

MRS. SHIN: They lost the carpet shop because they couldn't pay their taxes. The money arrived too late.

SHUI TA: They could have come to me.

MRS. SHIN: People don't like coming to you.

SHUI TA: [*sits suddenly, one hand to his head*] I'm dizzy.

MRS. SHIN: After all, you *are* in your seventh month. But old Mrs. Shin will be there in your hour of trial! [*She cackles feebly.*]

SHUI TA: [*in a stifled voice*] Can I count on that?

MRS. SHIN: We all have our price, and mine won't be too high for the great Mr. Shui Ta! [*She opens* SHUI TA'*s collar.*]

SHUI TA: It's for the child's sake. All of this.

MRS. SHIN: "All for the child," of course.

SHUI TA: I'm so fat. People must notice.

MRS. SHIN: Oh no, they think it's 'cause you're rich.

SHUI TA: [*more feelingly*] What will happen to the child?

MRS. SHIN: You ask that nine times a day. Why, it'll have the best that money can buy!

SHUI TA: He must never see Shui Ta.

MRS. SHIN: Oh, no. Always Shen Te.

SHUI TA: What about the neighbors? There are rumors, aren't there?

MRS. SHIN: As long as Mr. Shu Fu doesn't find out, there's nothing to worry about. Drink this.
> [*Enter* YANG SUN *in a smart business suit, and carrying a businessman's briefcase.* SHUI TA *is more or less in* MRS. SHIN'*s arms.*]

YANG SUN: [*surprised*] I guess I'm in the way.

SHUI TA: [*ignoring this, rises with an effort*] Till tomorrow, Mrs. Shin.
> [MRS. SHIN *leaves with a smile, putting her new gloves on.*]

YANG SUN: Gloves now! She couldn't be fleecing you? And since when did you have a private life? [*taking a paper from the briefcase*] You haven't been at your desk lately, and things are getting out of hand. The police want to close us down. They say that at the most they can only permit twice the lawful number of workers.

SHUI TA: [*evasively*] The cabins are quite good enough.

YANG SUN: For the workers maybe, not for the tobacco. They're too damp. We must take over some of Mrs. Mi Tzu's buildings.

SHUI TA: Her price is double what I can pay.

YANG SUN: Not unconditionally. If she has me to stroke her knees she'll come down.

SHUI TA: I'll never agree to that.

YANG SUN: What's wrong? Is it the rain? You get so irritable whenever it rains.

SHUI TA: Never! I will never . . .

YANG SUN: Mrs. Mi Tzu'll be here in five minutes. *You* fix it. And Shu Fu will be with her. . . . What's all that noise?
> [*During the above dialogue,* WONG *is heard offstage, calling:* "The good

Shen Te, where is she? Which of you has seen Shen Te, good people? Where is Shen Te?" *A knock. Enter* WONG.]

WONG: Mr. Shui Ta, I've come to ask when Miss Shen Te will be back, it's six months now. . . . There are rumors. People say something's happened to her.

SHUI TA: I'm busy. Come back next week.

WONG: [*excited*] In the morning there was always rice on her doorstep—for the needy. It's been there again lately!

SHUI TA: And what do people conclude from this?

WONG: That Shen Te is still in Setzuan! She's been . . . [*He breaks off.*]

SHUI TA: She's been what? Mr. Wong, if you're Shen Te's friend, talk a little less about her, that's my advice to you.

WONG: I don't want your advice! Before she disappeared, Miss Shen Te told me something very important—she's pregnant!

YANG SUN: What? What was that?

SHUI TA: [*quickly*] The man is lying.

WONG: A good woman isn't so easily forgotten, Mr. Shui Ta.

[*He leaves.* SHUI TA *goes quickly into the back room.*]

YANG SUN: [*to the audience*] Shen Te's pregnant? So that's why. Her cousin sent her away, so I wouldn't get wind of it. I have a son, a Yang appears on the scene, and what happens? Mother and child vanish into thin air! That scoundrel, that unspeakable . . . [*The sound of sobbing is heard from the back room.*] What was that? Someone sobbing? Who was it? Mr. Shui Ta the Tobacco King doesn't weep his heart out. And where does the rice come from that's on the doorstep in the morning? [SHUI TA *returns. He goes to the door and looks out into the rain.*] Where is she?

SHUI TA: Sh! It's nine o'clock. But the rain's so heavy, you can't hear a thing.

YANG SUN: What do you want to hear?

SHUI TA: The mail plane.

YANG SUN: What?!

SHUI TA: I've been told *you* wanted to fly at one time. Is that all forgotten?

YANG SUN: Flying mail is night work. I prefer the daytime. And the firm is very dear to me—after all, it belongs to my ex-fiancée, even if she's not around. And she's not, is she?

SHUI TA: What do you mean by that?

YANG SUN: Oh, well, let's say I haven't altogether—lost interest.

SHUI TA: My cousin might like to know that.

YANG SUN: I might not be indifferent—if I found she was being kept under lock and key.

SHUI TA: By whom?

YANG SUN: By you.

SHUI TA: What could you do about it?

YANG SUN: I could submit for discussion—my position in the firm.

SHUI TA: You are now my manager. In return for a more . . . appropriate position, you might agree to drop the inquiry into your ex-fiancée's whereabouts?

YANG SUN: I might.

SHUI TA: What position *would* be more appropriate?

YANG SUN: The one at the top.

SHUI TA: My own? [*silence*] And if I preferred to throw you out on your neck?

YANG SUN: I'd come back on my feet. With suitable escort.

SHUI TA: The police?

YANG SUN: The police.

SHUI TA: And when the police found no one?

YANG SUN: I might ask them not to overlook the back room. [*ending the pretense*] In short, Mr. Shui Ta, my interest in this young woman has not been officially terminated. I should like to see more of her. [*into* SHUI TA's *face*] Besides, she's pregnant and needs a friend. [*He moves to the door.*] I shall talk about it with the water seller.

> [*Exit.* SHUI TA *is rigid for a moment, then he quickly goes into the back room. He returns with* SHEN TE's *belongings: underwear, etc. He takes a long look at the shawl of the previous scene. He then wraps the things in a bundle, which, upon hearing a noise, he hides under the table. Enter* MRS. MI TZU *and* MR. SHU FU. *They put away their umbrellas and galoshes.*]

MRS. MI TZU: I thought your manager was here, Mr. Shui Ta. He combines charm with business in a way that can only be to the advantage of all of us.

SHU FU: You sent for us, Mr. Shui Ta?

SHUI TA: The factory is in trouble.

SHU FU: It always is.

SHUI TA: The police are threatening to close us down unless I can show that the extension of our facilities is imminent.

SHU FU: Shui Ta, I'm sick and tired of your constantly expanding projects. I place cabins at your cousin's disposal; you make a factory of them. I hand your cousin a check; you present it. Your cousin disappears; you find the cabins too small and start talking of yet more—

SHUI TA: Mr. Shu Fu, I'm authorized to inform you that Miss Shen Te's return is now imminent.

SHU FU: Imminent? It's becoming his favorite word.

MRS. MI TZU: Yes, what does it mean?

SHUI TA: Mrs. Mi Tzu, I can pay you exactly half what you asked for your buildings. Are you ready to inform the police that I am taking them over?

MRS. MI TZU: Certainly, if I can take over your manager.

SHU FU: What?

MRS. MI TZU: He's so efficient.

SHUI TA: I'm afraid I need Mr. Yang Sun.

MRS. MI TZU: So do I.

SHUI TA: He will call on you tomorrow.

SHU FU: So much the better. With Shen Te likely to turn up at any moment, the presence of that young man is hardly in good taste.

SHUI TA: So we have reached a settlement. In what was once the good Shen Te's little shop we are laying the foundation for the great Mr. Shui Ta's twelve magnificent super tobacco markets. You will bear in mind that though they call me the Tobacco King of Setzuan, it is my cousin's interests that have been served . . .

VOICES: [*off*] The police, the police! Going to the tobacco shop! Something must have happened!

> [*Enter* YANG SUN, WONG, *and the* POLICEMAN.]

POLICEMAN: Quiet there, quiet, quiet! [*They quiet down.*] I'm sorry, Mr. Shui Ta, but there's a report that you've been depriving Miss Shen Te of her freedom. Not that I believe all I hear, but the whole city's in an uproar.

SHUI TA: That's a lie.

POLICEMAN: Mr. Yang Sun has testified that he heard someone sobbing in the back room.

SHU FU: Mrs. Mi Tzu and myself will testify that no one here has been sobbing.

MRS. MI TZU: We have been quietly smoking our cigars.

POLICEMAN: Mr. Shui Ta, I'm afraid I shall have to take a look at that room. [*He does so. The room is empty.*] No one there, of course, sir.

YANG SUN: But I heard sobbing. What's that? [*He finds the clothes.*]

WONG: Those are Shen Te's things. [*to crowd*] Shen Te's clothes are here!

VOICES: [*off, in sequence*]

—Shen Te's clothes!

—They've been found under the table!

—Body of murdered girl still missing!

—Tobacco King suspected!

POLICEMAN: Mr. Shui Ta, unless you can tell us where the girl is, I'll have to ask you to come along.

SHUI TA: I do not know.

POLICEMAN: I can't say how sorry I am, Mr. Shui Ta. [*He shows him the door.*]

SHUI TA: Everything will be cleared up in no time. There are still judges in Setzuan.

YANG SUN: I heard sobbing!

SCENE IXa———WONG's *den.*

> [*For the last time, the* GODS *appear to the water seller in his dream. They have changed and show signs of a long journey, extreme fatigue, and plenty of mishaps. The* FIRST *no longer has a hat; the* THIRD *has lost a leg; all three are barefoot.*]

WONG: Illustrious ones, at last you're here. Shen Te's been gone for months and today her cousin's been arrested. They think he murdered her to get the shop. But I had a dream and in this dream Shen Te said her cousin was keeping her prisoner. You must find her for us, illustrious ones!

FIRST GOD: We've found very few good people anywhere, and even they didn't keep it up. Shen Te is still the only one that stayed good.

SECOND GOD: If she *has* stayed good.

WONG: Certainly she has. But she's vanished.

FIRST GOD: That's the last straw. All is lost!

SECOND GOD: A little moderation, dear colleague!

FIRST GOD: [*plaintively*] What's the good of moderation now? If she can't be found, we'll have to resign! The world is a terrible place! Nothing but misery, vulgarity, and waste! Even the countryside isn't what it used to be. The trees are getting their heads chopped off by telephone wires, and there's such a noise from all the gunfire, and I can't stand those heavy clouds of smoke, and—

THIRD GOD: The place is absolutely unlivable! Good intentions bring people to the brink of the abyss, and good deeds push them over the edge. I'm afraid our book of rules is destined for the scrap heap—

SECOND GOD: It's people! They're a worthless lot!

THIRD GOD: The world is too cold!

SECOND GOD: It's people! They're too weak!

FIRST GOD: Dignity, dear colleagues, dignity! Never despair! As for this world, didn't we agree that we only have to find one human being who can stand the place? Well, we found her. True, we lost her again. We must find her again, that's all. And at once!

> [*They disappear.*]

SCENE X———*Courtroom.*

> [*Groups:* SHU FU *and* MRS. MI TZU; YANG SUN *and* MRS. YANG; WONG, *the* CARPENTER, *the* GRANDFATHER, *the* NIECE, *the* OLD MAN, *the* OLD WOMAN; MRS. SHIN, *the* POLICEMAN; *the* UNEMPLOYED MAN, *the* SISTER-IN-LAW.]

OLD MAN: So much power isn't good for one man.

UNEMPLOYED MAN: And he's going to open twelve super tobacco markets!

WIFE: One of the judges is a friend of Mr. Shu Fu's.

SISTER-IN-LAW: Another one accepted a present from Mr. Shui Ta only last night. A great fat goose.

OLD WOMAN: [*to* WONG] And Shen Te is nowhere to be found.

WONG: Only the gods will ever know the truth.

POLICEMAN: Order in the court! My lords the judges!

> [*Enter the* THREE GODS *in judges' robes. We overhear their conversation as they pass along the footlights to their bench.*]

THIRD GOD: We'll never get away with it, our certificates were so badly forged.

SECOND GOD: My predecessor's "sudden indigestion" will certainly cause comment.

FIRST GOD: But he *had* just eaten a whole goose.

UNEMPLOYED MAN: Look at that! *New* judges.

WONG: New judges. And what good ones!

> [*The* THIRD GOD *hears this, and turns to smile at* WONG. *The* GODS *sit. The* FIRST GOD *beats on the bench with his gavel. The* POLICEMAN *brings in* SHUI TA, *who walks with lordly steps. He is whistled at.*]

POLICEMAN: [*to* SHUI TA] Be prepared for a surprise. The judges have been changed.

> [SHUI TA *turns quickly round, looks at them, and staggers.*]

NIECE: What's the matter now?

WIFE: The great Tobacco King nearly fainted.

HUSBAND: Yes, as soon as he saw the new judges.

WONG: Does he know who they are?

> [SHUI TA *picks himself up, and the proceedings open.*]

FIRST GOD: Defendant Shui Ta, you are accused of doing away with your cousin Shen Te in order to take possession of her business. Do you plead guilty or not guilty?

SHUI TA: Not guilty, my lord.

FIRST GOD: [*thumbing through the documents of the case*] The first witness is the policeman. I shall ask him to tell us something of the respective reputations of Miss Shen Te and Mr. Shui Ta.

POLICEMAN: Miss Shen Te was a young lady who aimed to please, my lord. She liked to live and let live, as the saying goes. Mr. Shui Ta, on the other hand, is a man of principle. Though the generosity of Miss Shen Te forced him at times to abandon half measures, unlike the girl he was always on the side of the law, my lord. One time, he even unmasked a gang of thieves to whom his too-trustful cousin had given shelter. The evidence, in short, my lord, proves that Mr. Shui Ta was *incapable* of the crime of which he stands accused!

FIRST GOD: I see. And are there others who could testify along, shall we say, the same lines?

[SHU FU *rises.*]

POLICEMAN: [*whispering to* GODS] Mr. Shu Fu—a very important person.

FIRST GOD: [*inviting him to speak*] Mr. Shu Fu!

SHU FU: Mr. Shui Ta is a businessman, my lord. Need I say more?

FIRST GOD: Yes.

SHU FU: Very well, I will. He is Vice President of the Council of Commerce and is about to be elected a Justice of the Peace. [*He returns to his seat.*]

[MRS. MI TZU *rises.*]

WONG: Elected! *He* gave him the job!

[*With a gesture the* FIRST GOD *asks who* MRS. MI TZU *is.*]

POLICEMAN: Another very important person. Mrs. Mi Tzu.

MRS. MI TZU: My lord, as Chairman of the Committee on Social Work, I wish to call attention to just a couple of eloquent facts: Mr. Shui Ta not only has erected a model factory with model housing in our city, he is a regular contributor to our home for the disabled. [*She returns to her seat.*]

POLICEMAN: [*whispering*] And she's a great friend of the judge that ate the goose!

FIRST GOD: [*to the* POLICEMAN] Oh, thank you. What's next? [*to the Court, genially*] Oh, yes. We should find out if any of the evidence is less favorable to the defendant.

[WONG, *the* CARPENTER, *the* OLD MAN, *the* OLD WOMAN, *the* UNEMPLOYED MAN, *the* SISTER-IN-LAW, *and the* NIECE *come forward.*]

POLICEMAN: [*whispering*] Just the riffraff, my lord.

FIRST GOD: [*addressing the "riffraff"*] Well, um, riffraff—do you know anything of the defendant, Mr. Shui Ta?

WONG: Too much, my lord.

UNEMPLOYED MAN: What don't we know, my lord.

CARPENTER: He ruined us.

SISTER-IN-LAW: He's a cheat.

NIECE: Liar.

WIFE: Thief.

BOY: Blackmailer.

BROTHER: Murderer.

FIRST GOD: Thank you. We should now let the defendant state his point of view.

SHUI TA: I only came on the scene when Shen Te was in danger of losing what I had understood was a gift from the gods. Because I did the filthy jobs which someone had to do, they hate me. My activities were restricted to the minimum, my lord.

SISTER-IN-LAW: He had us arrested!

SHUI TA: Certainly. You stole from the bakery!

SISTER-IN-LAW: Such concern for the bakery! You didn't want the shop for your-self, I suppose!

SHUI TA: I didn't want the shop overrun with parasites.

SISTER-IN-LAW: We had nowhere else to go.

SHUI TA: There were too many of you.

WONG: What about this old couple. Were *they* parasites?

OLD MAN: We lost our shop because of you!

OLD WOMAN: And we gave your cousin money!

SHUI TA: My cousin's fiancé was a flyer. The money had to go to *him.*

WONG: Did you care whether he flew or not? Did you care whether she married him or not? You wanted her to marry someone else! [*He points at* SHU FU.]

SHUI TA: The flyer unexpectedly turned out to be a scoundrel.

YANG SUN: [*jumping up*] Which was the reason you made him your manager?

SHUI TA: Later on he improved.

WONG: And when he improved, you sold him to her? [*He points out* MRS. MI TZU.]

SHUI TA: She wouldn't let me have her premises unless she had him to stroke her knees!

MRS. MI TZU: What? The man's a pathological liar. [*to him*] Don't mention my property to me as long as you live! Murderer! [*She rustles off, in high dudgeon.*]

YANG SUN: [*pushing in*] My lord, I wish to speak for the defendant.

SISTER-IN-LAW: Naturally. He's your employer.

UNEMPLOYED MAN: And the worst slave driver in the country.

MRS. YANG: That's a lie! My lord, Mr. Shui Ta is a great man. He . . .

YANG SUN: He's this and he's that, but he is not a murderer, my lord. Just fifteen minutes before his arrest I heard Shen Te's voice in his own back room.

FIRST GOD: Oh? Tell us more!

YANG SUN: I heard sobbing, my lord!

FIRST GOD: But lots of women sob, we've been finding.

YANG SUN: Could I fail to recognize her voice?

SHU FU: No, you made her sob so often yourself, young man!

YANG SUN: Yes. But I also made her happy. Till he [*pointing at* SHUI TA] decided to sell her to you!

SHUI TA: Because you didn't love her.

WONG: Oh, no: it was for the money, my lord!

SHUI TA: And what was the money for, my lord? For the poor! And for Shen Te so she could go on being good!

WONG: For the poor? That he sent to his sweatshops? And why didn't you let Shen Te be good when you signed the big check?

SHUI TA: For the child's sake, my lord.

CARPENTER: What about *my* children? What did he do about them?
        [SHUI TA *is silent.*]

WONG: The shop was to be a fountain of goodness. That was the gods' idea. You came and spoiled it!

SHUI TA: If I hadn't, it would have run dry!

MRS. SHIN: There's a lot in that, my lord.

WONG: What have you done with the good Shen Te, bad man? She *was* good, my
    lords, she was, I swear it! [*He raises his hand in an oath.*]
THIRD GOD: What's happened to your hand, water seller?
WONG: [*pointing to* SHUI TA] It's all his fault, my lord, *she* was going to send me to
    a doctor—[*to* SHUI TA] You were her worst enemy!
SHUI TA: I was her only friend!
WONG: Where is she then? Tell us where your good friend is!
    [*The excitement of this exchange has run through the whole crowd.*]
ALL: Yes, where is she? Where is Shen Te? [*etc.*]
SHUI TA: Shen Te . . . had to go.
WONG: Where? Where to?
SHUI TA: I cannot tell you! I cannot tell you!
ALL: Why? Why did she have to go away? [*etc.*]
WONG: [*into the din with the first words, but talking on beyond the others*] Why not,
    why not? Why did she have to go away?
SHUI TA: [*shouting*] Because you'd all have torn her to shreds, that's why! My
    lords, I have a request. Clear the court! When only the judges remain, I will
    make a confession.
ALL: [*except* WONG, *who is silent, struck by the new turn of events*] So he's guilty?
    He's confessing! [*etc.*]
FIRST GOD: [*using the gavel*] Clear the court!
POLICEMAN: Clear the court!
WONG: Mr. Shui Ta has met his match this time.
MRS. SHIN: [*with a gesture toward the judges*] You're in for a little surprise.
    [*The court is cleared. Silence.*]
SHUI TA: Illustrious ones!
    [*The* GODS *look at each other, not quite believing their ears.*]
SHUI TA: Yes, I recognize you!
SECOND GOD: [*taking matters in hand, sternly*] What have you done with our good
    woman of Setzuan?
SHUI TA: I have a terrible confession to make: I am she! [*He takes off his mask, and
    tears away his clothes.* SHEN TE *stands there.*]
SECOND GOD: Shen Te!
SHEN TE: Shen Te, yes. Shui Ta *and* Shen Te. Both.
    Your injunction
    To be good and yet to live
    Was a thunderbolt:
    It has torn me in two
    I can't tell how it was
    But to be good to others
    And myself at the same time
    I could not do it
    Your world is not an easy one, illustrious ones!
    When we extend our hand to a beggar, he tears it off for us
    When we help the lost, we are lost ourselves
    And so
    Since not to eat is to die

Who can long refuse to be bad?
As I lay prostrate beneath the weight of good intentions
Ruin stared me in the face
It was when I was unjust that I ate good meat
And hobnobbed with the mighty
Why?
Why are bad deeds rewarded?
Good ones punished?
I enjoyed giving
I truly wished to be the Angel of the Slums
But washed by a foster mother in the water of the gutter
I developed a sharp eye
The time came when pity was a thorn in my side
And, later, when kind words turned to ashes in my mouth
And anger took over
I became a wolf
Find me guilty, then, illustrious ones,
But know:
All that I have done I did
To help my neighbor
To love my lover
And to keep my little one from want
For your great, godly deeds, I was too poor, too small.
    [*Pause.*]

FIRST GOD: [*shocked*] Don't go making yourself miserable, Shen Te! We're over-
    joyed to have found you!

SHEN TE: I'm telling you I'm the bad man who committed all those crimes!

FIRST GOD: [*using—or failing to use—his ear trumpet*] The good woman who did
    all those good deeds?

SHEN TE: Yes, but the bad man, too!

FIRST GOD: [*as if something had dawned*] Unfortunate coincidences! Heartless
    neighbors!

THIRD GOD: [*shouting in his ear*] But how is she to continue?

FIRST GOD: Continue? Well, she's a strong, healthy girl . . .

SECOND GOD: You didn't hear what she said!

FIRST GOD: I heard every word! She is confused, that's all! [*He begins to bluster.*]
    And what about this book of rules—we can't renounce our rules, can we?
    [*more quietly*] Should the world be changed? How? By whom? The world
    should *not* be changed! [*At a sign from him, the lights turn pink, and music
    plays.*][1]
    And now the hour of parting is at hand.
    Dost thou behold, Shen Te, yon fleecy cloud?
    It is our chariot. At a sign from me
    'Twill come and take us back from whence we came
    Above the azure vault and silver stars. . . .

---

[1] The rest of this scene has been adapted for the many American theatres that do not have "fly-space"
to lower things from ropes.

SHEN TE: No! Don't go, illustrious ones!

FIRST GOD: Our cloud has landed now in yonder field
From which it will transport us back to heaven.
Farewell, Shen Te, let not thy courage fail thee. . . .
[*Exeunt* GODS.]

SHEN TE: What about the old couple? They've lost their shop! What about the water seller and his hand? And I've got to defend myself against the barber, because I don't love him! And against Sun, because I do love him! How? How?
[SHEN TE's *eyes follow the* GODS *as they are imagined to step into a cloud which rises and moves forward over the orchestra and up beyond the balcony.*]

FIRST GOD: [*from on high*] We have faith in you, Shen Te!

SHEN TE: There'll be a child. And he'll have to be fed. I can't stay here. Where shall I go?

FIRST GOD: Continue to be good, good woman of Setzuan!

SHEN TE: I need my bad cousin!

FIRST GOD: But not very often!

SHEN TE: Once a week at least!

FIRST GOD: Once a month will be quite enough!

SHEN TE: [*shrieking*] No, no! Help!
[*But the cloud continues to recede as the* GODS *sing.*]

VALEDICTORY HYMN

> *What a rapture, oh, it is to know*
> *A good thing when you see it*
> *And having seen a good thing, oh,*
> *What rapture 'tis to flee it*
>
> *Be good, sweet maid of Setzuan*
> *Let Shui Ta be clever*
> *Departing, we forget the man*
> *Remember your endeavor*
>
> *Because through all the length of days*
> *Her goodness faileth never*
> *Sing hallelujah! Make Shen Te's*
> *Good name live on forever!*

SHEN TE: Help!

EPILOGUE

You're thinking, aren't you, that this is no right
Conclusion to the play you've seen tonight?[2]
After a tale, exotic, fabulous,

---

[2]*At afternoon performances:*
We quite agree, our play this afternoon
Collapsed upon us like a pricked balloon

A nasty ending was slipped up on us.
We feel deflated, too. We, too, are nettled
To see the curtain down and nothing settled.
How could a better ending be arranged?
Could one change people? Can the world be changed?
Would new gods do the trick? Will atheism?
Moral rearmament? Materialism?
It is for you to find a way, my friends,
To help good men arrive at happy ends.
You write the happy ending to the play!
There must, there must, there's got to be a way![3]

[3] When I first received the German manuscript of *Good Woman* from Brecht in 1945 it had no Epilogue. He wrote it a little later, influenced by misunderstandings of the ending in the press on the occasion of the Viennese première of the play. I believe that the Epilogue has sometimes been spoken by the actress playing Shen Te, but the actor playing Wong might be a shrewder choice, since the audience has already accepted him as a kind of chorus. On the other hand, it is not *Wong* who should deliver the Epilogue: whichever actor delivers it should drop the character he has been playing—E. B.

Tennessee Williams (1911–1983)

Cat on a Hot Tin Roof (1955)

For several years following World War II, the most successful American plays were written in a style that can be called modified realism. Tennessee Williams helped to popularize this style with *The Glass Menagerie* (1944) in which scenes and characters are called up out of the narrator-character's memory. The emphasis in this play, as in Williams' *A Streetcar Named Desire* (1949) and Arthur Miller's *Death of a Salesman* (1949), is on the psychological truth of character and situation played out in minimal and symbolic settings.

Cat on a Hot Tin Roof is in this tradition. The action, which is continuous, takes place in a bed-sitting room in a large plantation house in Mississippi. Within this restricted time and space, the characters are engulfed in mendacity—deception both of themselves and others. Two of the characters, Big Daddy and Brick, are forced to face truths that threaten the very core of their being: that Big Daddy is actually dying of cancer though he has been told he is free of it; and that Brick's friend Skipper loved him and died when Brick rejected him.

Brick's wife Maggie and his brother Gooper (along with Gooper's wife Mae) are primarily concerned with gaining control over Big Daddy's estate. Maggie, whose description of her position gives the play its title, seeks desperately to convince Brick to impregnate her because she believes a child will help overcome the doubts about Brick's reliability raised by his alcoholism. Ironically, it is a new deception, Maggie's false announcement that she is pregnant, that forces her to find the means to make Brick sleep with her (taking away his alcohol until he does so). Despite the play's denunciation of deception, the ending seems to condone Maggie's mendacity.

With its powerful psychological portraits, compelling conflicts, and its insights into a world dominated by self-interest, *Cat on a Hot Tin Roof* is an excellent example of postwar realism.

Tennessee Williams

Cat on a Hot Tin Roof

CHARACTERS

MARGARET

BRICK

MAE, *sometimes called Sister Woman*

BIG MAMA

DIXIE, *a little girl*

BIG DADDY

REVEREND TOOKER

GOOPER, *sometimes called Brother Man*

DOCTOR BAUGH, *pronounced "Baw"*

LACEY, *a Negro servant*

SOOKEY, *another*

Another little girl and two small boys

The set is the bed-sitting room of a plantation house in the Mississippi Delta. It is along an upstairs gallery that probably runs around the entire house; it has two pairs of very wide doors opening onto the gallery, showing white balustrades against a fair summer sky that fades into dusk and night during the course of the play. . . . The bathroom door, showing only pale-blue tile and silver towel racks, is in one side wall; the hall door in the opposite wall. Two articles of furniture need mention: a big double bed . . . ; and against the wall space between the two huge double doors upstage . . . a huge console combination of radio-phonograph (hi-fi with three speakers), TV set, and liquor cabinet, bearing and containing many glasses and bottles . . . . the walls below the ceiling should dissolve mysteriously into air; the set should be roofed by the sky. . . .

An evening in summer. The action is continuous, with two intermissions.

ACT ONE

At the rise of the curtain someone is taking a shower in the bathroom, the door of which is half open. A pretty young woman, with anxious lines in her face, enters the bedroom and crosses to the bathroom door.

MARGARET: [*shouting above roar of water*] One of those no-neck monsters hit me with a hot buttered biscuit so I have t' change!

> [MARGARET's *voice is both rapid and drawling. In her long speeches she has the vocal tricks of a priest delivering a liturgical chant, the lines are almost sung, always continuing a little beyond her breath so she has to gasp for another. Sometimes she intersperses the lines with a little wordless singing, such as* "DA-DA-DAAAA!"]
>
> [*Water turns off and* BRICK *calls out to her, but is still unseen. A tone of politely feigned interest, masking indifference, or worse, is characteristic of his speech with* MARGARET.]

BRICK: Wha'd you say, Maggie? Water was on s' loud I couldn't hearya. . . .

MARGARET: Well, I!—just remarked that!—one of th' no-neck monsters messed up m' lovely lace dress so I got t'—cha-a-ange. . . .

[*She opens and kicks shut drawers of the dresser.*]

BRICK: Why d'ya call Gooper's kiddies "no-neck monsters"?

MARGARET: Because they've got no necks! Isn't that a good enough reason?

BRICK: Don't they have any necks?

MARGARET: None visible. Their fat little heads are set on their fat little bodies without a bit of connection.

BRICK: That's too bad.

MARGARET: Yes, it's too bad because you can't wring their necks if they've got no necks to wring! Isn't that right, honey?

[*She steps out of her dress, stands in a slip of ivory satin and lace.*]

Yep, they're no-neck monsters, all no-neck people are monsters . . .

[*Children shriek downstairs.*]

Hear them? Hear them screaming? I don't know where their voice boxes are located since they don't have necks. I tell you I got so nervous at that table tonight I thought I would throw back my head and utter a scream you could hear across the Arkansas border an' parts of Louisiana an' Tennessee. I said to your charming sister-in-law, Mae, honey, couldn't you feed those precious little things at a separate table with an oilcloth cover? They make such a mess an' the lace cloth looks *so* pretty! She made enormous eyes at me and said, "Ohhh, noooooo! On Big Daddy's birthday? Why, he would never forgive me!" Well, I want you to know, Big Daddy hadn't been at the table two minutes with those five no-neck monsters slobbering and drooling over their food before he threw down his fork an' shouted, "Fo' God's sake, Gooper, why don't you put them pigs at a trough in th' kitchen?"—Well, I swear, I simply could have di-ieed!

Think of it, Brick, they've got five of them and number six is coming. They've brought the whole bunch down here like animals to display at a county fair. Why they have those children doin' tricks all the time! "Junior, show Big Daddy how you do this, show Big Daddy how you do that, say your little piece fo' Big Daddy, Sister. Show your dimples, Sugar. Brother, show Big Daddy how you stand on your head!"—It goes on all the time along, with constant little remarks and innuendos about the fact that you and I have not produced any children, are totally childless, and therefore totally useless!—Of course it's comical but it's also disgusting since it's so obvious what they're up to!

BRICK: [*without interest*] What are they up to, Maggie?

MARGARET: Why, you know what they're up to!

BRICK: [*appearing*] No, I don't know what they're up to.

[*He stands there in the bathroom doorway drying his hair with a towel and hanging onto the towel rack because one ankle is broken, plastered and bound. He is still slim and firm as a boy. His liquor hasn't started tearing him down outside. He has the additional charm of that cool air of detachment that people have who have given up the struggle. But now and then, when disturbed, something flashes behind it, like lightning in a fair sky, which shows that at some deeper level he is far from peaceful. Perhaps in a stronger light he would show some signs of deliquescence, but the fading, still warm, light from the gallery treats him gently.*]

MARGARET: I'll tell you what they're up to, boy of mine!—They're up to cutting you out of your father's estate, and—

[*She freezes momentarily before her next remark. Her voice drops as if it were somehow a personally embarassing admission.*]

—Now we know that Big Daddy's dyin' of—*cancer.* . . .

[*There are voices on the lawn below: long-drawn calls across distance.* MARGARET *raises her lovely bare arms and powders her armpits with a light sigh.*

[*She adjusts the angle of a magnifying mirror to straighten an eyelash, then rises fretfully saying:*]

There's so much light in the room it—

BRICK: [*softly but sharply*] Do we?

MARGARET: Do we what?

BRICK: Know Big Daddy's dyin' of cancer?

MARGARET: Got the report today.

BRICK: Oh . . .

MARGARET: [*letting down bamboo blinds which cast long, gold-fretted shadows over the room*]

Yep, got th' report just now . . . it didn't surprise me, Baby. . . .

[*Her voice has range and music; sometimes it drops low as a boy's and you have a sudden image of her playing boy's games as a child.*]

I recognized the symptoms soon's we got here last spring and I'm willin' to bet you that Brother Man and his wife were pretty sure of it, too. That more than likely explains why their usual summer migration to the coolness of the Great Smokies was passed up this summer in favor of—hustlin' down here ev'ry whipstitch with their whole screamin' tribe! And why so many allusions have been made to Rainbow Hill lately. You know what Rainbow Hill is? Place that's famous for treatin' alcoholics an' dope fiends in the movies!

BRICK: I'm not in the movies.

MARGARET: No, and you don't take dope. Otherwise you're a perfect candidate for Rainbow Hill, Baby, and that's where they aim to ship you—over my dead body! Yep, over my dead body they'll ship you there, but nothing would please them better. Then Brother Man could get a-hold of the purse strings and dole out remittances to us, maybe get power of attorney and sign checks for us and cut off our credit wherever, whenever he wanted! Son-of-a-bitch!—How'd you like that, Baby?—Well, you've been doin' just about ev'rything in your power to bring it about, you've just been doin' ev'erything you can think of to aid and abet them in this scheme of theirs! Quittin' work, devoting yourself to the occupation of drinkin'!—Breakin' your ankle last night on the high school athletic field: doin' what? Jumpin' hurdles? At two or three in the morning? Just fantastic! Got in the paper. *Clarksdale Register* carried a nice little item about it, human interest story about a well-known former athlete stagin' a one-man track meet on the Glorious Hill High School athletic field last night, but was slightly out of condition and didn't clear the first hurdle! Brother Man Gooper claims he exercised his influence t' keep it from goin' out over AP or UP or every god-dam "*P.*"

But, Brick? You still have one big advantage!

[*During the above swift flood of words,* BRICK *has reclined with contrapuntal leisure on the snowy surface of the bed and has rolled over carefully on his side or belly.*]

BRICK: [*wryly*] Did you *say* something, Maggie?

MARGARET: Big Daddy dotes on you, honey. And he can't stand Brother Man and Brother Man's wife, that monster of fertility, Mae; she's downright odious to him! Know how I know? By little expressions that flicker over his face when that woman is holding fo'th on one of her choice topics such as—how she refused twilight sleep!—when the twins were delivered! Because she feels motherhood's an experience that a woman ought to experience fully!—in order to fully appreciate the wonder and beauty of it! HAH!

[*This loud* "HAH!" *is accompanied by a violent action such as slamming a drawer shut.*]

—and how she made Brother Man come in an' stand beside her in the delivery room so he would not miss out on the "wonder and beauty" of it, either!—producin' those no-neck monsters. . . .

[*A speech of this kind would be antipathetic from almost anybody but* MARGARET; *she makes it oddly funny, because her eyes constantly twinkle and her voice shakes with laughter which is basically indulgent.*]

—Big Daddy shares my attitude toward those two! As for me, well—I give him a laugh now and then and he tolerates me. In fact!—I sometimes suspect that Big Daddy harbors a little unconscious "lech" fo' me. . . .

BRICK: What makes you think that Big Daddy has a lech for you, Maggie?

MARGARET: Way he always drops his eyes down my body when I'm talkin' to him, drops his eyes to my boobs an' licks his old chops! Ha ha!

BRICK: That kind of talk is disgusting.

MARGARET: Did anyone ever tell you that you're an ass-aching Puritan, Brick?

I think it's mighty fine that that ole fellow, on the doorstep of death, still takes in my shape with what I think is deserved appreciation!

And you wanta know something else? Big Daddy didn't know how many little Maes and Goopers had been produced! "How many kids have you got?" he asked at the table, just like Brother Man and his wife were new acquaintances to him! Big Mama said he was jokin', but that old boy wasn't jokin', Lord, no!

And when they infawmed him that they had five already and were turning out number six!—the news seemed to come as a sort of unpleasant surprise . . .

[*Children yell below.*]

Scream, monsters!

[*Turns to* BRICK *with a sudden, gay, charming smile which fades as she notices that he is not looking at her but into fading gold space with a troubled expression.*

[*It is constant rejection that makes her humor "bitchy."*]

Yes, you should of been at that supper table, Baby.

[*Whenever she calls him* "Baby" *the word is a soft caress.*]

Y'know, Big Daddy, bless his ole sweet soul, he's the dearest ole thing in the world, but he does hunch over his food as if he preferred not to notice anything else. Well, Mae an' Gooper were side by side at the table, direckly across from Big Daddy, watchin' his face like hawks while they jawed an' jabbered about the cuteness an' brilliance of th' no-neck monsters!

[*She giggles with a hand fluttering at her throat and her breast and her long throat arched.*

[*She comes downstage and re-creates the scene with voice and gesture.*]

And the no-neck monsters were ranged around the table, some in high chairs and some on th' *Books of Knowledge,* all in fancy little paper caps in honor of Big Daddy's birthday, and all through dinner, well, I want you to know that Brother Man an' his partner never once, for one moment, stopped exchanging pokes an' pinches an' kicks an' signs an' signals!—Why, they were like a couple of cardsharps fleecing a sucker.—Even Big Mama, bless her ole sweet soul, she isn't th' quickest an' brightest thing in the world, she finally noticed, at last, an' said to Gooper, "Gooper, what are you an' Mae makin' all these signs at each other about?"—I swear t' goodness, I nearly choked on my chicken!

[MARGARET, *back at the dressing table, still doesn't see* BRICK. *He is watching her with a look that is not quite definable—Amused? shocked? contemptuous?—part of those and part of something else.*]

Y'know—your brother Gooper still cherishes the illusion he took a giant step up on the social ladder when he married Miss Mae Flynn of the Memphis Flynns.

[MARGARET *moves about the room as she talks, stops before the mirror, moves on.*]

But I have a piece of Spanish news for Gooper. The Flynns never had a thing in this world but money and they lost that, they were nothing at all but fairly successful climbers. Of course, Mae Flynn came out in Memphis eight years before I made my debut in Nashville, but I had friends at Ward-Belmont who came from Memphis and they used to come to see me and I used to go to see them for Christmas and spring vacations, and so I know who rates an' who doesn't rate in Memphis society. Why, y'know ole Papa Flynn, he barely escaped doing time in the federal pen for shady manipulations on th' stock market when his chain stores crashed, and as for Mae having been a cotton carnival queen, as they remind us so often, lest we forget, well, that's one honor that I don't envy her for!—Sit on a brass throne on a tacky float an' ride down Main Street, smilin', bowin', and blowin' kisses to all the trash on the street—

[*She picks out a pair of jeweled sandals and rushes to the dressing table.*]

Why, year before last, when Susan McPheeters was singled out fo' that honor, y' know what happened to her? Y'know what happened to poor little Susie McPheeters?

BRICK: [*absently*] No. What happened to little Susie McPheeters?

MARGARET: Somebody spit tobacco juice in her face.

BRICK: [*dreamily*] Somebody spit tobacco juice in her face?

MARGARET: That's right, some old drunk leaned out of a window in the Hotel Gayoso and yelled, "Hey, Queen, hey, hey, there, Queenie!" Poor Susie looked up and flashed him a radiant smile and he shot out a squirt of tobacco juice right in poor Susie's face.

BRICK: Well, what d'you know about that.

MARGARET: [*gaily*] What do I know about it? I was there, I saw it!

BRICK: [*absently*] Must have been kind of funny.

MARGARET: Susie didn't think so. Had hysterics. Screamed like a banshee. They had to stop th' parade an' remove her from her throne an' go on with—

> [*She catches sight of him in the mirror, gasps slightly, wheels about to face him. Count ten.*]

—Why are you looking at me like that?

BRICK: [*whistling softly, now*] Like what, Maggie?

MARGARET: [*intensely, fearfully*] The way y' were looking at me just now, befo' I caught your eye in the mirror and you started t' whistle! I don't know how t' describe it but it froze my blood!—I've caught you lookin' at me like that so often lately. What are you thinkin' of when you look at me like that?

BRICK: I wasn't conscious of lookin' at you, Maggie.

MARGARET: Well, I was conscious of it! What were you thinkin'?

BRICK: I don't remember thinking of anything, Maggie.

MARGARET: Don't you think I know that—? Don't you—?—Think I know that—?

BRICK: [*coolly*] Know *what*, Maggie?

MARGARET: [*struggling for expression*] That I've gone through this—*hideous!*—*transformation*, become—*hard! Frantic!*

> [*Then she adds, almost tenderly:*]

—*cruel!!*

That's what you've been observing in me lately. How could y' help but observe it? That's all right. I'm not—thin-skinned any more, can't afford t' be thin-skinned any more.

> [*She is now recovering her power.*]

—But Brick? Brick?

BRICK: Did you say something?

MARGARET: I was *goin'* t' say something: that I get—lonely. Very!

BRICK: Ev'rybody gets that . . .

MARGARET: Living with someone you love can be lonelier—than living entirely *alone!*—if the one that y' love doesn't love you. . . .

> [*There is a pause.* BRICK *hobbles downstage and asks, without looking at her:*]

BRICK: Would you like to live alone, Maggie?

> [*Another pause: then—after she has caught a quick, hurt breath:*]

MARGARET: No!—God!—I wouldn't!

> [*Another gasping breath. She forcibly controls what must have been an impulse to cry out. We see her deliberately, very forcibly, going all the way back to the world in which you can talk about ordinary matters.*]

Did you have a nice shower?

BRICK: Uh-huh.

MARGARET: Was the water cool?

BRICK: No.

MARGARET: But it made y' feel fresh, huh?

BRICK: Fresher. . . .

MARGARET: I know something would make y' feel *much* fresher!

BRICK: What?

MARGARET: An alcohol rub. Or cologne, a rub with cologne!

BRICK: That's good after a workout but I haven't been workin' out, Maggie.

MARGARET: You've kept in good shape, though.

BRICK: [*indifferently*] You think so, Maggie?

MARGARET: I always thought drinkin' men lost their looks, but I was plainly mistaken.

BRICK: [*wryly*] Why; thanks, Maggie.

MARGARET: You're the only drinkin' man I know that it never seems t' put fat on.

BRICK: I'm gettin' softer, Maggie.

MARGARET: Well, sooner or later it's bound to soften you up. It was just beginning to soften up Skipper when—

   [*She stops short.*]

I'm sorry. I never could keep my fingers off a sore—I wish you *would* lose your looks. If you did it would make the martyrdom of Saint Maggie a little more bearable. But no such goddam luck. I actually believe you've gotten better looking since you've gone on the bottle. Yeah, a person who didn't know you would think you'd never had a tense nerve in your body or a strained muscle.

   [*There are sounds of croquet on the lawn below: the click of mallets, light voices, near and distant.*]

Of course, you always had that detached quality as if you were playing a game without much concern over whether you won or lost, and now that you've lost the game, not lost but just quit playing, you have that rare sort of charm that usually only happens in very old or hopelessly sick people, the charm of the defeated.—You look so cool, so cool, so enviably cool.

   [*Music is heard.*]

They're playing croquet. The moon has appeared and it's white, just beginning to turn a little bit yellow. . . .

   You were a wonderful lover. . . .

   Such a wonderful person to go to bed with, and I think mostly because you were really indifferent to it. Isn't that right? Never had any anxiety about it, did it naturally, easily, slowly, with absolute confidence and perfect calm, more like opening a door for a lady or seating her at a table than giving expression to any longing for her. Your indifference made you wonderful at lovemaking—*strange?*—but true. . . .

   You know, if I thought you would never, never, *never* make love to me again—I would go downstairs to the kitchen and pick out the longest and sharpest knife I could find and stick it straight into my heart, I swear that I would!

   But one thing I don't have is the charm of the defeated, my hat is still in the ring, and I am determined to win!

   [*There is the sound of croquet mallets hitting croquet balls.*]

—What is the victory of a cat on a hot tin roof?—I wish I knew. . . .

Just staying on it, I guess, as long as she can. . . .

   [*More croquet sounds.*]

Later tonight I'm going to tell you I love you an' maybe by that time you'll be drunk enough to believe me. Yes, they're playing croquet. . . .

Big Daddy is dying of cancer. . . .

What were you thinking of when I caught you looking at me like that? Were you thinking of Skipper?

[BRICK *takes up his crutch, rises.*]

Oh, excuse me, forgive me, but laws of silence don't work! No, laws of silence don't work. . . .

[BRICK *crosses to the bar, takes a quick drink, and rubs his head with a towel.*]

Laws of silence don't work. . . .

When something is festering in your memory or your imagination, laws of silence don't work, it's just like shutting a door and locking it on a house on fire in hope of forgetting that the house is burning. But not facing a fire doesn't put it out. Silence about a thing just magnifies it. It grows and festers in silence, becomes malignant. . . .

Get dressed, Brick.

[*He drops his crutch.*]

BRICK: I've dropped my crutch.

[*He has stopped rubbing his hair dry but still stands hanging onto the towel rack in a white towel-cloth robe.*]

MARGARET: Lean on me.

BRICK: No, just give me my crutch.

MARGARET: Lean on my shoulder.

BRICK: *I don't want to lean on your shoulder, I want my crutch!*

[*This is spoken like sudden lightning.*]

Are you going to give me my crutch or do I have to get down on my knees on the floor and—

MARGARET: *Here, here, take it, take it!*

[*She has thrust the crutch at him.*]

BRICK: [*hobbling out*] Thanks . . .

MARGARET: We mustn't scream at each other, the walls in this house have ears. . . .

[*He hobbles directly to liquor cabinet to get a new drink.*]

—but that's the first time I've heard you raise your voice in a long time, Brick. A crack in the wall?—Of composure?

—I think that's a good sign. . . .

A sign of nerves in a player on the defensive!

[BRICK *turns and smiles at her coolly over his fresh drink.*]

BRICK: It just hasn't happened yet, Maggie.

MARGARET: What?

BRICK: The click I get in my head when I've had enough of this stuff to make me peaceful. . . .

Will you do me a favor?

MARGARET: Maybe I will. What favor?

BRICK: Just, just keep your voice down!

MARGARET: [*in a hoarse whisper*] I'll do you that favor, I'll speak in a whisper, if not shut up completely, if *you* will do *me* a favor and make that drink your last one till after the party.

BRICK: What party?

MARGARET: Big Daddy's birthday party.

BRICK: Is this Big Daddy's birthday?

MARGARET: You know this is Big Daddy's birthday!

BRICK: No, I don't, I forgot it.

MARGARET: Well, I remembered it for you. . . .

> [*They are both speaking as breathlessly as a pair of kids after a fight, drawing deep exhausted breaths and looking at each other with faraway eyes, shaking and panting together as if they had broken apart from a violent struggle.*]

BRICK: Good for you, Maggie.

MARGARET: You just have to scribble a few lines on this card.

BRICK: You scribble something, Maggie.

MARGARET: It's got to be your handwriting; it's your present, I've given him my present; it's got to be your handwriting!

> [*The tension between them is building again, the voices becoming shrill once more.*]

BRICK: I didn't get him a present.

MARGARET: I got one for you.

BRICK: All right. You write the card, then.

MARGARET: And have him know you didn't remember his birthday?

BRICK: I didn't remember his birthday.

MARGARET: You don't have to prove you didn't!

BRICK: I don't want to fool him about it.

MARGARET: Just write "Love, Brick!" for God's—

BRICK: No.

MARGARET: You've *got* to!

BRICK: I don't have to do anything I don't want to do. You keep forgetting the conditions on which I agreed to stay on living with you.

MARGARET: [*out before she knows it*] I'm not living with you. We occupy the same cage.

BRICK: You've got to remember the conditions agreed on.

MARGARET: They're impossible conditions!

BRICK: Then why don't you—?

MARGARET: HUSH! Who is out there? Is somebody at the door?

> [*There are footsteps in hall.*]

MAE: [*outside*] May I enter a moment?

MARGARET: Oh, *you!* Sure. Come in, Mae.

> [MAE *enters bearing aloft the bow of a young lady's archery set.*]

MAE: Brick, is this thing yours?

MARGARET: Why, Sister Woman—that's my Diana Trophy. Won it at the intercollegiate archery contest on the Ole Miss campus.

MAE: It's a mighty dangerous thing to leave exposed round a house full of nawmal rid-blooded children attracted t'weapons.

MARGARET: "Nawmal rid-blooded children attracted t'weapons" ought t'be taught to keep their hands off things that don't belong to them.

MAE: Maggie, honey, if you had children of your own you'd know how funny that is. Will you please lock this up and put the key out of reach?

MARGARET: Sister Woman, nobody is plotting the destruction of your kiddies.—
Brick and I still have our special archers' license. We're goin' deer-huntin' on
Moon Lake as soon as the season starts. I love to run with dogs through
chilly woods, run, run leap over obstructions—
[*She goes into the closet carrying the bow.*]

MAE: How's the injured ankle, Brick?

BRICK: Doesn't hurt. Just itches.

MAE: Oh my! Brick—Brick, you should've been downstairs after supper! Kiddies
put on a show. Polly played the piano, Buster an' Sonny drums, an' then they
turned out the lights an' Dixie an' Trixie puhfawmed a toe dance in fairy
costume with *spahkluhs!* Big Daddy just beamed! He just beamed!

MARGARET: [*from the closet with a sharp laugh*] Oh, I bet. It breaks my heart that
we missed it!
[*She reenters.*]
But Mae? Why did y'give dawgs' names to all your kiddies?

MAE: *Dogs'* names?
[MARGARET *has made this observation as she goes to raise the bamboo
blinds, since the sunset glare has diminished. In crossing she winks at* BRICK.]

MARGARET: [*sweetly*] Dixie, Trixie, Buster, Sonny, Polly!—Sounds like four dogs
and a parrot . . . animal act in a circus!

MAE: Maggie?
[MARGARET *turns with a smile.*]
Why are you so catty?

MARGARET: 'Cause I'm a cat! But why can't *you* take a joke, Sister Woman?

MAE: Nothin' pleases me more than a joke that's funny. You know the real names
of our kiddies. Buster's real name is Robert. Sonny's real name is Saunders.
Trixie's real name is Marlene and Dixie's—
[*Someone downstairs calls for her.* "HEY, MAE!"—*She rushes to door,
saying:*]
Intermission is over!

MARGARET: [*as* MAE *closes door*] I wonder what Dixie's real name is?

BRICK: Maggie, being catty doesn't help things any . . .

MARGARET: I know! *WHY!*—Am I so catty?—'Cause I'm consumed with envy
an' eaten up with longing?—Brick, I've laid out your beautiful Shantung
silk suit from Rome and one of your monogrammed silk shirts. I'll put your
cuff links in it, those lovely star sapphires I get you to wear so rarely. . . .

BRICK: I can't get trousers on over this plaster cast.

MARGARET: Yes, you can, I'll help you.

BRICK: I'm not going to get dressed, Maggie.

MARGARET: Will you just put on a pair of white silk pajamas?

BRICK: Yes, I'll do that, Maggie.

MARGARET: *Thank* you, thank you *so much!*

BRICK: Don't mention it.

MARGARET: *Oh, Brick!* How long does it have t' go on? This punishment? Haven't
I done time enough, haven't I served my term, can't I apply for a—pardon?

BRICK: Maggie, you're spoiling my liquor. Lately your voice always sounds like
you'd been running upstairs to warn somebody that the house was on fire!

MARGARET: Well, no wonder, no wonder. Y'know what I feel like, Brick?

[*Children's and grown-ups' voices are blended, below, in a loud-but-uncertain rendition of "My Wild Irish Rose."*]
I feel all the time like a cat on a hot tin roof!

BRICK: Then jump off the roof, jump off it, cats can jump off roofs and land on their four feet uninjured!

MARGARET: Oh, yes!

BRICK: Do it!—fo' God's sake, do it . . .

MARGARET: Do what?

BRICK: Take a lover!

MARGARET: I can't see a man but you! Even with my eyes closed, I just see you! Why don't you get ugly, Brick, why don't you please get fat or ugly or something so I could stand it?
[*She rushes to hall door, opens it, listens.*]
The concert is still going on! Bravo, no-necks, bravo!
[*She slams and locks door fiercely.*]

BRICK: What did you lock the door for?

MARGARET: To give us a little privacy for a while.

BRICK: You know better, Maggie.

MARGARET: No, I don't know better. . . .
[*She rushes to gallery doors, draws the rose-silk drapes across them.*]

BRICK: Don't make a fool of yourself.

MARGARET: I don't mind makin' a fool of myself over you!

BRICK: I mind, Maggie. I feel embarrassed for you.

MARGARET: Feel embarrassed! But don't continue my torture. I can't live on and on under these circumstances.

BRICK: You agreed to—

MARGARET: I know but—

BRICK: —Accept that condition!

MARGARET: *I CAN'T! CAN'T! CAN'T!*
[*She seizes his shoulder.*]

BRICK: Let go!
[*He breaks away from her and seizes the small boudoir chair and raises it like a lion-tamer facing a big circus cat.*
[*Count five. She stares at him with her fist pressed to her mouth, then bursts into shrill, almost hysterical laughter. He remains grave for a moment, then grins and puts the chair down.*
[BIG MAMA *calls through closed door.*]

BIG MAMA: Son? Son? Son?

BRICK: What is it, Big Mama?

BIG MAMA: [*outside*] Oh, son! We got the most wonderful news about Big Daddy. I just had t' run up an' tell you right this—
[*She rattles the knob.*]
—What's this door doin', locked, faw? You all think there's robbers in the house?

MARGARET: Big Mama, Brick is dressin', he's not dressed yet.

BIG MAMA: That's all right, it won't be the first time I've seen Brick not dressed. Come on, open this door!
[MARGARET, *with a grimace, goes to unlock and open the hall door, as* BRICK

[*hobbles rapidly to the bathroom and kicks the door shut.* BIG MAMA *has disappeared from the hall.*]

MARGARET: Big Mama?

[BIG MAMA *appears through the opposite gallery doors behind* MARGARET, *huffing and puffing like an old bulldog. She is a short, stout woman; her sixty years and 170 pounds have left her somewhat breathless most of the time; she's always tensed like a boxer, or rather, a Japanese wrestler. Her "family" was maybe a little superior to* BIG DADDY'S, *but not much. She wears a black or silver lace dress and at least half a million in flashy gems. She is very sincere.*]

BIG MAMA: [*loudly, startling* MARGARET] Here—I come through Gooper's and Mae's gall'ry door. Where's Brick? *Brick*—Hurry on out of there, son, I just have a second and want to give you the news about Big Daddy.—I hate locked doors in a house. . . .

MARGARET: [*with affected lightness*] I've noticed you do, Big Mama, but people have got to have *some* moments of privacy, don't they?

BIG MAMA: No, ma'am, not in *my* house. [*without pause*] Whacha took off you' dress faw? I thought that little lace dress was so sweet on yuh, honey.

MARGARET: I thought it looked sweet on me, too, but one of m' cute little table partners used it for a napkin so—!

BIG MAMA: [*picking up stockings on floor*] What?

MARGARET: You know, Big Mama, Mae and Gooper's so touchy about those children—thanks, Big Mama . . .

[BIG MAMA *has thrust the picked-up stockings in* MARGARET's *hand with a grunt.*]

—that you just don't dare to suggest there's any room for improvement in their—

BIG MAMA: Brick, hurry out!—Shoot, Maggie, you just don't like children.

MARGARET: I do SO like children! Adore them!—well brought up!

BIG MAMA: [*gentle—loving*] Well, why don't you have some and bring them up well, then, instead of all the time pickin' on Gooper's an' Mae's?

GOOPER: [*shouting up the stairs*] Hey, hey, Big Mama, Betsy an' Hugh got to go, waitin' t' tell yuh g'by!

BIG MAMA: Tell 'em to hold their hawses, I'll be right down in a jiffy!

[*She turns to the bathroom door and calls out.*]

Son? Can you hear me in there?

[*There is a muffled answer.*]

We just got the full report from the laboratory at the Ochsner Clinic, completely negative, son, ev'rything negative, right on down the line! Nothin' a-tall's wrong with him but some little functional thing called a spastic colon. Can you hear me, son?

MARGARET: He can hear you, Big Mama.

BIG MAMA: Then why don't he say something? God Almighty, a piece of news like that should make him shout. It made *me* shout, I can tell you. I shouted and sobbed and fell right down on my knees!—Look!

[*She pulls up her skirt.*]

See the bruises where I hit my kneecaps? Took both doctors to haul me back on my feet!

[*She laughs—she always laughs like hell at herself.*]
Big Daddy was furious with me! But ain't that wonderful news?
[*Facing bathroom again, she continues:*]
After all the anxiety we been through to git a report like that on Big Daddy's birthday? Big Daddy tried to hide how much of a load that news took off his mind, but didn't fool *me.* He was mighty close to crying about it *himself!*
[*Goodbyes are shouted downstairs, and she rushes to door.*]
Hold those people down there, don't let them go!—Now, git dressed, we're all comin' up to this room fo' Big Daddy's birthday party because of your ankle.—How's his ankle, Maggie?
MARGARET: Well, he broke it, Big Mama.
BIG MAMA: I know he broke it.
[*A phone is ringing in hall. A Negro voice answers:* "Mistuh Polly's res'dence."]
I mean does it hurt him much still.
MARGARET: I'm afraid I can't give you that information, Big Mama. You'll have to ask Brick if it hurts much still or not.
SOOKEY: [*in the hall*] It's Memphis, Mizz Polly, it's Miss Sally in Memphis.
BIG MAMA: Awright, Sookey.
[BIG MAMA *rushes into the hall and is heard shouting on the phone:*]
Hello, Miss Sally. How are you, Miss Sally?—Yes, well, I was just gonna call you about it. *Shoot!*—
[*She raises her voice to a bellow.*]
Miss Sally? Don't ever call me from the Gayoso Lobby, too much talk goes on in that hotel lobby, no wonder you can't hear me! Now listen, Miss Sally. They's nothin' serious wrong with Big Daddy. We got the report just now, they's nothin' wrong but a thing called a—spastic! *SPASTIC!*—colon . . .
[*She appears at the hall door and calls to* MARGARET.]
—Maggie, come out here and talk to that fool on the phone. I'm shouted breathless!
MARGARET: [*goes out and is heard sweetly at phone*] Miss Sally? This is Brick's wife, Maggie. So nice to hear your voice. Can you hear *mine?* Well, *good!*— Big Mama just wanted you to know that they've got the report from the Ochsner Clinic and what Big Daddy has is a spastic colon. Yes. Spastic colon, Miss Sally. That's right, spastic colon. *G'bye, Miss Sally, hope I'll see you real soon!*
[*Hangs up a little before* MISS SALLY *was probably ready to terminate the talk. She returns through the hall door.*]
She heard me perfectly. I've discovered with deaf people the thing to do is not shout at them but just enunciate clearly. My rich old Aunt Cornelia was deaf as the dead but I could make her hear me just by sayin' each word slowly, distinctly, close to her ear. I read her the *Commercial Appeal* ev'ry night, read her the classified ads in it, even, she never missed a word of it. But was she a mean ole thing! Know what I got when she died? Her unexpired subscriptions to five magazines and the Book-of-the-Month Club and a LIBRARY full of ev'ry dull book ever written! All else went to her hellcat of a sister . . . meaner than she was, even!

[BIG MAMA *has been straightening things up in the room during this speech.*]

BIG MAMA: [*closing closet door on discarded clothes*] Miss Sally sure is a case! Big Daddy says she's always got her hand out fo' something. He's not mistaken. That poor ole thing always has her hand out fo' somethin'. I don't think Big Daddy gives her as much as he should.

[*Somebody shouts for her downstairs and she shouts:*]

I'm comin'!

[*She starts out. At the hall door, turns and jerks a forefinger, first toward the bathroom door, then toward the liquor cabinet, meaning: "Has Brick been drinking?"* MARGARET *pretends not to understand, cocks her head and raises her brows as if the pantomimic performance was completely mystifying to her.*

[BIG MAMA *rushes back to* MARGARET:]

Shoot! Stop playin' so dumb!—I mean has he been drinkin' that stuff much yet?

MARGARET: [*with a little laugh*] Oh! I think he had a highball after supper.

BIG MAMA: Don't laugh about it!—Some single men stop drinkin' when they git married and others start! Brick never touched liquor before he—!

MARGARET: [*crying out*] THAT'S NOT FAIR!

BIG MAMA: Fair or not fair I want to ask you a question, one question: D'you make Brick happy in bed?

MARGARET: Why don't you ask if he makes *me* happy in bed?

BIG MAMA: Because I know that—

MARGARET: *It works both ways!*

BIG MAMA: Something's not right! You're childless and my son drinks!

[*Someone has called her downstairs and she has rushed to the door on the line above. She turns at the door and points at the bed.*]

—When a marriage goes on the rocks, the rocks are *there*, right *there!*

MARGARET: *That's—*

[BIG MAMA *has swept out of the room and slammed the door.*]

—not—*fair* . . .

[MARGARET *is alone, completely alone, and she feels it. She draws in, hunches her shoulders, raises her arms with fists clenched, shuts her eyes tight as a child about to be stabbed with a vaccination needle. When she opens her eyes again, what she sees is the long oval mirror and she rushes straight to it, stares into it with a grimace and says:* "Who are you?"—*Then she crouches a little and answers herself in a different voice which is high, thin, mocking:* "I am Maggie the Cat!"—*Straightens quickly as bathroom door opens a little and* BRICK *calls out to her.*]

BRICK: Has Big Mama gone?

MARGARET: She's gone.

[*He opens the bathroom door and hobbles out, with his liquor glass now empty, straight to the liquor cabinet. He is whistling softly.* MARGARET's *head pivots on her long, slender throat to watch him.*

[*She raises a hand uncertainly to the base of her throat, as if it was difficult for her to swallow, before she speaks:*]

You know, our sex life didn't just peter out in the usual way, it was cut off short, long before the natural time for it to, and it's going to revive again, just as sudden as that. I'm confident of it. That's what I'm keeping myself attractive for. For the time when you'll see me again like other men see me. Yes, like other men see me. They still see me, Brick, and they like what they see. Uh-huh. Some of them would give their—

> Look, Brick!

> [*She stands before the long oval mirror, touches her breast and then her hips with her two hands.*]

How high my body stays on me!—Nothing has fallen on me—not a fraction. . . .

> [*Her voice is soft and trembling: a pleading child's. At this moment as he turns to glance at her—a look which is like a player passing a ball to another player, third down and goal to go—she has to capture the audience in a grip so tight that she can hold it till the first intermission without any lapse of attention.*]

Other men still want me. My face looks strained, sometimes, but I've kept my figure as well as you've kept yours, and men admire it. I still turn heads on the street. Why, last week in Memphis everywhere that I went men's eyes burned holes in my clothes, at the country club and in restaurants and department stores, there wasn't a man I met or walked by that didn't just eat me up with his eyes and turn around when I passed him and look back at me. Why, at Alice's party for her New York cousins, the best-lookin' man in the crowd—followed me upstairs and tried to force his way in the powder room with me, followed me to the door and tried to force his way in!

BRICK: Why didn't you let him, Maggie?

MARGARET: Because I'm not that common, for one thing. Not that I wasn't almost tempted to. You like to know who it was? It was Sonny Boy Maxwell, that's who!

BRICK: Oh, yeah, Sonny Boy Maxwell, he was a good end-runner but had a little injury to his back and had to quit.

MARGARET: He has no injury now and has no wife and still has a lech for me!

BRICK: I see no reason to lock him out of a powder room in that case.

MARGARET: And have someone catch me at it? I'm not that stupid. Oh, I might sometime cheat on you with someone, since you're so insultingly eager to have me do it!—But if I do, you can be damned sure it will be in a place and time where no one but me and the man could possibly know. Because I'm not going to give you any excuse to divorce me for being unfaithful or anything else. . . .

BRICK: Maggie, I wouldn't divorce you for being unfaithful or anything else. Don't you know that? Hell. I'd be relieved to know that you'd found yourself a lover.

MARGARET: Well, I'm taking no chances. No, I'd rather stay on this hot tin roof.

BRICK: A hot tin roof's 'n uncomfo'table place t' stay on. . . .

> [*He starts to whistle softly.*]

MARGARET: [*through his whistle*] Yeah, but I can stay on it just as long as I have to.

BRICK: You could leave me, Maggie.

> [*He resumes whistle. She wheels about to glare at him.*]

MARGARET: *Don't want to and will not!* Besides if I did, you don't have a cent to pay for it but what you get from Big Daddy and he's dying of cancer!

[*For the first time a realization of* BIG DADDY's *doom seems to penetrate to* BRICK's *consciousness, visibly, and he looks at* MARGARET.]

BRICK: Big Mama just said he *wasn't,* that the report was okay.

MARGARET: That's what she thinks because she got the same story that they gave Big Daddy. And was just as taken in by it as he was, poor ole things. . . .

   But tonight they're going to tell her the truth about it. When Big Daddy goes to bed, they're going to tell her that he is dying of cancer.

   [*She slams the dresser drawer.*]

—It's malignant and it's terminal.

BRICK: Does Big Daddy know it?

MARGARET: Hell, do they *ever* know it? Nobody says, "You're dying." You have to fool them. They have to fool *themselves.*

BRICK: Why?

MARGARET: *Why?* Because human beings dream of life everlasting, that's the reason! But most of them want it on earth and not in heaven.

   [*He gives a short, hard laugh at her touch of humor.*]

Well. . . . [*She touches up her mascara.*] That's how it is, anyhow. . . . [*She looks about.*] Where did I put down my cigarette? Don't want to burn up the home place, at least not with Mae and Gooper and their five monsters in it!

   [*She has found it and sucks at it greedily. Blows out smoke and continues:*]

So this is Big Daddy's last birthday. And Mae and Gooper, they know it, oh, *they* know it, all right. They got the first information from the Ochsner Clinic. That's why they rushed down here with their no-neck monsters. Because. Do you know something? Big Daddy's made no will? Big Daddy's never made out any will in his life, and so this campaign's afoot to impress him, forcibly as possible, with the fact that you drink and I've borne no children!

   [*He continues to stare at her a moment, then mutters something sharp but not audible and hobbles rather rapidly out onto the long gallery in the fading, much faded, gold light.*]

MARGARET: [*continuing her liturgical chant*] Y'know, I'm *fond* of Big Daddy, I am genuinely fond of that old man, I really *am,* you know. . . .

BRICK: [*faintly, vaguely*] Yes, I know you are. . . .

MARGARET: I've always sort of admired him in spite of his coarseness, his four-letter words, and so forth. Because Big Daddy *is* what he *is,* and he makes no bones about it. He hasn't turned gentleman farmer, he's still a Mississippi redneck, as much of a redneck as he must have been when he was just overseer here on the old Jack Straw and Peter Ochello place. But he got hold of it an' built it into th' biggest an' finest plantation in the Delta.—I've always *liked* Big Daddy. . . .

   [*She crosses to the proscenium.*]

Well, this is Big Daddy's last birthday. I'm sorry about it. But I'm facing the facts. It takes money to take care of a drinker and that's the office that I've been elected to lately.

BRICK: You don't have to take care of me.

MARGARET: Yes, I do. Two people in the same boat have got to take care of each other. At least you want money to buy more Echo Spring when this supply is exhausted, or will you be satisfied with a ten-cent beer?

Mae an' Gooper are plannin' to freeze us out of Big Daddy's estate because you drink and I'm childless. But we can defeat that plan. We're *going* to defeat that plan!

Brick, y'know, I've been so goddam disgustingly poor all my life!—That's the *truth*, Brick!

BRICK: I'm not sayin' it isn't.

MARGARET: Always had to suck up to people I couldn't stand because they had money and I was poor as Job's turkey. You don't know what that's like. Well, I'll tell you, it's like you would feel a thousand miles away from Echo Spring!—And had to get back to it on that broken ankle . . . without a crutch!

That's how it feels to be as poor as Job's turkey and have to suck up to relatives that you hated because they had money and all you had was a bunch of hand-me-down clothes and a few old moldly three-percent government bonds. My daddy loved his liquor, he fell in love with his liquor the way you've fallen in love with Echo Spring!—And my poor Mama, having to maintain some semblance of social position, to keep appearances up, on an income of one hundred and fifty dollars a month on those old government bonds!

When I came out, the year that I made my debut, I had just two evening dresses! One Mother made me from a pattern in *Vogue*, the other a hand-me-down from a snotty rich cousin I hated!

—The dress that I married you in was my grandmother's weddin' gown. . . .

So that's why I'm like a cat on a hot tin roof!

[BRICK *is still on the gallery. Someone below calls up to him in a warm Negro voice,* "Hiya, Mistuh Brick, how yuh feelin'?" BRICK *raises his liquor glass as if that answered the question.*]

MARGARET: You can be young without money, but you can't be old without it. You've got to be old *with* money because to be old without it is just too awful, you've got to be one or the other, either *young* or *with money*, you can't be old and *without* it.—That's the *truth*, Brick. . . .

[BRICK *whistles softly, vaguely.*]

Well, now I'm dressed, I'm all dressed, there's nothing else for me to do.

[*Forlornly, almost fearfully.*]

I'm dressed, all dressed, nothing else for me to do. . . .

[*She moves about restlessly, aimlessly, and speaks, as if to herself.*]

I know when I made my mistake.—What am I—? Oh!—my bracelets. . . .

[*She starts working a collection of bracelets over her hands onto her wrists, about six on each, as she talks.*]

I've thought a whole lot about it and now I know when I made my mistake. Yes, I made my mistake when I told you the truth about that thing with Skipper. Never should have confessed it, a fatal error, tellin' you about that thing with Skipper.

BRICK: Maggie, shut up about Skipper. I mean it, Maggie; you got to shut up about Skipper.

MARGARET: You ought to understand that Skipper and I—

BRICK: You don't think I'm serious, Maggie? You're fooled by the fact that I am saying this quiet? Look, Maggie. What you're doing is a dangerous thing to do. You're—you're—you're—

MARGARET: This time I'm going to finish what I have to say to you. Skipper and I made love, if love you could call it, because it made both of us feel a little bit closer to you. You see, you son of a bitch, you asked too much of people, of me, of him, of all the unlucky poor damned sons of bitches that happen to love you, and there was a whole pack of them, yes, there was a pack of them besides me and Skipper, you asked too goddam much of people that loved you, you—superior creature!—you godlike being!—And so we made love to each other to dream it was you, both of us! Yes, yes, yes! Truth, truth! What's so awful about it? I like it, I think the truth is—yeah! I shouldn't have told you. . . .

BRICK: [*holding his head unnaturally still and uptilted a bit*] It was Skipper that told me about it. Not you, Maggie.

MARGARET: I told you!

BRICK: After he told me!

MARGARET: What does it matter who—?

[BRICK *turns suddenly out upon the gallery and calls:*]

BRICK: Little girl! Hey, little girl!

LITTLE GIRL: [*at a distance*] What, Uncle Brick?

BRICK: Tell the folks to come up!—Bring everybody upstairs!

MARGARET: I can't stop myself! I'd go on telling you this in front of them all, if I had to!

BRICK: Little girl! Go on, go on, will you? Do what I told you, call them!

MARGARET: Because it's got to be told and you, you!—you never let me!

[*She sobs, then controls herself, and continues almost calmly.*]

It was one of those beautiful, ideal things they tell about in the Greek legends, it couldn't be anything else, you being you, and that's what made it so sad, that's what made it so awful, because it was love that never could be carried through to anything satisfying or even talked about plainly. Brick, I tell you, you got to believe me, Brick, I *do* understand all about it! I—I think it was—*noble!* Can't you tell I'm sincere when I say I respect it? My only point, the only point that I'm making, is life has got to be allowed to continue even after the *dream* of life is—all—over. . . .

[BRICK *is without his crutch. Leaning on furniture, he crosses to pick it up as she continues as if possessed by a will outside herself:*]

Why, I remember when we double-dated at college, Gladys Fitzgerald and I and you and Skipper, it was more like a date between you and Skipper. Gladys and I were just sort of tagging along as if it was necessary to chaperone you!—to make a good public impression—

BRICK: [*turns to face her, half lifting his crutch*] Maggie, you want me to hit you with this crutch? Don't you know I could kill you with this crutch?

MARGARET: Good Lord, man, d' you think I'd care if you did?

BRICK: One man has one great good true thing in his life. One great good thing which is true!—I had friendship with Skipper.—You are naming it dirty!

MARGARET: I'm not naming it dirty! I am naming it clean.

BRICK: Not love with you, Maggie, but friendship with Skipper was that one great true thing, and you are naming it dirty!

MARGARET: Then you haven't been listenin', not understood what I'm saying! I'm naming it so damn clean that it killed poor Skipper!—You two had something that had to be kept on ice, yes, incorruptible, yes!—and death was the only icebox where you could keep it. . . .

BRICK: I married you, Maggie. Why would I marry you, Maggie, if I was—?

MARGARET: Brick, don't brain me yet, let me finish!—I know, believe me I know, that it was only Skipper that harbored even any *unconscious* desire for anything not perfectly pure between you two!—Now let me skip a little. You married me early that summer we graduated out of Ole Miss, and we were happy, weren't we, we were blissful, yes, hit heaven together ev'ry time that we loved! But that fall you an' Skipper turned down wonderful offers of jobs in order to keep on bein' football heroes—pro football heroes. You organized the Dixie Stars that fall, so you could keep on bein' teammates forever! But somethin' was not right with it!—*Me included!*—between you. Skipper began hittin' the bottle . . . you got a spinal injury—couldn't play the Thanksgivin' game in Chicago, watched it on TV from a traction bed in Toledo. I joined Skipper. The Dixie Stars lost because poor Skipper was drunk. We drank together that night all night in the bar of the Blackstone and when cold day was comin' up over the lake an' we were comin' out drunk to take a dizzy look at it, I said, "SKIPPER! STOP LOVIN' MY HUSBAND OR TELL HIM HE'S GOT TO LET YOU ADMIT IT TO HIM!"—one way or another!

HE SLAPPED ME HARD ON THE MOUTH!—then turned and ran without stopping once, I am sure, all the way back into his room at the Blackstone. . . .

—When I came to his room that night, with a little scratch like a shy little mouse at his door, he made that pitiful, ineffectual little attempt to prove that what I had said wasn't true. . . .

[BRICK *strikes at her with crutch, a blow that shatters the gemlike lamp on the table.*]

—In this way, I destroyed him, by telling him truth that he and his world which he was born and raised in, yours and his world, had told him could not be told?

—From then on Skipper was nothing at all but a receptacle for liquor and drugs. . . .

—*Who shot Cock Robin? I with my*—

[*She throws back her head with tight shut eyes.*]

—*merciful arrow!*

[BRICK *strikes at her; misses.*]

Missed me!—Sorry,—I'm not tryin' to whitewash my behavior, Christ, no! Brick, I'm not good. I don't know why people have to pretend to be good, nobody's good. The rich or the well-to-do can afford to respect moral patterns, conventional moral patterns, but I could never afford to, yeah, but— I'm honest! Give me credit for just that, will you *please?*—Born poor, raised poor, expect to die poor unless I manage to get us something out of what

Big Daddy leaves when he dies of cancer! But Brick?!—*Skipper is dead! I'm alive!* Maggie the Cat is—

[BRICK *hops awkwardly forward and strikes at her again with his crutch.*]

—alive! I am alive, alive! I am . . .

[*He hurls the crutch at her, across the bed she took refuge behind, and pitches forward on the floor as she completes her speech.*]

—alive!

[*A little girl,* DIXIE, *bursts into the room, wearing an Indian war bonnet and firing a cap pistol at* MARGARET *and shouting:* "Bang, bang, bang!"

[*Laughter downstairs floats through the open hall door.* MARGARET *had crouched gasping to bed at child's entrance. She now rises and says with cool fury:*]

Little girl, your mother or someone should teach you—[*gasping*]—to knock at a door before you come into a room. Otherwise people might think that you—lack—good breeding. . . .

DIXIE: Yanh, yanh, yanh, what is Uncle Brick doin' on th' floor?

BRICK: I tried to kill your Aunt Maggie, but I failed—and I fell. Little girl, give me my crutch so I can get up off th' floor.

MARGARET: Yes, give your uncle his crutch, he's a cripple, honey, he broke his ankle last night jumping hurdles on the high school athletic field!

DIXIE: What were you jumping hurdles for, Uncle Brick?

BRICK: Because I used to jump them, and people like to do what they used to do, even after they've stopped being able to do it. . . .

MARGARET: That's right, that's your answer, now go away, little girl.

[DIXIE *fires cap pistol at* MARGARET *three times.*]

Stop, you stop that, monster! You little no-neck monster!

[*She seizes the cap pistol and hurls it through gallery doors.*]

DIXIE: [*with a precocious instinct for the cruelest thing*] You're *jealous!*—You're just jealous because you can't have babies!

[*She sticks out her tongue at* MARGARET *as she sashays past her with her stomach stuck out, to the gallery.* MARGARET *slams the gallery doors and leans panting against them. There is a pause.* BRICK *has replaced his spilt drink and sits, faraway, on the great four-poster bed.*]

MARGARET: You see?—they gloat over us being childless, even in front of their five little no-neck monsters!

[*Pause. Voices approach on the stairs.*]

Brick?—I've been to a doctor in Memphis, a—a gynecologist. . . .

I've been completely examined, and there is no reason why we can't have a child whenever we want one. And this is my time by the calendar to conceive. Are you listening to me? Are you? Are you LISTENING TO ME!

BRICK: Yes. I hear you, Maggie.

[*His attention returns to her inflamed face.*]

—But how in hell on Earth do you imagine—that you're going to have a child by a man that can't stand you?

MARGARET: That's a problem that I will have to work out.

[*She wheels about to face the hall door.*]

Here they come!
        [*The lights dim.*]
CURTAIN

ACT TWO

There is no lapse of time. MARGARET *and* BRICK *are in the same positions they held at the end of Act I.*

MARGARET: [*at door*]: *Here they come!*
        [BIG DADDY *appears first, a tall man with a fierce, anxious look, moving carefully not to betray his weakness even, or especially, to himself.*]
BIG DADDY: Well, Brick.
BRICK: Hello, Big Daddy.—Congratulations!
BIG DADDY: —Crap. . . .
        [*Some of the people are approaching through the hall, others along the gallery: voices from both directions.* GOOPER *and* REVEREND TOOKER *become visible outside gallery doors, and their voices come in clearly.*
        [*They pause outside as* GOOPER *lights a cigar.*]
REVEREND TOOKER: [*vivaciously*] Oh, but St. Paul's in Grenada has three memorial windows, and the latest one is a Tiffany stained-glass window that cost twenty-five hundred dollars, a picture of Christ the Good Shepherd with a Lamb in His arms.
GOOPER: Who give that window, Preach?
REVEREND TOOKER: Clyde Fletcher's widow. Also presented St. Paul's with a baptismal font.
GOOPER: Y'know what somebody ought t' give your church is a *coolin'* system, Preach.
REVEREND TOOKER: Yes, siree, Bob! And y'know what Gus Hamma's family gave in his memory to the church at Two Rivers? A complete new stone parish-house with a basketball court in the basement and a—
BIG DADDY: [*uttering a loud barking laugh, which is far from truly mirthful*] Hey, Preach! What's all this talk about memorials, Preach? Y' think somebody's about t' kick off around here? 'S that it?
        [*Startled by this interjection,* REVEREND TOOKER *decides to laugh at the question almost as loud as he can.*
        [*How he would answer the question we'll never know, as he's spared that embarrassment by the voice of* GOOPER's *wife,* MAE, *rising high and clear as she appears with* "DOC" BAUGH, *the family doctor, through the hall door.*]
MAE: [*almost religiously*]—Let's see now, they've had their *tyyy*-phoid shots, and their tetanus shots, their diphtheria shots and their hepatitis shots and their polio shots, they got *those* shots every month from May through September, and—Gooper? Hey! Gooper!—What all have the kiddies been shot faw?
MARGARET: [*overlapping a bit*] Turn on the hi-fi, Brick! Let's have some music t' start off th' party with!
        [*The talk becomes so general that the room sounds like a great aviary of chattering birds. Only* BRICK *remains unengaged, leaning upon the liquor cabinet with his faraway smile, an ice cube in a paper napkin with which*

he now and then rubs his forehead. He doesn't respond to MARGARET's *command. She bounds forward and stoops over the instrument panel of the console.*]

GOOPER: We gave 'em that thing for a third anniversary present, got three speakers in it.

[*The room is suddenly blasted by the climax of a Wagnerian opera or a Beethoven symphony.*]

BIG DADDY: *Turn that dam thing off!*

[*Almost instant silence, almost instantly broken by the shouting charge of* BIG MAMA, *entering through hall door like a charging rhino.*]

BIG MAMA: *Wha's my Brick, wha's mah precious baby!!*

BIG DADDY: *Sorry! Turn it back on!*

[*Everyone laughs very loud.* BIG DADDY *is famous for his jokes at* BIG MAMA's *expense, and nobody laughs louder at these jokes than* BIG MAMA *herself, though sometimes they're pretty cruel and* BIG MAMA *has to pick up or fuss with something to cover the hurt that the loud laugh doesn't quite cover.*

[*On this occasion, a happy occasion because the dread in her heart has also been lifted by the false report on* BIG DADDY's *condition, she giggles, grotesquely, coyly, in* BIG DADDY's *direction and bears down upon* BRICK, *all very quick and alive.*]

BIG MAMA: Here he is, here's my precious baby! What's that you've got in your hand? You put that liquor down, son, your hand was made fo' holdin' somethin' better than that!

GOOPER: Look at Brick put it down!

[BRICK *has obeyed* BIG MAMA *by draining the glass and handing it to her. Again everyone laughs, some high, some low.*]

BIG MAMA: Oh, you bad boy, you're my bad little boy. Give Big Mama a kiss, you bad boy, you!—Look at him shy away, will you? Brick never liked bein' kissed or made a fuss over, I guess because he's always had too much of it!

Son, you turn that thing off!

[BRICK *has switched on the TV set.*]

I can't stand TV, radio was bad enough but TV has gone it one better, I mean—[*plops wheezing in chair*]—one worse, ha ha! Now what'm I sittin' down here faw? I want t' sit next to my sweetheart on the sofa, hold hands with him and love him up a little!

[BIG MAMA *has on a black and white figured chiffon. The large irregular patterns, like the markings of some massive animal, the luster of her great diamonds and many pearls, the brilliants set in the silver frames of her glasses, her riotous voice, booming laugh, have dominated the room since she entered.* BIG DADDY *has been regarding her with a steady grimace of chronic annoyance.*]

BIG MAMA: [*still louder*] Preacher, Preacher, hey, Preach! Give me you' hand an' help me up from this chair!

REVEREND TOOKER: None of your tricks, Big Mama!

BIG MAMA: What tricks? You give me you' hand so I can get up an'—

[REVEREND TOOKER *extends her his hand. She grabs it and pulls him into her lap with a shrill laugh that spans an octave in two notes.*]

Ever seen a preacher in a fat lady's lap? Hey, hey, folks! Ever seen a preacher in a fat lady's lap?

[BIG MAMA *is notorious throughout the Delta for this sort of inelegant horseplay.* MARGARET *looks on with indulgent humor, sipping Dubonnet "on the rocks" and watching* BRICK, *but* MAE *and* GOOPER *exchange signs of humorless anxiety over these antics, the sort of behavior which* MAE *thinks may account for their failure to quite get in with the smartest young married set in Memphis, despite all. One of the negroes,* LACY *or* SOOKEY, *peeks in, cackling. They are waiting for a sign to bring in the cake and champagne. But* BIG DADDY's *not amused. He doesn't understand why, in spite of the infinite mental relief he's received from the doctor's report, he still has these same old fox teeth in his guts.* "This spastic thing sure is something," *he says to himself, but aloud he roars at* BIG MAMA:]

BIG DADDY: *BIG MAMA, WILL YOU QUIT HORSIN'?*—You're too old an' too fat fo' that sort of crazy kid stuff an' besides a woman with your blood pressure—she had two hundred last spring!—is riskin' a stroke when you mess around like that. . . .

BIG MAMA: *Here comes Big Daddy's birthday!*

[*Negroes in white jackets enter with an enormous birthday cake ablaze with candles and carrying buckets of champagne with satin ribbons about the bottle necks.*

[MAE *and* GOOPER *strike up song, and everybody, including the Negroes and* CHILDREN, *joins in. Only* BRICK *remains aloof.*]

EVERYONE: *Happy birthday to you.*
                                  Happy birthday to you.
                                  Happy birthday, Big Daddy—
[*Some sing:* "Dear, Big Daddy!"]
                                  Happy birthday to you.
[*Some sing:* "How old are you?"]
[MAE *has come down center and is organizing her children like a chorus. She gives them a barely audible:* "One, two, three!" *and they are off in the new tune.*]

CHILDREN: *Skinamarinka—dinka—dink*
                                  Skinamarinka—do
                                  We love you.
                                  Skinamarinka—dinka—dink
                                  Skinamarinka—do.
[*All together, they turn to* BIG DADDY.]
                                  Big Daddy, you!
[*They turn back front, like a musical comedy chorus.*]
                                  We love you in the morning;
                                  We love you in the night.
                                  We love you when we're with you,
                                  And we love you out of sight.
                                  Skinamarinka—dinka—dink
                                  Skinamarinka—do.
[MAE *turns to* BIG MAMA.]
                                  Big Mama, too!

[BIG MAMA *bursts into tears. The Negroes leave.*]

BIG DADDY: Now Ida, what the hell is the matter with you?

MAE: She's just so happy.

BIG MAMA: I'm just so happy, Big Daddy, I have to cry or something.
[*Sudden and loud in the hush:*]
Brick, do you know the wonderful news that Doc Baugh got from the clinic about Big Daddy? Big Daddy's one hundred percent!

MARGARET: Isn't that wonderful?

BIG MAMA: He's just one hundred percent. Passed the examination with flying colors. Now that we know there's nothing wrong with Big Daddy but a spastic colon, I can tell you something. I was worried sick, half out of my mind, for fear that Big Daddy might have a thing like—
[MARGARET *cuts through this speech, jumping up and exclaiming shrilly:*]

MARGARET: Brick, honey, aren't you going to give Big Daddy his birthday present?
[*Passing by him, she snatches his liquor glass from him.*
[*She picks up a fancily wrapped package.*]
Here it is, Big Daddy, this is from Brick!

BIG MAMA: This is the biggest birthday Big Daddy's ever had, a hundred presents and bushels of telegrams from—

MAE: [*at same time*] What is it, Brick?

GOOPER: I bet 500 to 50 that Brick don't *know* what it is.

BIG MAMA: The fun of presents is not knowing what they are till you open the package. Open your present, Big Daddy.

BIG DADDY: Open it you'self. I want to ask Brick somethin! Come here, Brick.

MARGARET: Big Daddy's callin' you, Brick.
[*She is opening the package.*]

BRICK: Tell Big Daddy I'm crippled.

BIG DADDY: I see you're crippled. I want to know how you got crippled.

MARGARET: [*making diversionary tactics*] Oh, look, oh, look, why, it's a cashmere robe!
[*She holds the robe up for all to see.*]

MAE: You sound surprised, Maggie.

MARGARET: I never saw one before.

MAE: That's funny.—*Hah!*

MARGARET: [*turning on her fiercely, with a brilliant smile*] Why is it funny? All my family ever had was family—and luxuries such as cashmere robes still surprise me!

BIG DADDY: [*ominously*] Quiet!

MAE: [*heedless in her fury*] I don't see how you could be so surprised when you bought it yourself at Loewenstein's in Memphis last Saturday. You know how I know?

BIG DADDY: I said, "Quiet!"

MAE: —I know because the salesgirl that sold it to you waited on me and said, "Oh, Mrs. Pollitt, your sister-in-law just bought a cashmere robe for your husband's father!"

MARGARET: Sister Woman! Your talents are wasted as a housewife and mother, you really ought to be with the FBI or—

BIG DADDY: QUIET!

[REVEREND TOOKER'S *reflexes are slower than the others'. He finishes a sentence after the bellow.*]

REVEREND TOOKER: [*to* DOC BAUGH]—the Stork and the Reaper are running neck and neck!

[*He starts to laugh gaily when he notices the silence and* BIG DADDY'S *glare. His laugh dies falsely.*]

BIG DADDY: Preacher, I hope I'm not butting in on more talk about memorial stained-glass windows, am I, Preacher?

[REVEREND TOOKER *laughs feebly, then coughs dryly in the embarrassed silence.*]

Preacher?

BIG MAMA: Now, Big Daddy, don't you pick on Preacher!

BIG DADDY: [*raising his voice*] You ever hear that expression "all hawk and no spit"? You bring that expression to mind with that little dry cough of yours, all hawk an' no spit. . . .

[*The pause is broken only by a short startled laugh from* MARGARET, *the only one there who is conscious of and amused by the grotesque.*]

MAE: [*raising her arms and jangling her bracelets*] I wonder if the mosquitoes are active tonight?

BIG DADDY: What's that, Little Mama? Did you make some remark?

MAE: Yes, I said I wondered if the mosquitoes would eat us alive if we went out on the gallery for a while.

BIG DADDY: Well, if they do, I'll have your bones pulverized for fertilizer!

BIG MAMA: [*quickly*] Last week we had an airplane spraying the place and I think it done some good, at least I haven't had a—

BIG DADDY: [*cutting her speech*] Brick, they tell me, if what they tell me is true, that you done some jumping last night on the high school athletic field?

BIG MAMA: Brick, Big Daddy is talking to you, son.

BRICK: [*smiling vaguely over his drink*] What was that, Big Daddy?

BIG DADDY: They said you done some jumping on the high school track field last night.

BRICK: That's what they told me, too.

BIG DADDY: Was it jumping or humping that you were doing out there? What were you doing out there at three A.M., layin' a woman on that cinder track?

BIG MAMA: Big Daddy, you are off the sick-list, now, and I'm not going to excuse you for talkin' so—

BIG DADDY: Quiet!

BIG MAMA: —*nasty* in front of Preacher and—

BIG DADDY: *QUIET!*—I ast you, Brick, if you was cuttin' you'self a piece o' poon-tang last night on that cinder track? I thought maybe you were chasin' poon-tang on that track an' tripped over something in the heat of the chase—'sthat it?

[GOOPER *laughs, loud and false, others nervously following suit.* BIG MAMA *stamps her foot, and purses her lips, crossing to* MAE *and whispering something to her as* BRICK *meets his father's hard, intent, grinning stare with a slow, vague smile that he offers all situations from behind the screen of his liquor.*]

BRICK: No, sir, I don't think so. . . .

MAE: [*at the same time, sweetly*] Reverend Tooker, let's you and I take a stroll on the widow's walk.

> [*She and the preacher go out on the gallery as* BIG DADDY *says:*]

BIG DADDY: Then what the hell were you doing out there at three o'clock in the morning?

BRICK: Jumping the hurdles, Big Daddy, runnin' and jumpin' the hurdles, but those high hurdles have gotten too high for me, now.

BIG DADDY: 'Cause you was drunk?

BRICK: [*his vague smile fading a little*] Sober I wouldn't have tried to jump the *low* ones. . . .

BIG MAMA: [*quickly*] Big Daddy, blow out the candles on your birthday cake!

MARGARET: [*at the same time*] I want to propose a toast to Big Daddy Pollitt on his sixty-fifth birthday, the biggest cotton planter in—

BIG DADDY: [*bellowing with fury and disgust*] I told you to stop it, now stop it, quit this—!

BIG MAMA: [*coming in front of* BIG DADDY *with the cake*] Big Daddy, I will not allow you to talk that way, not even on your birthday, I—

BIG DADDY: I'll talk like I want to on my birthday, Ida, or any other goddam day of the year and anybody here that don't like it knows what they can do!

BIG MAMA: You don't mean that!

BIG DADDY: What makes you think I don't mean it?

> [*Meanwhile various discreet signals have been exchanged and* GOOPER *has also gone out on the gallery.*]

BIG MAMA: I just know you don't mean it.

BIG DADDY: You don't know a goddam thing and you never did!

BIG MAMA: Big Daddy, you don't mean that.

BIG DADDY: Oh, yes, I do, oh, yes, I do, I mean it! I put up with a whole lot of crap around here because I thought I was dying. And you thought I was dying and you started taking over, well, you can stop taking over now, Ida, because I'm not gonna die, you can just stop now this business of taking over because you're not taking over because I'm not dying, I went through the laboratory and the goddam exploratory operation and there's nothing wrong with me but a spastic colon. And I'm not dying of cancer which you thought I was dying of. Ain't that so? Didn't you think that I was dying of cancer, Ida?

> [*Almost everybody is out on the gallery but the two old people glaring at each other across the blazing cake.*
> [BIG MAMA's *chest heaves and she presses a fat fist to her mouth.*
> [BIG DADDY *continues, hoarsely:*]

Ain't that so, Ida? Didn't you have an idea I was dying of cancer and now you could take control of this place and everything on it? I got that impression, I seemed to get that impression. Your loud voice everywhere, your fat old body butting in here and there!

BIG MAMA: Hush! The preacher!

BIG DADDY: Rut the goddam preacher!

> [BIG MAMA *gasps loudly and sits down on the sofa, which is almost too small for her.*]

Did you hear what I said? I said rut the goddam preacher!

[*Somebody closes the gallery doors from outside just as there is a burst of fireworks and excited cries from the children.*]

BIG MAMA: I never seen you act like this before and I can't think what's got in you!

BIG DADDY: I went through all that laboratory and operation and all just so I would know if you or me was boss here! Well, now it turns out that I am and you ain't—and that's my birthday present—and my cake and champagne!—because for three years now you been gradually taking over. Bossing. Talking. Sashaying your fat old body around the place I made! I made this place! I was overseer on it! I was the overseer on the old Straw and Ochello plantation. I quit school at ten! I quit school at ten years old and went to work like a nigger in the fields. And I rose to be overseer of the Straw and Ochello plantation. And old Straw died and I was Ochello's partner and the place got bigger and bigger and bigger and bigger and bigger! I did all that myself with no goddam help from you, and now you think you're just about to take over. Well, I am just about to tell you that you are not just about to take over, you are not just about to take over a goddam thing. Is that clear to you, Ida? Is that very plain to you, now? Is that understood completely? I been through the laboratory from A to Z. I've had the goddam exploratory operation, and nothing is wrong with me but a spastic colon—made spastic, I guess, by *disgust!* By all the goddam lies and liars that I have had to put up with, and all the goddam hypocrisy that I lived with all these forty years that we been livin' together!

Hey! Ida!! Blow out the candles on the birthday cake! Purse up your lips and draw a deep breath and blow out the goddam candles on the cake!

BIG MAMA: Oh, Big Daddy, oh, oh, oh, Big Daddy!

BIG DADDY: What's the matter with you?

BIG MAMA: *In all these years you never believed that I loved you??*

BIG DADDY: Huh?

BIG MAMA: *And I did, I did so much, I did love you!*—I even loved your hate and your hardness, Big Daddy!

[*She sobs and rushes awkwardly out onto the gallery.*]

BIG DADDY: [*to himself*] *Wouldn't it be funny if that was true. . . .*

[*A pause is followed by a burst of light in the sky from the fireworks.*]

BRICK! HEY, BRICK!

[*He stands over his blazing birthday cake.*]

[*After some moments,* BRICK *hobbles in on his crutch, holding his glass.*]

[MARGARET *follows him with a bright, anxious smile.*]

I didn't call you, Maggie. I called Brick.

MARGARET: I'm just delivering him to you.

[*She kisses* BRICK *on the mouth, which he immediately wipes with the back of his hand. She flies girlishly back out.* BRICK *and his father are alone.*]

BIG DADDY: Why did you do that?

BRICK: Do what, Big Daddy?

BIG DADDY: Wipe her kiss off your mouth like she'd spit on you.

BRICK: I don't know. I wasn't conscious of it.

BIG DADDY: That woman of yours has a better shape on her than Gooper's but somehow or other they got the same look about them.

BRICK: What sort of look is that, Big Daddy?

BIG DADDY: I don't know how to describe it but it's the same look.

BRICK: They don't look peaceful, do they?

BIG DADDY: No, they sure in hell don't.

BRICK: They look nervous as cats?

BIG DADDY: That's right, they look nervous as cats.

BRICK: Nervous as a couple of cats on a hot tin roof ?

BIG DADDY: That's right, boy, they look like a couple of cats on a hot tin roof. It's funny that you and Gooper being so different would pick out the same type of woman.

BRICK: Both of us married into society, Big Daddy.

BIG DADDY: Crap . . . I wonder what gives them both that look?

BRICK: Well. They're sittin' in the middle of a big piece of land, Big Daddy, twenty-eight thousand acres is a pretty big piece of land and so they're squaring off on it, each determined to knock off a bigger piece of it than the other whenever you let it go.

BIG DADDY: I got a surprise for those women. I'm not gonna let it go for a long time yet if that's what they're waiting for.

BRICK: That's right, Big Daddy. You just sit tight and let them scratch each other's eyes out. . . .

BIG DADDY: You bet your life I'm going to sit tight on it and let those sons of bitches scratch their eyes out, ha ha ha. . . .

But Gooper's wife's a good breeder, you got to admit she's fertile. Hell, at supper tonight she had them all at the table and they had to put a couple of extra leafs in the table to make room for them, she's got five head of them, now, and another one's comin'.

BRICK: Yep, number six is comin'. . . .

BIG DADDY: Brick, you know, I swear to God, I don't know the way it happens?

BRICK: The way what happens, Big Daddy?

BIG DADDY: You git you a piece of land, by hook or crook, an' things start growin' on it, things accumulate on it, and the first thing you know it's completely out of hand, completely out of hand!

BRICK: Well, they say nature hates a vacuum, Big Daddy.

BIG DADDY: That's what they say, but sometimes I think that a vacuum is a hell of a lot better than some of the stuff that nature replaces it with.

Is someone out there by that door?

BRICK: Yep.

BIG DADDY: Who?

[*He has lowered his voice.*]

BRICK: Someone int'rested in what we say to each other.

BIG DADDY: Gooper?—*GOOPER!*

[*After a discreet pause,* MAE *appears in the gallery door.*]

MAE: Did you call Gooper, Big Daddy?

BIG DADDY: Aw, it was you.

MAE: Do you want Gooper, Big Daddy?

BIG DADDY: No, and I don't want you. I want some privacy here, while I'm having a confidential talk with my son Brick. Now it's too hot in here to close them doors, but if I have to close those rutten doors in order to have a private talk with my son Brick, just let me know and I'll close 'em. Because I hate eaves-droppers, I don't like any kind of sneakin' an' spyin'.

MAE: Why, Big Daddy—

BIG DADDY: You stood on the wrong side of the moon, it threw your shadow!

MAE: I was just—

BIG DADDY: You was just nothing but *spyin'* an' you *know* it!

MAE: [*begins to sniff and sob*] Oh, Big Daddy, you're so unkind for some reason to those that really love you!

BIG DADDY: Shut up, shut up, shut up! I'm going to move you and Gooper out of that room next to this! It's none of your goddam business what goes on in here at night between Brick an' Maggie. You listen at night like a couple of rutten peekhole spies and go and give a report on what you hear to Big Mama an' she comes to me and says they say such and such and so and so about what they heard goin' on between Brick an' Maggie, and Jesus, it makes me sick. I'm goin' to move you an' Gooper out of that room, I can't stand sneakin' an' spyin', it makes me sick. . . .

> [MAE *throws back her head and rolls her eyes heavenward and extends her arms as if invoking God's pity for this unjust martyrdom; then she presses a handkerchief to her nose and flies from the room with a loud swish of skirts.*]

BRICK: [*now at the liquor cabinet*] They listen, do they?

BIG DADDY: Yeah. They listen and give reports to Big Mama on what goes on in here between you and Maggie. They say that—

> [*He stops as if embarrassed.*]

—You won't sleep with her, that you sleep on the sofa. Is that true or not true? If you don't like Maggie, get rid of Maggie!—What are you doin' there now?

BRICK: Fresh'nin' up my drink.

BIG DADDY: Son, you know you got a real liquor problem?

BRICK: Yes, sir, yes, I know.

BIG DADDY: Is that why you quit sports announcing, because of this liquor problem?

BRICK: Yes, sir, yes, sir, I guess so.

> [*He smiles vaguely and amiably at his father across his replenished drink.*]

BIG DADDY: Son, don't guess about it, it's too important.

BRICK: [*vaguely*] Yes, sir.

BIG DADDY: And listen to me, don't look at the damn chandelier. . . .

> [*Pause.* BIG DADDY's *voice is husky.*]

—Somethin' else we picked up at th' big fire sale in Europe.

> [*Another pause.*]

Life is important. There's nothing else to hold onto. A man that drinks is throwing his life away. Don't do it, hold onto your life. There's nothing else to hold onto. . . .

Sit down over here so we don't have to raise our voices, the walls have ears in this place.

BRICK: [*hobbling over to sit on the sofa beside him*] All right, Big Daddy.

BIG DADDY: Quit!—how'd that come about? Some disappointment?

BRICK: I don't know. Do you?

BIG DADDY: I'm askin' you, goddam it! How in hell would I know if you don't?

BRICK: I just got out there and found that I had a mouth full of cotton. I was always two or three beats behind what was goin' on on the field and so I—

BIG DADDY: Quit!

BRICK: [*amiably*] Yes, quit.

BIG DADDY: Son?

BRICK: Huh?

BIG DADDY: [*inhales loudly and deeply from his cigar; then bends suddenly a little forward, exhaling loudly and raising a hand to his forehead*]

—Whew!—ha ha!—I took in too much smoke, it made me a little lightheaded. . . .

[*The mantel clock chimes.*]

Why is it so damn hard for people to talk?

BRICK: Yeah. . . .

[*The clock goes on sweetly chiming till it has completed the stroke of ten.*]

—Nice peaceful-soundin' clock, I like to hear it all night. . . .

[*He slides low and comfortable on the sofa;* BIG DADDY *sits up straight and rigid with some unspoken anxiety. All his gestures are tense and jerky as he talks. He wheezes and pants and sniffs through his nervous speech, glancing quickly, shyly, from time to time, at his son.*]

BIG DADDY: We got that clock the summer we wint to Europe, me an' Big Mama on that damn Cook's Tour, never had such an awful time in my life, I'm tellin' you, son, those gooks over there, they gouge your eyeballs out in their grand hotels. And Big Mama bought more stuff than you could haul in a couple of boxcars, that's no crap. Everywhere she wint on this whirlwind tour, she bought, bought, bought. Why, half that stuff she bought is still crated up in the cellar, under water last spring!

[*He laughs.*]

That Europe is nothin' on earth but a great big auction, that's all it is, that bunch of worn-out places, it's just a big fire sale, the whole rutten thing, an' Big Mama wint wild in it, why, you couldn't hold that woman with a mule's harness! Bought, bought, bought!—lucky I'm a rich man, yes, siree, Bob, an' half that stuff is mildewin' in th' basement. It's lucky I'm a rich man, it sure is lucky, well, I'm a rich man, Brick, yep, I'm a mighty rich man.

[*His eyes light up for a moment.*]

Y'know how much I'm worth? Guess, Brick! Guess how much I'm worth!

[BRICK *smiles vaguely over his drink.*]

Close on ten million in cash an' blue-chip stocks, outside, mind you, of twenty-eight thousand acres of the richest land this side of the valley Nile!

[*A puff and crackle and the night sky blooms with an eerie greenish glow. Children shriek on the gallery.*]

But a man can't buy his life with it, he can't buy back his life with it when his life has been spent, that's one thing not offered in the Europe fire sale or in the American markets or any markets on earth, a man can't buy his life with it, he can't buy back his life when his life is finished. . . .

That's a sobering thought, a very sobering thought, and that's a thought that I was turning over in my head, over and over and over—until today. . . .

I'm wiser and sadder, Brick, for this experience which I just gone through. They's one thing else that I remember in Europe.

BRICK: What is that, Big Daddy?

BIG DADDY: The hills around Barcelona in the country of Spain and the children running over those bare hills in their bare skins beggin' like starvin' dogs with howls and screeches, and how fat the priests are on the streets of Barcelona, so many of them and so fat and so pleasant, ha ha!—Y'know I could feed that country? I got money enough to feed that goddam country, but the human animal is a selfish beast and I don't reckon the money I passed out there to those howling children in the hills around Barcelona would more than upholster one of the chairs in this room, I mean pay to put a new cover on this chair!

Hell, I threw them money like you'd scatter feed corn for chickens, I threw money at them just to get rid of them long enough to climb back into th' car and—drive away. . . .

And then in Morocco, them Arabs, why, prostitution begins at four or five, that's no exaggeration, why, I remember one day in Marrakech, that old walled Arab city, I set on a broken-down wall to have a cigar, it was fearful hot there and this Arab woman stood in the road and looked at me till I was embarrassed, she stood stock still in the dusty hot road and looked at me till I was embarrassed. But listen to this. She had a naked child with her, a little naked girl with her, barely able to toddle, and after a while she set this child on the ground and give her a push and whispered something to her.

This child come toward me, barely able t' walk, come toddling up to me and—

Jesus, it makes you sick t' remember a thing like this!

It stuck out its hand and tried to unbutton my trousers!

That child was not yet five! Can you believe me? Or do you think that I am making this up? I wint back to the hotel and said to Big Mama, "Git packed! We're clearing out of this country." . . .

BRICK: Big Daddy, you're on a talkin' jag tonight.

BIG DADDY: [*ignoring this remark*] Yes, sir, that's how it is, the human animal is a beast that dies but the fact that he's dying don't give him pity for others, no, sir, it—

—Did you say something?

BRICK: Yes.

BIG DADDY: What?

BRICK: Hand me over that crutch so I can get up.

BIG DADDY: Where you goin'?

BRICK: I'm takin' a little short trip to Echo Spring.

BIG DADDY: To where?

BRICK: Liquor cabinet. . . .

BIG DADDY: Yes, sir, boy—

[*He hands* BRICK *the crutch.*]

—the human animal is a beast that dies and if he's got money he buys and buys and buys and I think the reason he buys everything he can buy is that in the back of his mind he has the crazy hope that one of his purchases will be life everlasting!—Which it never can be. . . . The human animal is a beast that—

BRICK: [*at the liquor cabinet*] Big Daddy, you sure are shootin' th' breeze here tonight.

[*There is a pause and voices are heard outside.*]

BIG DADDY: I been quiet here lately, spoke not a word, just sat and stared into space. I had something heavy weighing on my mind but tonight that load was took off me. That's why I'm talking.—The sky looks diff'rent to me. . . .

BRICK: You know what I like to hear most?

BIG DADDY: What?

BRICK: Solid quiet. Perfect unbroken quiet.

BIG DADDY: Why?

BRICK: Because it's more peaceful.

BIG DADDY: Man, you'll hear a lot of that in the grave.

[*He chuckles agreeably.*]

BRICK: Are you through talkin' to me?

BIG DADDY: Why are you so anxious to shut me up?

BRICK: Well, sir, ever so often you say to me, "Brick, I want to have a talk with you," but when we talk, it never materializes. Nothing is said. You sit in a chair and gas about this and that and I look like I listen. I try to look like I listen, but I don't listen, not much. Communication is—awful hard between people an'—somehow between you and me, it just don't—

BIG DADDY: Have you ever been scared? I mean have you ever felt downright terror of something?

[*He gets up.*]

Just one moment. I'm going to close these doors. . . .

[*He closes doors on gallery as if he were going to tell an important secret.*]

BRICK: What?

BIG DADDY: Brick?

BRICK: Huh?

BIG DADDY: Son, I thought I had it!

BRICK: Had what? Had what, Big Daddy?

BIG DADDY: Cancer!

BRICK: Oh . . .

BIG DADDY: I thought the old man made out of bones had laid his cold and heavy hand on my shoulder!

BRICK: Well, Big Daddy, you kept a tight mouth about it.

BIG DADDY: A pig squeals. A man keeps a tight mouth about it, in spite of a man not having a pig's advantage.

BRICK: What advantage is that?

BIG DADDY: Ignorance—of mortality—is a comfort. A man don't have that comfort, he's the only living thing that conceives of death, that knows what it is. The others go without knowing, which is the way that anything living should go, go without knowing, without any knowledge of it, and yet a pig squeals, but a man sometimes, he can keep a tight mouth about it. Sometimes he—

[*There is a deep, smoldering ferocity in the old man.*]

—can keep a tight mouth about it. I wonder if—

BRICK: What, Big Daddy?

BIG DADDY: A whiskey highball would injure this spastic condition?

BRICK: No, sir, it might do it good.

BIG DADDY: [*grins suddenly, wolfishly*] Jesus, I can't tell you! The sky is open! Christ, *it's open again! It's open, boy, it's open!*

> [BRICK *looks down at his drink.*]

BRICK: You feel better, Big Daddy?

BIG DADDY: Better? Hell! I can breathe!—All of my life I been like a doubled-up fist. . . .

> [*He pours a drink.*]

—Poundin', smashin', drivin'!—now I'm going to loosen these doubled-up hands and touch things *easy* with them. . . .

> [*He spreads his hands as if caressing the air.*]

You know what I'm contemplating?

BRICK: [*vaguely*] No, sir. What are you contemplating?

BIG DADDY: Ha ha!—*Pleasure!*—pleasure with *women!*

> [BRICK's *smile fades a little but lingers.*]

Brick, this stuff burns me!—

—Yes, boy. I'll tell you something that you might not guess. I still have desire for women and this is my sixty-fifth birthday.

BRICK: I think that's mighty remarkable, Big Daddy.

BIG DADDY: Remarkable?

BRICK: *Admirable,* Big Daddy.

BIG DADDY: You're damn right it is, remarkable and admirable both. I realize now that I never had me enough. I let many chances slip by because of scruples about it, scruples, convention—crap. . . . All that stuff is bull, bull, bull!—It took the shadow of death to make me see it. Now that shadow's lifted, I'm going to cut loose and have, what is it they call it, have me a—ball!

BRICK: A ball, huh?

BIG DADDY: That's right, a ball, a ball! Hell!—I slept with Big Mama till, let's see, five years ago, till I was sixty and she was fifty-eight, and never even liked her, never did!

> [*The phone has been ringing down the hall.* BIG MAMA *enters, exclaiming:*]

BIG MAMA: Don't you men hear that phone ring? I heard it way out on the gall'ry.

BIG DADDY: There's five rooms off this front gall'ry that you could go through. Why do you go through this one?

> [BIG MAMA *makes a playful face as she bustles out the hall door.*]

Hunh!—Why, when Big Mama goes out of a room, I can't remember what that woman looks like, but when Big Mama comes back into the room, boy, then I see what she looks like, and I wish I didn't!

> [*Bends over laughing at this joke till it hurts his guts and he straightens with a grimace. The laugh subsides to a chuckle as he puts the liquor glass a little distrustfully down on the table.*
>
> [BRICK *has risen and hobbled to the gallery doors.*]

Hey! Where you goin'?

BRICK: Out for a breather.

BIG DADDY: Not yet you ain't. Stay here till this talk is finished, young fellow.

BRICK: I thought it was finished, Big Daddy.

BIG DADDY: It ain't even begun.

BRICK: My mistake. Excuse me. I just wanted to feel that river breeze.

BIG DADDY: Turn on the ceiling fan and set back down in that chair.

[BIG MAMA's *voice rises, carrying down the hall.*]

BIG MAMA: Miss Sally, you're a case! You're a caution, Miss Sally. Why didn't you give me a chance to explain it to you?

BIG DADDY: Jesus, she's talking to my old maid sister again.

BIG MAMA: Well, goodbye, now, Miss Sally. You come down real soon, Big Daddy's dying to see you! Yaisss, goodbye, Miss Sally. . . .

[*She hangs up and bellows with mirth.* BIG DADDY *groans and covers his ears as she approaches.*]

[*Bursting in:*]

Big Daddy, that was Miss Sally callin' from Memphis again! You know what she done, Big Daddy? She called her doctor in Memphis to git him to tell her what that spastic thing is! Ha-*HAAAA!*—And called back to tell me how relieved she was that—Hey! Let me in!

[BIG DADDY *has been holding the door half closed against her.*]

BIG DADDY: Naw I ain't. I told you not to come and go through this room. You just back out and go through those five other rooms.

BIG MAMA: Big Daddy? Big Daddy? Oh, Big Daddy!—You didn't mean those things you said to me, did you?

[*He shuts door firmly against her but she still calls.*]

Sweetheart? Sweetheart? Big Daddy? You didn't mean those awful things you said to me?—I know you didn't. I know you didn't mean those things in your heart. . . .

[*The childlike voice fades with a sob and her heavy footsteps retreat down the hall.* BRICK *has risen once more on his crutches and starts for the gallery again.*]

BIG DADDY: All I ask of that woman is that she leave me alone. But she can't admit to herself that she makes me sick. That comes of having slept with her too many years. Should of quit much sooner but that old woman she never got enough of it—and I was good in bed . . . I never should of wasted so much of it on her. . . . They say you got just so many and each one is numbered. Well, I got a few left in me, a few, and I'm going to pick me a good one to spend 'em on! I'm going to pick me a choice one, I don't care how much she costs, I'll smother her in—minks! Ha ha! I'll strip her naked and smother her in minks and choke her with diamonds! Ha ha! I'll strip her naked and choke her with diamonds and smother her with minks and hump her from hell to breakfast. *Ha aha ha ha ha!*

MAE: [*gaily at door*] Who's that laughin' in there?

GOOPER: Is Big Daddy laughin' in there?

BIG DADDY: Crap!—them two—*drips.* . . .

[*He goes over and touches* BRICK's *shoulder.*]

Yes, son. Brick, boy.—I'm—*happy!* I'm happy, son, I'm happy!

[*He chokes a little and bites his under lip, pressing his head quickly, shyly against his son's head and then, coughing with embarrassment, goes uncertainly back to the table where he set down the glass. He drinks and makes a grimace as it burns his guts.* BRICK *sighs and rises with effort.*]

What makes you so restless? Have you got ants in your britches?

BRICK: Yes, sir . . .

BIG DADDY: Why?

BRICK: —Something—hasn't happened. . . .

BIG DADDY: Yeah? What is that!

BRICK: [*sadly*]—the click. . . .

BIG DADDY: Did you say "click"?

BRICK: Yes, click.

BIG DADDY: What click?

BRICK: A click that I get in my head that makes me peaceful.

BIG DADDY: I sure in hell don't know what you're talking about, but it dis-
turbs me.

BRICK: It's just a mechanical thing.

BIG DADDY: What is a mechanical thing?

BRICK: This click that I get in my head that makes me peaceful. I got to drink till
I get it. It's just a mechanical thing, something like a—like a—like a—

BIG DADDY: Like a—

BRICK: Switch clicking off in my head, turning the hot light off and the cool
night on and—
     [*He looks up, smiling sadly.*]
—all of a sudden there's—peace!

BIG DADDY: [*whistles long and soft with astonishment; he goes back to* BRICK *and
clasps his son's two shoulders*] Jesus! I didn't know it had gotten that bad with
you. Why, boy, you're—*alcoholic!*

BRICK: That's the truth, Big Daddy. I'm alcoholic.

BIG DADDY: This shows how I—let things go!

BRICK: I have to hear that little click in my head that makes me peaceful. Usually
I hear it sooner than this, sometimes as early as—noon, but—
     —Today it's—dilatory. . . .
          —I just haven't got the right level of alcohol in my bloodstream yet!
     [*This last statement is made with energy as he freshens his drink.*]

BIG DADDY: Uh—huh. Expecting death made me blind. I didn't have no idea that
a son of mine was turning into a drunkard under my nose.

BRICK: [*gently*] Well, now you do, Big Daddy, the news has penetrated.

BIG DADDY: UH-huh, yes, now I do, the news has—penetrated. . . .

BRICK: And so if you'll excuse me—

BIG DADDY: No, I won't excuse you.

BRICK: —I'd better sit by myself till I hear that click in my head, it's just a
mechanical thing but it don't happen except when I'm alone or talking to
no one. . . .

BIG DADDY: You got a long, long time to sit still, boy, and talk to no one, but now
you're talkin' to me. At least I'm talking to you. And you set there and listen
until I tell you the conversation is over!

BRICK: But this talk is like all the others we've ever had together in our lives! It's
nowhere, nowhere!—it's—it's *painful,* Big Daddy. . . .

BIG DADDY: All right, then let it be painful, but don't you move from that chair!—
I'm going to remove that crutch. . . .
     [*He seizes the crutch and tosses it across room.*]

BRICK: I can hop on one foot, and if I fall, I can crawl!

BIG DADDY: If you ain't careful you're gonna crawl off this plantation and then, by Jesus, you'll have to hustle your drinks along Skid Row!

BRICK: That'll come, Big Daddy.

BIG DADDY: Naw, it won't. You're my son and I'm going to straighten you out; now that *I'm* straightened out, I'm going to straighten out you!

BRICK: Yeah?

BIG DADDY: Today the report come in from Ochsner Clinic. Y'know what they told me?

> [*His face glows with triumph.*]

The only thing that they could detect with all the instruments of science in that great hospital is a little spastic condition of the colon! And nerves torn to pieces by all that worry about it.

> [*A little girl bursts into room with a sparkler clutched in each fist, hops and shrieks like a monkey gone mad and rushes back out again as* BIG DADDY *strikes at her.*
>
> [*Silence. The two men stare at each other. A woman laughs gaily outside.*]

I want you to know I breathed a sigh of relief almost as powerful as the Vicksburg tornado!

BRICK: You weren't ready to go?

BIG DADDY: GO WHERE?—crap. . . .

—When you are gone from here, boy, you are long gone and no where! The human machine is not no different from the animal machine or the fish machine or the bird machine or the reptile machine or the insect machine! It's just a whole goddam lot more complicated and consequently more trouble to keep together. Yep. I thought I had it. The earth shook under my foot, the sky come down like the black lid of a kettle and I couldn't breathe!—Today!!—that lid was lifted, I drew my first free breath in—how many years?—*God!*—three. . . .

> [*There is laughter outside, running footsteps, the soft, plushy sound and light of exploding rockets.*
>
> [BRICK *stares at him soberly for a long moment; then makes a sort of startled sound in his nostrils and springs up on one foot and hops across the room to grab his crutch, swinging on the furniture for support. He gets the crutch and flees as if in horror for the gallery. His father seizes him by the sleeve of his white silk pajamas.*]

Stay here, you son of a bitch!—till I say go!

BRICK: I can't.

BIG DADDY: You sure in hell will, goddamn it.

BRICK: No, I can't. We talk, you talk, in—circles! We get no where, no where! It's always the same, you say you want to talk to me and don't have a ruttin' thing to say to me!

BIG DADDY: Nothin' to say when I'm tellin' you I'm going to live when I thought I was dying?!

BRICK: Oh—*that!*—Is that what you have to say to me?

BIG DADDY: Why, you son of a bitch! Ain't that, ain't that—*important?!*

BRICK: Well, you said that, that's said, and now I—

BIG DADDY: Now you set back down.

BRICK: You're all balled up, you—

BIG DADDY: I ain't balled up!

BRICK: You are, you're all balled up!

BIG DADDY: Don't tell me what I am, you drunken whelp! I'm going to tear this coat sleeve off if you don't set down!

BRICK: Big Daddy—

BIG DADDY: Do what I tell you! I'm the boss here, now! I want you to know I'm back in the driver's seat now!

[BIG MAMA *rushes in, clutching her great heaving bosom.*]

What in hell do you want in here, Big Mama?

BIG MAMA: Oh, Big Daddy! Why are you shouting like that? I just cain't *stainnnnnnnd*—it. . . .

BIG DADDY: [*raising the back of his hand above his head*] GIT!—outa here.

[*She rushes back out, sobbing.*]

BRICK: [*softly, sadly*] Christ. . . .

BIG DADDY: [*fiercely*] Yeah! Christ!—is right . . .

[BRICK *breaks loose and hobbles toward the gallery.*]

[BIG DADDY *jerks his crutch from under* BRICK *so he steps with the injured ankle. He utters a hissing cry of anguish, clutches a chair and pulls it over on top of him on the floor.*]

Son of a—tub of—hog fat. . . .

BRICK: Big Daddy! Give me my crutch.

[BIG DADDY *throws the crutch out of reach.*]

Give me that crutch, Big Daddy.

BIG DADDY: Why do you drink?

BRICK: Don't know, give me my crutch!

BIG DADDY: You better think why you drink or give up drinking!

BRICK: Will you please give me my crutch so I can get up off this floor?

BIG DADDY: First you answer my question. Why do you drink? Why are you throwing your life away, boy, like somethin' disgusting you picked up on the street?

BRICK: [*getting onto his knees*] Big Daddy, I'm in pain, I stepped on that foot.

BIG DADDY: Good! I'm glad you're not too numb with the liquor in you to feel some pain!

BRICK: You—spilled my—drink . . .

BIG DADDY: I'll make a bargain with you. You tell me why you drink and I'll hand you one. I'll pour you the liquor myself and hand it to you.

BRICK: Why do I drink?

BIG DADDY: Yea! Why?

BRICK: Give me a drink and I'll tell you.

BIG DADDY: Tell me first!

BRICK: I'll tell you in one word.

BIG DADDY: What word?

BRICK: DISGUST!

[*The clock chimes softly, sweetly.* BIG DADDY *gives it a short, outraged glance.*]

Now how about that drink?

BIG DADDY: What are you disgusted with? You got to tell me that, first. Otherwise being disgusted don't make no sense!

BRICK: Give me my crutch.

BIG DADDY: You heard me, you got to tell me what I asked you first.

BRICK: I told you, I said to kill my disgust!

BIG DADDY: DISGUST WITH WHAT!

BRICK: You strike a hard bargain.

BIG DADDY: What are you disgusted with?—an' I'll pass you the liquor.

BRICK: I can hop on one foot, and if I fall, I can crawl.

BIG DADDY: You want liquor that bad?

BRICK: [*dragging himself up, clinging to bedstead*] Yeah, I want it that bad.

BIG DADDY: If I give you a drink, will you tell me what it is you're disgusted with, Brick?

BRICK: Yes, sir, I will try to.

> [*The old man pours him a drink and solemnly passes it to him.*
> [*There is silence as* BRICK *drinks.*]

Have you ever heard the word "mendacity"?

BIG DADDY: Sure. Mendacity is one of them five-dollar words that cheap politicians throw back and forth at each other.

BRICK: You know what it means?

BIG DADDY: Don't it mean lying and liars?

BRICK: Yes, sir, lying and liars.

BIG DADDY: Has someone been lying to you?

CHILDREN: [*chanting in chorus offstage*]
> We want Big Dad-dee!
> We want Big Dad-dee!

> [GOOPER *appears in the gallery door.*]

GOOPER: Big Daddy, the kiddies are shouting for you out there.

BIG DADDY: [*fiercely*] Keep out, Gooper!

GOOPER: 'Scuse *me!*

> [BIG DADDY *slams the doors after* GOOPER.]

BIG DADDY: Who's been lying to you, has Margaret been lying to you, has your wife been lying to you about something, Brick?

BRICK: Not her. That wouldn't matter.

BIG DADDY: Then who's been lying to you, and what about?

BRICK: No one single person and no one lie. . . .

BIG DADDY: Then what, what then, for Christ's sake?

BRICK: —The whole, the whole—thing. . . .

BIG DADDY: Why are you rubbing your head? You got a headache?

BRICK: No, I'm tryin' to—

BIG DADDY: —Concentrate, but you can't because your brain's all soaked with liquor, is that the trouble? Wet brain!

> [*He snatches the glass from* BRICK's *hand.*]

What do you know about this mendacity thing? Hell! I could write a book on it! Don't you know that? I could write a book on it and still not cover the subject? Well, I could, I could write a goddam book on it and still not cover the subject anywhere near enough!!—Think of all the lies I got to put up with!—Pretenses! Ain't that mendacity? Having to pretend stuff you don't think or feel or have any idea of? Having for instance to act like I care for Big Mama!—I haven't been able to stand the sight, sound, or smell of that woman for forty years now!—even when I *laid* her!—regular as a piston. . . .

Pretend to love that son of a bitch of a Gooper and his wife Mae and those five same screechers out there like parrots in a jungle? Jesus! Can't stand to look at 'em!

Church!—it bores the bejesus out of me but I go!—I go an' sit there and listen to the fool preacher!

Clubs!—Elks! Masons! Rotary!—*crap!*

[*A spasm of pain makes him clutch his belly. He sinks into a chair and his voice is softer and hoarser.*]

You I *do* like for some reason, did always have some kind of real feeling for—affection—respect yes, always. . . .

You and being a success as a planter is all I ever had any devotion to in my whole life!—and that's the truth. . . .

I don't know why, but it is!

I've lived with mendacity!—Why can't *you* live with it? Hell, you *got* to live with it, there's nothing *else* to *live* with except mendacity, is there?

BRICK: Yes, sir. Yes, sir, there is something else that you can live with!

BIG DADDY: What?

BRICK: [*lifting his glass*] This!—Liquor. . . .

BIG DADDY: That's not living, that's dodging away from life.

BRICK: I want to dodge away from it.

BIG DADDY: Then why don't you kill yourself, man?

BRICK: I like to drink. . . .

BIG DADDY: Oh, God, I can't talk to you. . . .

BRICK: I'm sorry, Big Daddy.

BIG DADDY: Not as sorry as I am. I'll tell you something. A little while back when I thought my number was up—

[*This speech should have torrential pace and fury.*]

—before I found out it was just this—spastic—colon. I thought about you. Should I or should I not, if the jig was up, give you this place when I go—since I hate Gooper an' Mae an' know that they hate me, and since all five same monkeys are little Maes an' Goopers.—And I thought, No!—Then I thought, Yes!—I couldn't make up my mind. I hate Gooper and his five same monkeys and that bitch Mae! Why should I turn over twenty-eight thousand acres of the richest land this side of the valley Nile to not my kind?—But why in hell, on the other hand, Brick—should I subsidize a goddam fool on the bottle?—Liked or not liked, well, maybe even—*loved!*—Why should I do that?—Subsidize worthless behavior? Rot? Corruption?

BRICK: [*smiling*] I understand.

BIG DADDY: Well, if you do, you're smarter than I am, goddam it, because I don't understand. And this I will tell you frankly. I didn't make up my mind at all on that question and still to this day I ain't made out no will!—Well, now I don't *have* to. The pressure is gone. I can just wait and see if you pull yourself together or if you don't.

BRICK: That's right, Big Daddy.

BIG DADDY: You sound like you thought I was kidding.

BRICK: [*rising*] No, sir, I know you're not kidding.

BIG DADDY: But you don't care—?

BRICK: [*hobbling toward the gallery door*] No, sir, I don't care. . . .
Now how about taking a look at your birthday fireworks and getting some
of that cool breeze off the river?
> [*He stands in the gallery doorway as the night sky turns pink and green and
> gold with successive flashes of light.*]

BIG DADDY: *WAIT!*—Brick. . . .
> [*His voice drops. Suddenly there is something shy, almost tender, in his re-
> straining gesture.*]

Don't let's—leave it like this, like them other talks we've had, we've always—talked around things, we've—just talked around things for some
rutten reason, I don't know what, it's always like something was left not
spoken, something avoided because neither of us was honest enough with
the—other. . . .

BRICK: I never lied to you, Big Daddy.

BIG DADDY: Did I ever to *you?*

BRICK: No, sir. . . .

BIG DADDY: Then there is at least two people that never lied to each other.

BRICK: But we've never *talked* to each other.

BIG DADDY: We can *now.*

BRICK: Big Daddy, there don't seem to be anything much to say.

BIG DADDY: You say that you drink to kill your disgust with lying.

BRICK: You said to give you a reason.

BIG DADDY: Is liquor the only thing that'll kill this disgust?

BRICK: Now. Yes.

BIG DADDY: But not once, huh?

BRICK: Not when I was still young an' believing. A drinking man's someone who
wants to forget he isn't still young an' believing.

BIG DADDY: Believing what?

BRICK: Believing. . . .

BIG DADDY: Believing *what?*

BRICK: [*stubbornly evasive*] Believing. . . .

BIG DADDY: I don't know what the hell you mean by "believing" and I don't think
you know what you mean by "believing" but if you still got sports in your
blood, go back to sports announcing and—

BRICK: Sit in a glass box watching games I can't play? Describing what I can't do
while players do it? Sweating out their disgust and confusion in contests I'm
not fit for? Drinkin' a Coke, half bourbon, so I can stand it? That's no goddam good any more, no help—time just outran me, Big Daddy—got there
first. . . .

BIG DADDY: I think you're passing the buck.

BRICK: You know many drinkin' men?

BIG DADDY: [*with a slight, charming smile*] I have known a fair number of that
species.

BRICK: Could any of them tell you why he drank?

BIG DADDY: Yep, you're passin' the buck to things like time and disgust with "mendacity" and—crap!—if you got to use that kind of language about a thing, it's ninety-proof bull, and I'm not buying any.

BRICK: I had to give you a reason to get a drink!

BIG DADDY: You started drinkin' when your friend Skipper died.

> [*Silence for five beats. Then* BRICK *makes a startled movement, reaching for his crutch.*]

BRICK: What are you suggesting?

BIG DADDY: I'm suggesting nothing.

> [*The shuffle and clop of* BRICK's *rapid hobble away from his father's steady, grave attention.*]

—But Gooper an' Mae suggested that there was something not right exactly in your—

BRICK: [*stopping short downstage as if backed to a wall*] "Not right"?

BIG DADDY: Not, well, exactly *normal* in your friendship with—

BRICK: They suggested that, too? I thought that was Maggie's suggestion.

> [BRICK's *detachment is at last broken through. His heart is accelerated; his forehead sweat-beaded; his breath becomes more rapid and his voice hoarse. The thing they're discussing, timidly and painfully on the side of* BIG DADDY, *fiercely, violently on* BRICK's *side, is the inadmissible thing that Skipper died to disavow between them. The fact that if it existed it had to be disavowed to "keep face" in the world they lived in, may be at the heart of the "mendacity" that* BRICK *drinks to kill his disgust with. It may be the root of his collapse. Or maybe it is only a single manifestation of it, not even the most important. The bird that I hope to catch in the net of this play is not the solution of one man's psychological problem. I'm trying to catch the true quality of experience in a group of people, that cloudy, flickering, evanescent—fiercely charged!—interplay of live human beings in the thundercloud of a common crisis. Some mystery should be left in the revelation of character in a play, just as a great deal of mystery is always left in the revelation of character in life, even in one's own character to himself. This does not absolve the playwright of his duty to observe and probe as clearly and deeply as he* legitimately *can: but it should steer him away from "pat" conclusions, facile definitions which make a play just a play, not a snare for the truth of human experience.*
> [*The following scene should be played with great concentration, with most of the power leashed but palpable in what is left unspoken.*]

Who else's suggestion is it, is it *yours?* How many others thought that Skipper and I were—

BIG DADDY: [*gently*] Now, hold on, hold on a minute, son.—I knocked around in my time.

BRICK: What's that got to do with—

BIG DADDY: I said "Hold on!"—I bummed, I bummed this country till I was—

BRICK: Whose suggestion, who else's suggestion is it?

BIG DADDY: Slept in hobo jungles and railroad Y's and flophouses in all cities before I—

BRICK: Oh, *you* think so, too, you call me your son and a queer. Oh! Maybe that's why you put Maggie and me in this room that was Jack Straw's and Peter

Ochello's, in which that pair of old sisters slept in a double bed where both of 'em died!

BIG DADDY: *Now just don't go throwing rocks at—*

[*Suddenly* REVEREND TOOKER *appears in the gallery doors, his head slightly, playfully, fatuously cocked, with a practiced clergyman's smile, sincere as a bird call blown on a hunter's whistle, the living embodiment of the pious, conventional lie.*

[BIG DADDY *gasps a little at this perfectly timed, but incongruous, apparition.*]

—What're you lookin' for, Preacher?

REVEREND TOOKER: The gentleman's lavatory, ha ha!—heh, heh . . .

BIG DADDY: [*with strained courtesy*]—Go back out and walk down to the other end of the gallery, Reverend Tooker, and use the bathroom connected with my bedroom, and if you can't find it, ask them where it is!

REVEREND TOOKER: Ah, thanks.

[*He goes out with a deprecatory chuckle.*]

BIG DADDY: It's hard to talk in this place . . .

BRICK: Son of a—!

BIG DADDY: [*leaving a lot unspoken*]—I seen all things and understood a lot of them, till 1910. Christ, the year that—I had worn my shoes through, hocked my—I hopped off a yellow dog freight car half a mile down the road, slept in a wagon of cotton outside the gin—Jack Straw an' Peter Ochello took me in. Hired me to manage this place which grew into this one.—When Jack Straw died—why, old Peter Ochello quit eatin' like a dog does when its master's dead, and died, too!

BRICK: Christ!

BIG DADDY: I'm just saying I understand such—

BRICK: [*violently*] Skipper is dead. I have not quit eating!

BIG DADDY: No, but you started drinking.

[BRICK *wheels on his crutch and hurls his glass across the room shouting.*]

BRICK: YOU THINK SO, TOO?

BIG DADDY: *Shhh!*

[*Footsteps run on the gallery. There are women's calls.*

[BIG DADDY *goes toward the door.*]

Go way!—Just broke a glass. . . .

[BRICK *is transformed, as if a quiet mountain blew suddenly up in volcanic flame.*]

BRICK: You think so, too? You think so, too? You think me an' Skipper did, did, did!—*sodomy!*—together?

BIG DADDY: Hold—!

BRICK: That what you—

BIG DADDY: —*ON*—a minute!

BRICK: You think we did dirty things between us, Skipper an'—

BIG DADDY: Why are you shouting like that? Why are you—

BRICK: —Me, is that what you think of Skipper, is that—

BIG DADDY: —so excited? I don't think nothing. I don't know nothing. I'm simply telling you what—

BRICK: You think that Skipper and me were a pair of dirty old men?

BIG DADDY: Now that's—

BRICK: Straw? Ochello? A couple of—

BIG DADDY: Now just—

BRICK: —ducking sissies? Queers? Is that what you—

BIG DADDY: Shhh.

BRICK: —think?

> [*He loses his balance and pitches to his knees without noticing the pain. He grabs the bed and drags himself up.*]

BIG DADDY: Jesus!—Whew. . . . Grab my hand!

BRICK: Naw, I don't want your hand. . . .

BIG DADDY: Well, I want yours. Git up!

> [*He draws him up, keeps an arm about him with concern and affection.*]
>
> You broken out in a sweat! You're panting like you'd run a race with—

BRICK: [*freeing himself from his father's hold*] Big Daddy, you shock me, Big Daddy, you, you—*shock* me! Talkin' so—

> [*He turns away from his father.*]
>
> —casually!—about a—thing like that . . .
>
>   —Don't you know how people *feel* about things like that? How, how *disgusted* they are by things like that? Why, at Ole Miss when it was discovered a pledge to our fraternity, Skipper's and mine, did a, *attempted* to do a, unnatural thing with—
>
>   We not only dropped him like a hot rock!—We told him to git off the campus, and he did, he got!—All the way to—
>
> [*He halts, breathless.*]

BIG DADDY: —Where?

BRICK: —North Africa, last I heard!

BIG DADDY: Well, I have come back from further away than that, I have just now returned from the other side of the moon, death's country, son, and I'm not easy to shock by anything here.

> [*He comes downstage and faces out.*]
>
> Always, anyhow, lived with too much space around me to be infected by ideas of other people. One thing you can grow on a big place more important than cotton!—is *tolerance!*—I grown it.
>
> [*He returns toward* BRICK.]

BRICK: Why can't exceptional friendship, *real, real, deep, deep friendship!* between two men be respected as something clean and decent without being thought of as—

BIG DADDY: It can, it is, for God's sake.

BRICK: —*Fairies.* . . .

> [*In his utterance of this word, we gauge the wide and profound reach of the conventional mores he got from the world that crowned him with early laurel.*]

BIG DADDY: I told Mae an' Gooper—

BRICK: Frig Mae and Gooper, frig all dirty lies and liars!—Skipper and me had a clean, true thing between us!—had a clean friendship, practically all our lives, till Maggie got the idea you're talking about. Normal? No!—It was too rare to be normal, any true thing between two people is too rare to be normal. Oh, once in a while he put his hand on my shoulder or I'd put mine on his, oh, maybe even, when we were touring the country in pro football an' shared hotel rooms we'd reach across the space between the two beds and shake hands to say goodnight, yeah, one or two times we—

BIG DADDY: Brick, nobody thinks that that's not normal!

BRICK: Well, they're mistaken, it was! It was a pure an' true thing an' that's not normal.

[*They both stare straight at each other for a long moment. The tension breaks and both turn away as if tired.*]

BIG DADDY: Yeah, it's—hard t'—talk. . . .

BRICK: All right, then, let's—let it go. . . .

BIG DADDY: Why did Skipper crack up? Why have you?

[BRICK *looks back at his father again. he has already decided, without knowing that he has made this decision, that he is going to tell his father that he is dying of cancer. Only this could even the score between them: one inadmissible thing in return for another.*]

BRICK: [*ominously*] All right. You're asking for it, Big Daddy. We're finally going to have that real true talk you wanted. It's too late to stop it, now, we got to carry it through and cover every subject.

[*He hobbles back to the liquor cabinet.*]

Uh-huh.

[*He opens the ice bucket and picks up the silver tongs with slow admiration of their frosty brightness.*]

Maggie declares that Skipper and I went into pro football after we left Ole Miss because we were scared to grow up . . .

[*He moves downstage with the shuffle and clop of a cripple on a crutch. As* MARGARET *did when her speech became "recitative," he looks out into the house, commanding its attention by his direct, concentrated gaze—a broken, "tragically elegant" figure telling simply as much as he knows of "the Truth":*]

—Wanted to—keep on tossing—those long, long!—high, high!—passes that—couldn't be intercepted except by time, the aerial attack that made us famous! And so we did, we did, we kept it up for one season, that aerial attack, we held it high!—Yeah, but—

—that summer, Maggie, she laid the law down to me, said, Now or never, and so I married Maggie. . . .

BIG DADDY: How was Maggie in bed?

BRICK: [*wryly*] Great! the greatest!

[BIG DADDY *nods as if he thought so.*]

She went on the road that fall with the Dixie Stars. Oh, she made a great show of being the world's best sport. She wore a—wore a—tall bearskin cap! A "shako," they call it, a dyed moleskin coat, a moleskin coat dyed red!—Cut up crazy! Rented hotel ballrooms for victory celebrations, wouldn't cancel them when it—turned out—defeat. . . .

MAGGIE THE CAT! Ha ha!

[BIG DADDY *nods.*]

—But Skipper, he had some fever which came back on him which doctors couldn't explain and I got that injury—turned out to be just a shadow on the X-ray plate—and a touch of bursitis. . . .

I lay in a hospital bed, watched our games on TV, saw Maggie on the bench next to Skipper when he was hauled out of a game for stumbles, fumbles!—Burned me up the way she hung on his arm!—Y'know, I think that Maggie had always felt sort of left out because she and me never got any closer together than two people just get in bed, which is not much closer than two cats on a—fence humping. . . .

So! She took this time to work on poor dumb Skipper. He was a less-than-average student at Ole Miss, you know that, don't you?!—Poured in his mind the dirty, false idea that what we were, him and me, was a frustrated case of that ole pair of sisters that lived in this room, Jack Straw and Peter Ochello!—He, poor Skipper, went to bed with Maggie to prove it wasn't true, and when it didn't work out, he thought it *was* true!—Skipper broke in two like a rotten stick—nobody ever turned so fast to a lush—or died of it so quick. . . .

—Now are you satisfied?

[BIG DADDY *has listened to this story, dividing the grain from the chaff. Now he looks at his son.*]

BIG DADDY: Are *you* satisfied?

BRICK: With what?

BIG DADDY: That half-ass story!

BRICK: What's half-ass about it?

BIG DADDY: Something's left out of that story. What did you leave out?

[*The phone has started ringing in the hall. As if it reminded him of something,* BRICK *glances suddenly toward the sound and says:*]

BRICK: Yes!—I left out a long-distance call which I had from Skipper, in which he made a drunken confession to me and on which I hung up!—last time we spoke to each other in our lives. . . .

[*Muted ring stops as someone answers phone in a soft, indistinct voice in hall.*]

BIG DADDY: You hung up?

BRICK: Hung up. Jesus! Well—

BIG DADDY: Anyhow now!—we have tracked down the lie with which you're disgusted and which you are drinking to kill your disgust with, Brick. You been passing the buck. This disgust with mendacity is disgust with yourself.

You!—dug the grave of your friend and kicked him in it!—before you'd face truth with him!

BRICK: *His* truth, not *mine!*

BIG DADDY: His truth, okay! But you wouldn't face it with him!

BRICK: Who *can* face truth? Can *you?*

BIG DADDY: Now don't start passin' the rotten buck again, boy!

BRICK: *How about these birthday congratulations, these many, many happy returns of the day, when ev'rybody but you knows there won't be any!*

[*Whoever has answered the hall phone lets out a high, shrill laugh; the voice becomes audible saying:* "No, no, you got it all wrong! Upside down! Are you crazy?"

[BRICK *suddenly catches his breath as he realizes that he has made a shocking disclosure. He hobbles a few paces, then freezes, and without looking at his father's shocked face, says:*]

Let's, let's—go out, now, and—

[BIG DADDY *moves suddenly forward and grabs hold of the boy's crutch like it was a weapon for which they were fighting for possession.*]

BIG DADDY: Oh, no, no! No one's going out! What did you start to say?

BRICK: I don't remember.

BIG DADDY: "Many happy returns when they know there won't be any"?

BRICK: Aw, hell, Big Daddy, forget it. Come on out on the gallery and look at the fireworks they're shooting off for your birthday. . . .

BIG DADDY: First you finish that remark you were makin' before you cut off. "Many happy returns when they know there won't be any"?—Ain't that what you just said?

BRICK: Look, now. I can get around without that crutch if I have to but it would be a lot easier on the furniture an' glassware if I didn' have to go swinging along like Tarzan of th'—

BIG DADDY: FINISH! WHAT YOU WAS SAYIN'!

[*An eerie green glow shows in sky behind him.*]

BRICK: [*sucking the ice in his glass, speech becoming thick*] Leave th' place to Gooper and Mae an' their five little same little monkeys. All I want is—

BIG DADDY: "LEAVE TH' PLACE," did you say?

BRICK: [*vaguely*] All twenty-eight thousand acres of the richest land this side of the valley Nile.

BIG DADDY: Who said I was "leaving the place" to Gooper or anybody? This is my sixty-fifth birthday! I got fifteen years or twenty years left in me! I'll outlive *you!* I'll bury you an' have to pay for your coffin!

BRICK: Sure. Many happy returns. Now let's go watch the fireworks, come on, let's—

BIG DADDY: Lying, have they been lying? About the report from th'—clinic? did they, did they—find something?—*Cancer.* Maybe?

BRICK: Mendacity is a system that we live in. Liquor is one way out an' death's the other. . . .

[*He takes the crutch from* BIG DADDY'S *loose grip and swings out on the gallery leaving the doors open.*
[*A song, "Pick a Bale of Cotton," is heard.*]

MAE: [*appearing in door*] Oh, Big Daddy, the field hands are singin' fo' you!

BIG DADDY: [*shouting hoarsely*] BRICK! BRICK!

MAE: He's outside drinkin', Big Daddy.

BIG DADDY: *BRICK!*

[MAE *retreats, awed by the passion of his voice. Children call "Brick" in tones mocking* BIG DADDY. *His face crumbles like broken yellow plaster about to fall into dust.*
[*There is a glow in the sky.* BRICK *swings back through the doors, slowly, gravely, quite soberly.*]

BRICK: I'm sorry, Big Daddy. My head don't work any more and it's hard for me to understand how anybody could care if he lived or died or was dying or cared about anything but whether or not there was liquor left in the bottle and so I said what I said without thinking. In some ways I'm no better than the others, in some ways worse because I'm less alive. Maybe it's being alive that makes them lie, and being almost *not* alive makes me sort of

accidentally truthful—I don't know but—anyway—we've been friends . . .
—And being friends is telling each other the truth. . . .
[*There is a pause.*]
You told *me!* I told *you!*
[*A child rushes into the room and grabs a fistful of firecrackers and runs out again.*]
CHILD: [*screaming*] Bang, bang, bang, bang, bang, bang, bang, bang, bang!
BIG DADDY: [*slowly and passionately*]
CHRIST—DAMN—ALL—LYING SONS OF—LYING BITCHES!
[*He straightens at last and crosses to the inside door. At the door he turns and looks back as if he had some desperate question he couldn't put into words. Then he nods reflectively and says in a hoarse voice:*]
Yes, all lairs, all liars, all lying dying liars!
[*This is said slowly, slowly, with a fierce revulsion. He goes on out.*]
—Lying! Dying! Liars!
[*His voice dies out. There is a sound of a child being slapped. It rushes, hideously bawling, through room and out the hall door.*
[BRICK *remains motionless as the lights dim out and the curtain falls.*]
CURTAIN

ACT THREE

There is no lapse of time. MAE *enters with* REVEREND TOOKER.

MAE: Where is Big Daddy! Big Daddy?
BIG MAMA: [*entering*] Too much smell of burnt fireworks makes me feel a little bit sick at my stomach.—Where is Big Daddy?
MAE: That's what I want to know, where has Big Daddy gone?
BIG MAMA: He must have turned in, I reckon he went to baid. . . .
[GOOPER *enters.*]
GOOPER: Where is Big Daddy?
MAE: We don't know where he is!
BIG MAMA: I reckon he's gone to baid.
GOOPER: Well, then, now we can talk.
BIG MAMA: What *is* this talk, *what* talk?
[MARGARET *appears on gallery, talking to* DR. BAUGH.]
MARGARET: [*musically*] My family freed their slaves ten years before abolition, my great-great-grandfather gave his slaves their freedom five years before the War between the States started!
MAE: Oh, for God's sake! Maggie's climbed back up in her family tree!
MARGARET: [*sweetly*] What, Mae?—Oh, where's Big Daddy?!
[*The pace must be very quick. Great Southern animation.*]
BIG MAMA: [*addressing them all*] I think Big Daddy was just worn out. He loves his family, he loves to have them around him, but it's a strain on his nerves. He wasn't himself tonight, Big Daddy wasn't himself, I could tell he was all worked up.
REVEREND TOOKER: I think he's remarkable.
BIG MAMA: Yaisss! Just remarkable. Did you all notice the food he ate at that table? Did you all notice the supper he put away? Why, he ate like a hawss!

GOOPER: I hope he doesn't regret it.

BIG MAMA: Why, that man—ate a huge piece of cawn-bread with molasses on it! Helped himself twice to hoppin' john.

MARGARET: Big Daddy loves hoppin' john.—We had a real country dinner.

BIG MAMA: [*overlapping* MARGARET] Yais, he simply adores it! An' candied yams? That man put away enough food at that table to stuff a nigger *field* hand!

GOOPER: [*with grim relish*] I hope he don't have to pay for it later on. . . .

BIG MAMA: [*fiercely*] What's *that*, Gooper?

MAE: Gooper says he hopes Big Daddy doesn't suffer tonight.

BIG MAMA: Oh, shoot, Gooper says, Gooper says! Why should Big Daddy suffer for satisfying a normal appetite? There's nothin' wrong with that man but nerves, he's sound as a dollar! And now he knows he is an' that's why he ate such a supper. He had a big load off his mind, knowin' he wasn't doomed t'—what he thought he was doomed to. . . .

MARGARET: [*sadly and sweetly*] Bless his old sweet soul. . . .

BIG MAMA: [*vaguely*] Yais, bless his heart, where's Brick?

MAE: Outside.

GOOPER: —Drinkin' . . .

BIG MAMA: I know he's drinkin'. You all don't have to keep tellin' *me* Brick is drinkin'. Cain't I see he's drinkin' without you continually tellin' me that boy's drinkin'?

MARGARET: Good for you, Big Mama!
   [*She applauds.*]

BIG MAMA: Other people *drink* and *have* drunk an' will *drink*, as long as they make that stuff an' put it in bottles.

MARGARET: That's the truth. I never trusted a man that didn't drink.

MAE: Gooper never drinks. Don't you trust Gooper?

MARGARET: Why, Gooper, don't you drink? If I'd known you didn't drink, I wouldn't of made that remark—

BIG MAMA: *Brick?*

MARGARET: —at least not in your presence.
   [*She laughs sweetly.*]

BIG MAMA: *Brick!*

MARGARET: He's still on the gall'ry. I'll go bring him in so we can talk.

BIG MAMA: [*worriedly*] I don't know what this mysterious family conference is about.
   [*Awkward silence.* BIG MAMA *looks from face to face, then belches slightly and mutters, "Excuse me. . . ." She opens an ornamental fan suspended about her throat, a black lace fan to go with her black lace gown, and fans her wilting corsage, sniffing nervously and looking from face to face in the un-comfortable silence as* MARGARET *calls "Brick?" and* BRICK *sings to the moon on the gallery.*]
   I don't know what's wrong here, you all have such long faces! Open that door on the hall and let some air circulate through here, will you please, Gooper?

MAE: I think we'd better leave that door closed, Big Mama, till after the talk.

BIG MAMA: Reveren' Tooker, will *you* please open that door?!

REVEREND TOOKER: I sure will, Big Mama.

MAE: I just didn't think we ought t' take any chance of Big Daddy hearin' a word of this discussion.

BIG MAMA: I *swan!* Nothing's going to be said in Big Daddy's house that he cain't hear if he wants to!

GOOPER: Well, Big Mama, it's—

> [MAE *gives him a quick, hard poke to shut him up. He glares at her fiercely as she circles before him like a burlesque ballerina, raising her skinny bare arms over her head, jangling her bracelets, exclaiming:*]

MAE: *A breeze! A breeze!*

REVEREND TOOKER: I think this house is the coolest house in the Delta.—Did you all know that Halsey Banks' widow put air-conditioning units in the church and rectory at Friar's Point in memory of Halsey?

> [*General conversation has resumed; everybody is chatting so that the stage sounds like a big bird cage.*]

GOOPER: Too bad nobody cools your church off for you. I bet you sweat in that pulpit these hot Sundays, Reverend Tooker.

REVEREND TOOKER: Yes, my vestments are drenched.

MAE: [*at the same time to* DR. BAUGH] You think those vitamin B_{12} injections are what they're cracked up t' be, Doc Baugh?

DOCTOR BAUGH: Well, if you want to be stuck with something I guess they're as good to be stuck with as anything else.

BIG MAMA: [*at gallery door*] Maggie, Maggie, aren't you comin' with Brick?

MAE: [*suddenly and loudly, creating a silence*] I have a strange feeling, I have a peculiar feeling!

BIG MAMA: [*turning from gallery*] What feeling?

MAE: That Brick said somethin' he shouldn't of said t' Big Daddy.

BIG MAMA: Now what on earth could Brick of said t' Big Daddy that he shouldn't say?

GOOPER: Big Mama, there's somethin'—

MAE: NOW, WAIT!

> [*She rushes up to* BIG MAMA *and gives her a quick hug and kiss.* BIG MAMA *pushes her impatiently off as the* REVEREND TOOKER'S *voice rises serenely in a little pocket of silence:*]

REVEREND TOOKER: Yes, last Sunday the gold in my chasuble faded into th' purple. . . .

GOOPER: Reveren', you must of been preachin' hell's fire last Sunday!

> [*He guffaws at this witticism but the* REVEREND *is not sincerely amused. At the same time* BIG MAMA *has crossed over to* DR. BAUGH *and is saying to him:*]

BIG MAMA: [*her breathless voice rising high-pitched above the others*] In my day they had what they call the Keeley cure for heavy drinkers. But now I understand they just take some kind of tablets, they call them "Annie Bust" tablets. But *Brick* don't need to take *nothin'*.

> [BRICK *appears in gallery doors with* MARGARET *behind him.*]

BIG MAMA: [*unaware of his presence behind her*] That boy is just broken up over Skipper's death. You know how poor Skipper died. They gave him a big, big dose of that sodium amytal stuff at his home and then they called the ambulance and give him another big, big dose of it at the hospital and that and all of the alcohol in his system fo' months an' months an' months just proved too much for his heart. . . . I'm scared of needles! I'm more scared of a needle than the knife. . . . I think more people have been needled out of this world than—

[*She stops short and wheels about.*]

OH!—here's Brick! My precious baby—

[*She turns upon* BRICK *with short, fat arms extended, at the same time uttering a loud, short sob, which is both comic and touching.*

[BRICK *smiles and bows slightly, making a burlesque gesture of gallantry for* MAGGIE *to pass before him into the room. Then he hobbles on his crutch directly to the liquor cabinet and there is absolute silence, with everybody looking at* BRICK *as everybody has always looked at* BRICK *when he spoke or moved or appeared. One by one he drops ice cubes in his glass, then suddenly, but not quickly, looks back over his shoulder with a wry, charming smile, and says:*]

BRICK: I'm sorry! Anyone else?

BIG MAMA: [*sadly*] No, son. I *wish* you wouldn't!

BRICK: I wish I didn't have to, Big Mama, but I'm still waiting for that click in my head which makes it all smooth out!

BIG MAMA: Aw, Brick, you—BREAK MY HEART!

MARGARET: [*at the same time*] Brick, go sit with Big Mama!

BIG MAMA: I just cain't *staiiiiiiiii-nnnnnd*—it. . . .

[*She sobs.*]

MAE: Now that we're all assembled—

GOOPER: We kin talk. . . .

BIG MAMA: Breaks my heart. . . .

MARGARET: Sit with Big Mama, Brick, and hold her hand.

[BIG MAMA *sniffs very loudly three times, almost like three drum beats in the pocket of silence.*]

BRICK: You do that, Maggie. I'm a restless cripple. I got to stay on my crutch.

[BRICK *hobbles to the gallery door; leans there as if waiting.* MAE *sits beside* BIG MAMA, *while* GOOPER *moves in front and sits on the end of the couch, facing her.* REVEREND TOOKER *moves nervously into the space between them; on the other side,* DR. BAUGH *stands looking at nothing in particular and lights a cigar.* MARGARET *turns away.*]

BIG MAMA: Why're you all *surroundin'* me—like this? Why're you all starin' at me like this an' makin' signs at each other?

[REVEREND TOOKER *steps back startled.*]

MAE: Calm yourself, Big Mama.

BIG MAMA: Calm you'self, *you'self,* Sister Woman. How could I calm myself with everyone starin' at me as if big drops of blood had broken out on m' face? What's this all about, annh! What?

[GOOPER *coughs and takes a center position.*]

GOOPER: Now, Doc Baugh.

MAE: Doc Baugh?

BRICK: [*suddenly*] SHHH!—

[*Then he grins and chuckles and shakes his head regretfully.*]
—Naw!—that wasn't th' click.

GOOPER: Brick, shut up or stay out there on the gallery with your liquor! We got to talk about a serious matter. Big Mama wants to know the complete truth about the report we got today from the Ochsner Clinic.

MAE: [*eagerly*]—on Big Daddy's condition!

GOOPER: Yais, on Big Daddy's condition, we got to face it.

DOCTOR BAUGH: Well. . . .

BIG MAMA: [*terrified, rising*] Is there? Something? Something that I? Don't— Know?

> [*In these few words, this startled, very soft, question,* BIG MAMA *reviews the history of her forty-five years with* BIG DADDY, *her great, almost embarrassingly true-hearted and simple-minded devotion to* BIG DADDY, *who must have had something* BRICK *has, who made himself loved so much by the "simple expedient" of not loving enough to disturb his charming detachment, also once coupled, like* BRICK's, *with virile beauty.*
> [BIG MAMA *has a dignity at this moment: she almost stops being fat.*]

DOCTOR BAUGH: [*after a pause, uncomfortably*] Yes?—Well—

BIG MAMA: *I!!!*—want to—*knowwwwwwww. . . .*

> [*Immediately she thrusts her fist to her mouth as if to deny that statement.*
> [*Then, for some curious reason, she snatches the withered corsage from her breast and hurls it on the floor and steps on it with her short, fat feet.*]

—Somebody must be lyin'!—I want to know!

MAE: Sit down, Big Mama, sit down on this sofa.

MARGARET: [*quickly*] Brick, go sit with Big Mama.

BIG MAMA: *What is it, what is it?*

DOCTOR BAUGH: I never have seen a more thorough examination than Big Daddy Pollitt was given in all my experience with the Ochsner Clinic.

GOOPER: It's one of the best in the country.

MAE: It's *THE* best in the country—bar *none!*

> [*For some reason she gives* GOOPER *a violent poke as she goes past him. He slaps at her hand without removing his eyes from his mother's face.*]

DOCTOR BAUGH: Of course, they were ninety-nine and nine-tenths percent sure before they even started.

BIG MAMA: Sure of what, sure of what, sure of—*what?—what!*

> [*She catches her breath in a startled sob.* MAE *kisses her quickly. She thrusts* MAE *fiercely away from her, staring at the doctor.*]

MAE: Mommy, be a brave girl!

BRICK: [*in the doorway, softly*]

> "By the light, by the light,
> Of the sil-ve-ry mo-ooo-n . . ."

GOOPER: Shut up!—Brick.

BRICK: —Sorry. . . .

> [*He wanders out on the gallery.*]

DOCTOR BAUGH: But now, you see, Big Mama, they cut a piece off this growth, a specimen of the tissue and—

BIG MAMA: Growth? You told Big Daddy—

DOCTOR BAUGH: Now wait.

BIG MAMA: [*fiercely*] You told me and Big Daddy there wasn't a thing wrong with him but—

MAE: Big Mama, they always—

GOOPER: Let Doc Baugh talk, will yuh?

BIG MAMA: —little spastic condition of—
[*Her breath gives out in a sob.*]

DOCTOR BAUGH: Yes, that's what we told Big Daddy. But we had this bit of tissue run through the laboratory and I'm sorry to say the test was positive on it. It's—well—malignant. . . .
[*Pause.*]

BIG MAMA: —Cancer?! Cancer?!
[DR. BAUGH *nods gravely.*]
[BIG MAMA *gives a long gasping cry.*]

MAE and GOOPER: Now, now, now, Big Mama, you had to know. . . .

BIG MAMA: *WHY DIDN'T THEY CUT IT OUT OF HIM? HANH? HANH?*

DOCTOR BAUGH: Involved too much, Big Mama, too many organs affected.

MAE: Big Mama, the liver's affected and so's the kidneys, both! It's gone way past what they call a—

GOOPER: A Surgical risk.

MAE: —Uh-huh. . . .
[BIG MAMA *draws a breath like a dying gasp.*]

REVEREND TOOKER: Tch, tch, tch, tch, tch!

DOCTOR BAUGH: Yes, it's gone past the knife.

MAE: *That's why he's turned yellow, Mommy!*

BIG MAMA: *Git away from me, git away from me, Mae!*
[*She rises abruptly.*]
I want Brick! Where's Brick? Where is my only son?

MAE: Mama! Did she say "*only*" son"?

GOOPER: What does that make *me?*

MAE: A sober responsible man with five precious children!—*Six!*

BIG MAMA: I want Brick to tell me! Brick! Brick!

MARGARET: [*rising from her reflections in a corner*] Brick was so upset he went back out.

BIG MAMA: *Brick!*

MARGARET: Mama, let *me* tell you!

BIG MAMA: No, no, leave me alone, you're not my blood!

GOOPER: *Mama, I'm your son!* Listen to *me!*

MAE: Gooper's your son, Mama, he's your first-born!

BIG MAMA: Gooper never liked Daddy.

MAE: [*as if terribly shocked*] *That's not TRUE!*
[*There is a pause. The minister coughs and rises.*]

REVEREND TOOKER: [*to* MAE] I think I'd better slip away at this point.

MAE: [*sweetly and sadly*] Yes, Doctor Tooker, you go.

REVEREND TOOKER: [*discreetly*] Goodnight, goodnight, everybody, and God bless you all . . . on this place. . . .
[*He slips out.*]

DOCTOR BAUGH: That man is a good man but lacking in tact. Talking about people giving memorial windows—if he mentioned one memorial window, he must have spoke of a dozen, and saying how awful it was when somebody died intestate, the legal wrangles, and so forth.

[MAE *coughs, and points at* BIG MAMA.]

DOCTOR BAUGH: Well, Big Mama. . . .

[*He sighs.*]

BIG MAMA: It's all a mistake, I know it's just a bad dream.

DOCTOR BAUGH: We're gonna keep Big Daddy as comfortable as we can.

BIG MAMA: Yes, it's just a bad dream, that's all it is, it's just an awful dream.

GOOPER: In my opinion Big Daddy is having some pain but won't admit that he has it.

BIG MAMA: Just a dream, a bad dream.

DOCTOR BAUGH: That's what lots of them do, they think if they don't admit they're having the pain they can sort of escape the fact of it.

GOOPER: [*with relish*] Yes, they get sly about it, they get real sly about it.

MAE: Gooper and I think—

GOOPER: Shut up, Mae!—Big Daddy ought to be started on morphine.

BIG MAMA: Nobody's going to give Big Daddy morphine.

DOCTOR BAUGH: Now, Big Mama, when that pain strikes it's going to strike mighty hard and Big Daddy's going to need the needle to bear it.

BIG MAMA: I tell you, nobody's going to give him morphine.

MAE: Big Mama, you don't want to see Big Daddy suffer, you know you—

[GOOPER *standing beside her gives her a savage poke.*]

DOCTOR BAUGH: [*placing a package on the table*] I'm leaving this stuff here, so if there's a sudden attack you all won't have to send out for it.

MAE: I know how to give a hypo.

GOOPER: Mae took a course in nursing during the war.

MARGARET: Somehow I don't think Big Daddy would want Mae to give him a hypo.

MAE: You think he'd want *you* to do it?

[DR. BAUGH *rises.*]

GOOPER: Doctor Baugh is goin'.

DOCTOR BAUGH: Yes, I got to be goin'. Well, keep your chin up, Big Mama.

GOOPER: [*with jocularity*] She's gonna keep *both* chins up, aren't you, Big Mama?

[BIG MAMA *sobs.*]

Now stop that, Big Mama.

MAE: Sit down with me, Big Mama.

GOOPER: [*at door with* DR. BAUGH] Well, Doc, we sure do appreciate all you done. I'm telling you, we're surely obligated to you for—

[DR. BAUGH *has gone out without a glance at him.*]

GOOPER: —I guess that doctor has got a lot on his mind but it wouldn't hurt him to act a little more human. . . .

[BIG MAMA *sobs.*]

Now be a brave girl, Mommy.

BIG MAMA: It's not true, I know that it's just not true!

GOOPER: Mama, those tests are infallible!

BIG MAMA: Why are you so determined to see your father daid?

MAE: Big Mama!

MARGARET: [*gently*] I know what Big Mama means.

MAE: [*fiercely*] Oh, do you?

MARGARET: [*quietly and very sadly*] Yes, I think I do.

MAE: For a newcomer in the family you sure do show a lot of understanding.

MARGARET: Understanding is needed on this place.

MAE: I guess you must have needed a lot of it in your family, Maggie, with your father's liquor problem and now you've got Brick with his!

MARGARET: Brick does not have a liquor problem at all. Brick is devoted to Big Daddy. This thing is a terrible strain on him.

BIG MAMA: Brick is Big Daddy's boy, but he drinks too much and it worries me and Big Daddy, and, Margaret, you've got to cooperate with us, you've got to cooperate with Big Daddy and me in getting Brick straightened out. Because it will break Big Daddy's heart if Brick don't pull himself together and take hold of things.

MAE: Take hold of *what* things, Big Mama?

BIG MAMA: The place.

[*There is a quick violent look between* MAE *and* GOOPER.]

GOOPER: Big Mama, you've had a shock.

MAE: Yais, we've all had a shock, but . . .

GOOPER: Let's be realistic—

MAE: —Big Daddy would never, would *never*, be foolish enough to—

GOOPER: —put this place in irresponsible hands!

BIG MAMA: Big Daddy ain't going to leave the place in anybody's hands; Big Daddy is *not* going to die. I want you to get that in your heads, all of you!

MAE: Mommy, Mommy, Big Mama, we're just as hopeful an' optimistic as you are about Big Daddy's prospects, we have faith in *prayer*—but nevertheless there are certain matters that have to be discussed an' dealt with, because otherwise—

GOOPER: Eventualities have to be considered and now's the time. . . . Mae, will you please get my briefcase out of our room?

MAE: Yes, honey.

[*She rises and goes out through the hall door.*]

GOOPER: [*standing over* BIG MAMA] Now, Big Mom. What you said just now was not at all true and you know it. I've always loved Big Daddy in my own quiet way. I never made a show of it, and I know that Big Daddy has always been fond of me in a quiet way, too, and he never made a show of it, neither.

[MAE *returns with* GOOPER's *briefcase.*]

MAE: Here's your briefcase, Gooper, honey.

GOOPER: [*handing the briefcase back to her*] Thank you. . . . Of ca'use, my relationship with Big Daddy is different from Brick's.

MAE: You're eight years older'n Brick an' always had t'carry a bigger load of th' responsibilities than Brick ever had t'carry. He never carried a thing in his life but a football or a highball.

GOOPER: Mae, will y' let me talk, please?

MAE: Yes, honey.

GOOPER: Now, a twenty-eight thousand-acre plantation's a mighty big thing t'run.

MAE: Almost singlehanded.

> [MARGARET *has gone out onto the gallery, and can be heard calling softly to* BRICK.]

BIG MAMA: You never had to run this place! What are you talking about? As if Big Daddy was dead and in his grave, you had to run it? Why, you just helped him out with a few business details and had your law practice at the same time in Memphis!

MAE: Oh, Mommy, Mommy, Big Mommy! Let's be fair! Why, Gooper has given himself body and soul to keeping this place up for the past five years since Big Daddy's health started failing. Gooper won't say it, Gooper never thought of it as a duty, he just did it. And what did Brick do? Brick kept living in his past glory at college! Still a football player at twenty-seven!

MARGARET: [*returning alone*] Who are you talking about, now? Brick? A football player? He isn't a football player and you know it. Brick is a sports announcer on TV and one of the best-known ones in the country!

MAE: I'm talking about what he was.

MARGARET: Well, I wish you would just stop talking about my husband.

GOOPER: I've got a right to discuss my brother with other members of MY OWN family which don't include *you*. Why don't you go out there and drink with Brick?

MARGARET: I've never seen such malice toward a brother.

GOOPER: How about his for me? Why, he can't stand to be in the same room with me!

MARGARET: This is a deliberate campaign of vilification for the most disgusting and sordid reason on earth, and I know what it is! It's *avarice, avarice, greed, greed!*

BIG MAMA: *Oh, I'll scream! I will scream in a moment unless this stops!*

> [GOOPER *has stalked up to* MARGARET *with clenched fists at his sides as if he would strike her.* MAE *distorts her face again into a hideous grimace behind* MARGARET's *back.*]

MARGARET: We only remain on the place because of Big Mom and Big Daddy. If it is true what they say about Big Daddy we are going to leave here just as soon as it's over. Not a moment later.

BIG MAMA: [*sobs*] Margaret. Child. Come here. Sit next to Big Mama.

MARGARET: Precious Mommy. I'm sorry, I'm so sorry, I—!

> [*She bends her long graceful neck to press her forehead to* BIG MAMA's *bulging shoulder under its black chiffon.*]

GOOPER: How beautiful, how touching, this display of devotion!

MAE: Do you know why she's childless? She's childless because that big beautiful athlete husband of hers won't go to bed with her!

GOOPER: You jest won't let me do this in a nice way, will yah? Aw right—Mae and I have five kids with another one coming! I don't give a goddam if Big Daddy likes me or don't like me or did or never did or will or will never! I'm just appealing to a sense of common decency and fair play. I'll tell you the truth. I've resented Big Daddy's partiality to Brick ever since Brick was born, and the way I've been treated like I was just barely good enough to spit on and sometimes not even good enough for that. Big Daddy is dying of cancer, and it's spread all through him and it's attacked all his vital organs including the kidneys and right now he is sinking into uremia, and you all know what uremia is, it's poisoning of the whole system due to the failure of the body to eliminate its poisons.

MARGARET: [*to herself, downstage, hissingly*] *Poisons, poisons! Venomous thoughts and words! In hearts and minds!—That's poisons!*

GOOPER: [*overlapping her*] I am asking for a square deal, and I expect to get one. But if I don't get one, if there's any peculiar shenanigans going on around here behind my back, or before me, well, I'm not a corporation lawyer for nothing, I know how to protect my own interests.—*OH! A late arrival!*

[BRICK *enters from the gallery with a tranquil, blurred smile, carrying an empty glass with him.*]

MAE: Behold the conquering hero comes!

GOOPER: The fabulous Brick Pollitt! Remember him?—Who could forget him!

MAE: He looks like he's been injured in a game!

GOOPER: Yep, I'm afraid you'll have to warm the bench at the Sugar Bowl this year, Brick!

[MAE *laughs shrilly.*]

Or was it the Rose Bowl that he made that famous run in?

MAE: The punch bowl, honey. It was in the punch bowl, the cut-glass punch bowl!

GOOPER: Oh, that's right, I'm getting the bowls mixed up!

MARGARET: Why don't you stop venting your malice and envy on a sick boy?

BIG MAMA: *Now you two hush, I mean it, hush, all of you, hush!*

GOOPER: All right, Big Mama. A family crisis brings out the best and the worst in every member of it.

MAE: *That's* the truth.

MARGARET: *Amen!*

BIG MAMA: *I said, "hush!"* I won't tolerate any more catty talk in my house.

[MAE *gives* GOOPER *a sign indicating briefcase.*]

[BRICK's *smile has grown both brighter and vaguer. As he prepares a drink, he sings softly:*]

BRICK: *Show me the way to go home,*
            I'm tired and I wanta go to bed,
            I had a little drink about an hour ago—

GOOPER: [*at the same time*] Big Mama, you know it's necessary for me t'go back to Memphis in th' mornin' t'represent the Parker estate in a lawsuit.

[MAE *sits on the bed and arranges papers she has taken from the briefcase.*]

BRICK: [*continuing the song*]

            Wherever I may roam,
            On land or sea or foam.

BIG MAMA: Is it, Gooper?

MAE: Yaiss.

GOOPER: That's why I'm forced to—to bring up a problem that—

MAE: Somethin' that's too important t' be put off!

GOOPER: If Brick was sober, he ought to be in on this.

MARGARET: Brick is present; we're here.

GOOPER: Well, good. I will now give you this outline my partner, Tom Bullitt, an' me have drawn up—a sort of dummy—trusteeship.

MARGARET: Oh, that's it! You'll be in charge an' dole out remittances, will you?

GOOPER: This we did as soon as we got the report on Big Daddy from th' Ochsner Laboratories. We did this thing, I mean we drew up this dummy outline with the advice and assistance of the Chairman of the Boa'd of Directors of th' Southern Plantahs Bank and Trust Company in Memphis, C. C. Bellowes, a man who handles estates for all th' prominent fam'lies in West Tennessee and th' Delta.

BIG MAMA: Gooper?

GOOPER: [*crouching in front of* BIG MAMA] Now this is not—not final, or anything like it. This is just a preliminary outline. But it does provide a basis—a design—a—possible, feasible—*plan!*

MARGARET: Yes, I'll bet.

MAE: It's a plan to protect the biggest estate in the Delta from irresponsibility an'—

BIG MAMA: Now you listen to me, all of you, you listen here! They's not goin' to be any more catty talk in my house! And Gooper, you put that away before I grab it out of your hand and tear it right up! I don't know what the hell's in it, and I don't want to know what the hell's in it. I'm talkin' in Big Daddy's language now; I'm his *wife,* not his *widow,* I'm still his *wife!* And I'm talkin' to you in his language an'—

GOOPER: Big Mama, what I have here is—

MAE: Gooper explained that it's just a plan. . . .

BIG MAMA: I don't care what you got there. Just put it back where it came from, an' don't let me see it again, not even the outside of the envelope of it! Is that understood? Basis! Plan! Preliminary! Design! I say—what is it Big Daddy always says when he's disgusted?

BRICK: [*from the bar*] Big Daddy says "crap" when he's disgusted.

BIG MAMA: [*rising*] That's right—*CRAP!* I say *CRAP,* too, like Big Daddy!

MAE: Coarse language doesn't seem called for in this—

GOOPER: Somethin' in me is *deeply outraged* by hearin' you talk like this.

BIG MAMA: *Nobody's goin' to take nothin'!*—till Big Daddy lets go of it, and maybe, just possibly, not—not even then! No, not even then!

BRICK: *You can always hear me singin' this song,*
                    Show me the way to go home.

BIG MAMA: Tonight Brick looks like he used to look when he was a little boy, just like he did when he played wild games and used to come home all sweaty and pink-cheeked and sleepy, with his—red curls shining. . . .
    [*She comes over to him and runs her fat shaky hand through his hair. He draws aside as he does from all physical contact and continues the song in a whisper, opening the ice bucket and dropping in the ice cubes one by one as if he were mixing some important chemical formula.*]

BIG MAMA: [*continuing*] Time goes by so fast. Nothin' can outrun it. Death commences too early—almost before you're half acquainted with life—you meet with the other. . . .

Oh, you know we just got to love each other an' stay together, all of us, just as close as we can, especially now that such a *black* thing has come and moved into this place without invitation.

[*Awkwardly embracing* BRICK, *she presses her head to his shoulder.*

[GOOPER *has been returning papers to* MAE, *who has restored them to briefcase with an air of severely tried patience.*]

GOOPER: Big Mama? Big Mama?

[*He stands behind her, tense with sibling envy.*]

BIG MAMA: [*oblivious of* GOOPER] Brick, you hear me, don't you?

MARGARET: Brick hears you, Big Mama, he understands what you're saying.

BIG MAMA: Oh, Brick, son of Big Daddy! Big Daddy does so love you! Y'know what would be his fondest dream come true? If before he passed on, if Big Daddy has to pass on, you gave him a child of yours, a grandson as much like his son as his son is like Big Daddy!

MAE: [*zipping briefcase shut: an incongruous sound*] Such a pity that Maggie an' Brick can't oblige!

MARGARET: [*suddenly and quietly but forcefully*] Everybody listen.

[*She crosses to the center of the room, holding her hands rigidly together.*]

MAE: Listen to what, Maggie?

MARGARET: I have an announcement to make.

GOOPER: A sports announcement, Maggie?

MARGARET: Brick and I are going to—*have a child!*

[BIG MAMA *catches her breath in a loud gasp.*]

[*Pause.* BIG MAMA *rises.*]

BIG MAMA: Maggie! Brick! This is too good to believe!

MAE: That's right, too good to believe.

BIG MAMA: Oh, my, my! This is Big Daddy's dream, his dream come true! I'm going to tell him right now before he—

MARGARET: We'll tell him in the morning. Don't disturb him now.

BIG MAMA: I want to tell him before he goes to sleep, I'm going to tell him his dream's come true this minute! And Brick! A child will make you pull yourself together and quit this drinking!

[*She seizes the glass from his hand.*]

The responsibilities of a father will—

[*Her face contorts and she makes an excited gesture; bursting into sobs, she rushes out, crying.*]

I'm going to tell Big Daddy right this minute!

[*Her voice fades out down the hall.*

[BRICK *shrugs slightly and drops an ice cube into another glass.* MARGARET *crosses quickly to his side, saying something under her breath, and she pours the liquor for him, staring up almost fiercely into his face.*]

BRICK: [*coolly*] Thank you, Maggie, that's a nice big shot.

[MAE *has joined* GOOPER *and she gives him a fierce poke, making a low hissing sound and a grimace of fury.*]

GOOPER: [*pushing her aside*] Brick, could you possibly spare me one small shot of that liquor?

BRICK: Why, help yourself, Gooper boy.

GOOPER: I will.

MAE: [*shrilly*] Of course we know that this is—

GOOPER: *Be still, Mae!*

MAE: I won't be still! I know she's made this up!

GOOPER: Goddam it, I said to shut up!

MARGARET: Gracious! I didn't know that my little announcement was going to provoke such a storm!

MAE: *That* woman isn't *pregnant!*

GOOPER: Who said she was?

MAE: *She* did.

GOOPER: The doctor didn't. Doc Baugh didn't.

MARGARET: I haven't gone to Doc Baugh.

GOOPER: Then who'd you go to, Maggie?

MARGARET: One of the best gynecologists in the South.

GOOPER: Uh huh, uh huh!—I see. . . .

> [*He takes out pencil and notebook.*]

—May we have his name, please?

MARGARET: No, you may not, Mister Prosecuting Attorney!

MAE: He doesn't have any name, he doesn't exist!

MARGARET: Oh, he exists all right, and so does my child, Brick's baby!

MAE: You can't conceive a child by a man that won't sleep with you unless you think you're—

> [BRICK *has turned on the phonograph. A scat song cuts* MAE'S *speech.*]

GOOPER: *Turn that off!*

MAE: We know it's a lie because we hear you in here; he won't sleep with you, we hear you! So don't imagine you're going to put a trick over on us, to fool a dying man with a—

> [*A long drawn cry of agony and rage fills the house.* MARGARET *turns phonograph down to a whisper.*
> [*The cry is repeated.*]

MAE: [*awed*] Did you hear that, Gooper, did you hear that?

GOOPER: Sounds like the pain has struck.

MAE: Go see, Gooper!

GOOPER: Come along and leave these lovebirds together in their nest!

> [*He goes out first.* MAE *follows but turns at the door, contorting her face and hissing at* MARGARET.]

MAE: *Liar!*

> [*She slams the door.*
> [MARGARET *exhales with relief and moves a little unsteadily to catch hold of* BRICK'S *arm.*]

MARGARET: Thank you for—keeping still . . .

BRICK: Okay, Maggie.

MARGARET: It was gallant of you to save my face!

BRICK: —It hasn't happened yet.

MARGARET: What?

BRICK: The click. . . .

MARGARET: —the click in your head that makes you peaceful, honey?

BRICK: Uh-huh. It hasn't happened. . . . I've got to make it happen before I can sleep. . . .

MARGARET: —I—know what you—mean. . . .

BRICK: Give me that pillow in the big chair, Maggie.

MARGARET: I'll put it on the bed for you.

BRICK: No, put it on the sofa, where I sleep.

MARGARET: Not tonight, Brick.

BRICK: I want it on the sofa. That's where I sleep.

> [*He has hobbled to the liquor cabinet. He now pours down three shots in quick succession and stands waiting, silent. All at once he turns with a smile and says:*]
>
> *There!*

MARGARET: What?

BRICK: The *click.* . . .

> [*His gratitude seems almost infinite as he hobbles out on the gallery with a drink. We hear his crutch as he swings out of sight. Then, at some distance, he begins singing to himself a peaceful song.*
>
> [MARGARET *holds the big pillow forlornly as if it were her only companion, for a few moments, then throws it on the bed. She rushes to the liquor cabinet, gathers all the bottles in her arms, turns about undecidedly, then runs out of the room with them, leaving the door ajar on the dim yellow hall.* BRICK *is heard hobbling back along the gallery, singing his peaceful song. He comes back in, sees the pillow on the bed, laughs lightly, sadly, picks it up. He has it under his arm as* MARGARET *returns to the room.* MARGARET *softly shuts the door and leans against it, smiling softly at* BRICK.]

MARGARET: Brick, I used to think that you were stronger than me and I didn't want to be overpowered by you. But now, since you've taken to liquor—you know what?—I guess it's bad, but now I'm stronger than you and I can love you more truly!

> Don't move that pillow. I'll move it right back if you do!
>
> —Brick?
>
> [*She turns out all the lamps but a single rose-silk-shaded one by the bed.*]
>
> I really have been to a doctor and I know what to do and—Brick?— this is my time by the calendar to conceive!

BRICK: Yes, I understand, Maggie. But how are you going to conceive a child by a man in love with his liquor?

MARGARET: By locking his liquor up and making him satisfy my desire before I unlock it!

BRICK: Is that what you've done, Maggie?

MARGARET: Look and see. That cabinet's mighty empty compared to before!

BRICK: Well, I'll be a son of a—

> [*He reaches for his crutch but she beats him to it and rushes out on the gallery, hurls the crutch over the rail and comes back in, panting.*
>
> [*There are running footsteps.* BIG MAMA *bursts into the room, her face all awry, gasping, stammering.*]

BIG MAMA: Oh, my God, oh, my God, oh, my God, where is it?

MARGARET: Is this what you want, Big Mama?

[MARGARET *hands her the package left by the doctor.*]

BIG MAMA: I can't bear it, oh, God! Oh, Brick! Brick, baby!

[*She rushes at him. He averts his face from her sobbing kisses.* MARGARET *watches with a tight smile.*]

My son, Big Daddy's boy! Little Father!

[*The groaning cry is heard again. She runs out, sobbing.*]

MARGARET: And so tonight we're going to make the lie true, and when that's done, I'll bring the liquor back here and we'll get drunk together, here, tonight, in this place that death has come into. . . .

—What do you say?

BRICK: I don't say anything. I guess there's nothing to say.

MARGARET: Oh, you weak people, you weak, beautiful people!—who give up.— What you want is someone to—

[*She turns out the rose-silk lamp.*]

—take hold of you.—Gently, gently, with love! And—

[*The curtain begins to fall slowly.*]

I *do* love you, Brick, I *do!*

BRICK: [*smiling with charming sadness*] Wouldn't it be funny if that was true?

THE CURTAIN COMES DOWN

THE END

Samuel Beckett (1906–1989)

Happy Days (1961)

Several postwar dramatists (among them Samuel Beckett, Eugene Ionesco, and Jean Genet) were dubbed "absurdists" by Martin Esslin because their work conveyed "the sense that the certitudes and unshakable basic assumptions of former ages have been swept away, that they have been . . . discredited as cheap and somewhat childish illusions." Or, as Ionesco put it, "cut off from his religious, metaphysical, and transcendental roots, man is lost; all his actions become senseless, absurd and useless." Most absurdist plays, rather than telling a story, explore this human condition, in which characters seek to insulate themselves against the void by indulging in meaningless activities or abortive attempts at communication.

Beckett's *Happy Days* embodies most of the traits of absurdism. It has virtually abandoned action. The first act shows a woman, Winnie, trapped up to her waist in a mound of earth. She does not struggle against her physical entrapment but fills her days with a routine built around objects she keeps in a shopping bag; she speaks often to her husband, who for the most part remains unseen behind the mound and who responds only rarely. In the second act, Winnie is buried up to her neck and able to move only her eyes and mouth; at first she is not even sure that her husband is still alive, but eventually he crawls up the mound into her view. Despite her situation, Winnie remains determinedly cheerful; she speaks often of her blessings and the small things that will make this "another happy day." She never questions why she is in this situation, nor does she wonder at her isolation. She apparently accepts her lot as no more to be questioned than existence itself.

As in others of his plays, in *Happy Days* Beckett uses visual imagery to sum up his vision of the human condition. He shows human beings trapped in a symbolic landscape, cut off from all but the most minimal contact, passing time as best they can while waiting doggedly or hoping desperately for something that will give meaning to the moment or to life itself. Occasionally they reveal flashes of anxiety, but they quickly divert themselves with games, memories, and speculations. The plays explore a state of being rather than show a developing action.

Samuel Beckett

Happy Days

CHARACTERS

WINNIE, *a woman about fifty*
WILLIE, *a man about sixty*

ACT I

Expanse of scorched grass rising centre to low mound. Gentle slopes down to front and either side of stage. Back an abrupter fall to stage level. Maximum of simplicity and symmetry.
    Blazing light.
    Very pompier trompe-l'oeil backcloth to represent unbroken plain and sky receding to meet in far distance.
    Embedded up to above her waist in exact centre of mound, WINNIE. *About fifty, well preserved, blond for preference, plump, arms and shoulders bare, low bodice, big bosom, pearl necklet. She is discovered sleeping, her arms on the ground before her, her head on her arms. Beside her on ground to her left a capacious black bag, shopping variety, and to her right a collapsible collapsed parasol, beak of handle emerging from sheath.*
    To her right and rear, lying asleep on ground, hidden by mound, WILLIE.
    Long pause. A bell rings piercingly, say ten seconds, stops. She does not move. Pause. Bell more piercingly, say five seconds. She wakes. Bell stops. She raises her head, gazes front. Long pause. She straightens up, lays her hands flat on ground, throws back her head and gazes at zenith. Long pause.

WINNIE: [*gazing at zenith*] Another heavenly day. [*Pause. Head back level, eyes front, pause. She clasps hands to breast, closes eyes. Lips move in unaudible prayer, say ten seconds. Lips still. Hands remain clasped. Low.*] For Jesus Christ sake Amen. [*Eyes open, hands unclasp, return to mound. Pause. She clasps hands to breast again, closes eyes, lips move again in inaudible addendum, say five seconds. Low.*] World without end Amen. [*Eyes open, hands unclasp, return to mound. Pause.*] Begin, Winnie. [*Pause.*] Begin your day, Winnie. [*Pause. She turns to bag, rummages in it without moving it from its place, brings out toothbrush, rummages again, brings out flat tube of toothpaste, turns back front, unscrews cap of tube, lays cap on ground, squeezes with difficulty small blob of paste on brush, holds tube in one hand and brushes teeth with other. She turns modestly aside and back to her right to spit out behind mound. In this position her eyes rest on* WILLIE. *She spits out. She cranes a little further back and down. Loud.*] Hoo-oo! [*Pause. Louder.*] Hoo-oo! [*Pause. Tender smile as she turns back front, lays down brush.*] Poor Willie—[*examines tube, smile off*]—running out—[*looks for cap*]—ah well—[*finds cap*]—can't be helped—[*screws on cap*]—just one of those old things—[*lays down tube*]—another of those old things—[*turns towards bag*]—just can't be cured—[*rummages in bag*]—cannot be cured—

[*brings out small mirror, turns back front*]—ah yes—[*inspects teeth in mirror*]—poor dear Willie—[*testing upper front teeth with thumb, indistinctly*]—good Lord!—[*pulling back upper lip to inspect gums, do.*]—good God!—[*pulling back corner of mouth, mouth open, do.*]—ah well—[*other corner, do.*]—no worse—[*abandons inspection, normal speech*]—no better, no worse—[*lays down mirror*]—no change—[*wipes fingers on grass*]—no pain—[*looks for toothbrush*]—hardly any—[*takes up toothbrush*]—great thing that—[*examines handle of brush*]—nothing like it—[*examines handle, reads*]—pure . . . what?—[*Pause.*]—what?—[*lays down brush*]—ah yes—[*turns toward bag*]—poor Willie—[*rummages in bag*]—no zest—[*rummages*]—for anything—[*brings out spectacles in case*]—no interest—[*turns back front*]—in life—[*takes spectacles from case*]—poor dear Willie—[*lays down case*]—sleep for ever—[*opens spectacles*]—marvellous gift—[*puts on spectacles*]—nothing to touch it—[*looks for toothbrush*]—in my opinion—[*takes up toothbrush*]—always said so—[*examines handle of brush*]— wish I had it—[*examines handle, reads*]—genuine . . . pure . . . what?—[*lays down brush*]—blind next—[*takes off spectacles*]—ah well—[*lays down spectacles*]—seen enough—[*feels in bodice for handkerchief*]—I suppose—[*takes out folded handkerchief*]—by now—[*shakes out handkerchief*]—what are those wonderful lines—[*wipes one eye*]—woe woe is me—[*wipes the other*]—to see what I see—[*looks for spectacles*]—ah yes—[*takes up spectacles*]—wouldn't miss it—[*starts polishing spectacles, breathing on lenses*]—or would I?—[*polishes*]—holy light—[*polishes*]—bob up out of dark—[*polishes*]—blaze of hellish light. [*Stops polishing, raises face to sky, pause, head back level, resumes polishing, stops polishing, cranes back to her right and down.*] Hoo-oo! [*Pause. Tender smile as she turns back front and resumes polishing. Smile off.*] Marvelous gift—[*stops polishing, lays down spectacles*]—wish I had it—[*folds handkerchief*]—ah well—[*puts handkerchief back in bodice*]—can't complain—[*looks for spectacles*]—no no—[*takes up spectacles*]— mustn't complain—[*holds up spectacles, looks through lens*]—so much to be thankful for—[*looks through other lens*]—no pain—[*puts on spectacles*]—hardly any—[*looks for toothbrush*]—wonderful thing that—[*takes up toothbrush*]—nothing like it (*examines handle of brush*]—slight headache sometimes—[*examines handle, reads*]—guaranteed . . . genuine . . . pure . . . what?—[*looks closer*]—genuine pure . . . —[*takes handkerchief from bodice*]—ah yes—[*shakes out handkerchief*]—occasional mild migraine—[*starts wiping handle of brush*]—it comes—[*wipes*]—then goes—[*wiping mechanically*]—ah yes—[*wiping*]—many mercies—[*wiping*]—great mercies—[*stops wiping, fixed lost gaze, brokenly*]—prayers perhaps not for naught—[*Pause, do.*]—first thing—[*Pause, do.*]—last thing—[*head down, resumes wiping, stops wiping, head up, calmed, wipes eyes, folds handkerchief, puts it back in bodice, examines handle of brush, reads*]—fully guaranteed . . . genuine pure . . .—[*looks closer*]—genuine pure . . . [*Takes off spectacles, lays them and brush down, gazes before her.*] Old things. [*Pause.*] Old eyes. [*Long pause.*] On, Winnie. [*She casts about her, sees parasol, considers it at length, takes it up, and develops from sheath a handle of surprising length. Holding butt of parasol in right hand she cranes back and down to her right to hand over* WILLIE.] Hoo-oo! [*Pause.*] Willie! [*Pause.*] Wonderful gift. [*She strikes down at him with beak of para-*

sol.] Wish I had it. [*She strikes again. The parasol slips from her grasp and falls behind mound. It is immediately restored to her by* WILLIE'S *invisible hand.*] Thank you, dear. [*She transfers parasol to left hand, turns back front and examines right palm.*] Damp. [*Returns parasol to right hand, examines left palm.*] Ah well, no worse. [*Head up, cheerfully.*] No better, no worse, no change. [*Pause. Do.*] No pain. [*Cranes back to look down at* WILLIE, *holding parasol by butt as before.*] Don't go off on me again now, dear, will you please, I may need you. [*Pause.*] No hurry, no hurry, just don't curl up on me again. [*Turns back front, lays down parasol, examines palms together, wipes them on grass.*] Perhaps a shade off colour just the same. [*Turns to bag, rummages in it, brings out revolver, holds it up, kisses it rapidly, puts it back, rummages, brings out almost-empty bottle of red medicine, turns back front, looks for spectacles, puts them on, reads label.*] Loss of spirits . . . lack of keenness . . . want of appetite . . . infants . . . children . . . adults . . . six level . . . tablespoonfuls daily—[*head up, smile*]—the old style!—[*smile off, head down, reads*]—daily . . . before and after . . . meals . . . instantaneous . . . [*looks closer*] improvement. [*Takes off spectacles, lays them down, holds up bottle at arm's length to see level, unscrews cap, swigs it off head well back, tosses cap and bottle away in* WILLIE'S *direction. Sound of breaking glass.*] Ah that's better! [*Turns to bag, rummages in it, brings out lipstick, turns back front, examines lipstick.*] Running out. [*Looks for spectacles.*] Ah well. [*Puts on spectacles, looks for mirror.*] Musn't complain. [*Takes up mirror, starts doing lips.*] What is that wonderful line? [*Lips.*] Oh fleeting joys—[*lips*]—oh something lasting woe. [*Lips. She is interrupted by disturbance from* WILLIE. *He is sitting up. She lowers lipstick and mirror and cranes back and down to look at him. Pause. Top back of* WILLIE'S *bald head, trickling blood, rises to view above slope, comes to rest.* WINNIE *pushes up her spectacles. Pause. His hand appears with handkerchief, spreads it on skull, disappears. Pause. The hand appears with boater, club ribbon, settles it on head, rakish angle, disappears. Pause.* WINNIE *cranes a little further back and down.*] Slip on your drawers, dear, before you get singed. [*Pause.*] No? [*Pause.*] Oh I see, you still have some of that stuff left. [*Pause.*] Work it well in, dear. [*Pause.*] Now the other. [*Pause. She turns back front, gazes before her. Happy expression.*] Oh this is going to be another happy day! [*Pause. Happy expression off. She pulls down spectacles and resumes lips.* WILLIE *opens newspaper, hands invisible. Tops of yellow sheets appear on either side of his head.* WINNIE *finishes lips, inspects them in mirror held a little further away.*] Ensign crimson. [WILLIE *turns page.* WINNIE *lays down lipstick and mirror, turns towards bag.*] Pale flag.

> [WILLIE *turns page.* WINNIE *rummages in bag, brings out small ornate brimless hat with crumpled feather, turns back front, straightens hat, smooths feather, raises it towards head, arrests gesture as* WILLIE *reads.*]

WILLIE: His Grace and Most Reverend Father in God Dr. Carolus Hunter dead in tub.

> [*Pause.*]

WINNIE: [*gazing front, hat in hand, tone of fervent reminiscence*] Charlie Hunter! [*Pause.*] I close my eyes—[*she takes off spectacles and does so, hat in one hand, spectacles in other,* WILLIE *turns page*]—and am sitting on his knees again, in the back garden at Borough Green, under the horse-beech. [*Pause. She opens eyes, puts on spectacles, fiddles with hat.*] Oh the happy memories!

[*Pause. She raises hat towards head, arrests gesture as* WILLIE *reads.*]

WILLIE: Opening for smart youth.

[*Pause. She raises hat towards head, arrests gesture, takes off spectacles, gazes front, hat in one hand, spectacles in other.*]

WINNIE: My first ball! [*Long pause.*] My second ball! [*Long pause. Closes eyes.*] My first kiss! [*Pause.* WILLIE *turns page.* WINNIE *opens eyes.*] A Mr. Johnson, or Johnston, or perhaps I should say John*stone*. Very bushy moustache, very tawny. [*Reverently.*] Almost ginger! [*Pause.*] Within a toolshed, though whose I cannot conceive. We had no toolshed and he most certainly had no toolshed. [*Closes eyes.*] I see the piles of pots. [*Pause.*] The tangles of bast. [*Pause.*] The shadows deepening among the rafters.

[*Pause. She opens eyes, puts on spectacles, raises hat towards head, arrests gesture as* WILLIE *reads.*]

WILLIE: Wanted bright boy.

[*Pause.* WINNIE *puts on hat hurriedly, looks for mirror.* WILLIE *turns page.* WINNIE *takes up mirror, inspects hat, lays down mirror, turns towards bag. Paper disappears.* WINNIE *rummages in bag, brings out magnifying glass, turns back front, looks for toothbrush. Paper reappears, folded, and begins to fan* WILLIE'*s face, hand invisible.* WINNIE *takes up toothbrush and examines handle through glass.*]

WINNIE: Fully guaranteed ... [WILLIE *stops fanning*] ... genuine pure ... [*Pause.* WILLIE *resumes fanning.* WINNIE *looks closer, reads.*] Fully guaranteed ... [WILLIE *stops fanning*] ... genuine pure ... [*Pause.* WILLIE *resumes fanning.* WINNIE *lays down glass and brush, takes handkerchief from bodice, takes off and polishes spectacles, puts on spectacles, looks for glass, takes up and polishes glass, lays down glass, looks for brush, takes up brush and wipes handle, lays down brush, puts handkerchief back in bodice, looks for glass, takes up glass, looks for brush, takes up brush and examines handle through glass.*] Fully guaranteed ... [WILLIE *stops fanning*] ... genuine pure ... [*pause,* WILLIE *resumes fanning*] ... hog's [WILLIE *stops fanning, pause*] ... setae. [*Pause.* WINNIE *lays down glass and brush, paper disappears,* WINNIE *takes off spectacles, lays them down, gazes front.*] Hog's setae. [*Pause.*] That is what I find so wonderful, that not a day goes by—[*smile*]—to speak in the old style—[*smile off*]—hardly a day, without some addition to one's knowledge however trifling, the addition I mean, provided one takes the pains. [WILLIE'*s hand reappears with a postcard which he examines close to eyes.*] And if for some strange reason no further pains are possible, why then just close the eyes—[*she does so*]—and wait for the day to come—[*opens eyes*]—the happy day to come when flesh melts at so many degrees and the night of the moon has so many hundred hours. [*Pause.*] That is what I find so comforting when I lose heart and envy the brute beast. [*Turning towards* WILLIE.] I hope you are taking in—[*She sees postcard, bends lower.*] What is that you have there, Willie, may I see? [*She reaches down with hand and* WILLIE *hands her card. The hairy forearm appears above slope, raised in gesture of giving, the hand open to take back, and remains in this position till card is returned.* WINNIE *turns back front and examines card.*] Heavens, what are they up to! [*She looks for spectacles, puts them on and examines card.*] No *but this is just* genuine pure filth! [*Examines card.*] Make any nice-minded person want to vomit! [*Impatience of* WILLIE'*s fingers. She looks for glass, takes it up and examines card through glass. Long pause.*] What does the creature in the background think he's doing? [*Looks closer.*] Oh no really! [*Impatience of fingers. Last long look. She lays down glass, takes edge of card between right forefinger and thumb, averts head, takes nose between left forefinger and thumb.*] Pah! [*Drops card.*] Take it away! [WILLIE's *arm disappears. His hand reappears immediately, holding card.* WINNIE *takes off spectacles, lays them down, gazes before her. During what follows* WILLIE *continues to relish card, varying angles and distance from his eyes.*] Hog's setae. [*Puzzled expression.*] What exactly is a hog? [*Pause. Do.*] A sow, of course, I know, but a hog . . . [*Puzzled expression off.*] Oh well what does it matter, that is what I always say, it will come back, that is what I find so wonderful, all comes back. [*Pause.*] All? [*Pause.*] No, not all. [*Smile.*] No no. [*Smile off.*] Not quite. [*Pause.*] A part. [*Pause.*] Floats up, one fine day, out of the blue. [*Pause.*] That is what I find so wonderful. [*Pause. She turns towards bag. Hand and card disappear. She makes to rummage in bag, arrests gesture.*] No. [*She turns back front. Smile.*] No no. [*Smile off.*] Gently Winnie. [*She gazes front.* WILLIE's *hand reappears, takes off hat, disappears with hat.*] What then? [*Hand reappears, takes handkerchief from skull, disappears with handkerchief. Sharply, as to one not paying attention.*] Winnie! [WILLIE *bows head out of sight.*] What is the alternative? [*Pause.*] What *is* the al—[WILLIE *blows nose loud and long, head and hands invisible. She turns to look at him. Pause. Head reappears. Pause. Hand reappears with handkerchief, spreads it on skull, disappears. Pause. Hand reappears with boater, settles it on head, rakish angle, disappears. Pause.*] Would I had let you sleep on. [*She turns back front. Intermittent plucking at grass, head up and down, to animate following.*] Ah yes, if only I could bear to be alone, I mean prattle away with not a soul to hear. [*Pause.*] Not that I flatter myself you hear much, no Willie, God forbid. [*Pause.*] Days perhaps when you hear nothing. [*Pause.*] But days, too, when you answer. [*Pause.*] So that I may say at all times, even when you do not answer and perhaps hear nothing, something of this is being heard, I am not merely talking to myself, that is in the wilderness, a thing I could never bear to do—for any length of time. [*Pause.*] That is what enables me to go on, go on talking, that is. [*Pause.*] Whereas if you were to die—[*smile*]—to speak in the old style—[*smile off*]—or go away and leave me, then what would I do, what *could* I do, all day long, I mean between the bell for waking and the bell for sleep? [*Pause.*] Simply gaze before me with compressed lips. [*Long pause while she does so. No more plucking.*] Not another word as long as I drew breath, nothing to break the silence of this place. [*Pause.*] Save possibly, now and then, every now and then, a sigh into my looking glass. [*Pause.*] Or a brief . . . gale of laughter, should I happen to see the old joke again. [*Pause. Smile appears, broadens and seems about to culminate in laugh when suddenly replaced by expression of anxiety.*] My hair! [*Pause.*] Did I brush and comb my hair? [*Pause.*] I may have done. [*Pause.*] Normally I do. [*Pause.*] There is so little one *can* do. [*Pause.*] One does it all. [*Pause.*] All one can. [*Pause.*] 'Tis only human. [*Pause.*] Human nature. [*She begins to inspect mound, looks up.*] Human weakness. [*She resumes inspection of mound, looks up.*] Natural weakness. [*She resumes inspection of mound.*] I see no comb. [*Inspects.*] Nor any hairbrush. [*Looks up. Puzzled expression. She turns to bag, rummages in it.*]

The comb is here. [*Back front. Puzzled expression.*] Perhaps I put them back after use. [*Pause. Do.*] But normally I do not put things back, after use, no, I leave them lying about and put them back all together, at the end of the day. [*Smile.*] To speak in the old style. [*Pause.*] The sweet old style. [*Smile off.*] And yet . . . I seem . . . to remember . . . [*Suddenly careless.*] Oh well, what does it matter, that is what I always say, I shall simply brush and comb them later on, purely and simply, I have the whole—[*Pause. Puzzled.*] Them? [*Pause.*] Or it? [*Pause.*] Brush and comb it? [*Pause.*] Sounds improper somehow. [*Pause. Turning a little towards* WILLIE.] What would you say, Willie? [*Pause. Turning a little further.*] What would you say, Willie, speaking of your hair, them or it? [*Pause.*] The hair on your head, I mean. [*Pause. Turning a little further.*] The hair on your head, Willie, what would you say speaking of the hair on your head, them or it?

     [*Long pause.*]

WILLIE: It.

WINNIE: [*turning back front, joyfully*] Oh you are going to talk to me today, this is going to be a happy day! [*Pause. Joy off.*] Another happy day. [*Pause.*] Ah well, where was I, my hair, yes, later on, I shall be thankful for it later on. [*Pause.*] I have my—[*raises hand to hat*]—yes, on, my hat on—[*lowers hands*]—I cannot take it off now. [*Pause.*] To think there are times one cannot take off one's hat, not if one's life were at stake. Times one cannot put it on, times one cannot take it off. [*Pause.*] How often I have said, Put on your hat now, Winnie, there is nothing else for it, take off your hat now, Winnie, like a good girl, it will do you good, and did not. [*Pause.*] Could not. [*Pause. She raises hand, frees a strand of hair from under hat, draws it towards eye, squints at it, lets it go, hand down.*] Golden you called it, that day, when the last guest was gone—[*hand up in gesture of raising a glass*]—to your golden . . . may it never . . . [*voice breaks*] . . . may it never . . . [*Hand down. Head down. Pause. Low.*] That day. [*Pause. Do.*] What day? [*Pause. Head up. Normal voice.*] What now? [*Pause.*] Words fail, there are times when even they fail. [*Turning a little towards* WILLIE.] Is that not so, Willie? [*Pause. Turning a little further.*] Is not that so, Willie, that even words fail, at times? [*Pause. Back front.*] What is one to do then, until they come again? Brush and comb the hair, if it has not been done, or if there is some doubt, trim the nails if they are in need of trimming, these things tide one over. [*Pause.*] That is what I mean. [*Pause.*] That is all I mean. [*Pause.*] That is what I find so wonderful, that not a day goes by—[*smile*]—to speak in the old style— [*smile off*]—without some blessing—[WILLIE *collapses behind slope, his head disappears,* WINNIE *turns towards event*]—in disguise. [*She cranes back and down.*] Go back into your hole now, Willie, you've exposed yourself enough. [*Pause.*] Do as I say, Willie, don't lie sprawling there in this hellish sun, go back into your hole. [*Pause.*] Go on now, Willie. [WILLIE, *invisible, starts crawling left towards hole.*] That's the man. [*She follows his progress with her eyes.*] Not head first, stupid, how are you going to turn? [*Pause.*] That's it . . . right round . . . now . . . back in. [*Pause.*] Oh I know it is not easy, dear, crawling backwards, but it is rewarding in the end. [*Pause.*] You have left your Vaseline behind. [*She watches as he crawls back for Vaseline.*] The lid! [*She watches as he crawls back towards hole. Irritated.*] Not head first, I tell you! [*Pause.*] More to the right. [*Pause.*] The *right,* I said. [*Pause. Irritated.*] Keep your tail down, can't you! [*Pause.*] Now. [*Pause.*] There! [*All these directions loud. Now in her normal voice, still turned towards him.*] Can you hear me? [*Pause.*] I beseech you, Willie, just yes or no, can you hear me, just yes or nothing.

      [*Pause.*]

WILLIE: Yes.

WINNIE: [*turning front, same voice*] And now?

WILLIE: [*irritated*] Yes.

WINNIE: [*less loud*] And now?

WILLIE: [*more irritated*] Yes.

WINNIE: [*still less loud*] And now? [*A little louder.*] And now?

WILLIE: [*violently*] Yes!

WINNIE: [*same voice*] Fear no more the heat o' the sun. [*Pause.*] Did you hear that?

WILLIE: [*irritated*] Yes.

WINNIE: [*same voice*] What? [*Pause.*] What?

WILLIE: [*more irritated*] Fear no more.

      [*Pause.*]

WINNIE: [*same voice*] No more what? [*Pause.*] Fear no more what?

WILLIE: [*violently*] Fear no more!

WINNIE: [*normal voice, gabbled*] Bless you Willie I do appreciate your goodness I know what an effort it costs you, now you may relax I shall not trouble you again unless I am obliged to, by that I mean unless I come to the end of my own resources which is most unlikely, just to know that in theory you can hear me even though in fact you don't is all I need, just to feel you there within earshot and conceivably on the qui vive is all I ask, not to say anything I would not wish you to hear or liable to cause you pain, not to be just babbling away on trust as it is were not knowing and something gnawing at me. [*Pause for breath.*] Doubt. [*Places index and second finger on heart area, moves them about, brings them to rest.*] Here. [*Moves them slightly.*] Abouts. [*Hand away.*] Oh no doubt the time will come when before I can utter a word I must make sure you heard the one that went before and then no doubt another come another time when I must learn to talk to myself a thing I could never bear to do such wilderness. [*Pause.*] Or gaze before me with compressed lips. [*She does so.*] All day long. [*Gaze and lips again.*] No. [*Smile.*] No no. [*Smile off.*] There is, of course, the bag. [*Turns towards it.*] There will always be the bag. [*Back front.*] Yes, I suppose so. [*Pause.*] Even when you are gone, Willie. [*She turns a little towards him.*] You *are* going, Willie, aren't you? [*Pause. Louder.*] You *will* be going soon, Willie, won't you? [*Pause. Louder.*] Willie! [*Pause. She cranes back and down to look at him.*] So you have taken off your straw, that is wise. [*Pause.*] You do look snug, I must say, with your chin on your hands and the old blue eyes like saucers in the shadows. [*Pause.*] Can you see me from there I wonder, I still wonder. [*Pause.*] No? [*Back front.*] Oh I know it does not follow when two are gathered together—[*faltering*]—in this way—[*normal*]—that because one sees the other the other sees the one, life has taught me that . . . too. [*Pause.*] Yes, life I suppose, there is no other word. [*She turns a little towards him.*]

Could you see me, Willie, do you think, from where you are, if you were to raise your eyes in my direction? [*Turns a little further.*] Lift up your eyes to me, Willie, and tell me can you see me, do that for me, I'll lean back as far as I can. [*Does so. Pause.*] No? [*Pause.*] Well never mind. [*Turns back painfully front.*] The earth is very tight today, can it be I have put on flesh, I trust not. [*Pause. Absently, eyes lowered.*] The great heat possibly. [*Starts to pat and stroke ground.*] All things expanding, some more than others. [*Pause. Patting and stroking.*] Some less. [*Pause. Do.*] Oh I can well imagine what is passing through your mind, it is not enough to have to listen to the woman, now I must look at her as well. [*Pause. Do.*] Well it is very understandable. [*Pause. Do.*] One does not appear to be asking a great deal, indeed at times it would seem hardly possible—[*voice breaks, falls to a murmur*]—to ask less—of a fellow creature—to put it mildly—whereas actually—when you think about it—look into your heart—see the other—what he needs—peace—to be left in peace—then perhaps the moon—all this time—asking for the moon. [*Pause. Stroking hand suddenly still. Lively.*] Oh I say, what have we here? [*Bending head to ground, incredulous.*] Looks like life of some kind! [*Looks for spectacles, puts them on, bends closer. Pause.*] An emmet! [*Recoils. Shrill.*] Willie, an emmet, a live emmet! [*Seizes magnifying glass, bends to ground again, inspects through glass.*] Where's it gone? [*Inspects.*] Ah! [*Follows its progress through grass.*] Has like a little white ball in its arms. [*Follows progress. Hand still. Pause.*] It's gone in. [*Continues a moment to gaze at spot through glass, then slowly straightens up, lays down glass, takes off spectacles and gazes before her, spectacles in hand. Finally.*] Like a little white ball.

[*Long pause. Gesture to lay down spectacles.*]

WILLIE: Eggs.

WINNIE: [*arresting gesture*] What?
[*Pause.*]

WILLIE: Eggs. [*Pause. Gesture to lay down glass.*] Formication.

WINNIE: [*arresting gesture*] What!
[*Pause.*]

WILLIE: Formication.
[*Pause. She lays down spectacles, gazes before her. Finally.*]

WINNIE: [*murmur*] God. [*Pause.* WILLIE *laughs quietly. After a moment she joins in. They laugh quietly together.* WILLIE *stops. She laughs on a moment alone.* WILLIE *joins in. They laugh together. She stops.* WILLIE *laughs on a moment alone. He stops. Pause. Normal voice.*] Ah well what a joy in any case to hear you laugh again, Willie, I was convinced I never would, you never would. [*Pause.*] I suppose some people might think us a trifle irreverent, but I doubt it. [*Pause.*] How can one better magnify the Almighty than by sniggering with him at his little jokes, particularly the poorer ones? [*Pause.*] I think you would back me up there, Willie. [*Pause.*] Or were we perhaps diverted by two quite different things? [*Pause.*] Oh well, what does it matter, that is what I always say, so long as one . . . you know . . . what is that wonderful line . . . laughing wild . . . something something laughing wild amid severest woe. [*Pause.*] And now? [*Long pause.*] Was I lovable once, Willie? [*Pause.*] Was I ever lovable? [*Pause.*] Do not misunderstand my question, I am not asking you if you loved me, we know all about that, I am asking you if you found me lovable—at one stage. [*Pause.*] No? [*Pause.*] You can't? [*Pause.*] Well I admit it is a teaser. And you have done more than your bit already, for the time being, just lie back now and relax, I shall not trouble you again unless I am compelled to, just to know you are there within hearing and conceivably on the semi-alert is . . . er . . . paradise enow. [*Pause.*] The day is now well advanced. [*Smile.*] To speak in the old style. [*Smile off.*] And yet it is perhaps a little soon for my song. [*Pause.*] To sing too soon is a great mistake, I find. [*Turning towards bag.*] There is, of course, the bag. [*Looking at bag.*] The bag. [*Back front.*] Could I enumerate its contents? [*Pause.*] No. [*Pause.*] Could I, if some kind person were to come along and ask, What all have you got in that big black bag, Winnie? give an exhaustive answer? [*Pause.*] No. [*Pause.*] The depths in particular, who knows what treasures. [*Pause.*] What comforts. [*Turns to look at bag.*] Yes, there is the bag. [*Back front.*] But something tells me, Do not overdo the bag, Winnie, make use of it, of course, let it help you . . . along, when stuck, by all means, but cast your mind forward, something tells me, cast your mind forward, Winnie, to the time when words must fail—[*she closes eyes, pause, opens eyes*]—and do not overdo the bag. [*Pause. She turns to look at bag.*] Perhaps just one quick dip. [*She turns back front, closes eyes, throws out left arm, plunges hand in bag and brings out revolver. Disgusted.*] You again! [*She opens eyes, brings revolver front and contemplates it. She weighs it in her palm.*] You'd think the weight of this thing would bring it down among the . . . last rounds. But no. It doesn't. Ever uppermost, like Browning. [*Pause.*] Brownie . . . [*Turning a little toward* WILLIE.] Remember Brownie, Willie? [*Pause.*] Remember how you used to keep on at me to take it away from you? Take it away, Winnie, take it away, before I put myself out of my misery. [*Back front. Derisive.*] Your misery! [*To revolver.*] Oh I suppose it's a comfort to know you're there, but I'm tired of you. [*Pause.*] I'll leave you out, that's what I'll do. [*She lays revolver on ground to her right.*] There, that's your home from this day out. [*Smile.*] The old style! [*Smile off.*] And now? [*Long pause.*] Is gravity what it was, Willie, I fancy not. [*Pause.*] Yes, the feeling more and more that if I were not held—[*gesture*]—in this way, I would simply float up into the blue. [*Pause.*] And that perhaps some day the earth will yield and let me go, the pull is so great, yes, crack all round me and let me out. [*Pause.*] Don't you ever have that feeling, Willie, of being sucked up? [*Pause.*] Don't you have to cling on sometimes, Willie? [*Pause. She turns a little towards him.*] Willie.

[*Pause.*]

WILLIE: *Sucked* up?

WINNIE: Yes, love, up into the blue, like gossamer. [*Pause.*] No? [*Pause.*] You don't? [*Pause.*] Ah well, natural laws, natural laws, I suppose it's like everything else, it all depends on the creature you happen to be. All I can say for my part is that for me they are not what they were when I was young and . . . foolish and . . . [*faltering, head down*] . . . beautiful . . . possibly . . . lovely . . . in a way . . . to look at. [*Pause. Head up.*] Forgive me, Willie, sorrow keeps breaking in. [*Normal voice.*] Ah well what a joy in any case to know you are there, as usual, and perhaps awake, and perhaps taking all this in, some of all this, what a happy day for me . . . it will have been. [*Pause.*] So far.

[*Pause.*] What a blessing nothing grows, imagine if all this stuff were to start growing. [*Pause.*] Imagine. [*Pause.*] Ah yes, great mercies. [*Long pause.*] I can say no more. [*Pause.*] For the moment. [*Pause. Turns to look at bag. Back front. Smile.*] No no. [*Smile off. Looks at parasol.*] I suppose I might—[*takes up parasol*]—yes, I suppose I might . . . hoist this thing now. [*Begins to unfurl it. Following punctuated by mechanical difficulties overcome.*] One keeps putting off—putting up—for fear of putting up—too soon— and the day goes by—quite by—without one's having put up—at all. [*Parasol now fully open. Turned to her right she twirls it idly this way and that.*] Ah yes, so little to say, so little to do, and the fear so great, certain days, of finding oneself . . . left, with hours still to run, before the bell for sleep, and nothing more to say, nothing more to do, that the days go by, certain days go by, quite by, the bell goes, and little or nothing said, little or nothing done. [*Raising parasol.*] That is the danger. [*Turning front.*] To be guarded against. [*She gazes front, holding up parasol with right hand. Maximum pause.*] I used to perspire freely. [*Pause.*] Now hardly at all. [*Pause.*] The heat is much greater. [*Pause.*] The perspiration much less. [*Pause.*] That is what I find so wonderful. [*Pause.*] The way man adapts himself. [*Pause.*] To changing conditions. [*She transfers parasol to left hand. Long pause.*] Holding up wearies the arm. [*Pause.*] Not if one is going along. [*Pause.*] Only if one is at rest. [*Pause.*] That is a curious observation. [*Pause.*] I hope you heard that, Willie, I should be grieved to think you had not heard that. [*She takes parasol in both hands. Long pause.*] I am weary, holding it up, and I cannot put it down. [*Pause.*] I am worse off with it up than with it down, and I cannot put it down. [*Pause.*] Reason says, Put it down, Winnie, it is not helping you, put the thing down and get on with something else. [*Pause.*] I cannot. [*Pause.*] I cannot move. [*Pause.*] No, something must happen, in the world, take place, some change, I cannot, if I am to move again. [*Pause.*] Willie. [*Mildly.*] Help. [*Pause.*] No? [*Pause.*] Bid me put this thing down, Willie, I would obey you instantly, as I have always done, honoured, and obeyed. [*Pause.*] Please, Willie. [*Mildly.*] For pity's sake. [*Pause.*] No? [*Pause.*] You can't? [*Pause.*] Well I don't blame you, no, it would ill become me, who cannot move, to blame my Willie because he cannot speak. [*Pause.*] Fortunately I am in tongue again. [*Pause.*] That is what I find so wonderful, my two lamps, when one goes out the other burns brighter. [*Pause.*] Oh yes, great mercies. [*Maximum pause. The parasol goes on fire. Smoke, flames if feasible. She sniffs, looks up, throws parasol to her right behind mound, cranes back to watch it burning. Pause.*] Ah earth you old extinguisher. [*Back front.*] I presume this has occurred before, though I cannot recall it. [*Pause.*] Can you, Willie? [*Turns a little towards him.*] Can you recall this having occurred before? [*Pause. Cranes to look at him.*] Do you know what has occurred, Willie? [*Pause.*] Have you gone off on me again? [*Pause.*] I do not ask if you are alive to all that is going on, I merely ask if you have not gone off on me again. [*Pause.*] Your eyes appear to be closed, but that has no particular significance, we know. [*Pause.*] Raise a finger, dear, will you please, if you are not quite senseless. [*Pause.*] Do that for me, Willie, please, just the little finger, if you are still conscious. [*Pause. Joyful.*] Oh all five, you are a darling today, now I may continue with an easy mind. [*Back front.*] Yes, what ever occurred that did not occur before and yet . . . I wonder, yes, I confess I wonder. [*Pause.*] With the sun blazing so much fiercer down, and hourly fiercer, is it not natural things should go on fire never known to do so, in this way I mean, spontaneous like. [*Pause.*] Shall I myself not melt perhaps in the end, or burn, oh I do not mean necessarily burst into flames, no, just little by little be charred to a black cinder, all this—[*ample gesture of arms*]—visible flesh. [*Pause.*] On the other hand, did I ever know a temperate time? [*Pause.*] No. [*Pause.*] I speak of temperate times and torrid times, they are empty words. [*Pause.*] I speak of when I was not yet caught—in this way—and had my legs and had the use of my legs, and could seek out a shady place, like you, when I was tired of the sun, or a sunny place when I was tired of the shade, like you, and they are all empty words. [*Pause.*] It is no hotter today than yesterday, it will be no hotter tomorrow than today, how could it, and so on back into the far past, forward into the far future. [*Pause.*] And should one day the earth cover my breasts, then I shall never have seen my breasts, no one ever seen my breasts. [*Pause.*] I hope you caught something of that, Willie, I should be sorry to think you had caught nothing of all that, it is not every day I rise to such heights. [*Pause.*] Yes, something seems to have occurred, something has seemed to occur, and nothing has occurred, nothing at all, you are quite right, Willie. [*Pause.*] The sunshade will be there again tomorrow, beside me on this mound, to help me through the day. [*Pause. She takes up mirror.*] I take up this little glass, I shiver it on a stone—[*does so*]—I throw it away—[*does so far behind her*]—it will be in the bag again tomorrow, without a scratch, to help me through the day. [*Pause.*] No, one can do nothing. [*Pause.*] That is what I find so wonderful, the way things . . . [*voice breaks, head down*] . . . things . . . so wonderful. [*Long pause, head down. Finally turns, still bowed, to bag, brings out unidentifiable odds and ends, stuffs them back, fumbles deeper, brings out finally musical box, winds it up, turns it on, listens for a moment holding it in both hands, huddled over it, turns back front, straightens up and listens to tune, holding box to breast with both hands. It plays the waltz duet "I Love You So" from* The Merry Widow. *Gradually happy expression. She sways to the rhythm. Music stops. Pause. Brief burst of hoarse song without words—musical box tune—from* WILLIE. *Increase of happy expression. She lays down box.*] Oh this will have been a happy day! [*She claps hands.*] Again, Willie, again! [*Claps.*] Encore, Willie, please! [*Pause. Happy expression off.*] No? You won't do that for me? [*Pause.*] Well it is very understandable, very understandable. One cannot sing just to please someone, however much one loves them, no, song must come from the heart, that is what I always say, pour out from the inmost, like a thrush. [*Pause.*] How often I have said, in evil hours, Sing now, Winnie, sing your song, there is nothing else for it, and did not. [*Pause.*] Could not. [*Pause.*] No, like the thrush, or the bird of dawning, with no thought of benefit, to oneself or anyone else. [*Pause.*] And now? [*Long pause. Low.*] Strange feeling. [*Pause. Do.*] Strange feeling that someone is looking at me. I am clear, then dim, then gone, then dim again, then clear again, and so on, back and forth, in and out of someone's eye. [*Pause. Do.*] Strange? [*Pause. Do.*] No, here all is strange. [*Pause. Normal voice.*] Something says, Stop talking now, Winnie, for a minute, don't squander all your words for the day, stop talking and do something for a change, will you? [*She raises hands and holds them open before her eyes. Apostrophic.*] Do something! [*She closes hands.*] What claws! [*She turns to bag, rummages in it, brings out finally a nail file, turns back front and begins to file nails. Files for a time in silence, then the following punctuated by filing.*] There floats up—into my thoughts—a Mr. Shower—a Mr. and perhaps a Mrs. Shower—no—they are holding hands—his fiancée then more likely—or just some—loved one. [*Looks closer at nails.*] Very brittle today. [*Resumes filing.*] Shower— Shower—does the name mean anything—to you, Willie—evoke any reality, I mean—for you, Willie,—don't answer if you don't—feel up to it— you have done more—than your bit—already—Shower—Shower. [*Inspects filed nails.*] Bit more like it. [*Raises head, gazes front.*] Keep yourself nice, Winnie, that's what I always say, come what may, keep yourself nice. [*Pause. Resumes filing.*] Yes—Shower—Shower—[*stops filing, raises head, gazes front, pause*]—or Cooker, perhaps I should say Cooker, [*Turning a little towards* WILLIE.] Cooker, Willie, does Cooker strike a chord? [*Pause. Turns a little further. Louder.*] Cooker, Willie, does Cooker ring a bell, the name Cooker? [*Pause. She cranes back to look at him. Pause.*] Oh really! [*Pause.*] Have you no handkerchief, darling? [*Pause.*] Have you no delicacy? [*Pause.*] Oh, Willie, you're not eating it! Spit it out, dear, spit it out! [*Pause. Back front.*] Ah well, I suppose it's only natural. [*Break in voice.*] Human. [*Pause. Do.*] What *is* one to do? [*Head down. Do.*] All day long. [*Pause. Do.*] Day after day. [*Pause. Head up. Smile. Calm.*] The old style! [*Smile off. Resumes nails.*] No, done him. [*Passes on to next.*] Should have put on my glasses. [*Pause.*] Too late now. [*Finishes left hand, inspects it.*] Bit more human. [*Starts right hand. Following punctuated as before.*] Well anyway—this man Shower—or Cooker—no matter—and the woman—hand in hand—in the other hands bags—kind of big brown grips—standing there gaping at me—and at last this man Shower—or Cooker—ends in "er" anyway— stake my life on that—What's she doing? he says—What's the idea? he says—stuck up to her diddies in the bleeding ground—coarse fellow— What does it mean? he says—What's it meant to mean—and so on—lot more stuff like that—usual drivel—Do you hear me? he says—I do, she says, God help me—What do you mean, he says, God help you? [*Stops filing, raises head, gazes front.*] And you, she says, what's the idea of you, she says, what are you meant to mean? It is because you're still on your two flat feet, with your old ditty full of tinned muck and changes of underwear, dragging me up and down this fornicating wilderness, coarse creature, fit mate—[*with sudden violence*]—let go of my hand and drop for God's sake, she says, drop! [*Pause. Resumes filing.*] Why doesn't he dig her out? he says—referring to you, my dear—What good is she to him like that?— What good is he to her like that?—and so on—usual tosh—Good! she says, have a heart for God's sake—Dig her out, he says, dig her out, no sense in her like that—Dig her out with what? she says—I'd dig her out with my bare hands, he says—must have been man and—wife. [*Files in silence.*] Next thing they're away—hand in hand—and the bags—dim— then gone—last human kind—to stray this way. [*Finishes right hand, inspects it, lays down file, gazes front.*] Strange thing, time like this, drift up into the mind. [*Pause.*] Strange? [*Pause.*] No, here all is strange. [*Pause.*] Thankful for it in any case. [*Voice breaks.*] Most thankful. [*Head down. Pause. Head up. Calm.*] Bow and raise the head, bow and raise, always that. [*Pause.*] And now? [*Long pause. Starts putting things back in bag, toothbrush last. This operation, interrupted by pauses as indicated, punctuates following.*] It is perhaps a little soon—to make ready—for the night—[*stops tidying, head up, smile*]—the old style!—[*smile off, resumes tidying*]—and yet I do—make ready for the night—feeling it at hand—the bell for sleep—saying to my-self—Winnie—it will not be long now, Winnie—until the bell for sleep. [*Stops tidying, head up.*] Sometimes I am wrong. [*Smile.*] But not often. [*Smile off.*] Sometimes all is over, for the day, all done, all said, all ready for the night, and the day not over, far from over, the night not ready, far, far from ready. [*Smile.*] But not often. [*Smile off.*] Yes, the bell for sleep, when I feel it at hand, and so make ready for the night—[*gesture*]—in this way, sometimes I am wrong—[*smile*]—but not often. [*Smile off. Resumes tidy-ing.*] I used to think—I say I used to think—that all these things—put back into the bag—if too soon—put back too soon—could be taken out again—if necessary—if needed—and so on—indefinitely—back into the bag—back out of the bag—until the bell—went. [*Stops tidying, head up, smile.*] But no. [*Smile broader.*] No no. [*Smile off. Resumes tidying.*] I suppose this—might seem strange—this—what shall I say—this what I have said—yes—[*she takes up revolver*]—strange—[*she turns to put revolver in bag*]—were it not—[*about to put revolver in bag she arrests gesture and turns back front*]—were it not—[*she lays down revolver to her right, stops tidying, head up*]—that all seems strange. [*Pause.*] Most strange. [*Pause.*] Never any change. [*Pause.*] And more and more strange. [*Pause. She bends to mound again, takes up last object, i.e. toothbrush, and turns to put it in bag when her at-tention is drawn to disturbance from* WILLIE. *She cranes back and to her right to see. Pause.*] Weary of your hole, dear? [*Pause.*] Well I can understand that. [*Pause.*] Don't forget your straw. [*Pause.*] Not the crawler you were, poor darling. [*Pause.*] No, not the crawler I gave my heart to. [*Pause.*] The hands and knees, love, try the hands and knees. [*Pause.*] The knees! The knees! [*Pause.*] What a curse, mobility! [*She follows with eyes his progress towards her behind mound, i.e. towards place he occupied at beginning of act.*] Another foot, Willie, and you're home. [*Pause as he observes last foot.*] Ah! [*Turns back front laboriously, rubs neck.*] Crick in my neck admiring you. [*Rubs neck.*] But it's worth it, well worth it. [*Turns slightly towards him.*] Do you know what I dream sometimes? [*Pause.*] What I dream sometimes, Willie. [*Pause.*] That you'll come round and live this side where I could see you. [*Pause. Back front.*] I'd be a different woman. [*Pause.*] Unrecognizable. [*Turning slightly toward him.*] Or just now and then, come round this side just every now and then and let me feast on you. [*Back front.*] But you can't, I know. [*Head down.*] I know. [*Pause. Head up.*] Well anyway—[*looks at toothbrush in her hand*]—can't be long now—[*looks at brush*]—until the bell. [*Top back of* WILLIE's *head appears above slope.* WINNIE *looks closer at brush.*] Fully guaran-teed. . . . [*head up*] . . . what's this it was? [WILLIE's *hand appears with hand-kerchief, spreads it on skull, disappears.*] Genuine pure . . . fully guaranteed . . . [WILLIE's *hand appears with boater, settles it on head, rakish angle, disappears*]

... genuine pure ... ah! hog's setae. [*Pause.*] What is a hog exactly? [*Pause. Turns slightly towards* WILLIE.] What exactly is a hog, Willie, do you know, I can't remember. [*Pause. Turning a little further, pleading.*] What is a hog, Willie, please!
      [*Pause.*]

WILLIE: Castrated male swine. [*Happy expression appears on* WINNIE's *face.*] Reared for slaughter.
      [*Happy expression increases.* WILLIE opens newspaper, hands invisible. Tops of yellow sheets appear on either side of his head. WINNIE *gazes before her with happy expression.*]

WINNIE: Oh this *is* a happy day! This will have been another happy day! [*Pause.*] After all. [*Pause.*] So far.
      [*Pause. Happy expression off.* WILLIE *turns page. Pause. He turns another page. Pause.*]

WILLIE: Opening for smart youth.
      [*Pause.* WINNIE *takes off hat, turns to put it in bag, arrests gesture, turns back front. Smile.*]

WINNIE: No. [*Smile broader.*] No no. [*Smile off. Puts on hat again, gazes front, pause.*] And now? [*Pause.*] Sing. [*Pause.*] Sing your song, Winnie. [*Pause.*] No? [*Pause.*] Then pray. [*Pause.*] Pray your prayer, Winnie.
      [*Pause.* WILLIE *turns page.*]

WILLIE: Wanted bright boy.
      [*Pause.* WINNIE *gazes before her.* WILLIE *turns page. Pause. Newspaper disappears. Long pause.*]

WINNIE: Pray your old prayer, Winnie.
      [*Long pause.*]

CURTAIN

ACT II

Scene as before.
      WINNIE *embedded up to neck, hat on head, eyes closed. Her head, which she can no longer turn, nor bow, nor raise, faces front motionless throughout act. Movements of eyes as indicated.*
      Bag and parasol as before. Revolver conspicuous to her right on mound.
      Long pause.
      Bell rings loudly. She opens eyes at once. Bell stops. She gazes front. Long pause.

WINNIE: Hail, holy light. [*Long pause. She closes her eyes. Bell rings loudly. She opens eyes at once. Bell stops. She gazes front. Long smile. Smile off. Long pause.*] Someone is looking at me still. [*Pause.*] Caring for me still. [*Pause.*] That is what I find so wonderful. [*Pause.*] Eyes on my eyes. [*Pause.*] What is that unforgettable line? [*Pause. Eyes right.*] Willie. [*Pause. Louder.*] Willie. [*Pause. Eyes front.*] May one still speak of time? [*Pause.*] Say it is a long time now, Willie, since I saw you. [*Pause.*] Since I heard you. [*Pause.*] May one? [*Pause.*] One does. [*Smile.*] The old style! [*Smile off.*] There is so little one can speak of. [*Pause.*] One speaks of it all. [*Pause.*] All one can. [*Pause.*] I used to think ... [*Pause.*] ... I say I used to think that I would learn to talk alone. [*Pause.*] By that I mean to myself, the wilderness. [*Smile.*] But no. [*Smile broader.*] No no. [*Smile off.*] Ergo you are there. [*Pause.*] Oh no doubt you are dead like the others, no doubt you have died, or gone away and left me, like the others, it doesn't matter, you are there. [*Pause. Eyes left.*] The bag, too, is there, the same as ever, I can see it. [*Pause. Eyes right. Louder.*] The bag is there, Willie, as good as ever, the one you gave me that day . . . to go to market. [*Pause. Eyes front.*] That day. [*Pause.*] What day? [*Pause.*] I used to pray. [*Pause.*] I say I used to pray. [*Pause.*] Yes, I must confess I did. [*Smile.*] Not now. [*Smile broader.*] No no. [*Smile off. Pause.*] Then . . . now . . . what difficulties here, for the mind. [*Pause.*] To have been always what I am—and so changed from what I was. [*Pause.*] I am the one, I say the one, then the other. [*Pause.*] Now the one, then the other. [*Pause.*] Now the one, then the other. [*Pause.*] There is so little one can say, one says it all. [*Pause.*] All one can. [*Pause.*] And no truth in it anywhere. [*Pause.*] My arms. [*Pause.*] My breasts. [*Pause.*] What arms? [*Pause.*] What breasts? [*Pause.*] Willie. [*Pause.*] What Willie? [*Sudden vehement affirmation.*] My Willie! [*Eyes right, calling.*] Willie! [*Pause. Louder.*] Willie! [*Pause. Eyes front.*] Ah well, not to know, not to know for sure, great mercy, all I ask. [*Pause.*] Ah yes . . . then . . . now . . . beechen green . . . this . . . Charlie . . . kisses . . . this . . . all that . . . deep trouble for the mind. [*Pause.*] But it does not trouble mine. [*Smile.*] Not now. [*Smile broader.*] No no. [*Smile off. Long pause. She closes eyes. Bell rings loudly. She opens eyes. Pause.*] Eyes float up that seem to close in peace . . . to see . . . in peace. [*Pause.*] Not mine. [*Smile.*] Not now. [*Smile broader.*] No no. [*Smile off. Long pause.*] Willie. [*Pause.*] Do you think the earth has lost its atmosphere, Willie? [*Pause.*] Do you, Willie? [*Pause.*] You have no opinion? [*Pause.*] Well that is like you, you never had any opinion about anything. [*Pause.*] It's understandable. [*Pause.*] Most. [*Pause.*] The earth-ball. [*Pause.*] I sometimes wonder. [*Pause.*] Perhaps not quite all. [*Pause.*] There always remains something. [*Pause.*] Of everything. [*Pause.*] Some remains. [*Pause.*] If the mind were to go. [*Pause.*] It won't, of course. [*Pause.*] Not quite. [*Pause.*] Not mine. [*Smile.*] Now now. [*Smile broader.*] No no. [*Smile off. Long pause.*] It might be the eternal cold. [*Pause.*] Everlasting perishing cold. [*Pause.*] Just chance, I take it, happy chance. [*Pause.*] Oh yes, great mercies, great mercies. [*Pause.*] And now? [*Long pause.*] The face. [*Pause.*] The nose. [*She squints down.*] I can see it . . . [*squinting down*] . . . the tip . . . the nostrils . . . breath of life . . . that curve you so admired . . . [*pouts*] . . . a hint of lip . . . [*pouts again*] . . . if I pout them out . . . [*sticks out tongue*] . . . the tongue, of course . . . you so admired . . . if I stick it out . . . [*sticks it out again*] . . . the tip . . . [*eyes up*] . . . suspicion of brow . . . eyebrow . . . imagination possibly . . . [*eyes left*] . . . cheek . . . no . . . [*eyes right*] . . . no . . . [*distends cheeks*] . . . even if I puff them out . . . [*eyes left, distends cheeks again*] . . . no . . . no damask. [*Eyes front.*] That is all. [*Pause.*] The bag, of course . . . [*eyes left*] . . . a little blurred perhaps . . . but the bag. [*Eyes front. Offhand.*] The Earth, of course, and sky. [*Eyes right.*] The sunshade you gave me . . . that day . . . [*Pause.*] . . . that day . . . the lake . . . the reeds. [*Eyes front. Pause.*] What day? [*Pause.*] What reeds? [*Long pause. Eyes close. Bell rings loudly. Eyes open. Pause. Eyes right.*] Brownie, of course. [*Pause.*] You remember Brownie, Willie, I can see him. [*Pause.*] Brownie is there, Willie, beside me. [*Pause. Eyes front.*] That is all. [*Pause.*] What would I do without them? [*Pause.*] What would I do without them, when words fail? [*Pause.*] Gaze before me, with compressed lips. [*Long pause while she does so.*] I cannot. [*Pause.*] Ah yes, great mercies, great mercies. [*Long pause. Low.*] Sometimes I hear sounds. [*Listening expression. Normal voice.*] But not often. [*Pause.*] They are a boon, sounds are a boon, they help me . . . through the day. [*Smile.*] The old style! [*Smile off.*] Yes, those are happy days, when there are sounds. [*Pause.*] When I hear sounds. [*Pause.*] I used to think . . . [*Pause.*] . . . I say I used to think they were in my head. [*Smile.*] But no. [*Smile broader.*] No no. [*Smile off.*] That was just logic. [*Pause.*] Reason. [*Pause.*] I have not lost my reason. [*Pause.*] Not yet. [*Pause.*] Not all. [*Pause.*] Some remains. [*Pause.*] Sounds. [*Pause.*] Like little . . . sunderings, little falls . . . apart. [*Pause. Low.*] It's things, Willie. [*Pause. Normal voice.*] In the bag, outside the bag. [*Pause.*] Ah yes, things have their life, that is what I always say, *things* have a life. [*Pause.*] Take my looking glass, it doesn't need me. [*Pause.*] The bell. [*Pause.*] It hurts like a knife. [*Pause.*] A gouge. [*Pause.*] One cannot ignore it. [*Pause.*] How often . . . [*Pause.*] . . . I say how often I have said, Ignore it, Winnie, ignore the bell, pay no heed, just sleep and wake, sleep and wake, as you please, open and close the eyes, as you please, or in the way you find most helpful. [*Pause.*] Open and close the eyes, Winnie, open and close, always that. [*Pause.*] But no. [*Smile.*] Not now. [*Smile broader.*] No no. [*Smile off. Pause.*] What now? [*Pause.*] What now, Willie? [*Long pause.*] There is my story, of course, when all else fails. [*Pause.*] A life. [*Smile.*] A long life. [*Smile off.*] Beginning in the womb, where life used to begin, Mildred has memories, she will have memories, of the womb, before she dies, the mother's womb. [*Pause.*] She is now four or five already and has recently been given a big waxen dolly. [*Pause.*] Fully clothed, complete outfit. [*Pause.*] Shoes, socks, undies, complete set, frilly frock, gloves. [*Pause.*] White mesh. [*Pause.*] A little white straw hat with a chin elastic. [*Pause.*] Pearly necklet. [*Pause.*] A little picture book with legends in real print to go under her arm when she takes her walk. [*Pause.*] China blue eyes that open and shut. [*Pause. Narrative.*] The sun was not well up when Milly rose, descended the steep . . . [*Pause.*] . . . slipped on her nightgown, descended all along the steep wooden stairs, backwards on all fours, though she had been forbidden to do so, entered the . . . [*Pause.*] . . . tiptoed down the silent passage, entered the nursery and began to undress Dolly. [*Pause.*] Crept under the table and began to undress Dolly. [*Pause.*] Scolding her . . . the while. [*Pause.*] Suddenly a mouse—[*Long pause.*] Gently, Winnie. [*Long pause. Calling.*] Willie! [*Pause. Louder.*] Willie! [*Pause. Mild reproach.*] I sometimes find your attitude a little strange, Willie, all this time, it is not like you to be wantonly cruel. [*Pause.*] Strange? [*Pause.*] No. [*Smile.*] Not here. [*Smile broader.*] Not now. [*Smile off.*] And yet . . . [*Suddenly anxious.*] I do hope nothing is amiss. [*Eyes right, loud.*] Is all well, dear? [*Pause. Eyes front. To herself.*] God grant he did not go in head foremost [*Eyes right, loud.*] You're not stuck, Willie? [*Pause. Do.*] You're not jammed, Willie? [*Eyes front, distressed.*] Perhaps he is crying out for help all this time and I do not hear him! [*Pause.*] I do, of course, hear cries. [*Pause.*] But they are in my head surely. [*Pause.*] Is it possible that . . . [*Pause. With finality.*] No no, my head was always full of cries. [*Pause.*] Faint confused cries. [*Pause.*] They come. [*Pause.*] Then go. [*Pause.*] As on a wind. [*Pause.*] That is what I find so wonderful. [*Pause.*] They cease. [*Pause.*] Ah yes, great mercies, great mercies. [*Pause.*] The day is now well advanced. [*Smile. Smile off.*] And yet it is perhaps a little soon for my song. [*Pause.*] To sing too soon is fatal, I always find. [*Pause.*] On the other hand it is possible to leave it too late. [*Pause.*] The bell goes for sleep and one has not sung. [*Pause.*] The whole day has flown—[*smile, smile off*]—flown by, quite by, and no song of any class, kind, or description. [*Pause.*] There is a problem here. [*Pause.*] One cannot sing . . . just like that, no. [*Pause.*] It bubbles up, for some unknown reason, the time is ill chosen, one chokes it back. [*Pause.*] One says, Now is the time, it is now or never, and one cannot. [*Pause.*] Simply cannot sing. [*Pause.*] Not a note. [*Pause.*] Another thing, Willie, while we are on this subject. [*Pause.*] The sadness after song. [*Pause.*] Have you run across that, Willie? [*Pause.*] In the course of your experience. [*Pause.*] No? [*Pause.*] Sadness after intimate sexual intercourse one is familiar with, of course. [*Pause.*] You would concur with Aristotle there, Willie, I fancy. [*Pause.*] Yes, that one knows and is prepared to face. [*Pause.*] But after song . . . [*Pause.*] It does not last, of course. [*Pause.*] That is what I find so wonderful. [*Pause.*] It wears away. [*Pause.*] What are those exquisite lines? [*Pause.*] Go forget me why should something o'er that something shadow fling . . . go forget me . . . why should sorrow . . . brightly smile . . . go forget me . . . never hear me . . . sweetly smile . . . brightly sing . . . [*Pause. With a sigh.*] One loses one's classics. [*Pause.*] Oh not all. [*Pause.*] A part. [*Pause.*] A part remains. [*Pause.*] That is what I find so wonderful, a part remains, of one's classics, to help one through the day. [*Pause.*] Oh yes, many mercies, many mercies. [*Pause.*] And now? [*Pause.*] And now, Willie? [*Long pause.*] I call to the eye of the mind . . . Mr. Shower—or Cooker. [*She closes her eyes. Bell rings loudly. She opens her eyes. Pause.*] Hand in hand, in the other hands bags. [*Pause.*] Getting on . . . in life. [*Pause.*] No longer young, not yet old. [*Pause.*] Standing there gaping at me. [*Pause.*] Can't have been a bad bosom, he says, in its day. [*Pause.*] Seen worse shoulders, he says, in my time. [*Pause.*] Does she feel her legs? he says. [*Pause.*] Is there any life in her legs? he says. [*Pause.*] Has she anything on underneath? he says. [*Pause.*] Ask her, he says, I'm shy. [*Pause.*] Ask her what? she says. [*Pause.*] Is there any life in her legs. [*Pause.*] Has she anything on underneath. [*Pause.*] Ask her yourself, she says. [*Pause. With sudden violence.*] Let go of me for Christ sake and drop! [*Pause. Do.*] Drop dead! [*Smile.*] But no. [*Smile broader.*] No no. [*Smile off.*] I watch them recede. [*Pause.*] Hand in hand—and the bags. [*Pause.*] Dim. [*Pause.*] Then gone. [*Pause.*] Last human kind—to stray this way. [*Pause.*] Up to date. [*Pause.*] And now? [*Pause. Low.*] Help. [*Pause. Do.*] Help, Willie. [*Pause. Do.*] No? [*Long pause. Narrative.*] Suddenly a mouse . . . [*Pause.*] Suddenly a mouse ran up her little thigh and Mildred, dropping Dolly in her fright, began to scream—[*Winnie gives a sudden piercing scream*]—and screamed and screamed—[*Winnie screams twice*]—screamed and screamed and screamed and screamed till all came running, in their night attire, papa, mamma, Bibby and . . . old Annie, to see what was the matter . . . [*Pause.*] . . . what on earth could possibly be the matter. [*Pause.*] Too late. [*Pause.*] Too late. [*Long pause. Just audible.*] Willie. [*Pause. Normal voice.*] Ah well, not long now, Winnie, can't be long now, until the bell for sleep. [*Pause.*] Then you may close your eyes, then you must close your eyes—and keep them closed. [*Pause.*] Why say that again? [*Pause.*] I used to think . . . [*Pause.*] . . . I say I used to think there was no difference between one fraction of a second and the next. [*Pause.*] I used to say . . . [*pause*] . . . I say I used to say, Winnie, you are changeless, there is never any difference between one fraction of a second and the next. [*Pause.*] Why bring that up again? [*Pause.*] There is so little one can bring up, one brings up all. [*Pause.*] All one can. [*Pause.*] My neck is hurting me! [*Pause.*] Ah that's better. [*With mild irritation.*] Everything within reason. [*Long pause.*] I can do no more. [*Pause.*] Say no more. [*Pause.*] But I must say more. [*Pause.*] Problem here. [*Pause.*] No, something must move, in the world, I can't any more. [*Pause.*] A zephyr. [*Pause.*] A breath. [*Pause.*] What are those immortal lines? [*Pause.*] It might be the eternal dark. [*Pause.*] Black night without end. [*Pause.*] Just chance, I take it, happy chance. [*Pause.*] Oh yes, abounding mercies. [*Long pause.*] And now? [*Pause.*] And now, Willie? [*Long pause.*] That day. [*Pause.*] The pink fizz. [*Pause.*] The flute glasses. [*Pause.*] The last guest gone. [*Pause.*] The last bumper with the bodies nearly touching. [*Pause.*] The look. [*Long pause.*] I hear cries. [*Pause.*] Sing. [*Pause.*] Sing your old song, Winnie.

[*Long pause. Suddenly alert expression. Eyes switch right.* WILLIE'*s head appears to her right round corner of mound. He is on all fours, dressed to kill—top hat, morning coat, striped trousers, etc., white gloves in hand. Very long bushy white Battle of Britain moustache. He halts, gazes front, smooths moustache. He emerges completely from behind mound, turns to his left, halts, looks up at* WINNIE. *He advances on all fours towards centre, halts, turns head front, gazes front, strokes moustache, straightens tie, adjusts hat, advances a little further, halts, takes off hat and looks up at* WINNIE. *He is now not far from centre and within her field of vision. Unable to sustain effort of looking up he sinks head to ground.*]

WINNIE: [*mondaine*] Well this is an unexpected pleasure! [*Pause.*] Reminds me of the day you came whining for my hand. [*Pause.*] I worship you, Winnie, be mine. [*He looks up.*] Life a mockery without Win. [*She goes off into a giggle.*] What a getup, you do look a sight! [*Giggles.*] Where are the flowers? [*Pause.*] That smile today. [WILLIE *sinks head.*] What's that on your neck, an anthrax? [*Pause.*] Want to watch that, Willie, before it gets a hold on you. [*Pause.*] Where were you all this time? [*Pause.*] What were you doing all this time? [*Pause.*] Changing? [*Pause.*] Did you not hear me screaming for you? [*Pause.*] Did you get stuck in your hole? [*Pause. He looks up.*] That's right, Willie, look at me. [*Pause.*] Feast your old eyes, Willie. [*Pause.*] Does anything remain? [*Pause.*] Any remains? [*Pause.*] No? [*Pause.*] I haven't been able to look after it, you know. [*He sinks his head.*] You are still recognizable, in a way. [*Pause.*] Are you thinking of coming to live this side now . . . for a bit maybe? [*Pause.*] No? [*Pause.*] Just a brief call? [*Pause.*] Have you gone deaf, Willie? [*Pause.*] Dumb? [*Pause.*] Oh I know you were never one to talk, I worship you Winnie be mine and then nothing from that day forth only titbits from *Reynold's News.* [*Eyes front. Pause.*] Ah well, what

matter, that's what I always say, it will have been a happy day, after all, another happy day. [*Pause.*] Not long now, Winnie. [*Pause.*] I hear cries. [*Pause.*] Do you ever hear cries, Willie? [*Pause.*] No? [*Eyes back on* WILLIE.] [*Pause.*] Look at me again, Willie. [*Pause.*] Once more, Willie. [*He looks up. Happily.*] Ah! [*Pause. Shocked.*] What ails you, Willie, I never saw such an expression! [*Pause.*] Put on your hat, dear, it's the sun, don't stand on ceremony, I won't mind. [*He drops hat and gloves and starts to crawl up mound towards her. Gleeful.*] Oh I say, this is terrific! [*He halts, clinging to mound with one hand, reaching up with the other.*] Come on, dear, put a bit of jizz into it, I'll cheer you on. [*Pause.*] Is it me you're after, Willie . . . or is it something else? [*Pause.*] Do you want to touch my face . . . again? [*Pause.*] Is it a kiss you're after, Willie . . . or is it something else? [*Pause.*] There was a time when I could have given you a hand. [*Pause.*] And then a time before that when I did give you a hand. [*Pause.*] You were always in dire need of a hand, Willie. [*He slithers back to foot of mound and lies with face to ground.*] Brrum! [*Pause. He rises to hands and knees, raises his face towards her.*] Have another go, Willie, I'll cheer you on. [*Pause.*] Don't look at me like that! [*Pause. Vehement.*] Don't look at me like that! [*Pause. Low.*] Have you gone off your head, Willie? [*Pause. Do.*] Out of your poor old wits, Willie?
   [*Pause.*]

WILLIE: [*just audible*] Win.
   [*Pause.* WINNIE's *eyes front. Happy expression appears, grows.*]

WINNIE: Win! [*Pause.*] Oh this *is* a happy day, this will have been another happy day! [*Pause.*] After all. [*Pause.*] So far.
   [*Pause. She hums tentatively beginning of song, then sings softly, musical box tune.*]

> *Though I say not*
> *What I may not*
> *Let you hear,*
> *Yet the swaying*
> *Dance is saying,*
> *Love me dear!*
> *Every touch of fingers*
> *Tells me what I know,*
> *Says for you,*
> *It's true, it's true,*
> *You love me so!*

   [*Pause. Happy expression off. She closes her eyes. Bell rings loudly. She opens her eyes. She smiles, gazing front. She turns her eyes, smiling, to* WILLIE, *still on his hands and knees looking up at her. Smile off. They look at each other. Long pause.*]

CURTAIN

George C. Wolfe

The Colored Museum (1986)

The civil rights movement of the 1960s brought with it an increased concern for diversity in drama and theatrical production. One result was the greatly increased number of plays by and about African Americans. There are now a large number of skillful dramatists, as well as more than 200 African-American producing groups in the United States. Among the playwrights, George C. Wolfe has become one of the most influential, both through his writing and his work as a director and as head of the New York Shakespeare Festival.

Wolfe's *The Colored Museum* is conceived as a series of eleven exhibits of African-American history and life. In this way, Wolfe confronts audiences with behavior and attitudes reflecting both the oppressions of the past and the compromises and hopes of the present. In doing so, he alternates between (and sometimes combines) comic exposure and fierce defense. Some audiences have been offended by the play because they have failed to recognize the serious purpose of the humor. Wolfe satirizes black stereotypes to force African Americans to recognize that, even as they seek to escape stereotyping, they are living according to labels forced on them not only by others but also by themselves. Wolfe says that he wrote *The Colored Museum* "in order to undefine myself in relation to all these labels." He does not ask African Americans to forget their past; rather, he suggests, they should face it and move beyond it. As one of the characters in the final exhibit says: "I can't live inside yesterday's pain, but I can't live without it." A major concern of the play, then, is how African Americans can both honor and escape the baggage of the past.

The most interesting scene for those interested in theatre is *The Last Mama-on-the-Couch Play*, a satirical look at the familiar stereotypes of black drama that ends in a production number using "a myriad of black-Broadwayesque dancing styles" undercut by projected images of "coon performers," who in earlier times had presented song-and-dance shows demeaning to blacks but favored by whites. The final exhibit, *The Party*, brings together all the characters of the play, acknowledging the great variety, good and bad, of black experience, past and present. It suggests that the power of African Americans lies in the contradictions of their past. Taken all together, these eleven exhibits ask us to look at attitudes and stereotypes that have shaped important aspects of African-American sensibilities. It does so in a form both imaginative and entertaining.

George C. Wolfe

The Colored Museum

THE CAST———*An ensemble of five, two men and three women, all black, who per-form all the characters that inhabit the exhibits. (A little girl, seven to twelve years old, is needed for a walk-on part in* Lala's Opening.*)*

THE STAGE———White walls and recessed lighting. A starkness befitting a museum where the myths and madness of black/Negro/colored Americans are stored. Built into the walls is a series of small panels, doors, revolving walls, and compartments from which actors can retrieve key props and make quick entrances. A revolve is used, which allows for quick transitions from one exhibit to the next.

MUSIC———*All of the music for the show should be prerecorded. Only the drummer, who is used in* Git on Board, *and then later in* Permutations *and* The Party, *is live.*

There is no intermission.

THE EXHIBITS AND CHARACTERS

   Git on Board
      MISS PAT
   Cookin' with Aunt Ethel
      AUNT ETHEL
   The Photo Session
      GIRL
      GUY
   Soldier with a Secret
      JUNIE ROBINSON
   The Gospel According to Miss Roj
      MISS ROJ
      WAITER
   The Hairpiece
      THE WOMAN
      JANINE
      LAWANDA
   The Last Mama-on-the-Couch Play
      NARRATOR
      MAMA
      WALTER-LEE-BEAU-WILLIE-JONES
      LADY IN PLAID
      MEDEA JONES

Symbiosis
    THE MAN
    THE KID
Lala's Opening
    LALA LAMAZING GRACE
    ADMONIA
    FLO'RANCE
    THE LITTLE GIRL
Permutations
    NORMAL JEAN REYNOLDS
The Party
    TOPSY WASHINGTON
    MISS PAT
    MISS ROJ
    LALA LAMAZING GRACE
    THE MAN (*from* Symbiosis)

GIT ON BOARD

Blackness. Cut by drums pounding. Then slides, rapidly flashing before us. Images we've all seen before, of African slaves being captured, loaded onto ships, tortured. The images flash, flash, flash. The drums crescendo. Blackout. And then lights reveal MISS PAT, *frozen. She is black, pert, and cute. She has a flip to her hair and wears a hot pink miniskirt stewardess uniform.*

    She stands in front of a curtain which separates her from an offstage cockpit.

    An electronic bell goes "ding" and MISS PAT *comes to life, presenting herself in a friendly but rehearsed manner, smiling and speaking as she has done so many times before.*

MISS PAT: Welcome aboard Celebrity Slaveship, departing the Gold Coast and making short stops at Bahia, Port au Prince, and Havana, before our final destination of Savannah.

    Hi, I'm Miss Pat and I'll be serving you here in Cabin A. We will be crossing the Atlantic at an altitude that's pretty high, so you must wear your shackles at all times.

    [*She removes a shackle from the overhead compartment and demonstrates.*]
To put on your shackle, take the right hand and close the metal ring around your left hand like so. Repeat the action using your left hand to secure the right. If you have any trouble bonding yourself, I'd be more than glad to assist.

    Once we reach the desired altitude, the Captain will turn off the "Fasten Your Shackle" sign . . . [*She efficiently points out the "Fasten Your Shackle" signs on either side of her, which light up.*] . . . allowing you a chance to stretch and dance in the aisles a bit. But otherwise, shackles must be worn at all times.

    [*The "Fasten Your Shackle" signs go off.*]

MISS PAT: Also, we must ask that you please refrain from call-and-response singing between cabins as that sort of thing can lead to rebellion. And, of course, no drums are allowed on board. Can you repeat after me, "No drums." [*She gets the audience to repeat.*] With a little more enthusiasm, please. "No drums."

[*After the audience repeats it.*] That was great!

Once we're airborne, I'll be by with magazines, and earphones can be purchased for the price of your first-born male.

If there's anything I can do to make this middle passage more pleasant, press the little button overhead and I'll be with you faster than you can say, "Go down, Moses." [*She laughs at her "little joke."*] Thanks for flying Celebrity and here's hoping you have a pleasant takeoff.

[*The engines surge, the "Fasten Your Shackle" signs go on, and over-articulate Muzak voices are heard singing as* MISS PAT *pulls down a bucket seat and "shackles up" for takeoff.*]

VOICES: GET ON BOARD CELEBRITY SLAVESHIP
GET ON BOARD CELEBRITY SLAVESHIP
GET ON BOARD CELEBRITY SLAVESHIP
THERE'S ROOM FOR MANY A MORE

[*The engines reach an even, steady hum. Just as* MISS PAT *rises and replaces the shackles in the overhead compartment, the faint sound of African drumming is heard.*]

MISS PAT: Hi. Miss Pat again. I'm sorry to disturb you, but someone is playing drums. And what did we just say . . . "No drums." It must be someone in Coach. But we here in Cabin A are not going to respond to those drums. As a matter of fact, we don't even hear them. Repeat after me. "I don't hear any drums." [*The audience repeats.*] And "I will not rebel."

[*The audience repeats. The drumming grows.*]

MISS PAT: [*placating*] OK, now I realize some of us are a bit edgy after hearing about the tragedy on board The Laughing Mary, but let me assure you Celebrity has no intention of throwing you overboard and collecting the insurance. We value you!

[*She proceeds to single out individual passengers/audience members.*]

Why, the songs *you* are going to sing in the cotton fields, under the burning heat and stinging lash, will metamorphose and give birth to the likes of James Brown and the Fabulous Flames. And you, yes *you*, are going to come up with some of the best dances. The best dances! The Watusi! The Funky Chicken! And just think of what *you* are going to mean to William Faulkner.

All right, so you're gonna have to suffer for a few hundred years, but from your pain will come a culture so complex. *And*, with this little item here . . . [*She removes a basketball from the overhead compartment.*] . . . you'll become millionaires!

[*There is a roar of thunder. The lights quiver and the "Fasten Your Shackle" signs begin to flash.* MISS PAT *quickly replaces the basketball in the overhead compartment and speaks very reassuringly.*]

MISS PAT: No, don't panic. We're just caught in a little thunderstorm. Now the only way you're going to make it through is if you abandon your God and worship a new one. So, on the count of three, let's all sing. One, two, three . . .

NOBODY KNOWS DE TROUBLE I SEEN

Oh, I forgot to mention, when singing, omit the T-H sound. "The" becomes "de." "They" becomes "dey." Got it? Good!

NOBODY KNOWS . . .

NOBODY KNOWS . . .

Oh, so you don't like that one? Well then let's try another—

SUMMER TIME

AND DE LIVIN' IS EASY

Gershwin. He comes from another oppressed people so he understands.

FISH ARE JUMPIN' . . . come on.

AND DE COTTON IS HIGH.

AND DE COTTON IS . . . Sing, damnit!

> [*Lights begin to flash, the engines surge, and there is wild drumming.* MISS PAT *sticks her head through the curtain and speaks with an offstage* CAPTAIN.]

MISS PAT: What?

VOICE OF CAPTAIN: [*offstage*] Time warp!

MISS PAT: Time warp! [*She turns to the audience and puts on a pleasant face.*] The Captain has assured me everything is fine. We're just caught in a little time warp. [*Trying to fight her growing hysteria.*] On your right you will see the American Revolution, which will give the U.S. of A. exclusive rights to your life. And on your left, the Civil War, which means you will vote Republican until F.D.R. comes along. And now we're passing over the Great Depression, which means everybody gets to live the way you've been living. [*There is a blinding flash of light, and an explosion. She screams.*] Ahhhhhhhhh! That was World War I, which is not to be confused with World War II . . . [*There is a larger flash of light, and another explosion.*] . . . Ahhhhh! Which is not to be confused with the Korean War or the Vietnam War, all of which you will play a major role in.

> Oh, look, now we're passing over the sixties. Martha and the Vandellas . . . "Julia" with Miss Diahann Carroll . . . Malcolm X . . . those five little girls in Alabama . . . Martin Luther King . . . Oh no! The Supremes broke up! [*The drumming intensifies.*] Stop playing those drums! Those drums will be confiscated once we reach Savannah. You can't change history! You can't turn back the clock! [*To the audience.*] Repeat after me, "I don't hear any drums! I will not rebel! I will not rebel! I will not re—"

> [*The lights go out, she screams, and the sound of a plane landing and screeching to a halt is heard. After a beat, lights reveal a wasted, disheveled* MISS PAT, *but perky nonetheless.*]

MISS PAT: Hi. Miss Pat here. Things got a bit jumpy back there, but the Captain has just informed me we have safely landed in Savannah. Please check the overhead before exiting as any baggage you don't claim, we trash.

> It's been fun, and we hope the next time you consider travel, it's with Celebrity.

> [*Luggage begins to revolve onstage from offstage left, going past* MISS PAT *and revolving offstage right. Mixed in with the luggage are two male slaves/ and a woman slave, complete with luggage and I.D. tags around their necks.*]

MISS PAT: [*with routine, rehearsed pleasantness*]

Have a nice day. Bye bye.
Button up that coat, it's kind of chilly.
Have a nice day. Bye bye.
You take care now.
See you.
Have a nice day.
Have a nice day.
Have a nice day.

COOKIN' WITH AUNT ETHEL

As the slaves begin to revolve off, a low-down gut-bucket blues is heard. AUNT ETHEL, *a down-home black woman with a bandana on her head, revolves to center stage. She stands behind a big, black pot and wears a reassuring grin.*

AUNT ETHEL: Welcome to "Aunt Ethel's Down-Home Cookin' Show," where we explores the magic and mysteries of colored cuisine.

Today, we gonna be servin' ourselves up some . . . [*She laughs.*] I'm not gonna tell you. That's right! I'm not gonna tell you what it is till after you done cooked it. Child, on "The Aunt Ethel Show" we loves to have ourselves some fun. Well, are you ready? Here goes.

[*She belts out a hard-drivin' blues and throws invisible ingredients into the big, black pot.*]

FIRST YA ADD A PINCH OF STYLE
AND THEN A DASH OF FLAIR
NOW YA STIR IN SOME PREOCCUPATION
WITH THE TEXTURE OF YOUR HAIR

NEXT YA ADD ALL KINDS OF RHYTHMS
LOTS OF FEELING AND PIZAZZ
THEN HUNNY THROW IN SOME RAGE
TILL IT CONGEALS AND TURNS TO JAZZ

NOW YOU COOKIN'
COOKIN' WITH AUNT ETHEL
YOU REALLY COOKIN'
COOKIN' WITH AUNT ETHEL, OH YEAH

NOW YA ADD A HEAP OF SURVIVAL
AND HUMILITY, JUST A TOUCH
ADD SOME ATTITUDE
OOPS! I PUT TOO MUCH

AND NOW A WHOLE LOT OF HUMOR
SALTY LANGUAGE, MIXED WITH SADNESS
THEN THROW IN A BOX OF BLUES
AND SIMMER TO MADNESS

NOW YOU COOKIN'
COOKIN' WITH AUNT ETHEL, OH YEAH!

NOW YOU BEAT IT—REALLY WORK IT
DISCARD AND DISOWN
AND IN A FEW HUNDRED YEARS
ONCE IT'S AGED AND FULLY GROWN
YA PUT IT IN THE OVEN
TILL IT'S BLACK
AND HAS A SHEEN
OR TILL IT'S NICE AND YELLA
OR ANY SHADE IN BETWEEN

NEXT YA TAKE 'EM OUT AND COOL 'EM
'CAUSE THEY NO FUN WHEN THEY HOT
AND WON'T YOU BE SURPRISED
AT THE CONCOCTION YOU GOT

YOU HAVE BAKED
BAKED YOURSELF A BATCH OF NEGROES
YES YOU HAVE BAKED YOURSELF
BAKED YOURSELF A BATCH OF NEGROES
[*She pulls from the pot a handful of Negroes, black dolls.*]
But don't ask me what to do with 'em now that you got 'em, 'cause child,
that's your problem. [*She throws the dolls back into the pot.*] But in any case,
yaw be sure to join Aunt Ethel next week, when we gonna be servin' our-
selves up some chitlin quiche . . . some grits-under-glass,
AND A SWEET POTATO PIE
AND YOU'LL BE COOKIN'
COOKIN' WITH AUNT ETHEL
OH YEAH!
[*On* AUNT ETHEL's *final riff, lights reveal . . .*]

THE PHOTO SESSION

*. . . a very glamorous, gorgeous, black couple, wearing the best of everything and perfect
smiles. The stage is bathed in color and bright white light. Disco music with the chant:
"We're fabulous" plays in the background. As they pose, larger-than-life images of their
perfection are projected on the museum walls. The music quiets and the images fade
away as they begin to speak and pose.*

GIRL: The world was becoming too much for us.
GUY: We couldn't resolve the contradictions of our existence.
GIRL: And we couldn't resolve yesterday's pain.
GUY: So we gave away our life and we now live inside *Ebony Magazine.*
GIRL: Yes, we live inside a world where everyone is beautiful, and wears fabulous
  clothes.
GUY: And no one says anything profound.

GIRL: Or meaningful.

GUY: Or contradictory.

GIRL: Because no one talks. Everyone just smiles and shows off their cheekbones.
[*They adopt a profile pose.*]

GUY: Last month I was black and fabulous while holding up a bottle of vodka.

GIRL: This month we get to be black and fabulous together.
[*They dance/pose. The "We're fabulous" chant builds and then fades as they start to speak again.*]

GIRL: There are, of course, setbacks.

GUY: We have to smile like this for a whole month.

GIRL: And we have no social life.

GUY: And no sex.

GIRL: And at times it feels like we're suffocating, like we're not human anymore.

GUY: And everything is rehearsed, including this other kind of pain we're starting to feel.

GIRL: The kind of pain that comes from feeling no pain at all.
[*They then speak and pose with a sudden burst of energy.*]

GUY: But one can't have everything.

GIRL: Can one?

GUY: So if the world is becoming too much for you, do like we did.

GIRL: Give away your life and come be beautiful with us.

GUY: We guarantee, no contradictions.

GIRL/GUY: Smile/click, smile/click, smile/click.

GIRL: And no pain.
[*They adopt a final pose and revolve off as the "We're fabulous" chant plays and fades into the background.*]

A SOLDIER WITH A SECRET

Projected onto the museum walls are the faces of black soldiers—from the Spanish-American through to the Vietnam War. Lights slowly reveal JUNIE ROBINSON, *a black combat soldier, posed on an onyx plinth. He comes to life and smiles at the audience. Somewhat dim-witted, he has an easygoing charm about him.*

JUNIE: Pst. Pst. Guess what? I know the secret. The secret to your pain. 'Course, I didn't always know. First I had to die, then come back to life, 'fore I had the gift.

Ya see the Cappin sent me off up ahead to scout for screamin' yella bastards. 'Course, for the life of me I couldn't understand why they'd be screamin', seein' as how we was tryin' to kill them and they us.

But anyway, I'm off lookin', when all of a sudden I find myself caught smack dead in the middle of this explosion. This blindin', burnin', scaldin' explosion. Musta been a booby trap or something, 'cause all around me is fire. Hell, I'm on fire. Like a piece of chicken dropped in a skillet of cracklin' grease. Why, my flesh was justa peelin' off of my bones.

But then I says to myself, "Junie, if yo' flesh is on fire, how come you don't feel no pain!" And I didn't. I swear as I'm standin' here, I felt nuthin'.

That's when I sort of put two and two together and realized I didn't feel no whole lot of hurtin' 'cause I done died.

Well I just picked myself up and walked right on out of that explosion. Hell, once you know you dead, why keep on dyin', ya know?

So, like I say, I walk right outta that explosion, fully expectin' to see white clouds, Jesus, and my Mama, only all I saw was more war. Shootin' goin' on way off in this direction and that direction. And there, standin' around, was all the guys. Hubert, J.F., the Cappin. I guess the sound of the explosion must of attracted 'em, and they all starin' at me like I'm some kind of ghost.

So I yells to 'em, "Hey there Hubert! Hey there Cappin!" But they just stare. So I tells 'em how I'd died and how I guess it wasn't my time 'cause here I am, "Fully in the flesh and not a scratch to my bones." And they still just stare. So I took to starin' back.

[*The expression on* JUNIE's *face slowly turns to horror and disbelief.*]
Only what I saw . . . well I can't exactly to this day describe it. But I swear, as sure as they was wearin' green and holdin' guns, they was each wearin' a piece of the future on their faces.

Yeah. All the hurt that was gonna get done to them and they was gonna do to folks was right there clear as day.

I saw how J.F., once he got back to Chicago, was gonna get shot dead by this po-lice, and I saw how Hubert was gonna start beatin' up on his old lady which I didn't understand, 'cause all he could do was talk on and on about how much he loved her. Each and every one of 'em had pain in his future and blood on his path. And God or the Devil one spoke to me and said, "Junie, these colored boys ain't gonna be the same after this war. They ain't gonna have no kind of happiness."

Well right then and there it come to me. The secret to their pain.

Late that night, after the medics done checked me over and found me fit for fightin', after everybody done settle down for the night, I sneaked over to where Hubert was sleepin', and with a needle I stole from the medics . . . pst, pst . . . I shot a little air into his veins. The second he died, all the hurtin'-to-come just left his face.

Two weeks later I got J.F. and after that Woodrow . . . Jimmy Joe . . . I even spent all night waitin' by the latrine 'cause I knew the Cappin always made a late night visit and pst . . . pst . . . I got him.

[*Smiling, quite proud of himself.*] That's how come I died and come back to life. 'Cause just like Jesus went around healin' the sick, I'm supposed to go around healin' the hurtin' all these colored boys wearin' from the war.

Pst, pst. I know the secret. The secret to your pain. The secret to yours, and yours. Pst. Pst. Pst. Pst.

[*The lights slowly fade.*]

THE GOSPEL ACCORDING TO MISS ROJ

The darkness is cut by electronic music. Cold, pounding, unrelenting. A neon sign that spells out "THE BOTTOMLESS PIT" clicks on. There is a lone bar stool. Lights flash

on and off, pulsating to the beat. There is a blast of smoke and, from the haze, MISS ROJ
*appears. He is dressed in striped patio pants, white go-go boots, a halter, and cat-shaped
sunglasses. What would seem ridiculous on anyone else,* MISS ROJ *wears as if it were
high fashion. He carries himself with total elegance and absolute arrogance.*

MISS ROJ: God created black people and black people created style. The name's
Miss Roj . . . that's R.O.J. thank you and you can find me every Wednesday,
Friday, and Saturday nights at "The Bottomless Pit," the watering hole for
the wild and weary which asks the question, "Is there life after Jherri-curl?"
[*A* WAITER *enters, hands* MISS ROJ *a drink, and then exits.*]
Thanks, doll. *Yes,* if they be black and swish, the B.P. has seen them, which
is not to suggest the Pit is lacking in cultural diversity. Oh no. There are
your dinge queens, white men who like their chicken legs dark. [*He
winks/flirts with a man in the audience.*] And let's not forget, "Los Mucha-
chos de la Neighborhood." But the specialty of the house is The Snap
Queens. [*He snaps his fingers.*] We are a rare breed.
For, you see, when something strikes our fancy, when the truth comes
piercing through the dark, well you just can't let it pass unnoticed. No darling. You must pronounce it with a snap. [*He snaps.*]
Snapping comes from another galaxy, as do all snap queens. That's
right. I ain't just your regular oppressed American Negro. No-no-no! I am
an extraterrestrial. And I ain't talkin' none of that shit you seen in the
movies! I have real power.
[*The* WAITER *enters.* MISS ROJ *stops him.*]
Speaking of no power, will you please tell Miss Stingy-with-the-rum, that
if Miss Roj had wanted to remain sober, she could have stayed home and
drank Kool-aid. [*He snaps.*] Thank you.
[*The* WAITER *exits.* MISS ROJ *crosses and sits on bar stool.*]
Yes, I was placed here on Earth to study the life habits of a deteriorating society, and, child, when we talkin' New York City, we are discussing the
Queen of Deterioration. Miss New York is doing a slow dance with death,
and I am here to warn you all, but before I do, I must know . . . don't you just
love my patio pants? Annette Funicello immortalized them in "Beach Blanket Bingo," and I have continued the legacy. And my go-gos? I realize white
after Labor Day is very gauche, but as the saying goes, if you've got it, flaunt
it, if you don't, front it and snap to death any bastard who dares to defy you.
[*Laughing.*] Oh ho! My demons are showing. Yes, my demons live at the
bottom of my Bacardi and Coke.
Let's just hope for all concerned I dance my demons out before I
drink them out 'cause, child, dancing demons take you on a ride, but those
drinkin' demons just take you, and you find yourself doing the strangest
things. Like the time I locked my father in the broom closet. Seems the
liquor made his tongue real liberal and he decided he was gonna baptize me
with the word "faggot" over and over. Well, he's just going on and on with
"faggot this" and "faggot that," all the while walking toward the broom
closet to piss. So the demons just took hold of my wedgies and forced me to
kick the drunk son of a bitch into the closet and lock the door. [*Laughter.*]
Three days later I remembered he was there. [*He snaps.*]

[*The* WAITER *enters.* MISS ROJ *takes a drink and downs it.*]
Another!
      [*The* WAITER *exits.*]
[*Dancing about.*] Oh yes-yes-yes! Miss Roj is quintessential style. I cornrow the hairs on my legs so that they spell out M.I.S.S. R.O.J. And I dare any bastard to fuck with me because I will snap your ass into oblivion.

      I have the power, you know. Everytime I snap, I steal one beat of your heart. So if you find yourself gasping for air in the middle of the night, chances are you fucked with Miss Roj and she didn't like it.

      Like the time this asshole at Jones Beach decided to take issue with my coulotte-sailor ensemble. This child, this muscle-bound Brooklyn thug in a skin-tight bikini, very skin-tight so the whole world can see that instead of a brain, God gave him an extra thick piece of sausage. You know the kind who beat up on their wives for breakfast. Snap your fingers if you know what I'm talking about . . . Come on and snap, child. [*He gets the audience to snap.*] Well, he decided to blurt out when I walked by, "Hey look at da monkey coon in da faggit suit." Well, I walked up to the poor dear, very calmly lifted my hand, and. . . . [*He snaps in rapid succession.*] A heart attack, right there on the beach. [*He singles out someone in the audience.*] You don't believe it? Cross me! Come on! Come on!

      [*The* WAITER *enters, hands* MISS ROJ *a drink.* MISS ROJ *downs it. The* WAITER *exits.*]
[*Looking around.*] If this place is the answer, we're asking all the wrong questions. The only reason I come here is to communicate with my origins. The flashing lights are signals from my planet way out there. Yes, girl, even further than Flatbush. We're talking another galaxy. The flashing lights tell me how much time is left before the end.

      [*Very drunk and loud by now.*] I hate the people here. I hate the drinks. But most of all I hate this goddamn music. That ain't music. Give me Aretha Franklin any day. [*Singing.*] "Just a little respect. R.E.S.P.E.C.T." Yeah! Yeah!

      Come on and dance your last dance with Miss Roj. Last call is but a drink away and each snap puts you one step closer to the end.

      A high-rise goes up. You can't get no job. Come on everybody and dance. A whole race of people gets trashed and debased. Snap those fingers and dance. Some sick bitch throws her baby out the window 'cause she thinks it's the Devil. Everybody snap! *The New York Post.* Snap!

      Snap for every time you walk past someone lying in the street, smelling like frozen piss and shit and you don't see it. Snap for every crazed bastard who kills himself so as to get the jump on being killed. And snap for every sick muthafucker who, bored with carrying around his fear, takes to shooting up other people.

      Yeah, snap your fingers and dance with Miss Roj. But don't be fooled by the banners and balloons 'cause, child, this ain't no party going on. Hell no! It's a wake. And the casket's made out of stone, steel, and glass and the people are racing all over the pavement like maggots on a dead piece of meat.

      Yeah, dance! But don't be surprised if there ain't no beat holding you together 'cause we traded in our drums for respectability. So now it's just words. Words rappin'. Words screechin'. Words flowin' instead of blood 'cause you know that don't work. Words cracklin' instead of fire 'cause by the time a match is struck on 125th Street and you run to midtown, the flame has been blown away.

So come on and dance with Miss Roj and her demons. We don't ask for acceptance. We don't ask for approval. We know who we are and we move on it!

I guarantee you will never hear two fingers put together in a snap and not think of Miss Roj. That's power, baby. Patio pants and all.

[*The lights begin to flash in rapid succession.*]

So let's dance! And snap! And dance! And snap!

[MISS ROJ *begins to dance as if driven by his demons. There is a blast of smoke and when the haze settles,* MISS ROJ *has revolved off and in place of him is a recording of Aretha Franklin singing "Respect."*]

THE HAIRPIECE

As "Respect" fades into the background, a vanity revolves to center stage. On this vanity are two wigs, an Afro wig, circa 1968, and a long, flowing wig, both resting on wig stands. A black WOMAN *enters, her head and body wrapped in towels. She picks up a framed picture and after a few moments of hesitation, throws it into a small trash can. She then removes one of her towels to reveal a totally bald head. Looking into a mirror on the "fourth wall," she begins applying makeup.*

The wig stand holding the Afro wig opens her eyes. Her name is JANINE. *She stares in disbelief at the bald woman.*

JANINE: [*calling to the other wig stand*] LaWanda. LaWanda girl, wake up.

[*The other wig stand, the one with the long, flowing wig, opens her eyes. Her name is* LAWANDA.]

LAWANDA: What? What is it?

JANINE: Check out girlfriend.

LAWANDA: Oh, girl, I don't believe it.

JANINE: [*laughing*] Just look at the poor thing, trying to paint some life onto that face of hers. You'd think by now she'd realize it's the hair. It's all about the hair.

LAWANDA: What hair! She ain't go no hair! She done fried, dyed, de-chemicalized her shit to death.

JANINE: And all that's left is that buck-naked scalp of hers, sittin' up there apologizin' for being odd-shaped and ugly.

LAWANDA: [*laughing with* JANINE] Girl, stop!

JANINE: I ain't sayin' nuthin' but the truth.

LAWANDA/JANINE: The bitch is bald! [*They laugh.*]

JANINE: And all over some man.

LAWANDA: I tell ya, girl, I just don't understand it. I mean, look at her. She's got a right nice face, a good head on her shoulders. A good job, even. And she's got to go fall in love with that fool.

JANINE: That political quick-change artist. Everytime the nigga went and changed his ideology, she went and changed her hair to fit the occasion.

LAWANDA: Well at least she's breaking up with him.

JANINE: Hunny, no!

LAWANDA: Yes, child.

JANINE: Oh, girl, dish me the dirt!

LAWANDA: Well, you see, I heard her on the phone, talking to one of her girl-friends, and she's meeting him for lunch today to give him the ax.

JANINE: Well it's about time.

LAWANDA: I hear ya. But don't you worry 'bout a thing, girlfriend. I'm gonna tell you all about it.

JANINE: Hunny, you won't have to tell me a damn thing 'cause I'm gonna be there, front row, center.

LAWANDA: You?

JANINE: Yes, child, she's wearing me to lunch.

LAWANDA: [*outraged*] I don't think so!

JANINE: [*with an attitude*] What do you mean, you don't think so?

LAWANDA: Exactly what I said, "I don't think so." Damn, Janine, get real. How the hell she gonna wear both of us?

JANINE: She ain't wearing both of us. She's wearing me.

LAWANDA: Says who?

JANINE: Says me! Says her! Ain't that right, girlfriend?

    [*The* WOMAN *stops putting on makeup, looks around, sees no one, and goes back to her makeup.*]

JANINE: I said, ain't that right!

    [*The* WOMAN *picks up the phone.*]

WOMAN: Hello . . . hello . . .

JANINE: Did you hear the damn phone ring?

WOMAN: No.

JANINE: Then put the damn phone down and talk to me.

WOMAN: I ah . . . don't understand.

JANINE: It ain't deep so don't panic. Now, you're having lunch with your boy-friend, right?

WOMAN: [*breaking into tears*] I think I'm having a nervous breakdown.

JANINE: [*impatient*] I said you're having lunch with your boyfriend, right!

WOMAN: [*scared, pulling herself together*] Yes, right . . . right.

JANINE: To break up with him.

WOMAN: How did you know that?

LAWANDA: I told her.

WOMAN: [*stands and screams*] Help! Help!

JANINE: Sit down. I said sit your ass down!

    [*The* WOMAN *does.*]

JANINE: Now set her straight and tell her you're wearing me.

LAWANDA: She's the one that needs to be set straight, so go on and tell her you're wearing me.

JANINE: No, tell her you're wearing me.

    [*There is a pause.*]

LAWANDA: Well?

JANINE: Well?

WOMAN: I ah . . . actually hadn't made up my mind.

JANINE: [*going off*] What do you mean you ain't made up you mind! After all that fool has put you through, you gonna need all the attitude you can get and there is nothing like attitude and a healthy head of kinks to make his shit shrivel like it should!

   That's right! When you wearin' me, you lettin' him know he ain't gonna get no sweet-talkin' comb through your love without some serious resistance. No-no! The kink of my head is like the kink of your heart and neither is about to be hot-pressed into surrender.

LAWANDA: That shit is so tired. The last time attitude worked on anybody was 1968. Janine girl, you need to get over it and get on with it. [*To the* WOMAN.] And you need to give the nigga a goodbye he will never forget.

   I say give him hysteria! Give him emotion! Give him rage! And there is nothing like a toss of the tresses to make your emotional outburst shine with emotional flair.

   You can toss me back, shake me from side to side, all the while screaming, "I want you out of my life forever!!!" And not only will I come bouncing back for more, but you just might win an Academy Award for best performance by a head of hair in a dramatic role.

JANINE: Miss hunny, please! She don't need no Barbie doll dipped in chocolate telling her what to do. She needs a head of hair that's coming from a fo' real place.

LAWANDA: Don't you dare talk about nobody coming from a "fo' real place," Miss Made-in-Taiwan!

JANINE: Hey! I ain't ashamed of where I come from. Besides, it don't matter where you come from as long as you end up in the right place.

LAWANDA: And it don't matter the grade as long as the point gets made. So go on and tell her you're wearing me.

JANINE: No, tell her you're wearing me.

   [*The* WOMAN, *unable to take it, begins to bite off her fake nails, as* LAWANDA *and* JANINE *go at each other.*]

LAWANDA: Set the bitch straight. Let her know there is no way she could even begin to compete with me. I am quality. She is kink. I am exotic. She is common. I am class and she is trash. That's right. T.R.A.S.H. We're talking three strikes and you're out. So go on and tell her you're wearing me. Go on, tell her! Tell her! Tell her!

JANINE: Who you callin' a bitch? Why, if I had hands I'd knock you clear into next week. You think you cute. She thinks she's cute just 'cause that synthetic mop of hers blows in the wind. She looks like a fool and you look like an even bigger fool when you wear her, so go on and tell her you're wearing me. Go on, tell her! Tell her! Tell her!

   [*The* WOMAN *screams and pulls the two wigs off the wig stands as the lights go to black on three bald heads.*]

THE LAST MAMA-ON-THE-COUCH PLAY

A NARRATOR, *dressed in a black tuxedo, enters through the audience and stands center stage. He is totally solemn.*

NARRATOR: We are pleased to bring you yet another Mama-on-the-Couch play. A searing domestic drama that tears at the very fabric of racist America. [*He crosses upstage center and sits on a stool and reads from a playscript.*] Act One. Scene One.

[MAMA *revolves on stage left, sitting on a couch reading a large, oversized Bible. A window is placed stage right.* MAMA's *dress, the couch, and drapes are made from the same material. A doormat lays down center.*]

NARRATOR: Lights up on a dreary, depressing, but with middle-class aspirations tenement slum. There is a couch, with a Mama on it. Both are well worn. There is a picture of Jesus on the wall . . . [*A picture of Jesus is instantly revealed.*] . . . and a window which looks onto an abandoned tenement. It is late spring.

Enter Walter-Lee-Beau-Willie-Jones [SON *enters through the audience.*] He is Mama's thirty-year-old son. His brow is heavy from three hundred years of oppression.

MAMA: [*Looking up from her Bible, speaking in a slow manner.*] Son, did you wipe your feet?

SON: [*an ever-erupting volcano*] No, Mama, I didn't wipe me feet! Out there, every day, Mama, is the Man. The Man, Mama. Mr. Charlie! Mr. Bossman! And he's wipin' his feet on me. On me, Mama, every damn day of my life. Ain't that enough for me to deal with? Ain't that enough?

MAMA: Son, wipe your feet.

SON: I wanna dream. I wanna be somebody. I wanna take charge of my life.

MAMA: You can do all of that, but first you got to wipe your feet.

SON: [*as he crosses to the mat, mumbling and wiping his feet*] Wipe my feet . . . wipe my feet . . . wipe my feet . . .

MAMA: That's a good boy.

SON: [*exploding*] Boy! Boy! I don't wanna be nobody's good boy, Mama. I wanna be my own man!

MAMA: I know, son, I know. God will show the way.

SON: God, Mama! Since when did your God ever do a damn thing for the black man. Huh, Mama, huh? You tell me. When did your God ever help me?

MAMA: [*removing her wire-rim glasses*] Son, come here.

[SON *crosses to* MAMA, *who slowly stands and in an exaggerated stage slap, backhands* SON *clear across the stage. The* NARRATOR *claps his hands to create the sound for the slap.* MAMA *then lifts her clenched fists to the heavens.*]

MAMA: Not in my house, my house, will you ever talk that way again!

[*The* NARRATOR, *so moved by her performance, erupts in applause and encourages the audience to do so.*]

NARRATOR: Beautiful. Just stunning.

[*He reaches into one of the secret compartments of the set and gets an award, which he ceremoniously gives to* MAMA *for her performance. She bows and then returns to the couch.*]

NARRATOR: Enter Walter-Lee-Beau-Willie's wife, the Lady in Plaid.

[*Music from nowhere is heard, a jazzy pseudo-abstract intro as the* LADY IN PLAID *dances in through the audience, wipes her feet, and then twirls about.*]

LADY: She was a creature of regal beauty
who in ancient time graced the temple of the Nile

with her womanliness
But here she was, stuck being colored
and a woman in a world that valued neither.

SON: You cooked my dinner?

LADY: [*oblivious to* SON]
Feet flat, back broke,
she looked at the man who, though he be thirty,
still ain't got his own apartment.
Yeah, he's still livin' with his Mama!
And she asked herself, was this the life
for a Princess Colored, who by the
translucence of her skin, knew the
universe was her sister.
[*The* LADY IN PLAID *twirls and dances.*]

SON: [*becoming irate*] I've had a hard day of dealin' with the Man. Where's my damn dinner? Woman, stand still when I'm talkin' to you!

LADY: And she cried for her sisters in Detroit
Who knew, as she, that their souls belonged
in ancient temples on the Nile.
And she cried for her sisters in Chicago
who, like her, their life has become
one colored hell.

SON: There's only one thing gonna get through to you.

LADY: And she cried for her sisters in New Orleans
And her sisters in Trenton and Birmingham,
and
Poughkeepsie and Orlando and Miami Beach
and
Las Vegas, Palm Springs.
[*As she continues to call out cities, he crosses offstage and returns with two black dolls and then crosses to the window.*]

SON: Now are you gonna cook me dinner?

LADY: Walter-Lee-Beau-Willie-Jones, no! Not my babies.
[SON *throws them out the window. The* LADY IN PLAID *then lets out a primal scream.*]

LADY: He dropped them!!!!
[*The* NARRATOR *breaks into applause.*]

NARRATOR: Just splendid. Shattering.
[*He then crosses and after an intense struggle with* MAMA, *he takes the award from her and gives it to the* LADY IN PLAID, *who is still suffering primal pain.*]

LADY: Not my babies . . . not my . . . [*Upon receiving the award, she instantly recovers.*] Help me up, sugar. [*She then bows and crosses and stands behind the couch.*]

NARRATOR: Enter Medea Jones, Walter-Lee-Beau-Willie's sister.
[MEDEA *moves very ceremoniously, wiping her feet and then speaking and gesturing as if she just escaped from a Greek tragedy.*]

MEDEA: Ah, see how the sun kneels to speak

her evening vespers, exalting all
in her vision, even lowly tenement
long abandoned.

Mother, wife of brother, I trust
the approaching darkness finds you
safe in Hestia's bosom.

Brother, why wear the face of a man
in anguish. Can the argument of thine
feelings cause the shape of your
countenance to disfigure so?

SON: [*at the end of his rope*] Leave me alone, Medea.

MEDEA: [*to* MAMA]
    Is good brother still going on and on and on
    about He and The Man.

MAMA/LADY: What else?

MEDEA: Ah brother, if with our thoughts and
    words we could cast thine oppressors
    into the lowest bowls of wretched
    hell, would that make us more like the
    gods or more like our oppressors?

    No, brother, no, do not let thy rage
    choke the blood which anoints thy
    heart with love. Forgo thine darkened
    humor and let love shine on your
    soul, like a jewel on a young maiden's hand.
        [*Dropping to her knees.*]
    I beseech thee, forgo thine
    anger and leave wrath to the gods!

SON: Girl, what has gotten into you.

MEDEA: Julliard, good brother. For I am no
    longer bound by rhythms of race or
    region. Oh, no. My speech, like my
    pain and suffering, have become
    classical and therefore universal.

LADY: I didn't understand a damn thing she said, but girl you usin' them words.
        [LADY IN PLAID *crosses and gives* MEDEA *the award and everyone
        applauds.*]

SON: [*trying to stop the applause*] Wait one damn minute! This my play. It's about
    me and the Man. It ain't got nuthin' to do with no ancient temples on the
    Nile and it ain't got nuthin' to do with Hestia's bosom. And it ain't got
    nuthin' to do with you slappin' me across no room. [*His gut-wrenching best.*]
    It's about me. Me and my pain! My pain!

THE VOICE OF THE MAN: Walter-Lee-Beau-Willie, this is the Man. You have
    been convicted of overacting. Come out with your hands up.
        [SON *starts to cross to the window.*]

SON: Well now that does it.

MAMA: Son, no, don't go near that window. Son, no!

>   [*Gun shots ring out and* SON *falls dead.*]

MAMA: [*crossing to the body, too emotional for words*] My son, he was a good boy. Confused. Angry. Just like his father. And his father's father. And his father's father's father. And now he's dead.

>   [*Seeing she's about to drop to her knees, the* NARRATOR *rushes and places a pillow underneath her just in time.*]

If only he had been born into a world better than this. A world where there are no well-worn couches and no well-worn Mamas and nobody overemotes.

>   If only he had been born into an all-black musical.
>
>   [*A song intro begins.*]

Nobody ever dies in an all-black musical.

>   [MEDEA *and* LADY IN PLAID *pull out church fans and begin to fan themselves.*]

MAMA: [*singing a soul-stirring gospel*]
OH WHY COULDN'T HE
BE BORN
INTO A SHOW WITH LOTS OF SINGING
AND DANCING

I SAY WHY
COULDN'T HE
BE BORN

LADY: Go ahead, hunny. Take your time.

MAMA: INTO A SHOW WHERE EVERYBODY
IS HAPPY

NARRATOR/MEDEA: Preach! Preach!

MAMA: OH WHY COULDN'T HE BE BORN WITH THE CHANCE
TO SMILE A LOT AND SING AND DANCE
OH WHY
OH WHY

OH WHY
COULDN'T HE
BE BORN
INTO AN ALL-BLACK SHOW
WOAH-WOAH

>   [*The* CAST *joins in, singing do-wop gospel background to* MAMA's *lament.*]

OH WHY
COULDN'T HE
BE BORN
(HE BE BORN)
INTO A SHOW WHERE EVERYBODY
IS HAPPY

WHY COULDN'T HE BE BORN WITH THE CHANCE
TO SMILE A LOT AND SING AND DANCE
WANNA KNOW WHY
WANNA KNOW WHY

OH WHY
COULDN'T HE
BE BORN
INTO AN ALL-BLACK SHOW
A-MEN
  [*A singing/dancing, spirit-raising revival begins.*]
OH, SON, GET UP
GET UP AND DANCE
WE SAY GET UP
THIS IS YOUR SECOND CHANCE

DON'T SHAKE A FIST
JUST SHAKE A LEG
AND DO THE TWIST
DON'T SCREAM AND BEG
SON SON SON
GET UP AND DANCE

GET
GET UP
GET UP AND
GET UP AND DANCE—ALL RIGHT!
GET UP AND DANCE—ALL RIGHT!
GET UP AND DANCE!
  [WALTER-LEE-BEAU-WILLIE *springs to life and joins in the dancing. A
  foot-stomping, hand-clapping production number takes off, which encom-
  passes a myriad of black-Broadwayesque dancing styles—shifting speeds
  and styles with exuberant abandonment.*]
MAMA: [*bluesy*]
  WHY COULDN'T HE BE BORN INTO AN ALL-BLACK SHOW
CAST: WITH SINGING AND DANCING
MAMA: BLACK SHOW
  [MAMA *scats and the dancing becomes manic and just a little too desperate to
  please.*]
CAST: WE GOTTA DANCE
  WE GOTTA DANCE
  GET UP GET UP GET UP AND DANCE
  WE GOTTA DANCE
  WE GOTTA DANCE
  GOTTA DANCE!
  [*Just at the point the dancing is about to become violent, the cast freezes and
  pointedly, simply sings:*]

IF WE WANT TO LIVE
WE HAVE GOT TO
WE HAVE GOT TO
DANCE . . . AND DANCE . . . AND DANCE . . .

> [*As they continue to dance with zombie-like frozen smiles and faces, around them images of coon performers flash as the lights slowly fade.*]

SYMBIOSIS

The Temptations singing "My Girl" are heard as lights reveal a BLACK MAN *in corporate dress standing before a large trash can throwing objects from a Saks Fifth Avenue bag into it. Circling around him with his every emotion on his face is* THE KID, *who is dressed in a late-sixties street style. His moves are slightly heightened. As the scene begins the music fades.*

MAN: [*with contained emotions*]
> My first pair of Converse All-stars. Gone.
> My first Afro-comb. Gone.
> My first dashiki. Gone.
> My autographed pictures of Stokley Carmichael,
>   Jomo Kenyatta, and Donna Summer. Gone.

KID: [*near tears, totally upset*] This shit's not fair, man. Damn! Hell! Shit! Shit! It's not fair!

MAN: My first jar of Murray's Pomade.
> My first can of Afro-sheen.
> My first box of curl relaxer. Gone! Gone! Gone!
> Eldridge Cleaver's *Soul on Ice.*

KID: Not *Soul on Ice!*

MAN: It's been replaced on my bookshelf by *The Color Purple.*

KID: [*horrified*] No!

MAN: Gone!

KID: But—

MAN: Jimi Hendrix's "Purple Haze." Gone.
> Sly Stone's "There's A Riot Goin' On." Gone.
> The Jackson Five's "I Want You Back."

KID: Man, you can't throw that away. It's living proof Michael had a black nose.

MAN: It's all going. Anything and everything that connects me to you, to who I was, to what we were, is out of my life.

KID: You've got to give me another chance.

MAN: "Fingertips Part 2."

KID: Man, how can you do that? That's vintage Stevie Wonder.

MAN: You want to know how, Kid? You want to know how? Because my survival depends on it. Whether you know it or not, the Ice Age is upon us.

KID: [*jokingly*] Man, what the hell you talkin' about. It's ninety-five damn degrees.

MAN: The climate is changing, Kid, and either you adjust or you end up extinct. A sociological dinosaur. Do you understand what I'm trying to tell you? King Kong would have made it to the top if only he had taken the elevator.

Instead he brought attention to his struggle and ended up dead.

KID: [*pleading*] I'll change. I swear I'll change. I'll maintain a low profile. You won't even know I'm around.

MAN: If I'm to become what I'm to become, then you've got to go. . . . I have no history. I have no past.

KID: Just like that?

MAN: [*throwing away a series of buttons*] Free Angela! Free Bobby! Free Huey, Duey, and Louie! U.S. out of Vietnam. U.S. out of Cambodia. U.S. out of Harlem, Detroit, and Newark. Gone! . . . "The Temptations Greatest Hits!"

KID: [*grabbing the album*] No!!!

MAN: Give it back, Kid.

KID: No.

MAN: I said give it back!

KID: No. I can't let you trash this. Johnny man, it contains fourteen classic cuts by the tempting Temptations. We're talking, "Ain't Too Proud to Beg," "Papa Was a Rolling Stone," "My Girl."

MAN: [*warning*] I don't have all day.

KID: For God's sake, Johnny man, "My Girl" is the jam to end all jams. It's what we are. Who we are. It's a way of life. Come on, man, for old times sake. [*Singing.*]
I GOT SUNSHINE ON A CLOUDY DAY
BUM-DA-DUM-DA-DUM-DA-BUM
AND WHEN IT'S COLD OUTSIDE
Come on, Johnny man, you ain't "bummin'," man.
I GOT THE MONTH OF MAY
Here comes your favorite part. Come on, Johnny man, sing.
I GUESS YOU SAY
WHAT CAN MAKE ME FEEL THIS WAY
MY GIRL, MY GIRL, MY GIRL
TALKIN' 'BOUT

MAN: [*exploding*] I said give it back!

KID: [*angry*] I ain't givin' you a muthafuckin' thing!

MAN: Now you listen to me!

KID: No, you listen to me. This is the kid you're dealin' with, so don't fuck with me!
[*He hits his fist into his hand, and* THE MAN *grabs for his heart.* THE KID *repeats with two more hits, which causes the man to drop to the ground, grabbing his heart.*]

KID: Jai! Jai! Jai!

MAN: Kid, please.

KID: Yeah. Yeah. Now who's begging who. . . . Well, well, well, look at Mr. Cream-of-the-Crop, Mr. Colored-Man-on-Top. Now that he's making it, he no longer wants anything to do with the Kid. Well, you may put all kinds of silk ties 'round your neck and white lines up your nose, but the Kid is here to stay. You may change your women as often as you change your underwear, but the Kid is here to stay. And regardless of how much of your past that you trash, I ain't goin' no damn where. Is that clear? Is that clear?

MAN: [*regaining his strength, beginning to stand*] Yeah.

KID: Good. [*after a beat*] You all right, man? You all right? I don't want to hurt you, but when you start all that talk about getting rid of me, well, it gets me kind of crazy. We need each other. We are one . . .

> [*Before* THE KID *can complete his sentence,* THE MAN *grabs him around his neck and starts to choke him violently.*]

MAN: [*as he strangles him*] The . . . Ice . . . Age . . . is . . . upon us . . . and either we adjust . . . or we end up . . . extinct.

> [THE KID *hangs limp in* THE MAN'S *arms.*]

MAN: [*laughing*] Man kills his own rage. Film at eleven. [*He then dumps* THE KID *into the trash can, and closes the lid. He speaks in a contained voice.*] I have no history. I have no past. I can't. It's too much. It's much too much. I must be able to smile on cue. And watch the news with an impersonal eye. I have no stake in the madness.

> Being black is too emotionally taxing; therefore I will be black only on weekends and holidays.

> [*He then turns to go, but sees the Temptations album lying on the ground. He picks it up and sings quietly to himself.*]

I GUESS YOU SAY
WHAT CAN MAKE ME FEEL THIS WAY

> [*He pauses, but then crosses to the trash can, lifts the lid, and just as he is about to toss the album in, a hand reaches from inside the can and grabs hold of* THE MAN'S *arm.* THE KID *then emerges from the can with a death grip on* THE MAN'S *arm.*]

KID: [*smiling*] What's happenin'?

BLACKOUT

LALA'S OPENING

Roving follow spots. A timpani drum roll. As we hear the voice of the ANNOUNCER, *outrageously glamorous images of* LALA *are projected onto the museum walls.*

VOICE OF ANNOUNCER: From Rome to Rangoon! Paris to Prague! We are pleased to present the American debut of the one! The only! The breathtaking! The astounding! The stupendous! The incredible! The magnificent! Lala Lamazing Grace!

> [*Thunderous applause as* LALA *struts on, the definitive black diva. She has long, flowing hair, an outrageous lamé dress, and an affected French accent, which she loses when she's upset.*]

LALA: EVERYBODY LOVES LALA
EVERYBODY LOVES ME
PARIS! BERLIN! LONDON! ROME!
NO MATTER WHERE I GO
I ALWAYS FEEL AT HOME

OHHHH
EVERYBODY LOVES LALA
EVERYBODY LOVES ME
I'M TRES MAGNIFIQUE

AND OH SO UNIQUE
AND WHEN IT COMES TO GLAMOUR
I'M CHIC-ER THAN CHIC
[*She giggles.*]
THAT'S WHY EVERYBODY
EVERYBODY
EVERYBODY-EVERYBODY-EVERYBODY
LOVES ME
[*She begins to vocally reach for higher and higher notes, until she has to point to her final note. She ends the number with a grand flourish and bows to thunderous applause.*]

LALA: Yes, it's me! Lala Lamazing Grace and I have come home. Home to the home I never knew as home. Home to you, my people, my blood, my guts.

My story is a simple one, full of fire, passion, magique. You may ask how did I, a humble girl from the backwoods of Mississippi, come to be the ninth wonder of the modern world. Well, I can't take all of the credit. Part of it goes to him. [*She points toward the heavens.*]

No, not the light man, darling, but God. For, you see, Lala is a star. A very big star. Let us not mince words, I'm a fucking meteorite. [*She laughs.*] But He is the universe and just like my sister, Aretha la Franklin, Lala's roots are in the black church. [*She sings in a showy gospel style:*]
THAT'S WHY EVERYBODY LOVES
SWING LOW SWEET CHARIOT
THAT'S WHY EVERYBODY LOVES
GO DOWN MOSES WAY DOWN IN EGYPT LAND
THAT'S WHY EVERYBODY EVERYBODY LOVES
ME!!!
[*Once again she points to her final note and then basks in applause.*]
I love that note. I just can't hit it.

Now, before I dazzle you with more of my limitless talent, tell me something, America. [*Musical underscoring.*] Why has it taken you so long to recognize my artistry? Mother France opened her loving arms and Lala came running. All over the world Lala was embraced. But here, ha! You spat at Lala. Was I too exotic? Too much woman, or what?

Diana Ross you embrace. A two-bit nobody from Detroit, of all places. Now, I'm not knocking la Ross. She does the best she can with the little she has. [*She laughs.*] But the Paul la Robesons, the James la Baldwins, the Josephine la Bakers, who was my godmother you know. The Lala Lamazing Graces you kick out. You drive . . .
AWAY
I AM GOING AWAY
HOPING TO FIND A BETTER DAY
WHAT DO YOU SAY
HEY HEY
I AM GOING AWAY
AWAY
[LALA, *caught up in the drama of the song, doesn't see* ADMONIA, *her maid, stick her head out from offstage.*]

[*Once she is sure* LALA *isn't looking, she wheels onto stage right* FLO'RANCE, LALA'*s lover, who wears a white mask/blonde hair. He is gagged and tied to a chair.* ADMONIA *places him on stage and then quickly exits.*]

LALA: AU REVOIR—JE VAIS PARTIR MAINTENANT
JE VEUX DIRE MAINTENANT
AU REVOIR
AU REVOIR
AU REVOIR
AU REVOIR
A-MA-VIE

[*On her last note, she sees* FLO'RANCE *and, in total shock, crosses to him.*]

LALA: Flo'rance, what the hell are you doing our here looking like that. I haven't seen you for three days and you decide to show up now?

[*He mumbles.*]

I don't want to hear it!

[*He mumbles.*]

I said shut up!

[ADMONIA *enters from stage right and has a letter opener on a silver tray.*]

ADMONIA: Pst!

[LALA, *embarrassed by the presence of* ADMONIA *on stage, smiles apologetically at the audience.*]

LALA: Un momento.

[*She then pulls* ADMONIA *to the side.*]

LALA: Darling, have you lost your mind coming onstage while I'm performing? And what have you done to Flo'rance? When I asked you to keep him tied up, I didn't mean to tie him up.

[ADMONIA *gives her the letter opener.*]

LALA: Why are you giving me this? I have no letters to open. I'm in the middle of my American debut. Admonia, take Flo'rance off this stage with you! Admonia!

[ADMONIA *is gone.* LALA *turns to the audience and tries to make the best of it.*]

LALA: That was Admonia, my slightly overweight black maid, and this is Flo'-rance, my amour. I remember how we met, don't you, Flo'rance. I was sitting in a café on the Left Bank, when I looked up and saw the most beautiful man staring down at me.

"Who are you," he asked. I told him my name . . . whatever my name was back then. And he said, "No, that cannot be your name. Your name should fly, like Lala." And the rest is la history.

Flo'rance molded me into the woman I am today. He is my Svengali, my reality, my all. And I thought I was all to him, until we came here to America, and he fucked that bitch. Yeah, you fucked 'em all. Anything black and breathing. And all this time, I thought you loved me for being me. [*She holds the letter opener to his neck.*]

You may think you made me, but I'll have you know I was who I was, whoever that was, long before you made me what I am. So there! [*She stabs him and breaks into song.*]

OH, LOVE CAN DRIVE A WOMAN TO MADNESS
TO PAIN AND SADNESS
I KNOW
BELIEVE ME I KNOW
I KNOW
I KNOW

[LALA *sees what she's done and is about to scream but catches herself and tries to play it off.*]

LALA: Moving right along.

[ADMONIA *enters with a telegram on a tray.*]

ADMONIA: Pst.

LALA: [*anxious/hostile*] What is it now?

[ADMONIA *hands* LALA *a telegram.*]

LALA: [*excited*] Oh, la telegram from one of my fans and the concert isn't even over yet. Get me the letter opener. It's in Flo'rance.

[ADMONIA *hands* LALA *the letter opener.*]

LALA: Next I am going to do for you my immortal hit song, "The Girl Inside." But first we open the telegram. [*She quickly reads it and is outraged.*] What! Which pig in la audience wrote this trash? [*Reading*] "Dear Sadie, I'm so proud. The show's wonderful, but talk less and sing more. Love, Mama."

First off, no one calls me Sadie. Sadie died the day Lala was born. And secondly, my Mama's dead. Anyone who knows anything about Lala Lamazing Grace knows that my mother and Josephine Baker were French patriots together. They infiltrated a carnival rumored to be the center of Nazi intelligence, disguised as Hottentot Siamese twins. You may laugh but it's true. Mama died a heroine. It's all in my autobiography, *Voilà Lala!* So whoever sent this telegram is a liar!

[ADMONIA *promptly presents her with another telegram.*]

LALA: This had better be an apology. [*To* ADMONIA.] Back up, darling. [*Reading.*] "Dear Sadie, I'm not dead. P.S. Your child misses you." What? [*She squares off at the audience.*] Well, now, that does it! If you are my mother, which you are not. And this alleged child is my child, then that would mean I am a mother and I have never given birth. I don't know nothin' 'bout birthin' no babies! [*She laughs.*] Lala made a funny.

So whoever sent this, show me the child! Show me!

[ADMONIA *offers another telegram.*]

LALA: [*To* ADMONIA] You know you're gonna get fired! [*She reluctantly opens it.*] "The child is in the closet." What closet?

ADMONIA: Pst.

[ADMONIA *pushes a button and the center wall unit revolves around to reveal a large black door.* ADMONIA *exits, taking* FLO'RANCE *with her, leaving* LALA *alone.*]

LALA: [*laughing*] I get it. It's a plot, isn't it. A nasty little CIA, FBI kind of plot. Well let me tell you muthafuckers one thing, there is nothing in that closet, real or manufactured, that will be a dimmer to the glimmer of Lamé the star. You may have gotten Billie and Bessie and a little piece of everyone else who's come along since, but you won't get Lala. My clothes are too fabulous! My hair is too long! My accent too French. That's why I came home to America. To prove you ain't got nothing on me!

[*The music for her next song starts, but* LALA *is caught up in her tirade, and talks/screams over the music.*]

My mother and Josephine Baker were French patriots together! I've had brunch with the pope! I've dined with the queen! Everywhere I go I cause riots! Hunny, I am a star! I have transcended pain! So there! [*Yelling.*] Stop the music! Stop that goddam music.

[*The music stops.* LALA *slowly walks downstage and singles out someone in the audience.*]

Darling, you're not looking at me. You're staring at that damn door. Did you pay to stare at some fucking door or be mesmerized by my talent?

[*To the whole audience:*]

Very well! I guess I am going to have to go to the closet door, fling it open, in order to dispel all the nasty little thoughts these nasty little telegrams have planted in your nasty little minds. [*Speaking directly to someone in the audience.*] Do you want me to open the closet door? Speak up, darling, this is live. [*Once she gets the person to say "yes."*] I will open the door, but before I do, let me tell you bastards one last thing. To hell with coming home and to hell with lies and insinuations!

[LALA *goes into the closet and after a short pause comes running out, ready to scream, and slams the door. Traumatized to the point of no return, she tells the following story as if it were a jazz solo of rushing, shifting emotions.*]

LALA: I must tell you this dream I had last night. Simply magnifique. In this dream, I'm running naked in Sammy Davis Junior's hair. [*Crazed laughter.*]

Yes! I'm caught in this larger-than-life, deep, dark forest of savage, nappy-nappy hair. The kinky-kinks are choking me, wrapped around my naked arms, thighs, breast, face. I can't breathe. And there was nothing in that closet!

And I'm thinking if only I had a machete, I could cut away the kinks. Remove once and for all the roughness. But then I look up and it's coming toward me. Flowing like lava. It's pomade! Ohhh, Sammy!

Yes, cakes and cakes of pomade. Making everything nice and white and smooth and shiny, like my black/white/black/white/black behiney.

Mama no!

And then spikes start cutting through the pomade. Combing the coated kink. Cutting through the kink, into me. There are bloodlines on my back. On my thighs.

It's all over. All over . . . all over me. All over for me.

[LALA *accidentally pulls off her wig to reveal her real hair. Stripped of her "disguise" she recoils like a scared little girl and sings.*]

MOMMY AND DADDY
MEET AND MATE
THE CHILD THAT'S BORN
IS TORN WITH LOVE AND WITH HATE
SHE RUNS AWAY TO FIND HER OWN
AND TRIES TO DENY

WHAT SHE'S ALWAYS KNOWN
THE GIRL INSIDE

[*The closet door opens.* LALA *runs away, and a* LITTLE BLACK GIRL *emerges from the closet. Standing behind her is* ADMONIA.]

[*The* LITTLE GIRL *and* LALA *are in two isolated pools of light, and mirror each other's moves until* LALA *reaches past her reflection and the* LITTLE GIRL *comes to* LALA *and they hug.* ADMONIA *then joins them as* LALA *sings. Music underscored.*]

LALA: WHAT'S LEFT IS THE GIRL INSIDE
THE GIRL WHO DIED
SO A NEW GIRL COULD BE BORN

SLOW FADE TO BLACK

PERMUTATIONS

Lights up on NORMAL JEAN REYNOLDS. *She is very Southern/country and very young. She wears a simple faded print dress and her hair, slightly mussed, is in plaits. She sits, her dress covering a large oval object.*

NORMAL: My mama used to say, God made the exceptional, then God made the special, and when God got bored, he made me. 'Course she don't say too much of nuthin' no more, not since I lay me this egg.

[*She lifts her dress to uncover a large, white egg lying between her legs.*]

Ya see it all got started when I had me sexual relations with the garbage man. Ooowee, did he smell.

No, not bad. No! He smelled of all the good things folks never shoulda thrown away. His sweat was like cantaloupe juice. His neck was like a ripe-red strawberry. And the water that fell from his eyes was like a deep, dark, juicy-juicy grape. I tell ya, it was like fuckin' a fruit salad, only I didn't spit out the seeds. I kept them here, deep inside. And three days later, my belly commence to swell, real big like.

Well my mama locked me off in some dark room, refusin' to let me see light of day 'cause, "What would the neighbors think." At first I cried a lot, but then I grew used to livin' my days in the dark, and my nights in the dark. . . . [*She hums.*] And then it wasn't but a week or so later, my mama off at church, that I got this hurtin' feelin' down here. Worse than anything I'd ever known. And then I started bleedin', real bad. I mean there was blood everywhere. And the pain had me howlin' like a near-dead dog. I tell ya, I was yellin' so loud, I couldn't even hear myself. Noooooooo! Noooooo! Carrying on something like that.

And I guess it was just too much for the body to take, 'cause the next thing I remember . . . is me coming to and there's this big white egg layin' 'tween my legs. First I thought somebody musta put it there as some kind of joke. But then I noticed that all 'round this egg were thin lines of blood that I could trace to back between my legs.

[*Laughing.*] Well, when my mama come home from church she just about died. "Normal Jean, what's that thing 'tween your legs? Normal Jean, you answer me, girl!" It's not a thing, Mama. It's an egg. And I laid it.

She tried separatin' me from it, but I wasn't havin' it. I stayed in that dark room, huggin', holdin' onto it.

And then I heard it. It wasn't anything that coulda been heard 'round the world, or even in the next room. It was kinda like layin' back in the bath tub, ya know, the water just coverin' your ears . . . and if you lay real still and listen real close, you can hear the sound of your heart movin' the water. You ever done that? Well that's what it sounded like. A heart movin' water. And it was happenin' inside here.

Why, I'm the only person I know who ever lay themselves an egg before so that makes me special. You hear that, Mama? I'm special and so's my egg! And special things supposed to be treated like they matter. That's why every night I count to it, so it knows nuthin' never really ends. And I sing it every song I know so that when it comes out, it's full of all kinds of feelings. And I tell it secrets and laugh with it and . . .

[*She suddenly stops and puts her ear to the egg and listens intently.*]
Oh! I don't believe it! I thought I heard . . . yes! [*Excited.*] Can you hear it? Instead of one heart, there's two. Two little hearts just pattering away. Boom-boom-boom. Boom-boom-boom. Talkin to each other like old friends. Racin' toward the beginnin' of their lives.

[*Listening.*] Oh, no, now there's three . . . four . . . five, six. More hearts than I can count. And they're all alive, beatin' out life inside my egg.

[*We begin to hear the heartbeats, drums, alive inside* NORMAL's *egg.*]
Any day now, this egg is gonna crack open and what's gonna come out a be the likes of which nobody has ever seen. My babies! And their skin is gonna turn all kinds of shades in the sun and their hair a be growin' every which-a-way. And it won't matter and they won't care 'cause they know they are so rare and so special 'cause it's not everyday a bunch of babies break outta a white egg and start to live.

And nobody better not try and hurt my babies 'cause if they do, they gonna have to deal with me.

Yes, any day now, this shell's gonna crack and my babies are gonna fly. Fly! Fly!

[*She laughs at the thought, but then stops and says the word as if it's the most natural thing in the world.*]
Fly.
BLACKOUT

THE PARTY

Before we know what's hit us, a hurricane of energy comes bounding into the space. It is TOPSY WASHINGTON. *Her hair and dress are a series of stylistic contradictions which are hip, black, and unencumbered.*

Music, spiritual and funky, underscores.

TOPSY: [*dancing about*] Yoho! Party! Party! Turn up the music! Turn up the music!
Have yaw ever been to a party where there was one fool in the middle of the room, dancing harder and yelling louder than everybody in the entire place? Well, hunny, that fool was me!

Yes, child! The name is Topsy Washington and I love to party. As a matter of fact, when God created the world, on the seventh day, he didn't rest. No child, he P-A-R-T-I-E-D. Partied!

But now let me tell you 'bout this function I went to the other night, way uptown. And baby when I say way uptown, I mean way-way-way-way-way-way-way-way uptown. Somewhere's between 125th Street and infinity.

Inside was the largest gathering of black/Negro/colored Americans you'd ever want to see. Over in one corner you got Nat Turner sippin' champagne out of Eartha Kitt's slipper. And over in another corner, Bert Williams and Malcolm X was discussing existentialism as it relates to the shuffle-ball-change. Girl, Aunt Jemima and Angela Davis was in the kitchen sharing a plate of greens and just goin' off about South Africa.

And then Fats sat down and started to work them eighty-eights. And then Stevie joined in. And then Miles and Duke and Ella and Jimi and Charlie and Sly and Lightnin' and Count and Louie!

And then everybody joined in. I tell you all the children was just all up in there, dancing to the rhythm of one beat. Dancing to the rhythm of their own definition. Celebrating in their cultural madness.

And then the floor started to shake. And the walls started to move. And before anybody knew what was happening, the entire room lifted up off the ground. The whole place just took off and went flying through space—defying logic and limitations. Just a spinning and a spinning and a spinning until it disappeared inside of my head.

[TOPSY *stops dancing and regains her balance and begins to listen to the music in her head. Slowly we begin to hear it, too.*]

That's right, girl, there's a party goin' on inside of here. That's why when I walk down the street my hips just sashay all over the place. 'Cause I'm dancing to the music of the madness in me.

And whereas I used to jump into a rage anytime anybody tried to deny who I was, now all I got to do is give attitude, quicker than light, and then go on about the business of being me. 'Cause I'm dancing to the music of the madness in me.

[*As* TOPSY *continues to speak,* MISS ROJ, LALA, MISS PAT, *and* THE MAN *from* Symbiosis *revolve on, frozen like soft sculptures.*]

TOPSY: And here, all this time I been thinking we gave up our drums. But, naw, we still got 'em. I know I got mine. They're here, in my speech, my walk, my hair, my God, my style, my smile, and my eyes. And everything I need to get over in this world, is inside here, connecting me to everybody and everything that's ever been.

So, hunny, don't waste your time trying to label or define me.

[*The sculptures slowly begin to come to "life" and they mirror/echo* TOPSY'S *words.*]

TOPSY/EVERYBODY: . . . 'cause I'm not what I was ten years ago or ten minutes ago. I'm all of that and then some. And whereas I can't live inside yesterday's pain, I can't live without it.

[*All of a sudden, madness erupts on the stage. The sculptures begin to speak all at once. Images of black/Negro/colored Americans begin to flash—images of them dancing past the madness, caught up in the madness, being lynched,*] *rioting, partying, surviving. Mixed in with these images are all the characters from the exhibits. Through all of this* TOPSY *sings. It is a vocal and visual cacophony which builds and builds.*]

LALA: I must tell you about this dream I had last night. Simply magnifique. In this dream I'm running naked in Sammy Davis Junior's hair. Yes. I'm caught in this larger-than-life, deep, dark tangled forest of savage, nappy-nappy hair. Yes, the kinky kinks are choking me, are wrapped around my naked arms, my naked thighs, breast, and face, and I can't breathe and there was nothing in that closet.

THE MAN: I have no history. I have no past. I can't. It's too much. It's much too much. I must be able to smile on cue and watch the news with an impersonal eye. I have no stake in the madness. Being black is too emotionally taxing, therefore I will be black only on weekends and holidays.

MISS ROJ: Snap for every time you walk past someone lying in the street smelling like frozen piss and shit and you don't see it. Snap for every crazed bastard who kills himself so as to get the jump on being killed. And snap for every sick muthafucker who, bored with carrying about his fear, takes to shooting up other people.

MISS PAT: Stop playing those drums. I said stop playing those damn drums. You can't stop history. You can't stop time. Those drums will be confiscated once we reach Savannah, so give them up now. Repeat after me: I don't hear any drums and I will not rebel. I will not rebel!

TOPSY: [*singing*]
THERE'S MADNESS IN ME
AND THAT MADNESS SETS ME FREE
THERE'S MADNESS IN ME
AND THAT MADNESS SETS ME FREE
THERE'S MADNESS IN ME
AND THAT MADNESS SETS ME FREE
THERE'S MADNESS IN ME
AND THAT MADNESS SETS ME FREE
THERE'S MADNESS IN ME
AND THAT MADNESS SETS ME FREE

TOPSY: My power is in my . . .

EVERYBODY: *Madness!*

TOPSY: And my colored contradictions.

[*The sculptures freeze with a smile on their faces as we hear the voice of* MISS PAT.]

VOICE OF MISS PAT: Before exiting, check the overhead as any baggage you don't claim, we trash.

BLACKOUT

Milcha Sanchez-Scott (1955–)

Roosters (1987)

Like African-American, Latino drama has become increasingly well-known since the mid-1960s, when Luis Valdez achieved wide recognition with plays designed to help migrant farm workers gain better working conditions. Although the number of Latino playwrights thereafter grew significantly, few prior to the 1980s were female. Among recent Latina playwrights, Milcha Sanchez-Scott has been one of the most successful.

Sanchez-Scott's *Roosters,* first produced jointly by INTAR Hispanic Arts Center and the New York Shakespeare Festival in 1987, uses cockfighting as its central metaphor. Set in the desert Southwest, the major action focuses on a struggle between the father of a family, Gallo ("rooster"; "macho"), whose life is given meaning by cockfighting (winning at which in his eyes justifies any behavior, including cheating, con games, and even murder) and his son Hector, who wishes to escape the kind of life his father has led. Their struggle is focused on their rival claims to Zapata, a fighting cock. Eventually Gallo (apparently willing to kill his own son in order to gain possession of the rooster), using a stiletto, forces Hector to fight him.

Caught in this struggle between males are the three women of the family: Juana, Gallo's worn-down wife who supports the family, always deferring to her adored husband; Chata, Gallo's promiscuous sister; and Angela, Gallo's adolescent daughter who wears angel wings and clings to childhood and religion as buffers against hurt. Angela's faith is shattered when her father, after cajoling her into revealing the whereabouts of Zapata, abandons her after he recovers the rooster. During a superhuman effort to regain her faith, she levitates. The atmosphere of the play moves easily between realism and fantasy in the manner of Latino "magic realism." Overall, *Roosters* is a powerful play that has much to say about machismo, women, love, and psychological need in a male-dominated Latino culture.

Latino
Magic realm
—Milagro Beanfield
—Like Water for Chocolate
—La Bamba
—Selena

Developed and originally produced on the stage by INTAR Hispanic American Art Center in New York City in 1987.

Milcha Sanchez-Scott

Roosters

CHARACTERS

GALLO

ZAPATA

HECTOR

ANGELA

JUANA

CHATA

ADAN

SHADOW #1

SHADOW #2

SAN JUAN

TIME:——— *The Present*
PLACE:——— *The Southwest*

ACT ONE

SCENE I

Stage and house are dark. Slowly a narrow pinspot of light comes up. We hear footsteps. Enter GALLO, *a very, very handsome man in his forties. He is wearing a cheap dark suit, with a white open-neck shirt. He carries a suitcase. He puts the suitcase down. He faces the audience.*

GALLO: Lord Eagle, Lord Hawk, sainted ones, spirits and winds, Santa María Aurora of the Dawn. . . . I want no resentment, I want no rancor. . . . I had an old red Cuban hen. She was squirrel-tailed and sort of slab-sided and you wouldn't have given her a second look. But she was a queen. She could be thrown with any cock and you would get a hard-kicking stag every time.

I had a vision, of a hard-kicking flyer, the ultimate bird. The Filipinos were the ones with the pedigree Bolinas, the high flyers, but they had no real kick. To see those birds fighting in the air like dark avenging angels . . . well like my father use to say, "Son nobles . . . finos. . . ." I figured to mate that old red Cuban. This particular Filipino had the best. A dark burgundy flyer named MacArthur. He wouldn't sell. I began borrowing MacArthur at night, bringing him back before dawn, no one the wiser, but one morning the Filipino's son caught me. He pulled out his blade. I pulled out mine. I was faster. I went up on manslaughter. . . . They never caught on . . . thought I was in the henhouse trying to steal their stags. . . . It took time—refining, inbreeding, cross-breeding, brother to sister, mother to son, adding power, rapid attack . . . but I think we got him.

[GALLO *stands still for a beat, checks his watch, takes off his jacket and faces center stage. A slow, howling drumbeat begins. As it gradually goes higher in pitch and excitement mounts, we see narrow beams of light, the first light of dawn, filtering through chicken wire. The light reveals a heap of chicken feathers which turns out to be an actor/dancer who represents the rooster* ZAPATA. ZAPATA *stretches his wings, then his neck, to greet the light. He stands and struts proudly, puffs his chest and crows his salutation to the sun.* GALLO *stalks* ZAPATA, *as drums follow their movements.*]

Ya, ya, mi lindo . . . yeah, baby . . . you're a beauty, a real beauty. Now let's see whatcha got. [*He pulls out a switchblade stiletto. It gleams in the light as he tosses it from hand to hand.*] Come on baby boy. Show Daddy whatcha got.

[GALLO *lunges at* ZAPATA. *The rooster parries with his beak and wings. This becomes a slow, rhythmic fight-dance, which continues until* GALLO *grabs* ZAPATA *by his comb, bending his head backwards until he is forced to sit.* GALLO *stands behind* ZAPATA, *straddling him, one hand still holding the comb, the other holding the knife against the rooster's neck.*]

Oh yeah, you like to fight? Huh? You gonna kill for me baby boy? Huh?

[GALLO *sticks the tip of the knife into* ZAPATA. *The rooster squawks in pain.*]

Sssh! Baby boy, you gotta learn. Daddy's gotta teach you.

[GALLO *sticks it to* ZAPATA *again. This time the rooster snaps back in anger.*]

That's right beauty. . . . Now you got it. . . . Come on, come.

[GALLO *waves his knife and hand close to* ZAPATA's *face. The rooster's head and eyes follow.*]

Oh yeah . . . that's it baby, take it! Take it!

[*Suddenly* ZAPATA *attacks, drawing blood.* GALLO's *body contracts in orgasmic pleasure/pain.*]

Ay precioso! . . . Mi lindo. . . . You like that, eh? Taste good, huh? [*He waves the gleaming knife in a slow hypnotic movement which calms the rooster.*] Take my blood, honey. . . . I'm in you now. . . . Morales blood, the blood of kings . . . and you're my rooster . . . a Morales rooster. [*He slowly backs away from the rooster. He picks up his suitcase, still pointing the knife at* ZAPATA.] Kill. You're my son. Make me proud.

[GALLO *exits.* ZAPATA *puffs his chest and struts upstage. Lights go up a little on upstage left area as the rooster goes into the chicken-wire henhouse. He preens and scratches. Enter* HECTOR, *a young man of about twenty. He is very handsome. He wears gray sweatpants and no shirt. On his forehead is a sweatband. His hair and body are dripping wet. He has been running. Now he is panting as he leans on the henhouse looking at* ZAPATA.]

HECTOR: I saw what you did to those chicks. Don't look at me like you have a mind, or a soul, or feelings. You kill your young . . . and we are so proud of your horrible animal vigor. . . . But you are my inheritance . . . Abuelo's gift to me . . . to get me out. Oh, Abuelo, Grandfather . . . you should have left me your courage, your sweet pacific strength.

[*A ray of light hits downstage right. In a semi-shadow, we see a miniature cemetery, with small white headstones and white crosses. We see the profile of a young angel/girl with wings and a pale dress.* ANGELA *is kneeling next to*

a bare desert tree with low scratchy branches. She has a Buster Brown hair-
cut and a low tough voice. She is fifteen, but looks twelve.]
ANGELA: [*loudly*]
> Angel of God
> My Guardian Dear
> To whom God's love
> Commits me here
> Ever this day be
> At my side
> To light and guard
> To rule and guide
> Amen.
[*Her paper wings get caught in a tree branch.*] Aw, shit! [*She exits.*]

SCENE II

*As the light changes we hear the clapping of women making tortillas. Lights come up
full. Center stage is a faded wood-frame house, with a porch that is bare except for a
table and a few chairs. The house sits in the middle of a desert agricultural valley somewhere in the Southwest. Everything is sparse. There is a feeling of blue skies and space.
One might see off on the horizon tall Nopales or Century cactus.* JUANA, *a thin,
wornout-looking woman of thirty-five, comes out of the house. She is wearing a faded
housedress. She goes to mid-yard, faces front and stares out.*

JUANA: It's dry. Bone dry. There's a fire in the mountains . . . up near Jacinto Pass.
> [*The clapping stops for a beat, then continues. She starts to go back into the house,
> then stops. She sniffs the air, sniffs again, and again.*] Tres Rosas . . . I smell
> Tres Rosas. [*She hugs her body and rocks.*] Tres Rosas. . . . Ay, St. Anthony let
> him come home. . . . Let him be back.
>> [*The clapping stops.* CHATA *enters from the house. She is a fleshy woman of
>> forty, who gives new meaning to the word "blowsy." She has the lumpy face
>> of a hard boozer. She walks with a slight limp. She wears a black kimono, on
>> the back of which is embroidered in red a dragon and the words "Korea,
>> U.S.S. Perkins, 7th Fleet." A cigarette hangs from her lips. She carries a bowl
>> containing balls of tortilla dough.*] I smell Tres Rosas. . . . The brilliantine
>> for his hair. . . . He musta been here. Why did he go?
CHATA: Men are shit.
JUANA: Where could he be?
CHATA: First day out of jail! My brother never comes home first day. You should
> know that. Gotta sniff around . . . gotta get use to things. See his friends.
JUANA: Sí, that's right. . . . He just gotta get used to things. I'll feel better when I
> see him . . . I gotta keep busy.
CHATA: You been busy all morning.
JUANA: I want him to feel good, be proud of us. . . . You hear anything when you
> come in yesterday?
CHATA: Who's gonna know anything at the Trailways bus station?
JUANA: You ain't heard anything?
CHATA: Juanita, he knows what he's doing. If there was gonna be any trouble he'd
> know. Ay, mujer, he's just an old warrior coming home.

JUANA: Ain't that old.

CHATA: For a fighting man, he's getting up there.

> [JUANA *slaps tortillas.* CHATA *watches her.*]

Who taught you to make tortillas?

JUANA: I don't remember. I never make 'em. Kids don't ask.

CHATA: Look at this. You call this a tortilla? Have some pride. Show him you're a woman.

JUANA: Chata, you've been here one day, and you already—

CHATA: Ah, you people don't know what it is to eat fresh handmade tortillas. My grandmother Hortensia, the one they used to call "La India Condenada" . . . she would start making them at five o'clock in the morning. So the men would have something to eat when they went into the fields. Hijo! She was tough. . . . Use to break her own horses . . . and her own men. Every day at five o'clock she would wake me up. "Buenos pinchi días," she would say. I was twelve or thirteen years old, still in braids. . . . "Press your hands into the dough," "Con fuerza," "Put your stamp on it." One day I woke up, tú sabes, con la sangre. "Ah! So you're a woman now. Got your own cycle like the moon. Soon you'll want a man, well this is what you do. When you see the one you want, you roll the tortilla on the inside of your thigh and then you give it to him nice and warm. Be sure you give it to him and nobody else." Well, I been rolling tortillas on my thighs, on my nalgas, and God only knows where else, but I've been giving my tortillas to the wrong men . . . and that's been the problem with my life. First there was Emilio. I gave him my first tortilla. Ay Mamacita, he use to say, these are delicious. Aye, he was handsome, a real lady-killer! After he did me the favor he didn't even have the cojones to stick around . . . took my TV set, too. They're all shit . . . the Samoan bartender, what was his name . . .

JUANA: Nicky, Big Nicky.

CHATA: The guy from Pep Boys—

JUANA: Chata, you really think he'll be back?

CHATA: His son's first time in the pit? With "the" rooster? A real Morales rooster? Honey, he'll be back. Stop worrying.

JUANA: Let's put these on the griddle. Angela, Hector . . . breakfast.

SCENE III

ANGELA *slides out from under the house, wearing her wings. She carries a white box which contains her cardboard tombstones, paper and crayons, a writing tablet, and a pen. She, too, sniffs the air. She runs to the little cemetery and looks up, as* HECTOR *appears at the window behind her.*

ANGELA: Tres Rosas. . . . Did you hear? Sweet Jesus, Abuelo, Queen of Heaven, all the Saints, all the Angels. It is true. It is certain. He is coming, coming to stay forever and ever. Amen.

HECTOR: Don't count on it!

ANGELA: [*to Heaven*] Protect me from those of little faith and substance.

HECTOR: I'm warning you. You're just going to be disappointed.

ANGELA: [*to Heaven*] Guard me against the enemies of my soul.

HECTOR: Your butt's getting bigger and bigger!

ANGELA: And keep me from falling in with low companions.

HECTOR: Listen, little hummingbird woman, you gotta be tough, and grown-up today.

> [ANGELA *digs up her collection can and two dolls. Both dolls are dressed in nuns' habits. One, the St. Lucy doll, has round sunglasses. She turns a box over to make a little tea table on which she places a doll's teapot and cups.*]

ANGELA: As an act of faith and to celebrate her father's homecoming, Miss Angela Ester Morales will have a tea party.

HECTOR: No more tea parties.

ANGELA: Dancing in attendance will be that charming martyr St. Lucy.

HECTOR: He will not be impressed.

ANGELA: Due to the loss of her eyes and the sensitivity of her alabaster skin, St. Lucy will sit in the shade. [*She sits St. Lucy in the shade and picks up the other doll.*]

HECTOR: Who's that?

ANGELA: St. Teresa of Avignon, you will sit over here. [*She seats St. Teresa doll.*]

HECTOR: Just don't let him con you, Angela.

ANGELA: [*pouring pretend tea*] One lump or two, St. Lucy? St. Teresa has hyper-glycemia, and only takes cream in her tea. Isn't that right, St. Teresa?

HECTOR: He's not like Abuelo.

> [ANGELA *animates the dolls like puppets and uses two different voices as St. Lucy and St. Teresa.*]

ANGELA: [*as St. Teresa*] Shouldn't we wait for St. Luke?

HECTOR: Stop hiding. You can't be a little girl forever.

ANGELA: [*as St. Lucy*] St. Luke! St. Luke! Indeed! How that man got into Heaven I'll never know. That story about putting peas in his boots and offering the discomfort up to God is pure bunk. I happen to know he boiled the peas first.

HECTOR: I don't want you hurt. It's time to grow up.

ANGELA: [*as St. Teresa*] St. Lucy! I can only think that it is the loss of your eyes that makes you so disagreeable. Kindly remember that we have all suffered to be saints.

HECTOR: Are you listening to me, Angie?

ANGELA: [*as St. Lucy*] Easy for you to say! They took my eyes because I wouldn't put out! They put them on a plate. A dirty, chipped one, thank you very much indeed! To this day no true effort has been made to find them.

HECTOR: Excuse me! . . . Excuse me, St. Teresa, St. Lucy, I just thought I should tell you . . . a little secret . . . your hostess, Miss Angela Ester Morales, lies in her little, white, chaste, narrow bed, underneath the crucifix, and masturbates.

ANGELA: Heretic! Liar!

HECTOR: Poor Jesus, up there on the cross, right over her bed, his head tilted down. He sees everything.

ANGELA: Lies! Horrible lies!

HECTOR: Poor saint of the month, watching from the night table.

ANGELA: I hate you! I hate you! Horrible, horrible Hector.

JUANA: [*from offstage*] Breakfast!

> [HECTOR *leaves the window.* ANGELA *sits on the ground writing on a tombstone.*]

ANGELA: [*lettering a tombstone*] Here lies Horrible Hector Morales. Died at age twenty, in great agony, for tormenting his little sister.

JUANA: [*offstage*] You kids . . . breakfast!

HECTOR: [*pops up at window*] Just be yourself. A normal sex-crazed fifteen-year-old girl with a big gigantic enormous butt. [*He exits.*]

ANGELA: [*to Heaven*]

    Send me to Alaska
    Let me be frozen
    Send me a contraction
    A shrinking antidote
    Make me little again
    Please make my legs
    Like tiny pink Vienna sausages
    Give me back my little butt.

    [JUANA *and* CHATA *bring breakfast out on the porch and set it on the table.*]

JUANA: Angie! Hector! We ain't got all day.

    [ANGELA *goes to the breakfast table with the St. Lucy doll and the collection can.*]

And take your wings off before you sit at the table. Ain't you kids got any manners?

    [ANGELA *removes her wings, sits down, bows her head in prayer.* CHATA *stares at St. Lucy. St. Lucy stares at* CHATA. JUANA *shoos flies and stares at the distant fire.*]

I hope he's on this side of the fire.

CHATA: That doll's staring at me.

ANGELA: She loves you.

    [*Lights fade on the women, come up on the henhouse,* ADAN, *a young man of twenty, is talking to* ZAPATA—*now a real rooster, not the actor/dancer—and preparing his feed.*]

ADAN: Hola Zapata . . . ya mi lindo . . . mi bonito En Inglés. Tengo que hablar en English . . . pinchi English . . . verdad Zapata? En Español más romántico pero Hector say I must learned di English. [ZAPATA *starts squawking.*] Qué te pasa? Orita vas a comer.

    [HECTOR *enters.*]

HECTOR: English, Adan . . . English.

ADAN: No English . . . pinchi English.

HECTOR: Good morning, Adan.

ADAN: A que la fregada! . . . Okay this morning in the fields, I talk English pero this afternoon for fight I talk puro Español.

HECTOR: Good morning, Adan.

ADAN: Sí, sí, good morning, muy fine. . . . Hector el Filipino he say . . . [*He moves away from* ZAPATA, *so bird will not hear him.*] He say to tell you que Zapata no win. Porque Filipino bird fight more y your bird first fight y your first fight y you got no ex . . . ex . . .

HECTOR: Experience.

ADAN: Sí eso, he say you sell bird to him y no fight. . . . He say is not true Morales bird porque Gallo not here. El Filipino say if you fight bird . . . bird dead. If bird still alive after Filipino bird beat him. . . . Bird still dead porque nobody pay money for bird that lose.

HECTOR: But if he wins, everybody wants him.

ADAN: I say, ay di poor, poor Hector. His abuelo leave him bird. He can no sell. El Filipino say, "Good!" Inside, in my heart I am laughing so hard porque he not know Gallo gonna be here. We win, we make much money.

HECTOR: It's my bird, I have to do it myself.

ADAN: You tonto! You stupido! You mulo! Like donkey. . . . He help you, he the king . . . he you papa. For him all birds fight.

HECTOR: No!

ADAN: Why? Why for you do this? You no even like bird. Zapata he knows this, he feel this thing in his heart. You just want money to go from the fields, to go to the other side of the mountains . . . to go looking . . . to go looking for what? On the other side is only more stupid people like us.

HECTOR: How could you think I just wanted money? I want him to see me.

ADAN: Sorry. . . . I am sorry my friend. . . . I know. . . . I stay with you y we win vas a ver! Okay Zapata! We win y esta noche estamos tomando Coors, Ripple, Lucky Lager, unas Buds, Johnnie Walkers, oh sí, y las beautiful señoritas. [*He gives* ZAPATA *his food.*] Eat Zapata! Be strong.

HECTOR: I almost forgot, look what I have for you . . . fresh, warm homemade tortillas.

ADAN: Oh, how nice.

HECTOR: Yes, how nice. Aunt Chata made them.

ADAN: Oh, much nice.

HECTOR: Today she woke up at five o'clock, spit a green booger the size of a small frog into a wad of Kleenex. She wrapped her soiled black "7th Fleet" kimono around her loose, flaccid, tortured, stretch-marked body and put her fat-toed, corned yellow hooves into a pair of pink satin slippers. She slap-padded over to the sink, where she opened her two hippo lips and looked into the mirror. She looked sad. I looked at those lips . . . those lips that had wrapped themselves warmly and lovingly around the cocks of a million campesinos, around thousands upon thousands of Mexicanos, Salvadoreños, Guatemaltecos. For the tide of brown men that flooded the fields of this country, she was there with her open hippo whore's lips, saying, "Bienvenidos," "Welcome," "Hola," "Howdy." Those are legendary lips, Adan.

ADAN: Yes . . . muy yes.

HECTOR: What a woman, what a comfort. Up and down the state in her beat-up station wagon. A '56 Chevy with wood panels on the sides, in the back a sad, abused mattress. She followed the brown army of pickers through tomatoes, green beans, zucchinis, summer squash, oranges, and finally Castroville, the artichoke capital of the world, where her career was stopped by the fists of a sun-crazed compañero. The ingratitude broke her heart.

ADAN: Oh my gooseness!

HECTOR: She was a river to her people, she should be rewarded, honored. No justice in the world.

ADAN: Pinchi world. [*He and* HECTOR *look to mountains.*] You look mountains. In my country I look mountains to come here. I am here and everybody still look mountains.

HECTOR: I want to fly right over them.

ADAN: No, my friend, we are here, we belong . . . la tierra.

JUANA: [*from offstage*] Hector, I ain't calling you again.

> [*Lights up on the porch.* JUANA *and* CHATA *are sitting at the table.* ANGELA *is sitting on the steps. She has her wings back on. St. Lucy and the collection can are by her side. She is writing on her tablet.*]

JUANA: Oh Gallo, what's keeping you?

CHATA: Men are shit! That's all. And it's Saturday. When do they get drunk? When do they lose their money? When do they shoot each other? Saturdays, that's when the shit hits the fan.

> [*Enter* HECTOR *and* ADAN *with* ZAPATA *in a traveling carrier.*]

JUANA: It's because I'm so plain.

HECTOR: We're better off without him.

CHATA: Buenos días Adan. Un cafecito?

ADAN: Ah. Good morning, Mrs. Chata, no gracias, ah good morning, Mrs. Morales y Miss Angelita.

> [ANGELA *sticks out her collection can.* ADAN *automatically drops coins in.*]

JUANA: Angela!

ADAN: No, is good, is for the poor. Miss Angela, she good lady . . . eh, girl. [*He pats* ANGELA *on the head.*]

JUANA: Why don't you leave the bird, so your father can see him when he gets home.

HECTOR: He's my bird. He can see it later.

JUANA: I can't believe you would do this to your own father. Birds are his life . . . and he's so proud of you.

HECTOR: This is news. How would he know, he hasn't seen me in years.

JUANA: It isn't his fault.

HECTOR: It never is.

JUANA: Your father is with us all the time, he got his eye on us, he knows everything we're doing.

ANGELA: Everything!?

JUANA: I brag about you kids in my letters. . . . His friends they tell him what a smart boy you are . . . that you're good-looking like him. . . . He's proud. . . . "A real Morales," that's what he says.

HECTOR: And did he call me a winner? A champ? A prince? And did you tell him I was in the fields?

ANGELA: What did he say about me, Mama?

HECTOR: Nothing, you're a girl and a retard. What possible use could he have for you? Grow up!

CHATA: No, you grow up.

> [ANGELA *buries herself in* CHATA'*s lap.*]

JUANA: Hector, please, Hector, for me.

HECTOR: No, Mother. Not even for you.

JUANA: You give him a chance.

HECTOR: What chance did he give us? Fighting his birds, in and out of trouble. He was never here for us, never a card, a little present for Angela. He forgot us.

JUANA: You don't understand him. He's different.

HECTOR: Just make it clear to him. Abuelo left the bird to me, not to him, to me.

JUANA: Me, me, me. You gonna choke on this me, me. Okay, okay, I'm not going to put my nose in the bird business. I just ask you for me, for Angie, be nice to him.

HECTOR: As long as we all understand the "bird business," I'll be nice to him even if it kills me, Mother.

JUANA: Now you're feeling sorry for yourself. Just eat. You can feel sorry for yourself later.

HECTOR: Why didn't I think of that. I'll eat now and feel sorry for myself later.

JUANA: Now, you kids gotta be nice and clean, you papa don't like dirty people.

CHATA: Me, too, I hate dirty people.

JUANA: Angie, you take a bath.

HECTOR: Oh, Angela, how . . . how long has it been since you and water came together? [ANGELA *hits him.*] Oww!

JUANA: You put on a nice clean dress, and I don't wanna see you wearing no dirty wings.

HECTOR: Right, Angie, put on the clean ones.

JUANA: You say "please" and "excuse me" . . . and you watch your table manners. . . . I don't want to see any pigs at my table.

HECTOR: [*making pig noises*] What a delicious breakfast! Cold eggs, sunny-side up. How cheery! How uplifting! Hmm, hmmm! [*He turns so* ANGELA *can see him. He picks up eggs with his hands and stuffs them in his mouth.*] Look, Angela, refried beans in a delicate pool of congealed fat. [*Still making pig noises, he picks up gobs of beans, stuffs them into his mouth.*]

CHATA: A que la fregada! Hector, stop playing with your food. You're making us sick.

JUANA: [*looking at watch*] 7:20, you got ten minutes before work.

　　　　[HECTOR *drums his fingers on the table.*]

HECTOR: Nine minutes. . . . I will now put on the same old smelly, shit-encrusted boots, I will walk to the fields. The scent of cow dung and rotting vegetation will fill the air. I will wait with the same group of beaten-down, pathetic men . . . taking their last piss against a tree, dropping hard warm turds in the bushes. All adding to this fertile whore of a valley. At 7:30 that yellow mechanical grasshopper, the Deerfield tractor, will belch and move. At this exact moment, our foreman, John Knipe, will open his pig-sucking mouth, exposing his yellow, pointy, plaque-infested teeth. He yells, "Start picking, boys." The daily war begins . . . the intimidation of violent growth . . . the expanding melons and squashes, the hardiness of potatoes, the waxy purple succulence of eggplant, the potency of ripening tomatoes. All so smug, so rich, so ready to burst with sheer generosity and exuberance. They mock me. . . . I hear them. . . . "Hey Hector," they say, "show us whatcha got," and "Yo Hector we got bacteria out here more productive than you." . . . I look to the ground. Slugs, snails, worms slithering in the earth with such ferocious hunger they devour their own tails, flies oozing out larvae, aphids, bees, gnats, caterpillars their prolification only slightly dampened by our sprays. We still find eggsacks hiding, ready to burst forth. Their teeming life, their lust, is shameful . . . a mockery of me and my slender spirit. . . . Well it's time. . . . Bye Ma. [*He exits.*]

JUANA: [*yelling*] Hector! You gotta do something about your attitude. [*To herself.*] Try to see the bright side.

> [JUANA *and* CHATA *exit into the house, leaving* ANGELA *on the porch steps.* ADAN *runs up to her.*]

ADAN: Pssst! Miss Angelita! . . . di . . . di cartas?

ANGELA: Oh, the letters . . . that will be one dollar.

ADAN: One dollar! Adan very poor man. . . .

> [ANGELA *sticks the collection can out and shakes it.* ADAN *reaches into his pockets and drops coins into the can.*]

Oh, sí, you are very good.

> [ANGELA *puts on glasses and pulls out a letter.*]

ANGELA [*reading letter*] Adored Señora Acosta: The impulses of my heart are such that they encourage even the most cautious man to commit indiscretion. My soul is carried to the extreme with the love that only you could inspire. Please know that I feel a true passion for your incomparable beauty and goodness. I tremulously send this declaration and anxiously await the result. Your devoted slave, Adan.

ADAN: [*sighing*] Ay, que beautiful.

ANGELA: P.S. With due respect Señora, if your husband should be home, do not turn on the porch light.

ADAN: Ah, thank you . . . thank you very much.

> [ADAN *hurriedly exits.* ANGELA *gathers her St. Lucy doll and her collection can, and exits quickly.* CHATA *enters from the house wearing "colorful" street clothes. She looks around, then swiftly exits.* HECTOR *enters, picks up* ZAPATA, *hurries off.*]
>
> [*The stage darkens, as if smoke from the distant fire has covered the sun. Drum howls are heard. In the distance we hear a rooster crow and sounds of excited chickens as the henhouse comes to life.* GALLO *appears.*]

GALLO: Easy hens, shshsh! My beauties. [*He puts his suitcase down, cups his hands to his mouth, and yells to the house.*] Juana! Juana! Juana! [JUANA *opens the door.*] How many times, in the fever of homesickness, have I written out that name on prison walls, on bits of paper, on the skin of my arms. . . . Let me look at you . . . my enduring rock, my anchor made from the hard parts of the earth—minerals, rocks, bits of glass, ground shells, the brittle bones of dead animals.

JUANA: I never seen you so pale, so thin. . . .

GALLO: I'm home to rest, to fatten up, to breathe, to mend, to you.

JUANA: How long? How long will you stay?

GALLO: Here. Here is where I'll put my chair. . . . I will sit here basking in the sun, like a fat old iguana catching flies, and watching my grandchildren replant the little cemetery with the bones of tiny sparrows. Here. Here I will build the walks for my champions. Morales roosters. The brave and gallant red Cubans, the hard and high-kicking Irish Warhorses, the spirited high-flying Bolinas.

JUANA: Don't say nothing you don't mean . . . you really gonna stay?

GALLO: [*gently*] Here. Here is where I'll plant a garden of herbs. Blessed laurel to cure fright, wild marjoram for the agony of lovesickness, cempasuchie flowers for the grief of loneliness.

[GALLO *gently kisses* JUANA, *picks her up and carries her into the house. The door slams shut.* ANGELA *enters, her wings drooping behind her. She trips over* GALLO'*s suitcase. She examines it. She smells it.*]

ANGELA: Tres Rosas!

[ANGELA *looks at the house. She sits on the suitcase, crosses her arms over her chest as if she were ready to wait an eternity. The shadows of two strangers fall on her.*]

ANGELA: What do you want?

SHADOW #1: Where's Gallo?

ANGELA: Nobody's home to you, rancor.

SHADOW #2: Just go in, tell him we got something for him.

ANGELA: Nobody's home to you, resentment.

SHADOW #1: Who are you supposed to be?

ANGELA: [*holding St. Lucy doll*]
    I am the angel of this yard
    I am the angel of this door
    I am the angel of light
    I am the angel who shouts
    I am the angel who thunders

SHADOW #1: She is pure crazy.

SHADOW #2: Don't play with it, it's serious.

ANGELA: You are the shadow of resentment
    You are the shadow of rancor
    I am the angel of acid saliva
    I will spit on you.

SHADOW #1: There's time.

SHADOW #2: Yeah, later.

[ANGELA *spits. The shadows leave.* ANGELA *crosses her hands over her chest and looks to Heaven.*]

ANGELA: Holy Father. . . . Listen, you don't want him, you want me. Please take me, claim me, launch me and I will be your shooting-star woman. I will be your comet woman. I will be your morning-star woman.

SCENE IV

Lights become brighter. ANGELA *exits under the house. The door opens.* GALLO *comes out in T-shirt and pants and goes to his suitcase.* JUANA *comes to the door in slip and tight robe.*

GALLO: I never sent him to the fields.

JUANA: I know.

GALLO: I never said for you to put him there.

JUANA: No, you never said. . . .

GALLO: Then why is my son in the fields? [*They look at each other. He looks away.*]
    Don't look at me. I see it in your eyes. You blame me. Just like the old man.

JUANA: Abuelo never said a word against you.

GALLO: I never let him down with the birds, nobody could match me. They were the best.

JUANA: He knew that. . . .

GALLO: So, he left the bird to Hector.

JUANA: He wanted him out of the fields. We didn't know when you would be out or maybe something would happen to you.

GALLO: He let the boy into the fields, that was his sin. He allowed a Morales into the fields.

JUANA: He was old, tired, heartbroken.

GALLO: Heartbroken, he wasn't a woman to be heartbroken.

JUANA: His only son was in jail.

GALLO: Yes, we know that, the whole valley knows that. You . . . what did you do? Didn't you lay out your hand, succulent, bitch's teat at the breakfast table? So he would have the strength to stand behind a hoe, with his back bent and his eyes on the mud for ten hours a day.

JUANA: Hard work never killed anybody.

GALLO: Ay, mujer! Can't you think what you've done, you bowed his head down.

JUANA: What was I suppose to do? There ain't no other work here. I can't see anything wrong with it for a little while.

GALLO: The difference between them and us, is we never put a foot into the fields. We stayed independent—we worked for nobody. They have to respect us, to respect our roosters.

> [HECTOR *and* ADAN *enter. They are both very dirty.* HECTOR *has* ZAPATA, *in his carrier.* ADAN *has a carrier containing a second rooster.* GALLO *and* HECTOR *stare at each other.*]

Well . . . you are taller. This offshoot . . . this little bud has grown.

HECTOR: Yeah, well . . . that must be why you seem . . . smaller.

GALLO: Un abrazo!

HECTOR: I'm dirty, I'm sweaty.

GALLO: I see that.

HECTOR: I'm afraid I smell of the fields.

GALLO: Yes.

HECTOR: Of cheap abundant peon labor . . . the scent would gag you.

GALLO: It's going to kill you.

HECTOR: Mama says hard work never killed anyone . . . isn't that right, Mother?

JUANA: It's only for a little while. Your papa thinks that—

GALLO: I'll tell him what I think. Now what about those tamales you promised me?

JUANA: Ah sí, con permiso . . . I got some work in the kitchen.

ADAN: Oh sí, Mrs. Juana, los tamales . . . que rico.

JUANA: [*Smiling at* ADAN] I hope they're the kind you like. [*She exits into house.*]

GALLO: Hijo, you always take the bird with you into the fields?

HECTOR: No, not always.

GALLO: This bird has to look like he's got secrets . . . no one but us should be familiar with him.

HECTOR: This is Adan.

ADAN: Es un honor, Mr. El Gallo.

> [ANGELA *sticks her head out from under the house.* ADAN *and* GALLO *shake hands and greet each other.*]

GALLO: [*referring to* ZAPATA] Let him out . . . he needs a bigger carrier . . . he's a flyer.

ADAN: Como Filipino birds?

GALLO: Yes, but this baby boy, he's got a surprise. He's got a kick.

ADAN: Like Cuban bird?

GALLO: He'll fight in the air, he'll fight on the ground. You can put spurs or razors on that kick and he'll cut any bird to ribbons. You can put money on that.

ADAN: Hijo! Señor . . . how you know? He never fight. Maybe he only kick in cage.

GALLO: I know because I'm his papa. . . . [*Pointing to the other carrier.*] That your bird?

ADAN: Sí, pero no good . . . no fight. San Juan, he run away.

GALLO: I'll make him fight. Just let him out.

ADAN: Mr. El Gallo, you give this pendejo bird too much honor. Gracias Señor, pero this poor bird, he no can fight.

GALLO: Is it the bird, or you who will not fight?

HECTOR: The bird is too young. He doesn't want him to fight.

GALLO: I've never seen a bird that won't fight, but there are men who are cowards.

HECTOR: He is not a coward.

ADAN: This is true, pero I am not El Gallo. In my country all men who love di rooster know Mr. El Gallo. They tell of di famoso día de los muertos fight in Jacinto Park.

GALLO: Ah, you heard about that fight. You remember that fight, Hector?

HECTOR: No.

GALLO: First time you saw a real cockfight . . . Abuelo took you. . . . How could you forget your first cockfight? [*To* ADAN.] Go on, take your bird out. I'll make him fight.

> [GALLO *takes a drink from a bottle, then blows on* SAN JUAN. *As he does this, lights go down almost to black. Pinspot comes up center stage, as other lights come up to a dark red. During this process, we hear* GALLO'*s voice—"Ready," then a few beats later* "Pit!" *On this cue two dancer/roosters jump into the pinspot. This rooster dance is savage. The dancers wear razors on their feet. The* ZAPATA *dancer jumps very high. The poor* SAN JUAN *dancer stays close to the ground. Throughout the dance, we hear drums and foot-stomping. At every hit, there is a big drum pound. During the fight,* HECTOR *appears on the porch.*]

HECTOR: [*to himself*] It was in Jacinto Park . . . the crowd was a monster, made up of individual human beings stuck together by sweat and spittle. Their gaping mouths let out screams, curses, and foul gases, masticating, smacking, eager for the kill. You stood up. The monster roared. Quasimoto, your bird, in one hand. You lifted him high, "Pit!" went the call. "Pit!" roared the monster. And you threw him into the ring . . . soaring with the blades on his heels flashing I heard the mighty rage of his wings and my heart soared with him. He was a whirlwind flashing and slashing like a dark avenging angel then like some distant rainbow star exploding he was hit. The monster crowd inhaled, sucking back their hopes . . . in that vacuum he was pulled down. My heart went down the same dark shaft, my brains slammed against the earth's hard crust . . . my eyes clouded . . . my arteries gushed . . . my lungs collapsed. "Get up," said Abuelo, "up here with me, and you will see a miracle." You, Father, picked up Quasimoto, a lifeless pile of bloody feathers, holding his head oh so gently, you closed your eyes, and like a great wave receding, you drew a breath that came from deep within your ocean floor. I heard the stones rumble, the mountains shift, the topsoil move, and as your breath slammed on the beaches, Quasimoto sputtered back to life. Oh Papi, breathe on me.

> [ANGELA *appears and stands behind her brother. Her wings are spread very far out. Drums and stomping crescendo as* ZAPATA *brutally kills* SAN JUAN. *Blackout.*]

ACT TWO

SCENE I

Early afternoon. The table is set up in the middle of the yard in a festive way, with tablecloth, flowers, a bowl of peaches, and bottles of whiskey and wine. GALLO *is in the henhouse with* ADAN. HECTOR *is in the bathroom,* JUANA *and* CHATA *are in the kitchen.* ANGELA *is by the little cemetery writing on a tombstone.*

ANGELA: Here lies Angela Ester Morales died of acute neglect. Although she is mourned by many, she goes to a far, far, better place, where they have better food.

> [ANGELA *slides under the house as* JUANA *comes out wearing a fresh house-dress and carrying a steaming pot.*]

JUANA: [*yelling*] Hector! Angela! You kids wash up, it's time to eat.

> [JUANA *hurries back into the house, almost knocking* CHATA *down as she comes out with a tray of tortillas. She is heavily made up, wearing tight clothes, dangling earrings, high-heeled shoes. A cigarette dangles from her mouth.*]

CHATA: Why are you eating out here?

JUANA: He wants it. Says he don't wanta hide in the house.

CHATA: Begging for trouble.

JUANA: What can I do, he's the man. [*She goes into the house.*]

CHATA: Ah, they're all shit! Just want trouble. Soup's on!

> [CHATA *pours herself a quick shot of whiskey, shoots it down and makes a face.* JUANA *comes out with another pot.*]

JUANA: You better tell 'em that the food's ready. [CHATA *goes to henhouse.*] Hector!

HECTOR: [*coming out on porch*] What?

JUANA: It's time to eat . . . you look real nice, honey. Makes me proud to have your papa see you all dressed up.

HECTOR: Okay. Okay. Don't make a big deal about it. I just don't want him to think—

JUANA: I just feel so happy—

HECTOR: I just don't want him to think—

JUANA: Hijito! You love your papa . . . don't you?

HECTOR: Mother!

JUANA: I know you a little mad at him . . . pero when he comes home it's like the
sun when it—

HECTOR: Shshshsh!

[CHATA, GALLO, *and* ADAN *come out of the henhouse.*]

GALLO: We have to sharpen and polish those spurs. I want them to flash.

JUANA: [*to* GALLO] The food's ready . . . we fixed what you like . . . mole, rice, fri-
jolitos . . . tamales.

GALLO: Tamales estilo Jalisco!

CHATA: [*looking* HECTOR *over*] Ay Papi que rico estás! [HECTOR *quickly sits down.*]
Honey! You gonna have to beat all them women off with a stick, when they
see you and that rooster tonight.

ADAN: No worry, Hector, I be there . . . down you mujeres, women leave de Mr.
Hector and me alone. . . . Ay Mama! [*He has a giggling fit.*]

GALLO: [*kissing* JUANA] It's wonderful to be in love . . . to be touched by the
noble fever.

CHATA: Ah, you're better off with a touch of typhoid.

JUANA: I . . . gracias al Señor que . . . my whole family is here. [*She looks around.
She yells.*] Angela! Angie!

HECTOR: Mom!

JUANA: Where is she? Where is your sister?

HECTOR: Talking to the saints! I don't know.

[JUANA *gets up, goes to the spot where* ANGELA *slides under the house, gets
down on her hands and knees and yells.*]

JUANA: Angela! Angela! You leave them saints alone. You hear me!

[*As everybody looks at* JUANA, ANGELA *comes from behind the house and
tiptoes toward the henhouse.* HECTOR *is the only one to see her. Using hand
signals, she pleads to him to be quiet.* JUANA *peers under the house.*]

Angie! Honey . . . your mama worked for days to fix this food and now it's
getting cold. [*To* GALLO.] You should see how sweet she looks when she's all
dressed up. [*To under the house.*] You ain't got no manners . . . ain't even said
hello to your father. [*To* GALLO.] She prays a lot . . . and she's got real pretty
eyes.

CHATA: [*to* GALLO] She's sorta . . . the bashful type . . . you know.

JUANA: [*to* GALLO] And she ain't spoiled.

CHATA: [*taking a drink*] Nah, all them kids smell like that.

JUANA: [*to under the house*] Angie!

GALLO: Juana, leave her alone.

JUANA: Okay. Angie, I'm gonna ignore you, 'cause you spoiled my day, this day
that I been looking forward to for years and years and now you making me
look like a bad mama, what's your papa gonna think of us.

GALLO: Juana, she'll come out when she's ready.

[JUANA *goes back to the table.*]

CHATA: Maybe was them roosters fighting got her scared.

ADAN: Poor San Juan.

GALLO: Adan, drink up and I'll see you get one of our famous Champion Morales
birds.

HECTOR: What famous Champion Morales birds?

GALLO: The ones I paid for dearly, the ones I came home to raise . . . isn't that right, mi amor?

JUANA: Yes . . . you see, honey, your papa's gonna stay home . . . raise birds . . . I think Abuelo would want that.

GALLO: And after they see our bird tonight . . . see, first I want them to think it's just you and the bird up there. After the bets are down, I'll take over and they're gonna know we got roosters. A toast . . .

> [*As* GALLO *stands up, everybody raises a glass, except* HECTOR. ANGELA *tiptoes from the henhouse carrying* ZAPATA. *She goes behind and under the house. Only* HECTOR *sees her.*]

To the finest fighting cocks ever to be seen. [*He slides bottle to* HECTOR.]

HECTOR: [*sliding bottle back.*] No.
> [*Pause.*]

GALLO: Too good to drink with your old man.

HECTOR: I only drink with people I trust.

CHATA: Me . . . I drink with anybody. Maybe that's my problem.

GALLO: I am your father.

HECTOR: Yes. You are my father.

CHATA: I like it better when I drink alone. Ya meet a better class of people that way.

HECTOR: But it's my bird. Abuelo left it to me.

GALLO: Abuelo was my father, and you are my son. I see no problem. Now let's eat.

HECTOR: Mother!

JUANA: Let's eat, honey, and we can talk about it later.

ADAN: Ay the mole muy delicious . . . the mole muy rico . . . the mole muy beautiful y Mrs. Juana. Today, you look beautiful, like the mole.

GALLO: Hm, sabroso, exquisito.

JUANA: I bet you been in plenty of fancy places got better food than this.

GALLO: This is home cooking, I know that your hands made it . . . These . . . these are the hands of a beautiful woman. . . .

HECTOR: Ha! Bullshit.

GALLO: We say your mother is beautiful and you call it bullshit! I find that very disrespectful.

JUANA: Hijo, you're right . . . it's just the way people talk, I know I ain't beautiful.

GALLO: I say you are beautiful.

ADAN: Sí, muy beautiful.

GALLO: Ya ves! . . . If your son doesn't have the eyes, the soul, the imagination to see it . . . it's his loss.

HECTOR: That's right. I just can't seem to stretch my imagination that far.

GALLO: This is an insult to your mother.

HECTOR: It's the truth. That is a plain, tired, worn-out woman.

GALLO: Shut up.

HECTOR: The hands of a beautiful woman! Those aren't hands, they're claws because she has to scratch for her living.

JUANA: Please, Hector, let him say what he wants . . . I know I ain't beautiful. It don't go to my head.

HECTOR: But it goes to your heart which is worse. Did he ever really take care of you? Did he ever go out and work to put food on the table, to buy you a dress? All he has is words, and he throws a few cheap words to you and you come to life. Don't you have any pride?

GALLO: Your mother has great courage to trust and believe in me.

HECTOR: Stupidity!

GALLO: You know nothing!

HECTOR: You don't seem to realize that it is my rooster. And that after the fight, depending on the outcome, I will sell him or eat him. I have made a deal with the Filipinos.

JUANA: Ay, Hector! You've spoiled everything. All this food . . . I worked so hard . . . for this day.

GALLO: You're not selling anything to anybody. This is nothing to joke about.

HECTOR: I don't want to spend my life training chickens to be better killers. And I don't want to spend my whole life in this valley. Mother, Aunt Chata, excuse me.

CHATA: Ah? . . . O sí hijo pase . . . sometimes Hector can be a real gentleman.
            [HECTOR *starts to leave.*]

GALLO: Son! . . . You have no courage, no juice . . . you are a disgrace to me.

JUANA: Ay, Gallo, don't say that to him.

HECTOR: Do you think I care what you think . . . Father.

JUANA: Hijo no . . . for me, just once for me. I don't wanna be alone no more.

HECTOR: What about me? You have me, you'll always have me, I'll work, I've always worked, I can take care of you. I won't leave you.

JUANA: It ain't the same, honey.

HECTOR: Yeah. . . . He comes first for you, he will always come first.

GALLO: If you sell that bird, it will be over your dead body.

HECTOR: You can't stop me.
            [*Exit* HECTOR. CHATA *takes a plate of food and bowl of peaches to the under-the-house area and tries to tempt* ANGELA *out.*]

GALLO: He doesn't seem to realize . . . coward . . . too bad.
            [GALLO *goes to the henhouse.* JUANA *starts to follow him.*]

JUANA: Talk to him . . . he's a good boy . . . if you just talk . . . [*Seeing* ADAN *still eating.*] Is it good? You really like it?

ADAN: Hm! Sabroso!

CHATA: Come on, Angie . . . it's real good.
            [GALLO *returns running.*]

GALLO: He's gone . . . the bird is gone. . . .

ADAN: Yo no see nada, nada.

JUANA: He'll bring it back, he's a good boy. He's just a little upset . . . you know.

GALLO: Nobody fools with my roosters. Not even this over-petted, over-pampered viper you spawned. Go and pray to your Dark Virgin. You know what I'm capable of.
            [*Exit* GALLO. ADAN *stops eating and tries to comfort* JUANA *as she puts her head down on the table and cries.*]

ADAN: No cry, no cry, Mrs. Juana. Di women cry y Adan, he not know what to do. [JUANA *cries louder.*] Ay, Mrs. Juana, for sure di flowers will die . . . di trees will be torn from di ground, freshness will leave di morning, softness will leave di night . . . [JUANA's *cries increase.*] Ay Dios! [*From his pocket, he brings out the letter* ANGELA *wrote for him. He crosses himself.*] Mrs. di Juana . . . [*Reading with great difficult.*] Di . . . impulses . . . of my . . . heart . . . are such . . . [*Throwing letter aside.*] A que la fregada! Mrs. Juana, Adan have mucho amor for you. My heart break to see you cry. I will not a breathe. when you no cry then I will breathe.

> [ADAN *takes a big breath and holds it. Slowly* JUANA *stops crying and lifts her head.* ADAN, *suffering some discomfort, continues to hold his breath.*]

JUANA: I been dreaming. Nothing's gonna change. I gotta face facts.

> [ADAN *lets his breath out in a great whoosh.* ANGELA *pops out from under the house and takes a peach from* CHATA's *hand. She stares at the peach with great intensity.*]

CHATA: Angie, ain't it nice to have the family all together again?

ANGELA: There is no pit in this peach. It is hollow. Instead of the pit, there is a whole little world, a little blue-green crystal-clear ocean, with little schools of tiny darting silver fish. On a tiny rock sits a mermaid with little teenie-weenie kinky yellow hair. A tiny sun is being pulled across a little china-blue sky by teenie-weenie white horses with itty-bitty wings. There is an island with tiny palm trees and tiny thatched hut. Next to the hut stand a tiny man and woman. She is wearing flowers and leaves. He is wearing one single leaf. On their heads are little bitty halos. In their arms is a little bitsy baby. He isn't wearing anything.

CHATA: Let me see . . . [*Looking at peach.*] I can't see dick!

BLACKOUT.

SCENE II

Later in the afternoon. CHATA *sits on the porch steps, her legs spread out, fanning her-self.* JUANA *sits on a straight-back chair, her hands folded on her lap. She rocks herself gently. She watches* ANGELA, *who is sitting on the ground drawing circles in the dirt and humming softly. The circles get deeper and deeper.*

CHATA: It's hot . . . I am waiting for a cool breeze. . . .

ANGELA: Uh ha uh ha uh ha uh haa.

CHATA: Aire fresco . . . come on, cool breeze, come right over here.

ANGELA: Uh ha uh ha uh haa.

CHATA: Women! We're always waiting.

> [ANGELA *hums for a beat, then there is silence for a beat.*]

JUANA: It's because I'm so plain.

CHATA: Ah, you just work too much.

JUANA: Plainness runs in my family. My mother was plain, my grandmother was plain, my great-grandmother—

CHATA: It was the hard times . . . the hard work that did it.

JUANA: My Aunt Chona was the plainest.

CHATA: I don't remember her.

JUANA: The one with the crossed eyes and the little mustache.

CHATA: Ay, Juanita, that woman had a beautiful soul, sewing those little tiny outfits for the statues of the saints. That woman was a saint.

JUANA: She's the one told on you that time you was drinking beer with them sailors at the cockfight.

CHATA: Disgusting old bitch!

[ANGELA *hums for a beat as she continues drawing circles.*]

JUANA: I get up at six, I brush my teeth, no creams, no lotions, what they gonna do for me? I work, that's all. I take care of people and I work. People look at me, they know that's all I do. I ain't got no secrets. No hidden gardens. I keep busy, that's what I do. Don't stop, that's what I say to myself. Don't stop, 'cause you're not pretty enough, exciting enough, smart enough to just stand there.

ANGELA: Mama, I don't wanna be plain.

CHATA: Honey, you're too colorful to be plain.

ANGELA: Yeah, that's what I thought.

CHATA: Your mama forgets . . . those years when her heart was filled with wild dreams when she use to weave white star jasmine vines in her hair and drive all the men crazy.

JUANA: It ain't true . . . she was the one always getting me in trouble.

CHATA: I wasn't the one they called Juanita la Morenita Sabrosita.

JUANA: Oh, Chata. We was young girls together . . . in the summer, at Jacinto Park . . . cockfights, fistfights, the music. At night we would jump out of our bedroom windows in our party dresses. With our good shoes in one hand, our hearts in the other, we ran barefoot through the wet grass, above us all the stars twinkling go, go, go.

CHATA: Nothing could stop us . . . we had a short time being girls.

JUANA: Now, all I am is an old hag.

CHATA: It ain't true.

JUANA: Sí, it's true enough. I carry burdens, I hang sheets, I scrub, I gather, I pick up, "Here sit down," "I'll wash it," "Here's fifty cents," "Have my chair," "Take my coat," "Here's a piece of my own live flesh"!

CHATA: Es la menopause, that's what it is. You getting it early. I knew this woman once, use to pull out her hair.

JUANA: I don't care, I don't want any stories, I don't care what happens to Fulano Mangano . . . I just wanna stand still, I wanna be interesting, exciting enough to stand still.

CHATA: Ay, mujer!

JUANA: And I want to look like I got secrets.

CHATA: Juana!

JUANA: Don't call me Juana. Juana is a mule's name.

CHATA: Ah, you're crazy! That new gray hen, the kids named her Juana. See, they think of you.

JUANA: A gray hen! An old gray hen, that's all I am. An old gray hen in a family of roosters. No more! I want feathers, I wanna strut, too. I wanna crow.

ANGELA: Mama!

JUANA: Don't! Don't call me "Mama." I am not Mama . . . I am . . . I am that movie star, that famous dancer and heartbreaker "Morenita Sabrosita" . . .

and now if my fans will excuse me I'm gonna take a bath in champagne, eat cherry bonbons and paint my toenails. [*She goes into the house.*]

CHATA: [*to* JUANA] We got champagne?

[CHATA: *goes into the house as* ANGELA *goes to the little cemetery and puts up a new tombstone.*]

ANGELA: [*printing on tombstone*] Here lies Juana Morales. Beloved Wife of El Gallo, Blessed Mother to Angela and Horrible Hector. Died of acute identity crisis sustained during la menopause.

SCENE III

Lights go down, as ANGELA *sits on her box/table at the little cemetery. The long shadows of men fall on* ANGELA *and the cemetery.*

SHADOW #1: There's that spooky kid. You go, brother.

SHADOW #2: Ah, it's just a weird kid. Hey! You! Kid!

[ANGELA *does not acknowledge them.*]

SHADOW #1: Call her "Angel."

SHADOW #2: Hey, Angel.

[ANGELA *looks up.*]

SHADOW #1: See what I mean.

SHADOW #2: Listen kid, tell your old man, we got business to discuss.

SHADOW #1: Yeah, and you make sure he gets the message.

ANGELA: My old man, my Holy Father, my all powerful Father, sees no problems. If there are problems, I am the angel of this yard. I am the comet. I am the whirlwind. I am the shooting stars. Feel my vibrance.

SHADOW #1: I feel it, right behind my ears, like . . . like . . .

ANGELA: Locust wings.

SHADOW #1: Let's get outta here.

SHADOW #2: Tell Gallo some pals dropped by to settle an old score.

SHADOW #1: Come on!

SHADOW #2: [*voice trailing off*] Hey! That kid don't scare me, see.

SHADOW #1: [*voice trailing off*] I'm telling ya, my ears hurt.

[*Exit shadows. Lights go back up.* ANGELA *folds her hands in prayer.*]

ANGELA: Holy Father, please help me, I feel the illumination, the fever of grace slipping away. I need to know that you are with me, that you take an interest in my concerns. Send me a little demonstration, a sign. Any sign . . . I don't care. Stigmata, visions, voices, send an angel, burn a bush. . . . I am attracted to levitation . . . but you choose . . . I'll just lay here and wait.

[ANGELA *lies on the ground waiting. After a few beats* HECTOR *enters. He slowly walks up to* ANGELA *and looks down on her for a beat.*]

HECTOR: What are you doing?

ANGELA: [*sitting up*] Ohhh . . . you're no sign.

HECTOR: What is going on?

ANGELA: Weird, shady men came here looking for Gallo. Two of them. They were not polite.

HECTOR: I see. . . . So your reaction is to lay stretched out on the dirt instead of going into the house.

ANGELA: Hector, please, I am scared. . . . I wanted a sign.

    [HECTOR *sits down next to* ANGELA.]

HECTOR: Hey, you're the shooting-star woman, you can't be scared.

ANGELA: I am scared. Really scared. If I grow up will I still be scared? Are grown-ups scared?

HECTOR: Always scared, trembling . . . cowering . . . this . . . this second, now . . . this planet that we are sitting on is wobbling precariously on its lightning path around the sun and every second the sun is exploding . . . stars are shooting at us from deep distant space, comets zoom around us, meteor rocks are being hurled through distances we measure in light . . . this very earth which we call our home, our mother, has catastrophic moods, she keeps moving mountains, receding oceans, shifting poles, bucking and reeling like an overburdened beast trying to shake us off. . . . Life is violent.

ANGELA: You're scared about the fight . . . huh?

HECTOR: No. Whatever happens, Papi will still only care about the rooster. That's his son, that's who gets it all.

ANGELA: Maybe if we gave him the rooster he'd stay here and be happy.

HECTOR: He has to stay for us, not the rooster . . . Angela . . . you . . . you were great taking the rooster.

ANGELA: He kept killing the little chicks. How could he do that, Hector? He's their papa.

HECTOR: Training. Look, Angela, you're the angel of this yard. You keep a close guard on that rooster. Don't let anyone near him . . . promise me.

ANGELA: Yes.

HECTOR: That's a real promise now. No crossed fingers behind your back.

ANGELA: I promise already. [*She spreads her hands out in front of her, then kisses the tip of her thumb.*] May God strike me dumb, make me a plain whiny person and take away my gift of faith. Forever and ever, throughout my mortal years on earth, and throughout the everlasting fires of hell. Amen. Satisfied?

HECTOR: Yes.

ANGELA: Gee, maybe I should have given myself a little leeway, a little room for error.

    [CHATA *enters from the house with a bottle and glass.*]

HECTOR: Too late now. Can't take it back.

CHATA: Oh, oh, look who's here. Angie, your mama needs some cheering up, a nice hug, an angel's kiss, maybe a little song.

ANGELA: Litany to the Virgin. That's her favorite. [*She exits.*]

CHATA: Men are shit. Pure shit.

HECTOR: And you're still drinking.

CHATA: Stay outta my drinking. You hurt your mama, Hector.

HECTOR: Too bad.

CHATA: Ay Dios, what a man he is now.

HECTOR: Yeah, well, what about you? Didn't you break Abuelo's heart when you became a whore?

CHATA: They called me the encyclopedia of love. You want to turn a few pages? Your Aunt Chata could show you a few things.

HECTOR: You're disgusting.

CHATA: Is that what fascinates you, honey? Is that why I always find you peeping at me, mirrors at the keyhole, your eyeballs in the cracks, spying when I'm sleeping, smelling my kimono.

HECTOR: You're drunk.

CHATA: I ain't drunk, honey.

HECTOR: You drink too much. It's not . . . good for you . . . it makes you ugly.

CHATA: Ain't none of your business. Don't tell me what to do, Hector.

HECTOR: I have to, it's for your own good.

CHATA: You got nothing to say about it, you ain't my man, and you ain't your mama's man. The sooner you learn that the better . . . take your bird, leave it, eat or sell it, but get out of here. [HECTOR *stands alone in the yard, as she goes to the door. She turns. They look at each other.*] What are you hanging around here for? Go on! Get out! It ain't your home anymore. [*She takes a broom and shoos* HECTOR *from the yard.*] Shoo! Shoo! You don't belong here, it ain't your place anymore.

HECTOR: Stop it, stop it, stop it.
> [HECTOR *goes to the outside boundary of the yard, where he falls to his knees and buries his face in his hands, as* CHATA *comes slowly up behind him.*]

CHATA: I feel like I'm tearing my own flesh from my bones. . . . He's back. Honey, we got too many roosters in this yard.

HECTOR: Did you sleep with my father? Did he yearn for you as you slept in your little white, chaste, narrow bed? Did he steal you when you were dreaming?

CHATA: [*embracing him*] Shshsh . . .

HECTOR: I'm not like him.

CHATA: You're just like him, so handsome you make my teeth ache.

HECTOR: Whore, mother, sister, saint-woman, moon-woman, give me the shelter of your darkness, fold me like a fan and take me into your stillness, submerge me beneath the water, beneath the sea, beneath the mysteries, baptize me, bear me up, give me life, breathe on me.
> [CHATA *enfolds him as the lights fade. We hear* ANGELA *reciting the litany.*]

ANGELA: [*offstage*] She is the Gate of Heaven, the Mystical Rose, the Flower of Consolation, the Fire of Transcendence, and the Queen of Love.

SCENE IV

Lights come up to indicate that time has passed. ANGELA *is alone in the yard. She sniffs the air.*

ANGELA: Tres Rosas!
> [ANGELA *slides under the house as* GALLO *enters. He sees a brief flash of* ANGELA *from the corner of his eye. He walks slowly into the yard. He stops by the little cemetery and reads the tombstones. Feeling the urge for a drink, he goes to the table and has a shot. He sits.*]

GALLO: Acute neglect? . . . uh-huh . . . I thought I felt a little spirit, slight, delicate . . . yes, I feel it. A little tenderness . . . a little greenness . . . [*Examining the ground.*] What's this? Tracks . . . little tiny paws . . . there . . . [*Following tracks.*] and there . . .

[GALLO *pretends to be following tracks to the porch. Then with one great leap he jumps in the opposite direction, surprising the hell out of* ANGELA, *and pulls her from under the house by her heels.*]

Ah, ha!

ANGELA: Shit! Hey! You're ripping my wings! You shithead! Put me down! Don't touch me!

[GALLO *puts* ANGELA *down, throws his hands up to indicate he won't touch her. They stand and stare at each other.* ANGELA *goes to the little cemetery, never taking her eyes off* GALLO. *They continue to stare for a beat, then* ANGELA *looks up to Heaven, slapping her hands together in prayer.*]

There is a person here trying to con me, but I don't con that easy.

GALLO: [*slapping his hands in prayer*] There is a person here who swallows saints but defecates devils.

ANGELA: [*to Heaven*] He comes here smelling of rosas using sweet oily words . . . it's phony, it's obnoxious, it's obscene . . . I wanna throw up.

GALLO: I came here to see my baby, my little angel, my little woman of the shooting stars, my light delicate splendorous daughter. But she is as light, as delicate, as splendid as an angel's fart.

ANGELA: Angels do not fart. They do not have a digestive system. That's why they can all scrunch together on the head of a pin.

GALLO: Oh . . . I only come with my love—

ANGELA: You only came with words . . . well, where were these words on my birthday, Christmas, my saint's day? Where's my Easter outfit, my trip to Disneyland, the orthodontist. . . . You owe me.

GALLO: Sweet Jesus. . . . What a monster! I owe you . . . but Angela! Angela! Angela! How many times have I written that name on prison walls. On bits of paper, on the skin of my arms.

ANGELA: [*to Heaven*] He's hopeless! You write everybody's name on your arms.

GALLO: Women like to know that they're on your flesh.

ANGELA: I am not a woman. I'm your baby daughter. You said so yourself.

GALLO: I'm afraid . . . fathers to daughters . . . that's so delicate. I don't know . . . what to do . . . help me, Angela. How do I know what to do?

ANGELA: Instinct! Ain't ya got no instinct? Don't you feel anything?

GALLO: [*moving closer to* ANGELA] When you were a little baby, you were a miracle of tiny fingers and toes and dimples and you had a soft spot on the top of your head.

ANGELA: I still have it, see.

GALLO: I wanted to take you into my arms and crush you against my chest so that I could keep you forever and nobody, and nothing, could ever, ever hurt you because you would be safe . . . my little offshoot, my little bud, my little flower growing inside my chest.

ANGELA: Papi . . .

GALLO: Sí, sí, hijita. Your papi's here.

ANGELA: And Papi, these men come all the—

GALLO: [*holding* ANGELA] Shshsh . . . it's nothing, nothing and you thought I forgot about you . . . well, it just hurt too much, do you understand?

ANGELA: You had to pull down some hard time and the only way to survive was to cut off all feelings and become an animal just like the rest of them.

GALLO: Well, something like that. Honey, you know what I wish—

ANGELA: Papa, did the lights really go down when they put the people in the electric chair?

GALLO: Angela, what a. . . . Honey, you know what I wish—

ANGELA: Did they force you to make license plates? Hector and I would look real close at the ones that started with a G. We thought you made them. "What craftsmanship!" Hector used to say.

GALLO: Don't you have any normal interests?

ANGELA: Like what?

GALLO: Like swimming . . . you know what I wish? That we could take a trip and see the ocean together.

ANGELA: I've never seen the ocean. When?

GALLO: Just you and me. Laying on our bellies, feeding the seagulls, riding the waves.

ANGELA: I can't swim.

GALLO: I will teach you, that's what fathers are for—

ANGELA: [*to Heaven*] Angels and saints, did you hear? My father's going to teach me to swim!

GALLO: Now Angela, I didn't promise.

ANGELA: But you said—

GALLO: I want to but I have to hurry and fix things. I have to find Hector, talk to him and find that rooster fast before Hector sells him. Honey, you pray to St. Anthony, your prayers are powerful . . . unless . . . St. Anthony, he listen to you?

ANGELA: [*crossing her fingers*] Hey, we're like that.

GALLO: Ask St. Anthony, Angela . . . then we can go to the ocean.

ANGELA: Truly, Papi? Just you and me? And will you stay with us forever and ever?

GALLO: Wild horses couldn't drag me away.

ANGELA: Close your eyes. Tony! Tony! Look around, Zapata's lost and can't be found.[*She goes under the house, gets* ZAPATA, *and gives him to* GALLO.] I found him, Papi, he was—

GALLO: Ya lindo, ya. [*To bird.*] Papa's got you now. Angela, you keep quiet now, honey, this is our secret.

ANGELA: What about Hector?

GALLO: I'm going to talk to Hector now. You go inside and get all dressed up. So I can be proud of my girl. I'll pick you up after the fight. [*He exits.*]

ANGELA: Your girl! [*Singing.*] We are going to the ocean, we are going to the sea, we are going to the ocean to see what we can see . . .
      [ANGELA *goes into the house. We hear cha-cha music.*]

CHATA: [*offstage*] One, two . . . not like that . . . I'm getting tired . . . what time's "Zorro" on?

JUANA: [*offstage*] No, no. . . . Just one more. [*Singing.*] Cha, cha, cha, que rico, . . . cha, cha, cha. . . . Ay, I could do it all night.
      [*Enter* GALLO *running, breathing hard. He has* ZAPATA's *carrier. He goes to the door and yells.*]

GALLO: Juana! Juana!
      [JUANA *and* CHATA *come to the door.*]

I need money . . . and my stuff. I gotta leave . . . something's come up. . . . Do you hear me? I need money now.

JUANA: I hear ya . . . you ain't even been here a day and already you're gone . . . nothing's going to change with you . . . nothing. I was having fun, dancing, remembering old times, do you know how long—

GALLO: I don't have time for this, just give me the money.

JUANA: I ain't got any!

CHATA: I got some. [*She goes in the house.*]

GALLO: The Filipino, somebody told him about the bird. Oh, ya, ya my little hen, don't you ruffle those pretty feathers, I'll be back.

JUANA: No, you always gonna be running.

GALLO: If it was just me, I'd stay. You know that, Juana? You know I'd stay, but I got the bird to think of, gotta hide him, breed him good, soon as I get some good stags I'll come home . . . this is just a little setback.

[CHATA *returns with suitcase and money.*]

JUANA: You know how long it's been since I went dancing?

CHATA: Here, you're gonna need this. [*Gives him the suitcase.*] And this is all the cash I got.

[ANGELA *enters as* GALLO *counts the money. She is dressed in a red strapless dress made tight by large visible safety pins, high heels, and a great deal of heavy makeup and jewelry. The effect is that of a young girl dressed like a tart for a costume party. She carries a suitcase, purse, and her collection can.*]

GALLO: Is this all you got?

ANGELA: [*shaking the can*] Don't worry, Papa, I got my donation-can money. [*They all stare at her for a beat.*]

JUANA and CHATA: Angela?!!

JUANA: Angie, you got on your mama's old party dress.

CHATA: Yeah, and all my jewelry . . . where you going?

ANGELA: Papa, didn't you hear me? I have money. [*She shakes the can.*]

GALLO: Oh honey, don't you look pretty . . . now you got a little bit too much lipstick on, let your mama wipe some off.

ANGELA: Are we leaving now?

JUANA: Gallo!

GALLO: Shshsh Juana . . . Angela, I gotta talk to your mama for a few minutes. You go in the house and I'll come and get you.

ANGELA: Are you sure?

GALLO: Don't you trust me, Angie?

CHATA: Come on, Angie, I'll show you how to draw eyebrows. First you draw a straight line across your forehead and then spit on your finger and rub out the middle. Let's go in and try it.

ANGELA: Really, Aunt Chata, I'm not a child, you don't have to patronize me.

CHATA: Okay, I'll give you the low-down on blow-jobs.

[ANGELA *and* CHATA *go into the house.*]

Now, don't tell your mama . . .

GALLO: Juana, keep her in the house until I leave.

JUANA: You promised to take her with you?

GALLO: I had to get the bird. I said I would take her to the ocean.

JUANA: Ay bruto! How could you do it?

GALLO: How was I to know this would happen . . . and Juanita, it hurts me to say this but that kid is crazy . . .

JUANA: No, no, Señor, she is not crazy and I ain't gonna let you call her crazy. She got the spirit they broke in me. I ain't gonna let it happen to her.

GALLO: Shshsh! Don't get so excited. It isn't important.

JUANA: It's important . . . it's her spirit, her soul and you ain't gonna stomp on it . . . you hear me.

[ADAN *enters running.*]

ADAN: Mr. El Gallo . . . bad men! Mucho bad, y mucho ugly. Looking for you y Zapata. All ober they look for you . . . Big Nicky's, Castro Fields, Don Pancho's. . . . You leave, Mr. El Gallo. You go far away. I take you. I go for my truck.

GALLO: You are a good friend, Adan, and my new partner.

ADAN: Oh, thank you, Mr. El Gallo. I am proud. But is better I come back here to Mrs. Juana y Hector.

JUANA: Thank you, Adan.

GALLO: We better hurry.

ADAN: Sí, sí, I come back with truck. [*He exits.*]

[JUANA *goes into the house.* HECTOR *enters as* GALLO *starts to pack his suitcase.*]

HECTOR: [*seeing* ZAPATA] You must have really sold her a bill of goods to get Zapata.

GALLO: Look, there's trouble . . . the Filipino send you?

HECTOR: No, how could you think I would work for him, but I came to get Zapata.

GALLO: You're the one told him about the bird.

HECTOR: Yes. I made a deal with the Filipino. He'll leave you alone if I give him the rooster.

GALLO: That's a lie and you fell for it.

HECTOR: No, he is an honorable man, we were here unprotected for seven years and he never bothered us. It's his bird, Papi.

GALLO: No, I paid seven years of my life for this baby.

HECTOR: And he lost his son. It's the right thing to do.

[*A truck horn is heard.* ANGELA *comes out of the house with her suitcase,* JUANA *and* CHATA *follow after her.*]

ANGELA: Papa? Are we leaving now, Papa?

JUANA: Angie! No!

HECTOR: So that's it . . . Angela, get back in the house.

ANGELA: I'm going with him, Hector.

HECTOR: Get back in the house, nobody's going anywhere.

ANGELA: No! I don't have to listen to you anymore. You're not my father.

JUANA: Angie . . . he's not going to the ocean . . . he can't take you.

[*We hear the sound of* ADAN's *truck. The horn is heard as* GALLO *starts backing away, picking up* ZAPATA's *carrier.*]

ANGELA: Papi, wait for me! Papa, you promised.

GALLO: You're all grown up now, you don't need your old man.

CHATA: Hector!

> [GALLO *turns, tries to run out.* ANGELA *grabs him knocking* ZAPATA's *carrier out of his hand.* HECTOR *picks up the carrier.*]

ANGELA: No, Papa, we need you and Mama needs you, we've been waiting, and waiting, you can't leave, you promised me.

JUANA: They'll kill you, Gallo.

GALLO: [*throwing* ANGELA *off*] Stop sucking off me. I got nothing for you.

ANGELA: [*beating her fists on the ground.*] No, no, Papa! You promised me! . . . Oh, Hector. . . . No, no, I promised Hector.

> [*Drums begin as punctuation of the pounding of* ANGELA's *fists on the ground. Lights change. A special on* ANGELA *and another on* GALLO *and* HECTOR *come up, as shadows appear.* ANGELA *sees them.*]

Ah. . . . Holy Father, Abuelo.

GALLO: [*to* HECTOR] Give me that bird.

ANGELA: Saints, Angels, Mama.

JUANA: [*trying to pick up* ANGELA] Come on, Angie, get up.

GALLO: [*to* HECTOR] What do you want?

HECTOR: You, alive, Papi.

CHATA: Careful, Hector.

ANGELA: I've lost my faith. I am splintered.

GALLO: [*imitating* HECTOR] You Papi. . . . Give me life. . . . Make me a man. [*He whips out his stiletto.*] This is how you become a man. [*The drums get louder. We hear howling.*] Come on, baby boy, show Daddy whatcha got.

JUANA: Are you crazy! That's your son!

ANGELA: I am cast down! Exiled!

> [GALLO *stalks* HECTOR *as drums follow their movements.*]

JUANA: Oh Gallo, you're killing your own children.

CHATA: Move, Hector, don't think, move!

GALLO: Oh yeah, mi lindo, you like to fight . . . eh?

JUANA: No, stop them! Please, please stop this.

ANGELA: Fallen from the light, condemned to the mud, to the shadows.

GALLO: You gotta learn, baby boy.

CHATA: Look at him, Hector. He's getting old, his hand is shaking . . . take the knife! Stay down, old warrior. Stay down.

ANGELA: Alone and diminished. This loneliness is unendurable.

JUANA: Hector!

HECTOR: Do I have it? Is this what you want me to be . . .

ANGELA: [*looking to Heaven*]
My brains are slammed against the earth's hard crust.
My eyes are clouded.
My arteries gush
My lungs collapsed.

HECTOR: [*letting go of* GALLO] No! I am your son.
> [*Drums and cries stop.*]

ANGELA: Holy Father, Abuelo, Hector, breathe on me.
> [*Celestial sound as a white narrow shaft of light falls on* ANGELA. *She levitates, her wings spreading. Only* CHATA *and* JUANA *see this.*]

HECTOR: [*taking a deep breath*] Oh sweet air! [*He gets the rooster and sees* ANGELA.] Angela!

ADAN: [*rushing in*] I am here, I have truck . . . [*Seeing* ANGELA, *he crosses himself.*] Ay Dios. [*He kneels.*]

JUANA: [*at* GALLO'*s side*] Gallo, look!

GALLO: Did you see the hands on that kid, just like steel, never seen finer hands . . . [*Seeing* ANGELA.] Sweet Jesus, my beautiful monster. [*He crosses himself.*]

CHATA: No, it ain't true.

HECTOR: [*standing before* ANGELA *holding the rooster*] Oh sweet hummingbird woman, shooting star, my comet, you are launched.

ANGELA: Abuelo, Queen of Heaven, All the Saints, All the Angels. It is true, I am back. I am restored. I am . . . Hector, take me with you.

HECTOR: Everywhere. . . . Over the mountains, up to the stars.

ANGELA: To the very edge.

ADAN: Hector! Angelita! You take Adan. [*He goes to* ANGELA.]

CHATA: [*looking at* ANGELA] Shit happens . . . been happening all my life, that's all I know.

JUANA: [*holding* GALLO *like the Pietà*] We seen it, Gallo, with our own eyes.

ANGELA: [*to* HECTOR *and* ADAN] And I want my doorstep heaped with floral offerings . . . and . . .

[HECTOR, ADAN, *and* ANGELA *freeze.* CHATA *removes the flower from her hair and holds it in her hand, trying to decide what to do. She freezes.*]

GALLO: Ay, Juanita, I had a vision of a hard-kicking flyer . . . [*He yawns.*] the ultimate bird, noble, fino. [*He falls asleep.*]

[JUANA *looks at* GALLO, *smiles, then looks out half-smiling.*]

END OF PLAY

David Henry Hwang (1957–)

M. Butterfly (1988)

Although Asian characters have a long history in American drama and films, they have been reduced, for the most part, to a limited number of stereotypes: dutiful houseboy, inscrutable detective, wise Confucian patriarch, treacherous dragon lady, or submissive doll-bride. Around 1965, Asian-American playwrights began to rebel against such depictions. Of these playwrights, David Henry Hwang has been the most successful, and his *M. Butterfly* is probably the best known of all Asian-American plays.

The title *M. Butterfly* immediately associates Hwang's play with *Madame Butterfly* (Giacomo Puccini's opera) and its emphasis on the submissive doll-bride. Hwang uses this association to focus attention on issues of race, gender, and politics. Overall, he argues that Westerners have viewed "Orientals" (both individuals and nations) as submissively "feminine," willing to be dominated by the aggressive, "masculine" West. Hwang fuses this perception with a real-life story in which a French diplomat carried on a twenty-year relationship with a Beijing Opera performer of female roles (and a spy for the Chinese government) without, he testified, recognizing that the performer was male. Hwang's play focuses on the diplomat Gallimard's attempt to understand and to explain to himself and the audience his relationship with the performer Song Liling.

Perhaps the most distinguishing feature of *M. Butterfly* is its theatricality— its acknowledgement that the place of the action is the stage, where ideas and events are examined rather than re-created in detail. Gallimard, and sometimes other characters, addresses the audience directly. In some scenes, multiple places and times blend; at no time is there an attempt to represent a scene illusionistically. This fluidity allows the action to move freely through space and time. The most striking visual feature is the use in several scenes of Chinese theatrical conventions, a device that reinforces the differences between East and West. Overall, *M. Butterfly* is a complex play, both in its personal and ideational dimensions.

David Henry Hwang

M. Butterfly

CHARACTERS

KUROGO
RENE GALLIMARD
SONG LILING
MARC/MAN 2/CONSUL SHARPLESS
RENEE/WOMAN AT PARTY/GIRL IN MAGAZINE
COMRADE CHIN/SUZUKI/SHU-FANG
HELGA
M. TOULON/MAN 1/JUDGE

SETTING——*The action of the play takes place in a Paris prison in the present, and in recall, during the decade 1960 to 1970 in Beijing, and from 1966 to the present in Paris.*

ACT ONE

SCENE I

M. GALLIMARD's *prison cell. Paris. Present.*

Lights fade up to reveal RENE GALLIMARD, *65, in a prison cell. He wears a comfortable bathrobe, and looks old and tired. The sparsely furnished cell contains a wooden crate upon which sits a hot plate with a kettle and a portable tape recorder.* GALLIMARD *sits on the crate staring at the recorder, a sad smile on his face.*

Upstage SONG, *who appears as a beautiful woman in traditional Chinese garb, dances a traditional piece from the Peking Opera, surrounded by the percussive clatter of Chinese music.*

Then, slowly, lights and sound cross-fade; the Chinese opera music dissolves into a Western opera, the "Love Duet" from Puccini's Madame Butterfly. SONG *continues dancing, now to the Western accompaniment. Though her movements are the same, the difference in music now gives them a balletic quality.*

GALLIMARD *rises, and turns upstage towards the figure of* SONG, *who dances without acknowledging him.*

GALLIMARD: Butterfly, Butterfly . . .
  [*He forces himself to turn away, as the image of* SONG *fades out, and talks to us.*]
GALLIMARD: The limits of my cell are as such: four-and-a-half meters by five. There's one window against the far wall; a door, very strong, to protect me from autograph hounds. I'm responsible for the tape recorder, the hot plate, and this charming coffee table.

When I want to eat, I'm marched off to the dining room—hot, steaming slop appears on my plate. When I want to sleep, the light bulb turns itself off—the work of fairies. It's an enchanted space I occupy. The French—we know how to run a prison.

But, to be honest, I'm not treated like an ordinary prisoner. Why? Because I'm a celebrity. You see, I make people laugh.

I never dreamed this day would arrive. I've never been considered witty or clever. In fact, as a young boy, in an informal poll among my grammar school classmates, I was voted "least likely to be invited to a party." It's a title I managed to hold onto for many years. Despite some stiff competition.

But now, how the tables turn! Look at me: the life of every social function in Paris. Paris? Why be modest? My fame has spread to Amsterdam, London, New York. Listen to them! In the world's smartest parlors. I'm the one who lifts their spirits!

[*With a flourish,* GALLIMARD *directs our attention to another part of the stage.*]

SCENE II

A party. Present.

Lights go up on a chic-looking parlor, where a well-dressed trio, two men and one woman, make conversation. GALLIMARD *also remains lit; he observes them from his cell.*

WOMAN: And what of Gallimard?

MAN 1: Gallimard?

MAN 2: Gallimard!

GALLIMARD: [*to us*] You see? They're all determined to say my name, as if it were some new dance.

WOMAN: He still claims not to believe the truth.

MAN 1: What? Still? Even since the trial?

WOMAN: Yes. Isn't it mad?

MAN 2: [*laughing*] He says . . . it was dark . . . and she was very modest!
[*The trio break into laughter.*]

MAN 1: So—what? He never touched her with his hands?

MAN 2: Perhaps he did, and simply misidentified the equipment. A compelling case for sex education in the schools.

WOMAN: To protect the national security—the Church can't argue with that.

MAN 1: That's impossible! How could he not know?

MAN 2: Simple ignorance.

MAN 1: For twenty years?

MAN 2: Time flies when you're being stupid.

WOMAN: Well, I thought the French were ladies' men.

MAN 2: It seems Monsieur Gallimard was overly anxious to live up to his national reputation.

WOMAN: Well, he's not very good-looking.

MAN 1: No, he's not.

MAN 2: Certainly not.

WOMAN: Actually, I feel sorry for him.

MAN 2: A toast! To Monsieur Gallimard!
WOMAN: Yes! To Gallimard!
MAN 1: To Gallimard!
MAN 2: Vive la différence!
> [*They toast, laughing. Lights down on them.*]

SCENE III

M. GALLIMARD's *cell.*

GALLIMARD: [*smiling*] You see? They toast me. I've become patron saint of the socially inept. Can they really be so foolish? Men like that—they should be scratching at my door, begging to learn my secrets! For I, Rene Gallimard, you see, I have known, and been loved by . . . the Perfect Woman.

> Alone in this cell, I sit night after night, watching our story play through my head, always searching for a new ending, one which redeems my honor, where she returns at last to my arms. And I imagine you—my ideal audience—who come to understand and even, perhaps just a little, to envy me.

> [*He turns on his tape recorder. Over the house speakers, we hear the opening phrases of* Madame Butterfly.]

GALLIMARD: In order for you to understand what I did and why, I must introduce you to my favorite opera: *Madame Butterfly.* By Giacomo Puccini. First produced at La Scala, Milan, in 1904, it is now beloved throughout the Western world.

> [*As* GALLIMARD *describes the opera, the tape segues in and out to sections he may be describing.*]

GALLIMARD: And why not? Its heroine, Cio-Cio-San, also known as Butterfly, is a feminine ideal, beautiful and brave. And its hero, the man for whom she gives up everything, is—[*he pulls out a naval officer's cap from under his crate, pops it on his head, and struts about*]—not very good-looking, not too bright, and pretty much a wimp: Benjamin Franklin Pinkerton of the U.S. Navy. As the curtain rises, he's just closed on two great bargains: one on a house, the other on a woman—call it a package deal.

> Pinkerton purchased the rights to Butterfly for one hundred yen—in modern currency, equivalent to about . . . sixty-six cents. So, he's feeling pretty pleased with himself as Sharpless, the American consul, arrives to witness the marriage.

> [MARC, *wearing an official cap to designate* SHARPLESS, *enters and plays the character.*]

SHARPLESS/MARC: Pinkerton!
PINKERTON/GALLIMARD: Sharpless! How's it hangin'? It's a great day, just great. Between my house, my wife, and the rickshaw ride in from town, I've saved nineteen cents just this morning.
SHARPLESS: Wonderful. I can see the inscription on your tombstone already: "I saved a dollar, here I lie." [*He looks around.*] Nice house.
PINKERTON: It's artistic. Artistic, don't you think? Like the way the shoji screens slide open to reveal the wet bar and disco mirror ball? Classy, huh? Great for impressing the chicks.

SHARPLESS: "Chicks"? Pinkerton, you're going to be a married man!

PINKERTON: Well, sort of.

SHARPLESS: What do you mean?

PINKERTON: This country—Sharpless, it is okay. You got all these geisha girls running around—

SHARPLESS: I know! I live here!

PINKERTON: Then, you know the marriage laws, right? I split for one month, it's annulled!

SHARPLESS: Leave it to you to read the fine print. Who's the lucky girl?

PINKERTON: Cio-Cio-San. Her friends call her Butterfly. Sharpless, she eats out of my hand!

SHARPLESS: She's probably very hungry.

PINKERTON: Not like American girls. It's true what they say about Oriental girls. They want to be treated bad!

SHARPLESS: Oh, please!

PINKERTON: It's true!

SHARPLESS: Are you serious about this girl?

PINKERTON: I'm marrying her, aren't I?

SHARPLESS: Yes—with generous trade-in terms.

PINKERTON: When I leave, she'll know what it's like to have loved a real man. And I'll even buy her a few nylons.

SHARPLESS: You aren't planning to take her with you?

PINKERTON: Huh? Where?

SHARPLESS: Home!

PINKERTON: You mean, America? Are you crazy? Can you see her trying to buy rice in St. Louis?

SHARPLESS: So, you're not serious.

> [*Pause.*]

PINKERTON/GALLIMARD: [*as* PINKERTON] Consul, I am a sailor in port. [*as* GALLIMARD] They then proceed to sing the famous duet, "The Whole World Over."

> [*The duet plays on the speakers.* GALLIMARD, *as* PINKERTON, *lip-syncs his lines from the opera.*]

GALLIMARD: To give a rough translation: "The whole world over, the Yankee travels, casting his anchor wherever he wants. Life's not worth living unless he can win the hearts of the fairest maidens, then hotfoot it off the premises ASAP." [*He turns towards* MARC.] In the preceding scene, I played Pinkerton, the womanizing cad, and my friend Marc from school . . . [MARC *bows grandly for our benefit.*] played Sharpless, the sensitive soul of reason. In life, however, our positions were usually—no, always—reversed.

SCENE IV

École Nationale. Aix-en-Provence. 1947.

GALLIMARD: No, Marc, I think I'd rather stay home.

MARC: Are you crazy?! We are going to Dad's condo in Marseille! You know what happened last time?

GALLIMARD: Of course I do.

MARC: Of course you don't! You never know. . . . They stripped, Rene!

GALLIMARD: Who stripped?

MARC: The girls!

GALLIMARD: Girls? Who said anything about girls?

MARC: Rene, we're a buncha university guys goin' up to the woods. What are we gonna do—talk philosophy?

GALLIMARD: What girls? Where do you get them?

MARC: Who cares? The point is, they come. On trucks. Packed in like sardines. The back flips open, babes hop out, we're ready to roll.

GALLIMARD: You mean, they just–?

MARC: Before you know it, every last one of them—they're stripped and splashing around my pool. There's no moon out, they can't see what's going on, their boobs are flapping, right? You close your eyes, reach out—it's grab bag, get it? Doesn't matter whose ass is between whose legs, whose teeth are sinking into who. You're just in there, going at it, eyes closed, on and on for as long as you can stand. [*Pause.*] Some fun, huh?

GALLIMARD: What happens in the morning?

MARC: In the morning, you're ready to talk some philosophy. [*Beat.*] So how 'bout it?

GALLIMARD: Marc, I can't . . . I'm afraid they'll say no—the girls. So I never ask.

MARC: You don't have to ask! That's the beauty—don't you see? They don't have to say yes. It's perfect for a guy like you, really.

GALLIMARD: You go ahead . . . I may come later.

MARC: Hey, Rene—it doesn't matter that you're clumsy and got zits—they're not looking!

GALLIMARD: Thank you very much.

MARC: Wimp.

> [MARC *walks over to the other side of the stage, and starts waving and smiling at women in the audience.*]

GALLIMARD: [*to us*] We now return to my version of *Madame Butterfly* and the events leading to my recent conviction for treason.

> [GALLIMARD *notices* MARC *making lewd gestures.*]

GALLIMARD: Marc, what are you doing?

MARC: Huh? [*Sotto voce.*] Rene, there're a lotta great babes out there. They're probably lookin' at me and thinking, "What a dangerous guy."

GALLIMARD: Yes—how could they help but be impressed by your cool sophistication?

> [GALLIMARD *pops the* SHARPLESS *cap on* MARC's *head, and points him offstage.* MARC *exits, leering.*]

SCENE V

M. GALLIMARD's *cell.*

GALLIMARD: Next, Butterfly makes her entrance. We learn her age—fifteen . . . but very mature for her years.

> [*Lights come up on the area where we saw* SONG *dancing at the top of the play. She appears there again, now dressed as Madame Butterfly, moving to the "Love Duet."* GALLIMARD *turns upstage slightly to watch, transfixed.*]

GALLIMARD: But as she glides past him, beautiful, laughing softly behind her fan, don't we who are men sigh with hope? We, who are not handsome, nor brave, nor powerful, yet somehow believe, like Pinkerton, that we deserve a Butterfly. She arrives with all her possessions in the folds of her sleeves, lays them all out, for her man to do with as he pleases. Even her life itself—she bows her head as she whispers that she's not even worth the hundred yen he paid for her. He's already given too much, when we know he's really had to give nothing at all.

[*Music and lights on* SONG *out.* GALLIMARD *sits at his crate.*]

GALLIMARD: In real life, women who put their total worth at less than sixty-six cents are quite hard to find. The closest we come is in the pages of these magazines. [*He reaches into his crate, pulls out a stack of girlie magazines, and begins flipping through them.*] Quite a necessity in prison. For three or four dollars, you get seven or eight women.

    I first discovered these magazines at my uncle's house. One day, as a boy of twelve. The first time I saw them in his closet . . . all lined up—my body shook. Not with lust—no, with power. Here were women—a shelf-ful—who would do exactly as I wanted.

[*The "Love Duet" creeps in over the speakers. Special comes up, revealing, not* SONG *this time, but a pinup girl in a sexy negligee, her back to us.* GAL-LIMARD *turns upstage and looks at her.*]

GIRL: I know you're watching me.

GALLIMARD: My throat . . . it's dry.

GIRL: I leave my blinds open every night before I go to bed.

GALLIMARD: I can't move.

GIRL: I leave my blinds open and the lights on.

GALLIMARD: I'm shaking. My skin is hot, but my penis is soft. Why?

GIRL: I stand in front of the window.

GALLIMARD: What is she going to do?

GIRL: I toss my hair, and I let my lips part . . . barely.

GALLIMARD: I shouldn't be seeing this. It's so dirty. I'm so bad.

GIRL: Then, slowly, I lift off my nightdress.

GALLIMARD: Oh, god. I can't believe it. I can't—

GIRL: I toss it to the ground.

GALLIMARD: Now, she's going to walk away. She's going to—

GIRL: I stand there, in the light, displaying myself.

GALLIMARD: No. She's—why is she naked?

GIRL: To you.

GALLIMARD: In front of a window? This is wrong. No—

GIRL: Without shame.

GALLIMARD: No, she must . . . like it.

GIRL: I like it.

GALLIMARD: She . . . she wants me to see.

GIRL: I want you to see.

GALLIMARD: I can't believe it! She's getting excited!

GIRL: I can't see you. You can do whatever you want.

GALLIMARD: I can't do a thing. Why?

GIRL: What would you like me to do . . . next?

    [*Lights go down on her. Music off. Silence, as* GALLIMARD *puts away his magazines. Then he resumes talking to us.*]

GALLIMARD: Act Two begins with Butterfly staring at the ocean. Pinkerton's been called back to the U.S., and he's given his wife a detailed schedule of his plans. In the column marked "return date," he's written "when the robins nest." This failed to ignite her suspicions. Now, three years have passed without a peep from him. Which brings a response from her faithful servant, Suzuki.

    [COMRADE CHIN *enters, playing* SUZUKI.]

SUZUKI: Girl, he's a loser. What'd he ever give you? Nineteen cents and those ugly Day-Glo stockings? Look, it's finished! Kaput! Done! And you should be glad! I mean, the guy was a woofer! He tried before, you know—before he met you, he went down to geisha central and plunked down his spare change in front of the usual candidates—everyone else gagged! These are hungry prostitutes, and they were not interested, get the picture? Now, stop slathering when an American ship sails in, and let's make some bucks—I mean, yen! We are broke!

    Now, what about Yamadori? Hey, hey—don't look away—the man is a prince—figuratively, and, what's even better, literally. He's rich, he's handsome, he says he'll die if you don't marry him—and he's even willing to overlook the little fact that you've been deflowered all over the place by a foreign devil. What do you mean, "But he's Japanese"? You're Japanese! You think you've been touched by the whitey god? He was a sailor with dirty hands!

    [SUZUKI *stalks offstage.*]

GALLIMARD: She's also visited by Consul Sharpless, sent by Pinkerton on a minor errand.

    [MARC *enters, as* SHARPLESS.]

SHARPLESS: I hate this job.

GALLIMARD: This Pinkerton—he doesn't show up personally to tell his wife he's abandoning her. No, he sends a government diplomat . . . at taxpayers' expense.

SHARPLESS: Butterfly? Butterfly? I have some bad—I'm going to be ill. Butterfly, I came to tell you—

GALLIMARD: Butterfly says she knows he'll return and if he doesn't she'll kill herself rather than go back to her own people. [*Beat.*] This causes a lull in the conversation.

SHARPLESS: Let's put it this way . . .

GALLIMARD: Butterfly runs into the next room, and returns holding—

    [*Sound cue: a baby crying.* SHARPLESS, *"seeing" this, backs away.*]

SHARPLESS: Well, good. Happy to see things going so well. I suppose I'll be going now. Ta ta. Ciao. [*He turns away. Sound cue out.*] I hate this job. [*He exits.*]

GALLIMARD: At that moment, Butterfly spots in the harbor an American ship— the *Abramo Lincoln!*

    [*Music cue: "The Flower Duet."* SONG, *still dressed as Butterfly, changes into a wedding kimono, moving to the music.*]

GALLIMARD: This is the moment that redeems her years of waiting. With Suzuki's help, they cover the room with flowers—

[CHIN, *as* SUZUKI, *trudges onstage and drops a lone flower without much enthusiasm.*]

GALLIMARD: —and she changes into her wedding dress to prepare for Pinkerton's arrival.

[SUZUKI *helps Butterfly change.* HELGA *enters, and helps* GALLIMARD *change into a tuxedo.*]

GALLIMARD: I married a woman older than myself—Helga.

HELGA: My father was ambassador to Australia. I grew up among criminals and kangaroos.

GALLIMARD: Hearing that brought me to the altar—

[HELGA *exits.*]

GALLIMARD: —where I took a vow renouncing love. No fantasy woman would ever want me, so, yes, I would settle for a quick leap up the career ladder. Passion, I banish, and in its place—practicality!

But my vows had long since lost their charm by the time we arrived in China. The sad truth is that all men want a beautiful woman, and the uglier the man, the greater the want.

[SUZUKI *makes final adjustments of Butterfly's costume, as does* GALLIMARD *of his tuxedo.*]

GALLIMARD: I married late, at age thirty-one. I was faithful to my marriage for eight years. Until the day when, as a junior-level diplomat in puritanical Peking, in a parlor at the German ambassador's house, during the "Reign of a Hundred Flowers," I first saw her . . . singing the death scene from *Madame Butterfly.*

[SUZUKI *runs offstage.*]

SCENE VI

German ambassador's house. Beijing. 1960.

*The upstage special area now becomes a stage. Several chairs face upstage, representing seating for some twenty guests in the parlor. A few "diplomats"—*RENEE, MARC, TOULON—*in formal dress enter and take seats.*

GALLIMARD *also sits down, but turns towards us and continues to talk. Orchestral accompaniment on the tape is now replaced by a simple piano.* SONG *picks up the death scene from the point where Butterfly uncovers the hara-kiri knife.*

GALLIMARD: The ending is pitiful. Pinkerton, in an act of great courage, stays home and sends his American wife to pick up Butterfly's child. The truth, long deferred, has come up to her door.

[SONG, *playing Butterfly, sings the lines from the opera in her own voice— which, though not classical, should be decent.*]

SONG: "Con onor muore/ chi non puo serbar/ vita con onore."

GALLIMARD: [*Simultaneously*] "Death with honor/ Is better than life/ Life with dishonor."

[*The stage is illuminated; we are now completely within an elegant diplomat's residence.* SONG *proceeds to play out an abbreviated death scene.*

[*Everyone in the room applauds. Song, shyly, takes her bows. Others in the room rush to congratulate her.* GALLIMARD *remains with us.*]

GALLIMARD: They say in opera the voice is everything. That's probably why I'd never before enjoyed opera. Here . . . here was a Butterfly with little or no voice—but she had the grace, the delicacy . . . I believed this girl. I believed her suffering. I wanted to take her in my arms—so delicate, even I could protect her, take her home, pamper her until she smiled.

[*Over the course of the preceding speech,* SONG *has broken from the upstage crowd and moved directly upstage of* GALLIMARD.]

SONG: Excuse me. Monsieur . . . ?

[GALLIMARD *turns upstage, shocked.*]

GALLIMARD: Oh! Gallimard. Mademoiselle . . . ? A beautiful . . .

SONG: Song Liling.

GALLIMARD: A beautiful performance.

SONG: Oh, please.

GALLIMARD: I usually—

SONG: You make me blush. I'm no opera singer at all.

GALLIMARD: I usually don't like *Butterfly*.

SONG: I can't blame you in the least.

GALLIMARD: I mean, the story—

SONG: Ridiculous.

GALLIMARD: I like the story, but . . . what?

SONG: Oh, you like it?

GALLIMARD: I . . . what I mean is, I've always seen it played by huge women in so much bad makeup.

SONG: Bad makeup is not unique to the West.

GALLIMARD: But, who can believe them?

SONG: And you believe me?

GALLIMARD: Absolutely. You were utterly convincing. It's the first time—

SONG: Convincing? As a Japanese woman? The Japanese used hundreds of our people for medical experiments during the war, you know. But I gather such an irony is lost on you.

GALLIMARD: No! I was about to say, it's the first time I've seen the beauty of the story.

SONG: Really?

GALLIMARD: Of her death. It's a . . . pure sacrifice. He's unworthy, but what can she do? She loves him . . . so much. It's a very beautiful story.

SONG: Well, yes, to a Westerner.

GALLIMARD: Excuse me?

SONG: It's one of your favorite fantasies, isn't it? The submissive Oriental woman and the cruel white man.

GALLIMARD: Well, I didn't quite mean . . .

SONG: Consider it this way: what would you say if a blonde homecoming queen fell in love with a short Japanese businessman? He treats her cruelly, then goes home for three years, during which time she prays to his picture and turns down marriage from a young Kennedy. Then, when she learns he has remarried, she kills herself. Now, I believe you would consider this girl to be a deranged idiot, correct? But because it's an Oriental who kills herself for a Westerner—ah!—you find it beautiful.

[*Silence.*]

GALLIMARD: Yes . . . well . . . I see your point . . .

SONG: I will never do Butterfly again, Monsieur Gallimard. If you wish to see some real theatre, come to the Peking Opera sometime. Expand your mind.

[SONG *walks offstage.*]

GALLIMARD: [*to us*] So much for protecting her in my big Western arms.

SCENE VII

M. GALLIMARD's *apartment. Beijing. 1960.*

GALLIMARD *changes from his tux into a casual suit.* HELGA *enters.*

GALLIMARD: The Chinese are an incredibly arrogant people.

HELGA: They warned us about that in Paris, remember?

GALLIMARD: Even Parisians consider them arrogant. That's a switch.

HELGA: What is it that Madame Su says? "We are a very old civilization." I never know if she's talking about her country or herself.

GALLIMARD: I walk around here, all I hear every day, everywhere is how *old* this culture is. The fact that "old" may be synonymous with "senile" doesn't occur to them.

HELGA: You're not going to change them. "East is east, west is west, and . . ." whatever that guy said.

GALLIMARD: It's just that—silly. I met . . . at Ambassador Koening's tonight— you should've been there.

HELGA: Koening? Oh god, no. Did he enchant you all again with the history of Bavaria?

GALLIMARD: No. I met, I suppose, the Chinese equivalent of a diva. She's a singer in the Chinese opera.

HELGA: They have an opera, too? Do they sing in Chinese? Or maybe—in Italian?

GALLIMARD: Tonight, she did sing in Italian.

HELGA: How'd she manage that?

GALLIMARD: She must've been educated in the West before the Revolution. Her French is very good also. Anyway, she sang the death scene from *Madame Butterfly.*

HELGA: *Madame Butterfly!* Then I should have come. [*She begins humming, floating around the room as if dragging long kimono sleeves.*] Did she have a nice costume? I think it's a classic piece of music.

GALLIMARD: That's what *I* thought, too. Don't let her hear you say that.

HELGA: What's wrong?

GALLIMARD: Evidently the Chinese hate it.

HELGA: She hated it, but she performed it anyway? Is she perverse?

GALLIMARD: They hate it because the white man gets the girl. Sour grapes if you ask me.

HELGA: Politics again? Why can't they just hear it as a piece of beautiful music? So, what's in their opera?

GALLIMARD: I don't know. But, whatever it is, I'm sure it must be *old.*

[HELGA *exits.*]

SCENE VIII

Chinese opera house and the streets of Beijing. 1960.
   The sound of gongs clanging fills the stage.

GALLIMARD: My wife's innocent question kept ringing in my ears. I asked around, but no one knew anything about the Chinese opera. It took four weeks, but my curiosity overcame my cowardice. This Chinese diva—this unwilling Butterfly—what did she do to make her so proud?
   The room was hot, and full of smoke. Wrinkled faces, old women, teeth missing—a man with a growth on his neck, like a human toad. All smiling, pipes falling from their mouths, cracking nuts between their teeth, a live chicken pecking at my foot—all looking, screaming, gawking . . . at her.
   [*The upstage area is suddenly hit with a harsh white light. It has become the stage for the Chinese opera performance. Two dancers enter, along with* SONG. GALLIMARD *stands apart, watching.* SONG *glides gracefully amidst the two dancers. Drums suddenly slam to a halt.* SONG *strikes a pose, looking straight at* GALLIMARD. *Dancers exit. Light change. Pause, then* SONG *walks right off the stage and straight up to* GALLIMARD.]

SONG: Yes. You. White man. I'm looking straight at you.

GALLIMARD: Me?

SONG: You see any other white men? It was too easy to spot you. How often does a man in my audience come in a tie?
   [SONG *starts to remove her costume. Underneath, she wears simple baggy clothes. They are now backstage. The show is over.*]

SONG: So, you are an adventurous imperialist?

GALLIMARD: I . . . thought it would further my education.

SONG: It took you four weeks. Why?

GALLIMARD: I've been busy.

SONG: Well, education has always been undervalued in the West, hasn't it?

GALLIMARD: [*laughing*] I don't think it's true.

SONG: No, you wouldn't. You're a Westerner. How can you objectively judge your own values?

GALLIMARD: I think it's possible to achieve some distance.

SONG: Do you? [*Pause.*] It stinks in here. Let's go.

GALLIMARD: These are the smells of your loyal fans.

SONG: I love them for being my fans, I hate the smell they leave behind. I, too, can distance myself from my people. [*She looks around, then whispers in his ear.*] "Art for the masses" is a shitty excuse to keep artists poor. [*She pops a cigarette in her mouth.*] Be a gentleman, will you? And light my cigarette.
   [GALLIMARD *fumbles for a match.*]

GALLIMARD: I don't . . . smoke.

SONG: [*lighting her own*] Your loss. Had you lit my cigarette, I might have blown a puff of smoke right between your eyes. Come.
   [*They start to walk about the stage. It is a summer night on the Beijing streets. Sounds of the city play on the house speakers.*]

SONG: How I wish there were even a tiny cafe to sit in. With cappuccinos, and men in tuxedos and bad expatriate jazz.

GALLIMARD: If my history serves me correctly, you weren't even allowed into the clubs in Shanghai before the Revolution.

SONG: Your history serves you poorly, Monsieur Gallimard. True, there were signs reading "No dogs and Chinamen." But a woman, especially a delicate Oriental woman—we always go where we please. Could you imagine it otherwise? Clubs in China filled with pasty, big-thighed white women, while thousands of slender lotus blossoms wait just outside the door? Never. The clubs would be empty. [*Beat.*] We have always held a certain fascination for you Caucasian men, have we not?

GALLIMARD: But . . . that fascination is imperialist, or so you tell me.

SONG: Do you believe everything I tell you? Yes. It is always imperialist. But sometimes . . . sometimes, it is also mutual. Oh—this is my flat.

GALLIMARD: I didn't even—

SONG: Thank you. Come another time and we will further expand your mind.

[SONG *exits.* GALLIMARD *continues roaming the streets as he speaks to us.*]

GALLIMARD: What was that? What did she mean, "Sometimes . . . it is mutual"? Women do not flirt with me. And I normally can't talk to them. But tonight, I held up my end of the conversation.

SCENE IX

GALLIMARD's *bedroom. Beijing. 1960.*
    HELGA *enters.*

HELGA: You didn't tell me you'd be home late.

GALLIMARD: I didn't intend to. Something came up.

HELGA: Oh? Like what?

GALLIMARD: I went to the . . . to the Dutch ambassador's home.

HELGA: Again?

GALLIMARD: There was a reception for a visiting scholar. He's writing a six-volume treatise on the Chinese revolution. We all gathered that meant he'd have to live here long enough to actually write six volumes, and we all expressed our deepest sympathies.

HELGA: Well, I had a good night, too. I went with the ladies to a martial arts demonstration. Some of those men—when they break those thick boards—[*She mimes fanning herself.*] whoo-whoo!

[HELGA *exits. Lights dim.*]

GALLIMARD: I lied to my wife. Why? I've never had any reason to lie before. But what reason did I have tonight? I didn't do anything wrong. That night, I had a dream. Other people, I've been told, have dreams where angels appear. Or dragons, or Sophia Loren in a towel. In my dream, Marc from school appeared.

[MARC *enters, in a nightshirt and cap.*]

MARC: Rene! You met a girl!

[GALLIMARD *and* MARC *stumble down the Beijing streets. Night sounds over the speakers.*]

GALLIMARD: It's not that amazing, thank you.

MARC: No! It's so monumental, I heard about it halfway around the world in my sleep!

GALLIMARD: I've met girls before, you know.

MARC: Name one. I've come across time and space to congratulate you. [*He hands* GALLIMARD *a bottle of wine.*]

GALLIMARD: Marc, this is expensive.

MARC: On those rare occasions when you become a formless spirit, why not steal the best?

[MARC *pops open the bottle, begins to share it with* GALLIMARD.]

GALLIMARD: You embarrass me. She . . . there's no reason to think she likes me.

MARC: "Sometimes, it is mutual"?

GALLIMARD: Oh.

MARC: "Mutual"? "Mutual"? What does that mean?

GALLIMARD: You heard!

MARC: It means the money is in the bank, you only have to write the check!

GALLIMARD: I am a married man!

MARC: And an excellent one, too. I cheated after . . . six months. Then again and again, until now—three hundred girls in twelve years.

GALLIMARD: I don't think we should hold that up as a model.

MARC: Of course not! My life—it is disgusting! Phooey! Phooey! But, you—you are the model husband.

GALLIMARD: Anyway, it's impossible. I'm a foreigner.

MARC: Ah, yes. She cannot love you, it is taboo, but something deep inside her heart . . . she cannot help herself . . . she must surrender to you. It is her destiny.

GALLIMARD: How do you imagine all this?

MARC: The same way you do. It's an old story. It's in our blood. They fear us, Rene. Their women fear us. And their men—their men hate us. And, you know something? They are all correct.

[*They spot a light in a window.*]

MARC: There! There, Rene!

GALLIMARD: It's her window.

MARC: Late at night—it burns. The light—it burns for you.

GALLIMARD: I won't look. It's not respectful.

MARC: We don't have to be respectful. We're foreign devils.

[*Enter* SONG, *in a sheer robe. The "One Fine Day" aria creeps in over the speakers. With her back to us,* SONG *mimes attending to her toilette. Her robe comes loose, revealing her white shoulders.*]

MARC: All your life you've waited for a beautiful girl who would lay down for you. All your life you've smiled like a saint when it's happened to every other man you know. And you see them in magazines and you see them in movies. And you wonder, what's wrong with me? Will anyone beautiful ever want me? As the years pass, your hair thins and you struggle to hold onto even your hopes. Stop struggling, Rene. The wait is over. [*He exits.*]

GALLIMARD: Marc? Marc?

[*At that moment,* SONG, *her back still towards us, drops her robe. A second of her naked back, then a sound cue: a phone ringing, very loud. Blackout, followed in the next beat by a special up on the bedroom area, where a phone now sits.* GALLIMARD *stumbles across the stage and picks up the phone.*

Sound cue out. Over the course of his conversation, area lights fill in the vicinity of his bed. It is the following morning.]

GALLIMARD: Yes? Hello?

SONG: [*offstage*] Is it very early?

GALLIMARD: Why, yes.

SONG: [*offstage*] How early?

GALLIMARD: It's . . . it's 5:30. Why are you—?

SONG: [*offstage*] But it's light outside. Already.

GALLIMARD: It is. The sun must be in confusion today.

> [*Over the course of* SONG'*s next speech, her upstage special comes up again. She sits in a chair, legs crossed, in a robe, telephone to her ear.*]

SONG: I waited until I saw the sun. That was as much discipline as I could manage for one night. Do you forgive me?

GALLIMARD: Of course . . . for what?

SONG: Then I'll ask you quickly. Are you really interested in the opera?

GALLIMARD: Why, yes. Yes, I am.

SONG: Then come again next Thursday. I am playing *The Drunken Beauty.* May I count on you?

GALLIMARD: Yes. You may.

SONG: Perfect. Well, I must be getting to bed. I'm exhausted. It's been a very long night for me.

> [SONG *hangs up; special on her goes off.* GALLIMARD *begins to dress for work.*]

SCENE X

SONG LILING'*s apartment. Beijing. 1960.*

GALLIMARD: I returned to the opera that next week, and the week after that . . . she keeps our meetings so short—perhaps fifteen, twenty minutes at most. So I am left each week with a thirst which is intensified. In this way, fifteen weeks have gone by. I am starting to doubt the words of my friend Marc. But no, not really. In my heart, I know she has . . . an interest in me. I suspect this is her way. She is outwardly bold and outspoken, yet her heart is shy and afraid. It is the Oriental in her at war with her Western education.

SONG: [*offstage*] I will be out in an instant. Ask the servant for anything you want.

GALLIMARD: Tonight, I have finally been invited to enter her apartment. Though the idea is almost beyond belief, I believe she is afraid of me.

> [GALLIMARD *looks around the room. He picks up a picture in a frame, studies it. Without his noticing,* SONG *enters, dressed elegantly in a black gown from the twenties. She stands in the doorway looking like Anna May Wong.*]

SONG: That is my father.

GALLIMARD: [*surprised*] Mademoiselle Song . . .

> [*She glides up to him, snatches away the picture.*]

SONG: It is very good that he did not live to see the Revolution. They would, no doubt, have made him kneel on broken glass. Not that he didn't deserve such a punishment. But he is my father. I would've hated to see it happen.

GALLIMARD: I'm very honored that you've allowed me to visit your home.

> [SONG *curtsies.*]

SONG: Thank you. Oh! Haven't you been poured any tea?

GALLIMARD: I'm really not—

SONG: [*to her offstage servant*] Shu-Fang! Cha! Kwai-lah!
[To GALLIMARD.] I'm sorry. You want everything to be perfect—

GALLIMARD: Please.

SONG: —and before the evening even begins—

GALLIMARD: I'm really not thirsty.

SONG: —it's ruined.

GALLIMARD: [*sharply*] Mademoiselle Song!
[SONG *sits down.*]

SONG: I'm sorry.

GALLIMARD: What are you apologizing for now?
[*Pause;* SONG *starts to giggle.*]

SONG: I don't know!
[GALLIMARD *laughs.*]

GALLIMARD: Exactly my point.

SONG: Oh, I am silly. Lightheaded. I promise not to apologize for anything else tonight, do you hear me?

GALLIMARD: That's a good girl.
[SHU-FANG, *a servant girl, comes out with a tea tray and starts to pour.*]

SONG: [*to* SHU-FANG] No! I'll pour myself for the gentleman!
[SHU-FANG, *staring at* GALLIMARD, *exits.*]

SONG: No, I . . . I don't even know why I invited you up.

GALLIMARD: Well, I'm glad you did.
[SONG *looks around the room.*]

SONG: There is an element of danger to your presence.

GALLIMARD: Oh?

SONG: You must know.

GALLIMARD: It doesn't concern me. We both know why I'm here.

SONG: It doesn't concern me, either. No . . . well, perhaps . . .

GALLIMARD: What?

SONG: Perhaps I am slightly afraid of scandal.

GALLIMARD: What are we doing?

SONG: I'm entertaining you. In my parlor.

GALLIMARD: In France, that would hardly—

SONG: France. France is a country living in the modern era. Perhaps even ahead of it. China is a nation whose soul is firmly rooted two thousand years in the past. What I do, even pouring the tea for you now . . . it has . . . implications. The walls and windows say so. Even my own heart, strapped inside this Western dress . . . even it says things—things I don't care to hear.
[SONG *hands* GALLIMARD *a cup of tea.* GALLIMARD *puts his hand over both the teacup and* SONG's *hand.*]

GALLIMARD: This is a beautiful dress.

SONG: Don't.

GALLIMARD: What?

SONG: I don't even know if it looks right on me.

GALLIMARD: Believe me—

SONG: You are from France. You see so many beautiful women.

GALLIMARD: France? Since when are the European women—?

SONG: Oh! What am I trying to do, anyway?!
> [SONG *runs to the door, composes herself, then turns towards* GALLIMARD.]

SONG: Monsieur Gallimard, perhaps you should go.

GALLIMARD: But . . . why?

SONG: There's something wrong about this.

GALLIMARD: I don't see what.

SONG: I feel . . . I am not myself.

GALLIMARD: No. You're nervous.

SONG: Please. Hard as I try to be modern, to speak like a man, to hold a Western woman's strong face up to my own . . . in the end, I fail. A small, frightened heart beats too quickly and gives me away. Monsieur Gallimard, I'm a Chinese girl. I've never . . . never invited a man up to my flat before. The forwardness of my actions makes my skin burn.

GALLIMARD: What are you afraid of? Certainly not me, I hope.

SONG: I'm a modest girl.

GALLIMARD: I know. And very beautiful. [*He touches her hair.*]

SONG: Please—go now. The next time you see me, I shall again be myself.

GALLIMARD: I like you the way you are right now.

SONG: You are a cad.

GALLIMARD: What do you expect? I'm a foreign devil.
> [GALLIMARD *walks downstage.* SONG *exits.*]

GALLIMARD: [*to us*] Did you hear the way she talked about Western women? Much differently than the first night. She does—she feels inferior to them—and to me.

SCENE XI

The French embassy. Beijing. 1960.
> GALLIMARD *moves towards a desk.*

GALLIMARD: I determined to try an experiment. In *Madame Butterfly,* Cio-Cio-San fears that the Western man who catches a butterfly will pierce its heart with a needle, then leave it to perish. I began to wonder: had I, too, caught a butterfly who would writhe on a needle?
> [MARC *enters, dressed as a bureaucrat, holding a stack of papers. As* GALLIMARD *speaks,* MARC *hands papers to him. He peruses, then signs, stamps, or rejects them.*]

GALLIMARD: Over the next five weeks, I worked like a dynamo. I stopped going to the opera, I didn't phone or write her. I knew this little flower was waiting for me to call, and, as I wickedly refused to do so, I felt for the first time that rush of power—the absolute power of a man.
> [MARC *continues acting as the bureaucrat, but he now speaks as himself.*]

MARC: Rene! It's me!

GALLIMARD: Marc—I hear your voice everywhere now. Even in the midst of work.

MARC: That's because I'm watching you—all the time.

GALLIMARD: You were always the most popular guy in school.

MARC: Well, there's no guarantee of failure in life like happiness in high school. Somehow I knew I'd end up in the suburbs working for Renault and you'd be in the Orient picking exotic women off the trees. And they say there's no justice.

GALLIMARD: That's why you were my friend?

MARC: I gave you a little of my life, so that now you can give me some of yours [*Pause.*] Remember Isabelle?

GALLIMARD: Of course I remember! She was my first experience.

MARC: We all wanted to ball her. But she only wanted me.

GALLIMARD: I had her.

MARC: Right. You balled her.

GALLIMARD: You were the only one who ever believed me.

MARC: Well, there's a good reason for that. [*Beat.*] C'mon. You must've guessed.

GALLIMARD: You told me to wait in the bushes by the cafeteria that night. The next thing I knew, she was on me. Dress up in the air.

MARC: She never wore underwear.

GALLIMARD: My arms were pinned to the dirt.

MARC: She loved the superior position. A girl ahead of her time.

GALLIMARD: I looked up, and there was this woman . . . bouncing up and down on my loins.

MARC: Screaming, right?

GALLIMARD: Screaming, and breaking off the branches all around me, and pounding my butt up and down into the dirt.

MARC: Huffing and puffing like a locomotive.

GALLIMARD: And in the middle of all this, the leaves were getting into my mouth, my legs were losing circulation, I thought, "God. So this is *it?*"

MARC: You thought that?

GALLIMARD: Well, I was worried about my legs falling off.

MARC: You didn't have a good time?

GALLIMARD: No, that's not what I—I had a great time!

MARC: You're sure?

GALLIMARD: Yeah. Really.

MARC: 'Cuz I wanted you to have a good time.

GALLIMARD: I did.
       [*Pause.*]

MARC: Shit. [*Pause.*] When all is said and done, she was kind of a lousy lay, wasn't she? I mean, there was a lot of energy there, but you never knew what she was doing with it. Like when she yelled "I'm coming!"—hell, it was so loud, you wanted to go "Look, it's not that big a deal."

GALLIMARD: I got scared. I thought she meant someone was actually coming. [*Pause.*] But, Marc?

MARC: What?

GALLIMARD: Thanks.

MARC: Oh, don't mention it.

GALLIMARD: It was my first experience.

MARC: Yeah. You got her.

GALLIMARD: I got her.

MARC: Wait! Look at that letter again!
       [GALLIMARD *picks up one of the papers he's been stamping, and rereads it.*]

GALLIMARD: [*to us*] After six weeks, they began to arrive. The letters.
> [*Upstage special on* SONG, *as Madame Butterfly. The scene is underscored by the "Love Duet."*]

SONG: Did we fight? I do not know. Is the opera no longer of interest to you? Please come—my audiences miss the white devil in their midst.
> [GALLIMARD *looks up from the letter, towards us.*]

GALLIMARD: [*to us*] A concession, but much too dignified. [*Beat; he discards the letter.*] I skipped the opera again that week to complete a position paper on trade.
> [*The bureaucrat hands him another letter.*]

SONG: Six weeks have passed since last we met. Is this your practice—to leave friends in the lurch? Sometimes I hate you, sometimes I hate myself, but always I miss you.

GALLIMARD: [*to us*] Better, but I don't like the way she calls me "friend." When a woman calls a man her "friend," she's calling him a eunuch or a homosexual. [*Beat; he discards the letter.*] I was absent from the opera for the seventh week, feeling a sudden urge to clean out my files.
> [*Bureaucrat hands him another letter.*]

SONG: Your rudeness is beyond belief. I don't deserve this cruelty. Don't bother to call. I'll have you turned away at the door.

GALLIMARD: [*to us*] I didn't. [*He discards the letter, bureaucrat hands him another.*] And then finally, the letter that concluded my experiment.

SONG: I am out of words. I can hide behind dignity no longer. What do you want? I have already given you my shame.
> [GALLIMARD *gives the letter back to* MARC, *slowly. Special on* SONG *fades out.*]

GALLIMARD: [*to us*] Reading it, I became suddenly ashamed. Yes, my experiment had been a success. She was turning on my needle. But the victory seemed hollow.

MARC: Hollow?! Are you crazy?

GALLIMARD: Nothing, Marc. Please go away.

MARC: [*exiting, with papers*] Haven't I taught you anything?

GALLIMARD: "I have already given you my shame." I had to attend a reception that evening. On the way, I felt sick. If there is a God, surely he would punish me now. I had finally gained power over a beautiful woman, only to abuse it cruelly. There must be justice in the world. I had the strange feeling that the ax would fall this very evening.

SCENE XII

Ambassador TOULON's *residence. Beijing. 1960.*
> *Sound cue: party noises. Light change. We are now in a spacious residence.*
TOULON, *the French ambassador, enters and taps* GALLIMARD *on the shoulder.*

TOULON: Gallimard? Can I have a word? Over here.

GALLIMARD: [*to us*] Manuel Toulon. French ambassador to China. He likes to think of us all as his children. Rather like God.

TOULON: Look, Gallimard, there's not much to say. I've liked you. From the day you walked in. You were no leader, but you were tidy and efficient.

GALLIMARD: Thank you, sir.

TOULON: Don't jump the gun. Okay, our needs in China are changing. It's embarrassing that we lost Indochina. Someone just wasn't on the ball there. I don't mean you personally, of course.

GALLIMARD: Thank you, sir.

TOULON: We're going to be doing a lot more information-gathering in the future. The nature of our work here is changing. Some people are just going to have to go. It's nothing personal.

GALLIMARD: Oh.

TOULON: Want to know a secret? Vice-Consul LeBon is being transferred.

GALLIMARD: [*to us*] My immediate superior!

TOULON: And most of his department.

GALLIMARD: [*to us*] Just as I feared! God has seen my evil heart—

TOULON: But not you.

GALLIMARD: [*to us*]—and he's taking her away just as . . . [*to* TOULON] Excuse me, sir?

TOULON: Scare you? I think I did. Cheer up, Gallimard. I want you to replace LeBon as vice-consul.

GALLIMARD: You—? Yes, well, thank you, sir.

TOULON: Anytime.

GALLIMARD: I . . . accept with great humility.

TOULON: Humility won't be part of the job. You're going to coordinate the revamped intelligence division. Want to know a secret? A year ago, you would've been out. But the past few months, I don't know how it happened, you've become this new aggressive, confident . . . thing. And they also tell me you get along with the Chinese. So I think you're a lucky man, Gallimard. Congratulations.

> [*They shake hands.* TOULON *exits. Party noises out.* GALLIMARD *stumbles across a darkened stage.*]

GALLIMARD: Vice-consul? Impossible! As I stumbled out of the party, I saw it written across the sky: There is no God. Or, no—say that there is a God. But that God . . . understands. Of course! God who creates Eve to serve Adam, who blesses Solomon with his harem but ties Jezebel to a burning bed—that God is a man. And he understands! At age thirty-nine, I was suddenly initiated into the way of the world.

SCENE XIII

SONG LILING'S *apartment. Beijing. 1960.*
> SONG *enters, in a sheer dressing gown.*

SONG: Are you crazy?

GALLIMARD: Mademoiselle Song—

SONG: To come here—at this hour? After . . . after eight weeks?

GALLIMARD: It's the most amazing—

SONG: You bang on my door? Scare my servants, scandalize the neighbors?

GALLIMARD: I've been promoted. To vice-consul.

> [*Pause.*]

SONG: And what is that supposed to mean to me?

GALLIMARD: Are you my Butterfly?

SONG: What are you saying?

GALLIMARD: I've come tonight for an answer: are you my Butterfly?

SONG: Don't you know already?

GALLIMARD: I want you to say it.

SONG: I don't want to say it.

GALLIMARD: So, that is your answer?

SONG: You know how I feel about—

GALLIMARD: I do remember one thing.

SONG: What?

GALLIMARD: In the letter I received today.

SONG: Don't.

GALLIMARD: "I have already given you my shame."

SONG: It's enough that I even wrote it.

GALLIMARD: Well, then—

SONG: I shouldn't have it splashed across my face.

GALLIMARD: —if that's all true—

SONG: Stop!

GALLIMARD: Then what is one more short answer?

SONG: I don't want to!

GALLIMARD: Are you my Butterfly? [*Silence; he crosses the room and begins to touch her hair.*] I want from you honesty. There should be nothing false between us. No false pride.
  [*Pause.*]

SONG: Yes, I am. I am your Butterfly.

GALLIMARD: Then let me be honest with you. It is because of you that I was promoted tonight. You have changed my life forever. My little Butterfly, there should be no more secrets: I love you.
  [*He starts to kiss her roughly. She resists slightly.*]

SONG: No . . . no . . . gently . . . please, I've never . . .

GALLIMARD: No?

SONG: I've tried to appear experienced, but . . . the truth is . . . no.

GALLIMARD: Are you cold?

SONG: Yes. Cold.

GALLIMARD: Then we will go very, very slowly.
  [*He starts to caress her; her gown begins to open.*]

SONG: No . . . let me . . . keep my clothes . . .

GALLIMARD: But . . .

SONG: Please . . . it all frightens me. I'm a modest Chinese girl.

GALLIMARD: My poor little treasure.

SONG: I am your treasure. Though inexperienced, I am not . . . ignorant. They teach us things, our mothers, about pleasing a man.

GALLIMARD: Yes?

SONG: I'll do my best to make you happy. Turn off the lights.
  [GALLIMARD *gets up and heads for a lamp.* SONG, *propped up on one elbow, tosses her hair back and smiles.*]

SONG: Monsieur Gallimard?

GALLIMARD: Yes, Butterfly?

SONG: "Vieni, vieni!"

GALLIMARD: "Come, darling."

SONG: "Ah! Dolce notte!"

GALLIMARD: "Beautiful night."

SONG: "Tutto estatico d'amor ride il ciel!"

GALLIMARD: "All ecstatic with love, the heavens are filled with laughter."

> [*He turns off the lamp. Blackout.*]

ACT TWO

SCENE I

M. GALLIMARD's *cell. Paris. Present.*
> *Lights up on* GALLIMARD. *He sits in his cell, reading from a leaflet.*

GALLIMARD: This, from a contemporary critic's commentary on *Madame Butterfly:* "Pinkerton suffers from . . . being an obnoxious bounder whom every man in the audience itches to kick." Bully for us men in the audience! Then, in the same note: "Butterfly is the most irresistibly appealing of Puccini's 'Little Women.' Watching the success of her humiliations is like watching a child under torture." [*He tosses the pamphlet over his shoulder.*] I suggest that, while we men may all want to kick Pinkerton, very few of us would pass up the opportunity to *be* Pinkerton.

> [GALLIMARD *moves out of his cell.*]

SCENE II

GALLIMARD *and Butterfly's flat. Beijing. 1960.*
> *We are in a simple but well-decorated parlor.* GALLIMARD *moves to sit on a sofa, while* SONG, *dressed in a chong sam, enters and curls up at his feet.*

GALLIMARD: [*to us*] We secured a flat on the outskirts of Peking. Butterfly, as I was calling her now, decorated our "home" with Western furniture and Chinese antiques. And there, on a few stolen afternoons or evenings each week, Butterfly commenced her education.

SONG: The Chinese men—they keep us down.

GALLIMARD: Even in the "New Society"?

SONG: In the "New Society," we are all kept ignorant equally. That's one of the exciting things about loving a Western man. I know you are not threatened by a woman's education.

GALLIMARD: I'm no saint, Butterfly.

SONG: But you come from a progressive society.

GALLIMARD: We're not always reminding each other how "old" we are, if that's what you mean.

SONG: Exactly. We Chinese—once, I suppose, it is true, we ruled the world. But so what? How much more exciting to be part of the society ruling the world today. Tell me—what's happening in Vietnam?

GALLIMARD: Oh, Butterfly—you want me to bring my work home?

SONG: I want to know what you know. To be impressed by my man. It's not the particulars so much as the fact that you're making decisions which change the shape of the world.

GALLIMARD: Not the world. At best, a small corner.
[TOULON *enters, and sits at a desk upstage.*]

SCENE III

French embassy. Beijing. 1961.

GALLIMARD *moves downstage, to* TOULON'S *desk.* SONG *remains upstage, watching.*

TOULON: And a more troublesome corner is hard to imagine.

GALLIMARD: So, the Americans plan to begin bombing?

TOULON: This is very secret, Gallimard: yes. The Americans don't have an embassy here. They're asking us to be their eyes and ears. Say Jack Kennedy signed an order to bomb North Vietnam, Laos. How would the Chinese react?

GALLIMARD: I think the Chinese will squawk—

TOULON: Uh-huh.

GALLIMARD: —but, in their hearts, they don't even like Ho Chi Minh.
[*Pause.*]

TOULON: What a bunch of jerks. Vietnam was *our* colony. Not only didn't the Americans help us fight to keep them, but now, seven years later, they've come back to grab the territory for themselves. It's very irritating.

GALLIMARD: With all due respect, sir, why should the Americans have won our war for us back in '54 if we didn't have the will to win it ourselves?

TOULON: You're kidding, aren't you?
[*Pause.*]

GALLIMARD: The Orientals simply want to be associated with whoever shows the most strength and power. You live with the Chinese, sir. Do you think they like Communism?

TOULON: I live in China. Not with the Chinese.

GALLIMARD: Well, I—

TOULON: *You* live with the Chinese.

GALLIMARD: Excuse me?

TOULON: I can't keep a secret.

GALLIMARD: What are you saying?

TOULON: Only that I'm not immune to gossip. So, you're keeping a native mistress. Don't answer. It's none of my business. [*Pause.*] I'm sure she must be gorgeous.

GALLIMARD: Well . . .

TOULON: I'm impressed. You have the stamina to go out into the streets and hunt one down. Some of us have to be content with the wives of the expatriate community.

GALLIMARD: I do feel . . . fortunate.

TOULON: So, Gallimard, you've got the inside knowledge—what *do* the Chinese think?

GALLIMARD: Deep down, they miss the old days. You know, cappuccinos, men in tuxedos—

TOULON: So what do we tell the Americans about Vietnam?

GALLIMARD: Tell them there's a natural affinity between the West and the Orient.

TOULON: And that you speak from experience?

GALLIMARD: The Orientals are people, too. They want the good things we can give them. If the Americans demonstrate the will to win, the Vietnamese will welcome them into a mutually beneficial union.

TOULON: I don't see how the Vietnamese can stand up to American firepower.

GALLIMARD: Orientals will always submit to a greater force.

TOULON: I'll note your opinions in my report. The Americans always love to hear how "welcome" they'll be. [*He starts to exit.*]

GALLIMARD: Sir?

TOULON: Mmmm?

GALLIMARD: This . . . rumor you've heard.

TOULON: Uh-huh?

GALLIMARD: How . . . widespread do you think it is?

TOULON: It's only widespread within this embassy. Where nobody talks because everybody is guilty. We were worried about you, Gallimard. We thought you were the only one here without a secret. Now you go and find a lotus blossom . . . and top us all. [*He exits.*]

GALLIMARD: [*to us*] Toulon knows! And he approves! I was learning the benefits of being a man. We form our own clubs, sit behind thick doors, smoke— and celebrate the fact that we're still boys. [*He starts to move downstage, towards* SONG.] So, over the—

[*Suddenly* COMRADE CHIN *enters.* GALLIMARD *backs away.*]

GALLIMARD: [*to* SONG] No! Why does she have to come in?

SONG: Rene, be sensible. How can they understand the story without her? Now, don't embarrass yourself.

[GALLIMARD *moves down center.*]

GALLIMARD: [*to us*] Now, you will see why my story is so amusing to so many people. Why they snicker at parties in disbelief. Please—try to understand it from my point of view. We are all prisoners of our time and place. [*He exits.*]

SCENE IV

GALLIMARD *and Butterfly's flat. Beijing. 1961.*

SONG: [*to us*] 1961. The flat Monsieur Gallimard rented for us. An evening after he has gone.

CHIN: Okay, see if you can find out when the Americans plan to start bombing Vietnam. If you can find out what cities, even better.

SONG: I'll do my best, but I don't want to arouse his suspicions.

CHIN: Yeah, sure, of course. So, what else?

SONG: The Americans will increase troops in Vietnam to 170,000 soldiers with 120,000 militia and 11,000 American advisors.

CHIN: [*writing*] Wait, wait. 120,000 militia and—

SONG: —11,000 American—

CHIN: American advisors. [*Beat.*] How do you remember so much?

SONG: I'm an actor.

CHIN: Yeah. [*Beat.*] Is that how come you dress like that?

SONG: Like what, Miss Chin?

CHIN: Like that dress! You're wearing a dress. And every time I come here, you're wearing a dress. Is that because you're an actor? Or what?

SONG: It's a . . . disguise, Miss Chin.

CHIN: Actors, I think they're all weirdos. My mother tells me actors are like gamblers or prostitutes or—

SONG: It helps me in my assignment.

> [*Pause.*]

CHIN: You're not gathering information in any way that violates Communist Party principles, are you?

SONG: Why would I do that?

CHIN: Just checking. Remember: when working for the Great Proletarian State, you represent our Chairman Mao in every position you take.

SONG: I'll try to imagine the Chairman taking my positions.

CHIN: We all think of him this way. Good-bye, comrade. [*She starts to exit.*] Comrade?

SONG: Yes?

CHIN: Don't forget: there is no homosexuality in China!

SONG: Yes, I've heard.

CHIN: Just checking. [*She exits.*]

SONG: [*to us*] What passes for a woman in modern China.

> [GALLIMARD *sticks his head out from the wings.*]

GALLIMARD: Is she gone?

SONG: Yes, Rene. Please continue in your own fashion.

SCENE V

Beijing. 1961–63.

> GALLIMARD *moves to the couch where* SONG *still sits. He lies down in her lap, and she strokes his forehead.*

GALLIMARD: [*to us*] And so, over the years 1961, '62, '63, we settled into our routine, Butterfly and I. She would always have prepared a light snack and then, ever so delicately, and only if I agreed, she would start to pleasure me. With her hands, her mouth . . . too many ways to explain, and too sad, given my present situation. But mostly we would talk. About my life. Perhaps there is nothing more rare than to find a woman who passionately listens.

> [SONG *remains upstage, listening, as* HELGA *enters and plays a scene downstage with* GALLIMARD.]

HELGA: Rene, I visited Dr. Bolleart this morning.

GALLIMARD: Why? Are you ill?

HELGA: No, no. You see, I wanted to ask him . . . that question we've been discussing.

GALLIMARD: And I told you, it's only a matter of time. Why did you bring a doctor into this? We just have to keep trying—like a crapshoot, actually.

HELGA: I went, I'm sorry. But listen: he says there's nothing wrong with me.

GALLIMARD: You see? Now, will you stop—?

HELGA: Rene, he says he'd like you to go in and take some tests.

GALLIMARD: Why? So he can find there's nothing wrong with both of us?

HELGA: Rene, I don't ask for much. One trip! One visit! And then, whatever you want to do about it—you decide.

GALLIMARD: You're assuming he'll find something defective!

HELGA: No! Of course not! Whatever he finds—if he finds nothing, we decide what to do about nothing! But go!

GALLIMARD: If he finds nothing, we keep trying. Just like we do now.

HELGA: But at least we'll know! [*Pause.*] I'm sorry. [*She starts to exit.*]

GALLIMARD: Do you really want me to see Dr. Bolleart?

HELGA: Only if you want a child, Rene. We have to face the fact that time is running out. Only if you want a child. [*She exits.*]

GALLIMARD: [*to* SONG] I'm a modern man, Butterfly. And yet, I don't want to go. It's the same old voodoo. I feel like God himself is laughing at me if I can't produce a child.

SONG: You men of the West—you're obsessed by your odd desire for equality. Your wife can't give you a child, and *you're* going to the doctor?

GALLIMARD: Well, you see, she's already gone.

SONG: And because this incompetent can't find the defect, you now have to subject yourself to him? It's unnatural.

GALLIMARD: Well, what is the "natural" solution?

SONG: In Imperial China, when a man found that one wife was inadequate, he turned to another—to give him his son.

GALLIMARD: What do you—? I can't . . . marry you, yet.

SONG: Please. I'm not asking you to be my husband. But I am already your wife.

GALLIMARD: Do you want to . . . have my child?

SONG: I thought you'd never ask.

GALLIMARD: But, your career . . . your—

SONG: Phooey on my career! That's your Western mind, twisting itself into strange shapes again. Of course I love my career. But what would I love most of all? To feel something inside me—day and night—something I know is yours. [*Pause.*] Promise me . . . you won't go to this doctor. Who is this Western quack to set himself as judge over the man I love? I know who is a man, and who is not. [*She exits.*]

GALLIMARD: [*to us*] Dr. Bolleart? Of course I didn't go. What man would?

SCENE VI

Beijing. 1963.
Party noises over the house speakers. RENEE *enters, wearing a revealing gown.*

GALLIMARD: 1963. A party at the Austrian embassy. None of us could remember the Austrian ambassador's name, which seemed somehow appropriate. [*To* RENEE.] So, I tell the Americans, Diem must go. The U.S. wants to be respected by the Vietnamese, and yet they're propping up this nobody seminarian as her president. A man whose claim to fame is his sister-in-law imposing fanatic "moral order" campaigns? Oriental women—when they're good, they're very good, but when they're bad, they're Christians.

RENEE: Yeah.

GALLIMARD: And what do you do?

RENEE: I'm a student. My father exports a lot of useless stuff to the Third World.

GALLIMARD: How useless?

RENEE: You know. Squirt guns, confectioner's sugar, Hula Hoops . . .

GALLIMARD: I'm sure they appreciate the sugar.

RENEE: I'm here for two years to study Chinese.

GALLIMARD: Two years?

RENEE: That's what everybody says.

GALLIMARD: When did you arrive?

RENEE: Three weeks ago.

GALLIMARD: And?

RENEE: I like it. It's primitive, but . . . well, this is the place to learn Chinese, so here I am.

GALLIMARD: Why Chinese?

RENEE: I think it'll be important someday.

GALLIMARD: You do?

RENEE: Don't ask me when, but . . . that's what I think.

GALLIMARD: Well, I agree with you. One hundred percent. That's very farsighted.

RENEE: Yeah. Well, of course, my father thinks I'm a complete weirdo.

GALLIMARD: He'll thank you someday.

RENEE: Like when the Chinese start buying Hula Hoops?

GALLIMARD: There's a billion bellies out there.

RENEE: And if they end up taking over the world—well, then I'll be lucky to know Chinese, too, right?

     [Pause.]

GALLIMARD: At this point, I don't see how the Chinese can possibly take—

RENEE: You know what I *don't* like about China?

GALLIMARD: Excuse me? No—what?

RENEE: Nothing to do at night.

GALLIMARD: You come to parties at embassies like everyone else.

RENEE: Yeah, but they get out at ten. And then what?

GALLIMARD: I'm afraid the Chinese idea of a dance hall is a dirt floor and a man with a flute.

RENEE: Are you married?

GALLIMARD: Yes. Why?

RENEE: You wanna . . . fool around?

     [Pause.]

GALLIMARD: Sure.

RENEE: I'll wait for you outside. What's your name?

GALLIMARD: Gallimard. Rene.

RENEE: Weird. I'm Renee, too. [*She exits.*]

GALLIMARD: [*to us*] And so, I embarked on my first extra-extramarital affair. Renee was picture perfect. With a body like those girls in the magazines. If I put a tissue paper over my eyes, I wouldn't have been able to tell the difference. And it was exciting to be with someone who wasn't afraid to be seen completely naked. But is it possible for a woman to be *too* uninhibited, *too* willing, so as to seem almost too . . . masculine?

     [*Chuck Berry blares from the house speakers, then comes down in volume as* RENEE *enters, toweling her hair.*]

RENEE: You have a nice weenie.

GALLIMARD: What?

RENEE: Penis. You have a nice penis.

GALLIMARD: Oh. Well, thank you. That's very . . .

RENEE: What—can't take a compliment?

GALLIMARD: No, it's very . . . reassuring.

RENEE: But most girls don't come out and say it, huh?

GALLIMARD: And also . . . what did you call it?

RENEE: Oh. Most girls don't call it a "weenie," huh?

GALLIMARD: It sounds very—

RENEE: Small, I know.

GALLIMARD: I was going to say, "young."

RENEE: Yeah. Young, small, same thing. Most guys are pretty, uh, sensitive about that. Like, you know, I had a boyfriend back home in Denmark. I got mad at him once and called him a little weeniehead. He got so mad! He said at least I should call him a great big weeniehead.

GALLIMARD: I suppose I just say "penis."

RENEE: Yeah. That's pretty clinical. There's "cock" but that sounds like a chicken. And "prick" is painful, and "dick" is like you're talking about someone who's not in the room.

GALLIMARD: Yes. It's a . . . bigger problem than I imagined.

RENEE: I—I think maybe it's because I really don't know what to do with them—that's why I call them "weenies."

GALLIMARD: Well, you did quite well with . . . mine.

RENEE: Thanks, but I mean, really *do* with them. Like, okay, have you ever looked at one? I mean, really?

GALLIMARD: No, I suppose when it's part of you, you sort of take it for granted.

RENEE: I guess. But, like, it just hangs there. This little . . . flap of flesh. And there's so much fuss that we make about it. Like, I think the reason we fight wars is because we wear clothes. Because no one knows—between the men, I mean—who has the bigger . . . weenie. So, if I'm a guy with a small one, I'm going to build a really big building or take over a really big piece of land or write a really long book so the other men don't know, right? But, see, it never really works, that's the problem. I mean, you conquer the country, or whatever, but you're still wearing clothes, so there's no way to prove absolutely whose is bigger or smaller. And that's what we call a civilized society. The whole world run by a bunch of men with pricks the size of pins. [*She exits.*]

GALLIMARD: [*to us*] This was simply not acceptable.

[*A high-pitched chime rings through the air.* SONG, *dressed as Butterfly, appears in the upstage special. She is obviously distressed. Her body swoons as she attempts to clip the stems of flowers she's arranging in a vase.*]

GALLIMARD: But I kept up our affair, wildly, for several months. Why? I believe because of Butterfly. She knew the secret I was trying to hide. But, unlike a Western woman, she didn't confront me, threaten, even pout. I remembered the words of Puccini's *Butterfly:*

SONG: "Noi siamo gente avvezza/ alle piccole cose/ umili e silenziose."

GALLIMARD: "I come from a people/ Who are accustomed to little/ Humble and silent." I saw Pinkerton and Butterfly, and what she would say if he were unfaithful . . . nothing. She would cry, alone, into those wildly soft sleeves, once full of possessions, now empty to collect her tears. It was her tears and her silence that excited me, every time I visited Renee.

TOULON: [*offstage*] Gallimard!

[TOULON *enters.* GALLIMARD *turns towards him. During the next section,* SONG, *up center, begins to dance with the flowers. It is a drunken dance, where she breaks small pieces off the stems.*]

TOULON: They're killing him.

GALLIMARD: Who? I'm sorry? What?

TOULON: Bother you to come over at this late hour?

GALLIMARD: No . . . of course not.

TOULON: Not after you hear my secret. Champagne?

GALLIMARD: Um . . . thank you.

TOULON: You're surprised. There's something that you've wanted, Gallimard. No, not a promotion. Next time. Something in the world. You're not aware of this, but there's an informal gossip circle among intelligence agents. And some of ours heard from some of the Americans—

GALLIMARD: Yes?

TOULON: That the U.S. will allow the Vietnamese generals to stage a coup . . . and assassinate President Diem.

[*The chime rings again.* TOULON *freezes.* GALLIMARD *turns upstage and looks at Butterfly, who slowly and deliberately clips a flower off its stem.* GALLIMARD *turns back towards* TOULON.]

GALLIMARD: I think . . . that's a very wise move!

[TOULON *unfreezes.*]

TOULON: It's what you've been advocating. A toast?

GALLIMARD: Sure. I consider this a vindication.

TOULON: Not exactly. "To the test. Let's hope you pass."

[*They drink. The chime rings again.* TOULON *freezes.* GALLIMARD *turns upstage, and* SONG *clips another flower.*]

GALLIMARD: [*to* TOULON] The test?

TOULON: [*unfreezing*] It's a test of everything you've been saying. I personally think the generals probably will stop the Communists. And you'll be a hero. But if anything goes wrong, then your opinions won't be worth a pig's ear. I'm sure that won't happen. But sometimes it's easier when they don't listen to you.

GALLIMARD: They're your opinions, too, aren't they?

TOULON: Personally, yes.

GALLIMARD: So we agree.

TOULON: But my opinions aren't on that report. Yours are. Cheers.

[TOULON *turns away from* GALLIMARD *and raises his glass. At that instant* SONG *picks up the vase and hurls it to the ground. It shatters.* SONG *sinks down amidst the shards of the vase, in a calm, childlike trance. She sings softly, as if reciting a child's nursery rhyme.*]

SONG: [*repeat as necessary*] "The whole world over, the white man travels, setting anchor, wherever he likes. Life's not worth living, unless he finds, the finest maidens, of every land . . ."

[GALLIMARD *turns downstage towards us.* SONG *continues singing.*]

GALLIMARD: I shook as I left his house. That coward! That worm! To put the burden for his decisions on my shoulders!

    I started for Renee's. But no, that was all I needed. A schoolgirl who would question the role of the penis in modern society. What I wanted was revenge. A vessel to contain my humiliation. Though I hadn't seen her in several weeks, I headed for Butterfly's.

[GALLIMARD *enters* SONG's *apartment.*]

SONG: Oh! Rene . . . I was dreaming!

GALLIMARD: You've been drinking?

SONG: If I can't sleep, then, yes, I drink. But then, it gives me these dreams which—Rene, it's been almost three weeks since you visited me last.

GALLIMARD: I know. There's been a lot going on in the world.

SONG: Fortunately I am drunk. So I can speak freely. It's not the world, it's you and me. And an old problem. Even the softest skin becomes like leather to a man who's touched it too often. I confess I don't know how to stop it. I don't know how to become another woman.

GALLIMARD: I have a request.

SONG: Is this a solution? Or are you ready to give up the flat?

GALLIMARD: It may be a solution. But I'm sure you won't like it.

SONG: Oh well, that's very important. "Like it"? Do you think I "like" lying here alone, waiting, always waiting for your return? Please—don't worry about what I may not "like."

GALLIMARD: I want to see you . . . naked.

[*Silence.*]

SONG: I thought you understood my modesty. So you want me to—what—strip? Like a big cowboy girl? Shiny pasties on my breasts? Shall I fling my kimono over my head and yell "ya-hoo" in the process? I thought you respected my shame!

GALLIMARD: I believe you gave me your shame many years ago.

SONG: Yes—and it is just like a white devil to use it against me. I can't believe it. I thought myself so repulsed by the passive Oriental and the cruel white man. Now I see—we are always most revolted by the things hidden within us.

GALLIMARD: I just mean—

SONG: Yes?

GALLIMARD: —that it will remove the only barrier left between us.

SONG: No, Rene. Don't couch your request in sweet words. Be yourself—a cad—and know that my love is enough, that I submit—submit to the worst you can give me. [*Pause.*] Well, come. Strip me. Whatever happens, know that you have willed it. Our love, in your hands. I'm helpless before my man.

[GALLIMARD *starts to cross the room.*]

GALLIMARD: Did I not undress her because I knew, somewhere deep down, what I would find? Perhaps. Happiness is so rare that our mind can turn somersaults to protect it.

    At the time, I only knew that I was seeing Pinkerton stalking towards his Butterfly, ready to reward her love with his lecherous hands. The image sickened me, pulled me to my knees, so I was crawling towards her like a worm. By the time I reached her, Pinkerton . . . had vanished from my heart. To be replaced by something new, something unnatural, that flew in the face of all I'd learned in the world—something very close to love.

[*He grabs her around the waist; she strokes his hair.*]

GALLIMARD: Butterfly, forgive me.

SONG: Rene . . .

GALLIMARD: For everything. From the start.

SONG: I'm . . .

GALLIMARD: I want to—

SONG: I'm pregnant. [*Beat.*] I'm pregnant. [*Beat.*] I'm pregnant. [*Beat.*]

GALLIMARD: I want to marry you!

SCENE VII

GALLIMARD *and Butterfly's flat. Beijing. 1963.*

> *Downstage,* SONG *paces as* COMRADE CHIN *reads from her notepad. Upstage,* GALLIMARD *is still kneeling. He remains on his knees throughout the scene, watching it.*

SONG: I need a baby.

CHIN: [*from pad*] He's been spotted going to a dorm.

SONG: I need a baby.

CHIN: At the Foreign Language Institute.

SONG: I need a baby.

CHIN: The room of a Danish girl . . . What do you mean, you need a baby?!

SONG: Tell Comrade Kang—last night, the entire mission, it could've ended.

CHIN: What do you mean?

SONG: Tell Kang—he told me to strip.

CHIN: *Strip?!*

SONG: Write!

CHIN: I tell you, I don't understand nothing about this case anymore. Nothing.

SONG: He told me to strip, and I took a chance. Oh, we Chinese, we know how to gamble.

CHIN: [*writing*] ". . . told him to strip."

SONG: My palms were wet, I had to make a split-second decision.

CHIN: Hey! Can you slow down?!

> [*Pause.*]

SONG: You write faster, I'm the artist here. Suddenly, it hit me—"All he wants is for her to submit. Once a woman submits, a man is always ready to become 'generous.'"

CHIN: You're just gonna end up with rough notes.

SONG: And it worked! He gave in! Now, if I can just present him with a baby. A Chinese baby with blond hair—he'll be mine for life!

CHIN: Kang will never agree! The trading of babies has to be a counterrevolutionary act!

SONG: Sometimes, a counterrevolutionary act is necessary to counter a counterrevolutionary act.

> [*Pause.*]

CHIN: Wait.

SONG: I need one . . . in seven months. Make sure it's a boy.

CHIN: This doesn't sound like something the Chairman would do. Maybe you'd better talk to Comrade Kang yourself.

SONG: Good. I will.

[CHIN *gets up to leave.*]

SONG: Miss Chin? Why, in the Peking Opera, are women's roles played by men?

CHIN: I don't know. Maybe, a reactionary remnant of male—

SONG: No. [*Beat.*] Because only a man knows how a woman is supposed to act.

[CHIN *exits.* SONG *turns upstage, towards* GALLIMARD.]

GALLIMARD: [*calling after* CHIN] Good riddance! [*to* SONG] I could forget all that betrayal in an instant, you know. If you'd just come back and become Butterfly again.

SONG: Fat chance. You're here in prison, rotting in a cell. And I'm on a plane, winging my way back to China. Your president pardoned me of our treason, you know.

GALLIMARD: Yes, I read about that.

SONG: Must make you feel . . . lower than shit.

GALLIMARD: But don't you, even a little bit, wish you were here with me?

SONG: I'm an artist, Rene. You were my greatest . . . acting challenge. [*She laughs.*] It doesn't matter how rotten I answer, does it? You still adore me. That's why I love you, Rene. [*She points to us.*] So—you were telling your audience about the night I announced I was pregnant.

[GALLIMARD *puts his arms around* SONG's *waist. He and* SONG *are in the position they were in at the end of Scene 6.*]

SCENE VIII

Same.

GALLIMARD: I'll divorce my wife. We'll live together here, and then later in France.

SONG: I feel so . . . ashamed.

GALLIMARD: Why?

SONG: I had begun to lose faith. And now, you shame me with your generosity.

GALLIMARD: Generosity? No, I'm proposing for very selfish reasons.

SONG: Your apologies only make me feel more ashamed. My outburst a moment ago!

GALLIMARD: Your outburst? What, about my request?!

SONG: You've been very patient dealing with my . . . eccentricities. A Western man, used to women freer with their bodies—

GALLIMARD: It was sick! Don't make excuses for me.

SONG: I have to. You don't seem willing to make them for yourself.

[*Pause.*]

GALLIMARD: You're crazy.

SONG: I'm happy. Which often looks like crazy.

GALLIMARD: Then make me crazy. Marry me.

[*Pause.*]

SONG: No.

GALLIMARD: What?

SONG: Do I sound silly, a slave, if I say I'm not worthy?

GALLIMARD: Yes. In fact you do. No one has loved me like you.

SONG: Thank you. And no one ever will. I'll see to that.

GALLIMARD: So what is the problem?

SONG: Rene, we Chinese are realists. We understand rice, gold, and guns. You are a diplomat. Your career is skyrocketing. Now, what would happen if you divorced your wife to marry a Communist Chinese actress?

GALLIMARD: That's not being realistic. That's defeating yourself before you begin.

SONG: We must conserve our strength for the battles we can win.

GALLIMARD: That sounds like a fortune cookie!

SONG: Where do you think fortune cookies come from?

GALLIMARD: I don't care.

SONG: You do. So do I. And we should. That is why I say I'm not worthy. I'm worthy to love and even to be loved by you. But I am not worthy to end the career of one of the West's most promising diplomats.

GALLIMARD: It's not that great a career! I made it sound like more than it is!

SONG: Modesty will get you nowhere. Flatter yourself, and you flatter me. I'm flattered to decline your offer. [*She exits.*]

GALLIMARD: [*to us*] Butterfly and I argued all night. And, in the end, I left, knowing I would never be her husband. She went away for several months—to the countryside, like a small animal. Until the night I received her call.

        [*A baby's cry from offstage.* SONG *enters, carrying a child.*]

SONG: He looks like you.

GALLIMARD: Oh! [*Beat; he approaches the baby.*] Well, babies are never very attractive at birth.

SONG: Stop!

GALLIMARD: I'm sure he'll grow more beautiful with age. More like his mother.

SONG: "Chi vide mai/ a bimbo del Giappon . . ."

GALLIMARD: "What baby, I wonder, was ever born in Japan"—or China, for that matter—

SONG: ". . . occhi azzurrini?"

GALLIMARD: "With azure eyes"—they're actually sort of brown, wouldn't you say?

SONG: "E il labbro."

GALLIMARD: "And such lips!" [*He kisses* SONG.] And such lips.

SONG: "E i ricciolini d'oro schietto?"

GALLIMARD: "And such a head of golden"—if slightly patchy—"curls?"

SONG: I'm going to call him "Peepee."

GALLIMARD: Darling, could you repeat that because I'm sure a rickshaw just flew by overhead.

SONG: You heard me.

GALLIMARD: "Song Peepee"? May I suggest Michael, or Stephan, or Adolph?

SONG: You may, but I won't listen.

GALLIMARD: You can't be serious. Can you imagine the time this child will have in school?

SONG: In the West, yes.

GALLIMARD: It's worse than naming him Ping Pong or Long Dong or—

SONG: But he's never going to live in the West, is he?
      [*Pause.*]

GALLIMARD: That wasn't my choice.

SONG: It is mine. And this is my promise to you: I will raise him, he will be our child, but he will never burden you outside of China.

GALLIMARD: Why do you make these promises? I want to be burdened! I want a scandal to cover the papers!

SONG: [*to us*] Prophetic.

GALLIMARD: I'm serious.

SONG: So am I. His name is as I registered it. And he will never live in the West.
      [SONG *exits with the child.*]

GALLIMARD: [*to us*] It is possible that her stubbornness only made me want her more. That drawing back at the moment of my capitulation was the most brilliant strategy she could have chosen. It is possible. But it is also possible that by this point she could have said, could have done . . . anything, and I would have adored her still.

SCENE IX

Beijing. 1966.
   A driving rhythm of Chinese percussion fills the stage.

GALLIMARD: And then, China began to change. Mao became very old, and his cult became very strong. And, like many old men, he entered his second childhood. So he handed over the reins of state to those with minds like his own. And children ruled the Middle Kingdom with complete caprice. The doctrine of the Cultural Revolution implied continuous anarchy. Contact between Chinese and foreigners became impossible. Our flat was confiscated. Her fame and my money now counted against us.
      [*Two dancers in Mao suits and red-starred caps enter, and begin crudely mimicking revolutionary violence, in an agitprop fashion.*]

GALLIMARD: And somehow the American war went wrong, too. Four hundred thousand dollars were being spent for every Viet Cong killed; so General Westmoreland's remark that the Oriental does not value life the way Americans do was oddly accurate. Why weren't the Vietnamese people giving in? Why were they content instead to die and die and die again?
      [TOULON *enters.*]

TOULON: Congratulations, Gallimard.

GALLIMARD: Excuse me, sir?

TOULON: Not a promotion. That was last time. You're going home.

GALLIMARD: What?

TOULON: Don't say I didn't warn you.

GALLIMARD: I'm being transferred . . . because I was wrong about the American war?

TOULON: Of course not. We don't care about the Americans. We care about your mind. The quality of your analysis. In general, everything you've predicted here in the Orient . . . just hasn't happened.

GALLIMARD: I think that's premature.

TOULON: Don't force me to be blunt. Okay, you said China was ready to open to Western trade. The only thing they're trading out there are Western heads. And, yes, you said the Americans would succeed in Indochina. You were kidding, right?

GALLIMARD: I think the end is in sight.

TOULON: Don't be pathetic. And don't take this personally. You were wrong. It's not your fault.

GALLIMARD: But I'm going home.

TOULON: Right. Could I have the number of your mistress? [*Beat.*] Joke! Joke! Eat a croissant for me.

> [TOULON *exits.* SONG, *wearing a Mao suit, is dragged in from the wings as part of the upstage dance. They "beat" her, then lampoon the acrobatics of the Chinese opera, as she is made to kneel onstage.*]

GALLIMARD: [*simultaneously*] I don't care to recall how Butterfly and I said our hurried farewell. Perhaps it was better to end our affair before it killed her.

> [GALLIMARD *exits.* COMRADE CHIN *walks across the stage with a banner reading: "The Actor Renounces His Decadent Profession!" She reaches the kneeling* SONG. *Percussion stops with a thud. Dancers strike poses.*]

SONG: I want to serve the people!

> [*Dancers regain their revolutionary smiles, and begin a dance of victory.*]

CHIN: What?!

SONG: I want to serve the people!!

> [*Dancers unveil a banner: "The Actor Is Rehabilitated!"* SONG *remains kneeling before* CHIN, *as the dancers bounce around them, then exit. Music out.*]

SCENE X

A commune. Hunan Province. 1970.

CHIN: How you planning to do that?

SONG: I've already worked four years in the fields of Hunan, Comrade Chin.

CHIN: So? Farmers work all their lives. Let me see your hands.

> [SONG *holds them out for her inspection.*]

CHIN: Goddamn! Still so smooth! How long does it take to turn you actors into good anythings? Hunh. You've just spent too many years in luxury to be any good to the Revolution.

SONG: I served the Revolution.

CHIN: Served the Revolution? Bullshit! You wore dresses! Don't tell me—I was there. I saw you! You and your white vice-consul! Stuck up there in your flat, living off the People's Treasury! Yeah, I knew what was going on! You two . . . homos! Homos! Homos! [*Pause; she composes herself.*] Ah! Well . . . you will serve the people, all right. But not with the Revolution's money. This time, you use your own money.

SONG: I have no money.

CHIN: Shut up! And you won't stink up China anymore with your pervert stuff. You'll pollute the place where pollution begins—the West.

SONG: What do you mean?

CHIN: Shut up! You're going to France. Without a cent in your pocket. You find your consul's house, you make him pay your expenses—

SONG: No.

CHIN: And you give us weekly reports! Useful information!

SONG: That's crazy. It's been four years.

CHIN: Either that, or back to rehabilitation center!

SONG: Comrade Chin, he's not going to support me! Not in France! He's a white man! I was just his plaything—

CHIN: Oh yuck! Again with the sickening language? Where's my stick?

SONG: You don't understand the mind of a man.

[*Pause.*]

CHIN: Oh no? No, I don't? Then how come I'm married, huh? How come I got a man? Five, six years ago, you always tell me those kind of things, I felt very bad. But not now! Because what does the Chairman say? He tells us *I'm* now the smart one, you're now the nincompoop! *You're* the blockhead, the harebrain, the nitwit! You think you're so smart? You understand "The Mind of a Man"? Good! Then *you* go to France and be a pervert for Chairman Mao!

[CHIN *and* SONG *exit in opposite directions.*]

SCENE XI

Paris. 1968–70.

GALLIMARD *enters.*

GALLIMARD: And what was waiting for me back in Paris? Well, better Chinese food than I'd eaten in China. Friends and relatives. A little accounting, regular schedule, keeping track of traffic violations in the suburbs. . . . And the indignity of students shouting the slogans of Chairman Mao at me—in French.

HELGA: Rene? Rene. [*She enters, soaking wet.*] I've had a . . . a problem. [*She sneezes.*]

GALLIMARD: You're wet.

HELGA: Yes, I . . . coming back from the grocer's. A group of students, waving red flags, they—

[GALLIMARD *fetches a towel.*]

HELGA: —they ran by, I was caught up along with them. Before I knew what was happening—

[GALLIMARD *gives her the towel.*]

HELGA: Thank you. The police started firing water cannons at us. I tried to shout, to tell them I was the wife of a diplomat, but—you know how it is . . . [*Pause.*] Needless to say, I lost the groceries. Rene, what's happening to France?

GALLIMARD: What's—? Well, nothing, really.

HELGA: Nothing?! The storefronts are in flames, there's glass in the streets, buildings are toppling—and I'm wet!

GALLIMARD: Nothing! . . . that I care to think about.

HELGA: And is that why you stay in this room?

GALLIMARD: Yes, in fact.

HELGA: With the incense burning? You know something? I hate incense. It smells so sickly sweet.

GALLIMARD: Well, I hate the French. Who just smell—period!

HELGA: And the Chinese were better?

GALLIMARD: Please—don't start.

HELGA: When we left, this exact same thing, the riots—

GALLIMARD: No, no . . .

HELGA: Students screaming slogans, smashing down doors—

GALLIMARD: Helga—

HELGA: It was all going on in China, too. Don't you remember?!

GALLIMARD: Helga! Please! [*Pause.*] You have never understood China, have you? You walk in here with these ridiculous ideas, that the West is falling apart, that China was spitting in our faces. You come in, dripping of the streets, and you leave water all over my floor. [*He grabs* HELGA's *towel, begins mopping up the floor.*]

HELGA: But it's the truth!

GALLIMARD: Helga, I want a divorce.

[*Pause.* GALLIMARD *continues, mopping the floor.*]

HELGA: I take it back. China is . . . beautiful. Incense, I like incense.

GALLIMARD: I've had a mistress.

HELGA: So?

GALLIMARD: For eight years.

HELGA: I knew you would. I knew you would the day I married you. And now what? You want to marry her?

GALLIMARD: I can't. She's in China.

HELGA: I see. You want to leave. For someone who's not here, is that right?

GALLIMARD: That's right.

HELGA: You can't live with her, but still you don't want to live with me.

GALLIMARD: That's right.

[*Pause.*]

HELGA: Shit. How terrible that I can figure that out. [*Pause.*] I never thought I'd say it. But, in China, I was happy. I knew, in my own way, I knew that you were not everything you pretended to be. But the pretense—going on your arm to the embassy ball, visiting your office and the guards saying, "Good morning, good morning, Madame Gallimard"—the pretense . . . was very good indeed. [*Pause.*] I hope everyone is mean to you for the rest of your life. [*She exits.*]

GALLIMARD: [*to us*] Prophetic.

[MARC *enters with two drinks.*]

GALLIMARD: [*to* MARC] In China, I was different from all other men.

MARC: Sure. You were white. Here's your drink.

GALLIMARD: I felt . . . touched.

MARC: In the head? Rene, I don't want to hear about the Oriental love goddess. Okay? One night—can we just drink and throw up without a lot of conversation?

GALLIMARD: You still don't believe me, do you?

MARC: Sure I do. She was the most beautiful, et cetera, et cetera, blasé blasé.

[*Pause.*]

GALLIMARD: My life in the West has been such a disappointment.

MARC: Life in the West is like that. You'll get used to it. Look, you're driving me away. I'm leaving. Happy, now? [*He exits, then returns.*] Look, I have a date tomorrow night. You wanna come? I can fix you up with—

GALLIMARD: Of course. I would love to come.

[*Pause.*]

MARC: Uh—on second thought, no. You'd better get ahold of yourself first.

[*He exits;* GALLIMARD *nurses his drink.*]

GALLIMARD: [*to us*] This is the ultimate cruelty, isn't it? That I can talk and talk and to anyone listening, it's only air—too rich a diet to be swallowed by a mundane world. Why can't anyone understand? That in China, I once loved, and was loved by, very simply, the Perfect Woman.

[SONG *enters, dressed as Butterfly in wedding dress.*]

GALLIMARD: [*to* SONG] Not again. My imagination is hell. Am I asleep this time? Or did I drink too much?

SONG: Rene?

GALLIMARD: God, it's too painful! That you speak?

SONG: What are you talking about? Rene—touch me.

GALLIMARD: Why?

SONG: I'm real. Take my hand.

GALLIMARD: Why? So you can disappear again and leave me clutching at the air? For the entertainment of my neighbors who—?

[SONG *touches* GALLIMARD.]

SONG: Rene?

[GALLIMARD *takes* SONG's *hand. Silence.*]

GALLIMARD: Butterfly? I never doubted you'd return.

SONG: You hadn't . . . forgotten—?

GALLIMARD: Yes, actually, I've forgotten everything. My mind, you see—there wasn't enough room in this hard head—not for the world *and* for you. No, there was only room for one. [*Beat.*] Come, look. See? Your bed has been waiting, with the Klimt poster you like, and—see? The xiang lu [incense burner] you gave me?

SONG: I . . . I don't know what to say.

GALLIMARD: There's nothing to say. Not at the end of a long trip. Can I make you some tea?

SONG: But where's your wife?

GALLIMARD: She's by my side. She's by my side at last.

[GALLIMARD *reaches to embrace* SONG. *Song sidesteps, dodging him.*]

GALLIMARD: Why?!

SONG: [*to us*] So I did return to Rene in Paris. Where I found—

GALLIMARD: Why do you run away? Can't we show them how we embraced that evening?

SONG: Please. I'm talking.

GALLIMARD: You have to do what I say! I'm conjuring you up in *my* mind!

SONG: Rene, I've never done what you've said. Why should it be any different in your mind? Now split—the story moves on, and I must change.

GALLIMARD: I welcomed you into my home! I didn't have to, you know! I could've left you penniless on the streets of Paris! But I took you in!

SONG: Thank you.

GALLIMARD: So . . . please . . . don't change.

SONG: You know I have to. You know I will. And anyway, what difference does it make? No matter what your eyes tell you, you can't ignore the truth. You already know too much.

[GALLIMARD *exits.* SONG *turns to us.*]

SONG: The change I'm going to make requires about five minutes. So I thought you might want to take this opportunity to stretch your legs, enjoy a drink, or listen to the musicians. I'll be here, when you return, right where you left me.

[SONG *goes to a mirror in front of which is a wash basin of water. She starts to remove her makeup as stagelights go to half and houselights come up.*]

ACT THREE

SCENE I

A courthouse in Paris. 1986.

As he promised, SONG *has completed the bulk of his transformation, onstage by the time the houselights go down and the stagelights come up full. He removes his wig and kimono, leaving them on the floor. Underneath, he wears a well-cut suit.*

SONG: So I'd done my job better than I had a right to expect. Well, give him some credit, too. He's right—I was in a fix when I arrived in Paris. I walked from the airport into town, then I located, by blind groping, the Chinatown district. Let me make one thing clear: whatever else may be said about the Chinese, they are stingy! I slept in doorways three days until I could find a tailor who would make me this kimono on credit. As it turns out, maybe I didn't even need it. Maybe he would've been happy to see me in a simple shift and mascara. But . . . better safe than sorry.

That was 1970, when I arrived in Paris. For the next fifteen years, yes, I lived a very comfy life. Some relief, believe me, after four years on a fucking commune in Nowheresville, China. Rene supported the boy and me, and I did some demonstrations around the country as part of my "cultural exchange" cover. And then there was the spying.

[SONG *moves upstage, to a chair.* TOULON *enters as a judge, wearing the appropriate wig and robes. He sits near* SONG. *It's 1986, and* SONG *is testifying in a courtroom.*]

SONG: Not much at first. Rene had lost all his high-level contacts. Comrade Chin wasn't very interested in parking-ticket statistics. But finally, at my urging, Rene got a job as a courier, handling sensitive documents. He'd photograph them for me, and I'd pass them on to the Chinese embassy.

JUDGE: Did he understand the extent of his activity?

SONG: He didn't ask. He knew that I needed those documents, and that was enough.

JUDGE: But he must've known he was passing classified information.

SONG: I can't say.

JUDGE: He never asked what you were going to do with them?

SONG: Nope.
> [*Pause.*]

JUDGE: There is one thing that the court—indeed, that all of France—would like to know.

SONG: Fire away.

JUDGE: Did Monsieur Gallimard know you were a man?

SONG: Well, he never saw me completely naked. Ever.

JUDGE: But surely, he must've . . . how can I put this?

SONG: Put it however you like. I'm not shy. He must've felt around?

JUDGE: Mmmmm.

SONG: Not really. I did all the work. He just laid back. Of course we did enjoy more . . . complete union, and I suppose he *might* have wondered why I was always on my stomach, but. . . . But what you're thinking is. "Of course a wrist must've brushed . . . a hand hit . . . over twenty years!" Yeah. Well, Your Honor, it was my job to make him think I was a woman. And chew on this: It wasn't all that hard. See, my mother was a prostitute along the Bundt before the Revolution. And, uh, I think it's fair to say she learned a few things about Western men. So I borrowed her knowledge. In service to my country.

JUDGE: Would you care to enlighten the court with this secret knowledge? I'm sure we're all very curious.

SONG: I'm sure you are. [*Pause.*] Okay, Rule One is: Men always believe what they want to hear. So a girl can tell the most obnoxious lies and the guys will believe them every time—"This is my first time"—"That's the biggest I've ever seen"—or *both*, which, if you really think about it, is not possible in a single lifetime. You've maybe heard those phrases a few times in your own life, yes, Your Honor?

JUDGE: It's not my life, Monsieur Song, which is on trial today.

SONG: Okay, okay, just trying to lighten up the proceedings. Tough room.

JUDGE: Go on.

SONG: Rule Two: As soon as a Western man comes into contact with the East— he's already confused. The West has sort of an international rape mentality towards the East. Do you know rape mentality?

JUDGE: Give us your definition, please.

SONG: Basically, "Her mouth says no, but her eyes say yes."
> The West thinks of itself as masculine—big guns, big industry, big money—so the East is feminine—weak, delicate, poor . . . but good at art, and full of inscrutable wisdom—the feminine mystique.
> Her mouth says no, but her eyes say yes. The West believes the East, deep down, *wants* to be dominated—because a woman can't think for herself.

JUDGE: What does this have to do with my question?

SONG: You expect Oriental countries to submit to your guns, and you expect Oriental women to be submissive to your men. That's why you say they make the best wives.

JUDGE: But why would that make it possible for you to fool Monsieur Gallimard? Please—get to the point.

SONG: One, because when he finally met his fantasy woman, he wanted more than anything to believe that she was, in fact, a woman. And second, I am an Oriental. And being an Oriental, I could never be completely a man.
         [*Pause.*]
JUDGE: Your armchair political theory is tenuous, Monsieur Song.
SONG: You think so? That's why you'll lose in all your dealings with the East.
JUDGE: Just answer my question: Did he know you were a man?
         [*Pause.*]
SONG: You know, Your Honor, I never asked.

SCENE II

Same.

   Music from the "Death Scene" from Butterfly blares over the house speakers. It is the loudest thing we've heard in this play.

   GALLIMARD *enters, crawling towards* SONG's *wig and kimono.*

GALLIMARD: Butterfly? Butterfly?
         [SONG *remains a man, in the witness box, delivering a testimony we do not hear.*]
GALLIMARD: [*to us*] In my moment of greatest shame, here, in this courtroom—with that . . . person up there, telling the world. . . . What strikes me especially is how shallow he is, how glib and obsequious . . . completely . . . without substance! The type that prowls around discos with a gold medallion stinking of garlic. So little like my Butterfly.
         Yet even in this moment my mind remains agile, flip-flopping like a man on a trampoline. Even now, my picture dissolves, and I see that . . . witness . . . talking to me.
         [SONG *suddenly stands straight up in his witness box, and looks at* GALLIMARD.]
SONG: Yes. You. White man.
         [SONG *steps out of the witness box, and moves downstage towards* GALLIMARD. *Light change.*]
GALLIMARD: [*to* SONG] Who? Me?
SONG: Do you see any other white men?
GALLIMARD: Yes. There're white men all around. This is a French courtroom.
SONG: So you are an adventurous imperialist. Tell me, why did it take you so long? To come back to this place?
GALLIMARD: What place?
SONG: This theatre in China. Where we met many years ago.
GALLIMARD: [*to us*] And once again, against my will, I am transported.
         [*Chinese opera music comes up on the speakers.* SONG *begins to do opera moves, as he did the night they met.*]
SONG: Do you remember? The night you gave your heart?
GALLIMARD: It was a long time ago.
SONG: Not long enough. A night that turned your world upside down.
GALLIMARD: Perhaps.
SONG: Oh, be honest with me. What's another bit of flattery when you've already

given me twenty years' worth? It's a wonder my head hasn't swollen to the size of China.

GALLIMARD: Who's to say it hasn't?

SONG: Who's to say? And what's the shame? In pride? You think I could've pulled this off if I wasn't already full of pride when we met? No, not just pride. Arrogance. It takes arrogance, really—to believe you can will, with your eyes and your lips, the destiny of another. [*He dances.*] C'mon. Admit it. You still want me. Even in slacks and a button-down collar.

GALLIMARD: I don't see what the point of—

SONG: You don't? Well, maybe, Rene, just maybe—I want you.

GALLIMARD: You do?

SONG: Then again, maybe I'm just playing with you. How can you tell? [*Reprising his feminine character, he sidles up to* GALLIMARD.] "How I wish there were even a small cafe to sit in. With men in tuxedos, and cappuccinos, and bad expatriate jazz." Now you want to kiss me, don't you?

GALLIMARD: [*pulling away*] What makes you—?

SONG: —so sure? I take the words from your mouth. Then I wait for you to come and retrieve them. [*He reclines on the floor.*]

GALLIMARD: Why?! Why do you treat me so cruelly?

SONG: Perhaps I *was* treating you cruelly. But now—I'm being nice. Come here, my little one.

GALLIMARD: I'm not your little one!

SONG: My mistake. It's I who am *your* little one, right?

GALLIMARD: Yes, I—

SONG: So come get your little one. If you like. I may even let you strip me.

GALLIMARD: I mean, you were! Before . . . but not like this!

SONG: I was? Then perhaps I still am. If you look hard enough. [*He starts to remove his clothes.*]

GALLIMARD: What—what are you doing?

SONG: Helping you to see through my act.

GALLIMARD: Stop that! I don't want to! I don't—

SONG: Oh, but you asked me to strip, remember?

GALLIMARD: What? That was years ago! And I took it back!

SONG: No. You postponed it. Postponed the inevitable. Today, the inevitable has come calling.

[*From the speakers, cacophony:* Butterfly *mixed in with Chinese gongs.*]

GALLIMARD: No! Stop! I don't want to see!

SONG: Then look away.

GALLIMARD: You're only in my mind! All this is in my mind! I order you! To stop!

SONG: To what? To strip? That's just what I'm—

GALLIMARD: No! Stop! I want you—!

SONG: You want me?

GALLIMARD: To stop!

SONG: You know something, Rene? Your mouth says no, but your eyes say yes. Turn them away. I dare you.

GALLIMARD: I don't have to! Every night, you say you're going to strip, but then I beg you and you stop!

SONG: I guess tonight is different.

GALLIMARD: Why? Why should that be?

SONG: Maybe I've become frustrated. Maybe I'm saying "Look at me, you fool!" Or maybe I'm just feeling . . . sexy. [*He is down to his briefs.*]

GALLIMARD: Please. This is unnecessary. I know what you are.

SONG: Do you? What am I?

GALLIMARD: A—a man.

SONG: You don't really believe that.

GALLIMARD: Yes, I do! I knew all the time somewhere that my happiness was temporary, my love a deception. But my mind kept the knowledge at bay. To make the wait bearable.

SONG: Monsieur Gallimard—the wait is over.

> [SONG *drops his briefs. He is naked. Sound cue out. Slowly, we and* SONG *come to the realization that what we had thought to be* GALLIMARD'S *sobbing is actually his laughter.*]

GALLIMARD: Oh god! What an idiot! Of course!

SONG: Rene—what?

GALLIMARD: Look at you! You're a man! [*He bursts into laughter again.*]

SONG: I fail to see what's so funny!

GALLIMARD: "You fail to see—!" I mean, you never did have much of a sense of humor, did you? I just think it's ridiculously funny that I've wasted so much time on just a man!

SONG: Wait. I'm not "just a man."

GALLIMARD: No? Isn't that what you've been trying to convince me of?

SONG: Yes, but what I mean—

GALLIMARD: And now, I finally believe you, and you tell me it's not true? I think you must have some kind of identity problem.

SONG: Will you listen to me?

GALLIMARD: Why?! I've been listening to you for twenty years. Don't I deserve a vacation?

SONG: I'm not just any man!

GALLIMARD: Then, what exactly are you?

SONG: Rene, how can you ask—? Okay, what about this?

> [*He picks up Butterfly's robes, starts to dance around. No music.*]

GALLIMARD: Yes, that's very nice. I have to admit.

> [SONG *holds out his arm to* GALLIMARD.]

SONG: It's the same skin you've worshiped for years. Touch it.

GALLIMARD: Yes, it does feel the same.

SONG: Now—close your eyes.

> [SONG *covers* GALLIMARD'S *eyes with one hand. With the other,* SONG *draws* GALLIMARD'S *hand up to his face.* GALLIMARD, *like a blind man, lets his hands run over* SONG'S *face.*]

GALLIMARD: This skin, I remember. The curve of her face, the softness of her cheek, her hair against the back of my hand . . .

SONG: I'm your Butterfly. Under the robes, beneath everything, it was always me. Now, open your eyes and admit it—you adore me. [*He removes his hand from* GALLIMARD'S *eyes.*]

GALLIMARD: You, who knew every inch of my desires—how could you, of all people, have made such a mistake?

SONG: What?

GALLIMARD: You showed me your true self. When all I loved was the lie. A perfect lie, which you let fall to the ground—and now, it's old and soiled.

SONG: So—you never really loved me? Only when I was playing a part?

GALLIMARD: I'm a man who loved a woman created by a man. Everything else— simply falls short.

[*Pause.*]

SONG: What am I supposed to do now?

GALLIMARD: You were a fine spy, Monsieur Song, with an even finer accomplice. But now I believe you should go. Get out of my life!

SONG: Go where? Rene, you can't live without me. Not after twenty years.

GALLIMARD: I certainly can't live with you—not after twenty years of betrayal.

SONG: Don't be so stubborn! Where will you go?

GALLIMARD: I have a date . . . with my Butterfly.

SONG: So, throw away your pride. And come . . .

GALLIMARD: Get away from me! Tonight, I've finally learned to tell fantasy from reality. And, knowing the difference, I choose fantasy.

SONG: *I'm* your fantasy!

GALLIMARD: You? You're as real as hamburger. Now get out! I have a date with my Butterfly and I don't want your body polluting the room! [*He tosses* SONG*'s suit at him.*] Look at these—you dress like a pimp.

SONG: Hey! These are Armani slacks and—! [*He puts on his briefs and slacks.*] Let's just say . . . I'm disappointed in you, Rene. In the crush of your adoration, I thought you'd become something more. More like . . . a woman.

But no. Men. You're like the rest of them. It's all in the way we dress, and make up our faces, and bat our eyelashes. You really have so little imagination!

GALLIMARD: You, Monsieur Song? Accuse me of too little imagination? You, if anyone, should know—I am pure imagination. And in imagination I will remain. Now get out!

[GALLIMARD *bodily removes* SONG *from the stage, taking his kimono.*]

SONG: Rene! I'll never put on those robes again! You'll be sorry!

GALLIMARD: [*to* SONG] I'm already sorry! [*Looking at the kimono in his hands.*] Exactly as sorry . . . as a Butterfly.

SCENE III

M. GALLIMARD*'s prison cell. Paris. Present.*

GALLIMARD: I've played out the events of my life night after night, always searching for a new ending to my story, one where I leave this cell and return forever to my Butterfly's arms.

Tonight I realize my search is over. That I've looked all along in the wrong places. And now, to you, I will prove that my love was not in vain— by returning to the world of fantasy where I first met her.

[*He picks up the kimono; dancers enter.*]

GALLIMARD: There is a vision of the Orient that I have. Of slender women in chong sams and kimonos who die for the love of unworthy foreign devils. Who are born and raised to be the perfect women. Who take whatever punishment we give them, and bounce back, strengthened by love, unconditionally. It is a vision that has become my life.

[*Dancers bring the wash basin to him and help him make up his face.*]

GALLIMARD: In public, I have continued to deny that Song Liling is a man. This brings me headlines, and is a source of great embarrassment to my French colleagues, who can now be sent into a coughing fit by the mere mention of Chinese food. But alone, in my cell, I have long since faced the truth.

And the truth demands a sacrifice. For mistakes made over the course of a lifetime. My mistakes were simple and absolute—the man I loved was a cad, a bounder. He deserved nothing but a kick in the behind, and instead I gave him . . . all my love.

Yes—love. Why not admit it all? That was my undoing, wasn't it? Love warped my judgment, blinded my eyes, rearranged the very lines on my face . . . until I could look in the mirror and see nothing but . . . a woman.

[*Dancers help him put on the Butterfly wig.*]

GALLIMARD: I have a vision. Of the Orient. That, deep within its almond eyes, there are still women. Women willing to sacrifice themselves for the love of a man. Even a man whose love is completely without worth.

[*Dancers assist* GALLIMARD *in donning the kimono. They hand him a knife.*]

GALLIMARD: Death with honor is better than life . . . life with dishonor. [*He sets himself center stage, in a seppuku position.*] The love of a Butterfly can withstand many things—unfaithfulness, loss, even abandonment. But how can it face the one sin that implies all others? The devastating knowledge that, underneath it all, the object of her love was nothing more, nothing less than . . . a man. [*He sets the tip of the knife against his body.*] It is 19—. And I have found her at last. In a prison on the outskirts of Paris. My name is Rene Gallimard—also known as Madame Butterfly.

[GALLIMARD *turns upstage and plunges the knife into his body, as music from the "Love Duet" blares over the speakers. He collapses into the arms of the dancers, who lay him reverently on the floor. The image holds for several beats. Then a tight special up on* SONG, *who stands as a man, staring at the dead* GALLIMARD. *He smokes a cigarette; the smoke filters up through the lights. Two words leave his lips.*]

SONG: Butterfly? Butterfly?

[*Smoke rises as lights fade slowly to black.*]

END OF PLAY

Paula Vogel (1951–)

The Baltimore Waltz (1992)

The Baltimore Waltz is a play that deals with AIDS and impending death through various strategies that create distance from the reality. Although it is Carl, a gay man, who has AIDS, it is his heterosexual sister, Anna, a first-grade teacher, who is said to have contracted ATD, Acquired Toilet Disease, a fictional deadly disease transmitted to unmarried teachers by small children with whom they share toilet facilities. ATD is not sexually transmittable, however, and Anna decides to spend the rest of her doomed existence having sex as often as possible during the European tour she and Carl embark on (at least in her imagination; in actuality the entire play transpires in the Baltimore hospital where Carl is dying).

In the scenes that follow, as Carl and Anna make their way through several European countries, Anna is seen in a series of rather comic couplings with various partners and Carl in mysterious encounters with men carrying stuffed rabbits. Their final destination is Vienna with its vague promise of a cure through drugs and treatment by a strange doctor. The sense of intrigue and mystery is enhanced through references to Carol Reed's film, *The Third Man*, set in Vienna during the Cold War. The Vienna scenes are divided between Anna's encounter with Dr. Todesröcheln ("Deathrattle"), whose treatment is based on drinking one's own urine, and Carl's meeting with Harry Lime, his closest friend in college and now a purveyor of phony drugs. When Carl threatens to expose Harry, Carl is pushed to his death from a Ferris wheel. (There is a strong suggestion that Harry is the source of Carl's AIDS.) Carl's death shatters the fantasy and returns the action to the hospital room in which Carl has just died.

The Baltimore Waltz shows the loving concern of a sister for her brother, even to the extent of projecting a deadly disease onto herself. It also implies much about several aspects of the AIDS crisis. By replacing AIDS with ATD (a disease of heterosexual school teachers acquired from small children), the play suggests that AIDS should be looked at medically rather than through the lens of homophobia, which often blames the victims. The trip to Vienna is related both to the desperate willingness of those who are terminally ill to try any treatment, however farfetched, and the mysteries (even intrigues) in the pharmaceutical and medical professions over drugs and treatments for AIDS.

Relatively simple on the surface, *The Baltimore Waltz* is complex in its layering of reality and fantasy and in the implications of its intertwined references. It won an Obie Award for the Best Play in 1992, as well as an AT&T New Play Award.

Paula Vogel

The Baltimore Waltz

CHARACTERS

ANNA
CARL, *her brother*
THE THIRD MAN/DOCTOR, *who also plays:*
    HARRY LIME
    PUBLIC HEALTH OFFICIAL
    AIRPORT SECURITY GUARD
    GARÇON
    CUSTOMS OFFICIAL
    THE LITTLE DUTCH BOY AT AGE 50
    MUNICH VIRGIN
    RADICAL STUDENT ACTIVIST
    CONCIERGE
    DR. TODESRÖCHELN
    and all other parts

SETTING———The Baltimore Waltz *takes place in a hospital (perhaps in a lounge, corridor, or waiting room) in Baltimore, Maryland.*
NOTES——— *The lighting should be highly stylized, lush, dark, and imaginative, in contrast to the hospital white silence of the last scene. Wherever possible, prior to the last scene, the director is encouraged to score the production with music—every cliché of the European experience as imagined in Hollywood.*

    ANNA *might be dressed in a full slip/negligee and a trench coat.* CARL *is dressed in flannel pajamas and a blazer or jacket. The stuffed rabbit should be in every scene with Carl after Scene VI.* THE THIRD MAN *should wear latex gloves throughout the entire play.*

SCENE I

Three distinct areas on stage: ANNA, *stage right, in her trench coat, clutching the* Berlitz Pocket Guide to Europe; CARL, *stage left, wearing pajamas and blazer;* THE THIRD MAN/DOCTOR *in his lab coat and with stethoscope, is center.*

ANNA: [*reads from her book. Her accents are execrable*] "Help me please." Dutch: "Kunt U mij helpn, alstublieft?" "There's nothing I can do." French:—"I have no memory." [*Reading.*] "Il n'y a rien à faire." "Where are the toilets?" "Wo sind die Toiletten?" I've never been abroad. It's not that I don't want to—but the language terrifies me. I was traumatized by a junior high school French teacher and, after that, it was a lost cause. I think that's the reason I went into elementary education. Words like *bureau, bidet, Bildungsroman*

538

raise a sweat. Oh, I want to go. Carl—he's my brother, you'll meet him shortly—he desperately wants to go. But then, he can speak six languages. He's the head librarian of literature and languages at the San Francisco Public. It's a very important position. The thought of eight-hundred-year-old houses perched on the sides of mountains and rivers whose names you've only seen in the *Sunday Times* crossword puzzles—all of that is exciting. But I'm not going without him. He's read so much. I couldn't possibly go without him. You see, I've never been abroad—unless you count Baltimore, Maryland.

CARL: Good morning, boys and girls. It's Monday morning, and it's time for "Reading Hour with Uncle Carl" once again, here at the North Branch of the San Francisco Public Library. This is going to be a special reading hour. It's my very last reading hour with you. Friday will be my very last day with the San Francisco Public as children's librarian. Why? Do any of you know what a pink slip is? [*Carl holds up a rectangle of pink.*] It means I'm going on a paid leave of absence for two weeks. Shelley Bizio, the branch supervisor, has given me my very own pink slip. I got a pink slip because I wear this— [*He points to a pink triangle on his lapel.*] A pink triangle. Now, I want you all to take the pink construction paper in front of you, and take your scissors, and cut out pink triangles. There's tape at every table, so you can wear them, too! Make some for Mom and Dad, and your brothers and sisters. Very good. Very good, Fabio. Oh, that's a beautiful pink triangle, Tse Heng. Now before we read our last story together, I thought we might have a sing-along. Your parents can join in, if they'd like to. Oh, don't be shy. Let's do "Here we go round the Mulberry Bush." Remember that one? [*He begins to sing. He also demonstrates.*]

"Here we go round the Mulberry Bush, the Mulberry Bush, the Mulberry Bush; Here we go round the Mulberry Bush, so early in the morning."

"This is the way we pick our nose, pick our nose, pick our nose; This is the way we pick our nose, so early in the morning."

Third verse! [*He makes a rude gesture with his middle finger.*]

"This is the way we go on strike, go on strike, go on strike; this is the way we go on strike, so early in the—"

What, Mrs. Bizio? I may leave immediately? I do not have to wait until Friday to collect unemployment? Why, thank you, Mrs. Bizio.

Well, boys and girls, Mrs. Bizio will take over now. Bear with her, she's personality-impaired. I want you to be very good and remember me. I'm leaving for an immediate vacation with my sister on the east coast, and I'll think of you as I travel. Remember to wear those pink triangles. [*To his supervisor.*] I'm going. I'm going. You don't have to be rude. They enjoyed it. We'll take it up with the union. [*Shouting.*] In a language you might understand, up-pay ours-yay!

ANNA: It's the language that terrifies me.

CARL: Lesson Number One: Subject position. I. Je. Ich. Ik. I'm sorry. Je regrette. Es tut mir leid.

ANNA: But we decided to go when the doctor gave us his verdict.

DOCTOR: I'm sorry.

CARL: I'm sorry.

DOCTOR: There's nothing we can do.

ANNA: But what?

CARL How long?

ANNA: Explain it to me. Very slowly. So I can remember. Excuse me, could you tell me again?

DOCTOR: There are exudative and proliferative inflammatory alterations of the endocardium, consisting of necrotic debris, fibrinoid material, and disintegrating fibroblastic cells.

CARL: Oh, sweet Jesus.

DOCTOR: It may be acute or subacute, caused by various bacteria: streptococci, staphylococci, enterococci, gonococci, gram negative bacilli, etc. It may be due to other micro-organisms, of course, but there is a high mortality rate with or without treatment. And there is usually rapid destruction and metastases.

CARL: Anna—

ANNA: I'm right here, darling. Right here.

CARL: Could you explain it very slowly?

DOCTOR: Also known as Löffler's syndrome, i.e., eosinophilia, resulting in fibroblastic thickening, persistent tachycardia, hepatomegaly, splenomegaly, serous effusions into the pleural cavity with edema. It may be Brugia malayi or Wuchereria bancrofti—also known as Weingarten's syndrome. Often seen with effusions, either exudate or transudate.

ANNA: Carl—

CARL: I'm here, darling. Right here.

ANNA: It's the language that terrifies me.

SCENE II

CARL: Medical Straight Talk: Part One.

ANNA: So you're telling me that you really don't know?

DOCTOR: I'm afraid that medical science has only a small foothold in this area. But of course, it would be of great benefit to our knowledge if you would consent to observation here at Johns Hopkins—

CARL: Why? Running out of laboratory rats?!

ANNA: Oh, no. I'm sorry. I can't do that. Can you tell me at least how it was . . . contracted?

DOCTOR: Well—we're not sure, yet. It's only a theory at this stage, but one that seems in great favor at the World Health Organization. We think it comes from the old cultus ornatus—

CARL: Toilet seats?

ANNA: Toilet seats! My God. Mother was right. She always said—

CARL: And never, ever, in any circumstances, in bus stations—

ANNA: Toilet seats? Cut down in the prime of youth by a toilet seat?

DOCTOR: Anna—I may call you Anna?—you teach school, I believe?

ANNA: Yes, first grade. What does that have—

DOCTOR: Ah, yes. We're beginning to see a lot of this in elementary schools. Anna—I may call you Anna? With assurances of complete confidentiality—we need to ask you very specific questions about the body, body fluids, and body functions. As mature adults, as scientists and educators. To speak frankly—when you needed to relieve yourself—where did you make wa-wa?

ANNA: There's a faculty room. But why—how—

DOCTOR: You never, ever used the johnny in your classroom?

ANNA: Well, maybe once or twice. There's no lock, and Robbie Matthews always tries to barge in. Sometimes I just can't get the time to—surely you're not suggesting that—

DOCTOR: You did use the facilities in your classroom? [*The* DOCTOR *makes notes from this.*]

CARL: Is that a crime? When you've got to go, you've got to—

ANNA: I can't believe that my students would transmit something like this—

DOCTOR: You have no idea. Five-year-olds can be deadly. It seems to be an affliction, so far, of single schoolteachers. Schoolteachers with children of their own develop an immunity to ATD . . . Acquired Toilet Disease.

ANNA: I see. Why hasn't anybody heard of this disease?

DOCTOR: Well, first of all, the Centers for Disease Control doesn't wish to inspire an all-out panic in communities. Secondly, we think education on this topic is the responsibility of the NEA, not the government. And if word of this pestilence gets out inappropriately, the PTA is going to be all over the school system demanding mandatory testing of every toilet seat in every lavatory. It's kindling for a political disaster.

ANNA: [*taking the* DOCTOR *aside.*] I want to ask you something confidentially. Something that my brother doesn't need to hear. What's the danger of transmission?

DOCTOR: There's really no danger to anyone in the immediate family. You must use precautions.

ANNA: Because what I want to know is . . . can you transmit this thing by . . . by doing—what exactly do you mean by precautions?

DOCTOR: Well, I guess you should do what your mother always told you. You know, wash your hands before and after going to the bathroom. And never lick paper money or coins in any currency.

ANNA: So there's no danger to anyone by . . . what I mean, Doctor, is that I can't infect anyone by—

DOCTOR: Just use precautions.

ANNA: Because, in whatever time this schoolteacher has left, I intend to fuck my brains out.

DOCTOR: Which means, in whatever time is left, she can fuck her brains out.

SCENE III

CARL *and the* DOCTOR.

CARL: [*agitated*] I'll tell you what. If Sandra Day O'Connor sat on just one infected potty, the media would be clamoring to do articles on ATD. If just one grandchild of George Bush caught this thing during toilet training, that would have been the last we had heard about the space program. Why isn't someone doing something?! I'm sorry. I know you're one of the converted. You're doing . . . well, everything you can. I'd like to ask you something in confidence, something my sister doesn't need to hear. Is there any hope at all?

DOCTOR: Well, I suppose there's . . . always hope.

CARL: Any experimental drugs? Treatments?

DOCTOR: Well, they're trying all sorts of things abroad. Our hands are tied here by NIH and the FDA, you understand. There is a long-shot avenue to explore, nothing, you understand, that I personally endorse, but there is an eighty-year-old urologist overseas who's been working in this field for some time—

CARL: We'll try anything.

DOCTOR: His name is Dr. Todesröcheln. He's somewhat unorthodox, outside the medical community in Vienna. It's gonna cost you. Mind you, this is not an endorsement.

ANNA: You hear the doctor through a long-distance corridor. Your ears are functioning, but the mind is numb. You try to listen as you swim towards his sentences in the fluorescent light in his office. But you don't believe it at first. This is how I'd like to die: with dignity. No body secretions—like Merle Oberon in "Wuthering Heights." With a somewhat becoming flush, and a transcendental gaze. Luminous eyes piercing the veil of mortal existence. The windows are open to the fresh breeze blowing off the moors. Oh. And violins in the background would be nice, too. [*Music: violins playing Strauss swell in the background.*]

SCENE IV

The Phone Call.

THE THIRD MAN: Lesson Number Two: Basic dialogue. The phone call. Hello, I would like to speak to Mr. Lime, please.

CARL: Entschuldigen Sie, bitte—operator? Operator? Hello? Güten Tag? Kann ich bitte mit Herrn Lime sprechen? Harry? Harry? Wie geht es dir?! Listen, I . . . can you hear . . . no, I'm in Baltimore . . . yeah, not since Hopkins . . . no, there's—well, there is something up. No, dear boy, seriously—it's my sister. ATD.

THE THIRD MAN: ATD? Jesus, that's tough, old man. You've got to watch where you sit these days. She's a sweet kid. Yeah. Yeah. Wait a second. [*Offstage.*] Inge? Inge, baby? Ein Bier, bitte, baby. Ja. Ja. You too, baby. [*Pause.*] Okay. Dr. Todesröcheln? Yeah, you might say I know him. But don't tell anybody I said that. There's also a new drug they've got over here. Black market. I might be able to help you. I said "might." But it's gonna cost you. [*Cautiously, ominously.*] Do you still have the rabbit?

CARL: I'll bring the rabbit.

THE THIRD MAN: Good. A friend of mine will be in touch. And listen, old man . . . if anybody asks you, you don't know me. I'll see you in a month. You know where to find me.

THE THIRD MAN and CARL: [*simultaneously*] Click.

SCENE V

THE THIRD MAN: Lesson Number Three: Pronouns and the possessive case. I, you, he, she, and it. They and we. Yours, mine, and ours.

VOICE OF ANNA: There's nothing I can do. There's nothing you can do. There's nothing he, she, or it can do. There's nothing we can do. There's nothing they can do.

ANNA: So what are we going to do?

CARL: Start packing, sister dear.

ANNA: Europe? You mean it?

CARL: We'll mosey about France and Germany, and then work our way down to Vienna.

ANNA: What about your job?

CARL: It's only a job.

ANNA: It's a very important job! Head of the entire San Francisco Public—

CARL: They'll hold my job for me. I'm due for a leave.

ANNA: Oh, honey. Can we afford this?

CARL: It's only money.

ANNA: It's your money.

CARL: It's our money.

SCENE VI

THE THIRD MAN: Lesson Four: Present tense of *faire*. What are we going to do? Qu'est-ce qu'on va faire?

ANNA: So what are we going to do?

CARL: We'll see this doctor in Vienna.

ANNA: Dr. Todesröcheln?

CARL: We have to try.

ANNA: A urologist?

CARL: He's working on a new drug.

ANNA: A European urologist?

CARL: What options do we have?

ANNA: Wait a minute. What are his credentials? Who is this guy?

CARL: He was trained at the Allgemeines Krankenhaus during the Empire.

ANNA: Yeah? Just what was he doing from, say, 1938 to 1945? Research?

CARL: It's best not to ask too many questions. There are people who swear by his work.

ANNA: What's his specialty?

CARL: Well, actually, he's a practitioner of uriposia.

ANNA: He writes poems about urine?

CARL: No. He drinks it.

ANNA: I'm not going.

CARL: Let's put off judgment until we arrange a consultation . . . my god, you're so messy. Look at how neat my suitcase is in comparison. You'll never find a thing in there.

ANNA: I refuse to drink my own piss for medical science. [CARL *grabs a stuffed rabbit and thrusts it in* ANNA's *suitcase.*]

ANNA: What are you doing?

CARL: We can't leave bunny behind.

ANNA: What is a grown man like you doing with a stuffed rabbit?

CARL: I can't sleep without bunny.

ANNA: I didn't know you slept with . . . stuffed animals.

CARL: There's a lot you don't know about me.

SCENE VII

THE THIRD MAN: Lesson Five: Basic dialogue. At the airport. We are going to Paris. What time does our flight leave? Nous allons à Paris. Quelle est l'heure de depart de notre vol? [THE THIRD MAN *becomes an* AIRPORT SECURITY GUARD.]

AIRPORT SECURITY GUARD: Okay. Next. Please remove your keys and all other metallic items. Place all belongings on the belt. Next. [CARL *and* ANNA *carry heavy luggage.* CARL *halts.*]

CARL: Wait. I need your suitcase. [*He opens* ANNA's *luggage and begins to rummage around.*]

ANNA: Hey!

CARL: It was a mess to begin with. Ah—[*He retrieves the stuffed rabbit.*] There.

ANNA: Are you having an anxiety attack?

CARL: You hold it. [*He and* ANNA *stamp, sit, and stand on the baggage.* CARL *manages to relock the bag.*]

ANNA: What is wrong with you?

CARL: X-rays are bad for bunny.

AIRPORT SECURITY GUARD: Next. Please remove all metallic objects. Keys. Eyeglasses. Gold fillings. Metallic objects?

CARL: Go on. You first. [ANNA *passes through, holding the stuffed rabbit.* CARL *sighs, relieved.* CARL *passes through. The* AIRPORT SECURITY GUARD *stops him.*]

AIRPORT SECURITY GUARD: One moment please. [*The* AIRPORT SECURITY GUARD *almost strip searches him. He uses a metallic wand which makes loud, clicking noises. Finally, he nods. He hands* ANNA *and* CARL *their bags, still suspiciously looking at* CARL.]

ANNA: Okay, bunny—Paris, here we come!

SCENE VIII

THE THIRD MAN: [*simultaneously with* CARL's *next lines*] Lesson Six. Direct pronouns. I am tired. And my sister looks at herself in the mirror.

CARL: Sixième Leçon: Pronoms—compléments directs. Je suis fatigué. Et ma soeur—elle se regarde dans la glace. [CARL *climbs into a double bed with the stuffed rabbit.* ANNA *stares into a mirror.* THE THIRD MAN, *apart, stands in their bedroom.*]

THE THIRD MAN: The first separation—your first sense of loss. You were five— your brother was seven. Your parents would not let you sleep in the same bed anymore. They removed you to your own bedroom. You were too old, they said. But every now and then, when they turned off the lights and went downstairs—when the dark scared you, you would rise and go to him. And he would let you nustle under his arm, under the covers, where you would fall to sleep, breathing in the scent of your own breath and his seven-year-old body.

CARL: Come to bed, sweetie. Bunny and I are waiting. We're going to be jet-lagged for a while. [ANNA *continues to stare in the mirror.*]

ANNA: It doesn't show yet.

CARL: No one can tell. Let's get some sleep, honey.

ANNA: I don't want anyone to know.

CARL: It's not a crime. It's an illness.

ANNA: I don't want anybody to know.

CARL: It's your decision. Just don't tell anyone . . . what . . . you do for a living. [ANNA *joins* CARL *in the bed. He holds her hand.*]

ANNA: Well, there's one good thing about travelling in Europe . . . and about dying.

CARL: What's that?

ANNA: I get to sleep with you again.

SCENE IX

CARL: Medical Straight Talk: Part Two. [THE THIRD MAN *becomes a* PUBLIC HEALTH OFFICIAL.]

PUBLIC HEALTH OFFICIAL: Here at the Department of Health and Human Services we are announcing Operation Squat. There is no known cure for ATD right now, and we are recognizing the urgency of this dread disease by recognizing it as our 82nd national health priority. Right now ATD is the fourth major cause of death of single schoolteachers, ages 24 to 40 . . . behind school buses, lockjaw, and playground accidents. The best policy, until a cure can be found, is of education and prevention. [ANNA *and* CARL *hold up posters of a toilet seat in a circle with a red diagonal slash.*] If you are in the high-risk category—elementary school teachers, classroom aides, custodians, and playground drug pushers—follow these simple guides. [ANNA *and* CARL *hold up copies of the educational pamphlets.*]

PUBLIC HEALTH OFFICIAL:

Do: Use the facilities in your own home before departing for school.

Do: Use the facilities in your own home as soon as you return from school.

Do: Hold it.

Don't: Eat meals in public restrooms.

Don't: Flush lavatory equipment and then suck your digits.

If absolutely necessary to relieve yourself at work, please remember the Department of Health and Human Services ATD slogan: Don't sit, do squat.

SCENE X

Music: accordion playing "La vie en rose." ANNA *and* CARL *stroll.*

CARL: Of course, the Left Bank has always been a haven for outcasts, foreigners, and students, since the time that Abelard fled the Île de la Cité to found the university here—

ANNA: Oh, look. Is that the Eiffel Tower? It looks so . . . phallic.

CARL: And it continued to serve as a haven for the avant-garde of the Twenties, the American expatriate community that could no longer afford Montparnesse—

ANNA: My god, they really do smoke Gauloise here.

CARL: And, of course, the Dada and Surrealists who set up camp here after World War I and their return from Switzerland—[THE THIRD MAN, *in a trench coat and red beret, crosses the stage.*]

ANNA: Are we being followed?

CARL: Is your medication making you paranoid? [*Pause.*] Now, over here is the famous spot where Gertrude supposedly said to her brother Leo—[THE THIRD MAN *follows them.*]

ANNA: I know. God is the answer. What is the question?—I'm not imagining it. That man has been trailing us from the Boulevard St. Michel.

CARL: Are you getting hungry?

ANNA: I'm getting tired.

CARL: Wait. Let's just whip around the corner to the Café St. Michel where Hemingway, after an all-night bout, threw up his shrimp heads all over Scott's new suede shoes—which really was a moveable feast. [THE THIRD MAN *is holding an identical stuffed rabbit and looks at them.*]

ANNA: Carl! Carl! Look! That man over there!

CARL: So? They have stuffed rabbits over here, too. Let's go.

ANNA: Why is he following us? He's got the same—

CARL: It's your imagination. How about a little dejeuner? [ANNA *and* CARL *walk to a small table and chairs.*]

SCENE XI

GARÇON: [*with a thick Peter Sellers French accent*] It was a simple bistro affair by French standards. He had le veau Prince Orloff, she le boeuf a la mode—a simple dish of haricots verts, and a Médoc to accompany it all. He barely touched his meal. She mopped the sauces with the bread. As their meal progressed, Anna thought of the lunches she packed back home. For the past ten years, hunched over in the faculty room at McCormick Elementary, this is what Anna ate: on Mondays, pressed chipped chicken sandwiches with mayonnaise on white; on Tuesdays, soggy tuna sandwiches; on Wednesdays Velveeta cheese and baloney; on Thursdays, drier pressed chicken on the now stale white bread; on Fridays, Velveeta and tuna. She always had a small wax envelope of carrot sticks or celery, and a can of Diet Pepsi. Anna, as she ate in the bistro, wept. What could she know of love?

CARL: Why are you weeping?

ANNA: It's just so wonderful.

CARL: You're a goose.

ANNA: I've wasted over thirty years on convenience foods. [*The* GARÇON *approaches the table.*]

GARÇON: Is everything all right?

ANNA: Oh God. Yes—yes—it's wonderful.

CARL: My sister would like to see the dessert tray. [ANNA *breaks out in tears again. The* GARÇON *shrugs and exits. He reappears a few minutes later as* THE THIRD

MAN, *this time with a trench coat and blue beret. He sits at an adjacent table and stares in their direction.*]

ANNA: Who is that man? Do you know him? [CARL *hastily looks at* THE THIRD MAN.]

CARL: No, I've never seen him before. [THE THIRD MAN *brings the stuffed rabbit out of his trench coat.*]

ANNA: He's flashing his rabbit at you. [CARL *rises.*]

CARL: Excuse me. I think I'll go to les toilettes.

ANNA: Carl! Be careful! Don't sit! [CARL *exits.* THE THIRD MAN *waits a few seconds, looks at* ANNA, *and then follows* CARL *without expression.*] What is it they do with those rabbits? [*A split second later, the* GARÇON *reenters with the dessert tray.* ANNA *ogles him.*]

GARÇON: Okay. We have la crème plombière pralinée, un bavarois à l'orange, et ici we have une Charlotte Malakoff aux Framboises. Our specialité is le gateau de crêpes à la Normande. What would mademoiselle like? [ANNA *has obviously not been looking at the dessert tray.*]

ANNA: [*sighing*] Ah, yes. [*The* GARÇON *smiles.*]

GARÇON: Vous êtes Américaine? This is your first trip to Paris?

ANNA: Yes.

GARÇON: And you do not speak at all French?

ANNA: No. [*The* GARÇON *smiles.*]

GARÇON: [*suggestively*] Bon. Would you like la specialité de la maison?

SCENE XII

CARL: Exercise: La Carte. La specialité de la maison.

Back at the hotel, Anna sampled the Garçon's specialité de la maison while her brother browsed the Louvre. [ANNA *and the* GARÇON *are shapes beneath the covers of the bed.* CARL *clutches his stuffed rabbit.*]

Jean Baptiste Camille Corot lived from 1796 to 1875. Although he began his career by studying in the classic tradition, his later paintings reveal the influence of the Italian style.

ANNA: [*muffled*] Ah! Yes!

GARÇON: [*also muffled*] Ah! Oui!

CARL: He traveled extensively around the world, and in the salon of 1827 his privately lauded techniques were displayed in public.

ANNA: Yes—oh, yes, yes!

GARÇON: Mais oui!

CARL: Before the Academy had accepted realism, Corot's progressive paintings, his clear-sighted observations of nature, revealed a fresh almost spritely quality of light, tone, and composition.

ANNA: Yes—that's right—faster—

GARÇON: Plus vite?

ANNA: Faster—

GARÇON: Encore! Plus vite!

ANNA: Wait!

GARÇON: Attends?

CARL: It was his simplicity, and his awareness of color that brought a fresh wind into the staid Academy—

GARÇON: Maintenant?

ANNA: Lower—faster—lower—

GARÇON: Plus bas—plus vite—plus bas—

CARL: He was particularly remembered and beloved for his championing the cause of younger artists with more experimental techniques, bringing the generosity of his advancing reputation to their careers.

ANNA: Yes—I—I—I—I—!

GARÇON: Je—je! Je! Je! [*Pause.*]

CARL: In art, as in life, some things need no translation.

GARÇON: Gauloise?

CARL: For those of you who are interested, in the next room are some stunning works by Delacroix.

SCENE XIII

Back at the Hotel.

CARL: Lesson Seven: Basic vocabulary. Parts of the body. [CARL, *slightly out of the next scene, watches them.* ANNA *sits up in bed. The* GARÇON *is asleep beneath the sheet.*]

ANNA: I did read one book once in French. *Le Petit Prince.* Lying here, watching him sleep, I look at his breast and remember the Rose with its single, pathetic thorn for protection. And here—his puckered red nipple, lying poor and vulnerable on top of his blustering breast plate. It's really so sweet about men. [*She kisses the* GARÇON'*s breast. The* GARÇON *stirs.*]

GARÇON: Encore?

ANNA: What is the word—in French—for this? She fingers his breast.

GARÇON: For un homme—le sein. For une femme—la mamelle.

ANNA: Sein?

GARÇON: Oui, sein.

ANNA: [*She kisses his neck.*] And this?

GARÇON: Le cou.

ANNA: Et ici?

GARÇON: Bon. Decollette—[ANNA *begins to touch him under the sheet.*]

ANNA: And this? [*The* GARÇON *laughs.*]

GARÇON: S'il vous plaît . . . I am tickling there. Ah, Les couilles.

ANNA: Culle?

GARÇON: Non. Couilles. Le cul is something much different. Ici c'est le cul.

ANNA: Oh, yes. That's very different.

GARÇON: [*taking her hand under the sheet*] We sometimes call these also Le Quatrième État. The Fourth Estate.

ANNA: Really? Because they enjoy being "scooped"?

GARÇON: Bein sur.

ANNA: And this?

GARÇON: Ah. Ma Tour Eiffel. I call it aussi my Charles DeGaulle.

ANNA: Wow.

GARÇON: My grandfather called his Napoléon.

ANNA: I see. I guess it runs in your family.

GARÇON: [*modestly*] Oui. Grand-mère—qu'est-ce que c'est le mot en anglais? Her con—here—ici—do you know what I am meaning?

ANNA: You're making yourself completely clear—

GARÇON: We called hers the Waterloo de mon grand-père—[ANNA *digs under the sheet more.*]

ANNA: And this? [*The* GARÇON *is scandalized.*]

GARÇON: Non. There is no word en Français. Pas du tout.

ANNA: For this? There must be—

GARÇON: Non! Only the Germans have a word for that. [CARL *enters and casually converses with* ANNA. *Startled, the* GARÇON *covers himself with the sheet.*]

CARL: Hello, darling. Are you feeling better? [CARL *walks to the chair beside the bed and removes the* GARÇON's *clothing.*]

ANNA: Yes, much. I needed to lie down. How was the Louvre? [*The* GARÇON *carefully rises from the bed and takes his clothing from* CARL, *who is holding them out. He creeps cautiously stage left and begins to pull on his clothes.*]

CARL: Oh, Anna. I'm so sorry you missed it. The paintings of David were amazing. The way his paintbrush embraced the body—it was just incredible to stand there and see them in the flesh.

ANNA: Ah yes—in the flesh. [*She smiles at the confused* GARÇON.]

CARL: Well, sweetie. It's been a thoroughly rewarding day for both of us. I'm for turning in. How about you? [*The* GARÇON *is now fully dressed.*]

ANNA: Yes, I'm tired. Here—I've warmed the bed for you. [*She throws back the sheet.*]

CARL: Garçon—l'addition!

ANNA: [*to the* GARÇON] Merci beaucoup. [ANNA *blows him a kiss. The* GARÇON *takes a few steps out of the scene as* CARL *climbs into bed.*]

SCENE XIV

THE THIRD MAN: Anna has a difficult time sleeping. She is afflicted with night thoughts. According to Elizabeth Kubler-Ross, there are six stages the terminal patient travels in the course of her illness. The first stage: Denial and Isolation. [THE THIRD MAN *stays in the hotel room and watches* CARL *and* ANNA *in the bed. They are sleeping, when* ANNA *sits upright.*]

ANNA: I feel so alone. The ceiling is pressing down on me. I can't believe I am dying. Only at night. Only at night. In the morning, when I open my eyes, I feel absolutely well—without a body. And then the thought comes crashing in my mind. This is the last spring I may see. This is the last summer. It can't be. There must be a mistake. They mixed the specimens up in the hospital. Some poor person is walking around, dying, with the false confidence of my prognosis, thinking themselves well. It's a clerical error. Carl! I can't sleep. Do you think they made a mistake?

CARL: Come back to sleep—[CARL *pulls* ANNA *down on the bed to him, and strokes her brow. They change positions on the bed.*]

THE THIRD MAN: The second stage: Anger. [ANNA *sits bolt upright in bed, angry.*]

ANNA: How could this happen to me! I did my lesson plans faithfully for the past ten years! I've taught in classrooms without walls—kept up on new audio-visual aids—I read *Summerhill!* And I believed it! When the principal assigned me the job of the talent show—and nobody wants to do the talent show—I pleaded for cafeteria duty, bus duty—but no, I got stuck with the talent show. And those kids put on the best darn show that school has ever seen! Which one of them did this to me? Emily Baker? For slugging Johnnie MacIntosh? Johnnie MacIntosh? Because I sent him home for exposing himself to Susy Higgins? Susy Higgins? Because I called her out on her nosepicking? or those Nader twins? I've spent the best years of my life giving to those kids—it's not—

CARL: Calm down, sweetie. You're angry. It's only natural to be angry. Elizabeth Kubler-Ross says that—

ANNA: What does she know about what it feels like to die?! Elizabeth Kubler-Ross can sit on my face! [CARL *and* ANNA *change positions on the bed.*]

THE THIRD MAN: The third stage: Bargaining.

ANNA: Do you think if I let Elizabeth Kubler-Ross sit on my face I'll get well? [CARL *and* ANNA *change positions on the bed.*]

THE THIRD MAN: The fourth stage: Depression. [CARL *sits on the side of the bed beside* ANNA.]

CARL: Anna—honey—come on, wake up.

ANNA: Leave me alone.

CARL: Come on, sweetie . . . you've been sleeping all day now, and you slept all yesterday. Do you want to sleep away our last day in France?

ANNA: Why bother?

CARL: You've got to eat something. You've got to fight this. For me.

ANNA: Leave me alone. [CARL *lies down beside* ANNA. *They change positions.*]

THE THIRD MAN: The fifth stage: Acceptance. [ANNA *and* CARL *are lying in bed, awake. They hold hands.*]

ANNA: When I'm gone, I want you to find someone.

CARL: Let's not talk about me.

ANNA: No, I want to. It's important to me to know that you'll be happy and taken care of after . . . when I'm gone.

CARL: Please.

ANNA: I've got to talk about it. We've shared everything else. I want you to know how it feels . . . what I'm thinking . . . when I hold your hand, and I kiss it . . . I try to memorize what it looks like, your hand . . . I wonder if there's any memory in the grave?

THE THIRD MAN: And then there's the sixth stage: Hope. [ANNA *and* CARL *rise from the bed.*]

CARL: How are you feeling?

ANNA: I feel good today.

CARL: Do you feel like travelling?

ANNA: Yes. It would be nice to see Amsterdam. Together. We might as well see as much as we can while I'm well—

CARL: That's right, sweetie. And maybe you can eat something—

ANNA: I'm hungry. That's a good sign, don't you think?

CARL: That's a wonderful sign. You'll see. You'll feel better when you eat.

ANNA: Maybe the doctor in Vienna can help.

CARL: That's right.

ANNA: What's drinking a little piss? It can't hurt you.

CARL: Right. Who knows? We've got to try.

ANNA: I'll think of it as . . . European lager.

CARL: Golden Heidelberg. [CARL *and* ANNA *hum/sing the drinking song from* The Student Prince.]

SCENE XV

THE THIRD MAN: And as Anna and Carl took the train into Holland, the seductive swaying of the TEE-train aroused another sensation. Unbeknownst to Elizabeth Kubler-Ross, there is a seventh stage for the dying. There is a growing urge to fight the sickness of the body with the health of the body. The seventh stage: Lust. [ANNA *and* CARL *are seated in a train compartment.* CARL *holds the stuffed rabbit out to* ANNA.]

ANNA: Why?

CARL: Just take it. Hold it for me. Just through Customs.

ANNA: Only if you tell me why.

CARL: Don't play games right now. Or we'll be in deep, deep do-do. [ANNA *reluctantly takes the stuffed rabbit and holds it.*]

ANNA: You're scaring me.

CARL: I'm sorry, sweetie. You're the only one I can trust to hold my rabbit. Trust me. It's important.

ANNA: Then why won't you tell me—?

CARL: There are some things you're better off not knowing.

ANNA: Are you smuggling drugs? Jewels?

CARL: [*whispers*] It's beyond measure. It's invaluable to me. That's all I'll say. [*In a louder tone.*] Just act normal now.

CUSTOMS OFFICIAL: Uw paspoort, alstublieft. [ANNA *and* CARL *give him their passports.* CARL *is nervous.* ANNA *smiles at the* CUSTOMS OFFICIAL *a bit lasciviously.*] Have you anything to declare?

ANNA: [*whispering*] Yes—captain, I'm smuggling contraband. I demand to be searched. In private. [*The* CUSTOMS OFFICIAL *blushes.*]

CUSTOMS OFFICIAL: Excuse me?

ANNA: Yes. I said—waar is het damestoilet?

CUSTOMS OFFICIAL: Oh . . . I thought . . . [*The* CUSTOMS OFFICIAL *giggles.*]

ANNA: Yes?

CUSTOMS OFFICIAL: First left. [*The* CUSTOMS OFFICIAL *returns their passports.*] Have a pleasant stay. [ANNA *waves bunny's arm goodbye. The* CUSTOMS OFFICIAL *looks at her, blushes again, and retreats.* CARL *relaxes.*]

CARL: You're good at this. Very good.

ANNA: When in Holland, do like the Dutch . . . Mata Hari was Dutch, you know.

SCENE XVI

CARL: Questions sur le Dialogue. Est-ce que les hommes Hollandais sont comme les Français? Are Dutch men like the French? [ANNA *and* THE LITTLE

DUTCH BOY AT AGE 50. *He wears traditional wooden shoes, trousers, and vest. His Buster Brown haircut and hat make him look dissipated.*]

THE LITTLE DUTCH BOY AT AGE 50: It was kermis-time, the festival in my village. And I had too much bier with my school friends, Piet and Jan. Ja. Soo— Piet thought we should go to the other dyke with cans of spray paint, after the kermis. So we went.

Here in Noord Brabant there are three walls of defenses against the cruelty of the North Sea. The first dyke is called the Waker—the Watcher; the second dyke is de Slaper—the Sleeper; and the last dyke, which had never before been tested, is known as the Dromer—the Dreamer.

And when we got to the Dreamer, Piet said to me: "Willem, you do it." Meaning I was to write on the walls of the Dreamer. This is why I was always in trouble in school—Piet and Jan would say, "Willem, you do it," and whatever it was—I would do it.

Soo—I took up a can of the paint and in very big letters, I wrote in Dutch that our schoolmaster, Mijnheer Van Doorn, was a gas-passer. Everyone could read the letters from far away. And just as I was finishing this, and Piet and Jan were laughing behind me, I looked—I was on my knees, pressed up against the dyke—and I could see that the wall of the Dreamer was cracking its surface, very fine little lines, like a goose egg when it breaks from within.

And I yelled to my friends—Look! And they came a bit closer, and as we looked, right above my head, a little hole began to peck its way through the clay. And there was just a small trickle of water. And Jan said: "Willem, put your thumb in that hole." And by that time, the hole in the dyke was just big enough to put my thumb in. "Why?" I asked of Jan. "Just do it," he said. And so I did.

And once I put my thumb in, I could not get it out. Suddenly we could hear the waves crashing as the Sleeper began to collapse. Only the Dreamer remained to hold off the savage water. "Help me!" I yelled to Jan and Piet—but they ran away. "Vlug!" I cried—but no one could hear me. And I stayed there, crouching, with my thumb stuck into the clay. And I thought what if the Dreamer should give in, too. I thought how the waves would bear my body like a messenger to the Village. How no one would survive the Flood. Only the church steeple would remain to mark the place where we had lived. How young we were to die. [*Pause.*]

Have you ever imagined what it would be like to be face to face with death?

ANNA: Yes—yes, I have.

THE LITTLE DUTCH BOY AT AGE 50: And have you ever prayed for deliverance against all hope?

ANNA: I—no. I haven't been able to get to that stage. Yet.

THE LITTLE DUTCH BOY AT AGE 50: But the Dreamer held. And finally there came wagons with men from the village, holding lanterns and sand and straw. And they found me there, strung up by my thumb, beside the big black letters: Mijnheer Van Doorn is een gas-passer. And they freed me and said I was a hero, and I became the boy who held back the sea with his thumb.

ANNA: Golly. You were very brave.

THE LITTLE DUTCH BOY AT AGE 50: I was stupid. Wrong place, wrong time.

ANNA: How long ago did this happen?

THE LITTLE DUTCH BOY AT AGE 50: [*sadly*] Let us just say it happened a long time ago.

ANNA: You've faced death. I wish my brother were here to meet you.

THE LITTLE DUTCH BOY AT AGE 50: Where is he? Wo ist dein bruder?

ANNA: Oh, he stayed in Amsterdam to see the Rijksmuseum and the Van Gogh Museum.

THE LITTLE DUTCH BOY AT AGE 50: And you did not go? You should see them, they are really fantastic.

ANNA: Why? What's the use? I won't remember them, I'll have no memory.

THE LITTLE DUTCH BOY AT AGE 50: So you are an American?

ANNA: Yes.

THE LITTLE DUTCH BOY AT AGE 50: So, do you want to sleep with me? All the women touristen want to sleep with the little Dutch boy who put his thumb in the dyke.

ANNA: Do you mind so much?

THE LITTLE DUTCH BOY AT AGE 50: [*shrugs*] Nee. It's a way to make a living, is it niet?

ANNA: [*quietly*] Let's go then.

SCENE XVII

CARL: Répétez. En Français. Where is my brother going? Où va mon frère? Bien.

ANNA: I had just returned from my day trip and left the Central Station. The sun sparkled on the waters of the canal, and I decided to walk back to the hotel. . . . Just then I saw my brother. [CARL *enters in a trench coat, sunglasses, holding the stuffed rabbit.*] I tried to catch up with Carl, dodging bicycles and pedestrians. And then, crossing the Amstel on the Magere Brug, he appeared. [THE THIRD MAN *enters, in a trench coat, sunglasses, and with black gloves, holding a stuffed rabbit.*] I trailed them from a discrete distance. [THE THIRD MAN *and* CARL *walk rapidly, not glancing at each other.* CARL *stops;* THE THIRD MAN *stops a few paces behind.* CARL *walks;* THE THIRD MAN *walks.* CARL *stops;* THE THIRD MAN *stops. Finally, they face each other and meet. Quickly, looking surreptitiously around,* CARL *and* THE THIRD MAN *stroke each other's stuffed rabbits. They quickly part and walk off in opposite directions.* ANNA *rushes to center stage, looking in both directions.*] I tried to follow the man in the trench coat, and crossed behind him over the Amstel, but I lost sight of him in the crowd of men wearing trench coats and sunglasses. I want some answers from my brother. Whatever trouble he's in, he has to share it with me. I want some answers back at the hotel. He's going to talk.

SCENE XVIII

CARL: Questions sur le dialogue. You must learn. Sie müssen lernen. [ANNA *enters the empty hotel room. On the bed, propped up on pillows, lies a stuffed rabbit.*]

ANNA: Carl? Carl? Are you back? Carl? [ANNA *stops and looks at the stuffed rabbit.*]

CARL: [*from the side*] You were not permitted to play with dolls; dolls are for girls.

You played with your sister's dolls until your parents found out. They gave you a stuffed animal—a thin line was drawn. Rabbits were an acceptable surrogate for little boys. You named him Jo-Jo.

    You could not sleep without him. Jo-Jo traveled with you to the seashore, to the hotel in New York City when you were seven, to your first summer camp. He did not have the flaxen plastic hair of your sister's Betsy-Wetsy, but he had long, furry ears, soft white on one side, pink satin inside. He let you stroke them. He never betrayed you. He taught you to trust in contact. You will love him always. [ANNA *moves towards the stuffed rabbit.*]

ANNA: My brother left you behind, did he? Alone at last. Okay, bunny, now you're going to talk. I want some answers. What have you got that's so important? [*Just as* ANNA *reaches for the stuffed rabbit,* THE THIRD MAN *(in trench coat, sunglasses and black gloves) steps out into the room.*]

THE THIRD MAN: [*threateningly*] I wouldn't do that, if I were you. [ANNA *screams in surprise.*] Now listen. Where is your brother? I have a message for him. Tell him he's running out of time. Do you understand? [ANNA, *scared, nods.*] Good. He'd better not try to dupe us. We're willing to arrange a swap—his sister for the rabbit. Tell him we're waiting for him in Vienna. And tell him he'd better bring the rabbit to the other side. [THE THIRD MAN *leaves.* ANNA, *shaken, sits on the bed and holds the stuffed rabbit. She strokes it for comfort.* CARL *enters, in a frenzy. He carries his stuffed rabbit.* ANNA *stares as* CARL *tosses the decoy rabbit away.*]

CARL: Don't ask me any questions. I can't tell you what's happening. Are you able to travel? Good. We have to leave Amsterdam tonight. There's a train in an hour. We'll go to Germany. Are you packed?

SCENE XIX

ANNA and THE THIRD MAN: [*simultaneously*] Wann geht der nächste Zug nach Hamburg? [*German band music swells as* ANNA *and* CARL *sit in their railroad compartment, side by side.* ANNA, *pale, holds the stuffed rabbit in her lap.*]

CARL: Ah, Saxony, Bavaria, the Black Forest, the Rhineland . . . I love them all. I think perhaps now would be a good time to show the slides.

ANNA: I'm so sorry. I hate it when people do this to me.

CARL: Nonsense. People like to see slides of other people's trips. These are in no particular order. We'll only show a few, just to give a taste of the German countryside.

ANNA: Carl took over two hour's worth of slides.

CARL: If you'll just dim the lights, please. [THE THIRD MAN *wheels in the projector and operates it throughout the travelogue.*]

CARL: Well, Bonn's as good a place to start as anywhere. This is the view from our snug little hotel we stayed in. The gateway to the Rhine, the birthplace of Beethoven, and the resting place of Schumann.

    [*Slide: the view of downtown Baltimore from the Ramada Inn near Johns Hopkins Hospital, overlooking the industrial harbor.*]

ANNA: Looks a lot like Baltimore to me.

CARL: My sister jests. As you can see in the slide, one night we splurged and stayed in a rather dear inn near the Drachenfels mountains, where Lord Byron had sported.

[*Slide: a close-up of the balcony railing looking into the Ramada Inn hotel room.*]

ANNA: [*dead-panned*] This is the room I slept in while I stayed with my brother Carl.

[*Slide: gutted ruins of inner-city Baltimore near the Jones-Fall Expressway; rubble and obvious urban blight.*]

CARL: Alas, poor Köln. Practically wiped out by airplane raids during World War II, and yet, out of this destruction, the cathedral of Köln managed to survive—one of the most beautiful Gothic churches in the world, with a superb altar painted by the master artist of Köln, Stefan Lochner.

[*Slide: an impoverished storefront church, a black evangelical sect in Baltimore.*]

Let's see—what do we have next?

[*Slide: a Sabrett's hotdog cart with its blue and orange umbrella in front of Johns Hopkins Hospital.*]

Oh, yes. Let's talk about the food. Whereas I snapped mementoes of the regal pines of the Black Forest, Anna insisted on taking photos of everything she ate.

ANNA: I can remember things I feel.

CARL: Well, then, let's talk about the food. Germany has a more robust gustatory outlook than the delicate palate of France. The Germans positively celebrate the pig from snout to tail. I could not convince Anna to sample the Sulperknochen, which is a Rheingau concoction of ears, snout, tail, and feet.

ANNA: Ugh.

[*Slide: a close-up of vender placing a hotdog on a bun and lathering it with mustard; there are canned sodas in a wide variety.*]

CARL: And of course, everything is washed down with beer.

[*Slide: ANNA sipping a Bud Lite.*]

ANNA: It was delicious.

CARL: Enough of food. May we talk about culture, sister, dear? Next slide, please.

[*Slide: the Maryland National Armory; the state penitentiary.*]

Ah, Heidelberg. Dueling scars and castles. Spectacular ruin which serves as the locale for open-air concerts and fireworks . . .

[*Slide: the Baltimore smokestack.*]

. . . and by a quaint cable car, you can reach the peak at Königstuhl, two thousand feet high, with its breathtaking view of the Neckar Valley.

[*Slide: the Bromo Seltzer tower in Baltimore.*]

[*Slide: the interstate highway viewed from the tower.*]

Every cobblestoned street, every alleyway, was so pristine and clean.

[*Slide: the row houses on Monument Street.*]

[*Slide: a corridor of Hopkins Hospital, outside the basement laboratories.*]

Wasn't it, Anna?

ANNA: [*deadpan*] Yes. Sterile.

[*Slide: a hospital aide washing the floor.*]

CARL: Even the Black Forest looked swept. We splurged once again and stayed at the Waldhorn Post here, outside of Wildbad.

[*Slide: exterior of Johns Hopkins Hospital.*]

The hotel dates back to 1145—the chef there is renowned for his game dishes.

[*Slide:* ANNA *in front of a vending machine dispensing wrapped sandwiches in the Hopkins Hospital cafeteria.*]

ANNA: I wasn't too hungry.

CARL: I was ravenous.

[*Slides: Route 95 outside the harbor tunnel; the large toll signs are visible.*]

Let's see—the Romantic Road . . . Die Romantishe Strasse . . . a trek through picture-book Bavaria and the Allgau Alpen . . . Füssen to Würzburg.

ANNA: Honey, perhaps they've seen enough. It's hard to sit through this many—

CARL: Wait. Just one more. They've got to see Neuschwanstein, built by mad King Ludwig II. It's so rococco it's Las Vegas.

[*Slide: the castle at Disneyland.*]

I believe that Ludwig was reincarnated in the twentieth century as Liberace. Wait a moment, that's not the castle.

ANNA: Yes, it is.

CARL: [*upset*] It looks like—how did that get in here?

ANNA: I don't know which castle you're referring to, but it's definitely a castle.

[*Slide: a close-up of the castle, with a large Mickey Mouse in the picture.*]

CARL: That's not funny, Anna! Are you making fun of me?

ANNA: Don't get upset.

[*Slide: Donald Duck has joined Mickey Mouse with tourists.*]

CARL: I went to Europe. I walked through Bavaria and the Black Forest. I combed through Neuschwanstein! I did these things, and I will remember the beauty of it all my life! I don't appreciate your mockery!

ANNA: It's just a little—

CARL: You went through Germany on your back. All you'll remember are hotel ceilings. You can show them your Germany—

[*He rushes off, angry.*]

ANNA: Sometimes my brother gets upset for no apparent reason. Some wires cross in his brain and he—I'm sorry. Lights, please. [THE THIRD MAN *wheels the projector offstage.*]

I would like to show you my impressions of Germany. They were something like this—

SCENE XX

In Munich.

ANNA *is under the sheet beside the* MUNICH VIRGIN, *who is very young.*

ANNA: Are you comfortable?

MUNICH VIRGIN: Ja, ja . . . danke.

ANNA: Good. Have you been the bellhop here for a long time?

MUNICH VIRGIN: Not so very long a time. My vater owns the hotel, and says I must learn and work very hard. Soon I will be given the responsibility of the front desk.

ANNA: My. That's exciting. [*Pause.*] Are you cold?

MUNICH VIRGIN: Nein. Just a . . . klein nervos. My English is not so very good.

ANNA: Is this your first time? You always remember your first time. [*Pause.*] I'm very honored. [*Pause.*]

    Listen. I'm a schoolteacher. May I tell you something? A little lesson? When you're a much older man, and you've loved many women, you'll be a wonderful lover if you're just a little bit nervous . . . like you are right now. Because it will always be the first time.

MUNICH VIRGIN: You are a very nice woman.

ANNA: The human body is a wonderful thing. Like yours. Like mine. The beauty of the body heals all the sickness, all the bad things that happen to it. And I really want you to feel this. Because if you feel it, you'll remember it. And then maybe you'll remember me.

SCENE XXI

ANNA *and the* MUNICH VIRGIN *rise.* CARL *gets into the bed with his stuffed rabbit.* ANNA *gets ready to leave.*

THE THIRD MAN: Conjugations of the verb *verlassen.* To leave, to abandon, to forsake. The present tense.

CARL: Are you leaving me alone?

ANNA: Yes. Just for a little while. I need to take a walk. I'm restless. It's perfectly safe.

CARL: Okay, sweetie. Don't be too long. Bunny and I are ready for bed.

ANNA: I won't stay out long. I'll be right back.

THE THIRD MAN: The future tense of the verb *verlassen.*

CARL: Will you be leaving me alone again tonight? I'm ready for bed.

ANNA: I will be leaving you alone. Just for a little while.

CARL: Who will it be tonight? The bellhop? The desk clerk? Or the maitre d'?

ANNA: Don't be mean. You said you didn't make judgments.

CARL: I don't. I just want to spend time with you.

ANNA: I'll be back in time for a bedtime story.

THE THIRD MAN: The past tense of the verb *verlassen.*

CARL: Again? Again? You left me alone last night. And the night before.

ANNA: I can't help it. I've been a good girl for the past thirty years. Now I want to make up for lost time.

CARL: And what am I supposed to do while you're out traipsing around with every Thomas, Dieter, und Heinrich?

ANNA: Hug bunny.

THE THIRD MAN: There are three moods of the verb *verlassen:* the indicative, the imperative, and the subjunctive. Anna and Carl are never in the same mood.

CARL: Leave me alone.

ANNA: Carl, don't be like that.

CARL: Why? It doesn't matter what I want. You are going to leave.

ANNA: I never stay out very long.

CARL: All I can say is if this establishment charges us for room service, they've got some nerve—

ANNA: I've got to take what opportunities come along—

CARL: I wish you wouldn't go—

ANNA: Please understand. I don't have much time. I spend as much time with you as I can, but while I still have my health . . . please?

SCENE XXII

THE THIRD MAN: As children they fought.
CARL: We never fought, really.
ANNA: Not in a physical way. He was a sickly child.
CARL: She was very willful.
ANNA: No rough-housing. But he knew all of my weak points. My secret openings. He could be ruthless.
CARL: She'd cry at the slightest thing.
ANNA: He has a very sharp tongue.
CARL: But when one of you is very sick, you can't fight. It's not fair. You've got to hold it in. We never fight.
ANNA: But we had a doozy in the hotel room in Berlin.
CARL: Well, my god, Anna, even though you're sick, I have the right to get angry.
ANNA: We'd been traveling too long. We were cranky. The rooms were closing in.
CARL: I'm just saying that we should spend a little more time together. I don't get to see you alone enough. You're always restless.
ANNA: Fine. You go out without me for a change.
CARL: I'm going out for a walk.
ANNA: [*starting to weep*] I don't care.
CARL: When she was little, this would be the time I'd bribe her. With a comic book or an ice cream. I always had pennies saved up for these little contingencies.
ANNA: But sometimes, for the sake of my pride, I would be inconsolable. I would rush off and then feel just awful alone. Why didn't I take the bribe? [*To* CARL.] I'm going out.
CARL: To fuck?
ANNA: No, dear. The passive voice is used to emphasize the subject, to indicate the truth of the generalization. I'm going out. To get fucked.

SCENE XXIII

Music: Kurt Weill. ANNA *goes over to a small cabaret table. There is a telephone on the table. The* RADICAL STUDENT ACTIVIST *sits at another identical table, smoking, watching her.*

ANNA: I'm going to enjoy Berlin without him. I'll show him. I'm going to be carefree, totally without scruples. I'll pretend I've never taught first-graders. [*Beat.*] I'm going to have a perfectly miserable time. [*The* RADICAL STUDENT ACTIVIST *picks up the telephone. The telephone at* ANNA's *table rings.*] Oh my goodness. My miserable time is calling me. [ANNA *picks up the phone.*] Yes?
RADICAL STUDENT ACTIVIST: Are you alone, Fräulein?
ANNA: Well, uh, actually—yes, I am.
RADICAL STUDENT ACTIVIST: Gut. Du willst mal richtig durchgefickt werden, ja?

ANNA: I'm sorry. I don't speak a word of German. [*The* RADICAL STUDENT ACTIVIST *laughs.*]

RADICAL STUDENT ACTIVIST: Ja. Even better. I said, would you like to get fucked?

ANNA: Do you always come on to single women like that?

RADICAL STUDENT ACTIVIST: Would you like it better if I bought you tall drinks with umbrellas? Told to you the stories of how hard a time my parents had during the war? Tell you how exciting I find foreign women, how they are the real women, not like the pale northern mädchen here at home? How absolutely bourgeois.

ANNA: I see. Why do you come here?

RADICAL STUDENT ACTIVIST: I don't come here for the overpriced drinks. I come here because of the bored western women who come here, who leave their tired businessmen husbands in the hotel rooms behind.

ANNA: You're cute. In a hostile way.

RADICAL STUDENT ACTIVIST: Fucking is a revolutionary act.

ANNA: Your hovel or my hotel?

SCENE XXIV

In the hotel room. ANNA, *awake, lies in the middle of the bed. To her left,* CARL *sleeps, curled up. To her right, the* RADICAL STUDENT ACTIVIST, *curled on her breast, slumbers.* ANNA *is awake with an insomniacal desperation.*

ANNA: [*singing softly*] Two and two are four; four and four are eight; eight and eight are sixteen; sixteen and sixteen are thirty-two—

RADICAL STUDENT ACTIVIST: [*groggy*] Wo ist die Toilette?
    [*The* RADICAL STUDENT ACTIVIST *rises and stumbles stage left.*]

ANNA: In love-making, he's all fury and heat. His North Sea pounding against your Dreamer. And when you look up and see his face, red and huffing, it's hard to imagine him ever having been tiny, wrinkled, and seven pounds. That is, until afterwards. When he rises from sleep and he walks into the bathroom. And there he exposes his soft little derriere, and you can still see the soft baby flesh. [*As the* RADICAL STUDENT ACTIVIST *comes back into the room.*] I've got to put a name to that behind. What's your name? Wie heissen Sie? [*The* RADICAL STUDENT ACTIVIST *starts dressing in a hurry.*]

RADICAL STUDENT ACTIVIST: Auf Wiedersehn. Next thing you'll ask for my telephone number.

ANNA: No, I won't. I was just curious—

RADICAL STUDENT ACTIVIST: Ja, ja . . . und then my sign of the zodiac. I'll get cards from Hallmark und little scribblings like "I'll never forget the night we shared."

ANNA: Forget it.

RADICAL STUDENT ACTIVIST: There is something radical in two complete strangers committing biological necessity without having to give into bourgeois conventions of love, without breeding to produce workers for a capitalist system, without the benediction of the church, the family, the bosses—

ANNA: I have something to confess to you. I lied to you.

RADICAL STUDENT ACTIVIST: About what?

ANNA: I'm not here on business. I don't specialize in corporate takeovers. I don't work on Wall Street. I only told you that because I thought that was what you wanted to hear.

RADICAL STUDENT ACTIVIST: Okay. So you do estate planning? Income tax?

ANNA: No. You just committed a revolutionary act with a first-grade schoolteacher who lives in low-income housing. And I'm tired. I think you should go.

RADICAL STUDENT ACTIVIST: And your husband?

ANNA: Not too loud. And he's not my husband. He's my brother. A maiden librarian for the San Francisco Public. [*As the* RADICAL STUDENT ACTIVIST *starts to leave.*] And by the way—the missionary position does not a revolution make. [*The* RADICAL STUDENT ACTIVIST *leaves.* ANNA, *depressed, lies down.* CARL *rises from the bed.*]

SCENE XXV

CARL: And as she lay in the bed, sleepless, it swept over her—the way her classroom smelled early in the morning, before the children came. It smelled of chalk dust—

THE THIRD MAN: It smelled of Crayola wax, crushed purple and green—

CARL: The cedar of hamster cage shavings—

THE THIRD MAN: The sweet wintergreen of LePage's paste—

CARL: The wooden smell of the thick construction paper—

THE THIRD MAN: The spillings of sticky orange drink and sour milk—

THE THIRD MAN and CARL: [*simultaneously*] And the insidious smell of first-grader pee.

CARL: It smelled like heaven.

ANNA: And the first thing I did each morning was put up the weather map for today on the board under the flag. A bright, smiling sun, or Miss Cloud or Mr. Umbrella. On special days I put up Suzy Snowflake. And when I opened my desk drawer, scattered like diamonds on the bottom were red, silver and gold stars. [*Beat.*] I want to go home. Carl, I want to go home.

CARL: Soon, sweetie. Very soon.

ANNA: I've had enough. I've seen all of the world I want to see. I want to wake up in my own bed. I want to sit with you at home and we'll watch the weather. And we'll wait.

CARL: We've come so far. We have to at least go to Vienna. Do you think you can hold out long enough to meet Dr. Todesröcheln?

[ANNA, *miserable and homesick, nods.*] That a girl. I promise you don't have to undertake his . . . hydrotherapy unless you decide to. I have a friend in Vienna, a college chum, who might be able to get us some of the black-market stuff. It's worth a shot.

ANNA: Then you'll take me home?

CARL: Then I'll take you home.

SCENE XXVI

Music: the zither theme from The Third Man. CARL *and* ANNA *stand, with their luggage, in front of a door buzzer.*

CARL: First we'll just look up Harry and leave our bags here. Then we'll cab over to Dr. Todesröcheln. [CARL *rings the buzzer. They wait.* CARL *rings the buzzer again. They wait. An aging* CONCIERGE *comes out.*]
Entschuldigung. Wir suchen Harry Lime? Do you speak English?

CONCIERGE: Nein. Ich spreche kein Englisch. [CARL *and the* CONCIERGE *start to shout as if the other one was deaf.*]

CARL: Herr Lime? Do you know him? Herr Harry Lime?

CONCIERGE: Ach. Ach. Ja, Herr Harry Lime. You come . . . too spät.

CARL: He's gone? Too spat?

CONCIERGE: Fünf minuten too spät. Er ist tot—

CARL: What?

CONCIERGE: Ja. Ein auto mit Harry splatz-machen auf der Strasse. Splatz!

ANNA: Splatz!?

CARL: Splatz?! [*It dawns on* CARL *and* ANNA *what the* CONCIERGE *is saying.*]

CONCIERGE: Ja, ja. Er geht über die strasse, und cin auto . . . spppllllaattz!

ANNA: Oh, my god!

CONCIERGE: [*gesturing with hands*] Ja. Er hat auch eine rabbit. Herr rabbit auch— sppllaattz! They are . . . diggen ein grab in den Boden. Jetz.

CARL: Now? You saw this happen?

CONCIERGE: Ja. I . . . saw it mit meinen own Augen. Splatz. [*As he exits.*] "Splatzen, splatzen, über alles . . ."

CARL: Listen, darling. I want you to take a cab to the doctor's office.

ANNA: Where are you going?

CARL: Ich verlasse. I'll find out what happened to Harry.

ANNA: I wish you wouldn't leave . . .

CARL: I'll come back. Okay?

SCENE XXVII

ANNA *climbs onto a table and gathers a white paper sheet around her. She huddles.*

ANNA: Some things are the same in every country. You're scared when you see the doctor, here in Vienna just like in Baltimore. And they hand you the same paper cup to fill, just like in America. Then you climb onto the same cold metal table, and they throw a sheet around you and you feel very small. And just like at home, they tell you to wait. And you wait. [*As* ANNA *waits, dwarfed on the table, the scene with* HARRY LIME *and* CARL *unfolds.* The Third Man *theme music up.*]

SCENE XXVIII

On the Ferris wheel in the Prater.
CARL *holds the stuffed rabbit closely.*

CARL: I just came from your funeral.

HARRY LIME: I'm touched, old man. Was it a nice funeral?

CARL: What are you doing? Why are we meeting here?

HARRY LIME: It's best not to ask too many questions. The police were beginning to do that. It's extremely convenient, now and then in a man's career, to die.

I've gone underground. So if you want to meet me, you have to come here. No one asks questions here.

CARL: Can you help us? [HARRY LIME *at first does not answer. He looks at the view.*]

HARRY LIME: Where is your sister? She left you alone?

CARL: She's—she needs her rest.

HARRY LIME: Have you looked at the view from up here? It's quite inspiring. No matter how old I get, I always love the Ferris wheel.

CARL: You were my closest friend in college.

HARRY LIME: I'll be straight with you. I can give you the drugs—but it won't help. It won't help at all. Your sister's better off with that quack Todesröcheln—we call him the Yellow Queen of Vienna—she might end up drinking her own piss, but it won't kill her.

CARL: But I thought you had the drugs—

HARRY LIME: Oh, I do. And they cost a pretty penny. For a price, I can give them to you. At a discount for old times. But you have to know, we make them up in my kitchen.

CARL: Jesus.

HARRY LIME: Why not? People will pay for these things. When they're desperate, people will eat peach pits, or aloe, or egg protein—they'll even drink their own piss. It gives them hope.

CARL: How can you do this?

HARRY LIME: Listen, old man, if you want to be a millionaire, you go into real estate. If you want to be a billionaire, you sell hope. Nowadays the only place a fellow can make a decent career of it is in Mexico and Europe.

CARL: That's . . . disgusting.

HARRY LIME: Look. I thought you weren't going to be . . . sentimental about this. It's business. You have to have the right perspective. Like from up here . . . the people down on the street are just tiny little dots. And if you could charge 1,000 dollars, wouldn't you push the drugs? I could use a friend I can trust to help me.

CARL: When we were at Hopkins together, I thought you were God. You could hypnotize us into doing anything, and it would seem . . . charming. "Carl, old man," you'd say, "Just do it." Cutting classes, cribbing exams, shoplifting, stupid undergraduate things—and I would do it. Without knowing the consequences. I would do it.

THE THIRD MAN: Oh, you knew the consequences, old man. You knew. You chose not to think about them.

CARL: I've grown old before my time from the consequences. I'm turning you in.

HARRY LIME: I wouldn't do that, old man. [HARRY LIME *pats a bulge on the inside of his trench coat.*] By the time you hit the ground, you'll be just a tiny little dot. [CARL *and* HARRY LIME *look at each other, waiting.*]
And I think you have something I want. The rabbit, bitte.

CARL: No. You're not getting it. I'm taking it with me. [HARRY LIME *puts his arms in position for a waltz and begins to sway, seductively.*]

HARRY LIME: Come on, give it up. Come to my arms, my only one. Dance with me, my beloved, my sweet—[CARL *takes the stuffed rabbit and threatens to throw it out the window of the Ferris wheel. A Strauss waltz plays very loudly, and* HARRY LIME *and* CARL *waltz-struggle for the rabbit.* CARL *is pushed and* HARRY LIME *waltzes off with the rabbit.*]

SCENE XXIX

Meanwhile, back at DOCTOR TODESRÖCHELN.

ANNA: You begin to hope that the wait is proportionate to the medical expertise. My God. My feet are turning blue. Where am I? An HMO?

The problem with being an adult is that you never forget why you're waiting. When I was a child, I could wait blissfully unaware for hours. I used to read signs and transpose letters, or count tiles in the floor. And in the days before I could read, I would make up stories about my hands—Mr. Left and Mr. Right. [*Beat.*] Mr. Left would provoke Mr. Right. Mr. Right would ignore it. The trouble would escalate, until my hands were battling each other to the death. [*Beat.* ANNA *demonstrates.*] Then one of them would weep. Finally, they became friends again, and they'd dance—[ANNA*'s two hands dance together; she is unaware that* DR. TODESRÖCHELN *has entered and is watching her. He clears his throat. He wears a very dirty lab coat with pockets filled with paper and a stale doughnut. He wears a white fright wig and glasses. He also wears one sinister black glove. With relish, he carries a flask of a golden liquid.*] Oh, thank goodness.

DR. TODESRÖCHELN: Ja. So happy to meet you. Such an interesting specimen. I congratulate you. Very, very interesting.

ANNA: Thank you.

DR. TODESRÖCHELN: We must have many more such specimens from you—for the urinocryoscopy, the urinometer, the urinoglucosometer, the uroacidimeter, uroazotometer, and mein new acquirement in der laboratorium—ein urophosphometer.

ANNA: My goodness. [DR. TODESTROCHELN *has put the flask down on a table. Quietly, his left hand reaches for it; the right hand stops the left.*]

DR. TODESRÖCHELN: Ja. Nowadays, we have learned to discover the uncharted mysteries of the fluids discharged through the urethra. We have been so primitive in the past. Doctors once could only analyze by taste and smell— but thanks to the advancement of medical science, there are no limits to our thirst for knowledge.

ANNA: Uh-huh. [DR. TODESRÖCHELN*'s left hand seizes the flask. Trembling, with authority, his right hand replaces the flask on the table, and soothes the left hand into quietude.*]

DR. TODESRÖCHELN: So much data has been needlessly, carelessly destroyed in the past—the medical collections of Ravensbrück senselessly annihilated— and that is why, as a scientist, I must be exacting in our measurements and recordings.

ANNA: What can I hope to find out from these . . . specimens?

DR. TODESRÖCHELN: Ah, yes—the layman must have his due! Too much pure research und no application makes Jack . . . macht Jack . . . [DR. TODESRÖCHELN *loses his train of thought.*]

Fräulein Anna—I may call you Fräulein Anna?—Let us look at the body as an alchemist, taking in straw and mud und schweinefleisch and processing it into liquid gold which purifies the body. You might say that the sickness of the body can only be cured by the health of the body. To your health! [*His left hand seizes the flask in a salute, and raises the flask to his lips. In time, the right hand brings the flask down. A brief struggle. It appears the flask might spill, but at last the right hand triumphs.*]

ANNA: You know, even though I really grew up in the suburbs of Baltimore, I like to think of myself as an open-minded person—

DR. TODESRÖCHELN: The ancient Greeks knew that the aromatic properties of the fluid could reveal the imbalances of the soul itself . . . [*The left hand sneaks towards the flask.*]

ANNA: I'm always very eager to try new foods, or see the latest John Waters film—

DR. TODESRÖCHELN: —its use in the purification rites of the Aztecs is, of course, so well known that it need not be mentioned—[*The hand has grasped the flask and begins to inch it off the table.*]

ANNA: And whenever I meet someone who cross-dresses, I always compliment him on his shoes or her earrings—

DR. TODESRÖCHELN: It is the first golden drop that marks the infant's identity separate from the womb—[*The hand has slipped the flask beneath the table; his right hand is puzzled.*]

ANNA: But still, it's important to know where your threshhold is . . . and I think we're coming dangerously close to mine . . .

DR. TODESRÖCHELN: Until the last precious amber releases the soul from the body—ashes to ashes, drop to drop—excuse me—[*His left hand, with the flask, swings in an arc behind his body; he swivels his body to the flask, his back turned to us; we can hear him drink in secrecy. With his back turned . . .*] Ahhh . . . [*He orders himself. Composed, he turns around to face* ANNA *again, and demurely sets down the flask. Its level is noticeably lower.* ANNA *is aghast.*]

I can sense your concern. I have been prattling on without regard to questions you must surely have—

ANNA: Is that your real hair?

DR. TODESRÖCHELN: Of course, I can not promise results, but first we must proceed by securing more samples—

ANNA: I don't believe that's your real hair.

DR. TODESRÖCHELN: I will need first of all twenty-four hours of your time for a u(r)ononcometry—

ANNA: [*increasingly scared*] You look familiar to me—

DR. TODESRÖCHELN: Although I can tell you from a first taste—er, test, that your uroammonica level is high—not unpleasantly so, but full-bodied—

ANNA: Oh, my god . . . I think I know who you are . . . you're . . . you're . . . [ANNA *rises to snatch his toupee.* DR. TODESRÖCHELN *suddenly stands, menacing. And the light changes.*]

DR. TODESRÖCHELN: WO IST DEIN BRUDER? [*He takes off his wig and glasses and appears as the* DOCTOR *in the first scene, peeling off the black gloves to reveal latex gloves underneath.*]

You fool! You left your brother in the room alone! WO IST DEIN BRUDER?

> *Music:* The Emperor Waltz *plays at a very loud volume.* ANNA, *frightened, races from the doctor's office to the hotel room. We see* CARL, *lying stiff beneath a white sheet. To the tempo of the Strauss,* ANNA *tries to wake him. He does not respond.* ANNA *forces him into a sitting position, the stuffed rabbit clenched beneath his arm.* CARL *remains sitting, stiff, eyes open, wooden. Then he slumps.* ANNA *raises him again. He remains upright for a beat, and begins to fall.* ANNA *stops him, presses his body against hers, pulls his legs over the bed, tries to stand him up. Frozen, his body tilts against hers. She tries to make him cross the floor, his arms around her neck. She positions him in a chair, but his legs are locked in a perpendicular angle and will not touch the floor. He mechanically springs forward. Then, suddenly, like the doll in E. T. A. Hoffman, the body of* CARL *becomes animated, but with a strange, automatic life of its own, and faltering, falls back to the bed. There is the sound of a loud alarm clock; the* DOCTOR *enters, and covers* CARL *with a sheet. Then he pulls a white curtain in front of the scene, as the stage lights become, for the first time, harsh, stark, and white.*]

SCENE XXX

In the hospital lounge.
The DOCTOR *holds the stuffed rabbit and travel brochures in his hands. He awkwardly peels off his latex gloves.*

DOCTOR: I'm sorry. There was nothing we could do.

ANNA: Yes. I know.

DOCTOR: I thought you might want to take this along with you. [*The* DOCTOR *hands* ANNA *the stuffed rabbit.*]

ANNA: [*to the stuffed rabbit*] There you are! [ANNA *hugs the stuffed rabbit and sees the* DOCTOR *watching her.*]
   It's Jo-Jo. My brother's childhood rabbit. I brought it to the hospital as a little surprise. I thought it might make him feel better.

DOCTOR: Sometimes little things become important, when nothing else will help—

ANNA: Yes. [*They pause and stand together awkwardly.*] At least Carl went in his sleep. I guess that's a blessing.

DOCTOR: If one has to die from this particular disease, there are worse ways to go than pneumonia.

ANNA: I never would have believed what sickness can do to the body. [*Pause.*] Well, Doctor, I want to thank you for all you've done for my brother.

DOCTOR: I wish I could do more. By the way, housekeeping found these brochures in your brother's bedside table. I didn't know if they were important. [ANNA *takes the brochures.*]

ANNA: Ah, yes. The brochures for Europe. I've never been abroad. We're going to go when he gets—[ANNA *stops herself. With control.*] I must learn to use the past tense. We would have gone had he gotten better.

DOCTOR: Anna—may I call you Anna?—I, uh, if there's anything I can do—

ANNA: Thank you, but there's nothing you can do—
DOCTOR: I mean, I really would like it if you'd call me for coffee, or if you just
     want to talk about all this—[*The* DOCTOR *trails off.* ANNA *looks at him. She
     smiles. He squirms.*]
ANNA: You're very sweet. But no, I don't think so. Not now. I feel it's simply not
     safe for me right now to see anyone. Thanks again and goodbye.
          [ANNA *starts to exit. The* DOCTOR, *wistful, watches her go. The lighting be-
          gins to change back to the dreamy atmosphere of the first scene. Softly, a
          Strauss waltz begins.* CARL, *in uniform, perfectly well, waits for* ANNA.
          They waltz off as the lights dim.]

END OF PLAY

Credits